CW00474270

# A Raj Collection

OUP India's Omnibus collection offers readers a comprehensive coverage
of works of enduring value, woven together by a new introduction,
attractively packaged for easy reference and reading.

Other publications by Saros Cowasjee

FICTION
*Stories and Sketches*
*Goodbye to Elsa*
*Nude Therapy*
*The Last of the Maharajahs* (screenplay)
*The Assistant Professor*
*Modern Indian Fiction* (ed.)
*Modern Indian Short Stories* (ed.)
*Stories from the Raj* (ed.)
*More Stories from the Raj and After* (ed.)
*When the British Left* (ed.)
*The Raj and After* (ed.)
*Women Writers of the Raj* (ed.)
*Orphans of the Storm: Stories on the Partition of India* (ed.)
*The Best Short Stories of Flora Annie Steel* (ed.)
*The Oxford Anthology of Raj Stories* (ed.)
*The Mulk Raj Anand Omnibus*

CRITICISM
*Sean O'Casey: The Man Behind the Plays*
*O'Casey*
*'Coolie': An Assessment*
*So Many Freedoms: A Study of the Major Fiction of
    Mulk Raj Anand*
*Author to Critic: The Letters of Mulk Raj Anand* (ed.)
*Studies in Indian and Anglo-Indian Fiction*

'A Question of Control'

# A Raj Collection

ON THE FACE OF THE WATERS
FLORA ANNIE STEEL

SIRI RAM—REVOLUTIONIST
EDMUND CANDLER

INDIGO
CHRISTINE WESTON

THE WILD SWEET WITCH
PHILIP MASON

*Edited, with an Introduction, by*
SAROS COWASJEE

OXFORD
UNIVERSITY PRESS

# OXFORD
UNIVERSITY PRESS

YMCA Library Building, Jaì Singh Road, New Delhi 110 001

Oxford University Press is a department of the University of Oxford. It
furthers the University's objective of excellence in research, scholarship, and
education by publishing worldwide in

Oxford  New York
Auckland  Cape Town  Dar es Salaam  Hong Kong  Karachi
Kuala Lumpur  Madrid  Melbourne  Mexico City  Nairobi  New Delhi
Shanghai  Taipei  Toronto

With offices in
Argentina  Austria  Brazil  Chile  Czech Republic  France  Greece  Guatemala
Hungary  Italy  Japan  South Korea  Poland  Portugal  Singapore
Switzerland  Thailand  Turkey  Ukraine  Vietnam

Oxford is a registered trademark of Oxford University Press
in the UK and in certain other countries

Published in India
by Oxford University Press, New Delhi

© Saros Cowasjee and Oxford University Press 2005

The moral rights of the author have been asserted
Database right Oxford University Press (maker)
First published 2005

All rights reserved. No part of this publication may be reproduced,
stored in a retrieval system, or transmitted, in any form or by any means,
without the prior permission in writing of Oxford University Press, or as
expressly permitted by law, or under terms agreed with the appropriate
reprographics rights organization. Enquiries concerning reproduction outside
the scope of the above should be sent to the Rights Department, Oxford
University Press, at the address above

You must not circulate this book in any other binding or cover and you must
impose this same condition on any acquirer

ISBN 0 19 566500 7

Typeset in 9.5/11.5 Palatino by Laser Print Craft
Printed by De Unique, New Delhi 110 018
Published by Manzar Khan, Oxford University Press
YMCA Library Building, Jai Singh Road, New Delhi 110 001

# Editor's Note

A *Raj Collection* is a companion volume to *The Oxford Anthology of Raj Stories*. The latter brings together, in one volume, some of the finest short stories of the Raj by Anglo-Indian* writers; the former attempts to bring, under one cover, four outstanding Raj novels not readily available. The period covered by these novels is from the time of Kipling to Indian Independence in 1947. Most of us are familiar with the novels of Kipling, Forster, and Orwell, and no doubt they make the top rung of not only Raj fiction but of English fiction in general. But what about fiction by Flora Annie Steel (a contemporary of Kipling) or Christine Weston or Philip Mason? Even if they fall short of the masters in the art of story telling, their portrayals of India are equally compelling and haunting. And they add immensely to a more comprehensive picture of India under British rule.

We have reproduced here the texts of the four novels as they first appeared. A few printers' errors have been silently corrected and, on occasions, the spelling of Indian words standardized if they varied within the same text. Apart from that, we have been scrupulous in letting the original texts stand as they were, not even italicizing those Indian words which are conventionally italicized. However, all words in the Glossary, whether italicized or not in the texts, have been italicized. Though a large number of Indian words have entered standard English, not all of them have gained equal currency in written and spoken English. There is also the question of audience: some readers may be more familiar with Indian words and phrases than others. Taking these factors into account, we have included in the Glossary some Indian words which may seem a trifle unnecessary to devotees of Anglo-Indian literature but, hopefully, not to all readers.

It is a pleasure to thank those who have made this work possible. My first thanks go to Oxford University Press and its editors for commissioning this volume, my next to Russell & Volkening (New York), and Gillon Aitken Associates (London) respectively for permission to reprint Christine Weston's *Indigo* and Philip Mason's

*The term 'Anglo-Indian' is explained on the first page of the Introduction.

*The Wild Sweet Witch.* I must also thank my own university—an institution whose help I have taken so much for granted over the years that acknowledging it now seems more routine than it should. I also owe thanks to Rachael Corkill for her Preface to *Siri Ram— Revolutionist,* written by her grandfather, Edmund Candler, to Sarah Irons for her Preface to *The Wild Sweet Witch,* a work by her father, Philip Mason, to Lady Violet Powell for her Preface to *On the Face of the Waters* by Flora Annie Steel, and to Christine Weston for her Foreword to *Indigo.* Lastly, but in no way less, I wish to express gratitude to John Chamberlain, Richard Harvey, M.K. Naik, Aydon Charlton, and Gillian Murad for going through my Introduction and other textual material and making valuable suggestions. My work would have been the poorer without their contribution.

# CONTENTS

# Introduction

As a genre, Raj fiction or Anglo-Indian fiction (the terms are used interchangeably) began with Rudyard Kipling and ended when India won Independence in 1947. Both these dates are in a sense arbitrary, for we find fiction by Anglo-Indian* writers long before Kipling established himself on the literary scene with *Plain Tales from the Hills* and *Soldiers Three* (both in 1888). Similarly, scores of novels about India, set during the British rule and revealing many of the characteristics of the period, continued to appear long after Independence. The most distinctive, perhaps, is Paul Scott's *The Raj Quartet* (1966–75). Written some twenty years after the events, the four volumes cover the period from the Quit India riots of 1942 to the partitioning of the country in 1947. Largely ignored in the author's lifetime, the *Quartet* is a minor epic that mirrors a spectrum of British views of India from Kipling to Independence.

The first Anglo-Indian novel, *The Disinterested Nabob*, was published anonymously in 1785. Between that date and the arrival of Kipling a hundred years later, few novelists have survived as more than mere names. The earliest of them is William Browne Hockley, who held a judgeship in Bombay. Taking advantage of the vogue for the criminal hero popular in English fiction at the time, he published *Pandurang Hari, or Memoirs of a Hindoo* in 1826. In itself little more than a picaresque novel of treachery and corruption, its importance lay in that it served as a model for Colonel Meadows Taylor's more famous first novel, *The Confessions of a Thug* (1839). Hockley's other work of note is *Tales of the Zenana* (1827), a collection of witty tales he heard from his servants and which he put together in the manner of the *Arabian Nights*.

Meadows Taylor came out to India at the age of fifteen and spent several years in the service of the Nizam of Hyderabad. Not only did he know India better than any of his contemporaries, but moving

---

*The term 'Anglo-Indian' was applied originally to the British in India, and only later to people of British and Indian descent. Here it is used in its original meaning. For more information, see Frank Anthony's *Britain's Betrayal in India* (1969).

among Indians he was relatively free from many of their prejudices. Apart from the realistic *Confessions of a Thug*, Taylor's other novels such as *Tippoo Sultan* (1840), *Tara* (1863), *Seeta* (1872), and *A Noble Queen* (1878) are all romances. But romances somehow are not regarded strictly as Raj fiction even when written by Anglo-Indian writers during the years of British rule. The same applies to historical novels set in the past, like those by L.H. Myers. Even the Raj stalwart Flora Annie Steel's Mogul studies such as *A Prince of Dreamers* (1908), *King Errant* (1912), *Mistress of Men* (1917), and *The Builders* (1928) find little place in studies of Raj fiction. Though nestled within the corpus of Anglo-Indian literature, Raj fiction's defining feature is that it is set in the present and that in one way or another it reflects the British presence in India. In nine cases out of ten, the protagonist is an Englishman whose interaction with his own people, and even more so with Indians, is a corollary of his belonging to the ruling class. Kipling offers abundant examples of this and so do a host of prominent Raj writers like Flora Annie Steel, Alice Perrin, Maud Diver, Leonard Woolf, Edmund Candler, E.M. Forster, Edward Thompson, and George Orwell.

Of authors preceding Kipling, William Delafield Arnold, brother of the poet Matthew Arnold, stands out among Raj novelists with his single book *Oakfield, or Fellowship in the East* (1854). Described by E.M. Forster as a 'disquieting book', it offers withering criticism of the members of British officialdom—their slack morals, their drunkenness, and their debauchery. The British are also pilloried by Iltudus Thomas Prichard in *The Chronicles of Budgepore* (1870) and by Sir Henry Stuart Cunningham in *The Chronicles of Dustypore* (1875). However, both these novelists make use of genial satire and have little of the moral intensity and despair that runs through Arnold's work. All the same, *Oakfield* remains the single most important work of the pre-Kipling era. Its emphasis on the cultural incompatibility of the British and the Indian minds was to become a dominant theme in many of the novels that followed its publication. Its failure to win readership was largely owing to the fact that it gave a scathing portrait of the British rulers on the one hand with no compensatory love for India or the Indians on the other. Its fierce moral intensity proved too much even for the smug Victorians and few read it today for enjoyment.

For most readers, Rudyard Kipling (1865–1936) marks the beginning of Raj fiction. Born in Bombay in 1865, his principal years in India were from 1882 to 1889 when he worked on the staff of the *Civil and Military Gazette* and then the Allahabad *Pioneer*. The impression of these seven years in India provided him with much of the material for his vast body of writings on the Raj. Many of his short stories and verses first appeared in local journals and were subsequently published in book form by A.H. Wheeler in its 'Indian Railway Library' series. The year 1888 was particularly bountiful, for apart from *Plain Tales from the Hills* and *Soldiers Three*, it saw the publication of *In Black and White, Under the Deodars, The Phantom Rickshaw*, and *Wee Willie Winkie*. British editions of these books appeared soon after Kipling left India, and new titles were added such as *Life's Handicap* (1891), *Barrack-Room Ballads* (1892), *The Day's Work* (1898), and, finally, *Kim* (1901). *Kim*, unlike its creator, has no detractors and is by common consent one of Anglo-India's finest novels. But it is a novel out of character with much of Kipling's other writing and in any discussion of Kipling and the Raj, is silently pushed aside.

In 1907 Kipling was awarded the Nobel Prize for Literature—the first to an English writer. Other works followed, set in countries around the world, but nothing caught the British public imagination as strongly as his Indian verse and stories. It was a period when Britain was going through an expansionistic phase, and Kipling was the prophet of British imperialism. His uncompromising belief that it was Britain's God-given duty to govern India and civilize its people fitted perfectly with the British ideology of the day. Later, liberal politics at home, and the rise of nationalism abroad, manifested the chauvinism of Kipling's outlook. As time passed, his detractors began to outnumber his admirers but, oddly, his popularity with the reading public endured. George Orwell drew attention to this strange paradox when he wrote, 'During five literary generations every enlightened person has despised him, and at the end of that time nine-tenths of those enlightened persons are forgotten and Kipling is in some sense still there.'

Kipling is a complex and puzzling character who is loved and hated in the extreme. The question that concerns us primarily here is: Why is Kipling looked upon as the starting point of Raj fiction when there are several other novelists who precede him? To this is tied another question: What gives Kipling this unique position among Anglo-Indian writers? Indians have never had much use for him, and in Britain and the United States he has failed to command serious critical attention despite approbation from formidable critics such as Henry James, T.S. Eliot, Edmund Wilson, and C.S. Lewis. And yet to think of Anglo-Indian fiction is to think of Kipling.

It is true that a large amount of Kipling's Indian writing is marred by vulgarity, cruelty, and what Lionel Trilling called his 'mindless imperialism'. And it is these qualities that have got in the way of an objective assessment of his works. There is a tendency to dismiss Kipling out of hand for his politics with no effort to acknowledge his immense literary gifts: the variety and range of his characters, his sharp observation, and his multifaceted portrait of India. Attempts to rehabilitate him began with Eliot's *A Choice of Kipling's Verse* (1942), followed by two widely acclaimed critical studies: Charles Carrington's *Rudyard Kipling: His Life and Work* (1955) and J.M.S. Tompkin's *The Art of Rudyard Kipling* (1959). A third book, complementing the above two, appeared in 1975. Titled *Kipling: The Glass, The Shadow and The Fire*, it was by the last of the Raj novelists, Philip Mason. No two writers could be more different in their politics and approach to India than Mason and Kipling. That Mason should see real merit in Kipling as a writer is not only a tribute to both men but also shows the strong influence Kipling has had on Anglo-Indian writers of different persuasions.

There are several factors that make Kipling the starting point in a study of Raj fiction. His work is rooted in the present; so much so that even the Mutiny of 1857, which ushered in direct rule from Britain, receives scant attention. The present gave immediacy to his writing, and the fact that he chose the short story form (which had been ignored by Anglo-Indian writers until then) made him easily accessible to his readers. There were no Anglo-Indian intelligentsia as such. The bulk of Kipling's readers were officials within the civil and military branches of the British administration who applauded his portrayals of themselves. Also, in plotting his stories, Kipling laid new emphasis on the interaction between the British rulers and their Indian subjects. Such interaction, sparse in pre-Mutiny fiction, became with Kipling a major theme. In this he was not always successful because of his pro-Raj leanings, which often led to a distorted and unsympathetic portrayal of Indians. His numerous successors and imitators fared no better, and not till we come to E.M. Forster's *A Passage to India* (1924) do we find a fully realized Indian character in Raj fiction.

Kipling's influence on the Raj and Raj fiction was not wholly beneficial. His stories and verses became prescribed reading for young civil servants and military personnel drafted for service in India. Kipling's imperialism, his arrogance, his racial prejudice, and disdain for certain classes of Indians could hardly have provided healthy precepts for those assigned the task of governing India. As for his influence on later fiction, he swayed a whole school of writers who took their political views and especially their attitude towards Indians from him. A good many of them were women, and among them Flora Annie Steel and Alice Perrin were the most gifted. Like Kipling, Steel and Perrin excelled in the short story rather than in novel writing, and both shared Kipling's interests—ranging from a firm belief in Britain's imperial role to a love of the occult and the mysterious. Bhupal Singh in *A Survey of Anglo-Indian Fiction* (revised 1975) devotes an entire chapter to writers who imitated Kipling and those who felt his influence. Many of them are unrecognizable names today, recalled only by critics and historians to demonstrate Kipling's enormous influence on Anglo-Indian fiction.

\* \* \* \*

Allen Greenberger in his study *The British Image of India* (1969) divides Anglo-Indian writers into three periods: The Era of Confidence, 1880–1910; The Era of Doubt, 1910–35; and The Era of Melancholy, 1935–60. Such a division has obvious difficulties as Greenberger himself acknowledges: authors who began writing in one period often continued to write in the same vein in the next period. Then there are authors like Edmund Candler who underwent a change in thinking over the years, making it difficult to assign them to any one period. Still, some categorization is necessary if we are to bring order to this large body of fiction. Greenberger's division is useful, but since we are concerned with fiction written strictly during the British rule in India, I would change the dates of The Era of Melancholy to 1935–47. Fiction written after 1947, but set in India during the Raj, could be placed in a fourth period which we could call 'The Era of Nostalgia and Revaluation'. The fourth period is in many ways a continuation of The Era of Melancholy except that there is now a sense of irreparable loss. An empire has vanished and Britain's claim to world power is at stake. There is a belated attempt on the part of the rulers to acknowledge past mistakes, to re-examine some of their actions, and to woo India as if she were an ill-treated mistress. Even the 'heat and dust' of India, a long-standing complaint, seems for once to be forgotten.

Though the fourth period does not fall within our scope, many of the writers of this period were either former colonialists or were born and raised in India. Jon Godden was born in Bengal, John Masters in Calcutta, and M.M. Kaye in Simla. Paul Scott, the most distinguished of them all, wrote his *Quartet* and *Staying On* (1977) long after Independence, yet drew chiefly on his recollections of India during World War II. J.G. Farrell and Valerie Fitzgerald have also had strong ties with India and in their respective novels, *The Siege of Krishnapur* (1971) and *Zemindar* (1981), show a deep feeling for the country and its people. But to many Indians, the change of heart comes too late and the portrait of Hindu India as depicted by Kipling still galls.

Accepting Greenberger's framework without the restrictions imposed by dates, Anglo-Indian fiction shows a movement from confidence in the Raj to a mood of doubt and despair. This transition is more visible in the short story than in the novel, as I illustrated in my Introduction to *The Oxford Anthology of Raj Stories* (1998) by placing Kipling's 'The Head of the District' (1891) alongside George Orwell's 'Shooting an Elephant' (1936). Kipling's argument is clear, and it is one that comes up repeatedly in his writings: the British are brave and resourceful and ordained to rule. Given what the Indians are, the British have no choice in the matter—they must rule India even if they do not want to. Orwell, standing at the other end of the spectrum, questions the very ethics of one country governing another and describes the British Raj as an 'unbreakable tyranny'. In a ceaseless effort to impress those whom he governs, the white man begins to wear a mask, 'and his face grows to fit it'. Thus, in essence, the ruler becomes the ruled. In ruling others, it is his own freedom he destroys.

Kipling is the chief exponent of The Era of Confidence. He expresses faith in the continuance of British rule in India more strongly than any writer before him or after. The ideal British hero of this period is portrayed as firm, masculine, daring, a born leader of men who, to use a phrase of one of Kipling's lesser imitators, Ethel M. Dell, 'works like an ox'. The Indians, with few exceptions, are portrayed as unpleasant. Though in life they may have filled more varied roles, in much of early fiction they appear as cooks, bearers, *ayahs, fakirs*, and frequently as thugs and thieves. If an Indian is shown in a position of authority, like the Bengali Deputy Commissioner in 'The Head of the District', it is only to reveal how inept he is at exercising that authority. The class of Indians with whom the British felt comfortable, and even admired, were those who accepted a subservient role and looked upon them as *mai-baap*. The illiterate peasant, the trusting soldier, and the domestic servant belong to this class. They were depicted as grown-up children who needed the care and supervision of their English nurse. The image of Indians as children fitted in perfectly with the British view of themselves as leaders and their unselfish desire to do good to the Indian people.

Jawaharlal Nehru summed up this philanthropic British attitude with amused irritation in his *An Autobiography* (1936): 'Like the Inquisitors of old, they [the British] were bent on saving us regardless of our desire in the matter.'

Apart from characterization, the fiction of this period manifests other recognizable features such as an indisputable cultural gulf between the two peoples, the British disapproval of intermarriage, a preference for the Muslims over the Hindus, the ridicule of the Bengali and the Western-educated Indian, the dismissal of the nationalist as a person of no consequence, and the ignoring of the Christian missionary and his work. Though missionaries were among the first whites to come to the subcontinent, they became increasingly unpopular as the British hold on the country grew stronger. The missionary was either frowned upon for becoming half-Indian himself in his quest to convert the heathens, as in Alice Perrin's *Idolatry* (1909), or for failing to understand the people among whom he served, as in Kipling's story 'Lispeth'. The real reason, however, lay deeper. How was the British ruler to insist on his racial superiority—the very keystone to governing India—in the midst of the missionary's prattle about Christian love and equality of all before God? The missionary was blamed for undoing the work of the Raj when in actual fact the services rendered by him (through schools, hospitals, dispensaries) did much to curb the rising antagonism the Raj engendered. Anglo-Indian fiction has been reluctant to give the missionary his due, and not till we come to Edward Thompson (himself a missionary) in the 1920s do we find a missionary as a central figure in Raj fiction.

The principal writers of this period are all women: Flora Annie Steel, Maud Diver, Alice Perrin, and Sara Jeannette Duncan. Though they differ somewhat in their attitude towards Indians, they stand united in their imperial dream—the British right to rule India. Steel spent twenty-two years in India and came to know Indians and their customs as no wife of an English officer had ever done. She had a large circle of Indian friends, but by temperament she was an authoritarian and considered British rule a dire necessity. This is seen in *The Potter's Thumb* (1894), *The Host of the Lord* (1900), and in many of her short stories. She is completely against intermarriage between Indians and whites, and except for *Voices in the Night* (1900), shuns it even as a topic for fiction. In this respect she differs from Maud Diver who in *Lilamani* (1910) shows a union between an Englishman and an Indian girl. But this is a union between ideal people under ideal conditions with ideal results and should not be mistaken for the author's blanket approval of cohabitation. Though somewhat more liberal in her attitude towards Indians, Diver was also a firm believer in the Raj, as demonstrated by her soldier heroes in her Frontier trilogy *Captain Desmond V.C.* (1907), *The Great Amulet* (1908), and *Desmond's Daughter* (1916). Alice Perrin, the daughter of a general, does not overtly express fascination for the soldier or the civilian administrator. Her novels are primarily about Anglo-Indian life in the *mofussil*. But like other writers of this group, she advocates 'racial purity' and looks on cohabitation as unnatural. In *The Stronger Claim* (1903) she shows the catastrophic outcome of a mixed marriage between an Englishman and a Eurasian woman. Perrin is best in her short stories and her 'The White Tiger' is a splendid allegory of the British desire to hold on to her Indian Empire to the very end.

It is a little puzzling that a writer of Sara Jeannette Duncan's importance should be absent from Greenberger's study of Anglo-Indian fiction as well as from similar studies by Benita Parry, Roshna Singh, and others. Of Duncan's ten books on India, the last two, *Set in Authority* (1906) and *The Burnt Offering* (1909), are as good as anything Maud Diver wrote and incomparably better than the fiction of other women writers like Bithia M. Croker, F.E. Penny, and E.W. Savi. All of Duncan's Indian novels were published during The Era of Confidence and taken together they provide an exhaustive portrait of the Anglo-Indian community. *The Burnt Offering* has the additional distinction of presenting a balanced picture of the current political situation in India and of introducing an Indian nationalist—a composite portrait of Bal Gangadhar Tilak and Aurobindo Ghose—as a central character. She does, however, make the claim that the Indians are not yet ready for self-government. Her sympathies are with the rulers, and some of her best writings deal with the hardships of their life in India. Separation from children was perhaps the greatest hardship Anglo-Indian parents had to endure (for reasons of health and education, children as a rule were sent back to England at an early age). Duncan's 'A Mother in India' is the most poignant expression of this separation and, by virtue of this long short story alone, she deserves a place in the history of Anglo-Indian fiction.

* * * *

The Era of Confidence gives way to the less cohesive Era of Doubt. Greenberger sees three groups of writers in this period. The first group consists of supporters of the Raj who, owing to lack of confidence, react aggressively to anything that threatens British dominance in India. With the rise of liberalism, these writers no longer feel secure in their imperial quest and are often on the defensive. They search for new reasons to justify Britain's continued presence in India. Novels such as Maud Diver's *Siege Perilous* (1924) and Talbot Mundy's *King of the Khyber Rifles* (1917) raise the bogey that India needs Britain to defend her frontier from foreign incursions. The second group comprises writers who disapprove of British colonialism and denounce the very concept of Empire. Forster, Orwell, Leonard Woolf, and Edward Thompson make the backbone of this group and together raise Raj fiction to a higher plane. The third group is composed of writers who vacillate between the supporters of the Raj and those who proscribe it. They express doubt about the existence of any meaningful relationship between the two very different peoples.

A noticeable feature of The Era of Doubt is the entrance into Anglo-Indian fiction of previously neglected categories of Indians. The *mali*, the *khidmutgar*, the *dhobi*, are still there (there can be no Anglo-Indian fiction without them), but we now meet Indian judges, lawyers, doctors, teachers, administrators, and senior civil servants in numbers rarely found before. Though the treatment they receive might leave us uneasy, it is often more generous than that meted out to their white counterparts in anti-Raj novels. (Let us not forget the outcry with which Anglo-India greeted Forster's portrayal of the rulers in *A Passage to India*.) But the most significant development in Anglo-Indian fiction is the induction of the Indian nationalist. Except for Sara Duncan's *The Burnt Offering*, the nationalist was fleetingly mentioned in novels of the 1910s but portrayed for the first time in some depth in Edmund Candler's *Siri Ram—Revolutionist* (1912).

Up to this time the nationalist was either decried as a person of little consequence or held up to ridicule. But the political unrest following the division of Bengal in 1905 had brought the national movement into focus and Candler in *Siri Ram—Revolutionist* makes a frontal attack to show that revolutionaries such as Siri Ram are basically cowards and self-seekers, and the Raj can take care of them. His faith in England's power to govern, however, changed in the decade that followed. In *Abdication* (1922) he reached the conclusion that India was 'a festering sore' and the British rule 'a positive calamity'. Understanding between the two races was no longer a possibility and the only alternative left to the British was to abdicate and get out of India. The blame for the failure he placed mostly on the Indians, but held that Britain had played into the hands of the nationalists by agreeing to political reforms. Candler was not alone in holding this view. Many writers who believed in British rule were assailed with doubts and fear at its continuance, but none threw in the towel as Candler did. Maud Diver, for one, foresaw the need for a closer relationship between the two races if the Raj were to continue, but she did not envisage an independent India. She kept depicting nationalists as maniacs, and in *Ships of Youth* (1931) called the concept of an Indian nation a 'political fairy-tale'.

Though Candler felt 'that neither white men nor brown contributed to the tranquillity of the other', the search for under-standing and friendship between the British and the Indians became the single most important topic with emerging Anglo-Indian novelists. This also led to a more sympathetic portrayal of the nationalist and a more critical review of the Anglo-Indian who took his status for granted. This is nowhere better demonstrated than in Edward Thompson's Indian trilogy, *An Indian Day* (1927), *A Farewell to India* (1931), and *An End of the Hour* (1938). After serving as a teaching missionary in Bengal for eight years, Thompson returned to Britain in 1923 with the aim, to quote Benita Parry, of 'humanizing an inhuman situation . . . [and] making the British Empire a more generous and moral institution, and the British–Indian relationship a more compassionate one.' An indefatigable writer, he wrote *The Other Side of the Medal* (1925) to 'atone' for Britain's persistent castigation of Indians for the horrors of the Mutiny of 1857. In this polemical though scholarly study, Thompson documents the 'devilish cruelties' practised by both sides and not by the Indians alone, as claimed by most British historians.

Another author who took India seriously and studied Indian civilization was Dennis Kincaid, a judicial member of Bombay Presidency from 1928 until his tragic death by drowning in 1937. The satiric vein that runs through his highly readable *British Social Life in India, 1608–1937* (published posthumously in 1938) shows where his political sympathies lie, though in his five Indian novels he makes few pronouncements on the efficacy or failure of British administration. *Durbar* (1933), however, presents a political officer, Major Hilton, who is simply marking time in the feudal state of Krishnagad and longing for the day he can go back to England. His wife Dorothy, like many other Anglo-Indian women in Raj fiction, is full of contempt for most Indians. But it is in the novel *Their Ways Divide* (1936) that Kincaid treats the theme of friendship between English and Indians. The theme immediately brings to mind Forster's *A Passage to India* and Kincaid's book suffers in comparison. The relationship between Naru and Edward is beset with difficulties rooted in race and culture and the two move apart, as the title suggests, never to meet again. In Thompson's view there is something elemental about India, something inexplicable, which seems to make friendship between the races difficult to achieve. The liberal Kincaid—much to his discomfort—would perhaps agree with this.

E.M. Forster's influence on Anglo-Indian fiction has been as strong as that of Kipling, but with one exception. Kipling's stories created bad blood between the races by continually running down the Indians, while Forster's *A Passage to India* brought the two peoples together, momentarily, no doubt, by showing the way to a lasting friendship. There has not been an Anglo-Indian writer of note who has escaped Forster's influence, and every novel published since *A Passage to India* is measured against the yardstick that Forster provided. Thompson and Kincaid faced strong competition but did not fare badly, the uncompromising Orwell held his own with *Burmese Days* (1935), and Christine Weston and Philip Mason came close enough to Forster's achievement to earn a permanent place in Raj fiction. Their respective novels, *Indigo* (1943) and *The Wild Sweet Witch* (1947), are accordingly included in this volume.

Forster is the novelist of human decency. What matters most to him is how people behave with one another. He is anti-Raj, not because imperialism leads to economic exploitation but because it destroys human relations—it creates barriers that make friendship impossible. Two years prior to the publication of his masterpiece he had written in *The Nation and the Athenaeum*, 'Never in history did ill-breeding contribute so much towards the dissolution of an Empire.' *A Passage to India* bears this out. When Ronny, the City Magistrate, tells his mother that he is in India to do a difficult job and not to be pleasant, Forster observes:

His words without his voice might have impressed her [Ronny's mother], but when she heard the self-satisfying lilt of them, when she saw the mouth moving so complacently and competently beneath the little red nose, she felt, quite illogically, that this was not the last word on India. One touch of regret—not the canny substitute but the true regret from the heart—would have made him a different man, and the British Empire a different institution.

*A Passage to India* is a highly complex novel. The relationship between Aziz and Fielding is undoubtedly influenced by the prevailing political conditions, but it is also influenced by a host of smaller conflicts within each character of which they are but dimly aware. Would Indian freedom alone bring in the promised friendship between the two people? There is no clear answer to this. Political freedom is the first prerequisite to friendship between people, but it is not all. There are other issues as well—cultural and racial—of which Forster is well aware. The novel ends on a note of qualified optimism.

*Burmese Days* (1934) also has the relationship between the rulers and the natives as one of its primary themes. In an essay titled 'Why I Write', Orwell said, 'I write . . . because there is some lie I want to expose, some fact to which I want to draw attention, and my initial concern is to get a hearing.' It is in the light of this statement that *Burmese Days* should be approached. The lie he wants to expose is the fallacy of the 'White Man's Burden' as popularized by Kipling. The white man's burden, as Orwell sees it, is simply greed for self-enrichment in the guise of civilizing the world. The fact to which Orwell wants to draw attention is the evil of imperialism as manifest in the Raj with all its accompanying immorality, hypocrisy, injustice, and economic exploitation. No real friendship is possible between the oppressor and the oppressed; besides, the oppressor in exercising his power destroys his own freedom. Colonization is self destructive—there is not a white character in the novel who emerges unscathed.

Orwell's admission that his initial concern is to get a hearing accounts for the crystal clarity of his writing. He does not concern himself with 'mysteries' or 'muddles' as Forster does nor leave them for his readers to resolve. In *Burmese Days* there are no ever-deepening caves, no 'bou-oum' or self-generating echoes. There is Burma, the country itself, dark, sinister, mysterious, but as vividly sketched as its judicial representative—the rascal U Po Kyin. There are the whites, less than a dozen, etched in fine detail and completely distinct from one another. Each of them represents a type who came out to India: from soldiers to civil administrators to merchants to missionaries. The preciseness of language and certainty of mind, coupled with Orwell's hatred of imperialism, make this novel the single most explosive attack on the Raj.

It should, however, be borne in mind that Orwell's anti-Raj stance does not stem from his love of either the Burmese or the Indians. Like the pro-Raj writers, he is primarily concerned with the effect of British rule on the British themselves. Kipling and Maud Diver felt that the Empire was valuable chiefly in that it provided the British with an opportunity for self-development and brought out the best qualities in them. Orwell and, to a lesser degree, Leonard Woolf, felt that the Empire was evil, for among other things it debased the British character. Neither group (with the exception of Forster and Edward Thompson) was interested in Indians for their own sake. It is therefore not surprising that those who opposed the Raj did not necessarily show Indians as being any better than those who supported the Raj. Only in the third period, when the end of the Raj was in sight, were Indians generally shown in a better light.

\* \* \* \*

The Era of Melancholy, the third and last period of the Raj, covers only some twelve years, from 1935 to 1947. A good slice of this was taken up by World War II when very little fiction was published in Britain. Old Raj hands such as F.E. Penny and E.W. Savi, who had begun their writing careers in The Era of Confidence, continued to write their second-rate romances, with occasional swipes at the Indian nationalists and the freedom movement. They sailed through The Era of Doubt into The Era of Melancholy with unconcealed indifference to the changing world around them, producing between them over a hundred novels of which not even one is read today. It is not surprising that impatient critics dismiss Anglo-Indian fiction, apart from Kipling, Forster, Orwell, and a couple of others, as worthless. This is certainly not the case, as this anthology shows.

In this Era, no new themes were introduced, but there is an expansion of certain themes that had already been present in The Era of Doubt. The introduction of the Government of India Act of 1935 (allowing a federal structure with popular responsible government in the provinces) made it all too clear that the Empire was coming to an end. It profoundly affected the attitude of the rulers, and the need for friendship and understanding with the Indians took added importance. Thompson's *The End of the Hour* (1938), Rumer Godden's *Breakfast with the Nikolides* (1942), and the much later *Kingfishers Catch Fire* (1953) bear testimony to this. Even the imperialist John Masters bitterly admitted the need for a change of heart. Writing about the Mutiny in *Nightrunners of Bengal*, four years after Independence, Masters said that the cycle of hatred then existing between the British and the Indians could have only been broken by love, 'and there was no love'. The notion that the Empire might have lasted longer had the British treated the Indians with affection is an oversimplification. It fails to recognize the determination on the part of educated Indians to run their own affairs. The British failure to recognize this longing for self-rule has much to do with their portrayal of Indian nationalists as self-seekers.

Any new development that took place in The Era of Melancholy owed itself to the realization that the British rule in India had run its course. It mattered little whether one was pro-Raj or anti-Raj, since the Raj would soon be a matter of the past. A certain sadness of spirit gripped writers as they looked within themselves to see what had gone wrong. Self-examination led to self-censure, and India gathered about itself a new attractiveness (sentimental perhaps) that Anglo-Indian writers had not known before. England no longer seemed the home they wanted to return to, and a free India was unlikely to welcome them. They found themselves tossed between two worlds and belonging to neither. Their predicament reminded them of the Eurasians who also, though for a different reason, found themselves devoid of a country and a home. A fresh look at the Eurasian after years of thoughtless abuse became imminent.

The Eurasian community had seen better days in the times of the lavish, earthy nabobs of the early eighteenth century. Anglo-native alliances were then taken for granted and the children accepted as the natural by-product of a prosperous Empire. But this process gradually began to erode so that by the time the British Parliament took over administration of the country from John's Company in 1858, concubinage between the two races was strongly resented and the offspring of such alliance treated with scorn. It became fashionable with writers to present the Eurasian community unfavourably. Even some of the titles, such as Irene Burn's *The Border Line* (1916) and E.W. Savi's *Neither Fish Nor Fowl* (1924) speak of the Eurasian's unenviable situation in life. The community was supposed to have imbibed the worst traits of both races, the Europeans and the Indians, and its members were frequently referred to as 'blackie-whites'. The men were shown to lack moral fibre; they were drawn as obsequious and ingratiating towards the English and contemptuous towards the pure Indians. The Eurasian women were admittedly beautiful, but passionate and unscrupulous and always manoeuvring to capture an Englishman for a husband. So strong was the prejudice against this community that even the anti-Raj humanist George Orwell reserved his most bitter scorn for the two Eurasians, Francis and Samuel, in *Burmese Days*. 'It's perfectly vile', wrote Edward Thompson in *An Indian Day*, 'the way we have treated the Eurasian. We brought them into existence, and then we tread them underfoot and despise them.'

The Eurasians that appear in the fiction of this period are still stereotyped, but there is an attempt to understand the complexity of their situation. One of the earlier novels to do so was Miss Tennyson

Jesse's *The Lacquer Lady* (1929); among the later are Rumer Godden's *The Lady and the Unicorn* (1937), and to a lesser degree Louis Bromfield's *The Rains Came* (1937) and Joseph Hitrec's *Son of the Moon* (1948). John Masters' *Bhowani Junction* (1954), set in the time of the transfer of power, is perhaps the deepest study of the Eurasian psyche. It deals with the pretensions of a people who look on England as their home and despise India and the Indians. In the political climate of the Raj this attitude is not wholly surprising. Masters brings out, with sympathy and understanding, the bitterness they feel, and the injustice of the ridicule to which they have been subjected. That the best novel on the Eurasian should have been written by an imperialist is not surprising, for the Eurasian was an imperial creation.

As time to hand over power to the Indians approached, the British attitude towards the Hindus and the nationalists went through a radical change. With a Hindu-Muslim ratio of three to one, it was apparent that the successor government would be made up mostly of Hindus. Readjusting the perception of the Hindus in the light of the new political situation became necessary. Until now the Muslims were preferred to the Hindus, partly because of the similarity between Christianity and Islam and partly because they came to India, like the British themselves, as a conquering people. The Muslims were also thought to be more manly and more trustworthy. On the other hand, the Hindus, and specially the Bengalis, were viewed as effete, trouble-makers and idolators with their hybrid caste system. This view persisted in Anglo-Indian fiction until almost the time of Edward Thompson who, in his portrayal of the magistrate Kamalakanta Neogyi and Sadhu Jayananda in *An Indian Day*, did much to correct the imbalance. But it was left to the writers of this period, specially the Godden sisters, to popularize Hindu beliefs and spirituality. Rumer Godden in *The River* (1946) tries to capture the timelessness which is the essence of Hinduism, and Jon Godden in *The Seven Islands* (1950) awakens the readers' respect for the Hindu through her narration of a priest's devotion and sacrifice.

Much to the chagrin of the rulers, the nationalists could no longer be dismissed as cowardly rabble-rousers, bent on spreading disaffection among people for personal advancement. The India Act of 1935 had already approved of a future Indian Federation, and the 1937 elections had brought Indian government into the provinces. Except for a few conservative Englishmen who thought the Empire would somehow find a way to survive, it was an accepted fact that its end was in sight. To continue showing the nationalist as selfish and cowardly was not only false, but it served no immediate British purpose. Thus for the first time we are presented with nationalists who are also patriots, however mistaken they might be in their goal and methods. The stereotypical nationalists conceived earlier continued to appear in the novels but they were now joined, if not replaced, by a better breed of men. The leadership and personality of Mahatma Gandhi, Jawaharlal Nehru, and Maulana Azad had much to do with the new face given to nationalists. Gandhi had already entered fiction as a character in Candler's *Abdication* and Thompson's *A Farewell to India* and had been mentioned by name in many others. Though often found fault with by the defenders of the Raj, Gandhi's integrity and courage had rarely been questioned. It is integrity and courage, in the midst of human failings, that define nationalists in the better novels of this period—in Christine Weston's *Indigo* and Philip Mason's *The Wild Sweet Witch*.

## On the Face of the Waters

*On the Face of the Waters* has been hailed by critics as one of the best novels dealing with the Indian Mutiny, and the Mutiny itself—to use a phrase of Flora Annie Steel—as 'an epic of the [British] race'. A century or more has passed since these two claims were first made. Today, in the light of the facts available and our more sober perception of events, few would bestow epic dimensions on the Mutiny. But *On the Face of the Waters* still holds a dominant position among the eighty or so novels reputed to have been written on the Mutiny during the Raj. Long out of print, its chief competitors are novels written since 1947 by English men and women: John Masters' *Night Runners of Bengal*, M.M. Kaye's *Shadow of the Moon* (1957), Valerie Fitzgerald's *Zemindar,* and, more importantly, J.G. Farrell's *The Siege of Krishnapur* which won its author the Booker Prize. These novels depict events with far greater objectivity than those written during the Raj, though they continue to present the story from the British perspective with a Briton as the central character. This is understandable. What is surprising is that, apart from Manohar Malgonkar's *The Devil's Wind* (1972), there has been no rendering of the Mutiny by Indian writers in English, even though it has now been enshrined by academic historians like V.D. Savarkar and Nandalal Chatterji as India's 'First War of Independence'. The reason may be that many people still look on the Mutiny as a British phenomenon displaying British heroism, while on the Indian side there are few known heroes besides the Rani of Jhansi and Tantia Tope whom the British have done much to denigrate.

A few words on the Mutiny may not be out of place here, even though Steel provides us in her novel an impartial account of the events that led up to the rebellion and its aftermath in Delhi. Discontent and disillusionment with British policy with regard to the annexation of territories, the mistreatment of sepoys, the disrespect for popular and religious sentiments were simmering in the Indian people long before 1857. What signalled the revolt was the issuing of new cartridges supposed to have been greased with cow and pig fat (the cow being sacred to the Hindus and the pig impure to the Muslims). The paper end of the cartridges had to be bitten before use, thus making it seem to both Hindu and Muslim sepoys that they were being forced to commit sacrilege. The first shot in protest was fired on 29 March at Barrackpore by a sepoy, Mangal Pande, at his adjutant. Pande missed his target and was hanged the next day, but his name became legendary and was simultaneously honoured and despised. The Indians looked on him as a hero while the British held him in derision and began calling all mutineers 'Pandis'.

The next important event of the Mutiny took place at Meerut on 10 May. The sepoys at the station rose in support of eighty-five of their comrades who had earlier been court-martialled and humiliated for refusing to accept the new cartridges. The rebel sepoys set fire to the cantonment and carried out indiscriminate looting and killing. They freed their eighty-five comrades from prison, and the next day marched to Delhi. In Delhi, they repeated their vicious killing of the Europeans, and then forced their way into the palace. They acknowledged the feeble Bahadur Shah as Emperor and made him their symbol and focus of revolt. By June the rebellion had spread to Cawnpore, the scene of some of the most heinous crimes committed during the Mutiny. Nana Sahib, the arch villain to the British mind, offered the besieged English safe passage to Allahabad and then reneged, occasioning a slaughter that included many women and children. Other well-known sieges were those of Lucknow, Jhansi, and Gwalior and these, along with those of Delhi and Cawnpore, provide the plot or setting for almost all the Mutiny novels.

Though vastly outnumbered, the British were able to defeat the mutineers by their tenacity and superior military strategy. Thus far it is a British epic and there is much grandeur in it. But the swiftness and ferocity with which retribution followed make it one of the darkest chapters in British imperial history. They inflicted on their defeated foe, and often on innocent civilians, the very horror that had been their lot, and more. Shamshul Islam provides in his *Chronicles of the Raj* (1979) a spectacular account of violence of a kind also recorded by historians and diarists:

> While rebel sepoys were blown to death from the mouth of the cannons, civilians were hanged on a mass scale. There was hardly a tree without a corpse hanging on its branches; volunteer hanging parties went out into the districts, and amateur executioners found delight in finishing the Indians off 'in an artistic manner' such as the figure of eight—these executions were known as 'Colonel Neill's hangings'.

So strong was the feeling of hate that savagery such as this was accepted as rightful revenge. But with revenge went an arrogance focused on teaching the Indians a lesson that they would not easily forget. It was similar arrogance that led General Dyer to fire on an un-armed crowd of 5000 at Jallianwala Bagh in 1919, killing and woun-ding some 1500 people. British rule had to be maintained, and to the rulers of the day there seemed no better way than to strike terror in the hearts of potential rebels.

Long after the last rebel sepoy had vanished, the cry for revenge lingered on in the British and Indian presses. The relationship bet-ween the British and the Indians reached a new low as stories of Indian atrocities gained circulation—especially those of the raping of European women by the mutineers. The rape charges were largely unfounded, as the distinguished historian Sir George Otto Trevelyan argued in *Cawnpore* (1865), but they became a fixity in the minds of the British in India. So too in the minds of the early Mutiny fiction writers who, while claiming historical accuracy, contradicted the facts as recorded by their own historians. Novel after novel was strung out on the rape—or near rape—of white women by Indians. The theme suited the British notion of the mutineers as barbarians and themselves as saviours, and it helped legitimize some of their vindictive behaviour towards their enemy. Self-induced as much of the fear was, it was genuinely believed and became in time a part of the total British recorded experience in India. Forster's *A Passage to India* and Paul Scott's *The Raj Quartet* bear this out. In Orwell's *Burmese Days*, Mrs Lackersteen's nightmare of 'being raped by a procession of jet-black coolies with rolling white eyeballs', though ill-founded, was not an uncommon fear among European women in India.

The Mutiny led to a spate of novels cast in the form of chivalric romances, starting with Edward Money's *The Wife and the Ward, or A Life's Error* (1859). By the time Queen Victoria was crowned Empress of India in 1878, Mutiny fiction was well on its way to becoming an accepted literary sub-genre. At the turn of the century there was a solid body of fictional and historical writing on the subject. The early novels were mostly by people who had witnessed or participated in quelling the uprising, while the later novels were by writers who claimed to have assiduously studied the facts surrounding the Mutiny. In both cases, the resultant portraits were gory and sensational, or, to put it in the words of one critic, 'a technicolor nightmare'. The authors' intent, too, with rare exceptions such as Meadows Taylor's *Seeta* (1872), remained much the same: to show British heroism in the face of Indian treachery and deceit.

With the writer's sympathy established firmly on the side of his own people and his perception of the mutineers unaltered, his ingenuity is seriously curtailed. Though the love story in the novel may be his own invention, he feels compelled to observe the stereotypical patterning which the genre of chivalric romance demands. There are also the political demands imposed by Anglo-India, in which racism plays no small part. Thus all too often we have a white woman in distress, a black or brown villain, and a white hero. The action is predetermined: the woman has to be rescued, the villain punished, the hero rewarded—possibly with a wife or a V.C. (Victoria Cross), or both. It would not be idle to speculate how many V.C.s were handed out for courage in Mutiny novels during the period of the Raj. One of the recipients was Major Herbert Erlton in Steel's *On the Face of the Waters*, a hero without the flamboyance we have come to associate with chivalric romances.

At the outbreak of the Indian Mutiny in 1857, Flora Annie Steel was living at Burnside, Scotland, with her family. Stories of the horrors committed by the mutineers spread throughout Great Britain and the call for revenge penetrated even the nurseries and the school rooms. Flora, a mere child of ten, 'burnt and hanged and tortured the Nana Sahib in effigy many times'. Forty years later, she was to write what remains to this day one of the most engaging novels on the Mutiny.

*On the Face of the Waters* is planned and structured with great care. It is divided into five books of more or less equal length. Each book has six chapters, except for Book II which has seven. Book I opens with the words 'Going! Going! Gone!' in Lucknow in March 1856, fourteen months before the start of the Mutiny. The deposed King of Oude's menagerie is being auctioned, and among the spectators are Major Erlton and his mistress Alice Gissing. It is not long before we meet the Major's wife, Kate, and a cashiered soldier and adventurer, Jim Douglas. These four are the principal British characters of the novel, and Steel's purpose is to show through them the insular and unenviable life the British live in India. They are, as she is to remind us later in the novel, 'strangers and exiles', cut off from their homeland by distance and from India by race and culture. They have little understanding of or communication with the people they govern, a fact not to be underestimated while looking for causes that led to the Mutiny.

Book II transplants us to Delhi, six months later. Each of the first five chapters is structured so as to provide five distinct portraits of Delhi and its surroundings—the Palace, the City, the Ridge, the Village, and the Residency. Steel's descriptions of the ornate fort palace, the Emperor deprived of all regality save his high-sounding honorifics, the ambitious Queen promising her octogenarian husband yet another heir (he has already fathered sixty!), the scores of scheming courtiers and idle followers, all are presented with a fine irony. Equally compelling is her portrayal of the city where some of the Muslim nobility dwell, rich in idleness and dreams but short on cash. But it is her recollection of the Delhi Ridge, 'not unlike some huge spiny saurian, basking in the sunlight', that sends Steel into raptures of praise for the finest record of English 'pluck and perseverance the world is ever likely to see'. The book ends with the sepoys in Meerut, a garrison town forty miles north of Delhi, spurred to premature action by a harlot's sneer: 'We of the bazaar kiss no cowards'. Women's taunts play a determining role in this novel. It is Alice Gissing's laugh of derision that prompts Major Erlton to pay fifty rupees for a useless cockatoo; it is Queen Zeenat Maihl's scornful defiance that puts courage into the dithering crowd; and it is Tara's taunt that hastens Kate Erlton to the bedside of the ailing Jim Douglas.

In Book III, the events following the uprising in Meerut are funnelled into a single day as the mutineers arrive in Delhi and hail Bahadur Shah as their leader. The six chapters are divided into Night, Dawn, Daylight, Noon, Sunset, and Dusk, a brilliant device to crystallize and give shape to the chaos and disorder immediately following the uprising. The Book acts as a summing up of what has preceded it and portends what is to come. Books IV and V deal with the English struggle to regain Delhi, the outcome of which is never in doubt. The arrival of John Nicholson on the scene provides the English with the leadership they had lacked, and Delhi is taken. But Nicholson himself is fatally wounded and the novel ends with his exhortation to his soldiers, 'Come on, men! Come on!' The words hark back to the opening words of the novel, 'Going! Going! Gone!'. Both the opening and the concluding words are highly symbolic: the former signifying the end of a feudal and decadent era, the latter opening up a new horizon for the Raj.

Flora Annie Steel's handling of characters is no less adroit than
her handling of the plot. All her major characters are rounded, and
though they may share the same traits, no two characters are alike.
For instance, both Jim Douglas and Major Erlton are gamblers and
lack probity. But here the similarities end, for the two are as different
in their attitudes towards women and the native population as they
are in their appearances. Even minor characters are sharply individualized, be it the unwieldy figure of Mahboob Ali, Chief Eunuch and
Prime Minister, or Ahsan-Oolah, the philosopher physician with a
passion for gold, or Hussan Askuri, the priest and miracle monger
who leads 'the last of the Moghuls [Bahadur Shah] by the nose'.
Only the Hindu widow, Tara, with her unrequited love for Douglas,
seems to be lacking in complexity. A reason for this may be that
Steel wants to uphold the commonly held Anglo-Indian notion that
an Indian woman is a sensual and emotional creature whose single-
minded devotion to the man she loves—especially if he be a
Westerner—is fraught with danger. Had Steel depicted Tara as
Douglas's lover or mistress, she might have been a more attractive
character than the forlorn and envious woman she is shown to be.
But this Steel could not do, for she was adamantly against marriage
and concubinage between the two races. Douglas had already erred
once in having an Indian mistress, Zora, and Steel could not permit
her hero to err a second time.

Of the four British characters, three are shown as dissolute when
we first make their acquaintance. But as so often in Anglo-Indian
fiction, characters under the stress of a great moment rise above
their frailties to meet a common challenge. At the end of the day, like
the ordinary folk in W.B. Yeats's 'Easter', they are 'changed, changed
utterly'. There is Major Erlton involved in a passionate liaison with
Alice Gissing, for whose sake he has already destroyed his marriage
and is now prepared to wreck his military career. There is Alice
Gissing, the vibrant and seductive young wife of a military contractor.
She has been married twice, the first time to a man for his good
looks and the second time to a man for his money, and she is quite
ready for a third wedding. There is Jim Douglas, an ex-jockey and
horse trader now spying for the English, who is unsure of what he
wants from life. The Mutiny changes their lives completely and
brings out in each a goodness we had least suspected. A sense of
duty reasserts itself in Major Erlton and he dies fighting (the death of
Alice, no doubt, being a contributing factor). Alice Gissing, who has
buried her own child and no longer cares for children, gives her life
protecting a neighbour's child. And Jim Douglas, much as he

wanted to see action in battle, foregoes his dreams in order to offer protection to the wife of a man he does not respect. Douglas's sacrifice is the greatest of all. The safety of their women and children was foremost in the British mind throughout their stay in India. It was the protection of women and children that hampered them in their initial fight with the mutineers; it was the massacre of women and children by the mutineers that broke all restraint and led them to savage rebuttal.

'I honestly like my hero, Jim Douglas', wrote Steel in her autobiography *The Garden of Fidelity* (1929). And she endows him with a virtue which she considered to be most important in any man: 'never to hold his tongue regarding error'. Thus through Douglas she voices many of her own strong opinions on both the rulers and the ruled. That he is unconventional, has kept an Indian mistress, and moves freely among all shades of Indians make his criticism of the natives seem unprejudiced. On the other hand, that he is British by birth and upbringing gives him the right to censure his own people for obvious misdemeanours. His opposite number on the female side is the Bohemian Alice Gissing, and it is a pity that the two never come in close contact. Alice, with her zest for life, stands in sharp contrast to Kate Erlton, who in her person reveals many of the hardships of Anglo-Indian women in India. The meeting of the two women over who should possess Major Erlton makes spirited reading. Moments later, Alice dies at the hands of a fanatic. The first victim of the Mutiny, Alice is also a major loss to the novel. Her early death deprives the book of its most fascinating character and leaves the reader wondering what shape the human drama might have taken had she lived. If Steel were not so committed to historical accuracy, she might have brought about a confrontation between the two most lively and notorious characters in the novel—Alice Gissing and Prince Abool-Bukr. The result would not have been disappointing.

Steel claims that her account of 'the sham court of Delhi' and its 'picturesque group of schemers and dupes' is presented without 'a single touch of fancy'. If this sounds somewhat of an exaggeration, Daya Patwardhan's patiently researched study of the novelist, *A Star of India* (1963), shows that much of Steel's boast finds support in published diaries and historical records. While preparing to write the novel, Steel visited the homes of the descendents of Bahadur Shah in Delhi, and it was here that she designed her four historical studies 'on the most royal dynasty the world has ever seen'. Her deep-rooted fascination with the Moguls enables her to portray the octogenarian Emperor with all his foibles and yet allows him to retain a good measure of sympathy. Superstitious, vacillating, feeble beyond his apparent years, he has not lost all his dreams of an empire. He composes couplets, even as Nero fiddled while Rome burnt, and insists on decorum from his tawdry court. He is surrounded by intriguers, but none so clever as his chief queen, Zeenut Maihl, who wants her son Jewan Bakht recognized as the heir-apparent. A restless contriver, the queen is, in Steel's words, a 'mixture of personal ambition for her son, and real patriotism for her country'. But this 'real patriotism' is never brought to the forefront; we are still decades away from the British admitting the existence of anything like a true Indian patriot.

Among the chief claimants to the throne is the profligate Prince Mirza Abool-Bukr. He lacks ambition and is 'content to be the best musician in Delhi, the boldest gambler, the fastest liver'. He is certainly the last as he reels around in a drunken stupor, singing lewd songs and swearing to kill all the infidels. His guardian angel is his aunt, the widowed Newâsi Begum, who has left the palace to live austerely in the city. She works tirelessly to bring order into her nephew's dishevelled life, and collapses in a dead faint when he is betrayed and murdered by the English. She is the most endearing character in the book, though like the other Indian characters she shows no real development. The charm of the characters of the 'sham court at Delhi' lies in their ability to resist development, to maintain against all odds their original form and shape. And Steel presents this defiance of change, the dreaming of the old dream, as the cause for the end of the Mogul empire.

In the 'Author's Note', Steel tells us that 'the reader may rest assured that every incident bearing in the remotest degree on the Indian Mutiny, or on the part which real men took in it, is scrupulously exact, even to the date, the hour, the scene, the weather. Nor have I allowed the actual actors in the great tragedy to say a word regarding it which is not to be found in the account of eyewitnesses, or in their own writings.'

The novel was the result of painstaking research the author had conducted in India. Despite a couple of minor slips that are of little consequence, reviewers and critics were unanimous in praising Steel for her accurate portrayal of historical events. Some readers may, however, feel that in adhering too closely to the events of history, she may have lost something in the way of artistry. In the first half of the novel, human interest is well maintained, but in the latter half Steel's fidelity to historical details (such as providing the hour, the date, the very weather) seems to take the forefront. The characters are not forgotten: they are all there, but they seem to have lost some of their magic. Steel's inclusion of a dozen footnotes to convince us of her historical accuracy, and the presence of two appendices, do not add to our enjoyment.

One may well ask what constitutes historical accuracy. Is it simply an objective presentation of events as seen by an outsider? Steel's accounts of the various events of the Mutiny are certainly accurate, but the same cannot be said when it comes to assessing the people and motives that underlie the events. Benita Perry reminds us in *Delusions and Discoveries* that Steel, after having provided good reasons for the rebellion, abandons them and treats the uprising 'as an aimless and meaningless explosion, a reversion to barbarism, a contest between forces of light and powers of darkness.' She refers to the rebel sepoys as 'murderers' and the civilians who follow them as 'rabble and refuse'. Terms such as 'courage', 'bravery', 'pluck', 'perseverence', are reserved solely for the English, and the word 'revenge' is elevated to sound almost like a creed. In one place Steel tells us of a battle where the Indians lost more than a thousand men, the English but one. Factual as that may be, she does not tell us that many on the Indian side were armed with primitive weapons like swords, spears, pickaxes, and spades. Professor Hira Lal Gupta in his article 'The Revolt of 1857 and Its Failure' cites the lack of weaponry as the most important cause of the failure of the Mutiny.

Excepting Edward Thompson, no Anglo-Indian writer worked harder than Flora Annie Steel to know India and its people. She made numerous friends among Indians, and towards the end of her stay was referred to as *Madr Mihr-ban* (Mother of Mercy). Yet all this must not blind us to the facts that she was steeped in British imperial pride, and that she was an elitist who believed 'that the best form of Government is a beneficient Autocracy'. She could not understand the Indian aspiration for freedom, and through her spokesperson, Douglas, calls the mutineers 'children—simple, ignorant, obstinate'. Here, too, she may claim to be following history closely, for the noted historian of the period William Henry Fitchett attributed the uprising to the mutinous state of mind of people who 'had the petulance and the ignorance of children'. Besides, there is also the oft-quoted phrase of Kipling—'Half devil and half child'—to support her characterization of Indians.

It is to Mrs Steel's credit that despite her belief that there is no effective substitute for British rule in India, she makes no excuses for the failure of the rulers and the part they played in bringing about the Mutiny. The causes of the Mutiny were manifold, not the least being British arrogance, greed, and self-complacency. She brings this out in the opening scene of the novel where the King of Oude's property is being auctioned with no regard for Indian feelings:

The King, for some unsatisfactory reason, had been ousted from his own. His goods and chattels were being sold. The valuable ones had been knocked down for a mere song—just to keep up the farce of sale—to the *Huzoors*. The rubbish—lame elephants and such like—was being sold to them [the public]; more or less against their will, since who could forbear bidding sixpence for a whole leviathan?

Among the rubbish is a cockatoo for which Major Erlton offers fifty rupees just to outbid a native, and then walks away with the bird without paying for it. Mrs Kate Erlton's carriage, too, has been bought at an auction, and the best of the British households have been refurbished with plundered goods. The Residency, 'the prettiest place in Delhi', is bursting in splendour with looted goods that 'belonged to some potentate or another, dead, banished, or annexed'. But it is the self-complacency of the rulers of which Steel is most critical. She blames them for ignoring Indian sensibilities and mindlessly provoking the soldiers to the point of revolt. The notion that the sepoys would never mutiny against their officers shows the extent to which the rulers had lost touch with the country they governed.

*On the Face of the Waters* should not be read simply as history in fictional form. Nor should it be read to determine how fair or unfair its author has been to the Indian cause. It should be read, first and foremost, as a work of art. Few can miss Steel's immense power of observation and her ability to paint pictures in every shade and colour, be it the quiet of the countryside, the hustle and bustle of the Palace, the colours and smells of the city, or the din and noise of battle. Though writing of war, she sees no glory in violence (despite her adulation of John Nicholson) and stands for the sanctity of all living things. This is brought out in a touching little scene in Book II. Close to a village, the English have arranged a hunt. A girl is worried about the safety of her pet:

'Think you they will come our way and kill our deer as they did once?' asked a slender slip of a girl anxiously. Her tame fawn had lately taken to joining the wild ones when they came at dawn to feed upon the wheat.
'God knows,' replied one beside her. 'They will come if they like, and kill if they like. Are they not the masters?'

In these artless words there is severe censure of the British in India; in these words lie also the germ of what led to the Mutiny.

## SIRI RAM—REVOLUTIONIST

Though the Mutiny was crushed and the perpetrators hanged in large numbers to make an example of them, the invulnerability of the Raj could no longer be taken for granted. The growing insecurity of the rulers began to be reflected in the novelists' portrayal of the nationalist. Edmond Candler, in *Siri Ram—Revolutionist: A Transcript from Life, 1907–1910*, was among the first to depict a nationalist as a serious threat to contend with. A possible challenge to British rule draws from Skene, Principal of Gandeshwar College and the author's *alter ego*, the following comments: 'The country is ours after all, and we won it as fairly as countries ever have been won. There is no question of handing it over. When the Indians are strong enough to govern it, they will be strong enough to take it, and they won't ask us.'

The notion that 'the country is ours' has been expressed by other imperialist writers like Maud Diver and John Masters and is at the root of the British dislike of the nationalist. During Kipling's time the nationalist was ignored in Anglo-Indian fiction and there was seemingly no discussion of him outside Kipling's own story, 'The Enlightenment of Pagett, M.P'. Later, he was dismissed as not being representative of the real India, the argument being that the average Indian had no use for him and wanted the British to rule them. When that stand became no longer defensible, and the nationalist had made his presence felt unmistakably, he was portrayed in an unfriendly light. At his best he was shown as a vain and foolish young man exploited by minds sharper than his own. At his worst he was a criminal and a seditionist trying to oust a legitimate and benign government. So strong was the prejudice that even the most saintly of nationalist leaders, Mohandas Karamchand Gandhi, did not escape unscathed. Maud Diver in *The Singer Passes* (1934) suggests that he is in the pay of wealthy Indians, and Kathrine Mayo in her short story 'The Widow' castigates Gandhi for hypocrisy, for 'spreading hatred and destruction while preaching non-violence'. John Rivett-Carnac of the Indian Police is quoted in *Plain Tales from the Raj* (1975) as saying, 'I never allowed anyone to shout Gandhi without giving him six on the bottom with a stick.' Such sentiments explain why Gandhi succeeded and Rivett-Carnac and his kind had to say goodbye to the Raj.

Candler portrays Siri Ram as a weak and excitable village lad who is exhilarated by nationalist propaganda. His dream of glory and martyrdom make him an easy tool in the hands of the conspirators. Soon after he is expelled from college for an anti-British speech, he is flattered into accepting the position of a 'scapegoat prison-editor', that is, taking on the responsibility for a seditious issue of a paper prepared by others. He is sentenced to two years rigorous imprisonment. On his release, his flagging loyalties are once more aroused by his cunning comrades who work behind the scenes. He is feted and feasted and given the 'honour' of shooting Merivale, the District Magistrate who had earlier convicted him. He is assured that the assassination will ignite a countrywide revolution against the British and that his victorious friends will come and free him from jail. Siri Ram kills Merivale, and in turn is sentenced to death. In prison, he waits for words of the promised revolution and, despairing, takes poison. A storm that had been gathering outside spends itself in a few drops of rain, an apt symbol of Siri Ram and his futile crusade against the British.

The novel is subtitled *A Transcript from Life, 1907–1910* and deals with the violence that followed the partitioning of Bengal by Lord Curzon in 1905. Candler was at this time Principal of Mohindra College in the princely state of Patiala (in the Punjab), and he draws on his own knowledge of the secret societies in which students were active. Some of the characters and incidents are taken from real life, and a reading of Valentine Chirol's *Indian Unrest* (1910) shows how close to the facts this novel is. Merivale is based on the Collector of Nasik, affectionately called 'Pundit' Jackson, who was, like Merivale, shot dead on the eve of his departure. Merivale is presented with a laudatory poem called 'Valedictory Verses', very much as Jackson is presented with an ode written in Marathi at a reception organized to bid him farewell. Merivale's murderer, Siri Ram, has distinct affinities with Jackson's murderer, Anant Lakshman Kanhare. Chirol describes Kanhare as the product 'both of the Western education which we [the British] have imported into India and of the religious revivalism which underlies the present political agitation.' And this is exactly how Candler views Siri Ram. Swami Narasimha has a good deal of the magnetism of Bal Gangadhar Tilak, Father of Indian Unrest. But Tilak was not an anarchist as Narasimha is portrayed to be, though he did espouse extreme measures to drive out the English and restore the glories of Hindu India. Tilak's paper, *Kesari*, like the *Kali Yuga* in the novel, published inflammatory articles for which Tilak himself was more than once convicted and imprisoned. *Siri Ram—Revolutionist*, though set in the Punjab, attempts to chronicle the nationalist uprisings in Bengal and the Deccan during the years 1907–10.

The novel aims to show how simple and thoughtless young men were skilfully recruited by seditionists to perform acts of terrorism. Siri Ram has all the prerequisites for the job. He is discontented, ill-educated, and given to fantasies of grandeur. Proud to be called a 'political missionary', he is readily taken in by demagogy of the kind he finds in pamphlets given to him by the Swami: 'There was no crime which the English had not inflicted upon his Motherland, no indignity which his people had not suffered at their hands.' The Swami perceives him as 'a tool that needed careful sharpening, and one easily blunted. . . .' Mohan Roy, one of the Swami's trusted lieutenants, sums up Siri Ram even better: ' "He is a goat," he said to the Swami. "He may be useful for a sacrifice, but you will have to lead him right up to the altar." ' Cruel words, but nonetheless true.

Siri Ram has at least one merit: he stands his trial manfully and does not give away any of the conspirators. He is, as the author puts it ironically, 'a most competent scapegoat'. But most of the other revolutionaries lack even this negative virtue. Banarsi Das is described as 'a vain, meddling, town-bred youth, superficially cocksure and alert, inwardly dense as the mud of Mograon'. Ramji Das, the secretary of a political organization masquerading as the 'Students' Improvement Club', is a fat *bunnia* with 'three chins and three paunches'. Even though he has amassed a huge fortune under the protection of the British, he is now out to kill them. And there is Dr Hari Gopi, 'the moderate', who rejects the shedding of blood but accepts administering poison as a fair compromise. It is this wholesale derision that leads one to suspect that Candler is not being fair to the revolutionaries.

But he is not altogether unfair either. Candler's depiction of Swami Narasimha, though critical, is objective. Hobbs, Commander of a British Regiment, dubs him 'a mischievous agitator. A canting, hypocritical humbug.' There is some truth here. He has come from Bengal (the hotbed of seditionists), and under an assumed name is spreading disaffection among the people. His associates are members of the Arya Samaj, and he is using their rallying call 'Back to the Vedas' as ground-bait to captivate unthinking youth and poison them with hatred of the British. 'Sacrifice' is the keyword of his utterances, and he makes his exhortations doubly effective by astutely mingling politics with religion. ' "Sacrifice yourself to the shrine [of Kali]," he tells Siri Ram. "Without bloodshed, the worship of the Goddess cannot be accomplished." ' No Western reader can miss the

Christian imagery of purification by blood sacrifice placed in a pagan context.

There is, however, more to the Swami than Hobbs perceives. In the very opening of the novel he is presented as a fragile little man, 'a palpable ascetic', standing alone on a platform and holding his audience spellbound. As the story progresses, we learn something of his past: his personal magnetism, his erudition, the psychic force that led him to be lionized in the drawing rooms of Europe and America. A chance insult by an Englishman (as so often is the case in Anglo-Indian fiction) had set his dormant nationalism on fire. He returned home, says Candler, convinced 'that his people could not become regenerate until they were free, a much more dangerous doctrine than that they could not be free until they became regenerate.'

Aloof, remote, the Swami conducts a wide-ranging campaign against the British from his mountain hideout in the Himalayas. His doctrine is as simple as it is brutal: Englishmen must be sacrificed at the altar of Independence; Kali, the black goddess of death, must be appeased with 'a white goat'. What does it matter if a thousand Siri Rams were to die in the process? Disinterested reformers must die too, for they stem the tide. Narasimha, alas, is as hollow as Kurtz in Conrad's *Heart of Darkness* (1902). But unlike Kurtz, he has never looked into himself, never passed judgement on his own soul. And the reader's judgement of the Swami, despite the Swami's many accomplishments, must be severe. But for once the author remains absolved of any bias or predisposition. The character is completely convincing.

Apart from the distinction of introducing the nationalist in Anglo-Indian fiction in a major way, Candler is possibly among the first writers to bring the British Club into Anglo-Indian fiction. Orwell in *Burmese Days* describes the European Club as 'the spiritual citadel, the real seat of the British power, the Nirvana for which native officials and millionaires pine in vain'. The Club in Gandeshwar is nowhere near reaching this status, for Indian demands for membership became a major issue only in the late 1920s and early 1930s. Candler's Club is a place where the rulers can, so to speak, 'let their hair down', and plan strategies to keep the nationalists in check. It is a place their womenfolk frequent for lack of anything better. When Merivale returns to the Club from the plague-infested village, the card-loving Chaplain's wife accosts him:

'Why, it is Mr Merivale!' she gasped; 'where have you been all these months? Famine, wasn't it?'

Merivale explained that it was plague.

'But how romantic! Is it near here? And have they plague carts and red crosses on the doors? I suppose it is all dirt; clean people don't get it, do they?'

'We lost Captain Chauncey in the I.M.S.'

'But oh, how dreadful! He had to go near them, of course, hadn't he?'

The Englishwomen in India have been harshly portrayed by most male writers of the Raj. Whatever the reason, and there are a few that hold good, the portrayal is often as one-sided as that of the Indians themselves. We are told little or nothing of the thousands of women who came out to India and served the people as missionaries, nurses, and social workers. Their contribution was no less than that of the rulers, but it was one without glamour. And the Raj was glamorous.

Travel and adventure drew Candler to India in 1896. He decided on teaching as a career because it would provide him the leisure to write, and during his twenty years in the East he held various teaching positions in Bengal and the Punjab. But he never came to love India. In fact, the more he saw of violence (he lost his left hand during an affray in Tibet), the more he loved England 'for its physical and spiritual tranquillity'. But physical India stirred him sufficiently to draw from him some memorable portraits of the landscape. His short story 'Mecca', set in the swamps of Bengal, is a case in point; Siri Ram's long trek to Amarnath to see the Swami is another.

Though Candler came to view the Raj differently towards the end of his stay in India, his attitude towards Indians, that they were an inferior people, remained unchanged. Liberty, he believed, was for those who deserve it, and the Indians did not deserve it. In *Siri Ram—Revolutionist*, he came close to Kipling in his general distaste for most educated Indians, and in his admiration for the British rulers in India. He portrays the British men in India as upright and dedicated people who 'have always tried to do the straight and disinterested thing'. When plague sweeps through Siri Ram's village, Merivale and the English doctor, Chauncey, risk their lives to save the simple and devout people. Merivale carries Siri Ram's sister, Shiv Dai, in his own arms to the hospital after her father has abandoned her and Siri Ram is afraid to touch her for fear of contracting the disease. It is a favourite device of the pro-Raj writers to depict the British as more caring of the Indians than the Indians are of each other. In *The Great Amulet* (1908), Maud Diver shows an English master rushing to the aid of his *punkah* coolie who has been stricken by cholera, while the household servants stand and watch disapprovingly.

For all its pro-Raj biases, *Siri Ram—Revolutionist* is a landmark novel dealing with the first phase of Indian unrest following the Mutiny. With insight and objectivity, Candler has exposed the true nature of anarchism, though he may have failed to see the generous impulse behind the freedom movement. His novel firmly established Indian nationalism as a major theme in Anglo-Indian fiction, and since its publication there has not been a novel of significance that did not deal with Indian nationalism in one form or the other.

## INDIGO

Soon after reading *Indigo*, E.M. Forster wrote to Christine Weston: 'I enjoyed it very much. The reviewers were likely to compare us—they love comparisons for it means less work for them—but I think it is true that we have the same sort of feeling for India.'

What sort of feeling? It is the feeling of friendship and goodwill towards India that is common to Forster's *A Passage to India* and *Indigo* and not so much characters and incidents that reviewers have so diligently pointed out. Granted, Bertie Wood's experience in the Terai jungles approximates that of Adela Quested in Forster's Marabar Caves and Hardyal's conversion to nationalism has a strong resemblance to Aziz's own. Granted, too, the final message of both authors is the same, namely, that 'love never has and never will transcend politics . . . not until politics have broken down the barriers which transcend love'. But Weston's up-country civil station of Amritpore is very unlike Forster's Chandrapore. Here there is no European Club that plays a pivotal role as in *A Passage to India*, nor is there a tribe of particularly odious sahibs and memsahibs whom we meet in Forster's pages. There is only the canal engineer Aubrey Wall, who betrays the worst traits of the ruling class and, as one reviewer puts it, demonstrated in his person how 'the conqueror remains a thwarted exile in the house of the conquered'.

*Indigo* is set in the United Provinces where Christine Weston was born and where she spent the first nineteen years of her life. It opens at the turn of the twentieth century and closes soon after the start of World War I. Part I is almost entirely devoted to the coming of age of Jacques de St Remy and his attachment to two boys of his own age: John Macbeth, a classmate and the son of an English army colonel, and Hardyal, the son of a pro-British Hindu lawyer, soon to leave for England to study and to absorb English culture. There is also Mrs Lyttleton, the widow of a general in her seventies, who was once the mistress of Jacques' father, and who now holds the son in a complex emotional tie. There is the new arrival from England,

Macbeth's cousin Bertie Wood, whom Jacques proposes to marry. Battling against them all for Jacques' undivided attention is his domineering mother, Madame de St Remy, the owner of an indigo plantation. But for all her efforts, she comes in the end no closer to possessing him than when she first began.

In Part II, politics begins to put a strain on the friendships of youth, and in Part III irreparable damage is done. Hardyal returns from England but he is no longer the boy he was two years ago. Though still warm towards Jacques, he occasionally appears cold and aloof towards others. He has given up his 'Englishness' and is moving towards self-identity. His recognition of the courage and patriotism of Salim, an impoverished lawyer and family friend, kindles his own latent nationalistic impulses, but it is the reading of Wall's letter (which Hardyal had stolen from its owner) that delivers the final blow to Hardyal's serenity. The letter reveals not only Wall's murder of an innocent servant but his abysmal contempt for all Indians. Wall writes to Mrs Lyttleton:

There is, in me, something which makes it impossible to 'believe' in Indians. You have assured me fiercely that they are human beings, but I have known horses and dogs almost as human, and I have loved them better. You will resent this, you will hate me for saying it, but let me say it, for I must. I do not believe in Indians, I do not hold with the sentimentality of treating dark people as one treats even the lowest, the humblest white. I do not believe that there will ever be equality of races . . . between them and ourselves there can be only one relationship, the relationship of our mastery over them.

The reading of this letter is the turning point in Hardyal's life. This is shown not by anything he says or does, but in his quiet deference to the reactionary Salim. With Salim he attends a political rally to hear the much revered Jagnath Singh whom the British fear. The scene is reminiscent of the arrival of Gandhi at a rally in Candler's *Abdication*, and even more so in Mulk Raj Anand's *Untouchable* (1935). There is the same variegated crowd, the excitement, the suspense, the legends surrounding the speaker, and the plangent cries of 'Jagnath Singh ki jai!' that drown every other sound. But while in *Untouchable* the Mahatma carries the day, in this novel the meeting is called off at the last minute, a very clever device, for it puts the focus back on Hardyal, who is badly mauled by the police. As Hardyal lies recovering in a jail cell, his anglicized father tells Jacques that Hardyal 'may never again bring himself to take a white man for granted'.

Friendship, its worth, and how it can be destroyed by adverse political conditions, is only one aspect of this many-faceted novel. *Indigo* is full of insights which must be supplemented by the reader's own awareness and sensitivity. Weston, by introducing a French boy's friendship with an Indian, adds depth and complexity to the theme of race relations beyond what is found in the works of Forster, Orwell, and Edward Thompson. The English attitude seems all the more absurd when contrasted with that of the French: Jacques finds it quite natural to regard an Indian as his best friend, and Madame de St Remy is completely at home in her adopted country. It is the English she objects to: 'They never submerge their identity, as we are willing to submerge ours, in the soil and culture of a foreign land', she tells her mentor Father Sebastien. Her strictures on the English are as severe as those of the arch-revolutionary Salim, and they bite deeper as they come from one who is not a party to the British–Indian conflict, and happens also to be a white.

It would be a mistake, though, to take Madame de St Remy's criticism at face value or to believe that India would have fared better under French rule. She is right, however, when she says that the French submerge themselves more readily to the culture of the land they live in. French novels set in Algeria, Cambodia, Indo-China, and countries that once constituted the French empire are proof of that. But Madame de St Remy's dislike of the English has a lot to do with her detestation of the two English women who strive to take control of her son—the embattled Mrs Lyttleton and the outgoing, lively, Bertie Wood. Madame de St Remy's character is full of contradictions, though she would have been scandalized had anyone told her so. She likens the Raj to the moneylender Ramdatta, and yet herself works in close association with the moneylender and with a goal not very different from his. She prides herself on accepting India as her home, but she is 'simply not interested in natives as human beings'. Cold, impervious, she looms large in the pages of the book as a powerful matriarchal figure, fighting all and sundry for what she believes to be the preservation of her brood.

Hardyal's conversion to nationalism is handled with great sophistication, and a demand is made on the reader's intelligence to perceive the subtle undercurrents that shape Hardyal's thinking. The initial process must have begun in England and is possibly the result of some unfortunate experiences. But of these we are told nothing; Hardyal is extremely reluctant to speak of his days in England. When he steps off the boat he is dressed in English clothes and looks as one who could pass for a sunburnt English boy. He is full of enthusiasm, but a chance encounter with an obnoxious Englishman unsettles him.

Back home in Amritpore, he appears thoughtful, poised, and more orthodox than ever before. His acceptance of an arranged marriage surprises Jacques, and Hardyal tells him that it is not 'easy to throw aside the traditions of many thousand years'. But the perceptive reader will see in the act Hardyal's attempt to distance himself from the British. Hardyal's conversion to nationalism symbolizes the conversion of those of the Indian elite who approached Britain with hope and longing to assimilate her way of life and who returned disillusioned. His acquired nationalism is not simply the result of personal humiliation at the hands of the English but one of collective shame at the treatment of all Indians. Hardyal may well have been modelled on the young Jawaharlal Nehru (the author knew the Nehru family. See 'Author's Note'), and in Ganpat Rai, Hardyal's father, there are traces of Jawaharlal's father, Motilal Nehru.

*Indigo* has a host of compelling characters. We have seen something of Hardyal and Madame de St Remy. The other principal characters are Jacques and Macbeth. Jacques is the most finely drawn. When he was a child, his father had wished that his son would grow up to be 'ambitious' and 'ruthless' so that he might suffer less. But these are the very qualities that are lacking in him. Suffering seems to be his birthright and from the very start we see him fighting to preserve himself from the self-righteous onslaught of his mother and the religious fanaticism of his sister. He goes into a confessional and comes out confessing, 'nothing is sin, a sin is nothing . . . nothing . . . nothing'. One by one he loses to death or to parting those whom he loves. In the end there remains only Hardyal to whom his loyalty is, as Diana Trilling says, 'as luminous and ineffectual as everything else in his character'.

John Macbeth possesses none of the loyalties that we find in Jacques or Hardyal. Like his colonel father, 'booted, spurred, armed against a world unarmed', his first kinship is with the Raj. Though he grows up to shed some of the prejudices against 'educated natives' and 'howling niggers', he remains a stolid specimen of the men England sent out to rule India. He is honest, dedicated, hardworking, even intelligent in a way, but he is oblivious to everything that lies beyond his circle of interest. He does not even pretend to understand Indian aspirations; nationalists, like Salim and Jagnath, are to him revolutionaries, trouble-makers, and as a police officer he wants no trouble in his district. For Hardyal, who suffers serious injuries to save his life, Macbeth has sympathies, genuine sympathies, but no gratitude. He embodies many of the qualities that kept the Empire going as long as it did; he also has the faults that led to its inevitable collapse.

Among the other characters indispensable to the plot are Mrs
Laura Lyttleton and Aubrey Wall. They embody the two extremes of
British attitudes towards India. Mrs Lyttleton had come to India
when quite young, with her mind made up to accept her adopted
country. Because she had never fought India, India in turn had
preserved her from the bitterness of exile and the frustrations of the
usurper. Aristocratic by birth and temperament, it never occurred to
her that she had anything to lose by adapting to the Indian way of
life. She took to native dress, ate native food, and spoke the native
language as fluently as her own. Direct and forthright, she makes
no secret of her affection for Jacques. Her meeting with Madame de
St Remy, where she is prepared to barter her land for the right of
Jacques to visit her whenever he chooses, is one of the highlights of
the novel. A friend of every Indian, as Ganpat Rai is a friend of
every white man, she had India in her bones. And she knew that
'her bones would remain in India to sweeten, a little, some corner of
its tortured soil'.

Aubrey Wall, a canal engineer, is a composite picture of the civil
engineer in Alice Perrin's short story 'The Rise of Ram Din' and the
timber merchant Ellis in George Orwell's *Burmese Days*. Like the civil
engineer, Wall is given to the abusing and senseless beating of
servants; like Ellis, if only a little less, he detests the natives with a
vengeance that has few parallels in Anglo-Indian fiction. There is
only one relationship he can foresee with Indians and that is of
'mastery over them'. He calls India a 'bloody country' and admits
that he is here for reasons of bread and butter alone. Memories of his
home in Sussex intensify his loneliness. The inacessibility of the
familiar world he grew up in makes him hate his exile. He seeks
solace from his disappointments in bouts of drinking and the
occasional fling with prostitutes. But 'even in the self-effacement of
debauchery he is bitterly conscious of the difference between himself
and them, for the dark skin was aromatic with it.'

Some of the minor characters are no less memorable than the
major ones. Among them is Hanif, Madame de St Remy's servant,
who is as dissolute as his mistress is austere. His death at the
hands of a Hindu mob, while all decked up and scented following a
visit to a brothel, makes chilling reading. There is the moneylender,
Ramdatta, but without the proverbial evil associated with his kind.
He too has 'his code of honour', he reminds Jacques as he tells him
of the extent to which Madame had allowed herself to sink into
debt. But the most arresting of them all is Jacques' sister Gisele:

lithe, golden-haired, blue-eyed, mature at the age of fifteen. Adult and childlike at the same time, she is at one moment looking for snakeskins 'with the eye-holes complete', and the next searching for love in the arms of a middle-aged man and beseeching him to take her 'somewhere, anywhere'. In the name of God she tortures her brother and begs him to sacrifice his friendship with Mrs Lyttleton. With morbid tears she weeps over the dead baby of a coolie whom she has dressed in her old doll's clothes and holds close to her breast. She watches the parents of the child dig a grave at the edge of the compound and exhorts them to dig 'deeper, deeper'. A phantom figure, we finally lose sight of her in a convent, beloved of the nuns and sanctiminious as ever. Though her appearance is brief, she is the most enigmatic character in the book.

In a portrait of India as comprehensive as *Indigo* with its English and French, Hindus and Muslims, a large starving peasantry and the few excessively well-to-do, the Eurasian could hardly be omitted. Weston's portrayal of Boodrie is real and reminds us of the Eurasian driver Harris in *A Passage to India*. Born of a white father and a Hindu mother, he should have been instrumental in bringing the English and the Indians together, but such is the division between the two races that Boodrie and his kind are considered excommunicate. 'Swine! I can't stand these half-castes', says Wall on seeing Boodrie drive past in a dog-cart. Even Jacques, who is completely free of prejudice of any kind, finds Boodrie difficult to accept, not because he is 'half-and-half, black-and-white', but because of his 'zebra personality'. Boodrie, when unobserved, 'slid into the path of least resistance and went native with a vengeance, but on public occasions he remained offensively, pervasively *white*, an ubiquitous reminder of man's sexual democracy, despised by the natives and deplored by the whites.' Weston is one with Forster and Thompson in implying that the Eurasian does not deserve the treatment meted out to him, but then he has done little to improve his lot. One must remember, however, that the Eurasian of today (now termed Anglo-Indian) has completely assimilated into Indian society and is a loyal and respected citizen.

*Indigo* is written with compassionate awareness of the social, political, racial, and religious issues that dominate the subcontinent. The writing itself is precise, meditative, and replete with modulations and insights. Alone among the women writers of the Raj, Weston had a genuine fondness for India which she describes as a 'brown kindly land'. But she is no sentimentalist. She is acutely aware of the filth and disease and starvation that is India; she is equally aware of what Jacques calls the 'turgid vitality' of its inhabitants who survive every misfortune.

## THE WILD SWEET WITCH

'Here at last is your book, built up from all we remember together', wrote Philip Mason in the copy of *The Wild Sweet Witch* he gave to his wife, Mary. In this inscription lies the author's chief purpose in writing this novel, and the pitfalls that must be avoided by trying to read in it more than the author intended. Teresa Hubel's choice of this novel in her study *Whose India?* (1996) to illustrate British nostalgia is based on the faulty assumption that the book 'is a lament for Britain's lost power in India'. Far from it. On the question of granting India independence, Mason is as forthright as Forster himself. His Deputy Commissioner, Christopher Tregard, pulls the rug from beneath the feet of his countrymen who want to stay on in India because a segment of the Indian people so desire it. This is what he tells his wife Susan:

'. . . it seems to me wrong for us, the English, as a people, to take refuge behind the peasant and say we must stay because he wants us. Every people must express itself through its vocal classes . . . and the vocal classes in India want us to go. It is true they're out of touch with the peasant, but that is just because we're here. It is a thing which can't right itself so long as we are here.'

Mason is among the most honest of Raj writers, and through Tregard he admits that he would rather be, despite his immense fondness for Garhwal, in the English countryside and among his own people. Furthermore, in words that remind one of Orwell, he tells Susan, '. . . the good we can do has to be balanced against the harm to our own lives. And for me, the point is approaching when the balance tips over against staying.' But Orwell looked upon the Raj as a device of economic exploitation, while for Mason it was an institution that would lead India to its rightful place among free nations. It was his contention that Indian freedom had always been the professed aim of the British Parliament, though it may not always have been borne in mind by the majority of the British in India.

Hubel, however, is perfectly justified in calling the novel 'a eulogy of the ICS' (Indian Civil Service). Mason himself was for twenty years a member of this illustrious service, and was later to write *The Guardians* (1954), the finest study of the ICS from its inception in 1858 to the end of the Raj. The ICS made the very hub of British administration in India, the day-to-day governance being carried out by the District Magistrate, often referred to as the Deputy Commissioner. It was expected that these men would consider themselves as Guardians in the sense Plato would have them in his *Republic*: 'All who are in any place of command in so far as they are indeed rulers, neither consider nor enjoin their own interest but that of the subjects on behalf of whom they exercise their craft.' The three Deputy Commissioners in *The Wild Sweet Witch* approximate Plato's concept of the 'Guardian'—more of a philosophical ideal than a plausible reality—and are thus too much like each other. This is my only complaint against the book, and it seems Mason was prepared for criticism of this sort. In his Foreword to the novel he acknowledges that the portrait of Mr Bennett and his successors may appear too kind to the reader, but then he can only write from his own experiences. 'Perhaps I have been lucky in the people I have known and the visitors who write books after a six months' stay have been unlucky,' he says.

By 'visitors' he no doubt had Forster in mind. And this mild rebuke of Forster is not without its point. Mason admired *A Passage to India*, describing it as 'brilliantly and delicately written', but he disapproved of Forster's wholesale portrayal of the British officials of Chandrapore with irony verging on disgust. In *The Wild Sweet Witch* he sets out to correct the imbalance by showing three totally dedicated Deputy Commissioners. Much in the same way, he portrays the wives of the last two Deputy Commissioners, Margaret Upton and Susan Tregard, as women entirely devoted to helping their husbands to fulfil their official duties. He seems to imply that the successful running of a district requires teamwork of both husband and wife. In his portrayal of the two women he may also be answering those novelists who have blamed the presence of the memsahib for creating bad blood between the Indians and the whites. Forster, with his obnoxious memsahibs, would certainly be counted among them.

Set in the far reaches of the Garhwal hills in northern India, *The Wild Sweet Witch* recalls the three happy years the author spent as Deputy Commissioner of Garhwal district. His autobiography, *A Shaft of Sunlight: Memories of a Varied Life* (1978), reveals his sense of duty and his affection for the country he serves. For the Garhwalis he has a special place in his heart, and in the chapter 'Kingdom in the Mountains' he praises them for their simplicity, fidelity, courage, and endurance. In this chapter he also tells us why, at the age of thirty and after having served in capitals like Lucknow and Delhi, he found the job of Deputy Commissioner the most satisfying:

Walking among mountains was what Mary and I liked better than anything
else—but there was much more to it than that. To be inaccessible is to be
independent; instructions from the Government arrive late and are often so
quaintly out of the question that they can be disregarded. Ministers do not
come to see you. And in Garhwal, just because it was remote, power had so
long been centred in the District Officer's hands that he had a prestige that in
the rest of India was a thing of the past.

Mason enjoyed power. He was, in his own words, 'the product of
an imperial society'. But the power he sought was not part of any
imperial design, but to help the people—to provide the rough and
ready justice on the spot which the Garhwalis sought above all else.
On one occasion he had a woman with a putrefying leg placed
under arrest so that she could be forcibly sent to a hospital. He
admits he had no right to do this, but the people told him he was a
king in Garhwal and it was no use being a king if he could not
sometimes break the law.

The three Deputy Commissioners in *The Wild Sweet Witch* are a
coalescence of people whom Mason knew and some of whom he
portrays in *The Guardians*. However, in each of them there is
something of Mason himself. Mr Bennett expresses some of Mason's
own love of the mountains, and his orderly, Kalyanu, is no doubt
based on Mason's own orderly Kalyan, who filled him in on many
of the tales about bears and man-eating panthers. Hugh Upton,
physically the very opposite of Mason, shows Mason's administrative
sagacity and the fine line he had to steer between loyalty to the
British government and his own sense of what is right and what is
wrong. Christopher Tregard, who has some traits of Michael
Nethersole (District Magistrate of Bareilly in 1930 while the author
was a subdivisional officer there), comes closest to Mason in his
love of Garhwal, in his exercise of personal rule, and in facing
candidly the fact that the time to leave India had come. Tregard is an
example of the best of the ICS, of whom there were as many in India
as there were of Forster's arrogant Turtons and Heaslops, but at
whose existence Forster never so much as hinted. Susan Tregard
and Margaret Upton have qualities to be found in the author's wife
Mary, who loved Garhwal and the Garhwalis as much as her
husband did and to whom this book is fittingly dedicated.

A character of compelling interest is Jodh Singh. Like his creator,
Mason, he is honest and loves power, and like Mason he wishes to
use it for the well-being of his fellow countrymen. After graduating

from Lucknow University, he returns to his home district in Garhwal to find himself leading a campaign against forced labour. His
initial success (more the result of Hugh Upton's intervention with
the authorities concerned than of his own initiatives) wins him
popularity and convinces him of his mission to lead his people out
of a mental and political morass. Though sincere and full of life and
enthusiasm, his ideas are half-baked and impractical. He is quick
tempered and highly emotional, and in matters of everyday intrigue
he is no match for political adventurers like the Congressite Ram
Prashad Singh or the wily Brahmins such as Ram Dat and Uma Nand.
He first falls victim to a whispering campaign as a creature who
changes into a man-eating panther by night, and is ironically saved
by the very man he is out to denounce—Hugh Upton. Some years
later he is falsely accused of complicity in a murder, loses his mind
completely, goes on a killing spree, and is eventually shot by the
police. But despite the violence towards the end, Jodh Singh is a
character of noble and tragic dimensions.

With *The Wild Sweet Witch*, we have come a long way since
Candler portrayed a nationalist in *Siri Ram—Revolutionist*. Candler
depicted his protagonist as a foolish, excitable young lad, given to
dreams of glory and martyrdom. Mason depicts Jodh Singh as brave
and totally unselfish, but emotional and immature. (Unfortunately,
the British had taken it upon themselves to determine when India
would be mature enough for self-government.) Jodh Singh is a
definite advance on nationalists as generally shown in Raj fiction,
and also on those portrayed by Mason himself in *Call the Next
Witness* (1945) and *The Island of Chamba* (1950). In addition, Mason
reveals with considerable insight that the real enemies of Indian
aspirations are not the British but Indian customs, ignorance, superstitions, and divisions in Indian society itself. The last is perhaps as
true today as it was when the novel was first published. Cornered
and betrayed by his own people, Jodh Singh finally puts his trust in
Christopher Tregard. It is no small irony that it falls on Tregard to
order the police to shoot Jodh Singh.

*The Wild Sweet Witch* is skilfully plotted. Though divided into
three parts, and spread over several years, 1875, 1923, and 1938,
the novel is closely knit by its theme and a judicious use of imagery
and symbolism. Jodh Singh's elation at the abolition of corvee
(unpaid labour) in Part II has a close parallel to the rejoicing of his
grandfather, Kalyanu, at killing his first bear in Part I. Jodh Singh's
failure at leading a procession, with a Dom on horseback, in Part II
has its counterpart in Kalyanu being badly mauled when tackling

his second bear, also in Part I. Both grandfather and grandson are carried away by the enthusiasm attending their initial successes and both, as a result, overreach themselves and blunder in their second attempts. Mr Bennett's saving the life of Kalyanu in Part I corresponds with Hugh Upton's efforts to protect Jodh Singh in Part II when he is suspected by the villagers of becoming a man-eating panther. Such is the spell cast by suspicion and fear that even Jodh Singh half believes the stories told about him, and in Part III he develops many of the traits of the animal he was earlier said to become. The panther imagery is worked out with minute care, and Jodh Singh's final rage and collapse completes the analogy. But what most unifies the novel is its setting, the varied yet unchanging face of the Himalayas.

M.K. Naik in his very knowledgeable survey of Anglo-Indian fiction, *Mirrors on the Wall* (1991), writes that only those who have subdued their first impressions of India's 'heat and dust' are open to the charms of the Indian landscape. The Nilgiri hills in the south have reminded many an Englishman of home, but nothing has captivated the British imagination as the Himalayas in the north. S.J. Duncan in *The Simple Adventures of a Memsahib* (1893) cannot find words to describe its beauty and majesty, and Gordon Casserly in *The Elephant God* (1920) goes into raptures over the Kanchenjunga peaks. But it was left to Philip Mason to capture the mountains, not merely in their solitary grandeur, but as the natural habitat of the Garhwalis who were as much a part of it as its rocks and ferns and streams:

In one place up there in the high alps there was a low cliff of grey stone, with the heavenly blue of the Himalayan poppy growing here and there in the crevices. Beneath this cliff were caves, not deep, but sheltered from rain and wind, with encircling walls built to keep off wild beasts and to throw back the warmth of the fire; it was here that the colony from Bantok made their headquarters. Here they sat at night with the sheep huddled round them, telling stories of ghosts and gods and godlings and warlocks who turned at night into bears or panthers. The fire shone back from the eyes of the sheep; it flickered on the ruddy faces of the men, their long hair hanging out from under round caps of unbleached wool. Men and sheep alike smelt of damp wool, and there was the raw bitter smell of wood-smoke, the drip of water outside the mist, and the small sounds of the sheep stamping or changing their ground.

The book abounds in sharp, descriptive details of this kind. It is evocative of the sights, smells, and the sound of the Himalayas as no other Raj novel I have read. Though it arouses a strong sense of nostalgia, it is not for a vanished Empire but for a remote corner of

India and its lovable people who had failed to keep step with changing times. The novel, above all, is a firm handshake and goodbye to India by a man who came to govern the country and was not disappointed to see it win freedom.

UNIVERSITY OF REGINA                                              SAROS COWASJEE
REGINA, CANADA

# On the Face of the Waters*
## Flora Annie Steel

* First published by William Heinemann
London 1896

# CONTENTS

4 • CONTENTS

# Preface

Oxford's choice to reissue *On the Face of the Waters* not only rescues a neglected masterpiece but brings back to public notice a novel from which many others concerned with India may be said to descend. Its author, Flora Annie Webster, sixth in a family of eleven children, was born at Sudbury Park, Harrow, Middlesex, on 2 April 1847. Mostly self-educated, she had talents for both music and painting. She also possessed an assertive personality and raised the cry 'I can do that' at any challenge in arts and crafts. At the age of twenty she married Henry Steel of the Indian Civil Service and with him sailed to India, after a childhood and girlhood mostly spent in the Lowlands and Highlands of Scotland.

In the spirit of 'I can do that' she faced the problems posed by a new life in the Indian subcontinent. For twenty years she followed her husband into camp on his tours of his district; she opened clinics for women and children and particularly she set up schools for girls as well as boys wherever she happened to find herself. Her education had been mostly acquired by reading in a library books which included a collection of medical works. These gave her the confidence to doctor the inhabitants of the stations to which her husband was posted. Her medicine chest was more elaborate in its contents than the basic 'amateur's pharmacopoeia' of grey powder, castor oil, and ipecacuanha, which, by the standards of the day, was essential in the home. It was during her work among the villages of the Punjab that she invariably received the philosophical answer to any question as to the causes of the Mutiny of 1857—'God knows! He sent a Breath into the world'. This was the idea, a caprice of an inscrutable Deity, which gave Mrs Steel both the theme and the title of her masterpiece.

In the meantime, for two decades, she pursued her work for education. Frequently she found herself fighting a war on two fronts. On one side the forces of Government were arrayed against her. Whenever she thought that injustice, prejudice or parsimony were hampering schemes she felt to be beneficial, she never hesitated to speak her mind. On one occasion when Government had failed to uproot Mrs Steel from Lahore by posting her husband to an outlying station, the Secretary to the Lieutenant Governor appealed to Henry

Steel. Flora was conducting a campaign against academic corruption in the newly-instituted University of the Punjab, and, distressed by the scandal, the Secretary wailed to her husband, 'Can't you keep your wife in order?' An amused 'Take her for a month and try', was all the change he got.

Equally in her dealings with Indians, Flora met with many prejudices and frustrations in matters of health and education. Curiously enough it was her energetic promoting of amateur theatricals which first obliged her to break through the shell which isolated the majority of memsahibs and their Indian servants from any real contact with the life of towns and villages. Flora wished for certain materials outside the run of a memsahib's requirements. Faced with the incomprehension of the bearer sent on this errand in the bazaar, she got a phrase-book which she used to such good effect that she never again accepted that her wishes were impossible to fulfil. With the complexities of Indian religions and with the difficulties of caste distinctions, she displayed more sympathy and patience than she sometimes showed towards her own countrymen. She might use gentle mockery, but she accepted even the most brutally extreme cults as having a basis in the human struggle towards the perfection of the Infinite.

When Henry Steel retired he left behind him the pleasant reputation as having been 'the Sahib who planted gardens', for his fingers were of the greenest. Flora Annie Steel was remembered with equal love and respect. When the time came to leave Kasur, the station at which she had first begun her medical and educational work, the inhabitants asked if she would accept a present. The rules on such an occasion forbade the acceptance of gifts to prevent the possibility of corruption, but an exception was made for Mrs Steel. The gift itself was a large brooch of mixed jewels, each one contributed from the bangles and necklaces of those she had nursed and taught. When she had recovered from the tears that flowed at such a tribute, Flora christened this brooch her Star of India. It was from here that Mrs Daya Patwardhan chose the title *A Star of India* for her very informative study of Flora Annie Steel.

Even at the time of her first arrival, Flora's mind had been full of stories of the Mutiny of 1857. These ideas germinated until, with some success as a novelist and writer of short stories to her credit, she set herself to paint her chosen subject on the widest possible canvas. The few restraints she had been prepared to accept as the wife of a serving Indian Civil Servant had, by her husband's retirement, ceased to impede her. In 1894 she returned to India to think herself back, as it were, into her Indian skin. This she achieved by spending two months in Kasur where she had first learned to love her Indian neighbours. Then she acquired more local colour by spending a week in the household of a Hindu family in Lahore. A tyrannical widowed sister of the owner ruled the family. Herself something of a despot, Mrs Steel was fascinated by the widow's dictatorial habit of inventing taboos by which the family were perpetually kept off balance.

Delhi was less familiar to Mrs Steel than was Lahore, so her next move was to learn the intricacies of its byways. Even more important was her approach to her old enemy the Punjab Government for permission to consult the sealed boxes of papers relating to the Mutiny which had not been examined or even sorted. First-hand material had not been lacking, for in an age of letter writing, accounts of horrors and heroism had been plentiful. No one before Flora, however, had the influence or the initiative to examine the official archives. After a bureaucratic pause, permission was granted, even to the extent of allowing her to take the boxes to her hotel bedroom.

Without the photographic methods of later days, Flora had to rely on her own handwritten notes, aware that a strong force of military historians would be waiting to shoot her down over the smallest slip. The archives themselves were enthralling. Besides reports from official departments there were secret messages concealed in quills and in one case even in a piece of *chapatti*, that unleavened bread whose baking had a mysterious influence on the spread of the Mutiny. Subsequent writers have found her an authority to be relied upon. More than one has absorbed from Flora the material for best-sellers—grandchildren, it might be said, of *On the Face of the Waters*.

Readers must judge for themselves which sections of her masterpiece were nearest to Flora's own heart. For example, her admiration for John Nicholson equalled the hero worship of Nicholson's own Multani Horsemen. Regarding their duty to be to him alone, they retreated to the hills when their leader was dead and their desire for loot satisfied. Famous as administrator of the Punjab, Nicholson was, of course, a historical character, as were the dissolute but attractive Mirza Abool-Bukr and his virtuous aunt by marriage, the princess known as Newâsi. Flora was obviously attracted by Abool-Bukr, and blamed his moral collapse largely on his estrangement from Newâsi.

Of the characters created by the author's imagination far and away, the most vivid are Major Erlton, a rider of crooked races, and Alice Gissing, with whom he is conducting an adulterous affair. Mrs Erlton, who has failed to take root in India, consoles herself in religion for her husband's general unreliability. The beginning of the Mutiny coincides with Major Erlton writing a letter to tell his wife that he is leaving her for Alice Gissing. Although tragedy is moving fast upon the actors, there is comedy in Mrs Erlton's inability to understand that her husband's mistress is pregnant. Alice Gissing, with her mop of golden curls, her baby face, and her tough courage is so brilliantly drawn that her early departure from the scene can only be regretted.

Well aware that she had worked to the best of her own high standard, Flora was disconcerted when the publisher of her earlier novels turned down *On the Face of the Waters*. It was hinted to her that the book was weak in its writing, but it can be suspected that there was nervousness at the idea of publishing a book in which the faults on both sides in the Mutiny were so uncompromisingly set out. Fortunately Mrs Steel had not only confidence in her own work, but another publisher, William Heinemann, up her sleeve. Heinemann had already made friends with Flora and brought out *On the Face of the Waters* with justified enthusiasm. Its author recorded that thirty-three years later the novel had never gone out of print and was still selling. It is agreeable to reflect that Flora Annie Steel's great novel will again be appearing in the country to which she gave so much of herself and from which she gained so much in return.

The Chantry, Somerset, UK                                    Violet Powell

# Author's Note

A word of explanation is needed for this book, which, in attempting to be at once a story and a history, probably fails in either aim.

That, however, is for the reader to say. As the writer, I have only to point out where my history ends, my story begins, and clears the way for criticism. Briefly then, I have not allowed fiction to interfere with fact in the slightest degree. The reader may rest assured that every incident bearing in the remotest degree on the Indian Mutiny, or on the part which real men took in it, is scrupulously exact, even to the date, the hour, the scene, the very weather. Nor have I allowed the actual actors in the great tragedy to say a word regarding it which is not to be found in the accounts of eyewitnesses, or in their own writings.

In like manner, the account of the sham court at Delhi—which I have drawn chiefly from the lips of those who saw it—is pure history; and the picturesque group of schemers and dupes—all of whom have passed on their account—did not need a single touch of fancy in its presentment. Even the story of Abool-Bukr and Newâsi is true; save that I have supplied a cause for an estrangement, which undoubtedly did come to a companionship of which none speak evil. So much for my facts.

Regarding my fiction. An Englishwoman was concealed in Delhi, in the house of an Afghan, and succeeded in escaping to the Ridge just before the siege. I have imagined another; that is all. I mention this because it may possibly be said that the incident is incredible.

And now a word for my title. I have chosen it because when you ask an uneducated native of India why the Great Rebellion came to pass, he will, in nine cases out of ten, reply, 'God knows! He sent a Breath into the World.' From this to a Spirit moving *On the Face of the Waters* is not far. For the rest I have tried to give a photograph—that is, a picture in which the differentiation caused by colour is left out—of a time which neither the fair race nor the dark one is ever likely quite to forget or to forgive.

That they may come nearer to the latter is the object with which this book has been written.

F.A. Steel

# BOOK I

## Thistledown and Gossamer

# 1

## Going! Going! Gone

'Going! Going! Gone!'

The Western phrase echoed over the Eastern scene without a trace of doubt in its calm assumption of finality. It was followed by a pause, during which, despite the crowd thronging the wide plain, the only recognizable sound was the vexed yawning purr of a tiger impatient for its prey. It shuddered through the sunshine, strangely out of keeping with the multitude of men gathered together in silent security; but on that March evening of the year 1856, when the long shadows of the surrounding trees had begun to invade the sunlit levels of grass by the river, the lately deposed King of Oude's menagerie was being auctioned. It had followed all his other property to the hammer, and a perfect Noah's Ark of wild beasts was waiting doubtfully for a change of masters.

'Going! Going! Gone!'

Those three cabalistic words, shibboleth of a whole hemisphere's greed of gain, had just transferred the proprietary rights in an old tusker elephant for the sum of eighteenpence. It is not a large price to pay for Leviathan, even if he be lame, as this one was. Yet the new owner looked at his purchase distastefully, and even the auctioneer sought support in a gulp of brandy and water.

'Fetch up them pollies, Tom,' he said in a dejected whisper to a soldier, who, with others of the fatigue party on duty, was trying to hustle refractory lots into position. 'They'll be a change after elephants—go off lighter like. Then there's some of them La Martiniery boys comin' down again as ran up the fightin' rams this mornin'— Wonder wot the 'ead master said! But boys is allowed birds, and Lord knows we want to be a bit brisker than we 'ave bin with *guj-putti*. But there! it's slave-drivin' to screw bids for beasts as eats hunderweights out of poor devils as 'aven't enough for themselves, or a notion of business as business.'

He shook his head resentfully yet compassionately over the impassive dark faces around. He spoke as an auctioneer; yet he gave expression to a very common feeling which in the early fifties, when the commercial instincts of the West met the uncommercial ones of the East in open market for the first time, sharpened the antagonism of race immensely—that inevitable antagonism when the creed of one people is that Time is Money, of the other that Time is Naught.

From either standpoint, however, the auction going on down by the river Goomtee was confusing; even to those who, knowing the causes which had led up to it—the unmentionable atrocities, the crass incapacity on the one hand, the unsanctioned treaties, and craze for civilization on the other—were conscious of a distinct flavour of Sodom and Gomorrah, the Ark of the Covenant, and the Deluge all combined, as they watched the just and yet unjust retribution going on. But such spectators were few, even in the outer fringe of English onlookers pausing in their evening drive or ride to gratify their curiosity. The long reports and replies regarding the annexation of Oude which filled the office boxes of the elect were unknown to them, so they took the affair as they found it. The King, for some reason satisfactory to the authorities, had been exiled, majesty being thus vested in the representatives of the annexing race: that is in themselves—a position which comes naturally to most Englishmen.

To the silent crowds closing round the auctioneer's table the affair was simple also. The King, for some unsatisfactory reason, had been ousted from his own. His goods and chattels were being sold. The valuable ones had been knocked down for a mere song—just to keep up the farce of sale—to the *Huzoor*s. The rubbish—lame elephants and such like—was being sold to them; more or less against their will, since who could forbear bidding sixpence for a whole leviathan? That this was in a measure inevitable, that these new-come *sahibs* were bound to supply their wants cheaply when a whole *posse* of carriages and horses, cattle and furniture was thrown on an otherwise supplied market, did not, of course, occur to those who watched the hammer fall to that strange new cry of the strange new master. When does such philosophy occur to crowds? So when the waning light closed each day's sale and the people drifted back citywards over the boat-bridge they were no longer silent. They had tales to tell of how much the barouche and pair, or the Arab charger had cost the King when he bought it. But then Wajeed Ali, with all his faults, had never been a bargainer. He had spent his revenues right royally, thus giving ease to many. So one could tell of a purse of gold flung at a beggar, another of a life pension granted to a tailor for inventing a new way of sewing spangles to a waistcoat; for there had been no lack of the insensate munificence in which lies the oriental test of royalty, about the King of Oude's reign.

Despite this talk, however, the talkers returned day after day to watch the auction; and on this, the last one, the grassy plain down by the Goomtee was peaceful and silent as ever save for the occasional cry of an affrighted hungry beast. The sun sent golden gleams over the short turf worn to dustiness by crowding feet, and the long curves of the river, losing themselves on either side among green fields and mango trees, shone like a burnished shield. On the opposite bank, its minarets showing fragile as cut paper against the sky, rose the Chutter Munzil—the deposed King's favourite palace. Behind it, above the belt of trees dividing the high Residency gardens from the maze of houses and hovels still occupied by the hangers-on to the late Court, the English flag drooped lazily in the calm floods of yellow light. For the rest, were dense dark groves following the glistening curve of the river, and gardens gravely gay in pillars of white *chum-baeli* creeper and cypress, long prim lines of latticed walls, and hedges of scarlet hibiscus. Here and there above the trees, the dome of a mosque or the minaret of a mausoleum told that the town of Lucknow, scattered yet coherent, lay among the groves; the most profligate town in India which, by one stroke of an English pen, had just been deprived of the *raison-d'être* of its profligacy, and been bidden to live as best it could in cleanly, court-less poverty.

So, already, there were thousands of workmen in it, innocent enough panderers in the past to luxurious vice, who were feeling the pinch of hunger from lack of employment; and there were those past employers also, deprived now of pensions and offices, with a bankrupt future before them. But Lucknow had a keener grievance than these in the new tax on opium, the drug which helps men to bear hunger and bankruptcy. So, as the auctioneer said, it was not a place in which to expect brisk bidding for wild beasts with large appetites; but the parrots roused a faint interest, and the crowd laughed suddenly at the fluttering screams of a red - and blue macaw, as it was tossed from hand to hand on its way to the surprised and reluctant purchaser who had bid a farthing for it out of sheer idleness.

'Another mouth to feed, Shumshu!' jeered a fellow-butcher, as he literally flung the bird at a neighbour's head. 'Rather he than I,' laughed the recipient, continuing the fling. '*Ari!* Shumshu, take thy baby. Well caught, brother! but what will thy house say?'

'That I have made a fat bargain,' retorted the big coarse owner coolly as he wrung the bird's neck, and twirled it, a quivering tuft of bright feathers and choking cries, above his head. 'Thou'lt buy no meat at a farthing a pound, even from *my* shop I'll swear, and this bird weighs two, and is delicate as chicken.'

The laugh which answered the sally held a faint scream, not wholly genuine in its ring. It came from the edge of the crowd, where two

English riders had paused to see what the fun was about.

'Cruel devils, arn't they, Allie?' said one, a tall fair man whose good looks were at once made and marred by heaviness of feature. 'Why! you've turned pale despite the rouge!' His tone was full of not over-respectful raillery, his bold bloodshot eyes met his companion's innocent-looking ones with careless admiration.

'Don't be a fool, Erlton,' she replied promptly; and the even, somewhat hard pitch of her voice did not match the extreme softness of her small, childish face. 'You know I don't rouge; or you ought to. And it *was* horrible, in its way.'

'Only what your ladyship's cook does to your ladyship's fowls,' retorted Major Erlton. 'You don't *see* it done, that's all the difference. It is a cruel world, Mrs Gissing, the sex is the cruellest thing in it, and you, as I'm always telling you, are the cruellest of your sex.'

His manner was detestable, but little Mrs Gissing laughed again. She had not a fine taste in such matters; perhaps because she had no taste for them at all. So, in the middle of the laugh, her attention shifted to the big white cockatoo which formed the next lot. It had a most rumpled and dejected appearance as it tried to keep its balance on the ring, which the soldier assistant swung backwards and forwards boisterously. 'Do look at that ridiculous bird!' she exclaimed, 'did you ever see any creature look so foolish?'

It did, undoubtedly, with its wrinkled grey eyelids closed in agonized effort, its clattering grey beak bobbing rhythmically towards its scaly grey legs. It roused the auctioneer from his depression, into beginning in grand style—'Now then, gentlemen! This is a real treat, indeed! A cockatoo old as Methusalem and twice as wise. It speaks I'll be bound. Says 'is prayers—look at 'im genyflexing! and may be he swears a bit like the rest of us. Any gentleman bid a rupee!—a eight annas?—a four annas? Come, gentlemen!'

'One anna,' called Mrs Gissing, with a coquettish nod to the big Major, and a loud aside—'Cruel I may be to you, sir, but I'll give that to save the poor brute from having its neck wrung.'

'Two annas!' There was a stress of eagerness in the new voice which made many in the crowd look whence it came. The speaker was a lean old man wearing a faded green turban, who had edged himself close to the auctioneer's table, and stood with upturned eyes watching the bird anxiously. He had the face of an enthusiast, keen, remorseless, despite its look of ascetic patience.

'Three annas!' Alice Gissing's advance came with another nod at her big admirer.

'Four annas!' The reply was quick as an echo.

A vexed surprise showed on the pretty babyish face. 'What an impertinent wretch! Eight annas—do you hear!—Eight annas!'

The auctioneer bowed effusively. 'Eight annas bid for a cockatoo as says—' he paused cautiously, for the bidding was brisk enough without exaggeration—'Eight annas once—twice—Going! going—'

'One rupee!'

Mrs Gissing gave a petulant jag to her rein. 'Oh come away, Erlton, my charity doesn't run to rupees.'

But her companion's face, never a very amiable one, had darkened with temper. 'D—n the impudent devil,' he muttered savagely, before raising his voice to call—'Two rupees!'

'Five!' There was no hesitation still; only an almost clamorous anxiety in the worn old voice.

'Ten!' Major Erlton's had lost its first heat, and settled into a dull decision which made the auctioneer turn to him, hammer in hand. Yet the echo was not wanting.

'Fifteen!'

The Englishman's horse backed as if its master's hand lay heavy on the bit. There was a pause, during which that shuddering cough of the hungry tiger quavered through the calm flood of sunshine, in which the crowd stood silently, patiently.

'Fifteen rupees,' began the auctioneer reluctantly, his sympathies outraged, 'Fifteen once, twice—'

Then Alice Gissing laughed. The woman's laugh of derision which is responsible for so much.

'Fifty rupees,' said Major Erlton at once.

The old man in the green turban turned swiftly; turned for the first time to look at his adversary, and in his face was intolerant hatred mingled with self-pity; the look of one who, knowing that he has justice on his side, knows also that he is defeated.

'Thank *you* sir' caught up the auctioneer. 'Fifty once, twice, thrice. Hand the bird over, Tom. Put it down, sir, I suppose with the other things?'

Major Erlton nodded sulkily. He was already beginning to wonder why he had bought the brute. Meanwhile Tom, still swinging the cockatoo derisively, had jumped from the table into the crowd round it as if the sea of heads was non-existent; being justified of his rashness by its prompt yielding of foothold as he elbowed his way outward, shouting for room goodnaturedly, and answered by swift smiles and swifter obedience. Yet both were curiously silent; so that Mrs Gissing's voice, wondering what on earth Herbert was going to do with the creature now that he had bought it, was distinctly audible.

'Give it to you, of course,' he replied moodily. 'You can wring its neck if you choose, Allie. You are cruel enough for that I daresay.' The thought of the fifty rupees wasted was rankling fiercely. Fifty rupees! when he would be hard put to it for a penny if he didn't pull off the next race. Fifty rupees! because a woman laughed!

But Mrs Gissing was laughing again. 'I shan't do anything of the kind. I shall give it to your wife, Major Erlton. I'm sure she must be dull all alone; and then she loves prayers!' The absolute effrontery of the speech was toned down by her indifferent expression. 'Here, sergeant!' she went on, 'hold the bird up a bit higher, please, I want to see if it is worth all that money. Gracious! what a hideous brute!'

It was, in truth, save for the large gold-circled eyes, like strange gems, which opened suddenly as the swinging ceased. They seemed to look at the dainty little figure, taking it in; and then, in an instant, the dejected feathers were afluff, the wings outspread, the flame-coloured crest, unseen before, was raised like a fiery flag as the bird gave an ear-piercing scream.

'*Deen! Deen! Futteh Mahomed.*' (For the Faith! For the Faith! victory to Mahomed.)

The war cry of the fiercest of all faiths was unmistakable; the first two syllables cutting the air, keen as a knife, the last with the blare as of a trumpet in them. And following close on their heels came an indescribable sound, like the answering vibration of a church to the last deep organ-note. It was a faint murmur from the crowd till then so silent.

'Damn the bird! Hold it back, man! Loosen the curb, Allie, for God's sake! or the brute will be over with you.'

Herbert Erlton's voice was sharp with anxiety as he reined his own horse savagely out of the way of his companion's, which, frightened at the unexpected commotion, was rearing badly.

'All right,' she called; there was a little more colour on her child-like face, a firmer set of her smiling mouth: that was all. But the hunting crop she carried fell in one savage cut after another on the startled horse's quarters. It plunged madly, only to meet the bit and a dig of the spur. So, after two or three unavailing attempts to unseat her, it stood still with pricked ears and protesting snorts.

'Well sat, Allie! By George you can ride! I do like to see pluck in a woman; especially in a pretty one.' The Major's temper and his fears had vanished alike in his admiration. Mrs Gissing looked at him curiously.

'Did you think I was a coward?' she asked lightly; and then she laughed. 'I'm not so bad as all that. But look! There is your wife coming along in the new victoria—it's an awfully stylish turnout, Herbert, I wish Gissing would give me one like it. I suppose she has been to church. It's Lent or something isn't it? Anyhow she can take that screaming beast home.'

'You're not'—, began the Major; but Mrs Gissing had already ridden up to the carriage, making it impossible for the solitary occupant to avoid giving the order to stop. She was rather a pale woman who leant listlessly among the cushions.

'Good-evening, Mrs. Erlton,' said the little lady; 'been, as you see, for a ride. But we were thinking of you and hoping you would pray for us in church.'

Kate Erlton's eyebrows went up as they had a trick of doing when she was scornful. 'I am only on my way thither as yet,' she replied; 'so that now I am aware of your wishes I can attend to them.'

The obvious implication roused the aggressor to greater recklessness. 'Thanks! but we really deserve something, for we have been buying a parrot for you. Erlton paid a whole fifty rupees for it because it said its prayers and he thought you would like it!'

'That was very kind of Major Erlton—'—there was a fine irony in the title—'but, as he knows, I'm not fond of things with gay feathers and loud voices.'

The man listening moved his feet restlessly in his stirrups. It was too bad of Allie to provoke these sparring matches; foolish too, since Kate's tongue was sharp when she chose to rouse herself.

'If you don't want the bird,' he interrupted shortly, 'tell the groom to wring its neck.'

Mrs Gissing looked at him, her reproachful blue eyes perfect wells of simplicity. 'Wring its neck! How can you, when you paid all that money to save it from being killed? That is the real story, Mrs Erlton; it is indeed—'

He interrupted his wife's quick glance of interest impatiently. 'The main point being that I had, or shall have to pay fifty rupees—which I must get. So, I must be off to the racecourse if I don't want to be posted. I ought to have been there a quarter of an hour ago; should have been but for that confounded bird. Are you coming, Mrs Gissing, or not?'

'Now, Erlton!' she replied, 'don't be stupid. As if he didn't know, Mrs Erlton, that I am every bit as much interested as he is in the match with that trainer man!—what's his name, Erlton?—Greyman—isn't it? I have endless gloves on it, sir, so of course I'm coming to see fair play.'

Major Erlton shot a rapid glance at her, as if to see what she really meant; then muttered something angrily about chaff as, with a dig of his heels, he swung his horse round to the side of hers.

Kate Erlton watched their figures disappear behind the trees, then turned indifferently to the groom who was waiting for orders with the cockatoo; but she started visibly in finding herself face to face with a semicircle of spectators which had gathered about the figure of an old man in a faded green turban who stood close beside the groom, and who, seeing her turn, salaamed, and with clasped hands began an appeal of some sort. So much she gathered from his bright eyes, his tone; but no more, and so all unconsciously she drew back to the furthest corner of the carriage, as if to escape from what she did not understand and therefore did not like. That, indeed, was her attitude towards all things native; though at times, as now, she felt a dim regret at her own ignorance. What did he want? What were they thinking of, those dark incomprehensible faces closing closer and closer round her? What could they be thinking of? Uncivilized, heathen, as they were— tied to hateful horrible beliefs and customs—unmentionable thoughts! So the innate repulsion of the alien overpowered her dim desire to be kind.

'Drive on!' she called in her clear soft voice, 'drive on to the church.'

The grooms, new taken from royal employ—for the victoria had been one of the spoils of the auction—began their arrogant shouting to the crowd; the coachman, treating it also in royal fashion, cut at his horses regardless of their plunging. So, after an instant's scurry and flurry, a space was cleared, and the carriage rolled off. The old man, left standing alone, looked after it silently for a moment, then flung his arms skyward.

'O God, reward them! reward them to the uttermost!' he cried. The appeal, however, seemed too indefinite for solace, and he turned for closer sympathy to the crowd. 'The bird is mine, brothers! I lent it to the King, to teach him the Cry-of-Faith that I had taught it. But the *Huzoors* would not listen, or they would not understand. It was a little thing to them! So I brought all I had, thinking to buy mine own again. But yonder hell-doomed infidel hath it for nothing—for he paid nothing; and here—here is *my* money!' He drew a little bag from his breast and held it up with shaking hand.

'For nothing?' echoed the crowd, seizing on what interested it most. 'For sure he paid nothing.'

The murmur, spreading from man to man in doubt, wonder, assertion, was interrupted by a voice with the resonance and calm in it of one accustomed to listeners. 'Nay! not for nothing. Have patience. The bird may yet give the Great Cry in the house of the thief. I Ahmed-oolah, the dust of the feet of the Most High, say it. Have patience. God settles the accounts of men.'

'It is the Moulvie,' whispered some, as the gaunt hollow-eyed speaker moved out of the crowd, a good head-and-shoulders taller than most there. 'The Moulvie from Fyzabad. He preaches in the big Mosque tonight, and half the city goes to hear him.'

The whispering voices formed a background to that recurring cry of the auctioneer, 'Going! Going! Gone!' as lot after lot fell to the hammer, while the crowd listened to both, or drifted citywards with the memory of them lingering insistently.

'Going! Going! Gone!' What was going? Everything, if tales were true; and there were so many tales nowadays. Of news flashed faster by wires than any, even the Gods themselves, could flash it; of carriages, fire-fed, bringing God knows what grain from God knows where! Could a body eat of it and not be polluted? Could the children read the school books and not be apostate? Burning questions these, not to be answered lightly. And as the people, drifting homewards in the sunset, asked them, other sounds assailed their ears—the long-drawn chant of the call to prayer from the Mahomedan mosques, the clashings of gongs from the Hindoo temples, the solitary clang of the Christian church bell; diverse, yet similar in this, that each called Life to face Death, not as an end, but as a beginning. Called with more insistence than usual in the church, where a special missionary service was being held, at which a well-known worker in the vineyard was to give an address on the duty of a faithful soldier of Christ in a heathen land; with greater authority in the mosque also, where the Moulvie was to lay down the law for each soldier of the faith in an age of unbelief and change. Only in the Hindoo temples the circling lights flickered as ever, and there was neither waxing nor waning of worship as mortality drifted in, and drifted out, hiding the rude stone symbol of regeneration with their chaplets of flowers—the symbol of Life-in-Death, of Death-in-Life—the cult of the Inevitable.

There was no light in these dark shrines, save the circling cresset; none, save the dim reflection of dusk from white marble, in the mosque where the Moulvie's sonorous voice sent the broad Arabic vowels rebounding from dome to dome. But in the church there was a blaze of lamps, and the soldierly figure at the reading desk showed clear to the men and women listening leisurely in the cushioned pews. Yet the words were stirring enough; there was no lack of directness in him. Kate Erlton, resting her chin on her hand, kept her eyes on the speaker closely as his voice rose in a final confession of the faith that was in him.

'I conceive it is ever the hope and aim of a true Christian that his Lord should make him the happy instrument of rescuing his neighbour from eternal damnation. In this belief I find it my duty to be instant in season and out of season, speaking to all, sepoys as well as civilians, making no distinction of persons or place, since with the Lord there are no such distinctions. In temporal matters I act under the orders of my earthly superior, but in spiritual matters I own no allegiance save to

Christ. So, in trying to convert my sepoys, I act as a Christian soldier under Christ, and thus, by keeping the temporal and spiritual capacities in which I have to act clearly under their respective heads, I render unto Caesar the things that are Caesar's, to God the things that are God's'.[1]

There was a little rustle of satisfaction and relief from the pews, the hymn closing the service went with a swing, and the congregation, trooping out into the scented evening air, fell to admiring the address.

'And he looked so handsome and soldierly, didn't he?' said one voice with a cadence of sheer comfortableness in it, as the owner nestled back into a barouche.

'Quite charming!' assented another. 'And to think of a man like that, brave as a lion, submitting to be hustled off his own parade ground because his sepoys objected to his preaching. It is an example to us all!'

'I wouldn't give much for the discipline of his regiment,' began Kate Erlton, impulsively, then paused, certain of her hearers, uncertain of herself; for she was of those women who use religion chiefly as an anodyne for the heartache, leaving her intellect to take care of itself; with the result that it revenged itself, as now, by sudden flashes of reason which left her helpless before her own common sense.

'My dear Mrs Erlton!' came a shocked coo, 'discipline or no discipline, we are surely bound to fight the good— Gracious heavens! what *is* that?'

It was the cockatoo; roused from a doze by the movement of Kate's carriage towards the church-door, it had dashed at once into the war cry—'*Deen! Deen! Futteh Mahomed!*'

The appositeness of the interruption, however, was quite lost on the ladies, who were too ignorant to recognize it; so their alarm ended in a laugh, and the suggestion that the bird would be a noisy pet.

Thus, with worldly gossip coming to fill the widening spaces in their complacent piety, they drove homewards together where the curving river shimmered faintly in the dark, or through scented gardens where the orange-blossom showed as faintly among the leaves, like stardust on a dark sky.

But Kate Erlton drove alone as she generally did. And as she drove, her mind diverted listlessly to the semicircle of dark faces she had left unanswered. What had they wanted? Nothing worth hearing, no doubt! Nothing was worth much in this weary land of exile where the heart-hunger for one little face and voice gnawed at your vitality day and night; for Kate Erlton set down all her discontent to the fact that

[1]From Colonel Wheler's defence.

she was separated from her boy. Yet she had sent him home of her own free will to keep him from growing up in the least like his father; and she had stayed with that father simply to keep him within the pale of respectability for the boy's sake. That was what she told herself. She allowed nothing for her own disappointments; nothing for the keen craving for sentiment which lay behind her refinement. All she asked from fate was that the future might be no worse than the past; so that she could keep up the fiction to the end.

And as she drove, a sudden sound made her start, for—soldier's wife though she was—the report of a rifle always set her heart a-beating. Then from the darkness came a long-drawn howl; for over on the other side of the river they were beginning to shoot down the hungry beasts which all through the long sunny day had found no master.

The barter of *their* lives was complete. The last 'Going! Going! Gone!' had come, and they had passed to settle the account elsewhere. So, amid this dropping fire of kindly-meant destruction, the night fell soft and warm over the shimmering river, and the scented gardens with the town hidden in their midst.

# 2

## Home, Sweet Home!

'Y ou sent for me, I believe, Mrs Erlton.'

'Yes, Mr Greyman, I sent for you.'

Both voices came reluctantly into the persistent cooing of doves which filled the room, for the birds were perched among a coral begonia overhanging the verandah. But the man had so far the best of it in the difficult interview which was evidently beginning, in that he stood with his back to the French window through which he had just entered; his face, therefore, was in shadow. Hers, as she paused, arrested by surprise, faced the light. For Kate Erlton, when she sent for James Greyman in the hopes of bribing him to silence regarding the match which had been run the evening before between his horse and her husband's, had not expected to see a gentleman in the person of an ex-jockey, trainer, and general hanger-on to the late King's stables. The diamonds with which she had meant to purchase honour lay on the table; but this man would not take diamonds. What would he take? She scanned his face anxiously, yet with a certain relief in her disappointment; for the clean-shaven contours were fine, if a trifle stern; and the mouth, barely hidden by a slight moustache, was thin-lipped, well cut.

'Yes! I sent for you,' she continued—and the even confidence of her own voice surprised her,—'I meant to ask how much you would want to keep this miserable business quiet; but now—' She paused, and her hand, which had been resting on the centre table, shifted its position to push aside the jewel-case; as if that were sufficient explanation.

'But now?' he echoed formally, though his eyes followed the action. She raised hers to his, looking him full in the face. They were beautiful eyes, and their cold grey blue, with the northern glint of steel in it, gave James Greyman an odd thrill. He had not looked into eyes like these for many a long year; not since, in a room just like this one, homely and English in every twist and turn of foreign flowers and furniture, he had ruined his life for a pair of eyes, as coldly pure as these, to look at. He did not mean to do it again.

'But now I can only ask you to be kind, and generous. Mr Greyman!—I want you to save my husband from the disgrace your claim must bring—if you press it.'

Once more the monotonous cooing from outside filled the darkness and the light of the large lofty room. For it was curiously dark in the raftered roof and the distant corners; curiously light in the great bars of golden sunshine slanting across the floor. In one of them James Greyman stood, a dark silhouette against an arch of pale blue sky, wreathed by the climbing begonia. He was a man of about forty, looking younger than his age, taller than his real height, by reason of his beardless face and the extreme ease and grace of his figure. He was burnt brown as a native by constant exposure to the sun; but as he stooped to pick up his glove which had slipped from his hold, a rim of white showed above his wrist.

'So I supposed; but why should I save him?' he said briefly. The question, thus crudely put, left her without reply for a minute; during which he waited. Then, with a new tinge of softness in his voice, he went on: 'It was a mistake to send for me. I thought so at the time, though, of course, I had no option save to come. But now—'

'But now?' she echoed in her turn.

'There is nothing to be done save to go away again.' He turned at the words, but she stopped him by a gesture.

'Is there not?' she asked, 'I think there is, and so will you if you understand—if you will wait and let me speak.' His evident impatience

made her add quickly—'You can at least do so much for me, surely?'
There was a quiver in her voice now, and it surprised her as her
previous calm had done; for what was this man to her that his
unkindness should give pain?

'Certainly,' he said, pausing at once; 'but I understand too much,
and I cannot see the use of raking up details. You know them—or
think you do. Either way they do not alter the plain fact that I cannot
help—because I would not if I could. That sounds brutal; but,
unfortunately, it is true. And it is best to tell the truth, as far as it can
be told.'

A faint smile curved her lips. '*That* is not far. If you will wait *I* will
tell you the truth to the bitter end.'

He looked at her with sudden interest, for her pride attracted him.
She was not in the least pretty; she might be any age from five-and-
twenty to five-and-thirty; and she—well! she was a lady. But would
she tell the truth? Women, even ladies, seldom did; still he must wait
and hear what she had to say.

'I sent for you,' she began, 'because, knowing you were an
adventurer, a man who had had to leave the army under a cloud—in
disgrace—'

He started at her blankly. Here was the truth about himself at any
rate!

'I thought, naturally, you would be a man who would take a bribe.
There are diamonds in that case; for money is scarce in this house.' She
paused, to gain firmness for what came next, 'I was keeping them for
the boy. I have a son in England and he will have to go to school soon;
but I thought it better to save his father's reputation instead. They are
fine diamonds'—she drew the case closer and opened it—the sunshine,
streaming in, caught the facets of the stones, turning them to liquid
light—'You needn't tell me they are no use,' she went on quickly, as he
seemed about to speak, 'I am not stupid; but that has nothing to do
with the question. I want you to save my husband—don't interrupt
me, please, for I do want you to understand, and I will tell you the
truth. You asked me why? and you think, no doubt, that he does not
deserve to be saved. Do you think I do not know that? Mr Greyman! a
wife knows more of her husband than any one else can do; and I have
known for so many years.'

A sudden softness came to her hearer's eyes. That was true at any
rate. She must know many things of which she could not speak, and a
sort of horror at what she must know, with a man like Major Erlton as
her husband, held him silent.

'Yet I have saved him so far,' she went on, 'but if what happened
yesterday becomes public property all my trouble is in vain. He will

have to leave the regiment—'

'He is not the first man, as you were kind enough to mention just now,' interrupted James Greyman, 'who has had to leave the army under a cloud. He would survive it—as others have done.'

'I was not thinking of him at all,' she replied quietly, 'I was thinking of my son; my only son.'

'There are other only sons also, Mrs Erlton,' he retorted, 'I was my mother's, but I don't think the fact was taken into consideration by the court-martial. Why should I be more lenient? You have come to the wrong person when you come to me for charity or consideration. None was shown to me.'

'Perhaps because you did not need it,' she said quickly.

'Not need it—?'

'Many a man falls under the shadow of a cloud blamelessly. What do they want with charity?'

He rose swiftly, and so, facing the light again, stood looking out into. 'I am obliged to you,' he said after a pause. 'Whether you are right or wrong doesn't affect the question from which we have wandered. Except—' he turned to her again with a certain eagerness— 'Mrs Erlton! You say you are prepared to tell the truth to the bitter end. Then for Heaven's sake let us have it for once in our lives. You never saw me before, nor I you. It is not likely we shall ever meet again. So we can speak without a past or a future tense. You ask me to save your husband from the consequences of his own cheating. I ask why? Why should I sacrifice myself? Why should I suffer? for, mark you, there were heavy bets—'

'There are the diamonds,' she interrupted, pointing to them; their gleam was scarcely brighter than her scornful eyes.

He gave a half-smile. 'Doubtless there are the diamonds! I can have my equivalent, so far, if I choose; but I don't choose. It does not suit me personally; so that is settled. I can't do this thing, then, to please myself. Now, let us go on. You are a religious woman, I think, Mrs Erlton—you have the look of one. Then you will say that I should remember my own frailty, and forgive as I would be forgiven. Mrs Erlton! I am no better than most men, no doubt, but I never remember cheating at cards or pulling a horse as your husband does—it is the brutal truth between us, remember. And if you tell me I'm bound to protect a man from the natural punishment of a great crime because I've stolen a pin, I say you are wrong. That theory won't hold water. If our own faults, even our own crimes, are to make us tender over these things in others, there must be—what, if I remember right, my Colenso used to call an arithmetical progression in error—until the Day of Judgment; for the odds on sin would rise with every crime. I don't believe in mercy, Mrs Erlton. I never did. Justice doesn't need it. So let us leave religion alone too, and come to other things—altruism—charity—what you will. Now, who will benefit by my silence? Will you? 'You said just now that a wife knows more of her husband than a stranger can. I well believe it. That is why I ask you to tell me frankly, if you really think that a continuance of the life you lead with him can benefit you?' He leant over the table, resting his head on his hand, his eyes on hers, and then added in a lower voice, 'The brutal truth, please. Not as woman to man, or for the matter of that, woman to woman; but soul to soul, if there be such a thing.'

She turned away from him and shook her head. 'It is for the boy's sake,' she said in muffled tones. 'It will be better for him, surely.'

'The boy,' he echoed, rising with a sense of relief. She had not lied, this woman with the beautiful eyes; she had simply shut the door in his face. 'You have a portrait of him, no doubt, somewhere. I should like to see it. Is that it on the mantelpiece?'

He walked over to a coloured photograph, and stood looking at it silently, his hands—holding his hunting crop—clasped loosely behind his back. Kate noticed them even in her anxiety; for they were noticeable, nervous, fine-cut hands, matching the figure.

'He is not the least like you. He is the very image of his father,' came the verdict. 'What right have you to suppose that anything you or I can do now will overcome the initial fact that the boy is your husband's son, any more than it will ease you of the responsibility of having chosen such a father for the boy?'

She gave a quick cry, more of pain than anger, and hid her face on the table in sudden despair.

'You are very cruel,' she said, indistinctly.

He walked back towards her, remorseful at the sight of her miserable self-abasement. He had not meant to hit so hard, being accustomed himself to facing facts without flinching.

'Yes! I am cruel; but a life like mine doesn't make a man gentle. And I don't see how this trivial concealment of fact—for that is all it would be—can change the boy's character or help him. If I did—' he paused, 'I should like to help you if I could, Mrs Erlton, if only because you—you refused me charity! But I cannot see my way. It would do no one any good. Begin with me. I'm not a religious man, Mrs Erlton. I don't believe in the forgiveness of sins. So my soul—if I have one—wouldn't benefit. As for my body? At the risk of you offering me diamonds again,'—he smiled charmingly—'I must mention that I should lose—how much is a detail—by concealment. So I must go out of the question of benefit. Then there is you—'

He broke off to walk up and down the room thoughtfully, then to pause before her. 'I wish you to believe,' he said, 'that I want really to understand the truth, but I can't, because I don't know one thing. I don't know if you love your husband—or not?'

She raised her head quickly with a fear behind the resentment of her eyes. 'Put me outside the question too. I have told you that already. It is the simplest, the best way.'

He bowed cynically. She came no nearer to truth than evasion.

'If you wish it, certainly. Then there is the boy. You want to prevent him from realizing that his father is a—let us twist the sentence—what his father is. You have, I expect, sent him away for this purpose. So far good. But will this concealment of mine suffice? Will no one else blab the truth? Even if concealment succeeds all along the line, will it prevent the boy from following in his father's steps if he has inherited his father's nature as well as his face? Wouldn't it be a deterrent in that case to know early in life that such instincts can't be indulged with impunity in the society of gentlemen? You will never have the courage to keep the boy out of your life altogether as you are doing now. Sooner or later you will bring him back, he will bring himself back, and then, on the threshold of life, he will have an example of successful dishonesty put before him. Mrs Erlton! You can't keep up the fiction always; so it is better for you, for me, for him, to tell the truth—and I mean to tell it.'

She rose swiftly to her feet and faced him, thrusting her hair back from her forehead passionately, as if to clear away aught that might obscure her brain.

'And for my husband?' she asked. 'Have you no word for him? Is he not to be thought of at all? You asked me just now if I loved him, and I was a coward. Well! I do not love him—more's the pity, for I can't make up the loss of that to him anyhow. But there is enough pity in his life without that. Can't you see it? The pity that such things should be in life at all. You called me a religious woman just now. I'm not, really. It is the pity of such things without a remedy that drives me to believe, and the pity of it which drives me back again upon myself, as you have driven me now. For you are right! Do you think I can't see the shame? Do you think I don't know that it is too late—that I should have thought of all this before I called my boy's nature out of the dark? And yet—' her face grew sharp with a pitiful eagerness, she moved forward and laid her hand on his arm—'It is all so dark! You said just now that I couldn't keep up the fiction; but need it be a fiction always? What do we know? God gives men a chance sometimes. He gives the whole world a chance sometimes of atoning for many sins. A Spirit moves on the Waters of life bringing something to cleanse and heal. It may be moving now. Give my husband his chance, Mr

Greyman, and I will pray that, whatever it is, it may come quickly.'

He had listened with startled eyes; now his hand closed on hers in swift negation.

'Don't pray for that,' he said, in a quick low voice, 'it may come too soon for some of us, God knows—too soon for many a good man and true!' Then, as if vexed at his own outburst, he drew back a step, looking at her with a certain resentment.

'You plead your cause well, Mrs Erlton, and it is a stronger argument than you perhaps guess. So let him have this chance that is coming. Let us all have it, you and I into the bargain. No! don't be grateful, please, for he may prove himself a coward, amongst other things. So may I, for that matter. One never knows until the chance comes for being a hero—or the other thing.'

'When the chance comes we shall see,' she said, trying to match his light tone. 'Till then, goodbye—you have been very kind.' She held out her hand but he did not take it.

'Pardon me! I have been very rude, and you—' he paused in his half-jesting words, stooped over her outstretched hand and kissed it.

Kate stood looking at the hand with a slight frown after his horse's hoofs died away; and then with a smile she shut the jewel case. Not that she closed the incident also; for full half-an-hour later she was still going over all the details of the past interview; and everything in it seemed to hinge on that unforeseen appeal of hers for a chance of atonement, on that unpremeditated, strange suggestion that a Spirit might even then be moving on the face of the Waters; until, in that room, gay with English flowers, and peaceful utterly in its air of security, a terror seized on her, body and soul. A causeless terror, making her strain eyes and ears as if for a hint of what was to come and make cowards or heroes of them all.

But there was only the flowerful garden beyond the arched verandah, only the soft gurgle of the doves. Yet she sat with quivering nerves till the sight of the gardener coming as usual with his watering pot made her smile at the unfounded tragedy of her imaginings.

As she passed into the verandah she called to him, in the jargon which served for her orders, not to forget a plentiful supply to the heartsease and the sweet peas; for she loved her poor clumps of English annuals more than all the scented and blossoming shrubs which, in those late March days, turned the garden into a wilderness of strange perfumed beauty. Her cult of home was a religion with her; and if a visitor remarked that anything in her environment was reminiscent of the old country, she rejoiced to have given another exile what was to her as the shadow of a rock in a thirsty land.

So, her eye catching something barely up to western mark in the pattern of a collar her tailor was cutting for her new dress, she crossed over to where he squatted in the further corner of the verandah.

'That isn't right. Give me something to cut—here! this will do.'

She drew a broad sheet of native paper from the bundle of scraps beside him, and began on it with the scissors, too full of her idea to notice the faint negation of the man's hand. 'There!' she said after a few deft snippings, 'that is new fashion.'

'*Huzoor!*' assented the tailor submissively as, apparently from tidiness, he put away the remainder of the paper, before laying the new-cut pattern on the cloth.

His mistress looked down at it critically. There was a broad line of black curves and square dots right across the pattern suggestive of its having been cut from a title-page. But to her ignorance of the Persian character they were nothing but curves and dots, though the tailor's eyes read clearly in them 'The Sword is the Key of Heaven.' For he, in company with thousands of other men, had been reading the famous pamphlet of that name; reading it with that thrill of the heart-strings which has been the prelude to half the discords and harmonies of history. Since, quaintly enough, those who may hope to share your heaven are always friends, those who can with certainty be consigned to hell, your enemies.

'That is all right,' she said. 'Cut it well on the bias, so that it won't pucker.'

As she turned away, she felt the vast relief of being able to think of such trivialities again after the strain and stress of the hours since her husband had come home from the racecourse, full of excited maledictions on the mean, underhand bribery and spying which might make it necessary for him to send in his papers—if he could. Kate had heard stories of a similar character before; since Major Erlton knew by experience that she had his reputation more at heart than he had himself, and that her brain was clearer, her tact greater than his. But she had never heard one so hopeless. Unless this jockey Greyman, who, her husband said, was so mixed up with native intrigue as to have any amount of false evidence at his command, could be silenced, her labour of years was ruined. So, long after her husband had gone off to his bed to sleep soundly, heavily, after the manner of men, Kate had lain awake in hers after the manner of women, resolving to risk all, even to a certain extent honesty, in order to silence this man, this adventurer—who no doubt was not one whit better than her husband.

And now? As her mind flashed back over that interview the one thing that stood out above all others was the bearing, the deference of the man as he had stooped to kiss her hand. For the life of her, she— who protested even to herself that such things had no part in her life—

could not help a joy in the remembrance; a quick recognition that here was a man who could put romance into a woman's life. The thought was one, however, from which to escape by the first distraction at hand. This happened to be the cockatoo, which, after a bath and plentiful food, looked a different bird on its new perch.

'Pretty, pretty poll,' she said hastily with tentative white finger tickling its crest. The bird, in high good humour, bent its head sideways and chuckled inarticulately; yet to an accustomed ear the sound held the cadence of the Great Cry, and the tailor, who had heard it given wrathfully, looked up from his work.

'O Miffis Erlton!' what a boo'ful new polly,' came a silvery lisp. She turned with a radiant smile to greet her next door neighbour's little boy, a child of about three years old, who, pathetically enough, was a great solace to her child-bereft life.

'Yes, Sonny, isn't it lovely?' she said, her slim white hand going out to bring the child closer; 'and it screams splendidly. Would you like to hear it scream?'

Sonny, clinging tightly to her fingers, looked doubtful. 'Wait till muv'ver comth, muv'ver's comin' to zoo esectly. Sonny's always flightened wizout hith muvver.'

At which piece of diplomacy, Kate, feeling light-hearted, caught the little white-clad golden-curled figure in her arms and ran out with it into the garden smothering the laughing face with kisses as she ran.

'Sonny's a little goose to be "flightened," ' came her glad voice between the laughs and the kisses. 'He ought never to be "flightened" at all, because no one in all the wide, wide world would ever hurt a good little childie like Sonny-kin—No one! No one! No one!'

She had set the little fellow down among the flowers by this time, being in good sooth breathless with his weight; and now, continuing the game, chased him with pretence booings of 'No one! No one!' about the pansy bed and so round the sweet peas; until, in delicious terror, he shrieked with delight, and chased her back between her chasings.

It was a pretty sight, indeed, this game between the woman and the child. The gardener paused in his watering, the tailor at his work; and even the native orderly going his rounds with the brigade order-book grinned broadly, so adding one to the kindly dark faces watching the chasing of Sonny.

'My dear Kate! How can you?' The querulous voice broke in on the booings, and made Mrs Erlton pause and think of her loosened hairpins. The speaker was a fair diaphanous woman, the most solid-looking part of whose figure, as she dawdled up the path, was the large white umbrella she carried. 'Here am I melting with the heat!

What I shall do next year if George is transferred to Delhi, I don't know. He says we shan't be able to afford the hills. And he has the dogcart at some of those eternal court-martials. I wonder why the sepoys give so much trouble nowadays. George says they're spoilt. So I came to see if you'd drive me to the band; though I'm not fit to be seen. I was up half the night with baby. She is so cross, and George will have it she must be ill; as if children didn't have tempers! Lucky you, to have your boy at home; and yet you go romping with other people's. I wouldn't; but then I look horrid when I'm hot.'

Kate laughed. She did not, and as she rearranged her hair seemed to have left years of life behind her. 'I can't help it,' she said. 'I feel so ridiculously young myself sometimes—as if I hadn't lived at all, as if nothing belonged to me, and I was really somebody else. As if—' She paused abruptly in her confidences, and, to change the subject, turned to the group behind Mrs Seymour. It consisted of an ayah holding a toddler by the hand, and a tall orderly in uniform carrying a year-old baby in his arms—such a languid little mortal as is seldom seen out of India, where the swift, sharp fever of the changing seasons seems to take the very life from a child in a few hours. The fluffy golden head in its limp white sun-bonnet rested inert against the orderly's scarlet coatee, the listless little legs drooped helplessly among the burnished belts and buckles.

'Poor little chick! Let me have her a bit, orderly,' said Kate, laying her hand caressingly on the slack dimpled arm; but baby, with a fretful whine, nestled her cheek closer into the scarlet. A shade of satisfaction made its owner's dark face less impassive, and the small, sinewy, dark hands held their white burden a shade tighter.

'She *is* so cross,' complained the mother. 'It has been so all day. She won't leave the man for an instant. He must be sick of her, though he doesn't show it. And she used to go to the ayah; but do you know, Kate, I don't trust the woman a bit. I believe she gives opium to the child, so that she may get a little rest.'

Kate looked at the ayah's face with a sudden doubt. 'I don't know,' she said slowly. 'I think they believe it is a good thing. I remember when Freddy was a baby—'

'Oh I don't believe they ever think that sort of thing,' interrupted Mrs Seymour. 'You never can trust the natives you know. That's the worst of India. Oh! how I wish I was back in dear old England with a real nurse who would take the children off my hands.'

But Kate Erlton was following up her own doubt. 'The children trust them—' she began.

'My dear Kate! you can't trust children either. Look at Baby! It gives me the shudders to think of touching Bij-rao, and see how she cuddles up to him,' replied Mrs Seymour, as she dawdled on to the house. Then, seeing the bed of heartsease, she paused to go into raptures over them; they were like English ones, she said.

The puzzled look left Kate's face. 'I sent some home last mail,' she replied in a sort of hushed voice, 'just to show them that we were not cut off from everything we care for—not everything.'

So, as if by one accord, these two Englishwomen raised their eyes from the pansy bed, and passing by the flowering shrubs, the encircling tamarind trees framing the cosy homelike house, rested them on the reddening gold of the western sky. Its glow lay on their faces, making them radiant.

But baby's heavy lids had fallen at last over her heavy eyes as she lay in the orderly's arms, and he glanced at the ayah with a certain pride in his superior skill as a nurse.

# 3

# The Great Gulf Fixed

It was a quaint house in the oldest quarter of the city of Lucknow, where odd little groves linger between the alleys, so that men pass, at a step, from evil-smelling lanes to cool, scented retreats, dark with orange and mango-trees; where birds flutter, and squirrels loll yawning through the summer days, as if the great town were miles away.

It was in the furthest corner of such a flowerless shady garden that the house reared its lessening storeys and projecting eaves above its neighbours. The upper half of it was not unlike an Italian villa in its airiness, its balustraded roof, its green jalousies; but the lower portion was unmistakably Indian. It was a perfect rabbit warren of dark cells, crushed in on each other causelessly; the very staircase, though but two feet wide, having to fold itself away circumspectly so as to find space to creep upwards. But no one lived below, and the dark twists and turns of the brick ladder mattered little to Zora-*bibi* who lived in the pleasant pavilions above; for she had scarcely ever left them since the day, nearly eight years past, when James Greyman had installed her there with all the honour possible to the situation. Which was, briefly, that he had bought the slip of a girl from a house of ill-fame, as he would have bought a horse, or a flowerpot, or anything else which he thought would make life pleasanter to him. He had paid a long price for her, not only because she was beautiful, but because he pitied the delicate-looking child—for she was little more—just about to enter a profession to which she was evidently a recruit kidnapped in early infancy; as so many are in India. Not that his pity would have led him to buy her if she had been ugly, or even dark; for the creamy ivory tint of her skin satisfied his fastidiousness quite as much as did the hint of a soul in her dark dreamy eyes. Romance had perhaps had more to do with his purchase than passion; restless, reckless determination to show himself that he had no regrets for the society which had dispensed with his, had had more than either. For he had begun to rent the pleasant pavilions after a few years of adventurous roving had emphasized the gulf fixed between him and his previous life, and forced his pride into leading his present one as happily as he could.

As for the girl, those eight years of pure passion on the house-tops had been a dream of absolute content. It was so even now when she lay dying, as so many secluded women do, of a slow decline. To have flowers and fruit brought to her, to find no change in his tenderness because she was too languid to amuse him, to have him wait upon her and kiss away her protests; all this made her soft warm eyes softer, warmer. It was so unlike anything she had ever heard or dreamt of; it made her blind to the truth, that she was dying. How could this be so when there was no hint of change, when life still gave her all she cared for? She did not, to be sure, play tricks with him like a kitten, as she used to; but that was because she was growing old—nearly one and twenty!

'She is worse today. I deem her close to freedom, Soma, so I have warned the death-tender,' said a tall woman, as she straightened the long column of her throat to the burden of a brass water-pot, new-poised on her head, and stepped down from the low parapet of the well which stood in one corner of the shady grove. Sometimes its creaking Persian wheel moaned over the task of sending runnels of water to the thirsty trees; but today it was silent, save for an intermittent protest when the man—who was lazily leaning his back against the yoke—put out his strength so as to empty an extra water-can or two into the trough for the woman's use. He was in the undress uniform of a sepoy, and as he also straightened himself to face the speaker, the extraordinary likeness between them in face and figure stamped them as twins. It would have been difficult to give the palm to either for superior height or beauty; and in their perfection of form they might have stood as models of the mythical race-founders whose names they bore. For Tara Devi and Soma Chund were Rajpoots of the single Lunar or Yadubansi tribe. She was dressed in an endless scarf of crimson wool, which with its border of white and yellow embroidery hung about her in admirable folds. The gleam of the water-pot matched the dead gold circlets on the brown wrists and ankles; for Tara wore her savings thus, though she had no right to do so, being a widow. But she had been eight years in James Greyman's service; and for more than eight she had been bound to him by the strangest of ties. He had been the means of saving her from her husband's funeral pyre; in other words of preventing her from being a saint, of making her outcaste utterly. Since none, not even other widows, would eat or drink with a woman rejected by the very gods on the threshold of Paradise. Such a mental position is well-nigh incomprehensible to Western minds. It was confusing, even to Tara herself; and the mingling of conscious dignity and conscious degradation, gratitude, resentment, attraction, repulsion, made her a puzzle even to herself at times.

'The master will grieve,' replied Soma; his voice was far softer than his sister's had been, but it had the effect of hardening hers still more.

'What then?' she asked; 'man's sorrow for a woman passes; or even if it pass not, bears no fruit here, or hereafter. But I, as *thou knowest, Soma,* would have burnt with my love. *But for thee,* as thou knowest, I would have been *suttee (lit.* virtuous). *But for thee* I should have found, ay! and given salvation.'

She passed on with a sweep of full drapery, bearing her water-pot as a queen might her crown, leaving Soma's handsome face full of conscience-stricken amaze. His sister—from whom, despite her degradation, he had not been able to dissociate himself utterly—had never before rounded on him for his share in her misfortune; but in his heart of hearts he had admitted his responsibility at one moment, scorned it the next. True, he had told his young lieutenant that his brother-in-law was going to be burnt, as an excuse for not accompanying him after black-buck one morning; but who would have dreamt that this commonplace remark would rouse the *Huzoor's* curiosity to see the obsequies of a high-caste Rajpoot, and so lead, incidentally, to a file of policemen and the neighbouring magistrate dragging the sixteen-year old widow from the very flames?—when she was drugged, too, and quite happy—when the wrench was over, even for him, and she, to all intents, was a saint scattering salvation on seven generations of inconstant males! Much as he loved Tara, the little twin sister who, so the village gossips used to tell, had left the Darkness for the Light of Life still clasping his hand, how could he have done her such an injury? As a Rajpoot how could he have brought such a scandalous dishonour on any family?

But being also a soldier, as his fathers had been before him, and so leavened unconsciously by much contact with Europeans, he could not help admiring Tara's pluck in refusing to accept the life of a dog which was all that was left to her among her own people. And he had been grateful to the *Huzoor,* as she was, for giving her good service where he could see her; though he would not for worlds have touched the hand which had lain in his from the beginning of all things. It was unclean now.

Still he could not forget the gossip's story any more than he could forget that James Greyman had been his lieutenant, and that together they had shot over half Hurreeana. So when he passed through Lucknow on his way to spend his leave in his wife's village, he always gave a day or two of it to the quaint garden-house.

And now Tara had definitely accused him of ruining her life! Anger, born of a vague remorse, filled him as he watched her disappear up the plinth. If it was anybody's fault it was the *Huzoor's;* or rather of the *Sirkar* itself who, by high-handed interference with venerable customs, made it possible for a poor man, by a mere slip of the tongue, to injure one bound to him by the closest of ties.

'It will leave us naught to ourselves soon,' he muttered sulkily as he went out to the doorstep to finish polishing the master's sword; that being a recognized office during these occasional visits, which, as it occurred to him in his discontent, would be still more occasional if among other things the *Sirkar,* now that Oude was annexed, took away the extra leave due to foreign service. They had said so in the regiment; and though he was too tough to feel pinpricks in advance, he had sneered with others in the current jest that the maps were tinted red— *i.e.* shown to be British territory—by savings stolen from the sepoy's pocket.

It was very quiet on the paved slope leading up from the alley to the carved door beyond the gutter. The lane was too narrow for wheeled traffic, the evening not sufficiently advanced for the neighbours to gather in it for gossip. But every now and again a veiled figure would sidle along the further wall, passing good-looking Soma with a flurried shuffle. Whereat, though he knew these ghostly figures to be old women on their way to market, he cocked his turban more awry, and curled his mustachios nearer his eyes; from no set purpose of playing the gay Lothario, but for the honour of the regiment, and because War and Women go together, East and West.

After a time, however, the workmen began to dawdle past from their work, and some of them, remembering Soma, paused to ask him the latest news—a stranger in a native city being equivalent to an evening paper. And, of course, there were questions as to what the regiment thought of this and that. But Soma's replies were curt. He never relished being lumped in as a simple Rajpoot with the rest of the

Rajpoots, for he was inordinately proud of his tribe. That was one reason why he stood aloof, as he did, from much that went on among his comrades. He drilled, it is true, between two of them who were entered as he was—that is to say, as a Rajpoot—on the roster; but the three were, in reality, as wide apart as the Sun, the Moon, and the Fire from which they respectively claimed descent. They would not have intermarried into each other's families for all the world and its wealth: a causeless differentiation which makes, and must make, a people who cling to it incomprehensible to a race which boasts, as a check to pride or an encouragement to humility, that all men are born of Adam, and which seeks no hallmark for its descendants save the stamp of the almighty dollar.

Soma, therefore, polishing his master's sword sulkily, grew irritable also; especially when the frequenters of the opium and hemp shops began, with wavering steps and lack-lustre eyes, to loaf homewards for the evening meal which would give them strength for another dose. There were many such habitual drug-takers in the quarter; for it was largely inhabited by poor claimants to nobility who, having nothing to do, had time for dreams. That was why people from other quarters flocked to this one at sundown for gossip; since it is to be had at its best from the opium-eater, whose imagination is stimulated, his reason dulled, beyond the power of discriminating even his own truth or falsehood. One of these, a haggard, sallow fellow in torn muslin and ragged embroidery, stopped with a heavy-lidded leer beside Soma.

'So, brother, back again!' he said with the maudlin gravity of a hemp-smoker; 'and thou lookest fat. The bone-dust must agree with thee.'

It was if a bomb had fallen. The Hindoo bystanders, recognizing the rumour that ground bones were mixed with Commissariat flour, drew back from the Rajpoot instinctively; the Mohamedans smiled on the sly. Soma himself had in a moment one sinewy hand on the half-drunk creature's throat, the other brandishing the fresh-polished sword.

'Bone-dust thyself, and pigs-meat too, foul-mouthed slayer of sacred kine!' he gasped, carrying the war into the enemy's country. 'Thou beast! Unsay the lie!'

His indignation, showing that he appreciated the credence some might be disposed to give to the accusation, only made the Hindoos look at each other. The Mohamedans, however, dragged him from the swaying figure of the accuser, who, after all, was one of themselves.

'Heed him not!' they chorused appeasingly. 'Tis drug-shop talk, and every sane man knows that for dreams. Lo! his sense is clean gone as horns from a donkey! Sure, thy mother ate chillies in her time for thou to be so hot-blooded. It is not morning, brother, because a hen crows, and a snake is but a snake, and goes crooked even to his own home!'

These hoarded saws, with physical force superadded, left Soma reduced to glaring and renewed claims for a retraction of the insult.

The hemp-smoker looked at him mournfully. 'Would'st have me deny God's truth?' he hiccupped. 'Lo! I say not thou did'st eat it. Thou say'st not, and who am I to decide between a man and his stomach, even though he looks fat? Yet this all know, that as bird fattens his tail shrinks, and honour is nowhere nowadays. But this I say for certain. Let him eat who will, there is bone-dust in the flour—there is bone-dust in the flour—'

He lurched from a supporter's hold and drifted down the lane, half-chanting the words.

Some glared, now, at those doubtful faces which remained. ''Tis a lie, brothers! But there, 'tis no use wearing the red coat nowadays when all scoff at it. And why not? when the *Sirkar* itself mocks our rights. I tell thee at the father-in-law's village, but now, a man who titled me *Sahib* last year puffed his smoke in my face this. And wherefore not? May not every scoundrel nowadays drag us to court and set us a-bribing underlings as the common herd have to do? We, soldiers of Oude, who had a Resident of our own always, and—'

'Nothing lasts for always, save God,' said a long-bearded bystander, interrupting Soma's parrot-roll of military grievances. 'As the Moulvie said last night at our mosque, it is well He remains ever the same, giving the same plain orders once and for all. So none of the faithful can mistake. God is Might and Right. All the rest is change.'

'*Wah! wah!*' murmured some respectfully; but the Rajpoot's scowl lost its fierceness in supercilious indifference.

'That may suit the Moulvie. It may suit thee and thine, *syyed-jee*,' he replied, with a shrug of the shoulders. 'It suits not me nor mine, being of a different race. We are Rajpoots, and there is no change possible to that. We are ever the same.'

The pride in his voice and manner reflected but faintly the inconceivable pride in his heart. Yet he was on the alert, salaaming cheerfully, as James Greyman came riding with a clatter down the alley, and without drawing bridle, passed through the low gateway into the dark garden heavy with the perfume of orange-blossom. His arrival ended the incident, for Soma followed him quickly, and in obedience to his curt order to see the groom rub down the horse while it waited as it had been a breather round the racecourse, walked off with it towards the well. It was such an opportunity for ordering other men about as natives dearly love; so that the more autocratic a master is, the better pleased they are to gain dignity by serving him.

James Greyman, meanwhile, had paused on the plinth to give a low whistle and look upwards to the terraced roof. And as he did so his face was full of weariness, and yet of impatience. He had been telling himself that he was a fool ever since he had left Kate Erlton's drawing-room half-an-hour before, and even his mad gallop round the steeplechase course had not effaced the curious sense of compulsion which had made him promise to let her husband go scot-free. Even now, when he waited with that dread at his heart—which of late had been growing stronger day by day—for the answer which Zora loved to make to his signal, his fear lest the Great Silence had fallen between them was lost in the recollection that, if it were so, his freedom had come too late. He hated himself for thus bracketing death and freedom together, but for all that he would not blind himself to its truth. Now that his profession had gone with the King's exile, Zora was, indeed, the only tie to a life which had grown distasteful to him; and when the Great Silence came, as come it must, he had made up his mind to leave James Greyman behind, and go home to England. He was nearing forty, and though the spirit of reckless adventure was fading, the ambitions of his youth seemed to be returning—as they so often do when the burden and heat of passion passes. He was tired of perpetual sunshine. The thought of the cold mists on the hill tops, the wild storms on the west coast, haunted him. He wanted to see them again. Above all, he wanted to hear himself called by his own familiar name, not by the one he had assumed. It had seemed brutal to dream of all this sometimes, while little Zora still lay in his arms smiling contentedly; but it was inevitable. And so, while he waited, watching with the dread growing at his heart for the flutter of the tinsel veil, the half-heard whisper 'Khush amud-eed' (welcome), it was inevitable also that the remembrance of his promise to Kate Erlton should invade, and as it were desecrate, his real regret for the silence that seemed to grow deeper every second. It had come too late—too late! There could be no solace in freedom now. That other silence in regard to Major Erlton's misdeeds meant the loss of every penny he had scraped together for England. He might have to sell up almost everything he possessed in order to pay his racing bets honourably; and that he must do, or he gave away his only hope of recouping his bad luck. Why had he promised? Why had he given up a certainty for that vague chance of which he had spoken, he scarcely knew why, to these cold blue Northern eyes with the glint of steel. The remembrance brought a passionate anger at himself. Was there anything in the world worth thinking of now, with that silence new-fallen upon him, except the soft warm eyes which were perhaps closed for ever? So, with a quick step, he passed up the stairs and gave his signal knock at the door which led on to the terraced roof.

Tara, opening it, answered his look with finger to her lip, and a warning glance to the low string-bed set close to the arches of the summer-house so as to catch the soft-scented breeze. He stepped over to it lightly and looked down on the sleeper; but the relief passed from his face at what he saw there. It could only be a question of hours now.

'Why did'st not send before?' he asked in a low voice. 'I bid thee send if she were worse and she needed me.' Once more the anger against that other woman came uppermost. What was she to him that she should filch even half-an-hour from this one who loved him? He might so easily have come earlier—and then the promise would not have been made! Was he utterly heartless, that this thought would come again and again?

'She slept,' replied Tara coldly. 'And sleep needs naught. Not even Love's kisses. It is nigh the end though, master, as thou seest; so I have warned mother Jewuni the death-tender.' She had spoken so far as if she desired to make him wince; now the pain on his face made her add hurriedly: 'She hath not suffered, *Huzoor*, she hath not complained. Had it been so I would have sent. But sleep is rest.'

She passed on to a lower roof softening her echoing steps with a quaint crooning lullaby:

My breast is rest
And rest is Death.
Ye who have breath
Say which is best?
Death's Sleep is rest!

Was it so? As he stood, still looking down on the sleeper, something in the lack of comfort, of all the refinements and luxuries which seem to belong by right to the sickness of dear ones in the West, smote him suddenly with a sense of deprivation, of division. And though he told himself that Death came in far more friendly fashion out there in the sunlight, where you could hear the birds, watch the squirrels, and see the children's kites go sailing overhead in the blue sky; still the bareness of it seemed somehow to reveal the great gulf between his complexity, his endless needs and desires, and the simplicity of that human creature drifting to death, almost as the animals drift, without complaint, without fears, or hopes. It seemed so pitiful. The slender figure, still gay in tinsel and bright draperies, all cuddled up on the quilt, its oval face resting hardly on the thin arm where the bracelets hung so loosely, had an uncared-for look. It seemed alone, apart; as far from Death in its nearness to Life, as it was from Life in its closeness to Death. In swift pity he stooped to risk an awakening by gathering it into his warm friendly arms—it would at least feel the beating of another human heart when it lay there—it would at least be more comfortable than on the bare, hard, pillowless bed.

But he paused. How could he judge? How dare he judge even for that wasted body, which, despite its softness, had never known half the luxuries he claimed? So he left her lying as he had so often seen her sleep, all curled up on herself like a tired squirrel, and passing to the parapet leant over it looking moodily down into the darkening orange-trees. Their heavy perfume floated upwards reminding him of many another night in spring time spent with Zora upon this terraced roof.

And suddenly his hand fell heavily in a gesture of sheer anger.

Before God! it had been unfair—this idyll on the housetops. The world had held no more for her save her passion for him, pure in its very perfection. His for her had been but a small part of his life. It never was more than that to a man, in reality, and so this sort of thing must always be unfair. That she had been content made it worse, not better. Poor little soul! drifting away from the glow and the glamour.

A resentment for her, more than for himself, made him go to where Tara sat gossiping with her fellow-servant on the other roof and bid them wait downstairs. If the silence were indeed about to fall, if the glow and the glamour were going, then she and he might at least be alone once more beneath the coming stars; alone in the soft scented darkness which had so often seemed to clasp them closer to each other as they sat in it like a couple of children whispering over a secret.

Closer! As he leant over the parapet his keen eyes stared down into the half-seen city spreading below him. Wide, tree-set, full of faint sounds of life; the wreaths of smoke from thousands of hearths rising to obscure it from his view; obscuring it hopelessly with their tale of a life utterly apart from any he could lead. Even there on the housetop he had only pretended to lead it. It was not she, drifting to death so contentedly, who was alone! It was he. Yet some men he had known had seemed able to combine the two lives. They had been content to think half-caste thoughts, to rear up a tribe of half-caste children; while he? How many years was it since he had seen Zora weeping over a still little morsel of humanity, his child and hers, that lay in her tinselled veil? She had wept, mostly because she was afraid he might be angry because his son had never drawn breath, and he had comforted her. He had never told her of the relief it was to him, of the vague repulsion which the thought of a child had always brought with it. One could not help these things; and, after all, she had only cared because she was afraid he cared. She did not crave for motherhood either. It was the glow and the glamour that had been the bond between them—nothing else. And, thank Heaven! she had never tired of it, would never see him tire of it—since Death would come before that now.

A chiming clash of silver made him turn quickly. She had awakened, and seeing him by the parapet, had set her small feet to the ground, and now stood trying to steady herself by her thin, wide-spread arms.

'Zora! wait! I am coming,' he cried, starting forward. Then he paused, speech and action arrested by something in her look, her gesture.

'Let me come,' she murmured, her breath gone with the effort. 'I can come. I must be able to come. My lord is so near—so near.'

A fierce pity made him stand still. 'Surely thou canst come,' he answered. 'I will stay here.'

As she stood, with parted lips, waiting for a glint of strength ere she tried to walk, her swaying figure, the brilliance of her eyes, the heaving of her delicate throat, cut him to the very heart for her sake more than for his own. Then the jingle of her silver anklets rose again in irregular cadence, to cease at the next pillar where she paused, steadying herself against the cold stone to regain her breath.

'Surely, I can come; and he so near,' she murmured wistfully, half to herself.

'Thou art in too great a hurry, sweetheart. There is plenty of time. The stars are barely lit, and star-time is ever our time.'

He set his teeth over the words; but the glow and the glamour should not fail her yet. He would take her back with him, while he could, to the past which had been so full of it.

'Come slower, my bird, I am waiting,' he said again as the jingling cadence ceased once more.

'It is so strange,' she gasped; 'I feel so strange.' And even in the dim light he could see a vague terror, a pitiful amaze in her face. That must not be. That must be stopped. 'And it *is* strange,' he answered quickly. 'Strange, indeed, for me to wait like a king, when thou art my queen!'

A faint smile drove the wonder away, a faint laugh mingled with the chiming and clashing. She was like a wounded bird, he thought, as he watched her; a wounded bird fluttering to find shelter from death.

'Take care! Take care of the step!' he cried, as a stumble made him start forward; but when she recovered herself blindly he stood still once more, waiting. Let her come if she could. Let her keep the glamour.

Keep it! She had done more than that. She had given it back to him at its fullest, as, close at hand, he saw her radiant face, and his outstretched hands met hers warm and clasping. The touch of them made him forget all else, he drew her close to him passionately. She gave a smiling sob of sheer content, raising her face to meet his kisses.

'I have come,' she whispered. 'I have come to my king.' Her voice ended like a sigh. Then there was silence, a fainter sigh, then silence again.

'Zora!' he called with a sudden dread at his heart. 'What is it—Zora! Zora!'

Half-an-hour afterwards, Tara Devi, obeying her master's summons, found him standing beside the bed, which he had dragged out under the stars, and flung up her arms to give the wail for what she saw there.

'Hush!' he said sternly, clutching at her shoulder. 'I will not have her disturbed.'

Tara looked at him wonderingly. 'There is no fear of that,' she replied clearly, loudly, 'none shall disturb Zora again. She hath found *that* freedom in the future. For the rest of us, God knows! The times are strange. So let her have her right of wailing, master. She will feel silent in the grave without the voices of her race.'

He drew his hand away sharply; even in death a great gulf lay between him and the woman he had loved.

So the death wail rang out clamorously through the soft dark air.

# 4

# Tape and Sealing-wax

I can't think,' said a good-looking middle-aged man as he petulantly pushed aside a pile of official papers, 'where Dashe picks these things up. I never come across them. And it is not as if he were in a big station or—or in the swim in any way.' He spoke fretfully, as one might who, having done his best, has failed. And he had grounds for this feeling, since the fact that the different district-officer named Dashe was not in the swim, must clearly have been due to his official superiors; the speaker being one of them.

Fortunately however for England, these diffident sons of hers cannot always hide their lights under bushels. As the biographies of many Indian statesmen show, some outsider notices a gleam of common-sense amid the gloom, and steers his course by it. Now Mr Dashe's intimate knowledge of a certain jungle tract in his district, had resulted in a certain military magnate bagging three tigers. From this, to a reliance on his political perceptions is not so great a jump as might appear; since a man acquainted with the haunt of every wild beast in his jurisdiction, may be credited with knowledge of other dangerous inhabitants. So much so that the military magnate being impressed by some casual remarks, had asked Mr Dashe to put down his views on paper, and had passed them on to a great political light.

It was he who sat at the table looking at a broadsheet printed in the native character, as if it were a personal affront. The military magnate, who had come over to discuss the question, was lounging in an easy-chair with a cheroot. They were both excellent specimens of Englishmen. The civilian a trifle bald, the soldier a trifle grey; but one glance was sufficient to judge them neither knaves nor fools.

'That's the proclamation you're at now, isn't it?' asked the military magnate looking up; 'I'm afraid I could only make out a word here and there. That's the worst of Dashe. He's so deuced clever at the vernaculars himself that he imagines other people—'

The political, who had earned his first elevation from the common herd to the Secretariat by a nice taste in Persian couplets suitable for *durbar* speeches, smiled compassionately:

'My dear sir! This is not even *shikust* (broken character). It is lithographed, and plain sailing to any one not a fool—I mean to any one on the civil side, of course—you soldiers have not to learn the language. But I have a translation here. As this farrago of Dashe's must go to Calcutta in due course, I had one made for the Governor-General's use.'

He handed a paper across the table, and then turned to the next paragraph of the jeremiad.

The military magnate laid down his cigar, took up the document, and glanced at it apprehensively; resumed his cigar, and settled himself in his chair. It was a very comfortable one and matched the office-room, which being in the political light's private house, was under the supervision of his wife, who was a notable woman. Her portrait stood in the place of honour on the mantelpiece and it was flanked by texts; one inculcating the virtue of doing as you would be done by, the other the duty of doing good without ceasing. Both rather dangerous maxims, when you have to deal with a different personal and ethical standard of happiness and righteousness. There was also a semicircle of children's photographs—of the kind known as positives—on the table round the official ink-pot. When the sun shone on their glasses, as it did now through a western window, they dazzled the eyes. May be it was their hypnotizing influence, which inclined the father of the family towards treating every problem which came to that office-table, as if the first desideratum was their welfare, their approbation; not, of course, as his children, but as the representative Englishmen and women of the future. Yet he was filled with earnest desires to do his duty by those over whom he had been set to rule, and as he read, his sense of responsibility was simply portentous, and his pen, scratching fluently in comments over the half margin, was full of wisdom. This sound was the only one in the room save, occasionally, voices raised eagerly in the rehearsal going on in the drawing-room next door. It was a tragedy in aid of an orphan asylum in England which the notable wife was getting up; and once her voice could be heard distinctly, saying to her daughter, 'Oh Elsie, I'm sure you could die better than that!'

Meanwhile the military magnate was reading:

'I, servant of God, the all-powerful, and of the prophet Mahomed—to whom be all praise. I, *Syyed* Ahmed-Oolah, the dust of the feet of the descendants of *Huzrut Ameer-Oolah-Moomereen-Ali-Moortuza*, the Holy.' He shifted uneasily, looked across the table, appeared discouraged by that even scratching and went on.

'I, *Syyed* Ahmed, after preferring my salaams and the blessings of Holy War, to all believers of the sect of Sheeahs or the sect of Sunnees alike, and also to all those having respectful regards to the Faith, declare that I, the least of servants in the company of those waiting on the Prophet, did by the order of God receive a Sword of Honour, on condition that I should proclaim boldly to all the duty of combining to drive out Infidels. In this, therefore, is there great Reward; as is written in the Word of God, since His Gracious Power is mighty for success. Yea! and if any fail, will they not be rid of all the ends of this evil world, and attain the Joys and Glories of Martyrdom? So be it. A sign is ever sufficient to the intelligent, and the Duty of a servant is simply to point the way.'

When he had finished he laid the document down on the table, and for a minute or so continued to puff at his cigar. Then he broke silence with that curious constraint in his tone, which most men assume when religious topics crop up in general conversation. 'I wonder if this—this paper is to be considered the sign, or'—he hesitated for a moment, then, the cadence of the proclamation being suggestive, he finished his sentence to match—'or look we for another?'

'Another!' retorted his companion irritably, 'according to Dashe the whole of India is one vast sign-post! He seems to think we in authority are blind to this. On the contrary, there is scarcely one point he mentions which is not, I say this confidentially of course, under inquiry. I have the files in my confidential box here and can show them to you now—No! by the way the head-clerk has the key—that proclamation had to be translated, of course. But, naturally, we don't proclaim this on the house-tops. We might hurt people's feelings, or give rise to unfounded hopes. As for these bazaar rumours Dashe retails with such zest, I confess I think it undignified for a district-officer to give any heed to them. They are inevitable with an ignorant population, and we, having the testimony of a good conscience'—he glanced almost unconsciously at the mantelpiece—'should disregard these ridiculous lies. Of course every one—every one in the swim that is—admits that the native army is most unsettled. And as Sir Charles Napier declared, mutiny is the most serious danger in the future; in fact, if the first symptoms are not grappled with, it may shake the very foundations. But we are grappling with it, just as we are grappling, quietly, with the general distrust. That was a most mischievous paragraph, by the way, in the *Christian Observer*, jubilant over the alarm created by those first widow remarriages the other day. So was that in *The Friend of India*, calling attention to the fact that a regular prayer was offered up in all the mosques for the Restoration of the Royal Family. We don't want these things *noticed*. We want to create a feeling of security by ignoring them. That is our policy. Then as for Dashe's political news it is all stale! That story, for instance, of the Embassy from Persia, and of the old King of Delhi having turned a Sheeah—'

'That has something to do with saying Amen, hasn't it?' interrupted the military magnate, with the air of one determined to get at the bottom of things at all costs to himself.

The political light smiled in superior fashion. 'Partially; but politically—as a gauge I mean to probable antagonism—Sheeahs and Sunnees are as wide apart as Protestants and Papists. The fact that the Royal Family of Oude are Sheeahs, and the Delhi one Sunnee, is our safeguard. Of course the old king's favourite wife, Zeenut Maihl, is an Oude woman, but I don't credit the rumours. I had it carefully inquired into, however, by a man who has special opportunities for that sort of work. A very intelligent fellow, Greyman by name. He has a black wife or—or something of that sort, which, of course helps him to understand the natives better than most of us who—er—who don't—you understand—'

The military magnate, having a sense of humour, smiled to himself. 'Perfectly,' he replied, 'and I'm inclined to think that perhaps there is something to be said for a greater laxity.' In his turn he glanced at the mantelpiece, and paused before that immaculate presence. 'The proclamation, however,' he went on hurriedly, 'appears to me a bit dangerous. Holy War is awkward, and a religious fanatic is a tough subject even to regulars.' He had seen a rush of *Ghâzees* once and the memory lingered.

'Undoubtedly. And as we have pointed out again and again to your Department, here and at home, the British garrisons are too scattered. These large accessions of territory have put them out of touch with each other. But that again is being grappled with. In fact, personally, I believe we are getting on as well as can be expected—' He glanced here at the semicircle of children as if the phrase were suggestive—'We are doing our best for India and the Indians. Now here, in Oude, things are wonderfully ship-shape already. Despite Jackson and Gubbins' tiffs over trifles they are both splendid workers, and Lucknow was never so well governed as it is today.'

'But about the proclamation,' persisted his hearer. 'Couldn't you get some more information about it? That Greyman for instance.'

'I'm afraid not. He refused some other work I offered him not long ago; said he was going home for good. I sometimes wish I could. It is a thankless task slaving out here and being misunderstood, even at home; being told in so many words that the very system under which we were recruited has failed. Poor old Haileybury! I only hope competition will do as well, but I doubt it; these new fellows can never have the old *esprit de corps;* won't come from the same class! One of the Rajah's people was questioning me about it only this morning—they read the English newspapers, of course—"So we are not to have *Sahibs* to rule over us," he said, looking black as thunder. "Any *krani*'s (*lit.* low-caste English) son will do, if he has learnt enough." I tried to explain—' Here a red-coated orderly entering with a card, the speaker broke off into angry inquiries why he was being disturbed contrary to orders.

'The *Sahib* bade me bring it,' replied the man, as if that were sufficient excuse. His master looking at the card tossed it over the table to the soldier, who exclaimed—'Talk of the devil! He may as well come in, if you don't mind.'

So James Greyman was ushered in, and remained standing between the civilian and the soldier; for it is not given to all to have the fine perceptions of the native. The orderly had unhesitatingly classed the visitor as a 'gentleman to be obeyed'; but the Political Department knew him only as a reliable source of information.

'Well, Greyman! Have you brought any more news?' asked the civilian, in a tone intended to impress the Military Department with the fact that here was one grapnel out of the many which were being employed in bringing truth to the surface, and securing safety. But the soldier, after one brief look at the newcomer, sat up and squared his own shoulders a bit.

'That depends, sir,' replied James Greyman quietly, 'whether it pays me to bring it or not. I told you last month that I could not undertake any more work, because I was leaving India. My plans have changed; and to be frank, I am rather hard up. If you could give me regular employment I should be glad of it.' He spoke with the utmost deliberation, but the incisive finality of every word, taking his hearer unprepared, gave an impression of hurry, and left the civilian breathless. James Greyman, however, having said what he had come to say, said no more. During the past week he had had plenty of time to make up his mind, or rather to find out that it was made up; for he recognized frankly that he was acting more on impulse than reason. After he had buried poor little Zora away in accordance with the customs of her people, and paid his racing bets and general liabilities,—to do which he had found it necessary to sell most things, including the very horse he had matched against Major Erlton's,—he had suddenly found out, rather to his own surprise, that the idea of starting again on the old lines was utterly distasteful to him. In a lesser degree this second loss of his future and severing of ties in the past, had had the same effect upon him as the previous one. It had left him reckless, disposed to defy all he had lost, and prove himself superior to ill-luck. Then being, by right of his Celtic birth, imaginative, in a way superstitious, he had again and again found himself thrown back, as it were, upon Kate Erlton's appeal for that chance, to bring which the Spirit might be, even now, moving on the waters. It was that, that only, with its swift touch on his own certainty that a storm was brewing, which had made him yield his point; which had forced him into yielding by an unreasoning assent to her suggestion that it might bring a chance of atonement with it. And now, in calm deliberation, he confessed that he might find his chance in it also; a better chance, maybe, than he would have had in England. It would be his only one, at any rate, for some time to come; since those grey-blue northern eyes with the glint of steel in them had, by a few words, changed the current of his life. The truth was unpalatable, but as usual he did not attempt to deny it. He simply cast round for the best course in which to flow towards that tide in the affairs of men which he hoped to take at its flood; and political employment, briefly, spy's work, seemed as good as any for the present.

'Regular employment,' echoed the civilian, recovering from his sense of hurry. 'You mean, I presume, as a news-writer.'

'As a spy, sir,' interrupted James Greyman.

The political light disregarded the suggestion. 'Your acquirements, of course, would be suitable enough; but I fear there are no native courts without one at present. And the situation hardly calls for excess expenditure. But of course, any isolated *douceur*—'

His hearer smiled. 'Call it payment, sir. But I think you must find job-work in secret intelligence rather expensive. It produces such a crop of mare's-nests; at least so I have found.'

The suspicion of equality in the remark made the official mount his high horse, deftly.

'Really we have so many reliable sources of information, Mr Greyman,' he began, laying his hand as if casually on the papers before him. The action was followed by James Greyman's keen eyes.

'You have the proclamation there, I see,' he said cheerfully. 'I thought it could not be much longer before the police or some one else became aware of its existence. The Moulvie himself was here about a week ago.'

'The Moulvie—what Moulvie?' asked the military magnate eagerly. The civilian, however, frowned. If confidential work were to be carried out on those lines, something, even if it were only ignorance, must be found out.

'The Moulvie of Fyzabad,' began James Greyman.

'And who—?'

'My dear sir,' interrupted the other pettishly; 'we really know all about the Moulvie of Fyzabad. His name has been on the register of suspects for months.' He rose, crossed to a bookshelf, and coming back processionally with two big volumes, began to turn over the pages of one.

'M—Mo—Ah! *Ma*, no doubt. That is correct, though transliteration is really a difficult task—to be consistent, yet intelligible in a foreign language is—No. It must be under F in the first volume. *F; Fy*. Just so! Here we are. "*Fyzabad, Moulvie of—fanatic, tall, medium colour, mole on inside of left shoulder*." This the man, I think?'

'I was not aware of the mole, sir,' replied James Greyman drily, 'but he is a magnificent preacher, a consistent patriot, a born organizer; and he is now on his way to Delhi.'

'To Delhi?' echoed the civilian pettishly. 'What can a man of the stamp you say he is, want with Delhi? A sham court, a miserable pantaloon of a king, the prey of a designing woman who flatters his dotage. I admit he is the representative of the Moghul dynasty, but its record for the last hundred and fifty years is bad enough surely to stamp out sentiment of that sort.'

'Prince Charles Edward was not a very admirable person, nor the record of the Stuarts a very glorious one, and yet my grandfather—' James Greyman pulled himself up sharply, and seeing an old prayer-book lying on the table, which, with the alternatives of a bottle of Ganges water and a copy of the *Koran*, lay ready for the discriminate swearing of witnesses, finished his sentence by opening the volume at a certain Office, and then placing the open book on the top of the Proclamation. 'It will be no news to you, sir, that prayers of that sort are being used in all the mosques. Of course here, in Lucknow, they are for my late master's return. But if anything comparable to the '15 or the '45 were to come, Delhi must be the centre. It is the lens which would focus the largest area, the most rays; for it appeals to greed as well as good, to this world as well as the next.'

'Do you think it a centre of disaffection now, Mr Greyman?' asked the military magnate with an emphasis on the title.

'I do not know, sir. Zeenut Maihl, the Queen, has court intrigues, but they are of little consequence.'

'I disagree,' protested the political. 'You require the experience of a lifetime to estimate the enormous influence—'

'What do you consider of importance then?' interrupted the soldier rather cavalierly, leaning across the table eagerly to look at James Greyman. There was an instant's silence, during which those voices rehearsing were clearly audible. The tragedy had apparently reached a climax.

'That; and this.' He pointed to the Proclamation, and small fragment of something which he took from his waistcoat pocket and laid beside the paper. The civilian inspected it curiously, the soldier, leaving his chair, came round to look at it also. The sunny room was full of peace and solid security as those three Englishmen, with no lack of pluck and brains, stood round the white fragment.

'Looks like bone,' remarked the soldier.

'It is bone, and it was found, so I heard in the bazaar today, at the bottom of a commissariat flour-sack—'

James Greyman was interrupted by a relieved pshaw! from the political light.

'The old story, eh, Greyman! I wonder what next these ignorant fools—'

'When the ignorant fools happen to be drilled soldiers, and, in Bengal, outnumber our English troops by twenty-four to one,' retorted James Greyman sharply, 'it seems a work of supererogation to ask what they will do next. If I were in their place—However, if I may tell you how that came into my hands you will perhaps be able to grasp the gravity of the situation.'

'Won't you take a chair?' asked the soldier quickly.

James Greyman glanced at the political. 'No, thanks, I won't be long. There is a class of grain carriers called Bunjâras. They keep herds of oxen, and have carried supplies for the Royal troops since time immemorial. They have a charter engraved on a copper breastplate. I've only seen a copy, for the original Jhungi and Bhungi lived ages ago in Rajpootana. It runs so:-

'While Jhungi Bhungi's oxen
Carry the army's corn,

House-thatch to feed their flocks on,
House-water ready drawn.
Three murders daily shriven,
These rights to them are given,
While Jhungi Bhungi's oxen
Carry the army's corn.'

'Preposterous,' murmured the civilian. 'That's at an end anyhow.'

'Naturally; for they no longer carry the corn. The method is too slow, too Eastern for our commissariat. But the Oude levies used to employ them. So did I at the stables. This is over also, and when I last saw my *tanda*—that's a caravan of them, sir—they were sub-contracting under a rich Hindoo firm which was dealing direct with the Department. They didn't like it.'

'Still you can't deny that the growth of a strong, contented commercial class with a real stake in the country—' began the civilian hurriedly.

'That sounds like the home-counties or a vestry board,' interrupted his hearer drily. 'The worst of it, in this case, being that you have to get your content out of the petty dealers like these Bunjâras. I came upon one yesterday telling a select circle of admirers, in the strictest confidence of course, lest the *Sirkâr* should kill him for letting the cat out of the bag, that he had found that bit of bone at the bottom of a Commissariat sack he bought to mend his own. The moral being, of course, that it was safer to buy from him. But he was only half through when I, knowing the scoundrel, fell on him and thrashed him for lying. The audience approved, and assented to his confession that it was a lie; but only to please me, the man with the stick. And as for Jhungi, he will tell the tale with additional embellishments in every village to which the caravan goes; unless some one is there to thrash him if he does.'

'Scoundrel,' muttered the soldier, angrily.

'Or saint,' added James Greyman. 'He will be that when he comes to believe in his own story of having burnt the sack rather than use it. That won't be long. Then he will be much more dangerous. However, if there is no place vacant for me, sir—'

'If you would not mind waiting a minute,' began the military magnate, with a hasty look at the political.

James Greyman bowed, and retired discreetly to the window. It looked out upon just such another garden as Kate Erlton's, and the remembrance provoked the cynical question as to what the devil he was doing in that galley? Racing was a far safer way of making money than acting as a spy—to no purpose possibly, at least so far as his own chance was concerned.

Yet five minutes after, when the political was writing him out a safe conduct in the event of his ever getting into difficulties with the authorities, he interrupted the scratching of the pen to say, suddenly.

'If you would make it out in my own name, sir, I should prefer it. James Sholto Douglas, late of the—th Regiment.'

'Him!' said the military magnate thoughtfully when the new *employé* in the Secret Intelligence Department left the room. 'So that is Jim Douglas, is it? I thought he was a service man by the set of his shoulders. Jim Douglas. I remember his case when I was in the A.-G.'s office.'

'What was it?' asked the civilian curiously.

'Oh, a woman, of course. I forget the details; she was the wife of his major, a drunken beast. There was something about a blow, and she didn't back him up; saved her reputation, you understand. But he was an uncommonly smart officer, I know that.'

# 5

# Bravo!

The Gissings' house stood in a large garden; but though it was wreathed with creepers, and set with flowers after the manner of flowerful Lucknow, there was no cult of pansies or such like English treasures here. It was gay with that acclimatized tangle of poppies and larkspur, marigold, mignonette, and corn cockles which Indian gardeners love to sow broadcast in their cartwheel mud-beds; '*power of flowers*,' as they call the mixed seeds they save for it from year to year.

In the big dark dining-room also—where Alice Gissing, looking half her years in starched white muslin, and blue ribbons, sat at the head of the table—there was no cult of England. Everything was frankly, staunchly of the nabob-and-pagoda-tree style; for the Gissings preferred India, where they were received into society, to England, where they would have been out of it.

It had been one those heavy luncheons, beginning with many meats and much bottled beer, ending with much madeira and many cigars, which sent the insurance rate for India up to war risks in those days.

And there was never any scarcity of the best beer at the Gissings, seeing that he had the contract for supplying it to the British troops. His wife, however, preferred solid-looking porter with a creamy head to it, and a heavy odour which lingered about her pretty smiling lips. It was a most incongruous drink for one of her appearance; but it never seemed to affect either her gay little body or her gay little brain. The one remained youthful, slender; the other brightly, uncompromisingly clear.

She had been married twice. Once in extreme youth to a clerk in the Opium Department, who owed the good looks which had attracted her to a trace of dark blood. Then she had chosen wealth in the person of Mr Gissing. Had he died, she would probably have married for position; since she had a catholic taste for the amenities of life. But he had not died, and she had lived with him for ten years in good-natured toleration of all his claims upon her. As a matter of fact, they did not affect her in the least, and in her clear, high voice, she used to wonder openly why other women worried over matrimonial troubles, or fussed over so slight an encumbrance as a husband. In a way she felt equal to more than one, provided they did not squabble over her. That was unpleasant, and she not only liked things to be pleasant, but had the knack of making them so; both of the man whose name she bore, and whose house she used as a convenient spot wherein to give luncheon parties, and to the succession of admirers who came to them and drank her husband's beer.

He was a vulgar creature, but an excellent business man, with a knack of piling up the rupees which made the minor native contractors, whose trade he was gradually absorbing, gnash their teeth in sheer envy. For the Western system of risking all to gain all was too much opposed to the Eastern one of risking nothing to gain little, for the hereditary merchants to adopt it at once. They have learnt the trick of fence and entered the lists successfully since then; but in 1856 the foe was new. So they fawned on the shrewd despoiler instead, and curried favour by bringing his wife fruits and sweets, with something costlier hidden in the oranges or sugar drops. Alice Gissing accepted everything with a smile; for her husband was not a Government servant; the contracts, however, being for Government supplies, the givers did not discriminate the position so nicely. They used to complain that the *Sirkar* robbed them both ways, much to Mr Gissing's amusement, who, as a method of self-glorification, would allude to it at the luncheon parties where many men came who, between the intervals of badinage with the gay little hostess, could talk with authority on most affairs. They did not bring their wives with them, but Alice Gissing did not seem to mind that; she did not get on with women.

'So they complain I rob them, do they?' he said loudly, complacently, to the men on either side of him. 'My dear Colonel! an

Englishman is bound to rob a native if that means creaming the market, for they haven't been educated, sir, on those sound commercial principles which have made England the first nation in the world. Take this flour contract they are howling about. I'm beer by rights, of course, and, by George, I'm proud of it! Your men, Colonel, can't do without beer, England can't do without soldiers; so my business is sound. But why shouldn't I have my finger in any other pie which holds money? These hereditary fools think I shouldn't, and they were trying a ring, sir. Ha! ha! an absurd upside-down d—d oriental ring, based on utterly rotten principles. You can't keep up the price of a commodity because your grandfather got that price! They ignored the facility of transport given by roads, etc.; ignored the right of Government to benefit—er—slightly—by these outlays. Commerce isn't a selfish thing, sir, by gad! If you don't consider your market a bit, you won't find one at all. So I stepped in, and made thousands; for the Commissariat, seeing the saving here, of course asked me to contract for other places. It serves the idiots uncommon well right; but it will benefit them in the end. If they're to face Western nations they must learn—er—the—the morality of speculation.' He paused, helped himself to another glass of madeira, and added in an unctuous tone, 'but till they do, India's a good place.'

'Is that Gissing preaching morality?' asked his wife, in her clear high voice. The men at her end of the table had had their share of her, she thought, and those others might be getting bored by her husband.

'Only the morality of business,' put in a coarse-looking fellow who, having been betwixt and between the conversations, had been drinking rather heavily. 'There's no need for you to join the ladies as yet, Mrs Gissing.'

Major Erlton, at her right hand, scowled, and the boy on her left flushed up to the eyes. He was her latest admirer, and was still in the stage when she seemed an angel incarnate. Only the day before he had wanted to call out a cynical senior who had answered his vehement wonder as to how a woman like she was could have married a little beast like Gissing, with the irreverent suggestion that it might be because the name rhymed with kissing.

In the present instance she heeded neither the scowl nor the flush, and her voice came calmly: 'I don't intend to, Doctor. I mean to send you into the drawing-room instead. That will be quite as effectual to the proprieties.'

Amid the laugh, Major Erlton found opportunity for an admiring whisper that she had got the brute well above the belt that time. But the boy's flush deepened; he looked at his goddess with pained perplexed eyes.

'The morality of speculation or gambling,' retorted the doctor, speaking slowly and staring at the delighted Major angrily, 'is the art of winning as much money as you can—conveniently. That reminds me, Erlton; you must have raked in a lot over that match.'

A sudden dull red showed on the face whose admiration Alice was answering by a smile.

'I won a lot also,' she interrupted hastily. 'Thanks to your tip, Erlton. You never forget your friends.'

'No one could forget you—there is no merit'—began the boy, hastily, then paused before the publicity of his own words, and bewildered by the smile now given to him. Herbert Erlton noted the fact sullenly. He knew that for the time being all the little lady's personal interest was his; but he also knew that was not nearly so much as he gave her. And he wanted more, not understanding that if she had had more to give she would probably have been less generous than she was; being of that class of women who sin because the sin has no appreciable effect on them, but leaves them strangely, inconceivably unsoiled. This imperviousness, however, being, as a rule, considered the man's privilege only, Major Erlton failed to understand the position, and so, feeling aggrieved, turned on the lad.

'I'll remember you next time if you like, Mainwaring,' he said, 'but some one has to lose in every game. I'd grasped that fact before I was your age, and made up my mind it shouldn't be me.'

'Sound commercial morality!' laughed another guest. 'Try it, Mainwaring, at the next *Gymkhâna*. By the way, I hear that professional, Greyman, is off, so amateurs will have a chance now; he was a devilish fine rider.'

'Rode a devilish fine horse, too,' put in the unappeased doctor. 'You bought it, Erlton, in spite—'

'Yes! for fifteen hundred,' interrupted the Major, in unmistakable defiance. 'A long price, but there was hanky-panky in that match. Greyman tried fussing to cover it. You never can trust professionals. However, I *and my friends* won, and I shall win again with the horse. Take you evens in gold *mohurs* for the next—' There was always a sledgehammer method in the Major's fence, and the subject dropped.

The room was heavy with the odours of meats and drinks. Dark as it was, the flood of sunshine streaming into the verandah outside where yellow hornets were buzzing and the servants washing up the dishes, sent a glare even into the shadows. Neither the furniture nor appointments of the room owed anything to the East—for Indian art was, so to speak, not as yet invented for English folk—yet there was a strange unkennedness about their would-be familiarity which suddenly struck the latest exile, young Mainwaring.

'India is a beastly hole,' he said, in an undertone— 'things are so different—I wish I were out of it.' There was a note of appeal in his young voice; his eyes, meeting Alice Gissing, filled—to his intense dismay—with tears. He hoped she might not see them; but she did, and leant over to lay one kindly be-ringed little hand on the table quite close to his.

'You've got liver,' she said, confidentially. 'India is quite a nice place. Come to the assembly tonight, and I will give you two extras—whole ones. And don't drink any more madeira, there is a good boy. Come and have coffee with me in the drawing-room instead; that will set you right.'

Less has set many a boy hopelessly wrong. To do Alice Gissing justice, however, she never recognized such facts; her own head being quite steady. But Major Erlton understood the possible results perfectly, and commented on them when, as a matter of course, his long length remained lounging in an easy chair after the other guests had gone, and Mr Gissing had retired to business. People, from the *Palais Royale* playwrights downwards—or upwards—always poke fun at the husband in such situations; but no one gibes at the man who succeeds to the cut-and-dried necessity for devotion. Yet there is surely something ridiculous in the spectacle of a man playing a conjugal part without even a sense of duty to give him dignity in it. As a matter of fact the curse of the commonplace comes as quickly to Abelard and Heloise as it does to Darby and Joan. So Major Erlton, lounging and commenting, might well have been Mrs Gissing's legal owner.

'Going to make a fool of that lad now, I suppose, Allie,' he said. 'Why the devil should you when you don't care for boys?'

She came to stand in front of him like a child, her hands behind her back, but her china-blue eyes had a world of shrewdness in them. 'Don't I? Do you think I care for men either? I don't. You just amuse me, and I've got to be amused. By the way, did you remember to order the cart at five sharp? I want to go round the fair before the Club.'

If they had been married ten times over, their spending the afternoon together could not have been more of a foregone conclusion; there seemed, indeed, no choice in the matter. And they were prosaically punctual, too; at 'five sharp' they climbed into the high dogcart boldly, in face of a whole *posse* of servants, dressed in the nabob and pagoda-tree style with silver crests in their pith turbans and huge monograms on their breastplates; old-fashioned servants with the most antiquated notions as to the needs of the *sahib logue,* and a fund of passive resentment for the least change in the inherited routine of service—changes which they referred to the fact that the new-fangled *sahibs* were not real *sahibs.* But the heavy little and big breakfasts, the unlimited beer, the solid dinners, the milk punch and brandy *pâni*, all had their appointed values in the Gissings' house; so the servants watched their mistress with approving smiles. And on Mondays there was always a larger *posse* than usual to see the old Mai—who had been Alice Gissing's ayah for years and years—hand up the bouquet which the gardener always had ready, and say, 'My salaams to the missy-*baba*.' Mrs Gissing used to take the flowers just as she took her parasol or her gloves. Then she would say, 'All right,' partly to the ayah, partly to her cavalier, and the dogcart, or buggy, or mail-phaeton—whichever it happened to be—would go spinning away. For the old Mai had handed the flowers into many different turnouts, remaining always on the steps ready, with the authority of age and long service, to crush any frivolous remarks newcomers might make. But the destination of the bouquet was always the same; and that was to stand in a peg tumbler at the foot of a tiny white marble cross in the cemetery. Mrs Gissing put a fresh offering in it every Monday, going through the ceremony with a placid interest; for the date on the cross was far back in the years. Still, she used to speak of the little life which had come into and gone from hers when she was yet a child herself, with a certain self-possessed plaintiveness born of long habit.

'I was barely seventeen,' she would say, 'and it was a dear little thing. Then Saumarez was transferred, and I never returned to Lucknow till I married Gissing. It was odd wasn't it, marrying twice to the same station. But, of course, I can't ask him to come here, so it is doubly kind of you; for I couldn't come alone, it is so sad.'

Her blue eyes would be limpid with actual tears; yet as she waited for the return of the tumbler, which the watchman always had to wash out, she looked more like some dainty figure on a cracker than a weeping Niobe. Nevertheless, the admirers whom she took in succession into her confidence, thought it sweet and womanly of her never to have forgotten the dead baby, though they approved of her dislike to live ones. Some of them, when their part in the weekly drama came upon them—as it always did—in the first flush of their fancy for the principal actress in it, began by being quite sentimental over it. Herbert Erlton did. He went so far once as to bring an additional bouquet of pansies from his wife's pet bed; but the little lady had looked at it with plaintive distrust. Pansies withered so soon, she said, and as the bouquet had to last a whole week, something less fragile was better. Indeed, the gardener's bouquets, compact, hard, with the blossoms all jammed into little spots of colour among the protruding sprigs of privet, were more suited to her calm permanency of regret than the passionate purple posy which looked so pathetically out of place in the big man's coarse hands. She had taken it from him, however, and strewn the already drooping flowers about the marble. They looked lovely, she had said, though the others were best, as she liked everything to be tidy because she had been very, very fond of the poor little dear. Saumarez had never been kind, and it had been so pretty; dark like its father, who had been a very handsome man. She had cried for days, then, though she didn't like children now. But she would always remember this one, always! The old Mai and she often talked of it; especially when she was dressing for a ball, because the gardener brought bouquets for them also.

Major Erlton, therefore, gave no more pansies, and his sentiment died down into a sort of irritable wonder what the little woman would be at. The unreality of it all struck him afresh on this particular Monday, as he watched her daintily removing a few fallen petals. So he left her to finish her task while he walked about. The cemetery was a perfect garden of a place, with rectangular paths bordered by shrubs which rose from a tangle of annual flowers like that around the Gissings' house. This blossoming screen hid the graves for the most part; but in the older portions great, domed erections—generally safeguarding an infant's body—rose above it more like summer-houses than tombs. Herbert Erlton preferred this part of the cemetery, for it was less suggestive than the newer portion, and he was one of those wholesome hearty animals, to whom the very idea of death is horrible. So hither, after a time, she came, stepping daintily over the graves, and pausing an instant on the way to add a sprig of mignonette to the rosebud she had brought from a bush beside the cross—it was a fine healthy bush which yielded a constant supply of buds suitable for buttonholes. She looked charming, but he met her with a perplexed frown.

'I've been wondering, Allie,' he said, 'what you would have been like if that baby had lived. Would you have cared for it?'

Her eyes grew startled. 'But I do care for it! Why should I come if I didn't? It isn't amusing I'm sure; so I think it very unkind of you to suggest—'

'I never suggested anything,' he protested. 'I know you did—that you do care. But if it had lived—' he paused as if something escaped his mental grasp—'Why, I expect you would have been different somehow; and I was wondering—'

'Oh! don't wonder, please, it's a bad habit,' she replied, suddenly appeased. 'You will be wondering next if I care for you. As if you didn't know that I do.' She was pinning the buttonhole into his coat methodically, and he could not refuse an answering smile; but the puzzled look remained.

'I suppose you do, or you wouldn't—' he began slowly, then a sudden emotion showed in face and voice. 'You slip from me somehow, Allie,—slip like an eel. I never get a real hold—Well! I wonder if women understand themselves? They ought to, for nobody else can, that's one comfort.'

Whether he meant he was no denser than previous recipients of rosebuds, or that mankind benefited by failing to grasp feminine standards was not clear; and Mrs Gissing was more interested in the fact that the mare was growing restive. So they climbed into the high dogcart again, and took her a quieting spin down the road. The fresh wind of their own speed blew in their faces, the mare's feet scarcely seemed to touch the ground, the trees slipped past quickly, the palm-squirrels fled chirrupping. He flicked his whip gaily at them in boyish fashion as he sat well back, his big hand giving to the mare's mouth. Hers lay equably in her lap, though the pace would have made most women clutch at the rail.

'Jolly little beasts, ain't they, Allie?'

'Jolly altogether; jolly as it can be,' she replied with the frank delight of a girl. They had forgotten themselves innocently enough; but one of the men in a dog cart, past which they flashed, put on an outraged expression.

'Erlton and Mrs Gissing again!' he fussed. 'I shall tell my wife to cut her. Being in business ourselves we have tried to keep square. But this is an open scandal. I wonder Mrs Erlton puts up with it. I wouldn't.'

His companion shook his head. 'Dangerous work saying that. Wait till you are a woman. I know more about them than most, being a doctor, so I never venture on an opinion. But, honestly, I believe most women—that little one ahead into the bargain—don't care a button one way or the other. And, for all our talk, I don't believe we do either, when all is said and done.'

'What is said and done?' asked the other peevishly.

There was a pause. The lessening dog cart with its flutter of muslin, its driver sitting square to his work, showed on the hard white road which stretched like a narrowing ribbon over the empty plain. Far ahead a little devil of wind swept the dust against the blue sky like a cloud. Nearer at hand lay a cluster of mud hovels, and—going towards it before the dog cart—a woman was walking along the dusty side of the road. She had a bundle of grass on her head, a baby across her hip, a toddling child clinging to her skirts. The afternoon sun sent their shadows conglomerately across the white metal.

'Passion, Love, Lust, the attraction of sex for sex,—what you will,' said the doctor, breaking the silence. 'Nothing is easier knocked out of a man, if he is worth calling one—a bugle call, a tight corner—God

Almighty!—they're over that child! Drive on like the devil, man, and let me see what I can do.'

There is never much to do when all has been done in an instant. There had been a sudden causeless leaving of the mother's side, a toddling child among the shadows, a quick oath, a mad rear as the mare, checked by hands like a vice for strength, snapped the shafts as if they had been straws. No delay, no recklessness; but one of these iron-shod hoofs as it was flung out, had caught the child full on the temple, and there was no need to ask what that curved blue mark meant, which had gone crashing into the skull.

Alice Gissing had leapt from the dog cart and stood looking at the pitiful sight with wide eyes.

'We couldn't do anything,' she said in an odd hard voice, as the others joined her. 'There was nothing we could do. Tell the woman, Herbert, that we couldn't help it.'

But the Major, making the still plunging mare a momentary excuse for not facing the ghastly truth, had, after one short, sharp exclamation—almost of fear—turned to help the groom; so there was no sound for a minute save the plunging of hoofs on the hard ground, the groom's cheerful voice lavishing endearments on his restless charge, and a low animal-like whimper from the mother, who, after one wild shriek, had sunk down in the dust beside the dead child, looking at the purple bruise dully, and clasping her living baby tighter to her breast. For it, thank the gods! was the boy. That one with the mark on its forehead only the girl.

Then the doctor, who had been busy with deft but helpless hands, rose from his knees, saying a word or two in Hindustani which provoked a whining reply from the woman.

'She admits it was no one's fault,' he said. 'So, Erlton, if you will take our dog cart—'

But the Major had faced the position by this time. 'I can't go. She is a camp follower, I expect, and I shall have to find-out,—for compensation and all that. If you would take Mrs Gissing—' His voice, steady till then, broke perceptibly over the name; its owner looked up sharply, and going over to him laid her hand on his arm.

'It wasn't your fault,' she said, still in that odd hard voice. 'You had the mare in hand; she didn't stir an inch. It is a dreadful thing to happen, but—' she threw her head back a little, her wide eyes narrowed as a frown puckered her smooth forehead, 'it isn't as if we could have prevented it. The thing bad to be.'

She might have been the incarnation of Fate itself as she glanced down at the dead child in the dust, at the living one reaching from its mother's arms to touch its sister curiously, at the slow tears of the mother herself as she acquiesced in the eternal fitness of things; for a girl more or less was not much in the mud hovel, where she and her man lived hardly, and the *Huzoors* would doubtless give rupees in exchange, for they were just. But the tears came faster when, with conventional wailing the women from the clustering huts joined her, while the men, frankly curious, listened to the groom's spirited description of the accident.

'You had better go, Allie; you do no good here,' said the Major almost roughly. He was anxious to get through with it all—he was absorbed in it.

So the man who had said he was going to tell his wife to cut Mrs Gissing, had to help her into the dog cart.

'It was horrible, wasn't it?' she said suddenly when, in silence, they had left the little tragedy far behind them. 'We were going a frightful pace, but you saw he had the mare in hand. He is awfully strong you know.' She paused, and a reflectively-complacent smile stole to her face. 'I suppose you will think it horrid,' she went on; 'but it doesn't feel to me like killing a human being, you know. I'm sorry, of course, but I should have been much sorrier if it had been a white baby. Wouldn't you?'

She set aside his evasion remorselessly. 'I know all that! People say, of course, that it is wicked not to feel the same towards people whether they're black or white. But we don't. And they don't either. They feel just the same about us because we are white. Don't you think they do?'

'The antagonism of race—' he began sententiously, but she cut him short again; this time with an irrelevant remark.

'I wonder what your wife would say if she saw me driving in your dog cart?'

He stared at her helplessly. The one problem was as unanswerable as the other.

'You had better drive round the back way to the Fair,' she said considerately. 'Somebody there will take me off your hands. Otherwise you will have to drive me to the Club; for I'm not going home. It would be dreadful after that horrid business. Besides, the Fair will cheer me up. One doesn't understand it, you know, and the people crowd along like figures on a magic-lantern slide. I mean that you never know what's coming next, and that is always so jolly, isn't it?'

It might be, but the man with the wife felt relieved when, five minutes afterwards, she transferred herself to young Mainwaring's buggy. The boy, however, felt as if an angel had fluttered down from the skies to the worn broken-springed cushion beside him; an angel to be guarded from humanity—even her own.

'How the beggars stare,' he said, after they had walked the horse for a space through the surging crowds. 'Let us get away from the grinning apes.' He would have liked to take her to paradise and put flaming swords at the gate.

'They don't grin,' she replied curtly, 'they stare like Bank-holiday people stare at the wild beasts in the Zoo. But let us get away from the watered road, the policemen, and all that. That's no fun. See, go down that turning into the middle of it; you can get out that way to the river road afterwards if you like.'

The bribe was sufficient; it was not far across to peace and quiet, so the turn was made. Nor was the staring worse in the irregular lane of booths and stalls down which they drove, and though the air was full of throbbings of tomtoms, twangling of *sutara*s, intermittent poppings, and fizzings of squibs, the unchecked crowd was strangely silent despite the numberless children carried shoulder high to see the show. But it was also strangely insistent; going on its way regardless of the shouting groom.

'Take care,' said Mrs Gissing lightly, 'don't run over another child. By the way, I forgot to tell you—the Fair was so funny—but Erlton ran over a black baby. It wasn't his fault a bit, and the mother, luckily, didn't seem to mind; because it was a girl, I expect. Aren't they an odd people? One really never knows what will make them cry or laugh.'

Something was apparently amusing them at that moment, however, for a burst of boisterous merriment pealed from a dense crowd near a booth pitched in an open space.

'What's that?' she cried sharply. 'Let's go and see.'

She was out of the dog cart as she spoke, despite his protest that it was impossible—that she must not venture.

'Do you imagine they'll murder me?' she asked with an *insouciant* incredulous laugh. 'What nonsense! Here, good people, let me pass, please!'

She was by this time in the thick of the crowd, which gave way instinctively, and he could do nothing but follow, his boyish face stern with the mere thought her idle words had conjured up. Do her any injury? Her dainty dress should not even be touched if he could help it! But the sightseers, most of them peasants beguiled from their fields for this Festival of Spring, had never seen an English lady at such close quarters before, if, indeed, they had ever seen one at all. So, though they gave way they closed in again, silent, but insistent in their curiosity; while, as the centre of attraction came nearer, the crowd in front became denser, more absorbed in the bursts of merriment. There was ring of licence in them which made young Mainwaring plead hurriedly—

'Mrs Gissing!—Don't—please don't.'

'But I want to see what they're laughing at,' she replied; and then, in perfect mimicry of the groom's familiar cry, her high clear voice echoed over the heads in front of her: *'Hut! Hut! Ari bhaiyan! Hut!'*

They turned to see her gay face full of smiles, joyous, confident, sympathetic, and the next minute the cry was echoed with approving grins from a dozen responsive throats.

'Stand back, brothers! Stand back!'

There were quick hustlings to right and left, quick nods and smiles, even broad laughs full of good fellowship; so that in no time she found herself at the innermost circle, with a clear view of the central space, of the cause of the laughter; it made her give a faint gasp and stand transfixed. Two white-masked figures, clasped waist to waist, were waltzing about tipsily. One had a curled flaxen wig, a muslin dress distended by an all too visible crinoline giving full play to a pair of prancing brown legs. The other wore an old staff uniform, cocked hat and feather complete. The flaxen curls rested on the tarnished epaulette, the unembracing arms flourished brandy bottles.

It was a vile travesty; and the Englishwoman turned instinctively to the Englishman as if doubtful what to do, how to take it; but the passion on his boyish face seemed to make things clear—to give her the clue, and she gripped his hand hard.

'Don't be a fool!' she whispered fiercely. 'Laugh! It's the only thing to do.' Her own rang out shrill above the uncertain stir in the crowd, taken aback in its merriment.

But something else rose above it also. A single word—

'Bravo!'

She turned like lightning to the sound, her cheeks for the first time aflame, but she could see no one in the circle of dark faces whom she could credit with the exclamation. Yet she felt sure she had heard it.

'Bravo!' Had it been said in jest or earnest, in mockery or— Young Mainwaring interrupted the problem by suggesting that as the maskers had run away into a booth, where he could not follow and give them the licking they deserved because of her presence, it might be as well for her to escape further insult by returning to the buggy. His tone was as full of reproach as that of a lad in love could be, but Mrs Gissing was callous. She declared she was glad to have seen what she had seen. Englishmen did drink and Englishwomen waltzed. Why then, shouldn't the natives poke fun at both habits if they chose? They themselves could laugh at other things. And laugh she did, recklessly, at everything and everybody for the remainder of the drive. But underneath her gaiety she was harping on that 'Bravo!' And suddenly, as they drove by the river, she broke in on the boy's prattle to say excitedly: 'I have it! It must have been the one in the Afghan cap who said "Bravo!" He was fairer than the rest. Perhaps he was an Englishman disguised. Well! I should know him again if I saw him.'

'Him? who—what? Who said bravo!' asked the lad. He had been too angry to notice the exclamation at the time.

She looked at him quizzically. 'Not you—you abused me. But some one did—or didn't'— here her little slack hands resting in her lap clasped each other tightly. 'I rather wish I knew. I'd rather like to make him say it again. Bravo! Bravo!'

And then, as if at her own mimicry, she returned to her childish unreasoning laugh.

# 6

# The Gift of Many Faces

Mrs Gissing had guessed right. The man in the Afghan cap was Jim Douglas, who found the disguise of a frontiersman the easiest to assume, when, as now, he wanted to mix in a crowd. And he would have said 'Bravo' a dozen times over if he had thought the little lady would like to hear it, for her quick denial of the possibility of insult had roused his keenest admiration. Here had spoken a dignity he had not expected to find in one whom he only knew as a woman Major Erlton delighted to honour. A dignity lacking in the big brave boy beside her; lacking, alas! in many a big brave Englishman of greater importance. So he had risked detection by that sudden 'Bravo.' Not that he dreaded it much. To begin with, he was used to it, even when he posed as an out-lander, for there was a trick in his gait, not to be orientalized, which made policemen salute gravely as he passed disguised to the tent, and there was ignorance of some one or another of the million shibboleths which divide men from each other in India; shibboleths too numerous for one lifetime's learning, which require to be born in the blood, bred in the bone. In this case, also, he had every intention of asserting his race by licking some of the offenders when the show was over; for he happened to know one of them; having indeed licked him a few days before over a certain piece of bone. So, as the crowd, accepting the finale of one amusement placidly, drifted away to see another, he walked over to the tent in which the discomfited caricaturists had found refuge. It was a tattered old military bell-tent, bought most likely with the tattered old staff uniform at some auction. As he lifted the flap the sound of escaping feet made him expect a stern chase; but he was mistaken. Two figures rose with the start of studied surprise and salaamed profoundly as he entered. They were both stark naked save for a waist cloth, and Jim Douglas could not resist a quick glance round for the discarded costumes. They were nowhere to be seen; being hidden, probably, under the litter of properties strewing the squalid green-room. Still of the identity of the man he knew Jim Douglas had no doubt, and as this one was also the nearest, he promptly seized him by both shoulders and gave him a sound western kick, which would have been followed by others if the recipient had not slipped from his hold like an eel; for Jhungi, Bunjâra and general vagrant, habitually oiled himself from head to foot after the manner of his profession as a precaution against such possible attempts at capture.

His assailant, grasping this fact, at any rate, did not risk dignity by pursuit, though the man stood salaaming again within arm's length.

'You scoundrel!' said Jim Douglas with as much severity as he could command before the mixture of deference and defiance, innocence, and iniquity, in the sharp cunning face before him. 'Wasn't the licking I gave you before enough?'

Jhungi superadded perplexity to his other show of emotions. 'The *Huzoor* mistakes,' he said, with sudden cheerful understanding. 'It was the miscreant Bhungi, my brother, whom the *Huzoor* licked. The misbegotten idler who tells lies in the bazaar about bones and sacks. So his skin smarts, but my body is whole. Is it not so, Father Tiddu?'

The appeal to his companion was made with curious eagerness, and Jim Douglas, who had heard this tale of the ill-doing double before, looked at the witness to it with interest. That this man was or was not Jhungi's co-offender he could not say with certainty, for there was a remarkable lack of individuality about both face and figure when in repose; and save for the faint frostiness of sprouting grey hairs on a shaven cheek and skull he might have been any age. But the nickname of Tiddu, or cricket, was immediately explained by the jerky angularity of his actions.

'Of a truth it was Bhungi,' he said in a well-modulated but creaky voice. 'Time was when liars, such as he, fell dead. Now they don't even catch fevers, and if they do, the *Huzoor*s give them bitter powder and start them lying again. So, since one dead fish stinks a whole tank, virtuous Jhungi, being like as two peas in a pod, suffers an ill-name. But Bhungi will know what it means to tell lies when he stands before his Creator. Nevertheless in this world the master being enraged—'

'Not so, Father Tiddu,' interrupted Jhungi glibly, 'the *Huzoor* is but enraged with Bhungi. And rightly. Did not we hide our very faces for shame while he mimicked the noble people? Did we not try to hold him when he fled from punishment— as the *Huzoor* no doubt heard—'

Jim Douglas without a word slipped his hand down the man's back. The wales of a sound hiding were palpable; so was his wince as he dodged aside to salaam again.

'The *Huzoor* is a male judge,' he said admiringly. 'No black man could deceive him. This slave has certainly been whipped. He fell among liars who robbed him of his reputation. Will the *Huzoor* do likewise? On the honour of a Bunjâra 'tis Bhungi whom the *Huzoor* beats. He gives Jhungi bitter powders when he gets the fever. And even Bhungi but tries to earn a stomachful as he can, when the *Huzoor*s take his trade from him.'

'The world grows hollow, to match a man's swallow,' quoted Tiddu affably.

The familiar by-word of poverty, the quaint mingling of truth and falsehood, daring and humility, in Jhungi's plea roused both Jim Douglas's sense of humour, and the sympathy—which with him was always present—for the hardness and squalidness of so many of the lives around him.

'But you can surely earn the stomachful honestly,' he said, anger passing into irritation. 'What made you take to this trade?' He kicked at a pile of properties, and in so doing disclosed the skeleton of a crinoline; Jhungi, with a shocked expression, stooped down and covered it up decorously.

'Because it is my trade,' he replied; 'the *Huzoor* must surely have heard of the Many-faced Tribe of Bunjâras? I am of them.'

'Lie not, Jhungi!' interrupted Tiddu calmly, 'he is but my apprentice, *Huzoor*, but I—' he paused, caught up a cloth, gave it one dexterous twirl round him, squatted down, and there he was, to the life, a veiled woman watching the stranger with furtive, modest eye. 'But I,' came a round feminine voice full of the feminine inflections, 'am of the thousand-faced people who wander to a thousand places. A new place, a new face. It makes a large world, *Huzoor*, a strange world.' There was a melancholy cadence in his voice, which added interest to the sheer amaze which Jim Douglas was feeling. He had heard the legend of the Many-faced Tribe, had even seen clever actors claiming to belong to it, and knew how the Stranglers deceived their victims, but anything like this he had never credited, much less seen. He himself, though he knew to the contrary, could scarcely combat the conviction, which seemed to come to him from that one furtive eye, that a woman sat within those folds.

'But how?' he began in perplexity, 'I thought the Baharupas[1] never went in caravans.'

Tiddu resumed the cracked voice and let the smile become visible, and, as if by magic, the illusion disappeared. 'The *Huzoor* is right. We are wanderers. But in my youth a woman tied me to one place one face; women have the trick, *Huzoor*, even if they are wanderers themselves. This one was, but I loved her; so after we had burnt her and her fellow-wanderer together hand-in-hand, according to the custom, so that they might wander elsewhere but not in the tribe, I lingered on. He was the father of Jhungi, and the boy being left destitute I taught him to play; for it needs two in the play as in life — the man and the woman, or folks care not for it. So I taught Jhungi—'

'And brother Bhungi?' suggested his hearer dryly.

A faint chuckle came from the veil. 'And Bhungi. He plays well, and hath beguiled an old rascal with thin legs and a fat face like mine into playing with him. Some, even the *Huzoor* himself, might be beguiled into mistaking Siddu for Tiddu. But it is a tom cat to a tiger. So, being warned, the *Huzoor* will give no unearned blows; yet if he did, are not two kicks bearable from the milch-cow?' As he spoke he angled out a hand impudently for an alms with the beggars' cry of '*Alakh*,' to point his meaning.

It was echoed by Jhungi, who, envious of Tiddu's holding the boards, as it were, had in sheer devilry and desire not to be outdone, taken up the disguise of a mendicant. It was a most creditable performance, but Tiddu dismissed it with a wave of the hand.

'*Bullah!*' he said, contemptuously, "tis the refuge of fools. There is not one true beggar in fifty, so the forty-and-nine false ones go free of detention as the potter's donkey. Even the *Huzoor* could do better—had I the teaching of him.'

He leant forward, dropping his voice slightly, and Jim Douglas narrowed his eyes as men do when some unbidden idea claims admittance to the brain.

'You?' he echoed; 'what could you teach me?'

Tiddu rose, let fall the veil to decent dignified drapery, and fixed his eyes full on the questioner. They were luminous eyes, differing from Jhungi's beady ones, as the fire-opal differs from the diamond.

'What could I teach?' he re-echoed, and his tone, monotonously distinct to Jim Douglas, seemed inaudible to others, judging by Jhungi's impassive face. 'Many things. For one, that the Baharupas are not mimics only; they have the Great Art. What is it? God knows. But what they will folk to see, that is seen; that and no more.'

[1]*Lit.* many faced.

Jim Douglas laughed derisively. Animal magnetism and mesmerism were one thing; this was another.

'The *Huzoor* thinks I lie; but he must have heard of the doctor *sahib* in Calcutta who made suffering forget to suffer.'

'You mean Dr Easdale.[1] Did you know him? Was he a pupil of yours?' came the cynical question.

Tiddu's face became expressionless. 'Perhaps; but this slave forgets names. Yet the *Huzoor*s have the Gift sometimes; the Baharupas have it not always—though the father's hoard goes oftenest to the son. Now, if, by chance, the *Huzoor* had the gift and could use it, there would be no need for policemen to salute as he passes; no need for the drug-smokers to cease babbling when he enters. So the *Huzoor* could find out what he wants to find out; what he is paid to find out.'

His eyes met Jim Douglas's surprise boldly.

'How do you know I want to find out anything?' asked the latter, after a pause.

Tiddu laughed. 'The *Huzoor* must find a turban heavy, and there is no room for English toes in a native shoe; folk seek not such discomfort for naught.'

Jim Douglas paused again; the fellow was a charlatan, but he was consummately clever; and if there was anything certain in this world it was the wisdom of forgetting Western prejudices occasionally in dealing with the East.

'Send that man away,' he said curtly, 'I want to talk to you alone.'

But the request seemed lost on Tiddu. He folded up the veil impudently, and resumed the thread of the former topic. 'Yet Jhungi plays the beggar well, for which Fate be praised, since he must ask alms elsewhere if the *Huzoor* refuses them; for the purse is empty,'—here he took a leathern bag from his waistband and turned it inside out—'by reason of the *Huzoor*'s dislike to good mimics. So thou must to the temples, Jhungi, and if thou meetest Bhungi give him the *sahib*'s generous gift; for blows should not be taken on loan.'

Jhungi, who all this time had been telling his beads like the best of beggars, looked up with some perplexity; whether real or assumed Jim Douglas, in that hotbed of deception, felt it was impossible to say.

'Bhungi?' echoed the former, rising to his feet. 'Ay! that will I, if I meet him. But God knows as to that. God knows if Bhungi—'

'The purse is empty,' repeated Tiddu in a warning voice, and Jhungi, with a laugh, pulled himself and his disguise together, as it were, and passed out of the tent; his beggar's cry, '*Alakh! Alakh!*' growing fainter and fainter while Tiddu and Jim Douglas looked at each other.

[1]Who started the Mesmeric Hospital.

'Jhungi-Bhungi—Bhungi-Jhungi,' jeered the Baharupa, suddenly, jingling the names together. 'Which be which, as he said, God knows, not man. That is the best of lies. They last a body's lifetime, so the *Huzoor* may as well learn old Tiddu's—'

'Or Siddu's?'

'Or Siddu's,' assented the mountebank, calmly. 'But the *Huzoor* cannot learn to use his Gift from that old rascal. He must come to the Many-faced one, who is ready to teach it.'

'Why?'

Tiddu abandoned mystery at once

'For fifty rupees, *Huzoor*; not a *pice* less; now, in my hand.'

Was it worth it? Jim Douglas decided instantly that it might be. Not for the Gift's sake; of that he was incredulous; but Tiddu was a consummate actor and could teach many tricks worth knowing. Then in this roving commission to report on anything he saw and heard to the military magnate, it would suit him for the time to have the service of an arrant scoundrel. Besides, the pay promised him being but small, the wisdom of having a second string to the bow of ambition had already decided him on combining inquiry with judicious horse-dealing; since he could thus wander through villages buying, through towns selling, without arousing suspicion; and this life in a caravan would start him on these lines effectively. Finally, this offer of Tiddu's was unsought, unexpected, and, ever since Kate Erlton's appeal, Jim Douglas had felt a strange attraction towards pure chance. So he took out a note from his pocket book and laid it in the Baharupa's hand.

'You asked fifty,' he said, 'I give a hundred; but with the branch of the *neem*-tree between us two.'

Tiddu gave him an admiring look. 'With the sacred "*Lim ke dagla*" between us, and Mighty Murri-am herself to see it grow,' he echoed. 'Is the *Huzoor* satisfied?'

The Englishman knew enough of Bunjâra oaths to be sure that he had, at least, the cream of them; besides, a hundred rupees went far in the purchase of good faith. So that matter was settled, and he felt it to be a distinct relief, for during the last day or two he had been casting about for a fair start rather aimlessly. In truth, he had underrated the gap little Zora's death would make in his life, and had been in a way bewildered to find himself haunting the empty nest on the terraced roof in forlorn, sentimental fashion. The sooner, therefore, that he left Lucknow the better. So, as the Bunjâra had told him the caravan was starting the very next morning, he hastily completed his few preparations, and having sent Tara word of his intention, went, after the moon had risen, to lock the doors on the past idyll and take the key of the garden-house back to its owner; for he himself had always lodged, in European fashion, near the Palace.

The garden, as he entered it, lay peaceful as ever; so utterly unchanged from what he remembered it on many balmy moonlit nights, that he could not help looking up once more, as if expectant of that tinsel flutter, that soft welcome, 'Khushâmudund Huzrut.' Strange! So far as he was concerned the idyll might be beginning; but for her? All unconsciously, as he paused, his thought found answer in one spoken word—the Persian equivalent for 'it is finished,' which has such a finality in its short syllable—'Khutm.'

'Khutm.' The echo came from Tara's voice, but it had a ring in it which made him turn, anticipating some surprise. She was standing not far off, below the plinth as he was, having stepped out from the shadow of the trees at his approach, and she was swathed from head to foot in the white veil of orthodox widowhood, which encircled her face like a cere cloth. Even in the moonlight he could see the excitement in her face, the glitter in the large, wild eyes.

'Tara!' he exclaimed sharply, his experience warning him of danger, 'what does this mean?'

'That the end has come; the end at last,' she cried, theatrically, every fold of her drapery, though she stood stiff as a corpse, seeming to be instinct with fierce vitality.

He changed his tone at once, perceiving that the danger might be serious. 'You mean that your service is at an end,' he said quietly. 'I told you that some days ago. Also that your pay would be continued because of your goodness to her—to the dead. I advised your returning north, nearer your own people, but you are free to go or stay. Do you want anything more? If you do, be quick, please, for I am in a hurry.' His coolness, his failure to remark on the evident meaning of her changed dress, calmed her somewhat.

'I want nothing,' she replied sullenly. 'A suttee wants nothing in this world, and I am suttee. I have been the master's servant for gratitude's sake—now I am the servant of God for righteousness' sake.' So far she had spoken as if the dignified words had been pre-arranged; now she paused in a sort of wistful anger at the indifference on his face. The words meant so much to her, and, as she ceased from them, their controlling power seemed to pass also, and she flung out her arms wildly, then brought them down in stinging blows upon her breasts.

'I am suttee. Yes! I am suttee! Reject me not again, ye Shining Ones! Reject me not again.'

The cry was full of exalted resolve and despair. It made Jim Douglas step up to her, and seizing both hands, hold them fast.

'Don't be a fool, Tara!' he said sternly. 'Tell me, sensibly, what all this means. Tell me what you are going to do.' His touch seemed to scorch her, for she tore herself away from it vehemently; yet it seemed also to quiet her, and she watched him with sombre eyes for a minute ere replying.

'I am going to Holy Gunga. Where else should a *suttee* go? The Water will not reject me as the Fire did, since, before God! I am *suttee*. As the master knows'—her voice held a passionate appeal,—'I have been *suttee* all these long years. Yet now I have given up all—all!'

With a swift gesture, full of womanly grace, but with a sort of protest against such grace in its utter abandonment and self-forgetfulness, she flung out her arms once more. This time to raise the shrouding veil from her head and shoulders. Against this background of white gleaming in the moonlight, her new-shaven skull showed death-like, ghastly. Jim Douglas recoiled a step, not from the sight itself, but because he knew its true meaning; knew that it meant self-immolation if she were left to follow her present bent. She would simply go down to the Ganges and drown herself. An inconceivable state of affairs, beyond all rational understanding; but to be reckoned with, nevertheless, as real, inevitable.

'What a pity!' he said, after a moment's pause had told him that it would be well to try and take the starch out of her resolution by fair means or foul, leaving its cause for future inquiry. 'You had such nice hair. I used to admire it very much.'

Her hands fell slowly, a vague terror and amaze came to her eyes. He pursued the advantage remorselessly. 'Why did you cut it off?' He knew of course, but his affected ignorance took the colour, the intensity from the situation, by making her feel her *coup de théâtre* had failed.

'The *Huzoor* must know,' she faltered, anger and disappointment and vague doubt in her tone, while her right hand drew itself over the shaven skull as if to make sure there was no mistake. 'I am *suttee*—' the familiar word seemed to bring certainty with it, and she went on more confidentially. 'So I cut it all off and it lies there, ready, as I am, for purification.'

She pointed to the upper step leading to the plinth where, as on an altar, lay all her worldly treasures, arranged carefully with a view to effect. The crimson scarf she had always worn was folded—with due regard to the display of its embroidered edge—as a cloth, and at either end of it lay a pile of trumpery personal adornments, each topped and redeemed from triviality by a gold wristlet and anklet. In the centre, set round by fallen orange-blossoms rose a great heap of black hair, snakelike in glistening coils. The simple pomposity of the arrangement was provocative of smiles, the wistful eagerness of the face watching its effect on the master was provocative of tears. Jim Douglas feeling inclined for both, chose the former deliberately; he even managed a derisive laugh as he stepped up to the altar and laid sacrilegious hands on the hair. Tara gave a cry of dismay, but he was too quick for her, and dangled a long lock before her very eyes, in jesting, but stern decision.

'That settles it, Tara. You can go to Gunga now if you like, and bathe and be as holy as you like. But there will be no Fire or Water. Do you understand?'

She looked at the hand holding the hair with the oddest expression, though she said obstinately, 'I shall drown if I choose.'

'Why should you choose?' he asked. 'You know as well as I that it is too late for any good to you or others. The Fire or Water should have come twelve years ago. The priests won't say so of course. They want fools to help them in this fuss about the new law. Ah! I thought so! They have been at you, have they? Well, be a fool if you like, and bring them pennies at Benares as a show. You cannot do anything else. You can't even sacrifice your hair really, so long as I have this bit—' He began to roll the lock round his finger, neatly.

'What is the *Huzoor* going to do with it?' she asked, and the oddness had invaded her voice.

'Keep it,' he retorted. 'And by all those thirty thousand and odd gods of yours, I'll say it was a love-token if I choose. And I will if you are a fool.' He drew out a small gold locket attached to the Brahminical thread he always wore, and began methodically to fit the curl into it, wondering if this cantrip of his—for it was nothing more—would impress Tara. Possibly. He had found such suggestions of ritual had an immense effect, especially with the women-kind who were for ever inventing new shackles for themselves; but her next remark startled him considerably.

'Is the *bibi*'s hair in there too?' she asked. There was a real anxiety in her tone, and he looked at her sharply, wondering what she would be at.

'No,' he answered. In truth it was empty; and had been empty ever since he had taken a fair curl from it many years before—a curl which had ruined his life. The memory making him impatient of all feminine subtleties, he added roughly, 'It will stay there for the present; but if you try *suttee* nonsense I swear I'll tie it up in a cowskin bag, and give it to a sweeper to make broth of.'

The grotesque threat, which suggested itself to his sardonic humour as one suitable to the occasion, and which in sober earnest was terrible to one of her race, involving as it did eternal damnation, seemed to pass her by. There was even, he fancied, a certain relief in the face watching him complete his task; almost a smile quivering about her lips. But when he closed the locket with a snap, and was about to slip it back to its place, the full meaning of the threat, of the loss—or of something beyond these—seemed to overtake her; an unmistakable terror, horror, and despair swept through her. She flung herself at his feet, clasping them with both hands.

'Give it me back, master,' she pleaded wildly. 'Hinder me not again! Before God I am *suttee*! I am *suttee*!'

But this same Eastern clutch of appeal is disconcerting to the average Englishman. It fetters the understanding in another sense, and smothers sympathy in a desire to be left alone. Even Jim Douglas stepped back from it with something like a bad word. She remained crouching for a moment with empty hands, then rose in scornful dignity.

'There was no need to thrust this slave away,' she said proudly. 'Tara, the Rajputni, will go without that. She will go to Holy Gunga and be purged of inmost sin. Then she will return and claim her right of *suttee* at the master's hand. Till then he may keep what he stole.'

'He means to keep it,' retorted the master savagely, for he had come to the end of his patience. 'Though what this fuss about *suttee* means I don't know. You used to be sensible enough. What has come to you?'

Tara looked at him helplessly, then wrapping her widow's veil round her, prepared to go in silence. She could not answer that question even to herself. She would not even admit the truth of the old tradition, that the only method for a woman to preserve constancy to the dead was to seek death itself. That would be to admit too much. Yet that was the truth, to which her despair at parting pointed, even to herself. Truth? No! it was a lie! She would disprove it in life, if she was prevented from doing so by death. So, without a word, she gathered up the crimson drapery and what lay on it; then with these pathetic sacrifices of all the womanhood she knew tight clasped in her widow's veil, she paused for a last salaam.

The incomprehensible tragedy of her face irritated him into greater insistence.

'But what *is* it all about?' he reiterated. 'Who has been putting these ideas into your head? Who has been telling you to do this? Is it Soma, or some devil of a priest?'

As he waited for an answer the floods of moonlight threw their shadows together to join the perfumed darkness of the orange trees: the city, half asleep already, sent no sound to invade the silence.

'No! master. It was God.'

Then the shadow left his and disappeared with her among the trees. He did not try to call her back. That answer left him helpless.

But as, after climbing the stairs, he passed slowly from one to another of the old familiar places in the pleasant pavilions, the mystery of such womanhood as Tara Devi's and little Zora's oppressed him. Their eternal cult of purely physical passion, their eternal struggle for perfect purity and constancy, not of the soul, but the body, their worship, alike of sex and He who made it, seemed incomprehensible. And as he turned the key in the lock for the last time, he felt glad to think that it was not likely the problem would come into his life again despite the long lock of black hair he carried with him. It was an odd keepsake, but if he was any judge of faces, his cantrip had served his purpose, and Tara would not commit suicide while he held that hostage.

So, having scant leisure left, he hurried through the alleys to return the key. They were almost deserted; the children at this hour being asleep, the men away lounging in the bazaars. But every now and again a formless white figure clung to a corner shadow to let him pass, a white shadow itself, recalling the mystery he had been glad to leave unsolved; for he knew these were women taking this only opportunity for a neighbourly visit. Old or young, pretty or ugly? What did it matter? They were women, born temptresses of virtuous men, and they were proud of the fact; even the poor old things long past their youth! There was a chink in a door he was about to pass; a chink an inch wide with a white shadow behind it. A woman was looking out. What sort of a woman, he wondered idly? Suddenly the chink widened, a hand crept through it, beckoning. He could see it clearly in the moonlight; an old wrinkled hand, delicately old, delicately wrinkled, inconceivably thin, but with the pink henna stain of the temptress still on palm and fingers. A hand with the whole history of seclusion written on it. He crossed over to it, and heard a hurried breathless whisper.

'If the *Huzoor* would listen for the sake of any woman he loves.'

It was an old voice, but it sent a thrill to his heart. 'I am listening, mother,' He replied, 'for the sake of the dead.'

'God send her grave peace, my son!' came the voice less hurriedly. 'It is not much for listening. I am pensioner, *Huzoor*. The king gave me three rupees, but now he is gone and the money comes not. If the *Huzoor* would tell those who send it that Ashrâf-un-Nissa-Zainub-i-Mahal—the *Huzoor* may know my name, being as my father and mother—wants it. That is all, *Huzoor*.'

It was not much, but Jim Douglas could supplement the rest. Here was evidently a woman who had lived on bounty, and who was starving for the lack of it. There were hundreds in her position, he knew, even amongst those whose pensions had been guaranteed; for they had not been paid as yet. The papers were not ready, the tape not tied, the sealing wax not sealed.

'It will not be for long, *Huzoor,* and it is only three rupees. I was watching for a neighbour to borrow corn, if I could, and seeing the *Huzoor*—'

'It is all right, mother,' he interrupted reassuringly. 'I was coming to pay it. Hold the hand straight and I will count it in. Three rupees for three months; that is nine.'

The chink of the silver had a background of blessings, and Jim Douglas walked on, thinking what a quaint commentary this little incident was on his puzzle. 'Ashrâf-un-Nissa-Zainub-i-Mahal.' 'Honour-of-women and Ornament-of-Palaces.' If the King-paymaster had thought twice about such things, the poor old lady might not have been starving. He was the real culprit; for three months' delay was not long for sanctions, references, for all the paraphernalia and complex machinery of our Government. But a case like this did infinite harm. He looked up into the star-sprinkled riband of sky between the narrowing housetops, and wondered from how many unseen hearths and unheard voices the cry, *'How long, oh Lord! How long,'* was rising? But even to his listening ear there was no sign, no sound; and as he went on through the bazaars, the crowds were passing and repassing contentedly upon the trivial errands of life, and the twinkling cressets in the shops showed faces eager only after a trivial loss or gain.

And the world of Lucknow was apparently awakening contentedly to a new day, when, before dawn, he passed out of it disguised by Tiddu as a deaf-and-dumb driver to the bullock which carried the tattered bell-tent and the tattered staff uniform. It was still dark, but there was a sense of light in the sky, and the hum of the housewives' quern, early at work over the coming day's bread, filled the air like swarming bees. The spectral white shadows of widow-drudges were already at work on the creaking well-gear, and the swish of their reed brooms could be heard behind screening walls.

But on the broad white road beyond the bazaars, the fresh perfume of the dew-steeped gardens drifted with the faint breeze which heralds the dawn. And down the road, heard first, then dimly seen against its whiteness, came a band of chanting pilgrims to the Holy River.

*'Hurri Gunga! Hurri Gunga! Hurri Gunga!'*

Jim Douglas, swerving his bullock to give them room, wondered if Tara were amongst them. What if she were? That lock of her hair went with *him.* So, with a smile, he swerved the bullock back again. There was a hint of a gleaming river-curve through the lessening trees now, and that big black mass to his left must be the Bailey-guard gate. He could see a faint white streak like a sentry beside it, so it must be close on gunfire. Even as the thought came, a sudden rolling boom filled the silence, and seemed to vibrate against the archway. And hark! from within the Residency, and from far Dilkhusha, the clear glad notes of the *reveille* answered the challenge, while close at hand the clash of arms told they were changing guards. Then—though he could not see it—the English flag must be rising beyond the trees to float over the city during the coming day.

For one day more, at least!

# BOOK II

The Blowing of the Bubble

# 1

## In the Palace

It was a day in late September. Nearly six months, therefore, had gone by since Jim Douglas had passed the Bailey-guard at gunfire, and the English flag had risen behind the trees to float over Lucknow. It floated there now, serenely, securely, with an air of finality in its folds; for folk were becoming accustomed to it. At least so said the official reports, and even Jim Douglas himself could trace no waxing in the tide of discontent; it neither ebbed nor flowed, but beat placidly against the rocks of offence.

But at Delhi there was one corner of the city over which the English flag did not float. It lay upon the eastern side above the river, where four rose-red fortress walls hemmed in a few acres of earth from the march of Time himself, and safe-guarded a strange survival of sovereignty in the person of Bahâdur Shâh, last of the Moghuls; an old man past eighty years of age, who dreamt a dream of power among the golden domes, marble colonnades, and green gardens, with which his ancestors had crowned the eastern wall.

The sun shone hotly, steamily, within those four enclosing walls, save on that eastern edge where the cool breezes from the plains beyond, blew through open arches and latticed balconies. For the rest, the palace-fort—shut in from all outside influence—was like some tepid, teeming breeding-place for strange forms of life unknown to purer, clearer atmospheres.

It was at the Lahore gate of this Delhi palace, that on this late September day a tawdry palanquin, followed by a few tawdry retainers, paused before a cavernous arch ending the quaint lofty vaulted tunnel which led inwards for some fifty yards or more to another barrier. Here an old man in spectacles sat writing hurriedly.

'Quick, fool, quick! Read, and let me sign,' called the huge unwieldy figure in the palanquin, as the bearers, panting under their gross burden, shifted shoulders. Mahboob Ali, Chief Eunuch and Prime Minister, groaned under the jolt; it was a foretaste of many to be endured ere he reached the Resident's house, miles away on the northern edge of the river. Yet he had to endure them, for important negotiations were on foot between the Survival and Civilization. The heir-apparent to those few acres where the sun stood still had died, had been poisoned some said; and another had to be recognized. There was no lack of claimants; there never was a lack of claimants to anything within those walls, where every one strove to have the first and last word with the Civilization which supported the Survival. And here was he, Mahboob, Prime Minister, being delayed by a miserable scrivener!

'Read, pig! read,' he reiterated, laying his puffy hand on his jewelled sword-hilt; for he was still within the gate, therefore a despot. A few yards further he would be a dropsical old man; no more.

'Your slave reads!' faltered the editor of the Court Journal. 'Mussamât Hâfzan's record of the women's-apartments being late to-day, hath delayed—'

''Twas in time enough, uncle, if thou wouldst make fewer flourishes,' retorted a woman's voice; it was nothing but a voice by reason of the voluminous Pathan veil covering the small speaker.

'Curse thee for a misbegotten hound!' bawled Mahboob. 'Am I to lose the entrance fee I paid Gâmu, the *Huzoor*'s orderly for first interview—when money is so scarce too! Read as it stands, idiot—'tis but an idle tale at best.'

The last was an aside to himself as he lay back in his cushions; for, idle though the tale was undoubtedly, it suited him to be its Prime Minister. The editor laid down his pen hurriedly, and the polished Persian polysyllables began to trip over one another, while their murmurous echo—as if eager to escape the familiar monotony—sped from arch to arch of the long tunnel, which was lit about the middle by side arches through which the sunlight streamed in a broad band of gold across the red stone causeway.

The attributes of the Almighty having come to an end, the reader began on those of Bahâdur Shâh, Father of Victory, Light of Religion, Polestar and Defender of the Faith—

'Faster, fool, faster,' came the fat voice.

The spectacled old man swallowed his breath, as it were, and went on at full gallop through the uprisal and bathing of Majesty, through feelings of pulses and reception of visitors, then slowed down a bit over the recital of dinner; for he was a *gourmet*, and his tongue loved the very sound of dainty dishes.

'May your grave be spat upon!' shouted the Chief Eunuch. 'So none were poisoned by it what matters the food? Pass on—'

'The Most Exalted then said his appointed prayers,' gasped the reader. 'The Light-of-the-World then slept his usual sleep. On awakening, the physician Ahsan-Oolah—'

Mahboob sat up among his cushions. 'Ahsan-Oolah! he felt the royal pulse at dawn also—'

'The Most Noble forgets,' interrupted a voice with the veiled venom of a partisan in its suavity. 'The King—may his enemies die!—Took a cooling draught yesterday and requires all the care we can give him.'

'The King, Meean-*sahib*, needs nothing save the prayers of the holy priest, who has piously made over long years of his own life to prolong his Majesty's, retorted Mahboob, scowling at the speaker who wore the Moghul dress, proclaiming him a member of the royal family. There was no lack of such in the palace-fort, for though Bahâdur Shâh himself, being more or less of a saint, had contented himself with some sixty children, his ancestors had sometimes run to six hundred.

The Meean-*sahib* laughed scornfully as he passed inwards, and muttered that those who went forth with the dog's trot might return with the cat's slink, since the great question had yet to be settled. Mahboob's scowl deepened, the very audacity of the interruption rousing a fear lest the king's eldest son, Mirza Moghul, whose partisan the speaker was, might have some secret understanding with Civilization. All the more need for haste.

'Read on, fool! Who told thee to stop?'

'The Princess Farkhoonda Zamâni entered by the Delhi gate—'

Mahboob gave a scornful laugh in his turn. 'To visit the Mirza's house, no doubt. Let her come—a pretty fool! Yet she had wiser stay where she hath chosen to live, instead of being princess one day and plain Newâsi the next. There are enough women without her in the palace!'

So it seemed, to judge by the stream of female names and titles belonging to the curtained dhoolies which had passed and repassed the barriers, upon which the editor launched his tongue; but Mahboob, as Chief Eunuch, knew the value of such information and cut it short with a sneer.

'If that be all! quick! the pen, and I will sign.'

A bystander, also in the Moghul dress, laughed broadly at the well-worn innuendo on the possibilities of curtained dhoolies in intrigue. 'Thou art right, Mahboob,' he said, 'God only knows—'

—'His own work,' chuckled the Keeper of Virtue. 'And the Devil made most of the women here. Now pigs! Can'st not start? Am I to be kept here all day?'

As the litter went swaying out between the presented arms of the sentries, the white chrysalis of a Pathan veil stepped lamely down into the causeway. 'That, seeing there is no news, will be something to amuse the queen withal,' came the sharp voice.

'There may be news enough, when that fat pig returns, to make it hard to amuse thy mistress, Mussamat Hâfzan, suggested another bystander.

The chrysalis paused. 'My mistress! Nay, *sahib*! Hâfzan is that to herself only. I am for no one save myself. I carry news, and the more the better for my trade. Yet I have not had a real good day for gifts of gratitude from my hearers, since Prince Fukrud-deen, the heir-apparent, died.' There was a reckless cynicism in her voice, and he of the Moghul dress broke in hotly:

'Was poisoned, thou meanest, by—'

Hâfzan's shrill laugh rang through the arches.

'No names, Mirza-*sahib*, no names! And 'tis no news surely to have folk poisoned in the fort; as thou would'st know ere long, may be, if Hâfzan were spiteful. But I name no names—not I! I carry news, that is all.'

So, with a limp, showing that the woman within was a cripple, the formless figure passed along the tunnel through the inner barrier, and so across the wide courtyard where the public hall of audience stood blocking the eastern end. It was a massive, square, one-storied building, with a remorseless look in its plain expanse of dull red stone, pierced by toothed arches which yawned darkly into a redder gloom, like monstrous mouths agape for victims. Past this, with its high-set fretted marble *baldaquin* showing dimly against the end wall—whence a locked wicket gave sole entrance from the palace to this seat of justice or injustice—the Pathan veil flitted like a ghost; so, through a narrow passage guarded by the king's own body-guard, into a different world—a cool breezy world of white and gold, and blue, clasping a garden set with flowers and fruit, with blue sky, white marble colonnades, and golden domes vaulting and zoning the burnished leaves of the orange trees, where the green fruit hung like emeralds above a tangle of roses and marigolds, chrysanthemums and crimson amaranth. Hâfzan paused among them for a second; then, all unchallenged by any, passed on up the steps of the marble platform, which lies between the Baths and the Private Hall of Audience; that marvellous building where the legend, cunningly circled into the decorations, still tells the visitor again and again that, '*If earth holds a haven of bliss, /It is this, it is this, it is this.*'

Here on the platform, Hâfzan paused again to look over the low parapet. The wide eastern plains stretched away to the pale blue horizon before her, and the curving river lay at her feet edging the high bank faced with stone, which forms the eastern defence of the palace-fort. Thus the levels of the ground within touch the very top of the wall, so that the domes and colonnades and green gardens, when seen from the opposite side of the stream, cut clear upon the sky, like a castle in the air at all times; but in the sun-settings, when they show in shades of pale lilac, with the huge dome of the great mosque bulging like a big bubble into the golden light behind them, as a veritable Palace-of-Dreams.

She looked northward, first, along the sheer face of the rosy retaining wall to its trend westward at the Queen's favourite bastion, where a balconied summer-house was set overhanging the moat between the fort itself and the isolated citadel of Selimgarh; which, jutting out into the river, partially hid the bridge of boats spanning the stream beyond. Then she looked southward. Here was the sheer face of rosy wall again, but it was crowned close at hand by the colonnade and projecting eaves of the Private Hall of Audience. Further on it was broken by the carved *corbeilles* of the king's balcony, and it ended abruptly at a sudden eastward turn of the river, so giving a view of rolling rocky hillocks sweeping up to the horizon where—faint and far like a spear-point—the column of the Kutb showed on a clear day. The Kutb! That splendid promise, never fulfilled—that first minaret of the great mosque that never was, and never will be built—the symbol of the undying dream of Mohammedan supremacy that never came, that never can come to pass.

As she paused, a troop of women laden with cosmetics and combs and quaint baskets containing endless aids to beauty, came shuffling out of the baths, gossiping and chattering shrilly, and clanking heavy anklets as they came. And with them, a heavy perfumed stream suggestive of warm indolence, luxury, sensuality, passed out into the garden.

'What! done already?' called Hâfzan in surprise.

'Already!' echoed a bold-faced trollop pertly, '*Ari*, sister, Art grown a loose-liver? Sure this is Friday, and the King, good man, bathes apart, religiously! So we be religious too, matching his humour. That is the way with us women!'

An answering giggle met the sally.

'Thou art an impudent hussy, Goloo!' said Hâfzan angrily. 'And the Queen—where is she?'

'In the mosque praying for patience—in the summer-house playing games—in the King's room coaxing him to belief—in the vestibule feeding her son with lollipops—he likes them big, and sweet, and lively, and of his own choosing does the prince, as I know to my cost.' Here a general titter broke in on the unabashed recital.

'*Loh*! leave Hâfzan to find out what the queen does elsewhere,' suggested another voice. 'We speak not of such things.'

'Then speak lower of others,' retorted Hâfzan. 'Walls have echoes, sister, and thy mistress would fare no better than others if thy talk reached Zeenut Maihl's ears.'

'Tell her, spy! if thou wilt,' replied the woman carelessly. 'We have friends on our side now as thou mayst understand mayhap ere nightfall when the answer comes.'

Hâfzan laughed. 'Thou hast more faith in friends than I. *Loh*! I trust none within these four walls. And out of them but few.'

So saying she limped back into the garden, giving a glance as she passed it into the Pearl Mosque, which showed like a carven snowdrift against the blue of the sky, the green of the trees. Finding none there, she went straight to the Queen's favourite summer-house on the northern bastion. It was a curious fatality which made Zeenut Maihl choose it, since all her arts, all her cunning, could scarcely have told her that it would ere long be a watch-tower, whence the chance of success or failure could be counted. For the white road beyond the bridge of boats, and trending eastward to the packed population of Oude, to Lucknow, to all that remained of vitality in the Mohammedan dream, was to be ere long like a living growing branch to which she, the spider, hung by an invisible thread spinning her cobwebs, seemingly in mid-air.

'Hush!' The whispered monition made Hâfzan pause in the screened archway till the game was over. It was a sort of dumb crambo, and a most outrageous *double entendre* had just brought a smile to the broad heavy face of a woman who lay among cushions in the alcoved balcony. This was Zeenut Maihl, who for nearly twenty years had kept her hold upon the King, despite endless rivals. She was dark-complexioned, small-eyed, with a curious lack of eyebrows which took from her even vivacity of expression. But it was a man with experience in many wives who remarked that favour is deceitful and beauty is vain, for he knew, no doubt, that in polygamy, the victory always goes to the most unscrupulous fighter. Zeenut Maihl, at any rate, secured hers by ever-recurring promises of another heir to her octogenarian husband; a flattery to which his other wives either could not or would not stoop. But the trick served the Queen's purpose in more ways than one. Her oft-recurring disappointments could have but one cause—witchcraft; so on such occasions, with her paid priest, Hussan Askuri, saying prayers for those *in extremis* at her bedside, Zeenut Maihl's enemies went down like ninepins; and she rose from her bed of sickness with a board cleared of dangerous rivalry. For none in that hot-bed of shams felt secure enough to get into grips with her. Ahsan-Oolah the physician might have—she had cried quarter from his keen fence before now—but he did not care to take the trouble; for he was a philosopher, content to let his world go to the devil its own way, so long as it did not interfere with his passionate greed of gold.

And this master-passion being shared by Zeenut Maihl they hoisted the flag of truce for the most part against mutual spoliations. So the Queen played her game unmolested, as she played dumb-crambo; at which her servants, separated like their betters into cliques, tried to out do each other.

'Wâh!' said the set who were jubilant over the *double entendre*. 'That is the best today.'

'If you like it, a clod is a betel nut,' retorted the leader of another set, 'I'll wager to beat it easily.'

The Queen frowned. There was too much freedom in this speech of Fâtma's to suit her.

'And I will be the judge,' she said with a cruel smile, 'since Fâtma must be taught better manners.'

Fâtma—a woman older than the rest—salaamed calmly; and the fact made the other clique look at each other uneasily. What certainty gave her such confidence as she plucked a grey hair from her own head, and placed it on the black velvet cushion which lay at the Queen's feet?

'That is my riddle,' she said. 'Let the world guess it, and honour the real giver of it.'

What could it be? Even the Queen raised herself in curiosity; a sign in itself of commendation.

'Sure I know not,' she began musingly, when Fâtma sprang to her feet in theatrical appeal.

'Not so, Ornament of Palaces!' she cried. 'This may puzzle the herd; it is plain to the mother of Princes. It lies too lowly now for recognition, but in its proper place—' She snatched the hair from the cushion, and, with a flourish, laid it on the head of a figure which appeared as if by magic behind her; a figure dressed as a young Moghul Prince, and wearing all the crown jewels.

'My son, Jewan!' cried the Queen, starting angrily; the adverse clique taking their cue from her tone shrieked modestly, and scrambled for their veils.

Fâtma salaamed to the very ground.

'No! Mother of Princes, 'tis but my riddle—the heir-apparent.'

Zeenut Maihl paused, bewildered for an instant; then in the figure she recognized the features of a favourite dancing girl, saw the pun, and laughed uproariously, delightedly. The English sentry on the drawbridge leading to Selimgurh, might have heard her had there been one, but within the last month the right to use the citadel as a private entry to the palace had been given to the king; for it enabled him to cross the bridge of boats without the long circuit by the Calcutta gate of the city.

'A gold *mohur* for that to Fâtma!' she cried, 'and a post nearer my person. I need such wits sorely.' As she spoke she rose to her feet, the smiles fading from her face as she looked out along that white eastward streak; for the jest had brought her back to earnest, to that mixture of personal ambition for her son, and real patriotism for her country which kept her a restless intriguer. 'I need men too,' she muttered. 'Not dissolute idle weathercocks or doting old pantaloons! There are plenty of them yonder.' So she stood for a second, then turned like lightning on her attendants, and seeing Hâfzan, who had unveiled at the door, she gave a cry of pleasure. ' 'Tis well thou hast come,' she said, beckoning to her, 'for thou must know. God! if I were free to come and go, what could I not compass? But here, in this smothering veil—' She flung even the gauze apology for one which she wore from her, and stood with smooth, bare head, and fat bare arms, her quaint little pigtail dangling down her broad back; not a romantic figure truly, but one in its savage temper, strength, obstinacy, to be reckoned with. 'What time'—she went on rapidly—'does the King receive his initiates?'

'At five,' replied Hâfzan. Seen without its veil, also, her figure showed more shrunken than ill-formed, and her pale thin face would have been beautiful but for its look of permanent ill-health. 'The ceremony of saintship begins then.'

'Saints!' echoed the Queen, with a hard laugh, 'I would make them saints and martyrs, too, were I free. Quick, woman! pen and ink? And stay!—Fâtma's puzzle hath driven all else from my head—What time was't that Hussan Askuri was bidden to come?'

'The saint-born comes at four,' replied Hâfzan, ceremoniously, 'so as to leave leisure ere the Chief Eunuch's return with the answer.'

Zeenut Maihl's face was a study. 'The answer! My answer lies there in Fâtma's riddle—take two gold *mohur*s for it, woman, it hath given me new life—Write, Hâfzan, to the chamberlain, that the disciples must pass the southern window of the king's private room ere they leave the palace. And call my litter; I must see Hussan Askuri ere I meet him at the King's.'

An hour afterwards, with bistre marks below her eyes, and delicate hints of causeful, becoming languor in face and figure, she was waiting in the cluster of small dark rooms on the other side of the marble fountain-set aqueduct which flows under a lace-like marble screen to the very steps of the Hall of Audience; waiting the King's return from the latticed balcony overhanging the river, where he always spent the heats of the day.

'Is all prepared?' she asked anxiously, as a glint of light from a lifted curtain warned her of the King's approach.

'All is prepared,' echoed a hollow artificial voice. The speaker was a tall heavily-built man with long grey beard, big bushy grey eyebrows, and narrow forehead. A dangerous man to judge by the mixed spirituality and sensuality in his face, a man who could imagine evil, and make himself believe it good. This was Hussan Askuri, the priest and miracle-monger, who led the last of the Moghuls by the nose; not a difficult task, for Bahâdur Shâh, who came tottering across the intervening sunlit space, was but a poor creature. The first impression he gave was of extreme old age; evident in the sparse hair, the high hollow cheeks, the waxy skin, the purple glaze over the eyes. The next was of a feebleness beyond even his apparent years. He seemed fibreless, mind and body. Yet released at the door of privacy from his eunuch's supporting hands, he ambled gaily enough to a seat, and exclaimed vivaciously—

'A moment! A moment! good priest and physician. My mind first; my body after. The gift is on me. I feel it working, and the historian must write of me more as poet than king.'

'As the king of poets, sire,' suggested Hussan Askuri pompously.

Bahâdur Shâh smiled fatuously. 'Good! Good! I will weave that thought with mine into perfumed poesy.' He raised one slender hand for silence, and with the fingers of the other continued counting feet laboriously, until with a sigh of relief, he declaimed—

Bahâdur Shâh, sure all the world will know it,
Was poet more than king, yet king of poets.

Zeenut Maihl gave a cry of admiration. 'Quick! *Pir-sahib*, quick!' she exclaimed. 'Such a gem must not be lost.'

'But 'tis yet to be polished,' began the King complacently.

'That is the office of the scribe,' replied Hussan Askuri, as he drew out his ink-horn. He was by profession an ornamental writer, and gained great influence with the old poetaster by gathering up the royal fragments and hiding their lameness amid magnificent curves and flourishes.

'And now, *Pir-sahib*,' continued the Queen, with a look of loving anxiety at her lord, 'for this strange ailment of which I spoke to you—'

The King's face lost its self importance, as if he had been suddenly recalled to unpleasant memory. ' 'Tis naught of import,' he said hastily. 'The Queen will have it I start and sweat of nights. But this is only the timorous dread of one in her condition. I am well enough.'

'My lord, *Pir-sahib*, hath indeed renewed his youth through thy pious breathing of thine own life into his mouth—as time will show'— murmured the Queen with modest downcast look. 'But last night he muttered in his sleep of enemies—'

Bahâdur Shâh gave a gasp of dismay. 'Of enemies! Nay!—Did I truly? Thou didst not tell me this.'

'I would not distress my lord till fear was over. Now that the pious priest, who hath the ear of the Almighty—'

Hussan Askuri, who had stepped forward to gaze at the King, began to mutter prayers. ' 'Tis that cooling draught of Ahsan-Oolah's stands in the way,' he gasped, his hands and face working as if he were in deadly conflict with an unseen foe. 'No carnal remedy—Ah! God be praised! I see, I see! The eye of faith opens—*Hai!* venomous beast, I have thee!' With the words he rushed to the King's couch, and scattering its cushions, held up at arm's length a lizard; held by the tail, it seemed in the semi-darkness to writhe and wriggle.

'*Ouée! Umma!*' yelled the Great Moghul, shrinking to nothing in his seat, and using after his wont the woman's cry—sure sign of his habits.

'Fear not!' cried the priest. 'The mutterings are stilled, the sweats dried! And thus will I deal also with those who sent it.' He flung his captive on the ground and stamped it underfoot.

'Was it—was it a *bis-cobra*, think you?' faltered the King. He had hold of Zeenut Maihl's hand like a frightened child.

The priest shook his head. 'It was no carnal creature', he said in a hollow chanting voice. 'It was an emissary of evil made helpless by prayer. Give Heaven the praise'—Bahâdur Shâh began on his creed promptly, but the priest frowned—'Through his servant,' he went on. 'Since day and night, night and day, I pray for the King. And I see visions, I dream dreams. Last night, while my lord muttered of enemies, Hussan Askuri saw a flood coming from the West, and on its topmost wave, upon a raft of faithful swords, as on a throne sate—'

'With due respect,' came voices from the curtained door. 'The disciples await initiation in the Hall of Audience.'

Hussan Askuri and the Queen exchanged looks. The interruption was unwelcome, though strangely germane to the subject.

'I will hear thee finish the dream afterwards,' fussed the King rising in a bustle, for he prized his saintship next to his poetry. 'I must not keep my pupils from grace. Hast the kerchiefs ready, Zeenut?' There was something almost touching in the confidence of his appeal to her. It was that of a child to its mother, certain of what it demanded.

'All things are ready,' she replied tartly, with a meaning and vexed look at the miracle-monger; for they had meant to finish the dream before the initiation.

'A goodly choice,' said the royal saint, as he looked over the tiny silk squares, each embroidered with a text from the Koran which she took out of a basket. 'But I need many, *Pir-sahib.* Folk come fast, of late, to have the way of virtue pointed by this poor hand. And thou hast more in the basket, I see, Zeenut, ready against—'

'They are but begun,' put in the Queen, hastily covering the basket. 'Nor will they, likely, be needed; since the leave-season passes, and 'tis the soldiers who come most to be disciples to the Defender of their Faith.'

'I am the better pleased,' replied the King with edifying humility. 'This summer hath too many pupils as it is. Come! *Pir-sahib*, and support me through mine office with real saintship.'

As the curtain fell behind them Zeenut Maihl crossed swiftly to the crushed lizard and raised it gingerly.

'No carnal creature,' she repeated. It was not; only a deft piece of patchwork. Yet it, or something else, made her shiver as she dropped the tell-tale remains into the basket. This man Hussan Askuri sometimes seemed to her own superstition a saint, sometimes to her clear head, a mere sinner; she was not quite certain of anything about him save that his delusions, his dreams, his miracles, suited her purpose equally, whether they were false or true.

So she crossed over again to a marble lattice and peered through a convenient peephole towards the audience hall, which rose across an intervening stretch of platform in white shadow, and whiter light. She could not see or hear much; but enough to show her that everything was going on the same as usual. The disciples, most of them in full uniform, went up and down the steps calmly, and the wordy exordium on the cardinal virtues went on and on. How different it might be, she thought, if she had the voice. She would rouse more than those faint '*Wâh Wâhs!*' She would make the fire come to men's eyes. In a sort of pet with her own helplessness, she moved away and so, through another room, went to stand at another lattice. It looked south over a strip of garden, and there was an open square left in the tracery through which a face might peer, a hand might pass. And as she stood she counted the remaining kerchiefs in the basket she still held. They were all of bright green silk and bore in the same lettering the Great Cry: '*Deen! Deen! Futteh Mahomed!*'

As dangerous a woman this, as Hussan Askuri was a man; as dangerous, both of them, to peaceful life, as the fabled *bis-cobra*, at the idea of which the foolish old king had cried, '*Ouée, Umma!*' like any woman.

And now at last that wordy exordium must be over, for, along the garden path, came the clank of accoutrements. Zeenut Maihl's listless figure seemed galvanized to sudden life, there was a flutter of green at the open square, and her voice followed the shower of silk—

'These banners from the Defender to his soldiers.'

But as she spoke, a stir of excitement, a subdued murmur of expectation reached her ear from outside, and, leaning forward, she caught a glimpse of a swinging litter coming along the path. Mahboob returned already! Vexatious, indeed, when she had turned and planned everything so as to be sure of having the king in her apartments when the answer arrived. Now others would know it before she did—unless!—the thought obliterated all others, and she flew back to the further lattice. The king, returning from the initiation, had paused in the middle of the platform at the sight of the approaching litter, and his courtiers, as if by instinct, had grouped themselves round him, leaving him the central figure. The cruel sunlight streamed down on the tawdry court, on the worn out old man.

The pause while the fat eunuch was helped from his litter seemed interminable to the woman behind the lattice. She could have screamed to him for the answer, could have had at his fat carcass with her hands for its slowness. But the old king had better blood in his veins. He stood quietly, his tawdry court around him; behind him the marble, and gold, and mosaics of his ancestors.

'What news, slave?' he asked boldly.

'None, Light of the Faithful,' replied the chief eunuch.

'None!' The semi circle closed in a little, every face full of disappointed curiosity.

'I have a letter for the Lord of the World with me. Its substance is this. The *Sirkar* will recognize no heir. During the lifetime of our Great Master—whose life be prolonged for ever—the *Sirkar* will make no promise of any kind, either to His Majesty, or to any other member of the royal family. It is to remain as if there were no succession.'

No succession! Above the sudden murmur of universal surprise and dissent, a woman's cry of inarticulate rage came from behind the lattice. The king turned towards the sound instinctively. 'I must to the queen,' he murmured helplessly, 'I must to the queen.'

# 2

# In the City

Come, beauty, rare, divine,

Thy lover like a vine
With tendril arms entwine;

Lay rose red lips to mine,
Bewildering as wine.

The song came in little insistent trills and quaverings, and quaint recurring cadences, which matched the insistency of the rhymes. The singer was a young man of about three and twenty, and as he sang, seated on a Persian rug on the top of a roof, he played an elaborate symphony of trills and cadences to match, upon a tinkling *saringi*. He was small, slight, with a bright vivacious face smooth shaven, save for a thin moustache trimmed into a faint fine fringe. His costume marked him as a dandy of the first water, and he smelt horribly of musk.

The roof on which he sate was a secluded roof, protected from view, even from other roofs, by high latticed walls, its only connection with the world below it being by a dizzy brick ladder of a stair climbing down fearlessly from one corner. Across the further end stretched a sort of verandah, enclosed by lattice and screens. But the middle arch being open showed a blue and white striped carpet, and a low reed stool. Nothing more, though a sweet voice came from its unseen corner.

'Art not ashamed, Abool, to come to my discreet house among godly folk and sing lewd songs? Will they not think the ill of me? And if thou comest drunken horribly with wine, as thou didst last week, claiming audience of me, thine aunt, not all that title will save me from aspersion. And if I lose this calm retreat, whither shall poor Newâsi go?'

'Nay, kind one!' cried Prince Abool-Bukr, 'that shall never be.' So saying he cast away the tinkling *saringi* and from the litter of musical instruments around him, laid impulsive hands on a long-necked fiddle with a cello tone in it. 'I would sing psalms to please mine aunt,' he went on in reckless gaiety, 'but that I know none. Will pious Saadi suit your sober neighbours, since love-lorn Hâfiz shocks them? But no! I can never stomach his sentimental sanctity, so back we go to the wisest of all poets.'

The high thin tenor ran on without a break into a minor key, and a stanza of the Great Tentmakers. And as it quivered and quavered over the illusion of life, a woman's figure came to lean against the central arch, and look down on the singer with kindly eyes.

They were the most beautiful eyes in the world. Such is the consensus of opinion among all who ever saw them. Judged, indeed, by this standard, the Princess Farkhoonda Zamâni, alias Newâsi Begum, the widow of one of the king's younger sons, must have had that mysterious charm which is beyond beauty. But she was beautiful also, though smallpox had left its marks upon her. Chiefly, however, by a thickening of the skin, which brought an opaque pallor to it, giving her oval face a look of carved ivory. In truth, this memento of the past tragedy, which at the age of thirteen had brought her, the half-wedded bride, to death's door, and sent her fifteen-year-old bridegroom from the festival to the grave, enhanced, rather than detracted, from her beauty. Her lips were reddened after the fashion of court women, her short-sighted hazel eyes, were heavily blackened with antimony; but she wore no jewels, and her graceful sweeping Delhi dress was of deadest, purest white, embroidered in finest needlework round hems and seams, and relieved only by the lighter folds of her white lace-like veil. For she had forsworn colours when she fled from court-life and its many intrigues for an alliance with the charming widow, and, on the plea of a call to a religious and celibate life, had taken up her abode in the Mufti's Alley. This was a secluded little lane off the bazaar which lies to the south of the Jumma Mosque, where a score or two of the Mohammedan families connected with the late chief magistrate of the city lived, decently, respectably, respectedly. To do this, having sometimes to close the gate at the entrance of the alley, and so shut out the wicked world around them. That whole quarter of the city, however, held many such learned, well-born, well-doing folk. Hussan Askuri's house lay within a stone's throw, Ahsan-Oolah's not far off, and, all about, tall windowless buildings rose, standing sentinel blindly over the naughtiness. But they had eyes within, and ears also; so the hands belonging to them were held up in horror over the doings of the Survival, and—despite race and religion—an inevitably reluctant, yet inevitably firm adherence was given to Civilization. Even the womenfolk on the high roofs knew something of the mysterious woman across the sea, who reigned over the *Huzoor*s and made them pitiful to women, and Farkhoonda Zamâni read the London news with great interest, in the newspaper which Abool-Bukr used to bring her regularly. Hers was the highest roof of all, save one at the back of her verandah room; so close to it indeed that the same *neem*-tree touched both.

It was not a quarter, therefore, in which the leader of the fastest set in the palace might have been expected to be a constant visitor. But he was; and the decorous alley put up with his songs patiently. Partly, no doubt, for his aunt's sake; more for his own charm of manner, which always gained him a consideration better men might have lacked. Being the late heir-apparent's eldest son, he was certain of succeeding to the throne if he outlived all his uncles; for the claims of the elder generation are, by Moghul law, paramount over those of the younger. Now, since the inevitable harking back to the eldest branch after years of power enjoyed by the junior ones which this plan necessitates, is responsible for half the wars and murders which mark an Indian succession, some of these learned progressive folk admitted tentatively that the western plan was better; and that if Prince Abool-Bukr were only other than he was, he might as well succeed now as later on.

The idea now and again roused a like ambition in the young idler, but as a rule he was content to be the best musician in Delhi, the boldest gambler, the fastest liver. Yet through all, he kept his hold on one kind woman's hand; and those who knew the prince and princess, have never a word to say against the friendship which led to that singing of Omar Khayyâm upon the latticed roof.

'Life could be better than that for thee, nephew, didst thou but choose,' said her soft voice, interrupting the cynicism, while her delicate fingers, touching the singer's shoulder as if in reproof, lingered there tenderly. He bent his smooth cheek impulsively to caress the hand so close to it, with a frank, boyish action. The next moment, however, he had started to his feet, the minor tone changed to a dance measure, then ended in a wild discord and a wilder laugh. Her use of the word nephew was apt to rouse his recklessness, for she was but a month or two older than he.

'Thou canst not make me other than I was born,' he began; but she interrupted him quickly.

'Thou wast born of good parts enough, God knows.'

'But my father deemed me fool, therefore I was brought up in a stable, mine aunt; and sang in brothels ere I knew what the word meant. So 'tis sheer waste time to interview my scandalized relations as thou dost, and beg them to take me serious. By all the courtesans in the Thunbi bazaar, Newâsi, I take not myself so. Nor am I worse than the holy, pious aunt: I take paradise now, and leave hell to the last. They choose the other way; and make a better bargain for pleasure than I, seeing that the astrologers give me a short life, a bloody death.'

Newâsi caught her hand back to another resting place above her heart. 'A—a bloody death,' she echoed, 'who—who told the lie?'

Prince Abool-Bukr shook his head with a kindly smile. 'Oh! heed it not, kind lady. Such is the fashion with soothsayers nowadays. The heavens are black with portents. Some one's cow hath three calves, some one's child hath ten noses and a tail. Fire hath come from heaven—thou thyself didst tell me some such wind-sucker's tale—or from hell more likely—'

'Nay! but it is true,' she interrupted eagerly; 'I had it from the milkwoman, who comes from the village, where the *suttee*—'

'The mouse began to gnaw the rope. The rope began to bind the ox. The ox began—,' hummed the prince irreverently.

Newâsi stamped her foot. 'But it *is* true, scoffer! There is a festival of it today in some idol temple—may it be defiled! The widow would have burnt, after sinful custom, but was prevented by the *Huzoors*. And rightly. Yet, God knows—seeing the poor soul had to burn sometime through being an idolater—they might have let her burn with her love—'

Abool laughed softly. 'And yet thou wilt have naught of Hâfiz— Hâfiz the love-lorn! Verily, Newâsi, thou art true woman!'

She ignored the interruption.—'So, being hindered, she went to Benares, and there this fire fell on her through prayer, and burnt hands and feet—'

'But not her face,' cried Prince Abool, thrumming the muted strings and making them sound like a tom-tom. 'I'll wager my best pigeon, not her face, if she be a good-looking wench! And since fire follows on other things beside prayer, she was a fool not to get it, like me, through pleasure instead. To burn a virgin! What a dreary tale! Look not so shocked, Newâsi! a man must enjoy these presents, when folk around him waste half the time in dreaming of a future—of something better to come—as thou dost. . . .' He paused, and a soft eager ring came to his voice. 'If thou couldst only forget all that—forget who I might be in the years to come—forget what thou wouldst have been had my respected uncle not preferred peace to pleasure—for it never came to pass, remember, it never came to pass—then we two, you and I,'—he paused again, perhaps at the sudden shrinking in her eyes, and gave a restless laugh. 'As 'tis, the present must suffice,' he added lightly, 'and even so thou dost mourn for what I might be if the grace of God took me unawares. Thou hast caught the dreaming trick, mayhap, from the Prince of Dreamers yonder.'

He moved over to the outer parapet and waved his hand towards Hussan Askuri's house. Then his vagrant attention turned swiftly to something which he could see in a peep of bazaar visible from this new point of view.

'Three, four, five trays of sweetstuffs! and one of milk and butter,' he cried eagerly, 'and by my corn-merchant's bill—which I must pay soon or starve—the carriers are palace folk! Is there, by chance, a marriage in the clan? Why didst not tell me before, Newâsi? then I could have gone as musician and earned a few rupees.'

He gave a flourish of his bow, so drawing forth a lugubrious wail from the long-necked fiddle.

'No marriage that I wot of,' she replied, smiling fondly over his heedless gaiety. 'The trays will be going to the *Pir-sahib*'s house. They have gone every Thursday these few weeks past, ever since the queen took ill on hearing the answer about the heirship. She vowed it then every week, so that the holy man's prayer might bring success to our cousin of Persia in this war—God save the very dust of it from the winds of misfortune so long as dust and wind exist!'—She added piously.

Prince Abool-Bukr turned round on her sharply with anxiety in his face. 'So! Thou too canst quote the proclamation like other fools—a fool's message to other fools. Where didst thou see it?'

Newâsi looked at him disdainfully. 'Can I not read, nephew, and are there many in Delhi as heedless as thou? Why, even the Mufti's people discuss such things.'

He shrugged his shoulders. 'Ay! they will talk. Gossip hath a double tongue and wings too, nowadays. In old time the first tellers of a tale had forgot it ere the last hearer heard it; now the whole world is agog in half-an-hour. But it means naught—even this heirship. Who cares in Delhi? None!—out of the palace, none! Not even I. Yet mischief may come of it; so have naught to do with dreamings, Newâsi, if only for my sake. Remember the old saw, "Weevils are ground with the corn."'

'Thou canst scarce call thyself that, Abool, and thou so near the throne,' she said, still more coldly.

'Have me what pleaseth thee, kind one,' he replied, a trifle impatiently; 'but remember also that "the body is slapped in the killing of mosquitoes."' Then suddenly, an odd change came to his mobile face. It grew strained, haggard, his voice had a growing tremor in it. 'Lo! I tell thee, Newâsi, that Sheeah woman Zeenut Maihl in her plots for that young fool her son will hang the lot of us. I swear I feel a rope round my neck each time I think of her. I who only want to be let live as I like—not to die before my time—die and lose all the love and the laughter—die mayhap in the sunlight—die when there is no need; I seem to see it—the sunlight—and I helpless—helpless!'

He hid his face in his shuddering hands as if to shut out some sight before his very eyes.

'Abool! Abool! What is 't, dear? Look not so strange,' she cried, stretching out her hand towards him, yet standing aloof as if in vague alarm. Her voice seemed to bring him back to realities; he looked up with a reckless laugh.

''Tis the wine does it,' he said. 'If I lived sober—with thee, mine aunt—these terrors would not come. Nay! be not frightened. Hanging is a bloodless death, and that would confound the soothsayer; so it cuts both ways. And now, since I must have more wine or weep, I will leave thee, Newâsi.'

'For the bazaar?' she asked reproachfully.

'For life and laughter. Lo! Newâsi, thou thyself wouldst laugh at those new-come Bunjâra folk I told thee of, who imitate the *sahibs* so well. But for their eyes'—here he nodded gaily to some one below—

'They should get one of the Mufti's folk to play,' he added, his attention as usual following the first lead. 'Saw you ever such blue ones as the boy has yonder?'

Newâsi, drawing her veil tighter, stepped close to his side and peered gingerly.

'His sister's are as blue, his cousin's also. It runs in the blood, they say. I cannot like them. Dost thou not prefer the dark also?'

She raised hers to his innocently enough, then shrank back from the sudden passion of admiration she saw blazing in them. Shrank so that her arm touched his no longer. The action checked him, made him savage.

'I like black ones best,' he said insolently, 'big black staring eyes such as my mother swears my betrothed has to perfection. Thou hast not seen her yet, Newâsi; so thou canst keep me company in imagining them languishing with love. They will not have to languish long for—hast thou heard it?—The King hath fixed the wedding.' He paused, then added in a low, cruel voice, 'Art glad, Newâsi?'

But her temper could be roused too, and her heart had beat in answer to his look, in a way which ended calm. 'Ay!' she said, 'it will stop this farce of coming thither for study and learning—as today—without a line scanned.'

'Thou dost study enough for both, as thou art virtuous enough for both,' he retorted. 'I am but flesh and blood, and my small brain will hold no more than it can gather from bazaar tongues.'

—'Of lies, doubtless—'

'Lies if thou wilt. But they fill the mind as easily as truth, and fit facts better. As the lie the courtesans tell of my coming hither fits fact better than thy reason. Dost know it? Shall I tell it thee?'

'Yea! tell it me', she answered swiftly, her whole face ablaze with anger, pride, resentment. His matched it, but with a vast affection and admiration added which increased his excitement. 'The lie, did I say?' he echoed, 'nay! the truth. For why do I come? Why dost let me come? Answer me in truth?' There was an instant's silence, then he went on recklessly: 'What need to ask? We both know. And shy, in God's name, having come—come to see thy soft eyes, hear thy soft voice, know thy soft heart, do I go away again like a fool?—I who take pleasure elsewhere as I choose. I will be a fool no longer. Nay! do not struggle. I will but force thee to the truth. I will not even kiss thee—God knows there are women and to spare for that—there is but one woman whom Abool-Bukr cares—' he broke off, flung the hands he had seized away from him with a muttered curse, and stepped back from her, calming himself with an effort. 'That comes of making me in earnest for once. Did I not warn thee it was not wise?' he said, looking at her almost reproachfully, as she stood trying to be calm also, trying to hide the beating of her heart.

''Tis not wise, for sure, to speak foolishness,' she murmured, attempting unconsciousness. 'Yet do I not understand—'

He shook his delicate hand in derisive denial. 'Why the Princess Farkhoonda refuses to marry? Nay! Newâsi, we are two fools for our pains. That is God's truth between us. So now for lies in the bazaar.'

'Peace go with thee.' There was a sudden regret, almost a wistful entreaty in the farewell she sent after him. There was none in his reply, given with a backward look as his gay figure went downwards dizzily. 'Nay! Peace stays ever with thee.'

It was true. Those other women of whom he had spoken gave him kisses galore, but this one gave him more, and it was a refinement of sensuality, in a way, to go as he had come. But Newâsi went back to her books with a sigh, telling herself that her despondency was due to Abool's hopeless lack of ambition. If he would only show his natural parts, only let these new rulers see that he had the makings of a king in him! As for the other foolishness, if the old King would give his consent—if it were made clear that she was not really—She pulled herself up with a start, said a prayer or two, and went on with *The Mirror of Good Behaviour*, through which she was wading diligently. The writer of it had not been a beautiful woman, widowed before she was a wife, but his ideals were high.

Abool-Bukr meanwhile was already in a house with a wooden balcony. There were many such in the Thunbi bazaar, giving it an airiness, a cleanliness, a neatness it would otherwise have lacked. But Gul-anâri's was the biggest, the most patronized; not only for the tired heads which looked out unblushingly from it, but for the news and gossip always to be had there. The lounging crowds looked up and asked for it, as they drifted backwards and forwards aimlessly, indifferently, among the fighting quails in their hooded cages, the dogs snarling in the filth of the gutters, while a mingled scent of musk, and drains, and humanity steamed through the hot sunshine. Sometimes a corpse lay in the very roadway awaiting burial, but it provoked no more notice than a passing remark that Nargeeza or Yasmeena had been a good one while she lasted; for there was a hideous, horrible lack of humanity about the Thunbi bazaar, even in the very women themselves, with their foreheads narrowed by plastered hair to a mere wedge above a bar of continuous eyebrow, their lips crimsoned in unnatural curves, their teeth reddened with *pân* or studded with gold wire, their figures stiffened to artificial prominence. It was as if humanity, tired of its own beauty, sought the lack of it as a stimulant to jaded sensuality.

'*Allâh!* the old stale stories,' yawned Gul-anâri from the broad sheet of native newspaper whence, between the intervals of some of Prince Abool-Bukr's worst songs, she had been reading extracts to her illiterate clients; that being a recognized attraction in her trade. 'Persia! Persia! nothing but Persia! Who cares for it? I dare swear none. Not even the woman Zeenut herself, for all her pretence of sympathy with Sheeahs, who—'

'Have a care, mistress!' interrupted an arrogant-looking man, who showed the peaked Afghan cap below a regimental turban. He was a sergeant in a Pathân company of the native troops cantooned outside Delhi on the Ridge, and had been bickering all the afternoon with a Rajpoot of the 38th N.I., who had ousted him in his hostess's easy affections. He was therefore in an evil temper, ready to take offence at a word. 'I am of the north—a Sheeah myself, and care not to hear them miscalled. And I have those who would back me,' he continued, glaring at the Rajpoot who sate in the place of honour beside the stout syren; 'for yonder in the corner is another hill-tiger.' He pointed to a man who had just thanked one of the girls in Pushtoo for a glass of sherbet she handed him.

'Hill-cat rather!' giggled Gul-anâri. 'He brought me this one, but yesterday, from a caravan new-come to the *serai*—' she stroked the long fur of a Persian kitten on her lap—'And when I asked for news could not give them. He scarce knew enough Urdu for the settling of prices.'

A coarse joke from the Rajpoot, suggesting that he had found few difficulties of that sort in the Thunbi bazaar, made the sergeant scowl still more and swear that he would get Mistress Gul-anâri the news for mere love; whereat he called over, in Pushtoo, to the man in the corner, who, however, took no notice.

'He is as deaf as a lizard!' giggled Gul-anâri, enjoying the rejected one's discomfiture. 'Get my friends the corporal here to yell at him for thee, sergeant. His voice goes further than thine!'

The favoured Rajpoot squeezed the fat hand nearest to him. 'Go up and pluck him by the beard,' he suggested vaingloriously, 'then we might see a Pathân fight for once.'

'Thou wouldst see a fair one, which is more than thou canst among thine own people.'

'Peace! Peace!' cried the courtesan, smiling to see both men look round for a weapon. 'I'll have no bloodshed here. Keep that for the future.' She dwelt on the last word meaningly, and it seemed to have a soothing effect, for the sepoys contented themselves with scowls again.

'The future?' echoed a grey-beard who had been drinking cinnamon tea calmly. 'God knows there will be wars enough in it. Didst hear Meean-*sahib*?—I have it on authority—that Jarn Larnce is to give

Peshawur to Dost Mahomed and take Rajpootana instead; take it as
Oude was taken, and Sambalpore, and Jhansi, and all the others.'

'Even so,' assented a quiet-looking man in spectacles. 'When the last
Lât-sahib went, he got much praise for having taken five kingdoms and
given them to the Queen. The new one was told he must give more.
This begins it.'

'Let us see what we Rajpoots say first,' cried the corporal fiercely.
''Tis we have fought the Sirkar's battles, and we are not sheep to be
driven against our own.'

Gul-anâri leered admiringly at her new lover. 'Nay! the Rajpoots are
men! and 'twas his regiment, my masters, who refused to fight over
the sea, saying it was not in the bond. Ay! and gained their point.'

'That drop has gone over the sea itself,' sneered a third soldier. 'The
bond is altered now. Go we must, or be dismissed. The Thakoor-jee
would not be so bold now, I warrant.'

The Rajpoot twirled his moustache to his very eyes and cocked his
turban awry.

'Ay would I! and more, if they dare touch our privilege.'

Gul-anâri leered again, rousing the Pathân sergeant to mutter curses;
and—as if to change the subject—crossed over to the man in the corner,
lay insolent hands on his shoulder, and shout a question in his ear. The
man turned, met the arrogant eyes bent on him calmly, and with both
hands salaamed profusely but slowly with a sort of measured rhythm.
Apparently he had not caught the words and was deprecating
impatience. His hands were fine hands, slender, well-shaped, and he
wore a metal ring on the seal-finger. It caught the light as he salaamed.

'Louder, man, louder!' gibed the corporal. But the sergeant did not
repeat the question; he stood looking at the upturned face awaiting an
answer.

'Maybe he is Belooch, his speech not mine,' he said suddenly, yet
with a strange lack of curiosity in his tone. There was a faint quiver, as
if some strain were over in the face below, and the silence was broken
by a rapid sentence.

'Yea! Belooch!' he went on in a still more satisfied tone, 'I know it
by the twang. So there is small use in bursting my lungs.'

Here Prince Abool-Bukr, who had been dozing tipsily, his head
against his fiddle, woke, and caught the last words. 'Ay, burst! burst
like the royal kettle-drums of mine ancestors. Yet will I do my poor
best to amuse the company and—and instruct them in virtue.'
Whereupon, with much maudlin emotion, he thrummed and thrilled
through a lament on the fallen fortunes of the Moghuls written by that
King of Poets his Grandpapa. Being diffuse and didactic, it was met
with acclamations, and Abool, being beyond the stage of

discrimination, was going on to give an *encore* of a very different nature, when a wild clashing of cymbals and hooting of conches in the bazaar below sent every one to the balcony. Every one save Abool—who, deprived of his audience, dozed off against his fiddle again—and the man from the corner who looked down at the handsome drunken face as he passed it and muttered in English 'Poor devil! He rode honest enough always—but—'

"'Tis the holy Hindu widow to whom God sent fire on her way to the festival,' came the Rajpoot's arrogant voice from the balcony. 'A saint indeed! I know her brother, one Soma, a Yadubânsi Rajpoot in the 11th, new-come to Meerut.'

The clashings and brayings were luckily loud enough to hide an irrepressible exclamation. The next instant the man from the corner was half-way down the dark stairs, tearing off cap, turban, beard, and pausing at the darkest corner to roll his baggy northern drawers out of sight, and turn his woollen green shawl inside out, thus disclosing a cotton lining of ascetic ochre tint. It was the work of a second, for Jim Douglas had been an apt pupil. So, with a smear of ashes from one pocket, a dab of turmeric and vermilion from another—put on as he finished the stairs—he emerged into the street disguised as a mendicant—the refuge of fools, as Tiddu had called it. The easiest dress, however, to assume at an instant's notice, and in this case the best for the procession which Jim Douglas meant to join. So—careless and hurried though his get-up was—he set the very thought of detection from him as he edged his way among the streaming crowd; for in that, so he told himself, lay the Mysterious Gift. To be—briefly—even in your inmost thoughts, the personality you assumed—that was the secret. Somehow or another it impressed those around you, and even if a challenge came there was no danger if the challenger could be isolated—brought close, as it were, to your own certainty. To this, so it seemed to him—the Many-faced one vehemently protesting—came all Tiddu's mysterious instructions, which nevertheless he followed religiously. For, be they what they might, they had never failed him during those six months; save once, when, watching a horse-race, he had lost—or rather recovered himself—in the keen interest it awakened. Then his neighbours had edged from him and stared, and he had been forced into slipping away and changing his personality; for it was one of Tiddu's maxims that you should always carry that with you which made such change possible. To be many-faced, he said, made all faces more secure by taking from any the right of permanence. Jim Douglas therefore joined the procession boldly, and forced his way to the very front of it where the red-splashed figure of Durga Devi was being carried shoulder-high. It was garlanded with flowers and censed by swinging censers, and behind it, with wide spread arms to show her sacred scars, walked Tara. She was naked to the waist, and the scanty ochre-tinted cloth folded about her middle was raised so as to show the burns upon her lower limbs. The sunlight gleaming on its magnificent bronze curves showed a seam or two upon her breast also. No more. As Abool-Bukr had prophesied, her face, full of wild spiritual exaltation, was unmarred and, with the shaven head, stood out bold and clear as a cameo.

'Jai! Jai! Durga mai ke jai' (victory to Mother Durga).

The cry came incessantly from her lips, and was echoed not only by the procession, but by the spectators. So from many a fierce throat beside the corporal's—who from Gul-anâri's balcony shouted it frantically—that appeal to the Great Death Mother, implacable, athirst for blood, came to light the sordid life of the bazaar with a savage fire for something unknown—horribly unknown—that lay beyond that life. Even the Mahomedans, though they spat in the gutter at the idol, felt their hearts stir; felt that if miracles were indeed abroad, their God— the only true One—would not shorten His Hand either.

'Jai! Jai! Durga mai ke jai.'

The cry met with a sudden increase of volume as—the procession passing into the wider space before the big mosque—it was joined by a band of widows, who in rapturous adoration flung themselves before Tara's feet so that she might walk over them if need be, yet somehow touch them.

'Pigs of idolaters!' muttered one of a group standing on the mosque steps; a group of men unmistakable in their flowing robes and beards.

'Peace, *Kazi-sahib!*' came a mellow voice. 'Let God judge when the work is done. *"The clay is base, and the potter mean, yet the pot helps man to wash and be clean."*'

The speaker, a tall, gaunt man, rose a full head above the others, and Jim Douglas's keen eyes, taking in everything as they passed, recognized him instantly. It was the Moulvie of Fyzabad; but as it was partly to hear what he had to say when he was preaching, partly to find out how the people viewed the question of the heirship which had brought Jim Douglas to Delhi, he was not surprised at the sight.

And now the procession reaching the Dareeba—that narrowest of lanes hedged by high houses—received a momentary check. For down it, preceded by grooms with waving yak tails, came the Resident's buggy. He was taking a lady to see the picturesque sights of the city. This was one, with a vengeance, as the red-splashed figure of the Death-Goddess jammed itself in the gutter to let the aliens pass, so getting mixed up with a Mohammedan signboard. And the crowd following it—an ignorant crowd agape for wonders,—stood for a minute, hemmed in, as it were, between the buggy in front and the mosque behind, with the group of Moulvies on its steps.

> Fire worship for a hundred years,
> A century of Christ and tears,
> Then the True God shall come again
> And every infidel be slain,

quoted he of Fyzabad under his breath, and the others nodded. They knew the prophecy of Shah N'amut-oolah well. It was being bandied from mouth to mouth in those days; for the Mohammedan crowd was also agape for wonders.

# 3

# On the Ridge

'Amelly Klistmus to zoo, Miffis Erlton! An' oh! they's suts a lot of boo'ful boo'ful sings in a velandah.'

Sonny's liquid lisp said true. On this Christmas morning the verandah of Major Erlton's house on the Ridge of Delhi was full of beauties to childish eyes. For he, being on special duty regarding a scheme for cavalry remounts and having Delhi for his winter headquarters, found plenty of contractors, agents, troopers, and dealers, eager to be remembered by one who might probably have a voice in much future patronage. So there were trays on trays of oranges and apples, pistachios, almonds, raisins, round boxes of Cabul grapes, all decked with flowers. And on most of them, as the surest bid for recognition, lay a trumpery toy of sorts for the Major *Sahib*'s little unknown son, whose existence could, nevertheless, not be ignored by these gift-bringers, to whom children are the greatest gift of all.

And so, as they waited with a certain child like complacency in their own offerings for the recipients' tardy appearance, they had smiled on little Sonny Seymour as he passed them on his way to give greeting to his dearest Mrs Erlton. For the Seymours had had the expected change to Delhi, and Sonny's mother was now complaining of the climate, and the servants, and the babies, in one of the houses within the Kashmir gate of the city; a fact which took from her the grievance regarding dog carts, since it lay within a walk of her husband's office. Thus some of the smiles had not simply been given to a child, but to a child whose father was a *sahib* known to the smiler; and one broad grin had come because Sonny had paused to say, with the quaint precision with which all English children speak Hindustani—

'*Ai! Bij Rao! tu kyon aie?*' (Oh, Bij Rao, why are you here?)

The orderly's face, which Mrs Seymour had said gave her the shivers, had beamed over the recognition; he had risen and saluted, explaining gravely to the *chota sahib* that he came from Meerut, because the Major-*sahib* was now his *sahib* for the time. Sonny had nodded gravely as if he understood the position perfectly, and passed on to the drawing-room, where Kate Erlton was sticking a few sprigs of holly and mistletoe round the portrait of another fair-haired boy; these same sprigs being themselves a Christmas offering from the Parsee merchant, who had a branch establishment at a hill station. He sent for them from the snows every year as a delicate attention to his customers. But this year something still more reminiscent of home had come with them—a real spruce fir for the Christmas Tree which Kate Erlton was organizing for the school children. The Tree in itself was new to India in those days, and she had suggested a still greater innovation; namely, that all children of parents employed in Government offices or workshops should be invited, not only those with pretensions to white faces. For Kate, being herself far happier and more contented than she had been nine months before when she begged that last chance from Jim Douglas, had begun to look out from her own life into the world around her with greater interest. In a way, it seemed to her that the chance had come. Not tragically, as Jim Douglas had hinted, but easily, naturally, in this special duty, which had removed her husband both from Alice Gissing, and his own past reputation.

It had sent him to Simla, where people are accepted for what they are; and here his good looks, his good-natured, devil-may-care desire for amusement, had made him a favourite in society, and his undoubted knowledge of cavalry requirements stood him in good stead with the authorities. So he had come down for the winter to Delhi on a new track altogether. To begin with, his work interested him and made him lead a more wholesome life. It took him away from home pretty often, so lessening friction; for it was pleasant to return to a well-ordered house after roughing it in out stations. Then it took him into the wilds where there was no betting or card-playing. He shot deer and duck instead, and talked of caps and charges, instead of colours and tricks. To his vast improvement; for though the slaying instinct may not be admirable in itself, and though the hunter may rightly have been branded from the beginning with the mark of Cain, still the shooter or fisher generally lives straighter than his fellows. For murder is not the most heinous of crimes; not even in regard to the safety and welfare of the community.

So Kate had begun to have those pangs of remorse which come to women of her sort at the first symptom of regeneration in a sinner; pangs of pitiful consideration for the big, handsome fellow who could behave so nicely when he chose; vague questionings as to whether the past had not been partly her fault; whether if this were the chance she ought not to forget and forgive—many things?

He looked very handsome as he lounged in, dressed spick and span in full uniform for church parade. And she, poised on a chair, her dainty ankles showing, looked spick and span also in a pretty new dress. He noticed the fact instantly.

'A merry Christmas, Kate!' Here! give me your hand and I'll help you down.'

How many years was it since he had spoken like that, with a glint in his eyes, and she had had that faint flush in her cheek at his touch? The consciousness of this stirring among the dry bones of something they had both deemed dead, made her set to shaking some leaves from her dress, while he, with an irrelevantly boisterous laugh, stooped to swing Sonny to his shoulders. 'You here, jackanapes!' he cried. 'A merry Christmas. Come and get a sweetie—you come too, Kate, the beggars will like to see the _mem_. By Jove! what a jolly morning.'

A foretaste of the winter rains had fallen during the night, leaving a crisp new-washed feeling in the air, a heavy rime-like dew on the earth, and the sky—of a pale blue, yet colourful—vaulted the wide expanse cloudlessly. And from the verandah of the Erlton's house the expanse was wide, indeed; for it stood on the summit of the Ridge at its extreme northern end. The end, therefore, furthest from the city, which, nearly three miles away, blocked the widening wedge of densely wooded lowland lying between the rocky range and the river. The Ridge itself was not unlike some huge spiny saurian, basking in the sunlight; its tail in the river, its wider, flatter head, crowned by Hindoo Rao's house, resting on the groves and gardens of the Subz-mundi or Green Market, a suburb to the west of the town. It is a quaint fanciful spot this Delhi Ridge even without the history of heroism crystallized into its very dust—a red dust which might almost have been stained by blood—a dust which matches that history, since it is formed of isolated atoms of rock, glittering, perfect in themselves, like the isolated deeds which went to make up the finest record of pluck and perseverance the world is ever likely to see. Perseverance and pluck which sent more Englishmen to die cheerfully in that red dust than in the defences and reliefs of Lucknow, Cawnpore, and the subsequent campaigns all combined. Let the verdict on the wisdom of those months of stolid endurance be what it may, that fact remains.

This quaintness of the Ridge lies in its individuality. Not eighty feet above the river, its gradients so slight that a driver scarce slackens speed at its steepest, there is never a mistake possible as to where it begins or ends. Here is the river bed founded on sand; there, cleaving the green with rough red shoulder, is the rock.

From the verandah, then, its stony spine split by a road like a parting, it trended south-west, so giving room between it and the river for the rose-lit, lilac-shaded of the town, with the big white bubble of the Jumma mosque in its midst and the delicate domes fringing the palace gateways showing like strings of pearls on the blue sky. Beyond them a bright dazzle of gold among the green of the Garden-of-Grapes marked that last sanctuary of a dying dynasty upon the city's eastern wall.

The cantonments lay to the back of the house on the western slope of the Ridge, and on the plain beyond. This also was a widening wedge of green wooded land cut off from the rest of the plain by a tree-set overflow canal. The Ridge, therefore, formed the backbone of a triangle protected by water on two sides; while on the third lay the city and its suburbs. But—to carry out the image of the lizard—a natural outwork lay like a huge paw on either side of the head—on the river side the spur of Ludlow Castle, on the canal side the General's mound.

A brisk breeze was fluttering the flag on the tower cresting the Ridge a few hundred yards from the house, and as Major Erlton stepped into the verandah, a puff of white smoke curled citywards, and the roll of the time-gun reverberated among the rocks.

'By jingo! I must hurry up if I'm to have breakfast before church,' he exclaimed, as the circle of gift-bringers, who had been waiting nearly half-an-hour, rose simultaneously with salaams and good wishes. The sudden action made a white cockatoo perched in the corner raise its flame-coloured crest and begin to prance.

'Naughty Poll! Bad Poll!' came Sonny's mellifluous lisp from the Major's shoulder. 'Zoo mufn't make a noise and innerupt.'

The admonition made the bird smooth its ruffled temper and feathers. Not that there was much to interrupt, the Major's halting acknowledgments being of the briefest; partly because of breakfast, partly from lack of Hindustani, mostly from the inherent insular horror of a function.

'Thank God! that's over,' he said piously, when the last tray had been emptied on the miscellaneous pile round which the servants were already hovering expectantly, and the last well-wisher had disappeared. 'Still it was nice of them to remember Freddy,' he added, looking at the toys—'Wasn't it, wife?'

She looked up almost scared at the title. 'Very,' she replied, with a faint quiver in her voice. 'We must send some home to him, mustn't we?'

The pronoun of union made the Major in his turn feel embarrassed. He sought refuge once more in Sonny.

'You must have your choice first, jackanapes!' he said, swinging the child to the ground again. 'Which is it to be? A box of soldiers or a monkey on a stick?'

'Fanks!' replied Sonny with honest dignity, 'but I'se gotted my plesy already. She's give-ded me the polly—be-tos it 'oves me dearly.'

Kate answered her husband's puzzled look with a half-apology. 'He means the cockatoo. I thought you wouldn't mind, because it was so dreadfully noisy. And it never screams at him. Sonny! give Polly an apple and show Major Erlton how it loves you.'

The child, nothing loth to show off, chose one from the heap and went over fearlessly to the vicious bird; the servants pausing to look admiringly. The cockatoo seized it eagerly, but only as a means to draw the little fellow's arm within reach of its clambering feet and the next moment it was on the narrow shoulder dipping and sidling among the golden curls.

'See how it 'oves me,' cried Sonny, his face all smiles.

Major Erlton laughed good-temperedly at the pretty sight and went in to breakfast.

Then the dog cart came round. It was the same one in which the Major had been used to drive Alice Gissing. But this Christmas morning he had forgotten the fact, as he drove Kate instead, with Sonny—who was to be taken to church as a great treat—crushing the flounces of her pretty dress. Yet the fresh wind blew in their faces keenly, and the Major, pointing with his whip to the scudding squirrels said, 'Jolly little beasts, aren't they, Kate?' just as he had said it to Alice Gissing. What is more, she replied that it was jolly altogether with much the same enjoyment of the mere present as the other little lady had done; for the larger part of life is normal, common to all.

So they sped past the rocks and trees swiftly, down and down, till with a rumble they were on the drawbridge, through the massive arch of the Kashmir gate, into the square of the main-guard. The last clang of the church bell seemed to come from the trees overhanging it, and in the ensuing silence a sharp click of the whip sounded like a pistol crack. The mare sped faster through the wooden gate into the open. To the left the Court House showed among tall trees, to the right Skinner's House. Straight ahead, down the road to the Calcutta gate and the boat bridge, stood the college, the telegraph office, a dozen or so of bungalows in gardens, and the magazine shouldering the old cemetery; quite a colony of western ways and works within the city wall, clinging to it between the water-bastion and the Calcutta gate.

Close at hand in a central plot of garden, circled by roads, was the church, built after the design of St Paul's; obtrusively occidental, crowned by a very large cross.

As the mare drew up among the other carriages, the first notes of the Christmas hymn pealed out among the roses and the poinsettias, the glare, and the green. It was not a Christmas environment; but the festival brings its own atmosphere with it to most people, and Major Erlton, admiring his wife's rapt face, remembered his own boyhood as he sang a rumbling Gregorian bass of two tones and a semi-tone:

O come, all ye faithful! Joyful and triumphant.

The words echoed confidently into the heart of the great Mohammedan stronghold, within earshot almost of the rose-red walls of the palace—that survival of all the vices Christianity seeks to destroy.

'They have a new service tonight,' yawned the chaplain's groom to others grouped round a common pipe. 'I, who have served *padrés* all my life—the pay is bad but the kicks less—saw never the like. 'Tis a queer tree hung with lights, and toys to bribe the children to worship it. They wanted mine to go, but their mother is pious and would not. She says 'tis a spell.'

'Doubtless!' assented a voice. 'The spell Kali's priest, who came from Calcutta seeking aid against it, warned us of—the spell which forces a body to being Christian against his will.'

A scornful cluck came from a younger, smarter man. 'Trra! a trick that for offerings, Dittu. The priest came to me also, but I told him my master was not that sort. He goes not to church except on the Big Day.'

'But the *mem*?' asked a new speaker enviously. ''Tis the *mem*s do the mischief to please the *padrés*; just as our women do it to please the priests. My *mem* reads prayers to her ayah.'

'Paremeshwar be praised!' ejaculated the man to whom the pipe belonged. 'My master keeps no *mem*, but the other sort. Though as for the ayah it matters not, she has no caste to lose.'

There was a grunt of general assent. The remark crystallized the whole question to unmistakable form. So long as a man could get a pull from his neighbour's pipe and have a right to one in return, the master might say and do what he chose. If not; then—?

An evil-faced man, who still smarted from a righteous licking given him that morning for stealing his horse's grain, put his view of what would happen in that case plainly.

'*Bullah!*' sneered a bearded Sikh orderly waiting to carry his master's prayer-book. 'You Poorbeahs can talk glibly of change. And why not? seeing it is but a change of masters to born slaves. Oil burns to butter! butter to oil!'

The evil face scowled. 'Thou wilt have to shave under thy master anyhow, Gooroo-*jee*! Ay! and dock thy pigtail too.'

This allusion to a late ruling against the Nazarite customs of the newly-raised Sikh levies might have led to blows—the bearded one being a born fighter—if, the short service coming to an end, the masters had not trooped out, pausing to exchange Christmas greetings ere they dispersed.

'Never saw Mrs Erlton looking so pretty,' remarked Captain Seymour to his wife, as, with the restored Sonny between them, they moved off to their own house, which stood close by, plumb on the city wall. He spoke in a low voice, but Major Erlton happened to be within earshot. He turned complacently to identify the speaker, then looked at his wife to see if the remark was true. Scarcely; at least to Herbert Erlton's quickened recollection of the girl he had married. Yet she looked distinctly creditable, even desirable, as she stood, the centre of a little group of men and women eager to help her with the Christmas tree. It struck him suddenly, not in the least unpleasantly, that of late his wife had had no lack of aides-de-camp, and that one, Captain Morecombe—the pick of the lot—seemed to have little else to do; a symptom which the Major could explain from his own experience, and which made him smile; he being of those who admire women for being admired.

'I have arranged about the conjuror, Mrs Erlton,' said Captain Morecombe, who was, indeed, quite ready to do her behests; 'that sweep, Prince Abool-Bukr,—who is coming, by the way, to see the show—has promised me the best in the bazaar. And some Bunjâra fellows who act, and that sort of business.'

'Better find out first what they do act,' put in young Mainwaring, who chafed under the superior knowledge which the Captain claimed as interpreter to the Staff. 'I saw some of those brutes in Lucknow last spring, and—'

'Oh! there is no fear,' retorted the other with a condescending smile. 'The Prince is no fool, and he is responsible. It will most likely be something extremely instructive. Now, Mrs Erlton, I will drive you round to the College and you can show me anything else you want done. I can drive you home afterwards.'

'Don't think we need trouble you, thanks, Morecombe,' said a voice behind. 'I'll drive my wife. I'll stay as long as you like, Kate; and I can stick things high up, you know.'

There was no appeal in her husband's tone, but Kate, looking up at his great height, felt one; and with it came a fresh spasm of that self-reproach. As she had knelt beside him in church she had been asking herself, if she was not unforgiving; if it was not hard on him?

'That will be a great help,' she said soberly.

So Mrs Seymour, coming in daintily when the hard work was over to put a Father Christmas on the topmost shoot, wondered plaintively how she could have managed it without Major Erlton, and threw so much soft admiration into her pretty eyes, that he could scarcely fail to feel a fine fellow. He was in consequence a better one for the time being; so that he insisted on returning in the afternoon to hand the tea and cake, when he made several black-and-tan matrons profusely apologetic and proud at having the finest gentleman there to wait upon them. For the Major was a very fine animal, indeed. As Alice Gissing had told him frankly, over and over again, his looks were his strong point.

The larger portion of the guests were of this black-and-tan complexion; of varying shades, however, from the unmistakably pure-blooded native Christian, to the pasty-faced baby with all the yellow tones of skin due to its pretty languid mother, emphasized by the ruddiness of the English father who carried it.

They came chiefly from Duryagunj; a quarter of the city close to the Palace, between the river and the Thunbi bazaar. It had once been the artillery lines, and now its pleasant garden-set houses were occupied by clerks, contractors, overseers, and such like. Then later on, for the sports and games, came a contingent of College lads, speaking English fluently, and younger boys clinging affrightedly to their father's hand as he smirked and bowed to the special master for whose favour he had perhaps braved bitter tears of opposition from the women at home. The mission school sent orderly bands, and there was a ruck of servants' children, who would have gone to the gates of hell for a gift.

'You will tire yourself to death, Kate,' called her husband, as, quite in his element, he handicapped the boys for the races. He spoke in a half-satisfied, half-dissatisfied tone, for though her success pleased him, he fancied she looked less dainty, less attractive.

'Come and see the play,' suggested Captain Morecombe, who did not seem to notice anything amiss. 'It will be a rest, and we needn't light up yet awhile.'

'I'm going wis zoo', said Sonny confidently, escaping from his ayah as they passed; so, with the child's hand in hers, Kate went on into the long narrow verandah which had been enclosed by tent-walls as a theatre. Open to the sunlight at the entrance, it was dark enough to make a swinging lamp necessary at the further end. There was no stage, no scenery, only a coarse cotton cloth with indistinguishable shadows and lights on it hung over a rope at the very end. The place was nearly empty. A few native lads squatted in front, a bench or two held a sprinkling of half-castes, and at the entrance a group of English ladies and gentlemen waited for the performance to begin, laughing and talking the while.

'You look quite done,' said Captain Morecombe tenderly, as Kate sank back in the arm-chair he placed for her halfway down, where a chink of light and air came through a slit in the canvas.

'I didn't feel tired before,' she replied dreamily. 'I suppose it is the quiet, and the giving in.—Tell me about the play, please,' she went on more briskly. 'If I don't know something of the plot before it begins, I shall not understand.'

'I expect you will,' he began; but at that moment a cry for Captain Morecombe arose, and to his infinite anger he had to go off and interpret for the Colonel and Prince Abool-Bukr who had just arrived. Kate, to tell truth, felt relieved. After the clamour outside, and the constant appeals to her, the peace within was delightful. She leant back, with Sonny in her arms, feeling so disposed for sleep that her husband's loud voice coming through the chink startled her.

'Can't possibly take that into consideration. The race must be run on the runners' own merits only.'

He was only, she knew, laying down the law of handicaps to some dissentient; but the words thrilled her. Poor Herbert! What had *his* merits been? And then she wondered how long it had been since she had thought of him thus, by his Christian name, as it were. Would it be possible—

'It's a story of Fate, really,' said one of the spectators at the entrance, to the ladies who were with him—his voice was clearly audible in a sudden hush which had come to the dim verandah that grew dimmer and dimmer to the end, despite the swinging lamp—'A sort of miracle play, called *The Lord of Life, and the Lord of Death*. Yama and Indra of course. I saw it two days ago, and one of the actors is the best pantomimist I ever saw.—That's the man now.'

Kate turned her eyes instinctively to the open space which was to do duty as a stage. The play had begun. It must have been going on while she was thinking, for a scene was in full swing. A scene? That was a misnomer when there was no scenery, nothing but that strange dim curtain with its indefinite lights and shadows. Or was there some meaning in the dabs and splashes after all? Was that a corn merchant's shop? Yes, there were the gleaming pots, the cavernous shadows, the piled baskets of flour and turmeric and pulse, the odd little strings of dried cocoanuts and pipe cups, the blocks of red rock-salt. And that— she gave an odd little sigh of certainty—was the corn merchant himself selling flour, with a weighted balance, to a poor widow. What magnificent pantomime it was! And what a relief that it was pantomime, so leaving her no whit behind any one in comprehension, but the equal of all the world, as far as this story was concerned. And it was unmistakable. She seemed to hear the chink of money, to see the juggling with the change, the substitution of inferior flour for that chosen, the whole give and take of cheating, till the ill-gotten gain was clutched tight, and the robbed woman turned away patiently, unconsciously.

An odd doubtful murmur rose among the squatting boys, checked almost as it began; for the shadowy curtain behind wavered, seemed to grow dimmer, to curve in cloud-like festoons, and then disclosed a sitting figure. There was a burst of laughter from the entrance.

'Rum sort of God, isn't he?' came the voice again.

But from the front rose an uneasy whisper. 'Yama! Sri Yama himself; look at his noose!'

Viewed without reference to either remark, the figure, if quaint, almost ludicrous, did not lack dignity. There was impassiveness in the pea-green mask below the mitre-like gilt tiara, and impressiveness in the immovability of the pea-green hands folded on the scarlet draperies.

'He answers to Charon, you know,' went on the voice once more. 'I suppose it means that the *buniya-jee* will need all his ill-gotten gain to pay the fare to Paradise.'

Did it mean that, Kate wondered, as she leant back clasping Sonny tighter in her arms, or was it only to show that Fate lay behind the daily life of every man? Then what a farce it was to talk of chance. Yet she had pleaded for chance once, till she had gained it.

'*Let him have his chance. Let us all have our chance. You and I into the bargain.*' You and I! What made her think of that now?

A snigger from the lads in front roused her to a new scene; a serio-comic dispute, evidently, between a termagant of a mother-in-law and a tearful daughter. Kate found herself following it closely enough, even smiling at it, but Sonny shifted restlessly on her knee. 'I 'ikes a funny man,' he said plaintively. 'Tell a funny man to came again, Miffis Erlton.'

'I expect he will come soon, dear,' she replied, conscious of a foolish awe behind her own words. But this time, as the termagant triumphed and the dutiful daughter-in-law wept over her baking, the figure that showed wore a white mask, the rainbow-hued garments were hung with flowers, and the white hands held a particoloured bow.

The boys nodded and smiled. 'Sri Indra himself,' they said. 'Look at his bow!'

'Who is Indra, Mr Jones?' asked a feminine voice from behind.

'Lord of Paradise. And that is the whole show. It goes on and on. Some of the scenes are awfully funny, but they wouldn't act the funniest ones here. And they all end with the green or white dummy; so it gets a bit monotonous. Shall we go and look at the conjurors now?'

The voices departed; once more to Kate's relief. She felt that the explanation spoilt the play. And that was no dummy! She could see the same eyes through the mask—curious, steady, indifferent eyes—the eyes of a Fate indifferent as to what mask it wore. So the play went on and on. Some of the Eurasians slipped away, but the boys remained ready with awe or rejoicing, while Kate sat by the chink through which the light came more and more dimly as the day darkened. She scarcely noticed the actors; she waited dreamily for the Lord of Life or the Lord of Death—for there was never any doubt as to which was coming; but the child in her lap waited indiscriminately for the funny man. The thought of the contrast struck her, making her smile. Yet, after all, the difference only lay in the way you looked at life. There was no possibility of change to it; the Great Handicap was run on its own merits. And then, like an unseen hand brushing away the cobwebs which of late had been obscuring the unalterable facts, like a wave collapsing her house of sand, came the memory of words which at the time they were spoken had made her cry out on their cruelty. 'What possible right have you or I to suppose that anything you or I can do now will alter the initial fact?' If he—that stranger who had stepped in and laid rude touch on her very soul—had been the Lord of Life or Death himself, could he have been more remorseless? And what possessed her that she should think of him again and again? that she should wonder what his verdict would be on those vague thoughts of compromise—

'Mrs Erlton! Mrs Erlton! everything is ready. Everybody is waiting! I have been hunting for you everywhere. It never occurred to me you would be here after all this time. Why! you are almost alone?' Captain Morecombe's aggrieved regret was scarcely appeased by her hurried excuse that she believed she had been half-asleep; for the Christmas tree was lit to its topmost branch, the guests admitted, the drawings begun.

Perhaps it was the sudden change from dark to light, silence to clamour, which gave Kate Erlton the dazed look with which she came into that circle of radiant faces where Prince Abool-Bukr was clapping his hands like a child and thinking—as he generally did when his pleasures could be shared by virtue—of how he would describe it all to Newâsi Begum on her roof. He drew a spotless white lamb as his gift; Major Erlton its fellow, and the two men compared notes in sheer laughter, broken English, and shattered Hindustani. And through the fun and the pulling of crackers, Kate, who recovered herself rapidly, flitted here and there, arranging, deciding, setting the ball a-rolling. There was a flush on her cheek, a light in her eyes which forced other eyes to follow her, even among the packed prying faces, peeping from every door and window at the strange sight, the strange spell. One pair of eyes in particular belonging to a slight, clean-shaven man standing beside two others who carried bundles in their hands. They were the actors in the now forsaken drama of Life and Death. One of them, however, had evidently seen a Christmas tree before, since he suddenly called out in the purest English—

'The top branch on the left has caught! Put it out, some one!'

The sound of his own voice seemed to discomfit him utterly. He looked round him, then realizing that the crowd was too dense for the speaker to be accurately located save by his immediate neighbours, gave a half-apologetic sign to the older of his two companions and slipped away. They followed obediently, but once outside Tiddu shook his head at his pupil.

'The *Huzoor* will never remember to forget. He will get into trouble some day,' he said reproachfully.

'Not if I stick to playing Yama and Indra,' replied Jim Douglas with a shrug of his shoulders. 'The Mask of Fate is apt to be inscrutable.' He made the remark chiefly for his own benefit; for he was thinking of the strange chance of meeting those cold blue-grey eyes again in that fashion. Beautiful eyes, brilliant eyes! Then he smiled cynically. The chance he had given had evidently borne fruit. She seemed quite happy, and there was no mistaking the look on her owner's heavy face; so the heroics had meant nothing, and he had given up his chance for a vulgar kiss-and-make-it-up-again!

It was too dark to see that look on Major Erlton's face, but it was there, as, carrying Kate off which a certain air of proprietorship from the compliments which had grown stale, they went to find the dog cart, which, in deference to the mare's nerves, had been told to await them in a quiet corner of the compound.

'You did it splendidly, Kate!'

His voice came contentedly through the soft darkness which hid the easy arm which slipped to her waist, the easy smiling face which bent to kiss hers.

'Oh, don't! Please don't!' The cry, almost a sob, was unmistakable. So was the start which made her stumble over an unseen edging to the path. Even Herbert Erlton with his blunted delicacy could not misjudge it. He stood silent for a moment, then gave a short hard laugh.

'You haven't hurt yourself, I expect,' he said drily, 'so there's no harm done. I'll call that fellow with the lantern to give us a light.'

He did, and the vague shadow preceded by a swinging star turned out to be young Mainwaring on his pony, with the groom carrying a lantern.

'Mrs Erlton,' cried the lad slipping to the ground, 'what luck! The very person I wanted. I was going round by your house on the chance of catching you, as it was useless trying to get in a quiet word this afternoon. I want to ask if you know any houses to let! I had a letter this morning from Mrs Gissing asking me to look out one for her.'

'For her?' The echo came in a dull voice; Kate had scarcely recovered from her own recoil, from a vague doubt of what she had done.

'Yes! Her husband had to go home on business and won't be out till May. So, as the new people at Lucknow seem a poor lot, and she has old friends at Delhi—' a remembrance that some of these old friendships must be an unwelcome memory to his hearer made the boy pause. But the man, smarting with resentment, had no such scruples— what was the use of them?

'Coming here, is she?' he echoed. 'Then we may hope to have some fun in this deadly-lively stuck-up place. I say, Mainwaring, would you mind driving my wife home and lending me your pony to gallop round to the mess. I must go there, and as it is getting late there is no use dragging Mrs Erlton all that way. And she has a big Christmas dinner on, haven't you, Kate?'

As the young fellow climbed up into the dog cart beside her, Kate Erlton knew that one chance had gone irretrievably, irrevocably. Would there be another? Suddenly in the darkness she clasped her hands tight and prayed that there might be—that it might come soon!

And round them as they drove slowly to gain the city gate, the half-seen crowd which had gathered to see the strange spell, were drifting homewards to spread the tale of it from hearth to hearth.

# 4

# In the Village

The winter rains had come and gone, leaving a legacy of gold behind them. Promise of future gold in the emerald sea of young wheat, guerdon of present gold in the mustard blossom curving on the green, like the crests of waves curve upon a wind swept

Northern Sea. Far and near, wide as the eye could reach, there was nothing to be seen save this—a waving sea of green wheat crested by yellow mustard. But in the centre, whence the eye looked, stood a human ant-hill; for the congeries of mud alleys, mud walls, mud roofs, forming the village, looked from a little distance like nothing else. Viewed broadly, too, it was simply Earth made plastic by the Form-bringer, Water, hardened again by the Sun-fire; the triple elements combined into a shell for labouring life. Like most villages in Northern India this one stood high on its own ruins, girt round by shallow glistening tanks which were at once its cradle and its grave. From them the mud for the first and last house had been dug, to them the periodical rains of August washed back the village bit by bit.

There was scarcely a sign of life in the sky-encircled plain. Scarcely a tree, scarcely a landmark. Nothing far or near to show that aught lay beyond the pale horizon. The crisp cold air of a mid-January dawn held scarcely a sound, for the village was still asleep. Here and there, maybe, some one was stirring, but with that deliberate calm which comes to those who by virtue of early rising have the world to themselves. Here and there, too, in the high stone enclosures serving at once as a protection to the village and a cattle-fold, some goat, impatient to be roaming, bleated querulously; but these sights and sounds only seemed to increase the stillness, the silence surrounding them. It is a scene which to most civilized eyes is oppressive in its self-centred isolation, its air of remoteness. The isolation of a community self-supporting, self-sufficing, the remoteness of a place which cares not if, indeed, there be a world beyond its boundaries. And this one, type of many alike in most things—above all in steadfast self-absorption—shall be left nameless. We are in the village, that is enough.

Suddenly an odd clamorous wail rang from among the green corn, and a band of grey crane which had been standing knee-deep in the wheat rose awkwardly and headed, arrow-shaped, for the great Nujjufgurh *jheel* which they wotted of below the horizon; in this displaying a wider outlook than the villagers who toiled and slept within sight of those fields, while the birds left them at dawn for the sedgy stretches of another world.

At the sound, a man who had been crouching half-asleep against a mud wall, rose to his feet and peered drowsily over the fields. Something, he knew, must have startled the grey crane; and he was the village watchman; as his father had been before him, as his son, please God, would be after him. He carried a short spear hung with jingles as his badge of office, and he leant upon it lazily as he looked out into the grey dawn. Then he wrapped his blanket closer round him, and walked leisurely to meet a solitary figure coming towards him, threading its way by an invisible path through the dew-hung sea of wheat.

'*Ari*, brother,' he called mildly, when he reached earshot, 'is it well?'

'It is well,' came the answer. So he waited, leaning on his spear until the new-comer stood beside him, his large legs glistening and the folds of his drooping blanket frosted with the dew. In one hand he, also, held a watchman's spear; in the other one of those unleavened cakes, round and flat like a pancake, which form the daily bread alike of rich and poor. This he held out, saying briefly—

'For the elders. From the South to the North. From the East to the West.'

'Wherefore?' The brief reply held vague curiosity; no more. The cake had already changed hands, unchallenged.

'God knows. It came to us from Goloowallah with the message as I gave it. Thy folk will pass it on?'

'Likely; when the day's work is done. How go the crops thy way? Here, as thou seest, 'tis God's dew on God's grain.'

'With us also. There will be marriages galore this May.'

'Ay! if this bring naught.' The speaker nodded towards the cake which now lay on the ground between them, for they had inevitably squatted down to take alternate pulls at a pipe. 'What can it bring?'

'God knows,' replied the host in his turn. So the two, with that final reference in their minds, sat looking dully at the *chupatti* as if it were some strange wild fowl. Sat silently as men will do over a pipe, till a clinking of anklets and a chatter of feminine voices came round the corner, and the foremost woman of the troop on their way to the tank drew her veil close swiftly at sight of a stranger. Yet her voice came as swiftly.

'What news, brother? What news?'

'None for thee, Mother Kirpo,' answered the resident watchman tartly. ''Tis for the elders.'

The titterings and tossings of veiled heads at this snub to the worst gossip in the village, ended in an expectant pause as a very old woman, with a fine-cut face which had long since forsworn concealment, stepped up to the watchmen, and squatting down beside them raised the cake in her wrinkled hands.

'From the North to the South or the South to the North. From the East to the West or the West to the East. Which?' she asked, nodding her old head.

'Sure it was so, mother,' replied the stranger surprised. 'Dost know aught?'

'Know?' she echoed, 'I know 'tis an old tale—an old tale.'

'What is an old tale, mother?' asked the women eagerly, as,

emboldened by the presence of the village spey-wife, they crowded round, eyeing the cake curiously.

She gave a scornful laugh, let the *chupatti* drop, and rising to her feet passed on to the tank. It suited her profession to be mysterious, and she knew no more than this, that once, or at most twice in her long life, such a token had come peacefully into the village, and passed out of it with its message as peacefully.

'Mai Dhunnoo knows something, for sure,' commented a deep-bosomed mother of sons as the troop followed their chaperon's lead, closer serried than before, and full of whispering surmise. 'The gods send it mean not small pox. I will give curds and sugar to thee, Mâta-jee, each Friday for a year! I swear it for safety to the boys.'

'He slipped in a puddle and cried "Hail to the Ganges", retorted her neighbour, an ill-looking woman blind of one eye. She had been the richest heiress in the village, and was in consequence the wife of the handsomest young man in it; a childless wife into the bargain. 'Boys do not fill the world, Veru—not even thine! Their welfare will not set tokens a-going. It needs some real misfortune for that.'

'Then thy life is safe for sure,' began the other hotly, when a peacemaker intervened.

'Wrangle not, sisters! All are naked when their clothes are gone; and the warning may be for us all. Mayhap the Toorks are coming once more—Mai Dhunnoo said 'twas an old tale—God send we be not all reft from our husbands.'

'That would I never be,' protested the heiress, provoking uproarious titterings among some girls.

'No such luck for poor Ramo,' whispered one. 'And she sonless too!'

'He shaved for the heat, and then the hail fell on his bald pate,' quoted the prettiest callously. 'Serve him right, say I. He, at least, had two eyes.'

The burst of laughter following this sally made the peacemaker, who, as the wife of the head man, had authority, turn in rebuke. 'Twas no laughing matter to Jâtnis, as they were, who did so much of the field-work, that a token, may be of ill, should come to the village when the harvest promised so well. The revenue had to be paid, small pox or no small pox, Toork or no Toork. And was not one of the *Huzoors* in camp already giving one eye to the look of the crops, and the other to the shooting of wild things? Could they not hear the sound of his gun for themselves if they listened instead of chattering? And truly enough, in the pause which came to mirth, there echoed from the pale northern horizon, beyond which lay the big *jheels*, a shot or two, faint and far; for all that dealing death to some of God's creatures. And these listeners dealt death to none; their faith forbade it.

'Think you they will come our way and kill our deer as they did once?' asked a slender slip of a girl anxiously. Her tame fawn had lately taken to joining the wild ones when they came at dawn to feed upon the wheat.

'God knows,' replied one beside her. 'They will come if they like, and kill if they like. Are they not the masters?'

So the final reference was in the women's minds also, as, while the muddy water strained slowly into their pots through a filtering corner of their veils, they raised their eyes curiously, doubtfully, to the horizon which held the master. It had held him always. To the north or to the south, the east or the west. Mohammedan, Mahratta, Christian. But always coming over the far horizon and slaying something. In old days husbands, brothers, fathers. Nowadays the herds of deer which the sacredness of life allowed to have their full of the wheat unchecked, or the peacocks who spread their tails, securely vainglorious, on the heaps of corn upon the threshing floors.

So the unleavened cake stayed in the village all day long, and when the slant shadows brought leisure, the headman's wife baked two cakes, one for the north, the other for the west, and Dittu the old watchman, and the embryo watchman his son, set off with them to the next village west and north, since that was the old custom. So much must be done because their fathers had done it; for the rest who could tell?

Nevertheless, as the messengers passed through the village street where the women sat spinning, many paused to look after them, with a vague relief that the unknown, unsought, had gone out of their life. Then the moon rose peacefully, and one by one the sights and sounds of that life ceased. The latest of all was the hum of a mill in one of the poorest houses, and a snatch of a harvest-song in murmuring accompaniment.

> When the sickle meets the corn,
> From their meeting joy is born;
> When the sickle smites the wheat
> Care is conquered, sorrow beat.

'Have a care, sister, have a care!' came that rebuking voice from the headman's house close by. 'Wouldst bring ill-luck on us all, that grinding but millet thou singest the song of wheat?'

And thereinafter there was no song at all, and sleep settled on all things peacefully. The token had come and gone, leaving the mud shell, and the labouring life within it as it had been before. Curiously impassive, impassively curious. There was one more portent in the sky, one more mist on the dim horizon. That was all.

So through the dew-hung fields the mysterious message sped west and south.

Sent by whom? And wherefore?

The question was being asked by the masters in desultory fashion as they sat round a bonfire, which blazed in the centre of the Resident's camp, on the banks of the great *jheel*. It was a shooting camp, a standing camp, lavish in comfort. The white tents were ranged symmetrically on three sides of a square, and, in the moonlight, shone almost as brightly as the long levels of water stretching away on the fourth side to the sedgy brakes and isolated palms of the snipe marshes. Behind rose a heavy mass of burnished foliage, and in front of the big mess-tent the English flag drooped from its mast in the still night air. Nearer the *jheel* again the bonfire flashed and crackled, sending a column of smoke and sparks into the star-set sky. The ground about it was spread with carpets and Persian rugs, and here, in luxurious armchairs, the comfortably-tired sportsmen were lounging after dinner, some of them in mess uniform, some in civilian black, but all in decorous dress; for not only was the Brigadier present, but also a small sprinkling of ladies wrapped in fur cloaks above their evening fineries. Briefly, it was a company more suitable to the *foyer* of a theatre than this barbaric bonfire. But the whole camp, with its endless luxury, stood out in keen contrast with the sordid savagery of a wretched hamlet which lay half-hidden behind the trees.

The contrast struck Jim Douglas, who for that evening only, happened to be the Resident's guest; for having been on the *jheel* in a very different sort of camp when the Resident's had invaded his solitude, the usual invitation to dine had followed as a matter of course; as it would have followed to any white face with pretensions to be considered a gentleman's. He had accepted it, because, every now and again, a desire 'to chuck' as he expressed it, and go back to the ordinary life of his class came over him. This mood had been on him persistently ever since the Yama and Indra incident, so that, for the time being, he had dismissed his scoundrels and given up spying in disgust. He had, he told himself, wasted his time, and the military magnate was justified in politely dispensing with his further services. There was, in truth, no need for them so far as he could see. There was plenty of talk, plenty of discontent, but nothing more. And what there was any one could observe and gauge, for there was no mystery, no concealment; the whole affair was invertebrate utterly, except every now and again when you came upon the track of the Moulvie of Fyzabad. It was conceivable that the aspect might change, but for the present he was sick of the whole thing, ambition and all. Horse-dealing was better. So he had established himself in a small house in Duryagunj, started a stable, and then taken a holiday in a shooting *pâl* among the *jheel*s and jungles, where in his younger days he had spent so much of his time.

Thus, after eating a first-class dinner, he was smoking a first-class cigar, and—being a stranger to every one there—thinking his own thoughts, when the Resident's voice came from the other side of the fire which, with its dancing flame-light distorting every feature in myriad variation, disguised rather than revealed the faces seen by it.

'You have bagged one or two in your district, haven't you, Ford?'

'What, sir? Bustard?' inquired the Collector of the next district, who had come over his border for a day or two's shoot, and who had been engrossed in sporting talk with his neighbour. There was a laugh from the other side of the fire.

'No! these *chupatties*. The Brigadier was asking me if they were as numerous as they are further south, and Fraser, here, said none had come into the Delhi district as yet.'

'One came today into the hamlet behind the tents,' said Jim Douglas quietly. 'I met the man bringing it; a watchman from over the border in Mr Ford's district.'

Half-a-dozen faces turned to the voice which spoke so confidently, and then asked in whispers who the man was? But there was nothing in the whispered replies to warrant that tone of imparting information to others, and a man in black clothes seemed to resent it, for he appealed to the Resident rather fulsomely.

'It will be in the reports tomorrow, no doubt, sir. For myself I attach no importance to it. The custom is an old one; I remember observing it in Muttra when small pox was bad. But I should like to have your opinion; you ought to know, if any one does.'

The compliment was no idle flattery. None had a better right to it than Sir Theophilus Metcalfe, whose illustrious name had been a power in Delhi for two generations, and whose uncle had been one of India's most distinguished statesmen. So there was a hush for his reply.

'I can't say,' he answered deliberately. 'Personally I doubt the dissatisfaction ever coming to a head. There is a good deal of course; but of late, so it has seemed to me, it is quieting down. People are getting tired of fermenting. As for the causes of the disaffection it is patent. We can't, simply, do the work we are doing without making enemies of those whose vested interests we have to destroy. We may have gone ahead a little too fast; but that is another question. As for the army, I've no right to speak of it, but it seems to me it has been allowed to get out of hand, out of touch. It will need care to bring it into discipline, but I don't anticipate trouble. Its mixed character is our safeguard. It would be hard for even a good leader to hit on a general grievance which would touch both the army and the civil population, Hindoos and Mohammedans—and as a matter of fact they have no leader at all.'

'Have you ever come across the Moulvie of Fyzabad, sir?' remarked Jim Douglas again. 'If I had the power I would shoot him like a mad dog. But for the rest I quite agree.'

Here a stir behind them distracted both his attention and the attention of those who were listening to this authoritative voice with bated breath.

'Is that the post? Oh! how delightful,' chorused the ladies, and more than one added plaintively, 'I wonder if the English mail is in.'

'Let's bet on it. Sir Theophilus to hold the stakes,' cried a young fellow who had been yawning through the discussion. But the subject was too serious for such light handling, to judge by the eager faces which crowded round while the red-coated *chuprassies* poured the contents of the bags into a heap on the carpet at their master's feet. There is always a suspense about that moment of search among the bundles of official correspondence, the files, the cases which fill up the camp mail, for the thin packet of private letters which is the only tie between you and the world; but when hopes of home news is superadded, the breath is apt to come faster. And so a scene, trivial in itself, points an inexorable finger to the broad fact underlying all our Indian administration, that we are strangers and exiles.

'Not in!' announced the Resident, studiously cheerful. 'But there are heaps of letters for everybody. Did the *memsahib* come in the carriage, Gâmoo?' he added, as he sorted out the owners.

'*Huzoor!*' replied the head orderly, who was also his master's factotum, thrusting the remainder back in the bags. 'And the Major *sahib* also. According to order, refreshments are being offered.'

'Glad Erlton could come,' remarked a voice to its neighbour. 'We want another good shot badly.'

'And Mrs Gissing is awfully good company too,' assented the neighbour. Jim Douglas who was sitting on the other side looked up quickly; the juxtaposition of the names surprised him after what he had seen, or thought he had seen, at Christmas time.

'Is that Mrs Gissing from Lucknow?' he asked.

'I believe so. She is a stranger here. Seems awfully jolly, but the women don't like her. Do you know anything of her?'

Jim Douglas hesitated. He could have easily satisfied the ear evidently agog for scandal; but what, after all, did he know of her? What did he know of his own experience? It seemed to him as if she stood there, defiantly dignified, asking him the question, her china-blue eyes flashing the childish face set and stern.

'Personally I know little,' he replied, 'but that little is very much to her credit.'

As he relapsed into silence and smoke, he felt that she had once more walked boldly into his consciousness and claimed recognition. She had forced him to acknowledge something in her which corresponded with something in him. Something unexpected. If Kate Erlton's eyes with their cold glint in them had flashed like that, he would not have wondered; but they had not. They had done just the reverse. They had softened; they had only looked heroic. Underneath the glint which had sent him on a wild-goose chase had lain that common place indefinable womanhood, sweet enough, but a bit sickly, which could be in any woman's eyes if you fancied yourself in love with her. It had lain in the eyes belonging to the golden curl, in poor little Zora's eyes, might conceivably lie in half a dozen others.

'By George!' came an eager voice from the group of men who were reading their letters by the light of a lamp held for the purpose by a silent bronze image of a man in uniform. 'I have some news here which will interest you, sir. There has been a row at Dum-Dum about the new Enfield cartridges.'

'Eh! what's that?' asked the Brigadier, looking up from his own correspondence. 'Nothing serious, I hope.'

'Not yet, but it seems curious by the light of what we were discussing, and what Mr—er—Capt—'

'Douglas,' suggested the owner of the name, who at the first words had sat up to listen intently. His face had a certain anticipation in it— almost an eagerness.

'Thanks. It's a letter from the musketry depôt. Shall I read it, sir?'

The Brigadier nodded, one or two men looked up to listen, but most went on with their letters or discussed the chances of slaughter for the morrow.

'There is a most unpleasant feeling abroad respecting these new cartridges, which came to light a day or two ago in consequence of a high-caste Sepoy refusing to let a lower caste workman drink out of his cup. The man retorted that as the cartridges being made in the Arsenal were smeared with pig's grease and cow's fat there would soon be no caste left in the army. The Sepoy complained, and it came out that this idea is already widely spread. Wright denied the fact flatly at first, but found out that large quantities of beef-tallow *had* been indented for by the Ordnance. And that, of course, made the men think he had lied about it. Bontein, the chief, has wisely suggested altering the drill, since the men say they will not bite the cartridges. If they do, their relations won't eat with them, when they go home on leave. You see, with this new rifle it is not really necessary to bite the cartridge at all, so it would be a quite natural alteration, and get us out of the difficulty without giving in. The suggestion has been forwarded, and if it could be settled sharp would smother the business; but what with duffers and—' the reader broke off, and a faint smile showed even on the Brigadier's face as the former skipped hurriedly to find something safer—'Old General Hearsey, who knows the natives like a book, says there is trouble in it. He declares that the Moulvie of Fyzabad— whoever that may be—' the faces looked at Jim Douglas curiously, but he was too eager to notice it—'is at the bottom of the *chupatties* we hear are being sent round up-country; but that he is in league also with the Brahmins in Calcutta—especially the priests at Kali's shrine—over *suttee* and widow remarriage and all that. However, all I know is that both Hindoos and Mohammedans in my classes are in a blue funk about the cartridges, and swear even their wives won't live with them if they touch them.'

'The common grievance,' said Jim Douglas, in the silence that ensued. 'It alters the whole aspect of affairs.'

'Prepare to receive cavalry!' yawned the man who had suggested betting on the chance of the home-mail. What was the use of a week's leave on the best snipe *jheel* about, if it was to be spent in talking shop?

'No!' cried the man in black, not unwilling to change the subject of which he had not yet official cognizance. 'Prepare to receive ladies. There is Mrs Gissing, looking as fresh as paint!'

She looked fresh, indeed, as she came forward; her curly hair, rough when fashionable heads were smooth, glistening in the firelight, the fluffy swansdown on her long coat framing her childish face softly. Behind her, heavy, handsome, came Major Erlton with the half-sheepish air men assume when they are following a woman's lead.

'Here I am at last, Sir Theophilus,' she began, in a gay artificial voice as she passed Jim Douglas, who stood up, pushing his chair aside to give more room. 'I'm *so* glad Major Erlton managed to get leave. I'm such a coward! I should have died of fright all by myself in that long, lonely—'

'Keep still!' interrupted a peremptory voice behind her, as a pair of swift unceremonious arms seized her round the waist, and by sheer force dragged her back a step, then held her tight-clasped to something that beat fast despite the calm tone. 'Kill that snake, some one! There, right at her feet! It isn't a branch. I saw it move. Don't stir, Mrs Gissing, it's all right.'

It might be, but the heart she felt beat hard; and the one beneath his hand gave a bound and then seemed to stand still, as the sticks and staves, hastily caught up, smote furiously on her very dress, so close did certain death lie to her. There was a faint scent of lavender about that dress, about her curly hair, which Jim Douglas never forgot; just as he never forgot the passionate admiration which made his hands relax to an infinite tenderness, when she uttered no cry, no sound—when there was no need to hold her, so still did she stand, so absolutely in unison with the defiance of Fate which kept him steady as a rock. Surely no one in all his life, he thought, had ever stood so close to him, yet so far off!

'God bless my soul! My dear lady, what an escape!' The hurried faltering exclamation from a bystander heralded the holding up of a long limp rope of a thing hanging helplessly over a stick. It was the signal for a perfect babel. Many had seen the brute, but had thought it a branch, others had similar experiences of drowsy snakes scorched out of winter quarters in some hollow log, and all crowded round Mrs Gissing loud in praise of her coolness. Only she turned quickly to see who had held her—and found Major Erlton.

'The brute hasn't touched you, has he?' he began huskily, then broke into almost a sob of relief, 'My God! what an escape.'

She glanced at him with the faint distaste which any expression of strong emotion shown towards her by a man always provoked, and gave one of her high irrelevant laughs.

'Is it? I may die a worse death. But I want *him*—where is he?'

'Slipped away from your gratitude, I expect,' said the Collector. 'But I'll betray him. It was the man who knew about the *chupatties*, Sir Theophilus; I don't know his name.'

'Douglas,' said the host. 'He is in camp a mile or two down the *jheel*. I expect he has gone back. He seemed a nice fellow.'

Mrs Gissing made a *moue*. 'I would not have been so grateful as all that! I would only have said "Bravo" to him.' Her own phrase seemed to startle her, she broke off with a sudden wistful look in her wide blue eyes.

'My dear Mrs Gissing, have a glass of wine; you must indeed,' fussed the Brigadier. But the little lady set the suggestion aside.

'Douglas!' she repeated. 'I wonder where he comes from? Does any one know a Douglas?'

'James Sholto Douglas,' corrected the host. 'It's a good name.'

'And I knew a good fellow of that name once; but he went under,' said an older man.

'About what?' Alice Gissing's eyes challenged the speaker, who stood close to her.

'About a woman, my dear lady.'

'Poor dear! Erlton, you must fetch him over to see me tomorrow morning.' She said it with infinite verve, and her hearers laughed.

'Him!' retorted some one. 'How do you know it's the same man?'

She nodded her head gaily. 'I've a fancy it is. And I am bound to be nice to him anyhow.'

She had not the chance, however. Major Erlton riding over before breakfast to catch him, found nothing but the square-shaped furrow surrounding a dry vacant spot which shows where a tent has been. For Jim Douglas was already on his way back to Delhi, on his way back to more than Delhi if he succeeded in carrying out a plan which had suggested itself to him when he heard of General Hearsey's belief that the priests conducting the agitation against widow remarriage and the abolition of *suttee* were leagued with the Mohammedan revival. Tara, the would-be saint, was still in Delhi. He had not sought her out before, being in truth angry with the woman's duplicity, and not wanting to run the risk of her chattering about him. Now, as he had said, the whole position was changed. He had no common hold upon her, and might through her get some useful hints as to the leading men in the movement. She must have seen them when the miracle took place at Benares. The thought made him smile rather savagely. Decidedly she would not care to defy his tongue—from saint to sinner would be too great a fall.

So at dusk that very evening he was back in his mendicant's disguise, begging at a doorway in one of the oldest parts of Delhi; an insignificant doorway in an insignificant alley. But there was a faded wreath of yellow marigolds over the architrave, a deeper hollow in the stone threshold—sure signs both, that something to attract worshipping feet lay within. Yet at first sight the court into which you entered, after a brief passage barred by blank wall, was much as other courts. It was set round with high irregular houses, perfect rabbit-warrens of tiny rooms, slips of roof, and stairs; all conglomerate, yet distinct. Some reached from within, some from without, some from neighbouring roofs, and some, heaven knows how! possibly by wings after the fashion of the purple pigeons cooing and sidling on the purple brick cornices. In one corner, however, stood a huge *peepul*-tree, and partly shaded by this, partly attached to an arcaded building of two stories, was a small squalid-looking black stone Hindoo temple. It was not more than ten feet square, triply recessed at each corner, and with a pointed spire continuing the recesses of the base; a sort of hollow monolith raised on a plinth of three steps. In its dark windowless sanctuary, open to the outside world by a single arch, stood a polished black stone, resting on a polished black stone cup, like a large acorn; for this was the oldest Shivâla in Delhi, and in the rabbit-warrens surrounding this survival of Baal worship lived and lodged *yogis*, beggars, saints, half the insanity, and sacerdotalism of Delhi. It was not a place into which to venture rashly; so Jim Douglas sat at the gate begging, while the clashings and brayings and drummings echoed out into the alley. For the sevenfold circling of the Lamps was going on, and if Tara did not pass to this evening service from outside, she most likely lived within—that she lodged near the temple, he knew.

So as he sat waiting, watching, the light faded, the faint smell of incense grew fainter, the stream of worshippers coming to take the holy water in which the God had been washed slackened. Then by twos and threes the Brahmins and *yogis*—the Dean and Chapter, as it were— passed out clinking half-pennies, and carrying the offertory in kind, tied up in handkerchiefs.

The service was over, and Tara must therefore live in a lodging reached from within. And now, when the coast was clearing, he might still have opportunity of tracing her. So he rose and walked in boldly, disappointed to find the courtyard was almost empty already. There were only a few stragglers, mostly women, and they in the white shroud of widows; but even in the gloom and shadow he could see the tall figure he sought was not among them, and he was about to slip away when, following their looks, he caught sight of another figure crouching on the topmost step of the plinth, right in front of the sanctuary door, so that it stood faintly outlined against the glimmer of the single cresset, which, raised on the heap of half-dead flowers within showed them and nothing more.

He drew back hastily into the empty arcade, and waited for the widows' lingering bare feet—scarcely heard even on those echoing stones—to pass out and leave him and Tara alone. For it was Tara; that he knew though her face was turned from him.

The feet lingered on, making him fear lest some of the mendicants who must lodge in these arcades should return, after almsgiving time, and find him there. And as they lingered he thought how he had best make himself known to the devotee, the saint. It must be something dramatic, something to tie her tongue at once, something to bring home to her his hold upon her. The locket! He slipped it from his neck and stood ready. Then, as the last flutter of white disappeared, he stepped noiselessly across the court.

And so, suddenly, between the rapt face and the dim light on which its eyes were fixed, hung a dangling gold oval, and the Englishman bending over the woman's shoulder from behind, could see the amaze flash to her face. His other hand was ready with the clutch of command, his tongue with a swift threat; but she was too quick for him; she was round at his feet in an instant, clasping them.

'Master! Master!'

Jim Douglas recoiled from that touch once more; but with a half-shamed surprise, regret, almost remorse. He had meant to threaten this woman, and now—

She was up again, eager excited. 'Quick! The *Huzoor* is not safe here. They may return any moment. Quick! Quick! *Huzoor*, follow me.'

And as, blindly, he obeyed, passing rapidly through a low doorway and so up a dark staircase, he slipped the locket back to its place with a sort of groan. Here was another woman to be reckoned with, and though the discovery suited his purpose, and though he knew himself to be as safe as her woman's wit could make him, he wondered irritably if there was anything in the world into which this eternal question of sex did not intrude. And then, suddenly, he seemed to feel Alice Gissing's heartbeat beneath his hand; there had been no womanhood in that touch.

So he passed on. And next morning he was on his way southwards. Tara had told him what he wanted to know.

# 5

# In the Residency

'Strawberries! Oh! how delightful.'

Kate Erlton looked with real emotion at a plate of strawberries and cream which Captain Morecombe had just handed to her. 'They are the first I have ever seen in India,' she went on in almost pathetic explanation of her apparent greed. 'Where could Sir Theophilus have got them?'

'Meerut,' replied her cavalier with a kindly smile. 'They grow up-country. But they put one in mind of home, don't they?' He turned away, almost embarrassed, from the look in her eyes, and added, as if to change the subject, 'The Resident does it splendidly, does not he?'

There could be no two opinions as to that. The park-like grounds were kept like an English garden, the house was crammed from floor to ceiling with works of art, the broad verandahs were full of rare plants, and really valuable statuary. That towards the river, on the brink of which Metcalfe House stood, gave on a balustraded terrace which was in reality the roof of a lower storey excavated, for the sake of coolness, in the bank itself. Here, amongst others, was the billiard room from the balcony of which you could see along the curved stone embankment of the river to the Koodsia garden, which lay between Metcalfe Park and the rose-red wall of the city. It was an old pleasure-ground of the Moghuls, and a ruined palace, half-hidden in creepers, half-lost in sheet luxuriance of blossom still stood in its wilderness of forest trees and scented shrubs. It was a very different style of garden from that over which Kate Erlton looked, as it undulated away in lawns and drives between the Ridge and the river.

'Yes!' she said, 'it always reminds me of England but for that—' She pointed to the dome of a Mohammedan tomb which curved boldly into the blue sky close to the house.

'Yet that is the original owner,' replied her companion. 'There is rather an odd story about that tomb, Mrs Erlton. It is the burial place of the great Akbar's foster-brother. Most likely he was a cowherd by caste, for their women often go out as nurses, and the land about here all belonged to these Goojers as they are called. But when we occupied Delhi, a civilian—one Blake—fancied the tomb as a house, added to it, and removed the good gentleman's grave stone to make room for his dining-table—a hospitable man, no doubt, as the Resident is now. But the Goojers objected, appealed to the Government agent. In vain. Curiously enough both those men were, shortly afterwards, assassinated.'

'You don't mean to connect—'began Kate in a tone of remonstrance.

Captain Morecombe laughed. 'In India, Mrs Erlton, it is foolish to try and settle which comes first, the owl or the egg. You can't differentiate cause and effect when both are incomprehensible. But if I were Resident I should insure myself and my house against the act of God and the Queen's enemies.'

'But this house—' she protested.

'Is built on the site of a Goojer village, and they were most unwilling to sell. One could hardly believe it now, could one? Come and see the river terrace. It is the prettiest place in Delhi at this time of the year.'

He was right; for the last days of March, the first ones of April, are the crown and glory of a Northern Indian garden. Perhaps because there is already that faint hint of decay which makes beauty more precious. Another short week and the flower-lover going the evening round will find many a sun-weary head in the garden. But on this glorious afternoon, when the Resident was entertaining Delhi in right residential fashion, there was not a leaf out of place, a blade of grass untrimmed. Long lines of English annuals in pots bordered the broad walks evenly, the scentless gardenia festooned the rows of cypress in disciplined freedom, the roses had not a fallen petal, though the palms swept their long fringes above them boldly, and strange perfumed creepers leapt to the branches of the forest trees. In one glade, beside an artificial lake, some ladies in gay dresses were competing for an archery prize. On a brick dais close to the house the band of a native regiment was playing national airs, and beside it stood a gorgeous marquee of Kashmir shawls with silver poles and Persian carpets; the whole—stock and block—having belonged to some potentate or another, dead, banished, or annexed. Here those who wished for it found rest in English chairs or oriental divans; and here, contrasting with their host and his friends, harmonizing with the Kashmir shawl marquee, stood a group of guests from the palace. A perfect bevy of princes, suave, watchful, ready at the slightest encouragement to crowd round the Resident, or the Commissioner, or the Brigadier, with noiseless white-stockinged feet. Equally ready to relapse into stolid indifference when unnoticed. Here was Mirza Moghul the king's eldest son and his two supporters, all with lynx eyes for a sign, a hint, of favour or disfavour. And here—a sulky sickly looking lad of eighteen— was Jewan Bukt, Zeenut Maihl's darling, dressed gorgeously and blazing with jewels which left no doubt as to who would be the heir-apparent if she had her way. Prince Abool-Bukr however, scented, effeminate, watched the proceedings with bright eyes; giving the ladies unabashed admiration and after a time actually strolling away to listen to the music. Finally, however, drifting to the stables to gamble with the grooms over a quail fight. Then there were lesser lights. Ahsan-Oolah the physician, his lean plausible face and thin white beard suiting his black gown and skull-cap, discussed the system of Greek medicine with the Scotch surgeon, whose fluent, trenchant Hindustani had an Aberdonian twang. Then there was Elahi Buksh, whose daughter was widow of the late heir-apparent; a wily man, dogging the Resident's steps with persistent adulation, and watched uneasily by all the other factions. A few rich bankers curiously obsequious to the youngest ensign, and one or two pensioners owing their invitations to loyal service made up the company, which kept to the Persian carpets so as to avoid the necessity for slipping on and off the shoes which lay in rows under Gâmoo the orderly's care, and the consequent necessity for continual fees. For Gâmoo piled up the shekels until his master, after the mutiny, had reluctantly to hang him for extorting blood, as well as shoe-money.

They were a curious company, these palace guests, aliens in their own country, speaking to none save high officials, caring to speak to none, and waiting with ill-concealed yawns for the blunt dismissal or the ceremonious leave-taking after a decent space of boredom due to their rank.

'I wonder they come,' said Mrs Erlton, passing on rapidly to escape from the loud remarks of two of her countrywomen who were discussing Jewan Bukt's jewels as if the wearer, standing within a yard of them, was a lay figure: as indeed he was to them.

'Why does any one come?' asked Captain Morecombe airily, as he followed her across the terrace, and, leaning over the balustrade, looked down at the sand-banks and streams below. 'So far as I am concerned,' he went on, 'the reason is palpable. I came because I knew you would be here, and I like to see my friends.'

He was in reality watching her to see how she received the remark, and something in her face made him continue casually. 'And there, I should say, are some other people who have similar excuse for temporary aberration.' He pointed to the figures of a man and a woman who were strolling towards the Koodsia along a narrow path which curved below the embanking wall, and his sentence ended abruptly. He turned hastily to lean his back on the parapet and look park-wards, adding lightly, 'And there are two more, and two more! In fact most people really come to see other people.'

But Kate Erlton was proud. She would have no evasion, and the past three months since Christmas Day had forced her to accept facts.

'It is my husband and Mrs Gissing,' she said, looking towards the strolling figures. 'I suppose he is seeing her home. I heard her say not long ago she was tired. She hasn't been looking strong lately.'

The indifference, being slightly overdone, annoyed her companion. No man likes having the door slammed in his sympathetic face. 'She is looking extremely pretty though,' he replied coolly. 'It softens her somehow. Don't you agree with me?'

There was a pause ere Kate Erlton replied; and then her eyes had found the far horizon instead of those lessening figures.

'I do. I think she looks a better woman than she did—somehow.' She spoke half to herself with a sort of dull wonder in her voice. But the keenness of his, shown in his look at her, roused her reserve instantly. To change the subject would be futile; she had gone too far to make that possible if he wished otherwise, without that palpable refusal which would in itself be confession. So she asked him promptly if he would mind bringing her a glass of iced water, cup, anything, since she was thirsty after the strawberries; and when he went off reluctantly, took her retreat leaning over the balustrade, looking out to the eastern plains beyond the river; to that far horizon which in its level edge looked as if all or nothing might lie behind it. A new world, or a great gulf!

Three months! Three months since she had given up that chance, such as it was, on Christmas Day. And now her husband was honestly, truly in love with Alice Gissing. Would he have been as honestly, as truly in love with her if—if she could have forgotten? Had this really been his chance, and hers? Had it to come, somehow? She did not attempt to deny facts; she was too proud for that. It seemed incredible, almost impossible—but *this* was no Lucknow flirtation, no mere sensual *liaison* on her husband's part. He was in love. The love which she called real love, which, given to her, would, she admitted, have raised her life above the mere compromise from which she had shrunk. But he had never given it to her. Never. Not even in those first days. And now, if that chance had gone, what remained? What disgrace might not the future hold for her boy's father with a man like Mr Gissing, in a country where the stealing of a man's wife from him was a criminal offence? Thank heaven! Herbert was too selfish to risk—she turned and fled, as it were, for that cause for gratitude to find refuge in the certainty that Alice Gissing, at least, would not lose her head. But the chance! the chance was gone.

'Miffes Erlton,' came a little silvery voice behind her. 'Oh Miffes Erlton! He's give-ded me suts a boo'ful birdie.'

It was Sonny clasping a quail in both dimpled hands. His bearer was salaaming in rather a deprecatory manner, and a few paces off, strolling back from the stables with a couple of young bloods like himself, was Prince Abool-Bukr. All three with a furtive eye for Kate Erlton's face and figure.

'He give-ded it to me be-tos it tumbied down, and everbody laughed,' went on Sonny confidently. 'And so I is do-ing to comfit birdie, and 'ove it.'

'Sonny!' exclaimed Kate, suddenly aghast, 'What's that on your frock—down your arm?'

It was blood. Red, fresh-spilt blood! She was on her knees beside him in an instant coaxing, comforting, unclasping his hands to see where they were hurt. The bird fell from them fluttering feebly, leaving them all scarlet-stained with its heart's blood, making Sonny shriek at the sight, and hide face and hands in her muslin skirts. She stood up again, her cheeks ablaze with anger, and turned on the servant.

'How dare you! How dare you give it to the *chota-sahib*? How dare you?'

The man muttered something in broken English and Hindustani about a quail-fight, and not knowing the bird was dying when the Mirza gave it; accompanying his excuses with glances of appeal to Prince Abool-Bukr, who at Sonny's outburst, had paused close by. Kate's eyes following the bearer's, met those bright, dark, cruel ones, and her wrath blazed out again. Her Hindustani, however, being unequal to a lecture on cruelty to animals she had to be content with looks. The prince returned them with an indifferent smile for a moment, then with a half-impatient shrug of his shoulders, he stepped forward, lifted the dying quail gingerly between finger and thumb, and flung it over the parapet into the river.

'*Ab khutm piyâree, tussulli rukhiye!*' (Now is it finished, dear one; take comfort!) he said consolingly, looking at Sonny's golden curls. The liquid Urdu was sheer gibberish to the woman, but the child turned his head half-doubtfully, half-reassured. Abool-Bukr's face softened instantly.

'*Mujhe muaâf. Murna sub ke hukk hai*' (Excuse me; death is the right of all), he said with a graceful salaam as he passed on.

So the water Captain Morecombe brought back was used for a different purpose than quenching pretended thirst; and the bringer, hearing Kate's version of the story, hastily asked Sonny—who by this time was holding out chubby hands cheerfully to be dried and prattling of dirty birdies—what the Prince had said. The child, puzzled for an instant, smiled broadly.

'He said it was deaded all light.'

Kate shivered. The incident had touched her on the nerves, taking the colour from the flowers, the brightness from the sunshine.

'Come and have a turn,' suggested Captain Morecombe, 'they have begun dancing in the saloon. It will change the subject.'

But as she took his arm, she said in rather a tremulous voice, 'There is such a thing as a Dance of Death, though.'

'My dear lady,' he laughed, 'it is a most excellent pastime. And one can dance anywhere, on the edge of a volcano even, if one doesn't smell brimstone.'

Kate, however, found otherwise, and when the waltz was over, announced her intention of going off to take Sonny home, and see Mrs Seymour and the new baby. But in this her cavalier saw difficulties. The mare was evidently too fresh for a lady to drive, and Major Erlton returning might need the dog cart. It would be far better for him to drive her in his, so far, and afterwards let the Major know he had to call for her. Kate assented wearily. Such arrangements were part of the detail of life, with a woman neglected, as she was, by her husband; she could not deliberately avoid them, and yet keep the unconsciousness her pride claimed. How could she, when there were twenty men in society to one woman? Twenty—for the most part—gentlemen, quite capable of gauging a woman's character? So Captain Morecombe drove her to the Seymours' house on the city wall by the Water bastion. There were several houses there, set so close to the rampart that there was barely room for a paved pathway between their back verandahs and the battlement. In front of them lay a metalled road and shady gardens; and at the end of this road stood a small bungalow towards which Kate Erlton looked involuntarily. There was a horse waiting outside it. It was her husband's charger. He must have arranged to have it sent down; arranged, as it were, to leave her in the lurch, and a sudden flash of resentment made her say, as she got down at the Seymours' house, 'You had better call for me in half an hour; that will be best.'

Captain Morecombe flushed with sheer pleasure. Kate was not often so encouraging. But as he drove round to wait for her at a friend's house, close to the *Delhi Gazette* press, he, too, noticed the Major's charger, and swore under his breath. Before God it was too bad! But if ever there were signs of a coming smash they were to be seen here; for Erlton, after years of scandal had lost his head—it seemed incredible, but there was a Fate in such things from which mortal man could not escape.

And as he told himself this tale of Fate—the man's excuse for the inexcusable which will pass current gaily until women combine in refusing to accept it for themselves—another man at the back of the little house past which he was driving, was telling it to himself also. For a great silence had fallen between Major Erlton and Alice Gissing after she had told him something, to hear which, he had arranged to come home with her for a quiet talk. And, in the silence, the hollow note of the wooden bells upon the necks of the cattle grazing below the battlement, over which he leant, seemed to count the slow minutes. Quaintest, dumbest of all sounds, lacking vibration utterly, yet mellow, musical, to the fanciful ear, with something of the hopeless persistency of Time in its recurring beat.

Alice Gissing was not a fanciful woman, but as she lay back in her long cane chair, her face hidden in its pillows as if to shut out something unwelcome, her foot kept time to the persistency on the pavement, till, suddenly, she sat up and faced round on her silent companion.

'Well,' she said, impatiently. 'Well! what have you got to say?'

'I—I was thinking,' he began, helplessly, when she interrupted him.

'What *is* the use of thinking? That won't alter facts. As I told you, Gissing will be back in a month or so; and then we must decide.'

Major Erlton turned quickly. 'You can't go back to him, Allie, you weren't considering that surely. You can't—not—not *now*.' His voice softened over the last words; he turned away abruptly. His face was hidden from her so.

She looked towards him strangely for a second, covered her face with her hands for another, then, changing the very import of the action, used them to brush the hair back from her temples; so, clasping them behind her head, leant back on the pillows, and looked towards him again. There was a reckless defiance in her attitude and expression, but her words did not match it.

'I suppose I can't,' she said drearily, 'and I suppose you wouldn't let me go away by myself either.'

Once more he turned. 'Go!' he echoed, quickly. 'Where would you go?'

'Somewhere!'—The recklessness had invaded her voice now—'Anywhere! Wherever women do go in these cases. To the devil perhaps.'

He gave a queer kind of laugh; this spirited effrontery had always roused his admiration. 'I daresay,' he replied, 'for I'm not a saint, and you have got to come with me, Allie. You must. I shall send in my papers, and by-and-by, when all the fuss is over'—here he gave a fierce sigh—'for I expect Gissing will make a fuss, we can get married and live happily ever after.'

She shook her head. 'You'll regret it. I don't see how you can help regretting it!'

He came over to her, and laid his big broad hand very tenderly on her curly hair. 'No! I shan't, Allie,' he replied in a low, husky voice, 'I shan't, indeed. I never was a good hand at sentiment and that sort, but I love you dearly—dearly. All the more—for this that you've told me. I'd do anything for you, Allie. Keep straight as a die, dear, if you wanted it. And I wasn't regretting—it—just now. I was only thinking how strange—'

'Strange!' she interrupted, almost fiercely. 'If it is strange to you, what must it be to me? My God! I wonder if any man will ever understand what this means to a woman? All the rest seems to pass her by, to leave no mark—I—I—never cared. But this! Herbert! I feel sometimes as if I were Claude's wife again—Claude's wife so full of hopes and fears. And I dream of him too. I haven't dreamt of him for years, and I learnt to hate him before he died, you know. I have gone back to that old time, and nothing seems different. Nothing at all! Isn't that strange? And the old Mai—she has gone back, too—sees no difference either. She treats me just as she did in those old, old days. She fusses round, and cockers me up, and talks about it. There! she is coming now with smelling-salts or sal volatile or something! Oh! Go away, do, Mai, I don't want anything except to be left alone!'

But the old ayah's untutored instincts were not to be so easily smothered. Her wrinkled face beamed as she insisted on changing the dainty laced shoes for easy slippers, and tucked another pillow into the chair. The *mem* was tired, she told the Major with a respectful salaam, after her long walk; the faint resentment in her tone being entirely for the latter fact.

'You see, don't you?' said Mrs Gissing, with bright reckless eyes, when they were alone once more. 'She doesn't mind. She has forgotten all the years between, forgotten everything. And I—I don't know why—But there! What is the use of asking questions? I never can answer even for myself. So we had better leave it alone for the present. We needn't settle yet awhile, and there is always a chance of something happening.'

'But you said your husband would be back,' he began.

'In a month—but we may all be dead and buried in a month,' she interrupted. 'I only told you now, because I thought you ought to know soon, so as not to be hurried at the last. It means a lot, you see, for a man to give up his profession for a woman; and it isn't like England, you know—' she paused, then continued in an odd half-anxious voice, her eyes fixed on him inquiringly as he stood beside her. 'I shouldn't be angry, remember, Herbert, if—if you didn't.'

'Allie! What do you mean? Do you mean that you don't care?' His tone was full of pained surprise, his hand scarcely a willing agent as she drew it close to caress it with her cheek.

'Care? of course I care. You are very good to me, Herbert, far nicer to me than you are to other people. And I can't say "no" if you decide on giving up for me. I *can't* now. I see that. Only don't let us be in a hurry. As that big fat man in the tight satin trousers said to the Resident to-day, when he was asked what the people in the city thought of the fuss down country "*Delhi dur ust.*"'

'*Delhi dur ust?* What the devil does that mean?' asked the Major, his brief doubt soothed by the touch of her soft cheek. 'You are such a clever little cat, Allie! You know a deuced sight more than I do. How you pick it up I can't think.'

She gave one of her inconsequent laughs. 'Don't have so many men anxious to explain things to you as I have, I expect, sir! But if you ever spoke to a native here—which you don't—you'd know *that*. Even my old Mai says it—they all say it when they don't want to tell the truth, or be hurried, and that is generally. "Delhi is far," they say. Dr Macintyre translates it as "It's a far cry to Lochawe;" but I don't understand that; for it was an old King of Delhi who said it first. People came and told him an enemy had crossed his border. '*Delhi dur ust,*" says he. Can't you see him, Herbert? An old Turk of a thing with those tight satin trousers! Then they told him the enemy was in sight. '*Delhi dur ust,*" said he. And he said it when they were at the gate—he said it when their swords—' the dramatic instinct in her was strong, and roused her into springing to her feet and mimicking the thrust. '*Delhi dur ust.*'

Her gay mocking voice rang loud. Then she laid her hand lightly on his arm. 'Let us say it too, dear,' she said almost sharply. 'I won't think—yet. "*Delhi dur ust.*"'

The memory of the phrase went with him when he had said good-bye, and was pacing his charger towards the Post Office. But it only convinced him that the Delhi of his decision was reached; he would chuck everything for Allie.

It was by this time growing dusk, but he could see two figures standing in the verandah of the Press Office, and one of them called him by name. He turned in at the gate to find Captain Morecombe reading a proof-sheet by the light of a swinging lamp; for Jim Douglas drew back into unrecognizable shadow as he approached. He had purposely kept out of Major Erlton's way during his occasional returns to Delhi, and as he stepped back now he asked himself if he hated the big man most for his own sake, or for Kate's, or for that other little woman's. Not that it mattered a jot, since he hated him cordially on all three scores.

'Bad news from Barrackpore, Erlton,' said the captain, 'and as I have to drive Mrs Erlton home I thought you might take it round to the Brigadier's. At least if you have no objection, Douglas?'

'None. The telegram is all through the bazaar by now. You can't help it if you employ natives.'

'Through the medium of a private telegram,' read Captain Morecombe, 'the following startling news has reached our office. On Sunday (the 29th March) about 4.30 P.M., a Brahmin Sepoy of the 34th N.I.'—That's the missionary fellow Wheler's regiment, of course—'went amuck, and rushing to the quarter-guard with his musket, ordered the bugler to sound the assembly to all who desired to keep the faith of their fathers. The guard, ordered to arrest him, refused. The whole regiment being, it is said, in alarm at the arrival that morning of the first detachment of British troops, detailed to keep order during the approaching disbandment of the 19th for mutiny; rumour having it that all sepoys then refusing to become Christians would be shot down at once. The mutineer, who had been drinking hemp, actually fired at Sergeant-major Hewson, providentially missing him; subsequently he fired at the adjutant, who, after a hand-to-hand scuffle with the madman, in which Hewson joined, only escaped with his life through the aid of a faithful Mohammedan orderly. Until, and, indeed, after Colonel Wheler the Commandant arrived on the parade ground, the mutineer marched up and down in front of the guard, flourishing his musket and calling for his comrades to join him. The Colonel, therefore, ordered the guard to advance and shoot the man down. The men made show of obedience, but after a few steps they refused to go on, unless accompanied by a British officer. On this, Colonel Wheler, considering the risk needless with an unreliable guard already half-mutinous, rode off to report his failure to the Brigadier who had halted on the further side of the parade ground. At this juncture (abut 5.30 P.M.) matters looked most serious. The 43rd N.I. had turned out, and were barely restrained from rushing their bells of arms by the entreaties of their native officers. The 34th, beyond control altogether, were watching the mutineer's unchecked defiance with growing sympathy. Fortunately at this moment General Hearsey commanding the Division rode up, followed by his two sons as *aides*. Hearing what had occurred from the group of officers awaiting further developments, he galloped over to the guard, ordered them to follow him, and made straight for the mutineer; shouting back, "Damn his musket, sir!" to an officer who warned him it was loaded. But seeing the man kneel to take him, he called to his son, "If I fall, John, rush in and put him to death somehow." The precaution was, providentially, unnecessary, for the mutineer, seeing the remaining officers join in this resolute advance, turned his musket on himself. He is not expected to live. Adjutant Baugh, a most promising young officer is, we regret to say, dangerously wounded.'

'Treacherous black devils! I'd shoot 'em down like dogs—the lot of them,' said Major Erlton savagely. He had slipped from his horse and now stood in the verandah overlooking the proof, his back to Jim Douglas. Perhaps it was the closer sight of his enemy's face which roused the latter's temper; anyhow he broke into the conversation with that nameless challenge in his voice which makes a third person nervous—

'It is a pity you were not at Barrackpore. They seem to have been in need of a good pot-shot—even of an officer to be potted at—till Hearsey came to the front.'

Captain Morecombe turned quickly to put up his sword as it were. 'By the way, Erlton,' he said hastily, 'I don't think you know Douglas, though you tried to see him at Nujjufghur after he saved Mrs Gissing from that snake.'

But Jim Douglas's temper grew, partly at his own fatuity in risking the now inevitable encounter—and he had a vile uncontrollable temper when he was in the wrong.

'Major Erlton and I have met before,' he interrupted turning to go; 'but I doubt if he will recognize me. Possibly his horse may.'

He paused as he spoke before the Arab which stood waiting. It whinnied instantly, stretching its head towards its old master. Major Erlton muttered a startled exclamation, but regained his self-possession instantly. 'I beg your pardon—Mr—er—Douglas I think you said, Morecombe; but I did not recognize you—'

The pause was aggressive to the last degree.

'Under that name, you mean,' finished Jim Douglas, white with anger at being so obviously at a disadvantage. 'The fact is, Captain Morecombe, that as the late King of Oude's trainer I called myself James Greyman. I sold that Arab to Major Erlton under that name, and under—well—rather peculiar circumstances. I am quite ready to tell them if Major Erlton thinks them likely to interest the general public.'

His eyes met his enemy's fiercely, getting back now full measure of sheer, wild, vicious temper. Everything else had gone to the winds, and they would have been at each other's throats gladly; scarcely remembering the cause of quarrel, and forgetting it utterly with the first grip, as men will do to the end of time.

Then the Major, being less secure of his ground since fighting was out of the question, turned on his heel. 'So far as I'm concerned,' he said, 'the explanation is sufficient. Give the devil his due and every man his chance.'

The innuendo was again unmistakable; but the words reminded Jim Douglas of an almost-forgotten promise, and he bit his lips over the necessity for silence; but in that—as he knew well—lay his only refuge from his own temper; it was silence, or speech to the uttermost.

'If you have quite done with the proof, Captain Morecombe,' he said very ceremoniously.

'Certainly, certainly. Thanks for letting me see it,' interrupted the Captain, who had been looking from one to the other doubtfully, as most men do even when their dearest friends are implicated, if the cause of quarrel is a horse. 'It is a serious business,' he went on hurriedly, to help the diversion. 'After all the talk and fuss, this cutting down of an officer—'

'Is first blood,' put in Jim Douglas. 'There will be more spilt before long.

'Disloyal scoundrels!' growled Major Erlton wrathfully. 'Idiots! As if they had a chance!'

'They have none. That's the pity of it,' retorted his adversary as he rode off quickly.

Ay! that was the pity of it! The pity of blood to be spilt needlessly. The thought made him slacken speed, as if he were on the threshold of a graveyard, though he could not foresee the blood to be spilt so wantonly in that very garden-set angle of the city, so full now of the scent of flowers, the sounds of security. From far came the subdued hum which rises from a city in which there is no wheeled traffic, no roar of machinery, only the feet of men, their tears, their laughter, to assail the irresponsive air. Nearer, among the scattered houses hidden by trees, rose children's voices playing about the servants' quarters.

Across the now empty playground of the college, the outlines of the church showed faintly among the fret of branches upon the dull red sky which a cloudless sunset leaves behind it; and through the open arch of the Kashmir gate, the great globe of the full moon grew slowly from the ruddy earth-haze. Then loud and clear came the chime of seven from the mainguard gong, and the rattle of arms dying into silence again. The peace of it all seemed unassailable, the security unending.

'*Delhi dur ust!*'

The words were called across the road in a woman's voice, making him turn to see a shadowy white figure outlined against the dark arches of a verandah close upon the road. He reined up his horse almost involuntarily, remembering as he did so that this was Mrs Gissing's house.

'I beg your pardon—' he began.

'I beg yours,' came the instant reply. 'I mistook you for a friend. Good night!'

'Good night!'

As he paced his horse on, choosing the longer way to Duryagung, by the narrow lanes clinging to the city wall, the remembrance of that frank good night lingered with him. *For a friend!* What a name to call Herbert Erlton! Poor little soul! The thought, by its very intolerableness, drove him back to the other roused by her first words—

'*Delhi dur ust.*'

True! Even this Delhi lying before his very eyes was far from him. How would it take the news which by now, as he had said, must have filtered through the bazaar? He could imagine that. He knew also, that the Palace folk must all be discussing the Resident's garden party, with a view to their own special aims and objects. But what did they think of the outlook on the future? Did they also say '*Delhi dur ust*'?

One of them was saying it on a roof close by. It was Abool-Bukr, who on his way home had given himself the promised pleasure of retailing his virtuous afternoon's experiences to Newâsi; for his two-months-wed bride had not broken *him* of his habit of coming to his kind one, though it had made *her* graver, more dignified. Still she broke in on his thick assertion—for he had drunk brandy in his efforts to be friendly with the *sahibs*—that he had seen an Englishwoman of her sort, with the quick query:

'Like me! How so?'

He laughed mischievously. 'And thou art not jealous of my wife!— or sayest thou art not! She was but like thee in this, aunt, that she is of the sort who would have men better than God made them—'

'No worse, thou meanest,' she replied.

He shook his head. 'Women, Newâsi, are as the ague. A man is ever being made better or worse till he knows not if he be well or ill. And both ways God's work is marred, a man driven from his right fate—'

'But if a man mistakes his fate as thou dost. Abool,' she persisted. 'Sure, if Jewun Bukht with the evil woman, Zeenut—'

He started to his feet, thrusting out lissome hands wildly as if to set aside some thought. 'Have a care, Newâsi, have a care!' he cried. 'Talk not of that arch plotter, arch dreamer. Nay! not arch dreamer! 'tis thou that dreamest most. Dreamest of war without blood, men without passion, me without myself! Was there not blood on my hands ere ever I was born—I Abool-Bukr of the race of Timoor—kings, tyrants, by birth and trade?—The blood of those who stood in my father's way and my father's fathers. I tell thee there is too much tinder yonder—' he pointed to where, across the flat chequers of moonlit roofs, inlaid by the shadows of the intersecting alleys, the cupolas of the Palace gates rose upon the sky. 'There is too much tinder here'—he struck his own breast fiercely, 'for such fiery thoughts. Why canst not leave me alone, woman?'

She drew back coldly. 'Do I ask thee to come hither—Thy wife—'

He gave a half-maudlin laugh. 'Nay, I mean not that! Sure thou art very woman, Newâsi! That is why I love mine aunt! That is why I come to see her—that—'

She interrupted him hastily, but her eyes grew soft, her voice trembled.

'And I do but goad thee for thine own good, Abool. These are strange times. Even the Mufti *sahib*—'

'Ah! defend me from his wise saws. I know the ring of them too well as 'tis. Even that I endure—for mine aunt's sake. Though, by the faith, if he and others of his kidney waylay me as they do much longer, I will have a rope-ladder to thy roof and scandalize them all. I can stomach thy wisdom, dear; none else. So tell them that Abool-Bukr can quote saws as well as they. Tell them he lives for Pleasure and Pleasure lives in the present. For the rest, "*Delhi dur ust! Delhi dur ust*".

His reckless unrestrained voice rang out over the roofs, and into the alley below where Jim Douglas was telling himself, that with his finger on the very pulse of the city he had failed to count its heart-beats.

He looked up quickly. '*Delhi dur ust.*' All the world seemed to be saying it that night; though the first blood had been shed in the quarrel.

# 6

# The Yellow Fakeer

The days passed to weeks, the weeks to a month, after that shedding of first blood, and no more was spilt, save that of the shedders. Two of them were duly hanged, the regiment ordered to be disbanded. For the rest, though causeless fires broke out in every cantonment, though a Sikh orderly divulged to his master some tale of a concerted rising, though the dread of the greased cartridge grew to a perfect panic, even Jim Douglas, with his eyes wide open, was forced to admit that, so far as any chance of action went, the reply might still be 'Delhi dur ust'. The sky was dark indeed, there were mutterings on the horizon; but he and others remembered how often in India, even when rain is due, the clouds creep up and up day by day, darker and more lowering, until the yellowing crops seem to grow greener in sheer hope of the purple pall above them. And then some unseen Hand juggles those portentous rain-clouds into the daily darkness of night, and some dawn rises clear and dry to show, in its fierce blaze of sunlight, how the yellow has gained on the green.

So, day by day, the impression grew amongst the elect, that the storm signals would pass; that the best policy was to tide over the next few months somehow. In pursuance of which a sepoy who ventured to draw attention to the state of feeling in one regiment was publicly told he need expect no promotion.

But there were dissentients to this policy, apparently. Anyhow, in the end of April Colonel Carmichael Smyth, commanding the 3rd Bengal Cavalry at Meerut, returned from leave one evening, and ordered fifteen men from each troop to be picked out to learn the use of the new cartridge next morning, and then went to bed comfortably. The men, through their native officers, appealed to their captain for delay, saying they were neither prepared to take nor to refuse the cartridges, old or new. No answer was given them. They marched to the parade obediently at sunrise, and eighty-five of the ninety men picked from a picked regiment for smartness and intelligence refused to take the cartridges, even from their Colonel's or the Adjutant's hand. Their own troop officers were not present. They were at once tried by a court-martial of native officers, some of whom came from the regiments at Delhi—but thirty odd miles off along a broad, level, driving road. They were sentenced to ten years penal servitude, and a parade of all troops was ordered for sunrise on the 9th of May, to put the sentence into force.

So the night of the 8th found Jim Douglas riding over from Delhi in the cool to see something which, if anything could, ought to turn mere talk into action. It had brought a new sound into the air already; the clang of cold iron upon hot, rising from the regimental smithy where the fetters for the eighty-five were being forged. A cruel sound at best, proclaiming the indubitable advantage of coolness and hardness over glow and plasticity. Cruel indeed when the hardness and insistency go to the forging of fetters for emotion and ignorance.

Clang! Clang! Clang!

The sound rang out into the hot airless night, rang out into the gusty dawn; for it takes time to forge eight-five pairs of shackles. Rang out to where a mixed guard of the 11th and 20th Regiments of Native Infantry were waiting round the tumbrils for the last fetter. The grey of dawn showed the rest piled on the tumbrils, showed two English officers on horseback talking to each other a little way off, showed the faces of the guard dark and lowering like the dawn itself.

'*Loh*! sergeant-*jee*! there is the last,' said the master-armourer cheerfully. His task was done, at any rate.

Soma took it from him silently, and flung it on the others almost fiercely; it settled among them with a clank. His regiment, the 11th, had but newly come to Meerut, and therefore had as yet no ties of personal comradeship with the eighty-five; but fetters for any sepoys were enough to make the pulse beat full and heavy.

'The last! thank Heaven,' said the captain, giving his bridle rein a jag. 'All right forward, Jones! Then fall in, men. Quick march! We are late enough as it is.'

The disciplined feet fell in without a waver, the tumbrils moved on with a clank and a creak.

Quick march! Soma's mind, fair reflection of the minds of all about him, was full of doubt. Was that indeed the last fetter, or did Rumour say sooth when it told of others being secretly forged? Who could say in these days, when the *Huzoors* themselves had taken to telling lies. Not his *Huzoors* as yet; his Colonels and Captains and Majors, even the little *sahib*, who laughed over his own mistakes on parade, told the truth still. But the others lied. Lied about enlistment, about prize-money and leave, about those cartridges. At least, so the men in the 20th said; the sergeant marching next to him behind the tumbril most of all.

"Tis but three weeks longer, comrade,' said this man suddenly in a low whisper. They were treading the dim deserted outskirts of the cantonment bazaar, and Soma looked round nervously at the officers behind. Had they heard? He frowned at the speaker and made no reply. He gave a deaf ear, when he could, to the talk in the 20th; but that was not always, for its sepoys were part of the Bengal army. That army, which was not—as a European army is—a mere chance collection of men divided from each other in the beginning and end of life, associated loosely with each other in its middle, and using military service as a make shift; but, to a great extent, a guild, following the profession of arms by hereditary custom from the cradle to the grave.

Quick march! A woman, early astir, peered at the little procession through the chink of a door, and whispered to an unseen companion behind. What was she saying? What, by implication, would other women, who peeped virtuously—women he knew—say of his present occupation? That he was a coward to be guarding his comrades' fetters? No doubt; since others with less right would say it too; all the miserable disreputable riff-raff, for instance, which had drifted in from the neighbourhood to see the show. The bazaar had been full of it these three days past. Even the sweepers, pariahs, out castes, would snigger over the misfortunes of their betters—as those two ahead were doubtless sniggering already as they drew aside from their slave's work of sweeping the roadway, to let the tumbrils pass; drew aside with mock deference, leaving scantiest room for the twice-born following them. So scant, indeed, that the outermost tip of a reed broom, flourished in insolent salaam, touched the Rajpoot's sleeve. It was the veriest brush, no more than a fly's wing could have given; but the half-stifled cry from Soma's lips meant murder—nothing less. His disciplined feet wavered, he gave a furtive glance at his companions. Had they seen the insult? Could they use it against him?

'Eyes front there; forward!' came the order from behind, and he pulled himself together by instinct and went on.

'Only three weeks longer, brother!' said that voice beside him meaningly; and a dull rage rose in Soma's heart. So it had been seen. It might be said of him, Soma, that he had tamely submitted to a defiling touch. He did not look round at his officers this time. They might hear if they chose, the future might hold what it chose. Mayhap they had seen the insult and were laughing at it. They were not his *Huzoors*; they belonged to the man at his side who had the right to taunt him. As a matter of fact, they were discussing the chances of their ponies in next week's races; but Soma, lost in a great wrath, a great fear, made it, inevitably, the topic of the whole world.

Hark! The bugle for the Rifles to form; they were to come to the parade loaded with ball cartridge. And that rumble was the Artillery, loaded also, going to take up their position. By-and-bye, the Carabineers would sweep with a clatter and a dash to form the third side of the hollow square, whereof the fourth was to be a mass of helpless dark faces, with the eighty-five martyrs and the tumbrils in the middle. Soma had seen it all in general orders, talked it over with his dearest friend, and called it tyranny. And now the tumbrils clanked past a little heap of smouldering ashes, that but the day before had been a guard-house. The lingering smoke from this last work of the incendiary drifted northward, after the fetters, making one of the officers cough. But he went on talking of his ponies, true type of the race which lives to make mistakes, and dies to retrieve them.

'Quick march!' he called, as the feet before him lingered.

Streams of spectators bound for the show began to overtake them, ready with comments on what Soma guarded. And on the broad white Mall, dividing the native half of cantonments and the town of Meerut from the European portion, more than one carriage with a listless white-faced woman in it dashed by, on its way to see the show.

Quick march! Whatever else might be possible in the future, that was all now, midway between the barracks of the Rifles and the Carabineers, with the Church—mute symbol of the horror which day by day, month by month, had been closing in round the people—blocking the way in front. So they passed on to the wide northern parade ground, with that hollow square ready; three sides of it threatening weapons, the fourth of unarmed men, and in the centre the eighty-five picked men of a picked regiment.

The knot of European spectators round the flag listened with yawns to the stout General's exordium. The eighty-five being hopelessly, helplessly in the wrong by military law, there seemed no need to insist on the fact. And the mass of dark faces standing within range of loaded guns and rifles, within reach of glistening sabres, did not listen at all. Not that it mattered, since the units in that crowd had lost the power of accepting facts. Even Soma, standing to attention beside the tumbrils, only felt a great sense of outrage, of wrong, of injustice somewhere. And there was one Englishman, at least, rigid to attention also before his disarmed, dismounted, yet loyal troop, who must have felt it also, unless he was more than human. And this was Captain Craigie who, when his men appealed to him to save them—to delay this unnecessary musketry parade—had written in his haste to the Adjutant, 'Go to Smyth at once!'

'Go to Smyth!' and Smyth was his colonel! Incredible lack of official etiquette; repeated hardily, moreover.

'Pray don't lose a moment, but go to Smyth and tell him.'

What? Only 'that this is a most serious matter, and we may have the whole regiment in open mutiny in half-an-hour if it is not attended to.' Only that! So it is to be hoped that Captain Craigie had the official wigging for his unconventional appeal in his pocket as he shared his regiment's disgrace, to serve him as a warning—or a consolation!

And now, the pompous monotone being ended, the silence—coming after the clankings and buglings and trampings which had been going on since dawn—was almost oppressive. The three sides of steel, even the fourth of faces, however, showed no sign; they stood as stone while the eighty-five were stripped of their uniforms. But there was more to come. By the General's orders the leg-irons were to be riveted on one by one; and so, once more, the sound of iron upon iron recurred monotonously, making the silence of the intervals still more oppressive, for the prisoners at first seemed stunned by the isolation from even their as yet unfettered comrades. But suddenly from a single throat came that cry for justice, which has a claim to a hearing; at least, in the estimation of the people of India.

'*Dohai! Dohai! Dohai!*'

Soma gave a sort of sigh, and a faint quiver of expectation passed over the sea of dark faces.

Clang! Clang! The hammers, going on unchecked, were the only answer. Those three sides of stone had come to see a thing done, and it must be done—the sooner the better. But the riveting of eighty-five pairs of leg-irons is not to be done in a moment, and so the cry grew clamorous.

'*Dohai! Dohai!*' Had they not fought faithfully in the past? Had they not been deceived? Had they had a fair chance?

But the hammers went on as the sun climbed out of the dust-haze to gleam on the sloped sabres, glint on the loaded guns, and send glittering streaks of light along the rifles.

So the cry changed. Were their comrades cowards to stand by and see this tyranny and raise no finger of help? Oh! curses on them! 'Tis they were degraded, dishonoured. Curses on the Colonel who had forced them to this. Curses on every white face!—Curses on every face which stood by—

One, close to the General's flag, broke suddenly into passionate resentment. Jim Douglas drew out his watch, looked at it, and gathered his reins together. 'An hour and forty-five minutes already. I'm off, Ridgeway. I can't stand this d—d folly any more.'

'My dear fellow, speak lower! If the General—'

'I don't care who hears me,' retorted Jim Douglas recklessly as he steered through the crowd, followed by his friend. 'I say it is d—d inconceivable folly and tyranny. Come on, and let's have a gallop, for God's sake, and get rid of that devilish sound.'

The echo of their horses' resounding hoofs covered, obliterated it; the wind of their own swiftness seemed to blow the tension away. So, after a spin due north for a mile or two, they paused at the edge of a field where the oxen were circling placidly round on the threshing-floors, and a group of women were taking advantage of the gustiness to winnow. Their bare brown arms glistened above the falling showers of golden grain, their unabashed smiling faces showed against the clouds of golden chaff drifting behind them.

Jim Douglas looked at them for a moment, returned the salaam of the men driving the oxen and forking the straw, then turned his horse towards the cantonment again.

'It is nothing to them; that's one comfort,' he said. 'But they will have to suffer for it in the end I expect. Who will believe when the time comes that this'—he gave a backward wave of his hand—'went on unwitting of that?'—he gave a forward one.

His companion following his look to where, in the far distance, a faint cloud of dust telling of many feet hung on the horizon, said suddenly, as if the sight brought remembrance: 'By George! Douglas, how steady the sepoys stood, I half expected a row.'

'Steadier than I should,' remarked the other grimly. 'Well! I hope Smyth is satisfied. To return from leave and drive your regiment into mutiny in twelve hours is a record performance.'

His hearer who was a civilian gave a deprecating cough. 'That's a bit hard, surely. I happen to know that he heard while on leave some story about a concerted rising later on. He may have done it purposely, to force their hands.'

Jim Douglas shrugged his shoulders. 'Did he warn you what he was about to do? Did he allow time to prepare others for his private mutiny? My dear Ridgeway, it was put on official record two months ago that an organized scheme for resistance existed in every regiment between Calcutta and Peshawur; so Smyth might at least have consulted the colonels of the other two regiments at Meerut. As it is, the business has strained the loyalty of the most loyal to the uttermost; and we deserve to suffer, we do indeed.'

'You don't mince matters, certainly,' said the civilian drily.

'Why should anybody mince them? Why can't we admit boldly— the C.-in-C. did it on the sly the other day—that the cartridges are suspicious? that they leave the muzzle covered with a fat, like tallow? Why don't we admit it *was* tallow at first. Why not, at any rate, admit we are in a hole, instead of refusing to take the common precaution of having an ammunition waggon loaded up for fear it should be misconstrued into alarm? Is there no medium between bribing children with lollipops and torturing them—keeping them on the strain, under fire as it were, for hours watching their best friends punished unjustly?'

'Unjustly?'

'Yes. To their minds unjustly. And you know what forcible injustice means to children—and these are really children—simple, ignorant, obstinate'—

They had come back to cantonments again and were rapidly overtaking the now empty tumbrils going home, for the parade was over. Further down the road, raising a cloud of dust from their shackled feet, the eighty-five were being marched jail-wards under native escort.

'Well!' said the civilian drily, 'I would give a great deal to know what those simple babes really thought of us.'

'Hate us stock and block for the time. I should,' replied Jim Douglas. They were passing the tumbrils at the moment, and one of the guard, in sergeant's uniform, looked up in joyful recognition.

'*Huzoor*! It is I, Soma.'

The civilian looked at his companion oddly when, after a minute or two spent in answering Soma's inquiries as to where and how the master was to be found, Jim Douglas rode alongside once more.

'Out a bit; eh?' he said drily.

'Very much out; but they are a queer lot. Do you remember the story of the self-made American who was told his boast relieved the Almighty of a very great responsibility. Well, He is only responsible for one half of the twice-born. The other is due to humanity, to heredity, what you will! That is what makes these high caste men so difficult to deal with. They are twice-born—Yes! they are a queer lot.'

He repeated the remark with even greater fervour twelve hours later when, about midnight, he started on his return ride to Delhi; for though he had spent the whole day in listening, he had scarcely heard a word of blame for the scene which had roused him to wrath that morning. The sepoys had gone about their duties as if nothing had happened, and despite the undoubted presence of a lot of loose characters in the bazaar, there had been no disturbance. He laughed cynically to himself at the waste of a day which would have been better spent in horse-dealing. This, however, settled it. If this intolerable tyranny failed to rouse action there could be no immediate danger ahead. To a big cantonment like Meerut, the biggest in northern India, with two thousand British troops in it, even the prospect of a rising was not serious; at Delhi, however, where there were only native troops, it might have been different. But now he felt that a handful of resolute men ought to be able to hold their own anywhere against such aimless, invertebrate discontent. He felt a vague disappointment that it should be so, that the pleasant cool of night should be so quiet, so peaceful. They were a poor lot who could do nothing but talk!

As he rode through the station, the mess-houses were still alight, and the gay voices of the guests who had been dining at a large bungalow, bowered in gardens, reached his ears distinctly.

'It's the Sabbath already,' said one. 'Ought to be in our beds!'

'Hooray! for a Europe morning,' came a more boyish one breaking into a carol, '*Of all the days within the week, I dearly love—*'

'Shut up, Fitz!' put in a third, 'you'll wake the General!'

'What's the odds. He can sleep all day. I'm sure his buggy-charger needs a rest.'

'Do shut up, Fitz! The Colonel will hear you.'

'I don't care. It's Scriptural. *Thou and thy ox and thy ass—*'

'You promised to come to evening church, Mr Fitzgerald,' interrupted a reproachful feminine voice; 'you said you would sing in the choir.'

'Did I? Then I'll come. It will wake me up for dinner; besides, I shall sit next you.'

The last words came nearer, softer; Mr Fitzgerald was evidently riding home beside some one's carriage.

Pleasant and peaceful indeed! that clank of a sentry, here and there, only giving a greater sense of security. Not that it was needed, for here beyond cantonments, the houses of the clerks and civilians lay as peaceful, as secure. In the verandah of one of them, close to the road, a bearer was walking up and down crooning a patient lullaby to the restless fair-haired child in his arms.

No! truly there could be no fear. It was all talk! He set spurs to his horse and went on through the silent night at a hand-gallop, for he had another beast awaiting him half-way and he wished to be in Delhi by dawn. There was a row of tall trees bordering the road on either side, making it dark, and through their swiftly passing holes the level country stretched to the paler horizon like a sea. And as he rode, he sat in judgment in his thoughts on those dead levels and the people who lived in them.

Stagnant!—Featureless!—A dead sea!—A mere waste of waters without form or void! Not even ready for a spirit to move over them; for if that morning's work left them apathetic, the Moulvie of Fyzabad himself need preach no Voice of God. For *this,* surely—this sense of injustice to others, must be the strongest motive, the surest word to conjure with?—that dull dead beat of iron upon the fetters of others,—which he still seemed to hear,—the surest call to battle?

He paused in his thought, wondering if what he fancied he heard was but an echo from memory, or a real sound! Real; undoubtedly. It was the distant clang of the iron bells upon oxen. That meant that he must be seven or eight miles out, half-way to the next stage, so meeting the usual stream of night traffic towards Meerut. He passed two or three strings of large, looming, half-seen wains without drawing bridle, then pulled up almost involuntarily to a trot at the curiously even tread of a drove of iron-shod oxen, and a low chanted song from behind it. Bunjâra folk! The rough voice, the familiar rhythm of the hoofs, reminded him of many a pleasant night-march in their company.

'A good journey, brothers!' he called in the dialect. The answer came unerringly, dark though it was.

'The Lord keep the *Huzoor* safe!'

It made him smile as he remembered that, of course, a lone man trotting a horse along a high road at night was bound to be alien, in a country where horses are ambled and travellers go in twos and threes. So the rough, broad faces would be smiling over the surprise of a *sahib* knowing the Bunjâra talk; unless, indeed, it happened to be—The possibility of its being the *tanda* he knew had not occurred to him before. He pulled up and looked round. A breathless shadow was at his stirrup, and he fancied he saw a shadow or two further behind.

'The *Huzoor* has mistaken the road,' came Tiddu's familiar creak. 'Meerut lies to the north.'

Breathless as he was, there was the pompous mystery in his voice which always prefaced an attempt to extort money; and Jim Douglas, having no further use for the old scoundrel, did not intend to give him any, so he simulated an utter lack of surprise.

'Hullo, Tiddu!' he said. 'I had an idea it might be you. So you recognized my voice?'

The old man laughed. 'The *Huzoor* is mighty clever. He knows old Tiddu has eyes. They saw the *Huzoor*'s horse—a bay Wazeeri with a white star none too small, and all the luck-marks—waiting at the fifteenth milestone, by Begum-a-bad. But the *Huzoor*, being so clever, is not going to ride the Wazeeri to night. He is going to ride the Belooch he is on, back to Meerut, though the star on her forehead is too small for safety; my thumb could cover it.'

'It's a bit too late to teach me the luck-marks, Tiddu,' said Jim Douglas coolly. 'You want money, you ruffian; so I suppose you have something to sell. What is it? If it is worth anything, you can trust me to pay, surely.'

Tiddu looked round furtively. The other shadow, Jhungi or Bhungi, or both, perhaps—the memory made Jim Douglas smile—had melted away into the darkness. He and Tiddu were alone. The old man, even so, reached up to whisper.

''Tis the yellow fakeer, *Huzoor*! He has come.'

'The yellow fakeer!' echoed his hearer; 'who the devil is he? And why shouldn't he come, if he likes?'

Tiddu paused, as if in sheer amaze, for a second. 'The *Huzoor* has not heard of the yellow fakeer? The dumb fakeer who brings the speech that brings more than speech? *Wâh!*'

'Speech that is more than speech,' echoed Jim Douglas angrily, then paused in his turn; the phrase reminded him, vaguely, of his past thoughts.

Tiddu's hand went out to the Belooch's rein; his voice lost its creak and took a soft sing-song to which the mare seemed to come round of her own accord.

'Yea! Speech that is more than speech, though he is dumb. Whence he comes none know, not even I, the Many-faced. But I can see him when he comes, *Huzoor!* the others, not unless he wills to be seen. I saw him to night. He passed me on a white horse not half-an-hour agone, going Meerutwards. Did not the *Huzoor* see him? That is because he has learnt from old Tiddu to make others see, but not to see himself. But the old man will teach him this also if he is in Meerut by dawn. If he is there by dawn he will see the yellow fakeer who brings the speech that brings more than speech.'

The sing-song ceased; the Beloochi was stepping briskly back towards Meerut.

'You infernal old humbug!' began Jim Douglas.

'The *Huzoor* does not believe, of course,' remarked Tiddu, in the most matter-of-fact creak. 'But Meerut is only eight miles off. His other horse can wait; and if he does not see the yellow fakeer there is no need to open the purse-strings.'

The Englishman looked at his half-seen companion admiringly. He was the most consummate scoundrel! His blending of mystery and purely commercial commonplace was perfect—almost irresistible. There was no reason why he should go on; the groom, half-way, had his usual orders to stay till his master came. For the rest, it would be pleasant to renew the old pleasant memory—pleasant even to renew his acquaintance with Tiddu's guile, which struck him afresh each time he came across it.

He slipped from his horse without a word, and was about to pull the reins over her head so as to lead her, when Tiddu stopped short.

'Jhungi will take her to the rest-house, *Huzoor,* or Bhungi. It will be safer so. I have a clean cotton quilt in the bundle, and the Huzoor can have my shoes and rub his legs in the dust. That will do till dawn.'

He gave a jackal's cry, which was echoed from the darkness.

'Leave her so, *Huzoor!* She is safe,' said Tiddu; and Jim Douglas, as he obeyed, heard the mare whinny softly, as if to a foal, as a shadow came out of the bushes. Jhungi or Bhungi, no doubt.

Five minutes after, with a certain unaccountable pleasure, he found himself walking beside a laden bullock, one arm resting on its broad pack, his feet keeping step with the remittent clang of its bell. It was a strange dreamy companionship, as he knew of old; and once more the stars seemed, after a time, to twinkle in unison with the bell, he seemed to forget thought, to forget everything save the peaceful stillness around, and his own unresting peace.

So he and the laden beast went on as one living, breathing mortal, till the little shiver of wind came, which comes with the first paling of the sky. It was one of those yellow dawns, serene, cloudless, save for a puff or two of thin grey vapour low down on the horizon, looking as if it were smoke from an unseen censer swinging before the chariot of the Sun which heads the procession of the hours. He was so absorbed in watching the yellow light grow to those clouds no bigger than a man's hand, so lost in the strange companionship with the laden beast bound to the wheel of Life and Death as he was yet asking no question of the future, that Tiddu's hand and voice startled him.

'*Huzoor!*' he said.—'The yellow fakeer!'

They were close on the city of Meerut. The road, dipping down to cross a depression, left a bank of yellow dust on either side. And on the eastern one, outlined against the yellow sunrise, sat a motionless figure. It was naked, and painted from head to foot a bright yellow colour. The closed eyes were daubed over so as to hide them utterly, and on the forehead, as it is in the image of Shiva, was painted perpendicularly a gigantic eye, wide set, stony. Before it in the dust lay the beggar's bowl for alms.

'The roads part here, *Huzoor*,' said Tiddu. 'This to the city; that to the cantonments.'

As he spoke, a handsome young fellow came swaggering down the latter, on his way evidently to riotous living in the bazaar. Suddenly he paused, his hand went up to his eyes as if the rising sun were in them. Then he stepped across the road and dropped a coin into the beggar's bowl. Tiddu nodded his head gravely.

'That man is wanted, *Huzoor*. That is why he saw. Mayhap he is to give the word.'

'The word?' echoed Jim Douglas. 'You said he was dumb?'

'I meant the trooper, *Huzoor*. The fakeer wanted him. To give the word, mayhap. Some one must always give it.'

Jim Douglas felt an odd thrill. He had never thought of that before. Some one, of course, must always give the word, the speech which brought more than speech. What would it be? Something soul-stirring, no doubt; for Humanity had a theory that an angel must trouble the waters and so give it a righteous cause for stepping in to heal the evil.

But what a strange knack the old man had of stirring the imagination with ridiculous mystery! He felt vexed with himself for his own thrill, his own thoughts. 'He is a very ordinary *yogi, I* should say,'

he remarked, looking towards the yellow sunrise; but the figure was
gone. He turned to Tiddu again, with real annoyance. 'Well! Whoever
he is, he cannot want me. And I certainly saw him.'

'I willed the *Huzoor* to see!' replied Tiddu with calm effrontery.

Jim Douglas laughed. The man was certainly a consummate liar;
there was never any possibility of catching him out.

# 7

# The Word Went Forth

The Procession of the Hours had a weary march of it between the
yellow sunrise and the yellow sunset of the 10th of May 1857;
for the heavens were as brass, the air one flame of white heat.
The mud huts of the sepoy lines at Meerut looked and felt like bricks
baking in a kiln; yet the torpor which the remorseless glare of noon
brings even to native humanity was exchanged for a strange
restlessness. The doors stood open for the most part, and men
wandered in and out aimlessly, like swarming bees before the queen
appears. In the bazaar, in the city too, crowds drifted hither and thither,
thirstily, as if it were not the fast month of Rumzân when the
Mohammedans are denied the solace of even a drop of water till
sundown. Drifted hither and thither, pausing to gather closer at a hint
of novelty, melting away again, restless as ever.

Mayhap it was but the inevitable reaction after the stun and
stupefaction of Saturday, the sudden awakening to the result—namely,
that eighty-five of the best, smartest soldiers in Meerut had been set to
toil for ten years in shackles because they refused to be defiled—to
become apostate. On the other hand, the old Baharupa may have been
right about the yellow fakeer; the silent, motionless figure might have
set folk listening and waiting for the word. It was to be seen by all now
sitting outside the city; at least Jim Douglas saw it several times. Saw,
also, that the beggar's bowl was fuller and fuller; but the impossibility
of asserting that all the passers-by saw it, as he did, haunted him, once
the idea presented itself to his mind. It was always so with Tiddu's
mysteries; they were no more susceptible to disproof than they were to
proof. You could waste time, of course, in this case by waiting and
watching, but in the natural course of events half the passers-by would
go on as if they saw nothing, and only one in a hundred or so would
give alms. So what would be the good?

No one else, however, among the masters troubled themselves to find a cause for the restlessness; no one even knew of it. To begin with, it was a Sunday, so that even the bond of a common labour was slackened between the dark faces and the light. Then a mile or more of waste deserted land and dry watercourse lay on either side of the broad white road which split the cantonment into halves. So that the North knew nothing of what was going on in the South, and while men were swarming like bees in the sun on one side, on the other they were shut up in barracks and bungalows gasping with the heat, longing for the sun to set, and thanking their stars when the chaplain's *memo* came round to say that the evening service had been postponed for half-an-hour to allow the seething, glowing air to cool a little.

It was not the heat, however, which prevented Major Erlton from taking his usual *siesta*. It was thought. He had come over from Delhi on inspection duty a few days before and had intended returning that evening; but the morning's post had brought him a letter which upset all his plans. Alice Gissing's husband had come out a fortnight earlier than they had expected, and was already on his way up-country. The crisis had come, the decision must be made. It was not any hesitation, however, which sent the heavy handsome face to the big strong hands as he rested his elbows on a sheet of blank paper. He had made up his mind on the very day when Alice Gissing had first told him why she could not go back to her husband. The letter forwarding his papers for resignation was already sealed on the table beside him; and the surprise was rather a gain than otherwise. Alice could join him at Meerut now, and they could slip away together to Kashmir or any out of the way place where there was shooting. That would save a lot of fuss; and the fear of fuss was the only one which troubled the Major, personally. He hated to know that even his friends would wonder—for the matter of that those who knew him best would wonder most—why he was chucking everything for a woman he had been mixed up with for years? Yet he had found no difficulty in writing that official request; none in telling little Allie to join him as soon as she could. It was this third letter which could not be written. He took up the pen more than once, only to lay it down again. He began, 'My dear Kate,' once, only to tear the sheet to pieces. How could he call her his when he was going to tell her that she was his no longer—that the best thing she could do was to divorce him and marry some other chap to be a father to the boy?

The thought sent the head into the hands again; for Herbert Erlton was a healthy animal and loved his offspring by instinct. He had in truth, a queer upside-down notion of his responsibilities towards them. If the fates had permitted it he would have done his best by Freddy;

shown him the ropes, given him useful tips, stood by his inexperience, paid his reasonable debts—always supposing he had the wherewithal.

Then how was he to tell Kate all the ugly story. He had left her in his thoughts so completely, she had been so far apart from him for so many years now, that he hesitated over telling her the bare facts, just as—being conventionally a perfectly well-bred man—he would have hesitated how to tell them to any innocent woman of his acquaintance. Rather more so: for Kate—though she was sentimental enough, he told himself, for two—had never been sensible and looked things in the face. If she had, it might all have been different. Then with a rush came the remembrance that Allie did—that she knew him every inch and was yet willing to come with him. While he? He would stick through thick and thin to little Allie who never made a man feel a fool or a beast. Something in the last assertion seemed to harden his heart; he took up his pen and began to write:—

'My dear Kate,—I call you that because I can't think of any other beginning that doesn't seem foolish; but it means nothing, and I only want to tell you that circumstances over which we had no control' (he felt rather proud of this circumlocution for a circumstance due entirely to his volition) 'make it necessary for me to leave you. It is the only course open to me as a gentleman. Besides I want to, for I love Alice Gissing dearly. I am going to marry her, D.V., as soon as I can. Mr Gissing may make a fuss—it is a criminal offence, you see, in India— but we shall tide over that. Of course you could prevent me too, but you are not that sort. So I have sent in my papers. It is a pity, in a way, because I liked this work. But it is only a two-year appointment, and I should hate the regiment after it. For the rest, I am not such a fool as to think you will mind; except for the boy. It is a pity for him too, but it isn't as if he were a girl *and the other may be*. It will do no good to say I'm sorry. Besides I don't think it is all my fault, and I know you will be happier without me.—Yours sincerely,

Herbert Erlton.

'P.S.—It's no use crying over spilt milk. I believe you used to think I would get the regiment some day, but they would never have given it to me. I made a bit of a spurt lately but it couldn't have lasted to the finish, and after all, that is the win or the lose in a race.

H.E.'

The postscript was added after rereading the rest with an uncomfortable remembrance that it was the last letter he meant to write to her. Then he threw it ready for the post beside the others, and lay down feeling that he had done his duty. And as he dozed off his own simile haunted him. From start to finish! How few men rode straight all the way; and the poor beggars who came to grief over the last fence weren't so far behind those who came in for the clapping. It was the finish that did it; that was the win or the lose. But he would run straight with little Allie—straight as a die! So he lost consciousness in a glow of virtuous content with the future, and joined the whole of the northern half of Meerut in their noontide slumbers; for the future outlook, if not exactly satisfying, was not sufficiently dubious to keep it awake.

But in the southern half, humanity was still swarming in and out, waiting, listening. In one of the mud-huts, however, a company of men gathered within closed doors had been listening to some purpose; listening to an eloquent speaker, the accredited agent of a down-country organization. He had arrived in Meerut a day or two before, and had held one meeting after another in the lines, doing his utmost to prevent any premature action; for the fiat of the leaders was that there should be patience till the 31st of May. Then, not until then, a combined blow for India, for God, for themselves, might be struck with chance of success.

'Ameen!' assented one old man who had come with him—an old man in a huge faded green turban with dyed red hair and beard, and with a huge green waistband holding a curved scimitar—briefly, a *Ghazee* or Mohammedan fanatic, 'Patience all ye faithful till Sunday, the 31st of May. Then, while the hell-doomed infidels are at their evening prayer, defenceless, fall on them and slay. God will show the right! This is the Moulvie's word, sent by me his servant. Give the Great Cry, brothers, in the House of the Thief! Smite, ye of Meerut! and we of Lucknow will smite also!' His wild uncontrolled voice rolled on in broad Arabic vowels from one text to another.

'And we of Delhi will smite also,' interrupted the wearer of a rakish Moghul cap impatiently. 'We will smite for the Queen.'

'The Queen?' echoed an older man in the same dress. 'What hath the Sheeah woman to do with the race of Timoor?'

'Peace! peace! brothers,' put in the agent with authority. 'These times are not for petty squabbles. Let who be the heir, the King must reign.'

A murmur of assent rose; but it was broken in upon by a dissentient voice from a group of troopers at the door.

'Then our comrades are to rot in jail till the 31st? That suits not the men of the 3rd Cavalry.'

'Then let the 3rd Cavalry suit itself,' retorted the agent fearlessly. 'We can stand without them. Can they stand without us? Answer me, men of the 20th; men of the 11th.'

'There be not many of us here,' muttered a voice from a dark corner;

'and maybe we could hold our own against the lot of you.' It was Soma's, and the man beside him frowned. But the agent who knew every petty jealousy, every private quarrel of regiment with regiment, went on remorselessly. 'Let the 3rd swagger if it choose. The Rajpoots and Brahmins know how to obey the stars. The 31st is the auspicious day. That is the word. The word of the king, of the Brahmins, of India, of God!'

'The 31st! Then slay and spare not! It is *jehad! Deen! Deen! Futteh-Mahomed*,' said the *Ghazee*.

The cry, though a mere whisper, electrified the Mohammedans, and an older man in the group of dissentients at the door muttered that he could hold his troop, if others—who had risen to favour quicker than he—could hold theirs.

'I'll hold mine, Khân *sahib*, without thine aid,' retorted a very young smart-looking native officer angrily. 'That is if the women will hold their tongues. But, look you, my troop held the hardest hitters in the 3rd. And Nargeeza's fancy is of those in jail. Now Nargeeza leads all the other town-women by the nose; and that means much to men who be not all saints like *Ghazee-jee* yonder, who ties the two ends of life with a ragged green turban and a bloody banner!'

'And I see not why our comrades should stay yonder for three weeks, when there is but a native guard to hold them, and I and mine have made the *Sirkar* what it is,' put in a man with arrogance and insolence written on him from top to toe; a true type of the pampered Brahmin sepoy.

'Rescue them if thou wilt *Havildar-jee*,' sneered the agent. 'But the man who risks our plot will be held traitor by the Council. And the men of the 11th,' he added sharply, turning to the corner whence Soma's voice had come, 'may remember that also. They have had the audacity to stipulate for their Colonel's life.'

'For our officers' lives, *baboo-jee*,' came the voice again, bold as the agents. 'We of the 11th kill not men who have led us to victory. And if this be not understood I, Soma, Yadubansi, go straight to the Colonel and tell him. We are not butchers in the 11th, Oh! priest of Kâli!'

The agent turned a little pale. He did not care to have his calling known, and he saw at a glance that his challenger had the reckless fire of hemp in his eyes. He had indeed been drinking as a refuge from the memory of the sweeper's broom and from the taunts and threats which had been used to force him to join the malcontents. Such a man was not safe to quarrel with, nor was the audience fit for a discussion of that topic; there was already a stir in it, and mutterings that butchery was one thing, fighting another.

'Pay thy Colonel's journey home if thou likest, Rajpoot-*jee*,' he said with a sneer. 'Ay! and give him pension, too! All we want is to get rid of them. And there will be plenty of loot left when the pension is paid, for it is to be each man for himself when the time comes. Not share and share alike with every coward who will not risk his life in looting, as it is with the *Sirkar.*'

It was a deft red-herring to these born mercenaries and no more was said. But as the meeting dispersed by twos and threes to avoid notice, the agent stood at the door giving the word in a final whisper.

'Patience till the 31st.'

'Willst take a seat in our carriage, *Ghazee-jee,*' said a fat native officer as he passed out. ''Tis at thy service since thou goest to Delhi and we must return to night. God knows we have done enough to damn us at Meerut over this court-martial! But what would you? If we had not given the verdict for the *Huzoors* there would have been more of us in jail. So we bide our time like the rest. And tomorrow there is the parade to hear the sentence on the martyrs at Barrackpore. Do the *sahibs* think us cowards that they drive us so?—God smite their souls to hell!'

'He will, brother, He will. The cry shall yet be heard in the House of the Thief,' said the *Ghazee* fiercely, his eyes growing dreamy with hope. He was thinking of a sunset near the Goomtee more than a year ago, when he had bid every penny he possessed for his own, in vain.

'Well, come if thou likest,' continued the native officer. 'That camel of thine yonder is lame, and we have room. 'Twas Erlton *sahib*'s *dâk* by rights but he goes not; so we got it cheap instead of an *ekka.*'

'Erlton *sahib*'s!' echoed the fanatic, clutching at his sword. 'Ay! Ay!' he went on half to himself. 'I knew he was at Delhi, and the *mem* who laughed, and the other *mem* who would not listen. Nay! *Soubadar-jee*! I travel in no carriage of Erlton *sahib*'s. My camel will serve me.'

''Tis the vehicle of saints,' sneered the owner of the rakish Moghul cap. 'Verily when I saw thee mounted on it, *Ghazee-jee,* I deemed thee the Lord Ali.'

'Peace! scoffer,' interrupted the fanatic, 'lest I mistake thee for an infidel.'

The Moghul ducked hastily from a wild swing of the curved sword, and moved off swearing such firebrands should be locked up; they might set light to the train ere wise men had it ready.

'No fear!' said the smart young troop-sergeant of the 3rd. 'Who listens to such as he save those whose blood has cooled, and those whose blood was never hot? The fighters listen to women who can make theirs flame.'

Soma, who was drifting with them towards the drug-shops of the city, scowled fiercely. 'That may suit thee, Mussul man-*jee* who are

casteless, and can sup shares with sweeper women in the bazaar; but
the Rajpoot needs no harlot to teach him courage. The mothers of his
race have enough and to spare.'

'*Loh!* hark to him!' gibed the corporal of the 20th, who was sticking
to his prey like a leech. 'Ask him, *Havidar-jee*, if he prefers a sweeper's
broom to a sweeper's lips.'

There was a roar of laughter from the group.

Soma gave a beast-like cry, looked as though he were about to
spring, then—recognizing his own helplessness—flung himself away
from all companionship and walked home moodily. They had driven
him too far; he would not stand it. If that tale was spread abroad, he
would side with the *Huzoors* who did not believe such things—with
the Colonel who understood, like the Colonel before him who had
gone home on pension; for the 11th had a cult of their officers. And
these fools, his countrymen, thought to make him a butcher by threats;
sought to make him take revenge for what deserved revenge. For it
was the *Sirkar*'s fault—it was the *Sirkar*'s fault.

In truth a strange conflict was going on in this man's mind, as it
was in many another such as his, between inherited traditions, making
alike for loyalty and disloyalty. There was the knowledge of his
forbears' pride in their victories, in their *sahibs* who had led them to
victory, and the knowledge of their pride in the veriest jot or tittle of
ceremonial law. A dull painful amaze filled him that these two broad
facts should be in conflict; that those, whom in a way he felt to be part
of his life, should be in league against him. All the more reason, that,
for showing them who were the better men—for standing up fairly to
a fair fight. By all the delights of Swarga! he would like to stand up
fair, even to the master—the man who, in his presence, had shot three
tigers on foot in half-an-hour—the demi-god of his hunting yarns for
years—

And then, suddenly, he remembered that this hero of his might be
shot like a dog on the 31st at Delhi—would be shot, since he was
certain to be in the front of anything. Soma's heat-fevered, hemp-
drugged brain seized on the thought fiercely, confusedly. That must not
be! The master, at any rate, must be warned. He would go down when
the sun set, and see if he were still where he had been the day before;
and if not?—Why! then it must be two days leave to Delhi! He was not
going to butcher the master for all the sweeper's brooms in the world.
Fools! those others, to think to drive him, Soma, Chundrabansi! So he
flung himself on his string bed to sleep till the sunset came, and the
tyranny of heat be overpast.

But there was one, close by in the cantonment bazaar, who waited
for sunset with no desire for it to bring coolness. She meant it to bring

heat instead. And this was Nargeeza the courtesan. She was past the prime of everything save vice, a woman who, once all-powerful, could not hope for many more lovers; and hers, a man rich beyond most soldiers, lay in jail for ten years. No wonder, then, that as she lay half-torpid among a heap of tawdry finery in the biggest house of the lane set apart by regulation for such as she, there was all the venom of a snake in her drowsy brain. The air of the low room was deadly with a scent of musk and roses and orange-blossom-oil. The half-dozen girls and women who lounged in it, or in the balcony, were half undressed, their bare brown arms flung carelessly upon dirty mats and torn quilts. Their harvest time was not yet; that would come later when sun-setting brought the men from the lines. This then was the time for sleep. But Nargeeza, recognized head of the recognized regimental women, sat up suddenly and said sharply—

'Thou didst not tell me, Nasiban what Gulabi said. Is she of us?'

A drowsy lump of a girl stirred, yawned, and answered sullenly, 'Yea! Yea! she is of us. She claims our right to kiss no cowards—no cowards.'

The voice tailed off into sleep again, and Nargeeza lay back with a smile of content to wait also. So, after a time, folk began to stir in the bungalows. First in the rest-house, where, oddly enough, Jim Douglas occupied one end of the long low barrack of a place, and Herbert Erlton the other. The former having come back from the city in an evil temper to get something to eat before starting for Delhi, had found his horse, the Belooch, unaccountably indisposed; Jhungi, who had brought her there safely, professing entire ignorance of the cause, or, on pressure, suggesting the nefarious Bhungi. Tiddu asserting—with a calm assumption of superior knowledge, for which Jim Douglas could have kicked him—that the mare had been drugged. As if anybody could not tell that?—And that the drug had been opium. To which the old scoundrel had replied affably that in that case the effects would pass off during the night, and the mare be none the worse; no one be any the worse, since the Huzoor was quite comfortable in Meerut, and could *easily stay another day*. It was a nicer place than Delhi; there were more *sahibs* in it, and the presence of the *ghora logue* (*i.e.* English soldiers), kept every one virtuous.

His hearer looked at him sharply. Here was some other trick, no doubt, to cozen him out of another five rupees; for something, may be, as useless as the yellow fakeer. And there was really no reason for delay; it was only a case of walking the mare quietly. For the matter of that, the exercise would do her good, and help her to work off the effects of the drug. So he would start sooner, that was all. Nevertheless he gave an envious look at the Major's little Arab in the next stall. It would most likely be marching back to Delhi that night, and he would have given something to ride it again. But as he was returning from the stables, he learnt by chance that the Major's plans had been altered. An orderly was coming from his room with letters and a telegram, and knowing the man, Jim Douglas asked him to take one for him also, and so save trouble. It did not take long to write, for it only contained one word, 'No.' It was in reply to one he had received a few hours before from the military magnate, asking him to do some more work. And as the orderly stowed away the accompanying rupee carefully, Jim Douglas—waiting to make over the paper—saw quite involuntarily that the Major's telegram also consisted of the word, 'Come.' And he saw the name also; big, black, bold, in the Major's handwriting. 'Gissing, Delhi.'

He gave a shrug of his shoulders as he turned away to get ready for his start. So that was it; and even Kate Erlton had not benefited by his sacrifice. No one had benefited. There had been no chance for any of them.

'Come!' That ended Kate Erlton's hope of concealment, and the major's career. 'No!' That ended his own vague ambitions. Still, it was a strange chance in itself that those two laconic renunciations should go the same day by the same hand. No stranger telegrams, he thought, could have left Meerut, or were likely to leave it that night.

He was wrong, however. An hour or two later, the strangest telegram that ever came as sole warning to an Empire that its very foundation was attacked, left Meerut for Agra sent by the postmaster's niece.

'*The Cavalry*,' it ran, '*have risen, setting fire to their own houses besides having killed and wounded all European officers and soldiers they could find near the lines. If Aunt intends starting tomorrow, please detain her, as the van has been prevented from leaving the station.*'

For, as Jim Douglas paced slowly down the Mall towards Delhi, and Soma, his buckles gleaming, his belts pipe-clayed to dazzling whiteness, was swaggering through the bazaar on his way to the rest-house with his word of warning, another word—the word which would have given Jim Douglas the power for which he had longed—was being spoken in that lane of lust, where the time had come for which Nargeeza had waited all day. But *she* did not say it. It was only a big trollop of a girl hung with jasmine garlands, painted, giggling.

'We of the bazaar kiss no cowards,' she said derisively. 'Where are your comrades?'

The man to whom she said it, a young dissolute-faced trooper, dressed in the loose rakish muslins beloved of his class—the very man, perchance, who had gone citywards that morning, and drooped alms

into the yellow fakeer's bowl—stood for a second in the stifling
maddening atmosphere of musk and rose and orange-blossom; stood
before all those insolent allurements, baulked in his passion, checked in
his desires. Then, with an oath, he dashed from her insulting charms;
dashed into the street with a cry—

'To horse! To horse, brothers! To the jail! to our comrades!'

The word had been spoken. The speech which brings more than
speech, had come from the painted lips of a harlot.

The first clang of the church bell—which the chaplain had forgotten
to postpone—came faintly audible across the dusty plain, making other
men pause and look at each other. Why not? It was the hour of
prayer—the appointed time. Their comrades could be easily rescued—
there was but a native guard at the jail. And hark! from another pair of
painted derisive lips came the same retort, flung from a balcony.

'*Trra! We of the bazaar kiss no cowards!*'

'To horse! To horse! Let the comrades be rescued first; and then—'

The word had been spoken. Nothing so very soul-stirring after all.
No consideration of caste or religion, patriotism or ambition. Only a
taunt from a pair of painted lips.

# BOOK III

From Dusk to Dawn

# 1

# Night

'To the rescue! To the rescue!'

The cry was no more than that at first. To the rescue of the eighty-five martyrs, the blows upon whose shackles still seemed to echo in their comrades' ears. Even so, the cry heard by Soma as he passed through the bazaar meant insubordination—the greatest crime he knew—and sent him flying to his own lines to give the alarm. Sent him thence by instinct, oblivious of that promise for the 31st—or perhaps mindful of it and seeing in this outburst a mere riot—to his Colonel's house with twenty or thirty comrades clamouring for their arms, protesting that with them they would soon settle matters for the *Huzoor*s. But suspicion was in the air, and even the Colonel of the 11th could not trust all his regiment. Ready for church, he flung himself on his horse and raced back with the clamouring men to the lines.

And by this time there was another race going on. Captain Craigie's faithful troop of the 3rd Cavalry were racing after his shout of '*Dau-ro! bhai-yan Dau-ro!*' (Ride, brothers, ride!) towards the jail in the hopes of averting the rescue of their comrades. For, as the records are careful to say, he and his troop 'were dressed as for parade'—not a buckle or a belt awry—ready to combat the danger before others had grasped it, and swiftly without a thought, went for the first offenders. Too late! the doors were open, the birds flown.

What next was to be done? What but to bring the troop back without a defaulter—despite the taunts of escaping convicts, the temptations of comrades flushed by success—to the parade ground for orders. But there was no one to give them, for when the 3rd Cavalry led the van of mutiny at Meerut their Colonel was in the European cantonment as field officer of the week, and there he 'conceived it his duty to remain'. Perhaps rightly. And it is also conceivable that his absence made no difference since it is, palpably, an easier task to make a regiment mutiny than to bring it back to its allegiance.

Meanwhile the officers of the other regiments, the 11th and the 20th, were facing their men boldly; facing the problem how to keep them steady till that squadron of the Carabineers should sweep down followed by a company or two of the Rifles at the double, and turn the balance in favour of loyalty. It could not be long now. Nearly an hour had passed since the first wild stampede to the jail. The refuse and rabble of the town were by this time swarming out of it, armed with sticks and staves; the two thousand and odd felons released from the jails were swarming in, seeking weapons. The danger grew every second, and the officers of the 11th, though their men stood steady as rocks behind them counted the moments as they sped. For on the other side of the road, on the parade ground of the 20th regiment, the sepoys, ordered, as the 11th had been, to turn out unarmed, were barely restrained from rushing the bells by the entreaties of their native officers; the European ones being powerless.

'Keep the men steady for me,' said Colonel Finnis to his second in command; 'I'll go over and see what I can do.'

He thought the voice of a man loved and trusted by one regiment, a man who could speak to his sepoys without an interpreter, might have power to steady another.

'*Jai bahâduri!*' (Victory to courage!) muttered Soma under his breath as he watched his Colonel canter quietly into danger. And his finger hungered on that hot May evening for the cool of the trigger which was denied him.

'*Jai bahâduri!*' A murmur seemed to run through the ranks, they dressed themselves firmer, squarer. Colonel Finnis glancing back saw a sight to gladden any commandant's heart. A regiment steady as a rock, drawn up as for parade, absolutely in hand, despite that strange new sound in the air. The sound which above all others gets into men's brains like new wine. The sound of a file upon fetters—all sound of escape, of freedom, of licence! It had been rising unchecked for half-an-hour from the lines of the 3rd whither the martyrs had been brought in triumph. It was rising now from the bazaar, the city, from every quiet corner where a prisoner might pause to hack and hammer at his leg-irons with the first tool he could find.

What was one man's voice against this sound, strengthened as it was by the cry of a trooper galloping madly from the north shouting that the English were in sight? What more likely? Had not ample time passed for the whole British garrison to be coming with fixed bayonets and a whoop, to make short work of unarmed men who had not made up their minds?

That must be no longer!

'Quick! brothers. Quick! Kill! Kill! Down with the officers! Shoot ere the white faces come!'

It was a sudden wild yell of terror, of courage, of sheer cruelty. It drowned the scream of the Colonel's horse as it staggered under him. It drowned his steady appealing voice, his faint sob, as he threw up his hands at the next shot, and fell, the first victim to the Great Revolt.

It drowned something else also. It drowned Soma's groan of wild, half-stupefied, helpless rage as he saw his colonel fall,—the *sahib* who had led him to victory—the *sahib* whom he loved, whom he was pledged to save. And his groan was echoed by many another brave man in those ranks, thus brought face to face suddenly with the necessity for decision.

'Steady, men, steady!'

That call, in the alien voice, echoed above the whistling of the bullets as they found a billet here and there among the ranks; for the men of the 20th, maddened by that fresh murder, now shot wildly at their officers.

'Steady, men! Steady, for God's sake!'

The entreaty was not in vain; they were steady still. Ay, steady, but unarmed! Steady as a rock still, but helpless!

Helpless, unarmed! By all the gods all men worshipped, men could not suffer that for long, when bullets were whistling into their ranks!

So there was a waver at last in the long line. A faint tremble, like the tremble of a curving wave ere it falls. Then, with a confused roar, an aimless sweeping away of all things in its path, it broke as a wave breaks upon a pebbly shore.

'To arms, brothers! Quick! fire! fire!'

Upon whom?[1] God knows! Not on their officers, for these were already being hustled to the rear, hustled into safety.

'Quick, brothers, quick, kill, kill!'

The cry rose on all sides now, as the wave of revolt surged on. But there was none left to kill; for the work was done in the 20th lines, and no new white faces came to stem the tide; the two thousand and odd Englishmen who might have stemmed it being still on the parade-ground by the church, waiting for orders, for ammunition, for a General, for everything save—thank Heaven!—for courage.

---

[1] This question is one which must be asked as we look back through the years on this pitiful spectacle of the loyal regiment unarmed, facing the disloyal one shooting down its officers. Briefly, on whom would the seventy men of the 11th, who never left the colours, the hundred and twenty men who returned to them after the short night of tumult was over, have fired if a company of English troops had come up to turn the balance in favour of loyalty?

So the wave surged on, to what end it scarcely knew, leaving behind it groups of sullen, startled faces.

'Whose fault but their own?' muttered an old man fiercely, an old man whose son served beside him in the regiment, whose grandson was on the roster for future enlistment. 'Why were we left helpless as new born babes?'

'Why?' echoed a scornful voice from the gathering clusters of undecided men, waiting, with growing fear, hope, despair or triumph, for what was to come next: waiting, briefly, for the master to come, or not to come. 'Why? because they were afraid of us; because their time is past, *baba jee*. Let them go!'

Let them go! Incomprehensible suggestion to that brain worn stiff in the master's service; so, with a great numb ache in an old heart, an old body strode away, elbowing younger ones from its path savagely.

'Old Dhurma hath grown milksop,' jeered one spectator, 'that is with doing dry-nurse to his captain's babies.'

The words caught the old man's ear and sent a quick decision to his dazed face. The *baba logue*! Yes; they must be safeguarded; for ominous smoke began to rise from neighbouring roof-trees, and a strange note of sheer wild-beast ferocity grew to the confused roar of the drifting, shifting, still aimless crowd.

'Quick, brothers, quick! Kill, root and branch! Why dost linger? Art afraid? Afraid of cowards? Quick—kill every one!'

The cry, boastful, jeering, came from a sepoy in the uniform of the 20th, who with a face ablaze with mad exultation forced his way forward. There was something in his tone which seemed to send a shiver of fresh excitement through his comrades, for they paused in their strange tumult, paused and listened to the jeers, the reproaches.

'What! art cowards too?' he went on. 'Then follow me. For I began it—I fired the first shot—I killed the first infidel. I—'

The boast never ended, for above it came a quicker cry:

'Kill, kill, kill the traitor! Kill the man who betrayed us.'

There was a rush inwards towards the boastful, arrogant voice, the report of half-a-dozen muskets, and the crowd surged on to revolt over the body of the man who had fired the first shot of the mutiny.

For it was a strange crowd indeed. Most of it powerless for good or ill, sheep without a shepherd, wandering after the rabble of escaped convicts and the refuse of the bazaars as they plundered and fired the houses; joining in the licence helplessly, drifting inevitably to violence, so that some looked on curiously, unconcernedly, while others, maddened by the smell of blood, the sounds of murder, dragged helpless Englishmen and Englishwomen from their carriages and did them to death savagely.

But there were more like Soma, who, as the darkness deepened and the glare and the dire confusion and dismay grew, stood aloof from it voluntarily, waiting, with a certain callousness, to see if the master would come, or if folk said true when they declared his time was past, his day done.

Where was he? He should have come hours ago, irresistible, overwhelming. But there was no sign. Not a hint of resistance, save every now and again a clatter of hoofs through the darkness, an alien voice calling 'Mâro! Mâro!' to those behind him, and a fierce howl of an echo, 'Mâro! Mâro! Mâ-roh!' from the faithful troop. For Captain Craigie, finding none to help him, had changed his cry; it was 'kill, kill, kill!' now. And the faithful troop obeyed orders.

Soma when he heard it gave a great sigh. If there had been more of that sort of thing he would dearly have loved to be in it; but the other was butchery. So he wandered alone, irresolute; drifting northwards from the dire confusion and dismay, and crossing the Mall to question a sentry of his own regiment as to what had happened to the masters. But the man replied by eager questions as to what had happened to the servants? And then they both agreed that if the Two Thousand could not quell a riot it would be idle to help them, the Lord's hand being so palpably against them.

Nevertheless, half an hour afterwards the sentry still waited at his post, and the guard over the Treasury saluted as if nothing unusual was afoot to a group of Englishmen galloping past.

'Those men know nothing,' called Major Erlton to another man. 'It can't be so bad. Surely something can be done!'

'Something should have been done two hours ago,' came a sharp voice. 'However, the troops have started at last. If any one—'

The remainder was lost in the clatter. But more than one man's voice had been lost in those two hours at Meerut on the 10th of May 1857; indeed, everything seems to have been lost save—thank Heaven once more!—personal courage.

It was now near eight o'clock, and Soma, skulking by the Mall midway between the masters and the men, still irresolute, still uncertain, heard the first cry of 'to Delhi! to Delhi!' which, as the night wore on, was to echo so often along that road. The cry which came unbidden as the astounding success of the revolt brought thoughts of greater success in the future.

The moon was now rising to silver the dense clouds of smoke which hung above the pillars of flame, and give an additional horror of light to the orgies going on unchecked. It showed him a group of 3rd Cavalry troopers galloping madly down the Mall. It showed them the glitter of his buckles, making them shout again.

'To Delhi, brother, to Delhi!'

Not yet. He had not seen the upshot yet. He must go and see what was passing in the lines first. So he struck rapidly across the open as the quickest way. And then behind him, close upon him, came another clatter of hoofs, a very different cry.

'*Shâh bâsh! bhaiyân. Mâro! Mâro!*'

Remembering the glitter of his buckles, he turned and ran for the nearest cover. None too soon, for a Mohammedan trooper was after him, shouting '*Deen! Deen!* Death to the Hindoo pig!'—for any cry comes handy when the blood is up and there is a sabre in the hand. Soma had to double like a hare, and even so, when he paused to get his breath in a tangle of lime-bushes there was a graze on his cheek. He had judged his distance in one of those doubles a hair's-breadth too little. The faint trickle of blood sent a spasm of old inherited race hatred through him. The outcaste should know that the Hindoo pig shot straight. The means of showing this were not far to find in the track of the faithful troop. Five minutes after, Soma, with a musket dragged from beneath something which lay huddled up face down upon Mother Earth, was crouching in a belt of cover, waiting for the troop to come flashing through the glare seeking more work; for there had been yells and screams enough round that bungalow to stop looting there. And as it came, number seven bent lower to his saddle bow suddenly, then toppled over with a clang.

'Left wheel! clear those bushes,' came the order sharply. But Soma was too quick for that.

'Close up. Forward!' came the order again, as Captain Craigie's faithful troop went on, minus a man, and Soma, stumbling breathlessly in safety knew that the die was cast. There was that answering quiver in his veins which comes when like blood has been spilt. He knew his foe now; he could go to Delhi now. And hark! That was a regular rattle of musketry, at last—not the dropping fire of mere butchery—but a regular volley. He gripped his musket tighter and listened. If the battle had begun he must be in it. The air was full of cracklings and hissings—an inarticulate background to murderous yells, terrified screams, horrors without end; but no more volleys came to tell of retribution.

What did it mean? Soma held his breath hard. Hark! what was that? A louder burst of that recurring cry, 'to Delhi! to Delhi!' as the last stragglers of the 3rd Cavalry, escaping from the lines at the long-delayed appearance there of law and order, followed their comrades' example.

So that the Two Thousand coming down in force found nothing but the women and children; poor, frightened, terror-struck hostages, left behind, inevitably, in the unforeseen success.

But Soma, knowing nothing of this, waited—that grip on his musket slackening—for the next volley. But none came. Only, suddenly a bugle call.

*The retreat!*

Incredible! Impossible! Yes! Once, twice, thrice—*the retreat!* The masters were not going to fight at Meerut then, and he must try Delhi. So, turning swiftly, he cut into the road behind the cry.

'My God, Craigie! what's that? not the retreat, surely!' came a boyish voice from the clatter and rattle of the faithful troop.

'Don't know! Hurry up all you can, Clark! There's more of the devils needing cold steel yonder, and I'd like to see to my wife's safety as soon as I can. *Shâhbâsh bhaiyán! Dân-ro! Mâro!*'

'*Mâro—Mâ—ro—Mâ—roh!*' echoed the howl. What was the retreat to them when their Captain's voice called to them as brothers? It is idle to ask the question, but one cannot help wondering if the Captain's pocket still held the official wigging. For the sake of picturesque effect it is to be hoped it did.

Nevertheless it *was* the retreat. A council of officers had suggested that, since the mutineers were not in their lines, they might be looting European cantonments. So the Two Thousand returned thither, after firing that one volley into a wood, and then—finding all quiet to the north—proceeded to bivouac on the parade ground for the night. Not a very peaceful spot, since it was within sight and sound of blazing roof-trees, and plundering ruffians. The worst horrors of that night, we are told, can never be known. Perhaps some people beg to differ, holding that no horror can exceed the thought of women and children hiding like hares on that southern side, creeping for dear life from one friendly shadow to another, and finding help in dark hands when white ones failed them, within reach of that bivouac. But the faithful troop did good service, and many another band of independent braves also. Captain Craigie, finding leisure at last, found also—it is a relief to know—that some of his own men had sneaked away from duty to secure his wife's safety when they saw their Captain would not. And if anything can relieve the deadly depression which sinks upon the soul at the thought of that horrible lack of emotion in the north, it is to picture that very different scene on the south, when Captain Craigie, seeing his only hope of getting the ladies safely escorted to the European barracks lay in his troopers, brought the two Englishwomen out to them and said simply, 'Here are the *mems*! save them.'

And then the two score or so of rough men, swash bucklers by birth and training, flung themselves from their horses, cast themselves at those alien women's feet with tears and oaths. Oaths that were kept.

But, on the other side, people were more placid. One reads of

Englishmen watching 'their own sleeping children with gratitude in their hearts to God,' with wonderings as 'to the fate of their friends in the south,' with anticipations of 'what would befall their Christian brethren in Delhi on the coming morn, who, less happy than ourselves, had no faithful and friendly European battalions to shield them from the bloodthirsty rage of the sepoys.'

What, indeed? considering that for two hours bands of armed men had clattered and marched down that dividing road crying 'to Delhi, to Delhi'. But no warning of the coming danger had been sent thither; the confusion had been too great. And now, about midnight, the telegraph wires had been cut. Yet Delhi lay but thirty miles off along a broad white road, and there were horses galore and men ready to ride them. Men ready for more than that, like Captain Rosser of the Carabineers, who pleaded for a squadron, a field battery, a troop, a gun—anything with which to dash down the road and cut off that retreat to Delhi. But everything was refused. Lieutenant Mohler of the 11th offered to ride and at least give warning; but that offer was also set aside. And many another brave man, no doubt, bound to obey orders, ate his heart out in inaction that night, possessing himself in some measure of patience with the thought that the dawn *must* see them on that Delhi road.

But there was one man who owed obedience to none; who was free to go if he chose. And he did choose. Ten minutes after it dawned upon Herbert Erlton that no warning had been given, that no succour would be sent, he had changed horses for the game little Arab which had once belonged to Jim Douglas, and was off, to reach Delhi as best he could; for a woman slept in the very city itself, exposed to the first assault of ruffianism, whom he must save, if he could. So he set his teeth and rode straight. At first down the road, for the last of the fugitives had had a good hour's start of him, and he could count on four or five miles plain sailing. Then, since his object was to head the procession, and he did not dare to strike across country from his utter ignorance both of the way or how to ask it, he must give the road a half-mile berth or so, and keeping it as a guide, make his way somehow. There were bridges he knew where he must hark back to the only path, but he must trust to luck for a quiet interval.

The plan proved more difficult than he expected. More than once he found himself in danger from being too close to the disciplined tramp which he began to overtake about six miles out, and twice he lost himself from being too far away and mistaking one belt of trees for another. Still there was plenty of time if the Arab held out with his weight. The night was hot and stifling, but if he took it coolly till the road was pretty clear again he could forge ahead in no time; for the Arab had the heels of every horse in Upper India. Major Erlton knew this, and bent over to pat its neck with the pride of certainty with which he had patted it before many a race which it had won for him since it had lost one for Jim Douglas.

So he saved it all he knew; but he rode fifteen stone—and that, over jumps, must tell. There was no other way, however, that he knew of, by which an Englishman could head that procession of shouting black devils.

One headed it already, as it happened; though he was unaware of the supreme importance of the fact, ignorant of what lay behind him. Jim Douglas, who had left Meerut all unwitting of that rescue party on its way to the jail, was still about a mile from the half-way house where he expected to find his relay. He had had the greatest difficulty in getting the drugged mare to go at all at first, and more than once had regretted having refused old Tiddu's advice. She had pulled herself together a bit, but she was in a drip of sweat, and still shaky on her feet. Not that it mattered, he being close now to Begum-a-bad with plenty of time to reach Delhi by dawn.

He rather preferred to pace slowly, his feet out of the stirrups, his slight easy figure dressed, as it always was when in English costume, with the utmost daintiness, sitting well back in the saddle. For the glamour of the moonlight, the stillness of the night possessed him; everything so soundless save when the jackals began—there were a number of them about—A good hunting country—the memory of many a run in his youthful days, with a bobbery pack, came to him.— After all he had had the cream of life in a way.—Few men had enjoyed theirs more, for even this idle pacing through the stillness was a pleasure—Pleasure?—How many he had had! His mind, reverting from one to another, thought even of the owner of the golden curl without regret. She had taught him the religion of Love, the adoration of a spotless woman. And Zora, dear little Zora; had taught him the purity of passion. And then his mind went back suddenly to a scene of his boyhood—a boy of eighteen carrying a girl of sixteen who held a string of sea-trout midway in a wide deep ford. And he heard, as if it had been yesterday, the faint splash of the fish as they slipped one by one into the water, and felt the fierce fighting of the girl to be set down, his own stolid resistance, and listened to their mutual abuse of each other's obstinacy and carelessness. Yes! he would like to see his sisters once more, to know that pleasure again. Then his mind took another leap. Alice Gissing had not struggled in his hold, because she had been in unison with his ideal of conduct; but if she had not been, she would have fought as viciously, as unconsciously, as any sister. Alice Gissing who—He settled his feet into the stirrups sternly, thinking of that telegram with its one word 'Come,' which ended so many chances.

Hark! What was that? A clatter of hoofs behind! And something more, surely. A jingle, a jangle, familiar to his soldier's ears—cavalry at the gallop! He drew aside hastily into the shadow of the arcaded trees and waited.

Cavalry, no doubt; and the moon shone on their drawn sabres. By Heaven! Troopers of the 3rd!—Half-a-dozen or more!

'*Shâhbâsh*, brothers,' cried one as they swept past, 'we can breathe our beasts a bit at Begum-a-bad and let the others come up; no need to reach Delhi ere dawn. The Palace would be closed.'

Delhi! The Palace! And who were the others? That, if they were coming behind, could soon be settled. He turned the Belooch and trotted her back in the shadow, straining eyes and ears down the tree-fringed road which lay so still, so white, so silent.

Something was on it now, but something silent, almost ghost-like—an old man, muttering texts, on a lame camel which bumped along as even no earthly camel ought to bump. That could not be the 'others'?

No! Surely that was a thud, a jingle, a clatter, once more? and once more the glitter of cold steel in the moonlight—forty or fifty of the 3rd this time, with stragglers calling to others still further behind 'To Delhi! To Delhi! To Victory or Death'.

As he stood waiting for them all to pass ere he moved, his first thought was, that with all these armed men at Begum-a-bad there would be no chance of a remount. Then came a swift wonder as to what had happened. A row of some sort, of course, and these men had fled. Ere long, no doubt, a squadron of Carabineers would come rattling after them. No! That was not cavalry. That was infantry in the distance! Quite a number of men shouting the same cry—men of the 20th, to judge by what he could see. Then the row had been a big one! Still the men were evidently fugitives, and there was that in their recurring cry which told of almost hopeless, reckless enthusiasm.

And how the devil was he to get his remount? It was to be at the *serai* on the road side, the very place where these men would rest. Yet he must get to Delhi, he must get there sharp! The possibility that Delhi was unwarned did not occur to him; he only thought how he might best get there in time for the row which must come. Should he wait for the English troops to come up, and chance his remount being coolly taken by the first rebel who wanted one? Or, Delhi being not more than fifteen miles off across country, should he take the mare as far as she would go, leave her in some field, and do the rest on foot? He looked at his watch. Half past one! Say five miles in half-an-hour. The mare was good for that. Then ten miles, at five miles an hour. The very first glimmer of light should see him at the boat bridge if—if the mare could gallop five miles.

He must try her a bit slowly first. So, slipping across the broad white streak of road to the Delhi side, he took her slanting through the tall tiger grass—for they were close on a *nullah* which must be forded by a rather deep ford lower down, since the bridge was denied to him. About half a mile from the road he came upon the track suddenly, in the midst of high tamarisk jungle growing in heavy sand, and the next moment was on the shining levels of the ford. The mare strained on his hand, and he paused to let her have a mouthful of water. As she stood there, head down, a horseman at the canter showed suddenly, silently, behind him, not five yards away, his horse's hoofs deadened by the sand.

There was a hasty movement, an ominous click on both sides. But the moon was too bright for mistakes; the recognition was mutual.

'My God, Erlton!' he cried, as the other, without a pause, went on into the ford. 'What's up?'

'Is it fordable?' came the quick question, and as Jim Douglas for an answer gave a dig with his spurs, the Major slackened visibly; his eye telling him that the depth could not be taken, save at a walk.

'What's up?' he echoed fiercely. 'Mutiny! murder! I say, how far am I from Delhi?'

'Delhi!' cried Jim Douglas, his voice keen as a knife. 'By heaven! you don't mean they don't know—that they didn't wire—but the troops—'

'Hadn't started when I left,' said the Major with a curse. 'I came on alone. I say, Douglas,' he gave a sharp glance at the other's mount and there was a pause.

'My mare's beat—been drugged,' said Jim Douglas in the swish-swish of the water rising higher and higher on the horses' breasts, and there was a curious tone in his voice as if he were arguing out something to himself. 'I've a remount at the *serai*, but the odds are a hundred to one on my getting it. I'd given up the chance of it. I meant to take the mare as many miles across country as she'd go—more, perhaps—for she feels like falling at a fence, and walk the rest. I didn't know then—' he paused and looked ahead. The water, up to the girths, made a curious rushing sound, like many wings. The long shiny levels stretched away softly, mysteriously. The tamarisk jungle reflected in the water seemed almost as real as that which edged the shining sky. A white egret stood in the shallows; tall, ghostly.

'I thought it was only—a row.'

The voice ceased again, the breathings of the tired horses had slackened; there was no sound but that rushing, as of wings, as those two enemies rode side by side looking ahead. Suddenly Jim Douglas turned.

'You ride nigh four stone heavier than I do, Major Erlton.'

The heavy handsome face came round swiftly, all broken up with sheer passion.

'Do you suppose I haven't been thinking that ever since I saw your cursed face? And you know the country, and I don't. You know the lingo and I don't. And—and—you're a deuce sight better rider than I am, d—n you! But for all that, it's my chance, I tell you. My chance, not yours.'

A great surge of sympathy swept through the other man's veins. But the water was shallowing rapidly. A step or two and this must be decided.

'It's yours more than mine,' he said slowly, 'but it isn't ours, is it? It's the others, in Delhi.'

Herbert Erlton gave an old sound between a sob and an oath, a savage jag at the bridle as the little Arab, over-weighted, slipped a bit coming up the bank. Then, without a word, he flung himself from the saddle and set to work on the stirrup nearest him.

'How many holes?' he asked gruffly, as Jim Douglas, with a great ache in his heart, left the Belooch standing, and began on the other.

'Three; you're a good bit longer in the leg than I am.'

'I suppose I am,' said the Major, sullenly; but he held the stirrup for the other to mount.

Jim Douglas gathered the reins in his hand and paused.

'You had better walk her back. Keep more to the left; it's easier.'

'Oh! I'll do,' came the sullen voice. 'Stop a bit, the curb's too tight.'

'Take it off, will you? he knows me.'

Major Erlton gave an odd, quick, bitter laugh. 'I suppose he does. Right you are!'

He stood, putting the curb chain into his pocket, mechanically, but Jim Douglas paused again.

'Good bye! Shake hands on it, Erlton.'

The Major looked at him resentfully, the big coarse hand came reluctantly; but the touch of that other, like iron in its grip its determination, seemed to rouse something deeper than anger.

'The odds are on you,' he said, with a quiver in his voice. 'You'll look after her—not my wife, she's in cantonments—but in the city, you know.'

The voice broke suddenly. He threw out one hand in a sort of passionate despair, and walked over to the Beloochi.

'I'll do everything you could possibly do in my place, Erlton.'

The words came clear and stern, and the next instant the thud of the Arab's galloping hoofs filled the still night air. The sound sent a spasm of angry pain through Major Erlton. The chance had been his, and he had had to give it up because he rode three stone heavier—and curse it! knew only too well what a difference a pound or two might make in a race.

Nevertheless Jim Douglas had been right when he said the chance was neither his nor the Major's. For less than an hour afterwards, riding all he knew, doing his level best, the Arab put its foot in a rat hole just as his rider was congratulating himself on having headed the rebels; just as, across the level plain stretching from Ghazeabad to the only bridge over the Jumna, he fancied he could see a big shadowy bubble on the western sky—the dome of the Delhi mosque. Put its foot in a rat hole and came down heavily. The last thing Jim Douglas saw was—on the road which he had hoped to rejoin in a minute or two—a strange ghostlike figure. An old man on a lame camel, which bumped along as even no earthly camel ought to bump.

As he fell, the rushing roar in his ears which heralds unconsciousness seemed by a freak of memory to take a familiar rhythm—

*La! il-lah-il-ullaho! La! il-lah-il-ul-la-ho!*
(There is no god but God.)

# 2

# Dawn

The chill wind which comes with dawn swayed the tall grass beyond the river, and ruffling the calm stretches below the Palace wall died away again as an oldish man stepped out of a reed hut, built on a sandbank beside the boat-bridge, and looked eastwards. He was a *poojari*, or master of ceremonial at the bathing-place where, with the first streak of light, the Hindoos came to perform their religious ablutions. So he had to be up betimes in order to prepare the little saucers of vermilion and sandal and sacred gypsum needed in his profession; for he earned his livelihood by inherited right of hall-marking his fellow-creatures with their caste-signs when they came up out of the water. Thus he looked out over those eastern plains for the dawn, day after day.[1] And this dawn there was a cloud of dust no bigger than a man's hand upon the Meerut road. Some one was coming to Delhi.

---

[1] He looks for it still; this account is from his lips.

But some one was already on the bridge, for it creaked and swayed, sending little shivers of ripples down the calm stretches. The *poojari* turned and looked to see the cause; then turned eastward again. It was only a man on a camel with a strange gait, bumping noiselessly even on the resounding wood. That was all.

The city was still asleep; though here and there a widow was stealing out in her white shroud for that touch of the sacred river without which she would be indeed accursed. And in a little mosque hard by the road from the boat-bridge a *muazzin* was about to give the very first call to prayer with pious self-complacency. But some one was ahead of him in devotion, for, upon the still air, came a continuous rolling of chanted texts. The *muazzin* leant over the parapet, disappointed, to see who had thus forestalled him at heaven's gate; stared, then muttered a hasty charm. Were there visions about? The suggestion softened the disappointment, and he looked after the strange wild figure, half-seen in the shimmering, shadowy dawn-light, with growing and awed satisfaction. This was no mere mortal, this green-clad figure on a camel, chanting texts and waving a scimitar. A vision had been vouchsafed to him for his diligence; a vision that would not lose in the telling. So he stood up and gave the cry from full lungs.

'*Prayer is more than sleep! than sleep! than sleep!*'

The echo from the rose-red fortifications took it up first; then one chanting voice after another, monotonously insistent.

'*Prayer is more than sleep! than sleep! than sleep!*'

And the city woke to another day of fasting. Woke hurriedly, so as to find time for food ere the sun rose, for it was Rumzân, and one half of the inhabitants would have no drop of water till the sunset, to assuage the terrible drought of every living, growing thing beneath the fierce May sun. The backwaters lay like a steel mirror reflecting the grey shadowy pile of the palace, the *poojari*—waist-deep in them—was a solitary figure flinging water to the sacred airts, absorbed in a thorough purification from sin.

Then, from the serrated line of the Ridge came a bugle followed by the roll of a time gun. All the world was waking now; waking to give orders, to receive them, waking to mark itself apart with signs of salvation, waking to bow westwards and pray for the discomfiture of the infidel, waking to stand on parade and salute the royal standard of a ruler, hell-doomed inevitably, according to both creeds.

A flock of purple pigeons startled by the sound, rose like cloud flakes on the light grey sky above the glimmering dome of the big mosque, then flew westward towards the green fields and groves on the further side of the town. For the roll of the gun was followed by a reverberating roll, and groan, and creak, from the boat bridge. The little cloud on the Meerut road, had grown into five troopers dashing over the bridge at a gallop recklessly. The *poojari*, busy now with his pigments, followed them with his eyes as they clattered straight for the city gate. They were waking in the Palace by this time, for a slender hand set a lattice wide; perhaps from curiosity, perhaps simply to let in the cool air of dawn. It was a lattice in the women's apartments.

The *poojari* went on rubbing up the colours that were to bring such spiritual pride to the wearers, then turned to look again. The troopers, finding the city gate closed, were back once more clamouring for admittance through the low arched doorway leading from Selimgarh to the Palace. And as the yawning custodian fumbled for his keys, the men cursed and swore at the delay—for in truth they knew not what lay behind them. The Two Thousand from Meerut, or some of them, of course. But at what distance?

As a matter of fact only one Englishman was close enough to be considered a pursuer, and he was but a poor creature on foot, still dazed by a fall, striking across country to reach the Râj-ghât ferry below the city. For when Jim Douglas had recovered consciousness it had been to recognize that he was too late to be the first in Delhi, and that he could only hope to help in the struggle; and that tardily, for the Arab was dead lame.

So, removing its saddle and bridle to give it a better chance of escaping notice, he had left it grazing peacefully in a field and stumbled on riverwards, intending to cross it as best he could and so make for his own house in Duryagunj for a fresh horse and a more suitable kit. And as he plodded along doggedly he cursed the sheer ill-luck which had made him late.

For he *was* late.

The five troopers were already galloping through the Grape-garden towards the women's apartments and the king's sleeping-rooms.

Their shouts of 'The King! The King! Help for the martyrs! Help for the Holy War!' dumbfoundered the court *muazzim* who was going late to his prayers in the Pearl Mosque. The reckless hoofs sent a squatting bronze image of a gardener, threading jasmine chaplets for his gods peacefully in the pathway, flying into a rose bush.

'The King! The King! Help! Help!'

The women woke with the cry, confused, alarmed, surprised; save one or two who, creeping quickly to the Queen's room, found her awake, excited, calling to her maids.

'Too soon!' she echoed contemptuously. 'Can a good thing come too soon? Quick, woman—I must see the King at once—nay, I will go as I am if it comes to that.'

'The physician Ahsan-Oolah hath arrived as usual for the dawn pulse-feeling,' protested the shocked tirewoman.

'All the more need for hurry,' retorted Zeenut Maihl. 'Quick! Slippers and a veil! Thine will do, Fâtma; sure what makes thee decent—' she gave a spiteful laugh as she snatched it from the woman's head and passed to the door : but there she paused a second. 'See if Hafzân be below. I bid her come early, so she should be. Tell her to write word to Hussan Askuri to dream as he never dreamt before! And see—' her voice grew shriller, keener, 'the rest of you have leave. Go! cozen every man you know, every man you meet. I care not how. Make their blood flow! I care not wherefore, so that it leaps and bounds, and would spill other blood that checked it.' She clenched her hands as she passed on muttering to herself. 'Ah! if *he* were a man—if *his* blood were not chilled with age—if I had some one—'

She broke off into smiles; for in the anteroom she entered was, man or no man, the representative of the Great Moghul.

'Ah, Zeenut!' he cried in tones of relief. 'I would have sought thee.' The trembling shrunken figure in its wadded-silk dressing-gown paused and gave a backward glance at Ahsan-Oolah, whose shrewd face was full of alarm.

'Believe nothing, my liege!' he protested eagerly. 'These rioters are boasters. Are there not two thousand British soldiers in Meerut? Their tale is not possible. They are cowards fled from defeat, liars, hoping to be saved at your expense. The thing is impossible.'

The Queen turned on him passionately. 'Are not all things possible with God, and is not His Majesty the Defender of the Faith!'

'But not defender of five runaway rioters,' sneered the physician. 'My liege! Remember your pension.'

Zeenut Maihl glared at his cunning; it was an argument needing all her art to combat.

'Five!' she echoed, passing to the lattice quickly. 'Then miracles are about—the five have grown to fifty. Look, my lord, look! Hark! How they call on the Defender of the Faith.'

With reckless hand she set the lattice wide, so becoming visible for an instant; and a shout of 'the Queen, the Queen,' mingled with that other of 'the Faith! the Faith! Lead us, Oh! Ghazee-o-din-Bahâdur-shâh, to die for the faith.'

Pale as he was with age, the cry stirred the blood in the King's veins and sent it to his face.

'Stand back,' he cried in sudden dignity, waving both counsellors aside with trembling outstretched hands. 'I will speak mine own words.'

But the sight of him, rousing a fresh burst of enthusiasm left him no possibility of speech for a time. The Lord had been on their side, they cried. They had killed every hell-doomed infidel in Meerut! They would do so in Delhi if he would help! They were but an advanced guard of an army coming from every cantonment in India to swear allegiance to the Pâdishah. Long live the King! and the Queen!

In the dim room behind, Zeenut Maihl and the physician listened to the wild almost incredible tale which drifted in with the scented air from the garden, and watched each other silently. Each found in it fresh cause for obstinacy. If this were true, what need to be foolhardy?—Time would show, the thing come of itself without risk. If this were true, decisive action should be taken at once—and would be taken.

But the King, assailed, molested, by that rude interrupting loyalty— above all by that cry for the Queen—felt the Turk stir in him also. Who were these intruders in the sacred precincts, infringing the seclusion of the Great Moghul's women? Trembling with impotent passion, inherited from passions that had not been impotent, he turned to Ahsan-Oolah, ignoring the Queen, who, he felt, was mostly to blame for this outrage on her modesty. Why had she come there? Why had she dared to be seen?

'Your Majesty should send for the Captain of the Palace Guards and bid him disperse the rioters, and force them into respect for your royal person,' suggested the physician, carefully avoiding all but the immediate present, 'and your Majesty should pass to the Hall of Audience. The King can scarce receive the Captain-*sahib* here in presence of the Consort.' He did not add—'in her present costume'— but his tone implied it, and the King, with an angry mortified glance towards his favourite, took the physician's arm. If looks could kill, Ahsan-Oolah would not, he knew, have supported those tottering steps far; but it was no time to stick at trifles.

When they had passed from the anteroom Zeenut Maihl still stood as if half stupefied by the insult. Then she dashed to the open lattice again, scornful and defiant, dignified into positive beauty for the moment by her recklessness.

'For the Faith!' she cried in her shrill woman's voice, 'if ye are men, as I would *be*, to be loved of woman as I *am*, strike for the Faith!'

A sort of shiver ran through the clustering crowd of men below; the shiver of anticipation, of the marvellous, the unexpected. The Queen had spoken to them as men; of herself as woman. Inconceivable!— Improper of course—yet exciting. Their blood thrilled, the instinct of the man to fight for the woman rose at once.

'Quick, brothers! Rouse the guard! Close the gates! Close the gates!'

It was a cry to heal all strife within those rose-red walls, for the dearest wish of every faction was to close them against civilization; against those prying Western eyes and sniffing Western noses, detecting drains and sinks of iniquity. So the clamour grew, and faces which had frowned at each other yesterday sought support in each other's ferocity to day, and wild tales began to pass from mouth to mouth. Men, crowding recklessly over the flower-beds, trampling down the roses, talked of visions, of signs and warnings, while the troopers, dismounting for a pull at a pipe, became the centre of eager circles listening not to dreams, but deeds.

'Dost feel the rope about thy neck, sir Martyr?' said a bitter jeering voice behind one of the speakers; and something gripped him round the throat, then as suddenly loosed its hold, as a shrouded woman's figure hobbled on through the crowd. The trooper started up with an oath, his own hand seeking his throat involuntarily.

'Heed her not!' said a bystander hastily "tis the Queen's scribe, Hafzân. She hath a craze against men. One made her what she is. Go on! *Havildar-jee.* So thou did'st cut the *mem* down, and fling the babe—'

But the doer of the deed stood silent. He did in truth seem to feel the rope about his neck; and he seemed to feel it till he died—when it *was* there.

But Hafzân had passed on, and there were no more with words of warning; so the clamour grew and grew, till the garden swarmed with men ready for any deed.

Ahsan-Oolah saw this, and laid a detaining hand on the Captain of the Guard, who, summoned in hot haste from his quarters over the Lahore gate, came in by the private way, and proposed to go down and harangue the crowd.

'It is not safe, *Huzoor,*' he cried. 'My liege! detain him. These men by their own confession are murderers—'

The King looked from one to the other doubtfully. Some one must get rid of the rioters; yet the physician said truth—

—'And if aught befall,' added the latter craftily, 'your Majesty will be held responsible.'

The old man's hand fell instantly on the Englishman's arm: 'Nay, nay, *sahib*! go not. Go not, my friend! Speak to them from the balcony. They will not dare to violate it.'

So, backed by the sanctity of the Audience Hall of a dead dynasty, the Englishman stood and ordered the crowd to desist from profaning privacy, in the name of the old man behind him, whose power he, in common with all his race, hoped and believed to be dead. It was sufficient, however, to leave some respect for the royal person, and make the crowd disperse; but to little purpose so far as peace and quiet went, since the only effect was to send a leaven of revolt to every corner of the palace—and the palace was so full of malcontents, docked of power, privilege, pensions—of all that makes life in a palace worth living.

So the cry 'Close the gates' grew wider. The dazed old king clung to the Englishman's arm imploring him to stay; but now a messenger came running to say that the Commissioner-*sahib* had called, and left word that the *Captân* was to follow without delay to the Calcutta gate of the city. The courtiers, who had begun to assemble, looked at each other curiously; the disturbance, then, had spread beyond the palace. Could then, this amazing tale be true? The very thought sent them cringing round the old man, who might ere long be king indeed.

Yet as the captain dashed at a gallop past the sentries standing calmly at the Lahore gate, there was no sign of trouble beyond, and he gave a quick glance of relief back at those cool quarters of his over the arched tunnel where the chaplain, his daughter, and her friend were staying as his guests. He felt less fear of leaving them when he saw that the city was waking to life as always, buckling down quietly to the burden and heat of a new day. It was now past seven o'clock, and the sunlight, still cool, was bright enough to cleave all things into dark or light, shade or shine. Up on the Ridge, the brigade, after listening to the sentence on the Barrackpore mutineers was dispersing quietly; many of the men with that fiat of patience till the 31st in their minds, for the carriage-load of native officers returning from the Meerut court-martial had come into cantonments late the night before. On the roofs of the houses in the learned quarter women were giving the boys their breakfasts ere sending them off to school. The milk-women were trooping in city-wards from the country, the fruit-sellers and hawkers trooping out Ridge-ways as usual. The postman going his rounds had left letters, written in Meerut the day before, at two houses. And Kate Erlton returning from early church had found hers and was reading it with a scared face. Alice Gissing, however, having had that laconic telegram, had taken hers coolly. The decision had had to be made, since nothing had happened; and Herbert had the right to make it. For her part, she could make him happy; she had the knack of making most men happy, and she herself was always content when the people about her were jolly. So she was packing boxes in the back verandah of the little house on the city wall.

Thus she did not see the man who, between six and seven o'clock, ran breathlessly past her house, as a short-cut to the court-house from the bridge, taking a message from the toll-keeper to the nearest *Huzoor*, the Collector, who was holding early office, that a party of armed troopers had come down the Meerut road; that more could be seen coming, and would the *Huzoor* kindly issue orders—that first and final suggestion of the average native subordinate in any difficulty.

Armed men? That might mean much or nothing. Yet scarcely anything really serious, or warning would have been sent. The Commissioner, anyhow, must be told. So the Collector flung himself on his horse, which, in Indian fashion, was waiting under a tree outside the court-house, and galloped towards Ludlow Castle. No need for *that* warning, however, for just by the Kashmir gate he met the man he sought driving furiously down with a mounted escort to close the city gates. He had already heard the news.[1]

Gathering grave apprehensions from this hasty meeting, the Collector was off again to warn the Resident; then—still further—to beg help from cantonments. There was no delay here, no hesitation; simply a man on a horse doing his best for the future, leaving the present for those on the spot.

Nor was there delay anywhere. The Commissioner, calling by the way for the Captain of the Guard—the nearest man with men under him—was at the gate giving on the bridge of boats, by half-past seven. The Resident, calling on *his* way at the magazine for two guns to sweep the bridge, joined him there soon after. Too late. The enemy had crossed, and were in possession of the only ground commanding the bridge. Nothing remained but to close the gate and keep the city quiet till the columns of pursuit from Meerut should arrive; for that there was one upon the road no one doubted. The very rebels clamouring at the gate were listening for the sound of those following footsteps. The very fanatics, longing for another blow or two at an infidel, to gain Paradise withal, ere martyrdom was theirs, listened too; for during that moonlit night the certainty of failure had been as myrrh and hyssop deadening them to the sacrifice of life.

[1] How? His house lay a mile at least further off, and the Collector's office was on the only route a messenger could take. No record explains this. But the best ones mention casually that a telegram of warning came to Delhi in the early morning of the 11th. Whence? The wires to Meerut were cut. Lahore, Umballa, Agra, did not know the news themselves. Can the story—improbable in any other history, but in this record of fatal mistakes gaining a pathetic probability—which the old folk in Delhi tell be true? The story of a telegram sent *unofficially* from Meerut the night before, received while the Commissioner was at dinner, put unopened into his pocket, and *forgotten*.

Not susceptible of proof or disproof, it certainly explains three things:-
1. Whence the warning telegram came?
2. Why the Commissioner received information before a man a good mile nearer the source?
3. Why the Collector *at once* sought for military aid?

So the little knot of Englishmen, looking hopefully down the road, looked anxiously at each other, and closed the river gate; kept it closed, too, even when the 20th claimed admittance from their friends the guard within; for the 38th regiment, whose turn it was for city work, was also rotten to the core.

But they could not close that way through Selimgarh, though it, in truth, brought no trouble to the town. The men who chose it being intriguers, fanatics, the better class of patriots more anxious to entrench themselves for the struggle within walls, than to swarm into a town they could not hope to hold. But there were others of different mettle, longing for loot and licence. The 3rd Cavalry had many friends in Delhi, especially in the Thunbi bazaar; so they made for it by braving the shallow streams and shifting sandbanks below the eastern wall, and so gaining the Rajghât gate. Here, after compact with vile friends in that vile quarter, they found admittance and help. For what?

Between the bazaar and the palace lay Duryagunj, full of helpless Christian women and children; and so, 'Deen! Deen! Futteh Mahomed', the convenient cry of faith, was ready as, followed by the rabble and refuse once more, the troopers raced through the peaceful gardens, pausing only to kill the infidels they met. But like a furious wind gathering up all vile things in the street and carrying them along for a space, then dropping them again, the band left a legacy of licence and sheer murder behind it, while it sped on to loot.

But now the cry of 'Close the gates' rose once more, this time from the shopkeepers, the respectable quarters, the secluded alleys, the courtyards. And many a door was closed on the confusion and never opened again, *except to pass in bare bread, for four long months.*

'Close the gates! Close the gates! Close the gates!' The cry rose from the palace, the city, the little knot of Englishmen looking down the Meerut road. Yet no one could compass that closing. Recruits swarmed in through Selimgarh to the palace. Robbers swarmed in through the Rajghât gate to harry the bazaars. Only through the Kashmir gate, held by English officers and a guard of the 38th, no help came. The Collector arriving therein, hot from his gallop to cantonments, found more wonder than alarm; for death was dealt in Delhi by noiseless cold steel; and, since the main guard had to be kept, in order to secure retreat and safety to the European houses around it, no one had been able to leave it. Besides all around was still peaceful utterly; even the roar of growing tumult in the city had not reached it. Sonny Seymour was playing with his parrot in the verandah, Alice Gissing packing boxes methodically. The Collector galloping past as, scorning the suggestion that it was needless risk to go further, he replied briefly that he was the magistrate of the town and struck spurs to his horse, made some folk look up; that was all.

But he could scarcely make his way through the growing crowd, which, led by troopers, was beginning to close in behind the knot of waiting Englishmen, who, when they heard that some time must elapse ere they could hope for reinforcement, once more looked down the Meerut road. The guns could not be got ready, said the messenger, at a moment's notice; nor could the Kashmir-gate guard leave the post. But the 54th regiment should be down in about—In about what? No one asked; but those waiting faces listened as for a verdict of life and death—In about an hour.

An hour! And not a cloud of dust upon the Meerut road!

'They can't be long, though, now,' said the eldest there hopefully. 'And Ripley will bring his men down at the double. If we go into the guard-house we can hold our own till then, surely.'

'I can hold mine,' replied a young fellow with a rough-hewn, homely face. He gave a curt nod as he spoke to a companion, and together they turned back, skirting the wall, followed by an older, burlier man. They belonged to the magazine, and they were off to see the best way of holding their own. And they found it—found it for all time!

But fate had denied to those other brave men, the nameless something which makes men succeed together, or die together. Within half-an-hour they were scattered helplessly. The Resident, after seeking support from the city police for one whose name had been a terror to Delhi for fifty years, and finding insult instead, was flying for dear life through the Ajmere gate to the open country. The Commissioner, who, after seizing a musket from a wavering guard beside him and—with the first shot fired in Delhi—shooting the foremost trooper dead, seems to have lost hope with mutiny around the treason beside him, jumped into his buggy alone and drove off to those cool quarters above the Palace-gate as his nearest refuge. Their owner, the Captain, sought like refuge by flinging himself into the cover of the dry moat and creeping—despite injuries from the fall—along it, till some of his men, faithful so far, seeing him unable for more, carried him to his own room.

The Collector?—Strangely enough there is no record of what the Magistrate of the city did, thus left alone. He had been wounded by the crowd at first, and was no doubt weary after his wild gallopings. Still he, holding his own so far, managed to gain the same refuge, somehow. What else could he do alone? One thing we know he could not do. That is mount the broad, curving flight of shallow stone stairs leading to the cool upper rooms. So the chaplain helped him; the chaplain who had 'from an early hour been watching the advance of the Meerut mutineers through a telescope, and feeling there was mischief in the wind'.

Mischief indeed! and danger; most of all in those rose-red walls within which refuge had been sought. For the king was back in the women's apartments, listening to the queen's cozeners and Hussan Askuri's visions, when that urgent appeal to send dhoolies to convey the English ladies at the gate to the security of the harem, reached him—reached him in Ahsan-Oolah's warning voice of wisdom. And he listened to both the wheedling ambition and the crafty policy with a half-hearing for something beyond it of pity, honour, good faith; while Hafzân, pen in hand, sat with her large profoundly-sad eyes fixed on the old man's face, waiting—waiting.

'If they come here—out caste! infidel! I go,' said Zeenut Maihl.

'Thou shalt go with a bowstring about thy neck, woman, if I choose,' said the old king fiercely. 'Write! girl—the queen's dhoolies to the Lahore gate at once.'

So, through the swarm of pensioners quarrelling already over new titles and perquisites, through the groups of excited fanatics preparing for martyrdom about the Mosque, past Abool-Bukr, three parts drunk, boasting to ruffling blades of the European mistresses he meant to keep, the queen's dhoolies went swaying out of the precincts; all yielding place to them. And beyond, in the denser, more dangerous crowd without, they passed easily; for those tinsel-decked, tawdry canopies, screened with sodden musk and dirt-scented curtains, were sacred.

Sacred even to the refuse and rabble of the city, the dissolute eunuchs, the mob of retainers, palace guards, and blood-drunk soldiery who were surging through that long arched tunnel by the Lahore gate, hustling to get round that inside arch, and so, a few steps further, see the Commissioner standing at bay upon that wide curving red-stone stair that led upwards. Standing and thinking of the women above; of one woman mostly. Standing, facing the wild sea of faces, waiting to see if that last appeal for help had been heard.

'Room! Room! for the queen's dhoolies!'

The cry echoed above the roar of the crowd.

At last! He turned—to pass on the welcome news, perchance; but it was enough—that one waver of the stern face was enough to bring death. There was a rush—a cry—a clang of steel on stone—a fall—and then up those wide curving stairs, like fiends incarnate, jostled a mad crew elbowing each other, cursing each other, in their eagerness for that blow which would win Paradise!

There were four crowns of glory in the first room, where the chaplain, the Captain, and the two English girls fell side by side. One in the next, where the Collector and Magistrate, weary and wounded, still lay alone.

'Way! Way! for the queen's dhoolies!'

But they had come too late, as all things seemed to come too late on that fatal 11th of May.

Too late! Too late! The words dinned themselves into a horseman's brain, as he dashed out of the compound of a small house in Duryagunj and headed straight through the bazaar for the little house on the city wall by the Kashmir gate. And as he rode he shouted: '*Deen! Deen!*'

It was a convenient cry, and suited the trooper's dress he wore. He had had to shoot a man to get it, but he hoped to shoot many more when he had seen Alice Gissing in safety, and the Meerut column had come in. It could not be long now.

# 3

# Daylight

Three miles away Kate Erlton sat in her home-like, peaceful drawing-room, feeling dazzled. The sunshine, streaming through the open doors, seemed to stream into the very recesses of her mind as she sat, still looking at the letter which she had found half-an-hour before waiting for her beside a bunch of late roses which the gardener had laid on the table ready for her to arrange in the vases. The flowers were fading fast, and the dog cart, waiting outside to take her on to see a sick friend ere the sun grew hot, shifted to find another shadow; but she did not move.

She was trying to understand what it all meant; really—deprived of her conventional thoughts about such things. And one sentence in the letter had a strange fascination for her. 'I am not such a fool as to think you will mind. I know you will get on much better without me.'

Of course. She had, in a way, accepted the truth of this years ago. The fact must have been patent to him also all that time; and she had known that he accepted it.

But now, set down in black and white, it forced her into seeing—as she had never seen before—the deadly injury she had done to the man by not minding. And then the question came keenly—'Why had she not minded?' Because she had not been content with her bargain. She had wanted something else. What? The emotion, the refinement, the *fine-fleur* of sentiment. Briefly, what made *her* happy; what gave *her* satisfaction. It was only, then, a question between different forms of enjoyment; the one as purely selfish as the other. More so, in a way, for it claimed more and carried the grievance of denial into every detail of life. She moved restlessly in her chair, confused by this sudden daylight in her mind; laid down the letter, then took it up again and read another sentence.

'I believe you used to think that I'd get the regiment some day; but I shouldn't—after all, the finish is the win or the lose of a race.'

The letter went down on the table again, but this time her head went down with it to rest upon it above her clasped hands. Oh! the pity of it! the pity of it! Yet how could she have avoided standing aloof from this man's life as she had done from the moment she had discovered she did not love him?

Suddenly she stood up, pressing those clasped hands tight to her forehead as if to hold in her thoughts. The sunlight, streaming in, shone right into her cool grey eyes showing in a ray on the iris, as if it were passing into her very soul.

If she had been this man's sister, instead of his wife, could she not have lived with him contentedly enough, palliating what could be palliated, gaining what influence she could with him, giving him affection and sympathy? Why, briefly, had she failed to make him what Alice Gissing had made him—a better man? And yet Alice Gissing did not love him; she had no romantic sentiment about him. Did she really lay less stress—she, the woman at whom other women held up pious hands of horror—on that elemental difference between the tie of husband and wife and brother and sister than she, Kate Erlton did, who had affected to rise superior to it altogether? It seemed so. She had asked for a purely selfish gratification of the mind. And Alice Gissing? A strange jealousy came to her with the thought, not for herself, but for her husband—for the man who was content to give up everything for a woman whom he 'loved very dearly'. That was true. Kate had watched him for those three months, and she had watched Mrs Gissing too, and knew for a certainty the latter gave him nothing any woman might not have given him if she had been content to put her own claims for happiness, her own gratification, her own mental passion aside. So a quick resolve came to her. He must not give up the finish, the win or the lose of the race, for so little. There was time yet for the chance. She had pleaded for one with a man a year ago; she would plead for it with a woman to-day.

She passed into the verandah hastily, pausing involuntarily ere getting into the dog cart, before the still, sunlit beauty of that panorama of the eastern plains, stretching away behind the gardens which fringed the shining curves of the river. There was scarcely a shadow anywhere, not a sign to tell that three miles down that river the man with whom she had pleaded a year ago was straining every nerve to give her and himself a chance, and that within the rose-lit, lilac-shaded city, the chance of some had come and gone.

Nor, as she drove along the road intent on that coming interview in the hot little house upon the wall, was there any sign to warn her of danger. The Kashmir gate stood open, and the guard saluted as usual. Perhaps, had the English officers seen her, they might have advised her return, even though there was as yet no anticipation of danger—had there been one, the first thought would have been to clear the neighbouring bungalows. But they were in the main-guard, and she set down the stare of the natives to the fact that nine o'clock was unusually late for an English lady to be braving the May sun. The road beyond was also unusually deserted, but she was too busy searching for the winged words, barbed well, yet not too swift or sharp to wound beyond possibility of compromise, which she meant to use ere long, to pay any attention to her surroundings. She did not even catch the glimpse of Sonny, still playing with the cockatoo, as she sped past the Seymours' house, and she scarcely noticed the groom's '*Hut! teri, hut!*' (Out of the way! you there!) to a figure in a green turban, over which she nearly ran, as it came sneaking round a corner as if looking for something or some one; a figure which paused to look after her half-doubtfully.

Yet these same words, which came so readily to her imaginings, failed her, as set words will, before the commonplace matter-of-fact reality. If she could have jumped from the dog cart and dashed into them without preamble, she would have been eloquent enough; but the necessary inquiry if Mrs Gissing could see her, the ushering in as for an ordinary visit, the brief waiting, the perfunctory hand shake with the little figure in familiar white-and-blue were so far from the high-strung appeal in her thoughts that they left her silent, almost shy.

'Find a comfy chair, do,' came the high, hard voice. 'Isn't it dreadfully hot? My old Mai will have it something is going to happen. She had been *dikking* me about it all the morning. An earthquake, I suppose; it feels like it, rather. Don't you think so?'

Kate felt as if one had come already, as, quite automatically, she satisfied Alice Gissing's choice of 'a really—really comfy chair'.

How dizzily unreal it seemed! And yet not more so, in fact, than the life they had been leading for months past; knowing the truth about each other absolutely; pretending to know nothing. Well! the sooner that sort of thing came to an end, the better!

'I have had a letter from my husband,' she began, but had to pause to steady her voice.

'So I supposed, when I saw you,' replied Alice Gissing, without a quiver in hers. But she rose, crossed over to Kate, and stood before her, like a naughty child, her hands behind her back. She looked strangely young, strangely innocent in the dim light of the sunshaded room. So young, so small, so slight among the endless frills and laces of a loose morning wrapper. And she spoke like a child also, querulously, petulantly.

'I like you the better for coming, too, though I don't see what possible good it can do. He said in his letter to me he would tell you all about it, and if he has, I don't see what else there is to say, do you?'

Kate rose also, as if to come nearer to her adversary, and so the two women stood, looking boldly enough into each other's eyes. But the keenness, the passion, the pity of the scene had somehow gone out of it for Kate Erlton. Her tongue seemed tied by the tameness; she felt that they might have been discussing a trivial detail in some trivial future. Yet she fought against the feeling.

'I think there is a great deal to say; that is why I have come to say it,' she replied, after a pause. 'But I can say it quickly. You don't love my husband, Alice Gissing, let him go. Don't ruin his life.'

Bald and crude as this was in comparison with her imagined appeal, it gave the gist of it, and Kate watched her hearer's face anxiously, to see the effect. Was that by chance a faint smile? or was it only the barred light from the jalousies hitting the wide blue eyes?

'Love!' echoed Alice Gissing. 'I don't know anything about love. I never pretended to. But I can make him happy; you never did.'

There was not a trace of malice in the high voice. It simply stated a fact; but a fact so true that Kate's lip quivered.

'I know that as well as you do. But I think I could—now. I want you to give me the chance.'

She had not meant to put it so humbly; but, being once more the gist of what she had intended to say, it must pass. There was no doubt about the smile now. It was almost a laugh—that hateful, inconsequent laugh; but as if to soften its effect, a little jewelled hand hovered out as if it sought a resting-place on Kate's arm.

'You can't, my dear. It *is* so funny that you can't see that, when I, who know nothing about—about all that—can see it quite plainly. You are the sort of woman, Mrs Erlton, who falls in love—who must fall in love—who—don't be angry!—likes being in love, and is unhappy if she isn't. Now I don't care a rap for people to be thinking, and thinking, and thinking of me, nothing but me! I like them to be pleasant and pleased. And I make them so, somehow—' She shrugged her shoulders whimsically as if to dismiss the puzzle, and went on gravely, 'And you can't make people happy if you aren't happy yourself, you know, so there is no use in thinking you could.'

It was bitter truth, but Kate was too honest to deny it. There had always been the sense of grievance in the past, and the sense of self-sacrifice, at least, would remain in the future.

'But there are other considerations,' she began slowly. 'A man does not set such store by—by love and marriage as a woman. It is only a bit—'

—'A very small bit'—put in Mrs Gissing, with a whimsical face.

'A very small bit of his life,' continued Kate stolidly, 'and if my husband gives up his profession—'

Mrs Gissing interrupted her again; this time petulantly. 'I told him it was a pity—I offered to go away anywhere. I did, indeed! And I couldn't do more, could I? But when a man gets a notion of honour into his head—'

'Honour!' interrupted Kate in her turn, 'the less said about honour the better, surely, between you and me!'

The wide blue eyes looked at her doubtfully.

'I never can understand women like you,' said their owner. 'You pretend not to care, and then you make so much fuss over so little.'

'So little!' retorted Kate, her temper rising. 'Is it little that my boy should have to know this about his father?—about me?—You have no children, Mrs Gissing! If you had you would understand the shame better—Oh! I know about the baby and the flowers—who doesn't? But that is nothing. It was so long ago, it died so young, you have forgotten—'

She broke off before the expression on the face before her—that face with the shadowless eyes, but with deep shadows beneath the eyes and a nameless look of physical strain and stress upon it—and a sudden pallor came to her own cheek.

'So he hasn't told you,' came the high voice half-fretfully, half-pitifully. 'That was very mean of him; but I thought, somehow, he couldn't, by your coming here. Well! I suppose I must. Mrs Erlton—'

Kate stepped back from her defiantly, angrily. 'He has told me all I need, all I care to know about this miserable business. Yes! he has! You can see the letter if you like—there it is! I am not ashamed of it. It is a good letter, better than I thought he could write—better than you deserve. For he says he will marry you if I will let him! And he says he is sorry it can't be helped. But I deny that. It can, it must, it shall be helped! And when he says it is a pity for the boy's sake; but that it does not matter so much as if it was a girl—'

It was the queerest sound which broke in on those passionate reproaches. The queerest sound. Neither a laugh nor a sob, nor a cry;

but something compounded of all three, infinitely soft, infinitely tender.

'*And the other may be*,' said Alice Gissing in a voice of smiles and tears, as she pointed to the end of the sentence in the letter Kate had thrust upon her. 'Poor dear! What a way to put it! How like a man to think you could understand; and I wonder what the old Mai *would* say to its being—'

What did she say? What were the frantic words which broke from the frantic figure, its sparse grey hair showing, its shrivelled bosom heaving unveiled, which burst into the room and flung its arms round that little be-frilled white one as if to protect and shield it?

Kate Erlton gave a half-choked, half-sobbing cry. Even this seemed a relief from the incredible horror of what had dawned upon her, frightening her by the wild insensate jealousy it roused—the jealousy of motherhood.

'What is it? What does she say?' she cried passionately, 'I have a right to know!'

Alice Gissing looked at her with a faint wonder. 'It is nothing about *that*,' she said, and her face, though it had whitened, showed no fear. 'It's something more important. There has been a row in the city—the Commissioner and some other Englishmen have been killed, and she says we are not safe. I don't quite understand. Oh! don't be a fool, Mai!' she went on in Hindustani, 'I won't excite myself. I never do. Don't be a fool I say!' Her foot came down almost savagely and she turned to Kate. 'If you will wait here for a second, Mrs Erlton, I'll go outside with the Mai and have a look round, and bring my husband's pistol from the other room. You had better stay, really. I shall be back in a moment. And I daresay it's all the old Mai's nonsense—she is such a fool about me—nowadays.' Her white face, smiling over its own certainty of coming trouble, was gone, and the door closed, almost before Kate could say a word. Not that she had any to say. She was too dazed to think of danger to the little figure, which passed out into the shady back verandah perched on the city wall, looking out into the peaceful country beyond. She was too absorbed in what she had just realized to think of anything else. So this was what he had meant!— and this woman with her facile nature ready to please and be pleased with any one—this woman content to take the lowest place—had the highest of all claims upon him. This woman who had no right to motherhood, who did not know—

God in Heaven! What was that through the stillness and the peace? A child's pitiful scream. . . .

She was at the closed windows in an instant, peering through the slits of the jalousies; but there was nothing to be seen save a blare and blaze of sunlight on sun-scorched grass and sun-withered beds of flowers. Nothing!—stay!—Christ help us! What was that? A vision of white, and gold, and blue! White garments and white wings, golden curls and flaming golden crest, fierce grey-blue beak and claws among the fluttering blue ribbons—Sonny! His little feet flying and failing fast among the flower-beds. Sonny! still holding his favourite's chain in the unconscious grip of terror, while half-dragged, half-flying, the wide white wings fluttered over the child's head.

'*Deen! Deen! Futteh Mahomed!*'

That was from the bird terrified, yet still gentle.

'*Deen! Deen! Futteh Mahomed!*'

That was from the old man who followed fast on the child with long lance in rest like a pig-sticker's. An old man in a faded green turban with a spiritual relentless face.

Kate's fingers were at the bolts of the high French window—her only chance of speedy exit from that closed room. Ah! would they never yield?—And the lance was gaining on those poor little flying feet. Every atom of motherhood in her—fierce, instinctive, animal, fought with those unyielding bolts. . . .

What was that? Another vision of white, and gold, and blue, dashing into the sunlight with something in a little clenched right hand; childish itself in frills, and laces, and ribbons, but with a face as relentless as the old man's, as spiritual. And a clear confident voice rang above those discordant cries.

'All right, Sonny! All right, dear!'

On it went, swift and straight in the sunlight; and then came a pause to level the clenched right hand over the left arm coolly, and fire. The lance wavered. It was two feet further from that soft flesh and blood when Alice Gissing caught the child up, turned, and ran—ran for dear life to shelter.

'*Deen! Deen! Futteh Mahomed!*'

The cry came after the woman and child, and over them, released by Sonny's wild clutch at sheltering arms, the bird fluttered echoing the cry.

But one bolt was down at last, the next yielding. . . . Ah! who was that dressed like a native, riding like an Englishman, who leapt the high garden fence and was over among the flower-beds where Sonny was being chased? Was he friend or foe? No matter! since under her vehement hands the bolt had fallen, and Kate was out in the verandah. Too late! The flying sunlit vision of white and gold and blue had tripped and fallen. No! not too late. The report of a revolver rang out, and the cry of faith came only from the bird, for the fierce relentless face was hidden among the laces, and frills, and ribbons that hid the withered flowers.

But the lance? The lance whose perilous nearness had made that shot Jim Douglas's only chance of keeping his promise? He was on his knees on the scorched grass choking down the curse which rose as he saw a broken shaft among the frills and ribbons, a slow stream oozing in gushes to dye them crimson. There was another crimson spot, too, on the shoulder showing where a bullet, after crashing through a man's temples, had found its spent resting place. But as the Englishman kicked away one body, and raised the other tenderly from the unhurt child, so as not to stir that broken shaft, he wished that if death had had to come, he might have dealt it. To his wild rage, his insane hatred, there seemed a desecration even in that cold touch of steel from a dark hand.

But Alice Gissing resented nothing. She lay propped by his arms with those wide blue eyes still wide, yet sightless, heedless of Kate's horrified whispers, or the poor old Mai's frantic whimper. Until suddenly a piteous little wail rose from the half-stunned child to mingle with that ceaseless iteration of grief. 'Oh! meri buchchi murgyia!' (Oh, my girlie is dead!—Dead!)

It seemed to bring her back, and a smile showed on the fast-paling face.

'Don't be a fool, Mai. It isn't a girl; it's a boy. Take care of him, do, and don't be stupid. I'm all right.'

Her voice was strong enough, and Kate looked at Jim Douglas hopefully—she had recognized him at once, despite his dress, with a faint dead wonder as to why things were so strange to-day. But he could feel something oozing wet and warm over his supporting arm, and he knew the meaning of that whitening face; so he shook his head hopelessly, his eyes on those wide unseeing ones. She was as still, he thought, as she had been when he held her before. Then suddenly the eyes narrowed into sight, and looked him in the face curiously, clearly.

'It's you, is it?' came the old inconsequent laugh. 'Why don't you say Bravo!—Bravo!—Bra—'

The crimson rush of blood from her still-smiling lips, dyed his hands also, as he caught her up recklessly with a swift order to the others to follow, and ran for the house. But as he ran, clasping her close, close, to him, his whispered bravos assailed her dead ears passionately, and when he laid her on her bed, he paused even in the mad tumult of his rage, his anxiety, his hope for others, to kiss the palms of those brave hands ere he folded them decently on her breast, and was out to fetch his horse, and return to where Kate waited for him in the verandah, the child in her arms. Brave also; but the certainty that he had left the flood-level of sympathy and admiration behind him at the feet of a dead woman he had never known, was with him even in his hurry.

'I can't see any one else about as yet,' he said, as he reloaded hastily, 'and but for that fiend—that devil of a bird hounding him on—what did it mean?—not that it matters now'—he threw his hand out in a gesture .... impotent regret and turned to mount.

Kate shivered. What, indeed, did it mean? A vague recollection was adding to her horror. Had she driven away once from an incomprehensible appeal in that relentless face? when the bird—'

'Don't think, please,' said Jim Douglas, pausing to give her a sharp glance. 'You will need all your nerve. The troops mutinied at Meerut last night, and killed a lot of people. They have come on here, and I don't trust the native regiments. Go inside, and shut the door. I must reconnoitre a bit before we start.'

'But my husband?' she cried, and her tone made him remember the strangeness of finding her in that house. She looked unreliable, to his keen eye; the bitter truth might make her rigid, callous, and in such callousness lay their only chance.

'All right. He asked me to look after—her.'

He saw her waver, then pull herself together; but he saw also that her clasp on Sonny tightened convulsively, and he held out his arms.

'Hand the child to me for a moment,' he said briefly, 'and call that poor lady's ayah from her wailing.'

The piteous whimperings from the darkened rooms within ceased reluctantly. The old woman came with lagging step into the verandah, but Jim Douglas called to her in the most matter-of-fact voice.

'Here, Mai! Take your *mem*'s charge. She told you to take care of the boy, remember.' The tear-dim doubtful eyes looked at him half-resentfully, as he went on coolly: 'Now, Sonny, go to your ayah, and be a good boy. Hold out your arms to old ayah, who had had ever so many Sonnys—haven't you, ayah?'

The child, glad to escape from the prancing horse, the purposely rough arms, held out its little dimpled hands. They seemed to draw the hesitating old feet, step by step, till with a sudden fierce snatch, a wild embrace, the old arms closed round the child with a croon of content.

Jim Douglas breathed more freely. 'Now, Mrs Erlton,' he said, 'I can't make you promise to leave Sonny there; but he is safer with her than he could be with you. She must have friends in the city. You haven't *one*.'

He was off as he spoke, leaving her to that knowledge. Not a friend! No! not one. Still, he need not have told her so, she thought proudly, as she passed in and closed the doors as she had been bidden to do. But he had succeeded. A certain fierce dull resistance had replaced her emotion. So while the ayah, still carrying Sonny, returned to her dead mistress, Kate remained in the drawing-room, feeling stunned; too stunned to think of anything save those last words. Not a friend! Not one, saving a few cringing shop keepers, in all that wide city to whom she had ever spoken a word! Whose fault was that? Whose fault was it that she had not understood that appeal?—

A rattle of musketry quite close at hand roused her from apathy into fear for the child, and she passed rapidly into the next room. It was empty, save for that figure on the bed. The ayah with her charge had gone, closing the doors behind her; to her friends no doubt. But she, Kate Erlton, had none. The renewed rattle of musketry sent her to peer through the jalousies; but she could see nothing. The sound seemed to come from the open space by the church, but gardens lay between her and that, blocking the view. Still it was quite close; seemed closer than it had been. No doubt it would come closer and closer till it found her waiting there, without a friend. Well! Since she was not even capable of saving Sonny, she could at least do what she was told—she could at least die alone.

No! not quite alone! She turned back to the bed and looked down on the slender figure lying there as if asleep—for the ayah's vain hopes of lingering life had left the face unstained, and the folded hands hid the crimson below them. Asleep, not dead; for the face had no look of rest. It was the face of one who dreams still of the stress and strain of coming life.

So this was to be her companion in death; this woman who had done her the greatest wrong—What wrong? The question came dully. What wrong had she done to one who refused to admit the claims or rights of passion? What had she stolen, this woman who had not cared at all? Whose mind had been unsullied utterly? Only motherhood; and that was given to saint and sinner alike; and given rightly here, for those little hands were brave mother-hands. Kate put out hers softly and touched them. Still warm, still life-like, their companionship thrilled her through and through. With a faint sob, she sank on her knees beside the bed and laid her cheek on them. Let death come and find her there! Let the finish of the race, which was the win and the lose—

'Mrs Erlton! quick, please!'

Jim Douglas's voice calling to her from outside roused her from a sort of apathy into sudden desire for life; she was out in the verandah in a second.

'The game's up,' he said, scarcely able to speak from breathlessness, and his horse was in a white lather. 'I had to see to the Seymours first, and now there's only one chance I can think of—desperate at that.

Quick, your foot on mine—so—from the step—Now your hand. One! two! three! That's right.'

He had her on the saddle before him and was off through the gardens citywards at a gallop. 'The 54th came down from the cantonments all right,' he went on rapidly, 'but shot their officers at the church—the city scoundrels are killing and looting all about, but the main-guard is closed and safe as yet. I got Mrs Seymour there. I'll get you if I can. I'm going to ride through the thick of the devils now with you as my prisoner—do you see?—there at the turn. I'll hark back down the road—it's the only chance of getting through. Slip down a bit across the saddle bow. Don't be afraid. I'll hold as long as I can. Now scream—scream like the devil. No! let your arms slack as if you'd fainted—people won't look so much—that's better—that's capital— now—ready!' . . . .

He swerved his horse with a dig of the spur and made for the crowd which lay between him and safety. The words, describing the rape of the Sabine women, over the construing of which he remembered being birched at school recurred to him, as such idle thoughts will at such times, as he hitched his hand tighter on Kate's dress and scattered the first group with a coarse jest or two. Thank Heaven! she would not understand these, his only weapons, since cold steel could not be used, till it had to be used to *prevent* her understanding. Thank Heaven too! he could use both weapons fairly. So he dug in the spurs again and answered the crowd in its own kind, recklessly; a laugh, an oath, once or twice a blow with the flat of his sword. And Kate, with slack arms and closed eyes, lay and listened— listened to a sharper, angrier voice, a quick clash of steel, a shout of half-doubtful, half-pleased derision from those near, a jest, provoking a roar of merriment for one who meant to hold his own in love and war. Then there was a sudden bound of the horse; a faint slackening of that iron grip on her waist-belt. The worst of the stream was past; another moment and they were in a quiet street, another, and they had turned at right-angles down a secluded alley where Jim Douglas paused to pass his right hand, still holding his sword, under Kate's head and bid her lean against him more comfortably. The rest was easy. He would take her out by the Moree gate—the alleys to it would be almost deserted—so, outside the walls, to the rear of the Kashmir gate. They were already twisting and turning through the narrow lanes as he told her this. Then, with a rush and a whoop, he made for the gate, and the next moment they had the open country, the world, before them. How still and peaceful it lay in the sunshine! But the main-guard was the nearest, safest shelter, and so the galloping hoofs sped down the tree-set road along which Kate generally took her evening drive.

'And you?' she asked hurriedly as he set her down at the moat and bade her run for the wicket and knock, while he kept the drawbridge.

He shook his head. 'The reliefs from Meerut must be in soon. If they started at dawn, in an hour. Besides I'm off to the palace to see what has really happened; information's everything.'

She saw him turn, with a wave of his sword for farewell, as the wicket was opened cautiously, and then make for the Moree gate once more. As he rode he told himself there should be no further cause for anxiety on her account. De Tessier's guns were in the main-guard now, and reinforcements of the loyal 74th. They could hold their own easily till the Meerut people smashed up the palace. They could not be long now, and the city had not risen as yet. The bigger bazaars through which he cantered were almost deserted—every one had gone home. But at the entrance to an alley a group of boys clustered, and one ran out to him crying, 'Khân-*sahib*! What's the matter? Folk say people are being killed, but we want to go to school.'

'Don't,' said Jim Douglas as he passed on. He had seen the schoolmaster, stripped naked, lying on his back in the broad daylight as he galloped along the college road with Kate over his saddle-bow.

'*Ari*, brothers,' reported the spokesman. 'He said "*don't*" but he can know naught. He comes from outside. And we shall lose places in class if we stop, and others go.'

So in the cheerful daylight the school boys discussed the problem, school or no school; the Great Revolt had got no further than that—*as yet*.

But there was no cloud of dust upon the Meerut road, though straining eyes thought they saw one more than once.

# 4

# Noon

B ut if the schoolmaster of one school lay dead in the sunlight there was another, well able to teach a useful lesson, left alive; and his school remains for all time as a place where men may learn what men can do.

For about three hundred yards from the deserted college, about six from the main-guard of the Kashmir gate stood the magazine, to which the two young Englishmen, followed by a burlier one, had walked back quietly after one of them had remarked that he could hold his own; since there were gates to be barred, four walls to be seen to, and various other preparations to be made before the nine men who formed the garrison could be certain of thus holding their own. And their own meant much to others; for with the stores and the munitions of war safe, the city might rise, but it would be unarmed; but with *them* at the mercy of the rabble, every pitiful pillager could become a recruit to the disloyal regiments.

'The mine's about finished now, sir,' said Conductor Buckley, saluting gravely as he looked critically down a line ending in the powder magazine. 'And, askin' your pardon, sir, mightn't it be as well to settle a signal beforehand, sir; in case it's wanted? And, if you have no objection, sir, here's Sergeant Scully here, sir, saying he would look on it as a kind favour—'

A man with a spade glanced up a trifle anxiously for the answer as he went on with his work.

'All right! Scully shall fire it. If you finish it there in the middle by that little lemon tree, we shan't forget the exact spot. Scully must see to having the portfire ready for himself. I'll give the word to you, as your gun will be near mine, and you can pass it on by raising your cap. That will do, I think.'

'Nicely, sir,' said Conductor Buckley, saluting again.

'I wish we had one more man,' remarked the Head-of-the-nine, as he paused in passing a gun to look to something in its gear with swift professional eye. 'I don't quite see how the nine of us are to work the ten guns.'

'Oh! we'll manage somehow,' said his second in command, 'the native establishment—perhaps—'

George Willoughby, the Head-of-the-nine, looked at the sullen group of dark faces lounging distrustfully within those barred doors, and his own face grew stern. Well, if they would not work, they should at least stay and look on—stay till the end. Then he took out his watch.

'Twelve! The Meerut troops will be in soon—if they started at dawn—' there was the finest inflection of scorn in his voice.

'They must have started,' began his companion. But the tall figure with the grave young face was straining its eyes from the bastion they were passing; it gave upon the Bridge-of-boats and the lessening white streak of road. He was looking for a cloud of dust upon it; but there was none.

'I hope so,' he remarked as he went on. He gave a half-involuntary glance back, however, to the stunted lemon bush. There was a black streak by it, which might be relied upon to give aid at dawn, or dusk, or noon; high noon as it was now.

The chime of it echoed methodically as ever from the main-guard, making a cheerful young voice in the officer's room say, 'Well! the enemy is passing, anyhow. The reliefs can't be long—if they started at dawn.'

'If they had started when they ought to have started, they would have been here hours ago,' said an older man, almost petulantly, as he rose and wandered to the door, to stand looking out on the baking court where his men—the two companies of the 54th, who had come down under his charge after these under Colonel Ripley had shot down their officers by the church—were lounging about sullenly. These men might have shot him, also, but for the timely arrival of the two guns? might have shot at him, even now, but for those loyal 74th overawing them. He turned and looked at some of the latter with a sort of envy. These men had come forward in a body when the regiment was called upon by its commandant to give honest volunteers to keep order in the city. What had they had, which his men had lacked? Nothing that he knew of. And then, inevitably, he thought of his six murdered friends and comrades, officers apparently as popular as he, whose bodies were lying in the next room waiting for a cart to remove them to the Ridge; for even Major Paterson saddened, depressed as he was, looked forward to decent sepulture for his comrades by-and-by—by-and-by when the Meerut troops should arrive. And the half-dozen or more of women upstairs were comforting each other with the same hope, and crushing down the cry that it seemed an eternity, already, since they had waited for that little cloud of dust upon the Meerut road—but for the hope of which they might have gone Meerut-wards themselves; for the country was peaceful.

Even in Duryagunj, though by noon it was a charnel-house, the score or so of men who kept cowards at bay in a miserable store-house comforted themselves with the same thought; and women with the long languid eyes of one race, looked out of them with the temper and fire of the other, saying in soft staccato voices—'It will not-be long now. They will be here soon, for they would start at dawn.'

'They will come soon,' said a young telegraph clerk coolly, as he stood by his instrument hoping for a welcome *kling* of the bell; and sending, finally, that bulletin northwards which ended with the reluctant admission 'we must shut up.' Must indeed; seeing that some ruffians rushed in and sabred him with his hands still on the levers.

'They will be here soon,' agreed the compositors of the *Delhi Gazette* as they worked at the strangest piece of printing the world is ever likely to see. That famous Extra, wedged in between English election news, which told in bald journalese of a crisis, which became the crisis of their own lives before the whole edition was sent out.

But down in the palace Zeenut Maihl had been watching that white streak of road also, and as the hours passed, her wild impatience would let her watch it no longer. She paced up and down the queen's bastion like a caged tigress, leaving Hafzân to take her place at the lattice. No sign of an avenging army yet! Then the troopers' tale must be true! The hour of decisive action had come, it was slipping past, the king was in the hands of Ahsan-Oolah and Elahi Buksh—whose face was set both ways like the physician's. And she, helpless, half in disgrace, caged, veiled, screened, unable to lay hands on any one! Oh! why was she not a man? Why had she not a man to deal with? Her henna-stained nails bit into her palms as she clenched her hands, then in sheer childish passion tore off her hampering veil and rolling it into a ball flung it at the head of a drowsy eunuch in the outside arcade—the nearest thing to a man within her reach.

'No sign yet, Hafzân?' she asked fiercely.

'No sign, my Queen,' replied Hafzân with an odd derisive smile. If they did not come now, thought this woman with her warped nature, they would come later on; come and put a rope round the necks of men who had laid violent hands on women.

'Then I stop here no longer,' cried Zeenut Maihl recklessly; 'I must see somewhat of it or die. Quick, girls, my dhooli, I will go back to my own rooms. 'Twill at least bear me through the crowd, and the jogging will keep the blood from tingling from very stillness.'

So through the tawdry, dirty, musky curtains a woman's fierce eye watched the crowd hungrily, as the dhooli swung through it. It was a fierce crowd in its way, but it lacked cohesion. Like the world without those four rose-red walls, it was waiting for a Master. And the man who should have been master was taking cooling draughts, and composing couplets, so her spies brought word. There was no hope from him till she could lure him back from his vexation, and put some of her own energy into him. Who next was there, likely to do her bidding? Her eye, taking in all the strangeness of the scene—troopers stabling their horses in the colonnades—sepoys bivouacking under the trees—courtiers hurrying up and down the private steps, found none in all that crowd of place-hunters, boasters, enthusiasts, whom she could trust. The King's eldest son Mirza Moghul was the fiercest-tempered of them all, the only one whom she feared in any way; perhaps if she could get hold of him—?

As her dhooli swayed up the steps he was standing on them talking to Mirza Khair Sultan. She could have put out her hand and touched him; but even she did not dare convention enough for that. Nevertheless, the sight of him determined her. If the King did not come back to her by noon, she must lure the Mirza to her side.

'Thou art a fool, *Pir-jee*,' she said petulantly to Hussan Askuri, who, as father confessor, had entrance to the women's rooms, and was awaiting her. 'Thou hast no grip on the King when I am absent. Canst not even drive that slithering physician from his side?'

'Cooling draughts, seest thou, *Pir-jee*,' put in Hafzân maliciously, 'have tangible effects. Thy dreams—'

'Peace, woman!' interrupted the Queen sternly, "tis no time for jesting. Where sits the King now?'

'In the river balcony, Ornament-of-palaces,' replied Fâtma glibly, 'where he is not to be disturbed these two hours, so the physician says, lest the cooling draught—'

The Queen stamped her foot in sheer impotent rage.

'I must see some one! And Jewan Bukht my son? why hath he not answered my summons?'

'His Highness,' put in Hafzân gravely, 'was, as I came by just now, quarrelling in his cups with his nephew, the princely Abool-Bukr, regarding the Inspectorship-of-Cavalry; which office both desire—a weighty matter—'

'Peace! she-devil!' almost screamed the Queen. 'Can I not see, can I not hear for myself, that thy sharp wits must for ever drag the rotten heart to light? thou wilt go too far, some day, Hafzân, and then—'

'The Queen will have to find another scribe,' replied Hafzân meekly.

Zeenut Maihl glared at her, then rolled round into her cushions as if she were in actual physical pain. And hark! from the Lahore gate, as if nothing had happened, came the chime of noon. Noon! and nothing done. She sat up suddenly and signed to Hafzân for pen and ink. She would wait no longer for the King; she would at least try the Mirza.

'*This, to the most illustrious the Mirza Moghul, Heir-Apparent by right to the throne of Timoor,*'[1] she dictated firmly, and Hafzân looked up startled. 'Write on, fool,' she continued, 'hast never written lies before? *After salutation the Begum Zeenut Maihl—*' the humbler title came from her lips in a tone which boded ill for the recipient of the letter if he fell into the toils—'*seeing that in this hour of importance the King is sick, and by order of physicians not to be disturbed, would know if the Mirza, being by natural right the King's viceregent, desires the private seal to any orders necessary for peace and protection. Such signet being in the hands of the Queen—*' nay not that, I was forgetting—'*the Begum.*'

She gave an angry laugh as she lay back among her cushions and bid them send the letter forthwith. That should make him nibble. Not that she had the signet—the King kept that on his own finger; but if the Mirza came on pretence, or rather in hopes of getting it?—Why!

---

[1]There is no actual warranty for this letter; but it is certain that Zeenut Maihl made use of the signet several times.

then; if the proper order was given, and if she could ensure the aid of men to carry out her schemes, the signet should be got at somehow. The King was old and frail; the storm and stress might well kill him.

So her thoughts ranged from one plot to another as she waited for an answer. If this lure succeeded, she would but use the Heir-Apparent for a time. What use was there in plotting for him? He could die, as other heirs had died; and then the only person likely to put a spoke in her wheel was Abool-Bukr. He was teaching his young uncle the first pleasures of manhood, and might find it convenient to influence the boy against her. It would be well therefore to get hold of him also. That was not a hard task, and she sat up again without a moment's hesitation, and signed once more to Hafzân.

'Thy best flourishes,' she said with an evil sneer, 'for it goes to a rare scholar; to a fool for all that, who would have folk think nephews visit their aunts from duty! *"This to Newâsi loving and beloved, greeting. Consequent on the disturbances, the princely nephew Abool-Bukr lieth senseless here in the palace."*—Stare not, fool! senseless drunk he is by this time, I warrant—*"Those who have seen him think ill of him."'*—here she broke off into malicious enjoyment of her own wit—'Ay! and those who have but heard of him also! *"The course of events, however, being in the hands of heaven will be duly reported."*

She coiled herself up again on the cushions, an insignificant square homely figure draped in worn brocade and laden with tarnished jewelry—ill-matched strings of pearls, flawed emeralds, diamonds without sparkle. Yet not without a certain dignity, a certain symmetry of purpose, harmonizing with the arched and frescoed room in which she lay; a room beautiful in design and decoration, yet dirty, comfortless, almost squalid.

'Nay! not my, signature,' she yawned. 'I am too old a foe of the scholars; but a smudge o' the thumb will do. If I know aught of aunts and nephews, she will be too much flustered by the news to look at seals. And have word sent to the Delhi gate that the Princess Farkhoonda be admitted, but goes not forth again.'

Her hard voice ceased; there was no sound in the room save that strange hum from the gardens outside which at this hour of the day was generally wrapped in sun-drugged slumbers.

But the world beyond, towards which the old King's lustreless eyes looked as he lay on the river balcony, was sleepy, sun-drugged as ever. Through the tracery-set arches showed yellow stretches of sand and curving river, with tussocks of tall tiger-grass hiding the slender stems of the palm-trees which shot up here and there into the blue sky—blue with the yellow glaze upon it which comes from sheer sunlight. A row of *saringhi* players squatted in the room behind the balcony, thrumming softly, so as to hide that strange hum of life which reached even here. For the King was writing a couplet and was in difficulties with a rhyme for *cartouche* (cartridge); since he was a stickler for form, holding that the keynote of the lines should jingle. And this couplet was to epitomize the situation on the other side of the *saringhies*. *Cartouche? Cartouche?* Suddenly he sat up.

'Quick! send for Hussan Askuri; or stay!' he hesitated for an instant. Hussan Askuri would be with the Queen, and no one ever admired his couplets as she did. How many hours was it since he had seen her? And what was the use of making couplets, if you were denied their just meed of praise? 'Stay,' he repeated, 'I will go myself.'

It was a relief to feel himself on the way back to be led by the nose, and as they helped him across the intervening courtyard he kept repeating his treasure, imagining her face when she heard it.

> *Kuchch Chil-i-Room nahin kya, ya Shah-i-Roos, nahin*
> *Jo kuchch kya na sara se, so cartouche ne.*

A couplet, which, lingering still in the mouths of the people, warrants the old poetaster's conceit of it, and—dog-anglicized—runs thus—

> Nor Czar nor Sultan made the conquest easy,
> The only weapon was a cartridge greasy

'The Queen? Where is the Queen?' fumed the old man, when he found an empty room instead of instant flattery; for he was after all, the Great Moghul.

'She prays for the King's recovery,' said Fâtma readily. 'I will inform her that her prayer is granted.' But as she passed on her errand, she winked at a companion, who hid her giggle in her veil; for Grand Turk or not, the women hold all the trump cards in seclusion. So how was the old man to know that the one who came in radiant with exaggerated delight at his return, had been interviewing his eldest son behind decorous screens, and that she was thanking heaven piously for having sent him back to her apron-string in the very nick of time; sent him, and Hussan Askuri, and pen and ink, within reach of her quick wit.

'That is the best couplet my lord has done,' she said superbly. 'That must be signed and sealed.'

So must a paper be, which lay concealed in her bosom. And as she spoke she drew the signet ring lovingly, playfully from the King's finger and walked over to where the scribe sat crouched on the floor.

'Ink it well, *Pir-jee*,' she said, keeping her back to the King, 'the impression must be as immortal as the verse.'

Despite the warning, a very keen ear might have detected a double sound, as if the seal had needed a second pressure. That was all.

So it came about that, half an hour or so afterwards, the Head-of-the-nine at the magazine was looking contemptuously at a paper brought by the Palace Guards, and passed under the door, ordering its instant opening. George Willoughby laughed; but some of the Eight dashed people's impudence and cursed their cheek! Yet, after the laugh, the Head-of-the-nine walked over, yet another time, to that river bastion to look down at that white streak of road. How many times he had looked already, Heaven knows; but his grave face had grown graver, though it brightened again after a glance at the lemon bush. The black streak there would not fail them.

'In the King's name open!' The demand came from Mirza Moghul himself this time, for the Palace was without arms, without ammunition; and if they were to defend it according to the Queen's idea, against all comers till there was time for other regiments to rebel, this matter of the magazine was important. Abool-Bukr was with him, half-drunk, wholly incapable, but full of valour; for a scout sent by the Queen had returned with news that no English soldier was within ten miles of Delhi, and within the last half hour an ominous word had begun to pass from lip to lip in the city.

'*Helpless*!'

The masters were *helpless*. Past two o'clock and not a blow in revenge! *Helpless*! The word made cowards brave, and brave folk cowards. And many who had spent the long hours in peeping from their closed doors at each fresh clatter in the street, hoping it was the master, looked at each other with startled eyes.

*Helpless*! *Helpless*!

The echo of the thought reached the main-guard, still in touch with the outside world, whence, as the day dragged by, fresh tidings of danger drifted down from the Ridge where men, women, and children lay huddled helplessly in the Flagstaff Tower, watching the white streak of road. It seems like a bad dream, that hopeless, paralysing strain of the eyes for a cloud of dust.

But the echo won no way into the magazine, for the simple reason that it knew it was not helpless. It could hold its own.

'Shoot that man Kureem Buksh, please, Forrest, if he comes bothering round the gate again. He is really very annoying. I have told him several times to keep back; so it is no use his trying to give information to the people outside.'

For the Head-of-the-nine was very courteous. 'Scaling ladders?' he echoed, when a native superintendent told him that the princes, finding him obdurate, had gone to send some down from the palace. 'Oh! by all means let them scale if they like.'

Some of the Eight, hearing the reply, smiled grimly. By all means let the flies walk into the parlour; for if that straight streak of road was really going to remain empty, the fuller the four square walls round the lemon bush could be, the better.

'That's them sir,' said one of the Eight cheerfully, as a grating noise rose above the hum outside. 'That's the grapnels.' And as he turned to his particular gun of the ten, he told himself that he would nick the first head or two with his rifle and keep the grape for the bunches. So he smiled at his own little joke and waited. All the Nine waited, each to a gun, and of course there was one gun over, but, as the Head of them had said, that could not be helped. And so the rifle-triggers clicked, and the stocks came up to the shoulders; and then?—then there was a sort of laugh, and some one said under his breath, 'Well, I'm blowed!' And his mind went back to the streets of London, and he wondered how many years it was since he had seen a lamp-lighter. For up ropes and poles, on roofs and outhouses, somehow, clinging like limpets, running like squirrels along the top of the wall, upsetting the besiegers, monopolizing the ladders, was a rush, not of attack but of escape! Let what fool who liked scale the wall and come into the parlour of the Nine, those who knew the secret of the lemon-bust were off. No safety there beside the Nine! No life-insurance possible while that lay ready to their hand!

Would he ever see a lamplighter again? The trivial thought was with the bearded man who stood by his gun, the real self in him, hidden behind the reserve of courage, asking other questions too, as he waited for the upward rush of fugitives to change into a downward rush of foes worthy of good powder and shot.

It came at last—and the grape came too, mowing the intruders down in bunches. And these were no mere rabble of the city. They were the pick of the trained mutineers swarming over the wall to stand on the outhouse roofs and fire at the Nine; and so, pressed in gradually from behind, coming nearer and nearer, dropping to the ground in solid ranks, firing in platoons; thus by degrees hemming in the Nine, hemming in the lemon-bush.

But the Nine were busy with the guns. They had to be served quickly, and that left no time for thought. Then the smoke, and the flashes, and the yells, and the curses, filled up the rest of the world for the present.

'This is the last round, I'm afraid, sir; we shan't have time for another,' said a warning voice from the Nine, and the Head of them looked round quietly. The intruders were not more than forty yards now from the guns; there was barely time, certainly, unless they had had that other man! So he nodded, and the last round pealed out as recklessly, as defiantly, as if there had been a hundred to follow,—and a hundred thousand—a hundred million. But one of the gunners threw down his fuse ere his gun recoiled, and ran in lightly towards the lemon-tree, so as to be ready for the favour he had begged.

'We're about full up, sir,' came the warning voice again, as the rest of the Nine fell back amid a desultory rattle of small arms. The tinkle of the last church bell, as it were, warning folk to hurry up,—a last invitation to walk into the parlour of the Nine.

'We're about full up, sir,' came that one voice.

'Wait half a second,' came another, as the Head-of-the-nine ran to the river bastion for a last look down the white streak for that cloud of dust.

How sunny it was!—How clear!—How still!—That world beyond the smoke, beyond the flashes, beyond the deafening yells and curses. He gave one look at it, one short look—only one—then turned to face his own world, the world he had to keep. Full up indeed! No pyrotechnist could hope for better audience in so small a place.

'Now, if you please!'

Some one in the thick of the smoke and the flashes, the yells and the curses, heard and raised his cap—a last salute, as it were, to the school and the schoolmaster—a final dismissal to the scholars, a thousand of them or so, about to finish their lesson of what men can do to hold their own. And some one else, standing beside the lemon-bush, bent over that faithful black streak, then ran for dear life from the hissing of that snake of fire flashing to the powder magazine.

A faint sob, a whispering gasp of horror, came from the thousand and odd; but above it came a roar, a rush, a rending. A little puff of white smoke went skywards first, and then slowly, majestically, a great cloud of rose-red dust grew above the ruins, to hang—a corona glittering in the slant sunbeams—over the school, the schoolmasters, and the scholars.

It hung there for hours. To those who know the story it seems to hang there still,—a bloody pall for the many; for the Nine, a crown indeed.

# 5

## Sunset

'What's that?'

The question sprang to every lip; yet all knew the answer. The magazine had saved itself.

But in the main-guard, not six hundred yards off, where the very ground rocked and the walls shook, the men and women pent up since noon, looked at each other when the first shock was over, feeling that here was the end of inaction. Here was a distinct, definite challenge to Fate, and what would come of it? It was now close on four o'clock; the day was over, the darkness at hand. What would it bring them? If Meerut with its two thousand was so sore bested that it could not spare one man to Delhi, what could they, a mere handful, hope for— save annihilation?

Yet even Mrs Seymour only clasped her baby closer, and said nothing; for there was no lack of courage anywhere. And Kate, with another child in her arms, paused as she laid it down, asleep at last, upon an officer's coat, to feel a certain relief. If *they* were to fare thus, that bitter self-reproach and agonizing doubt for vanished Sonny was unavailing; his chance might well be better than theirs.

Well indeed! pent up as they were cheek-by-jowl with four hundred unstable sepoys, and with the ominously-rising hum of the unstable city on their unprotected rear. Up on the Flagstaff Tower crowning the extreme northern end of the Ridge, away from this hum, where Brigadier Graves had gathered together the remaining women and children, so as to guard them as best he could with such troops as he had remaining—many of them too unstable to be trusted city-wards— they were in better plight. For they had the open country round them; a country where folk could still go and come with fair chance of safety, since even the predatory tribes, always ready to take advantage of disorder, were still waiting to see what master the day would bring forth. And they had also the knowledge that something was being done, that they were not absolutely passive in the hands of Fate, after Dr Batson started in disguise to summon that aid from Meerut which would not come of itself. Above all, they had the decision, they had the power to act; while down in the main-guard they could but obey orders. Not that the Flagstaff Tower did much with this advantage; for it was paralysed by that straining of the eyes for a cloud of dust upon the Meerut road which was the damnation of Delhi. Yet even here that decisive roar, that corona of red dust brightening every instant as the sun dipped to the horizon, brought the conviction that something must be done at last. But what? Hampered by women and children, what could they do? If, earlier in the day, they had sent all the non-combatants off towards Kurnal or Meerut, with as many faithful sepoys as they could spare, arming everybody from the arsenal down by the river, they would have been free to make some forlorn hope— free, for instance, to go down *en masse* to the main-guard and hold it, if they could. That, even now, was what one man thought best, who, seven miles out from Delhi—returning from a reconnaissance of his own to see if help were on the way—saw that little puff of smoke, heard the roar, and watched the red corona grow to brightness.

But on the Ridge, men thought differently. The claims of those patient women and children seemed paramount, and so it was decided to get back the guns from the main-guard as a first step towards entrenching themselves for the night at the Tower. The men in the main-guard, however, looked at each other in doubt when the order reached them. Was the garrison going to be withdrawn altogether, leaving merely a forlorn hope to keep the gate closed as long as possible against the outburst of rabble, to whom it would be the natural and shortest route to cantonments? If so, surely it would have been better to send the women away first? Still the orders were clear, and so the gate was set wide and the guns rumbled over the drawbridge under escort of a guard of the 38th. That, at any rate, was good riddance of bad rubbish—though the wisdom of sending the guns in such charge was doubtful; yet how could the little garrison have afforded to give up even a single man of the still loyal 74th?—a company of whom had actually followed their captain to the ruins of the magazine to see if they could do anything, and returned, without a defaulter, to say that all was confusion—the dead lying about in hundreds, the enemy nowhere.

'How did the men behave, Gordon?' asked their commandant anxiously, getting his captain into a quiet corner. And the two men, both beloved of their regiment, both believing in it, both with a fierce wild hope in their hearts that such belief would be justified, looked into each other's faces for a moment in silence. There was a shadowing branch of *neem* overhead as they stood in the sunlight. A squirrel upon it was chippering at the glitter of their buckles; a kite overhead was watching the squirrel.

'I think they hesitated, sir,' said Captain Gordon quietly.

Major Abbott turned hastily, and looked through the open gate, past the lumbering guns, to the open country lying peaceful, absolutely peaceful, beyond. If he could only have got his men there—away from the disloyalty of the 38th guard, the sullen silence of the 54th—if he could only have given them something to do! If he could only have said 'Follow me!' they would have followed.

And Kate Erlton, who weary of the deadly inaction in the room above, had drifted down to the courtyard, stood close to the archway looking through it also, thinking, not for the first time that weary day, of Alice Gissing's swift, heroic death with envy. It was something to die so that brave men turned away without a word when they heard of it. But as she thought this, the look on young Mainwaring's face as he stood with others listening to her story, came back to her. It had haunted her all day, and more than once she had sought him out, not for condolence—he was beyond that—but for a trivial word or two; just a human word or two to show him remembered by the living. And now the impulse came to her again, and she drifted back—for there was no hurry in that deadly, deadly inaction—to find him leaning listlessly against a wall digging holes in the dry dust idly with the point of his drawn sword for want of something better whereon to use it. Such a young face, she thought, to be so old in its chill anger and despair. She went over to him swiftly, her reserve gone, and laid her hand upon his, holding the sword.

'Don't fret so, dear boy,' she said, and the fine curves of her mouth quivered. 'She is at peace.'

He looked at her in a blaze of fierce reproach. 'At peace! How dare you say so? How dare you think so—when she lies—there.'

He paused, impotent for speech before his unbridled hatred, then strode away indignantly from her pity, her consolation. And as she looked after him her own gentler nature was conscious of a pride, almost a pleasure in the thought of the revenge which would surely be taken sooner or later, by such as he, for every woman, every child killed, wounded—even touched. She was conscious of it, even though she stood aghast before a vision of the years stretching away into an æon of division and mutual hate.

A fresh stir at the gate roused her; a quick stir among a group of senior officers, recruited now by two juniors who had earned their right to have their say in any council of war. These were two artillery subalterns begrimed from head to foot, deafened, disfigured, hardly believing in their own safety as yet; looking at each other queerly, wondering if indeed they could be the Head-of-the-nine and his second in command, escaped by a miracle through the sally port in the outer wall of the magazine, and so come back by the drawbridge, as Kate Erlton had come, to join the refugees in the main-guard. Was it possible? And—and—what would the world say? That thought must have been in their minds. And, no doubt, a vain regret that they were under orders now, as they listened while Major Abbott read out those just received from cantonments. Briefly to take back the whole of the loyal 74th and leave the post to the 38th and the 54th—about a hundred and fifty openly disloyal men.

A sort of stunned silence fell on the little group, till Major Paterson of the 54th said quietly, officially, to Major Abbott. 'If you leave, sir, I shall have to abandon the post; I could not possibly hold it. Some of my men who have returned to the colours here might possibly fight were we to stick together. But with retreat, and the example of the 38th before them, they would not. I have, or I should have, lives in my charge when you are gone, and I warn you that I must use my own discretion in doing the best I can to protect them.'

'Paterson is right, Abbott,' put in the civil officer, who had stuck to his charge of the Treasury all day, and repelled the only attack made by the enemy during all those long hours. 'If I am to do any good, I must have men who will fight. I don't trust the 54th; and the 38th are clearly just biding their time. This retreat might have done six hours ago—might do now if it were general; but I doubt it.'

'Anyhow,' put in another voice, 'if the 74th are to go, they should take the women with them—they couldn't fare worse than they are sure to do here. I don't think the Brigadier can realize—'

'Couldn't you refer it?' asked some one; but the Major shook his head. The orders were clear—no doubt there was good cause for them—anyhow they must be obeyed.

'Then as civil officer in charge of the Government Treasury, I ask for quarter-of-an-hour's law. If by then—'

The eager voice paused. Whether the owner thought once more of that expected cloud of dust, or whether he meant to gallop to cantonments in hope of getting the order rescinded is doubtful. Whether he went or stayed doubtful also. But the fifteen minutes of respite were given, during which the preparations for departure went on, the men of the 38th aiding in them with a new alacrity. Their time had come. Only a few minutes now before the last fear of a hand-to-hand fight would be over, the last chance of the master turning and rending them gone. It lingered a bit, though, for rumbling wheels came over the drawbridge once more, and voices clamoured to be let in. The guns had returned. The gunners had deserted, said the escort insolently, and guns being in such case useless, they had preferred to rejoin their brethren; as for their officer, he had preferred to go on.

Kate Erlton, drawn from the inner room once again by the creaking of the gates, saw a look pass between one or two of the officers. And there stood the 74th, smart and steady, waiting for marching orders. There was no need to close the gates again, since time was up; the fifteen minutes had slipped by, bringing no help, just as the long hours had dragged by uselessly. So the gate stood open to the familiar, friendly landscape, all aglow with the rays of the setting sun. Close at hand, within a stone's throw, lay the tall trees and dense flowering thickets of the Koodsia gardens, where fugitives might have found cover. To the left were the ravines and rocks of the Ridge, fatal to mounted pursuit, and in the centre lay the road northwards, leading straight to the Punjâb, straight from that increasing roar of the city. There had been no attack as yet; but every soul within the main-guard knew for a certainty that the first hint of retreat would bring it.

How could it do otherwise? The decisive answer of the magazine, with its thousand-and-odd good reasons against the belief that the master was helpless, had died away. The refuse and rabble of the city had ceased to wander awestruck among the ruins, murmuring, 'What tyranny is here?'—that passive, resigned comment of the weaker brother in India. In the palace, too, they had recovered the shock of the mean trick of the Nine, who however must, thank Heaven, be all dead too.

So, as the gate stood open, and the sun streamed through it into the wide courtyard, glinting on the buckles and bayonets, Major Abbott's voice rose quietly. 'Are you ready, Gordon?' The drawbridge was clear of the guns now, clear of everything save the slant shadows.

'All ready, sir,' came the quiet reply.

'Number!' called the Commandant; but a voice at his right hand pleaded swiftly—'Don't wait for sections, *Huzoor!* Let us go!' and another at his left whispered, 'For God's sake, *Huzoor!* quick, get them out quick!'

Major Abbott hesitated a second, only a second; for the voices were the voices of good men and true, whom he could trust. 'Fours about! quick march!' he corrected, and a sort of sigh of relief ran down the regiment as it swung into position and the feet started rhythmically. Action at last!—At long last!

'Good bye, old chap,' said some one cheerfully, but Major Abbott did not turn. 'Good bye! Good bye!' came voices all round; steady quiet voices, as the disciplined tramp echoed on the drawbridge, and a bar of scarlet coats grew on the rise of the white road outside.

'Good bye, Gordon! Good bye!'

The tall figure in its red and gold was under the very arch, shining, glittering in the sunlight streaming through it. Another step or two and he would have been beyond it. But the time for goodbye had come. The time for which the 38th had been waiting all day. He threw up his arms and fell dead from his horse without a cry, shot through the

heart. The next instant the gate was closed, its creaking smothered in
the wild, senseless cry 'to kill, to kill, to kill,'—in a wild, senseless rattle
of musketry. For there was really no hurry; the handful of Englishmen
were helpless. Major Abbott and his men might clamour for re-entry at
the gate if they chose. They could not get in. Nor could the remnant of
the 74th, deprived of its loyal companions, and of the only two men
who seemed to have controlled it, do anything. The 54th were helpless
also by their own act; for they had pushed Major Paterson through the
gate before it closed.

So there was no one left even to try and stem the tide. No one to
check that beast-like cry.

'*Mâro! Mâro! Mâro!*'

But, in truth, it would have been a hopeless task. The game was up;
the only chance was flight. And two, foreseeing this for the last hour,
had already made good theirs by jumping from an embrasure in the
rampart into the ditch, while one, uninjured by the fall, had scrambled
up the counter-scarp, and was running like a hare for those same
thickets of the Koodsia.

'Come on! come on!' cried others, seeing their success. And then?—
And then the cries and piteous screams of women reminded them of
something dearer than life, and they ran back under a hail of bullets to
that upper room which they had forgotten for the moment. And
somehow, despite the cry of kill, despite the whistling bullets, they
managed to drag its inmates to the embrasure. But—oh! pathos and
bathos of poor humanity making smiles and tears come together!—The
women who had stared death in the face all day without a wink, stood
terrified before a twenty-feet scramble with a rope of belts and
handkerchiefs to help them. It needed a round shot to come whizzing
a message of certain death over their heads, to give them back a
courage which never failed again in the long days of wandering and
desperate need that were theirs ere some of them reached safety.

But Kate neither hesitated nor jumped. She had not the chance of
doing either. For that longing look of hers through the open gates had
tempted her to creep along the wall nearer to them; so that the rush to
close them jammed her into a corner against a door, which yielded
slightly to her weight. Quick enough to grasp her imminent danger,
she stooped instantly to see if the door could be made to yield further.
And that stoop saved her life, by hiding her from view behind the
crowd. The next moment she had pushed aside a log which had
evidently rolled from some pile within, and slipped sideways into a
dark outhouse. She was safe so far. But was it worth it? The impulse to
go out again and brave merciful death rose keen, until with a flash, the
memory of that escape through the crowd came back to her; she

seemed to hear the changing ready voice of the man who held her, to feel his quick instinctive grip on every chance of life.

Chance! There was a spell in the very word. A minute after logs jammed the door again, and even had it been set wide, none would have guessed that a woman full of courage, ay! and hope, crouched behind the piles of brushwood. So she lay hidden, her strongest emotion, strange to say, being a raging curiosity to know what had become of the others, what was passing outside? But she could hear nothing save confused yells, with every now and again a dominant cry of 'Deen Deen' or 'Jai Kali ma!' For faith is one of the two great passions which makes men militant. The other is sex. But as a rule it has no cry; it fights silently, giving and asking no words—only works.

So fought young Mainwaring, who, with his back to that same wall against which Kate had found him leaning, was using his sword to better purpose than digging holes in the dust; or rather had adopted a new method of doing the task! He had not tried to escape as the others had done; not from superior courage, but because he never even thought of it. When he was free to choose, how could he think of leaving those devils unpunished, leaving them unchecked to touch her dead body, while he lived? He gave a little faint sob of sheer satisfaction as he felt the first soft resistance, which meant that his sword had cut sheer into flesh and blood; for all his vigorous young life made for death, nothing but death. Was not she dead yonder?

So, after a bit, it seemed to him there was too little of it there—that it came too slowly, with his back to the wall and only those who cared to go for him within reach,—for the crowd was dense, too dense for loading and firing; dense with a hustling, horrified wonder, a confused prodding of bayonets. So, without a sound, he charged ahead, hacking, hewing, never pausing, not even making for freedom, but going for the thickest silently.

'Amuk! Saiya! A-muk.' The yell that he was mad, possessed, rang hideously as men tumbled over each other in their hurry to escape, in their hurry to have at this wild beast, this devil, this horror! And they were right. He was possessed. He was life instinct with death; fulfilled with but one desire—to kill, or to be killed quickly. . .

'Saiya! Amuk! Saiya!—Out of his way—out of his way! Amuk! Saiya! Fate is with him! The gods are with him! Saiya! Amuk!'

So, by chance, not method—so by sheer terror as well as hacking and hewing, the tall figure found itself, with but a stagger or two, outside the wooden gates, out on the city road, out among the gardens and the green trees. And then 'Hip, Hip, Hurray!' His ringing cheer rose with a sort of laugh in it. For yonder was her house!—Her house!

'Hip, hip, hurray!' As he ran—as he had run in races at school, his young face glad—the fingers on the triggers behind him wavered in sheer superstitious funk, and two troopers coming down the road wheeled back as from a mad dog. The scarlet coat with its gold epaulettes went crashing into a group red-handed with their spoil, out of it impartially into a knot of terrified bystanders, while down the lane left behind it by the hacking and hewing came bullet after bullet. The fingers on the triggers wavered, but some found a billet; one badly. He stumbled in the dust and his left arm fell oddly. But the right still hacked and hewed as he ran, though the crowd lessened; though it grew thin, too thin for his purpose—or else his sight was failing? But there, to the right, the devils seemed thicker again.

'Hip! hip! hooray!' No! Trees! Only trees to hew—a garden:— perhaps the garden about her house—then 'Hip, hip—'

He fell headlong on his face, biting the soft earth in sheer despite as he fell.

'Don't touch him, brothers!' said one of the two or three who had followed at a distance, as they might have followed a mad dog, which they hoped others would meet and kill. 'Provoke him not, or the demon possessing him many possess us. 'Tis never safe to touch till they have been dead a watch. Then the poison leaves them. Krishn-*jee*, save us! Saw you how he turned our lead?'

'He has eaten mine, I'll swear,' put in another sepoy boastfully, pointing gingerly with his booted foot to a round scorched hole in the red coat. 'The muzzle was against him as I fired.'

'And mine shall be his portion too,' broke in a new arrival breathlessly, preparing to fire at the prostrate foe; but the first speaker knocked aside the barrel with an oath.

'Not while I stand by, since devils choose the best men. As 'tis, having women in our houses 'twere best to take precautions.' He stooped down as he spoke, and muttering spells the while, raised a little heap of dust at the lad's head and feet and outstretched arms—a little cross of dust, as it were, on which the young body lay impaled.

'What is't?' asked a haughty-looking native officer, pausing as he rode by.

''Tis a hell-doomed who went possessed, and Dittu makes spells to keep him dead,' said one.

'Fool!' muttered the man. 'He was drunk, likely. They get like that, the cursed ones, when they take wine.' And he spat piously on the red coat as he passed on.

So they left the lad there lying face down in the growing gloom, hedged round by spells to keep him from harming women. Left him for dead.

But the scoffer had been right. He was drunk, but with the Elixir of

Life and Love which holds a soul captive from the clasp of Death for a space. So, after a time, the cross of dust gave up its victim; he staggered to his feet again; and stumbling, falling, rising to fall again, he made his way to the haven where he would be—to the side of a dead woman.

And the birds, startled from their roosting-places by the stumbling, falling figure, waited, fluttering over the topmost branches for it to pass, or paused among them to fill up the time with a last twittering song of good night to the day; for the sun still lingered in the heat-haze on the horizon as if loath to take its glow from that corona of red dust above the northern wall of Delhi; mute sign of the only protest made, as yet, by the Master against mutiny.

And now He had left the city to its own devices. The rebels were free to do as they liked. The three thousand disciplined soldiers, more or less, might have marched out, had they chosen, and annihilated the handful of loyal men about the Flagstaff Tower. But it was sunset— sunset in Rumzân. And the eyes of thousands, who had been deprived even of a drop of water since dawn, were watching the red globe sink in the west, hungrily thirstily. Their ears were attuned but to one sound—the firework signal from the big mosque telling that the day's fast was over. The very children on the roofs were watching, listening, so as to send shrill joyful news that day was done to their elders below, waiting with their water-pots ready in their hands.

Besides, in good truth, there was no set purpose from one end of the city to another. From the Palace to the meanest brothel which had belched forth its vilest to swell the tide of sheer rascality which had ebbed and flowed all day, the one thought was still, 'What does it mean? How long will it last? Where is the Master?'

So men ate and drank their fill first, then looked at each other almost suspiciously, and drifted away to do what pleased them best. Some to the palace to swell the turmoil of bellicose loyalty to the King—loyalty which sounded unreal, almost ridiculous, even as it was spoken. Others to plunder while they could. The bungalows had long since been rifled, the very church bells thrown down and broken—for the time had been ample even for wanton destruction; but the city remained, and while shops were being looted inside, the dispossessed Goojurs were busy over Metcalfe House, tearing up the very books in their revenge. The Flagstaff Tower lay not a mile away, almost helpless against attack, but no attack was made; there was in truth no stomach for cold steel in Delhi on the 11th of May 1857—no stomach for anything except safe murder, safe pillaging. Least of all was it to be found in the Palace, where men had given the rein to everything they possessed—to their emotions, their horses, their passions, their aspirations; stabling some in the King's gardens, some in dream-palaces, some in pigsties of sheer brutality; weeping maudlin tears over heaven-sent success, and boasting of their own prowess in the same breath; squabbling insanely over the partition of coming honours and emoluments.

Abool-Bukr, drunk as a lord, lurched about asserting his intention of being Inspector-General of the King's cavalry, and not leaving man, woman, or child of the hell-doomed alive in India. For he had been right when he had warned Newâsi to leave him to his own life, his own death—when he had shrunk from the inherited bloodstains on his hands, the inherited tinder in his breast. It had caught fire with the first spark, and there was fresh blood on his hands—the blood of a Eurasian boy who had tried to defend his sister from drunken kisses. Some one in the melée had killed the girl and finished the boy; the Prince himself being saved from greater crime by tumbling into the gutter and setting his nose a-bleeding; a catastrophe which had sent him back to the Palace partially sobered.

But Princess Farkhoonda Zamâni, safe-housed in the rooms kept for honoured visitors, knew nothing of this, knew little even of the disturbances; for she had been a close prisoner since noon—a prisoner with servants who would answer no questions, with trays of jewels and dresses as if she had been a bride. She sat in a flutter, trying to piece out the reason for this kidnapping. Was she to be married by force to some royal nominee? But why today? Why in all this turmoil, unless she was required as a bribe? The arch-plotter was capable of that. But to whom? One thing was certain, Abool-Bukr could know nothing of this—he would not dare, surely! Suddenly the hot blood tingled through every vein as she lay all unconsciously enjoying the return to the easeful idleness and luxury she had renounced. But if he did dare?—it was not mere anger which brought bewilderment to heart and brain, as she hid her face from the dim light which filtered in through the lattice—the dim, scented, voluptuous light from which she had fled once to purer air?

And not a hundred yards away from where she was trying to steady her bounding pulses, Abool-Bukr himself was bawling away at his favourite love-song to a circle of intimates, all of whom he had already provided with places on the civil list. His head was full of promises, his skin as full of wine as it could be, and he not be a mere wastrel unable to enjoy life; for Abool-Bukr gave care to this; since to be dead drunk was sheer loss of time.

> Ah mistress rare, divine
> Thy lover like a vine
> With tendril arms entwine.

Here his effort to combine gesture with song nearly caused him to fall of the steps, and roused a roar of laughter from some sepoys bivouacking under the trees hard by; but Mirza Moghul, passing hastily to an audience with the King, frowned. Today, he told himself, when none knew what might come, the Queen might have her way so far; but this idle drunkard must be got rid of soon. He would offend the pious to begin with, and then he could not be trusted. Who could trust a man who had been known to lure back his hawk because a bird's gay feathers shone in the sunshine?

But Ahsan-Oolah, dismissed by the Mirza's audience from feeling the royal pulse, paused as he passed, to recommend a cooling draught if the Inspector-General of Cavalry wanted to keep his head clear. It was the physician's panacea for excitement of all kinds; but an exhibition of steel would have done better on the 11th of May.

There was no one, however, to administer it to Delhi, and even the refugees in the Flagstaff Tower were beginning to give up hope of its arriving from Meerut. Those in the storehouse at Duryagunj still clung to the belief that succour must come somehow; but Kate Erlton behind the wood-pile knew that her hope lay only in herself.

For how could Jim Douglas, as he more than once passed through the now open and almost deserted Kashmir gate, in the hope, or rather the fear, of finding some trace of her, know that she was hidden within a few yards of him? or how could she distinguish the sound of his horse's hoofs from the hundreds which passed?

She must have escaped with the others, he concluded, as he galloped towards cantonments to see if she were there. But she was not. He had failed again, he told himself; failed through no fault of his own—for who could have foretold that madness of retreat from the gate?

So now, there was nothing to be done in Delhi save gather what information he could, give decent burial—if he could—to Alice Gissing's body, and, if no troops arrived before dawn, leave the city.

# 6

# Dusk

'I entreat you to leave, sir. Believe me there is nothing else to be done now. It will be dark in half an hour, and we shall need every minute of the night to reach Kurnal.'

It was said openly now by many voices. It had been hinted first when—the corona of red dust having just sprung to hide the swelling white dome of the distant mosque—a dismal procession had come slowly up the steep road to the tower with a ghastly addition to the little knot of white faces there; come very slowly, the drivers of the oxen whacking and gibing at them as if the cart held logs or refuse; as if the driving of it were quite commonplace. Yet in a way the six bodies of English gentlemen it had held were welcome additions; since it is something to see a dear face even when it is dead. But they were fateful additions, making the disloyal 38th regiment posted furthest from the Tower—partly commanded by it and the guns, in case of accident—shift restlessly. If others had done such work, ought not they to be up and doing? And now another procession came filing up from the city—the two guns returning from the Kashmir gate. They came on sullenly, slowly, yet still they came on; another few minutes and the refugees would have been the stronger, the chances of mutiny weaker. The 38th saw this. Their advanced picquet rushed out, drove off the gunners and the officers, and, fixing bayonets, forced the drivers to wheel and set off down the road again at a trot. And down the road, commanded by other guns, they went unchecked; for the refugees did not dare to give the order to fire, lest it should be disobeyed. The effect, we read, would probably have been '*that the guns would have been swung round and fired on the order-ers, and so not a European would have escaped to tell the tale; this catastrophe, however, was mercifully averted and the crisis passed over.*' It reads strangely, but there were women and children to think of; and few men are strong enough to say, must less to set down in black and white as John Nicholson did, that the protection 'of women and children in some crises is such a very minor consideration that it ceases to be a consideration at all'.

Still, it began to be patent to every one that there was little good in remaining in a place where they did not dare to defend themselves. There were carriages and horses ready; the road to Kurnal was still fairly safe. Would it not be better to retreat? But the Brigadier held out. He had, in deference partly to others, wholly for the sake of his helpless charges, weakened the city post. Why should he have done that if he meant to abandon his own? Then he was an old sepoy officer who had served boy and man in one regiment, rising to its command at last, and he was loath to believe that the 38th regiment, which had been specially commended to him by his own, would turn against him, if only he were free to handle it. And this hope gained colour from the fact, that to him personally and to his direct orders, the regiment was still cheerfully obedient.

So the waiting went on, and there were no signs of the 74th

returning. What had happened? Fresh disaster? The voices urging retreat grew louder.

'Have it your own way, gentlemen,' said the Brigadier at last. 'The women and children had better go, at any rate, and they will need protection; so let all retire who will, and in what way seems best to them. I stay here.'

So on foot, on horseback, in carriages, the exodus began forth with; hastening more rapidly when the first man to jump from the embrasure at the Kashmir gate arrived with that tale of hopeless calamity.

But still the Brigadier refused to join the rout. He had been hanging on the skirts of Hope all day, trying—wisely or unwisely—to shield women and children behind that frail shelter. So he had been tied hand and foot; now he would be free. True! the mystery of oncoming dusk made that red city in the distance loom larger, but a handful of desperate men unhampered, with plenty of ammunition, might surely hold such a post as the Flagstaff Tower till help arrived. He meant to try, at any rate. Then nearly half of the 74th had got away safely—they were long in turning up certainly—but when they came they would form a nucleus. The 54th were not all bad, or they would not have saved their Major. Even the 38th, if they could once be got away from the sight of weakness, from that ghastly cart with its mute witness to successful murder, might respond to a familiar commonplace order. They were creatures of habit, with drill born in the blood, bred in the bone.

'I stay here,' he said shortly; and said it again, even when neither the escaped officers nor the men turned up. He said it again, when the guns rolled off towards Meerut, leaving him face to face with a sprinkling of the 74th and 54th, and the great mass of the 38th sullen, but still obedient.

The sun, now some time set, had left a flaming pennant in the sky, barring it low down on the horizon with a blood-red glow marking the top of the dust-haze, and the quick chill of colour which in India comes with the lack of sunlight even while its heat lingers to the touch, had fallen upon all things. Upon the red Ridge, upon the distant line of trees marking the canal, and upon the level plain between them where all the familiar landmarks of cantonment life still showed clearly, despite the darkening sky. Guard-rooms, lines, bells-of-arms, wide parade-grounds—all the familiar surroundings of a sepoy's life, and behind them that red flare of a day that was done.

'There is no use, sir, in stopping longer,' said the brigade-major, almost compassionately, to the figure which sat its horse steadfastly, but with a despondent droop of the shoulders.

'No possible use, sir,' echoed the staff doctor kindly. The three were facing westward, for that vain hope of help from the east had been given up at last; and behind them, barely audible, was the faint hum of the distant city. A shaft of cormorants flying *jheel*-wards with barbed arrowhead, trailed across the purpling sky; below them the red pennant was fading steadily. The day was done. But to one pair of eyes there seemed still a hope, still a last appeal to something beyond east or west.

'Bugler! sound the assembly!'

The Brigadier's voice rang sharp over the plain and was followed, quick as an echo—quick from that habit of obedience on which so much depended—by the cheerful notes—

'*Come—to the colours! Come quick, come all—come quick, come all—come quick! Quick! Come to the colours!*'

Last appeal to honour and good faith, to memory and confidence! But they had passed with the day.

Yet not quite, for as the rocks and stones, the distant lines, the familiar landmarks gave back the call, a solitary figure, trim and smart in the uniform of the loyal 74th, fell in and saluted. In all that wide plain one man true to his salt, heroic utterly, standing alone in the dusk. A nameless figure, like many another hero. Yet better so, when we remember that but a few hours before his regiment had *volunteered to a man* against their comrades and their country!

So sepoy—, of company—, can stand there, outlined against the dying day upon the parade-ground at Delhi, as a type of others who might have stood there also, but for the lack of that cloud of dust upon the Meerut road.

Brigadier Graves wheeled his horse slowly northwards; but at the sight the sepoys of the 38th, still friendly to him personally, crowded round him urging speed. It was no place for him, they said. No place for the master.

Palpably not. It was time, indeed, for the thud of retreating hoofs to end the incident. So far, at any rate, as the master was concerned; the actual finale of the tragic mistake being a disciplined tramp, as the sepoy who had fallen in at the last Assembly, fell out again—at his own word of command—and followed the master doggedly.[1]

'God be praised!' said the 38th, as with curious deliberation they took possession of the cantonments. 'That is over! He has gone in safety, and we have kept the promise given to our brothers of the 56th not to harm him.' So, joined by their comrades from the city, they set guards and gave out rations, with double and treble doses of rum;

[1]He was killed fighting for us noon afterwards.

played the master, in fact, perfectly; until, in the darkness, a rumble arose upon the road, and one half of the actors fled citywards incontinently and the other half went to bed in their huts like good boys. But it was not the troops from Meerut at last. It was only their old friends the guns, once more brought back from the fugitives by comrades who had finally decided to stand by the winning side.

So the question has once more to be asked, 'What would have happened, if, even at that eleventh hour, there really *had* been a cloud of dust on the Meerut road?'

As it was, confidence and peace were restored. In the city, indeed, they had never been disturbed. It seemed weary, bewildered by the topsy-turviness of the day, desirous chiefly of sleep and dreams; so that Kate Erlton, peering out through a chink in the wood-store, felt that if she were ever to escape from the slow starvation which stared her in the face, she could choose no better time than this, when traffic had ceased, and the moon had not yet risen. She had settled that her best chance lay in creeping along the wall at first, then, taking advantage of the gardens, cutting across to that same sally-port through which the heroes of the magazine had told her they had made their escape. She did not know the exact situation, but she could surely find it. Besides, the ruins would most likely be deserted, and the other gates of the city, even if they were not closed for the night, as the gate here was, would be guarded. Once out of the city, she meant to make for the Flagstaff Tower; for, of course, she knew nothing of its desertion.

So she set the door ajar softly, and crept out. And as she did so, the whiteness of her own dress, even in the dense blackness, startled her, and roused the trivial wish that she had put on her navy-blue cotton instead, as she had meant to do that day. Strange! how a mere chance . . . the word was like a spur always, and she crept along the wall, hoping that the smoking flaring fire of refuse in the opposite corner round which the guards were sitting so as to be free of mosquitoes, might dazzle their eyes. It was her only chance, however, so she must risk it. Then suddenly, under her foot, she felt something long, curved, snakelike. It was all she could do not to scream; but she set her teeth, and trod down hard with all her strength, her heart beating wildly in the awful suspense. But nothing struck her, there was no movement. Had she killed it? Her hand went down in the dark with a terror in it lest her touch should light on the head—perhaps within reach of the fangs. But she forced herself to the touch, telling herself she was a coward, a fool—

Thank Heaven! It was no snake after all, only a rope; a rope that must have been used for tethering a horse, for here under her foot was straw, rustling horribly. No! not now—that was something soft. A blanket!—A horse's double blanket, dark as the darkness itself. Here was a chance, indeed! She caught it up, and paused deliberately in the darkest corner of the square, to slip off shoes and stockings, petticoats and bodices; then, in the scantiest of costumes, winding the long blanket round her, ayah's fashion, as a skirt and veil. Her face could be hidden by a modest down-drop over it, her white hands hidden away by the modest drawing of a fold across her mouth. Her feet, then, were the only danger, and the dust would darken them. She must risk that anyhow. So, boldly, she slipped out of the corner, and made for the gate, remembering, to her comfort, that it was not England where a lonely woman might be challenged all the more for her loneliness. In this heathen land, that down-dropped veil hedged even a poor grass-cutter's wife about with respect. What is more, even if she were challenged, her proper course would be to be silent and hurry on. But no one challenged her, and she passed on into the denser shadows of the church garden to regain her breath; for it had gone somehow. Why she knew not; she had not felt frightened. Then the question came, what next? Get to the magazine, somehow; but the strain of looking forward seemed far worse than the actual doing, so she went on without settling anything, save that she would avoid roads, and give the still-smoking roofless bungalows as wide a berth as possible, lest, in the dark, she should come on some dead thing—a friend perhaps. And with the thought came that of Alice Gissing. The house lay right on her path to the magazine. Surely she must be near it now. Was that the long sweep of its roof against the sky? If she could see so much, the moon must be rising, and she could have no time to lose. As she crept along through the garden, she wondered why the bungalow had not been burnt like the others. Perhaps the ayah's friends had saved it, or, perhaps, there had not been much to attract robbers in the little hired house. Or, perhaps—

Hark! She crouched back from the sound of voices close beside her, and doubled a bit; but they seemed to follow her. Yet straight ahead the trees ended, and she must brave the open space by the house itself; unless, indeed, she slipped by the row of servant's houses to the verandah, and so—through the rooms—gain the further side. Or she might hide in the house till these voices passed. There they were again! She made a breathless dash for the shadow, ran on till she found the verandah, and deciding to hide for a time, passed in at the first door— the door of the room where she had left Alice Gissing lying dead a few hours before. But it was too dark, as yet, to see if she lay there still, too dark to see even if the house had been plundered. It must have been, however, for the very floor-cloths were gone and the concrete struck cold to her feet. A sudden terror at the darkness, the emptiness, coming over her, she passed on rapidly to the faintly-glimmering square of the further door, seen through the intervening rooms. There were three of them; bedroom, drawing-room, dining-room, set in a row in Indian fashion, all leading into each other, all opening on to the verandah; the two end ones opening also into the side verandah. She could get out again, therefore, by this further door. But it was bolted; she undid the bolts, only to find it hasped on the outside. A feeling of being trapped seized upon her. She ran to the other door—hasped also! The drawing-room door?—firmer even than the others! But what a fool she was to feel so frightened, when she could always go out as she had come in, when the voices had passed? She stole back softly, knowing they must be just outside, and almost fancying, in her alarm, that she heard a step in the verandah. But there was the glimmering square of escape—open? No!—shut too!—shut from the outside.

Had they seen her and shut the door? And there, indeed, *were* footsteps! Loud footsteps and voices coming up the long flight of steps which led to the verandah from the road—coming straight, and she locked in, helpless.

She threw up her hands involuntarily at a bright flash in the verandah. Was it lightning? No! a pistol shot—a quick curse—a fall—a yell of rage—a rush of those feet upon the steps, and then another flash, another, and another! Then more curses and a confused clashing! She stood as if turned to stone, listening. Hark! down the steps surely, this time, came another rush, a cry, a scuffle, a fall: then, loud and unmistakable, a laugh! then silence.

Merciful heavens! what was it? What had happened? She shook at the door gently, but still there was silence. Then, gripping the woodwork she tried to peer out; but she could only see the bit of verandah in front of her which, being latticed in and hung with creepers, was very dark. The rest was invisible from within. She leant her ear on the glass and listened. Was that a faint breathing? 'Who's there?' she cried softly; but there was no answer. She sank down on the floor in sheer bewilderment and tried to think what to do, and after a time, a faint glimmer of the rising moon aiding her, she went round to every door and tried it again. They were all locked inside and out. And now she could see that the house had been pillaged to the uttermost. There was literally nothing left in it. Nothing to aid her fingers if she tried to open the doors. By breaking the upper panes of glass, of course, she could undo the top bolt, but how was she to reach the bottom ones behind the lower panels? And why—why had they been locked? Who had locked the one by which she had come in? What was there that needed protection in that empty house? Was there by chance some one else? Then, suddenly, the remembrance of what she had left lying in the end room hours before came back to her. She had forgotten it utterly in her alarm and she crept back to see if Alice Gissing still kept her company. The bed was gone, but by the steadily-growing glimmer of the moon she could see something lying on the floor in the very centre of the room. Something strangely orderly, with a look of care and tidiness about it; but not white—and *her* dress had been white—Kate knelt down beside it and touched the still figure gently. What had it been covered with? Some sort of network, fine—silken—crimson; an officer's sash surely! And now her eyes becoming accustomed to what lay before them, and the light growing, she saw that the curly head rested on an officer's scarlet coat. The gold epaulettes were arranged neatly on either side the delicate ears so as not to touch them. Who had done this? Then that step she had thought she heard in the verandah must have been a real one—some one must have been watching the dead woman—

She was at the door in an instant, rapping at a pane—'Herbert! Herbert! are you there? Herbert! Herbert!'

He might have done this thing! He might have come over from Meerut, for he had loved the dead woman, he had loved her dearly; but there was no answer. So, wrapping the blanket round her hand, she dashed it through the pane, and removing the glass, managed to crane out a little. She could see better now. Was that some one, or only a heap of clothes in the shadow of the corner by the inner wall? By this time the moonlight was shining white on the orange-trees on the further side of the road. She could see beyond them to the garden, but nothing of the road itself, nothing of the steep flight of steps leading down to it; for a balustrade set with pots which filled up all but the centre arch prevented that.

'Herbert!' she cried again louder; 'is that you?' But there was not a sound. God in Heaven! who lay there? dying or dead? . . .

Her helplessness broke down her self-control at last, and she crept back into the room, back to the old companionship, crying miserably. Ah! she was so tired, so weary of it all; so glad to rest! A sense of real physical relief came to her body as, for the first time for long, long hours, she let her muscles slacken; and to her mind as she let herself cry on, like a child, forgetting the cause of grief in the grief itself. Forgetting even *that* after a time in sheer rest; so that the moon, when it had climbed high enough to peep in through the closed doors, found her asleep, her arms spread out over the crimson net-work, her head resting on what lay beneath it. But she slept dreamfully, and once her voice rose in the quick anxious tones of those who talk in their sleep—

'Freddy! Freddy!' she called, 'save Freddy, some one! Never mind, ayah! He is only a boy, and the other, the other may. . . .'

Then her words merged into each other uncertainly, after the manner of dreamers, and she slept sounder. Soundest of all, however, in the cool before the dawn; so that she did not wake with a stealthy foot in the side verandah, a stealthy hand on the hasp outside; did not wake even when Jim Douglas stood beside her, looking down vexedly on the blanket-shrouded figure pillowed on the body he came to seek. For he had been delayed by a thousand difficulties, and though the shallow grave was ready dug in the garden, the presence of this native—even though a woman, apparently—must make his task longer. Was it a woman? One hand on his revolver, he laid the other on the sleeper's shoulder. His touch brought Kate to her feet blindly, without a cry, to meet Fate.

'My God! Mrs Erlton!' he cried, and she recognized his voice at once. Fate indeed! His chance and hers! His chance and hers!

She stood half stupefied by her dreams, her waking; but he, after his nature, was ready in a second for action, and broke in on his own wondering questions impatiently. 'But we are losing time.—Quick! you must get to some safer place before dawn. Twist that blanket right—let me, please. That will do. Now, if you will follow close, I must get you hidden somewhere for today. It is too near dawn for anything else. Come!'

She put out her hand vaguely, as if to stave his swift decision away, and, looking in her face, he recognized that she must have time, that he must curb his own energy.

'Then it was you who fired,' she said in a dull voice. 'You who shut me in here.—You who killed those voices.—Why didn't you answer when I called, when I thought it was Herbert?—It was very unkind— very unkind.'

He stared at her for a second, and then his hand went out and closed on hers firmly. 'Mrs Erlton! I'm going to save you if I can.— Come! I don't know what you're talking about, and there is no time for talk.—Come!'

Hand in hand, they passed into the side verandah, through which he had entered, and so—since the nearest way to the city lay down that flight of steps—to the front one.

'Take care,' he cried, half-stumbling himself, and forcing her to avoid something that lay huddled up against the wall. It was a dead man. And there, upon the steps which showed white as marble in the moonlight, were two others in a heap; a third lower down, ghastlier still, lying amid dark stains marring the whiteness, and with a gaping cut clearly visible on the shoulder.

But that still further down! Jim Douglas gave a quick cry, dropped Kate's hand, and was on his knees beside the tall, young figure—

coatless, its white shirt stiff with blood—which lay head downwards on the last steps as if it had pitched forward in some mad pursuit. As he turned it over on its back gently, the young face showed in the moonlight stern, yet still exultant, and the sword, still clenched in the stiff right hand, rattled on the steps.

'Mainwaring! I don't understand,' he said, looking up bewildered into Kate's face. The puzzle had gone from it; she seemed roused to life again.

'I understand now,' she said softly, and as she spoke she stooped and raised the boy's head tenderly in her hands. 'Don't let us leave him here,' she went on eagerly, hastily. 'Leave him there, beside—beside—*her*.'

Jim Douglas made no reply. He understood also dimly, and he only signed to her to take the feet instead. So together they managed to place that dead weight within the threshold and close the door.

Then Jim Douglas held out his hand again, but there was a new friendliness in its grip. 'Come!' he said—and there was a new ring in his voice—'the night is far spent, the day is at hand.'

It was true. As they stepped from the now waning moonlight into the shadow of the trees, the birds, beginning to dream of dawn, shifted and twittered faintly among the branches. And once, startling them both, there was a louder rustling from a taller tree, a flutter of broad white wings to a perch nearer the city, a half-sleepy cry of—

'*Deen! Deen! Futteh Mahomed!*'

'If I had time,' muttered Jim Douglas fiercely, 'I would go and wring that cursed bird's neck! But for it—' Kate's tighter clasp on his hand seemed like an appeal, and he went on in silence.

So, as they slipped from the gardens into the silent streets, the *muazzim*'s monotonous chant began from the shadowy minaret of the big mosque.

'Prayer is more than sleep!—than sleep!—than sleep!'

The night was far spent; the day was indeed at hand;—and what would it bring forth? Jim Douglas, with a sinking at his heart, told himself he could at least be thankful that one day was done.

# BOOK IV

## 'Such Stuff as Dreams are Made of'

# 1

## The Death-Pledge

The outer court of the palace lay steeped in the sunshine of noon. Its hot rose-red walls and arcades seemed to shimmer in the glare, and the dazzle and glitter gave a strange air of unreality, of instability to all things: to the crowds of loungers taking their *siesta* in every arcade and every scrap of shadow, to the horses stabled in rows in the glare and the blaze, to the eager groups of new arrivals which, from time to time, came in from the outer world by the cool, dark tunnel of the Lahore gate to stand for a second, as if blinded by the shimmer and glitter, before becoming a part of that silent, drowsy stir of life.

From an arch close to the inner entry to the precincts, rose a monotonous voice reading aloud. The reader was evidently the author also, for his frown of annoyance was unmistakable at a sudden diversion caused by the entry of a dozen or more armed men, shouting at the top of their voices: '*Pâdishâh, Pâdishâh!* We be fighters for the faith. *Pâdishâh!* a blessing, a blessing!'

A malicious laugh came from one of the listeners in the arcade—a woman shrouded in a Pathan veil.

''Tis as well his Majesty hath taken another cooling draught,' came her voice shrilly. 'What with writing letters for help to the *Huzoor*s to please Ahsan-Oolah and Elâhi Buksh, and blessing faith to please the Queen, he hath enough to do in keeping his brain from getting dizzy with whirling this way and that. Mayhap faith will fail first, since it is not satisfied with blessings. They are windy diet, and I heard Mahboob say an hour agone that there was too much faith for the Treasury. Lo! *moonshee-jee*, put that fact down among thy heroics—they need balance!'

'Sure, niece Hâfzan,' reproved the old editor of the Court Journal, 'I see naught that needs of. Syyed Abdulla's periods fit the case as peas fit a pod; they hang together—'

'As we shall when the *Huzoors* return,' assented the voice from the veil.

'They will return no more, woman!' said another. It belonged to a man who leant against a pilaster, looking dreamily out into the glare

where, after a brief struggle, the band of fighters for the faith had
pushed aside the timid doorkeepers and forced their way to the inner
garden. Through the open door they showed picturesquely, surging
down the path, backed by green foliage and the white dome of the
Pearl Mosque rising against the blue sky.

'The faith! the faith! We come to fight for the faith!'

[Their cry echoed over the drowsy, dreaming crowds, making men
turn over in their sleep; that was all.]

But the dreaminess grew in the face looking at the vista through the
open door till its eyes became like those Botticelli gives to his Moses—
the eyes of one who sees a promised land—the dreamy voice went
on—

'How can they return; seeing that He is Lord and Master? Changing
the Day to Darkness, the Darkness into Day. Holding the unsupported
skies, proving His existence by His existence, Omnipotent. High in
Dignity, the Avenger of His Faithful people.'

The old editor waggled his head with delighted approval; the
author fidgeted over an eloquence not his own; but Hâfzan's high
laugh rang cynically—

'That may be so, most learned divine; yet I, Hâfzan, the harem
scribe, write no orders nowadays for king or queen without the proviso
of "*writ by a slave in pursuance of lawful order and under fear of death*" in
some quiet corner. For I have no fancy, see you, for hanging, even if it
be in good company. But go on with thy leading article, *moonshee-jee*, I
will interrupt no more.'

'Thus by a single revolution of time the state of affairs is completely
reversed,[1] and the great and memorable event which took place four
days ago must be looked upon as a practical warning to the
uninformed and careless, namely the British officers and those who
never dreamt of the decline and fall of their government, but who have
now convincing proof of what has been written in the Indelible Tablets
by God. The following brief account, therefore, of the horrible and
memorable events is given here solely for the sake of those still
inclined to treat them as a dream. On Monday the 16th of Rumzân,
that holy month in which the Word of God came down to earth, and in
which, for all times, lies the Great Night of Power, the courts being
open early on account of the hot weather, the magistrate discharging
his wonted duties, suddenly the bridge toll-keeper appeared, informing
him that a few Toork troopers had first crossed the bridge—'

The dreamy-faced divine turned in sharp reproach. 'Not so, *Syyed-
jee*. The vision came first—the vision of the blessed Lord Ali seen by

---

[1]From the account in the native papers.

the *muazzim*. Would'st make this time as other times, and deny the miracles by which it is attested as of God?'

'Miracles,' echoed Hâfzan. 'I see no miracle in an old man on a camel.'

The divine frowned. 'Nor in a strange white bird with a golden crown, which hovered over the city giving the sacred cry? Nor in the fulfilment of Hussan Askuri's dream?'

Hâfzan burst into shrill laughter. 'Hussan Askuri! Lo! Moulvie Mahomed Ismail, didst thou know the arch dreamer as I, thou wouldst not credit his miracles. He dreams to the Queen's order as a bear dances to the whip. And as thou knowest, my mistress hath the knack of jerking the puppet-strings. She hath been busy these days, and even the Princess Farkhoonda—'

'What of the princess?' asked the news-writer, eagerly nibbling his pen in anticipation.

'Nay, not so!' retorted Hâfzan. 'I give no news nowadays, since I cannot set "*spoken under fear of death*" upon the words.'

She rose as she spoke, yet lingered, to stand a second beside the divine and say in a softer tone, 'Dreams are not safe, even to the pious as thou, Moulvie-*sahib*. A bird is none the less a bird because it is strange to Delhi and hath been taught to speak. That it was seen all know; yet, for all that, it may be one of Hussan Askuri's tricks.'

'Let it be so, woman,' retorted Mahomed Ismail almost fiercely. 'Is there not miracle enough and to spare without it? Did not the sun rise four days ago upon infidels in power? Where are they now? Were there not two thousand of them in Meerut? Did they strike a blow? Did they strike one here? Where is their strength? Gone! I tell thee—gone!'

Hâfzan laid a veiled clutch on his arm suddenly and her other hand, widening the folds of her shapeless form mysteriously, pointed into the blaze and shimmer of sunlight. 'It lies there, Moulvie-*sahib*, it lies there,' she said in a passionate whisper, 'for God is on their side.'

It was a pitiful little group to which she pointed. A woman, her mixed blood showing in her face, her Christianity in her dress, being driven along like a sheep to the shambles across the courtyard. She clasped a year-old baby to her breast and a handsome little fellow of three toddled at her skirts. She paused in a scrap of shade thrown by a tree which grew beside a small cistern or reservoir near the middle of the court, and shifted the heavy child in her arms, looking round, as she did so, with a sort of wild, fierce fear, like that of a hunted animal. The cluster of sepoys who had made their prisoner over to the palace guard turned hastily from the sight; but the guard drove her on with coarse gibes.

'The rope dangles close, Moulvie-*jee*,' came Hâfzan's voice again.

'Ropes, said I?—gentle ropes? Nay! only as the wherewithal to tie writhing limbs as they roast. If thou hast a taste for visions, pious one, tell me what thou seest ahead for the murderers of such poor souls?'

'Murderers,' echoed Mahomed Ismail swiftly; 'there is no talk of murder. 'Tis against our religion. Have I not signed the edict against it? Have we not protested against the past iniquity of criminals, and ignorant beasts, and vile libertines like Prince Abool-Bukr, who take advantage—'

'He was too drunk for much evil, learned one!' sneered Hâfzan, 'godly men do worse than he in their own homes, as I know to my cost. As for thine edict! Take it to the Princess Farkhoonda! She is a simple soul, though she holds the vilest liver of Delhi in a leash. But the Queen—the Queen is of a different mettle, as you edict-signers will find. There are nigh fifty such prisoners in the old cook-room now. Wherefore?'

'For safety. There are nigh forty in the city police station also.'

Hâfzan gathered her folds closer. 'Truly thou art a simple soul also, pious divine. Dost not think there is a difference, still, between the palace and the city? But God save all women, black or white, say I! Save them from men, and since we be all bound to Hell together by virtue of our sex, then will it be a better place than Paradise by having fewer men in it.'

She flung her final taunts over her shoulder at her hearers as she went limping off.

'Heed her not, most pious!' said her uncle apologetically. 'She hath been mad against men even since hers, being old and near his end, took her, a child, and—'

But Moulvie Mahomed Ismail was striding across the courtyard to the long, low, half-ruinous shed in which the prisoners were kept.

'Have they proper food, and water?' he asked sharply of the guard, 'the King gave orders for it.'

'It comes but now!' replied the sergeant glibly, pointing to a file of servants bearing dishes which were crossing the courtyard from the royal kitchens. The Moulvie gave a sigh of relief, for Hâfzan's hints had alarmed him. These same helpless prisoners lay on his conscience, since he and his like were mainly responsible for the diligent search for Christians which had been going on during the last few days; for it was not to be tolerated that the faithful should risk salvation by concealing them. The proper course was plain, unmistakable. They should be given up to the authorities and be made into good Mohammedans; by persuasion if possible, if not, by force. In truth the Moulvie dreamt already of ninety and odd willing converts, as a further manifestation of divine favour. Perhaps more; though most of these ill-advised attempts at concealment must have come to an end by now.

They had indeed; those four days of peace, of hourly increasing religious enthusiasm for a cause so evidently favoured by High Heaven, had made it well nigh impossible to carry on a task, attempted by many when it seemed likely to last for a few hours only.

Even Jim Douglas told himself he must fail unless he could get help. He had succeeded so far, simply because—by a mere chance—he had, not one, but several, places of concealment ready to his hand without the necessity for taking any one into his confidence. For he had found it convenient in his work to have cities of refuge, as it were, where he could escape from curiosity or change a disguise at leisure. The shilling or so a month required for the rent of a room in some tenement house being more than repaid by the sense of security the possession gave him. It was to one of these, therefore, that he took Kate on the dawn of the 12th, leaving her locked up in it alone till night enabled him to take her on to another; so by constant change managing to escape suspicion. But as the days passed in miraculous peace, he recognized the hopelessness of continuing this life for long. To begin with, Kate's nerves could not stand it. She was brave enough, but she had an imagination, and what woman with that could stand being left alone in the dark for twelve hours at a time, never knowing if the slow starvation which would be her fate if anything untoward happened to him, had not already begun? He could not expect her to stand it, when three days of something far less difficult had left him haggard, his nerves unstrung; left him with the possibility looming in the future of his losing his self-control some day, and going madly for the whole world as young Mainwaring had done. Not that he cared for Kate's safety so much, as that the mere thought of failure roused a beast-like ferocity in him. So, as he wandered restlessly about the city, waiting in a fever of impatience for some sign of the world without those rose-red walls; waiting day by day, with a growing tempest of rage, for the night to return and let him creep up some dark stairs and assure himself of a woman's safety, he was piecing together a plan in case. Of what?—In case the stories he heard in the bazaars were true? No! that was impossible. How could the English have been wiped out of India? Yet as he saw the deserted shops being reopened in solemn procession by an old pantaloon on an elephant calling himself the Emperor, when he saw Abool-Bukr letting off squibs in general rejoicing over the re-establishment of Mohammedan empire; above all when he saw the tide of life returning to the streets, his mad desire to strike a blow and smash the sham was tempered by an almost unbearable curiosity as to what had really happened. But he dared not try and find out. Useless though he knew it was, he hung round the quarter where Kate lay concealed for the day, feeling a certain consolation in knowing that he was as close to her as he dared to be. Such a life was manifestly impossible, and so, bit by bit, his plan grew. Yet when it had grown, he almost shrank from it, so strange did it seem, in its linking of the past with the present. For Kate must pass as his wife—his sick wife, hidden, as Zora had been, on some terraced roof, with Tara as her servant; he, meanwhile, passing as an Afghan horse-dealer, kept from returning north, like others of his trade, by this illness in his house. The plan was perfectly feasible if Tara would consent; and Jim Douglas, though he ignored his own certainty, never really doubted that she would. He had not been born in the mist-covered mountains of the north for nothing. Their mysticism was part of his nature, and he felt that he had saved the Rajpootni for this; that for this, and this only, he had played that childish but successful cantrip with her hair. In a way, was not the pathetic idyll on the roof with little Zora but a rehearsal of a tragedy— a rehearsal without which he could not have played his part? Strange thread of fate, indeed, linking these women together! and though he shrank from admitting its very existence, it gave him confidence that the whole would hang together securely. So that when he sought Tara out, his only real doubt was whether it would be wiser to tell her the truth about Kate, or assert that she *was* his wife. He chose the latter as less risky, since, even if Tara refused aid, she would not overtly betray any one belonging to him.

But Tara did not refuse. To begin with, she could have refused nothing in the first joy of finding him safe when she had believed him dead like all the other *Huzoor*s. And then a vast confusion of love and pride and remorse, and fierce passionate denial of all three, led her into consent. If the *Huzoor* wanted her to help to save his wife why should she object?—though it was nothing to her if the *mem* was *his mem* or not. Jim Douglas, listening to the eager protest, wondered if he might not safely have saved himself an unnecessary complication. But then he wondered at many things Tara said and did; at her quick frown when he promised her both hair and locket as her reward; at the faint quiver amid the scorn with which she had replied that he would still want the latter for the *mem*'s hair; at her slow smile when he opened the gold oval to show the black lock still in sole possession. She had turned aside to look at the hearth-cakes she had been toasting when he came in, and then gone into the necessary details of arrangement in the most matter-of-fact way. Naturally the *Huzoor* had sought help from his servant. From whom else could he seek it? As for her saintship, there was nothing new in that. She had been *suttee* always as the master very well knew. So nothing she did for him, or he for her, could make *that* suffer. Therefore she would arrange as she had arranged for Zora. The *Huzoor* must rent a roof—roofs were safest—and she would engage a half-blind half-deaf old sweeper-woman she knew of. Perhaps another if need be. But the *Huzoor* need have no fear of such details if he gave her money. And this Jim Douglas had hidden in the garden of his deserted bungalow in Duryagunj; so that, in truth, it seemed as if the whole plan had been evolved for them by a kindly fate.

And yet Jim Douglas felt a keen pang of regret when, for the first time, he gave the familiar knock of those old Lucknow days at the door of a Delhi roof, and Tara opened it to him, dressed in the old crimson drapery, the gold bangles restored to her beautiful brown arms. He had brought Kate round during the previous night to the lodging he had managed to secure in the Mufti's quarter, and leaving her there alone, had taken the key to Tara; this being the safest plan, since everything could then be arranged in discreet woman's fashion before he put in an appearance.

And the task had been done well. The outside square or yard of parapeted roof which he entered lay conventional to the uttermost. A spinning-wheel here, a row of water-pots there, a mat, a reed stool or two, a cooking place in one corner, a ragged canvas screen at the inner doors. There was nothing to prepare him for finding an Englishwoman within; and Englishwoman with a faint colour in her wan cheeks, a new peace in her grey eyes, busy—Heaven save the mark!—in sticking some disjointed jasmine buds into the shallow saucer of a water-pot.

'Tara brought them strung on a string,' said Kate half-apologetically after her first welcome, as she noted his look. 'I suppose she meant me to wear them—with the other things—' she paused to glance down with a smile at her dress—'but it seemed a pity. They were like a new world to me—like a promise—somehow.'

He sat down on the edge of the string bed feeling a little dazed, and looked at her and her surroundings critically. It was a pleasant sunshiny bit of roof, vaulted by the still-cool morning sky. There was a little arcaded room at one end, and the topmost branches of a *neem* tree showed over one side. On the other, the swelling dome of the big mosque looked like a great white cloud, and in one corner was a sort of square turret, from the roof of which, gained by a narrow brick ladder, the whole city was visible; for it was the highest house in the quarter, higher even than the roof beside it, over which the same *neem* tree cast a shadow.

And as he looked, he thought idly that no dress in the world was more graceful than the Delhi dress with its billowy train and loose, soft, filmy veil. And Kate looked well in white—all in white. He pulled himself up sharply; but indeed memory was playing him tricks, and the stress and strain of reality seemed far from that slip of sun-saturated roof where a graceful woman in white was sticking jasmine buds into water. And suddenly the thought came that Zora would have worn the chaplets heedlessly—there would have been no sentimentality over withered flowers on her part.

'A promise?' he echoed half-bitterly. 'Well! one must hope so. And even if the worst comes, it will come easier here.'

She looked up at him reproachfully. 'Don't remind me of that, please,' she said hurriedly; 'I seem to have forgotten—here under the blue sky. I dare say it's very trivial of me, but I can't help it. Everything amuses me, interests me. It is so quaint, so new. Even this dress; it is hardly credible, but I wished so much for a looking-glass just now, to see how I looked in it.'

Her eyes met his almost gaily, and he felt an odd resentment in recognizing that Zora would have said the words as frankly.

'I have one here—in a ring,' he replied somewhat stiffly, with a vague feeling he had done all this before, as he untied the knot of a small bundle he had brought with him. 'It is not much use—for that sort of thing—I'm afraid,' he went on, 'but I think you had better have these: it is a great point—even for your own sake—to dress as well as play the part.'

Kate, with a sudden gravity, looked at the pile of native ornaments he emptied out on to the bed. Bracelets in gold and silver, anklets, odd little jewelled tassels for the hair, quaint silk-strung necklets and talismans.

'Here is the looking-glass,' he said choosing out a tiny round one set in filigree gold; 'you must wear it on your thumb—but it will barely go on my little finger,' he spoke half to himself, and Kate fitting on the ring, looked at him and set her lips.

'It is too small for me also,' she said, laying it down with a faint air of distaste. 'They are very pretty, Mr Greyman,' she added quickly, 'but I would rather not—unless it is really necessary—unless you think—'

He rose half-wearily, half-impatiently. 'I should prefer it; but you can do as you like. The jewels belonged to a woman I loved very dearly, Mrs Erlton. She was not my wife—but she was a good woman for all that. You need not be afraid.'

Kate felt the blood tingle to her face as she laid violent hands on the first ornament she touched. It happened to be a solid gold bangle. 'It is too small also,' she said petulantly, trying to squeeze her hand through it. 'Really it would be better—'

'Excuse me,' he replied coolly, 'if you will let me.' He drew the great carved knobs apart deftly, slipped her wrist sideways through the opening, and had them closed again in a second.

'You can't take it off at night, that is all,' he went on, 'but I will tell Tara to show you how to wear the rest. I must be off now and settle a thousand things.'

As he passed into the outer roof once more, Kate felt that flush, half of resentment, half of shame, still on her face. In such surroundings how trivial it was, and yet he had guessed her thought truly. Had he guessed also the odd thrill which the touch of that gold fetter gave her? Half-mechanically she tried to loosen it, to remove it, and then with an impatient frown desisted and began to put on the other bracelets. What did it matter, one way or the other? And then, becoming interested despite herself, she set to work to puzzle out uses and places for the pile.

Meanwhile Jim Douglas was dinning instructions into Tara's ear; but she also, he told himself angrily, was trivial to the last degree. And when finally he urged an immediate darkening of Kate's hair and a faint staining of the face to suit the only part possible with her grey eyes—that of a fair Afghan—he flung away in despair from the irrelevant remark: 'But the *mem* will never be so pretty as Zora; and besides she has such big feet.'

'Big feet!' He swore under his breath that all women were alike in this, that they saw the whole world through the medium of their sex; and *that* was at the bottom of all the mischief. Delhi had been lost to save women; the trouble had begun to please them. Even now, as far as he could see, resistance would collapse but for one woman's ambition; though despite the Queen and her plots, a hundred brave men or so might still be masters of Delhi if they chose, since it was still each for himself, and the devil take the hindmost with the mutineers. The certainty of this had made these long days of inaction almost beyond bearing to him; and as Jim Douglas passed out into the street he thought bitterly that here again a woman had stood in the way; since but for Kate, he could surely have forced Meerut into making reprisals by reporting the true state of affairs.

Yet every hour made these reprisals more difficult. Indeed, as he left the Mufti's quarter on that morning of the 16th of May, something was going on in the palace which ended indecision for many a man and left no chance of retreat. For Zeenut Maihl saw facts as clearly as Jim Douglas, and knew that the first tramp of disciplined feet would be the signal for scuttle, if a chance of escape remained.

And so this something was going on. By some one's orders of course; by whose is one of the unanswered questions of the Indian Mutiny.

The Queen herself was sitting with the King, amicably, innocently, applauding his latest couplet; which was in sober truth, one of his best:

God takes this dice-box world, shakes upside down,
Throws one defeat, and one a kingly crown.

He was beginning to feel the latter on his old head, which was so
diligently stuffed with dreams; but the Queen knew in her heart of
hearts that the fight for sovereignty had only just begun. So her mind
was chiefly occupied in a spiteful exultation at the thought of some
folk's useless terror when—this thing being done—they would find
their hands irrevocably on the plough. Ahsan-Oolah and Elâhi-Buksh,
for instance—their elaborate bridges would be useless; and Abool-Bukr
with his squibs and processions, Farkhoonda with her patter of virtue
and religion? If only for the sake of enmeshing this last victim Zeenut
Maihl would not have shrunk; since those three or four days of
cozening had left the Queen with a still more vigorous hate for the
Princess Farkhoonda who had fallen into the trap so easily, and who,
already, began to give herself airs and discuss the future on a plane of
equality. Pretty, conceited fool! who even now, so the spies said, was
waiting to receive the Prince, her nephew, for the first time since she
came to the Palace. The very fact that it *was* the first time seemed an
aggravation in the Queen's angry eyes, proving as it did a certain
reality in Farkhoonda's pretensions to decorum.

In truth they were very real to the Princess herself, and had been
gaining reality ever since that first deft suggestion of a possibility had
set her heart beating. The possibility, briefly, of the King choosing to set
aside that early marriage so tragically interrupted—choosing to declare
it no marriage and give his consent to another. Newâsi had indignantly
scouted the suggestion, had stopped her ears, her heart; but the
remembrance of it lingered, enervating her mind, and, as she waited
for the interview with the Prince, she felt vaguely that it was a very
different matter receiving him in these bride-like garments, in these
dim heavily-scented rooms, to what it had been under the clear sky in
her scholar's dress. Yet, as she stooped from mere habit, aroused by the
finery itself, to arrange her long brocaded train into better folds, she
gave something between a sigh and a laugh at the certainty of his
admiration. And after all, why should she not have it if the King—?

The sound of a distant shot made her start and pause, listening for
another. So she stood a slim figure ablaze with colour and jewels, a
figure with studied seductiveness in every detail of its dress; and she
knew that it was so. Why not? If—if he liked it so, and if the King—

Newâsi clasped her hands nervously and walked up and down the
dim room, Abool was late, and he had no right to be late on this his
first visit of ceremony to his aunt.

The Mirza-*sahib* was no doubt late, admitted her attendants, but the door keeper had reported a disturbance of some kind in the outer court which might be the cause of delay. A disturbance! Newâsi, a born coward, shrank from the very thought, though she felt that it could be nothing—nothing but one of the many brawls, the constant quarrels.—

God and His prophet! who—what was that? She recoiled with a scream of terror from the wild figure which burst in on her unceremoniously, which followed her retreat into the far corner, flung itself at her knees, clasping them, burying its face among her scented draperies. But by that time her terror was gone, and she stooped trying to free herself from those clinging arms—from the disgrace—from the outrage—from the drunken—

'Abool!' she cried fiercely, then turning to the curious tittering women, stamped her foot at them and bade them begone. And when they had obeyed, she beat her little hands against those clinging ones again with wild upbraidings, till suddenly they fell as if paralysed before the awful horror and dread in the face which rose from her fineries.

'Come, Newâsi!' stammered the white trembling lips, 'come from this hangman's den. Did I not warn thee? But thou hast put the rope round my neck—I who only wanted to live my own life, die my own death—Come! Come!'

He stumbled to his feet, but seemed unable to stir. So he stood looking at his hands stupidly.

Farkhoonda looked too, her face growing grey.

'What is't, Abool?' she faltered; 'what is't, dear?'

But she knew; it was blood, new shed, still wet.

He stood silent, gazing at the stains stupidly. 'I did not strike,' he muttered to himself, 'but I called; or did I strike? I—I—' He threw up his head and his words rushed recklessly in a high shrill voice, 'I warned thee! I told thee it was not safe. They were herded like sheep in the sunshine by the cistern, and the smell of blood rose up. It was in my very nostrils, for, look you, that first shot missed them and killed one of my men. I saw it. A round red spot oozing over the white—and they herded like sheep—'

'Who?' she asked faintly.

'I told thee; the prisoners, with the cry to kill above the cries of the children, the flash of blood-dulled swords above women's heads—and I—Nay! I warned thee, Newâsi, there was butcher *here*'—his blood-stained hands left their mark on his gay clothes.

'Abool!' she cried, 'thou didst not—'

'Did I?' he almost screamed. 'God! will it ever leave my sight? I gave the call, I ran in, I drew my sword. It spurted over my hands from a child's throat as I would have struck—or—or—did I strike?

Newâsi!' his voice had sunk again almost to a whisper, 'it was in its mother's arms,—she did not cry—she looked and I—I—' he buried his face in his hands— 'I came to thee.'

She stood looking at him for a moment, her hands clenched, her beautiful soft eyes ablaze; then recklessly she tore the jewels from her arms, her neck, her hair—

'So she has dared! Yea! Come! thou art right, Abool!' The words mixed themselves with the tinkle of bracelets as, flung from her in wild passion, they rolled into the corners of the room, with the chink of necklaces as they fell, with the rustle of brocade and tinsel as she tore them from her. 'She has killed them—the helpless fugitives, guests who have eaten the King's salt! She thinks to beguile us all—to beguile thee. But she shall not. It is not too late. Come! Come! Abool—thou shalt have all from me—yea! all, sooner than she should beguile thee thus— Come!'—

She had snatched an old white veil from its peg and wrapped it round her, as she passed rapidly to the door; but he did not move. So she passed back again as swiftly to take his hand, stained as it was, and lay her cheek to it caressingly.

'Thou didst not strike, dear, thou didst not! Come, dear, that she-devil shall not have thee—I will hold thee fast.'

Five minutes after a plain curtained dhoolie left the precincts and swayed past the Great Hall of Audience with its toothed red arches, looking as if they yawned for victims. The courtyard beyond lay strangely silent, despite the shifting crowd, which gathered and melted and gathered again round the little tree-shaded cistern where but the day before Hâfzan and the Moulvie had watched a mother pause to clasp her baby to softer, securer rest.

The woman and the child were at the cistern now, and the Rest had come. Softer, securer than all other rest, and the mother shared it; shared it with other women, other children.

But as the Princess Farkhoonda, fearful of what she might see, peeped through the dhoolie curtains, there was nothing to be seen save the shifting curious crowd, while in impartial sunshine streamed down on it, and those on whom it gazed.

So let the shifting crowding years with their relentless questioning eyes shut out all thought of what lay by the cistern, save that of rest and the impartial sunshine streaming upon it.

For as the beautiful soft eyes drew back relieved, a bugle rang through the arcades, echoed from the wall, floated out into the city. The bugle to set watch and ward, to close the gates; since the irrevocable step had been taken, the death-pledge made.

So the dream of sovereignty began in earnest behind closed gates.

But if women had lost Delhi, those who lay murdered about the little cistern had regained it. For Hâfzan had spoken truth; the strength of the *Huzoors* lay there.

The strength of the real Master!

# 2

# Peace! Peace!

There weeks had passed, and still the dream of sovereignty went on behind the closed gates, while all things shimmered and simmered in the fierce blaze of summer sunlight. The city lay— a rose-red glare dazzling to look at—beside the glittering curves of the river, and the deserted Ridge, more like a lizard than ever, sweltered and slept lazily, its tail in the cool blue water, its head upon the cool green groves of the Subz-mundi. And over all, lay a liquid yellow heat-haze blurring every outline, till the whole seemed some vast mirage.

And still here was no tidings of the master, no cloud of dust upon the Meerut road. None.

Amazing, incredible fact! Men whispered of it on the steps of the Great Mosque when, the last Friday of the fast coming round, its commination service brought many from behind closed doors to realize that by such signs of kingship as beatings of drums, firing of salutes, and levying of loans, Bahâdur Shâh really had filched the throne of his ancestors from the finest fighters in the world. Filched it without a blow, without a struggle, without even a threat, a defiance.

So here they were in a new world without posts or telegraphs, laws or order; time itself turned back hundreds of years and all power of progress vested absolutely in one old man, the Light of Religion, the Defender of the Faith, the Great Moghul! If that were not a miracle it came too perilously near to one for some folk's loyalty; and so they drifted palace-wards when prayers were over to swell the growing crowd of courtiers about the Dream-King. And even the learned and most loyal lingered on the steps to whisper, and call obscure prophecies and ingenious commentaries to mind, and admit that it was strange, wondrous strange, that the numerical values of the year should yield the anagram '*Ungrez tubbah shood ba hur soorut*,' briefly 'The British shall be annihilated'. For the oriental mind loves such trivialities.

244 • A RAJ COLLECTION

And, to all intents and purposes, the English were annihilated, during that short month of peace between the 11th of May and the 8th of June 1857; for Delhi knew nothing of the vain striving, the ceaseless efforts of the master to find tents and carriages, horses, ammunition, medicine, everything save, thank Heaven once more! courage, and the determination to be master still.

Even Soma admitted the miracle grudgingly; for he had so far bolstered up his disloyalty by thoughts of a fair fight. He had not, after all, gone to Delhi direct, but had cut across country to his own village near Hânsi, and had waited there, hoping to hear of a regular outbreak of hostilities before definitely choosing his side; and he was still waiting when, after a fortnight, his greatest chum in the regiment had turned up from Meerut. For Davee Singh had been one of the many sepoys of the 11th who had gone back to the colours after that one brief night of temptation was over. Soma had known this, and more than once as he waited, the knowledge had been as a magnet drawing him back to the old pole of thought; for that his chum should be led to victory and he be among the defeated, was probable enough to make Soma hate himself in anticipation.

But here was Davee Singh, a deserter like he was, sulkily uncommunicative to the village gossips, but to his fellow admitting fiercely that the latter had been right. The *Huzoor*s had forgotten how to fight. Meerut was quiet as the grave; but there was no word of Delhi, and folk said—What did they not say?

So these two, with a strange mixture of regret and relief in their hearts, set out for Delhi to see what was happening there; not knowing that many of their fellows were drifting from it, weary like themselves of inaction.

They had arrived there, two swaggering Rajpoots, in the midst of the thanksgivings and jollity of the Mohammedan Easter which followed on the last Friday of Fast; and they had fallen foul of it frankly. As frankly as the Mohammedans would have fallen foul of a Hindoo Saturnalia, or both Mohammedans and Hindoos would have fallen foul of the festivities in honour of the Queen's Birthday which, on this 25th of May 1857, were going on in every cantonment in India as if there were no such thing as mutiny in the world. So, annoyed with what they saw and heard, they joined themselves to other Rajpoot malcontents promptly. They sneered at the old pantaloon's procession—which was in truth a poor one though half the tailors in Delhi had been impressed to hurry up trappings and robes. Perhaps if Abool-Bukr had still been in charge of squibs and such like, it would have been better; but he was not. The order he had given to let the Princess Farkhoonda's dhoolie pass out, before the gates were closed on that day of the death-pledge, had been his last exercise of authority; for the next Court Journal contained the announcement that he was dismissed from his appointment. So he, hovering between the Thunbi bazaar and the Mufti's quarter, had nothing to do with the procession at which the Rajpoots sneered, criticizing Mirza Moghul the commander-in-chief's seat on a horse, and talking boastfully of the dead heroes, Vicramaditya and Pertap, as warlike Hindoos will. Until, about dusk, words came to blows amid a tinkling of anklets and a terrible smell of musk; for valour drifted as a matter of course to the wooden balconies of the Thunbi bazaar during the month of miracle; so that the inmates, coining money, called down blessings on the new *régime*.

Soma, however, with a cut over one eye sorely in need of a stitch, swore loudly when he could find none to patch him up save a doddering old *hakeem*, who proposed dosing him with paper pills inscribed with the name of Providence—an incredible remedy to one accustomed to all the appliances of hospitals and skilled surgery.

'Yea! no doubt he is a fool,' assented the other sepoys in frank commiseration, 'yet he is the best you will get. For see you, brother, the doctors belong to the *Huzoors*; so, many a brave man must expect to die needlessly, since those cursed dressers are not safe. There was one took the bottles and things and swore he could use them as well as any; and luck went with him until he gave five heroes who had been drunk the night before somewhat to clear their heads. By all the gods in Indra's heaven they were clear even of life in half-an-hour! So we fell on the dresser and cleared him too. Yea! fool or no fool, paper pills are safer!'

Jim Douglas, who, profiting by the dusk and confusion, had lingered by the group after recognizing Soma's voice, turned away with a savage chuckle; not that the tale amused him, but that he was glad to think six of the devils had gone to their account. For those long days of peace and enforced inaction had sunk him lower and lower into sheer animal hatred of those he dare not rebuke. He knew it himself, he felt that his very courage was becoming ferocity, and the thought that others—biding their time as he was—must be sinking into it also, filled him with fierce joy at the thought of future revenge. And yet, so far as he personally was concerned, those long days had passed quietly, securely, peacefully, and he could at any time climb out of all sight and sound of turmoil to a slip of sunlit roof where a woman waited for him with confidence and welcome in her eyes; with something obtrusively English, also, for his refreshment, since tragedy, even the fear of death, cannot claim a whole life, and Kate took to amusing herself once more by making her corner of the East as much

like the West as she dare. That was not much, but Jim Douglas's eye
noted the indescribable difference which the position of a reed stool,
the presence of a poor bunch of flowers, the little row of books in a
niche, made in the familiar surroundings. For there were books and to
spare in Delhi for the price of a few pennies. Jim Douglas might have
brought her a cartload of such *loot* had he deemed it safe; but he did
not, and so the library consisted of grammars and vocabularies from
which Kate learnt with a rapidity which surprised and interested her
teacher. In truth she had nothing else to do. Yet when he came, as he
often did, to find her absorbed in her work, her eyes dreamy with the
puzzles of tense, he resented it inwardly, telling himself, once more,
that women were trivial creatures. And life seemed trivial too, for in
truth his nerves were all jangled and out of tune with the desire to get
away from this strange shadow of a past idyll; to leave all womanhood
behind and fall to fighting manfully. So that often as he sat beside her,
patient outwardly, inwardly fretting to be gone even into the nightmare
of the city, his eye would fall on the circlet of gold he had slipped, out
of sheer arrogance and imperious temper, round that slender wrist, and
feel that somehow he had fettered himself hopelessly when, more than
a year past, he had given that promise. His chance and hers! Was this
all? One woman's safety! And she, following his eyes to the bangle,
would feel the thrill of its first touch once more, and think how strange
it was that his chance and hers were so linked together. But, being a
woman, her heart would soften instinctively to the man who sat beside
her, and whose face grew sterner and more haggard day by day; while
hers?—she could see enough of it even in the little looking-glass on her
thumb to recognise that she was positively getting fat! She tried to
amuse him by telling him so, by telling him many of the little
humorous touches which come even into tragic life, and he was quite
ready to smile at them. But only to please her. So day by day a silence
grew between them as they sat on the inner roof, while Tara span
outside, or watched them furtively from some corner. And the flare of
sunset—unseen behind the parapeted wall—would lie on the swelling
dome and spiked minarets of the Mosque, and make the paper kites,
flown in this month of May by half the town, look like drifting jewels;
fit canopy for the City of Dreams and for this strangest of dreams upon
the housetop.

'Has—has anything gone wrong?' she asked in desperation one day,
when he had sat moodily silent for a longer time than usual. 'I would
rather you told me, Mr Greyman.'

He looked at her vaguely surprised at the name; for he had almost
forgotten it. Forgotten utterly that she could not know any other. And
why should she? He had made the promise under that name; let them

stick to it so long as Fate linked their chances together.⎤

'Nothing; not for us at least,' he said, and then a sudden remorse at his own unfriendliness came over him. 'There was another poor chap discovered to-day;' he added in a softer tone. 'I believe that you and I, Mrs Erlton, must be the only two left now'

'I daresay,' she echoed a little wearily, 'they—they killed him I suppose.'

He nodded. 'I saw his body in the Bazaar afterwards. I used to know him a bit—a clever sort—'

'Yes—'

'Mixed blood, of course, or he could not have passed muster so long as a greengrocer's assistant—'

'Well—I would rather hear if you don't mind.'

His dark eyes met hers with a sudden eagerness, a sudden passion in them.

'What a little thing life is after all! He only said one word—only one. He was selling watermelons, and some brute tried to cheat first, and then cheeked him. And he forgot a moment and said: "*Chup-raho*," (be silent)—only that!—"*chup-raho*"! They were bragging of it—the devils—"*We knew he couldn't be a coolie*," they said, "*that is a master's word.*" My God! What wouldn't I give to say it sometimes! I could have shouted to them then: "*Chup-raho*, you fools! you cowards!" and some of them would have been silent enough—'

He broke off hurriedly, clenching his hands like a vice on each other, as if to curb the tempest of words.

'I beg your pardon,' he said after a pause, rising to walk away; 'I—I lose control—' he paused again and shook his head silently. Kate followed him and laid her hand on his arm; the loose gold fetter slipped to her wrist and touched him too.

'You think I don't understand,' she said with a sudden sob in her voice, 'but I do—you must go away—it isn't worth it—no woman is worth it.'

He turned on her sharply. 'Go? You know I can't. What is the use of suggesting it? Mrs Erlton! Tara is faithful, but she is faithful to me— only to me—you must see that surely—'

'If you mean that she loves you—worships the very ground you tread on,' interrupted Kate sharply, 'that is evident enough.'

'Is that my fault?' he began angrily; I happened—'

'Thank you, I have no wish to hear the story.'

The commonplace, second-rate, mock-dignified phrase came to her lips unsought, and she felt she could have cried in sheer vexation at having used it there—in the very face of Death as it were. But Jim Douglas laughed; laughed good-naturedly.

'I wonder how many years it is since I heard a woman say that? In another world surely,' he said with quite a confidential tone. 'But the fact remains that Tara protects you, as my wife, and if I were to go—'

Kate looked at him with a quick resentment flaming up in her face beneath the stain.

'I think you are mistaken,' she said slowly, 'I believe Tara would be better pleased if—if she knew the truth.'

'You mean if I were to tell her you are not my wife?' he replied quickly. 'Why?'

'Because I should be less of a tie to you—because,' she paused, then added sharply; 'Mr Greyman, I must ask you to tell her the truth, please. I have a right to so much, surely. I have my reasons for it, and if you do not, I shall.'

Jim Douglas shrugged his shoulders. 'In that case I had better tell her myself; not that I think it matters much one way or another, so long as I am here. And the whole thing from beginning to end is chance, nothing but chance.'

'Your chance and mine,' she murmured half to herself. It was the first time she had alluded openly to the strange linking of their fates, and he looked at her almost impatiently.

'Yes! your chance and mine; and we must make the best of it. I'll tell her as I go out.'

But Tara interrupted him at the beginning.

'If the *Huzoor* means that he does not love the *mem* as he loved Zora, that requires no telling, and for the rest what does it matter to this slave?'

'And it matters nothing to me either,' he retorted roughly, 'but of this be sure. Who kills the *mem* kills me, unless I kill first; and by Krishn, and Vishn, and the lot, I'd as lief kill you, Tara, as any one else, if you get in my way.'

A great broad flash of white teeth lit up her face as she salaamed, remarking that the *Huzoor*'s mother must have been as Kunti. And Jim Douglas understanding the complimentary allusion to the God visited mother of the Lunar race, wished as he went downstairs, that he was like the Five Heroes in one respect, at least, and that was in having only a fifth part of a woman to look after, instead of two whole ones who talked of love! So he passed out to listen, and watch, and wait, while the fire-balloons went up into the velvety sky, replacing the kites. For May is the month of marriages also, and night after night these false stars floated out from the Dream-City to form new constellations on the horizon for a few minutes and then disappear with a flare into the darkness—into the darkness whence the master did not come. Yet, as the month ended, villagers passing in with grain from Meerut averred that the masters were not all dead, or else God gave their ghosts a like power in cursing and smiting—which was all poor folk had to look to; since some had appeared and burnt a village.

Not all dead? The news drifted from market to market, but if it penetrated through the palace gates it did not filter through the new curtains and hangings of the private apartments where the King took perpetual cooling draughts, and wrote perpetual appeals for more etiquette and decorum. For nothing likely to disturb the unities of dreams was allowed within the precincts, where every day the old King sat on a mock peacock throne with a new cushion to it, and listened for hours to the high-flown letters of congratulation which poured in, each with its own little covering bag of brocade, from the neighbouring chiefs. And if, any day, there happened to be a paucity of real ones, Hussan Askuri could supply them, like other dreams, at so much a dozen; since nothing more costly than the brocade bag came with them. So that the Mahboob's face, as Treasurer, grew longer and longer over the dressmaker's and upholsterer's bills, and the Court Journal was driven into recording the fact that some one actually presented a bottle of *Pandamus odoratissimus* whatever that may be. Some subtle essence, mayhap, favourable to dreaminess; since, even in the month of peace, drugs were necessary to prevent awakening.

Especially when, on the 30th of May, a sound came over the distant horizon; the sound of artillery.

At last! at last! Jim Douglas who in sheer dread of his own growing despair had taken to spending all the time he dared in moody silence on that peaceful roof, started as if he had been shot, and was down the stairs seeking news. The streets were full of a silent, restless crowd, almost empty of soldiers. They had gone out during the night, he learnt, Meerut-wards; tidings of an army on the banks of the Hindun river, seven or eight miles out, having been brought in by scouts.

At last! at last! He wandered through the bazaars scarcely able to think, wondering only when the army could possibly arrive, feeling a mad joy in the anxious faces around him, lingering by the groups of men collected in every open space simply for the satisfaction of hearing the wonder and alarm in the words; 'So the master lives.'

He lived indeed! Listen! That was his voice over the eastern horizon! Kate, when he came back to the roof about noon, had never seen him in this mood before, and wondered at his fire, his gaiety, his youth. But the recognition brought a dull pain with it, in the thought that this was natural to the man; that gloomy moodiness the result of her presence.

'You are not afraid, surely?' he said suddenly, breaking off in the recital of some future event which seemed to him certain.

'No. I am only glad,' she replied slowly. 'It could not have lasted much longer. It is a great relief.'

'Relief,' he echoed, 'I wonder if you know the relief it is to me?' And then he looked at her remorsefully. 'I have been an awful brute, Mrs Erlton, but women can scarcely understand what inaction means to a man.'

Could they not? she wondered bitterly as he hastened off again, leaving her to long weary hours of waiting, until the red flush of sunset on the bubble dome of the mosque brought him back with a new look on his face—a look of angry doubt.

'The sepoys are coming in again,' he said, 'they claim a victory—but that, of course, is impossible. Still I don't understand, and it is so difficult to get any reliable information.'

'You should go out yourself—I believe it would be best for us both,' replied Kate, 'Tara—'

He shook his head impatiently. 'Not now. What is the use of risking all at the last. We can only have to wait till tomorrow. But I don't understand it, all the same. The sepoys say they surprised the camp— that the buglers were still calling to arms when their artillery opened fire. But so far as I can make out they have lost five guns, and from the amount of *bhang* they are drinking, I believe it was a rout. However, if you don't mind, I'll be off again—and—and don't be alarmed if I stay out.'

'I am not in the least alarmed,' she replied. 'As I have told you before, I don't think it is necessary you should come here at all.'

He paused at the door to glance back at her half-resentfully. To be sure she did not know that he had slept on its threshold as a rule; but anyhow, after eating your heart out over one woman's safety for three weeks, it was hard to be told that you were not wanted. But, thank Heaven! the end was at hand. And yet as he lingered round the watch-fires he heard nothing but boasting, and in more than one of the mosques thanksgivings were being offered up; while outside the walls volunteers to complete the task so well begun were assembling to go forth with the dawn and kill the few remaining infidels. Some drunk with *bhang*, more intoxicated by the lust of blood which comes with the first blow to fighting races like the Rajpoot. It had come to Soma, as, with fierce face seamed with tears, he told the tale again and again of his chum's gallant death. How Davee Singh, brother in arms, his boyhood's playmate, seeing some cowards of artillery-men abandoning a tumbril full of ammunition to the cursed *Mlechcha*'s, had leapt to it like a black-buck, and with a cry to Kali, Mother of Death, had fired his musket into it; so sending a dozen or more of the Hell-doomed to their place, and one more brave Rajpoot to Swarga!

'*Jai! Jai! Kâli mâ ki jai!*'

An echo of the dead man's last cry came from many a living one, as muskets were gripped tighter in the resolve to be no whit behind. A few more such heroes and the Golden Age would come again; the age of the blessed Pandâva, who forgot the cause in the quarrel.

And so for one day more, Jim Douglas strained his ears for that distant thunder on the horizon, while the people of the town, becoming more accustomed to it, went about their business, vaguely relieved at anything which should keep the sepoy's idle hands from mischief.

The red sunset glow was on the mosque again when he returned to the little slip of roof to find Kate working away at her grammars calmly. It was the best thing she could do, since every word she learnt was an additional safeguard; and yet the man could not help a scornful smile.

'It is a rout this time, I am sure,' he said; 'and yet there is no sign of pursuit. I cannot understand it; there seems a Fate about it!'

'Is that anything new?' she asked wearily, as she laid down her book, and with the certain precision which marked all her actions, saw that the water was really boiling before she made the tea. It was made in a *lota*, and drunk out of handleless basins, yet for all that it was western-made tea, strong and unspiced, with cream to put to it also, which she skimmed from a dish set in cold water in the coolest, darkest place she could find. It was dreamlike indeed, and Jim Douglas, drinking his tea, felt, that with his eyes shut, he might have dreamt himself in an English drawing-room.

'Nothing new,' he retorted, 'but it seems incomprehensible. Hark! That is a salute; for the victory, I suppose. Upon my soul I feel as if—as if I were a dream myself—as if I should go mad! Don't look startled— I shan't. The whole thing is a sham—I can see that. But why has no one the pluck to give the House-of-Cards a push and bring it about their ears? And what has become of the army at the Hindun? It took three days to march there from Meerut, I hear—not more than twenty-four miles. No! I cannot understand it. No wonder the people say we are all dead. I begin to believe it myself.'

He certainly heard the saying often enough to bring belief during the 1st and 2nd of June, when there was no more distant thunder on the horizon, and the whole town, steeped and saturated with sunshine, lay half-asleep, the soldiers drowsing off the effect of their drugs.

Dead? Yea! the masters were dead, and those who had escaped were in full retreat up the river; so at least said villagers coming in with supplies. But some one else who had come in with supplies also, sate crouched up like a grasshopper on a great pile of wool-be-tasselled sacks in the corn market and laughed creakily. 'Dead! not they. As the

*tanda* passed Kurnal four days agone the camping ground was white
as a poppy field with tents, and the soldiers like the flies buzzing
round them. And if folk want to hear more, I, Tiddu, Baharupa-Bunjâra
can tell tales beyond the Kashmir gate on the river island where the
bullocks graze.'

The creaking voice rose unnecessarily loud, and a man in the dress
of an Afghan who had been listening—his back to the speaker—moved
off with a surprised smile. Tiddu had proved his vaunted superiority in
this instance; though by what arts he had penetrated the back of a
disguise, Jim Douglas could not imagine. Still here was news indeed—
news which explained some of the mystery, since the seeming retreat
up the river had been, no doubt, for the purpose of joining forces. But
it was something almost better than news—it was a chance of giving
them. He had not dared, for Kate's sake, to risk any confederate as yet;
but here was one ready to hand—a confederate, too, who would do
anything for money.

So that night, he sate in tamarisk shadow on the river island talking
in whispers, while the monotonous clank of the bells hung on the
wandering bullocks sounded fitfully, the flicker of the watchfires
gleamed here and there on the half-dried pools of water, the fireflies
flashed among the bushes, and every now and again a rough, rude
chant rose on the still air.

'They have been there these ten days, *Huzoor*,' came Tiddu's
indifferent voice. 'They are waiting for the siege train. Nigh on three
thousand of them, and some black faces besides.'

Jim Douglas gave an exclamation of sheer despair. To him, living in
the House-of-Cards, the Palace-of-Dreams, such caution seemed
unnecessary. Still, the past being irretrievable, the present remained in
which by hook or by crook to get the letter he had with him, ready
written, conveyed to the army at Kurnal. And Tiddu, with fifty rupees
stowed away in his waistband, being lavish of promise and confidence,
there was no more to be done save creep back to the city, feeling as if
the luck had turned at last.

But the next morning he found the Thunbi bazaar in a turmoil of
talk. There were spies in the city. A letter had been found—written in
the Persian character, it is true—but with the devilish knowledge of the
West in its details of likely spots for attack, the indecision of certain
quarters in the city, its general unpreparedness for anything like
resistance. Who had written it? As the day went on the camps were in
uproar, the palace invaded, the dream disturbed by denouncings of
Ahsan-Oolah, the giver of composing draughts—Mahboob Ali, the
checker of the purse strings—even of Mirza Moghul, commander-in-
chief himself, who might well be eager to buy his recognition as heir

by treachery.

The net result of the letter being that, as Jim Douglas, with wrath in his heart, crept out at dusk to the low levels by the Water bastion, intent on having it out with Tiddu, he could see gangs of sepoys still at work by torchlight strengthening the bridge defence, and had to dodge a measuring party of artillery-men busy range-finding. His suggestions had been of use!

But the old Bunjâra took his fierce reproaches philosophically. ''Tis the miscreant Bhungi,' he assented mournfully. 'He is not to be trusted, but Jhungi having a tertian ague, I deemed a surer foot advisable. Yet the *Huzoor* need not be afraid. Even the miscreant would not betray *his* person; and for the rest, the Presence writes Persian like any court *moonshee.*'

The calm assumption that personal fear was at the bottom of his reproaches, made Jim Douglas desire to throttle the old man, and only the certainty that he dare not risk a row prevented him from going for the ill-gotten rupees at any rate. His thought, however, seemed read by the old rascal, for a lean protesting hand, holding a bag, flourished out of the darkness, and the creaking voice said magnificently—

'Before Murri-âm and the sacred *neem*, *Huzoor*, I have kept my bargain. As for Jhungi or Bhungi, did I make them that I should know the evil in them? But if the *Huzoor* suspects one who *holds his tongue*, let the bargain between us end.'

His hearer could not repress a smile at the consummate cunning of the speech. 'You can keep the money for the next job,' he said briefly; 'I haven't done with you yet, you scoundrel.'

A grim chuckle came out of the shadows as the hand went back into them.

'The *Huzoor* need not fret himself whatever happens. The end is nigh.'

It seemed as if it must be with three thousand British soldiers within sixty miles of Delhi; or less, since they might have marched during those five days. They might be at Delhi any moment. Three thousand men! Enough and to spare, even though in the last few days a detachment or two of fresh mutineers had arrived. Ah! if the blow had been struck sooner.—If—if—

Kate listened during those first days of June to many such wishes, despairs, hopes, from one whose only solace lay in words; since with relief staring him in the face, Jim Douglas crushed down his craving for action. There was no real need for it, he told her; it must involve risk, so they must wait—must sleep and dream like the city!

For, lulled by the delay, stimulated to fresh fancy by the new-comers, the townspeople went on their daily round monotonously, the sepoys boasted and drank *bhang*. And in the palace, the king, in new robes of state, sate on his new cushion and put the sign-manual to such trifles as a concession to a home-born slave that he might 'continue, as heretofore, a-tinning the royal sauce pans!' Though Mahboob Ali's face lengthened as he doled out something on account for faith and finery, and suggested that the army might at least be employed in collecting revenue somewhere. But the army grinned in the commander-in-chief's face, scorned laborious days, and—between the seductions of the Thunbi bazaar—gave peaceful citizens what one petitioner against plunder calls 'a foretaste of the Day of Judgment.'

But one soul in Delhi felt in every fibre of him that the Judgment had come—that atonement must be made.

'Thou wilt kill thyself with prayers and fastings and seekings of other folks' salvations, Moulvie-*sahib*,' said Hâfzan almost petulantly as, passing on her rounds, she saw Mahomed Ismail's anxious face, seeking audience with every one in authority, 'Thou hast done thy best. The rest is with God; and if these find death also, the blame will lie elsewhere.'

'But the blame of those, woman?' he asked fiercely, pointing with trembling finger to the little cistern shaded by the *peepul* tree.

Hâfzan gave a shrill laugh as she passed on.

'Fear not that either, learned one! This world's atonement *for that* will be sufficient for future pardon.'

It might be so, Mahomed Ismail told himself as he hurried off feverishly to another appeal. He had erred in ignorance there; but what of the forty prisoners still at the Kotwâli—forty stubborn Christians despite their dark skins? They were safe so far, but if the city were assaulted?—if some of the fresh, fiery-faithed new comers?—the doubt felt him no peace.

'If thou wilt swear Moulvie-*jee* on thine own eternal salvation that they are Mohammedans, or stake thy soul on their conversion,' jeered those who held the keys. A heavy stake, that! A solemn oath with forty stubborn Christians to deal with. No wonder Mahomed Ismail felt judgment upon him already.

But the stake was staked, the oath spoken on the 6th of June. The record of it is brief; but it stands as history in the evidence of one of the forty. 'We were released in consequence of a Moulvie of the name of Mahomed Ismail giving evidence that we were all Mohammedan; or that if any were Christian they would become Mohammedan.'

And it was given none too soon. For on the 6th of June as the sun set, a silhouette of a man on a horse stood clear against the red-gold in the west, looking down from the Ridge on Delhi. Looking down on the city bathed in the dreamy glamour of the slanting sunbeams; rose-red and violet-shadowed, with the great white dome hovering above the smoke wreaths, and a glitter of gold on the eastern wall, where backed by that arcaded view of the darkening Eastern plains, an old man sate listening to sentiments of fidelity from a pile of little brocaded bags.

It was Hodson of Hodson's Horse, reconnoitring ahead. So there was an Englishman on the Ridge once more as the paper kites came down on the 6th of June. But the fire balloons did not go up; for the night set in gusty and wet, giving no chance to new constellations.

Jim Douglas did not sleep at all that night, for Tiddu had brought word that the English were at Alipore, ten miles out; and nothing but the dread of needless risk kept him in Delhi. For any risk was needless when, to a certainty, the English flag would be flying over the city in a few hours.

And Hodson of Hodson's Horse—back at Alipore—slept late, for he lingered, weary and wet after his long ride, to write to his wife ere turning in, that 'if he had had a hundred of the Guides he could have gone right up to the city wall.'

But Mahomed Ismail slept peacefully, his work being over, and dreamt of Paradise.

# 3

# The Challenge

'For Gawd's sake, sir! don't say I'm unfit for dooty, sir,' pleaded a lad, who, as he stood to attention, tried hard to keep the sharp shivers of coming ague from the doctor's keen eyes. 'I'm all right, ain't I, mates? It ain't a bad sort o' fever at worst, as I oughter know, havin' it constant. It's go ter hell, an' lick the blood up fust as I'm fit for with Jack Pandy. That's all the matter—you see if it ain't, sir!'

He threw his fair curly head back, his blue eyes blazed with the coming fever light, but the bearded man next to him murmured, "Ee's all right, sir. 'Ee'll 'old 'is musket straight, never fear,' and the doctor walked on with a nod.

'They killed his girl at Meerut,' said his company officer in a whisper, and Herbert Erlton standing by set his teeth and glanced back, blue eye meeting blue eye with a sort of triumph.

For it was the 7th of June, and the blow was to be struck, the challenge given at last.

Nearly a month, thought Herbert Erlton, since *it* had happened. He had spent much of the time in bed, struck down with fever; for he had regained Meerut with difficulty, wounded and exhausted. And then it had been too late—too late for anything save to hang round hungrily in the hopes of that challenge to come, with many another such as he.

But it had come at last. The camp was ringing with cheers for the final reinforcement, every soul who could stand was coming out of hospital, and the air, new washed with rain, and cool, seemed to put fresh life, and with it a desire to kill, into the veins of every son of the cold North.

And now the dusk was at hand. The men, half-mad with impatience, laughed and joked over each trivial preparation. Yet, when the order came with midnight, weapons were never gripped more firmly, more sternly, than by those three thousand Englishmen marching to their long-deferred chance of revenge. And some, not able to march, toiled behind in hopes of one fair blow; and not a few, unable even for so much, slipped desperately from hospital beds to see at least one murderer meet with his reward.

For, to the three thousand marching upon Delhi that cool dewy night, sent—so they told themselves—for special solace and succour of the Right, there were but two things to be reckoned with in the wide world. Themselves—Men. Those others—Murderers.

The fireflies, myriad-born from the rain, glimmered giddily in the low marshy land, the steady stars shone over head, and Major Erlton looked at both indifferently as he rode, long-limbed and heavy, through the night whose soft silence was broken only by the jingle of spurs and the squelching of light gun-wheels in water logged ruts; save when— from a distance—the familiar tramp, tramp, of disciplined feet along a road came wafted on the cool wind, for the column in which he was doing duty moved along the canal bank so as to take the enemy, who held an entrenched position five miles from Alipore, in flank. But Herbert Erlton was not thinking of stars or fireflies; was not thinking of anything. He was watching for other lights, the twinkling cresset lights which would tell where the Murderers waited for that first blow. He did not even think of the cause of his desire; he was absorbed in the revenge itself, and a bitter curse rose to his lips, when just before dawn the roll of a gun and the startled flocks of birds flying westwards told him that others were before him.

'Hurry up, men! For God's sake hurry up!' The entreaty passed along the line where the troopers of the 9th Lancers were setting shoulders to the gun-wheels, and every one—men and officers alike— was listening with fierce regret to the continuous roll of cannon, the casual rattle of musketry, telling that the heavy guns were bearing the brunt of it so far.

'Hurry up, men! Hurry up. That's the bridge ahead! Then we can go for them!'

Hark! A silence; if silence it could be called, now that the shouts, and yells, and confused murmur of battle could be heard. But the guns were silent. And hark again! A ringing cheer! Bayonet work that, at last, at last! And yonder, behind the fireflies in the bushes?—Surely those were men in flight! Hurrah! Hurrah!

When Major Erlton returned from that wild charge it was to find that one splendid rush from the 75th Regiment had cleared the road to Delhi. The murderers had been swept from their shelter, their guns— some fighting desperately, others standing stupidly to meet death, and many with clasped hands and vain protestations of loyalty on their lips paying the debt of their race. But one man had paid some other debt, Heaven knows what; and the Rifle Brigade cleared the road to Delhi of an English deserter fighting against his old regiment.

It had not taken an hour; and now, as the yellow sun peered over the eastern horizon, a little knot of staff officers consulted what to do next.

What to do? Herbert Erlton and many another wondered stupidly what the deuce fellows could mean by asking the question when the jagged line of the Ridge lay not three miles off, and Delhi lay behind that? Could any sane person think that England had done its duty at sunrise, even though forty good men and true of the three thousand had dealt their first and last blow?

But if some did, there were not many; so, after a pause, the march began again. Westwards, by a forking road, to the flat head of the Lizard lying above the Subzmandi, eastward towards the tail and the old cantonment. And this time the bayonets went with the jingling spurs, and together they cleared the green groves merrily. Still, even so, it was barely nine o'clock when they met the eastward column again at Hindoo Rao's house and shook hands over their bloodless victory. For the westward force had lost seven men, the eastward but one; despite the fact that the retreating Murderers had attempted a rally in their old lines.

Nine o'clock! In seven hours the ten miles had been marched, the battle of Budli-ke-serai won, and below them lay Delhi. Within twelve hundred yards rose the Moree bastion, the extreme western point of that city face which, with the Kashmir gate jutting about its middle and the Water bastion guarding its eastern end must be the natural target of their valour—a target three-quarters of a mile long by twenty-four feet high.

Seven hours! And the Murderers had been driven into the city, while

the Men had gained 'twenty-six guns and the finest possible base for
the conduct of future operations'. The Ridge, the old cantonments were
once more echoing to the master's step, and the city-folk, as they
looked eagerly from the walls, had the first notice of defeat in the
smoke and flames of the sepoy lines which the English soldiers fired in
reckless revenge; reckless because the tents were not up, and they
might at least have been a shelter from the sun.

But the Delhi force, taken as a whole, was in no mood to think; and
so perhaps those at the head of it felt bound to think the more. There
was Delhi undoubtedly; but the rose-red walls with their violet
shadows looked formidable. And who could tell how many Murderers
it harboured? A thousand of them or thereabouts would return to
Delhi no more; but, even so, if all the regiments known to have
mutinied and come to Delhi were at their full strength, the odds must
still be close on four to one. And then there was the rabble, armed no
doubt from the larger magazine below the Flagstaff Tower, which, alas,
had found no Willoughby for its destruction on the 11th of May. And
then there was the May sun. And then—and then—

'What's up? When are we going on?' asked Major Erlton, sitting fair
and square on his horse in the shadow of the big trees by Hindoo
Rao's house, as an orderly officer rode past him.

'Aren't going on today. Chief thinks it safer not—these native
cities—'

He was gone, and Herbert Erlton without a word threw himself
heavily from his horse with a clatter and jingle of swords and
scabbards and Heaven knows what of all the panoply of war; so with
the bridle over his arm he stood looking out over the bloody city
which lay quiet as the grave. Only, every now and again, a white puff
of smoke followed by a dull roar came from a bastion like a salute of
welcome to the living, or a parting honour to the dead.

Was it possible? His eyes followed the familiar outline mechanically
till they rested half-unconsciously on some ruins beside the city wall.
Then with a rush memory came back to him, and as he turned
hurriedly to loosen his horse's girths, the tears seemed to scald his tired
angry eyes. Yet it was not the memory of Alice Gissing only, which sent
these unwonted visitors to Herbert Erlton's eyes; it was a wild,
desperate pity and despair for all women.

And as he stood there ignoring his own emotion, or at least hiding
it, one of the women whom he pitied was looking up with a certain
resentful eagerness at a man, who, from the corner turret of that roof in
the Mufti's quarter, was straining his eyes Ridge-ways.

'They must rest, surely,' she said sharply; 'you cannot expect them
to be made of iron—'; as you are, she was about to add, but withheld

even that suspicion of praise.

'Well! There goes the bugle to pitch tents anyhow,' retorted Jim Douglas recklessly. 'So I suppose we had better have our breakfast too—coffee and a rasher of bacon and a boiled egg or so. By God! it's incredible—it's—' He flung himself on a reed stool and covered his face with his hands for a second; but he was up facing her the next. 'I've no right to say these things—no one knows better than I how worse than idle it is to press others to one's own tether—I learned that lesson early, Mrs Erlton. But'—he gave a quick gesture of impotent impatience—'when the news first came in, the men who brought it ran in at the Kashmir and Moree gates in hundreds, and out at the Ajmere and Turkoman, calling that the masters had come back; and people were keeking round the doors hopefully. I tell you the very boys as I came in here were talking of school again—of holiday tasks, perhaps— Heaven knows! People were running in the streets—they will be walking now—in another hour they will be standing; and then!—Well! I suppose the General funks the sun. So I'll be off. I only came because I thought I had better be here in case; you see the men would have had their blood up, rushing the city—'

'And your breakfast?' she asked coldly, almost sarcastically; for he seemed to her so hard, so grudging, while her sympathies, her enthusiasms were red-hot for her new comers.

He laughed bitterly. 'I've learned to live on parched grain like a native, if need be, and I take opium too; so I shall manage.' He was back again to the turret, however, before two o'clock, curtly apologetic, calmer, yet still eager. The people, to be sure, he said, had given up keeking round their doors at every clatter, and the gates had been closed on deserters by the palace folk; but no one had thought of bricking them up, and after going round everywhere he doubted if there were more than seven or eight thousand real soldiers in Delhi. The 74th and 11th regiments had been slipping away for days, and numbers of men who had remained did not really mean to fight. Tiddu, who seemed to know everything, said that the mutineers had been very strongly entrenched at Budli-serai, so the resistance could not have been very dogged, or our troops could not have fought their way in before nine o'clock. Yes! since she pressed for an answer, the General might have been wise in waiting for the cool. Only he, personally, wished he had thought it possible, for then he would at any rate have tried to get a letter sent to the Ridge. Now it was too late.

And then suddenly, as he spoke, a fierce elation flashed to his face again at the sound of bugles, the roll of a gun from the Moree bastion; and he was up the stairs of the turret in a second, casting a half-humorous, wholly deprecating glance back at her.

'*A hare and a tortoise once*—I learned that at school—put it into Latin!' he said lightly, as the walls round them quivered to the reverberating rolls, thundering from the city wall.

Kate walked up and down the roof restlessly, passing into the outer one so as to be further from the eager sentinel and his criticisms. Tara was spinning calmly, and Kate wondered if the woman could be alive? Did she not know that brave men on both sides were going to their deaths? And Tara, from under her heavy eyelashes, watched Kate, and wondered how any woman who had brought Life into the world could fear Death. Did not the Great Wheel spin unceasingly? Let brave men, then, die bravely—even Soma. For she knew by this time that her brother was in Delhi, and by the master's orders had dodged his detection more than once. So the two women waited, each after her nature; while like the pulse of time itself, the beat of artillery shook the walls. It came so regularly that Kate, crouching in a corner weary of restless pacing to and fro, grew almost drowsy and started at a step beside her.

'A false alarm,' said Jim Douglas quietly; 'a sortie, as far as I could judge, from the Moree; easily driven back.'

His tone roused her antagonism instantly. 'Perhaps they are waiting for night.'

'There is a full moon—almost,' he replied; 'besides, there is fair cover up to within four hundred yards of the Cabul gate. They could rush that, and a bag or two of gunpowder would finish the business.'

'They could do that as well tomorrow,' she remarked hotly.

'I hope to God they won't be such fools as to try it!' he replied as hotly. 'If they don't come in to night they will have to batter down the walls, and then the city will go against them. What city wouldn't? It will rouse memories we can't afford to rouse. Who could? And every wounded man who creeps in today will be a centre of resistance by tomorrow. The women will hound others on to protect him. It is their way. You have always to allow for humanity in war. Well! we must wait and see.' He paused and rubbed his forehead vexedly. 'If I had known, I might have got out with the sortie; but I suppose I couldn't really—' He paused, shrugged his shoulders, and went out.

And Kate, as she sat watching the red flush of sunset grow to the dome, remembered his look at her with a half-angry pang. Why should she be in this man's way always? So the day died away in soft silence, and there on the housetop it seemed incredible that so much hung in the balance, and that down in the streets the crowds must be drifting to and fro restlessly. At least she supposed so. Yet, monotonous as ever, there was the evening cry of the *Muazzim* and the persistent thrumming of *toms-toms* and *saringis* which evening brings to a native city. It rose louder than usual from a roof hard by, where, so Tara told her, a princess of the blood royal lived; a great friend of Abool-Bukr's. The remembrance of little Sonny's hands all red with blood, and the cruel face smiling over an apology, made her shiver, and wonder as she often did with a desperate craving what the child's fate had been. Why had she let the old ayah take him? Why was he not here, safe; making life bearable? As she sat, the tears falling quietly over her cheeks, Tara came and looked at her curiously. 'The *mem* should not cry', she said consolingly, 'the *Huzoor* will save her somehow.'

For an instant Kate felt as if she would rather he did not. Then on the distance and the darkening air came a familiar sound: the evening bugle from the Ridge with its cheerful invitation—

'*Come-and-set-a-picquet-boys! come-and-keep-a-watch.*'

So some one else was within hail, ready to help! The knowledge brought her a vast consolation, and for the first time in that environment she slept through the night without wakening in deadly dreamy fear at the least sound.

Even the uproarious devilry of Prince Abool in the alley below did not rouse her, when about midnight he broke loose from the feverish detaining hold which Newâsi had kept on him by every art in her power during the day, lest the master returning should find the Prince in mischief. But now he lurched away with a party of young bloods who had come to fetch him, swearing that he must celebrate the victory properly; that but for a moment's weakness, fostered by a foolish, fearful woman, he might have led the cavalry. He wept maudlin tears over the thought, swearing he would yet show his mettle. He would not leave one Hell-doomed alive; and, suiting the action to the word, he began incontinently to search for fugitives in some open cow-yards close by, till the strapping dairymaids, roused from slumber, declared in revenge that they had seen a man slip down the culvert of the big drain. Five minutes afterwards Prince Abool, half-choked, half-drowned, was dragged from the sewer by his comrades, protesting feebly that he must have killed an infidel; else why did the blood smell so horribly?

But after that incident the city sank into the soundlessness, the stillness, of the hour before dawn, save for a recurring call of the watch bugles on wall and Ridge and the twinkling lights which burned all night in camp and court. For those two had challenged each other, and the fight was to the bitter end. What else could it be with a death-pledge between them? The townspeople might sleep, uncertain which side they would espouse, but between the Men and the Murderers the issue was clear.

And it remained so, even though the month-of-miracle lingered, and no assault came on the morrow, or the day after, or the day after that. So that the old King himself set his back to the wall and for once spoke as a king should. 'If the army will not fight without pay, punish it,' he said to the commander-in-chief. But it was only a flash in the pan, and he retired once more to the latticed marble balcony and set the sign-manual to a general fiat that 'those who would be satisfied with a trifle might be paid something'. Whereat Mahboob Ali shook his head, for there was not even a trifle in the privy purse.

As for the city people, their ears and tongues grew longer during those three days, when the sepoys, returning from the sorties and skirmishes, brought back tales of glorious victory, stupendous slaughter. Her man had killed fifteen *Huzoor*s himself, and there were not five hundred left on the Ridge, said Futteh-deen's wife to Pera-Khan's as they gossiped at the wall; and a good job too. When they were gone there would be an end of these sword-cuts and bullet wounds. Not a wink of sleep had she had for nights, yawned Zainub, what with thirsts and poultices! And on the steps of the mosque, too, the learned lingered to discuss the newspapers. So Bukht-Khân with 50,000 men was on his way to swear allegiance, and the Shah of Persia had sacked Lahôre, where *Jân Lârnce* himself had been caught trying to escape on an elephant and identified by wounds on his back. And the London correspondent of the *Authentic News* was no doubt right in saying the Queen was dumbfounded, while the St Petersburg one was clearly correct in asserting that the Czar was about to put on his crown at last. Why not, since his vow regarding it was at an end, with the passing of India from British supremacy?

So the dream went on; the little brocaded bags kept coming in; the stupendous slaughter continued.

Yet every night the Widow's Cruse of a Ridge echoed to the picquet bugles, and the court and the camp twinkled at each other till dawn.

A sort of vexed despairing patience came to Jim Douglas, and more than once he apologized to Kate for his moodiness, like a patient who apologizes to his nurse when unfavourable symptoms set in. He gave her what news he could glean—which was not much—for Tiddu had gone south for another consignment of grain. But on the morning of the 12th he turned up with a face clearer than it had been, and a friendlier look in his eyes.

'The Guides came into camp yesterday. Splendid fellows. They were at it hammer and tongs immediately, though that man Rujjub Ali, I told you of,—it was he who said Hodson was with the force—declares they marched from Murdân in twenty-one days. Over thirty miles a day! Well! they looked like it. I saw them ride slap up to the Cabul gate. And—and I saw some one else with them, Mrs Erlton. I wasn't sure at first if I had better tell you; but I think I had. I saw your husband.'

'My husband,' she echoed faintly. In truth the past seemed to have slipped from her. She seemed to have forgotten so much; and then suddenly she remembered that the letter he had written must still be in the pocket of the dress Tara had hidden away. How strange! She must find it, and look at it again.

Jim Douglas watched her curiously with a quick recognition of his own rough touch. Yet it could not be helped.

'Yes. He was looking splendid, doing splendidly. I couldn't help thinking—Well! I wish you could have seen him; you would have been proud'—

She interrupted him with swift, appealing hand. 'Oh!—Don't—please don't—what have I to do with it? Can't you see—can't you understand he was thinking of—of *her*! And doesn't she deserve it? While I—I—'

It was the first breakdown he had seen during those long weeks of strain, and he stood absolutely, wholly compassionate before it.

'My dear lady,' he said gently, as he walked away to give her time, 'if you good women would only recognize the fact which worse ones do, that most men think of many women in their lives, you would be happier. But I doubt if Major Erlton was thinking of any one in particular. He was thinking of the dead, and you are among them, for *him*; remember that'. 'Come,' he continued, crossing over to her again and holding out his hand. 'Cheer up! Aren't you always telling me it is bad for a man to have one woman on the brain, and think, think how many there may be to avenge by this time!'

His voice, sounding a whole gamut of emotion, a whole cadence of consolation, seemed to find an echo in her heart, and she looked up at him gratefully.

It would have found one also in most hearts upon the Ridge, where men were beginning to think with a sort of mad fury of women and children in a hundred places to which this unchecked conflagration of mutiny was spreading swiftly. What would become of Lucknow, Cawnpore, Agra, if something were not done at Delhi? if the challenge so well given were not followed up? And men elsewhere telegraphed the same question, until, half-heartedly, the General listened, finally gave a grudging assent, to a plan of assault urged by four subalterns.

What the details were matters little. A bag of gunpowder somewhere, with fixed bayonets to follow. A gamester's throw for sixes or deuce-ace, so said even its supporters. But anything seemed better than being a target for artillery practice five times better than their own, while the mutiny spread around them.

The secret was well kept as such secrets must be. Still the afternoon of the 12th saw a vague stir on the Ridge, and though even the fighting men turned in to sleep, each man knew what the midnight order meant which sent him fumbling hurriedly with belts and buckles.

'The city at last, mates! No more playin' ball,' they said to each other as they fell in, and stood waiting the next order under the stars; waiting with growing impatience as the minutes slipped by.

'My God! where is Graves?' fumed Hodson. 'We can't go on without him and his three hundred. Ride, some one, and see. The explosion party is ready, the Rifles safe within three hundred yards of the wall. The dawn will be on us in no time—Ride sharp!'

'Something has gone wrong,' whispered a comrade. 'There were lights in the General's tent and two mounted officers—there! I thought so! It's all up!'

All up indeed! For the bugle which rang out was the retreat. Some of those who heard it remembered a moonlight night just a month before when it had echoed over the Meerut parade ground; and if muttered curses could have silenced it the bugle would have sounded in vain. But they could not, and so the men went back sulkily, despondently to bed; back to inaction, back to target practice.

'Graves says he misunderstood the verbal orders, so I understand,' palliated a staff-officer in a mess tent whither others drifted to find solace from the chill of disappointment, the heat of anger. A tall man with hawk's eyes and sparse red hair paused for a moment ere passing out into the night again. 'I dislike euphemisms,' he said curtly. 'In these days I prefer to call a spade a spade. Then you can tell what you have to trust to.'

'Hodson's in a towering temper,' said an artillery man as he watched a native servant thirstily; 'I don't wonder. Well! here's to better luck next time.'

'I don't believe there will be a next time,' echoed a lad gloomily. And there was not, *for him*, the target practice settling that point definitely next day.

'But why the devil couldn't—' began another vexed voice, then paused. 'Ah! here comes Erlton from the General. He'll know. I say, Major—' he broke off aghast.

'Have a glass of something, Erlton!' put in a senior hastily 'you look as if you had seen a ghost, man!'

The Major gave an odd hollow laugh. 'The other way on—I mean—I—I can't believe it—but my wife—she—she's alive—she's in Delhi.' The startled faces around seemed too much for him; he sat down hurriedly and hid his face in his hands, only to look up in a second more collectedly, 'It has brought the whole d—d business home, somehow, to have her there.'

'But how?'—The eager voices got so far—no further.

'I nearly shot him—should have if he had not ducked, for the get-up was perfect. Some of you may know the man—Douglas—Greyman—a trainer chap, but, by God! a well-plucked one. He sneaked into my tent to tell. But I don't understand it yet, and he said he would come back and arrange. It was all so hurried, you see; I was due at the muster, and he was off, when he heard what was up, to see Graves—whom he knows. Oh curse the whole lot of them! Here, *khansâman!* brandy—anything!'

He gulped it down fiercely, for he had heard of more than life from Jim Douglas.

The latter meanwhile was racing down a ravine as his shortest way back to the city. His getting out had been the merest chance, depending on his finding Soma as sentry at the sally-port of the ruined magazine. He had instantly risked the danger of another confederate for the opportunity, and he was just telling himself with a triumph of gladness that he had been right, when a curious sound like the rustling of dry leaves at his very feet, made him spring into the air and cross the flat shelf of rock he was passing at a bound; for he knew what the noise meant. A true lovers' knot of deadly viper, angry at intrusion, lay there; the dry Ridge swarms with them. But, as he came down lightly on his feet again, something slipped from under one of them, and though he did not fall, he knew in a second that he was crippled; break or sprain, he knew instantly that he could not hope to reach the sally-port before Soma's watch was up. Yet he must get back to the city; for *this*—he had tried a step by this time with the aid of a projecting rock—might make it impossible to return for days if he did the easiest thing and crawled upwards again on hands and knees. That, then, was not to be thought of. The Ajmere gate, however, *might* be open for traffic; the Delhi one certainly was, morning and evening. The latter meant a round of nearly four miles, and endless danger of discovery; but it must be done. So he set his face westwards.

It was just twenty-four hours after this, that Tara, unable for longer patience, told Kate that she must lock herself in, while she went out to seek news of the master. Something must have happened. It was thirty-six hours since they had seen him, and if he was gone, that was an end.

Her face as she spoke was fierce, but Kate did not seem to care; she had in truth almost ceased to care of her own safety except for the sake of the man who had taken so much trouble about it. So she sat down quietly, resolved to open the locked door no more. They might break it in if they chose, or she could starve. What did it matter?

Tara meanwhile went, naturally, to seek Soma's aid—all other considerations fading before the master's safety; and so, of course, came instantly on the clue she sought. He had left the city, let out by Soma's own hands; hands which had never meant to let him in again—that being a different affair. And though he had said he would return, why should he? asked Soma. Whereupon Tara, to prove her ground for fear, told of the hidden *mem*. She would have told anything for the sake of the master. And Soma looked at her fierce face apprehensively.

'That is for afterwards!' she said curtly, impatiently. 'Now, we must make sure he is not wounded. There was fighting today. Come, thou can'st give the password and we can search before dawn if we take a light. That is the first thing.'

But as, cresset in hand, Tara stooped over many a huddled heap or long, still, stretch of limb, Kate, with a beating heart, was listening to the sound of some one on the stairs. The next moment she had flung the door wide at the first hint of the familiar knock.

'Where is Tara?' asked Jim Douglas peremptorily, still holding to the door jamb for support.

'She went—to look for you—we thought—what has happened?— What is the matter?' she faltered.

'Fool! as if that would do any good! Nothing's the matter, Mrs Erlton. I hurt my ankle, that's all.' He tried to step over the threshold as he spoke, but even that short pause from sheer dogged effort, had made its renewal an agony, and he put out his hand to her blindly. 'I shall have to ask you to help me—' he began, then paused. Her arm was round him in a second, but he stood still, looking up at her curiously, 'To—to help—' he repeated. Then she had to drag him forward by main force so that he might fall clear of the door, and enable her to close it swiftly; for who could tell what lay behind?

One thing was certain. That hand on her arm had almost scorched her—the ankle he had spoken of must have been agony to move. Yet there was nothing to be done save lay cold water to it, and to his burning head, settle him as best she could on a pillow and quilt as he lay, and then sit beside him waiting for Tara to return; for Tara could bring what was wanted.

But if Tara was never to return? Kate sat, listening to the heavy breathing broken by half-delirious moans, while the stars dipped and the grey of dawn grew to that dominant bubble of the mosque; and, as she sat, a thousand wild schemes to help this man—who had helped her for so long—passed through her brain, filling her with a certain gladness; until in the early dawn Tara's voice, calling on her, stole through the door.

It was still so dark that Kate, opening it with the quick cry—'He is here, Tara, he is here safe!' did not see the tall figure standing behind the woman's, did not see the menace of either face, did not see Tara's quick thrust of a hand backwards as if to check some one behind.

So she never knew that Jim Douglas, helpless, unconscious, had yet stepped once more between her and death; for Tara was on her knees beside the prostrate figure in a second, and Soma, closing the door carefully, salaamed to Kate with a look of relief in his handsome face. This settled the doubtful duty of denouncing hidden *Mlechchas*. How could that be done in a house where the master lay sick?

And he lay sick for days and weeks, fighting against sun-fever and inflammation, against the general strain of that past month of inaction, which, as Kate found with a pulse of soft pity, had sprinkled the hair about his temples with grey.

'He would die but for her,' said Tara gloomily, grudgingly, 'so she must live, Soma—'

'Nay! 'twas not I—' began her brother, then held his peace, doubtful if the disavowal was to his praise or blame; for duty was a puzzle to most folks in those hot lingering days of June when the Ridge and the City skirmished with each other and wondered mutually if anything were gained by it. Yet both Men and Murderers were cheerful, and Major Erlton going to see the hospital after that fifteen hours fight of the 23rd of June, when the centenary of Plassey, a Hindoo fast, and a Mahomedan festival, made the sepoys come out to certain victory in full parade uniform with all their medals on, heard the lad whose girl had been killed at Meerut say in an aggrieved tone, 'and the nigger as stuck me 'ad 'er Majesty's scarlet coatee on 'is d—d carcase, and a 'eap of medals she give him a blazin' on his breast—dash 'is impudence.'

So blue eye met blue eye again sympathetically; for that was no time to see the pathos of the story.

# 4

# Bugles and Fifes

There was a blessed coolness in the air, for the rains had broken, the molten heats of June had passed. And still that handful of obstinate aliens clung like barnacles to the bare red rocks of the Ridge. Clung all the closer because in one corner of it, beside the canal, they had become part of the soil itself in rows on rows of new-made graves. A strong rear guard this, what with disease and exposure superadded to skirmishes and target-practice. Yet, though not a gun in the city had been silenced, not a battery advanced a yard, the living garrison day after day dug these earthworks for the dead one, firm as if in silent resolve to yield no inch of foothold on those rocks until the Judgment Day, when Men and Murderers should pass together to the great settlement of this world's quarrels.

And yet those in command began to look at each other, and ask what the end was to be; for though, despite the daily drain, the Widow's Cruse grew in numbers as time went on, the city grew also, portentously.

Still the men were cheerful, the Ridge strangely unlike a war-camp in some ways; for the country to the rear was peaceful, posts came every day, and there was no lack even of luxuries. Grain merchants, deserting their city shops, set up amid the surer payments of the cantonment bazaar, and greed of gain brought hawkers of fruit, milk, and vegetables to run the gauntlet of the guns; while some poor folk living on their wits, when there was not a rag or a patch or a bit of wood left to be looted in the deserted bungalows, took to earning pennies by tracking the big shot as they trundled in the ravines, and bringing them to the masters who had need of them.

Between the rain-showers too, men, after the manner of Englishmen, began to talk of football matches, sky races, and bewail the fact of the racquet court being within range of walls. But some, like Major Reid—who never left his post at Hindoo Rao's house for three months—preferred to face the city always; to watch it as a cat watches a mouse to whom she means to deal death by and by. Herbert Erlton was one of these, and so the old *khânsaman* with whom Kate used to quarrel over his terribly Oriental ideas of Irish stew and such like—would bring him his lunch, sometimes his dinner, to the picquets. It was quite a dignified procession, with a cook-boy carrying a brazier, so that the *Huzoor*'s food should be hot, and the *bhisti* carrying a porous pot of water holding bottles, so that the *Huzoor*'s drink might be cool. The *khânsaman*—a wizened figure with many yards of waistband swathed round his middle—leading the way with the mint sauce for the lamb, or the mustard for the beefsteak. He used at first to mumble charms and vows for safe passage as he crossed the Valley of the Shadow—as a dip where round shot loved to dance was nicknamed by the men; but so many others of his trade were bringing cool drinks and hot food to the master that he soon grew callous to the danger, and grinned like the rest when a wild caper to dodge a trundling thundering ball made a fair-haired laddie remark sardonically to the caperer, 'It's well for you, my boy, that you haven't spilt my dinner!'

Perhaps it was, considering the temper of the times. Herbert Erlton, eating his lunch, sheltered from the pelting rain behind the low scarp which by this time scored the summit of the Ridge, smiled also. He was all grimed and smirched with helping young Light—the gayest dancer in Upper India—with his guns. He helped wherever he could in his spare time, for a great restlessness came over him when out of sight of those rose-red walls; they had a fascination for him since Jim Douglas's failure to return had left him uncertain what they held. So, when the day's work slackened, as it always did towards sunset, and—the rain clearing—he had drifted back to his tent for a bath and a change, he drifted out again along the central road, where those off duty were lounging, and the sick had their beds set out for the sake of company and cooler air. It was a quieter company than usual, for some two days before, the General himself had joined the rear guard by the canal; struck down by cholera, and dying with the half-conscious, wholly pathetic words on his lips, 'Strengthen the Right'.

And that very day the auctions of his and other dead comrade's effects had been held; so that more than one usually thoughtless youngster looked down, maybe, on a pair of shoes into which he had stepped over a grave.

Still it was an eager company, as it discussed Lieut. Hills' exploit of the morning, and asked for the latest bulletin of that reckless young fighter with fists against the swords.

'How was it?' asked the Major, 'I only heard the row. The beggars must have got clean into camp.'

'Right up to the artillery lines. You see it was so beastly misty and rainy, and they were dressed like the native vedette. So Hills, thinking them friends, let them pass his two guns, until they began charging the Carabineers; and then it was too late to stop 'em.'

'Why?'

'Carabineers—didn't stand, somehow—except their officer. So Hills charged instead. By George! I'd have given a fiver to see him do it! You know what a little chap he is—a boy to look at. And then—'

'And then,' interrupted the doctor who had been giving a glance at a ticklish bandage as he passed the bed round which the speakers had gathered, 'I think I can tell you in his own words; for he was quite cool and collected when they brought him in—said it was from bleeding so much about the head—'

A ripple of mirth ran through the listeners, but Major Erlton did not smile this time; the laugh was too tender.

'He said he thought if he charged it would be a diversion, and give time to load up. So he rode—Yes! I should like to have seen it too!—Slap at the front rank, cut down the first fellow, slashed the next over the face. Then the two following crashed into him, and down he went at such a pace that he only got a slice to his jacket and lay snug till the troop—a hundred and fifty or so—rode over him. Then—ha—ha! he got up and looked for his sword! Had just found it ten yards off, when three of them turned back for him. He dropped one from his horse, dodged the other who had a lance, and finally gashed him over the head. Number three was on foot—the man he'd dropped, he thinks, at first—and they had a regular set to. Then Hills' cloak, soaked with rain, got round his throat and half-choked him, and the brute managed to disarm him. So he had to go for him with his fists, and by punching merrily at his head managed all right till he tripped over his cloak and fell—'

'And then,' put in another voice eagerly, 'Tombs, his Major, who had been running from his tent through the thick of those charging devils, on foot, to see what was up that the Carabineers should be retiring, saw him lying on the ground, took a pot shot at thirty paces—and dropped his man!'

'By George, what luck!' commented some one; 'he must have been blown!'

'Accustomed to turnips, I should say,' remarked another, with a curiously even voice; the voice of one with a lump in his throat, and a slight difficulty in keeping steady.

'Did they kill the lot?' asked Major Erlton quickly.

'Bungled it rather, but it was all right in the end. They were a plucky set, though; charged to the very middle of the camp, shouting to the black artillery to join them—to come back with them to Delhi!'

'But they met with a pluckier lot!' interrupted the man who had suggested turnips. 'The black company wasn't ready for action. The white one behind it was; unlimbered, loaded. And the blackies knew it. So they called out to fire—fire at once—fire sharp—fire through them— Well! d—n it all, black or white I don't care, it's as plucky a thing as has been done yet—' he moved away, his hands in his pockets, attempting a whistle; perhaps to hide his trembling lips.

'I agree,' said the doctor gravely 'though it wasn't necessary to take them at their word. But somehow it makes that mistake afterwards all the worse.'

'How many of the poor beggars were killed, doctor?' asked an uneasy voice in the pause which followed.

'Twenty or so. Grass-cutters and such like. They were hiding in the cemetery from the troopers—who were slashing at every one; and our men pursuing the party which escaped over the canal bridge—made— made a mistake. And—I'm sorry to say there was a woman —'

'There have been too many mistakes of that sort,' said an older voice breaking the silence, 'I wish to God some of us would think a bit. What would our lives be without our servants, who, let us remember, outnumber us by ten to one? If they weren't faithful—'

'Not quite so many, Colonel,' remarked the doctor with a nod of approval. 'Twenty families came to the brigade-major today with their bundles, and told him they preferred the quiet of home to the distraction of camp. I don't wonder—'

'It is all their own fault,' broke in an angry young voice. 'Why did they—'

And so began one of the arguments, so common in camp, as to the right of revenge pure and simple; arguments fostered by the newspapers, where, every day, letters appeared from 'Spartacus', or 'Fiat Justitia', or some such *nom de plume*. Letters all alike in one thing, that they quoted texts of Scripture; notably one about a daughter of Babylon and the blessedness of throwing children on stones.

But Major Erlton did not stop to listen to it. The ethics of the question did not interest him, and in truth mere revenge was lost in him in the desire, not so much to kill, as to fight. To go on hacking and hewing for ever and ever. As he drifted on, smoking his cigar, he thought quite kindly of the poor devils of grass-cutters who really worked uncommonly well; just, in fact, as if nothing had happened. So did the old *khânsaman*, and the sweeper who had come back to him on his return to the Ridge, saying that the *Huzoor* would find the tale of chickens complete. And the garden of the ruined house near the Flagstaff Tower whither his feet led him unconsciously—as they often did of an evening—was kept tidy. The gardener—when he saw the tall figure approaching—going over to a rose-bush, which, now that the rain had fallen was new budding with white buds, and picking him a buttonhole. He sat down on the plinth of the verandah twiddling it idly in his fingers as he looked out over the panorama of the eastern plains, the curving river, and the city with the white dome of the mosque hanging unsupported above the smoke and mist wreaths. For now, at sunsetting, the sky was a mass of rose-red and violet cloud and a white steam rose from the dripping trees and the moist ground. It was a perfect picture. But he only saw the city. That, to him, was India. That filled his eye. The wide plains east and west, north and south— where the recent rain had driven every thought save one of a harvest to come, from the minds of millions—where the master meant simply the claimer of revenue—might have been non-existent so far as he, and his like, were concerned.

Yet even for the city he had no definite conception. He merely looked at it idly, then at the rosebud he held. And that reminding him of a certain white marble cross with 'Thy will be done' on it, he rose suddenly, almost impatiently. But there was no resignation in *his* face, as he wandered towards the batteries again with the white flower of a blameless life stuck in his old flannel coat, and a strange conglomerate of pity and passion in his heart; while the city—as the light faded— grew more and more like the clouds above it, rose-red and purple; until, in the distance, it seemed indeed a City of Dreams.

In truth it was so still, despite the clangour of bugles and fifes which Bukht Khân brought with him when, on the 1st of July, he crossed the swollen river in boats with five thousand mutineers. A square broad-shouldered man was Bukht Khân, with a broad face and massive beard; a massive sonorous voice also, to match. A man of the Cromwell type, of the church militant, disciplinarian to the back bone, believing in drill; yet with an eye to a Providence above platoon exercise. And there was no lack of soldiers to drill in Delhi by this time. They came in squads and battalions, to jostle each other in the streets and overflow into the camp on the southern side of the city—that furthest from the obstinate colony on the Ridge! But first they flung themselves against it in all the ardour of new brooms, and failing to sweep the barnacles away, subsided into the general state of dreaminess and drugs. For the bugles and fifes could always be disobeyed, on the plea that they were not sounded by the right commander-in-chief. There were three of them now. Bukht Khân the Queen's nominee, Mirza Moghul, and another son of the King's, Khair Sultân. So that Abool-Bukr's maudlin regrets for possible office became acute, and Newâsi's despairing hold on his hand had to gain strength from every influence she could bring to bear upon it. Even drunkenness and debauchery were safer than intrigue, in view of that vision of retribution which seemed to have left him, and taken to haunting her day and night. So she held him fast, and when he was not there wept and prayed, and listened hollow-eyed to a Moulvie who preached at the neighbouring mosque; a man who preached a judgment.

'Thou art losing thy looks, mine Aunt,' said the Prince to her one day; not unkindly; on the contrary, almost tenderly. 'Dost know, Newâsi, thou art more woman than most, for thou dost brave all things, even loss of good name—for I swear even these Mufti folk complain of thee—*for nothing*. None other I know would do it; and so I would not have it done—*for something*. Yet some day we shall quarrel over it; some day thy patience will go; some day thou wilt be as others, thinking of thyself; and then—'

'And then, nephew?' she asked coldly.

He laughed, mimicking her tone. 'And then I shall grow tired and go mine own way to mine own end.'

In the meantime, however, the thrummings and drummings went

on until Kate Erlton, watching a sick bed hard by, felt as if she must send round and beg for quiet. It seemed quite natural she should do so, for she was completely absorbed over that patient of hers, who, without being seriously ill, would not get better; who passed from one relapse of fever to another with a listless impatience, and now, nearly a month after he had stumbled over the threshold, lay barely convalescent. It had been a strange month. Stranger even than the previous one, when she had dragged through the lonely days as best she could, and he had wandered in and out restlessly, full of strain and stress. If even that had been a curious linking of their fates, what was this when she tended him day and night, when the weeks slipped by securely, almost ignorantly? For though Soma came every day to inquire after the master—standing at the door to salute to her, spick and span in full uniform—he brought no disturbing news.

It seemed to her, now, that she had known Jim Douglas all his life. And in truth she had learnt something of the real man during the few days of delirium consequent on the violent inflammation which set in on the injured ankle. But for the most part he had muttered and moaned in liquid Persian. He had always spoken it with Zora, who had been taught it as part of her attractions, and, no doubt, the jingle of the jewels as Kate tended him, brought reminiscence of that particular part of his life.

By the time he came to himself, however, she had removed all the fineries, finding them in the way; save the heavy gold bangle which would not come off—at least not without help. He used to watch it half-confusedly, at first, as it slipped up and down her arm, and wonder why she had not asked Tara to take it off for her; but he grew rather to like the look of it; to fancy that she had kept it on purpose; to be glad that she had—though it was distinctly hard when she raised him up on his pillows!—for, after all, fate linked them strangely, and he was grateful to her—very grateful.

'You are laughing at me,' she said one morning as she came up to his bed, with a tray improvised out of a brass platter, and found him smiling.

'I have been laughing at you all the morning, when I haven't been grumbling,' he replied, 'at you and the chicken-tea, and that little fringed business, to do duty as a napkin, I suppose, and the fly-paper—which isn't the least use, by the way, and I'm sure I could make a better one—and the mosquito net to give additional protection to my beauty when I fall asleep. Who could help laughing at it?'

She looked at him reproachfully. 'But it makes you more comfortable surely?'

'Comfortable,' he echoed, 'my dear lady! It is a perfect convalescent home!' But, in the silence which followed, his right hand clenched itself over a fold in the quilt unmistakably.

'If you will take your chicken-tea,' she replied cheerfully, despite a faint tremble in her voice, 'you will soon get out of it. And really, Mr Greyman, you don't seem to have lost any chance. Soma is not very communicative, but everything seems as it was. I never keep back anything from you. But, indeed, the chief thing in the city seems that there is no money to pay the soldiers. Do you know, I'm afraid Soma must *loot* the shops like the others. He seems to get things for nothing; though of course they are extraordinarily cheap. When I was a *mem* I used to pay twice as much for eggs.'

He interrupted her with a laugh that had a tinge of bitterness in it, 'Do you happen to know the story of the Jew who was eating ham during a thunderstorm, Mrs Erlton—?'

She shook her head, smiling, being accustomed by this time to his unsparing, rather reckless ridicule.

'—He looked up and said, "All this fush about a little bit of pork." So all this fuss has taught you the price of eggs! Upon my word! it is worse than the convalescent home!' He lay back on his pillows with a half-irritated weariness.

'I've learned more than that, surely'—she began.

'Learned!' he echoed sharply, 'you've learned everything, my dear lady, necessary to salvation. That's the worst of it! You chatter to Tara— I hear you when you think I'm asleep. You draw your veil over your face when the water-carrier comes to fill the pots as if you had been born on a housetop. You . . . Mrs Erlton!—If I were not a helpless idiot I could pass you out of the city tomorrow, I believe. It isn't your fault any longer. It's mine, and Heaven only knows how long—Oh! confound that thrumming and drumming. It gets on my nerves—*my nerves!*—pshaw!'

It was then that Kate declared that she would really send Tara—

'Mrs Erlton presents her compliments to the Princess Farkhoonda Zamâni, and will be obliged,' jested Jim Douglas; then paused, in truth more irritated than amused, despite the humour on his face. And suddenly he appealed to her almost pitifully, 'Mrs Erlton! if any one had told you it would be like this—your chance and mine—when the world outside us was alive—was struggling for life—would you— would you have believed it?'

She bent to push the chicken-tea to a securer position. 'No,' she said softly; then to change the subject, added, 'How white your hands are getting again! I must put some more stain on them, I suppose.' She spoke regretfully, though she did not mind putting it on to her own. But he looked at the whiteness with distinct distaste.

'It is with doing nothing and lying like a log. Well! I suppose I shall wake from the dream some day, and then the moment I can walk—'

'There will be an end of peace,' she interrupted, quite resolutely. 'I know it is very hard for you to lie still, but really you must see how much safer and smoother life has been since you were forced to give in to Fate—'

'And Kate—' he muttered crossly under his breath. But she heard it, and bit her lip to prevent a tender smile as she went off to give an order to Tara; for the vein of almost boyish mischief and light-hearted recklessness which showed in him at times, always made her think how charming he must have been before the cloud shadowed his life.

'The master is much better today, Tara,' she said cheerfully, 'I really think the fever has gone for good.'

'Then he will soon be able to take the *mem* away,' replied the woman quickly.

'Are you in such a hurry to get rid of me?' asked Kate with a smile, for she had grown fond of the tall stately creature with her solemn airs of duty, and absolute disregard of anything which came in its way. The intensity of the emotion which swept over the face, which was usually calm as a bronze statue, startled Kate.

'Of a truth I shall be glad to go back. The life of the *Huzoor*s is not my life, their death not my death.'

It was as if the woman's whole nature had recoiled, as one might recoil from a snake in the path, and a chill struck to Kate Erlton's heart, as she realized on how frail a foundation peace and security rested. A look, a word, might bring death. It seemed to her incredible that she should have forgotten this, but she had. She had almost forgotten that they were living in a beleaguered city, though the reverberating roll of artillery, the rush and roar of shells, and the crackle of musketry never ceased for more than a few hours at a time.

She was not alone, however, in her forgetfulness. Half Delhi had become accustomed to cannon, to bugles and fifes, and went on its daily round indifferently. But in the palace the dream grew ominously thin once or twice. For not a fraction remained in the Treasury, no effort to collect revenue had been made anywhere, and fat Mahboob, the only man who knew how to screw money out of a stone, lay dying of dropsy. And as he lay—the mists of personal interest in the future dispersing—he told his old master the King some home truths privately, while Ahsan-Oolah the physician, administering cooling draughts as usual, added his wisdom to the eunuch's. There was no hope where there was no money. Life was not worth living without a regular pension. Let the king secure his, and secure pardon while there was yet time, by sending a letter to the General on the Ridge, and offering to let the English in by Selimgarh and betray the city. When all was said and done, others had betrayed *him*, had forced *his* hand; so let him save himself if he could, quietly, without a word to any but Ahsan-Oolah. Above all, not a word to Zeenut Maihl, Hussan Askuri, and Bukht Khân—that Trinity of Dreams!

With which words of wisdom mayhap lightening his load of sins, the fat eunuch left the court once and for all. So the old king, as he sat listening to the quarrels of his commander-in-chief, had other consolation besides couplets, and when he wrote—

> No peace, no rest, since armies round me riot
> Life lingers yet, but ere long I shall die o't.

he knew—though his yellow, wax-like mask hid the knowledge from all—that a chance of escape remained.

The old king's letter reached the Ridge easily. (There was no difficulty in communication now. Spies were plentiful, and if Jim Douglas had been able to get about, he could have set Major Erlton's mind at rest without delay; but Soma positively refused to be a go-between—to do anything, in short, save secure the master's safety.) And the offer of betrayal arrived, when the man who held command of the Ridge felt uncertain of the future; all the more so because of the telegrams, the letters—almost the orders—which came pouring in to take Delhi—to take it at once! Early in the month, the Gamester's-throw of Assault had been revived with the arrival of reinforcements, only to be abandoned once more, within an hour of the appointed time, in favour of the Grip-of-Death. But now, though the whisper had gone no further than the General's tent, a third possibility was allowed—Retreat. The six thousand were dwindling day by day, the men were half-dead with picquet duty, wearied out with needless skirmishes, crushed by the tyranny of bugles and fifes.

If this betrayal, then, could be? There was no lack of desire to believe it possible; but Greathed of the politicals, and Sir Theophilus Metcalfe shook their heads doubtfully. Hodson, they said, had better be consulted. So the tall man with the blue hawk's eyes, who had lost his temper many times since that dawn of the 12th of June, when the first assault had hung fire, was asked for his opinion.

'We had a chance at the beginning,' he said. 'We could have a chance now, if there was some one who . . . but that is beside the question. As for *this*, it is not worth the paper it is written on. The king has no power to fulfil his promise. He is virtually a prisoner himself. That is the truth. But don't send an answer. Refer it, and keep him quiet.'

'And retreat?'

'Retreat is impossible, sir. It would lose us India.'

'Any news, Hodson?' asked Major Erlton, meeting the free lance as he rode back to his tent after his fashion, with loose rein and loose seat, unkempt, undeviating, with an eye for any and every advantage.

'None.'

'Any chance of—of anything?'

'None with our present chiefs. If we had Sir Henry Lawrence here it would be different.'

But Sir Henry Lawrence, having done his duty to the uttermost, already lay dead in the residency at Lucknow, though the tidings had not reached the Ridge. And still more direful tidings were on their way to bring July, that month of clouds and cholera, of flies and funerals, of endless buglings and fifings—to a close.

It came to the city first—came one afternoon when the King sat in the private Hall of Audience, his back towards the arcaded view of the eastern plains ablaze with sunlight, his face towards the garden, which, through the marble mosaic-traced arches, showed like an embroidered curtain of green, set with jewelled flowers. Above him on the roof circled the boastful legend—

> If earth holds a haven of bliss
> It is this—it is this—it is this.

And all around him, in due order of precedence, according to the latest army lists procurable in Delhi, were ranged the mutinous native officers—since half the king's sovereignty showed itself in punctilious etiquette. At his feet, below the peacock throne stood a gilded cage containing a cockatoo. For Hâfzan had been so far right in her estimate of Hussan Askuri's wonders that poor little Sonny's pet, duly caught, and with its crest dyed an orthodox green, had been used—like the stuffed lizard—to play on the old man's love of the marvellous. So, for the time being, the bird followed him in his brief journeyings from audience-hall to balcony, from balcony to bed.

The usual pile of brocaded bags lay below that again upon the marble floor, where a reader crouched, sampling the most loyal to be used as a sedative; for one would be needed ere long, since the commanders-in-chief were at war. They, Bukht Khân backed by Hussan Askuri, stood apart; and all the puritans and fanatics of the city; Mirza Moghul by his brother Khair Sultân, and most of the Northern Indian rebels who refused a mere ex-*soubadar*'s right to be better than they.

'Let the Light-of-the-World choose between us,' came the sonorous voice almost indifferently; in truth those secret counsels of Bukht Khân with the Queen—of which the palace was big with gossip—held small place, allowed small consideration for the puppet King.

'Yea! let the Pillar-of-State choose,' bawled the shrill voice of the Moghul, whose yellow, small-featured face was ablaze with passion. 'Choose between his son and heir and this low born upstart, this *soubadar* of artillery, this puritan by profession, this debaucher of King's—'

He paused, for Bukht Khân's hand was on his sword, and there was an ominous stir behind Hussan Askuri. Ahsan-Oolah, a discreet figure in black standing by the side of the throne, craned his long neck forward, and his crafty face wore an amused smile.

Bukht Khân laughed disdainfully at the Mirza's full stop. 'What I am, sire, matters little if I can lead armies to victory. The Mirza hath not led his, *as yet.*'

'Not led them?' interrupted an officious peace-bringer. 'Lo! the hell-doomed are reduced to five hundred; the colonels are eating their horses' grain, the captains are starving, and our shells cause terror as they cry "Coffin! coffin!" (*boccus! boccus!*)—'

'The Mirza could do as well as thou,' put in a partisan heedless of the tales—to which the King, however, had been nodding his head— 'if, as thou hast, he had money to pay his troops. The Begum Zeenut Maihl's hoards—'

The sword and the hand kept company again significantly. 'I pay my men by the hoard I took from the infidel, Meean-*jee*,' retorted the loud, indifferent voice. 'And when it is done I can get more. The palace is not sucked dry yet, nor Delhi either.'

The Meean, well known to have feathered his nest bravely, muttered something inaudible, but a stout, white-robed gentleman bleated hastily—

'There is no more money to be loaned in Delhi, be the interest ever so high.'

The broad face broadened with a sardonic smile. 'I borrow, banker-*jee*, according to the tenets of the faith—without interest! For the rest, five minutes in thy house with a spade and a string bed to hang thee on head down, and I pay every fighter-for-the-faith in Delhi his arrears!'

'*Wâh! Wâh!*' A fierce murmur of approval ran round the audience, for all liked that way of dealing with folk who kept their money to themselves.

'But, Khân-*jee*! there is no such hurry,' protested the keeper of peace, the promoter of dreams. 'The Hell-doomed are at the last gasp. Have not two commanders-in-chief had to commit suicide before their troops? And was not the third allowed by special favour of the Queen to go away and do it privately? This one will have to do it also, and then—'

'And a letter has but this day come in,' said a grave, clever looking man, interrupting the tale once more, 'offering ten lakhs; but as the writer makes stipulations, we are asking what treasury he means to loot, or if it is hidden hoards.'

Bukht Khân shrugged his shoulders. 'The Meean's or the banker's hoards are nearer,' he said brutally, 'and money we must have, if we are to fight as soldiers. Otherwise—' He paused. There was a stir at the entrance, where a news-runner had unceremoniously pushed his way in to flourish a letter in a long envelope, and pant—with vehement show of breathlessness.—'In haste! In haste! and *buksheesh* for the bringer.'

The King, who had been listening wearily to the dispute, thinking possibly that the paucity of commanders on the Ridge was preferable to the plethora of them at court, looked up indifferently. They came so often, these bearers of wonderful news; not so often as the little brocaded bags; but they had no more effect.

'Reward him, Keeper-of-the-Purse,' he said punctiliously, 'and read, slave. It is some victory to our troops, no doubt.'

There was a pause, during which people waited indifferently, wondering, some of them, if it was bogus news that was to come or not.

Then the Court *moonshee* stood up with a doubtful face. ''Tis from Cawnpore,' he murmured, forgetting decorum and etiquette; forgetting everything save the news that the Nâna of Bithoor had killed the two hundred women and children he had pledged himself to save.

Bukht Khân's hand went to his sword once more, as he listened, and he turned hastily to Hussan Askuri. 'That settles it as *thou* wouldst have it,' he whispered. 'It is Holy War, indeed, or defeat.'

But Mirza Moghul shrank as a man shrinks from the scaffold.

The old King stood up quickly; stood up between the lights looking out on the curtain of flowers. 'Whatever happens,' he said tremulously, 'happens by the will of God.'

His sanctimoniousness never failed him.

So on the night of the 23rd of August there was an unwonted stillness in the city, and the coming of day did not break it. The rain, it is true, fell in torrents, but many an attack had been made in rain before. There was none now. The bugles and fifes had ended, and folk were waiting for the drum ecclesiastic to begin. What they thought, meanwhile, who knows? Delhi held a hundred and fifty thousand souls, swelled to nigh two hundred thousand by soldiers; only this, therefore, is certain, that the thoughts must have been diverse.

But on the Ridge, when, after a few days, the tidings of Cawnpore reached it with certainty, there was but one opinion. It found

expression in a letter which the General wrote on the last day of July.
'It is my firm intention to hold my present position and resist attack to
the last. The enemy are very numerous, and may possibly break
through our entrenchments and overwhelm us, but the force will die at
its post.'

There were no talk of retirement now! The millions of peasants
ploughing their land peaceably in firm faith of a just master who
would take no more than his due, the thousands—even in the bloody
city itself—waiting for this tyranny to pass, were not to be deserted.
The fight would go on. The fight for law and order.

So the sanctimonious old King had said sooth, 'Whatever happens,
happens by the will of God.'

Those two hundred had not died in vain.

# 5

# The Drum Ecclesiastic

The silence of the city had lasted for seven days. And now, on the
1st of August, the dawn was at hand, and the rain which had
been falling all night had ceased, leaving pools of water about
the city walls. Still, smooth pools like plates of steel, dimly reflecting
the grey misty sky against which the minarets of the mosque showed
as darker streaks, its dome like a faint cloud.

And suddenly the silence ended. The first shuddering beat of a
royal salute vibrated through the heavy, dewy air, the first chord of
'God save the Queen,' played by every band in Delhi floated Ridge-
wards.

The cheek of it!

That phrase—no other, less trenchant, more refined—expressed
purely the feeling with which the roused six thousand listened from
picquet or tent, comfortable bed or damp sentry-go, to this topsy-
turveydom of anthems! The cheek of it! The very walls ought to fall
Jericho-wise before such sacrilegious music.

But in the city it sent a thrill through hearts and brains. For it
roused many a dreamer who had never felt the chill of a sword-hilt on
his palm to the knowledge that the time for gripping one had come.

Since this was Bukr-eed, the Great Day of Sacrifice. No common
Bukr-eed either, when the blood of a goat or a bull would worthily
commemorate Abraham's sacrifice of his best and dearest, but

something more akin to the old patriarch's devotion. Since on Bukr-eed, 1857, the infidel was to be sacrificed by the faithful, and the faithful by the infidel.

For the silence of seven days had been a silence only from bugles and fifes; the drum ecclesiastic had taken their place. The mosques had resounded day and night to the wild tirades of preachers, and even Mahomed Ismail—feeling that in religious war lay the only chance of forgiveness for past horrors—spent every hour in painting its perfections, in deprecating any deviation from its rule; the sword or the faith for men who fought; the faith, without the sword, for those who could not fight. But others were less scrupulous, their denunciations less guarded. So, as the processions passed through the narrow streets flaunting the green banner, half the Mohammedan population felt that the time had come to strike their blow for the faith without restriction; and Hussan Askuri dreamt dreams; and the Bird-of-Heaven—with its crest new-dyed for the occasion—gave the Great Cry viciously as it was paraded through jostling crowds in the Thunbi bazaar, where religion found recruits by the score, even among the women. Abool-Bukr, vaguely impressed by the stir, the colour, the noise, took to the green and swore to live cleanly; so that Newâsi's soft eyes shone as she repeated Mahomed Ismail's theories. They were very true, the Prince said; besides, this could be nothing but honest fighting since there were no women on the Ridge; whereupon she stitched away at his green banner fearlessly.

But in the Palace it needed all Bukht Khân's determination and Hussan Askuri's wily dreams to reconcile the old King to the breach of etiquette which the sacrifice of a camel, instead of a bull, by the royal hands involved; for the army—three-quarters Brahmin and Rajpoot—had been promised, as a reward for helping to drive out the infidel, that no sacred kine should be killed in Hindustan.

And others besides the King objected to the restriction. Old Fâtma, for instance, Shumsh-a-deen the seal-cutter's wife, as she swathed her husband's white beard with pounded henna leaves to give it the orthodox red dye.

'What matters it, woman?' he replied sternly, but with an odd quaver in his voice. 'There is a greater sacrifice than the blood of bulls and goats, and that I may yet offer this blessed Eed.'

'And mayhap, mother,' suggested the widowed, childless daughter-in-law, 'a goat will serve our turn better than a stirk this year: there will be enough for offering, and belike there may be no feasting.'

The old lady, high-featured, high-tempered, wept profusely between her railings at the ill-omened suggestion; but the old Turk admitted the possibility, with a strained wondering look in the eyes which had lost their keenness with graving texts. So, as the day passed, the women helped him faithfully in his bath of purification, and the daughter-in-law, having the steadiest hand, put the antimony into the old man's eyes as he squatted on a clean white cloth stretched in the centre of the odd little courtyard. She used the stylus she had brought with her to the house as a bride, and it woke past memories in the old brain, making the black-edged old eyes look at the wife of his youth with a wistful tenderness. For it was years since a woman had performed the kindly office—not since the finery and folly of life had passed into the next generation's hands. But old Fâtma thought he still looked as handsome as any as he finally stepped into the streets in his baggy trousers, with one green shawl twisted into a voluminous waistband, another into a turban, his flaming red beard flowing over his white tunic, and a curved scimitar—it was rather difficult to get out of its scabbard by reason of rust—at his side.

'Lo! here comes old Fâtma's Shumsha-deen,' whispered other women peeping through other chinks. 'He looks well for sure; better by far than Murriam's Faiz-Ahmud for all his new gold shoes!'

And those two, daughter and mother-in-law, huddled in unaccustomed embrace to see the last of their martyr through the only convenient crack, felt a glow of pitiful pride before they fell a-weeping and a-praying the old pitiful prayer of quarrellers that God would be good to His own.

There were thousands in Delhi about sun setting on the 1st of August who were praying that prayer, though there were hundreds who held aloof, talking learnedly of the 'House of Protection' as distinguished from the 'House of the Enemy', as they listened to the evening call to prayer. How could there be Holy War, when that had echoed freely during the British rule? And Mahomed Ismail, listening to their arguments feverishly, knew in his heart that they were right.

But the old 'Shumsha-deens' did not split hairs. So, as the sun set, they went forth in thousands and the gates were closed behind them; for they were to conquer or die. They were to hurl themselves recklessly on the low breast-works which now furrowed the long line of hill; above all, on that which had crept down its side to a ruined temple within seven hundred yards of the Moree bastion.

So, about the rising of the moon, two days from full, began such a cannonading and fusillading as was not surpassed even on that final day when the Ridge, taking similar heart of grace, was to fling itself against the city.

Major Erlton, off duty but on pleasure in the Sammy-house breastwork, said to his neighbour that they must be mad, as a confused wild rush burst from the Moree gate; six thousand or so of soldiers, and 'Shumsha-deens', with elephants, camels, field-pieces, distinct in the mixed mirk and moonlight! And behind them came a hail of shell and shot, with them a rain of grape and musket-balls. But above all the din and rattle could be heard two things. The cries of the *Muazzims* from the minarets, chanting to the four corners of earth and sky that 'Glory is for all and Heaven for those who bleed'; and an incessant bugling.

'It's that man in front,' remarked Major Erlton. 'Do you think we shall manage, Reid? There's an awful lot of them.'

Major Reid looked round on his little garrison of dark faces—for there was not an Englishman in the post; only a hundred quaint squat Ghoorkas, and fifty tall fair Guides from the Western frontier—'We'll do for just now, and I can send for the Rifles by-and-by. There's to be no pursuit, you know. The order's out. Ought to have been out long ago. Reserve your fire, men, till they come close up.'

And come close they did, while Walidâd Khân, fierce fanatic from Peshawur, and Gorakh-nâth, fiercer Buddhist from Nepâl, with fingers on trigger, called on them gibingly to come closer still—though twenty yards from a breastwork bristling with rifles was surely close enough for any one!

But it was not for the bugler who led the van, sounding assemblies, advances, doubles—anything which might stir the hearts behind.

'He has got a magnificent pair of bellows,' remarked an officer, who, after a time, came down with a hundred and fifty of the Rifles to aid that hundred and fifty natives in holding the post against six thousand and more of their countrymen.

'Splendid! he has been at it this hour or more,' said Major Erlton. 'I really think they are mad. They don't seem to aim or to care. There they are again!'

It was darker now, and Walidâd Khân from Peshawur and Gorakh-nâth from Nepâl, and Bill Atkins from Lambeth had to listen for that tootling of assemblies and advances to tell them when to fire blindly from the embrasures into the smoke and the roar and the rattle. So they fell to wondering among themselves if they had nicked the bugler that time. Once or twice the silence seemed to say they had; but after a bit the tootling began again, and a disappointed pair of eyes peeping curiously, recklessly, would see a dim figure running madly to the assault again.

'Plucky devil!' muttered Major Erlton as, with the loan of a rifle, he had his try. There was a look of hope on dark faces and white alike as they cuddled down to the rifle stocks and came up to listen. It was like shooting into a herd of does for the one royal head—and some of the sportsmen had tempers.

'*Shaitân-ke-butcha!* (Child of the devil),' muttered Walidâd-Khân, whereat Gorakh-nâth grinned from ear to ear.

'Wot cher laughin' at?' asked Bill Atkins, who had been indulging in language of his own, 'a feller can't 'it ghosts, An' 'ee's the piper as played afore Moses; that's what 'ee is.'

'Look sharp, men!' came the officer's warning. 'There's a new lot coming on. Wait, and let them have it!'

They did. The din was terrific. The incessant flashes lighting up the city, showed its roofs crowded with the families of absent 'Shumsha-deens'; so High Heaven must have been assailed, indeed, that night.

And even when dawn came it brought no Sabbath calm; only a fresh batch of martyrs. But they had no bugler. For with the dawn, some fierce frontiersman, jesting Cockney, or grinning Ghoorkha may have risked his life for a fair shot, in daylight, at the piper who played before Moses; anyhow, he played no more. Perhaps the lack of him, perhaps the torrents of rain which began to fall as the sun rose, quenched the fires of faith. Anyhow, by nine o'clock the din was over, the drum ecclesiastic ceased to beat, and the English, going out to count the dead, found the bugler lying close to the breastwork, his bugle still in his hand—a nameless hero save for that passing jest. But some one in the city no doubt mourned the piper who played before Moses, as they mourned other martyrs; more than a thousand of them.

Yet the Ridge, despite the faith, and fury, and fusillading, had only to dig one grave; for fourteen hours of what the records call 'unusual intrepidity'—(contemptuously cool equivalent for all that faith and fury)—had only killed *one infidel*.

Shumsha-deen's Fâtma, however, was as proud as if he had killed a hundred; for he had bled profusely for the faith, having been at the very outset of it all kicked by a camel and sent flying on to a rock to dream confused dreams of valour till the bleeding from his nose relieved the slight concussion of his brain, and enabled him to go home, much shaken, but none the worse. But many hundreds of women never saw their Shumsha-deens again, or if they saw them, only saw something to weep over and bind in white swaddling clothes and gold thread.

So by dark on the 2nd of August the sound of wailing women rose from every alley, and the men, wandering restlessly about the bazaars, listened to the sound of tattoo from the Ridge and looked at each other almost startled.

'*Go-to-bed-Tom! Go-to-bed-Tom! Drunk-or-sober-go-to-bed-Tom!*'

The Day of Sacrifice was over, and Tom was going to bed quietly as if nothing had happened! They did not know that three-quarters of the Toms had been in bed the night before, undisturbed by the martyrs' supreme effort; if they had, they might have wondered still more persistently what Providence was about.

But in the big Mosque, among the great white bars of moonlight slanting beneath the dome, one man knew. He stood, a tall white figure beneath a furled green banner, his arms outspread, his voice rising in fierce denunciation.

'Cursed[1] be they who did the deed, who killed *jehad*! Lo! I told you my dream in the past and ye would not believe. I tell it again that ye may know. It was dawn. And the Lord Christ and the Lord Mohammed sat over the World striving, each for His own, according to the Will of the Most High, who sets men's quarrels before the Saints in Heaven with a commander to each side. And I saw the Lord Christ weep, knowing that justice was on ours. So the fiat for victory went forth, and I slept. But I dreamed again and lo! it was eve with a blood-red sun-setting westwards. And the Lord Christ wept still, but the Lord Mahommed's voice rang loud and stern. "Reverse the fiat. Give the victory to the women and the children." So I woke. And it is true! is true! Cursed be they who killed *jehad*!'

The voice died away among the arches where, in delicate tracery, the attributes of the Great Creator were cut into changeless marble; Truth, Justice, Mercy,—all the virtues from which all religions make their God.

'He is mad,' said some; but for the most part men were silent as they drifted down the great flights of steps to the city leaving Mahomed Ismail alone under the dome.

'Didst expect otherwise, my Queen?' said Bukht Khân hardily. 'So did not I! But the end is gained. Delhi was not ours in heart and soul before. It is now. When the assault comes those who fought for faith will fight for their skins. And at the worst there is Lucknow for good Sheeahs, like the Queen and her slave. We have no tie here among these Sunnees who think only of their hoards.'

Zeenut Maihl shrank from him with her first touch of fear, for she had eight or nine lakhs of rupees hidden in that very house, and this man whom she had summoned to her aid bid fair to make flight necessary even for a woman. Had she ventured too much? Was there yet time to throw him over, to throw every one over and make her peace? She turned instinctively in her thoughts to one who loved money also, who also had hoards to save; and so, within half-in-hour of Bukht Khân's departure, Ahsan-Oolah was closeted with the Queen, who, after the excitement of the day, needed a cooling draught.

Most people in the Palace needed one that night, for by this time

---

[1]From a contemporaneous account.

almost all the possible permutations of confederacy had come about, with the result that—each combination's intrigue being known to the next—a general distrust had fallen upon all. In addition, there was now a fourth commander-in-chief; one Ghaus-Khân, from Neemuch, who declared the rest were fools.

In truth the Dream was wearing thin indeed within the Palace!

But on that peaceful little housetop in the Mufti's quarter it seemed more profound than ever; it seemed as if Fate was determined to leave nothing wanting to the strange unreal life that was being lived in the very heart of the city. Jim Douglas was almost himself again. A little lame, a little uncertain still of his own strength; and so, remembering a piece of advice given him by the old Baharupa never to attempt using the Gift when *he* was not strong enough for *it* to be strong, he had been patient beyond Kate's hopes. But on this 2nd of August, after lying awake all night listening to the roar and the din, he had insisted on going out when Soma did not turn up as usual to bring the news. He would not be long, he said—not more than an hour or two—and the attempt must be made some time; at no better one than now, perchance, since folk would be occupied in their own affairs.

'Besides,' he added with a smile, 'I'm ready to allow the convalescent home its due. While I've been kept quiet, the very thought of concealed Europeans has died out.'

'I don't know!' she interrupted quickly. 'It isn't long since Prince Abool-Bukr chased that blue-eyed boy of the Mufti's over the roofs thinking he was one—don't you remember I was so afraid he might climb up here?'

'That's the advantage of being up-top,' he replied lightly. 'Now, if anything were to happen, *you* could scramble down. But the Prince was drunk, and I won't go near his haunts—there isn't any danger—really there isn't!'

'I shall have to get accustomed to it even if there is,' she replied in the same tone. Jim Douglas paused at the door irresolutely—'Shall I wait till Tara returns?'

'No, please don't. She is not coming back till late. She grows restless if she does not go—and I am all right.'

In truth Tara had been growing restless of late. Kate, looking up from the game of chess—at which her convalescent gave her half the pieces on the board and then beat her easily—used to find those dark eyes watching them furtively. Zora Begum had never played *shatrïnj* with the master, had never read with him from books, had never treated him as an equal. And, strangely enough, the familiar companionship—inevitable under the circumstances—roused her jealousy more than the love-making on that other terraced roof had done. *That* she understood. *That* she could crush with her cry of *suttee*. But *this*—this which to her real devotion seemed so utterly desirable— what did it mean? So she crept away, when she could, to take up the saintly rôle as the only certain solace she knew for the ache in her heart.

Therefore Kate sat alone, darning Jim Douglas's white socks—which as a better-class Afghan he was bound to wear—and thinking as she did so how incredibly domestic a task it was! Still socks had to be darned, and with Tara at hand to buy odds and ends, and Soma with his knowledge of the *Huzoor*'s life ready to bring chess boards, and soap, and even a book or two, it seemed as if the roof would soon be a very fair imitation of home. So she sat peacefully; till, about dusk, hearing a footfall on the stairs halting with long pauses between the steps, her vexation at her patient's evident fatigue overcame her usual caution; and without waiting for his signal knock she set the door wide and stepped out on to the stairs to give him a hand if need be. And then out of the shadow of the narrow brick ladder came a strange voice panting breathlessly:

'*Salaam! mem-sahib.*' She started back, but not in time to prevent a bent figure with a bundle on its back from stumbling past her on to the roof; where, as if exhausted, it leant against the wall before slipping the bundle to the floor. It was an ordinary brown blanket bundle full of uncarded cotton, and the old woman who carried it was ragged and feeble; emaciated too beyond belief, as if cotton-spinning had not been able to keep soul and body comfortably together. Not a very formidable foe this—if foe it was. Why! surely she knew the face—

'I have brought Sonny back, *Huzoor*,' came the breathless voice.

Sonny! Kate Erlton gave a little cry. She recollected now. 'O ayah!' she began recklessly, 'what? where is he—'

The old woman stumbled to the door, closed the catch and then leant exhausted upon the lintel, sinking down slowly to a squatting position, her hand upon her heart. There was more in this than the fatigue of the stairs, Kate recognized.

'He is in the bundle, *Huzoor*. The *mem* did not know me. She will know the *baba*.'

Know him! As her almost incredulous fingers fumbled at the knots, her mind was busy with an adorable vision of white embroideries, golden curls, and kissable, dimpled milk and roses. So it was no wonder that she recoiled from the ragged shift and dark skin, the black close-cropped hair shaved horribly into a wide gangway from nape to forehead.

'O ayah!' she cried reproachfully, 'What have you done to Sonny *baba*!' For Sonny it was unmistakably, in the guise of a street urchin. A foolish remark to make doubtless, but the old Mai, most of whose life had been passed in the curling of golden curls, the prinking of mother's darlings, did not think it strange. She looked wistfully at her charge, then at Kate apologetically.

'It was safer, *Huzoor*. And at least he is fat and fresh. I gave him milk and *chikken-brât*.[1] And it was but a tiny morsel of opium just to make him quiet in the bundle.'

Something in the quavering old voice made Kate cross quickly to the old woman and kneel beside her.

'You have done splendidly, ayah, no one could have done better!'

But the interest had died from the haggard face. 'They said folk would be damned for it,' she muttered half to herself, 'but what could I do? The *mem*, my *mem*, said "take care of the boy." So I gave him *chikken-brât* and milk.' She paused, then looked up at Kate slowly. 'But I can grind and spin no more, *Huzoor*. My life is done. So I have brought him here—and—' she paused again for breath.

'How did you find me out?' asked Kate, longing to give the old woman some restorative, yet not daring to offer it; for she was a Mussulmâni.

The old Mai reached out a skeleton of a band, half-mechanically, to flick away a fluff of cotton wool from the still sleeping child's face. 'It was the *chikken-brât, Huzoor*. The *Huzoor* will remember the old mess *khansaman*? He did the *pagul khanas* (picnics) and *nautches* for the *sahib logue*. A big man with gold lace who made the cake at Christmas for the *baba*s and set fire to plum-puddens as no other *khansaman* did. And made *estârfit* turkeys and *sassets* (stuffed turkey and sausages)—and—' She seemed afloat on a Bagh-o-bahâr list of comestibles—a dream of days when, as ayah, she had watched many a big dinner go from the cook-room.

'But about *the chikken-brât*, ayah?' asked Kate with a lump in her throat; for the wasted figure babbling of old days was evidently close on death.

'*Huzoor*! Mungul Khân keeps life in him, these hard times, with the selling of eggs and fowls. So he, knowing me, said there was more *chikken-brât* than mine being made in the quarter. The *Huzoor* need have no fear. Mungul weeps every day and prays the *sahib*s may return, because his last month's account was not paid. A sweeper woman, he said, bought 'halflings,' saying they were for an Afghan's *bibi*. As if an Afghani would use three halflings in one day! No one but a *mem* making *chikken-brât* would do that. So I watched and made sure, against this day; for I was old, and I had not spun or ground for so long.'

[1]Chicken broth.

'You should have come before,' said Kate gently. 'You have worn yourself out.'

The old woman stumbled to her feet. 'My life was worn before, *Huzoor*. I am very old. I have put many boy-babies into the *mem*'s arms to make them forget their pain, and taken them from them to put the flowers round them when they were dead. He was safer with me speaking our language; with you he may remember. But I shall be dead, so I can do no more.'

'Wait, do wait till the *sahib* returns,' pleaded Kate.

The Mai paused, her hand on the latch. 'What have I to do with the *sahibs*, *Huzoor*? Mine were not much count. They made my *mem*s cry, or laugh; cry first, then laugh. It is bad for *mem*s. But my *mem* did not care, she only cared for the babies and so there was always a flower for the grave. Matadeen, the gardener, made it, and the big *Huzoor*—Erlton *sahib*—'

She ceased suddenly, and went mumbling down the stairs leaving Kate to close the door again and drop on her knees beside the sleeping child. Was he sleeping or had the opium . . . ? She gave a sigh of relief as—her hair tickling his cheek as she bent to listen—up came a chubby unconscious hand to brush the tickle away.

Sonny! It seemed incredible to her thought. The house would be a home indeed with his sweet 'Miffis Erlton' echoing through it. No! what the old Mai had said was true. There would be danger in English prattle. She must not tell him who she was. He must be kept as safe as that other child over across the seas whose empty place this one had partly filled—that other child who in all these storms and stress was, thank Heaven! so safe. She must deny herself that pleasure, and be content with this terribly-disfigured Sonny. Then she wondered if the dye came off as hers did; so with wet finger began trying the experiment on the child's cheek. A little; but perhaps soap and warm water might—She gathered Sonny in her arms and went over to the cooking-place. And there, to her unreasoning delight, after a space, was a square inch or so of milk and roses. It was trivial, of course; Mr Greyman would say womanish, but she *should* like to see the real Sonny just once! She could dye him again. So, with the sleeping child on her lap, she began soft dabbings and wipings on the forehead and cheeks. It was a fascinating task and she forgot everything else, till, as she began work on the nose, what with the tickling and the tepid-bathings dispelling the opium drowsiness, Sonny woke, and finding himself in strange arms began to scream horribly. And there she was, forgetful of caution amongst other things, kissing and cuddling the frightened child, asking him if he didn't know her and telling him he was a good little Sonnikins whom nobody in the world would hurt! At which juncture, with brain started in a new-old groove, he said amid lingering sobs:

'O Miffis Erlton! What *has* a-come of my polly?'

She recognized her slip in a second; but it was too late. And hark! There were steps on the stair, and Sonny was prattling on in his high, clear lisp! Not one step, but two—and voices—a visitor no doubt. Sometimes, to avoid suspicion, it was necessary to bring them in. She knew the routine. The modest claim for seclusion to her supposed husband in Persian, the leaving of the door on the latch, the swift retreat into the inner roof during the interval decorously allowed for such escape. All this was easy without Sonny. The only chance now was to stop his prattle, even by force, give the excuse that other women were within, and trust to a man's quickness outside.

Vain hope! Sonny wriggled like an eel, and just as the expected knock came evaded her silencing hand, so that the roof rang with outraged yells:

'Oh! 'oo's hurtin' me! Oo's hurtin' me!'

Without the words even, the sound was unmistakable; no native child was ever so ear-piercing, so wildly indignant. Kate, beside herself, tried soothings and force distractedly, in the midst of which an imperative voice called fiercely—

'Open the door quick, for God's sake! Anything's better than that.'

For the moment, it was doubtless; for Sonny's yells ended with victory; but another cry came sharp and short, as—the door giving under Kate's hasty fingers—two men tumbled over the threshold. Jim Douglas uppermost, his hands gripping the other's throat.

'Shut the door!' he gasped. 'Lock it. Then my revolver—no—a knife—no noise—quick. I can't hold—the brute long.'

Kate turned and ran mechanically, and the steel in her hand gleamed as she flew back. Jim Douglas, digging his knees into the ribs below them, loosened one hand cautiously from the throat and held it out, trembling, eager—

But Kate saw his face. It might have been the Gorgon's, for she stood as if turned to stone.

'Don't be a fool!' he panted—'give it me! It's the only—' a sudden twist beneath him sent his hand back to the throat. 'It's—it's death anyway—'

Death! What did that matter? she asked herself. Let it come, rather than murder!

'No!' she said suddenly, 'you shall not. It is not worth it.' The knife, flung backwards, fell with a clang, but the eyes which—though that choking grip on the throat made all things dim—had been fixed on its gleam, turned swiftly to those above them, and the writhing body lay still as a corpse; none too soon, for Jim Douglas was almost spent.

'A rope'—he muttered briefly, 'or stay, your veil will do.'

But Kate, trembling with the great passion and pity of her decision, had scarce removed it ere Jim Douglas, changing his mind, rose to his feet, leaving his antagonist free to do so likewise.

'Get up, Tiddu,' he said breathlessly, 'and thank the *mem* for saving your life. But the door's locked, and if you don't swear—'

'The *Huzoor* need not threaten,' retorted Tiddu far more calmly as he retwisted his rag of a turban. 'The Many-faced know gratitude. They do not fall on those who find them helpless and protect them.'

The thrust was keen, for in truth the old Baharupa had, not half-an-hour before, by sheer chance found his pupil in difficulties, and insisted on seeing him safe home and on his promising not to go out again till he was stronger; to both of which coercions Jim Douglas, in order to evade suspicion, had consented. Yet, but for Kate, he would have knifed the old man remorselessly; even now he felt doubtful of mercy.

Tiddu, however, saved him further anxiety by stepping close to Kate and salaaming theatrically.

'By Murri-âm and the *neem*, the *mem* is as my mother, the child as my child.'

So, for the first time, both he and Jim Douglas looked towards Sonny, who, with wide-planted legs and wondering eyes, had been watching Tiddu solemnly; the quaintest little figure with his red and white cheeks and black muzzle.

The old mime burst into a guffaw. 'Wâh! what a monkey-ling! Wâh! what a *tamâsha* (spectacle),' he cried, squatting down on his heels to look closer. In truth Sonny was like a hill baboon, especially when he smiled too—broadly, expectantly, at the familiar word.

'*Tamathâ-wallah!*' he said superbly, '*bunao tamâtha, juldi bunao!*' (make an amusement; make it quick).

Tiddu, a child himself like all his race in his delight in children, a child also in his capacity of sudden serenity, caught up Kate's fallen veil, and in an instant dashed into the hackneyed part of the daughter-in-law, while Kate and Jim Douglas stared; left behind, as it were, by this strange irresponsible pair—the mimic of life, and the child ignorant of what was mimicked. Tragedy a minute ago! Now farce! They looked at each other, startled, for sympathy.

'Make a funny man now,' came Sonny's confident voice, 'a funny man behind a curtain—a funny man—wif a gween face an' a white face, an' a lot of fwowers an' a bit o' tring.'

Tiddu looked round quickly at Jim Douglas. '*Wâh!*' he said, 'the little *Huzoor* has a good memory. He remembers the Lord of Life and Death.'

But Kate had remembered it too, and she also had turned to Jim Douglas passionately, almost accusingly. 'It was you! You were Fate— you—, —ah! I understand now!'

'Do you?' he answered with a frown. 'Then it's more than I do.' He walked away moodily towards the knife Kate had flung away, and stooped to pick it up. 'But you were right in what you did. It was an inspiration. Look there!'

He pointed to the old Baharupa, who was playing antics to amuse Sonny, who lisped, '*Thâ bâth!*' (bravo!) solemnly at each fresh effort. But Kate shivered. 'I did nothing. I thought I did; but it was Fate.'

'My dear lady,' he retorted with a kindly smile, 'it is all in the nature of dreams. The convalescent home is turned into a crèche. But we must transfigure the street urchin into the darling of his parent's hearts'—he paused, and looked at Kate queerly. 'I'll tell Tara to rig him out properly; and you must take off half the stain, you know, and leave some colour on his cheeks; for he must play the part as well as—' he laughed suddenly—'it is really more dream-like than ever!' he added. And Kate thought so too.

# 6

# Vox Humana

The five days following on the 2nd of August were a time of festivity for the Camp, a time of funerals for the City. There was a break in the rains, and on the Ridge the sunshine fell in floods upon the fresh green grass, and the air, bright and cool, set men's minds towards making the best of Nature's kindness; for she had been kind, indeed, to the faithful little colony, and few even of the seniors could remember a season so favourable in every way. And so the messes talked of games, of races; and men, fresh from seeing their fellows killed by balls on one side of the Ridge, joined those who on the other side were crying 'Well bowled!' as wickets went down before other balls.

But in the city the unswept alleys fermented and festered in the vapours and odours which rose from the great mass of humanity pent within the rose-red walls. For the gates had been closed strictly save for those with permits to come and go. This was Bukht Khân's policy. Delhi was to stand or fall as one man. There was to be no sneaking away while yet there was time. So the hundreds of sepoys protesting illness, hunger, urgent private affairs—every possible excuse for getting leave—were told that if they would not fight they could sulk. Starve they might, stay they should. The other commanders-in-chief, it is true, spent money in bribing mercenaries for one week's more fighting; but Bukht Khân only smiled sardonically. He had tried Bugles and Fifes, he had tried the Drum-ecclesiastic; he was now trying his last stop. The *vox humana* of self-preservation.

In the city itself, however, the preservation of life took for the present another form, and never within the memory of man had there been such a pounding of pestles and mortars over leaf-poultices. The sound of it rose up at dawn and eve like the sound of the querns, mingling with the *vox humana* of grief as the eastern and southern gates were set wide to let the dead pass out, and allow the stores for the living to pass in.

It formed a background to the gossip at the wells where the women met to draw water.

'Faiz Ahmed found freedom at dawn,' said one between her yawns. 'He was long in the throes. The *bibis* made a great wailing, so I could not even sleep since then. There are no sons, see you, and no money now the old man's annuity is gone.'

'*Loh*, sister!' retorted another, 'thou speakest as if death were a morsel of news to let dissolve on the tongue. There be plenty such soppets in Delhi, and if I know aught of wounds there will be another at nightfall. My mistress wastes time in the pounding of simples, and I waste time in waiting for them till my turn comes at the shop; for if it be not gangrened, I have no eyes.' The speaker jerked her pot to her shoulder deftly and passed down the alley.

'Juntu is wise in such matters,' said a worn-looking woman with sad eyes; 'I must get her to glance at my man's cut. 'Tis right to my mind—he will put naught but water to it after some foreign fashion—but who can tell these times?'

'Save that none pass their day, sister. Death will come of the Great Sickness, or the wound, as it chooses,' put in a half-starved soul who had to carry a baby besides her pot. 'The cholera rages in our alley. 'Tis the smell. None sweep the streets or flush the gutters now.'

'*Ari*, Fukra!' cried a fierce virago, 'thou art a traitor at heart! She bewails the pig-eating infidels who gave her man five rupees a month to bring water to the drains. *Ai teri!* If they saved one life from good cholera, have they not reft a hundred in exchange from widows and orphans? *Oo-ai-ie-ee!*'

Her howling wail, like a jackal's, was caught up whimperingly by the others; and so they passed on with their water-pots, to spread through the city the tale of Faiz Ahmed's freedom, Juntu's suspicions of gangrene, and Karima the butcher's big wife's retort. And, in the evening, folk gathered at the gates, and talked over it all again as the funerals passed out; old Faiz Ahmed in his new gold shoes looking better as a corpse, tied up in tinsel, than as a martyr, so the spectators agreed. Whereat *his* family had their glow of pride also.

Then, when the show was over, the crowd dispersed to pay visits of condolence, and raise that wailing *vox humana* in every alley.

Greatly to Jim Douglas's relief, for there was another voice difficult to keep quiet when the cool evenings came, and all Kate's replies in Hindustani would not beguile Sonny's tongue from English. He was the quaintest mother's darling now, in a little tinsel cap fringed with brown silk tassels hiding that dreadful gangway, anklets and bracelets on his bare corn-coloured limbs, the ruddy colour showing through the dye on his cheeks, his palms all henna-stained, his eyes blackened with *kohl*, and a variety of little tinsel and brocaded coatees ending far above his dimpled knees. There were little muslin and net ones too cunningly streaked with silver and gold, for Tara was reckless over the boy. She insisted, too, on a great black smudge on his forehead to keep away the evil eye; and Soma, coming now with the greatest regularity, brought odd little coral and grass necklets such as Rajpoot bairns ought to wear; while Tiddu, the child's great favourite, had a new toy every day for the little *Huzoor*. Paper whirligigs, cotton-wool bears on a stick, mud parrots and such like, whereat Sonny would lisp, '*Thâ-bâth*, Tiddu.' Though sometimes he would go over to Kate and ask appealingly, 'Miffis Erlton! What has a-come of my polly?'

Then she, startled into realities by the words, would catch him up in her arms, and look round as if for protection to Jim Douglas, who having overdone himself in the struggle with Tiddu, had felt it wiser to defer further action for a day or two; the more so because Tiddu had promised to help him to the uttermost if he would only be reasonable, and leave times and seasons to one who had ten times the choice that he had.

So he would smile back at Kate and say, 'It's all right, Mrs Erlton. At least as right as it can be. The lot of them are devoted to the child.'

Yet in his heart he knew there was danger in so many confederates. He felt that this incredibly peaceful home on the housetops could not last. Here he was looking at a woman who was not his wife, a child who was not his child, and feeling vaguely that they were as much a part of his life as if they were; as if, had they been so, he would have been quite contented—more contented than he had been on that other roof. He was, even now, more contented than he had been there. As he sat, his head on his hand, watching the pretty picture which Kate in Zora's jewels made with the be-tinselled, be-scented, be-decked child, he thought of his relief when years before he had looked at a still little morsel lying in Zora's veil. Had it been brutal of him? Would that dead baby have grown into a Sonny? Or was it because Sonny's skin was really white beneath the stain that he thought of him as something to be proud of possessing; of a boy who would go to school and be fagged and flogged and inherit familiar virtues and vices instead of strange ones?

'What are you thinking of, Mr Greyman? Do you want anything?' came Kate's kind voice.

'Nothing,' he replied, in the half-bantering tone he so often used towards her; 'I have more than my fair share of things already, surely! I was only meditating on the word ''*Om*''—the final mystery of all things.'

So, in a way, he was. On the mystery of fatherhood and mother-hood, which had had nothing to do with that pure idyll of romantic passion on the terraced roof at Lucknow, yet which seemed to touch him here, where there was not even love. Yet it was a better thing. The passion of protection, of absolute self-forgetfulness, seeking no reward, which the sight of those two raised in him, was a better thing than that absorption in another self. The thought made him cross over to where Kate sat with the child in her lap, and say gravely—

'The *crèche* is more interesting than the convalescent home; at least to me, Mrs Erlton! I shall be quite sorry when it ends.'

'When it ends?' she echoed quickly. 'There is nothing wrong, is there? Sonny has been so good, and that time when he was naughty the sweeper-woman seemed quite satisfied when Tara said he was speaking Pushtoo.'

'But it cannot last for all that,' he replied. 'It is dangerous. I feel it is. This is the 5th, and I am nearly all right. I must get Tiddu to arrange for Sonny first—then for you.'

'And you?' she asked.

'I'll follow. It will be safer, and there is no fear for me. I can't understand why I've had no answer from your husband. The letter went two days ago, and I am convinced we ought to have heard.'

The frown was back on his face, the restlessness in his brain; and both grew when in private talk with Tiddu the latter hinted at suspicions in the caravan which had made it necessary for him to be very cautious. The letter, therefore, had certainly been delayed, might never have reached. If no answer came by the morrow, he himself would take the opportunity of a portion of the caravan having a permit to pass out, and so ensure the news reaching the Ridge; trusting to get into the city again without delay, though the gates were very strictly kept. Nevertheless, in his opinion, the *Huzoor* would be wiser with patience. There was no immediate danger in continuing as they were, and the end could not be long if it was true that the great *Nikalseyn* was with the Punjâb reinforcements; since all the world knew that *Nikalseyn* was the prince of *sahibs*, having the gift, not only of being all things to all people, but of making all people be all things to him, which was more than the Baharupas could do.

In truth, the news that John Nicholson was coming to Delhi made even Jim Douglas hesitate at risking anything unnecessarily, so long as things went smoothly. As for the letter to Major Erlton, it was no doubt true that the number of spies sending information to the Ridge had made it difficult of late to send any, since the guards were on the alert.

It was so, indeed, even for the Queen herself, who had a missive she was peculiarly anxious should not fall into strange hands.

'There is no fear, Ornament-of-Palaces,' said Ahsan-Oolah urbanely; 'I will stake my life on its reaching.' He did not add that his chief reason for saying so was that a similar letter, written by the King, had been safely delivered by Rujjub Ali the spy, whose house lay conveniently near the physician's own, and from whom both the latter and Elâhi-Buksh heard authentic news from the Ridge; news which made them both pity the poor old pantaloon who, as they knew well, had been a mere puppet in stronger hands. And these two, laying their heads together in one of those kaleidoscope combinations of intrigue which made Delhi politics a puzzle even at the time, advised the King to use the *voix celeste* as an antidote to the *vox humana* of the city which was being so diligently fostered by the Queen and Bukht Khân. Let him say he was too old for this world, let him profess himself unable longer to cope with his coercers, and claim to be allowed to resign and become a fakeer! But the dreams still lingered in the old man's brain. He loved the brocaded bags, he loved the new cushion to the Peacock Throne; and though the cockatoo's crest was once more showing a yellow tinge through the green, the thought of *Jehâd* lingered sanctimoniously. But other folk in the palace were beginning to awake. Other people in Delhi besides Tiddu had heard that *Nikalseyn* was on his way from the Punjâb, and not even the rose-red walls had been able to keep out his reputation. Folk talked of him in whispers. The soldiers, unable to retreat, unwilling to fight, swore loudly that they were betrayed; that there were too many spies in the city. Of that there could be no doubt. Were not letters found concealed in innocent-looking cakes and such like? Had not one, vaguely suggesting that some cursed infidels were still concealed in the city, been brought in for reward by a Bunjâra who swore he had picked it up by chance? The tales grew by the telling in the Thunbi bazaar, making Prince Abool-Bukr, who had returned to it incontinently after the disastrous failure of faith on the 2nd, hiccup magnificently that, poor as he was, he would give ten golden *mohurs* to any one who set him on the track of a hell-doomed. Yea! folk might laugh, but he was good for tens till. Ay! and a rupee besides, to have the offer cried through the bazaar; so there would be an end to scoffers!

'What is't?' asked the languid loungers in the wooden balconies, as the drum came beating down the street.

'Only Abool offering ten *mohurs* for a Christian to kill,' said one.

'And he swore he had not a rupee when I danced for him but yesterday,' said another.

'He has to pay Newâsi, sister,' yawned a third.

'Then let her dance for him—I do it no longer,' retorted the grumbler.

So the crier and his drums passed down the scoffing bazaar. 'He will find many at that price,' quoth some, winking at their neighbours; for the Prince was a butt when in his cups.

Thus at earliest dawn next morning, the 7th of August, Tiddu gave a signal knock at the door of the roof, rousing Jim Douglas, who since the child's arrival had taken to sleeping across it once more.

'There is danger in the air, *Huzoor*,' he said briefly; 'they cried a reward for infidels in the bazaar yesterday. There is talk of some letter—'

'The child must go—go at once,' replied his hearer, alert in an instant; but Tiddu shook his head.

'Not till dark, *Huzoor*. The bullocks are to pass out with the moon, and he must pass out with them. In a sack, *Huzoor*. Say nothing till the last. Then—the *Huzoor* knows the cloth merchant's by the Delhi gate?'

Jim Douglas nodded.

'There is a court at the back. The bullocks are there, for we are taking cloth the Lâla wants to smuggle out; a length or two in each empty sack; for he hath been looted beyond limits. So he will have no eyes, nor the caravan either, for secret work in dark corners. Bring the boy drugged as he came here—the Rajpootni will carry the bundle as a spinner—to the third door down the lane. 'Tis an empty yard; I will have the bullock there with the half-load of raw cotton. We have two or three more as foils to the empty bags. Come as a Bunjâra, then the *Huzoor* can see the last of the child, and see old Tiddu's loyalty.'

The familiar whine came back to his voice; he could scarcely resist a thrust forward of his open hand. But dignity or no dignity, Jim Douglas knew that itching palm well, and said significantly—

'It will be worth a thousand rupees to you, Tiddu, if the child gets safe.'

A look of offended virtue came over the smooth face.

298 • A RAJ COLLECTION

'This slave is not thinking of money. The child is as his own child.'

'And the *mem* as your mother, remember,' put in the other quickly.

Tiddu hesitated. 'If his servant saves the *baba*, cannot the master save the lady?' he said, with the effrontery of a child trying how far he might go; but Jim Douglas's revolver was out in a second, and Tiddu with an air of injured innocence went on without a pause—

'The *mem* will be safe enough, *Huzoor*, when the child is gone; if the *Huzoor* will himself remain day and night to answer for the screened sick woman within. His slave will be back by dawn; and if he smells trouble, the *mem* must be moved in a dhoolie to another house, the Rajpootni must go home, and I will be mother-in-law. I can play the part, *Huzoor*.'

He could indeed! thought Jim Douglas. If Kate were to be safe anywhere, it would be with this old scoundrel with his thousand-faces, his undoubted gift for influencing the eyes of men. Three days of passing from one place to another, with him in some new character, and their traces must be lost. A good plan certainly!

'And there is no danger today?' he asked finally. Tiddu paused again, and his luminous eyes sought the *sahib's*. 'Who can say that, *Huzoor*, for a *mem*, in this city? But I think none. We can do no more, danger or not. And I will watch. And see, here is the dream-giver. The Rajpootni will know the dose for the child.'

The dream-giver! All that day the little screw of paper Tiddu had taken from his waist-belt lay in a fold of Jim Douglas's high-twined *pugri*, and its contents seemed to make him dull. Not that it mattered, since there was literally nothing to be done before dusk; for it would be cruel to tell Kate and keep her on tenter-hooks all day to no purpose. But after a while she noticed his dulness, and came over to where he sat, his head on his hand, in his favourite attitude.

'I believe you are going to have fever and ague again,' she said solicitously, 'do take some aconite; if we could only get some quinine, that would end the tiresome thing at once.'

He took some to please her, and because her suggestion gave him a reasonable excuse for being slack; but as he lounged about lazily, watching her playing with the boy, seeing her put him to sleep as the heat of the day came on, nothing the cheerful content with which she adapted herself to a simplicity of life unknown to her three months before, the wonder of the circumstances which had led to it faded in the regret that it should be coming to an end. It had been three months of incredible peace and goodwill; and today the peace and the goodwill seemed to strike him all the more keenly because he knew that in an hour or so at most he must disturb it. It seemed hard.

But something else began the task for him. About sunset, a sudden flash dazzled his eyes, and ere he grasped its vividness, the walls were rocking silently, and a second after a roar as of a thousand thunder claps deafened his ears. Kate had Sonny in her arms ere he could reach her, thrusting her away from the high parapet wall, which, in one already-cracked corner, looked as if it must come down; which did indeed crumble outwards, leaving a jagged gap half-way down its height, the *débris* falling with a rattle on the roof of the next house.

But ere the noise ended the vibration had passed, leaving him with relief on his face looking at a great mushroom of smoke and steam which had shot up into the sky.

'It is the powder-factory!' he exclaimed, using Hindustani for Tara's benefit as well, since she had rushed in from the outer court at the first hint of danger to cling round his feet. 'It is all over now, but it's lucky we were no nearer.'

As he spoke he was wondering if this would make any difference in Tiddu's plans for the night, since the powder factory had stood equi-distant between them and the Delhi gate. He wondered also what had caused the explosion. Not a shell certainly. The factory had purposely been placed at the furthest point from the Ridge. However, there was a fine supply of powder gone, and, he hoped, a few mutineers. But Kate's mind had reverted to that other explosion which had been the prologue to the three months of peace and quiet. Was this one to be the epilogue? A vague dread, a sudden premonition made her ask quickly—

'Can it mean anything serious? Can anything be the matter, Mr Greyman? Is anything wrong?'

It was a trifle early, he thought—she might have had another half hour or so of peace. But this was a good beginning, or rather a fitting end.

'And you have known this all day?' she said reproachfully when he told her the truth. 'How unkind of you not to tell me!'

'Unkind!' he echoed. 'What possible good—'

'I should have known it was the last day—I—I should have made the—the most of it.'

He felt glad of his own impatience of the sentimentality as he turned away, for in truth the look on her face hit him hard. It sent him to pace up and down the outer roof restlessly till the time for action came. Then he had a whispered consultation with Tara regarding the dose of raw opium safe for a child of Sonny's years.

'Are you sure that is not too much?' he asked anxiously.

Tara looked at the little black pellet she was rolling gravely. 'It is large, *Huzoor*, but it is for life or death; and if it was the *Huzoor*'s own son I would give no less.'

Once more the remembrance of the still little morsel in Zora's tinsel veil brought an odd compunction—for the very possibility of this strange child's death roused greater pain than that certainty had done. He felt unnerved at the responsibility; but Kate, looking up as he rejoined her, held out her hand without a tremor.

'Give it me, please,' she said, and her voice was steady also; 'he will take it best from me. I have some sugar here.'

The child, drowsy already with the near approach of bedtime, was in her lap, and rested his head on her breast, as with her arms still round him—her hands disguised the drug.

'It is a very large dose,' she said dully. 'I knew it must be; that's why I wanted to give it—myself. Sonny! Open your mouth, darling— it's quite sweet—there—swallow it quick—that's a good Sonny-kins.'

'You are very brave,' he said with a catch in his voice.

She glanced up at him for a second with a sort of scorn in her eyes. 'I knew he would take it from me,' she replied, and then, shifting the child to an easier position, began to sing in a half-voice—

There is a happy land—

'Far—farze—away,' echoed Sonny contentedly. It was his usual lullaby, chosen because it resembled a native air, beloved of ayahs.

And as she sang and Sonny's eyelids drooped, the man watched them both with a tender awe in his heart; and the other woman, crouching in the corner, watched all three with hungry, passionate eyes. Here, in this group of man, woman, and child, without a personal claim on each other, was something new, half-incomprehensible, wholly sweet.

'He is asleep now,' said Kate after a time. 'You had better take him.'

He stooped to obey, and she stooped also to leave a long, lingering kiss on the boy's soft cheek. It sent a thrill through the man as he recognized that in giving him the child she had given him more than kisses.

The feeling that it was so made him linger a few minutes afterwards at the door with a new sense of his responsibilities towards her to say—

'I wish I had not to leave you alone.'

'You will be back directly, and I shall be all right,' she said, pausing in her closing of the door, for Tara had already passed down the stair with her bundle.

'Shall I lock it outside?' he began. Tara and he had been used to do so in those first days when they left her.

She laid her hand lightly on his arm. 'Don't,' she said, 'don't get anxious about me again. What can happen in half-an-hour?'

He heard her slip the catch on the staple, however, before he ran downstairs. He was to take a different road to the Delhi gate from the quiet, more devious alleys which Tara would choose in her character of poor spinner carrying her raw stuff home. She was to await his arrival, to deposit the bundle somewhere close to the third door in the back lane by the cloth merchant's shop, leaving it to him to take inside, as if he were one of the caravan; this plan insuring two things—immunity from notice in the streets, and also in the yard. But, as Tara would be longer than he by a few minutes in reaching the tryst, he purposely went through a bit of the Thunbi bazaar to hear what he could of the explosion. He was surprised—a trifle alarmed—at the excitement. Crowds were gathered round many of the balconies, talking of spies, swearing that half the court was in league with the Ridge, and that, after all, Abool-Bukr might not have a wild goose chase.

'There will be naught but slops and slaps for him in *my* information, I'll swear,' said one, with a laugh. 'I'll back old Mother Sobrai to beat off a dozen princes.'

'And blows and bludgeons in *mine*,' chuckled another. 'I chose the house of Bahâdur, the single-stick player.'

And as, having no more time to lose, he cut across gate-wards, he saw down an alley a mob surging round Ahsan-Oolah the physician's house, and heard a passer-by say they had the traitor safe. It made him vaguely uneasy, since he knew that—when once the talk turns on hidden things—people, not to be behindhand in gossip, rake up every trivial doubt and wonder.

Still there was the file of bullocks waiting by the cloth merchant's as arranged. And as he passed into the lane a dim figure, scarce seen in the dark, slipped out of the further end. And there was the bundle. He caught it up as if it belonged to him, and after knocking gently at the third door pushed it open, knowing that he must show no hesitation. He found himself in a sort of outhouse or covered entrance, pitch dark save for a faintly lighter square showing an outlet, doubtless, into the yard beyond. He moved towards it, and stumbled over something unmistakable upon the floor. A man! He dropped the bundle promptly to be ready in case the sleeper should be a stranger. But there was no movement, and he knelt down to feel if it was Tiddu. A Bunjâra!—That also was unmistakable at the first touch—but the limpness was unmistakable too. The man was dead—still warm, but dead! By all that was unlucky!—not Tiddu surely! With the flint-and-steel in his waist cloth, he lit a tuft of cotton from the bundle as a torch.

It was Jhungi!—Jhungi with a knife in his heart!

'*Huzoor!*' came the familiar creak, as Tiddu, attracted by the sudden light, stole in from the yard beyond. 'Quick! there is no time to lose. Give me the bundle and go back.'

'Go back!' echoed Jim Douglas amazed.

'*Huzoor*! take off the Bunjâra's dress. I have a green turban and shawl here. The *Huzoor* must go back to the *mem* at once. There is treachery.'

Jim Douglas swore under his breath as he obeyed.

'I know not what, but the *mem* must not stay there. I heard him boasting before, and just now I caught him prying.'

'Who, Jhungi?'

Even at such a moment Tiddu demurred.

'The *Huzoor* mistakes. It is the miscreant Bhungi—Jhungi is virtuous—'

'You killed him then?' interrupted the hearer, putting the last touch to his disguise.

'What else could I do, *Huzoor*? I had only my knife. And it is not as if it were—Jhungi—'

But Jim Douglas was already out of the door, running through the dark deserted lanes while he dared, since he must walk through the bazaar. And as he ran he told himself that he was a fool to be so anxious. What could go wrong in half-an-hour?

What indeed!

As he stood five minutes after, staring into the dark emptiness of the roof, he asked himself again and again what could have happened? There had been no answer to his knock; the door had been hasped on the outside, yet the first glance as he entered made him realize that the place was empty of life. And though he had lit the cresset, with a fierce fear at what it might reveal, he could find no trace, even of a struggle. Kate had disappeared! Had she gone out? Impossible. Had Tara heard of the danger, returned and taken her elsewhere? Possible, but improbable. He passed rapidly down the stairs again. The storey below the roof, being reserved for the owner's use on his occasional visits to Delhi, was empty; the occupants of the second floor, pious folk, had fled from the city a day or two before; and when he paused to inquire on the ground floor to know if there had been any disturbance he found the door padlocked outside—sure sign that every one was out. Oh! why, he thought, had he not so padlocked that other door upstairs? He passed out into the street, beginning to realize that his task was over just as he had ceased to gird at it. There was nothing unusual to be seen. The godly folk about were beginning to close their gates for the night; and some paused to listen with an outraged air to the thrummings and drummings from the princess Farkhoonda's roof. And that was Abool-Bukr's voice singing—

O mistress rare, divine!

Then it could scarcely be he who had found Kate; besides, she might have met with friends in that quarter, where so many learned folk deemed the slaughter of women unlawful. But, he told himself, there was no use in speculating; he must find Tara first. He paused, however, to inquire from the cobbler at the corner; disturbance? echoed the man; not much more than usual; the Prince, who had passed in half-an-hour agone, being perhaps a bit wilder after his wild goose chase. Had not the Aga-*sahib* heard? The wags of the bazaar had taken up the offer made by the Prince; and his servants had sworn they were glad to get him to the Princess's, since they had been whacked out of half-a-dozen houses! He was safe now, however, for when he was of that humour Newâsi Begum never let him go till he was too drunk for mischief.

Then, thought Jim Douglas, it was possible that Jhungi might have given real information; still but one thing was certain—the roof was empty; the dream had vanished into thin air.

He did not know as he passed through the dim streets that their dream was over also, and that John Nicholson stood looking down from the Ridge on the shadowy mass of the town. He had posted in a hundred and twenty miles that day, arriving in time to hear the explosion of the magazine. The city's salute of welcome, as it were, to the man who was to take it.

He had been dining at the head quarters mess, taciturn and grave— a wet blanket on the jollity, and the Moselle cup, and the fresh cut of cheese from the new Europe-shop; and now, when others were calling cheery good nights as they passed to their tents, he was off to wander alone round the walls, measuring them with his keen kindly eyes. A giant of a man, biting his lips beneath his heavy brown beard, making his way once the rocks, sheltering in shadow, doggedly, moodily, lost in thought. He was parcelling out his world for conquest, settling already where to prick the bubble.

But, in a way, it was pricked already. For as he prowled about the palace walls, a miserable old man, *minus* even the solace of pulse-feeling and cooling draughts, was dictating a letter to Hâfzan the woman scribe. A miserable letter, to be duly sent next day to the commanders-in-chief, and forwarded by them to the volunteers of Delhi. A disjointed rambling effusion worthy of the shrunken mind and body which held but a rambling disjointed memory even of the advice given it.

'Have I not done all in my power to please the soldiery?' it ran. 'But it is to be deplored that you have, notwithstanding, shown no concern for my life, no consideration for my old age. The care of my health was in the hands of Ahsan-Oolah, who kept himself constantly informed of the changes it underwent. Now there is none to care for me but God, while the changes in my health are such as may not be imagined; therefore the soldiers and officers ought to gratify me and release the physician, so that he may come whenever he thinks it necessary to examine my pulse. Furthermore, the property plundered from his house belonged to the King, therefore it should be traced and collected and conveyed to our presence. If you are not disposed to comply, let me be conveyed to the Kutb shrine and employ myself as a sweeper of the Mosque. And if even this be not acceded I will still relinquish every concern and jump up from my seat. Not having been killed by the English, I will be killed by you; for I shall swallow a diamond and go to sleep. Moreover, in the plunder of the physician's house a small box containing our seal was carried away. No paper, therefore, of a date subsequent to the 7th August 1857 bearing our seal will be valid.'

A miserable letter indeed. The Dream of Sovereignty had come to an end with that salute of welcome to John Nicholson.

# BOOK V

## 'There Arose a Man'

# 1

## Forward

'Are you here on duty, sir?' asked a brief imperious voice. Major Erlton, startled from a half-dream as he sate listlessly watching the target practice from the Crow's Nest, rose and saluted. His height almost matched the speaker's, but he looked small in comparison with the indescribable air of dominant power and almost arrogant strength in the other figure. It seemed to impress him, for he pulled himself together smartly with a certain confidence, and looked, in truth, every inch a soldier.

'No, sir,' he replied as briefly, 'on pleasure.'

A distinct twinkle showed for a second in General Nicholson's deep-set hazel eyes. 'Then go to your bed, sir, and sleep. You look as if you wanted some.' He spoke almost rudely; but as he turned on his heel he added in a louder voice than was necessary had he meant the remark for his companion's ear only, 'I shall want good fighting men before long, I expect.'

If he did, he might reckon on one. Herbert Erlton was not good at formulating his feelings into definite thoughts, but as he went back to the peaceful side of the Ridge he told himself vaguely that he was glad Nicholson had come. He was the sort of man a fellow would be glad to follow, especially when he was dead-sick and weary of waiting and doing nothing—save get killed! Yes! he was a real good sort, and, as even the chaplain had said at mess, they hadn't felt quite so besieged on the Ridge these last two days since he came. And, by George! he had hit the right nail on the head. A man wasn't much good without sleep.

So, with a certain pride in following the advice, Major Erlton flung himself on his cot and promptly dozed off. In truth he needed rest. Sonny Seymour's safe arrival in camp two nights before, in charge of a Bunjâra, from whom even Hodson had been unable to extract anything—save that the Agha-*sahib* had forgotten a letter in his hurry, and that the *mem* was safe, or had been safe—had sent Major Erlton to watch those devilish walls more feverishly than ever. Not that it really mattered whether Kate was alive or dead, he told himself. No! he did not mean that, quite. He would be awfully glad—God! how glad! to know her safe. But it wouldn't alter other things, would not even alter them in regard to her. So, once more, he waited for the further news promised him, with a strange indifference, save to the thought that, alive or dead, Kate was within the walls—like another woman—like many women.

And now he was dreaming that he was inside them also, sword in hand.

There seemed some chance of it indeed, men were saying to each other, as they looked after John Nicholson's tall figure as it wandered into every post and picquet, asking brief questions, pleased with brief replies. Every now and again pausing, as it were, to come out of his absorption and take a sudden, keen interest in something beyond the great question. As when, passing the tents of the only lady in camp, he saw Sonny, who had been made over to her till he could be sent back to his mother who had escaped to Meerut; during which brief time he was the plaything of a parcel of subalterns who delighted in him, tinsel cap, anklets, and all. Major Erlton had at first rather monopolized the child, trying to find out something definite from him; but as he insisted that 'Miffis Erlton lived up in the 'ky wif a man wif a gween face, and a white face, and a lot of fwowers, and a bit of tring,' and spoke familiarly of Tiddu, and Tara, and Soma, without being able to say who they were, the Major had given it up as a bad job and gone back to the walls. So the subalterns had the child to themselves, and were playing pranks with him as the general passed by.

'Fine little fellow!' he said suddenly. 'I like to see children's legs and arms. Up in Bunnoo the babies were just like that young monkey. Real corn-colour. I got quite smitten with them and sent for a lot of toys from Lahore. Only I had to bar Lawrence from peg-tops, for I knew I should have got peg-topping with the boys, and that would have been fatal to my dignity. That is the worst of high estates. You daren't make friends, and you have to make enemies.'

The smile which had made him look years younger faded, and he was back in the great problem of his life—how to keep pace with his yoke-fellows, how to scorn consequences, and steer straight to independent action, without spoiling himself by setting his seniors and superiors in arms against him. He had never solved it yet. His career had been one long race with the curb on. A year before he had thrown up the game in disgust, and begged to be transferred from the Punjâb while he could go with honour; and even his triumphant march Delhi-wards—in which he found disaffection, disobedience, and doubt, and left fear, trembling, and peace—had been marred by much rebuking. So that once, nothing but the inner sense that pin-points ought not to let out the heart's blood, kept him at his post; and but two days before, on the very eve of that hundred-and-twenty mile rush to Delhi, he had written claiming definitely the right of an officer in his position to quarrel anybody's opinion, and asserting his duty of speaking out, no matter at what risk of giving offence.

And now, a man years younger than those in nominal command— he was but six-and-thirty,—and holding views diametrically opposed to theirs, he had been sent here, virtually, to take Delhi because those others could not. No wonder, then, that the question how to avoid collision puzzled him. Not because he knew that his appointment was in itself an offence, that some people affected to speak of him still as Mr Nicholson—that being his real rank—but because he knew in his heart of hearts that at any moment he might do something appalling. Move troops under some one else's command, without a reference, as he had done before during his career! Then, naturally, there must be 'ructions. He had a smile for the thought himself. Still, for the present, concord was assured; since, until his column arrived, the repose of the lion couching for a spring was manifestly the only policy; though it might be necessary to wag the tail a bit—to do more than merely forbid sorties and buglings. The fools, for instance, who harassed the Metcalfe House picquet, might be shown their mistake and made to understand that, if the Ridge called 'time!' for a little decent rest before the final round, it meant to have it. So he passed on his errand to inculcate Headquarters with his decision, leaving Sonny playing with the boys.

Meanwhile one of the garrison, at least, had found the benefit of his keen judgement. Herbert Erlton had passed from dreams of conflict to the real rest of unconscious sleep, oblivious of everything; even those rose-red walls.

But within them another man, haggard and anxious as he had been, was still allowing himself no rest in his search for Kate Erlton. Tara, as much at a loss as he, was helping him; for though at first she had been relieved at the idea of the *mem*'s disappearance, she had soon realized that the master ran more risk than ever in his reckless determination to find some trace of the missing woman. And Tiddu, who had returned, helped also. The *mem*, he said, must have found friends; must be alive. Such a piece of gossip as the discovery and death of an Englishwoman could not have been kept from the Thunbi bazaar. Then those who had passed from the roof had been calm enough to hasp the door behind them; that did not look like violence. If the *Huzoor* would only be patient and wait, something would turn up. There were other kindly folk in the city besides himself! But, in the meantime, he would do well to allow Soma to slip into the sulky indifference he seemed to prefer, and take no notice of him. It only meant that he, and half the good soldiers in Delhi, were mad with themselves for having chosen the losing side; for with *Nikalseyn* on the Ridge, what chance had Delhi?

This was rather an exaggerated picture; still it was a fairly faithful presentiment of the inward thoughts of many, who, long before this, had begun to ask themselves what the devil they were doing in that galley? Yet there they were, and there they must fight. Soma, however, was doubtful even of that. His heart positively ached as he listened to the tales told in the very heart of Delhi of the man whom other men worshipped—the man who took forts single-handed, and said that, given the powers of a provost-marshal, he would control a disobedient army in two days! The man who yoked bribe-taking *tahseeldar*s into the village well-wheel to draw water for the robbed *ryot*s, and set women of loose virtue, who came into his camp, to cool in muddy tanks. The man who flung every law-book on his office table at his clerks' heads, and then—with a kindly apologetic smile—paused while they replaced them for future use. The man who gave toys to children, and remorselessly hung two abettors of a vile murder, when he could not lay hands on the principal. The man, finally, who flogged those who worshipped him into promising adoration for the future to a very ordinary mortal of his acquaintance! Briefly the hero, the demi-god, who perhaps was neither, but, as Tiddu declared, had simply the greatest gift of all—the gift of making men what he wished them to be. Either way it was gall and wormwood to Soma—hero-worshipper by birth—that his side should have no such colossal figure to follow. So, sulky and sore, he held aloof from both sides, doing his bounden duty to both, and no more. Keeping guards when his fellows took bribes to fight, and agreeing with Tiddu, that since some others besides themselves knew of the roof, it was safer for the master to lock it up, and live for a time elsewhere.

So, all unwittingly, the only chance of finding Kate was lost. For what had happened was briefly this. Five minutes after Jim Douglas had left her, Prince Abool-Bukr, who had kept this *renseignement*—given him by a Bunjâra, who had promised to be in waiting and was not—to the last because it was close to the haven where he would he, had come roystering up the stairs, followed by his unwilling retainers suggesting that the Most Illustrious had really better desist from violating seclusion since they were all black and blue already. But, from sheer devilry and desire to outrage the quarter, which by its complaints had already brought him into trouble, the prince had begun battering at the door. Kate running to bar it more securely, saw that the hasp, carelessly hitched over the staple, was slipping—had slipped; and had barely time to dash into the inner roof ere the prince, unexpectant of the sudden giving way, tumbled headlong into the outer one. The fall gave her an instant more, but made him angry; and the end would have been certain, if Kate, seeing the new-made gap in the wall before her, had not availed herself of it. There was a roof not far below she knew—the *débris* would be on a slope perhaps—the blue-eyed boy had escaped by the roofs. All this flashed through her, as by the aid of a stool, which she kicked over in her scramble, she gained the top of the gap and peered over. The next instant she had dropped herself down some four feet; finding a precarious foothold on a sliding slope of rubble, and still clinging to the wall with her hands. If no one looked over, she thought breathlessly, she was safe! And no one did. The general air of decent privacy alarmed the retainers into remembering that two of their number had found death their reward for their master's last escapade in that quarter; so, after one glance round, they swore the place was empty, and dragged him off, feebly protesting that it was his last chance, and he had not bagged a single Christian.

Kate heard the door closed, heard the voices retreat downstairs, and then set herself to get back over the gap. It did not seem a difficult task. The slope on which she hung gave fair foothold, and by getting a good grip on the brick work, and perhaps displacing a brick or two in the crack lower down, as a step, she ought to get up easily. It was lucky the crack was there, she thought. In one way, not in another, for, as in her effort she necessarily threw all her weight on the wall, another bit of it gave way, she fell backwards, and so, half covered with bricks and mud, rolled to the roof below, which was luckily not more than eight or nine feet down. It was far enough, however, for the fall to have killed her; but, though she lay quite unconscious, she was not dead, only stunned, shaken, confused, unable absolutely to think. It was almost dawn, indeed, before she realized that her only chance of getting up again was in calling for help; and by that time the door above had been locked, and there was no one to hear her.

The few square yards of roof on to which she had rolled belonged to one of those box-like buildings, half-turrets, half-summer houses, which natives build here, there, and everywhere at all sorts of elevations, until the view of a town from a topmost roof resembles nothing so much as the piles of luggage awaiting the tidal train at Victoria. This particular square belonged to a tiny turret, which stood on a long narrow roof, belonging in its turn to an arcaded slip of summer-house standing on a square, and set round by high parapet walls. Quite a staircase of roofs! The one where she was had had a thatch set against the wall, but it had fallen in with the weight of bricks and mortar; still she might be able to creep between it and the wall for shelter. And on the slip of roof below, Indian corn was drying, during this break in the rains—rains which had filled a row of water-pots quite full. Since she could not make those above her hear, it would be as well, she thought, to secure herself from absolute starvation before broad daylight brought life to the wilderness of roofs around her; so she scrambled down a rough ladder of bamboo tied with string, and after a brief look into the square below, came back with some parched grain she had found in a basket, and a pot of water. She would not starve for that day. By this time it was dawn, and she crept into her shelter, listening all the while for a sound from above; every now and again venturing on a call. But there was no answer, and by degrees it came to her that she must rely on herself only for safety. She was not likely to be disturbed that day where she was, unless people came to repair the thatch; and under cover of night she might surely creep from roof to roof down to some alley. What alley? True, her goal now lay behind her, but these roofs, set at every angle, might lead her far from it. And how was she to know her own stair, her own house, from the outside? She had passed into it in darkness and never left it again. Then what sort of people lived in these houses through which she must creep like a thief? Murderers, perhaps. Still it was her only chance; and all that burning, blistering day, as she crouched between the thatch and the wall, she was bolstering up her courage for the effort. She could see the Ridge clearly from her hiding place. Ah! if she had only the wings of the doves—those purple pigeons which—circling from the great dome of the mosque—came to feast unchecked on the Indian corn! The people below, then, must be pious folk.

It was past midnight, and the silence of sleep had settled over the city before she nerved herself to the chance, and crept down among the corn. No difficulty in that; but to her surprise, a cresset was still burning in the arcaded verandah below, sending three bars of light across the square through which she must pass. It would be better to wait awhile; but an hour slipped by and still the light gleamed into the silence. Perhaps it had been forgotten. The possibility made her creep down the brick ladder, prepared to creep up again if the silence proved deceptive. But what she saw made her pause, hesitating. It was a woman reading from a large book held in a book rest. The Koran, of course. Kate recognized it at once, for just such another had been part of the necessary furniture of her roof. And what a beautiful face! Tender, refined, charming. Not the face of a murderess, surely?—surely it might be trusted? Those three months behind the veil had made Kate realize the emotionality of the East; its instinctive sympathy with the dramatic element in life. She remembered her sudden impulse in regard to the knife, and its effect on Tiddu; she felt a similar impulse towards confidence here. Besides, she knew that the doors might be locked below, and that her best chance might be to throw herself on the mercy of this woman.

The next moment she was standing full in the light close to the student, who started to her feet with a faint cry, gazing almost incredulously at the figure so like her own, save for the jewels gleaming among the white draperies.

'*Bibi*,' she faltered.

'I am no *bibi*,' interrupted Kate hurriedly in Hindustani. 'I am a Christian—but a woman like yourself—a mother. For the sake of yours—or the sake of your sons, if you are a mother too—for the sake of what you love best—save me.'

'A Christian! a *mem*!' In the pause of sheer astonishment the two women stood facing each other, looking into each other's eyes. Prince Abool-Bukr had been right when he said that Kate Erlton reminded him of the Princess Fârkhoonda Zamáni. Standing so, they showed strangely alike indeed, not in feature, but in type; in the soul which looked out of the soft dark, and the clear grey eyes.

'Save you?'—the faint echo was lost in a new sound, close at hand— a careless voice humming a song—a step coming up the dark stair.

O mistress rare, divine!

God and His Prophet! Abool himself! Newâsi flung her hands up in sheer horror. Abool! and this Christian here! The next instant with a fierce 'Keep still,' she had thrust Kate into the deepest shadow and was out to bar the brick ladder with her tall white grace. She had no time for thought. One sentence beat on her brain—'for the sake of what you love best, save me!' Yea! for *his* sake this strange woman must not be seen—he must not, should not guess she was there!

'Stand back, kind one, and let me pass,' came the gay voice carelessly. It made Kate shudder back into further shadow, for she knew now where she was; and but that she would have to pass those bars of light would have essayed escape to the roofs again.

But Newâsi stood still as stone on the first step of the stairs.

'Pass!' she repeated clearly, coldly. 'Art mad, Abool? that thou comest hither with no excuse of drunkenness and alone, at this hour of the night. For shame!'

Why, indeed, she asked herself wildly, had he come? He was not used to do so. Could he have heard? Had he come on purpose? There was a sound as if he retreated a step, and from the dark his voice came with a wonder in it.

'What ails thee, Newâsi?'

'What ails me!' she echoed. 'What I have lacked too long. Just anger at thy thoughtless ways. Go—'

'But I have that to tell thee of serious import that none but thou must hear. That which will please thee. That which needs thy kind wise eyes upon it.'

'Then let them see it by daylight, not now. I will not, Abool. Stand back, or I will call for help.'

The sound of retreat was louder this time, and a muttered curse came with it; but the voice had a trace of anxiety in it now—anxiety and anger.

'Thou dost not mean it, kind one; thou canst not! When have I done that which would make thee need help? Newâsi! be not a fool. Remember it is I, Abool; Abool-Bukr who has a devil in him at times!'

Did she not know it by this time? Was not that the reason why he must not find this Christian? Why she must refuse him hearing?— Though it was true that he had a right to be trusted! In all those long years, when had he failed to treat her tenderly, respectfully? As she stood barring his way, where he had never before been denied entrance, she felt as if she herself could have killed that strange woman for being there—for coming between them.

'Listen, Abool!' she said, stretching out her hands to find his in the dark. 'I mean naught, dear, that is unkind. How could it be so between me and thee? But 'tis not wise.' She paused, catching her breath in a faint sob. He could not see her face, perhaps if he had, he would have been less relentless.

'Wherefore? Canst not trust thy nephew, fair aunt?' The sarcasm bit deep.

'Nephew! A truce, Abool, to this foolish tale,' she began hotly, when he interrupted her.

'Of a surety, if the Princess Farkhoonda desires it! Yet would Mirza Abool-Bukr still like to know wherefore he is not received?'

His tone sent a thrill of terror through her, his use of the name he hated warned her that his temper was rising—the devil awakening.

'Canst not see, dear,' she pleaded, trying to keep the hands he would have drawn from hers—'folk have evil minds.'

He gave an ugly laugh. 'Since when hast thou begun to think of thy good name, like other women, Newâsi? But if it be so, if all my virtue—and God knows 'tis ill-got—is to go for naught, let it end.'

She heard him, felt him turn, and a wild despair surged up in her. Which was worst? To let him go in anger beyond the reach of her controlling hand mayhap—go to unknown evils—or chance this one? Since—since at the worst murder and death might be concealed!

God and His Prophet! What a thought. No! she would plead again—she would stoop—she would keep him at—at any price.

'Listen!' she whispered passionately, leaning towards him in the dark, 'dost ask since when I have feared for my good name? Canst not guess?—Abool! what—what does a woman, as I am, fear—save herself—save her own love—'

There was an instant's silence, and then his reckless jeering laugh jarred loud.

'So it has come at last! and there is another woman for kisses. That is an end indeed! Did I not tell thee we should quarrel over it some day? Well, be it so, Princess! I will take my virtue elsewhere.'

She stood as if turned to stone, listening to his retreating steps, listening to his nonchalant humming of the old refrain as he passed through the courtyard into the alley. Then, without a word, but quivering with passion, she turned to where Kate cowered, and dragged her by main force to the stairs where, a minute before, she had sacrificed everything for her. No! not for her, for him!

'Go,' she said bitterly. 'Go! and my curse go with you.'

Kate fled before the anger she saw but did not understand. Yet as she flew down the steep stairs she paused involuntarily to listen to the sound—a sound which needed no interpreter as the liquid Persian had done—of a woman sobbing as if her heart would break.

She had no time, however, even for wonder, and the next instant she was out in the alley, turning to the right. For the knowledge that it was the Princess Farkhoonda who had helped her, gave the clue to her position. But the house, the stair? How could she know it? She must try them one after another—since she would surely know the landing—the door she had so often opened and shut? Still it was perilously near dawn ere she found what she felt was the right one; but it was padlocked!

They must have gone; gone and left her alone!

For the first time, ghastly, unreasoning fear seized on her; she could have beaten at the door and screamed her claim to be let in; and even when the rush of terror passed, she sat stupidly on the step, not even wondering what to do next. Till suddenly she remembered that she had keys in her pocket. That of the inner padlock, certainly; perhaps of the outer one also, since Tara had given up using her duplicate altogether.

She had it; and five minutes after, having satisfied herself that the roof remained as it was—that it was merely empty for a time—she tried to feel grateful. But the loneliness, the dimness, were too much for her fatigue, her excitement. So once more the sound which needs no interpreter rose on the warm soft night.

It was two days after this that Tiddu held a secret consultation with Soma and Tara. The Agha-*sahib*, he said, was getting desperate. He was losing his head, as the *Huzoor*s did over women folk, and he must be got out of the city. It was not as if he did any good by staying in it. The *mem* was either dead, or safely concealed. There was no alternative, unless, indeed, she had already been passed out to the Ridge. There was talk of that sort among Hodson's spies, and he was going to utilize the fact and persuade the *Huzoor* to creep out to the camp and see. Soma could pass him out, and would not pass him in again; which was fortunate, since folk in addition to protecting masters had to make money, when every other corn-carrier in the place was coining it by smuggling gold and silver out of the city for the rich merchants! Tara, with a sudden fierce exultation in her sombre eyes, agreed. Let the *Huzoor* go back to his own life, she said; let him go to safety, and leave her free. As for the *mem*, the master had done enough for her. And Soma, sulky and lowering with the dull glow of opium in his brain— for the drug was his only solace now—swore that Tiddu was right. Delhi was no place for the master. And once out of it, the fighting would keep him; he knew him of old. As for the *mem*, he would not harm her, as Tara had once suggested he should. That dream was over. The *Huzoor*s were the true masters; they had men who could lead men; not princes in Kashmir shawls who could't understand a word of what you said, and mere *soubadar*s cocked up, but real *Colonell*s and *Generâl*s.

The result of this being that on the night of the 11th, between midnight and dawn, Jim Douglas, with that elation which came to him always at the prospect of action, prepared to slip out of the sally port by the Magazine, disguised as a sepoy. This was to please Soma. To please Tiddu, however, he wore underneath this disguise, the old staff-uniform from the theatrical properties. It reminded him of Alice Gissing, making him whisper another 'bravo' to the memory of the woman whom he had buried under the orange-trees in the crimson-netted shroud made of an officer's scarf.

Nevertheless Tiddu's remark that an English uniform would be the safest, once he was beyond the city, sent sadness flying, in its frank admission that the tide had turned.

Turned, indeed! The certainty came with a great throb of fierce joy as, half-an-hour afterwards, slipping past the gardens of Ludlow Castle, he found himself in the thick of English bayonets, and felt grateful for the foresight of the old staff uniform. They were on their way to surprise and take the picquet; not to defend but to attack.

The opportunity was too good to be lost. There was no hurry; he had arranged to remain three days on the Ridge, and he might not have another opportunity of a free fair fight.

He had forgotten every woman in the world, everything save the welcome silence before him as he turned and stole through the trees also, sword in hand.

By all that was lucky and well-planned! the picquet must be asleep! There was not a sound save the faint crackle of stealthy feet, almost lost in the insistent quiver of the cicalas. No! there was a challenge at last within a foot or two.

'Who—kum—dar?'

And swift as an echo a young voice beside him replied gibingly:

'It's me, Pandy! Take that.'

It's me! Just so; me with a vengeance. For the right attack and the left were both well up. There was a short, sharp volley, then the welcome familiar order. A cheer, a clatter, a rush and clashing with the bayonets. It seemed but half-a minute before Jim Douglas found himself among the guns, slashing at a dazed artillery-man who had a port-fire in his hand. So the artillery on either side never had a chance, and Major Erlton, riding up with the 9th Lancers as the central attack, found that bit of the fighting over. The picquet was taken, the mutineers had fled city-wards leaving four guns behind them; and against one of these, as the Major rode close to gloat over it, leant a man whom he recognized at once.

'My God! Douglas,' he said, 'where—where's Kate?—Where's my wife?'

It was rather an abrupt transition of thought, and Jim Douglas, who was feeling rather queer from something—he scarcely knew what— looked up at the speaker doubtfully.

'Oh! it is you, Major Erlton,' he said slowly. 'I thought—I mean I hoped she was here—if she isn't—why, I suppose I'd better go back.'

He took his arm off the gun and half-stumbled forward, when Major Erlton flung himself from his horse and laid hold of him.

'You're hit, man!—The blood's pouring from your sleeve. Here, off with your coat, sharp!'

'I can't think why it bleeds so?' said Jim Douglas feebly, looking down at a clean cut at the inside of the elbow from which the blood was literally spouting. 'It is nothing—nothing at all.'

The Major gave a short laugh. 'Take the go out of you a bit, though. I'll get a tourniquet on sharp, and send you up in a dhooli.'

'What an unlucky devil I am,' muttered Jim Douglas to himself, and the Major did not deny it. He was in a hurry to be off again with the party told to clear the Koodsia Gardens; which they did successfully before sunrise, when the expedition returned to camp cheering like demons and dragging in the captured guns, on which some of the wounded men sat triumphantly. It was their first real success since Budli-ke-serai, two months before; and they were in wild spirits.

Even the doctor, fresh from shaking his head over many a form lifted helplessly from the dhoolis, was jubilant as he sorted Jim

318 • A RAJ COLLECTION

Douglas's arm.

'Keep you here ten days or so, I should say. There's always a chance of its breaking out again till the wound is quite healed. Never mind! You can go into Delhi with the rest of us, before then.'

'Yoicks forward!' cried a wounded lad in the cot close by. The doctor turned sharply. 'If you don't keep quiet, Jones, I'll send you back to Meerut. And you too, Maloney. I've told you to lie still a dozen times.'

'Sure, docther dear, ye couldn't be so cruel,' said a big Irishman sitting at the foot of his bed so as to get nearer to a new arrival who was telling the tale of the fight. 'And me able-bodied and spoiling to be at me wurrk this three days.'

'It's a curious fact,' remarked the doctor to Jim Douglas as he finished bandaging him, 'the hospital has been twice as insubordinate since Nicholson came in. The men seem to think we are to assault Delhi tomorrow. But we can't till the siege train comes, of course. So you may be in at the death!'

Jim Douglas felt glad and sorry in a breath.

Finally he told himself he could let decision stand over for a day or two. He must see Hodson first, and find out if the letter he had had from his spies about an Englishwoman concealed in Delhi, referred to Kate Erlton.

# 2

# Bits, Bridles, and Spurs

The letter, however, did not refer to Kate; though, curiously enough, the Englishwoman it concerned had been, and still was concealed in an Afghân's house. Kate, then, had not been the only Englishwoman in Delhi. There was a certain consolation in the thought, since what was being done for one person by kindly natives might very well be done for another. Besides, removed as he was now from the fret and strain of actual search, Jim Douglas admitted frankly to Major Hodson that he was right in saying that Mrs Erlton must either have come to an end of her troubles altogether, or have found friends better able, perhaps, than he to protect her.

Regarding the first possibility, also, Major Hodson was sceptical. He had hundreds of spies in the city. Such a piece of good luck as the discovery of a Christian must have been noised abroad. They had not mentioned it; he did not, therefore, believe it had occurred. He would, however, enquire, and till the answer came it would be foolish to go back to the city. Jim Douglas admitted this also; but as the days passed, the desire to return increased; especially when Major Erlton came to see him, which he did with dutiful regularity. Jim Douglas could not help admiring him when he stood, stiff and square, thanking him as Englishmen thank their fellows for what they know to be beyond thanks.

'I am sure no one could have done more, and I know I couldn't have done a quarter so much—and I'm grateful,' he said awkwardly. Then with the best intentions, born from a real pity for the haggard man who sat on the edge of his cot looking as men do after a struggle of weeks with malarial fever, he added, 'And the luck has been a bit against you all the time, hasn't it?'

'As yet, perhaps,' replied Jim Douglas, feeling inclined then and there to start city-wards, 'but the game isn't over. When I go back—'

'Hodson says you could do no good,' continued the big man, still with the best intentions.

'I don't agree with him,' retorted the other sharply.

['Perhaps not—but—but I wouldn't, if I were you. Or—rather—*I* should, of course—only—you see it is different for me. She—' Major Erlton paused, finding it difficult to explain himself. The memory of that last letter he had written to Kate was always with him, making him feel she was not, in a way, his wife. He had never regretted writing it. He had scarcely thought what would happen if she came back from the dead, as it were, to answer it; for he hated thought.]Even now the complexity of his emotions irritated him, and he broke through them almost brutally. 'She was my wife, you see. But you had nothing to do with it; so you had better leave it alone. You've done enough already. And as I said before, I'm grateful.'

So he had stalked away leaving his hearer frowning. It was true. The luck had been against him. But what right had it to be so? Above all, what right had that big brutal fellow to say so? There he was going off to win more distinction, no doubt. He would end by getting the Victoria Cross, and confound him! from what people said of him, he would well deserve it.

While he? Even these two days had brought his failure home to him. And yet he told himself, that if he had failed to save one Englishwoman, others had failed to save hundreds. Fresh as he was to the facts, they seemed to him almost incredible. As he wandered round the Ridge inspecting that rear guard of graves, or sat talking to some of the thousand-and-odd sick and wounded in hospital, listening to endless tales of courage, pluck, sheer dogged resistance, he realized at what a terrible cost that armed force—varying from three to six thousand men—had simply clung to the rocks and looked at the city. There seemed enough heroism in it to have removed mountains; and coming upon him, not in the monotonous sequence of day-to-day experience, but in a single impression, the futility of it left him appalled. So did the news of the world beyond Delhi, heard, reliably, for the first time. Briefly, England was everywhere on her defence. It seemed to him as if from that mad dream of conquest within the city, he had passed to as strange a dream of defeat. And why? The fire— unchecked at first—had blazed up with fresh fuel in place after place and, left?—Nothing!—not a single attempt to wrest the government of the country from us; not even an organized resistance, when once the order to advance had been given. Had there been some mysterious influence abroad making men blind to the truth?

It was about to pass away if there had been, he felt, when on the 14th, he watched John Nicholson re-enter the Ridge at the head of his column. And many others felt the same, without in any way disparaging those who for long months of defence had borne the burden and heat of the day. They simply saw that Fate had sent a new factor into the problem, that the old order was changing; the Defence was to be Attack.

And why not, with that reinforcement of fine fighting men? Played in by the band of the 8th, amid cheering and counter-cheering, which almost drowned the music, it seemed fit—as the joke ran—if not to face hell itself, at any rate to take *Pandy-monium*. The 52nd Regiment looked like the mastiff to which its leader had likened it. The 2nd Sikhs were admittedly the biggest fellows ever seen. The wild Mooltânee Horse sat their lean Beloochees with the loose security of seat which tells of men born to the saddle.

Jim Douglas noted these things like his fellows; but what sent that thrill of confidence through him, was the look on many a face, as at some pause or turn, it caught a glimpse of the General's figure. It was that heroic figure itself, seen for the first time, riding ahead of all with no unconsciousness of the attention it attracted; but with a self-reliant acceptance of the fact—as far from modesty as it was from vanity—that here rode John Nicholson, ready to do what John Nicholson could do. But in the pale face, made paler by the darkness of the beard, there was more than this. There was an almost languid patience, as if the owner knew that the men around said to him, 'If ever there is a desperate deed to do in India, John Nicholson is the man to do it,' and was biding his time to fulfil their hopes.

The look haunted Jim Douglas all day, stimulating him strangely. Here was a man, he felt, who was in the grip of Fate, but who gave back the grip so firmly that his Fate could not escape him. Gave it back frankly, freely, as one man might grip another's hand in friendship. And then he smiled, thinking that John Nicholson's hand-clasp would go a long way in giving any one a help over a hard stile. If he had had a lead-over like that after the smash came; if even now? . . .Idle thoughts, he told himself; and all because the picturesqueness of a man's outward appearance had taken his fancy, his imagination. For all he knew, or was ever likely to know—He had been sitting idly on the edge of his cot in the tiny tent Major Erlton had lent him, having in truth nothing better to do, and now a voice from the blaze and blare of heat and light outside startled him.

'May I come in—John Nicholson?'

He almost stammered in his surprise; but without waiting for more than a word the General walked in, alone. He was still in full uniform; and surely no man could become it more, thought Jim Douglas involuntarily.

'I have heard your story, Mr Douglas,' he began in a sonorous but very pleasant voice. 'It is a curious one. And I was curious to see you. You must know so much'—he paused, fixed his eyes in a perfectly unembarrassed stare on his host's face, then said suddenly with a sort of old-fashioned courtesy: 'Sit you down again, please; there isn't a chair, I see, but the cot will stand two of us. If it doesn't it will be clearly my fault.' He smiled kindly—'Wounded too—I didn't know that.'

'A scratch, sir,' put in his hearer hastily, fighting shy even of that commiseration. 'I had a little fever in the city; that is all.'

The bright hazel eyes, with a hint of sunlight in them took rather an absent look. 'I should like to have done it myself. I've tried that sort of thing; but they always find me out.'

'I fancy you must be rather difficult to disguise,' began Jim Douglas with a smile, when John Nicholson plunged straight into the heart of things.

'You must know a lot I want to know. Of course I've seen Hodson and his letters; but this is different. First—Will the city fight?'

'As well as it knows how, and it knows better than it did.'

'So I fancied. Hodson said not. By the way, he told me that you declared his Intelligence department was simply perfect. And his accounts—I mean his information—wonderfully accurate.'

'I did, indeed, sir,' replied Jim Douglas, smiling again.

Nicholson gave him a sharp look. 'And he is a wonderfully fine soldier too, sir; one of the finest we have. Wilson is sending him out this afternoon to punish those Rânghars at Rohtuck—I don't know why I should present you with this information, Mr Douglas?'

'Don't you, sir?' was the cool reply; 'I think I do. Major Hodson may have his faults, sir, but the Ridge couldn't do without him. And I'm glad to hear he is going out. It is time we punished those chaps; time we got some grip on the country again.'

The General's face cleared. 'Hm,' he said, 'you don't mince matters; but I don't think we lost much grip in the Punjâb. And as for punishments! Do you know over two thousand have been executed already?'

'I didn't, sir; though I knew Sir John's hand was out. But, if you'll excuse me, we don't want the hangings now—they can come by and by. We want to lick them—show them we are not really in a blind funk.'

'You use strong language too, sir—very strong language.'

'I did not say we *were* in one,' began Jim Douglas eagerly, when a voice asking if General Nicholson were within interrupted him.

'He is,' replied the sonorous voice calmly. 'Come in, Hodson; and I hope you are prepared to fight.' The bright hazel eyes met Jim Douglas's with a distinct twinkle in them; but Major Hodson entering—a perfect blaze of scarlet and fawn and gold, loose, lank, lavish—gave the speech a different turn.

'I hope you'll excuse the intrusion, sir,' he said, saluting, as it were, loudly, 'but being certain I owed this piece of luck to your kind offices I ventured to follow you. And as for the fighting, sir, trust Hodson's Horse to give a good account of itself.'

'I do, Major, I do,' replied Nicholson gravely, despite the twinkle, 'but at present I want you to fight Mr Douglas for me. He suggests we are all in a blind funk.'

With any one else Jim Douglas might have refused this cool demand—for it was little else—that he should defend his statement against a man who in himself was a refutation of it, who was a type of the most reckless dare-devil courage and dash; but the thought of that umpire, ready to give an overwhelming thrust at any time, roused his temper and pugnacity.

'I'm not conscious of being in one myself,' said the Major, turning with a swing and a brief 'How do, Douglas?' He was the most martial of figures in the last-developed uniform of the Flamingoes, or the Ring-tailed Roarers, or the *Aloo Bokhâra*'s, as Hodson's levies were called indiscriminately during their lengthy process of dress-evolution: 'And what is more, I don't understand what you mean, sir!'

'General Nicholson does, I think,' replied the other. 'But I will go further than I did, sir,' he added, facing the General boldly: 'I only said that the natives thought we were in a blind funk. I now assert that they had a right to say so. We never stirred hand or foot for a whole month.'

'Oh! I give you in Meerut,' interrupted Hodson hastily. 'It was pitiable. Our leaders lost their heads.'

'Not only our leaders. We all lost them. From that moment to this it seems to me we have never been calm.'

'Calm!' echoed Hodson disdainfully, 'who wants to be calm? Who would be calm with those massacred women and children to avenge?'

'Exactly so. The horrors of those ghastly murders got on our nerves, and no wonder. We exaggerated the position from the first; we exaggerate the dangers of it now.'

'Of taking Delhi, you mean?' interrupted Nicholson drily.

Jim Douglas smiled. 'No, sir! Even you will find that difficult. I meant the ultimate danger to our rule—'

'There you mistake utterly,' put in Hodson magnificently. 'We mean to win—we admit no danger. There isn't an Englishman, or, thank heaven, an Englishwoman—'

'Is the crisis so desperate that we need levy the ladies?' asked his adversary sarcastically. 'Personally I want to leave them out of the question as much as I can. It is their intrusion into it which has done the mischief. I don't want to minimize these horrors: but if we could forget those massacres—'

'Forget them! I hope to God every Englishman will remember them when the time comes to avenge them! Ay! and make the murderers remember them too.'

'If I had them in my power today,' put in the sonorous voice, 'and knew I was to die tomorrow, I would inflict the most excruciating tortures I could think of on them with an easy conscience.'

'Bravo! sir,' cried Hodson, 'and I'd do executioner gladly.'

John Nicholson's face flinched slightly. 'There is generally a common hangman, I believe,' he said; then turned on Jim Douglas with bent brows: 'And you, sir?'

'I would kill them, sir, as I would kill a mad dog, in the quickest way handy; as I'd kill every man found with arms in his hands. Treason is a worse crime than murder to us now; and by God! if I tortured any one it would be the men who betrayed the garrison at Cawnpore. Yet even there, in our only real collapse, what has happened? It is reoccupied already—the road to it is hung with dead bodies—Havelock's march is one long procession of success. Yet we count ourselves beleaguered. Why? I can't understand it! Where has an order to charge, to advance boldly, met with a reverse? It seems to me that but for these massacres, this fear for women and children, we could hold our own gaily. Look at Lucknow—'

'Yes, Lucknow,' assented Hodson savagely—'Sir Henry, the bravest, gentlest, dead! Women and children pent up—by Heaven! it's sickening to think what may have happened'.

John Nicholson shot a quick glance at Jim Douglas.

'It proves my contention,' said the latter. 'Think of it! Fifteen hundred, English and natives, in a weak position with not even a palisade in some places between them and five times their number of trained soldiers backed by the wildest, wickedest, wantonest town rabble in India! What does it mean? Make every one of the fifteen hundred a paladin, and, by heaven! they *are* heroes.—Still, what does it mean?'

He spoke to the General, but he was silent.

'Mean?' echoed Hodson. 'Palpably, that the foe is contemptible. So he is. Pandy can't fight—'

'He fought well enough for us in the past. I know my regiment'—Jim Douglas caught himself up hard—'I believe they will fight for us again. The truth is that half, even of the army, does not want to fight, and the country does not mean fight at all.'

'Delhi?' came the dry voice again.

'Delhi is exceptional. Besides, it can do nothing else now. Remember we condemned it, unheard, on the 8th of June.'

'I told you that before, sir; didn't I?' Put in Hodson quickly. 'If we had gone in on the 11th, as I suggested'—

'You wouldn't have succeeded,' replied Jim Douglas coolly. Nicholson rose with a smile.

'Well, we are going to succeed now. So good-luck in the meantime, Hodson. Put bit and bridle on the Rânghars. Show them we can't have 'em disturbing the public peace, and kicking up futile rows. Eh—Mr Douglas?'

'No fear, sir!' said Hodson effusively. 'The Ring-tailed Roarers are not in a blind funk. I only wish that I was as sure that the politicals will keep order when we've made it. I had to do it twice over at Bhâgput. And it is hard, sir, when one has fagged horses and men to death, to be told one has exceeded orders—'

'If you served under me, Major Hodson,' said the General, with a sudden freeze of formality, 'that would be impossible. My instructions are always to do everything that can be done.'

Jim Douglas felt he could well believe it, as with a regret that the interview was over, he held the flap of the tent aside for the imperial figure to pass out. But it lingered in the blaze of sunshine after Major Hodson had jingled off.

'You are right in some things, Mr Douglas,' said the sonorous voice suddenly: 'I'd ask no finer soldiers than some of those against us. By-and-bye, unless I'm wrong, men of their stock will be our best war weapons; for, mind you, war is a primitive art and needs a primitive people. And the country isn't against us. If it were, we shouldn't be standing here. It is too busy ploughing, Mr Douglas; this rain is points in our favour. As for the women and children—poor souls'—his voice softened infinitely—'they have been in our way terribly; but—we shall fight all the better for that, by-and-bye. Meanwhile we have got to smash Delhi. The odds are bigger than they were at first. But Baird Smith will sap us in somehow, and then'—he paused, looking kindly at Jim Douglas, and said—'you had better stop and go in with—with the rest of us.'

'I think not, sir—'

'Why? Because of that poor lady? Woman again—eh?'

'In a way; besides, I have really nothing else to do.'

John Nicholson looked at him for a moment from head to foot; then said sharply—

'I don't know, sir. I give my personal staff plenty of work.'

For an instant the offer took his hearer's breath away, and he stood silent.

'I'm afraid not, sir,' he said at last, though from the first he had known what his answer must be. 'I—I can't, that's the fact. I was cashiered from the army fifteen years ago.'

General Nicholson stepped back a step, with sheer anger in his face. 'Then what do you mean, sir, by wearing Her Majesty's uniform?'

Jim Douglas looked down hastily on old Tiddu's staff properties, which he had quite forgotten. They had passed muster in the darkness of the tent, but here, in the sunlight, looked inconceivably worn, and shabby, and unreal. He smiled rather bitterly; then held out his sleeve to show the braiding.

'It's a General's coat, sir,' he said defiantly. 'God knows what old duffer it belonged to; but I might have worn it first instead of second-hand, if I hadn't been a d—d young one.'

The splendid figure drew itself together formally, but the other's pride was up too, and so for a minute the two men faced each other honestly, Nicholson's eyes narrowing under their bent brows.

'What was it? A woman, I expect.'

'Perhaps. I don't see that it matters.'

A faint smile of approval rather took from the sternness of the military salute. 'Not at all. That ends it, of course.'

'Of course.'

Not quite; for ere Jim Douglas could drop the curtain between himself and that brilliant, successful figure, it had turned sharply and laid a hand on his shoulder. A curiously characteristic hand—large, thin, smooth, and white as a woman's, with a grip in it beyond most men's.

'You have a vile habit of telling the truth to superior officers, Mr

Douglas. So have I. Shake hands on it.'

With that hand on his shoulder, that clasp on his, Jim Douglas felt as if he were in the grip of Fate itself, and following John Nicholson's example, gave it back frankly, freely. So, suddenly, the whole face before him melted into perfect friendliness. 'Stick to it, man—stick to it! Save that poor lady—or—or kill somebody! It's what we are all doing. As for the rest'—the smile was almost boyish—'I may get the sack myself before the General's coat. I'm insubordinate enough, they tell me—but I shall have taken Delhi first. So—so good-luck to you!'

As he walked away, he seemed to the eyes watching him bigger, more king-like, more heroic than ever; perhaps because they were dim with tears. But as Jim Douglas went off with a new cheerfulness to see Hodson's Horse jingle out on their lesson of peace, he told himself that the old scoundrel Tiddu had once more been right. *Nikalseyn* had the Great Gift. He could take a man's heart out and look at it, and put it back sounder than it had been for years. He could put his own heart into a whole camp and make it believe it was its own.

Such a clattering of hoofs and clinking of bits and bridles had been heard often before, but never with such gay light-heartedness. Only two days before a lesson had been given to the city. There had been no more harassing of picquets at night. Now the arm of the law was going coolly to reach out forty miles. It was a change indeed. And more than Jim Douglas watched the sun set red on the city wall that evening with a certain content in their hearts. As for him, he seemed still to feel that grip, and hear the voice saying, 'Stick to it, man, stick to it! save that poor lady or kill somebody. It's what we are all doing.'

He sat dreaming over the whole strange dream with a curious sense of comradeship and sympathy through it all, until the glow faded and left the city dark and stern beneath the storm-clouds which had been gathering all day.

Then he rose and went back to his tent cheerfully. He would run no needless risks; he would not lose his head, but as soon as the doctors said it was safe, he would find and save Kate, or—*kill somebody*. That was the whole duty of man.

Kate, however, had already been found, or rather she had never been lost; and when Tara, a few hours after Jim Douglas slipped out of the city, had gone to the roof to fetch away her spinning-wheel, and finding the door padlocked on the inside, had in sheer bewilderment tried the effect of a signal knock, Kate had let her in as if, so poor Tara told herself, it was all to begin over again.

All over again, even though she had spent those few hours of freedom in a perfect passion of purification, so that she might return to her saintship once more.

The gold circlets were gone already, her head was shaven, the coarse white shroud had replaced the crimson scarf. Yet here was the *mem* asking for the *Huzoor*, and setting her blood on fire with vague jealousies.

She squatted down almost helplessly on the floor answering all Kate's eager questions, until suddenly in the midst of it all she started to her feet, and flung up her arms in the old wild cry for righteousness, 'I am *suttee*! Before God! I am *suttee*!'

Then she had said with a gloomy calm, 'I will bring the *mem* more food and drink. But I must think. Tiddu is away; Soma will not help. I am alone; but I am *suttee*.'

Kate, frightened at her wild eyes, felt relieved when she was left alone, and inclined not to open the door to her again. She could manage, she told herself, as she had managed for a few days, and by that time Mr Greyman would have come back. But as the long hours dragged by, giving her endless opportunity of thought, she began to ask herself why he should come back at all. She had not realized at first that he had escaped; that he was safe; that he was, as it were, quit of her. But he was, and he must remain so. A new decision, almost a content, came to her with the suggestion. She was busy in a moment over details. To begin with, no news must be sent. Then, in case he were to return, she must leave the roof. Tara might do so much for her, especially if it was made clear that it was for the master's benefit. But Tara might never return. There had been that in her manner which hinted at such a possibility, and the stores she had brought in had been unduly lavish. In that case, Kate told herself, she would creep out some night, go back to the Princess Farkhoonda, and see if she would not help. If not, there was always the alternative of ending everything by going into the streets boldly and declaring herself a Christian. But she would appeal to these two women first.

And as she sat resolving this, the two women were cursing her in their inmost hearts. For there had been no bangings of drums or thrumming of *sutâra*s on Newâsi's roof these three days. Abool-Bukr had broken away from her kind detaining hand, and gone back to the intrigues of the Palace. So the Mufti's quarter benefited in decent quiet, during which the poor Princess began that process of weeping her eyes out, which left her blind at last. But not blind yet. And so she sate swaying gracefully before the book-rest on which lay the Word of her God, her voice quavering sometimes over the monotonous chant, as she tried to distil comfort to her own heart from the proposition that 'He is Might and Right.'

And far away in another quarter of the town Tara, crouched up before a mere block of stone, half-hidden in flowers, was telling her beads feverishly. '*Râm-Râm-Sita-Râm*!' That was the form she used for a whole tragedy of appeal and aspiration, remorse, despair, and hope. And as she muttered on, looking dully at the little row of platters she had presented to the shrine that morning—going far beyond necessity in her determination to be heard—the groups of women coming in to lay a fresh chaplet among the withered ones and give a '*jow*' to the deep-toned bell hung in the archway in order to attract the god's attention to their offering, paused to whisper among themselves of her piety; while more than once a widow crept close to kiss the edge of her veil, humbly.

It was balm indeed! It was peace. The *mem* might starve, she told herself fiercely, but she would be *suttee*. After all the strain, and the pain, and the wondering ache at her heart, she had come back to her own life. This she understood. Let the *Huzoors* keep to their own. This was hers.

The sun danced in motes through the branches of the peepul tree above the little shrine, the squirrels chirruped among them, the parrots chattered, sending a rain of soft little figs to fall with a faint sound on the hard stones, and still Tara counted her bead feverishly.

'*Râm-Râm-Sita-Râm, Râm-Râm-Sita-Râm.*'

'*Ari!* sisters! she is a saint indeed. She was here at dawn and she prays still,' said the women, coming in the lengthening shadows with odd little bits of feastings; a handful of cocoa-nut chips, a platter of flour, a dish of curds, or a dab of butter.

'*Râm-Râm-Sita-Râm!*'

And all the while poor Tara was thinking of the *Huzoor*'s face, if he ever found out that she had left the *mem* to starve. It was almost dark when she stood up, abandoning the useless struggle; so she waited to see the sacred Circling of the Lights and get her little sip of holy water before she went back to her perch among the pigeons, to put on the crimson scarf and the gold circlets again—since it was hopeless trying to be a saint till she had done what she had promised the *Huzoor* she would do. She must go back to the *mem* first.

But Kate, opening the door to her with eyes a-glitter, and a whole cut-and-dried-plan for the future, almost took her breath away, and reduced her into looking at the Englishwoman with a sort of fear.

'The *mem* will be *suttee* too,' she said stupidly, after listening awhile. 'The *mem* will shave her head and put away her jewels! The *mem* will wear a widow's shroud and sweep the floor, saying she comes from Bengal to serve the saint?'

'I do not care, Tara, how it is done. Perhaps you may have a better plan. But we must prevent the master from finding me again. He has done too much for me as it is; you know he has,' replied Kate, her eyes shining like stars with determination. 'I only want you to save him; that is all. You may take me away and kill me if you like; and if you won't help me to hide, I'll go out into the streets and let them kill me there. I will not have him risk his life for me again.'

'Râm-Râm-Sita-Râm,' said Tara under her breath. That settled it; and at dawn the next day Tara stood in her odd little perch above the shrine among the pigeons, looking down curiously at the *mem* who, wearied out by her long midnight walk through the city and all the excitement of the day, had dozed off on a bare mat in the corner, her head resting on her arm. Three months ago Kate could not have slept without a pillow; now, as she lay on the hard ground, her face looked soft and peaceful in sheer honest dreamless sleep. But Tara had not slept; that was to be told from the anxious strain of her eyes. She had sate out—since she returned home—on her two square yards of balcony in the waning moonlight, looking down on the unseen shrine, hidden by the tall peepul tree whose branches she could almost touch.

Would the *mem* really be *suttee*? she had asked herself again and again. Would she do so much for the master? Would she—would she really shave her head? A grim smile of incredulity came to Tara's face, then a quick, sharp frown of pain. If she did, she must care very much for the *Huzoor*. Besides, she had no right to do it! The *mem*s were never *suttee*. They married again many times. And then this *mem* was married to some one else. No! she would never shave her head for a strange man. She might take off her jewels, she might even sweep the floor. But shave her head? never!

But supposing she did?

The oddest jumble of jealousy and approbation filled Tara's heart. So, as the yellow dawn broke, she bent over Kate.

'Wake, *mem sahib!*' she said, 'wake. It is time to prepare for the day. It is time to get ready.'

Kate started up, rubbing her eyes, wondering where she was; as in truth she well might, for she had never been in such a place before. The long, low slip of a room was absolutely empty save for a reed mat or two; but every inch of it, floor, walls, ceiling, was freshly plastered with mud. That on the floor was still wet, for Tara had been at work on it already. Over each doorway hung a faded chaplet, on each lintel was printed the mark of a bloody hand, and round and about, in broad finger-marks of red and white, ran the eternal *Râm-Râm-Sita-Râm* in Sanskrit letterings. In truth, Tara's knowledge of secular and religious learning was strictly confined to this sentence. There was a faint smell of incense in the room, rising from a tiny brazier sending up a blue spiral flame of smoke before a two-inch-high brass idol with an elephant's head which sate on a niche in the wall. It represented Eternal Wisdom. But Kate did not know this. Nor in a way did Tara. She only knew it was Gunesh-*jee*. And outside was the yellow dawn, the purple pigeons beginning to coo and sidle, the quivering hearts of the peepul leaves.

'I have everything ready for the *mem*,' began Tara hurriedly, 'if she will take off her jewels.'

'You must pull this one open for me, Tara,' said Kate, holding out her arm with the gold bangle on it. 'The master put it on for me, and I have never had it off since.'

Tara knew that as well as she; knew that the master must have put it on, since *she* had not; had, in fact, watched it with jealous eyes over and over again. And there was the *mem* without it, smiling over the scantiness and intricacies of a coarse cotton shroud.

'There is the hair yet,' said Tara with quite a catch in her voice; 'if the *mem* will undo the plaits, I will go round to the old *poojârni's* and get the loan of her razor—she only lives up the next stair.'

'We shall have to snip it off first,' said Kate quite eagerly, for, in truth, she was becoming interested in her own adventures, now that she had, as it were, the control over them. 'It is so long'—she held up a tress as she spoke. It was beautiful hair; soft, wavy even, and the dye—unrenewed for days—had almost gone, leaving the coppery sheen distinct.

'She will never cut it off!' said Tara to herself as she went for the razor. No woman would ever shave her head willingly. Why! when she had had it done for the first time, she had screamed and fought. Her mother-in-law had held her hands, and—

She paused at the door as she re-entered, paralysed by what she saw. Kate had found the knife Tara used for her limited cooking, and, seated on the ground cheerfully, was already surrounded by rippling hair which she had cut off by clubbing it in her hand and sawing away as a groom does at a horse's tail.

Tara's cry made her pause. The next moment the Rajpootni had snatched the knife from her and flung it one way, the razor another, and stood before her with blazing eyes and heaving breast.

'It is foolishness!' she said fiercely. 'The *mem*s cannot be *suttee*. I will not have it.'

Kate stared at her. 'But I must—,' she began.

'There is no must at all,' interrupted Tara superbly; 'I will find some other way.' And then she bent over quickly, and Kate felt her hands upon her hair. 'There is plenty left,' she said with a sigh of relief. 'I will plait it up so that no one will see the difference.'

And she did. She put the gold bangle on again also, and by dawn the next day Kate found herself once more installed as a screened woman; but this time as a Hindu lady under a vow of silence and solitude in the hopes of securing a son for her lord through the intercession of old Anunda the Swâmi.

'I have told Sri Anunda,' said Tara with a new respect in her manner. 'I had to trust some one. And he is as God. He would not hurt a fly.' She paused, then went on with a tone of satisfaction, 'But he says the *mem* could not have been *suttee*, so that foolishness is well over.'

'But what is to be done next, Tara?' asked Kate, looking in astonishment round the wide old garden, arched over by tall forest trees, and set round with high walls, in which she found herself. In the faint dawn she could just see glimmering straight paths parcelling it out into squares: and she could hear the faint tinkle of the water runnels. 'I can't surely stop here.'

'The *mem* will only have to keep still all day in the darkest corner with her face to the wall,' said Tara. 'Sri Anunda will do the rest. And when Soma returns he must take the *mem* away before the thirty regiments come and the trouble begins.'

'Thirty regiments!' echoed Kate, startled.

'He and others have gone out to see if it is true. They say so in the Palace; but it is full of lies,' said Tara indifferently.

It was indeed. More than ever. But they began to need confirmation, and so there was big talk of action, and jinglings of bits and bridles and spurs in the city as well as in the camp. They were to intercept the siege train from Firozpur, they were to get round to the rear of the Ridge and over whelm it. They were to do everything save attack it in face.

And, meanwhile, other people besides Soma and such-like Sadducean sepoys had gone out to find the thirty regiments, and secret scouts from the Palace were hunting about for some one to whom they might deliver a letter addressed *'To the Officers, Subadars, Chiefs, and others of the whole military force coming from the Bombay Presidency.*

*'To the effect that the statement of the defeat of the Royal troops at Delhi is a false and lying fabrication contrived by contemptible infidels the English. The true story is that nearly eighty or ninety thousand organized Military Troops, and nearly ten or fifteen thousand regular and other Cavalry, are now here in Delhi. These troops are constantly engaged, night and day, in attacks on the infidels, and have driven back their batteries from the Ridge. In three or four days, please God, the whole Ridge will be taken, when every one of the base unbelievers will be sent to Hell. You are, therefore, on seeing this order, to use all endeavours to reach the Royal Presence, so, joining the Faithful, give proofs of zeal, and establish your renown. Consider this imperative.'*

But though they hunted high and low, east, north, south, and west, the Royal scouts found no one to receive the order. So it came back to Delhi, damp and pulpy; for the rains had begun again, turning great tracts of country into marsh and bog, and generally wetting the blankets in which the sepoys kept guard sulkily.

# 3

# The Beginning of the End

They drenched Kate Erlton also, despite the arcaded trees above her corner as she sate with her face to the wall in the wide old garden. At first her heart beat at each step on the walk behind her, but she soon realized that she was hidden by her vow, happed about from the possibility of intrusion by her penance. But not many steps came by her; they kept chiefly to the other end of the garden where Sri Anunda was to be found. It was a curious experience. There was a yard or two of thatch, screened by matting and supported by bamboos, leaning not far off against the wall; and into this she crept at night to find the indulgence of a dry blanket. At first she felt inclined to seek its shelter when the rain poured loudly on the leaves above her and fell thence in big blobs, making a noise like the little ripe figs when the squirrels shook them down; but the remembrance that such women as Tara performed like vows cheerfully kept her steady. And after a day or two she often started to find it was already noon or dusk, the day half-gone or done. Time slipped by with incredible swiftness in watching the squirrels and the birds, in counting the raindrops fall from a peepul leaf. And what a strange peace and contentment the life brought! As she sate after dark in the thatch, eating the rice and milk and fruit which Tara brought her stealthily, she felt, at times, a terrified amaze at herself. If she ever came through the long struggle for life, this surely would be the strangest part of the dream. Tara, indeed, used to remark with a satisfied smile that though the *mem* could not of course be *suttee*, still she did very well as a devoted and repentant wife. Sri Anunda could never have had a better penitent. And then, in reply to Kate's curious questions, she would say that Sri Anunda was a *Swâmi*. If the *mem* once saw and spoke to him she would know what that meant. He had lived in the garden for fifteen years. Not as a penance. A *Swâmi* needed no penance as men and women did; for he was not a man. Oh dear no! not a man at all.

So Kate, going on this hint of inhumanity, and guided by her conventional ideas of Hindoo ascetics, imagined a monstrosity, and felt rather glad than otherwise that Sri Anunda kept out of her way.

She was eager also to know how long she might have to stay in his garden. The vow, Tara said, lasted for fifteen days. Till then no one would question her right to sit and look at the wall; and by that time Soma would have returned, and a plan for getting the *mem* away to the Ridge settled. For the master was evidently not going to return to the city; perhaps he had forgotten the *mem*? Kate smiled at this, drearily, thinking that indeed he might; for he might be dead. But even this uncertainty about all things, save that she sate and watched the squirrels and the birds, had ceased to disturb her peace.

As a matter of fact, however, he was thinking of her more than ever, and with a sense of proprietorship that was new to him. Here by God's grace was the one woman for him to save; the somebody to kill, should he fail, needing no selection. There were enough enemies and to spare within the walls still, even though they had been melting away of late. But a new one had come to the Ridge itself, which, though it killed few, sapped steadily at the vigour of the garrison. This was the autumnal fever, bad at Delhi in all years, and worse than usual in this wet season; counterbalancing the benefit of the coolness and sending half a regiment to hospital one day and letting them out of it the next, sensibly less fit for arduous work. It claimed Jim Douglas, already weakened by it, and made his wound slow of healing.

'You haven't good luck certainly,' said Major Erlton, finding him with chattering teeth taking quinine dismally. 'I don't know how it is, but though I'm a lot thinner, this life seems to suit me. I haven't felt so fit for ages.'

He had not been so fit, in truth. It was a healthier, simpler life than he had led for many a long year; and ever since John Nicholson had bidden him go back to his tent and sleep, even the haggardness had left his face; the restlessness having been replaced by an eager certainty of success. He was coming steadily to the front too, so the Ridge said, since Nicholson had taken him up. And he had well deserved this, since there was not a better soldier; cool, stubborn, certain to carry out orders. The very man, in short, whom men like the General wanted; and if he stayed to the finish he would have a distinguished career before him.

But Herbert Erlton himself never thought of this; he hated thought instinctively, and of late had even given up thinking of the city. He never sate and watched the rose-red walls now. Perhaps because he was too busy. So he left that to Jim Douglas, who had nothing else to do, while he went about joyously preparing to accompany Nicholson in his next lesson of law and order.

For in the city it was becoming more and more difficult every day to make the lies pass muster, even in the Palace; and, in despair, the four commanders-in-chief had for once laid their heads together and concocted a plan for intercepting that siege train from Firozpur. So it was necessary that they should be taught the futility of such attempts. Not that even the Palace people really believed them possible. How could they? when almost every day, now, letters came to the Ridge

from some member or another of the Royal Family asking effusively
how he could serve the English cause. Only the old King, revising his
lists of precedence, listening still to brocaded bags, taking cooling
draughts, making couplets, being cozened by the Queen, and breathed
upon by Hussan Askuri, hovered between the policy of being the great
Moghul and a poor prisoner in the hands of fate. But the delights of
the former were too much for him as a rule, and he would sit and
finger the single gold coin which had come as a present from Oude, as
if he were to have the chance of minting millions with a similar
inscription.

'*Bahâdur Shâh Ghâzee has struck upon gold the coin of Victory.*'

Even in its solitary grandeur it had, in truth, a surpassing dignity of
its own in the phrase—'struck upon gold the coin of Victory.' So,
gazing at it, he forgot that it was a mere sample, sent, as the
accompanying brocaded bag said, with a promise to pay more when
more victory brought more gold. But Zeenut Maihl, as she looked at it,
thought with a vague fury of certain gold within reach, hidden in her
house, and of what was to become of these coins with John Company's
mark on them? For she still lingered in the palace. Other women had
fled, but she was wiser than they. She knew that, come what might, her
life was safe with the English as victors; so there was nothing but the
gold to think of. The gold, and Jewun-Bukht, her son. The royal signet
was in her possession altogether now, and sometimes the orders,
especially when they were for payment of money, had to go without it,
because '*the Queen of the World was asleep*'. But she did not dream. That
was over; though in a way she clung fiercely to hope. So Ghaus Khân
with the Neemuch Brigade, and Bukht Khân with the Bareilly Brigade,
and Khair Sultân with the scrapings and leavings of the regiments—
who, owning no leader of their own, did what was right in their own
eyes—set out to intercept the big guns; and Nicholson set out on the
dawn of the 25th to intercept them.

The rain poured down in torrents, the guns sank to their axles in
mud, the infantry slipped and slithered, the cavalry were blinded by the
mire from the floundering horses. So from daybreak till sunset the little
force, two thousand in all—more than one half of whom were natives—
laboured eighteen miles through swamps. At noon, it is true, they called
a halt nine miles out at a village where the women clustered on the
housetops in wild alarm, remembering a day—months back—when
they had clustered round an unleavened cake, and the head-man's wife
had bidden them listen to the master's gun over the far horizon.

They were to listen to it again that day. For the enemy was ten miles
further over the marshes; and it was but noon. The force, no doubt,
had been afoot since four; but General Nicholson was emphatically not

an eight-hour man. So the shovings and slitherings of guns and mortals began again cheerfully.

Still it was nigh on sundown when, across a deep stream flowing from the big marshes to the west, these contract-workers came on the job they were eager to finish ere nightfall; six thousand rebels of all arms holding three villages, a bastioned old *serai*, and a town. It was a strong position in the right angle formed by the stream and the flooded canal into which it flowed. Water—impassable save by an unknown ford in the stream, by a bridge held in force over the canal—on two sides of it. On the others dismal swamps. A desperately strong position to attack at sundown after eighteen miles slithering and shoving in the pouring rain; especially with unknown odds against you. Not less, anyhow, than three to one. But John Nicholson had a single eye; that is, an eye which sees one salient point. Here, it was that bridge to the left, leading back to safe shelter within the walls of Delhi. A cowardly foe must have no chance of using that bridge during silent night watches. So, without a pause, fifteen hundred of the two thousand waded breast-high across the stream to attack the six thousand, Nicholson himself riding ahead for a hasty reconnaissance; since the growing dusk left scant leisure for anything save action. Yet once more a glance was sufficient; and, ere the men, exposed to a heavy fire of grape in crossing the ford, were ready to advance, the orders were given.

There was a hint of cover in some rising ground before the old *serai*—the strongest point of the defence. He would utilize this, rush the position, change front, and sweep down on the bridge. That must not remain as a chance for cowards an instant longer than he could help; for Nicholson in everything he did seems never to have contemplated defeat.

So, flanked by the guns, supported by squadrons of the 9th Lancers and the Guides cavalry, the three regiments[1] marched steadily towards the rising ground, following that colossal figure riding, as ever, ahead. Till suddenly, as his charger's feet touched the highest ground, Nicholson wheeled and held up his hand to those below him.

'Lie down, men!' came his clear strong voice as he rode slowly along the line; 'lie down and listen to what I've got to say. It's only a few words.'

So, sheltered from the fire, they lay and listened. 'You of the 61st know what Sir Colin Campbell said to you at Chillianwallah. He said the same thing to others at the Alma. I say it to you all now. "*Hold your fire till within twenty or thirty yards of that battery, and then, my boys! we will make short work of it!*"'

[1] 61st, 1st Fusiliers, 2nd Punjabees.

Men cannot cheer lying on their stomachs, but the unmelodious grunt—'We will, sir, by God, we will!'—was as good as one.

Nicholson faced round on the *serai* again, and gave the order to the artillery. So, in sharp thuds widening into a roar, the flanking guns began work. Half a dozen round or so, and then the rider—motionless as a statue in the centre—looked back quickly, waved his sword, and went on. The men were up, after him, over the hillock, into the morass beyond, silently.

'Steady, men! steady with it. On with you! Steady!'

They listened to the clear sonorous voice once more, though there was no shelter now from the grape and canister, and musket balls; or rather only the shelter of that one tall figure ahead riding at a foot's-pace.

'Steady! Hold your fire! I'll give the word, never fear! Come on! Come on!'

So through a perfect bog they stumbled on doggedly. Here and there a man fell; but men will fall sometimes.

'Now then! Let them have it!'

They were within the limit. Twenty yards off lay the guns. There was one furious volley; above it one word answered by a cheer.

So at the point of the bayonet the *serai* was carried. Then without a pause the troops changed front with a swiftness unforeseen and swept on to the left.

'To Delhi, brothers! To Delhi!' The old cry, begun at Meerut, rose now with a new meaning as the panic-stricken guns limbered up and made for the bridge. Too late! Captain Blunt's were after them, chasing them. The wheel of the foremost, driven wildly, jammed; those following could not pull up. So, helter-skelter, they were in a jumble, out of which Englishmen helped the whole thirteen! The day, or rather the night, was won; for Nature's dark flag of truce hung even between the assailants and the few desperate defenders of the third village, who, with escape cut off, were selling their lives at a cost to the attackers of seventeen out of that total death-roll of twenty-five. But Nicholson knew his position sure, so he left night to finish the rout, and, with his men, bivouacked without food or cover among the marshes; for it was too dark to get the baggage over the ford. Yet the troops were ready to start at daybreak for an eighteen miles tramp back to the Ridge again. There was no talk of exhaustion now, as at Budli-ke-serai; so just thirty-six hours after they started, that is, just one hour for every mile of morass and none for the fight, they startled the Ridge by marching in again and clamouring for food. But Nicholson was in a towering temper. He had found that another brigade had been lurking behind the canal, and that if he had had decent information he might have smashed it, also, on his way home.

'He hadn't even a guide that he didn't pick up himself,' commented Major Erlton angrily. 'By George! how those niggers cave in to him! And his political information was all rot. If the General had obeyed instructions he would have been kicking his heels at Bahâdagurh still.'

'We heard you at it about two o'clock,' said a new listener. 'I suppose it was a night attack—risky business rather.'

Herbert Erlton burst into a laugh; but the elation on his face had a pathetic tenderness in it. 'That was the bridge, I expect. *He* blew it up before starting. *He* sat on it till then. Besides there were the wagons and tumbrils and things. *He* told Tombs to blow them up, too, for of course *he* had to bring the guns back, and *he* couldn't shove the lot.'

As he passed on, some of his listeners smiled.

'It's a case of possession,' said one to his neighbour.

'Pardon me,' said another, who had known the Major for years. 'It is a case of casting out. I wonder—' the speaker paused and shrugged his shoulders.

'Did you hear his name had gone up for the V.C.?' began his companion.

'Gone up! My dear fellow! It might have gone up fifty times over. But it isn't his pluck that I wonder at; it is his steadiness. He never shirks the little things. It is almost as if he had found a conscience.'

Perhaps he had. He was cheerful enough to have had the testimony of a good one, as, in passing, he looked in on Jim Douglas and met his congratulations.

'Bad shilling!' replied the Major, beautifully unconscious. 'So you've heard—and—hillo! what's up?' For Jim Douglas was busy getting into disguise.

'That old scoundrel Tiddu came in to camp with the news an hour ago,' said the latter, whose face was by no means cheerful. 'He was out carrying grain—saw the fugitives, and came in here, hoping for *backsheesh*, I believe. But—' Jim Douglas looked round rapidly at the Major—'I'm awfully afraid, Erlton, that he has not been in Delhi, to speak of, since I left. And I was relying on him for news—'

'There isn't any—is there?' broke in Major Erlton with a queer hush in his voice.

'None. But there may be. So I'm off at once. I couldn't have a better chance. The villain says the sepoys are slipping in on the sly in hundreds; for the palace folk—or at least the King—thinks the troops are still engaged, and is sending out reinforcements. So I shall have no trouble in getting through the gates.'

Major Erlton radiant, splashed from head to foot, covered at once with mud and glory, looked at the man opposite him with a curious deliberation.

'I don't see why you should go at all,' he said slowly. 'I wouldn't, if I—I mean I would rather you didn't.'

'Why?' The question came sharply.

'Do you want the truth?' asked Herbert Erlton with a sudden frown.

'Certainly.'

'Then I'll tell it, Mr Greyman—I mean Douglas—I—I'm grateful, but—damn me, sir, if—if want to be more so! I—I gave you my chance once—like a fool; for I might have saved her—'

The hard handsome face was all broken up with passionate regret, and the pity of it kept Jim Douglas silent for a moment; for he understood it.

'You might,' he said at last. 'But I don't interfere with you here. You can't save her—your wife, I mean—and if I fail you can always—'

'There is no need to tell me what to do then,' interrupted Major Erlton grimly. 'I'll do it without your help.'

He turned on his heel, then paused. 'It isn't that I'm ungrateful,' he repeated, almost with an appeal in his voice. 'And I don't mean to be offensive; only you and I can't—'

His own mental position seemed beyond him, and he stood for a moment irresolute. Then he held out his hand.

'Well! good bye. I suppose you mean to stick to it?'

'I mean to stick to it. Good bye.'

'And I must be off to my bed. Haven't slept a wink for two nights, and I shall be on duty to-morrow. Well! I believe I've as good a chance of seeing Kate here as you have of finding her there; but I can't prevent your going, of course.'

So he went off to his bed, and Jim Douglas, following Tiddu, who was waiting for him in the Koodsia Gardens, carried out his intention of sticking to it; while John Nicholson in his tent, forgetful of his advice to both of them, was jotting down notes for his despatch. One of them was. *'The enemy was driven from the serai with scarcely any loss to us, and made little resistance as we advanced.'* The other was *'Query? How many men in buckram? Most say seven or eight thousand. I think between three and four.'*

He had, indeed, a vile habit of telling the truth, even in despatches. So ended the day of Nujjufghur.

The next morning, the 27th, broke fine and clear. Kate Erlton waking with the birds found the sky full of light already, clear as a pale topaz beyond the over arching trees.

She stood after leaving her thatch, looking into the garden, lost in a sort of still content. It seemed impossible she should be in the heart of a big city. There was no sound but the faint rustling of the wet leaves drying themselves in the soft breeze, and the twitterings of squirrels and birds. There was nothing to be seen but the trees, and the broad paths rising above the flooding water from the canal-cut which ran at the further side.

And Sri Anunda had lived here for fifteen years; while she? How long had she been there? She smiled to herself, for, in truth, she had lost count of days altogether, almost of Time itself. She was losing hold of life. She told herself this, with that vague amaze at finding it so. Yes! She was losing her grip on this world without gaining, without even desiring, a hold on the next. She was learning a strange new fellowship with the dream of which she was a part, because it would soon be past; because the trees, the flowers, the birds, the beasts, were mortal as herself. A squirrel, its tail a-fluff, was coming down the trunk of the next tree in fitful half-defiant jerks, its bright eyes watching her. The corner of her veil was full of the leavings of her simple morning meal which she always took with her to scatter under the trees; and now, in sudden impulse, she sank down to her knees and held a morsel of plantain out temptingly.

Dear little mortal, she thought, with a new tenderness, watching it as it paused uncertain; until the consciousness that she was being watched in her turn made her look up; then pause, as she was, astonished, yet not alarmed, at the figure before her. It was neither tall nor short, dark nor fair, and it was wrapped from knee to shoulder in a dazzling white cloth draped like a Greek chiton, which showed the thin yet not emaciated curves of the limbs, and left the poise of the long throat bare. The head was clean-shaven, smooth as the cheek, and the face, destitute even of eyebrows, was softly seamed with lines and wrinkles which seemed to leave it younger, and brighter, as if in an eternity of smile-provoking content. But the eyes! Kate felt a strange shock, as they brought back to her the innocent dignity Raphael gave to his San-Sistine Bambino; for this was Sri Anunda—it could be no one else. In his hand he held a bunch of henna-blossom, the camphire of Scripture, the cypress of the Greeks; yellowish green, insignificant, incomparably sweet. He held it out to her, smiling, then laid it on her outstretched hand.

'The lesson is learnt, sister,' he said softly. 'Go in peace, and have no fear.'

The voice, musical exceedingly, thrilled her through and through. She knelt looking after him regretfully as, without a pause, he passed on his way. So that was a *Swâmi!* She went back to her corner—for already early visitors were drifting in for Sri Anunda's blessing—and with the bunch of henna-blossom on the ground before her sat thinking.

What an extraordinary face it was. So young, so old. So wise, so strangely innocent. Tara was right. It was not a man's face. Yet it could not be called angelic, for it was the face of a mortal. Yes! that was it, a mortal face immortal through its mortality—through the circling wheel of life and death. The strong perfume of the flowers reaching her, set her a-thinking of them. Did he always give a bunch when the penance was over and say the lesson was learnt? It was a significant choice, these flowers of life and death. For bridal hands had been stained with henna, and corpses embalmed with it for ages, and ages, and ages. Or was that 'peace go with you,' that 'have no fear' meant as an encouragement in something new? Had they been making plans? had anything happened? She scarcely seemed to care. So, as the cloudless day passed on, she sat looking at the henna-blossom and thinking of Sri Anunda's face.

But something *had* happened. Jim Douglas had come back to the city and Tara knew it. She had barely escaped his seeing her, and she felt she could not escape it long. And then, it seemed to her, the old life would begin again; for she would never be able to keep the truth from him. The *mem* might talk of deceit glibly; but if it came to telling lies to the master she would fail.

There was only one chance. If she could get the *mem* safely out of the city at once; then she could tell the truth without fear. The necessity for immediate action came upon her by surprise. She had ceased to expect the master's return, she had not cared personally for Kate's safety, and so had been content to let the future take care of itself. But now everything was changed. If Kate were not got rid of, sent out of the city, one of two things must happen. The master must be left to get her out as best he could, at the risk of his life; or she, Tara, must return to the old allegiance; return and sit by, while the *mem* in a language she did not understand, told the *Huzoor* how she had been willing to be *suttee* for him!

So while Kate sat looking at the henna-blossom, Tara sat telling herself that at all costs, all risks, she must be got out of the city that night. She, and her jewels. They were at present tied up in a bundle in Tara's room, but the *Huzoor* might think her a thief if the *mem* went without them. And another thing she decided. She would not tell the *mem* the reason of this sudden action. True, Kate had professed herself determined that the master should not risk his life for her again: but women were not—not always—to be trusted. For the rest, Soma must help.

She waited till dusk, however, before appealing to him, knowing that her only chance lay in taking him by storm, in leaving him no time for reflection. So, just as the lights were beginning to twinkle in the bazaars, she made her way, full of purpose, to the half-ruined sort of cell in the thickness of the wall not far from the sally-port, in which of late—since he had taken morosely to drugs,—he was generally to be found at this time, walking drowsily to his evening meal before going out.

She found him thus, sure enough, and began at once on her task. He must help. He could easily pass out the *mem*. That was all she asked of him. But his handsome face settled into sheer obstinacy at once. He was not going to help any one, he said, or harm any one, till they struck the first blow, and then they had better defend themselves. That was the end. And so it seemed; for after ten minutes of entreaty, he stood up with something of a lurch ere he found his feet, and bid her go. She only wasted her time and his, since he must eat his food ere he went to relieve the sentry at the sally-port.

She caught him up reproachfully, almost indignantly.

'Then thou art there, on guard! and it needs but the opening of a door, a thrusting of a woman out—to—*die*, perchance, Soma. Remember that!'

She spoke with a feverish eagerness, as if the suggestion had its weight with her, but he treated it contemptuously.

'*Loh!*' he said in scorn. 'What a woman's word! Thank the Gods I was not born one.'

The taunt bit deep, and Tara drew herself up angrily. So the brother and sister stood face to face, strangely alike.

'Was't not?' she retorted bitterly. 'The Gods know. Is there not woman in man, and man in woman, among those born at a birth? Soma! for the sake of that—do this for me—' It was her last appeal; she had kept it for the last, and now her sombre eyes were ablaze with passionate entreaty. 'See, brother! I claim it of you as a right. Thou didst take my sainthood from me once. Count this as giving it back again.'

'Back again?' echoed Soma thickly. 'What fool's talk is this?'

'Let it be fool's talk, brother,' she interrupted, with a strange intensity in her voice. 'I care not—thou dost not know; I cannot tell thee. But—but *this* will be counted to thee in restitution. Soma! think of it as my sainthood! Sure thou dost owe me it! Soma! for the sake of the hand which lay in thine.'

In her excitement she moved a step forward, and he shrank back instinctively. True, she was a saint in another way if those scars were true; but—at the moment, being angry with her, he chose to doubt, to remember—'Stand back!' he cried roughly, unsteadily. 'What do I owe thee? What claim hast thou?'

The question, the gesture outraged her utterly. The memory of a whole life of vain struggling after self-respect surged to her brain, bringing that almost insane light to her eyes. 'What?' she echoed fiercely—'this!' Ere he could prevent it, her hand was in his, gripping it like a vice.

'So in the beginning—so in the end!' she gasped, as he struggled with her madly. 'Tara and Soma hand in hand. Nay! I am strong as thou.'

She spoke truth, for his nerve and muscle were slack with opium; yet he fought wildly, striking at her with his left hand, until in a supreme effort she lost her footing, they both staggered, and he—as she loosed her hold—fell backwards, striking his head against a projecting brick in the ruined wall.

'Soma!' she whispered to his prostrate figure, 'art hurt, brother? Speak to me!'

But he lay still, and, with a cry, she flung herself on her knees beside him, feeling his heart, listening to his breathing, searching for the injury. It was a big cut on the crown of the head; but it did not seem a bad one, and she began to take his unconsciousness more calmly. She had seen folk like that before from a sudden fall, and they came to themselves, none the worse, after a while; but it would be scarcely in time for him to relieve guard. . . .

She stood up suddenly and looked round her. Soma's uniform hung on a peg, his musket stood in a corner.

Half-an-hour after this, Kate, waiting in the thatch for Tara to come as usual, gave a cry, more of surprise than alarm, as a tall figure, in uniform, stepped into the flickering light of the cresset.

'Soma!' she cried, 'what is it?'

A gratified smile came to the curled mustachios. 'Soma or Tara, it matters not,' replied a familiar voice. 'They were one in the beginning. Quick, *mem-sahib*. On with the jewels. I have a dark veil too for the gate.'

Kate stood up, her heart throbbing. 'Am I to go, then? Is that what Sri Anunda meant?'

'Sri Anunda! hath he been here?' Tara paused, sniffed, and once more those dark eyes met the light ones with a fierce jealousy. 'He hath given thee henna-blossom. I smell it; and he gives it to none but those who—So the Swâmi's lesson is learnt—and the disciple can go in peace!—' She broke off with a petulant laugh. 'Well! so be it. It ends my part. The *mem* will sleep among her own to night; Sri Anunda hath said it. Come—'

'But how? I must know how,' protested Kate.

The laugh rose again. 'Wherefore? The *mem* is Sri Anunda's disciple. For the rest, I will let the *mem* out through the little river-gate. There is a boat, and she can go in peace.'

There was something so wild, so almost menacing in Tara's face, that Kate felt her only hope was to obey. And, in good sooth, the scent of the henna-blossom she carried with her, tucked into her bosom, gave her, somehow, an irrational hope that all would go well as she followed her guide swiftly through the alleys and bazaars.

'The *mem* must wait here,' whispered Tara at last, pausing behind one of the ungainly mausoleums in what had been the old Christian cemetery. 'When she hears me singing Sonny-*baba*'s song, she must follow to the Water-gate. It is behind the ruins, there.'

Kate crouched down, setting her back, native fashion, against the tomb. And as she waited she wondered idly what mortal lay there; so, being strangely calm, she let her fingers stray to the recess she felt behind her. There should be a marble tablet there; and even in the dark she might trace the lettering. But the recess was empty, the marble having evidently been picked out. So it was a nameless grave. And the next? She moved over to it stealthily, then to the next. But the tablets had been taken out of all and carried off—for curry-stones most likely. So the graves were nameless; those beneath them mortals—nothing more. As she waited under the stars, her mind reverted to Sri Anunda and the Wheel of Life and Death. The immortality of mortality! Was that the lesson which was to let her go in peace?

She started from the thought as that native version of the 'Happy Land' came, nasally, from behind the ruins. As she passed them, a group of men were squatted gossiping round a hookah, and more than one figure passed her. But a woman with her veil drawn, and a clank of anklets on her feet, did not even invite a curious eye; for it was still early enough for such folk to be going home.

Then, as she passed down a flight of steps, a hand stole out from a niche and drew her back into a dark shadow. The next minute, with a low whisper, 'There is no fear! Sri Anunda hath said it. Go in peace!' she felt herself thrust through a door into darkness. But a feeble glimmer showed below her, and creeping down another flight of steps, she found herself outside Delhi, looking over the strip of low-lying land where in the winter the buffaloes had grazed beneath Alice Gissing's house, but which was now flooded into a still backwater by the rising of the river. And out of it the stunted *kikar* and tamarisks grew strangely, their feathery branches arching over it. But to the left, beyond the Water bastion, rose a mass of darker foliage—the Koodsia Gardens. Once there she would be beyond floods, and Tara had said there was a boat. Kate found it, moored a little further towards the river—a flat-bottomed punt, with a pole. It proved easier to manage than she had expected; for the water was shallow, and the trunks and branches of the trees helped her to get along, so that after a time she decided on keeping to that method of progress as long as she could. It enabled her to skirt the river bank, where there were fewer lights telling of watch-fires. Besides, she knew the path by the river leading to Metcalfe House. It might be under water now; but if she crept into the park at the ravine—if she could take the boat so far—she might manage to reach Metcalfe House. There was an English picquet there, she knew. So, as she mapped out her best way, a sudden recollection came to her of the last time she had been that river path, when her husband and Alice Gissing were walking down it, and Captain Morecombe—

Ah! was it credible? Was it not all a dream? Could this be real—could it be the same world?

She asked herself the question with a dull indifference as she struggled on doggedly.

But not more than two hours afterwards the conviction that the world had not changed came upon her with a strange pang as she stood once more on the terrace of Metcalfe House with English faces around her.

'By Heaven, it's Mrs Erlton!' she heard a familiar voice say. It seemed to her hundreds of miles away in some far, far country to which she had been journeying for years. 'Here! let me get hold of her—and fetch some water—wine—anything. How—how was it, sergeant?'

'In a boat, sir, coming hand over hand down at the stables. She sang out quite calmly she was an Englishwoman, and—'

'Then—then they touched their caps to me,' said Kate, making an effort, 'and so I knew that I was safe. It was so strange; it—it rather upset me. But I am all right now, Captain Morecombe.'

'We had better send up for Erlton,' said another officer aside; but Kate caught the whisper—

'Please not. I can walk up to cantonments quite well. And—I would rather have no fuss—I—I couldn't stand it.'

She had stood enough and to spare, agreed the little knot of men with a thrill at their hearts as they watched her set off in the moonlight with Captain Morecombe and an orderly. They were to go straight to the Major's tent; and if he was still at mess—which was more than likely, since it was only half-past nine—Captain Morecombe was to leave her there and go on with the news. There would be no fuss, of that she might be sure, said the latter, forbearing even to speak to her on the way, save to ask her if she felt all right.

'I feel as if I had just been born,' she said slowly. In truth, she was wondering if that spinning of the Great Wheel towards Life again brought with it this forlornness, this familiarity.

# 4

## At Last

No fuss indeed! Kate, as she sat in her husband's little tent waiting for him to come to her, felt that so far she might have arrived from a very ordinary journey. The bearer, it is true, who had been the Major's valet for years, had salaamed more profoundly than usual, had even put up a pious prayer, and expressed himself pleased; but he had immediately gone off to fetch hot water, and returning with it and clean towels, had suggested mildly that the *mem* might like to wash her face and hands. Kate, with a faint smile, felt there was no reason why she should not. She need not look worse than necessary. But she paused almost with a gasp at the familiar half-forgotten luxuries. Scented soap! a sponge—and there on the camp table was a looking-glass! She glanced down with a start at the little round one in the ring she wore; than went over to the other with its toilet cover, brushes, and combs, her husband's razors, gold studs in a box; and there was her own photograph in a frame, a Bible, and a prayer book—the latter things bringing her no surprise, no emotion of any kind. For they had always been fixtures on Major Erlton's dressing-table, mute evidences to no sentiment on his part, but simply to the bearer's knowledge of the proprieties and the ways of real *sahibs*. But other things she saw made her heart grow soft. The little camp bed, the simplicity, and hardness of everything in comparison with what her husband had been wont to demand of life; for he had always been a real prince, feeling the rose-leaf beneath the feather bed, and never stinting himself in comfort. Then the swords, and belts, and Heaven knows what panoply of war—not spick-and-span decorations as they used to be in the old days, but worn and used—gave her a pang. Well! he had always been a good soldier, they said.

And then, interrupting her thoughts, the old *khansâman* had come in, having taken time to array himself gorgeously in livery. The Father of the fatherless and orphan, he said, whimperingly, alluding to the fact that he had lost both parents—which, considering he was past sixty, was only to be expected—had heard his prayer. The *mem* was spared to Freddy-*baba*. And would she please to order dinner. As the Major-*sahib* dined at mess, her slave was unprepared with a roast. Fish also would partake of tyranny; but he could open a tin of Europe-soup, and with a chicken cutlet—Kate cut him short with a request for tea; by-and-by, when—when the Major-*sahib* should have come. And when she was alone again, she shivered and rested her head on her crossed arms

upon the table beside which she sat, with a sort of sob. This—Yes!—
This of all she had come through was the hardest to bear. This surge of
pity, of tenderness, of unavailing regret for the past, the present, the
future. What?—What could she say to him, or he to her, that would
make remembrance easier, anticipation happier?

Hark! there was his step!—His voice saying good night to Captain
Morecombe.

'I hope she will be none the worse,' came the reply. 'Good night,
Erlton—I'm—I'm awfully glad, old fellow.'

'Thanks!'

She stood up with a sickening throb at her heart. Oh! she was glad
too! So glad to see him, and tell him—

How tall he was, she thought with a swift recognition of his good
looks, as he came in, stooping to pass under the low entrance. Very tall,
and thin. Much thinner, and—and—different somehow—

'Kate!' He paused half a second, looking at her curiously—'Kate!
I'm—I'm—awfully glad.' He was beside her now, his big hands
holding hers; but she felt that she was further away from him than she
had been in that brief pause when she had half expected, half wished
him to take her in his arms and kiss her as if nothing had happened, as
if life were to begin again. It would have been so much easier; they
might have forgotten then, both of them. But now, what came, must
come without that chrism of impulse; must come in remembrance and
regret. *Awfully glad!* That was what Captain Morecombe had said. Was
there no more between them than that? No more between her and this
man, who was the father of her child. The sting of the thought made
her draw him closer, and with a sob rest her head on his shoulder.
Then he stooped and kissed her. 'I—I didn't know. I wasn't sure if
you'd like it,' he said, 'but I'm awfully glad, old girl, upon my life I
am. You must have had a terrible time.'

She looked up with a hopeless pain in her eyes. He was gone from
her again; gone utterly. 'It was not so bad as you might think,' she
answered, trying to smile. 'Mr Greyman did so much—'

'Greyman! You mean Douglas, I suppose?'

She stared for a second. 'Douglas? I don't know. I mean—' Then she
paused. How could she say, 'The man you rode against at Lucknow,'
when she wanted to forget all that; forget everything! And then a
sudden fear made her add hastily, 'He is here, surely—he came long
ago.'

Major Erlton nodded. 'I know; but his real name is Douglas; at least
he says so. Do you mean to say you haven't seen him? That he didn't
help you to get out?'

'You mean that—that he has gone back?' asked Kate faintly. Her

husband gave a low whistle. 'What a queer start; a sort of Box and
Cox. He went back to find you yesterday.'

Kate's hand went up to her forehead almost wildly. Then Tara must
have known. But why had she not mentioned it? Still, in a way, it was
best as it was; since once he heard she, Kate, had gone, he would
return. For Tara would tell him, of course.

These thoughts claimed her for the moment, and when she looked
up, she found her husband watching her curiously.

'He must have done an awful lot for you, of course,' he said shortly;
but I'd rather it had been any one else, and that's a fact. However, it
can't be helped. Hullo! here's the *khansâman* with some tea—thoughtful
of the old scoundrel, isn't it?'

'I—I ordered it,' put in Kate, feeling glad of the diversion. Major
Erlton laughed kindly. 'What, begun already! The old sinner's had a
precious easy time of it; but now—' he pulled himself up awkwardly,
and, as if to cover his hesitation, walked over to a box, and after
rummaging in it, brought out a packet of letters. 'Freddy's,' he said
cheerfully. 'He's all right. Jolly as a sandboy. I kept them—in—in
case—'

A great gratitude made the past dim for a moment. He seemed
nearer to her again. 'I can't look at them to night, Herbert,' she said
softly, laying her hand beside his upon them. 'I'm—I'm too tired.'

'No wonder. You must have your tea and go to bed,' he replied.
Then he looked round the tent. 'It isn't a bad little place, you'll find—
I'm on duty to night—so—so they'll manage, I daresay.'

'On duty,' she echoed, pouring herself out a cup of tea rather hastily.
'Where?'

'Oh! at the front. There is never anything worth going for now. We
are both waiting for the assault; that's the fact. But I shan't be back till
dawn, so—'

He was standing looking at her, tall, handsome, full of vitality; and
suddenly he lifted a fold of her tinsel-set veil and smiled.

'Jolly dress that for a fancy ball, and what a jolly scent it's got. It is
that flower, isn't it? You look awfully well in it, Kate! In fact, you look
wonderfully fit all round.'

'So do you!' she said hurriedly, her hand going up to the henna
blossom. There was a sudden quiver in her voice, a sudden fierce pain
in her heart. 'You—you look—'

'Oh! I,' he replied carelessly still with admiring eyes, 'I'm as fit as a
fiddle. I say! where did you get all those jewels? What a lot you have!
They're awfully becoming.'

'They are Mr Greyman's,' she said; 'they belonged to his—to—'
then she paused. But the contemptuously-comprehending smile on her

husband's face made her add quietly, 'to a woman—a woman *he loved very dearly*, Herbert.'

There was a moment or two of silence, and then Major Erlton went to the entrance, raised the curtain, and looked out. A flood of moonlight streamed into the tent.

'It's about time I was off,' he said after a bit, and there was a queer constraint in his voice. Then he came over and stood by Kate again.

'It isn't any use talking over—over things to night, Kate,' he said quietly. 'There's a lot to think of and I haven't thought of it at all. I never knew you see—if this would happen. But I dare say you have; you were always good at thinking. So—so you had better do it for both of us. I don't care, *now*. It will be what you wish, of course.'

'We will talk it over tomorrow,' she said in a low voice. She would not look in his face. She knew she would find it soft with the memory held in that one word,—*now*. Ah! how much easier it would have been if she had never come back! And yet she shrank from the same thought on his lips.

'There was always the chance of my getting potted,' he said almost apologetically. 'But I'm not. So—well! let's leave it for to-morrow.'

'Yes,' she replied steadily, 'for tomorrow.' He gathered some of his things together, and then held out his hand. 'Good night, Kate. I wouldn't lie awake thinking, if I were you. What's the good of it? We will just have to make the best of it for the boy. But I'd like you to know two things—'

'Yes—'

'That I couldn't forget, of course; and that—' he paused. 'Well! that doesn't matter. It's only about myself—and it doesn't mean much after all. So good night.'

As she moved to the door also—forced into following him by the ache in her heart, for him more than for herself—the jingle of her anklets made him turn with an easy laugh.

'It does't sound respectable,' he said; then, with a sudden compunction, he added, 'But the dress is much prettier than those dancing girls, and—by Heaven, Kate! you've always been miles too good for me; and that's the fact. Well!—let us leave it for tomorrow.'

Yes! For to-morrow she told herself, with a determination not to think as, dressed as she was, she nestled down into the strange softness of the camp bed, too weary of the pain and pity of this coming back even for tears. Yet she thought of one thing; not that she was safe, not that she would see the boy again—only of the thing he had been going to tell her about himself. What was it? She wanted to know; she wanted to know all—everything. 'Herbert! she whispered to the pillow, 'I wish you had told me—I want to know—I want to make it easier—

for—for us all.'

And so, not even grateful for her escape, she fell asleep dreamlessly.

It was dawn when she woke with the sound of some one talking outside. He had come back. No! that was not his voice. She sat up, listening.

'The servants say she is asleep. Some one had better go in and wake her. The doctor—'

'He's behind with the *dhooli*. Ah! there's Morecombe; he knows her.'

But there was no need to call her. Kate was already at the door, her eyes wide with the certainty of evil. There was no need even to tell her what had happened; for in the first rays of the rising sun, seen almost star-like behind a dip in the rocky ridge, she saw a little procession making for the tent.

'He—he is dead,' she said quietly. There was hardly a question in her tone. She knew it must be so. Had he not begged her to leave it till tomorrow? and this was tomorrow. Were not her eyes full of its rising sun, and what its beams held in their bright clasp?

'It seems impossible,' said some one in a low voice, breaking in on the pitiful silence. 'He always seemed to have a charmed life, and then, in an instant—when nothing was going on—this chance bullet.'

It did not seem impossible to her.

'Please don't make a fuss about me, doctor,' she pleaded in a tone which went to his heart when he proposed the conventional solaces. 'Remember I have been through so—so much already. I can bear it. I can, indeed, if I'm left alone with him—while it is possible. Yes! I know there is another lady, but I only want to be alone, with him.'

So they left her there beside the little camp bed with its new burden. There was no sign of strife upon him. Only that blue mark behind his ear among his hair. And his face showed no pain. Kate covered it with a little fine handkerchief she found folded away in a scented case she had made for him before they were married. It had Alice Gissing's monogram on it. It was better so, she told herself; he would have liked it. She had no flowers except the faded henna-blossom, but it smelt sweet as she tucked it under the hand which she had left half-clasped upon his sword. She might at least tell him so, she thought half-bitterly, that the lesson was learnt, that he might go in peace.

Then she sat down at the table and looked over their boy's letters mechanically; for there was nothing to think of now. The morrow had settled the problem. Captain Morecombe came in once or twice to say a word or two, or bring in other men, who saluted briefly to her as they passed to stand beside the dead man for a second, and then go out again. She was glad they cared to come; had begged that any might come who chose, as if she were not there. But at one visitor she looked curiously, for he came in alone. A tall man—as tall as Herbert, she thought—with a dark beard and keen kindly eyes. She saw them, for he turned to her with the air of one who has a right to speak, and she stood up involuntarily.

'His name was up for the Victoria Cross, madam,' said a clear resonant voice, 'as you may know; but that is nothing. He was a fine soldier—a soldier such as I—I am John Nicholson, madam—can ill spare. For the rest—he leaves a good name to his son.'

The sunlight streamed in for an instant on to the little bed and its burden as he passed out, and glittered on the sword and tassels. Kate knelt down beside it and kissed the dead hand.

'That was what you meant, wasn't it, Herbert?' she whispered. 'I wish you had told it me yourself, dear.'

She wished it often. Thinking over it all in the long days that followed, it came to be almost her only regret. If he had told her, if he had heard her say how glad she was, she felt that she would have asked no more. And so, as she went down every evening to lay the white rose-buds the gardener brought her upon his grave, she used to repeat—as if he could hear them—his own words. 'It is the finish that is the win or the lose of a race.'

That is what many a man was saying to himself upon the Ridge in the first week of September. For the siege train had come at last. The winning post lay close ahead, and they must ride all they knew. But those in command said it anxiously; for day by day the hospitals became more crowded, and cholera, reappearing, helped to swell the rear guard of graves, when the time had come for vanguards only.

Some men, however—amongst them Baird Smith and John Nicholson—took no heed of sickness or death. And these two, especially, looked into each other's eyes and said, 'When you are ready I'm ready.' Their seniors might say that an assault would be thrown on the hazard of a die. What of that—if men are prepared to throw sixes, as these two were? They had to be thrown, if India was to be kept; if this bubble of sovereignty was to be pricked, the gas let out.

In the city and the palace, also, men, feeling the struggle close, put hand and foot to whip and spur. But there was no one within the walls who had the seeing single eye, quick to seize the salient point of a position. Baird Smith saw it fast enough. Saw the thickets and walls of the Koodsia Gardens in front of him, the river guarding his left, a sinuous ravine—cleaving the hillside into cover—creeping down from the ridge on his right to within two hundred yards of the city wall; and that bit of the wall, between the Moree gate and the Water bastion, was its weakest portion—the curtain walls long, mere parapets, only wide enough for defence by muskets. So said the spies, though it seemed almost incredible to English engineers that the defence had not been strengthened by pulling down the adjacent houses and building a rampart for guns.

In truth there was no one to suggest it, and if it had been suggested there was no one to carry it out, for even now, at the last, the palace seethed with dissension and intrigue. Yet still the sham went on inconceivably. Jim Douglas, indeed, walking through the bazaars in his Afghan dress, very nearly met his fate through it. For he was seized incontinently and made to figure as one of the retinue of the Amir of Kabul's ambassador, who, about the beginning of September, was introduced to the private Hall of Audience as a sedative to doubtful dreamers, and a tonic to brocaded bags. Luckily for him, however, the men called upon to play the other part in the farce—chiefly cloth-merchants from Peshawur and elsewhere, whom Jim Douglas had dodged successfully so far—had been in such abject fear of being discovered themselves that they had no thought of discovering others. For Bahâdur Shâh had the dust and ashes of a Moghul in him still. Jim Douglas recognized the fact in the very obstinacy of delusion in the wax-like haggard old face looking with glazed, tremulous-lidded eyes at the mock mission; and in the faded voice accepting his vassal of Kabul's promise of help. It was an almost incredible scene, Jim Douglas thought; and given it, there was no limit to possibilities in this phantasmagoria of kingship. The white shadows of the marble arches with their tale of boundless power and wealth in the past, the wide plains beyond, the embroidered curtain of the sun lit garden, the curves of courtiers, most of them in the secret, no doubt; and below the throne these ragtag and bob tail of the bazaars—one of them at least a hell-doomed infidel—figuring away in borrowed finery—all this was as unreal as a magic lantern picture, and like it, was followed haphazard, without rhyme or reason, by the next on the slide; for, as he passed out of the presence, he heard the question of appointing a Governor to Bombay brought up and discussed gravely—that Province being reported to have sent in its allegiance *en bloc* to the Great Moghul.

The slides, however, were not always so dignified, so decorous. One came, a day or two afterwards, showing a miserable old pantaloon driven to despair because six hundred hungry sepoys would not behave according to strict etiquette, but, invading his privacy with threats, reduced him to taking his beautiful new cushion from the Peacock Throne and casting it among them.

'Take it,' he cried passionately, 'it is all I have left. Take it, and let me go in peace!' But the lesson he had to learn was not learnt by him as yet, so he had to remain; for once more the sepoys sent out word that there was to be no skulking. To do the Royal Family justice, however, they seem by this time to have given up the idea of flight. Even Abool-Bukr, forsaking drunkenness as well as that kind detaining hand, clung to his kinsfolk bravely, behaving in all ways as a newly-married young prince should, who looked towards filling the throne itself at some future time.[1]

The sepoys themselves had given up blustering, and many, like Soma, had taken to *bhang* instead; drugging themselves deliberately into indifference. The latter had recovered from the blow on the back of his head, which, however, as is so often the case, had for the time at any rate deprived him of all recollection of the events immediately preceding it. So, as Tara had restored his uniform before he was able to miss it, he treated her as if nothing had occurred—greatly to her relief.

The fact had its disadvantages, however, by depriving her of all corroborative evidence of the *mem* having really left the city. Thus Jim Douglas, warned by past experience, and made doubtful by Tara's strange reticences, refused to believe it. Her whole story, indeed, marred as it was by endless reserves and exaggerations, seemed incredible; the more so because Tiddu—who lied wildly as to his constant sojourn in Delhi—professed utter disbelief in it. So, after a few days unavailing attempt to get at the truth, Jim Douglas sent the old man off with a letter of inquiry to the Ridge, and waited for the answer.

Waited, like all Delhi, under the shadow of the lifted sword which hung above the city. A sword, held—behind a simulacrum of many— by one arm, sent for the purpose; for John Lawrence, being wise, knew that the shadow of that arm meant more even than the sword it held to the wildest half of the province under his control; a province trembling in the balance between allegiance and revolt; a province ready to catch fire if the extinguisher were not put upon the beacon light. And all India waited too. Waited to see that sword fall.

But a hatchet fell first. Fell in the lemon thickets and pomegranates of the walled old gardens outside the city, so that men who worked at the batteries still remember the sweet smell that went up from the crushed leaves; a welcome scent, for the Ridge, crowded now with eleven thousand troops, was not a pleasant abode. It was on Sunday the 6th of September that the final reinforcements came in, and on the 7th the men, reading General Wilson's order for the appointing of prize agents in each corps, and his assurance that all plunder would be divided fairly, felt as if they were already within the walls. The hospitals too were giving up their sick; those who could not be of use going to the

[1]His widow died last year, having spent thirty-eight years of her fifty-four in cherishing the memory of a saint upon earth.

rear, Meerut-wards; those fit for work to the front. And that night the first siege battery was traced and almost finished below the Sammy-house, while, under cover of this distraction on the right, the Koodsia Gardens and Ludlow Castle on the left were occupied by strong picquets.

But that first battery—only seven hundred yards from the Moree bastion—had a struggle for dear life. The dawn showed but one gun in position against all the concentrated fire of the bastion which, during the night, had been lured into a useless duel with the old defence-batteries above. Only one gun at dawn; but by noon—despite assault and battery—there were five, answering roar for roar. Then for the first time began that welcome echo—the sound of crumbling walls, the grumbling roll of falling stones and mortar. By sunset the gradually diminishing fire from the bastion had ceased, and the bastion itself was a heap of ruins. By this time the four guns in the left section of the battery were keeping down the fire from the Kashmir gate, and so protecting the real advance through the gardens.

That was the first day of the siege, and Kate Erlton—sitting in her little tent, which had been moved into a quiet spot, as she had begged to be allowed to stay on the Ridge until some news came of the man to whom she owed so much—thought with a shudder she could not help, of what it must mean to many an innocent soul shut up within those walls. It was bad enough here, where the very tent seemed to shake. It must be terrible down there beside the heating guns, in the roar and the rattle, the grime and the ache and strain of muscle. But in the city—even in Sri Anunda's garden—!

So, naturally enough, she wondered once more what could have become of the man who had gone back to find her nearly ten days before.

'May I come in? John Nicholson.'

She would have recognized the voice even without the name, for it was not one to be forgotten. Nor was the owner, as he stood before her, a letter in his hand.

'I have heard from Mr Douglas, Mrs Erlton,' he said. 'It is in the Persian character, so I presume it is no use showing it to you. But it concerns you chiefly. He wants to know if you are safe. I have to answer it immediately. Have you any message you would like to send?'

'Any message,' she echoed. 'Only that he must come back at once, of course.'

John Nicholson looked at her calmly.

'I shall say nothing of the kind,' he replied. 'It is best for a man to decide such matters for himself.'

She flushed up hotly. 'I had not the slightest intention of dictating to

Mr—Mr Douglas, General Nicholson; but considering how much he has already sacrificed for my sake—'

'You had better let him do as he likes, my dear madam,' interrupted the General, with a sudden kindly smile, which, however, faded as quickly as it came, leaving his face stern. 'He, like many another man, has sacrificed too much for women, Mrs Erlton; so if ever you can make up to him for some of the pain do so—he is worth it. Good bye. I'll tell him that you are safe; but that in spite of that, he has my permission to go ahead and kill—the more the better.'

She had not the faintest idea why he made this last remark; but it did not puzzle her, for she was occupied with his previous one. Sacrificed too much! That was true. He carried the scars of the knife upon him clearly. And the man who had just left her presence, who, for all his courtesy, had treated her so cavalierly? had he scars also? She was rather vexed with herself for feeling it, but a sudden sense of being a poor creature came over her. It flashed upon her that she could imagine a world without women—she was in one, almost, at that very moment—but not a world without men; and yet that ceaseless roar filling the air had more to do with women than men; it went more as a challenge of revenge, than as a stern recall to duty—

It was true. The men, working night and day in the batteries, thought little of men's rights, only of women's wrongs. Even General Wilson in his order had appealed to those under him on that ground only, urging them to spend life and strength freely in vengeance on murderers.

And they did. Down in the scented Koodsia Gardens the men seemed never to tire, never to shrink, though the shot from the city—not two hundred and fifty yards away—flew *pinging* through the trees above them; but the high wall gave cover, and so those off duty slept peacefully in the cool shade, or sat smoking on the river-terrace.

Thus, while the first battery, pounding away from the right at the Moree and Kashmir bastions, diverted attention, and the enemy, deceived by the feint, lavished a dogged courage in trying to keep up some kind of reply, a second siege battery in two sections was traced and made in front of Ludlow Castle five hundred yards from the Kashmir gate. By dawn on the 11th both sections were at work destroying the defences of the gate, and pounding away to breach the curtain wall beside it. So the roar was doubled, and the vibrations of the air began to quiver on the wearied ear almost painfully. Yet they were soon trebled, quadrupled. Trebled by a party of wide-mouthed mortars in the garden itself. Quadrupled by a wicked dare-devil; impertinent little company of six eighteen-pounders and twelve small mortars, which, with Medley of the Engineers as a guide, took advantage of a half-ruined house to creep within a hundred and sixty yards of the doomed walls, despite the shower of shell and bullets from it; for by this time the Murderers in the city had found out that the Men were at work at something in the scented thickets to the left. Not that the discovery hindered the work. The native pioneers who bore the brunt of it, digging and piling for the wicked little intruder, were working with the master, working with volunteers—officers and men alike—from the 9th Lancers and the Carabineers. So, when one of their number toppled over, they looked to see if he were dead or alive in order to sort him out properly. And if he was dead they would weep a few tears as they laid him in the row beside the others of his kind, before they went on with their work quietly; for, having to decide whether a comrade belonged to the dead or the living thirty-nine times one night, they began to get expert at it. So by the 12th, fifty guns and mortars flashed and roared, and the rumble of falling stones became almost continuous. Sometimes a shell would just crest the parapet, burst, and bring away yards of it at a time.

Up on the Ridge behind the siege batteries, when the cool of evening came on, every post was filled with sightseers watching the salvos, watching the game. And one, at least, going back to get ready for mess, wrote and told his wife at Meerut, that if she were at the top of the Flagstaff Tower, she would remain there till the siege was over—it was so fascinating. But they were merry on the Ridge in these days, and the messes were so full that guests had to be limited at one, till they got a new leaf in the table! Yet on the other slope of the Ridge, men were tumbling over like the stones in the walls. Tumbling over one after another in the batteries, all through the night of the 12th, and the day of the 13th.

Then at ten o'clock in the evening, men, sitting in the mess-tents, looked at each other joyfully, yet with a thrill in their veins, as the firing ceased suddenly. For they knew what that meant; they knew that down under the very walls of the city, friends and comrades were creeping, sword in one hand, their lives in the other, through the starlight, to see if the breaches were practicable.

But the city knew them to be so; and already the last order sent by the palace to Delhi was being proclaimed by beat of drum through the streets.

So, monotonously, the cry rang from alley to alley.

'Intelligence having just been brought that the infidel intend an assault to night, it is incumbent on all, Hindu and Mohammedan, from due regard to their faith, to assemble directly by the Kashmir gate, bringing iron picks and shovels with them. This order is imperative.'

Newâsi Begum, amongst others, heard it as she sat reading. She

stood up suddenly, overturning the book-rest and the Holy Word in her
haste; for she felt that the crisis was at hand. She had never seen
Abool-Bukr since the night, now a whole month past, when he had
taunted her with being one more woman ready for kisses. Her pride
had kept her from seeking him, and he had not returned. But now her
resentment gave way before her fears. She *must* see him—since God
only knew what might be going to happen!

True in a way. But up on the Ridge one man felt certain of one
thing. John Nicholson, with the order for an assault at dawn safe in his
hand, knew that he would be in Delhi on the 14th September—a day
earlier than he had expected.

# 5

# Through the Walls

It was a full hour past dawn on the 14th September ere that sudden
silence fell once more upon the echoing rocks of the Ridge and the
scented gardens. So, for a second, the twittering of birds in the
thickets behind them might have been heard by the men who with
fixed bayonets were jostling the roses and the jasmines. But they were
holding their breath—waiting, listening for something very different;
while in the ears of many, excluding all other sounds, lingered the
cadence of a text read by the chaplain before dawn in the church lesson
for the day.

'*Woe to the bloody city—the sword shall cut thee off.*'

For—to many—the coming struggle meant neither justice nor
revenge, but religion; it was Christ against Anti-Christ. So, whether for
revenge or faith they waited; a thousand down by the river opposite
the Water bastion; a thousand in the Koodsia facing the main breach,
with John Nicholson, first as ever, to lead it; a thousand more on the
broad white road fronting the Kashmir bastion, with an explosion
party ahead to blow in the gate, and a reserve of fifteen hundred to the
rear waiting for success. Briefly, four thousand five hundred men—
more than half natives—waiting for the assault, facing that half mile or
so of northern wall, and thus within touch of each other. Beyond, on
the western trend, were two thousand more—mostly untried troops
from Jumoo and a general muster of casuals—to sweep through the
suburbs and be ready to enter by the Cabul gate when it was opened
to them.

Above on the Ridge, six hundred sabres awaited orders. Behind it were three thousand sick in hospital, a weak defence, and that rear-guard of graves. And in front of all stood that tall figure with the keen eyes.

'Are you ready, Jones?' asked Nicholson, laying his hand on the last leader's shoulder. His voice and face were calm, almost cold.

'Ready, sir!'

Then, startling that momentary silence, came the bugle.

'*Advance!*'

With a cheer the Rifles skirmished ahead joyfully. The engineers posted in the furthest cover long before dawn—who had waited for hours, knowing that each minute made their task harder—rose waving their swords to guide the stormers towards the breach; then calmly, as if it had been dark not daylight, crested the *glacis* at a swift walk, followed by the laddermen in line. Behind, with a steady tramp, came the two columns bound for the breaches; but the third, upon the road, had to wait awhile, as, like greyhounds from a leash, a little company slipped forward at the double.

Home of the Engineers first with two sergeants, a native *havildar*, and ten Punjabee sappers, running lightly, despite the twenty-five pound powder bags they carried. Behind them, led by Salkeld, were the firing party and a bugler. All running under the hail of bullets, faster as they fell faster, as men run to escape a storm; but these courted it, though the task had been set for night, and it was now broad daylight.

What then? They could see better. See the outer gateway open, the footway of the drawbridge destroyed, the inner door closed save for the wicket.

'Come on,' shouted Home, and was across the bare beams like a boy, followed by the others.

Incredible daring! What did it mean? The doubt made the scared enemy close the wicket hastily. So against it, at the rebels' very feet, the powder bags were laid. True, one sergeant fell dead with his; but as it fell against the gates his task was done.

'Ready, Salkeld!—Your turn,' sang out young Home from the ditch, into which, the bags laid, the fuse set, he dropped unhurt. So, across the scant foothold came the firing party, its leader holding the portfire. But the paralysis of amazement had passed; the enemy, realizing what the audacity meant, had set the wicket-wide. It bristled now with muskets; so did the parapet.

'Burgess!—Your turn,' called Salkeld as he fell, and passed the portfire to the corporal behind him. Burgess, *alias* Grierson—some one perchance retrieving a past under a new name—took it, stooped, then with a half-articulate cry either that it was 'right' or 'out,' fell back into the ditch dead. Smith, of the powder-party—lingering to see the deed done—thought the latter, and, matchbox in hand, sprang forward, cuddling the gate for safety as he struck a light. But it was not needed. As he stooped to use it, the port-fire of the fuse exploded in his face, and, half-blinded, he turned to plunge headlong for escape into the ditch. A second after the gate was in fragments.

'Your turn, Hawthorne!' came that voice from the ditch. So the bugler, who had braved death to sound it, gave the advance. Once, twice, thrice, lest the din from the breaches should drown it. Vain precaution, not needed either; for the sound of the explosion was enough. That thousand on the road was hungering to be no whit behind the others, and with a wild cheer the stormers made for the gate.

But Nicholson was already in Delhi, though ten minutes had gone in a fierce struggle against an avalanche of shot and stone ere they could place a single ladder, ere he could slip into the ditch, and, calling on the 1st Bengal Fusiliers to follow, escalade the bastion, first as ever.

Even so, others were before him. Down at the Water bastion, though three-quarters of the laddermen had fallen and but a third of the storming party remained, twenty-five men of the 8th had gained the breach, and, followed by the whole column, were clearing the ramparts towards the Kashmir gate. Hence, again, without a check, joined by the left half of Nicholson's column, they swept the enemy before them like frightened sheep to the Moree gate; though in the bastion itself, the gunners stood to their guns and were bayoneted beside them. There, with a whoop, some of the wilder ones leapt to the parapet to wave their caps in exultation to the cavalry below, where, in obedience to orders, it was now drawn up, ready to guard the flank of the assault, despite the murderous fire from the Cabul gate, and the Burn bastion beyond it; the troopers sitting in their saddles, motionless, doing nothing, a mark for the enemy, yet still a wall of defence. So, leaving them to that hardest task of all—the courage of inaction—the victorious rush swept on to take the Cabul gate, to sweep past it up to the Burn bastion itself—the last bastion which commanded the position!

And then? Then the order came to retire and await orders at the Cabul gate. The fourth column after clearing the suburbs was to have been there ready for admittance, ready to support. It was not. And Nicholson was not there also, to dare and do all. He had had to pause at the Kashmir gate to arrange that the column which had entered through it should push on into the city, leaving the reserve to hold the points already won; and now, with the 1st Fusiliers behind him, he was fighting his way through the streets to the Cabul gate.

So, fearing to lose touch with those behind, over rating the danger, under estimating the incalculable gain of unchecked advance with an eastern foe, the leader of that victorious sweeping of the ramparts was content to set the English flag flying on the Cabul gate and await orders. But the men had to do something; so they filled up the time with plundering. And there were liquor shops about—Europe shops full of wine and brandy.

The flag had been flying over an hour when Nicholson came up. But by that time the enemy—who had been flying too—flying as far as the boat bridge in sheer conviction that the day was lost—had recovered some courage and were back, crowding the bastion and some tall houses beside it. And in the lane, three hundred yards long not ten feet wide leading to it, two brass guns—posted before bullet-proof screens—were ready to mow down the intruders.

Yet once more John Nicholson saw but one thing; the Burn bastion. Built by Englishmen, it was one of the strongest—the only remaining one, in fact, likely to give trouble. With it untaken a thorough hold on the city was impossible. Besides, with his vast knowledge of native character he knew that the enemy had expected it to be taken, and would construe caution into cowardice. Then he had the 1st Bengal Fusiliers behind him. He had led them into Delhi, they had fallen in his track in tens and fifties, and still they had come on—they would do this thing for him now. . . .

'We will do what we can, sir,' said their commandant, Major Jacob—but his face was grave.

'We will do what men can do, sir,' said the commandant of that left half of the column; 'but honestly, I don't think it can be done. We have tried it once.' His face was graver still.

'Nor I,' said Nicholson's brigade-major.

Nicholson, as he stood by the houses around the Cabul gate which had been occupied and plundered by the troops, looked down the straight lane again. It hugged the city wall on its right, its scanty width narrowed here and there by buttresses to some three feet. About a third of the way down was the first gun, placed beside a feathery *kikar* tree which sent a lace-like tracery of shadow upon the bullet proof screen. As far behind was the second. Beyond, again, was the bastion jutting out, and so forcing the lane to bend between it and some tall houses. Both were crowded with the enemy, and the screens held bayonets and marksmen. There was a gun in the wall close to the bastion, but to the left, citywards, in the low flat-roofed mud houses there seemed no trace of flanking foes.

'I think it can be done,' he said. He knew it must be done ere the palace could be taken. So he gave the order.

'*Fusiliers forward! officers to the front!*'

And to the front they were, with a cheer and a rush, overwhelming the first gun, within ten yards of the other. And one man was closer still, for Lieutenant Butler, pinned against that second bullet-proof screen by two bayonets thrust through the loopholes at him, had to fire his revolver through them also, ere he could escape this two-pronged fork.

But the fire of every musket on the bastion and the tall houses was centred on that second gun. Grape, canister, raked the narrow lane—made narrower by fallen Fusiliers—and forced those who remained to fall back upon the first gun—beyond that even. Yet only for a moment. Reformed afresh, they carried it a second time, spiked it, and pressed on.

*Officers still to the front!*

Just beyond the gun the commandant fell wounded to death. 'Go on, men, go on!' he shouted to those who would have paused to help him. 'Forward, Fusiliers!'

And they went forward, though at dawn two hundred and fifty men had dashed for the breach, and now there were not a hundred and fifty left to obey orders. Less! For fifty men and seven officers lay in that lane itself! Surely it was time now for others to step in—and there *were* others!—

Nicholson saw the waver, knew what it meant, and sprang forward sword in hand, calling on those others to follow. But he asked too much. Where the 1st Fusiliers had failed, none cared to try. That is the simple truth. The limit had been reached.

So for a minute or two he stood, a figure instinct with passion, energy, vitality, before men who—God knows with reason—had lost all three for the moment; a colossal figure beyond them, ahead of them, asking more than mere ordinary men could do. So a pitiful figure—a failure at the last!

'Come on, men! Come on, you fools—come on you—you—'

What the word was, which that bullet full in the chest arrested between heart and lips, those who knew John Nicholson's wild temper, his indomitable will, his fierce resentment at everything which fell short of his ideals, can easily guess.

'Lay me under that tree,' he gasped, as they raised him. 'I will not leave till the lane is carried. My God! Don't mind me—Forward, men, forward! It *can* be done.'

An hour or two afterwards a subaltern coming out of the Kashmir gate saw a *dhooli* deserted by its bearers. In it lay John Nicholson in dire agony; but he asked nothing of his fellows then save to be taken to hospital. He had learnt his lesson. He had done what others had set him to do. He had entered Delhi. He had pricked the bubble, and the gas was leaking out. But he had failed in the task he had set himself. The Burn bastion was still unwon, and the English force in Delhi, instead of holding its northern half up to the very walls of the palace, secure from flanking foes, had to retire on the strip of open ground behind the assaulted wall.

If, indeed, it had not to retire further still; for if one man had had his way it would have retired to the Ridge. Late in the afternoon, when fighting was over for the day, General Wilson rode round the new-won position, and, map in hand, looked despairingly towards the network of narrow lanes and alleys beyond. And he looked at something close at hand with even greater forebodings; for he stood in the European quarter of the town among shops still holding vast stores of wine and spirits which had been left untouched by that other army of occupation.

But what of this one? This product of civilization and culture and Christianity—these men who could give points to those others in so many ways, but might barter their very birthright for a bottle of rum? Yet even so the position must be held. So said Baird-Smith at the chief's elbow, so wrote Neville Chamberlain, unable to leave his post on the Ridge. And another man in hospital, thinking of the Burn bastion, thinking with a strange wonder of men who could refuse to follow, muttered under his breath, 'Thank God! I have still strength left to shoot a coward.'

And yet General Wilson in a way was right. Five days afterwards Major Hodson wrote in his diary: 'The troops are utterly demoralized by hard work and hard drink. For the first time in my life I have had to see English soldiers refuse repeatedly to follow their officers. Jacob, Nicholson, Greville, Speke were all sacrificed to this.'

A terrible indictment indeed, against brave men.

Yet not worse than that underlying the chief's order of the 15th, directing the provost-marshal to search for and smash every bottle and barrel to be found, and let the beer and wine, so urgently needed by the sick, run into the gutters; or his admission three days later that another attempt to take the Lahore gate had failed from 'the refusal of the European soldiers to follow their officers. One rush and it could have been done easily . . . we are still, therefore, in the same position to day as we were yesterday.'

So much for drink.

But the enemy luckily was demoralized also. It was still full of defence; empty of attack. For one thing attack would have admitted a reverse; and over on that eastern wall of the palace, in the fretted marble balcony overlooking the river there was no mention, even now, of such a word. Reverse! Had not the fourth column been killed to a man? Had not *Nikkalseyn* himself fallen a victim to valour? But Soma, and many a man of his sort, gave up the pretence with bitter curses at themselves. They had seen from their own posts that victorious escalade, that swift, unchecked herding of the frightened sheep. And they—intolerable thought!—were sheep also. They saw men with dark faces, no whit better than they—better!—The Rajpoot had at least a longer record than the Sikh!—led to victory while they were not led at all. So, brought face to face once more with the old familiar glory and honour, the old familiar sight of the master first—uncompromisingly, indubitably first to snatch success from the grasp of Fate, and hand it back to them—they thought of the past three months with loathing.

And as for *Nikkalseyn*'s rebuff? Soma, hearing of it from a comrade, hot at heart as he, went to the place, and looked down the lane as John Nicholson had done. By all the *Pandâvas*! a place for heroes indeed! Ah! if he had been there, he would have stayed there somehow. He walked up and down it moodily, picturing the struggle to himself; thinking with a curious anger of those men on the housetops, and in the bastion, taking pot-shots at the unsheltered men below. That was all there would be now. They might drive the masters back for a time, they might inveigle them into lanes and reduce their numbers by tens and fifties; and, men of his sort, might make a brave defence here and there. . . .

Defence! Soma wanted to attack. Attracted by the faint shade of the *kikar* tree he sat down beneath it, resting against the trunk, looking along the lane once more, just as a day or two before John Nicholson had rested for a space. And the irony of failure entered into this man's heart also, because there was none to lead. And with the master there had been none to follow.

Suddenly he rose, his mind made up. If that was so, let him go back to the plough; it also was a hereditary trade.

That night, without a word to any one, leaving his uniform behind him, he started along the Rohtuck road for his ancestral village. But he had to make a *detour* round the suburbs, for, despite that annihilation spoken of in the palace, they were now occupied by the English. Yet but very little headway had been made in securing a firmer hold within the city itself.

'You can't, till the Burn bastion is taken and the Lahore gate secured,' said Nicholson from his dying bed, whence, growing perceptibly weaker day by day, yet with mind clear and unclouded, he watched and warned. The single eye was not closed yet, was not even made dim by death. It saw still, what it had seen on the day of the assault—what it had coveted then and failed to reach.

But it was not for five days after this failure that even Baird-Smith recognized the absolute accuracy of this judgment, and, against the Chief's will, obtained permission to sap through the shelter of the intervening houses till they could tackle the bastion at close and commanding quarters, without asking the troops to face another lane. So on the morning of the 19th, after a night of storm and rain cooling the air incredibly, the pick-axe began what rifles and swords had failed to do. By nightfall a tall house was reached, whence the bastion could be raked fore and aft. Its occupants, recognizing this, took advantage of the growing darkness to evacuate it. Half-an-hour afterwards the master-key of the position was in English hands; rather unsteady ones, however, for here gain the troops—once more the 8th, the 75th, the Sikh infantry, and that balance of the Fusiliers—had found more brandy.

'*Poisoned, sir?*' said one thirsty trooper, flourishing a bottle of Exshaw's Number One before the eyes of his Captain, who, as a last inducement to sobriety, was suggesting danger. '*Not a bit of it. Capsules all right.*'

But this time England could afford a few drunk men. The bastion was gone, and by the Turkoman and Delhi gates half the town was going. And not only the town. Down in the palace men and women, with fumbling hands and dazed eyes, like those new roused from dreams, were snatching at something to carry with them in their flight.

Bukht Khân himself stood facing the Queen in her favourite summer-house, alone, save for Hâfzan, the scribe, who lingered, watching them with a certain malice in her eyes. She had been right. Vengeance had been coming. Now it had come.

'All is not lost, my Queen,' said Bukht Khân, with hand on sword. 'The open country lies before us, Lucknow is ours—come!'

'And the King, and my son,' she faltered. The dull glitter of her tarnished jewellery seemed in keeping with the look on her face. There was something sordid in it. Sordid, indeed, for behind that mask of wifely solicitude and maternal care lay the thought of her hidden treasure.

'Let them come too. Naught hinders it.'

True. But the gold, the gold!

After he had left her, impatient of her hesitation, a sudden terror seized her, lest he might have sought the King, lest he might persuade him.

'My bearers—woman! Quick!' she called to Hâfzan. 'Quick, fool! my *dhooli*!' But even dhooli-bearers have to fly when vengeance shadows the horizon, and in that secluded corner none remained.

Every one was busy elsewhere—or from sheer terror clustered together where soldiers were to be found.

'The Ornament-of-Palaces can walk,' said Hâfzan, still with that faint malice in her face. 'There is none to see, and it is not far.'

So, for the last time, Zeenut Maihl left the summer-house whence she had watched the Meerut road; left it on foot, as many better women, as unused to walking as she, were leaving Delhi with babies on their breasts and little children toddling beside them. Past the faint outline of the Pearl Mosque, through the cool damp of the watered garden with the moon shining overhead, she stumbled laboriously; then up the steps of the Audience-Hall towards a faint light by the Throne. The King sate on it, almost in the dark; for the oil cressets on a trefoil stand only seemed to make the shadows blacker. They lay thick upon the roof, blotting out that circling boast. Before him stood Bukht Khân, his hand still on his sword, broad, contemptuously bold. But on either side of the shrunken figure, half lost in the shadows also, were other counsellors. Ahsan-Oolah, wily as ever, Elâhi Buksh, the time-server, who saw the only hope of safety in prompt surrender.

'Let the Pillar-of-Faith claim time for thought,' the latter was saying. 'There is no hurry. If the *soubadar-sahib* is in one, let him go—'

Bukht Khân broke in with an ugly laugh, 'Yea, Mirza-*sahib*, I can go, but if I go the army goes with me. Remember that. The King can keep the rabble. I have the soldiers.'

Bahâdur Khân looked from one to the other helplessly. Whether to go—risk all—endure a life of unknown discomfort at his age, or remain, alone, unprotected, he knew not.

'Yea! that is true. Still there is no need for hurry,' put in the physician, with a glance at Elâhi Buksh. 'Let my master bid the *soubadar* and the army meet him at the tomb of Humayon tomorrow morning. 'Twill be a more seemly time to leave than now, like a thief in the night.'

Bukht Khân gave a sharp look at the speaker, then laughed again. He saw the game. He scarcely cared to check it.

'So be it. But let it be before noon. I will wait no longer.'

As he passed out hastily he almost ran into a half-veiled figure, which—with another behind it—was hugging one of the pillars, peering forward, listening. He guessed it for the Queen, and paused instantly.

''Tis thy last chance, Zeenut Maihl,' he whispered in her ear. 'Come if thou art wise.'

The last. No! not that! The last for sovereignty perhaps, but not for hidden treasure. Half an hour afterwards, a little procession of Royal *dhoolies* passed out of the palace on their way to Elâhi Buksh's house beside the Delhi gate, and Ahsan-Oolah walked beside the Queen's. He had gold also to save, and he was wise; so she listened, and as she listened she told herself that it would be best to stay. Her life was safe, and her son was too young for the punishment of death. As for the King, he was too old for the future to hold anything else.

Hâfzan watched her go, still with that half-jeering smile, then turned back into the empty palace. Even in the outer court it was empty, indeed, save for a few fanatics muttering texts; and within the precincts, deserted utterly, silent as the grave. Until, suddenly, from the Pearl Mosque a voice came, giving the call to prayer; for it was not far from dawn.

She paused, recognizing it, and leaving the marble terrace where she had been standing, looking river-wards, walked over to the bronze-studded door, and peered in among the white arches of the Mosque for what she sought.

And there it was, a tall, white figure looking westward, its back towards her, its arms spread skywards. A fanatic of fanatics.

'Thou art not wise to linger here, Moulvie *sahib*,' she called. 'Hast not heard? The Burn-bastion is taken. The King and Queen have fled. The English will be here in an hour or so, and then—'

'And then there comes judgment,' answered Mahomed Ismail, turning to look at her sternly. 'Doth not it lie within these walls? I stay here, woman, as I have stayed.'

'Nay, not here,' she argued in conciliatory tones. 'It lies yonder, in the outer court, by the trees shadowing the little tank. Thou canst see it from the window of my uncle's room. And he hath gone—like the others. 'Twere better to await it there.'

She spoke as she would have spoken to a madman. And, indeed, she held him to be little else. Here was a man, who had saved forty infidels, whose reward was sure; and who must needs imperil it by lingering where death was certain; must needs think of his battered soul instead of his body! Mahomed Ismail came and stood beside her, with the curious acquiescence in regard to details which is so often seen in men mastered by one idea.

'It may be better so, sister,' he said dreamily. ''Tis as well to be prepared.'

Hâfzan's hard eyes melted a little, for she had a real pity for this man who had haunted the palace persistently, and lost his reason over his conscience.

If she should once get him into her uncle's room, she would find some method of locking him in, of keeping him out of mischief. For herself, being a woman, the *Huzoor*s were not to be feared.

'Yea! 'tis as well to be near,' she said as she led the way.

And the time drew near also; for the dawn of the 20th September had broken ere, with the key of the outer door in her bosom, she retired into an inner room, leaving the Moulvie saying his prayers in the other. Already the troops, recovered from their unsteadiness, had carried the Lahore gate and were bearing down on the Mosque. They found it almost undefended. The circling flight of purple pigeons, which at the first volley flew westward, the sun glistening on their iridescent plumage, was scarcely more swift than the flight of those who attempted a feeble resistance. And now the palace lay close by. With it captured, Delhi was taken. Its walls, it is true, rose unharmed, secure as ever, hemming in those few acres of God's earth from the march of time; but they were strangely silent. Only now and again a puff of white smoke and an unavailing roar told that some one, who cared not even for success, remained within.

So powder bags were brought, and Home of the Engineers sent for, that he might have the honour of lighting the fuse which gave entry to the last stronghold; for there was no hurry now; no racing now under hailstorms, and over tight ropes. Calmly, quietly, the fuse was lit, the gate shivered to atoms, and the long red tunnel with the gleam of sunlight at its end lay before the men who entered it with a cheer. Then, here and there rose guttural Arabic texts, ending in a groan. Here and there the clash of arms. But not enough to rouse Hâfzan, who, long ere this, had fallen asleep after her wakeful night. It needed a touch on her shoulder for that, and the Moulvie's eager voice in her ear.

'The key, woman! The key—give it! I need the key.'

Half-dazed by sleep, deceived by the silence, she put her hand mechanically to her bosom. His followed hers; he had what he sought, and was off. She sprang to her feet recognizing some danger, and followed him.

'He is mad! He is mad!' she cried, as her halting steps lingered behind the tall white figure which made straight for a crowd of soldiers gathered round the little tank. There were other soldiers here, there, everywhere in the rose-red arcades around the wide sun lit court; soldiers with dark faces and white ones, seeking victims, seeking plunder. But these in the centre were all white men, and they were standing, as men stand to look at a holy shrine, upon the place where, as the spies had told them, English women and children had been murdered.

So towards them, while curses were in all hearts and on some lips, came the tall white figure with its arms outspread, its wild eyes aflame.[1]

'O God of Might and Right! Give judgment now, give judgment now.'

[1]This incident is imaginary.

The cry rolled and echoed through the arcades: to alien ears even as those other cries which had ended in a groan.

'He is mad—he saved them—he is mad!' gasped the maimed woman behind; but her cry seemed no different either to those unheeding, uncomprehending ears. . . .

So the tall white figure lay on its face, half a dozen bayonets in its back, and half a dozen more were after Hâfzan.

'Stick him! Stick him! A man in disguise. Remember the women and children. Stick the coward!' She fled shrieking—shrill, feminine shrieks; but the men's blood was up. They could not hear, they would not hear; and yet the awkwardness of that flying figure made them laugh horribly.

'Don't 'ustle 'im! Give 'im time! There's plenty o' run in 'im yet, mates. Lord! 'e'd get first prize at 'Ackney Wick 'e would.'

Some one else, however, had got it at Harrow not a year before, and was after the reckless crew. Almost too late—not quite. Hâfzan, run to earth against a red wall, felt something on her back, and gave a wild yell. But it was only a boy's hand.

'My God! sir, I've stuck you!' faltered a voice behind, as a man stood rigid, arrested in mid-thrust.

'You d—d fool!' said the boy. 'Couldn't you hear it was a woman? I'll—I'll have you shot—oh, hang it all! Drag the creature away, some one—get out, do!'

For Hâfzan, as he stood stanching the blood from the slight wound, had fallen at his feet and was kissing them frantically.

But even that indignity was forgotten as the stained handkerchief answered the flutter of something which at that moment caught the breeze above him.

It was the English flag.

The men, forgetting everything else, cheered themselves hoarse—cheered again when an orderly rode past waving a slip of paper sent back to the General with the laconic report:

'*Blown open the gates! Got the palace!*'

But Hâfzan, her veil up to prevent mistakes, limped over to where the Moulvie lay, turned him gently on his back, straightened his limbs, and closed his eyes. She would have liked to tell the truth to some one, but there was no one to listen. So she left him there before the tribunal to which he had appealed.

# 6

# Rewards and Punishments

So the strain of months was over on the Ridge. Delhi was taken; the Queen's health was being drunk night after night in the palace of the Moghuls. But there was one person to whom the passing days brought a growing anxiety. This was Kate Erlton; for there was no tidings of Jim Douglas. None.

At first she had comforted herself with the idea that he was still, for some reason or another, keeping to the yet unconquered part of the city; that he was obliged to do so being impossible, the long files of women and children seeking safety and passing through the Ridge fearlessly, precluding that consolation. Still it was conceivable he might be busy, though it seemed strange he should have sent no word. So, like many another in India at that time, she waited, hoping against hope, possessing her soul in patience. She had no lack of occupation to distract her. How could there be for a woman, when close on twelve hundred men had come back from the city dead or wounded?

But now the 21st of September was upon them. The city was occupied, the work was over. Yet Captain Morecombe, coming back from it, shook his head. He had spent time and trouble in the search, but had failed—failed even, from Kate's limited ideas of their locality, to find either Tara's lodging or the roof in the Mufti's quarter. She could have found them herself, she said almost pathetically; but of course that was impossible now, and would be so for some time to come.

'I am afraid it is no use, Mrs Erlton,' said the Captain kindly. 'There is not a trace to be found, even by Hodson's spies. Unless he is shut up somewhere, he—he must be dead. It is so likely that he should be; you must see that. Possibly before the siege began. Let us hope so.'

'Why?' she asked quickly. 'You mean that there have been horrible things done of late?—things like that poor English soldier who was found chained outside the Kashmir gate as a target for his fellows? Have there? I would so much rather know the worst—I used always to tell Mr Douglas so—it prevents one dreaming at night.' She shivered as she spoke, and the man watching her felt his heart go out towards her with a throb of pity. How long, he wondered irrelevantly, would it take her to forget the miserable tragedy, to be ready for consolation?

'Yes, there have been terrible things on both sides,' he replied, interrupting himself hastily with a sort of shame. 'There always are. You can't help it when you sack cities. The Goorkhas had the devil in them when I was down in the Mufti's quarter. They shot dozens of helpless learned people in the Chelon-ke-kucha—one who coached me up for my exams. And about twelve women in the house of a "Professor of Arabic"—so he styled himself—jumped down the well to escape—their own fears chiefly. For the men wanted loot, nothing else. That is the worst of it. The whole story from beginning to end seems so needless. It is as if Fate—'

She interrupted him quietly, 'It has been Fate. Fate from beginning to end.'

He sat for an instant with a grave face, then looked up with a smile. 'Perhaps. It's rather *a propos des bottes*, Mrs Erlton, but I wanted to ask you a question. Hadn't you a white cockatoo, once? When you first came here. I seem to recollect the bird making a row in the verandah when I used to drive up.'

Her face grew suddenly pale, she sat staring at him with dread in her eyes. 'Yes!' she replied with a manifest effort, 'I gave it to Sonny Seymour because—because it loved him—' she broke off, then added swiftly, eagerly, 'What then?'

'Only that I found one in the palace today. There is a jolly marble-latticed balcony overlooking the river. The King used to write his poetry there, they say. Well! I saw a brass cage hanging high up on a hook—there has been no loot in the precincts, you know, for the Staff has annexed them—I thought the cage was empty till I took it down from sheer curiosity, and there was a dead cockatoo.'

'Dead!' echoed Kate, with a quick smile of relief. 'Oh! how glad I am it was dead.'

Captain Morecombe stared at her. 'Poor brute!' he said under his breath 'it was skin and bone. Starved to death. I expect they forgot all about it when they got really frightened. They are cruel devils, Mrs Erlton.'

The Major had used the self-same words to Alice Gissing eighteen months before, and in the same connection. But, perhaps fortunately for Kate in her present state of nervous strain, that knowledge was denied to her; even so the coincidence of the bird itself absorbed her.

'It had a yellow crest,' she began.

'Oh! then it couldn't have been yours,' interrupted Captain Morecombe rather relieved, for he saw that he had somehow touched on a hidden wound. 'This one was green; yellowish green. I daresay the King kept pets like the Oude man—'

'It is dead, anyhow,' said Kate hurriedly.

And the knowledge gave her an unreasoning comfort. To begin with, it seemed to her as if those fateful white wings, which had begun to overshadow her world on that sunny evening down by the Goomtee river, had ceased to hover over it. And then this rounding of the tale—

for that the bird was little Sonny's favourite she did not doubt—made
her feel that Fate would not leave that other portion of it unfinished.
The inevitable sequence would be worked out somehow. She would
hear something. So once more she waited like many another; waiting
with eyes strained past the last known deed of gallantry for the end
which surely must have been nobler still. When that knowledge came,
she told herself, she would be content.

There was yet another thing which held her to hope even more than
this; it was the remembrance of John Nicholson's words, 'If ever you
have a chance of making up'. They seemed prophetic; for he who
spoke them was so often right. Men talking of him as he lingered,
watching, advising, warning, despite dire agony of pain and
drowsiness of morphia, said there was none like him for clear insight
into the very heart of things.

Yet he, as he lay without a complaint, was telling himself he had
been blind. He had sought more from his world than there was in it.
And so, though the news of the capture of the Burn-bastion brought a
brief rally, he sank steadily.

But Hodson coming into his tent to tell him of the safe capture of
the King and Queen upon the 21st at Humayon's tomb, found him
eager to hear all particulars. So eager, that when the Sirdars of the
Mooltanee Horse (a regiment he had practically raised), who sat
outside in dozens waiting for every breath of news about their fetish,
would not keep quiet, he emphasized his third order by a revolver
bullet through the wall of the tent; greatly to their delight since, as they
retired further off, they agreed that *Nikkalseyn* was *Nikkalseyn* still; and
surely death dare not claim one so full of life?

Even Hodson smiled in the swift silence through which the
labouring breath of the dying man could be heard.

'Well, sir,' he went on, 'as I was saying, I got permission, thanks to
you, to utilize my information—'

'You mean Rujjub Ali's and that sneak Elâhi-Buksh's, I suppose,' put
in Nicholson, 'it was sharp work. The King only went to Humayon's
tomb yesterday. They must have had it all cut and dried before, surely?'

'The Queen has been trying to surrender on terms some time back,
sir,' replied Hodson hastily. ''She has a lot of treasure—eight lakhs, the
spies tell me—and is anxious to keep it. However, to go on. After
stopping with Elâhi-Buksh that night—no doubt, as you say, pressure
was put on them then—they went off, as agreed, to meet Bukht Khân,
but refused to go with him. Of course the promise of their lives—'

'Then you were negotiating already?'[1]

'Not exactly—but—but I couldn't have done without the promise unless Wilson had agreed to send out troops, and he wouldn't. So I had to give in, though personally I would a deal rather have brought the old man in dead, than alive. Well, I set off this morning with fifty of my horse and sent in the two messengers while I waited outside. It was nearly two hours before they came back, for the old man was hard to move. Zeenut Maihl was the screw, and when Bahâdur Shâh talked of his ancestors and wept, told him he should have thought of that before he let Bukht Khân and the army go. In fact she did the business for me; but she stipulated for a promise of life from my own lips. So I rode out alone to the causeway by the big gate—it is a splendid place, sir, more like a mosque than a tomb—and drew up to attention. Zeenut Maihl came out first, swinging along in her curtained *dhooli* and Rujjub, who was beside me, called out her name and titles decorously. I couldn't help feeling it was a bit of a scene, you know—my being there, alone, and all that. Then the King came in his *palkee*; so I rode up, and demanded his sword. He asked if I were Hodson-*sahib bahadur*, and if I would ratify the promise? So I had to choke over it, for there were two or three thousand of a crowd by this time. Then we came away. It was a long five miles at a footpace, with that crowd following us until we neared the city. Then they funked. Besides, I had said openly I'd shoot the King like a dog, despite the promise, at the first sign of rescue. And that's all, except that you should have seen the officers' face at the Lahore gate when he asked me what I'd got in tow, and I said calmly, "Only the King of Delhi". So that is done.'

'And well done,' said Nicholson, briefly, reaching out a parched right hand. 'Well done, from the beginning to the end.'

Hodson flushed up like a girl, 'I'm glad to hear you say so, sir,' he replied as nonchalantly as he could, 'but personally, of course, I would rather have brought him in dead.'

Even that slight action, however, had left Nicholson breathless, and the only comment for a time came from his eyes; bright questioning eyes, seeking now with a sort of pathetic patience to grasp the world they were leaving, and make allowances for all shortcomings.

'And now for the Princes,' said Hodson. 'Did you write to Wilson, sir?'

Nicholson nodded, 'I think he'll consent. Only—only don't make any more promises, Hodson. Some of them must be hung; they deserve death.'

[1](Hodson in his diary says that the promise was virtually given *two* days before the capture, which was on the 21st. It must therefore have been given on the 19th. *Most likely* in Elâhi-Buksh's house; if so on Hodson's own authority. *Query*. Was he there in person?)

His hearer gave rather an uneasy look at the clear eyes, and remarked sharply, 'You thought they deserved more than hanging once, sir.'

The old imperious frown of quick displeasure at all challenge came to John Nicholson's face, then faded into a half smile. 'I was not so near death myself. It makes a difference. So good bye, Hodson. I mayn't see you again.' He paused; his smile grew clearer, and strangely soft. 'No news, I suppose, of that poor fellow Douglas, who didn't agree with us?'

'None, sir; I warned him it was useless and foolhardy to go back, when my information—'

'No doubt,' interrupted the dying man gently. 'Still, I'd have gone in his place.' He lay still for a moment, then murmured to himself. 'So he is on the way before me. Well! I don't think we can be unhappy after death. And, as for that poor lady—when you see her, Hodson, tell her I am sorry—sorry she hadn't her chance.' The last words were once more murmured to himself and ended in silence.

Kate Erlton, however, did not get the message which would, perhaps, have ended her lingering hope. Major Hodson was too busy to deliver it. Permission to capture the princes was given him that very night, and early next morning he set off to Humayon's tomb once more, with his two spies, his second in command, and about a hundred troopers; a small party indeed, to face the four or five thousand palace refugees who were known to be in hiding about the tomb, waiting to see if the princes could make terms like the King had done. But Hodson's orders were strict. He was to bring in Mirza Moghul and Khair Sultân, ex-commanders-in-chief, and Abool-Bukr, heir presumptive, unconditionally, or not at all.

The morning was deliciously cool and crisp, full of that promise of winter, which in its perfection of climate consoles the Punjâbee for six months of purgatory. The sun sent a yellow flood of light over the endless ruins of ancient Delhi which here extend for miles on miles. It was a nasty country for skulking enemies; but Hodson's pluck and dash were equal to anything, and he rode along with a heart joyous at his chance, and full of determination to avail himself of it and gain renown.

Some one else, however, was early astir on this the 22nd of September, so as to reach Humayon's Tomb in time to press on to the Kutb, if needs be. This was the Princess Farkhoonda Zamâni. Ever since that day, now more than a week past, when the last message to the city had warned her that the supreme moment for the House of Timoor was at hand, and she had started from her study of Holy Writ, telling herself piteously that she must find Prince Abool-Bukr—must, at all sacrifice to pride, seek him, since he would not seek her—must warn him and keep his hand in hers again—she had been distracted by the impossibility of carrying out her decision. For, expecting an immediate sack of the town, the Mufti's people had barricaded the only exit bazaar-wards, and when, after a day or two, she did succeed in creeping out, it was to find the streets unsafe, the palace itself closed against all. But now, at least, there was a chance. Like all the royal family, she knew of these two spies, Rujjub-Ali and Mirza Elâhi-Buksh, who was saving his skin by turning Queen's evidence. She knew of Hodson-*sahib*'s promise to the King and Queen. She knew that Abool-Bukr was still in hiding with the arch-offenders, Mirza Moghul and Khair Sultân, at Humayon's tomb. Such an association was fatal; but if she could persuade him to throw over his uncles, and go with her; and if, afterwards, she could open negotiations with the Englishmen, and prove that Abool-Bukr had been dismissed from office on the very day of the death-challenge and had been in disgrace ever since—had even been condemned to death by the King, as he had been once; surely she might yet drag her dearest from the net into which Zeenut Maihl had lured him—with what bait she scarcely trusted herself to think! The first thing to be done, therefore, was to persuade Abool to come with her to some safer hiding. She would risk all; her pride, her reputation, his very opinion of her, for this. And surely a man of his nature was to be tempted. So she put on her finest clothes, her discarded jewels, and set off about noon in a *ruth*—a sort of *dhoolie* on wheels, drawn by oxen, gay with trappings, and set with jingling bells. They let her pass at the Delhi gate, after a brief look through the curtains, during which she cowered into a corner without covering her face, lest they might think her a man, and stop her.

'By George! that was a pretty woman,' said the English subaltern, who passed her, as he came back to the guardroom. 'Never saw such eyes in my life. They were as soft, as soft as—well! I don't know what. And they looked, somehow, as if they have been crying for years, and—and as if they saw—saw something, you know.'

'They saw you—you sentimental idiot—that's enough to make any woman cry,' retorted his companion. And then the two, mere boys, wild with success and high spirits, fell to horse play over the insult.

Yet the first boy was right. Newâsi's eyes had seen something day and night, night and day, ever since they had strained into the darkness after Prince Abool-Bukr when he broke from her kind detaining hand and disappeared from the Mufti's quarter. And that something was a flood of sunlight holding a figure, as she had seen it more than once, in a wild unreasoning paroxysm of sheer terror. It seemed to her as if she could hear those white lips gasping once more over the cry which brought the vision. 'Why did'st not let me live mine own life, die mine own death? But to die—to die needlessly—to die in the sunlight perhaps.'

There was a flood of it now outside the *ruth* as it lumbered along by the jail, not a quarter of a mile yet from the city gate. Half-shivering she peeped through the gay patchwork curtains to assure herself it held no horror.

God and his Holy Prophet! What was that crowd on the road ahead? No: not ahead; she was in it, now, so that the oxen paused, unable to go on; a crowd, a cluster of spear-points, and then, against the jail wall, an open space round another *ruth*, an Englishman on foot, three figures stripped—No; not three! only two, for one had fallen as the crack of a carbine rang through the startled air. Two?—But one, now—and that. . . .

Oh! saints have mercy! the vision! the vision! It was Abool, dodging like a hare, begging for bare life—seeking it, at last, out of the sunshine, under the shadow of the *ruth* wheels.

'Abool! Abool!' she screamed. 'I am here. Come! I am here.'

Did he hear the kind voice? He may have, for it echoed clear before the third and final crack of the carbine. So clear that the driver, terrified lest it should bring like punishment on him, drove his goad into the oxen; and the next instant they were careering madly down a side road, bumping over watercourses and ditches. But Newâsi felt no more buffetings. She lay huddled up inside, as unconscious as that other figure which, by Major Hodson's orders, was being dragged out from under the wheels and placed upon it beside the two other corpses for conveyance to the city. And none of all the crowd, ready—so the tale runs—to rescue the princes lest death should be their portion in the future, raised voice or hand to avenge them now that it had come so ruthlessly, so wantonly. Perhaps the English guard at the Delhi gate cowed them, as it had cowed those who the day before had followed the King so far, then slunk away.

So the little *cortège* moved on peacefully; far more peacefully than the other *ruth*, which, with *its* unconscious burden, was racing Kutb-wards as if it was afraid of the very sunshine. But the Princess Farkhoonda, huddled up in all her jewels and fineries, had forgotten even that—forgotten even that vision seen in it.

Hodson, however, as he rode at ease behind the dead princes seemed to court the light. He gloried in the deed, telling himself that 'in less than twenty-four hours he had disposed of the principal members of the House of Timoor'; so fulfilling his own words written weeks before, 'If I get into the palace, the House of Timoor will not be worth five minutes purchase, I ween'—telling himself also, that in shooting down with his own hand, men who had surrendered without stipulations to his generosity and clemency—surrendered to a hundred troopers when they had five thousand men behind them—he 'had rid the earth of ruffians'—telling himself that he was 'glad to have had the opportunity, and was game to face the moral risk of praise or blame.'

He got the former unstintingly from most of his fellows as, in triumphant procession, the bodies were taken to the chief police station, there to be exposed, so say the eye-witnesses, 'In the very spot where, four months before, Englishwomen had been outraged and murdered, in the very place where their helpless victims had lain.'

A strange perversion of the truth, responsible, perhaps, not only for the praise, but for the very deed itself. So Mahomed Ismail's barter of his truth and soul for the lives of the forty prisoners at the Kotwâli counted for nothing in the judgment of this world.

But Hodson lacked either praise or blame from one man. John Nicholson lay too near the judgment of another world to be disturbed by vexed questions in this; and when the next morning came, men, meeting each other said, sadly, 'He is dead'.

The news, brought to Kate Erlton by Captain Morecombe when he came over to report another failure, took the heart out of even *her* hope.

'There is no use in my staying longer, I'm afraid,' she said quietly; 'I am only in the way. I will go back to Meerut; and then home—to the boy.'

'I think it would be best,' he replied kindly. 'I can arrange for you to start tomorrow morning. You will be the better for a change; it will help you to forget.'

She smiled a little bitterly; but when he had gone she set to work, packing up such of her husband's things as she wished the boy to have with calm deliberation; and early in the afternoon she went over to the garden of her old house to get some fresh flowers for what would be her last visit to that rearguard of graves; to take, also, her last look at the city, and watch it grow mysterious in the glamour of sunset.

Seen from afar it seemed unchanged. A mass of rosy-light and lilac-shadow, with the great white dome of the Mosque hanging airily above the smoke-wreaths. Yet the end had come to its four months' dream as it had come to hers. Rebellion would linger long, but its stronghold, its very *raison d'être*, was gone. And Memory would last longer still; yet surely it would not be all bitter? Hers was not. Then with a rush of real regret she thought of the peaceful roof, of old Tiddu, of the Princess Farkhoonda—Tara—Soma—of Sri Anunda in his garden. Was she to go home to safe, smug England, live in a suburb, and forget? Forget all but the tragedy! Yet even that held beautiful memories. Alice Gissing under young Mainwaring's scarf, while he lay at her feet. Her husband leaving a good name to his son. Did not these things help to make the story perfect? No! not perfect; and with the remembrance her eyes filled with sudden tears. There would always be a blank for her in the record. The Spirit which had moved on the Face of the Waters, bringing their chance of Healing and Atonement to so many, had left hers in the shadow. She had learnt her lesson. Ah! yes; she had learnt it. But the chance of using it?. . .

As she sat on the plinth of the ruined verandah, watching the city growing dim through the mist of her tears, John Nicholson's words came back to her once more, 'If ever you have the chance'; but it would never come now—never!

She started up wildly at the clutch of a brown hand on her wrist, a brown hand with a circlet of dead gold above it.

'Come!' said a voice behind her; 'come quick! he needs you.'

'Tara!' she gasped—'Tara! Is—is he alive then?'

'He would not need the *mem* if he were dead,' came the swift reply. Then with her wild eyes fixed on another gold circlet upon the wrist she held, Tara laughed shrilly. 'So the *mem* wears it still. She has not forgotten. Women do not forget, white or black'—With a strange stamp of her foot she interrupted herself fiercely—'Come, I say, come!'

If there had been doubts as to the Rajpootni's sanity at times in past days, there was none now. A glance at her face was sufficient. It was utterly distraught, the clutch on Kate's arm utterly uncontrolled; so that, involuntarily, the latter shrank back.

'The *mem* is afraid,' cried Tara exultantly. 'So be it! I will go back and tell the master. Tell him I was right and he wrong, for all the English he chattered. I will tell him the *mem* is not *suttee*—how could she be—'

The old taunt roused many memories, and made Kate ready to risk anything. 'I am coming, Tara—but where?' She stood facing the tall figure in crimson, a tall figure also, in white, her hands full of the white roses she had gathered.

Tara looked at her with that old mingling of regret and approbation, jealousy, and pride. 'Then she must come at once. He is dying—may be dead ere we get back.'

'Dead!' echoed Kate faintly. 'Is he wounded then?'

A sort of sombre sullenness dulled the excitement of Tara's face. 'He is ill,' she replied laconically. Suddenly, however, she burst out again: 'The *mem* need not look so! I have done all—all she could have done. It is his fault. He will not take things. The *mem* can do no more; but I have come to her, so that none shall say, "Tara killed the master." So come. Come quick!'

Five minutes after Kate was swinging city-wards in a curtained *dhooli* which Tara had left waiting on the road below, and trying to piece out a consecutive story from the odd jumble of facts, and fancies, and explanations which Tara poured into her ear between her swift abuse of the bearers for not going faster, and her assertion that there was no need to hurry. The *mem* need not hope to save the *Huzoor*, since everything had been done. It seemed, however, that Tiddu had taken back the letter telling of Kate's safety, and that in consequence of this the master had arranged to leave the city in a day or two, and Tiddu— born liar and gold grubber, so the Rajpootni styled him—had gone off at once to make more money. But on the very eve of his going back to the Ridge, Jim Douglas had been struck down with the Great Sickness, and after two or three days, instead of getting better, had fallen—as Tara put it—into the old way. So far Kate made out clearly; but from this point it became difficult to understand the reproaches, excuses, pathetic assertions of helplessness, and fierce declarations that no one could have done more. What was the use of the *Huzoor*'s talking English all night when even a *suttee* could not go out because every one was being shot in the streets? Besides, it was all obstinacy. The master could have got well if he had tried. And who was to know where to find the *mem*? Indeed, if it had not been for Sri Anunda's gardener, who knew all the gardener folk, of course, she would not have found the *mem* even now; for she would never have known which house to inquire at. Not that it would have mattered, since the *mem* could do nothing—nothing!—nothing—

Kate, looking down on the bunch of white flowers which she had literally been too hurried to think of laying aside, felt her heart shrink. They were rather a fateful gift to be in her hands now. Had they come there of set purpose, and would the man who had done so much for her be beyond all care save those pitiful offices of the dead? Still, even that was better than that he should lie alone, untended. So, urged by Tara's vehement upbraidings, the *dhooli*-bearers lurched along, to stop at last. It seemed to Kate as if her heart stopped also. She could not think of what might lie before her as she followed Tara up the dark, strangely-familiar stair. Surely, she thought, she would have known it among a thousand. And there was the step on which she had once crouched terror-stricken, because she was shut out from shelter within; but now Tara's fingers were at the padlock, Tara's hand set the door wide.

Kate paused on the threshold, feeling, in truth, dazed once more at the strange familiarity of all things. It seemed to her as if she had but just left that strip of roof a-glow with the setting sun, the bubble dome of the Mosque beginning to flush like a cloud upon the sky. But Tara, watching her with resentful eyes, put a different interpretation on the pause, and said quickly—

'He is within. The *mem* was away, and it was quieter. But the rest is all the same—there is nothing forgotten—nothing.'

Kate, however, heard only the first words, and was already across the outer roof to gain the inner one. Tara, still beyond the threshold, watched her disappear, then stood listening for a minute, with a face tragic in its intensity. Suddenly a faint voice broke the silence, and her hands, which had been tightly clenched, relaxed. She closed the door silently, and went downstairs.

Meanwhile Kate, on the inner roof, had paused beside the low string bed set in its middle, scarcely daring to look at its burden, and so put hope and fear to the touchstone of truth. But as she stood hesitating, a voice, querulous in its extreme weakness, said in Hindustani—

'It is too soon, Tara; I don't want anything; and—and you needn't wait—thank you.'

He lay with his face turned from her, so she could stand, wondering how best to break her presence to him, noting with a failing heart the curious slackness, the lack of contour even on that hard string bed. He seemed lost, sunk in it; and she had seen that sign so often of late that she knew what it meant. One thing was certain, he must have food— stimulants if possible—before she startled him. So she stole back to the outer roof, expecting to find Tara there, and Tara's help. But the roof lay empty, and a sudden fear lest, after all, she had only come to see him die, while she was powerless to fight that death from sheer exhaustion which seemed so perilously near, made her put down the bunch of flowers she held with an impatient gesture. What a fool she had been not to think of other things!

But as she glanced round, her eye fell on a familiar earthenware basin, kept warm in a pan of water over the ashes. It was full of 'chikken-brât', and excellent of its kind too. Then in a niche stood milk and eggs—a bottle of brandy, arrowroot—everything a nurse could wish for. And in another, evidently in case the brew should be condemned, was a fresh chicken ready for use. Strange sights these to bring tears of pity to a woman's eyes; but they did. For Kate, reading between the lines of poor Tara's confusion, began to understand the tragedy underlying those words she had just heard—

'*I don't want anything, Tara. And you needn't wait, thank you.*' She seemed to see, with a flash, the long long days which had passed, with that patient, polite negative coming to chill the half-distraught devotion.

He must take something now, for all that. So, armed with a cup and spoon, she went back, going round the bed so that he could see her.

'It is time for your food, Mr Greyman,' she said quietly; 'when you have taken some, I'll tell you everything. Only you must take this first.' As she slipped her hand under him, pillow and all, to raise his head slightly, she could see the pained, puzzled expression narrow his eyes as he swallowed a spoonful. Then with a frown he turned his head from her impatiently.

'You must take three,' she insisted; 'you must, indeed, Mr Greyman. Then I will tell you—everything.'

His face came back to hers with the faintest shadow of his old mutinous sarcasm upon it, and he lay looking at her deliberately for a second or two. 'I thought you were a ghost,' he said feebly at last; 'only they don't bully. Well! let's get it over.'

The memory of many such a bantering reply to her insistence in the past sent a lump to her throat and kept her silent. The little low stool on which she had been wont to sit beside him was in its old place, and half mechanically she drew it closer, and resting her elbow on the bed as she used to do, looked round her, feeling as if the last six weeks were a dream. Tara had told truth. Everything was in its place. There were flowers in a glass, a spotless fringed cloth on the brass platter. The pity held in these trivial signs brought a fresh pang to her heart for that other woman.

But Jim Douglas, lying almost in the arms of death, was not thinking of such things.

'Then Delhi must have fallen,' he said suddenly in a stronger voice. 'Did Nicholson take it?'

'Yes,' she replied quietly, thinking it best to be concise and give him, as it were, a fresh grip on facts. 'It has fallen. The King is a prisoner, the princes have been shot, and most of the troops move on tomorrow towards Agra.'

Her words epitomized the situation beyond the possibility of doubt, and he gave a faint sigh. 'Then it is all over. I'm glad to hear it. Tara never knew anything; and it seemed so long.'

Had she known and refused to tell, Kate wondered? or in her insane absorption had she really thought of nothing but the chance Fate had thrown in her way of saving this man's life? Yes! it must have been very long. Kate realized this as she watched the spent and weary face before her, its bright hollow eyes fixed on the glow which was now fast fading from the dome. 'All over!' he murmured to himself. 'Well! I suppose it couldn't be helped.'

She followed his thought unerringly; and a great pity for this man who had done nothing, where others had done so much, surged up in her and made her seek to show his fate no worse than others. Besides, this discouragement was fatal, for it pointed to a lack of that desire for life which is the best weapon against death. She might fail to rouse him, as those had failed who, but a day or two before, had sent a bit of red ribbon representing the Victoria Cross to the dying Salkeld—the hero of the Kashmir gate—and only gained in reply a faint smile and the words, 'They will like it at home.' Still she would try.

'Yes, it is over!' she echoed, 'and it has cost so many lives uselessly. General Nicholson lost his trying to do the impossible—so people say.'

Jim Douglas still lay staring at the fading glow. 'Dead!' he murmured. 'That is a pity. But he took Delhi first. He said he would.'

'And my husband,' she began.

He turned then, with curiously patient courtesy. 'I know. Nicholson wrote that in his letter. And I have been glad—glad he had his chance, and—and—made so much of it.'

Once more she followed his thought; and knew that, though he was too proud to confess it, he was saying to himself that he had had his chance too and had done nothing. So she answered him as if he had spoken.

'And you had your chance of saving a woman,' she said, with a break in her voice, 'and you saved her. It isn't much, I suppose. It counts as nothing to you. Why should it? But to me—' she broke off, losing her purpose for him in her own bitter regret and vague resentment. 'Why didn't you let them kill me, and then go away,' she went on almost passionately, 'it would have been better than saving me to remember always that I stood in your way—better than giving me no chance of repaying you for all—ah! think how much! Better than leaving me alone to a new life—like—like all the others have done.'

She buried her face on her arm as it rested on the pillow with a sob. This, then, was the end, she thought, this bitter unavailing regret for both.

So for a space there was silence while she sat with her face hidden, and he lay staring at that darkening dome. But suddenly she felt his hot hand find hers; so thin, so soft, so curiously strong still in its grip.

'Give me some more wine or something,' came his voice consolingly. 'I'll try and stop—if I can.'

She made an effort to smile back at him, but it was not very successful. His, as she fed him, was better; but it did not help Kate Erlton to cheerfulness, for it was accompanied by a murmur that the *chikken-brât* was very different from Tara's stuff. So she seemed to see a poor ghost glowering at them from the shadows, asking her how she dared take all the thanks. And the ghost remained long after Jim Douglas had dozed off; remained to ask, so it seemed to Kate Erlton,

every question that could be asked about the mystery of womanhood
and manhood.

But Tara herself asked none when in the first grey glimmer of dawn
she crept up the stairs again and stood beside the sleepers. For Kate,
wearied out, had fallen asleep crouched up on the stool, her head
resting on the pillow, her arm flung over the bed to keep that touch on
his hand which seemed to bring him rest. Tara, once more in her
widow's dress, looked down on them silently, then threw her bare
arms upwards. So for a second she stood, a white-shrouded appealing
figure against that dark shadow of the dome which blocked the paling
eastern sky. Then stooping, her long, lissome fingers busied themselves
stealthily with the thin gold chain about the sick man's neck; for there
was something in the locket attached to it which was hers by right
now. Hers, if she could have nothing else; for she was *suttee—suttee!*

The unuttered cry was surging through her heart and brain, rousing
a mad exultation in her, when half-an-hour afterwards she re-entered
the narrow lane leading to the arcaded courtyard with the black old
shrine hiding under the tall *peepul* tree. And what was that hanging
over the congeries of roofs and stairs, the rabbit warnen of rooms and
passages where her pigeon-nest was perched? A canopy of smoke, and
below it leaping flames. There were many wanton fires in Delhi during
those first few days of licence, and this was one of them; but already, in
the dawn, English officers were at work giving orders, limiting the
danger as much as possible.

'We can't save that top bit,' said one at last, then turned to one of
his fatigue party. 'Have you cleared everybody out, sergeant, as I told
you?'

'Yes, sir! it's quite empty.'

It *had* been so five minutes before. It was not now; for that canopy
of smoke, those licking tongues of flame, had given the last touch to
Tara's unstable mind. She had crept up and up, blindly, and was now
on her knees in that bare room set round with her one scrap of culture,
ransacking an old basket for something which had not seen the light
for years—her scarlet, tinsel-set, wedding dress. Her hands were
trembling, her wild eyes blazed like fires themselves.

And below, men waited calmly for the flames to claim this, their last
prize; for the turret stood separated from the next house.

'My God!' came an English voice, as something showed suddenly
upon the roof. 'I thought you said it was empty—and that's a woman!'

It was. A woman in a scarlet, tinsel-set dress, and all the poor
ornaments she possessed upon her widespread arms. So, outlined
against the first sun ray she stood, her shrill chanting voice rising
above the roar and rush of the flames.

*'Oh! Guardians eight, of this world and the next. Sun, Moon, and Air, Earth, Ether, Water, and my own poor soul bear witness! Oh! Lord of death, bear witness that I come. Day, Night, and Twilight say I am suttee.'*

There was a louder roar, a sudden leaping of the flames, and the turret sank inwardly. But the chanting voice could be heard for a second in the increasing silence which followed.

'Shiv-*jee* hath saved His own,' said the crowd, looking towards the unharmed shrine.

And over on the other side of the city, Kate Erlton, roused by that same first ray of sunlight, was looking down with a smile upon Jim Douglas before waking him. The sky was clear as a topaz, the purple pigeons were cooing and sidling on the copings. And in the bright, fresh light she saw the gold locket lying open on the sleeper's breast. She had often wondered what it held, and now—thinking he might not care to find it at her mercy—stooped to close it.

But it was empty.

The snap, slight as it was, roused him. Not however to a knowledge of the cause, for he lay looking up at her in his turn.

'So it is all over,' he said softly, but he said it with a smile.

Yes! It was all over. Down on the parade ground behind the ridge the bugles were sounding, and the men who had clung to the red rocks for so long were preparing to leave them for assault elsewhere.

But one man was taking an eternal hold upon them; for John Nicholson was being laid in his grave. Not in the rearguard however, but in the van, on the outermost spur of the Ridge abutting on the city wall, within touch almost of the Kashmir gate. Being laid in his grave—by his own request—without escort, without salute; for he knew that he had failed.

So he lies there facing the city he took. But his real grave was in that narrow lane within the walls where those who dream can see him still, alone, ahead, with yards of sheer sunlight between him and his fellow-men.

Yards of sheer sunlight between that face with its confident glance forward, that voice with its clear cry, 'Come on, men, come on,' and those—the mass of men—who with timorous look backwards hear in that call to go forward nothing but the vain regret for things familiar that must be left behind—

'Going, going, gone!'

So, in a way, John Nicholson stands symbol of the many lives lost uselessly in the vain attempt to go forward too fast.

Yet his voice echoes still to the dark faces and the light alike—

'Come on, men! Come on!'

# BOOK VI

## Appendices

# Appendix A
### (Enclosed in Appendix B)

*From* A. Dashe, *Collector and Magistrate of Kiyalpore, to* R. Tape, Esq., *Commissioner and Superintendent of Kwâbabad.*
   *Fol. No O.*

*Dated 11th May 1858*

Sir,—In reply to your No. 103 of the 20th April requesting me to report on the course of the Mutiny in my district, the measures taken to suppress it, and its effects, if any, on the judicial, executive, and financial work under my charge, I have the honour to enclose a brief statement, which for convenience sake I have drafted under the usual headings of the annual report which I was unable to send in till last week. I regret the delay, but the pressure of work in the English office due to the revising of forfeiture and pension lists made it unavoidable.—I have the honour, etc., etc.,

A. Dashe, *Coll. and Magte.*

*Introductory Remarks*[1]—So far as my district is concerned, the late disturbances have simply been a military mutiny. At no time could they be truthfully called a rebellion. In the outlying posts, indeed, the people knew little or nothing of what was going on around them, and even in the towns resistance was not thought of until the prospect of any immediate suppression of the mutiny disappeared.

The small force of soldiers in my district of course followed the example of their brethren. Nothing else could be expected from our position midway between two large cantonments; indeed the continuous stream of mutinous troops which passed up and down the main road during the summer had a decidedly bad effect.

I commenced to disperse the disturbers of the public peace on the 21st May. These were largely escaped felons from the Meerut jail; and

[1]Every statement in this supposed report has been gleaned from a real one, or from official papers published at the time. I am responsible for nothing but—very occasionally—the wording.

the fact that they were quite indiscriminate in their lawlessness enabled me to rally most of the well-doing people on my side. I hanged a few of the offenders, and having enlisted a small corps with the aid of some native gentlemen (whose names I append for reference), sent it out under charge of my assistant (I myself being forced throughout the whole business to remain at headquarters and keep a grip on things) to put down some Goojurs and other predatory tribes who took occasion to resort to their ancestral habits of life.

No real opposition, however, was ever met with; but in June (after our failure to take Delhi by a *coup de main* became known) there was an organized attempt to seize the Treasury. Fortunately I had some twenty or thirty of my new levy in headquarters at the time, so that the attempt failed and I was able to bring one or two of the ringleaders (one, I regret to say, a man of considerable importance in my district), to justice.

I subsequently made several applications to the nearest cantonment for a few European soldiers to escort my treasure—some two lakhs—to safer quarters. But this, unfortunately, could not be granted to me, so I had to keep a strong guard of men over the money, who might have been more useful elsewhere.

Until the fall of Delhi matters remained much the same. Isolated bands of marauders ravaged portions of my district, often, I regret to say, escaping before punishment could be meted out to them. The general feeling was one of disquiet and alarm to both Europeans and natives. My table attendant, for instance, absented himself from dinner one day, sending a substitute to do his work, under the belief that I had given orders for a general slaughter of Mahommedans that evening. I had done nothing of the kind.

After the fall of Delhi, as you are aware, the mutinous fugitives, some fifty or sixty thousand strong, marched southwards in a compact body and caused us much alarm. But after camping on the outskirts of my district for a few days, they suddenly disappeared. I am told they dispersed during one night, each to his own home. Anyhow they literally melted away, and the public mind seemed to become aware that the contest was over, and that the struggle to subvert British rule had ignominiously failed. Matters therefore assumed a normal aspect, but I believe that there is more shame, sorrow, and regret in the hearts of many than we shall probably ever have full cognizance of, and that it will take years for the one race to regain its confidence, the other its self-respect.

*Civil Judicature*—The courts were temporarily suspended for a week or two; after that original work went on much as usual, but the appellate work suffered. There was an indisposition both to institute and hear appeals, possibly due to the total eclipse of the higher appellate courts. I myself had little leisure for civil cases.

*Criminal Justice*—There has been far less crime than usual during the past year. Possibly because much of it had necessarily to be treated summarily and so did not come on the record. I am inclined to believe, however, that petty offences really are fewer when serious crime is being properly dealt with.

*Police*—The less said about the behaviour of the police the better. The force simply melted away; but as it was always inefficient its absence had little effect. Save, perhaps, in a failure to bring up those trivial offences mentioned in the last para.

*Jail*—The jail was happily preserved throughout; for the addition of four or five hundred felons to the bad characters of my district might have complicated matters. I was peculiarly fortunate in this, since I learn that only nine out of the forty-three jails in the Province were so held.

*Revenue (Sub-head, Land)*—The arrears under this head are less than usual, and there seems no reason to apprehend serious loss to Government.

*(Opium)*—There has, I regret to say, been considerable detriment to our revenue under this head, due to the fact that the smuggling of the drug is extremely easy, owing to its small bulk, and that the demand was greater than usual.

*(Stamps)*—The revenue here shows an increase of Rs 72,000. I am unable to account for this, unless the prevailing uncertainty made the public mind incline towards what security it could compass in the matter of bonds, agreements, etc.

*(Salt and Customs)*—This department shows a very creditable record. My subordinates, with the help of a few volunteers, were able to maintain the Customs line throughout the whole disturbances. Its value as a preventative of roving lawlessness cannot be overestimated. Four hundred and eighty-two smugglers were punished, and the Customs brought in Rs 33,770 more than in 1856. But the work done by this handful of isolated European patrols—with only a few natives under them—to the cause of law and order, cannot be estimated in money.

*Education*—The higher education went on as usual. Primary instruction suffered. Female schools disappeared altogether.

*Public Works*—Many things combined to stop anything like a vigorous prosecution of new public works, and those in hand were greatly retarded.

*Post-Office*—The work in this department suffered occasional lapses owing to the murder of solitary runners by lawless ruffians, but the service continued fairly efficient. An attempt was made, by the

388 • A RAJ COLLECTION

confiscation of sepoys' letters, to discover if any organized plan of attack or resistance was in circulation, but nothing incriminatory was found, the correspondence consisting chiefly of love-letters.

*Financial*—At one time the necessary cash for the pay of establishments ran short, but this was met by bills upon native bankers, who have since been repaid.

*Hospitals*—The dispensaries were in full working order throughout the year, and the number of cases treated—especially for wounds and hurts, many of them grievous—above the average.

*Health and Population*—Both were normal, and the supply of food grains ample. Markets strong, and well supplied throughout. Some grain stores were burnt, some plundered; but, as a rule, if A robbed B, B in his turn robbed C. So the matter adjusted itself. In many cases also, the booty was restored amicably when it became evident that Government could hold its own.

*Agriculture*—Notwithstanding the violence of contest, the many instances of plundered and burnt villages, the necessary impressment of labour and cattle, and the licence of mutineers consorting with felons, agricultural interests did not suffer. Ploughing and sowing went on steadily, and the land was well covered with a full winter crop.

*General Remarks*—Beyond these plundered and burnt villages, which are still somewhat of an eyesore, though they are recovering themselves rapidly, the only result of the Mutiny to be observed in my district is that money seems scarcer, and so the cultivators have to pay a higher rate of interest on loans.

There are, of course, some empty chairs in the district durbar. I append a list of their late occupants also, and suggest that the vacancies might be filled from the other list, as some of those gentlemen who helped to raise the levy have not yet got chairs.

In regard to future punishments, however, I venture to suggest that orders should be issued limiting the period during which mutineers can be brought to justice. If some such check on malicious accusation be not laid down we shall have a fine crop of false cases, perjuries, etc., since the late disturbances have, naturally, caused a good many family differences. In view of this also, I believe it would be safest, in the event of such accusations in the future, to punish the whole village to which the alleged mutineer belongs, by a heavy fine rather than to single out individuals as examples. In a case like the present it is extremely difficult to measure the exact proportion of guilt attachable to each member of the community, and, even with the very greatest care, I find it is not always possible to hang the right man. And this is a difficulty which will increase as time goes on.

# Appendix B

Dear Mrs Erlton,—I can scarcely believe that two whole years have passed since I helped you to decorate a Christmas-tree in the Government College here. Those long months before the walls, and those others of wild chase after vanishing mutineers over half India seem to belong to some one else's existence now that I—and the world around me—are back in the commonplaces of life. I was down today helping the chaplain's wife with another tree—she has a very pretty sister, by the way, just out from England—and I almost fancied, as I looked into the dim screened verandah where we are going to have an entertainment, that I could see you sitting there with little Sonny Seymour on your lap as I found you that afternoon half asleep when that interminable play about the Lord of Life and Death (wasn't it?) had been too much for you.

Well, I can only hope that Mr Douglas's health and the pleasures of that Scotch home, of which you wrote me such a delightful description, will allow of your returning to India sometime and giving me a sight of you again.

Meanwhile I am reminded that I sent you off a small parcel by last mail which I trust may arrive before the wedding—as this should do— and convey to you the kindly remembrances of friends many thousand miles away. Not that you will need to be reminded. I fancy that few who went through the Indian Mutiny will ever need to have the faces and places they saw there recalled to their memory. Terrible as it was at the time, I myself feel that I would not willingly forget a single detail. So, being certain that it holds your interest, your imagination also, I am enclosing something for you to read. Can you not imagine the Silent and Diffident Dashe writing it? I can, and the careful way in which he would order the gallows to be removed, and lay down his sword in favour of his pen at the earliest opportunity. You see he favours Clemency Canning. So do most of us out here except those who have not yet recovered their nerves. I remember hearing Hodson—sad, wasn't it? his death over a needless piece of dare-devilry—very angry

over something Mr Douglas said about our all being in a blind funk. I
am afraid it was true of a good many. Not Dashe, however; he kept his
district together by sheer absence of fear, and so did many another.
This report, then, will carry you on in the story, as it were, since you
left us. As you will see, it is all over except the shouting; except
honours and hanging. Regarding these, two items may interest you.
Bukt-Khân escaped the latter, escaped even the exile which, as you
know, overtook the King and Queen; but his fate was—if tales be
true—quite satisfactory. He was over-ridden by his own soldiers in a
rout. Concerning honours; when the troopers of the 9th Lancers were
called on for a nominee to receive the V.C. they sent up the name of
the regimental *bhistie*. What is more, they refused to amend their
selection on the ground that if he didn't get it no one else deserved it.
So it wasn't given. Government has very little tact. Have you heard of
the British soldier chalking up '*Delhi taken and India saved for Rs 30/8/*
*6*' on the walls of the palace? That is the amount of *batta;* but I think
the promised prize-money will be given eventually. For the rest, there
is not much to tell. You remember our old mess khansaman Mungal
Khan? He turned up, *with his bill,* and out of pure delight insisted on
feasting us so lavishly that we had to make him moderate his
transports. Even with *batta* and prize-money we should all have been
bankrupt, like the Royal Family. I can't help pitying it. Of course we
have pensioned the lot, but I expect precious little hard cash gets to
some of those wretched women. One of them, no less a person than the
princess Farkhoonda Zamâni—that beast Abool-Bukr's ally—has set up
a girls' school in the city. If she had only befriended you instead of
turning you out to find your own fate, she would have done better for
herself. Talking of friends and foes, it is rather amusing to find the
villages full of men busy at their ploughs with a suspicioulsy military
set about the shoulders, who, according to their own showing, never
wore uniform or doffed it before the Mutiny began. I was much struck
with one of these defaulters the other day; a big Rajpoot, who, but for
his name, might have stood for the Laodicean sepoy you told me
about. But names can be changed, so can faces; and that reminds me
that I had a petition from that old scoundrel Tiddu the other day—you
know I have been put on to civil work lately, and shall end, I suppose,
by being a Commissioner as well as a Colonel—he has had a grant of
land given him for life, and he now wants the tenure extended in
favour of one Jhungi, who, he declares, helped you in your marvellous
escape. It seems there was another brother, one Bhungi, who—but I
own to being a little confused in the matter. Perhaps you can set me
straight. Meanwhile, I have pigeon-holed the Jhungi-Bhungi claim until
I hear from you. The old man was well, and asked fervently after

Sonny, who, by the way, goes home from Lucknow in the spring. I expect the Seymours are about the only family in India which came out of the business unscathed; yet they were in the thick of it. Truly the whole thing was a mystery from beginning to end. I asked a native yesterday if he could explain it, but he only shook his head and said the Lord had sent a 'breath into the land.' But the most remarkable thing to my mind about the whole affair is the rapidity with which it proved the stuff a man was made of. You can see that by looking into the cemeteries. India is a dead level for the present; all the heads that towered above their fellows laid low. Think of them all! Havelock, Lawrence, Outram—the names crowd to one's lips; but they seem to begin and end with one—Nicholson!

Well, good bye! I have not wished you luck—that goes without saying; but tell Douglas I'm glad he had his chance.—Ever yours truly,

CHARLES MORECOMBE

# Siri Ram—Revolutionist*

## A Transcript from Life
## 1907–1910

### Edmund Candler

* First published by Constable & Company Limited
London 1912

# CONTENTS

# Preface

The beginning of 1912 found Edmund Candler hard at work as Principal of Mohindra College in the Indian princely state of Patiala. This was the year that *Siri Ram—Revolutionist* was published. Candler's personal letters to his family in England show that he had been working on the novel for over a year, as and when he could spare the time from his College work. *Siri Ram* was his first novel, and he decided to publish it anonymously for reasons which he explained to his brother Henry:

My book [of short stories, *The General Plan*, published in 1911] has fallen flat. I believe if I had published it anonymously—say by Macmillan, it would have been a success. It is partly Blackwood's [the publisher's] want of initiative & partly perhaps that having a reputation in one line is a bar to being taken seriously in another. . . . *Siri Ram*, tract as it is, ought to go better—being anonymous. (9.7.11)

The genesis of *Siri Ram* went back as far as 1909, when Candler wrote to his sister Katherine in England:

I only have the abstract theme of it & no plot. I could write it without a European in it, but Blackwood & his readers demand a girl with pink cheeks & fair hair—but how to mix such up with seditionists. The only Indians they ever speak to are servants. (30.12.09)

As I have indicated above, the novel was originally intended for Blackwood, whom Candler intended to ask about its suitability for serialization. However, while feeling loyal to that firm, whose principal, William Blackwood, had been very friendly and supportive to him over the years, he blamed the disappointing reception of his last two books at least in part on the way Blackwood had launched them ('. . . he only gets books now on his *name* and he won't *push* them . . .'). And in the end he gave the publication to Constable through William Meredith (son of the novelist George Meredith), who had approached him to write something for them after his wife had been affected by one of the stories in *The General Plan*.

Candler's developing attitude to *Siri Ram* is revealed in his letters to Katherine, with whom he corresponded regularly. Although he originally described it as his 'sedition book', he told her that the abstract theme was 'the relations between pale and brown folk'. (2.3.11) Later, in the course of the writing, he became depressed about it, at one point feeling it was 'perfunctory'. On 11 June 1911 he wrote to Katherine:

*Siri Ram*'s effort only teaches me that like many better men I haven't a ghost of a faculty for writing a novel. Something ought to run right through the book holding the reader in suspense—but I haven't got the 'something' or any idea of connecting separate pictures.

On 9 July he wrote to Henry, ' . . . it is degenerating into a political tract'. However, by November he felt more confident: 'I feel now the construction & writing of it are all right. It is well-knit together, & the Indian characters, Siri Ram, Narasimha Swami, Ramji Das, Mohan Roy, Banarsi Das, Lachmi Chand, are fairly individualized—although the English folk stand for one type.' (6.11.11)

The novel is set in 1907–10 and is subtitled 'A Transcript from Life'. Candler had lived and worked in the Punjab throughout those years and had personal knowledge of the political background. The main British character, the College Principal, Skene, is drawn on his own experience as Principal of Mohindra College. For instance, the opening—where Skene reluctantly attends an evening lecture to students of Gandeshwar College by Swami Narasimha instead of playing tennis at the Club—mirrors his own preferences as to how he should spend his spare time. 'Skene had been deeply interested in the Swami', but afterwards 'he breathed the air of the Club with relief. He had not spoken to an Englishman all day.'

The years from 1907 to 1910 were those when the names of Bal Gangadhar Tilak and Aurobindo Ghose, as mouthpieces of Indian nationalism, were on the lips of anyone who professed to know anything about India. After the unpopular partition of Bengal in 1905, public protests, including boycotts of foreign goods and student disturbances, took place there. At the same time, the list of deeds of violence aimed at Britons in Bengal and the Deccan, which had started in 1897 with the murder of two British officials at Poona, grew longer. In April 1908 a Mrs and Miss Kennedy were killed at Muzafferpur by a bomb intended for the Magistrate, Mr Kingsland. Other bomb explosions followed in Calcutta, and four attempts were made on the life of the Lieutenant Governor of Bengal. Candler was mindful of all this while writing his novel.

Meanwhile trouble, partly agricultural in origin, broke out in the Punjab, where successful irrigation schemes undertaken by the Government had led to the settlement of areas formerly too dry for cultivation. These are the 'canal colonies' referred to in *Siri Ram*. Proposed changes in the landholding arrangements in these colonies, although intended to benefit the tenant-farmers, coincided with an increased land-assessment and a sudden rise in irrigation rates, and proved so unpopular that the Government came to fear insurrection in the Army, in which many of the tenants' relatives were enlisted. As a result, the proposals were dropped. But the damage had been done, adding fuel to other causes of discontent. There was a serious riot at Rawalpindi on 2 May 1907, and on 9 May, the day before the Fiftieth Anniversary of the Mutiny, Lala Lajpat Rai, a Congress member well known in Lahore as a member of the Arya Samaj, was deported without charge or trial under the powers of an old Regulation. Ajit Singh (not a member of the Samaj), who had started an 'Indian Patriots' Association' to press agricultural grievances, was similarly deported. While it is not clear that the deportations referred to in *Siri Ram* are intended to refer to the actual deportations which took place in May 1907, they did lead to consequences very relevant to the book's later fortunes, including a libel suit instigated by Lala Lajpat Rai.

The publication of the book in 1912 went relatively unnoticed at first, but eventually caused quite a stir in India. *The Pioneer* carried a lively exchange of letters between the author and a Mr Andrews, in the course of which Andrews described the novel as 'an offence to every Indian who reads it'. Candler, in turn, charged Andrews with mis-representing the Pundit's address to the Gurukul as presented in Part IV of the novel.

In writing *Siri Ram*, Candler must have been aware of the sensitive nature of his material, but can hardly have expected a libel suit. In his private letters of 1913 he mentions the possibility of bankruptcy if the action were successful, but he was loth to 'knuckle under', as he put it. George Blackwood (the nephew of William Blackwood who had meanwhile died) wrote to Candler on 30 March 1914:

I have seen something about the excitement which your book *Siri Ram* has created in India, and I hope the libel action has been squashed and the book put in circulation again.

He wrote again on 4 June 1914:

I wonder how the trouble with *Siri Ram* has progressed, and if the book is still withdrawn from sale? I trust it is not giving you personally a lot of bother.

This shows that Blackwood had not been offended by Candler's decision to place the book with Constable, and the firm was probably quite pleased to have escaped legal involvement as its publisher. Candler continued to write for Blackwood until his death in 1926. The new edition of the novel which appeared in 1914 did contain some changes, though Candler's final word on this matter was to his brother Henry in a letter dated 18 May 1914: '*The Prakash* (an Arya vernacular newspaper) is still hammering away at me. Still, I am glad I wrote *Siri Ram*.'

Aldenham, Herts, U.K.                                     Rachael Corkill

# PART I

## The College

And he said, as he counted his beads and smiled,
'God smite their souls to the depth of hell!'

SIR ALFRED LYALL

# 1

S kene's resolution nearly failed him as he was driving to the meeting in the city. His pony wanted to turn into the Club gates, and a similar inclination nearly swung him round. He pulled up a moment to watch the tennis-four in which he ought to have been playing. It was a keen game, and he drove on reluctantly, feeling that he had been foolish to commit himself. What is life worth if one is immured from five to seven under a roof listening to talk? And it was the beginning of the cold weather. Exercise in the interval between work and dinner is as essential to an Englishman as air; but for the native of India talk is the only recreation—at a meeting if possible; if not, at his own or a neighbour's house. The Indian has no hobby. He is incapable of being bored.

For three years Skene had been pestered to preside at meetings, or 'to grace' some 'occasion' with his 'august presence'. But he was lamentably wanting in public spirit. This was only the second time he had undertaken to attend a gathering at Gandeshwar. He had shocked Lala Ram Prasad, 'the energetic secretary' of the municipality, by saying that anything that needed to be said publicly might be said in a dozen words. His students did not sympathize with this trait in their Principal. Some of them he used to herd off to cricket and football in the evenings, but the majority were more voluble than their elders. The more active-minded, if they did anything at all, were happiest at a meeting, reading or listening to addresses, votes of confidence, memorials, resolutions—oceans of verbiage leading nowhither.

So while Lala Ram Prasad was haranguing the citizens in the Town Hall, saying that every right-minded and self-respecting individual viewed with horror and detestation the revolting and heinous crime of some bloodthirsty and abandoned anarchist, Banarsi Das would be declaiming at the College that it behoved each and every young man to shun the ways of wickedness and violence as they would the deadly adder and the hissing serpent.

The pony made an effort to turn down a side lane to the polo ground, but Skene held him citywards with grim humour, thinking of the last meeting he had attended three years before in a Gothic façade of red bricks with the ends of the girders protruding from the wall. He remembered the crowded hall, his ineffable weariness and the smell of tightly-packed humanity with the thermometer at 104°F in the shade.

Every face set in a mould of serious complacency that made it seem the wildest dream in the world that any one of them could ever possibly connive at an end. They spoke for hours, and all the while he knew, and every one else knew, that nothing would be done to promote the worthy end in view beyond the expression of its desirability in the same sequence of platitudes. Still it was an opportunity for the ingenious application of strange idiom.

Skene hardened himself with the thought that it was his business to hear Narasimha Swami. No doubt it would be physically exhausting, but most of his students would be there, and he was interested to see the little superman who had gained such an extraordinary influence over the youth of India and to discover if possible where his magnetism lay. The Swami was going to give a religious address to the young men in Gandeshwar, and all the Europeans in the station had been invited. The man was known to be a dangerous agitator, but he was too clever to be run down. He was identified with the spiritual side of the revolutionary movement in the same way as Tilak was with the political. His influence in the north of India rivalled that of Arabindo Ghose in Bengal, and it was the more dangerous as the material he had to work upon was hardier and more robust.

When Skene arrived, the Swami had begun his address. As he had expected, there was only one other European present, a missionary; but the hall was crammed with natives, among whom he recognized many of his students and professors. Nearly all the Hindus of the college were there and a sprinkling of Sikhs. It took him some seconds to realize that the meeting was different from anything he had imagined. He was in an atmosphere of intense excitement. He saw a thin, fragile little man standing alone on a platform, a palpable ascetic. And out of this weak frame issued a volume of sound which rang true with a genuine message. The Swami was informed with a spirit which seemed to shake him like a gust of wind. Sometimes, when he paused and threw out his arms and held them motionless after some burst of eloquence, you could see his thin, salmon-coloured shift vibrate with inward emotion like a dragon-fly's wing. The young men were spellbound by it. Not a word would he utter until the quivering was still. The outstretched hand thrust the question home at them as the thunder in which it had been delivered died away. He seemed to be waiting for one of them to answer him, but no answer was possible.

At last his hands dropped to his sides in the hush, and a sad, mirthless smile stole into his eyes, more eloquent than any declamation. Every young man in the hall knew that he had been weighed and found wanting, as if the Swami had cried aloud, 'Of course I know it all—I have always known it. And yet . . .'

Then, before the faint, irresistible appeal was raised again that was to swell into an organ note, every young man knew that he was forgiven, that there was hope, individually and for all.

Theatrical! Skene felt it was too harsh a word. This little husk of humanity, with his shrunken limbs and his bright eyes sunk deep in their sockets, was the most spiritual-looking man he had seen. Yet he felt somehow that the speech was disingenuous. There had not been a word about politics. The few allusions to Government, the British, and the Christians had been moderate and natural. Yet there was more in it all than met the ear. He felt that a message had been conveyed to the young men that had passed over his head, and that they had responded.

After that vibrating silence the address became purely scriptural. The high, passionate ring died out of it, and for twenty minutes the Swami spoke in a hushed whisper, which penetrated every corner, as if he had just come through a hidden door through which he was going to lead them. But first he must prepare them for the sacred mysteries that lay the other side. In another moment he would hold back the curtain. The Samajists believed that they were in the presence of a man who had seen what he was speaking of. It was impossible that they should not, for the slow, deliberate accents were conveyed in just that pitch of voice raised above a whisper which compels the belief of every soul in the room. The pauses were impressive for the fulness behind, the dammed-up welling stream, to be distributed when all channels were prepared but now withheld. The restraint was as effective as the Swami's control of the spirit that had seemed about to possess his feeble frame in the earlier part of the speech. He was telling them to go back to the Vedas.

'Go back to the Vedas', he said; 'they contain all wisdom. Modern youths smile at them. "Wild fantasies", you call them. Ah, do not believe this. I myself was a young man and a scoffer once like some of you. But I have come to understand that the sayings of the Hindu religion are not false. I realize more and more the signs and symbols by which it has spoken. It is my will to take you with me that way. To help you to see those lights, to listen to those voices. You will hear in them the voice of the initiated speaking to the ignorant in fables. You are proud of the knowledge you are carrying away from your schools and colleges—Physics, Chemistry, Electricity, Evolution. That is well. Glean what you can from your new teachers. But remember that in their search for truth they are groping now through the accumulated wisdom of centuries towards a plane of knowledge which the ancient Vedantists took at a leap. How? By conquest of the flesh; by victory over self; by communion with the spirits; by the realization of the Infinite.'

Again the hushed voice, the vibrating pause, the tremulous shift, the bright eyes sunk in their sockets.

'Now I am going to prove to you that the wildest dreams of modern Science were known to the Rishis.

'Take first three simple truths—the date of the Creation, the origin of sex, the magnetism of the earth.

'How many years is it since the last Pralaya—the last obscuration of life on the planet? I do not mean the first beginnings of life which we read of in the Book of Genesis in the Christian Bible. Genesis speaks of four thousand years since the Spirit, that is God, informed chaos and created the earth. Turn to the Vedas, you will find a date that harmonizes more with scientific investigation—nineteen million years; not since the first creation but since the last Pralaya. And here, too, modern Science with its carefully sifted data tells us of cataclysms, upheavals, submergences, corresponding with our Vedic Manvantara and Pralaya, earth-periods of energy and rest.

'And what do the Vedas teach you of the origin of sex? Not the Christian conception that mankind was always sexual, male and female, as you read in the Bible, from the beginning. Science tells us that is not so. In all forms of life there is first the a-sexual, then the bi-sexual, then the sexual. The Rishis knew this, but how were the ignorant to understand? It had to be explained to them in the parables which some of you in your ignorance despise.

'Then again, what of the magnetism of the earth? You are told in the Vedas, when you sleep, to lie with your head and feet north and south. "Why not east and west?" you say. "Is not this all of a piece with the other mummery? Superstitious charlatanism—or at the least mere forms and rules, a ritual to impress barbarians?" Ah! do not think it, my dear young friends! There is no babble in the Vedas. Believe me, it is wrong to lie east and west. Those grand old men, your ancestors, who found God in Nature, knew this. The properly sensitized body cannot sleep so. Many of us Indians cannot now. But we have lost our finer physical faculties. Like our souls they have become deadened. We are no longer attuned to the Universe. The old Rishis needed no compass. They felt the north in their veins. And when they stretched themselves out to sleep, their blood pulsed freely to the heart, and every nerve and vein and cell played in harmony with the mysterious current that pervades the earth and links it with the stars. It is against nature to sleep athwart this current. Thus we pervert our organism, as we have perverted our souls. Both are vessels which God has filled with the Essence of life which we spill and squander every day we live.

'In Europe a few years back Science proclaimed with great blare of trumpets the Magnetism of the Earth, the Circulation of the Blood. Dear young men, we are a fallen people. Thousands of years ago your ancestors, whose word you despise, knew these secrets, the fringe of which you are now inheriting with an alien culture. They did not publish them in intellectual pride—pride, indeed, is a modern birth—but every simple rule of life which they inculcated upon the people was inspired by these laws—laws which you now call mysterious, though to the old sages they were the facts of life which came without seeking. Free of the dross, the deceits, the illusions of the world, they were attuned to the Infinite. They could read the book of Nature, the orderings of life. The flesh did not enchain them. They communed with spirits. They dwelt in the future and the past. The beginning and the end were revealed to them, from the first dim consciousness that informed matter to the ranging soul of man losing itself in the Infinite. The first groupings of the atoms, the energies that controlled them, and the part each electron played in the cosmic process upon which their fleeting lives were reflected as in a dream. And they have enshrined these truths in their sacred, obscure books for you to read. Ah! Go back to the Vedas. You will find all wisdom there.'

Skene watched his students. Siri Ram, Banarsi Das, Lachmi Chand, the trio whom he believed to be most affected by political unrest, were clearly in the toils. His eyes did not deceive him. Siri Ram was glowing with the spiritual pride of his race. But he was perplexed. What of the present? How were the Hindus to take the place they should inherit by their ancient wisdom? Where was their power and strength?

Skene listened in vain for a breath of political discontent, but there was no hint of it. Only a few words about indolence and indifference, the need to send out teachers, the loss to the religion through apathy and disunion. But at these obvious truisms there was a stir in the assembly, 'a little noiseless noise among the leaves', and the lecture was ended.

# 2

Skene had been deeply interested in the Swami, but he breathed the air of the Club with relief. He had not spoken to an Englishman all day. As he drove into the gates the impish, uniformed little boys in red caps were taking down the tennis nets, and the few men who had been playing were putting on their sweaters or drifting off to the bridge room or library. He was warmed by the way they greeted him. Working among Orientals makes a man observant of his own people: he notices distinctive traits, which folk at home take as a matter of course, with the acute perception of a foreigner. Skene enjoyed the atmosphere of friendly, personal chaff in which he found himself. He liked the easy way the Briton has of putting away serious things and his horror of the profession of a code. It was a relief to be among people who never 'inaugurated' or 'promoted' or 'ameliorated' anything, though they did more honest work in a day than a regiment of propagandists.

No one looking at the two men who joined him would have known that either of them had a thought outside polo or bridge or golf, yet Hobbs commanded a regiment, and Innes was Commissioner of the District. Their work was part of their tissue, and tradition sat lightly on them. Merivale, the smooth-faced little civilian on the chair, would have disowned an 'ideal' as hotly as the imputation of having shot a pigeon sitting, and Innes, who had just fought a famine, had been overheard by his secretary profanely 'damning causes' while waiting to receive a deputation.

Skene, upon cross-examination, pleaded guilty to having attended a seditious meeting. His defence was curiosity. He deprecated the argument that he, *quâ* Principal of a college, was himself a sedition-monger and an instiller of radical and subversive ideas into the callow young.

Hobbs demolished Narasimha in a few forcible phrases: 'A mischievous agitator. A canting, hypocritical humbug. His religion is all eyewash. Besides, these educated college fellows are not the men the people want.'

The others laughed. It was the voice of the old school whose rule was comfortably paternal. There was no sophistry in it. 'Treat 'em well, but no damned nonsense.' A soothing echo to the modern official who moves in intricacies and knots. It would not have occurred to any of them to discuss 'legitimate aspirations' with Hobbs, but Moon, a young Cambridge missionary, who was standing near, overhead him and politely remonstrated.

'I beg your pardon, sir, but I was at the lecture. There was really not a word of sedition in it. Narasimha is absolutely *pucca*.'

Hobbs stared at him.

'Do a lot of good if we strung a few of those fellows up. Save trouble in the end.'

Merivale intervened humanely.

'They didn't invite Englishmen to give themselves away. That was all a blind, of course. What do you think was said afterwards?' He appealed to Dean. 'I suppose you had a man there.'

'The lecture was probably only ground-bait,' the policeman said. 'Did he say anything about the English?'

'Yes, but in praise only.'

'Did he say anything about our unity?'

Moon had to admit that he did.

'Then you may be quite sure that it was sedition. That is an old trick. They harp on the absence of co-operation. No doubt Narasimha lauded the English in this respect, and said that they trusted one another and hung together in an emergency in a way the Indians cannot do. And he flattered us by telling the meeting to take a leaf out of our book. But what did he mean? You are fifty times stronger than the British if you combine your forces. Combine them, then, and kick them out.'

'I really think you are mistaken in Narasimha,' Moon objected. 'He has often been over to the Mission. My impression is that he is a deeply religious man, very sincere and single-minded, and he is doing a lot of good here.'

'A good bit too single-minded. My dear fellow, I have his record in the office. The man has all the instincts of a wolf. He has been home and all that, taken a degree, sipped tea in Bayswater drawing-rooms, read papers to the Asiatic Society, lectured in America; but he is a Bengali Lingayat still, and always will be. They draw their religion from the Tantras. They are just as fanatical as Wahabis, and far more bloodthirsty. I know the breed.'

'Talking about wolves,' Hobbs interrupted, yawning, 'have you seen that borzoi of Mrs Lee's?'

'Don't ride him off,' Merivale whispered. 'I want to hear about this fellow. What is he doing among the Arya Samaj?'[1]

'You may well ask. That is what damns him more than anything. They have nothing on earth in common. They are at opposite poles. Cats and dogs. Nothing would induce him to hunt with that pack but common hunger.'

'The blood of an Englishman.'

'Of course. The union is political. His mission is to introduce the Bengal system into the Punjab. You know Narasimha is not his real name. He adopted it for convenience. You can't pin the man down to any dogma. He'll take what suits him from anywhere.'

Moon, remembering the Swami's 'Back to the Vedas' cry, which is the rallying-point of the Aryas, began to feel uncomfortable. Hobbs

[1]See note at conclusion of volume.

and Dean were drawn off to the bridge room, and he gravitated towards Skene, hoping for sympathy there. But Skene would not expatiate on Swaraj.

'I don't like talking about the fitness or unfitness of Indians for self-government,' he said. 'It sounds too much like cant. The country is ours after all, and we won it as fairly as countries ever have been won. There is no question of handing it over. When the Indians are strong enough to govern it, they will be strong enough to take it, and they won't ask us. But I don't think it will be in our time.'

'But you wouldn't retard them?'

'Of course not. Let them make themselves fit. I do not respect a man who is not a nationalist.'

'Then you respect Narasimha Swami?'

'Certainly I respect him. He is doing what he thinks the straight thing—the term is relative—for his country, but it is our business to draw his teeth. If we hesitate on account of some vague humanitarian principles we are not playing the game. But I'm tired of politics. Let's play bridge.'

Moon did not play. He went off wrapped up in ethical difficulties, and Skene was glad to be left alone. He lay back in a long chair in the verandah, ordered a drink, and watched his own kind. It amused him to compare the people he worked with and the people he played with. The people he worked with had no interests. Their minds were fallow when they were hitched off the particular routine that earned them a living. It soothed him and made him feel at home to spend the evening with his countrymen, though their preoccupations were little more logical, or creditable, if you analysed them, than the Indian's apathy. Nevertheless the plunge from one to the other was refreshing.

The door of the ladies' and men's bridge room opened into the verandah where he was sitting, and his chair commanded a view of two tables at close quarters. At one a woman with a stern, careworn face under a picture hat garlanded with sweet-peas reviewed her cards with evident perplexity. Her partner, Mrs O'Shaughnessy, was making furtive dabs at a plate of chipped potatoes which she shared with a very solid, gruff-voiced lady with three chins. The fourth, a heavy, sub-bovine girl with sloe eyes, enjoyed a plate to herself owing to Dummy's preoccupation, and was making headway with it. When she had cleared the *débris* she asked—

'Did any one declare?'

'I left it to Sweet-peas.' Mrs O'Shaughnessy's rich provincial brogue decorated the commonplace. Spurred by her sally the sad, equine-faced lady looked up solemnly and made it spades.

The other table was more aristocratic, but there was less *bonhomie*.

Skene heard the acid voice of the chaplain's wife, a palpable loser—

'I thought you were weak and weak.'

'So I am.'

'Then why discard a spade?'

'Wasn't it a club? I think it was.'

'And didn't you see my call?'

The demure, frightened little mouse-like lady did not know what a call was, but she dared not admit it. In the meanwhile she had forgotten to ask if she might play. After a long pause the accusing silence of her partner awakened her to the new dilemma.

'Oh yes, please. I am sorry. I mean, may I play?' and she began to lay her cards on the table.

'You are not Dummy.'

'Oh no, of course not, how stupid!'

The chaplain's wife, with an expression of infinite forbearance, asked the dealer if she claimed that the cards were exposed. She did not, and Dummy laid her hand upon the table. Three aces and a suit of six, and they only wanted the odd. The little person was very near tears, feeling that the acerbity of the chaplain's wife implicated her somehow unfairly in the failure. Skene was sure that the padre's lady was mentally cancelling an order for a ham, or a new hat for one of the children. Even at those low points it meant that the padre would have to keep the lampshade in the dining-room, which was already in rags, another month. He was sorry for them both.

An uproar at the other table drew his attention to the more plebeian group. Sweet-peas had revoked. Mrs O'Shaughnessy was hurling recriminations on her head. 'You ought to look at your cards before you lay them on the table,' she said, and with much unnecessary movement and calculated equilibrium of the back of her head she gathered up her skirts and swept out of the room.

The gruff lady with the three chins asked the sub-bovine girl to put the score in the box on the plea that she would not have time to change. As she waddled out of the room the Commissioner's wife, Dummy with the three aces, turned to the chaplain's wife and said—

'I didn't know people like that dressed for dinner.'

'Did you see the good lady's hat?'

'Yes, and she played tennis in it.'

There was a rush and a roar in the passage, and the folding door swung open to emit half-a-dozen juvenile middle-aged men. 'Been weighing O'Shaughnessy,' one of them shouted to Skene as he passed. 'Eighteen stone without the brogue.'

Skene smiled to think that two hundred thousand of these folk ruled three hundred million of the others by virtue of the vitality that was in them.

Narasimha Swami was saying much the same thing to his young men.

After the lecture a few earnest and religious youths were presented. Siri Ram was called up by his teacher. The Guru spoke to him apart.

'Are you a patriot?' he asked. 'Do you love your country?'

Siri Ram testified his love.

'Are you prepared for sacrifice?'

Siri Ram was prepared for sacrifice.

'The youth of a nation are blessed, for in them lie its power and salvation. Youth is selfless; it does not calculate peril. In youth godliness first manifests itself; the perfection of manliness is attained. Who but young men have ever purified religion with their blood, baring their breasts to the sword of the oppressor? In every country oppressed and trodden underfoot by an alien government it is the community of young men who have conquered resistance and oppression, created a new nation, and reanimated the spirit of their fathers and their pride of race.'

The Swami fixed Siri Ram with a compassionate appraising eye. The boy hung his head.

'Is not the army of our young men the Nrsinha, the Vahara, the Kalki incarnation of Vishnu, which is to rid India of the Mlecchas? Do you wish to be enrolled in that army? Are you aware that independence is at hand?'

Siri Ram wished to serve in the ranks, to be part of the coming incarnation of the god Vishnu. Thus the humblest is beatified.

'The sword which is unsheathed for the protection of right in the name of religion is invincible, but the weapon in the hands of a persecutor has no power at all. For who can destroy the seed of liberty when it has germinated in the blood of a patriot? To-day our religion is still of martyrdom; tomorrow it will be of victory. Consider, what are the numbers of our oppressors?'

'Less than two million.'

'What are the numbers of our countrymen?'

'Three hundred million.'

'Oh, glorious is the heritage of our young men! The country is yours. If a thousand of you here and there cherish the desire of independence in your hearts, then in a single day you can bring English rule to an end. But there is the price. Are you strong enough to pay it?'

The Swami did not wait for Siri Ram's assurances. He turned to a heap of books by his side and chose six unbound pamphlets in Urdu, and bade the boy take them and consider and weigh them before he did anything in haste. If in a month's time he felt the true fire which could not be extinguished he must offer himself again, and a task would be allotted him proportionate to his love and zeal. He should pray to be worthy of the highest crown. In the meantime he must take his companions aside and instil into them true religious and political ideas. But he must work undergound. There must be no open movement in the College. Students must be compliant and appear to imbibe the opinions of Government. Premature divulgence would injure the Cause. There must be no general action till the flame had spread. For a little time it must burn secretly in hidden places until the conflagration became so great that it would consume all that was opposed to it.

'The saints of to-day are the guardians of the flame of liberty. Sacrifice yourself at that shrine. Without bloodshed the worship of the goddess cannot be accomplished.'

Siri Ram felt that these words, delivered by the Swami with such slow, solemn earnestness, were the formula of initiation. He departed swollen with pride. He slept ill that night in the boarding-house. His mind was distracted as he lay awake among his companions who were still slaves—slaves of the English, slaves of their families, slaves of their own pleasures. One of them had a portrait of the King from an illustrated paper pinned over his bed. Siri Ram got up and tore it from the wall. He felt himself steeped in anarchy. Remembering with what sacrifice the goddess of Independence must be worshipped, he pricked his hand with a nib and licked the blood. He did not know how to use a gun or a sword, yet he was dedicated.

When he fell asleep he was thinking of Kamala Kanta in the Shop of Fame—where nothing could be seen for the deep darkness. Kamala was calling to the vendor, but no voice could be heard; only the infinite roar of thunder, falling rocks and cannon striking terror into the hearts of all. In the faint light outside over the door he could read, 'The Shop of Fame. For Sale, Eternal Glory. Price, Life.'

# 3

Siri Ram was seven when his father's bullock cart and a neighbour's borrowed for the occasion took him and his parents to Gandeshwar. He had never, save once when he was a sleeping infant, been far from Mograon before that memorable journey; he had not even thought of exploring the cart track which connected it with the trunk road. He travelled in the hind cart with his mother under the red campanula-shaped purdah, and she held him at the parting of the curtains, whence he looked out stolidly on the world for the first time. The groaning of the unoiled wheels and the rattling of the brass pots as the cart jolted in and out of the permanent rut were his lullaby for three days. Then he passed through a city gate where men were counting money and under the bastions of a fort. The carts traversed a network of narrow streets full of strange shops and temples, and serais with intricately-carved doors and fretted windows, and houses with flaming pictures daubed on the walls, of Rajahs, and tigers, and peacocks, and gods without animation or perspective.

An English boy at such a time would have been restless, darting from one side of the cart to the other, or looking over his shoulder through the opposite chink afraid of missing something better on the other side of the road; but Siri Ram surveyed the traffic, dreamily content with what was thrown in front of his eye. He saw a camel-sowar with his bright belt and rifle, riding the largest and cleanest camel he had ever seen, with bells jingling on its knees and chest, and a bridle studded with cowrie shells and favours. He passed through the metal bazaar, a whole street of shops, where spectacled old men sat in dark recesses hammering bowls and cauldrons of copper and brass. He saw a young blood on horseback with a falcon on his wrist; and in the square in front of the fort by the big cannon the cart had to pull up to let a Maharajah's bodyguard sweep by, forty straight square-set men in green who passed on their cream-white chargers like one wave. In the street by Siva's temple Siri Ram saw more fakirs and holy men than he had seen in his life, some in ashen nakedness, and some in salmon-coloured shifts with bowls and staves and leopards' skins and matted hair. A shock-headed madman lurched along the street beside the cart, slowly revolving one arm and crying out with every revolution that he was the father of a devil. Beggars with lopped limbs and features all awry, with no eyes or one, and that often webbed or wounded, with twisted lips or mouth like a fleshy ring into which the snout has fallen, squatted under the walls crying aloud for alms and stretching out their bowls with their hands in supplication. Then, strangest of all, a carriage drawn by two grey horses passed in front of them down a side street, and Siri Ram had a momentary vision of the white-and-pink face of a brazenly unabashed woman who leant back on her cushions laughing in the eye of all the world, the man by her side. She wore a black hat with a white plume in it, and the shape reminded Siri Ram of the large, shallow vessel in which his sister pounded turmeric. Yet it was worn on the head. Before the carriage had passed, his mother drew the purdah to with a modest, frightened movement and murmured 'English.' It was Siri Ram's first sight of them.

The next morning Siri Ram was taken to the great towered building which played so important a part in his life. The College was a landmark for miles. It so dominated the country that it left an impression even on the dull brain of his father, Mool Chand, who on an earlier journey had been led to remark that if he sent his son to school anywhere it should be at Gandeshwar under Iskeen Sahib. Thus it happened that Skene was the first Englishman whom the boy saw at close quarters.

The white world did not trouble him much in those early days. His first encounter with the dominant race was one morning when his class was invaded by a sudden, strange, violent man. Siri Ram did not know it, but the lesson he was attending was designed to explain the physical features of the earth. The teacher had drawn a series of cones on the blackboard like the teeth of a saw, and he was leading the class in a kind of chanted litany.

'What are these?'

'Mountains.'

'What are mountains?'

'Mountains are steep.'

'What are plains?'

'Plains are low.'

'What are these?'

'Mountains.'

Siri Ram saw the teacher's back stiffen as he raised his voice to catch the sure response.

'What are these?'

'Mountains.'

'Stand!'

The boys leapt up. Action in the hall was paralysed. The hot, red man filled the space between the two classes. He was speaking to Siri Ram's teacher, evidently displeased. Then he swung round to the class.

'Has any boy here ever seen a mountain?' he asked.

'Has any boy seen a mountain?' the teacher repeated. 'Those who have seen mountains hold up their hands. . . .Yes, it is very bad, no doubt, after all. Every boy ought to have seen a mountain. Teaching must be accompanied by observation, of course. Eye must work with brain. Other methods are wrong. In future. . . .'

But these scraps of training-school reminiscence did not pacify the sudden violent man. He stood there staring stonily at the class, very angry, it seemed, because no one had ever seen a mountain. Stillness and silence prevailed. At last Siri Ram shuffled forward. There was something in the boy that responded to an appeal. He held out his hand.

'That is right. You have seen a mountain. Tell us about it. Where was it?'

'Mountains are steep,' he shrilled.

'The Principal Sahib asks you: Have you seen—?'

But the Principal Sahib waved him aside. Wrath was clearly dissolved. He had been seen to smile. At the same time a volcanic sound issued from his inside which puzzled everybody.

'Bring the class after you,' he said. 'I will show you all the mountains.'

When the dreadful man's back was turned the urchins laughed and chattered as they followed him down the corridors and up a flight of stone steps of the roof. It was a funny thing this being taken on the roof by the Principal Sahib instead of sitting in the class.

'There are the mountains,' he said.

Siri Ram looked over the parapet and saw dark purple masses on the far north-eastern horizon lifted out of the clouds, palpable earth, with a white rim of snow on them. Rain had fallen in the night, and the wind blew keenly from the hills.

Had none of them ever seen it before? They did not know. Some said they had.

The Principal told them about the snow and how the rivers were formed in the mountains and cut their channels out into the plains, and then on into the sea where the water was salt and no one could drink it. Then he announced a game. 'Some of us will stand on the roof,' he said, 'which is the mountain, and we will make a river; and some of us will stand by the water pipe underneath, which is the plain, and see what the river does when it comes down; but first we will make a bed of sand for it to flow through.' When the parties were divided Siri Ram saw him go up to a huge water butt and overturn it unaided. They were not quick enough to escape the deluge as they ran to the parapet to see what would happen.

They did not return to their classes that day, for the red man, dreadful no more, declared in a loud voice that there should be cricket.

'Not play cricket? They must play cricket, they must play to-day—now.'

'The Principal Sahib has ordered a contest of cricket. The competition will be the First and Second Primary on the one side and the Third Primary on the other. He has also said with honourable condescension that he will present a bat to the boy who makes the greatest number of runs.'

Few of them were big enough or strong enough to hit the ball so far as to make a real run. But there were overthrows. Siri Ram stood in his fixed place in a kind of dream and made ineffectual dives at the ball when it came his way. It was his first initiation into the barbarous rites of his oppressors. The Principal himself umpired. His thick, sunburnt neck, broad shoulders and bulging calves, which seemed to stretch out his wide trousers, made him appear the impersonation of force. Siri Ram stared at him. He did not brood or think in those days, but this strange, unexplained phenomenon waylaid his rambling attention as often as his eye fell on the space it filled so amply. It was a memorable visitation, and there were many such. Everything was all mixed-up and topsy-turvy when the Englishman impinged on their lives. No one knew what would happen next.

Siri Ram remembered one dreadful morning in the Fourth Primary. It was three years after this encounter. Nihal Singh had thrown a pellet of modelling clay across the classroom and it had hit Abdul Hamid in the eye and set him howling. The teacher was demanding that the boys in the quarter whence the missile issued should betray the culprit, and they had all left their benches and were dancing round him when the Principal entered upon the pandemonium like a hawk on a parliament of sparrows. The Headmaster was called in with his cane. First the noisy were chastised. Then those who bore false witness, and all palpable fabricators of untruth. Two canes were broken upon these before the inquisition passed into an inspection of exercises. Siri Ram was called up, and watered his desk with tears when he discovered that he, too, was to receive six stinging cuts for saying that he had left his torn copybook in an almirah and a rat had eaten it. It was the first time he had suffered intentional physical hurt, and he burned with resentment. The pellet thrower had not been dealt such harsh measure. It was a full hour before the boys discovered that the statement of unembellished fact paid better than the aptest embroidery. So after a time a kind of starveling truth emerged born of loss and pain. There was a feeling that the Principal had cheated, that he was angry at his failure to detect the mischief-maker at the start and was avenging himself promiscuously. For how should it enter their heads that deceit and evasion assimilated with their mother's milk and inculcated indirectly every day by the teachers themselves meant anything that was not creditable. It was etiquette among the schoolmasters to talk a great deal about truth and lies as if they did not admire the cleverness of the deceit they practised at home; but every one knew that the importance of the verbal distinction was only make-believe on the teachers' part to help them to find out things. So the injustice of the chastisement rankled the more.

Apart from these invasions of the Principal, five years in the primary department passed uneventfully enough. Siri Ram was taught natural history through the medium of object lessons. He learnt to sew patterns of animals on cardboard with coloured threads, to model fruit in clay, and to draw goats and hares with stripes and collars. His decorative instinct survived the matter-of-fact accuracy of the kindergarten. In the fourth and fifth primary he learnt a little English. In the first middle he was taught composition. He sent a copy of one of his first exercises to his father, and the village writer translated it.

'My dear Poppa,
'I much glade seeing Gandeshwar College. I cannot write because it each part made with a very beauty, two minarets on it both wings and its entrance has its name and date in which it estobelished upon its forehead. When I have seen the College I went in boarding-house there were all studdents very gentlemen and good they received me with a so love that I was their friend. All studdents here are civilized. When at last I leave it but my mind not say me that I leave it, please keep in this schole. I saw many things good because I had never see any things like these in our school teachers are very regular and punctual and they wish that our schole do more progress also they are all B.A. or F.A. trained nowadays I have good head master.
                                        'Your lovely son,
                                          'Siri Ram.'

It was in the First Middle that Siri Ram ventured on his earliest propaganda. A Cow Agitator had moved the first stirrings of a cause in him. He bought a sheet of foolscap in the bazaar for the twelfth of a penny, and he cut it into small slips, on which he inscribed this warning—

'The sky says
that sav the cows unless you should die plese save the cows.'

These he posted in yellow envelopes, unstamped and curiously addressed, to servants of the Crown.

As Siri Ram progressed in the collegiate school, English became almost a hobby with him. Copybook headings and tags from his moral reader were translated into his essays and his daily speech. He became attached to particular words and idioms. There is safety in the made phrase. One cannot go far wrong when one is talking of 'shuffling off one's mortal coil,' or of being 'brought to books,' or 'being made to eat the humble pie'. So Siri Ram and his companions made free with the language of the hated barbarian. No one ever died at Gandeshwar; they 'shuffled off their mortal coil amidst the unsuppressed wails of their family members and all their nears and dears'. And no one ever improved; they 'made up the deficiency'. That was a phrase which permeated to the College and disturbed the equanimity of Skene. It was supposed to still all manner of reproach; to make idleness and ignorance of no account, and to turn defeat into victory. When Puran Singh fell a lap behind in the half-mile race at the College sports, Ram Sarup would pant after him on the other side of the ropes, crying out to him to 'make up the deficiency'.

In this way Siri Ram got a grip of the language, which was the one asset which had stuck to him in the ten years' course from the infants' class to the entrance, whence he passed into the College. His mind had broadened very little during all these years. His moral code was drawn from certain vague formulas which had as little to do with his daily life as the culture which he was supposed to assimilate from his textbooks in the College. And no coercing had seduced him into cricket or football or any of the games which might have brought him into genial relationship with the healthier-minded of his companions.

## 4

By the time Siri Ram had read two years in the College he had become a typical product of the age. His father was an orthodox Jat Hindu, or, as his classmate, Banarsi Das, would have said, 'an ignorant steeped in the Cimmerian darkness.' His associates were members of the Arya Samaj, whose religious ideals might have helped him had they not been perverted into gall by his teachers for temporal ends. Religion in his circle had come to mean something approaching a deification of the early Hindus, and an assumption that the same stuff was latent in the modern youth of the country, and only needed a spark to kindle it into the divine fire. Against the sacred names of Rama and Arjun and Bhima were inscribed the names of such modern martyrs as Tilak, and Kanhya Lal and Kudiram Bose who murdered the English ladies at Mozaffarpur. History was going to repeat itself. The English were the Asuras again, who ravaged the Motherland, which was now in the birth pangs of a new breed of dragon slayers who were to rid her of the evil. So the religious man was the man who most execrated the English, who most forswore English rule, and English piece-goods and English everything except ideas and idioms and the itinerant Labour Member and his political catchwords.

Skene felt that the patriotism underlying all this might have been good if there had been any clean courageous note in it; but the cant and conscious misinterpretation of facts sickened him. Still there was pathos enough in some of its manifestations. A Hindu strong man brought his circus to Gandeshwar, and he was apotheosized. He rode an elephant in the streets, preceded by bands and lictors. Rajahs summoned him and sent him gifts. Ladies threw strings of pearls to him from behind the purdah in the circus. The coolies in the bazaar whispered that he was another incarnation of Vishnu. And that, allowing for the difference of Aryan enlightenment, was very much what the students believed. They garlanded him and addressed him, and asked him to speak to them; and he raised his hoarse voice in their midst, swaying like an elephant in the pangs of articulation. They looked on the man as a revival, as a witness of their ancient strength, and an earnest of deliverance. And they lifted weights, wielded clubs, broke stones on their chests, and stood on one another's abdomens for weeks after he had gone.

Skene was the only Englishman whom Siri Ram had spoken to, and somehow his general abhorrence of the race was mitigated in the individual. It was true that the Principal was a flesh-eater, and his belly was a tomb, and he had other disgusting habits inseparable from a race given to 'bloodthirst and matter-worship'. But he had a way with him. He gave himself no airs; he had nothing of what Banarsi Das used to call 'the false pride and unreal haughtiness of the Englishman'. Most of the students liked him. He always appeared genuinely pleased to meet them outside the College, when he would stop and talk to them and ask them questions. He knew them all personally by name, and he remembered things they had said and done. He poked fun at them good-naturedly. His anger was sudden and unreasonable, but the storm passed quickly, and his smile was embracing. His lectures partook of the nature of a conversation, and he was always ready to answer any question on earth, relevant or irrelevant, for he felt that it was something to the good if a student took an interest in anything. He liked them unaffectedly. And there was much to like in their gentleness and natural dignity and patience and tact, and in their responsiveness to any kindness. He felt drawn to the cricket and football team. He could talk to them on common ground, and he coached them in both games and kept alive their flickering keenness. A mutual cause made them allies; he could count on their loyalty. They had dash and spirit when their blood was up and things were going well, but they had no backbone. At the slightest reverse they went to pieces and became limp and apathetic, and they had to be inflated again like their own footballs. It was uphill work.

In the lecture room common ground was harder to seek; for their English textbooks meant unthinking drudgery to the bulk of the students and offence to the intelligent few, among whom was the morose group typified by Siri Ram. Nothing but direct moral teaching could appeal to their sombre reason. The modern books they read must have been incomprehensible even if they could have had enough English to appreciate the subtleties of meaning. They read wantonness into the badinage of Lamb. Thackeray sinned by condoning too much. Shelley and Keats were frank sensualists. Even Stevenson in his canoe shocked them, for ever waving his handkerchief at unknown maidens on the bank. Nor could fiction, romantic or realistic, have any point for them, as it offered a criticism of an existence as remote from their own as cobwebs in the moon. The mischief of it was, as critics of education were always pointing out, that the books bore no conceivable relation with the students' own lives. The Universities were accused of grafting an alien culture, substituting foreign for indigenous ideas. 'Not at all,' was Skene's caustic comment. 'We supplant nothing. We fill a vacuum. For what culture or ideas would the like of Siri Ram gather from his own people?'

There is a popular fallacy that the Indian is imaginative. Nothing is farther from the truth. In spite of his habit of inaccuracy he is the most literal prosaic soul alive. Logic, philosophy, ethics he can understand, even humour when it touches his experience; but there is no film in his mind that is responsive to poetic fancy. Imagination means much the same to him as multiplication. It is a kind of magnifying glass through which he sees a swollen universe. The imaginative man is the man who thinks in crores and hecatombs and holocausts, in Kalpas of time and vast compartments of space. The light play of fancy does not touch him. Yet Siri Ram and Banarsi Das were made to wrestle with Shelley and Keats in a book of selections prescribed—or *pro*scribed, as Skene would have said—for the first arts. Skene protested, but the Syndicate insisted upon 'culture'. So the spirit of Adonais was tortured and expired in his presence every day, and he was a paid accessory.

On the morning of the day when the Swami lectured to them upon the eternal truths hidden in the Vedas, Siri Ram and Banarsi Das had been construing the 'Ode to the Nightingale'. Siri Ram read out each stanza nasally, and at the end Banarsi Das 'consulted' the notes. Then he interpreted

> O for a beaker full of the warm South,
> Full of the true, the blissful Hippocrene,
> With beaded bubbles winking at the brim
> And purple stained mouth;
> That I might drink and leave the world unseen
> And with thee fade away into the forest dim.

The comments in the notes did not help them to the spirit of the piece. Still the central idea was clear. The poet wished to forget the world and to be with the nightingale in the forest. The means to this end were definitely expressed. Firstly, a long draught of wine; secondly, oblivion. Banarsi Das interpreted.

'The poet desired that he might drink the warm wine of South in a peg full of true fountain of Moses. He said that after intoxicating myself with above-mentioned wine I shall totally forget everything and be with you in the jungle.'

It was a fairly creditable effort for an F.A. student. The only bad blunder lay in the interpretation of 'the blissful Hippocrene', and that was due to a misprint in a locally annotated edition.

In the lecture room afterwards Skene discovered that the distinction between sensuousness and sensuality was too subtle for them, and his honest efforts to indicate a line of demarcation failed. The lover of the nightingale was debauched, it seemed, and the only reason why he did not eat the bird after all, when he had pursued it into the forest and caught it, was that it was not good to eat.

> Thou wast not born for death, immortal bird,
> No hungry generations tread thee down.

'Nightingale is not the game-bird for table,' Banarsi Das translated. 'Therefore the hungry sportsmen spare to tread on it.'

Skene did not even smile. His sense of humour was long ago dried at the roots. He could still enjoy a parody of Owen Seaman, but this living among inverted ideals had parched up the true well of mirth. He had to live six months away from the College, he told himself, before he could replenish it. And when he found himself defining the particular kind of humour which he could no longer appreciate he shuddered at the bear's-hug of pedantry which loomed over him like a persistent nightmare, and he swore roundly to his dog for half-an-hour in the language of an Elizabethan bargee.

His students had unearthed a Hindu annotator who had analysed the ingredients of English humour, and who pointed out all the passages in the textbooks which came or seemed to come under this head, so that they could tabulate them to a nicety. Skene came upon the scent of the mischief when he was reading Adonais with them. He had set the clearest-tongued to read the stanza beginning—

> He hath outsoared the shadow of our night,
> Envy and calumny and hate and pain,
> And that unrest which men miscall delight
> Can touch him not and torture not again.

when Banarsi Das rose darkling from his seat and said—
'Sir, are not these lines humorous?'

'Good God,' Skene began, but the youth caught him on the recoil.

'The humour lies in incongruity. Poet speaks of 'that unrest which men miscaall dee-light.' '

But it did not need Banarsi Das's discovery of a humorist in Shelley to show Skene how little their textbooks brought his students into touch with his world.

His struggle with Keats' 'Ode to a Nightingale' was Siri Ram's last adventure in the fields of English literature. When he awoke the morning after the lecture he picked up his textbook from force of habit and found himself reading a poem about a little girl and a sparrow's nest.

> She looked at it as if she feared it,
> Still wishing, dreading to be near it.

He threw the book aside. The piece was so simple he did not give it another thought. If any one had asked him the meaning of the lines, he would have said that the European sparrow is a ferocious bird, and that Emmeline was afraid to provoke it by going too near its nest. And he might have added, if there were any consequence in his broodings, some general reflections about European truculence in men and sparrows. There was plenty of material for it in the heap of pamphlets by his side which the Swami had given him. Siri Ram squatted at the end of his bed with his blanket pulled about his ears poring over them. There was no crime which the English had not inflicted upon his Motherland, no indignity which his people had not suffered at their hands. The Imperial Government was pictured as the monkey in the fable dividing a morsel of cheese between two cats. In spite of the scales, a specious show of justice behind which the hungry maw went on grinding, she swallowed the whole chunk herself. Then the story of Naboth's vineyard was adapted with advantages. Here was literature which Siri Ram could understand. He could be vastly allegorical over the wrongs of his country. History was retold, not as it was taught in the schools, but with coloured patches and all the statistics of fraud which made it clear how the hated foreigners were seated in authority. Here was set down the bribe to a rupee which each traitor had been paid as the price of his country. This was soothing to pride. It was not a question of three hundred thousand against three hundred million after all. His country had been filched from him by trickery and cunning.

One book described how a demon had drained the country of its wealth, sucked away the trade and industries from the people, and swallowed up all the products of the earth. Then, dropping allegory, figures were cited from which Siri Ram learnt that crores of rupees realized out of the earnings of Indians in their homes were sent to Europe every year, and that millions of white devils luxuriated in idleness upon them. The Indians, driven like cattle at the plough, sweated in the eye of the sun, while these pestilent *feringhi*s squandered the fruits of their toil.

Another pamphlet elaborated the colour grievance with some eloquence. It was written in America, and addressed to Indian soldiers. They were taunted with being cowards and dupes and slaves, submissive to insult, living like animals, content with their miserable lot. Every point inflamed an old sore. Their very blackness was counted an offence.

'Miserable Indian soldier! Your eyes have grown pale, subsisting on pulse and *chapatti*s. The redness and glow of your faces has faded. The prisoners of other nations are treated better than you. They have at least one meal a day. But you? Through bad pig-like diet your faces have become clay-coloured and mud-like. This is the reason the English call you black. You and the English belong to the same Aryan race. If they had given you the same food as their own soldiers you would not be so black and ugly. The negroes in this country are given the same pay as the American; but you, wretched and miserable, are paid for colour and not for service.'

Siri Ram had fallen on a textbook for 'Political Missionaries'. It was the first of a series of guides to disaffection, and it taught how to seduce the Indian Army. A second described how native soldiers had won England an empire, and how they had been treated. A third appealed to the worst passions of the Sikhs, calling upon them to drive out the British, whom they accused of lack of faith after the Second Sikh War and in their agreement with Dhulip Singh. It was made to appear that it was due to the Sikh support alone that the British Government had weathered the Mutiny, and that if this prop were removed the fabric must collapse. As Siri Ram read, he saw himself a missionary among soldiers. With this fuel to command he would have more power in the lines at Multan and Umballa than the red-headed, Satan-like, beef-eating English Colonels. He was a brand already lighted. The grizzled, bearded faces of the Khalsa[1] already shone, fired by his eloquence. In a year or two it would not be safe for an Englishman to set his foot upon the sacred soil of Bharat Mata. Or if they were admitted it would be to pay a poll-tax and a landing fee of a hundred pounds like the Chinese in New Zealand, and to travel in reserved compartments on the railway—reserved, oh, how differently!—lest *they* should pollute, because the *alien* was offensive

---

[1]Sikh community

and the carnivorous effluvium of him repulsive to sensitive noses.

But the next pamphlet took Siri Ram into a village, and he saw himself a pale-eyed Sadhu sitting by a well. The tillers of the soil, lean, vacuous, intense, encompassed him. The husbandmen gaped to hear how they had been deceived, as he discovered to them the Satanic craft of the English in every affliction of their lives. They learnt how the *feringhis* were afraid that the Indians were becoming too many, and how grain was being taken out of the country that there might be famine, and wells were being poisoned to spread the plague, and trains were being wrecked to reduce the numbers of the people. Already they were killing off the cows in the big cities. Soon children would cry out in vain for milk and curds, and a poor man would not find a bullock for his plough.

There was a special series with agonizing illustrations devoted to the slaughter of the cow. Milton could not have described the savage truculence of the butcher. Blake could not have captured the helpless innocence of the calf as its mother's scarlet blood spurted over its white coat, and it lifted a gentle protestant eye as the knife was raised again.

Siri Ram saw himself playing many parts in the village and the camp, and the mills and the bazaar; but in every environment he was reminded that missionary work was but a preparation. Sacrifice was needed, and the last sacrifice of all. It always came to that in the end. If one in five hundred gave up his life, the poisonous stock would be extirpated; the country would be freed. The cost was small at any reckoning. Every year hundreds of thousands were taken away by plague and fever and famine and cholera in the Punjab alone. Tomorrow Siri Ram and his companions might be summoned by the smallpox goddess. Would it not be better to die like heroes to-day? But who would accompany him? Siri Ram looked round the dormitory and saw little hope there. None certainly in Ram Sarup, the bunniah's son. He was not inflammable. *Ghee* and molasses clogged his aspirations, if ever he had any. Nor in Hashmat Ali; Muhammadans were not to be trusted with these secret matters. There was even less hope in Puran Singh. He was captain of the cricket, an ally, if anything, of the Satan-like Mlecchas. He would rather defeat Government College by one wicket than drive all the English into the sea. As Siri Ram's eyes searched his bed he saw the torn edge of the King's portrait protruding underneath, and he remembered how he had stripped the almanac from the wall in his passion the night before. And there was the bloodstain on his shirt where he had pricked his arm with a nib. He felt a little frightened at his work and the collision it must involve.

Siri Ram slept in his clothes. In the chill of the morning he had drawn his blanket and his stained quilt over his ears, and he sat motionless, brooding, like a bird on the edge of a tank, insensible to the thick reek of his companions' breath in the air-proof room and the perfume of stale hookah smoke and sweat-sodden clothes. The windows and doors were closed hermetically, as the boy's mind to true values. Pride and apprehension coursed dully through him, merged in a vague stream. He saw the handcuffs, and the Court with its splendid publicity, and the gallows; and he saw the crown beyond—his portrait handed round among the faithful, or in the zenana painted upon mirrors, or stamped upon home-spun shirts and pantaloons, an exhibit to incite children, and possibly, when the English were gone, a statue in the square. He fumbled in his locker and produced a small blurred hand-glass and gazed at himself with solemn admiration. His companions awoke and saw him regarding his sullen swart features in dumb ecstasy, but it provoked no remark or surprise in that matter-of-fact crew. An Englishman observing him at the moment would have divined an intense wobbly soul given to moods and sullenness and passion; and there might have come the suggestion of a marish pool with the scum disturbed in the centre in such a way that there could be no resettling of the viscous stuff or clearing of it away to the edges. But Siri Ram was enamoured of the image. He felt that his eye 'pried through the portage of his head'. He thought of Swami Dyanand, and believed that his lips had caught the straightened-bow curve of the evangelist, though his eyes had not the calm. He was engrossed in the lines of the chin and thinking of the obscure inky reproductions of them on a thousand cheap pill-boxes and parcels from druggists' stores, when he was rudely disturbed by Puran Singh standing over him.

'Why you have torn my picture?'

'It fell.'

Siri Ram was taken unawares; the hero was dormant in him. Siri Ram was frail and weak; Puran Singh was tall and strong, five foot ten to the cord which bound his plaited hair. He was taller and stronger than many of the English Siri Ram had seen. It was for the like of him to save the country. But he was a slave. He laughed and played with the *feringhi*s and joined in their games, and because the Principal cared for him like one of his ponies, the foolish young man was pliant and obedient like a beast trained to the shaft or yoke. Some thought of this kind was struggling for utterance in Siri Ram when he blurted out in reply to thick recriminations—

'You are horse. You are bullock.'

'You are monkey. You will be beaten.'

'You are slave to worship white King.'

'You are ill-begotten bastard. Why you tear my picture? I will tear your book.'

Puran Singh snatched a copy of the Vedic magazine from Siri Ram's table and tore it in halves. Siri Ram, blind with indignation, seized an Indian club and raised it with a parody of menace; but Puran Singh wrested it from him and threw him back upon the bed. He struck his head against the table edge as he fell, breaking the skin at the back of his ear. He picked himself up with no little dignity and made a martyr's exit, aglow with this witness-bearing. It was a step.

He found Banarsi Das in his cubicle. Lachmi Chand had already joined him. His grievance, distorted already, precipitated the campaign.

# PART II

## The Village

Or, where old-eyed oxen chew
Speculation with the cud,
Read their pool of vision through
Back to hours when mind was mud.

GEORGE MEREDITH

# 1

Skene's tennis four was broken up again. The horoscope of Siri Ram was dark reading; sinister influences threatened him on two sides. Merivale had marching orders at twelve hours' notice to the Harpur district where Magraon, our hero's village, lay. Plague was suspected at Mehlgahla nearby, and it was said that the villagers were dying off like rats. Chauncey in the I.M.S. was detailed from Jullundur to work with him, and they met at a small wayside station, whence they rode out to Mehlgahla, fifteen hours on camels over ruts and sand.

They found a suppressed panic. The villagers were gathered in a conclave by the well outside the wall, and greeted the Englishmen suspiciously. It was a huddled, sinister crowd, darkly secretive, and fearing the meddling Sahib-log more than the plague itself. They denied all pestilence and fever.

'What are the flames at the ghat?' Merivale asked, alighting from his camel. 'I am told the pyres are burning night and day.'

'Death walks among us at all times,' the headman said, and he unfolded an embroidered tale of misadventure. An old woman had been bitten by a snake. A little girl had fallen down a well. A centenarian had crawled home from his pilgrimage to the Ganges at Hardwar, and his heart had ceased beating on the threshold of his home.

'We sprinkled the Gunga water he brought with him on his pyre,' an old man with a goat's face added circumstantially.

'He died religiously,' the headman added.

'Why are the Granthis reading the Book?' Merivale asked, and pointed to the village gate, whence a melancholy religious drone issued like an incantation. Merivale knew that it was a *path*, the reading of the scriptures from end to end, and that it was for no ordinary visitation. Two priests of the Khalsa sat side by side in an alcove of the arch. One intoned with the rapid dignity that priests alone attain. The other stared at the ground at his feet, looking like a physician who has been given a charge and waits the decree of the Almighty, confident that he has done his part.

'Why are they reading the Granth?' Merivale repeated.

'The Lumbadar of Razian has been near death, and he wishes to appease God. He has ordered the *path* in five villages.'

Merivale called for the chowkidar to bring the village register of births and deaths. After many mischances the chronicles were found. Merivale scanned them.

'Where is the snakebite, and the drowned child, and the religiously dying pilgrim?'

The chowkidar mumbled a bewildered protest, resentful that his registers had played him such a trick. Then there rose a woman's wailing within the walls, a measured rhythmic ululation. Chauncey looked at Merivale. 'We had better go in,' he said. 'Perhaps we may hear something.'

The crowd followed them sullenly; one or two ran on quickly in front, casting furtive looks over their shoulders. The headman and the chowkidar followed on their heels. As they passed, the Granthi on duty in the arch did not raise his head. His companion eyed them steadfastly with a patient remote gaze as one regards some unexplained phenomenon, to which one has become accustomed from time to time. He waved his holy peacock-feather chauri over the book. Merivale had never seen such repose in movement. The oval beard, the far-seeking eyes under the turban wound in three flat plaits put him in mind of a priest in an old picture.

A figure was moving in the heat haze at the end of the street; it was one of the men who had run on in front tearing down the threaded neem leaves hung from house to house over the way to avert calamity. Then they passed some tell-tale funeral meats on the threshold of one of the first houses inside the gate. But they did not stop at these. They were guided by the woman's cries to the *mohalla*, where the trouble was the heaviest. Here they found her in her small mud-paved courtyard opening on the street, a poor uncomely hag, with unloosened hair grey with age and grit, squatting on her haunches and swaying backwards and forwards, crooning—

> 'Ahyee! Ahyee! I am accursed, abandoned.
> The fields lie untilled; the fruit of the earth perishes.
> He is gone who protected me, who looked to the tillage,
> He is gone whom I bore with pain, and nurtured motherly.'

She wailed to a measure. It was a prescribed dirge. The simple words were not her own. They had been sung with variations by widows and mothers and orphans for ages untold—maybe on the Scythian steppes in the background of time, before the earliest Jat shepherd descended through the western passes into the Punjab. But the pathos was true. If the words had been spontaneous they could not have betrayed a deeper grief.

Merivale entered the courtyard and stood by her side until the lament was finished. Then he asked her gently, 'What is the matter, Mother?'

> 'Ahyee! Ahyee! I am accursed, abandoned!
> The fields are untilled . . . .'

She rose and fumbled with some sticks for fuel and wailed her story intermittently. It was her son. He had died of a fever three days ago with a raging sore under his arm.

Merivale turned to the headman. 'Is this your centenarian, your Gunga water-bringer?' he asked.

'Certainly it occurs to me after consideration that the pilgrim in question may have died at an earlier date.'

'Enough! Enough! The doctor Sahib and I have come to rid you of this pest. We must purge the village, or you will all die like the house-rats in the drain. Come, now. Help to save yourselves.'

The headman salaamed. 'The Sahib is lord and master. Whatever he wishes will be done.'

But this time-worn formula did not hide the sullen obstruction in the man's face. It was an angry, menacing crowd that dogged their steps in the search. In the first house they entered they found a corpse hidden away in a granary with the bubo on the groin. It must have been concealed by one of the furtive forerunners. They searched every house in that *mohalla* and every stack and courtyard. The pest had fallen on the village like a flail. As they stumbled out of one death chamber into the *haveli* they heard a splash in the well and found the parched, scabby, thirst-maddened rats stretched limply on the stone coping. There was no scurry at their approach. Some lay where they had died with the smell of the water in their nostrils; others slid forward and dropped over, one by one, into the well—a prudent suicide. Chauncey, looking over the edge, saw the surface covered with their distended bellies and fattened paws, and to his horror he saw the upturned face of a woman with her lips parted and her hair floating among them. He learnt that a Ramdasia's wife, driven by the same mad thirst as they, had leapt to her repose on the noon of the day before.

In another dark hovel they barked their shins against a charpoy. They could see nothing in the gloom at first, but Chauncey knew they were in the presence of a corpse. Near at hand they could hear children's voices. As the darkness dwindled and revealed the long, low-raftered room, they unfolded the sheet from the figure on the bed and found a woman with the bubo behind the ear. On a charpoy beyond, where the passage led off to the stall of the cow, there was a man lying unconscious with his face uncovered. His eyes were open

and staring, and devoid of intelligence; but for a momentary twitching
of the legs he might have been dead. Then, as they watch, he is shaken
by a spasm of breathing, hurried, noisy, laboured, ending in a rattle in
the throat and the last quiet.

It was only then that they discovered that the children were in the
passage leading out of the chamber—three little urchins playing
unconcernedly within reach almost of their parents' clay, two little girls
and a boy making mud pies, shirtless, trouserless little mites, naked
but for their little open coats covering the back to the buttocks. A small
girl was playing with a sieve. She had made a circle in the dust with
the rim of it, and was piecing out a coloured wheel with marigold
petals and chili-pods and red powder for the spokes. Beside her were
the ruins of a mud Persian well which she had just fashioned with
care, the water still oozing out of the trough, the clay jar overturned by
the infant's foot which was now menacing a segment of the wheel. It
was her shrill protest that had merged with the rattle of the dying man.
Looking up now from her serious employment, and seeing Merivale
and Chauncey standing over her, she shrank to the wall, crying out in
alarm to her mother, who could listen to her no more. Then she
toddled into the empty room, looking back at the Englishmen
suspiciously over her shoulder.

Merivale came out of that house a tyrant. He cared not for man or
law. He *was* law. He might have had sealed orders in his pocket to
frame new codes every day to meet each new emergency. One thing
only mattered. The village had to be evacuated, the houses disinfected,
segregation camps and hospital camps built. He saw the work at his
feet and leapt at it. Responsibility warmed him like wine. The pitfalls
all round, the dozen different ways that offered themselves every day
of being 'broke' for playing the game, the official inquiries, the radical
on his hind legs in the House, the glimpse of the tethered civilian
scapegoat with his own smooth features, half-amused, half-protesting—
these were the blind fences youth loves to take with a stout horse
under him on fresh October mornings before the leaf is off the hedges,
when the first nip is in the air. 'We must go the whole hog,' he said to
Chauncey. 'It is no good tinkering at it.'

## 2

Through the heat of the morning they were moving out the sick.
Chauncey had marked out a hospital camp in a mango clump
round a well a quarter of a mile from the gate. And on the other

side of the village he had laid out the health and segregation camp, giving every caste its own quarter outside pollution distance, as in their homes. The Jats were in the centre, and the Kamins, or serfs, in detached camps all round, according to their degree; and the untouchables, the sweepers and the hide-defiled cobblers, farthest from the shade and the well.

In the meanwhile Merivale had started the evacuation. The sick were carried out on their beds by their relatives, who were forced to lend a sullen hand. As the first detachment filed through the streets Merivale was met with sour looks. The men were removed without much palaver, but when it came to the women's turn it looked like a riot. The first to go was an old hag; Merivale saw to that. He knew the '*purdah*' cry would be raised; it was inevitable. But in the beldam's case it would be the precedent only they feared, and what it might lead to. No one cared enough for the old lady to make a stand on her behalf, and it was with a poor heart that the nearest of kin intervened—

'No, Sahib. Do not move her. She is only a woman, and an old one. Let her stay. An old dame is worth half a pice, and it costs two pice to have her head shaved.'

The headman muttered something about the sanctity of *purdah*, and his fear of a disturbance if the women were touched. But Merivale answered so that all might hear.

'I understood that in the villages women went with their heads uncovered. But, perhaps, when they get to a certain age—'

The beldam was in the grip of the pest and beyond understanding, or Merivale's chivalry might have lost him his point. His coarse jest raised a laugh, and in a few minutes the poor old bundle was being carried out.

A woman had been moved. It was the thin edge of the wedge. Merivale knew how thin, and that it was touch and go whether the whole village might not be up in arms. He had sent for fifty military police from Jullundur to form a cordon round the place, but they could not reach Mehlgahla for three days. The thing was started now, and there was no turning back. Nothing could save him but his own pluck and initiative and his good star. Defeat was disgrace. If the village stirred to the point of riot it must at least be saved. Government would not brook a burning sore, a hundred illegalities, the *purdah* violated, authority defied, prestige half-mast high, or lower, and an enduring precedent for resistance. But when everything was over, and the villagers responsive and reconciled, as they must be, and turning to the Englishman, as they always do, in a tight place, however jealously they may assert their rights in fair weather, authority might wink at

Merivale's 'You see, sir, we had to save these men: they were dying off like rats; but of course they didn't like it.' Yet even this might mean a good deal of grumbling and little thanks.

Chauncey left his assistant in the camp and met Merivale at the gate. The beldam had been deposited, and a younger woman, heavily veiled, was being borne through the street. An angry man strode beside the litter crying out that foreigners were dogs, and calling on the bearers to stop. As the crowd pressed in, the man grasped the charpoy, and the bearers laid it down in the street. It seemed that every voice in Mehlgahla was raised at once. The headman was invisible. A gang was issuing from a side alley armed with sticks. A brick struck the arch by Chauncey's head. 'They are going for us,' he shouted to Merivale. 'We must attack, or we won't have a chance.'

As they ran through the gate, a youth lifted an arm to bar their way. 'We do not want you here,' he said, and flung a disgusting insult at them. Chauncey knocked him down. The two sprang on the crowd, clearing a lane with their sticks. In a moment they had the street to themselves. The tide had receded to where the litter lay on the ground abandoned by the bearers. The side alleys leading to the *mohalla*s were crowded with curious peeping faces. The young Jat who had encountered Chauncey's right arm lay on the ground as if dead. Chauncey stooped over him and felt his pulse. 'Shamming,' he cried to Merivale, and looking up he saw a providential waterman at the mouth of one of the alleys with a bulging skin on his back.

'Bring water quickly,' he cried to him. 'The young man has swooned.'

The whole waterskin was emptied on the Jat's face, and he bore it with shut eyes and clenched teeth, lying still. 'Another!'

He endured it manfully without the twitch of a limb. 'Another!' But he opened his eyes to the spout of the third, leapt to his feet, and fled, the most animated thing in Mehlgahla.

The little scene had been observed by all, and Merivale and Chauncey, bent double with laughter in the middle of the road, infected the crowd with their merriment. The hostile space filled with grinning faces, and for the moment there was no talk of sticks.

The headman appeared from nowhere, the offending youth behind, pushed forward by the elders, expecting swift judgment and the gaol. He threw himself at the Sahib's feet, imploring pardon. But Merivale laughed again at the sight of him.

'Give him this to heal his pate,' he said Fluellen-like. 'The *tamasha* was worth it. I am not in court here.' His jolly laugh and his composure were worth all the penalties of the law.

'Now to work,' he said. 'I do not wish to offend you, but the Sircar has ordered me to help you to save your own lives.'

This raised another laugh, which was only half protesting, and the headman, seeing that it was a moment in which he might publicly discover himself on the side of authority, said that he had sent for the *budmash* who had stopped the litter, if it were the Sahib's pleasure that he should be punished.

'No. Let all be forgotten. The present danger must be met quickly, and we will work together bearing no grudges.'

The litter was already moving, and by two o'clock the sick, man, woman and child, were all in the plague camp. But the trouble was not over. The Sahib had ordered that every soul, sick or hale, must leave the village within twenty-four hours, and take with them what was needful for six weeks' stay in camp. All the afternoon, while Merivale was erecting huts and shelters for the sick, he was plagued with deputations. Now it was a farmer—

'Sahib, how can we do this thing? If we keep our cattle out at night they will die. How can we take out *turi* in one day to feed them for six. weeks? Also the *turi* will be blown about by the wind and destroyed in different ways, and without cattle we will starve. Moreover, if they do not die they will be stolen.'

Then the bunniah—

'Sahib, I am a poor man. How can I remove my property in so short a time? I cannot pay for the labour. The food I have prepared to keep hunger from my poor children—and by your honour's grace they are many—the jars of treacle and the jars of *ghee* if they be taken out into the sun they will be spoilt. You are my father and mother, and would grieve if the little ones perished. Permit me to enter the village every third day and withdraw sufficient for the hour. Also there are moneys'—the fat man lowered his voice—'not of my own, but in my keeping—God knows I am a poor man. Moneys advanced for my shop, and now by my thrift and your honour's protection the advance with interest is almost ready to be paid. If I take this into the fields it will be stolen; if I leave it in the house it will also be stolen.'

Then the carpenter—

'Sahib, we have laid up wood for two seasons, deodar and shisham, timber of price. If we abandon it, it will be burnt or stolen. You are our lord and master. Of your mercy do not condemn us.'

Then the chamar—

'Nourisher of the poor! If we go out into the fields we leave our tanning. Without labour day by day we cannot subsist, but if it is our lord's pleasure—'

All were heard with patience and dismissed. The farmer was told that the Sircar would be responsible for every head of cattle that was lost. He could get the *turi* in, in time and stack it himself after the manner of his forefathers, so that it was not blown about by the wind. The bunniah was ordered to bring his shop into camp. The carriers would be paid, and the property that he left behind locked and sealed and a watchman put over it. Merivale would be responsible for everything left in the village. A special chowkidar would be given the carpenters for their wood. The chamars might go daily to their yard which lay outside the walls. But no one might enter the village save the watchmen, when once it was cleared. Any man else who passed the gate would be sent to the gaol to labour there without reward. In three days the police would arrive from Jullundur to keep the cordon. In the meanwhile the two Englishmen held patriarchal sway.

The pest was new in the Punjab. Merivale had never seen a plague case before; Chauncey had been through a bare month's training in Bombay; so they worked by the light of nature. They understood the people, which was the main thing. A strong hardy stock, assertive of their own rights, men of the toughest fibre, innocent of nerves, with little or no physical fear, but helpless as cattle when there was no one to lead them. Merivale laughed to think of their heads bobbing at the end of the alleys off the street after the fracas of the morning. Each of these lanes was a *cul-de-sac* leading to its own *mohalla* from which there was no exit, so that the village was honeycombed into different cells, the symbol of the Hindu's perpetual instinct of segregation, fear, suspicion, distrust of his neighbour, shrinking into himself. Had it been otherwise Merivale and Chauncey would never have seen Mehlgahla. They certainly would not have turned the village out into the fields. Yet it was done, and the peasants helped. In a few days the best of them had fallen into line and lent an ungrudging hand. And it was no small thing for these folk, separated as they were from their sick friends, terrified by European medicines, their privacy disturbed, their roofs broken down to let in the purging air, their lares and penates and their very clothes soaked in the distressful phenyl, business at a standstill, the village cordoned round with police, and the harvest stayed while they assisted in these real evils and many more imaginary ones, born of their superstitions, which haunted them as persistently.

Chauncey worked day and night between the camps and the village. The purging of Mehlgahla was an epic task. He was followed everywhere by two men, always at his elbow, with lantern, keys, chisel and hammer, spare locks and pots of paint, tongs for dead rats, and kerosene oil and straw to burn them in. In the camps the very donkeys and goats were disinfected and plunged in their carbolic bath. And the villagers soon spoke of 'phnail' as if it had always been a household property. The faint sting of it in their purifying baths gave them the confidence of a spell, and it became known that no one who had performed this rite was afterwards stricken down.

The disinfecting of the houses was more difficult. In many there was not an air-hole even, and the roofs had to be breached to let in the sun. Every crevice and rat-hole was scoured with phenyl, all the chests and the cupboards which were let into the wall, and the granaries and stalls for the cattle. For if the work was not thorough, if a rat-flea survived, the whole business was undone. What faith would the people have in the Sahibs and their *mantras* if the pest sprang up again in their steps?

It was the most unpleasant part of their campaign. Nothing was so much resented or so provocative to the peace. There was hardly a peasant who did not protest, though Merivale paid on the spot for any damage that was done. For the first day or two he picked his way warily through chattis of carbolic and the villagers' great iron cauldrons brimming with phenyl. Happily the disinfectant left no stain. The women's clothes, a blaze of embroidered flower-work, were laid on charpoys over the dun earth like a swarm of butterflies settling on a clay bank, and the relentless squirt played over all. The holy Granth in its rich silk wrappings alone was spared, but for another ordeal—to warp and blister on the roof in the sun. There were genuine grievances and misadventures. Chauncey never forgot an old hag who clung to his feet sobbing, clutching his ankles with her bony fingers and refusing to be removed. In the end she whimpered for leave to go on to the roof for the last time before it was broken in. She clambered up the rough tree-trunk ladder feebly and still sobbing, and, gaining the top, she measured five spans with her fingers from the smoke-hole to the east in a line with the neem tree in the *haveli*. Then, with furtive looks to either side, she broke the surface of the caked mud and grubbed out her hoard—two or three rupees and some annas and pies. It was her secret purse, hidden away from her good man against some mysterious need of her own.

The work in the camps was no less heavy. Merivale had called in some *gharamis* from a neighbouring village to build up rude shanties, huts of reed matting nailed on a wooden frame, in place of the four stakes over which they had stretched their blankets, and he made the people help so that in a day or two they were able to build their own camp. It was his business, too, to see that the women suffered as little as need be. He provided grinding and spinning wheels for them, and took care of their jewellery. And when they complained of hunger he issued paper vouchers daily for two or three annas on his own authority. These were accepted by the bunniah, who exchanged them for grain on Merivale's word that the Sircar would honour them.

So in the grip of the plague with their back to the wall, the villagers turned to Merivale as to a Providence. And his respect for them grew daily. He admired the magnificent calm with which they took their bludgeonings, and he was happy in their trust.

## 3

In twenty days they had left Mehlgahla to a staff of subordinates, every house disinfected and the village ringed in with police. By this time a large encampment had sprung up with nurses and apothecaries and babus, and assistants and all manner of stores. The sick were dead or recovering in the hospital camp. Those who had escaped infection were bringing in their harvest. The women were spinning and grinding corn. And the villagers knew the work had been good. Thirty-two had died in the three days before the evacuation and two only in all the days afterwards.

Innes, the Commissioner, paid a flying visit to the camp. He sanctioned evacuation 'with tactful persuasion where necessary'. Merivale was all attentive deference, but he had done the work already, and the Commissioner knew it, and was glad to have a man. The only thing that had given Merivale any real uneasiness was his budget; but he was given a liberal grant, and the vouchers and compensation were passed with merely formal objections—just the official salve and break on the wheel. The Commissioner agreed with him that it was worth it.

Mehlgahla was saved. It was but one battle in a campaign which the Englishmen fought all through the hot weather. For the plague goddess was multi-cephalous. Barbers and pilgrims and leech women and sadhus had carried her germs about before ever Merivale had set foot in Mehlgahla, and for the next six months he and Chauncey scoured the ravaged land searching out her tracks and exterminating them as best they might. Other citadels held out and capitulated, and bands of deputies were left behind to see that the work they had set afoot was carried out. The peasants were her allies as often as not; and when it became known that these cranky Sahibs were offering rewards to the man who first laid information of her presence in any new spot, corpses were introduced surreptitiously, and the vicious circle by which the goddess revolved was set spinning anew. Twice this trick was played, and the informer betrayed by a counter-informer and sentenced duly.

Everywhere Merivale found the relatives of the sick of every age and degree sitting round the bed. Thus the ball was set rolling. But in one or two small villages where the men were merely decimated, the women perished almost to a soul. Here, it seems, an idea had spread abroad that the suffering could be eased if all the women in the village bore their small share of it. So the good wife called the cobbler woman in to open her bubo, and every gossip who came to condole with her touched the sore with the edge of her sheet, hoping to carry off a little of the pain. Sacrifice and charity met Merivale at the door where he had expected selfishness and indifference.

As the weeks passed the work grew, but it became easier. The fear of the peasants became more rational. One day Merivale came upon a village that was evacuating of itself; the people were literally running out. Soon it became the rule for the villagers to help; only the crabbed few lurked in their houses until they were made to budge. They had a wide beat, a hundred-mile point from east to west and stretching north almost to the foot of the Himalaya. One day they would be galloping off to a newly-infected village; the next returning on their tracks to inspect a camp they had left behind.

Siri Ram's village was inside the wide-infected circle. The pest had laid its tentacles all round, but spared Mograon. Merivale and Chauncey inspected it and reported it immune. They had speech with the old patriarch, Mool Chand, the boy's father, who told them about his son in Gandeshwar under 'Iskeen Sahib', and showed them his horoscope, a sad one, and a blurred photograph of a College group in which Siri Ram's thin, melancholy, resentful visage was decipherable. And there was a book which Skene had given him as a prize. Then he unrolled the boy's matriculation certificate from its tin case and held it upside down, scanning it curiously. He spoke of Siri Ram with qualified pride, a little puzzled at the unaccustomed product. He was a queer, sage lad, he said; but he had lost in reverence, and when at home he would sit alone idly brooding.

All the while they were talking Shiv Dai, the conspirator's small sister, watched the Englishmen with wide-open eyes. She did not speak or smile. When they rose Merivale felt in his pocket and produced a tiny hand-mirror and a coloured rag-book, which she accepted with the serious grace of a lady of quality.

Mool Chand showed them the dark recesses of his home. It was like every other dwelling in that mud world. You went through the gate into the *haveli*, a cramped courtyard strewn with cow fodder, save where a little mud wall divides off a square for cooking. The mud floor here is scrupulously polished; the five brass vessels, as scrupulously clean, are laid beside the chula where the pulse is being cooked for the family, or some sort of herbal concoction for the cow. The ashes of the fire under the pot are invisible for the intense glare. In the shrine-like cupboard of clay let into the wall and protruding like a peaked cowl, the boiled smoked milk is kept all day immune from the sun. From the sacred hearth you creep through a low door into a long, low, mud-walled room with a roof of beams and twigs caked with clay pierced sometimes with a smoke hole to let out the smoke or to let in a shaft of light. Coming in out of the sun you have to wait awhile before you can see what is round you, the chattis of water propped against the wall, the second hearth for winter cooking, the cupboard for grain, the square chest for clothes, the charpoys laid against the wall, the low, square, six-inch stool of matted twine where the housewife sits tending the fire. A minute will have passed before the geometrically designed peacocks in their bas-relief of clay take shape out of the gloom.

An open door leads into a darker chamber beyond for the cow, almost as comfortable, and a chamber beyond that for the *turi*, its provender. The cow walks through the dwelling room to reach the outside, picking her way through the urchins sleeping on the floor. Yet there is an instinct of cleanliness followed everywhere to a certain point. The floor is a composition of mud and cow-dung plastered into smooth polished surface—'lepai'ed' as they call it, and brushed carefully. The hearth outside is lepai'ed, and sometimes the part of the *haveli* nearest the threshold. The greater part of the housewife's life is taken up with lepai-ing. The faint warm smell of it pervades the village, and is not unpleasant. Apart from the little shisham wood that is needed for the props and doors and beams, and the little brass for the hearth, mud and cow-dung supply every need and elegance of the home. Every house is the same, built of mud inside and out, and there is little that does not shade into that hue from Mool Chand's skin to the rubble by the well and the banyan trees outside the village. The crumpled leaves of the neem, the garbage heap, the plough, every utensil in the house or the street except the brass cooking things is the colour of dust or mud. The cow, the buffalo, the cat, the children, the pig, the sleeping pariah dog, all more or less prostrated by the sun, look as if they had been modelled out of the different strata of discoloured clay in the blistered, cracked hollow which has served for the village pond. 'Dust to dust' is easy to understand in Mograon. Every hour of the villagers' lives is a text for that sermon. Eye and mouth and nostril inform the brain of little else. The stages between being gathered out of the clay and being gathered into it are so little distinguishable that birth and death and toil and sleep and resignation are part of the same slow-moving dream in which different states merge indifferently. Nowhere does life look so much like some phase of an excrescence exuded from the earth, a hummock of gritty soil disturbed by ants of the same hue. As you watch, you cannot distinguish the insect from the particle of clay it is carrying to the new earthworks on the path, which the first wayfarer will crush just as the plague goddess will plant a careless foot on Mograon and pass on.

If a child of this clay is ever stirred to think at all, it is only natural that it should be of first and last things, of first things when there is still a little sap in him; of last things only too soon, at an age when a boy in England is getting some grip of life. Think of Siri Ram in his mud hutch reading of beaux and coquettes and of Belinda's toilet, and the conquests of Blanche Amory and Ethel Newcome. Think of him among the clay and the cow-dung under the eternal blistering sun spelling out 'The Rape of the Lock'.

> Whether the nymph shall break Diana's law,
> Or some frail china jar receive a flaw,
> Or stain her honour, or her new brocade,
> Forget her prayers, or miss a masquerade,
> Or lose her heart, or necklace, at a ball,
> Or whether Heav'n has doom'd that Shock must fall.

Siri Ram knew one kind of man and woman only, one kind of food, one kind of house, and one kind of thought born of physical urgency or the puzzle of being. An Englishman or woman was nothing to him but a violent gross phenomenon. Yet the mill of his mind was set slowly grinding on Thackeray and Pope and Stevenson as an introduction to life.

For hours of every day in his first College vacation he would squat under the air-hole mumbling each dainty passage like a *mantra,* as if light came that way, with the same unintelligent sing-song cadence. Heaven knows with what dim, vague suggestions or stirrings of the heart he read of that bevy of girls on the river bank at Précy, corseted and ribboned, a company of coquettes under arms, that convinced the Cigarette and the Arethusa at once of being fallible males; or how in his mud hutch where children and kine were procreated indifferently, and flea-bitten rats ran over both, he visualized the foremost of the three Graces of Origny Sainte-Benoîte, she of the neat ankles, more of a Venus than a Diana, who leapt on to a tree trunk and kissed her hand to the canoeists and called to them to come back, or whether it was through any pangs of thwarted appetite that he crushed the persistent cockroach between the leaves of his book in the middle of the passage where Stevenson conjures up his visionary menu of oyster-patties and Sauterne at Compiègne.

One can imagine the astonishment of Merivale when a much-bethumbed copy of *An Inland Voyage* dropped out of the chest in Mool Chand's house on to the floor. He could conceive the husks of wit and grace and laughter, words without the spirit, solid chunks of Nuttall and Webster, all baked into the mind like flowers in a child's mud pie. For in Mograon mud doesn't stop at matter; it permeates mind. The spirit that informs the dust here has something of its hue and consistency, coarsened to sustain the resisting dross, like the little, soft crabs that move the clay about in the bed of an estuary. Education is supposed to quicken it, and it does beyond doubt, but the early phases of the process are too ugly to dwell on. Here and there a father, moved by the same self-protective evolutionary instinct that assimilates crustaceans to some new strata laid open by a river current, sends his son to school and the boy becomes an F.A., and perhaps afterwards a B.A. The Hobbs half of Anglo-India resents the hybrid and all dabbling in organic chemistry for such ends, but there is no doubt that the B.A., however clumsily or absurdly contrived, is a better man in the end than the untortured product of sunburnt clay, though at first sight he may not appear as lovable.

Mool Chand, you would say, is a dear old man, slow-moving, slow-speaking, patient, strong, enduring, unbent in adversity. He is like an old prophet, clear-eyed, grizzled in the sun, the brow and beard of Abraham, the gestures of an apostle. He salaams with a submissive dignity, raising both hands. The Commissioner loves him as his horse. But he would leave his aunt, or his little girl, at a pinch, to die in her plague-bed alone. The odds against that sort of thing increase with a lad's grade in school or college, though grace is at first perfunctory. Skene could give you the exact statistics of it.

But Mool Chand did not consider the formative influences of Gandeshwar. He sent Siri Ram there as one invests a bit of money in a life insurance. As an F.A. he would be worth thirty rupees a month, as a B.A. from fifty to eighty any day in the week, whereas the whole profits of Mool Chand's land might be covered by three hundred rupees in a good year. Knowing nothing of the vagaries of enlightenment, the Jat looked on his son as a safe investment. He did not know that Siri Ram, rejected of coordinated progress, was already drifting home, pledged to his shameful and unremunerative campaign. He was indeed contemplating how much his heir could contribute in three years towards the expenses of his small sister's marriage when the young patriot was trudging darkly out of Gandeshwar, the personified bankruptcy of his father's hopes.

But worse ills awaited his house.

# 4

Siri Ram and Banarsi Das and Lachmi Chand found consolation in the pamphlets of the Swami. If any beam of happiness could enter Siri Ram's head it must radiate from some such pyramidical grievance as this. Siri Ram had been building in the air, loose architecture which impressed few of his companions. But here was a substantial fabric, plinth on plinth of cunning masonry. A monumental grievance. And they were to put the apex on it so that the blindest must see; the most subservient, sycophantic, shoe-licking slave of the English must understand how the Indians were being deceived.

Siri Ram had never dreamt of such body for his vapourings. He was almost drunk with it and his late witness-bearing. He was for calling all the students together that very day and persuading them to take an oath never to wear any foreign cloth, never to salaam to an Englishman, never to let a chance go by of instilling true political ideas into the people. The unfolding of the ideas would be their province. Then he would call for volunteers among the true patriots who were willing to take the life of an Englishman. Siri Ram had forgotten the Swami's advice to work underground.

'You must not worship goddess in open manner,' Banarsi Das reminded him; 'in this way the cabal will be bruited to extremities. It will be bruited to Comorin and to similar city in north of map, and you would be expelled the University. English people are very cunning.'

Banarsi Das had already made up his mind to serve the goddess as a schoolmaster, a safer if less glorious part. He was not a man of blood.

Lachmi Chand was also for deliberation.

'Siri Ram is awfully a hasty gentleman,' he said; 'he is like the individual who sits on the branch of some tree with axe in his hand and cuts the root at the trunk, by which he is probable to fall down.'

Banarsi Das was in sympathy with this criticism. Neither he nor Siri Ram saw the weakness of Lachmi Chand's metaphor. The Swami's warning came into the conspirator's mind, to appear to imbibe the opinions of Government until the day of awakening should come, and so he capitulated.

'First let us know what is in these books,' Lachmi Chand continued. 'Then when some patriot is sent to gaol let us hold a meeting. We would know what to say.'

The occasion fell opportunely before many days had passed, when the two Punjabi seditionists were deported for tampering with the Sikh regiments and stirring up trouble in the canal colonies.

They met in the boarding-house reading-room to discuss Justice, as

Banarsi Das announced, hoping to discourage students who cared nothing about politics, and who might be a danger to them, yet fearing to make the thing too secret lest it should attract scoffers like Puran Singh. Whatever happened there was no fear of any student betraying them.

The hour was six on a sultry May evening, a time when no abstract question would have kept an English youth indoors. Siri Ram was in the chair, Banarsi Das on his right, Lachmi Chand on his left, and all down the long benches of the reading table a company of capped and turbaned youths, with here and there a red fez. Many waited in the verandah and courtyard outside, whence they would drop in at any time of the proceedings, for it was the custom at Gandeshwar for every one to wait for some one else to begin. In this case the cause had begotten initiative, and the dawdlers missed the opening of Banarsi Das's speech.

Politics was a hobby with this young man; he was drawn to it as a means to the self-assertion which was his only need in life. Speech was his forte. He had none of Siri Ram's burning sincerity, no rankling bitterness in his heart. He was a vain, meddling, town-bred youth, superficially cocksure and alert, inwardly dense as the mud of Mograon, which had not mixed its melancholy with his clay. In the College he was half leader, half clown, and spoke glibly with an inconsequent, muddle-headed stream of verbiage which impressed his companions. No argument could take the bottom out of his conceit, and his temerity led him into paths of eloquence which delighted Skene, and bred a kind of amused liking in him for the youth as a rather pathetic type of the hybrid we are responsible for. And the liking was reciprocated. Banarsi Das was flattered by the interest the Principal took in him. He was human enough after all. He could not have endured the sight of a weapon, and it would have made him quite sick to see a drop of blood shed, whether of an Englishman or any one else. This did not impair his sanguinary declamation.

Called upon by the chair, Banarsi Das rose with a self-assured air, his little brown cap pushed back over his short-cropped hair, and smiling under his spectacles like a swimmer about to take the stream and conscious of his strength.

'Gentlemen, it is not enough for us to place upon record our loathing and detestation of the cowardly and dastardly crime of British Government, who have removed this high-souled and noble-spirited patriot out of our middle to rot in chains somewhere else. Poet has said, 'Stone bars do not make prison'. No, they do not make prison for soul. This is familiar to you. We are met here for a great purpose. Gentlemen, we are potent if we are unanimous to make the English not to stay in this country.

'The English are jungly and weak. By union only they have attained empire. Gentlemen, I put question to you, are they as plentiful as the blackberries and ants upon the seashore? No, they are not as plentiful. As Emerson says, The Englishman is a 'rarer avis' in this country. It is easy to muzzle him and to turn him into sea.

'Why he is ruling over us? Why you are afraid of Englishmen? They are not gods but men like yourselves, or rather monsters who have ravaged Sita-like beauty of your country. If there be any Rama among you, let him come forth to bring back your Sita.'

Banarsi Das paused to mark the effect of his appeal. His vanity was satisfied.

'Who are Englishmen?' he went on; 'how they have become our rulers? They have not taken India by sword. They have thrown noose of dependence round us by cunning. The ornament of a man is a weapon, but they have taken all these away from us. Now are all Indians worthless, they have become timid and afraid eunuchs. They are worse than women. They are accounted criminals for using the article of their native country.

'Gentlemen, when I look upon foreign-made things my whole body catches fire. I wish to kill one of these Satans who defile sugar with the bones of pig and cow and any dead animal to make Hindus and Muhammadans faithless alike.

'Are we to be taught courage by Bengal—'

Banarsi Das was skilfully preparing the meeting for the Swadeshi vow. When he sat down after a moving peroration, the forty students still in the room took it without demur. It was a formula in language less impressive than his own.

'I swear this very day in the presence of my Guru (or my priest or in the name of the goddess of Independence) never to wear any foreign-made cloth or to eat any foreign-made food or to keep money in English banks or to purchase any promissory notes. Also that I will consider every Indian, whatever his caste or creed, as my real brother, and that I will sacrifice myself for my country and devise means to uproot the enemy by secret bands, and to ruin the Feringhi all at once after making preparations for a suitable date which can fall within ten years if we work as one people.'

This was strong meat for the novices, but none save a red fez or two dared refuse or slink out of the room. One hysterical youth stood up, stripped his wilaiti shirt off his back, tore it into shreds, flung it on the floor, and buttoned his coat over a naked breast.

The milder Lachmi Chand followed with his religious appeal. He was a gentle, patient-looking youth with a sad face, and his melancholy was vested in the spiritual decay of the Aryans. Political dependence did not distress him so much as the cause of it, the falling away of his people from the ancient stock whom he saw telescopically magnified. Giants in stature and in soul striding over the mountains to occupy their birthright, men whose strength lay in their nearness to God, and who spent three parts of their lives in serving Him, giving a fourth part only to the family and the home. He spoke always of the Golden Country and the Aryan revival and the Lahore Samaj. The deported martyr was his text.

'India's golden land has not lost all her heroes. They are springing up in our midst, though brutal imprisonments reduce them to skeletons. The English are making us forget our old faith, they are making us forget our old learning, they are leading us along the path of sin. It is shame for them to think that with swords and guns they can shut in the Vedas. It is shame for them to think that with bricks and stones they can lock in the truth. What is that truth? It is the truth that consoled people hundreds of thousands of years before the Koran and the Bible, when the ancestors of these demons were in disgusting state of barbarism. The truth that gave light to the people lakhs of years before Zoroaster. They are fools who believe they can lock in the Vedas.'

Siri Ram rose with a bundle of notes, but he did not look at them. He had learnt his speech too well. He kept his eyes strained upon the wall, as if he saw the goddess of Independence materialized there above his companions' heads. First he drew a picture of the innocent patriot condemned without a trial to rot in chains, and his family members and nears and dears weeping and disconsolate. Then he expatiated upon the barbarity and injustice of the English, dwelling particularly on the slaughter of cows, and the deliberate impoverishment of the land that they might hold it the more easily. 'A dragon is sucking the life-blood of our Bharat Mata,' he cried. 'She is weeping. Her wound is ours. Shall we sit still at our meals amid laughter and merrymaking without care? Or shall we not rather give up our pleasures and smear our bodies with ashes every day until we have rescued her and trampled the demon under our foot?'

Then he went through the Swami's pamphlets one by one, all the old lies about the economic drain, which he half believed, and the perverted history of the occupation. How the English took the country step by step with fraud and broken faith, and how the native army won an empire for them and were despised and downtrodden for their pains. When he had probed every old sore and added new venom to race-hatred with the catchwords of the hour he began to repeat the names of the patriot heroes of the world, coupling Nana Sahib with

Garibaldi. And this brought him to the Mutiny of '57, and the impending anniversary of it which the English were preparing for themselves.

'Thirty crores will not be idle. They will wash the land again in blood, and not an English head will rise from the slaughter-pit. Our country was the crown of all countries, and was called the Golden Land. Her hour has come again. Drums are beating. Heroes and martyrs are preceding. See to Sivaji, and Napoleon Bonaparte, and other heroes in Germany and France. See to Japan. Take only a life for a life. If one thousand sacrifice themselves—'

But here a gross impersonation of British force blocked the door at Siri Ram's back. The students shuffled to their feet, and he saw in their faces what had happened. Turning round, he looked into the large, inquiring eyes of Skene. For a moment not a word was said. An irresponsible youth at the far end of the room slipped out at the door opposite, betraying his guilt. The rest stood their ground shamefacedly.

# 5

'What does this mean?' Skene asked. But Siri Ram only looked at him with shifty defiance, too confused to speak.Banarsi Das, entering the breach, explained glibly—

'Sir, we held meeting of Students' Improvement Society. The aim of Society is to provide lecture and discussion of moral and religious problem. It also serves purpose of English B. paper by improving idioms and etiquettes.'

'I know too much about what is going on,' Skene interrupted. 'I have been suspecting it for some time, and I'm afraid some of you must suffer. Now stay here and listen to me. You have been taught a great deal about the English lately, haven't you? They are cruel, unjust, cunning, godless, selfish, matter-worshippers, bloodthirsty—you see, I know your textbooks—and it is your duty as patriots to hate them. How many English have you met?'

The conspirators were silent.

'You know me, and perhaps some officers who have come here to play cricket. Now you must judge people by how you find them, not by what professional politicians tell you. Ask your fathers and grandfathers what dealings they have had with the English, and whether they have found them honest, true, and sympathetic, and ready to give of their very best to the people, no matter of what caste or creed.

'Mind you, I am not here to defend the English; we are strong enough to take care of ourselves. Stronger, indeed, than we were fifty years ago.' Here Skene looked at Siri Ram. 'Only it is better that we should be friends when we have to work together, and not go about with bitter, suspicious thoughts in our hearts.

'I'll tell you about these canal colonies some other time. Government, as you know, have turned hundreds of thousands of acres of desert land into cultivation, and they have given this land free of charge to cultivators, and the only conditions they have put upon the tenure are framed to preserve the property in the families it is intended for, so that it may pass from father to son, and not be whittled away, as too often happens, by usurers and lawyers.

'Well, your deportee and his friends have been let loose among these folk like snakes in Eden, and they have maddened them with lies and misrepresentations until they are on the point of rebellion. These are the firebrands that have been removed or, as your newspapers say, 'spirited away to rot in chains without trial'. Any other Government would have hanged them on the nearest tree. But you may be quite sure they will be well cared for in prison, and released as soon as it is safe.

'But this is only a side issue. What I wish you to understand is how we have won India, and with what right and justice we hold it. I know all about these seditious leaflets that have been circulated among you. I have seen them myself. We must have these charges sifted above ground. Bring the pamphlets to me. I will expose each lie and distortion of fact, point by point. You may ask me as many questions as you like, I won't be angry. And when I have done, I think you will agree with me that the British have been straight and honourable in their dealings with you. Clive played one dirty trick, it is true, and we are all ashamed of it. It is a single black blot in an otherwise clean record, the blacker because it is so utterly foreign to the national character and traditions that Englishmen become hot to-day when they think of it. But for that, you will find that the English have always tried to do the straight and disinterested thing.

'India for the Indian nation is a fine rallying cry, and I don't wonder it appeals to you. But a nation is not merely a geographical term; it implies a compact people, united and inspired by common aims and traditions. India, as you know, is not one people any more than Europe is one people. If ever she does become one, with a genuine sense of nationality, and the courage and unselfishness to defend it without any thought of individual interest or class privilege, she will be strong enough to take the reins from us, and no shame to us to drop them, seeing that it is we who have taught her to drive. But you are not going the right way to work. You must look facts in the face. Every one respects an honest nationalist, but you must *be* the thing first before you can enjoy its privileges. No nation was ever built on lies.

'Don't think I want you to believe that India is a distressful burden which we bow under from a sense of duty only. I hate cant. India is as much the property of the English as the estate of one of your zemindars is the property of the landlord whose ancestor won it by the sword, or was given it for service. Tell your zemindar he must divide his property among his tenants because they are becoming fit to manage it themselves, and hear what he will say. Yet this is what some of our politicians are saying about India. It is quite true that if we left the country, each community would be at the other's throat. This is one good reason for our staying. But it is not *the* reason. We are here because it is our country. Incidentally it happens to be our way to recognize our obligations to our tenants as no other rulers have done or are ever likely to.'

Skene had never talked politics to his students before. He shrank from it; for, when all is said and done, the case resolves itself in the end to the privilege of the weak to be ruled by the strong, and this is a very difficult thing for an Englishman to say without suspicion of brutality or pride. Skene was not pleased with his effort. In some of the students' faces he fancied he saw intelligent sympathy, but others were sheepish and sullen, obstinately grieved, as he might well have been if the situation had been reversed. He felt that he had bungled it somehow, but anything was better than saying nothing. Only he wished that one of them would speak. It would be so easy to put the case to them if they were not Indians.

Clive once behaved like a Bengali politician, and it left a stain on our honour like a drop of ink in a phial of pure water. But where was the diplomatist in their ranks who would have behaved like Admiral Watson?

It was impossible to suggest the shadow of the thought.

In the meanwhile there were Siri Ram, Banarsi Das, and Lachmi Chand to be dealt with. Skene passed sentence on the spot. He expelled Siri Ram from the University, and he rusticated Banarsi Das and Lachmi Chand for a year.

'I am sorry for you,' he said, 'but you must go. I have warned you once, and I can't have the College spoilt like this. I will help you as far as I can because I think you have been misled, and really believe the mischievous lies which your heads have been stuffed with. Anyhow I hope that you are too honest to circulate charges which you know are false. Banarsi Das and Lachmi Chand may rejoin the College after a year provided there is nothing new against them. And you, Siri Ram, come to my office tomorrow morning at ten, and I'll see what I can do for you.'

As Skene left the boarding-house, the suppressed murmur of the students became an angry babel. It had been one of the most depressing moments he had known in Gandeshwar. For the first few years, his relations with his pupils had been friendly and unstrained, but he had gradually become aware of a hostile element which was part of the growing trouble all over India. On the whole he was rather glad that things had come to a head, for it might relieve the charged atmosphere. Everything depended on his personality. If the students ceased to like him he could do nothing with them.

As he crossed the football field, the cloud in his mind lightened. The College were playing a regimental team, and he reached the corner flag just in time to see Puran Singh take a neat pass from the half-back, dribble through to front of goal with the ball at his feet, and make a clean shot along the ground just inside the posts. The cheering all round was like a tonic. He could have slapped Puran Singh on the back.

'Shabash, Puran Singh,' he shouted. 'That is better than lifting it over the bar, isn't it?'

Puran Singh beamed when he saw the Principal had been watching his feat, and every one laughed at Skene's chaffing allusion to a match against Government College, lost by a high, wild kick in the air when Puran Singh had the goal at his mercy. Skene had taught him after that to shoot clean and low in front of goal with a straightened instep or with the side of his foot.

'You are playing tennis with me tomorrow against the regiment. Don't forget.'

'Thank you, sir.'

Skene was almost pleased with the way things were going when he reached the Club and met Dean the policeman coming down the steps.

'You got hold of the right men,' he said. 'Thanks for the information. I've fired one out and rusticated the other two. Had to do it, but I am devilish sorry for them. Children all three.'

'What is the expelled youth going to do? I'd keep an eye on him.'

'I was thinking of sending him to Everitt in the XIXth. He wants a clerk on his own.'

'That's the man on the mule transport registration in the Hills, isn't it?'

'Yes. He has to trek half the year at the back of beyond, and his Babu stays down at headquarters in Sialkote. Government won't sanction another clerk.'

'I shouldn't risk it. He can do a lot of harm in those little States.'

'Are they touched?'

'You haven't heard of Blimba? People wondered where the resurrected Dhandora leaflets came from. Well, they had a small press up there. There were only two Babus in the State, but they worked it all right, and sent five hundred copies every week into Simla in *khiltas* covered with apricots and pomegranates.

'They had the time of their lives. The little Rajah man hates the English. He was fed up with his salute, and thought it a huge joke. There was no fear of a surprise. You can see the white road winding seven miles through the pines into Blimba, and a topee or a policeman's cap would have sent the whole warren skedaddling down the khud, press and all.'

Skene learnt a lot about sedition before dinner. Dean turned back into the Club with him, and they sat on a garden seat overshadowed by hibiscus and duranta, while he unfolded the schemes of the extremist gang in Lahore.

It was the most complicated organization, and the police believed that the whole body of the Arya Samaj was involved in the nexus, so that every postal and telegraph clerk and every subordinate on the railway knew exactly what he had to do on the day of reckoning. Many Aryas, of course, cared nothing for politics, but those who were well-disposed to Government dared not betray their associates if they would, so it was impossible to say how many knew what was going on in the inner ring.

'And the best of it is,' Dean went on, 'in some of these centres they have got a register in which they have booked all the best appointments for the fraternity after we have been wiped out. They have done us the honour to preserve our system, and the salaries will stand as they are. A hospital assistant at Jullundur on eight rupees a month will be P.M.O. of the Sirhind Brigade, and a Jemadar of the Nth Punjabis is to be Station Staff Officer at Dalhousie.'

'And who is to command the Division?'

'That is still in the lucky bag. The General is not nominated yet. They have chucked in a few Muhammadans just to look well, but they daren't give the command to one, and they daren't give it to a Sikh or a Dogra, as they know the Pathans would be at their throats.'

'And the Constitution?'

'A limited Monarchy. The beggars have had the impudence to approach Nepaul.'

'Pharaoh's feet, what a muddle! What wouldn't I give to be at the first Parliament! It would be almost worth being a disembodied spirit.'

'Yes, I dare say. This paper Empire won't do much harm, but they are doing a lot of real mischief. Take the Hills alone. They are working them pretty thoroughly with their political missionaries as they call them.'

Skene learnt that young men in the guise of Sannyasis were being sent to every little hill State and Zemindari ostensibly as pilgrims to visit Gangotri or Kedarnath, or to circumambulate Kailas, or to scatter flowers on Siva's frozen spring in the ice caves of Amarnath, but in reality to spread the tale that the white throne was tottering in Hindustan, that Englishmen were held of no account, and that all lonely Sahibs who visited the solitudes of the mountains should be done away with singly. That Sahibs fallen over cliffs, or shaken from rope bridges, or shot in ambush could tell no tale, and that merit and reward would fall to their assassins in this world and the next.

'If you sent Siri Ram you would be playing into their hands,' Dean said. 'Everitt wouldn't have the ghost of an idea what was going on.'

'Poor little devil,' Skene thought. 'He has no luck.'

But Siri Ram's horoscope was cast in sadder lines than Skene knew. A day or two after Merivale's visit, the pest had fallen on Mograon like a flail. It broke out in Uttam Singh, the headman's house, and Shiv Dai, Siri Ram's little sister, must have caught it when she was combing Uttam Singh's wife's hair. A leech-woman from Mehlgahla had brought it into the village. She had got through somehow in the early days unsuspected at the time before the cordon was formed, and passed from village to village putting leeches on the buboes of the sick and trailing the plague after her. In three days Mool Chand's *mohalla* was decimated. The rats crept out of their holes and lay dying in the street and in the houses, indifferent to man, and the fleas swarmed over them till they were cold, and then sought warmer pasture.

Siri Ram's mother had been one of the first stricken, and lay unconscious several days, but survived, and rose a crazy skeleton from her bed. Then his little sister, Shiv Dai, lay in the toils. When Mool Chand felt the gland on her groin, a smooth, round, movable tumour like an egg, he thought her doomed; the little girl was so thin and frail. For two days she lay unconscious almost, with her eyes half-closed, sleepless, restless, for ever moving her arms and legs, raising her knee slowly and then straightening it out again and moaning in her pain. Soon she passed into a stage of muttering delirium. She tried to fling herself off her bed, and Mool Chand tied her down with his turban. The presence of death was felt everywhere. Day and night the wailing of mourners rose from the houses all round. Soon Mool Chand's neighbours were all running out into the fields. The fear gripped him, and he felt that he, too, must go. He put some chapattis and water by Shiv Dai's bed, more to appease the lemures of the hearth than for any good it might do her, and he shambled out into the street supporting his wife.

He left the corn in the locker and the milk in the alcove by the hearth, and the square chest with the family clothes. He drove the cow out before him and left Shiv Dai alone to die. 'If she is to die, why disturb her?' he said. 'And if she lives—' He thought of the sorrow in the house when the woman-child was born, and the coming marriage expenses. It would be three years before Siri Ram, a full-blown B.A., could contribute.

He did not know that Siri Ram had been expelled from the College after all his outlay, and that he was an unmarketable product and a source of insecurity to quiet folk rather than profit.

## 6

Merivale was back on his tracks at Mehlgahla again. There had been no rain, but the moon was barely visible for the dense air, and not a star was to be seen. The villagers were drooping like sick crows, sprawling on their charpoys, and pitched forward on their haunches like birds on a bough, suspiring for air. But there was not a breath anywhere.

After a hard day Merivale had arrived in Mehlgahla before his tent and kit. The villagers came out to meet him. Some clutched at his feet and knees and greeted him as their saviour. They brought him warm smoked milk and eggs and *chapattis*. He dined off them. Then he braced himself to go round the camp. The quarantine was nearly over, and the plague had not touched a soul since he left. The unaffected pleasure of everybody at the merest glimpse of him kept him upright, and he had a smile and a joke for them all in spite of the trouble he had to keep on his feet. For the clogging air had to be resisted, and Merivale had not had more than three hours' broken sleep any night of the week.

He lay on the rickety charpoy he had borrowed from the headman, watching the moon, waiting for the haze to clear which filled his throat and nose and eyes with hot particles of grit. Yet he dreaded the moon more, for he could not sleep under her malignant rays, and cover was stifling. She was an enemy in Mehlgahla, red, bloody, passionate, exacting, exhaling weariness. Not the same Cynthia who swims over quickening hazel copses and primrose dells at home, and peeps into dimpled becks breasting cool clouds. Cynthia and Diana there, silvery and chaste; here a bronze pan of fire, phantom of the destroyer, the reverse of Durga's shield, more malignant than the Sun-god because stealthier and more insidious in her embrace. Merivale felt sick inwardly to think of the primroses glimmering palely in a meadow he knew well by an old ivied church in Devon under the caressing moonlight. On hot-weather nights he always thought of the old country in the freshness of spring.

He shut his eyes to a hot wave of air that flickered over him. But darkness was hotter, and he opened them soon to watch the brazen sphere slowly concentrating her light—and her heat, it seemed—as the mist thinned. In the coppery haze the hot, gritty stars glowed dully like exhausted embers. The night sky of June burnt itself into his mind through those interminable hot-weather vigils. Corvus and Corona and Scorpio and Bootes were sparks that added their rays to his fire-pit. It was only at Mehlgahla that he came to know the constellations, but he had the map in his head long afterwards. Sometimes even by lakes and above cool mountains Scorpio would unfold her scaly length for him over the segregation camp, and a feeling would come to him that if he wanted to inspect the cordon he must steer for the plough.

He was waiting for the last star of Scorpio to rise above the mango clump when he heard the creaking of bullock carts in a rutty lane. It was his belated camp. He recognized the heavy, premeditated tramp of his new orderly, who was conscious of the dignity of boots and lifted them with pain like an honourable burden. Merivale called the man to him and told him to take his meal at once and go to sleep, and pitch tents in the morning. Then as an afterthought he asked him if there were any news.

'The plague is at Mograon. Many have died, and there is great fear. The people all went out before midnight yesterday.'

'Is it far?'

'Perhaps eighteen miles.'

'You need not unload the carts. We go there tomorrow.'

A chaprassi arrived as he spoke, dragging his feet wearily. Wishing to be of some account, he supplemented the orderly's tale.

'Ah, Sahib, and they have left one woman behind.'

'They have, have they? Then we go tonight.'

Merivale sat up on his charpoy and thought of means. Both his ponies were dead beat, and one had not come in from the last stage. He sent to the headman for camels, and in a few minutes he was swinging through the night again. The hair and saddle of the brute were hotter than his bed, and when once he was mounted the sleep he had sought so long came uninvited, and he found it hard to throw off his drowsiness. A fall to earth might mean a broken limb, so he hung on and began to think he was swimming through a hot sea in which sleep was death, and port the scene of more toil, with sleep perhaps afterwards. Every time the camel lurched forward he breasted a wave, and in this mood his spirit became numb, and he ceased to care for anything, feeling like a bit of flotsam, cast here and there by the waves as he watched the strange veering pilot neck of the camel, so dainty and so gross and so eternally indifferent, swaying between him and the last star of Scorpio.

After five or six hours of this travail, the leading camel pulled up and swerved round alongside of him, and the driver waved his whip at a clump of trees on the right and called out in his profoundly melancholy voice, 'Mograon'.

There was a small plank over a nullah, by crossing which Merivale would save half a mile. He sent the camels round and took the footpath, and in a few minutes found himself alone in the deserted village. The sky was now clear, and, in the intense moonlight, the shadows of the posts and eaves and the thin kikar leaves lay etched in the white street with pin-point clearness. The doors of all the houses were chained and barred. The place was abandoned. There was no sound save the tread of the retreating camels beyond the nullah, and not a stir save where a furtive pariah slunk by with its shadow double. The very dogs, affected by the ghostly silence of the place, would not bark.

Merivale recognized the house in which the old Jat had given him milk and spoken of his first-born, the morose Gandeshwar student who brooded in his holidays—for choice on the nature of God and of necessity upon the coquettes of Precy and the Graces of Origny Sainte-Benoîte. It was a favourite passage he had come upon in Siri Ram's book so unexpectedly discovered in that mud world, and the picture rose again in his mind as he sat down on the threshold for very weariness, and wondered how he was going to find the woman they had left behind, and whether she would be alive or dead.

His head kept falling sideways against the door post as sleep captured him, and he almost forgot his errand, dreaming all the while of the girl on the tree stump so fresh and clean and cool and far away, waving her hand to the Arethusa and Cigarette. He saw the willows dripping over the stream and heard the church bells of Pont. Then, falling forwards on to the step, he thrust a hand forward to save himself, and clutched something cold and dead. It was a plague rat. He left the infested corner and wandered down the alley looking for an open door or some sign of life.

Under a neem tree in the next street he came upon a huddled figure crouching over a drain. It was an old woman, who turned an emaciated face to him in the moonlight. She had been sobbing tearlessly. Merivale awoke her from her sad dreams.

'Why, Mother! What is the matter? Why do you stay here alone?'

'Why should I go? I shall not find my sons there.'

'When did you last eat anything?'

'It may have been the day before yesterday.'

'You should come now. Can you walk? We will look after you in the camp tomorrow'.

'They said 'Come,' but I would not. What should I gain there?'

'It is better to live than to starve.'

'If it is fated that I am to die, I shall die like the others.'

Merivale tried to explain that there was no need to die, but she was unconvinced, and his argument sounded vain to himself. The wisdom learnt of suffering upsets all values. She knew her own plight best, and the saving of the poor old thing could only be perfunctory. He asked her about her sons. Two had died in one night. He learnt that there was no one else left in the village save the small daughter of Mool Chand in the next *mohalla*. But it was probable that she too was dead.

He left the old woman with words of sympathy and the promise to return—vain utterances, he knew, in the face of such sorrow—and he made his way back to the Jat's house near which he had slept. He found the door of the *haveli* locked, and wrenched the rivet open with the broken yoke of a plough. The inner door was ajar, and as he entered he heard the girl's voice calling for her mother, and thanked God he was not too late. He struck a match and found a tiny clay lamp in an alcove of the wall—a wick floating in oil—and he lighted it. Shiv Dai lay still, her large black eyes open and staring. She looked at him without fear or wonder, too exhausted for either. She called for her mother again, feebly looking at the door, and mumbled of her thirst. Did she know her parents had abandoned her? He took the empty bowl by her side and filled it from the chatti in the *haveli*, and she drank from his hand, defiled as the vessel was by his touch. He felt her wrist. The fever had left her. Then he unloosened the turban by which she was bound to the bed. Mool Chand had not thought of untying it before he left, though he had been careful to lock the door. 'I am going to take you to your mother,' he said. But it is doubtful if Shiv Dai heard or understood. He lifted her wasted little body in his arms, and carried her into the street and out of the village. He hoped to see the camp-fires of the plague fugitives from the embankment above the nullah.

Merivale ran into a clerkly youth on the plank across the nullah. He was astonished to see a brown cap and cropped hair at that hour and place.

To his salaam 'Who are you?' the lad answered in English—

'I am the son of an agriculturist of this village. I come now from

Gandeshwar College.'

'Who is your father?'

'He is cultivator.'

'It is you who read Stevenson, *The Inland Voyage,* isn't it? You are Mool Chand's son?'

'Ye—es, no doubt after all.'

'Then this is your sister. She is recovering from plague. They left her behind in the village.'

'Certainly that is very ba-ad. It is the duty of every one—'

Siri Ram was answering the indignation in the Englishman's voice, but Merivale cut him short.

'Take her,' he said, holding out the tiny frail bundle, 'while I go and find out the camp.'

Siri Ram hesitated. 'Sir, if you would put her on the ground,' he said, 'it would be more sateesfactory.'

'Afraid of infection! Well, some one will have to look after her till we fix up a hospital camp. Stay with her, anyhow, until I come back.'

Merivale laid her gently on the earth. Siri Ram said he would stay. He watched the retreating form of the civilian with inward bitterness.

Here was a man risking his life and forfeiting his sleep to save an Indian girl abandoned by her own people, and he was pleasant in his speech and there was no pride in him. Siri Ram did not put the whole case to himself like this, for he hated the Englishman and felt ashamed and uncomfortable in his presence.

It never occurred to him to analyse his sense of uneasiness or to sift prejudice from fact; for if he had, he might have found in Merivale the practical contradiction of his most cherished grievances. And the man was the type of the race. The only questions Siri Ram asked himself were: 'Why is this hated foreigner here at all? How is he superior to the Aryans? Is it his white skin that gives him authority to come to my village and send my people here and there and meddle with their affairs, and to carry my sister about in his arms as if she were of no account?'

Also it was a bitter thought that his father, Mool Chand, an ignorant who knew nothing about Mill and Burke and John Morley and advanced liberal thought, would greet the *feringhi* salaaming with both hands, with tears in his eyes, as if the English were the divinely appointed guardians of the Bharat Mata.

Siri Ram would not go with Merivale and Shiv Dai to his father. Greatly wavering, he was resolute in that. He feared the rage of the rude cultivator. Somehow he had half known that he would not see his parents again when he left Gandeshwar led by an undefined homing instinct to his village. He would have liked to see the house and the cow and to speak to his mother and to visit all his old haunts again, but he could not explain his new life to anybody. They would be very angry, and they would not understand.

He made up his mind to go away and write to them, but first he must learn what had happened to his father and mother. The dreadful thought came to him that he might have to stay and perform their funeral rites.

Dawn broke at last, and Siri Ram could hear the distant camp of the villagers wakening. A speck of dust advanced from the direction in which Merivale had disappeared. Soon it disclosed a boy driving a donkey with baskets on its back to collect the humble offerings of the cow for the domestic hearth. Siri Ram learnt from the urchin that his mother had been stricken, but had recovered, and that Mool Chand was well. So there was no need to stay. He turned to Shiv Dai, but could not make her understand anything. She was awake, but half crazy, it seemed. He reasoned with himself that the English pig would soon come back, and that no harm could come to her now in the daylight. Then he turned wearily on his tracks to Gandeshwar, hungry and sad at heart in spite of his mission.

In a few days Mool Chand received a letter from his son in Urdu, and he summoned the village writer to read it.

'The Bharat Mata calls, so it behoves me not to stay at home any more. Is this the time to stay at College? Now do I leave College, but not my learning. I leave my home and relatives, and perhaps I do this for ever. I shall again return to Gandeshwar, but not to my home in this life if I cannot finish my work. I am going alone, and must go alone if no one follows hearing me. Many will say many things. Parents and sister will weep, but it will not do if I look to them any more. What do I fear, and where is my sorrow, when I am going into the lap of her who is the mother of three hundred millions of men.'

The three conspirators had put their heads together over it. They had drunk deep of the well of Bengal. The Swami did not sow seed in waste ground. And he knew it was not in vain that he watched the zigzag path to his cave every day for the dejected face of Siri Ram.

# 7

Shiv Dai lived, and the old hag whom Merivale found in the gutter was restored to her folk to see another summer, but Chauncey was sickening of the plague and at death's door.

The two had taken war risks all the while. The serum—then in its tentative stage, a disputed prophylactic—did not arrive from Bombay until three weeks after they had started their campaign, and Chauncey's work was so exacting he could not spare the day or two needed to lie up after the inoculation. There had always been some new outbreak to grapple with, and as soon as he had got the pest under in one village and organized the camps he was off to another.

Merivale got the news in Mograon, and he arrived just in time. Chauncey had come in from the segregation camp looking well, the hospital assistant told him, but he felt cold in his joints. Soon he was very sick and the ague shook him. He lay on his bed holding his forehead, and for hours he would not utter a word except now and then to ask for Merivale with laboured and hesitating speech, breathing painfully. Merivale, when he came, was not sure that Chauncey recognized him. He tried to say something, but stopped in the middle of his sentence with a blank look, and turned over on his side. He threw off his sheet and kept his arm away from the gland in his armpit, and when Merivale brought him water he poured some of it over his body.

Merivale sat by his side all night trying to soothe his restlessness, his own wits sunk in exhaustion. From time to time Chauncey muttered incoherently. His pain was pitiful. One could see the straining of his heart. At the end he beckoned to Merivale to lean over him, and gasped out as if each syllable were an intolerable strain—

'Get inoculated, old man. This is hell.'

Merivale pressed his hand. 'Don't talk,' he said, 'if it hurts,' and he let a tear fall on his burning wrist. Chauncey clutched his friend's palm as if he had spoken.

'Thanks!' he said. And Merivale knew it was his farewell. Soon a heavy drowsiness fell on him which deepened into a coma, from which he never woke.

Merivale was tired out. He had kept himself going somehow through those long nights, but now exhaustion acted on him like an opiate, easing his distress. The whole thing seemed like some vague, remote nightmare. Only Chauncey had gone, and they were building a stone over his grave at Mehlgahla.

The saddest part of it was that he was almost the last to die—one of those 'dropping cases', as the doctors call them, which come in the dogdays at the end of the visitation when the sun seems to burn the virus out once for all.

Merivale had now only to stay and wind up. It was all routine office work, disbanding the camps, paying the bunniahs, allotting compensation. Things went very smoothly in the villages. Chauncey and Merivale had laughed over the bilious comments of the vernacular Press and their echoes in Parliament, but now Chauncey was dead they jarred on his friend.

He had been 'the fatted doctor', and Merivale 'the fat-salaried bureaucrat', and between them they had swallowed up half the collection which might have fed the poor. 'Every Indian knows,' shrieked the *Sahaik*, 'that the plague is a pest brought by the English, and is due to the poverty of the people and their physical weakness, caused by the miserable condition to which they have been reduced.'

'The plague is a disease which thrives specially amidst poverty,' cries our philosophical Radical in the House, 'and its fresh outbreak in India on a large scale is in itself a warning against optimism, plague being now endemic under our rule.' Whence he argues with glum satisfaction that all is not so well with our great Eastern Dependency as some would have us believe.

'How do the bureaucrats explain the pest?' shrilled the *Koel*. 'They lay it to the door of the poor harmless rat, just as they attribute malaria, which was never so rife as under their rule, to the innocent mosquito.' Whence the unphilosophic revolutionist goes on to hint what was being openly proclaimed by itinerant 'missionaries' in the villages, that the plague patients were being poisoned in the hospitals, and Government was making deliberate attempts to spread the disease.

'Only a question of degree,' Merivale observed. 'The spirit is the same. Each goes as far as he dare. Listen to this—

' "The cunning English are preparing a fluid which they pretend to be charmed, and this is to be squirted into the poor through a hole made in the arm. Thousands of gallons of this mixture, which contains all kinds of pollution destructive to caste, are being distributed among the villages, and lakhs of rupees are going into the pockets of English shopkeepers and chemists. In the same way lakhs' worth of quinine is being sold to poor Indians that English manufacturers may fatten." '

It was *The Koel* that described how a body of pampered bureaucrats sat in the clouds on the heights of Simla under the name of a Commission, drinking wine and brandy, and dancing with half-clothed women, and how in the interests of debauchery they devised means to develop the trade in drugs and to deceive the poor. The tax gatherers were busy, for one night's orgy would impoverish a village for a year.

Chauncey had sent the cutting to Merivale with a picture of Higgins, his precise, Presbyterian, bald-headed P.M.O., waving an empty brandy bottle at his *dècolletèe* vis-a-vis. The blameless, vacant head of old Fooks in the Secretariat protruded from under a neighbouring chair where he lay supine.

But Merivale could not wax merry over these things any more. When the mail came in he was surprised to find that there was quite a pother at Home about Chauncey and himself, and that Mehlgahla had become a household word. He had never realized the bitterness, and meanness, and ignorance of the Little England group in the House before. The same agitators who had screamed in the Punjab Press had written in more moderate terms to Radical Members of Parliament who were known to be sympathetic.

Dr Byleman asked the Under Secretary of State whether it was true that Mr Merivale, a Punjab civilian, and Captain Chauncey of the Indian Medical Service had forcibly entered the houses of high-caste villagers during the plague operations and violated the privacy of the zenana; and whether such profanation of the Indian reverence for home and women would be tolerated by the Government.

The Under Secretary of State said that full inquiries were being made into the case. He understood that *purdah* was not observed as a rule in Jat villages.

Dr Byleman rose a second time in the same week and asked whether the charges had been substantiated, and if so, whether under the circumstances the two officers would be retained in the Service.

The case cropped up in one way or another once or twice a week. The home Radical papers made capital out of it with their headlines of 'outrage' and 'violence' and the 'high-handed insolence of Anglo-Indian officialdom'. And every little rag in Bengal and Poona and Madras echoed the cry, and every schoolboy who read believed. For how could the charges be false if they were brought by the English against their own people? Dr Byleman had reason for elation. He had knocked more nails into the coffin of our prestige than anybody could count.

Perhaps the only district in which the charges did not harm was in Mehlgahla itself and in the villages round. Political 'missionaries' were sent there, but they did no good. Mool Chand only looked perplexed when it was explained to him that his house had been forcibly entered and the privacy of his zenana outraged.

'But the Sahib saved my little daughter,' he said. The truth of it was, the people were grateful. They were too stupid to understand their own wrongs. Merivale cannot go through that country now without a pageant, and Chauncey's grave is honoured like a shrine. They buried him on a mound outside Mehlgahla, as he had wished, and built an obelisk over his tomb, and the people scatter marigolds at the foot as they pass. It was Innes, the Commissioner of the District, who said, 'He is doing good work even in his grave.' Thousands died, but the villagers did not doubt that Merivale and Chauncey saved the Punjab from a far greater scourge.

Government, however, took the hint from the agitators. Nowadays methods are changed. There is no searching of houses or general disinfection or forced evacuation. Inoculation and health camps are the rule. Persuasion is discouraged, and the plague rages with little check. In the Punjab the villagers have learnt to evacuate for themselves. And perhaps the new system is as well. It would be impossible for any one to do what Merivale and Chauncey did without their tact and sympathy and knowledge of the people. The breed that yap at Westminster—to use Hobbs' phrase—would make the most unholy mess of it.

The rains had broken, and a stray Memsahib or two had come down from the Hills when Merivale found himself again in the Club. It was more by luck than any sparing of himself that he survived, presumably to increase 'the pampered annuitants of Cheltenham and Whitehall'. He had not spoken to an Englishman since Chauncey died, and he hungered for his kind. The first person he saw was the equine-faced lady, Mrs O'Shaughnessy's partner, in her huge black picture hat. The mould of the superstructure was the same; only roses had displaced sweet-peas. Merivale made a dive down a side passage to escape her, and almost ran into the Chaplain's wife.

'Why, it is Mr Merivale!' she gasped; 'where have you been all these months? Famine, wasn't it?'

Merivale explained that it was plague.

'But how romantic! Is it near here? And have they plague carts and red crosses on the doors? I suppose it is all dirt; clean people don't get it, do they?'

'We lost Captain Chauncey in the I.M.S.'

'But oh, how dreadful! He had to go near them, of course, hadn't he?'

Merivale was grateful to the Providence which made the lady answer her own questions.

'And what is Government going to do?' she went on. 'Teach them to be clean, I suppose. Prevention is so much better than cure, isn't it?'

But Merivale couldn't wait to bandy eternal truths with the padre's wife. Besides, he was afraid she would ask him to play Badminton, and he was a pitiful prevaricator.

'I've got to go and write a report on it,' he said, and made a gesture of escape as if the pen and ink lay ready for him on the table, and the chaprassie waited at the door. 'Shall I send you a copy of the Blue book?' he called back, when he had a safe start.

'Oh, thank you, that would be so ni-ice.'

The Chaplain's wife regarded his retreating back sadly. Badminton had been in her mind. She reflected that Mr Merivale was not quite at his ease in ladies' society. 'It's a pity,' she thought, 'because he is such a nice man. It must be because he is so much in the jungle.' And she began to devise plots for his socialization of which he was happily unaware.

A thirst for cold drinks and human companionship drove him along the passage to the men's Bridge room. He saw Skene and Hobbs through the glass door playing at the familiar corner table. And there were several strange faces. A new regiment had come in since he left. He pushed the door open slowly with that little catch of joy and excitement with which one surprises old friends, and he stood on the mat waiting for one of them to look up.

'Merivale!'

'Hullo, Skene! Hullo, Colonel!'

'Killed the plague?'

'Scotched it, I hope.'

'Had much *dik?*'

'Bit of a swat. Good chaps, though, these Jats. Behaved well.'

'Come and cut in. You're dining with me tonight. Boy! Four whiskies and sodas, and bring plenty of ice.'

Thus was Merivale restored to the lap of civilization with little comment, but much inward relish. Skene had heard something of his plague adventures from Innes, but he knew it would be difficult to make him talk. Little by little, perhaps, by leading questions, he might piece out a story.

'Did you see they had been baiting you in the House?' he asked, when the rubber was finished.

'Dr Byleman, yes.'

'It's a compliment to be yapped at by that rabble,' Hobbs observed.

Skene thought of the pariahs at the tail of his bulldog in the bazaar. But metaphor was not in his line.

'How many questions has he asked?'

'Five, I think. It won't do me any harm. He leaves Chauncey out now.'

'Wonderful delicacy!'

'It ought to be a good advertisement if the sun-dried bureaucrat has a sense of humour.'

'Did you see the question in yesterday's *Pioneer?* Dr Byleman asked the Under Secretary of State if the food in Alipur gaol was strictly vegetarian, or whether it was true that the Brahmin anarchist under trial for the Houghly bomb outrage had been made to eat rice cooked in fat.'

'Put up to it by a native rag. If a schoolboy in the bazaar writes Byleman an anonymous letter, he'll get up on his hind legs about it in the House. And the sedition-mongers know it.'

'Why don't they snub them?'

'Can't afford it. Means votes.'

'It is a mistake to hang these anarchists,' Hobbs interrupted. 'They like it. A martyr's crown, and all that. A life sentence is the thing. Solitary confinement. And take 'em out once a month on the anniversary and give 'em a dozen with the cat. Just a little reminder.'

Merivale laughed. It was jolly to hear the old fellow again. But Hobbs' partner, a very young subaltern, ventured—

'But, sir, wouldn't that be a bit mediæval?'

Hobbs glared at him.

'Mediæval? Common sense! Humanity! Take the glory out of them. Ridicule is the only thing that kills. You'd soon stop it.'

'What has happened to Narasimha Swami?' Merivale asked.

'Disappeared. "Spirited away", as the Radical papers say of the deportees. No one has seen him since he came here. He gave the police the slip.'

'I believe they've got enough against him for the Andamans.'

'The High Court would quash it,' Hobbs said.

'He got at your students, didn't he, Skene?'

Skene nodded. 'One or two, but they've gone.'

'By the way,' Merivale said, 'I ran against one of your hopefuls in his village. An odd youth not particularly endowed with the family affections, I should say. He read Stevenson.'

'Where was it?'

'Mograon.'

'That would be Siri Ram. What has happened to him?'

'Gone clean off like our friend Narasimha. His father is an old Jat farmer, a nice old fellow. He counted on the youth to support the whole family in a year, and he is naturally cut up.'

'I had to expel him, you know. He was one of Narasimha Swami's victims. He wouldn't come to me for a job.'

'Here's Dean, he can probably tell you where Siri Ram is.'

Merivale greeted the policeman with laconic warmth.

'Have you got Siri Ram on your register?' Skene asked.

'Yes, he is in the city somewhere now.'

'Better keep an eye on him,' Hobbs said. 'He'll be pinking one of us soon.'

'He has never seen a firearm,' said Skene. 'He couldn't hit a tree.'

'It is easy enough to jab a revolver into any one in a crowd and pull the trigger, isn't it, Dean?'

Dean laughed. He would have been dead if a certain revolver had not jammed.

'I always tell you, Skene,' Hobbs went on. 'It's all you College fellows. You turn out anarchists as quick as sausages in Chicago. They ought to stop education. Shut up all the schools and use the savings to police the district where the trouble is. By Gad, I wish I were Viceroy—'

Skene's explosive rumble of a laugh startled every one in the room.

'Come along and dine,' he said. 'I am jolly glad you are not.'

# PART III

## The Cave

'I asked a wild yogi
With dust in his hair
As thin as a bogey
And cross as a bear,
But this funny old fogey
Did nothing but stare.
If you meet a wild yogi'
Dear children, beware.

SANTA CLAUS' GEOGRAPHY

# 1

The goatherds of Zojpal would come and peep at Narasimha. Great was his reputation for occult power. He could project himself across the valley, they said, render himself invisible or dual, pass through a chink in the wall, and endure a month without food. The bowls of milk, the handfuls of grain, the little bundles of firewood they placed in front of the cave were often found untouched in the morning.

He would sit for hours, his eyes fixed on two pebbles at his feet, restraining his breath until the material world slipped away from him and his spirit floated in ether, looking down indifferently upon his shrunken body and his bowl and his staff and the grey sheep beside the stream as passing phenomena detached for the moment as the atoms cohere in the dance of matter and are reflected in the glass of illusion. Soon nothing objective would remain, and he would be drawn to the centre of light, conscious only of the rush and beat of wings as he was swept along with the eternal energy which informs all life.

Power and influence came out of these trances. The Swami owed much of his magnetism to them and the extraordinary hold he had upon the affections and imagination of his countrymen. Long ago before he visited Europe he had practised Yoga at Ujjain. Then he had studied the Vedanta philosophy nine years at Benares. Thus he became a kind of superman in his own country. Images of him carved in wood and stone and cast in metal were sold in the idol shops of Kashi, where he had a great name for piety and transcendental power.

When he went to Europe, the extreme forms of yoga asceticism which he had practised at Ujjain had left their print on his character and his face. He had a great deal of what is called in the jargon of the séance psychic force. He was of the stuff that founds sects among impressionable people, and in any other country than England he would have had disciples to apotheosize him. As it was, he became something of a lion. He addressed societies and sipped tea in fashionable boudoirs; romantic hostesses felt that he brought more of the mystery and repose of the East into their drawing-rooms than a shelf-ful of bronze Buddhas, and more than one emotional woman, English and Russian and American, embarrassed him with chelaship. A spirtualistic lady in Notting Hill literally knelt at his feet and offered herself to him wholly.

At Cambridge he lectured on Sanskrit and Indian philosophy. He spent two years on the Continent, and learnt to speak French and German and Russian and Italian fluently. He was six months at Göttingen. Then he went to the States and preached Vedantism. He was a figure in the West, and he found himself in danger of becoming the centre of a coterie of faddists, seekers after a new thing, women and degenerates, who would make him their Guru and call themselves Hindus. Esoteric was a word they were fond of using, though they would not have wasted an hour on the subtlest of philosophers if it had suddenly been made the State religion, or if they had been born under its orthodox sway. The Swami measured them and went his way.

In the end he took more from the West than he gave it. He never lost his transcendentalism, but his spirit became tempered like a sword, his ideals were crystallized. He remembered that the Vedas and all that they stood for were embodied in his own people. Gradually his flame-like energy became narrowed and concentrated into a cause. Nationalism became a religion with him.

The Swami was proud of his race and the stock to whom the eternal verities had been revealed, and in whose heart alone truth could germinate. When Narasimha's history became known, the Englishmen who had met him in the West could not associate the dreamer and mystic with the revolutionist who pulled the strings of the Bharat Red Flag Society. But the Swami was an anarchist because he believed that his people could not become regenerate until they were free, a much more dangerous doctrine than that they could not be free until they became regenerate. He had no scruples. He would sacrifice a thousand Siri Rams and foster a nursery of young murderers. And no service rendered to his people could lessen his hate of the English. The most disinterested reformers must go with the others; they were, in fact, more dangerous because they stemmed the tide, and he would devote them and the Hobbses, the 'martial-law-and-no-damned-nonsense-wallahs', indifferently to the bomb. His father, the Lingayat, would not have hesitated between a black and white goat at the altar, and Narasimha had a good deal of the old Lingayat in him yet; only the crude religious fanaticism of the sect had been diverted into politics. Dean was right. The man had all the instincts of a wolf. 'To sacrifice a white goat to Kali', that is, to dedicate an Englishman to the altar of independence, the ironical catchword of young Bengal, had emanated from him.

He had despised the English even before the demon of anarchy had entered into his head. He hated their materialism and insensibility. Save for a scholar or two whom he respected, his associates had been mostly shallow dabblers in the occult, keyhole peepers, without power of abnegation or self-forgetfulness. The yogi would sweep aside the curtain while they fumbled with the woof, seeking an interstice in the hope that the light behind might steal through somehow upon their blind eyes. The best of England, the true tempered steel of the country, he did not meet and could never have understood. And Demos was an unclean beast he could not touch, projected obliquely across his vision like the ugly figures on the frieze of a temple wall that one passes by. The monster was symbolized for him sometimes in his memory by a country bumpkin in cap and gown, who had brushed up rudely against him in the Petty Cury at Cambridge and called him 'a damned nigger'.

He had more in common with the Gaelic American of the Western States.

On his return to India Narasimha was irresistible. He had studied man in two hemispheres, and to the open appeal of mystic and reformer was added the hidden one of the revolutionary. He was the superman who alone could unite and direct the dissipated energies of the national spirit. He captured the imagination of the people. He preached to young Bengal, and he based his message on the teachings of Krishna to Arjun in the Bhagavad Gita. It was an insidious appeal, this doctrine of *yoga* by action and death in the discharge of one's own *dharma*, rousing passion by the creed which preaches freedom from passion and denounces anger and fear and all manner of attachment, and giving secret murder the sanction of divine law.

From Bengal Narasimha carried the message north, preaching to a hardier and more dogged, if less subtle and impressionable, stock. Among the young men who were being put into the mould was Siri Ram. The Swami knew that he would come.

Sometimes when he was exhausted by *yoga* Narasimha would walk knee-deep through meadows of fritillary and iris and yellow spurge to the frozen stream where the striped lizards flicked in and out of the crevice between the rock and the snow. He would look down on the marg speckled with grey stones and sheep while the eagles swept under him, swerving from his feet by the turn of a point of a feather. Or he would go down the valley to the last outpost of the silver birches which hung over the Zojpat stream. Here he would sit in a sunny belt of thyme which fringed the shadow of a lonely tree like a fairy ring, or in a warm, close-cropped hollow bright with forget-me-not and marjoram and meadow rue and turreted with the yellow spires of the mullein. Fritillaries and tortoise-shells lighted on his bowl; the murmur of bees soothed him into a trance. The silence and the space carried his mind far away until he was without attachment, at rest in *brahm*, and all the colour and life that danced and quivered before his eyes became a vague, illusory, opalescent gleam cast upon the plane his spirit traversed.

Narasimha's flight to Zojpal had fulfilled the religious bent of his mind. He was life-wear; he needed peace. For the last few years politics had been the most Sisyphean task. And he had not practised *yoga* since Ujjain. Once more he sat on the antelope skin, head erect, immovable, his gaze fixed steadily on his feet, controlling the incoming and outgoing breath, free of attachment, closing the passage to each sense. When the herdsmen brought him his bowl in the evening he would be performing the *pranayam,* and he would look at them without speech, or rather over and through them, and they would depart in awe.

As darkness gathered he climbed the mountain-side to perform another exercise, an unspiritual one—to prepare his physical escape. Every night he dug with the axe-head of his staff at the foot of a great rock. The herdsmen would have been frightened if they had seen the sprite-like little man delving in the moonlight as if he had found a passage to the unseen. The Swami was loosening a pinnacle of the cliff which held back a mass of tumbled shale, and if dislodged would precipitate an avalanche upon the cave.

## 2

Siri Ram did not go to Skene for help and advice when he returned from Mograon. He had dreams of personal as well as national independence. He did not want an appointment. He thought that if he gave himself up to the Cause, the Society might help him. It was not likely to be for long. Government offered board and a roof for conspirators. It might be Amritsar gaol; it might be the Andamans; he rather hoped that he would become a political deportee. There would be pride and glory in that as well as comfort. He could have forgiven the Imperial Government their 'barbarous unconstitutionalism' if this particular kind of martyrdom had fallen on himself. He brooded much on the future, but the gallows always loomed at the end of these vistas.

He lingered in the city several days, and the students visited him surreptitiously. He and Banarsi Das and Lachmi Chand got themselves photographed, singly and in a group, and he enjoyed the first taste of hero-worship. He was a conspirator and capable of hurt. That inert Leviathan, the Government, would soon receive a prick from him. He would have been flattered if he had known that the C.I.D. had a copy of his photograph. But his thoughts always returned to the Swami, who had disappeared so mysteriously and completely after his lectures at Gandeshwar. If he could find him he felt certain of being put on the right track.

Every morning he climbed the rickety stairs to the chamber of Ramji Das, the secretary of the Achar Sadhani or the 'Students' Improvement Club', as the local branch of the Bharat Red Flag Society was named. Ramji Das, the bunniah, lived in a kind of wooden doll's house above a druggist's shop in the bazaar. The ends of the iron girders protruded into the street, giving the flimsy second storey of wood built upon brick a much more substantial basis than it appeared to need. The balcony was painted in bright blue and yellow and green stripes, and roofed with strips of kerosene oil tins. The interior of the house was no more beautiful than the outside, and the fat bunniah who lurked within was a fitting complement to the dwelling.

Ramji Das was always sitting in the same corner. He would greet Siri Ram suavely, and seemed to encourage his coming, but said nothing directly helpful. They would talk politics. Economic grievances were the bunniah's forte, though he owed his great riches to British rule. Under no other Government could he have amassed wealth openly, nor achieved the three chins and three paunches which in his thrifty class always indicate immense reserves.

His grandfather would have been afraid to be so fat, lest he should become a too palpable object for loot, official and otherwise. But Ramji Das kept a bank openly, and sent his son to a technical school, and owed his security to the police and his growing business to improved communications.

Yet he sat on his oily mat and oozed venom and spleen.

'Do not use currency notes, Siri Ram.'

'No, I will not use.'

'It is easy to make a piece of paper and sell it for rupees fifty, or hundred, or thousand. By this means they take money away from the peoples of Hindustan. If they leave India we have then nothing left in our hand but pieces of paper.'

'I would rather leave the mineral wealth buried in the bowels of the mother,' Siri Ram remarked sententiously, 'than have it dug out by feringhis.'

'You have the true political ideas. You read the *Kali Yuga?*'

'Yes, I have written a letter to it.'

'You see this morning the death of poor Indians has risen from twenty-two to thirty-four per thousand under British Government?'

'Yes, I saw.'

'Do not forget that when you go to the villages. Also the poor have only one meal since the Mlecchas are come here. Remember that also. How does it sound? The ryots toil through hard times by tightening up their bellies.'

Siri Ram looked at the folds of the bunniah's paunch. He wore no shirt; he had ample breasts like a woman.

'You will see I am qualified to spread ideas of independence. Swamiji called me to him. He gave me books. I want to become political missionary.'

Siri Ram spoke almost pleadingly. He felt sure that Ramji Das knew where the Swami was hiding, but he could learn nothing from him. He had a feeling that Narasimha had discussed him with Ramji Das, and that he was part of a reserve force to be used in an emergency. But surely his witness-bearing and expulsion from the College had qualified him for the Cause.

One morning he noticed a difference in Ramji Das's manner which made him more hopeful. The bunniah admitted that he had heard from the Swami. The police were searching for him; there was evidence at last. An informer had implicated him in a political dacoity in Bengal. He was in a very safe place, hundreds of miles beyond the frontier, living in a cave amongst the ice and snow. But it was difficult to communicate with him.

The Society wanted a few young men who could be trusted like the youths who had devoted themselves in Bengal.

Siri Ram volunteered to go.

'You must be a very secret man. Can you be confeedential?'

Siri Ram could.

'Have you any money?'

Siri Ram had not.

'You have a father?'

'I have left him. He is pig-head, he will do nothing.'

Ramji Das considered his bulging calves. 'The Society is very poor,' he said, 'perhaps a subscreeption among friends. Your ticket to Rawalpindi. It will cost three rupees. After that you will beg.'

Siri Ram looked at him with inquiring wonder.

'You will go as Sadhu,' the bunniah explained. 'You will accompany the pilgrims on thorny path. Narasimha will meet you at Amarnath. You understand? You must be secret man. If you go in full blaze of public gaze it would not be poleetical. And use your cautions at Rawalpindi. Spies will be roaming there.'

Siri Ram was almost happy.

'You had better go to-night. The pilgrimage is starting, and if you go separate you will attract noteece. I will send quarter anna postcard to Jaganath in Rawalpindi—'

'Despatch homespun cloth, Sadhu-wear.' He will understand. I do not waste money on postal tickets. Besides, the police open letters.'

There was a scarcely perceptible twitching of the folds of the lower part of the bunniah's face, which in other men might have been a smile. It did not travel as far as his eye.

'You go to his shop in Sadar Bazaar. He will make you Sadhu. He receives all our young men.'

'And my ticket?' Siri Ram asked, 'who will pay?'

Very slowly the bunniah unfastened the knot in his loin-cloth and drew out three rupees and handed them reluctantly to Siri Ram one by one. Then he got up and waddled across the room to a safe in the corner. It was the first time Siri Ram had seen him on his legs. He took out a small parcel sewn up in oiled cloth.

'You will take care of thees,' he said, 'it is the Swami's dak. Eef you lose it, he and a number of others will be hanged before we kick bastard foreigners into sea.'

Siri Ram clutched the packet reverently.

'Narasimha is living in cave,' the bunniah continued. 'The pilgrims will pass under it two days before they reach to Amarnath. Do not leave the path or pay attention to it. Narasimha will come down. He will be walking with the pilgrims. The name of the place is—'

Ramji Das searched among some papers on the floor. ' "It is at Zojpal",' he read out slowly in Urdu, ' "below the goojar's track to Wardwan, two hundred paces south of the second bend in the path.' Narasimha is preecise.'

'Also if you hear that Narasimha has shaken off the coil,' the bunniah added as an afterthought, 'do not turn back. He may have another eencarnation.'

Again Siri Ram saw the tightening of the folds of flesh as if they had been moved by some involuntary twitching of a thread inside which held cheeks and chins together. He was shocked to hear the Swami spoken of so lightly. 'I do not understand,' he said.

'It is nothing at all. A mere sop in the pan, only do not return if you hear that Narasimha has breathed his latest. Also when you leave the railway station do not go straight to Jaganath's. Go first to the Hindu Ashram. You will find a brother there who will take you to the shop after it is dark. I will send him message in ciphers. Jaganath will give you the incognito—when you leave the shop you will be the Sadhu.'

As Siri Ram was descending the steps into the inner courtyard, Ramji Das called him back.

'Keep cautions,' he said. 'Remember 'Namaste' will open all the doors. I had forgotten,' he added, 'there is another young man, a poleetical missionary like yourself. Very clever. He was in this shop last week. You will look out for this young man, Mohan Roy, on the road. His bodical structure is very small; he has three golden nails in his front teeth; and he is fond of living in the English costume.'

Siri Ram was exalted. He was a political missionary at last. Ramji Das had styled him so. The Swami had remembered and trusted him and chosen him for this mission. He gripped the little packet in his coat.

# 3

When Siri Ram had left the shop of Jaganath he had discarded the sacred thread, and cut off the tuft of hair on his crown, and he wore the *rudraksha*, the necklace of beads, emblem of Siva.

Siri Ram ate away the miles slowly and with pain. His pilgrim muscles were of later growth; he dawdled by the road and spent the first night at the dusty village of Barakao, fourteen miles from the city. On the third evening he crawled painfully into Murree. These were the first hills he had seen since Skene pointed out the long, white line of the Himalayas that cold winter morning from the College roof. He might have seen that distant outline often, but Siri Ram was not an observant youth; he did not notice the different colours of the hills, the smoky blue of the pines under rain, the extraordinarily delicate, almost timid freshness of the young rice beneath the gathering storm-cloud. The Jhelum almost in flood raced by him. The white horses reared and plunged round the bends, tossing the great pine-logs forwards and sideways like splinters of wood, and the spray fell on the rocks at his feet. But he did not notice the timber or the freshets; he was conscious only of a volume of water and a noise in his head, and he remembered that the road had tunnelled in places through the rock. Yet he must have carried in his head some impression of a strange land, for at Baramulla he wrote to Banarsi Das: 'The sceneries of this happy valley have benefited me, the ambrosial retreats of nature are not far off.'

Truly he had entered a land different from anything he had ever seen. In the last few miles before Baramulla, the torrent had become a wide, unbroken stream; the valley broadened out in rich pasture-land. He might look in vain for the starved kikar and shisham of Mograon. Large, generous trees spread a bountiful shade on the well-nurtured land. Walnut and willows and elms enfolded snug villages. In the heat of noon Siri Ram would die under the thick foliage of the chenar. His daily tramp led him through straight poplar avenues. Mile upon mile of graceful, tapering white-stemmed trees from Patan to Srinagar. Snow glittered in the gap at the end of the long vista, and rocks seamed with frozen watercourses, a mesh of silver that disappeared in the black forest underneath. Lush marsh flowers twinkled in the ditch at his feet. The wraith of Nanga Parbat hung between earth and sky; the massive dromedary back of Haramokh and many a crenellated peak shut in the plain with firm buttresses.

Trees and flowers and snowy peaks were new to Siri Ram, if there can be new or old to such a mind. Day after day he marched dully on, the personification of a wrong, looking neither to left nor right, nor up nor down, wrapped solely in his broodings. For in abstraction or contemplation—call it what you will—he was already the perfect Sadhu.

Seventeen days after he had left Rawalpindi, he saw a low golden hill with a yellow fort scrambling over it, glowing in the slant rays of the sun and etched vividly against the hills which loomed dark under the storm-clouds. It was Hari Parbat, a landmark that even a Sadhu must see. Siri Ram learnt that he had reached Srinagar. The greater part of his journey was done. The cave of Amarnath where the Swami was to meet him lay among the glaciers to the north, now only eight marches distant.

He stayed two nights in Srinagar in the ancient serai of Bhairon Asthan, a three-storied, balconied, latticed caravanserai with windows fretted and carved, and a roof overgrown with moss and irises. The Mahunt had gone on to Amarnath, but Siri Ram met other pilgrims in the serai, the last few stragglers to be herded in the great camp that was gathering at Pahlgam.

On the road to Islamabad he overtook large camps of Sadhus. At Pampoor there were three hundred naked Vishnuites from Mooltan; at Avantipur a hundred and eighty Shivaites from Nepal, but he had speech with none of them. Then he met a group of musicians under a tree. A family of bangle-sellers went by, hung with their wares in long strings from head to foot and glittering like ringed serpents. A Muhammadan woman overtook him in a white *burka* with a purple crown, astraddle on a piebald tat hung with favours, her husband striding by the rein. Farther on he passed a group of Kashmir Pundits, hard, keen, unspiritual-looking men, priests and usurers in one. They sat by the roadside under the shade of a chenar in a ring of stone lingams—their spiritual ware—which were covered over with faded flowers and smeared with paint like blood.

An English subaltern rode by on his ambling Kashmir tat, a slim, keen, untroubled youth returning from first leave, his face and knees dark with the sun and snowdrift of Ladakh. As he passed, one of the spiritual robbers with the triple brand of Siva on his forehead advanced towards him from the shade, calling after him in a half insolent, half cringing voice.

'*Hum Padree hai.* Holy man. . . . All Sahibs give backsheesh.' The boy rode on without answer, a trifle perhaps added to the sum of his contempt. Siri Ram was ashamed.

The road left the river and stretched through a desert, stony plain under the parched hills, then joined it again, skirted by willows and sedges and flowering rushes. The scent of hot water-weed penetrated the shade; racing streamlets babbled of coolness. At noon the heat haze danced; the glare was blinding; and Siri Ram's throat and eyes were filled with dust. Light showers fell at sunset. Pearly mists rose out of the valley and hung in the jagged clefts of the hills, catching the slanting lights and etherealizing everything. But Siri Ram was not uplifted or depressed. Bharat Mata, the mother of whom he talked always, was an abstraction to him. To bask in her loveliness, to gaze on her physical beauty, gave him no thrill.

It was at Islamabad that Siri Ram met Mohan Roy. They had passed each other often on the road, but Siri Ram had forgotten to look out for the Bengali. He had been too engrossed in his own mission. Chance only revealed his fellow conspirator, or was it Mohan Roy's intuition? Siri Ram was sitting under a willow by the sacred spring of Ananti-Nag, when he looked up and saw the little man on the grass quite close to him eating a pear. He would not have noticed the Bengali even then if it had not been for the glint of gold in his teeth, which recalled somehow the rickety stairs over the druggist's shop and something Ramji Das had said to him about the road. There was a clue somewhere in teeth and gold. Siri Ram regarded the Bengali more closely, his grey chequered cotton trousers and coat, his bare head and short cropped hair, his glare spectacles and the necklace of tulsi beads, and the trifala, mark of Vishnu, on his forehead, made up a picture which seemed familiar. Suddenly Siri Ram remembered the conspirator he was to look out for on the road with three golden nails in his front teeth. Mohan Roy was grinning, he showed them clearly. Certainly his 'bodical structure' was small, and he was living in the English costume.

'Namaste,' said Siri Ram. It was the key to open all doors.

'Namaste,' said Mohan Roy.

'Ramji Das told me to look for you.' It was a safe thing to say. There are five thousand Ramji Dases in the Punjab.

'He told me, too, you might come after. You have the foreign letter?'

Siri Ram clutched his cloak nervously. They were silent a little. Then Siri Ram said awkwardly—

'You love Swaraj, is it not? Why you wear the *wilaiti* clothes?'

'I like these clothes,' Mohan Roy said. 'I would wear them if Shaitan made them.'

Siri Ram was angry.

'You belong to the cause of independence, do you not?' he asked.

'How do you define independence?'

'Certainly, it is fredom, liberty.'

'Yes, I belong. I am free—free to choose the clothes I wear and other things.'

Siri Ram did not understand badinage or the Bengali's inconsistencies. There was no life-weariness in this bright-eyed little man. He seemed to have a zest for pilgrimage. Though a rationalist and a philosopher, he spent half his days on the road, passing from shrine to shrine, and endured all manner of hardships in order to kneel before some monstrous image in a cave, or scatter flowers upon a lingam hidden away in the innermost recesses of the hills. And he did not even try to square his inclinations with his faith, as so many of the educated, emancipated, and orthodox do. Only he argued that his caste mark and trifala and his badges of pilgrimage, and the regularity of his wandering life from shrine to shrine threw off suspicion, and made his revolutionary work the easier. He even affected a sect and repeated a special version of the Gyatri, and had the symbols of Vishnu, the conch shell and the discus and the lotus and the club, branded on his right arm.

Siri Ram wondered. It had been the fashion in his hybrid student set to despise these things. The Aryas rejected them. When he left Gandeshwar he did not know the difference between a Sivaite and a Vishnuite. And his mistakes mattered little on the road, for there was room for every kind of anomaly in that motley pilgrim crew; men who put on the Sadhu's robe to escape the police or the discipline of work as well as the temptations of the world.

Mohan Roy had to be at Thaneswar for the eclipse and at Amritsar for the Dewali, and he would be at Hardwar during the Holi in the spring. He led a life of freedom with no one to annoy him except the plague inspection officers on the road. It was the true independence; Siri Ram was impressed. He sat under the willow for an hour listening to a tale of adventure, and when he took the road again he knew that the Bengali was reckless and daring, and indifferent to life. He had been tried often and found sufficient. When they left Islamabad they separated.

'We had better not be seen together,' Mohan Roy said, 'for if one of us is discovered it will be more difficult for the other.'

Siri Ram was proud of the dual 'we'. But he was soon overwhelmed with shame. Mohan Roy passed him on the road a mile outside the city.

'You had better take this,' he said, handing him the oiled cloth packet with a smile. 'You left it on the ground when you were feeding the fish.'

From Islamabad the pilgrims turned up the Lidar river, the loveliest, greenest, and sweetest-scented valley in the hills, past the blue springs of Bawan, where the pilgrims feed the holy carp, and the rock caves of Bomtzu, and the temple of the sun. It was a green world, and bubbling streams chattered among the poplars and walnut trees and ran underneath the road. The blue stars of the succory shone in the little grassy banks between the rice. Siri Ram might have seen a pageant of English flowers if he had had eyes for anything besides his wrongs, borage and milfoil and mullein and bladder campion and the tall lousewort which smells like a hayfield and beanfield in one. He slept that night on the terrace of the monastery at Eismakhan.

The next morning he passed through the walnut village of Patkote, before the sun had entered the valley, and by noon he had reached the great camp under the limestone cliffs of Pahlgam. Here he pitched his umbrella on a rock and sat, Sadhu-like, feeling more lonely among these seven thousand holy men than he had ever felt in his life.

His companions on either side, low-browed, naked, ash-strewn mendicants, sat motionless, with silent movements of the lips as if they had worked themselves into a trance. Half hypnotized by their stillness, half deafened by the roar of the torrent, Siri Ram sat dreaming through the hours in a sort of numb physical Nirvana.

Shivaites and Vishnuites, Sannyasis and Bairagis squatted in little groups, and drew circles round their fires, and when intoxicated enough with *charas*, beat any one who came within the ring.

At twilight a thick veil of smoke hung over the valley, but the Sadhus' cooking fire suggested spare diet. A ten-foot blaze on the bank opposite, the pyre of one of them, looked cheerier. Siri Ram became used to these beacons to the faithful at every camp.

The next morning he found himself in a strange human medley. It was a burning hot march up the valley to Tanin. The rocky path was a serpentining thread of black and white and yellow where the umbrellas of the faithful wound along the valley. The slaty-blue stream leapt between the dark pines below. Sometimes the track descended to it, and the torrent swirling by drove the fresh, icy spray across the six-foot path between the bank and the cliff. Siri Ram would have lingered here, but he was borne along in the human stream to Amarnath.

Troops of Sadhus of different sects followed the road with different kinds of staffs and pails and water jugs. There were men sick to death carried on coolies' backs. Old ladies in light palanquins with red-tented covers peeping through the folds, young ladies pulling the folds back, little girls curled up in baskets and half asleep; old women and young, plain and weather-beaten, drawn to the cave in the hope of motherhood, riding astride on peaked cloth saddles, their anxious husbands walking by the rein. Sadhinis who alone in all that crowd obey Diana's law, and who may not ride or be carried, striding along in one shift, saffron- or scarlet- or wallflower-coloured, tied in at the waist and opening in a modest V at the bosom. Siri Ram passed along among all these unheeding. It was one of his vows as a Sadhu that he must not look at or speak to a woman.

A mile below Tanin, a sheltered-snowdrift lay across the path. A Sadhu dislodged a chunk with the axe-head of his staff and carried it in his hand and moistened his lips with it, and every pilgrim who came after followed suit. It was the first snow Siri Ram had touched.

The next day the pilgrims left the forest. The zigzag up from Tanin was a trial of faith. Siri Ram panted up it for hours. At the top the path led through narrow defiles beneath the cliff, and he looked down upon the Zojpat tunnelling under the snow bridges a thousand feet beneath. He had soon passed the last straggling outpost of the birches. High up in the mountain above Zojpal, east of the goojars' track to Wardwan, Siri Ram looked for the Swami's cave in vain. He lingered by the stream until he met a cowherd tending his flock. He asked him if there was a hermit dwelling in the cave above the valley.

'The cave is destroyed, the hermit is dead,' the goojar told him.

'When did he die?' Siri asked, with a sinking heart.

'Nearly a month ago. Part of the hill fell down in the night. They found his drinking vessel and his cloak outside. They called to him in the morning, but there was no sound within. It is certain that he was crushed by the falling rock.'

The goojar pointed to a bare scar on the hillside, the track of an avalanche, and a heap of *débris* on a terrace where his flock were feeding.

'The cave was behind that,' he said.

Tears started to Siri Ram's eyes.

'Do not be distressed or turn back,' a voice said by his side in English. 'He had work to do. Eef he has kicked the bucket, he may have another eencarnation.'

Siri Ram started. It was the voice of the bunniah. Looking up, he met the ironic gaze of Mohan Roy.

'He told you, too?' he asked.

'Surely he told me.'

The Bengali stooped to drink from the spring in the rock. Then he went on, leaving Siri Ram to the cowherd and his perplexity.

That night they camped at Shisha Nag. Even Siri Ram was uplifted.

Flowers and fruits and trees, lights and shadows, the delicate greenery of the earth, left him unmoved. But here was the peace of the eternal. He recognized the hand of God at last, the region of the spirits. But at night the physical need of warmth gripped him. He sat up for hours shivering in his blanket. The image of Jupiter, a long red torch, lay in the shallow basin to the west. The moon rose above the Koh-i-noor and suffused the lake. The clean shadow of a rock cut the water in half with a line as clear as doom. Then the shadow of a hand was thrown upon the precipice, firm and sinister, pointing down the valley. It frightened the pilgrims; an excited chatter arose from the Sita-Ramis just as the camp was sinking into sleep. Whenever Siri Ram lifted his head from the blanket he saw the hand there, a palpable menace warning them back. It crept along the rock. Hours afterwards, when the moon was swimming overhead, it had disappeared. But Siri Ram was beyond wonder or fear or anything but cold.

In the morning all the pilgrims bathed in the lake.

The path rose from Shisha Nag and wound gently up to a pass still under snow. 'Man's country is passed,' they said, as they looked beyond; 'now we enter the country of the gods.' The last tree had been left a march behind; even the swart juniper had disappeared; the flowers became smaller and brighter. They had crossed the water-shed. The grey and buff and ochre rocks which hemmed in the valley became wilder and more fantastic. Splintered towers guarded the ravine. Streams flowed into the valley from the glaciers to the east, and the Sadhu who looked aside from the path might see the abode of the gods.

For what other purpose could these massive sky-communing mountains serve, approached by vast untrodden fields of snow, and visitable only to the eagles and the wandering spirits?

At last the road bends down into a valley which seems to be closed in on both sides in the far distance by a barren mountain too steep for snow to lie on. A small red path ascends it into the clouds. It is the end of all things save mist and shadow and ice and snow. Hidden somewhere in that tumbled chaos is the cave of Amarnath whence the divine creative energy proceeds which fashions mind and clay.

But Siri Ram thought only of one deity to whom he addressed his wrongs. At Panjitani, on the eve of Amarnath, he wrote the letter he had promised Lachmi Chand.

'May the goddess of Independence be pleased,' it began, 'I have given up all pleasures and smear my body with ashes every day. The water of this place is very bad. It conduces to shortness of breath. Also there are a great number of flowers whose smells create sickness among the pilgrims. I have a number of unpleasant feelings in my inside. But I do not care at all for the so-called bowels and other obscure parts if I can serve my mother. There are thousands of pilgrims here, but they are all nearly ignorants, and worship stalks and stones. I have conversed with some who are serving the mother. They are here performing her business. I hope I would meet the good man tomorrow, your understanding will tell you who I mean. He will not return soon. Government are looking at him with a black eye.'

Siri Ram had not scattered flowers on the lingam since he was a child, when his mother used to take him to a little shrine under a banyan tree near Mograon. Faded marigolds and hibiscus and greasy red paint smeared over the black stone always carried him back there. But there were no marigolds at Amarnath. He gathered the grey-blue harebell and purple geranium and the mauve heads of the wild onion instead. He thought of his classmates as he toiled up to the cave, Aryas and scoffers at superstition, who would affect ignorance of the very attributes of Vishnu or Siva, and if approached on any point of sect or Puranic lore would repeat some platitude about the oneness of God. But all things were honourable in the service of the Mother; so Siri Ram found himself drilled in the line; jammed in between a gross, low-caste, charas-smoking Bairagi, 'a very menial man,' who knew nothing of the Vedas and could not read or write, and a naked yogi, a husk of humanity, who, the pilgrims said, practised the last austerities, and had renounced even speech.

Siri Ram could not help being infected a little with the atmosphere of the place, and the magnetism of that rapt, inspiring crowd. It was a world unlike any he had dreamed of, savage and untamed, terrible in its rugged uncompromising bleakness. He had not thought of the surface of the earth as unapproachable to man anywhere. No wonder the superstitious people these valleys with spirits or the grosser manifestation of a personal God.

The strain on body and spirit began to tell. Siri Ram saw a Sadhini swoon by the road and the hospital Babu consign her to a basket in which she was borne quickly back to Panjitani from the very threshold of the god. An emaciated grey skeleton threw itself on the sharp stones and progressed to the cave by the *asthangam*, the progression of the eight members, dragging its heels to the spot where its forehead had rested in little jerks like a wounded caterpillar. The only flesh on the man was a pendulous goitre which trailed on the ground, a ninth member, lacerated by the sharp stones so that you might have tracked the man by his blood. The pilgrims stepped over him with half-envious wonder. As they approached the cave, the auspicious pigeons flew out, and they uttered a loud cry, which was repeated all down the line; for the birds were Shiv's messengers, and the Sadhus knew that the pilgrimage was acceptable and their travail not in vain.

The cave compelled wonder. The brow of the rock, its roof, could only have been conceived by a god for his dwelling-place. The solid shafts supporting it were built for eternity. Such a vault must shroud the Primal Cause, the green mysterious ice lingam in which all energy and force reside. Even Siri Ram, the rationalist fed on text-books and annotations, could have believed as he approached to scatter his flowers on the ice, that the cave was no mere haphazard design of the changing strata of the earth, but a mansion built by hands at the nod of Shiv.

In this atmosphere of the marvellous Siri Ram thought he heard the dumb man behind him speak. He believed that he was being addressed, and there was something familiar in the voice that stirred him, something bass and vibrant, brought up from the depths, disproportioned to the frame. He looked behind him. The eyes of the man, sunk in their sockets, stared straight in front with no sign of recognition, but the voice carried without a movement of the lips.

'Stay behind at the overhanging rock of Goojam.'

Siri Ram started. It was the voice of Narasimha. The Swami himself, but how changed! He had become a Lingayat mendicant, naked, ash-strewn, with the casket on his neck and the little tinkling bell on his arm. The flowing white prophet's beard had vanished. There was less pathos in the face without it, but more force. Siri Ram recognized the sad, earnest gaze which the Swami had fixed on the students at Gandeshwar. There was less appeal in it now; the chin and eye dictated. He looked thinner without the salmon shift, the quivering shell of a man. He had become a voice, an influence, an energy personified, like the lingam in the cave.

4

Siri Ram blinked downwards, fixing his eyes on the top of his nose, and thinking of nothing till his head swam, and he fell into something like a trance. Like Narasimha Swami he was life-weary. At times he almost forgot his dedication. The first days at Amarnath were the happiest he had known. Here abstraction was a merit, action a remote dream. He had never realized before how troublesome temporal cares had become. Here he could let go his hold on life. The escape from it was what he had needed all along. He felt born to Yoga. He watched Narasimha and imitated him always, believing that the Swami had escaped the mesh of desire.

Narasimha watched Siri Ram. He saw that he was not likely to carry anything to an end. He was a moody, impulsive youth, capable of resentment. There might be work in him of a kind at the proper moment, but he was a tool that needed careful sharpening, and one easily blunted; to be used, perhaps, and thrown away. He would not advertently betray a trust.

Narasimha warmed him with confidences. Under the snows of Amarnath the Gaelic-American-Indian plot gathered. Siva's mansion had become the Swami's office. The oiled cloth packet lay open at his feet; the floor was littered with his torn correspondence; envelopes with the American postmark fluttered on to the ice lingam. Siri Ram collected them in the evening with pious pride; there were letters from Paris and Dublin and Seattle and Portland and Los Angeles, envelopes with strange stamps—postal tickets Siri Ram called them. The cave had become the hub of the universe; the civilized world was conspiring with his master to set his country free. Sometimes Narasimha would hand the boy a private letter as carefully as he would lay a bit of juniper scrub on the dying embers. 'Read this, remember it, and burn it,' he would say. Siri Ram would read it and remember every word. Sometimes it would be a letter from an Indian in Paris or London, or an Irish professor in an American University, or some well-meaning Radical in the House of Commons.

'My dear Swami,' the professor wrote, 'the last mail brought sad news. The Rawalpindi *émeute* fell flat because the people were not ready. It was a little premature. You must have a day, a definite day, and fix it well ahead. Three years, four years, five years, ten years even, but we must all work steadily for that. All our forces in one channel, and let there be no leakage of energy in the meanwhile. We will send you the arms—you will distribute the men.

'A thousand fires will break out in one day—in a city where there are ten English there will be ten thousand desperadoes, and many of them will be armed. They need not even come to close quarters. You can leave the large cantonments, where the British troops are, alone. Your own army will come in when they see what you have done.

'Where shall the outbreak begin? Not in Peshawar or Rawalpindi; my friends here tell me that was a mistake, and the Pathans would take everything from you. Not in Delhi—the name is as sinister for us as for them. I hope you liked my leaflet to the Sikh regiment. The colour stigma was a good touch. It will sting them up. Read Garibaldi, Henderson's *Art of War*, and Hewitt's *Christianity and Civilisation in the East*, and make your young men read them. You know Bruce-Morton's little book, I see Sowaran Sing has translated it into Gurmukhi. It ought to have a good effect among the Sepoys. Ramji tells me the

Punjab University have set Seeley's *Expansion of England* for the F.A. course. That is a capital joke.'

Mohan Roy read it and smiled.

'They will be putting Ramji Das on the Textbook Committee,' he said.

Mohan Roy was always smiling. The more he smiled, the more resentful was Siri Ram's brooding. There can be no occasion for laughter, he thought, when the Mother is bleeding.

Mohan Roy laughed at the Labour Member's letter. He read it aloud slowly, with appreciative pauses and comments.

'He wishes to create suffragettes among our toiling sisters!

' "The labour movement is not a sex movement," he read; "you should not exclude women from any organization you may form in the future. They should sit side by side with you in Council. If you ask for benefits you must ask them both for women and men too." '

Mohan Roy smiled to think of the washer-women and the female mill-hands sitting beside the Swami voicing their wrongs.

'Ah, this is personal—most complimentary, I am sure.'

' "I enjoyed your friend Mr Mohan Roy's article in *The Eastern Review*. His generous tribute to our party's liberal interpretation of our obligations to your countrymen was much appreciated in political circles here; though the bureaucrats will not enjoy some of his strictures." '

'The very ideas of National Progress and National Advancement have come into being in India only after the spread of English education.' Such sentiments from the lips of an Indian patriot in these troubled times are most encouraging. I showed the article to Dr Byleman, who is going to pay a hurried visit to India next December. He wishes to study Indian questions on the spot, so that he may secure a thorough grasp of the difficult problems which are facing us at this parting of the ways. It may be hoped that on his return, his voice will carry even more authority in the House of Commons than it does at the present moment. He will be in Bengal three weeks. During this time he will require the services of a bright young Secretary who will be able to put him into touch with the inner life of the teeming millions of our great Eastern Dependency. He is especially anxious to study the question of the suffrage and representative government from inside. Dr Byleman was very much struck with your brilliant young friend's article, and I suggested to him that Mr Mohan Roy would be a very suitable young man for the work. Will you kindly ascertain if he is ready to accept the appointment? The salary would be at the rate of £20 a month; it will be provided out of party funds. Dr Byleman will be leaving Bombay early in January.'

'Yes, I accept,' Mohan Roy said with a grin. 'You may tell Dr Byleman Mohan Roy is willing.'

The Bengali's levity incensed Siri Ram. He saw nothing humorous in the letter. He had been told that Dr. Byleman, though a *feringhi*, was one of his country's saviours, like Tilak or Arabindo Ghose or Bepin Chandra Pal, with whom he fought in line. Good should come of his visit. Freedom, perhaps, without blood.

To the Swami all this talk of reform was so much meaningless patter. He was, if anything, opposed to it. He tolerated the meddling of sympathetic politicians because to detach himself from them too openly would be to show his hand. But he wanted no gifts, no concessions. They only delayed the millennium. The Indians must take everything for themselves. Repression was a dam against which the silent waters were gathering ready to burst.

He watched Siri Ram and understood his thoughts. He fed him with another scrap, a piece of brown paper, the outside of a bag, redolent of coarse sugar and the bunniah's shop. Siri Ram read.

' "Send a strong robust sepoy shirt to take charge from Mr Khaddar (homespun cloth), so that there may be no derangement in our store work." '

'Can you translate?' the Swami asked.

Siri Ram remembered the bunniah's postcard to Jaganath, in which he had been called 'homespun cloth, Sadhu wear'. With this clue he slowly interpreted the metaphor.

'Some patriot is leaving an employment where he is useful to the Society, and they are asking for another patriot, a bolder one, to take his place. No doubt it is some dangerous work.'

The Swami commended him.

No commendation was so sweet. He loved the cabalistic touch with its honeyed irony and the jargon of anarchists—'the bridegroom and the bride' for the destined victim and the bomb or pistol he was hurrying to meet. 'Marriage expenditure'—on picric acid and chlorate of potash! And the 'sweets prepared in every city and village in the land for the day of thanksgiving'. He himself would prepare 'the sweets'. or distribute them. He heard their deafening detonations in the thunder of the avalanche which awoke him from his dreams.

Sometimes Narasimha translated for him. The letters from the Secretary of the Red Flag Society in America were in cipher. One told of the export of five hundred revolvers packed in sewing machine cases and among condensed milk tins, booked through foreign houses in Bombay, and distributed among small retail merchants 'in sympathy with the Cause.' A cryptic letter from a Bengali in the Calcutta Customs advised him with the most extraordinary circumlocution of the receipt of seventy Browning Automatic Pistols and thirteen Derringers smuggled in by Chinamen through the Lascars of Penang.

Thus the Swami fed him day by day with just the scraps that were good for him, sufficient to keep his resentment warm and swell his pride and fill him with a sense of the strength of the organization behind him. It was only in the cave that he began to understand the magnitude of the scheme, the width of the web Narasimha was weaving. One day his imagination would be fired; then, the next, it all seemed so far away, so hopeless, and life so short and effort so exhausting. He fell back into the Yogi mood. He did not wish to live, but he did not wish to die violently.

The Swami watched him, and saw he was not ripe. Mohan Roy observed him with his caustic smile. 'He is a goat,' he said to the Swami. 'He may be useful for a sacrifice, but you will have to lead him right up to the altar.'

And he told the Swami of the meeting at Islamabad.

When Siri Ram saw the Swami and Mohan Roy talking together he was jealous. He hated the Bengali, who made him feel insufficient. He distrusted his humour, and was uncomfortable under his smile, and he felt that he was too familiar with the Swami. He had disliked him from the first, and had not forgiven him easily for finding the oiled cloth packet by the sacred tank. And he hated his English clothes. One day when his patience had been overtried by a long muttered conference from which he was excluded he broke out into passionate protest.

'Why you still wear *wilaiti* clothes,' he said, 'which are polluted with the blood and fat of animals? You swear by the Mother, and then you go and disobey her and defile her temples.'

Mohan Roy heard him with a smile. He only said: 'I like these clothes. I am habituated to them.'

Siri Ram got up sulkily and walked out of the cave. He sat brooding among the wild leeks and geraniums and dwarf willow scrub. The choughs sailed over him, crying plaintively. A russet-bosomed marmot sat up by her burrow over the snow-ridge and piped her shrill menace.

Siri Ram was tired of everything. He wanted to become a Sannyasi. Mohan Roy had smiled at his exercises in Yoga. The Bengali always smiled. Yet he had the ear of the Swami; he could hold his attention for hours. The Swami would sit silent listening while he talked, and Siri Ram would squat in the far corner of the cave watching the glint of the 'golden nails' in his teeth as if there was some occult spell in them. Sometimes the two would glance across with mutual understanding to where he sat by the small ice lingam of Ganesh, and he knew they were talking of him. Narasimha was always considerate. But Siri Ram felt that he took less interest in him than at first, and he attributed his diminished esteem to Mohan Roy, whom he hated.

He was counting the little pinnacles on the bluff of the cliff opposite, his resentment merged in dull abstraction, when he heard the Bengali's unwelcome voice behind him.

'I hope I do not intrude upon *Raja Yoga.* Or are you contemplating the beautiful scenery?'

Siri Ram did not speak. The Bengali seated himself on a stone by his side.

'No doubt you have already made the acquaintance of this lethal weapon?' he said.

Siri Ram saw that he held a dark black metal thing in his hand. He looked at it fascinated.

'It is revolver?' he said, with a question in his voice. It was the first he had seen out of a picture, though he had often held them in his dreams.

'You are cracked marksman, no doubt?'

'No. I have not used.'

'Take it. I will teach you. Patriots must learn to shoot.'

Siri Ram held out his hand. He was cold with fear, but he was ashamed to shrink. It lay in his open palm; he dared not press any part of it. Mohan Roy showed him how to grip it, and placed his first finger on the trigger-guard.

'Now,' he said. 'You see that *janwar* there.' And he pointed to the marmot, which still sat upright by her burrow, uttering her shrill warning pipe.

'Consider that is his Excellency. He is safe, as you are amateur. Point the deadly missile at his breast.'

Siri Ram took the revolver and held it out at arm's length. 'Do I look down pipe?' he said after a long pause.

'Yes. And put your finger on the hook underneath.'

Again there was a long pause. The revolver was not cocked, and Siri Ram dared not pull hard enough.

'I will lift the trigger,' Mohan Roy said. 'It will explode easier.'

Siri Ram took it a third time. Immediately there was a deafening explosion, which echoed through the narrow ravine like the roar of a distant avalanche. The bullet was thrown high up against the opposite cliff, and bits of splintered rock rolled slowly down to the ice roof of the stream. Mother marmot dived into her burrow as if she had been shot. There was a smell of burning. At the last moment Siri Ram had brought his left wrist up to the barrel to steady it, and his sleeve was burnt and his wrist singed. Drops of perspiration stood on his forehead.

'His Excellency has fled,' Mohan Roy said. 'Never mind. You will be cracked shot soon. Some of the volunteers only shoot touching.'

He went away smiling, and Siri Ram hated him more than ever.

The next morning when he woke in the cave he saw that Mohan Roy had gone, and he felt injured because he did not know why. All the morning the Swami was wrapt in an ecstatic trance, and afterwards when he spoke to Siri Ram he made no mention of the Bengali. Mohan Roy had vanished on some mysterious political errand, and he who at the first call had become a martyr to the Cause was left in the cold. Siri Ram was sunk in gloom. He could not understand in what way he was inferior to the dwarfish Bengali. In the evening when the Swami was stirring he approached him, awkward and self-conscious.

'I wish to practise Yoga,' he said.

'You have other work.'

'Have you work for me?'

'Proportionate to your love and zeal. You must have patience.'

'It is not diminished.'

'Your hour will come.'

Narasimha poked the fire with the axehead of his staff and stared fixedly into the ashes. Siri Ram knew that he must ask no more.

'Why do you wish to practise Yoga?' the Guru asked after a long pause.

'I want to become spiritual man.'

'You wish to escape from yourself?'

Siri Ram could not answer.

'I am a Yogi first of all for the Cause. I strengthen myself thus. By this means I can communicate with others hundreds of miles away. Today while you were gathering fuel I sent a message to Bengal. You can never attain this power.'

'Can Mohan Roy send air messages?'

'I can communicate with him'

Siri Ram knew at once that his spiritual hopes were vain.

'The true *Yog* is attained through concentration, not through abstraction. It is for the master, not for the servant. You have not the strength. It will be your part to act and obey. Your business is with the action now, not with the fruit. You will be found a task, and you will perform it. Nobly, I have no doubt.'

Once more Siri Ram felt drawn within the fold. Content shone in his eyes.

Narasimha observed him, and he remembered that he had neglected him. He had barely noticed him for days. Now he must make amends. He must lead the goat a little further on the path towards the altar.

'You wish to know why Mohan Roy has gone?'

Siri Ram started. The Swami read his mind always like a scroll.

'Mohan Roy has gone for two reasons. First he will discover whether my tracks are covered, whether I can safely go back. I must finish my work in Bengal. You know, it is believed that I have perished in a fall of stones. Afterwards he will find means to let me know. It will be difficult. He himself, I think, will not return.'

There was a note of deepened dejection and pathos in the Swami's voice which recalled the lecture at Gandeshwar.

'Why he will not come back?' Siri Ram asked.

'He will die, I think, but the future is not clear.'

Siri Ram gaped for more.

'You have heard of Ghulam Ali of the Criminal Investigation Department in Bengal. He has learnt too much; he is dangerous to the Cause. Mohan Roy has gone for that. He is clever and bold, but it will be difficult for him to escape.'

Siri Ram looked into the Swami's eyes and dropped his own. A cold fear crept over him.

'You wish me—' he began falteringly.

'No, you are not ripe for this work yet. Besides there is only this one, and Mohan Roy will not fail. You understand. We kill informers and spies only now, and we kill them because we must—not because we hate them, but because they hinder us. The Englishmen will fall later, all together. Perhaps your turn will come then. We want Government to sleep now. A sacrifice here and there does more harm than good. It prepares them, and it frightens the Liberals in England.'

'Will Byleman give us freedom without blood?' Siri Ram asked innocently.

'Do not hope it. Do not care for their gifts. Scorn them rather. They mean nothing to true patriots. The Mother can be delivered only by her own sons. But we must not frighten them yet. When they are frightened it is more difficult for us, because they do not hold Government back, they do not oppose the reactionaries. The army budget is increased; troops are quartered where we do not want them; it is more difficult in a hundred ways.'

Siri Ram thought of the Professor's letter. 'You must have a definite day and fix it well ahead. We will send you the arms. You will distribute the men.'

'Can you repeat it?' the Swami asked.

Siri Ram started. When the Guru looked at him intently he felt that a searching light was thrown upon his mind. Nothing could be hidden from Narasimha. Men's thoughts were naked for him to read.

'Ye-es. I have committed it to memory. 'Dear Swami, the last mail brought sad news. The Rawalpindi emmoot—' He droned it out word for word, as he would have repeated a page of annotator's stuff at Gandeshwar.

'That is well done. Keep it in your mind. We had decided on this course before you brought the Professor's letter. Remember. The awakening will come in one day. The sword of your country is in your hand. Shrink not. What if ye fall! There is no other door of admission into life after death.'

When Siri Ram fell asleep that night, the Sadhu was submerged in him. Again he was the conspirator and patriot.

The next week the snow lay lower on the mountains. Fuel was scarce and the cold intense. The ibex came down to within a bow-shot of the cave. Siri Ram wandered down the valley to collect juniper scrub, and climbed back over the frozen stream. The work was good for him. He brooded less, and often when he returned to his rice and mess of leeks thoroughly tired out he sank into a mood of something like passive cheerfulness. On these frosty evenings by the flickering fire in the cave, the Swami would devote an hour sometimes to his education.

At Amarnath Siri Ram learnt the whole of the Bhagavad Gita. He would chant it in the cave. Sometimes the Swami's full, rich voice would take up the hymns, vibrating with passion, and they would sing alternately, and then as the echoes died away, the Swami would become exalted, and he would preach to Siri Ram as if he were a great company, just as he had preached at Gandeshwar, as if all the youth of India were in the cave listening at his feet.

'Remember the teaching of Krishna to Arjun and you will not draw back. This dweller in the body is invulnerable. Slain, thou wilt obtain Swarga; victorious, thou wilt enjoy the earth; therefore stand up, resolute to fight.

'Shrink not from blood. Heed not the voice of the weaklings who chatter of 'rebellion'. You cannot commit this sin. Against whom can ye rebel? Tell me. Can a *feringhi* rule in Hindustan whose very touch, whose very shadow compels Hindus to purify themselves?

'Every patriot who removes one of these pale fiends from the sacred soil of Hindustan becomes a Saint.

'Listen to the sacred Shastras. It is in the young men alone that the salvation of the country lies. Blessed is your birthright. You are the Valki—the god is incarnated in you who will rid India of the Mlecchas.

'Come, offer your sacrifices before the altar in chorus, and let all white serpents perish in the flames ye are kindling even as the vipers perished in the serpent-slaying sacrifice of Janmayog.'

It was an impressive scene—this wraith of a man illumined by the dancing firelight which threw the shadow of his uplifted hand against the dark, dripping, buttressed rock above the lingam, a lighted husk, a bursting chrysalis, too weak almost to hold the straining spirit within. And the voice which issued from this shell was rich and vibrant, and it awoke echoes which beat along the massy roof of the cavern like lapping waves until they escaped into the eternal frosty silence of the starlight and the snow. And the message was delivered to the youth of the nation, to the Valki incarnation of Vishnu, which was personified in Siri Ram. It was enough to inspire the dullest and send him hot foot on any sacrifice.

But Siri Ram's hour had not yet come; the fire that the Swami had lighted in him must smoulder long. In the morning he was sent on a homely errand. He had to descend twenty miles to Zojpal to bring back white bark for the Swami's letters, and to find some empty gujar's hut for him to dwell in. For the time had come to abandon the cave. The snow was encroaching. Soon all exit from the valley would be blocked. The herdsmen below had already driven down their flocks, and the reign of the eternal stillness was already spreading wider, a sovereignty to be disturbed by no living voice until the snows melted in the margs in the spring.

Siri Ram slept in a gujar's empty stone hut and returned on the evening of the second day with the bark. As he approached he saw Narasimha standing in the entrance to the cave as if he expected him, and looking cold and thin. The Swami took the bark from Siri Ram with a quiet word of greeting, and sat down by the fire and wrote in cipher for an hour.

'Wrap this in your loin-cloth,' he said, 'and give it to Ramji Das. Go with the dawn.'

Then, seeing his chela's surprise and dismay, he added—

'Mohan Roy has been quick. He is dead. Both are dead. I had a message in the night.'

# PART IV

## 'The Kali-Yuga'

The determinate reason is but one in this mortal life,
Many-branched and endless are the thoughts of the irresolute.

*The Bhagavad Gita*

The man of perfect knowledge should not unsettle the foolish whose
knowledge is imperfect.

*The Bhagavad Gita*
(Mrs Besant's Translation)

# 1

Siri Ram did little in the cold weather for the Cause. The Swami's birch-bark letter to Ramji Das repeated Mohan Roy's estimate. He was wobbly and unstable. One could never tell what foolishness he might commit, undoing with one hand what he did with the other. But to Banarsi Das, still at a loose end, he was something of a hero. That glib youth tersely defined the progress of the three conspirators when he said, 'I am still seeking an employment. Lachmi Chand has become unpaid teacher in the Gurukul. And Siri Ram has taken the bitch between his teeth.'

When half his term of rustication was over, Banarsi Das approached Skene for pardon. First came the petition, a lengthy screed with capitals in red and the weightiest words in capitals. Skene was humbly reminded that he was a moral father. Banarsi Das solicited an opportunity of 'ameliorating' himself 'under his kind control'. 'I cannot thole this misfortune,' he added, 'I hope you would be my father. I think I have not gone worse than the prodigal son.' The conclusion showed signs of a maturer hand.

'In the end I beg to invite your kind attention to the notorious lines of Mr Shakespeare, Esq., and request that you would be kindly disposed to pardon me for the sake of the master who taught us this lesson—

'The Quality of Mercy is not Strained.'

Banarsi Das quoted the whole passage.

The position of the hybrid weighed heavily on Skene, for he understood the pathos of it more than most Englishmen. He was genuinely sorry for the youth, and he could not see what place there was for him and his fellows in the general scheme. Banarsi Das followed up the petition—which had been sped shaftlike in advance to penetrate official callousness, by a personal interview. He wanted to be recommended for a teachership. Skene told him to come back to the College after his year's rustication and start again with a clean slate. He would find an opening for him somewhere, but he advised him to give up the idea of educational work.

'You must see,' he explained, 'that with these ideas in your head you would be out of place in a school.'

But Banarsi Das did not see. Since he had been away from the College, his education had progressed on lines prescribed by the Students' Improvement Society. He had swallowed chunks of undigested history washed down with heady libations of political tracts.

'Sir,' he ventured, 'if you were an Early Briton would you not resist to the Romans? If you were an Italian would you not resist to Austrian tyrants?'

Skene smiled sadly.

'If I were an early Briton resisting the Romans, I should not think it reasonable to ask them for an appointment, certainly not an educational one.'

But this was vindictive evasiveness to Banarsi Das. He was really incapable of seeing a point turned against himself.

'I would not openly preach against Government,' he began.

'Where is Siri Ram?' Skene interrupted.

'Sir, he contemplated the adoption of the teaching profession. I hear he is walking in the Academe's groves with Mr Lachmi Chand.'

Banarsi Das shuffled his feet, self-consciously pleased at the successful delivery of so neatly-turned a trope. He watched for the effect of it in Skene's face, and noticed a slight muscular movement at the corner of his mouth which he took for approbation. The gift of eloquence atones for much.

He retired, not discomfited, and answered an advertisement in *The Tribune* for a Teachership in a Native State.

'Sir,

'I am young man of commanding appearance and winning personality. I have read up to F.A. I sometimes use the English costume. To enable you to get at the true idea of my managing capacity and other abilities I send under separate cover photo of myself in College group. The sixth one, second row, commencing from left, with crossing legs, head bare, and right hand grasping firmly with the wrist bone of the left is my own photo. I hope if you would kindly appoint me to situation under your kind control you would find me ornament who would pull on with you. A postal ticket of ½ an anna is sent herewith and intended for sharp reply.'

Skene was relieved to hear the news of Siri Ram. The Gurukul at Hardwar was perhaps the best melting-pot for him if he had the patience to endure it. The school is the nursery of the Arya Samaj, and its aim is the realization in modern life of the 'Back to the Vedas' cry. They believe that in the golden days, before Self was made a god, the Indians were lords of the earth and of themselves and of all knowledge. The Vedas were the repositories of all Science, and there was no modern revelation that did not lurk in some cryptic saying of the Rishis. And the conquest that this implied arose out of the conquest of Self. So long as they retained their courage and purity and austerity of mind, the splendour remained with them; when they became enmeshed in the web of delusion, given over to gratification of desire, it passed away.

The only way to recapture the lost heritage was a return to the discipline of life which made it possible. That was the truest and sanest form of patriotism, the only sure road to political independence, and better for body and soul than any wheedling of authority for privilege and concession. The wiser half of the Samaj—even the Aryas were divided—had the courage to face the fact which Skene had explained to his students, that they must be the thing before they could enjoy its privileges. If there is any health in this survival, Skene thought, nothing could fall out better for Siri Ram than that he should be caught up in it.

Lachmi Chand wrote happily from Kangri. The austerity of the life was in keeping with the deeply religious bent of his mind, for the ideal at the Gurukul was nothing less than a return to the old Bramacharya system of Vedic times. Lachmi Chand was Superintendent of a group of boys, and lived under the same discipline as his pupils, sharing their spare diet, sleeping on a plank bed, rising at four every morning, and bathing in the river and performing the same physical and devotional exercises. It was a sixteen-year course for the young Bramacharis, who were admitted in their eighth year, after which they were cut off from all outside influences, and not allowed to go to their homes or write to their parents or receive letters from them until they were twenty-five. They were eight years old when they took the vow of poverty, chastity, and obedience, and their guardians pledged themselves not to remove them.

Siri Ram did not feel drawn towards Hardwar. The life was too tedious and obscure, the fruition too remote, and the patience and self-discipline beyond his resources, though he would not have admitted it even to himself. But the months passed, and he was not called upon to do any desperate thing. The revolutionists were very quiet; there had been no political assassination since Mohan Roy had despatched Ghulam Ali in Hooghly railway station, winged a Moravian missionary and shot himself. All this time Siri Ram supported himself on twelve rupees a month by teaching the son of a cloth merchant in the bazaar. The prospect of the pedestal receded. He ascended the steps into Ramji Das's chamber almost daily, but that obese worthy blinked at him unconcernedly from his corner like an overfed spider, and gave him no material encouragement. If he was to remain a Nationalist, it seemed that he must fall into line with the band of silent workers whose sacrifice was unheeded, and whose names were never heard—a sad anti-climax for Siri Ram.

In the train he felt half afraid that he might be persuaded to stay at the Gurukul. Lachmi Chand expected it. His letter glowed with zeal and devotion. He spoke of the great anniversary when thousands would flock to the camp by the Ganges. Siri Ram was to meet him in the Punjab students' serai in time for the first day's celebration. Banarsi Das would be there, and they were to go to the *pandal* together to hear the lecture on 'Service and Sacrifice'.

It was the time of the Holi festival and the pilgrim train carried a double stream to Hardwar. Hordes of the enlightened were going to the anniversary, but the superstitious outnumbered them. Siri Ram found himself with three other Samajists jammed in a carriage full of his illiterate countrymen, priest-ridden idolaters groping in the dark and unconscious of their degradation. These simple folk were going to bathe in Mother Gunga and wash away their sins. It was an opportunity for missionary zeal.

They were a bewildered crowd, taxed and bullied by the police and the subordinate railway officials. Herds of them were penned in at every station, and not allowed to pass the barrier until they had paid some imaginary toll. Then the train would start off as they were clambering in, and they would be thrust back roughly by the guard to await another turn, perhaps twelve hours afterwards, when the weakest were likely to go to the wall again. Some of them had camped outside the station platform for two or three days.

A group of sad-eyed villagers ran in a dazed way beside a first-class carriage, staring blankly at the strange forbidden emptiness in which a subaltern reclined alone with his little bear-like dog and fishing rods and bedding. The boy, looking up, saw an old man's forlorn face just in time to pull him into the passage at the end of his carriage and make a sign to his three sons, laden with pots and pans and blankets and sugar-cane, to jump in behind as the train moved off. A disgusted official ran alongside protesting, but they were already squatting on the floor, stolid and expressionless, as if it were the most natural thing in the world, and secure until the next junction, where the subaltern found room for them in a carriage.

All these venturesome ones who hoped to reach Hardwar quickly by the iron road, performing a journey of weeks in one or two days, knew that they had submitted to an unseen agency which was all-powerful but perverse and capricious, and to be circumvented by rites which the policemen and ticket collectors alone understood. At every station there was confusion and bullying and apparent resentment that the pilgrims should take the train at all. It was 'Hat jao. Hat jao. Get out of the way. Make room'. Then the glib sedition-monger slipped in among them. They were ready to listen to any tale, though they had not taken it much amiss when they were mulcted at the barrier, knowing that every coveted door in Hindustan, whether of courts or shrines or offices, is guarded now as it always has been by some initiate priest or parawalla who is happily appeasable.

There were an old man and woman in Siri Ram's carriage who had come from their village with a concession for a party of twenty-four. The youth with the ticket had been lost in the crowd at the junction, and some of them had already been discovered and turned back. The old couple hoped to get through undetected. Their case was discussed in the frequent sidings.

'You will have to pay again,' a clerkly Sikh said to the old man.

'I cannot pay, and the paper was to take us all back.'

A tear rolled down the old woman's nose and broke on the quoit-like earring which covered her wrinkled face from ear to mouth.

'See how they treat you,' Siri Ram said. 'The Sircar only want your money. They don't care whether you see Hardwar or not.'

'Or whether you live or die,' the clerkly Sikh added.

One of the Samajists began to talk at the old man.

'Did you hear of the railway accident last week?' he said to Siri Ram. 'It was to kill off the black men. I heard it from a labourer who is working on the line. A red-faced man with white hair asked him to remove a rail, but he would not.'

Siri Ram recognized a trained hand, perhaps a Bharat Red Flag man. He tried the sitting sign, the thumb resting two seconds on the right knee, the first finger on the shinbone. The man repeated the sign on the left.

'It is these big trains they destroy most often killing hundreds at a time. There are too many black men, they say.'

'They will be enough to eat up the feringhis soon.'

'Whoever heard of an Englishman being destroyed in a railway accident?'

'Indeed, the road is better.'

The train drew up in a siding with a violent jerk, flinging the Samajists and pilgrims together pell-mell. Each man thought it was his end.

They reached Hardwar eighteen hours late. They had been shunted into sidings for every goods or passenger train that passed. The engine had jibbed and started and stopped dead as if it knew the cheapness of the human freight behind. The hustled carriages had charged into each other at intervals, and the couplings resisted with a straining and

clanking which might have awakened the dead. The pilgrims who had
been shaken together with violence all the night emerged in the
noonday heat instead of in the cool of the vigil.

2

The belated Samajists hurried off to the camp at Kangri, five miles
away, but Siri Ram was drawn with the superstitious into the
city. He loitered dreamily by the bathing ghat. He stood on the
bridge and looked down on the clear stream of the Ganges and the
crowds of pilgrims waist-deep in the cold water. He had been taken
there when a child by his mother, when he had been plunged in like
the little howling black-haired urchin, clasped to the breast of the
enormous matron underneath, lost almost against the ample folds of
the pale bosom. He watched the happy naked crowd with a kind of
envy, until he was drawn to the ghat and became one of them, dancing
youths, slim maidens, wizened old men, mountainous matrons,
wading out to Hari's Island temple. He circumambulated it with them,
and patted the stones, round and round in the ecstatic queue, and it
made him happy to feel the stream lapping his waist and the great
holy fish nosing his legs, as the Brahmins threw in the *atta* from the
bridge.

When he had bathed he sat on the Island in the dry breeze that
followed the stream, looking north to the woods where the River
Houses of the Chiefs ended in the scarlet dhak forest at the foot of the
hills. The tender green of a Shisham plantation in the river-bed spoke
of spring, while the sâl forest of the Sewaliks on either bank formed an
amphitheatre glinting with the red and gold of the turn of the year. In
the far background the purple mountains were lifted up, cleft by
Gunga. If Siri Ram marked them, it was only in a vague dreamy way
with an inner consciousness that he was in a land associated with the
beginnings of things, and a thrill of something like pride that he
walked in the country of his old gods. His day-dreams were rudely
disturbed.

'Why you have been bathing at the temple? You are superstitious.'

It was Shiv Narain, an acquaintance of his own Samaj. But Siri Ram
had no time to think of anything to say before the superior youth had
passed on and was lost in the crowd.

'Am I polytheistic heathen?' he asked himself. 'No, I was heated
and unclean. Why not in the waters of Ganges?' Then he remembered
a newspaper article he had read, and he wanted to run after Shiv

Narain to explain to him how the Ganges water had been analysed by Bengali chemists, and had been pronounced purer than any other water, having no germs but rather a virtue that destroyed them, so that those who were 'habituated' to bathe in it and drink of it lived healthily and attained a ripe old age.

'Sound mind may be had in the sound body, no doubt,' he muttered.

He thought of Swami-ji's lecture. It was another proof that the old Rishis knew by direct revelation what Western scientists have been groping after for thirty centuries in the dark. And they knew more.

'Yes, I am going back to the Vedas,' he said, with a reminiscence of Swami-ji. 'When I bathe in the Ganges I am obeying purely rationalistic principles of health, revealed to ancient sages, and inculcated by them upon ignorant masses in allegorical shape.'

But he found it hard to be esoteric all alone. The human throng appealed to him. He looked at the sea-green bottles for the holy water on the stalls, and the baskets and the lingams and the flowers for the shrines, and he thought he remembered being led by his mother past the shops when a tiny child, and he felt a faint regret that these things had ceased to mean anything for him. He wandered into the courtyard of Sarvvanath's temple, and he was nearly knocked down in the gate by a band of singing Sadhus, who had smeared one another all over with the scarlet paint and were emerging with a triumphant chant, dancing and swaying and posturing and waving their open palms, running at passers-by and daubing their clothes and faces, or pouring their brass lotahs full of the purple dye down their backs. Siri Ram shrank into a corner of the arcade and regarded them sadly. His sleeve was stained with carmine.

Before evening the stones of Hardwar and Kankhal were dyed red and purple, doorsteps and lintels, stalls and booths, even the sacred bulls were smeared so that one seemed to be looking at everything through crimson-stained glasses. And the companies of bacchanals came rolling out of the great houses, singing their indecent songs, leaping and beating drums with an inhuman flame-like glow on them like fiends in a devil's smithy.

The hours had slipped by. Siri Ram was due at the Gurukul at five. He had promised to meet Lachmi Chand and Banarsi Das in the Punjab Students' Camp and go with them to the *pandal* to hear the lecture on Service and Sacrifice; but the Pundit was half-way through his discourse when Siri Ram was passing the Mahatma's house at Kankhal, star-gazing as was his wont, looking up vacantly into the bare wintry twigs of the pipal and the green flowers of the mango and toon, whose fragrance scented the road.

At the end of the street, a cart track tilted down the bank of the river, where an unfinished causeway led over the Ganges bed towards the distant flag of the Gurukul. Here Siri Ram met another stream of people toiling home on foot, and in slow, labouring bullock-carts through the boulders and deep sand. These were the Aryan Protestants returning from the camp: a sombre-clad procession. In Kankhal the two streams mixed, the thread of grey and black was soon lost among the bacchanals—as a mountain stream debouches into a yellow silted torrent, and flows beside it a moment before its clear waters are merged in it. If Siri Ram had been given to parables he would have seen in the current from the Gurukul the beginnings of the Reformed Church which was to purge the nation, and in the opposing stream, the stains of superstition which were ultimately to be absorbed in the increasing volume which flowed from the direction of the Vedic flag. And he might have reproached himself with 'the unlit lamp, the ungirt loin'. As it was, he remembered that he had failed to keep his tryst with Lachmi Chand, and that he had lingered a whole day among the superstitious, attracted by their empty gawds, while he might have been listening to the discourse of the Pundit. He was ashamed of the vermilion stains on his coat, and he kept to the left of the track, so as to hide his sleeve as much as possible from the Reformers.

The sun was almost setting when he crossed the wattle bridge over the third channel and was near enough the flag to decipher the mystic *Om*. In the courtyard the young Bramacharis were sitting round the white fires, chanting their mantras, and casting their rice and *ghee* into the flames, just as their Aryan ancestors had done long ages ago, centuries before the Puranas, when they streamed across the Peninsula from the mountains in the full pride of their race, singing glad hymns as they camped among their herds by the river-side. It was the first time Siri Ram had seen the sacrifice of *Hôm*, the oldest surviving ritual in the world. 'It is no superstitious rite,' Lachmi Chand explained, 'but the symbol of purification. They keep no idols or lingams here, they do not worship stalks and stones. It was in this way the old Aryans used to purge the air.'

Lachmi Chand was already a devout convert. The Pundit's lecture, though it had offended most of the Samaj, had left a deep impression upon him. The gist of his dismal creed had been that the Indians had lost their country because they were not worthy of it. They had no character. They could not trust one another even in little things, not at all in great things. They had no sense of duty, responsibility, discipline, organization. And until they had developed these characteristics in the way Englishmen have done, they could not hope to do anything. They must wait for a new generation—a distant generation, when the system of Bramacharya which was being taught in the Gurukul had leavened the whole nation and recaptured some of its past glories, before they could dream even of Swaraj. In the meantime they must serve the British Government faithfully, and they must imitate the good qualities of Englishmen, and learn to speak the truth and depend on one another, and to do their duty for its own sake, wherever they were placed, apart from selfish motives, and they must be ready to forget their mutual differences when their country was in danger or in need of them.

In theory, the Pundit went on, no people were more thorough and systematic than the Indians. They could draw up schemes and societies, and rules of life, appoint leaders and office-bearers, and issue eloquent appeals towards union and nationalization. But in practice nothing came of it. Every new community was divided up into half-a-dozen different opposing factions before it had been in existence a month, according as its members were influenced by pride or greed or envy, or the hope of personal gain, or class privileges. Societies whose professed aim was solidarity afforded fresh examples of disintegration. Reformers who were always talking of self-effacement and national self-consciousness cared more for the glitter and prominence of their position at the head of their ineffectual factions than for any real good to the Cause. And this was not so much due to calculating selfishness as to lack of character and steadfastness. Young men were carried away by their dramatic sense and the heady and superficial emotions which quickly-assimilated ideas always bring to the surface. The ideal of Progress and national advancement which was on everybody's lips was a new cry which had not been heard in India before the spread of English education.

This was strong meat for the Samajists. Their leaders had talked a great deal about the degradation of the country, but always as due to British influence and education. The aim of their teaching was to impress the Bramacharis with the sense of their glorious national heritage, and to lead them back to it and away from the meretricious glitter of Western refinement. They believed that it would be India's part some day to rescue Europe from the slough of materialism into which she was sinking. This was to come in the age of universal Bramacharya.

So, as the Pundit continued, discontent grew louder. It was felt that he had exceeded decent bounds. He was destitute of national self-respect. Young men at the edge of the *pandal* interrupted loudly. Ready catchwords, some in English, often tags of textbook reminiscence, were exchanged. 'Sycophant, time-server, lick-spittle, subserviency, fouler of his nest'—and such burrs as stick to graduates who have struggled through the tangled idiom of our classics. It was a bitter draught, but there was worse to follow.

'It is not enough to found a Sabha or Samaj and call yourselves patriots. We must change ourselves before we can change others. It is because the Englishmen possess these qualities which we do not possess that a million of them are able to control three hundred lakhs of Indians just as one small boy can control a hundred sheep which nourish the blind life within the brain, because he is morally and intellectually on a higher plane than the dumb animals. And just as sheep cannot escape from the control of the boy as long as they are sheep, in the same way the Indians—'

But the Pundit was not allowed to finish his speech.

'He was drowned in stream of angry vocables discharged with torrential violence.' So Banarsi Das described the scene in his letter to a friend. The Pundit may have spoken sincerely. Or it may have been strategy, another way of rousing the young men against the English. His speech certainly had this effect on Siri Ram, though he only heard the diluted version from Lachmi Chand, who had taken it in literal earnest. But, disingenuous or not, it had incensed the Aryas.

Lachmi Chand took Siri Ram over the 'Academy', and showed him the Library and Laboratory and the huge cow-sheds and dormitories furnished only with plank beds. Then he took him to the great *pandal* where the meetings were held and the Visitors' Camp, a mile almost of whitewashed, tin-roofed sheds and thatched wattle outhouses. He had approached the Guru about his friend, and there was a humble office, almost menial, which Siri Ram might have at once. Lachmi Chand was full of zeal. Siri Ram had to run by his side to keep up with him. He was busy from morning to night, and at the next bell he had to be with his *brahmachari*s, a tender group of novices which he was shepherding.

As they strode back they met a continual stream of visitors going towards the river. Lachmi Chand took Siri Ram on to the roof of a shed and pointed to the plain where a sea of black and white-robed Aryas, swollen by tributaries from every side, extended for over a mile. 'It is the initiation ceremony of the first Muhammadan convert,' he said proudly. But somehow Siri Ram was not uplifted like his companion. He was strangely depressed. The mountains laboured with these birth pangs for so small a mouse. He thought of Narasimha Swami and Mohan Roy, and even longed for Amarnath, forgetting his jealous humours there. And all the while Lachmi Chand was informing and preparing him, as he panted by his side, talking as if he were already dedicated.

'We rise at four in response to the tintinnabulation of the bell. In winter it is four-thirty. After bathing there is drill. The exercises are very profitable to the body. Then *yagna* and *Agni Hotra*. Milk is at seven. Then teaching to ten-thirty. In the interval—'

Siri Ram was relieved at the thought of the interval. He admired rather than envied his friend's service. He wished to dream and moralize and talk until the hour of his call, and then to do his work all at once and with one stroke. Suddenly a bell 'tintinnabulated', interrupting his friend's discourse and his own apprehensions. Lachmi Chand started from him running, and calling back to him to be ready in the courtyard at four in the morning.

It would be wrong to say that Siri Ram slept on it. He knew already that he would drift along some other current. When he thought he was wondering whether to stay or not he was only wondering how he could escape without appearing lukewarm. He dreaded the routine and discipline of the place, but he had not the courage to admit his shrinking. In the end he did what most young men of his temperament would do. He said he would come, and went away meaning not to come. He persuaded himself that the machinery of the Gurukul was too slow, and that he would go back to Gandeshwar and do some desperate thing.

The next morning, having bathed with his charges, Lachmi Chand saw Siri Ram to the bridge, happy at the prospect of reclaiming his friend. He had the true pastoral spirit. They walked hand in hand.

'You will return in three days?' Lachmi Chand asked.

'Yes, I will return. I have a few businesses.'

'And your father? Are you going to Mograon?'

'I will write a letter. I shall not mind him.'

They unclasped hands. Siri Ram turned his back on the Vedic flag and pursued his vacillating path over the rough boulders of the old channel. Without raising his head he followed the line of least resistance, which would have brought him back to the island if Lachmi Chand had not called after him, pointing to the ford. Siri Ram swerved on to the track again. By the time he had become a wobbling black dot on the sand, Lachmi Chand knew in his heart that he would not come back.

## 3

A week after the anniversary at Gurukul Siri Ram was given his chance. Much frequenting of Ramji Das's staircase had brought him preferment. He was appointed acting scapegoat prison-editor of the *Kali-Yuga*. The post did not carry a salary, and it required no special gifts. The issue was prepared for the new Editor, who had to be on the spot when the press was raided, and claim responsibility. The reward was honourable confinement.

The *Kali-Yuga*,[1] as the name implied, was a political journal of a pessimistic turn. It was the policy of the gentlemen who financed the organ to sail as near the wind as possible, and occasionally to let the bark capsize, when they would throw some callow youth overboard to right her. Several immature patriots had already been sacrificed, while the nebulous authors of the enterprise escaped. But they did not get off scot-free. The press had been confiscated, and the profits had been inconsiderable. Still the sheet emerged in a new quarter under a new name—the *Kali-Yuga*, the present incarnation of the local spirit of disaffection, was also to go. The people needed waking up. A red-hot number had been prepared. The lamps in the temple of Independence were to be lighted again. It was a commination service, and Siri Ram was chosen High Priest.

The policy of the *Kali-Yuga* was opposed to Narasimha's method. The Swami wanted to let the Flame burn secretly. Ramji Das and his circle were for noise and advertisement. They were all for a panic. If one talks enough about revolution, they said, it will come. It was half the battle to get the people used to the idea, and a murder here and there, and a few flaming leaflets would go a long way. They liked to see officialdom agitated and suspicious. They chuckled at all open signs of uneasiness, talking with their tongue in their cheek of 'a flutter in the Anglo-Indian dovecotes'. That was a phrase that occurred two or three times in an issue in their most moderate organs. They felt that they had gained a point when any of the less responsible Anglo-Indian journals lent themselves to the scare, unable to resist a bid for sensationalism.

Siri Ram had wits enough to see that Narasimha would have condemned the *Kali-Yuga*. He remembered the Swami's conversation in the cave, and his warning that the time had not yet come to act, and that Government should sleep. Narasimha had never impressed his imagination so much as on that morning. He wished now that he could serve him, though his errands were perilous, rather than the pampered, worldly-looking bunniah. But no word had come of the Swami for months past. He had been ill in the mountains in the cold weather, and his name was not heard in the conspirators' talk so often as it had been.

The *Kali-Yuga* was not badly edited. Its harmony of tone and idea might have extracted admiration from a connoisseur. Hate had distorted its features into a kind of consistency. The notes,

[1]Era of Darkness.

correspondence, telegrams, leaders, even the advertisements and notices, were all the complement of one another, so that it had the physiognomy of an astutely edited London paper which comes out every day pervaded with some one idea, its features regular and proportionate, its expression set in the smirk or smile or frown demanded by the moment. It did not subscribe to Reuter, but items of European news which would interest Indians were telegraphed by a correspondent in Allahabad within an hour of their appearance in *The Pioneer.* The weekly London letter, by an Indian barrister in the Temple, which was taken up with India in Parliament and the sayings and doings of retired bureaucrats, generally narrowed down into an attack on Lord Curzon, who was still the 'Aunt Sally' of Indian journalists. Whenever 'His Ex-Magnificence' made an after-dinner speech or wrote a letter to *The Times,* the London correspondent's letter was full of it. The *Kali-Yuga* and a dozen other sheets were never tired of throwing mud at him. It was not strange that Siri Ram's next obsession, after his anti-cow-killing campaign in the school, should have been Lord Curzon, and that he should have come to regard him as the author of all evil. Whenever he saw the headlines: 'Cock-a-doodle-doo', 'The Prancing Proconsul', 'The Arch-Panjandrum', he longed to be an editor himself, and lacerate the feelings of ex-Viceroys. Ramji Das had warned the proprietor that Siri Ram was a strange, obstinate youth, and it might spoil everything if he were thwarted. So, as part of his reward over and above the glory of martyrdom, he was allowed one column for his own lucubrations. He had thought of giving a paragraph to Banarsi Das.

Siri Ram had often frequented the offices as an interested loiterer. He had nearly left a finger in the lithograph roller, and one day he had fallen into the machine for making ink. The premises of the *Kali-Yuga* took up three sides of a courtyard, and were approached by a remote alley, leading out of a *mohalla* in the bazaar. The rooms were small and cell-like and filled with tables of type, or stacks of superfluous forms and circulars, and dirty-looking paper which dry-rotted in every corner. In the yard one tripped over broken stone slabs for lithographs and the remains of prehistoric hand-presses. The third side of the building was taken up by the press, and the fourth by the engine, which also worked a flour-mill, the only one in Gandeshwar which did not belong to Ramji Das, for that astute capitalist was not going to be mixed up even indirectly with such machinery.

When Siri Ram's instructions were complete, he was left in the editorial chair. The portentous issue of the *Kali-Yuga,* for which he was to stand sponsor, was already in type save only his own column, which was still unfinished, an advertisement or two—payment uncertain—

and the telegrams from Allahabad. It was an eloquent appeal, an open bid for revolution, as defiant and outspoken as any document that had seen the light in the Punjab. The leaders opened with an appeal by Narasimha Swami: 'Which way does Salvation lie?' It was the work of an inspired fanatic, strong, nervous, impassioned, all trumpet-call and drumbeat, without a flourish to weaken it or a superfluous trope. The Swami had delivered the address at a secret meeting in Gandeshwar two years before, but held it too provocative at the time for publication. Now the Society decided that the moment for it had come, and the prophet's wishes were forgotten. The second article was in a different vein, bitter and cynical. Its text was a train outrage in which a young subaltern of a British regiment had deposited a portly Bengali grandee out of his carriage on to the platform of Howrah station. As ill-luck would have it, the gentleman was a member of the Viceroy's Legislative Council, and, as the *Kali-Yuga* pointed out, probably of much more ancient lineage than his ill-bred assailant. Beginning thus painfully in the right, the editor went on to enlarge upon the different law that held everywhere for 'black and white' in the face of Christian professions of brotherhood. He glanced off to the case of the Indians in the Transvaal, speaking of black men in mental inverted commas, and playing on the delicate theme with such skill that the brown-skinned man who read might well run amok at the first white face he saw. A white man could not read it without feeling guilty and sick. Siri Ram, to whom man's equality was an undebatable fact, rose in his chair as he read and called out to the foreman and the typesetters in his craving for indignant sympathy. But none of his staff had come.

The third article offered a salve to his inflamed resentment. It was headed, 'The Awakening of the Agricultural Classes', and it held out hints none too vague as to how the awakening might be completed. It ended with this sinister peroration—

'The *Feringhee* does not yet know us. He has long dealt with us, but no amount of familiarity has grown between him and us. Hidden amongst the mango groves of Plassey, without having even a semblance of battle, and by fraud, forgery and deceptive means, they have taken possession of Bharat Mata. That is why they fail to understand us. Now they have the audacity to tread on the tail of the cobra. The very sedition cases of which we now hear will start the 'fire'. *Feringhee*! let us tell you beforehand that you will soon know for yourself of how much each and every heart in Hindustan is capable. We know that you are thick-skinned, and cannot understand subtle words. The Indian now seeks to settle accounts with you. We thought of understanding one another's feelings in an altogether different way. But you would not let that be. You seek introduction to us by treading on our tail. Do whatever you please. Only remember the hideous cobra and its sting.'

The Notes and Comments were equally virulent. A new Honours list had just been published, and there was a caustic paragraph on the Indian gentlemen who had been given titles, which had come to mean 'nothing but the price of sycophancy and subservience'. More venom was spilt on the Anglophiles than on the English themselves. Muhammadans, who were counting on British favour and privileges over the Hindus, were warned to prepare themselves for that rude awakening which might come any moment without any notice or warning. To a letter published in the *Pioneer* from a native of a disaffected district upholding the justice and consideration of Government, the *Kali-Yuga* published a reply pointing out that the writer was a candidate for Government service, and that his application was still pending. Empire-Day celebrations brought down a shower of scornful gibes. The *Kali-Yuga* derided the 'Flunkeyism' of Lahore. As a lesson to 'Empire-Day-wallahs' it resuscitated a grievance which ought to have been 'an eye-opener to all who were not ashamed to take part in such—for Indians—meaningless demonstrations'.

Siri Ram read on fascinated. He did not notice the inconsistencies of his chiefs, the column of abuse evoked by the letter of a person 'whose opinion is of no consequence', and the demand for extradition and a trial in British Courts for the political suspects who were taking their chance before the tribunal of a native State.

It was not till noon, when the telegrams were coming in from Allahabad, that he began to realize that his foreman had failed him. He sent for the man, but the old press chowkidar returned half-an-hour later with the news that he was drunk. Siri Ram was in a desperate plight. The proof-reader had already made off, fearing to be involved in the prosecution. The editor was beyond call, making good a distant alibi. It was understood that no written word should pass between them. The drunken foreman was not his only stand-by. There were still three blank columns to fill; the mails north and south carrying the spawn of the *Kali-Yuga* to Bombay, Calcutta and Lahore passed through Gandeshwar between nine and ten in the night, and Siri Ram was left to see the complex business through with two or three gaping assistants who knew no English, and could not be trusted even to set type.

Responsibility, it is said, stiffens the most fibreless, and Siri Ram was responsible. He came to decisions and rose almost to initiative, investing himself with the dignity of office. He distributed the telegrams among the typesetters, he sent the chowkidar to the foreman again, praying him to awake from his drunken stupor, and he made up his mind to let the uncertain advertisements go and use the space for his own fiery rodomontade.

Three o'clock struck, the pressmen were still setting up the telegrams, the foreman had not listened to his prayer, when a bright idea struck him. He looked up 'Drunkenness' in the dingy old office Encyclopædia, and sent the chowkidar a third time with a note praying his debauched assistant 'for the love of the Almighty to take an emetic'. Then he began fumbling in the type boxes on the sloping tables. In five minutes he had set four words and bungled these, mixing up different sizes of type and putting them in backwards and upside down. In the middle of this he remembered Lord Curzon, and ran back to his den, hot all over with the fear that his lordship might escape his castigation.

The office to which he retired was little more than a pigeon-hole, littered with files and old proofs up to the small barred window which looked out on to the courtyard. Here he sat in state patching up for the hundredth time the long-considered attack upon 'His Ex-Magnificence,' which had been rejected of many editors and which he was now at last to father himself. It was a mosaic of the most haphazard kind; for Siri Ram had pieced together all the abusive catchwords of Indian journalism which had been levelled against his political *bêtenoir* since his retirement. And as all his most cherished epithets and phrases had been culled from different journals on different occasions, the result was the oddest mixture of 'moderate' and 'extreme', shrieks and playful irony in the same breath, the hysteria of the fanatic, and the sad smile of the injured friend. Siri Ram threw vitriol with the smirk of tolerance. He was the mentor and assassin in one.

'Who is Lord Curzon?' he asked. Lord Curzon was a 'Satan' and a 'high and dry imperialist' and a 'prancing pro-consul'. He was 'a sun-dried bureaucrat' and an 'Imperial Bounder'. He was a 'Judas', an 'Arch-Panjandrum', 'a superior Purzon' and 'the common Enemy of Man'. And he was a 'Barnum'. Siri Ram looked up 'Barnum' in Cassell's *Concise Dictionary*, and not finding it, he respected the word more, feeling certain that the shaft would tell.

He ended moderately, having learnt the trick of restraint in climax, a common device in the journals of his school, with its inimitable suggestion of tolerant aloofness and power withheld. He had intended to write—

'It is true we have not been accustomed to blow Lord Curzon's trumpet or to praise him with faint damns. Though it seems he has not learnt humility, his Lordship may now chew the cud of his thoughts for some days to come.'

But much of this pure salt was thrown away. The pressmen

blundered, and the dark Philippic through which he had held the torch to Curzonicide ended in an advertisement of Dr Huri Natn's pills.

Only see. A single dose will produce the desired effect in the marginally-noted diseases. Its effect is like thunderbolt.

The Proconsul, if these lines ever met his eyes, must have shuddered at the grim innuendo. Siri Ram cannot have been aware that they gave point to his eloquence. Had he perceived their extraminatory significance, he would have hesitated to add a word that might have restored the peace of mind of his lacerated victim. As it was, he inserted a slip in all the copies that had not gone to press.

'NOⱵION.

'We regret to say that by mistake of Pressman first eight pages of this journal were printed in a wrong order. The readers are requested to read such forms according to the number put on the head of the page, and not according to the place they at present occupy, as mistake has unfortunately been found out too late for the correction. The Editor begs to be excused for the inconvenience to our readers by the above-mentioned Pressman. Also in some parts of the columns the horse precedes cart. In each and every such case the readers would kindly do likewise. With some little trouble he may do the needful.

'Editor'

Siri Ram had no luck. Nevertheless he was filled with pride. When he discovered the mistake at the last moment, he thought that his Notice would make everything right. The foreman had arrived at six o'clock, touched perhaps by Siri Ram's appeal. He certainly looked as if he had tried the remedy. He spoke no word, but drifted solemnly round the press with injured gravity. The man had a drop of white blood in him which may have explained his debauched habits. He was extraordinarily competent. In a few minutes the engines were working, and the whole shed throbbed with the song of triumph. Siri Ram watched the advance and retreat of the rollers, certain and deliberate almost as fate. He had set them in motion, and they gave him a sense of power, of finality even, which he had never felt before. He listened to the rhythmic pulse of the crank. He stood by the press as the sheets were delivered, watching the birth of its prodigious issue with the pride of a parent.

# 4

Merivale tried Siri Ram, the 'Prison-editor' of the *Kali-Yuga*. The unhappy youth only presided at the birth of one issue, but he was a most competent scapegoat. He stood his trial manfully, and gave no one away. The prosecution found him obstinately loyal. He burnt every page of manuscript on the premises except his own incriminating essay, to which he owned up with pride. The police found him sitting beside the conflagration when they raided the office. It was Dean's first actual encounter with the youth. He told Merivale he had never seen any one so much on the defensive. Siri Ram rose up to confront them as if he expected to be led off to the gallows out of hand. At first his manner was an odd mixture of aggressiveness and 'funk'; then human pride crept in. Perhaps he felt that he had scored a point, and could afford to be generous. Before they had finished turning out the office, he had shown them one or two small details of the press on his own initiative, as if he had it in his mind to be hospitable.

In the street his manner was perfect. His friends had come to see him taken; hundreds of sympathizers lined the road. His face was bright and smiling; he looked as if he had expected an ovation, and bowed to the crowd with little jerks of the head which would have made Dean shriek with laughter if the whole thing had not been so pathetic.

He kept up this demeanour through the trial and forgot his sullen broodings. He had become positive, almost alert, as if for once he were on the winning side. When the Counsel for the Prosecution examined him after his statement in the hope that he might draw his instigators into the case, he hugged his criminality and quoted Mazzini and Garibaldi sententiously. The gaol as yet had no terrors for him.

The *Kali-Yuga* trial was followed with great interest in the Club. The confiscated issue with Siri Ram's Curzon article in it became a treasured possession, and every evening Merivale was expected to entertain his friends with new humours. He and Skene alone, perhaps, saw the true pathos of it.

Siri Ram an editor! Skene remembered the nightingale, the 'bird that lived in thicket', neglected of hungry sportsmen, and encouraged debauchery in poets. 'Can't you track the other fellows down?' he asked Merivale. He and Dean and Merivale and the very young subaltern were drinking tea in the verandah after a hard set of tennis. 'I suppose the whole thing was in type before they let him into the office.'

'Yes, but we can't get hold of them. I can only confiscate the press.'

'You'll let him off light?'

'Two years, perhaps. I can't make it less. The scapegoat ruse is too convenient.'

'He is a game little beggar. I didn't think he had it in him.'

'He plays up like all of them,' Dean said, 'when people are looking on. Hullo, here's the Colonel man.'

Hobbs approached Skene sadly.

'One of your fellows, isn't it? What did I tell you? I see they are going to have Board Schools now for the little sweeper boys.'

He laid a hand on Skene's broad shoulders with mock reproach, and tried to sway him backwards and forwards. The burly pedagogue rocked sympathetically.

'No place for a soldier. Eh, old man? We all know what you are going to say.'

'No. I'm damned if it is.'

'It may be soon.' Merivale was thinking of the enemy within the gate. 'Our own Press run the *Kali-Yuga* hard,' he said. 'Did you see that article in *The Planet*, 'Can we hold India? Probably not.' '

'That sort of sensation-mongering does more harm than Radical slop.'

'Of course. We couldn't play into their hands better. It is just what these agitators want—to make the people think we feel jumpy. Once let them think we are on the edge, and they'll try to push us over.'

'Do you think they'd put up a fight?' said the very young subaltern. 'I don't suppose they'd have a chance.'

'Not in the long run, perhaps. But we don't want another mutiny.'

'The sooner we have a little blood-letting the better,' Hobbs said. 'It'll quieten things down a bit. Come and play Bridge.'

Skene refused. 'I'm too sleepy,' he said. 'I'd revoke.'

Dean stayed with him, and they discussed the *Kali-Yuga*.

'Do you think Narasimha had anything to do with this?' Skene asked.

'No, not directly, though part of it reads like his style. You remember Mohan Roy?'

'The man who shot Ghulam Ali at Hooghly and blew his own brains out?'

'Yes, Siri Ram was seen with him in Kashmir, and Mohan Roy was here in Gandeshwar two days before he did it, asking about Narasimha Swami. He had just left him, but he wanted to find out if we knew anything.'

'The avalanche business was all a ruse, wasn't it?'

'Yes. Mohan Roy's visit was a feeler. The Swami sent him here to find out if it was safe for him to come back.'

'And he decided it was not?'

'I am not sure. Anyhow he is beyond harm now.'

'Have the Kashmir people caught him?'

'No. He is dying, I hear, up in the hills. Pneumonia after exposure.'

'That may be a ruse too.'

'I don't think so. Anyhow, he is an extraordinarily single-minded man. I can't help admiring him.'

'My students would follow him like the Pied Piper.'

'It's only natural. They love to see a superman among their own people. 'In Vishnu-land what avatar?' Yet I don't believe he made a single friend in Europe.'

'Talking about colour prejudice. Don't you think it is rather a misnomer? I mean the whole thing is chemical. You might as well talk of the prejudices of acids and alkaloids.'

'Simple as litmus paper.' Dean knocked the ashes out of his pipe and left his friend to his moralizings.

'Oh, Hades!' Skene muttered. 'Have I got liver?' And he reminded himself of the physical origin of depression and the inconstancy of humours. 'This is Tuesday,' he said. 'If history repeats itself I shall be smiling on Thursday at the forlornness of my condition, but I'm dashed if I see it now.'

The truth was, Skene was life-weary like Narasimha. He was tired, and the Siri Ram trial had made him think. He liked his young men. They were friendly and responsive, but he had become a little sceptical about his influence. He felt stale and off his work. It was like pumping air into a football with a huge puncture.

Skene did not turn to his own kind for comfort. The instinct of the wet blanket was too strong in him; he subsided into a long chair in the verandah and watched the crowd. He saw Mrs O'Shaughnessy stalk into the ladies' room followed by the Chaplain's wife, whom men called 'The Voucher', because of her suspicions and her great concern.

Skene would have laughed if he had known the common peril that had drawn these strange allies together. They were discussing the sub-bovine girl. The trouble was about the scores in the Ladies' Bridge box, of which the monthly account had just been posted on the wall.

'I know I was up at the end of the month,' the padre's lady was saying. 'It isn't safe to leave a chit with her when she loses. I'm sure she tears them up when she gets the chance.'

Here Mrs Innes, the Commissioner's wife, the '*burra-mem*'[1] of the station, passed through the room from the verandah, and was appealed to as an oracle.

[1]Great lady.

'I should be very careful another time,' she ventured graciously, with an air that indicated her aloofness.

'Another time indeed!' the Voucher sniffed when Mrs Innes was out of hearing. 'I refuse to play with the girl. The point is—can we put it right? Hadn't some one better speak to the Secretary?'

Here Mrs Waddilove, the gruff-voiced lady with the three chins, entered, following in Mrs Innes' wake, but was detached and initiated into the scandal. She recommended caution. It might have been a mistake. Perhaps she really forgot.

The Irishwoman's voice rose high in challenge. 'Forget! Don't you believe it, she's no chicken.'

Here the conversation became subtly disparaging. The girl was stripped of her sparse plumage. If she *had* been a chicken she would not have had a feather left. It was noted that she had been almost partnerless at the last dance, and the padre's wife was evidently glad.

'She has seventeen pads in her hair,' Mrs O'Shaughnessy screamed. 'Sweet-peas went to see her when she had influenza, and counted them.'

'Hssh!' the Voucher protested. The social sense in her warned the natural woman that she was being smirched. 'It is never safe to say anything in Gandeshwar,' she added, 'unless you are standing in the middle of the maidan.'

Mrs O'Shaughnessy looked uneasily at the door in the corner and through the jalousies at the much-partitioned verandah which was divided into recesses as if for perpetual 'sitting out'. A young subaltern was having tea with a dark-haired, Semitic-looking girl in a habit, whose air of nonchalance was meant to dispel the idea of an assignation. In the sudden hush, scraps of their conversation were borne across to the card-room.

'They're the limit,' the subaltern was saying. 'I don't mind padres as a rule, but any one can see he is a bit hairy about the heel.' He looked approvingly at his neat ankles, and socks which matched his tie. 'And she's all fluff and claw,' he added.

'All women are cats,' the habit agreed sweetly.

'Did you hear that?' Mrs O'Shaughnessy asked. 'The Passover girl. And talking of limits, too. Well, I'm O-P-H.'

But in the doorway she nearly ran into the dreamy, substantial young lady they had been discussing. The girl stood still to prevent a collision. She had the knack of looking sleepy and startled at the same time.

'I owe you two-eight,' she said stolidly.

The unexpected avowal nearly took their breath away.

'That's all right,' Mrs O'Shaughnessy said in her cheerful brogue.

'Come to tea here tomorrow, anyhow. You can have your revenge.'

'Thanks. I'm sorry I didn't put it in. I only found the chit last night in a book I was reading.'

Then she turned to the Chaplain's wife.

'And I owe you two-ten. Shall I put it in this month's account, or pay you now?'

'Oh, please don't bother. I had forgotten about it.' The wife of the 'man of God' spoke with laboured indifference. Then she added as an afterthought, 'Oh, I forgot. It *would* be convenient, if you don't mind. I've got to go into Spratt's on the way home about a lampshade.'

Skene witnessed the settling up, and remembered the lady's apt nickname. He tried to picture her in her husband's parish, if he ever had one.

'Gad, how India does spoil them,' was his inward comment. 'You wouldn't think they were the same breed. I wonder if they'd get any of the virtue back if they were transplanted.'

One of his recurrent fits of homesickness came on him with the thought of the Englishwomen he knew in their own country; women who worked and gardened and hunted and visited the poor. He thought of their fresh, untroubled, open-air faces; the peace and sympathy in their eyes, the tones of their voices, rich and deep as an old bell; the way they had of entering a cottage and talking to the folk inside. The memory was so vivid that he could see the path to the door with its phlox and sunflower borders and low box hedges. A girl on a moor came into the picture leaning against the wind like Diana of the Uplands, and a slim woman riding to a meet with her neck turned away from the blustering gusts of the east wind which flung the raindrops from the dead leaves into her face. And he thought of the insides of their homes, the new books on the table, the bowls of daffodils or snowdrops, the hostess sitting by the fire, a woman with a dozen different interests in life, who could work for a cause and keep her sense of humour at the same time.

Skene was like the sailor dedicated to the sea who never ceased to long for the wet furrow and the heath and pinewoods and the autumn coverts which shed their leaves all at once and at the proper time. He devoured books that smelt of the English soil, *Tess; Puck of Pook's Hill; Helbeck of Bannisdale.* He had a new novel by Mrs Humphry Ward under his arm. He would dine alone, inspect the College Boarding-house, and then give half the night to it. The women she drew were just the corrective he needed. The strong English air of the book inspired him. Pagan as he was, he could even envy Mrs Ward's clergymen. A scene in the story brought to his mind a particular church in the low meadows by a Norfolk river. A lime avenue led up to it from a road where there was a ruined priory; the old monks used to traverse the path daily to chant their hymns or catch the fat pike under the reeds. He remembered the sweet June scent in the air, the moths hovering among the blossoms, the snipe booming in the marshes, the barrier of sedge and flowering rush by the water's edge, and the streaks of red light reflected in the water, and broken by the rising fish as the sun set under dark clouds. He had envied the vicar of the place. 'I would captain the village cricket team,' he thought, 'and fish on Mondays and perhaps Thursdays, and go round every day bucking everybody up. Why shouldn't I? I could do it as well as any one else.' And there was nothing to stand in his way save a few words in the Creed and some films of dogma which he could not swear to, but for which he would have been as ready to die as Lyall's agnostic if a Mussulman captor had offered him Islam or the denial of his faith.

'By Gad,' he said as his reverie became articulate, 'I'd give my hat to be a Christian.'

His great rumble of a laugh echoed down the passage, and every one who heard was infected by it. Hobbs, playing Bridge in the next room, said, 'Listen to old Skene'. And the Chaplain's wife, looking up from *The Ladies' Field,* saw him sitting alone and grinning to himself. He met her envious stare, and remembered that she had started the train of thought. 'The most priest-like thing I can do,' he thought, with a weary smile, 'would be to go and see that poor little devil in gaol.'

## 5

Merivale convicted Siri Ram of conspiracy to deprive his Imperial Majesty the King Emperor of India of the sovereignty of British India, and of attempting to promote feelings of enmity and hatred between different classes of his subjects. He sentenced him to two years' rigorous imprisonment.

Every day during his trial he had been led by two policemen between the lock-up and the court along the same streets by which he had entered Gandeshwar with Mool Chand as a child peeping between the folds of his mother's purdah. He passed the Treasury where men were counting money, and under the bastions of the fort where the maimed beggars sat, along the street of the cloth merchants, and through the metal bazaar where the same grizzled, spectacled old men were hammering brass and copper in the dim recesses of their shops.

Public safety demanded that he should be handcuffed. At first he was attended by large and sympathetic crowds, but as the trial dragged on with constant interruptions, his friends grew indifferent. There were days when he did not meet a single student on the road. As he passed, the shopkeepers did not look up from their bales. Siri Ram tasted the bitterness of disillusion. Only on the day of his sentence there was a faint revival of zeal, some timid plaudits from the back of the crowd, which helped him for a time to wear his manacles and prison-clothes as a crown and garland.

But the utter dreariness and desolation of the place soon closed in on his spirit. In the daytime he ground corn with the other prisoners, and in the evening he was shut into one of a row of cells from which men looked at each other through bars across a courtyard like caged beasts. Beyond lay untilled, sandy spaces interrupted by the long, dormitory roofs with their tiaras of iron ventilators. On Sundays when Siri Ram kept his cell he could see the shadow of the watch-tower fall across them, and the everlasting kites over the roof of the kitchen and the white wings of the pigeons fluttering beyond the adobe walls. There was no other stimulus to the mind in that drab, dun-coloured world, save as he passed to and from the mill the glimpse of the condemned cells in a far distant corner with the little green-bordered pathway to the garden where the gallows stood.

This, then, was the scene of the exit he had pictured. Siri Ram had touched a condemned man. In the Registration Office where they had filed his record, and given him his prison cap and pyjamas, the convict in front of him had been a murderer who had torn the jewellery from a little girl and thrown her down a well. The details were entered on a small folded cardboard sheet with a green label like the one which held his own record, and he had seen the furtive-looking brute with his sullen, earthbound scowl limp through the porch and heard the bolt clang behind him. The murderer was alone now in one of those solitary cells by the garden, and in a few days he was to be taken out and destroyed with calculated violence. The saviours of his country died in the same way. It was gradually borne in on Siri Ram that the glory of martyrdom must be self-nurtured in solitude. He might be the mirror of patriots; his image might be enshrined in zenanas, his picture sold in the bazaar, but no reflected light could enter his cell; he could not read his achievement in the hard faces of the warders.

Solitary confinement at night alternated with periods in one of the dormitories, where he slept with casteless vagabonds, gipsies and eaters of snakes and crows. There was a whole gang of them in his ward, all sentenced in the same riot. He tried to proselytize among them, but when he spoke they would break out into a jargon he did not understand, or they would look at him with a passing concern as they might examine one of their own hobbled donkeys which browsed too near their earthen pots. All day he laboured with these men grinding corn, and in the evening he was mewed up with them. There were only three other 'literates' in the dormitory besides himself. Siri Ram had seen them arrive spick and span in clean raiment, their hair long and smooth, men sensible to refinement and courtesy. Now in their prison clothes they looked coarse and degraded with low cares, hardly distinguishable from the habitual convicts. They might have seen a similar change in Siri Ram if they had observed him at all, but they formed a sullen group apart, and did not respond to his tentative advances.

It was a relief almost to be in his cell again. Here he could brood, and it was all he wanted. Often he forgot his country's wrongs in his own. His burden had become intolerable. He hated Merivale, of whom he was always thinking. In the days when he frequented Ramji Das's staircase he and Banarsi Das had often seen the smooth-faced civilian driving past in his trap, spotlessly accoutred, cool, complacent, superior, masterful, infinitely remote. The young conspirators, newly fledged in liberal principles and the equality of man and inflated with a diet of Mill, would look up from some squalid clerkly threshold as he passed and hate him for material and abstract reasons. Siri Ram cursed him now in his cell, thinking of him as his inquisitor and judge, or as an alien parasite sucking the life-blood of his Bharat-Mata or perhaps with more bitter resentment, as he had seen him first in Mograon carrying his small sister Shiv Dai in his arms across the plank bridge.

Skene found him one Sunday afternoon in a black mood, squatting on his oblong bed of mud-plastered brick built into the floor, the size of a coffin. He would not rise or respond, but pretended to be wrapped in a religious trance. The depressing picture recurred to the Englishman for months afterwards.

As the days passed Siri Ram sought escape in Yoga; but it was more difficult in his prison cell than in Shiv's rock-hewn mansion under Amarnath. 'The dweller in the body is invulnerable,' he reminded himself, and recalled the rich tones of Narasimha in the cave. No message had come from the Swami for months before the trial. Siri Ram had heard that he was ill. Often as he lay in his narrow cell he thought of his guru wandering in the illimitable hills, and how sometimes when he was gathering juniper fuel he used to look for his salmon-coloured shift across the valley, a faint speck barely distinguishable from the lichen patches on the streaked rock. He and the marmots and the ravens were all part of that spirit-haunted ravine.

Siri Ram did not know that the Swami had left the gujar's hut in November, bitten by the cold, and drifted down the valley to Tanin and Patkote. The monks had found him insensible in the snow under the walnut trees at Eismakhan. They took him into the monastery, where he lay all the winter, his spirit at the ebb. It was not until the fruit-trees blossomed and the purple irises were flowering on the roof that he knew he was still capable of desire. His soul thirsted for the plains.

'I should be delusion-free,' he said; 'this wish is contact-born.' But the folk of the monastery took his longing for a behest. They had the palanquin of a lame Sadhini woman who had died at Amarnath. One morning his chela showed it to him and said, 'We will carry you to Hindustan.'

But the Swami demurred.

'He is at peace,' he said, 'into whom all desires flow and are still as rivers perish in the sea.'

'But see,' the chela continued, 'suffer me to lift you thus. You are no more burden than a small bird in its nest poised on the bough of a tree.'

Indeed, the Swami did not weigh more than a peasant's winter clothes. A boy might have carried him all day in a basket on his back.

So the next morning, when the air was warm, they bore him down the Lidar valley to the sacred spring of Anantinag. His carriers rested under the very same willow tree under which Siri Ram had met Mohan Roy when he left Ramji Das's oilskin packet in the grass. All the third day the great valley of Kashmir narrowed in front of them until it became a thin rift in the hills below the Banihal. The path rose gently through a rich country dotted with shady villages. Fat marsh flowers bordered the dykes, green lanes led off to hamlets on either side through willow avenues. The trees were all lopped of their twigs, which had been cut as winter provender for sheep when the snow was on the ground, and were stacked now in huge bundles, looking black and ugly, between the upright boughs to dry. They crossed the twelve rivulets that make the Jhelum and saw the bare red flank of Achibal in the east crowned with larch and pine, and beyond it the snows of the Brahma peaks and the Nun Kun. That evening they reached the orchard village of Vernag at the foot of the pass, and laid a bed for the Swami in one of the latticed chambers over the aqueduct in the old Mogul garden. The stream babbled under him all night as it leapt from the basin of the sacred spring chanting a mantra to him of continual life in death, ebbing and flowing and renewing, to which his tired spirit responded but not his mind.

In the morning the Swami appeared to be sinking. The ague had gripped him; he was chilled to the bone. The devoted chela, who had come with him from Eismakhan, carried him to the cloisters built in the rock wall of the spring; he spread a charpoy for him and stayed by him all day, dragging him over the flag-stones round the tank, pursuing the sun. The holy carp crowded to his shadow, expectant of grain, a wriggling, scrambling swarm. In the evenings he drew Narasimha into one of the cells and lighted a charcoal fire in the wicker-covered *kangar* by his feet.

It was weeks before the sun had strength to warm the Swami into life; he lay so still that the kingfishers perched on his bed and plumbed the clear spring from it. To his ranging mind, the flash of their dripping wings was merged in the iridescent gleam of Swarga.[1] In those days the spirit almost escaped its husk. The parcelling of the earth between the fat and lean was no more his concern. His mind was well poised. The particular was lost in the infinite. Siri Ram, Mohan Roy, Ramji Das were nothing more than busy spectres.

In the dark half of Bhadon he was able to sit out a little in the fruit gardens. He would walk a few steps and then rest his back against one of the ruined marble bridges that spanned the conduits, sunning himself like a lizard. And when his blood was warm, the desire came back to him to see the open stretches of the plains. He longed for the evening smells and cries of the villages, the sun rising and setting on a level with his eyes, the homing cattle, and the dust in their track caught in a web of light, and the dull red gleams of sunset flickering through the mango leaves like fairy lamps.

When he spoke of going, the chela obeyed; not that he thought that his guru had recovered sufficiently to move, but because he knew his heart was in the south, and that he would never be so strong again.

For safety's sake the Eismakhan monks had urged him to cross the frontier as a high-caste purdah lady, belonging to the household of a pundit in Jammu. But now the Swami would not.

'There is no need,' he said. 'They would not take me, seeing that I must leave this empty shell upon their hands. It would work them more ill than good.'

So he travelled openly along the unfrequented route. On the Banihal Pass he turned his back for the last time on the beauty of the snows. The pure white summits of Kolahoi, Haramokh, and Nanga Parbat fell behind the ridge, and the carriers dropped into a hot, bare, treeless valley. For three days they followed the Bechlari stream by Ramsu and Digdool to the Chenab. The path, which was cut out of the sheer rock, hung over the torrent, and pursued every tributary deep into the enfolding hills. The Swami lay with the curtain of the palanquin drawn back, steeped in the sun, his eyes burning with a quiet fire deep in their sockets. The narrow track was often blocked by gangs of road-

[1]Heaven

menders or drovers with their pack bullocks, carrying piece-goods into Kashmir, or herds of promontory goats standing on end and stretching out for the sparse blades of grass on the bright mica-strewn rock.

In the Chenab valley at Ramband they were almost on a level with the Punjab. The sand and blistering sun, the dry parched scent of the earth and the smell of cow-dung in the fires, the low pomegranate bushes rooted mysteriously in the hot, gritty soil made Narasimha feel that he was on the threshold of the plains. He who had attained Yoga was in the end earthbound.

He husbanded his spirit for the goal, coaxing the ebbing breath which strained to break its thin warped chrysalis shell. His tired brain revolved many images. Hour after hour in the garden at Vernag he had sat beside the conduits watching the water flow by, and now he felt like a weed in a stream sucked through a sluice. He was being drawn towards the land of his birth, his Bharat Mata, the womb of *avatars*, nurse of his spiritual life. Would the weak tissues of his mortal envelope hold together till he reached the gate? There was another spur to pass and fifty miles of devious mountain paths before he reached the foothills at Udhampur.

Two days afterwards on the Looralari ridge above Batot he saw the Sewaliks and the Plains glimmering beyond. The heat hung visibly over the valley. There were a few stunted firs and deodars on the top of the pass, and the carriers rested in the shade drawing in the last breath of mountain air.

They passed Chineni and Dramtal, and on the evening of the next day struck into the Sewaliks at Udhampur. After this they forded many torrents, and the Swami was sometimes lifted shoulder high. Between the streams the land was not rocky; it was a rock—unbroken for miles, save for an interstice here and there where a spring bubbled or a palm rose like a promise, or a patch of intense green caught the eye where the water lay shimmering in the scooped shallow depressions that made the oasis. Where the solid rock ended, crumbling, torn chasms fretted the earth, filled with the debris of the hills. The bearers toiled through these chasms which became wider and hotter and more boulder-strewn as they neared the plains.

The parched, gritty hillocks of loose sand, which looked as if they had been shovelled there from the refuse of some fire-pit and were still smouldering, refracted heat like Satan's marl. The Swami slept through these burning miles. His soul was comforted; he was entering the door of his escape. When his eyes opened they searched the south patiently, but there was always some obscuring ridge thrown between.

The hour came when his spirit was almost sped. In the intense heat of an August noon, the curtain of his palanquin was drawn aside, and the mortal husk of Narasimha was lifted up in his couch by pious hands. He saw a yellow fortress on a rock, the hold of Jammu, running out into the mist of the plains like a headland between an estuary and the sea. It was the gate of the Punjab.

A train of baggage camels swayed between him and the revetment, laden with neem branches for their evening meal, their uncouth necks hung with strings of coloured beads. The unsubstantial world rocked to the Swami in rhythm with their mincing steps. His eyes became dim. The fortress flickered and was blotted out; he had a sense of moving mountains. One of the beasts bent a nozzle over the litter, fastidious and inquisitive, scenting some dry provender. The driver struck the beast on the head, swearing volubly.

'It is enough,' the Swami said, raising himself on one arm. 'I have seen. Our caravan has made a bed with the dead in sleep.' Then he fell back into the arms of his chela.

# PART V

## The Sacrifice

And you shall see how the devil spends,
A fire God gave for other ends.

BROWNING

Siri Ram wondered why liberty was not sweet. The fruit he had pined for was insipid. There was no ovation for him at the gate; it seemed that no one cared for his goings and comings. Yet day after day, week after week, for eighteen months the end of his term had seemed to offer him a blessed rebirth. Then he had fallen ill; he had become too tired to care; his spirit was numbed. The gaol had made him less philosophical, and the presence of the English became more and more a personal wrong. His hate was concentrated on Merivale. On the day when his clothes were restored to him and the few rupees he had earned from the *Kali-Yuga*, when the door clanged behind him and he was free, he had never felt so much alone in his life.

His friends might have welcomed him, but his release was unexpected. Good conduct marks, little as he had sought them, had reduced his term by thirteen days. No one knew of his release except Ramji Das, who was in touch with tentacles of the Society everywhere, and had sent a scout along the road between the city and the gaol to intercept him. Siri Ram missed the bunniah's emissary. He went to a house frequented by Banarsi Das, but learnt that he had gone to his village. He drifted despondingly to the chamber above the drug shop in the bazaar. He did not love Ramji Das, but he did not know where else to go. He felt that he ought to be feted and garlanded, but that God hated him and that he was betrayed. The moment he laid a hand on the bannisters of the staircase in the courtyard, a servant ran out, crying excitedly—

'The door is closed. You must not come here.'

Siri Ram stood at the foot of the stairs bewildered. The sweets of liberty were turned to gall. 'Pity it is,' he murmured to the empty courtyard; 'he is afraid Government will look at him with a jaundiced eye. I am old tool after all, no doubt.'

He passed dejectedly into the street, wondering what in the world he was to do and where he was to go.

Ramji Das had not forgotten him. He and his confederates were awaiting him at that moment in another house which the Society frequented in a deserted quarter of the city. Siri Ram was no disused tool; he was still serviceable to the Cause. While he sat morosely brooding on an iron seat in the public gardens, they were discussing his worth, which to the bunniah's appraising eye was much enhanced. He remembered Mohan Roy's caustic comment. Siri Ram was a goat which might be useful for sacrifice, but he must be led right up to the altar.

'He is now at the very steps,' he thought. 'If we are careful we may lift him up between the knife and the stone.'

All were agreed that something must be done quickly, something that would be cried aloud from end to end of Hindustan. The lull had been too long. No white man had been sacrificed for seven months; the waverers would be becoming indifferent; the people must be shown their strength. And here was the inflammable, self-devoted Siri Ram coming out of gaol, ripe for murder, and marked out for it.

'He may be broken-spirited,' one of the conspirators, a too-cautious vakil, objected.

'I think not. He broods much. We shall see.'

'We must be careful with him.'

'He will come straight here. He will see no one alone.' Ramji Das was quietly persuasive. He put the lacquered stem of his hookah to his fat lips and inhaled. Then he added as an afterthought, 'We can make him think it is the day.' As he spoke he watched the effect of his strategy upon his lieutenants. His small dull eyes were quite expressionless in their fleshy folds. His chest and paunch heaved. Only the eyes were oddly still.

As the possibilities of the manœuvre began to dawn on the conspirators, they regarded the amorphous fat heap in the corner with increased respect. The vakil gaped in admiration. Dr Hari Chand, the least adventurous of the crew, was visibly excited. Here was generalship. If Siri Ram could be made to think it was the day nothing would stop him.

'He will not leave the house until the moment has come,' Ramji Das continued. 'When he enters the street you will keep him in view.'

'I have heard that he is timid and weak-willed,' the vakil said.

'It is true that he may bungle, but whom else will you find?'

'Even if he fails, the attempt will strike terror. In any case we gain.'

'Except for our danger.'

'He will not betray us.'

'But if they use violence.'

'You will see. I will provide against discovery.'

The overcautious one was persuaded.

'Let us leave all to Ramji Das,' Dr Hari Chand said. 'What time does the bridegroom start?'

'The mail to Bombay goes at ten in the night. He goes to his own Motherland. May he go farther.'

'Have you got the bride?'

Ramji Das produced a small revolver. 'It is a Browning Automatic,' he said. 'The zenana is full. It contains brides for six, and you may carry it concealed in your hand.'

His own flabby palm closed over it. He looked at his watch. 'Siri Ram ought to be here,' he said; 'we will receive him with honour. It will be best if he is elated. The Society will provide a Red Flag banquet.' He called a servant from below.

'Are the *balu-shahi* prepared? Do not forget the garlands.'

The word awoke Dr Hari Chand from his meditations. 'If we cannot have *the* day, let us at least have *a* day,' he said.

Every one knew what was in his mind. Bloodlessness was the hobby the Doctor rode. His theory was that liberty could be won by work among the depressed classes. In the public eye he was an honoured propagandist. He had lectured on the improvement of the condition of the poor; he was the author of pamphlets. After his speech on 'The Degradation of the Untouchables', the *Kali-Yuga* had called him the Wilberforce of the Punjab, and associated him with 'the moderate camp'. Still officialdom remained curiously unsympathetic. Ramji Das and his fellow opportunists had flirted with his ideas before he became one of them. Now he had met the Red Flag half way. He did not mind sacrifice if there were no blood. He objected to the idea of weapons or wounds on either side, but poison was a compromise.

They discussed Dr Hari Chand's day.

'What will you mix with the tonic pills?' the vakil asked.

'Hydrocyanic acid.' Being on scientific ground the Doctor forsook the vernacular. 'Even if a hundred taste they will be no more. We can despatch them from post offices where we have our own men; all officials will receive them the same morning. There will be a circular letter in the packet from some European drug-store saying, "Tonic Pills are sent you. Please state your experience after tasting." '

The vakil admired the plan, seeing in it the minimum of risk with the maximum of success. 'No one need fall into law's clutches,' he remarked in the speech of the hated foreigner.

Ramji Das did not think the Europeans would take the pills. He believed in surgery more than medicine, and said so, with a curious wrinkling of the cheek and chin which nearly travelled into a smile, but stopped short of the eye in a way which made the physician feel uncomfortable.

'I have the labels of Smith for the packets,' he said uneasily.

'It would be better to remove the informers and spies first,' the vakil suggested. 'If you strike terror into the traitor camp, the officials will be left helpless so that they cannot carry out their plans in any way.'

Meanwhile the bunniah's confidential agent had found Siri Ram. His '*Namaste*' startled the brooder on his seat in his melancholy dreams.

'Ramji Das sent me to you,' he said. 'Have you spoken to any one since you came out?'

Siri Ram gave him a sullen 'No.'

'Then you have not heard! Ramji Das will tell you all. The English are not long for here.'

Siri Ram's dull resentful stare lightened in a moment.

'I have been in the tomb,' he said. 'Tell me what has happened. Is the Swami here?'

'He is dead. But we must not be seen speaking here together. These are secret times. They have prepared to garland you. You are the hero in this city. There is a ticca ghari waiting for you by the lamp-post at the entrance to the vegetable bazaar opposite the Mori Gate. Get into it; the man will drive you to the place.'

As he walked away he added without looking round, 'I have come to this stall for betel nut. Go now without me.'

As the ghari rattled through the streets Siri Ram's self-respect came back to him and his devotion to the Cause, the keener for his own wrongs. Why had he doubted? He had been a hero all the time. He thought of the English falling singly and in bands or being led in chains to the prisons. He thought of Merivale shackled. There was retributive justice in that. Perhaps it would be possible to see him in his cell. Hope and doubt visited him in turn.

The ghari, after some seemingly aimless deviations, drew up in a silent, sunbaked square deserted in the heat of noon. The driver called to Siri Ram to alight, and, pointing to the mouth of an alley too narrow for wheels, drove off without waiting for his fare. Siri Ram was surprised to find the bunniah's agent loitering by a passage near the entrance. The man started walking as he approached, and beckoned him to follow. Siri Ram found himself in an unfamiliar quarter. They threaded a network of narrow passages where they could not walk abreast without treading on the garbage heaped against the wall. It was a *mohalla* of rich men's houses, presenting dead walls or barred windows to the street. The great brass-studded gateways of carved Shisham wood were closed or ajar, giving glimpses of the mysterious silent life within, a world of sleepy and drowsy capitulation to the invading sun. The pungent smells from the choked kennels thickening as they receded from the area of main thoroughfares told Siri Ram that they were approaching one of the city's endless *culs-de-sac*.

The guide paused by an archway with his hand on the wicket gate. Looking round, he asked Siri Ram if he knew the *mohalla* or the house.

Siri Ram did not.

They entered the spacious deserted *haveli* and felt their way up a corkscrew stair; the walls were smoothed and blackened with groping hands. Siri Ram heard voices in the upper storey. A door was thrown open, and he felt that he was among a company. To his surprise the room was dark. Figures were rising from the floor all round, approaching him, hailing him, strange familiar voices. Men were hanging wreaths of jasmine round his neck; he was almost overpowered with the sweet scent. He thought he recognized the fugitive Editor of the *Kali-Yuga*. Then he heard the throaty voice of Ramji Das. Even the bunniah, who for physical reasons was generally quiescent, upheaved himself pantingly to greet the restored hero.

'Welcome to our meedst, Siri Ram!' he said, relapsing into English. For with all his *swadeshi* and *swaraj* there was something Western and hybrid about the youth which even in the dark provoked that tongue.

He listened to sugared flattery, questions about his health, and his treatment in gaol, sweet compliments embalmed in affected ignorance or surprise, insinuations of the greater triumph imminent and the share in the fruition by those who had sown the seed.

His eyes were becoming accustomed to the gloom, and he was beginning to see the features of them dimly where a mote-shotten beam of light from a chink in the shutters hung across the room, when Ramji Das called out to the servant to show him the chamber where the food had been prepared, and he went off, impatient of the interlude, famished as he was.

He found the richest banquet spread on the floor. Beside the usual substantial messes there were flattering delicacies and sweets of every kind, *balu-shahi* and rose-scented *qala qund* and ice, and bottles of pink raspberryade and sherbets flavoured with strange essences from the aerated water shop in the bazaar. Siri Ram sat and ate and drank and wondered.

## 2

When he returned, the shutters had been thrown open, the room was light; the conspirators had gone; Ramji Das sat in a corner alone. Siri Ram was the first to speak.

'Can it be true that the end is so near?' he asked.

'It is true.'

'Who were the people who have gone?'

'They came to honour you. Also they came to learn if imprisonment had weakened your resolve, if it had reconciled you any more to the Mlecchas. Have you lost any of your boldness?'

Siri Ram said that he had not.

'We thought so. I said your body would be on fire. Also,' he added reflectively, 'it would not have been so easy for you to obtain a living wage. What were you going to do?'

Siri Ram did not know.

'You are a great patriot. Are you still ready to serve the Cause?'

'I am ready. But now?' The thought of the glory-proof gaol walls appalled him.

'All that you saw here just now have their bridegrooms to meet tonight. The troops will rise when the first Europeans fall.'

Siri Ram's heart throbbed. He remembered Narasimha's dream of the day of liberty, and he believed Ramji Das; or if he only half believed him he kept the doubt that would creep into his mind the other side of the threshold.

'Why was the room dark?' he asked inconsequently. He could not have explained why his mind lighted on this obscure detail in such a crisis of confused revelation. The bunniah looked at him curiously.

'The patriots always meet now in a darkened room,' he answered slowly. 'If one is taken it is easy to deny knowledge of the others. To the police, to the magistrate, to the judge the answer is always one: "The room was dark. I could not see." You could not see any of them?'

'No.'

'And they could not see you. You could not see me. You do not know what house you are in. You were taken here blindfolded.'

Siri Ram admitted the advantage of darkness to conspirators. The art of silence under cross-examination was simplified. It had not been so easy in the *Kali-Yuga* case.

'It has become our habit,' Ramji Das added, 'though to-day there was surely no need. Tomorrow we shall be answerable to no man.'

'Tell me. How will it burst out? How has it come so soon?'

'We have not been idle. The people are moving about the streets like angry wasps. Many of the Society are in gaol or in the Andamans.'

Ramji Das noticed an involuntary recoil in the scapegoat. 'But to-morrow they are the victors,' he added, seeing fear uppermost. It was necessary to draw the rope a little tighter.

'Siri Ram, if you are taken do not resist. The day of the trial may be fixed, but when the courts are held we shall be the judges. The prison doors will be thrown open, and those who have led the way —'

'If I am taken?' Siri Ram faltered. 'Do you mean tonight?'

The bunniah was impressively still. The pupils of his eyes were filmed with a dull moisture like wet beads; the streaky whites were almost hidden under the sagging lids.

'We have waited for you, Siri Ram,' he said. 'The organization is perfect. Tonight in every city young men will be ready. Hundreds of other officials will fall at the same time.'

'Other officials?'

'The fall of this tyrant will be a match to light the conflagration.'

'Which tyrant?'

'Who has oppressed you, Siri Ram?'

'Merivale?'

'We have preserved him for you.'

At the name Siri Ram's flickering resistance gave out. It was easier to yield; the current was too strong. He did not fully believe Ramji Das, who had been speaking strangely in a high-flown Urdu, and in a voice which sounded unnatural, like a wheezy parody of Narasimha. Still he snatched at the dream. What else was there left?

He barely listened as Ramji Das held forth on the honours in store, how the heroic sons of Bharat Mata would be garlanded and memorialized, and crowned as the saviours of their country, their persons sacred, the highest offices or the most retired leisure open to their choice. For the moment he thought only of himself and Merivale, oppressor and oppressed. The Cause had narrowed down to that.

Ramji Das unfolded the plot. Siri Ram should carry his revolver in a bunch of marigolds. The barrel in the centre would be concealed by the stalk of one thrust up to the calyx. His finger would be on the trigger inside the paper fold, so that he could hold it straight to Merivale's breast.

Siri Ram did not like the idea of the marigolds. Ramji Das found him obstinate.

'So many flowers will turn away the bullet,' he objected.

The bunniah reassured him.

'One little stalk in the barrel,' he said. 'It is nothing. Or it may be a hollow wreath.' He described the trial of Merivale who had been condemned by a court of patriots. He was to be executed by the man he had wronged, the innocent victim of his tyranny. That had been decided before the conspiracy had come to a head. By the laws of retribution Siri Ram had been chosen for the deed. He must employ the means that were most certain.

Siri Ram remembered the hint that Mohan Roy had given him, and asked the bunniah for a wafer of poison to conceal in his ear.

'I can give it, Siri Ram, but there is no need.'

Ramji Das watched his resistance ebb out. His fear was that the victim might become too limp. It was but a step to the sacrificial stone.

'You understand; it is funeral wreath. Marigolds are at the sacrifice.'

As the tension became less he relapsed into English again. He was more insidious and intriguing in that tongue. His spurious exaltation had not seemed natural.

The strange pair sat opposite each other all the afternoon. Siri Ram made one or two efforts to escape. He wanted to find Banarsi Das, to wander in old haunts, to see the streets and shops and the free crowd, but the bunniah's eye fascinated him. He could not turn his back on it.

Long minutes passed in silence. Ramji Das looked at him doubtfully. He feared his nerve, but not his loyalty.

'Siri Ram, is your body still on fire?'

'I will give my bones to the goddess like Dadhichi.'

He was thinking of the hero who offered his ribs to the gods to make a thunderbolt to slay the giant Britasura, but as he spoke he wished he were bearing witness before Narasimha. He did not like the bunniah's eye. Even in the dark he felt its watchful cynicism.

At seven a second meal was prepared. This time the bunniah shared it with him; he gorged noisily. Two thin wicks flickering in an earthen saucer were lighted in the niche above his head, and he was illumined fitfully like some triple-paunched idol in a cave. When he had finished he wiped his hands and sank back again into his vigilant repose. He spoke less and less. Siri Ram was hypnotized. Thoughts revolved like wheels in his head. He could not fix his mind or separate the sense of what he had to do, what he had been through, the reward and suffering, the heights and deeps before him. Every now and then the bunniah punctuated the silence with some slowly-delivered caution.

'Do not be at all premature, Siri Ram.' 'You have Browning Automatic?' 'Do not put your finger in paper handle in the street.'

It seemed almost midnight when the servant entered and called him to the door, and the bunniah quavered benedictions. Siri Ram followed the man down the corkscrew stair clenching his bouquet, and through the wicket gate into the street. A figure was waiting at the end of the alley with a lantern. He pursued the light, which paused and hovered like a will-o'-the-wisp, through a maze of turnings. Soon they crossed a familiar thoroughfare, and Siri Ram saw an Englishman in a white dinner jacket driving a dogcart, and looking confident and unconcerned though he was alone amidst thousands of Asiatics. His syce stood on the step behind and called rudely to the crowd to make way. Cold misgivings crept into Siri Ram's mind again as he followed his guide into another warren of alleys on the far side of the crossing. The echo of his lonely footsteps frightened him, and when he stopped to listen he thought he heard other footsteps following. He wanted to throw his garland into the gutter and hide, or run back into the open, lighted street.

# 3

As Siri Ram passed darkling through the streets, his intended victim was being feted at the Club. It was a stifling May evening, and the odd dozen Englishmen left in Gandeshwar had collected to give Merivale a send-off.

The hot weather grip was in the air. Every day the sun's tentacles let go their hold of the earth with more reluctance. Old night was like a worsted wrestler weakened with every new bout. There was no vigour in her. Darkness had ceased to be refreshing save for the half-hour before dawn.

The punkah-proof lamps on the table, the smell of the Khuskus tattis, the white dinner jackets all round, Merivale's furlough, awoke nostalgia in every one, and reminded them that for many weeks the pleasure of living would become more fugitive in Gandeshwar every day.

Skene and Merivale talked of home. They were both Devonshire men, and had the knack of remembering little things which one forgets—things which call up a picture.

'Do you remember what a basketful of trout looks like when you spill them on a bank of primroses?' Merivale asked.

Skene recalled the smell of hot mint in September stubble on a cub-hunting morning.

Merivale capped him with the purple fields of scabious by the Torridge.

Both thought of old Homer, and from purple fields their minds travelled to Asphodel—the Bog Asphodel on Dartmoor, the vivid green moss under the rose-coloured wilderness of ling, the stone circle in the mysterious hour of sunset with Yes Tor limned up behind it.

'You know Rattle Brook?' Skene asked.

'You are going to tell me about the snipe at the corner where it joins that other stream.'

If Skene had been a Frenchman he would have kissed Merivale. There is no endearment like that which grows out of the common love of earth. They tried to dovetail in their leave so that they might shoot there together. If Merivale got extension and Skene furlough combined with vacation they might do it.

Skene looked at his friend with envy. 'Good heavens, man! Do you know that in less than three weeks you will be walking on turf?'

'Where flowers grow on their stalks out of the grass, and are not shrivelled up.'

'And virtue oozes out of the earth.'

Merivale laughed. 'Old Jones says he is coming home for three months to get straight. He is fed up with this Municipal Inquiry.'

'Feeling a bit choked, I expect,' Skene muttered, with a confused image in his head of the compressed air in a diving-bell. He tugged at his collar, which had become pulp, and wondered how much crookedness and indirection the cursed clime was accountable for.

'How long do you think we could hang on to the country,' he said, 'if we stayed here and bred and reared our children in it?'

'Four generations, perhaps.'

'Human tissue couldn't stand more. It never has or will.'

'Not with education?' Dean suggested, looking across at Skene with friendly irony. The conversation had become general.

'No, not with education.'

'Here's an educationist who does not believe in education,' Hobbs broke in.

'Oh yes, I do. It must come, and it all helps, but it can't charge the battery.'

'It can't give fibre, you mean,' Merivale suggested. 'That only comes from the soil.'

'Exactly.'

Skene was not a pessimist. He believed that it would all pan out right in the end—after many incarnations—with the slow wave of evolution, though the line had unexpected kinks and curves in it. In the meantime his own particular concern was with the hybrid, the forced product.

'I'm tired of "whipping and wheedling the reluctant East",' he confessed to Merivale with a smile.

'Don't let your cubs get on your nerves,' Merivale said. 'They are all right. I like them better than the Mission crew with their self-conscious, bulging ideals. But about Dartmoor. Where shall we put up? Chagford?'

The two cronies fell to their Devonshire duet.

On Merivale's left Hobbs was instructing the very young subaltern across the table on the probable effects of the changed military situation in the case of another mutiny. Sedition and revolution were in the air. Skene caught snatches of the Colonel's argument. No guns. Shortage of ammunition. No cohesion. What could they do in the long run? They haven't got a navy, aeroplanes, wireless.

'What about education, sir; wouldn't that give them a better chance?'

'Whoever heard of education stiffening an Asiatic!' Hobbs, bawled out.

The boy steeped his prunes in his finger glass sadly and engaged his right-hand neighbour. A moment afterwards Skene heard him say in his high, assured voice—

'She's the vulgarest woman I have ever been seriously introduced to.'

His resonant laugh roused the table. Every one looked at him smiling, and began to laugh too, and to stamp on the floor and cry, 'Skene! A speech!' though Skene had never been known to make a speech in his life. He looked towards O'Shaughnessy at the other end of the table, hoping he had not heard. The Irishman caught his eye, happily unconscious, and lifted his glass: 'Here's to you, Skene.' The table rose and gave him the same musical honours they had given Merivale five minutes before. Then they sang 'Auld Lang Syne', and called to him again for a speech.

The big man met the demand with an evasion. He made a sign to Hobbs, and between them they picked up little Merivale and carried him round the room struggling on their shoulders and crying, 'Time! Time!'

'Time, what for? A speech?'

'Time for anything you like,' Skene panted; 'the bosun, the briny, chalk cliffs, hayfields, strawberries. Try to bear up.'

Other voices caught up the litany, vying with one another for what was homeliest.

'Trout.'

'Clover.'

'Soles.' Skene recognised the padre's unprofessional voice, and knew that he was innocent of the *double entendre*.

'Shrimps. Mixed bathing.'

'Mussels and cockles alive, alive, O!'

'Some one suppress that youth,' Merivale gasped. It was the very young subaltern. A digression was made towards the buttery hatch, through which the cub was thrust like a crumpled envelope. They carried Merivale to the porch and deposited him in Innes brougham.

The Club servants followed the jostling swaying crowd into the verandah. Abdul Karim and Mustafa Khan, greybeards of Islam, stood above the steps in their turbans and starched *chupkuns*, virginally white, and made solemn salutation. Mustafa approached with the gravity and gait of Abraham and the wisdom of all the Orient in his disillusioned eyes. The little old man, Mouse, of shrivelled dignity, who had never smiled, salaamed gently to his lord borne on high.

'Good-bye, Mouse,' Merivale called out in Hindustani. 'I should like to take you too.'

Mouse saluted again sadly, tenderly almost, but without elation.

You might have thought that Merivale Sahib, Judge and Protector of the Poor, was always carried thus on strong men's shoulders from room to room, his hair ruffled, his collar broken, his helpless feet dangling in the air.

# 4

Half Gandeshwar was at the station to see Merivale off. The Club disgorged its diners, and there were scores of his Indian friends. Native officialdom was there, magistrates, tehsildars, barristers, judges and minor folk, many of whom had come with addresses and applications, leaving things to the last after the manner of their kind. Some bore wreaths of threaded jasmine which they hung round his neck, and large bouquets of flowers without leaves packed into a tight ball. An old native physician squirted scent on to his coat. Chaprassies brought rupees on handkerchiefs, which he touched regally as if it were a king's healing. Lala Dwaka Das, M.A., Barrister-at-law, produced a framed illuminated address, a panegyric in high-flown Persian, in which the letters of Merivale's name were designed like a fish, and the verses that bespoke his virtues rose like smoke from a censer or curled up into geometrical rosebuds, or spread themselves like parrots flying. Then a Treasury clerk offered a scroll with a petition for increase of pay. Merivale glanced at it and handed it to Skene with a tired smile.

'The charming and fascinating way in which you magnetize your subordinates has been noticed by me. Sir, I do not wish to use studied and culpable flattery or to bandy Oriental adulation, but pity it is that the rumour of your departure has recently collected into dismal cloud of fact. But our loss, your gain.

> Happy have we met,
> Happy have we been,
> Happy may we part,
> And happy meet again.

'Your honour knows the narrowness of my hand. My motherless children and I are sitting in the corner of adversity guarding our empty pockets. I hope your grace would look sharp and do the needful by securing desired increment.'

Skene wondered if this were the composition of Banarsi Das.

Then a pitiful little old man with a stoop came up and presented a poem. He was a schoolmaster. The hair under his turban was white, and his birdlike face was puckered and wrinkled with the passive resistance of years. Merivale recognized him, and said the right words. He looked at the poem and saw that it was entitled 'Valedictory Verses', and that each stanza ended with the same burden—

> The greatest work of God on high,
> Is Mr Merivale kind.

The gentle old thing had the knack of looking only momentarily happy, as if bliss could be reflected but in the sunshine of Merivale's presence, and it were worth waiting for. His smile had survived two score years of the din and drudgery of schoolrooms, and he continued to make it appear that the sadness in it was half for his own distress, half for the passing of Merivale, his patron.

'My dear fellow,' Skene replied to an unsympathetic comment of Hobbs', 'he feels it, or thinks he does, and he thinks Merivale will like it, and he likes Merivale. It comes to the same thing.'

He mentally summed up the old man's position.

'Eighteen rupees a month—no rise for twenty-five years. Five children at school. Retires in six months on half-pay—that's nine rupees, what we pay for milk or bread or boots or socks, and he has to clothe himself and look clean. It's rot to talk of humbug. For the moment Merivale is his god. He stands for immanent power.' Skene turned to Merivale. 'Send him to me tomorrow. I have a vacancy on twenty-two rupees. That would mean he retires on eleven. He is no good, of course, but he can't do much harm in six months.'

Merivale explained the arrangement to the obsequious old man, who detached himself from the group with difficulty, his smile set permanent.

'Here is another,' Hobbs said. 'I'm d—d if I would stand it. Why do you let 'em dik you?'

'I wouldn't mind the show if we could fix them all up like that,' Merivale said, feeling that the pedagogue's smile would linger with him to Bombay.

Skene, seeing Lala Ram Prasad bearing down on them, intervened. 'Look here, old chap, you've had enough. We'd better ring you in.'

'No, it's all right, it's only for a few minutes. Here's Ram Prasad. He would be hurt if I did not speak to him, and he's a very decent little fellow. Works like a horse, if only he didn't *bukh* so much.'

A short and portly official approached with a step that suggested the consciousness of a grave charge.

'Mr Merivale,' he said, 'can you spare me a few minutes of your valuable time upon a matter of grave urgency?'

Merivale allowed himself to be led away, suspecting some municipal entanglement. They walked through the crowd conversing, until the Indian's discourse became a monologue of carefully chosen phrases. Merivale soon discovered that it was a matter that might have been left to this successor. Lala Ram Prasad had glanced off on to half-a-dozen side questions before they had reached the lonely end of the platform. He liked to listen to his own voice and monopolize an important official.

Merivale listened carelessly. He was thinking of the mile of trout fishing he had hired at home. There had been a drought in Devonshire the year before, and it was lucky his leave had been put off. The alders would want trimming a bit on the far bank.

They passed Mrs O'Shaughnessy in command of a hand-barrow laden with crates of cackling chickens. She smiled sympathetically as Merivale took off his hat. 'My husband is coming to see you off,' she called after him.

Lala Ram Prasad was delivering a sonorous indictment on a bogus claim for a building site on municipal ground.

They entered the dimly-lit spaces at the end of the station. The huddled groups of passengers became fewer. It was an interminable platform, stretching away almost to the distant signals. It might have been built for a metropolis. The passing trains were few, but all night long the cracked voice of a coolie was calling out, 'Line clear,' and aimless engines seemed to be eternally shunting goods trucks in the different sidings. Merivale wondered why they made these stations so big. At the far end humanity was packed thick, and there was a babel of shrill tongues, but the desert itself seemed to close in on the platform before the last lamp. A string of empty horse-boxes was drawn up on the right, the doors down on the coping littered with straw and hay. The smell was homelike, and sent Merivale's thoughts wandering back to the Torridge while Lala Ram Prasad blew his loud bassoon. Would the old pedagogue still be teaching the multiplication table while he waded in the cool stream? Was his pension all right? he wondered. He felt strangely depressed, wasting a deal of needless pity as was his wont. Then he remembered that his neck was hung with wreaths of flowers. What an absurd figure! An Englishman in a dress-suit garlanded like a beast for sacrifice.

As they turned back he saw another belated bouquet emerge into the lamplight from the direction of the empty horse-boxes, a huge garland of marigolds, massed like solid flesh as only Indians tie them. The youth behind this yellow ægis tacked towards him uncertainly out of the darkness with a reluctance that consorted oddly with his enormous signal of goodwill.

For a moment Merivale could not remember why the face was so familiar to him. The thought of the plague village came into his mind, and the tail of Scorpio and the long hot embankment beside the nulla, bridged by a plank. Then the court-house, and the tragi-comedy of the *Kali-Yuga*, and the pathetic defence of Siri Ram. What is this child of megrims doing here? Merivale asked himself. Is it irony or amendment or gratitude for Shiv Dai, or a tentative bid for favour? He dismissed each suggestion as it entered his head. The Municipal Secretary continued his harangue, clipping this syllable, rolling that, with the complacency of an artist.

'Regarding the lighting charges. The cost of illuminations to commemorate happy and auspicious occasion of His gracious King Emperor's . . .'

Merivale noticed that Siri Ram was clasping an iron pillar with his free hand, and stayed his approach as if resisting an invisible current. His attention wandered off to Mrs O'Shaughnessy, who was bending over her crate of fowls amongst the lumber on the platform where the goods van drew up. He had observed a bag of grain tied to the wicker-work of the lid and an empty tin pan, with the inscription 'Please feed us.' 'A little water, please.' 'We are thirsty too.' The Irishwoman was giving them a send-off herself. She scattered the grain and filled the water-pan, and tied up the bag again in a precise workmanlike way that was almost graceful. Merivale noticed that her corsetière had given her a shelf-like bust that protruded from the neck. He was the victim of one of those unaccountable waves of depression in which the ugly details of life gather at the threshold of the mind, crowding out comfort. He wondered why he was so unhappy. He was going home, yet somehow he did not believe in it, but felt like a goldfish in a globe as he circled round with Lala Ram Prasad in a current of futility.

Mrs O'Shaughnessy was closing in on him, and there was the feeling of Siri Ram with his absurd bouquet behind, a presentiment almost. All these things were soon to be shaken off; for the moment they demanded a pretence of consideration. Lala Ram Prasad had begun to discuss the drain by the Mori Gate and the removal of the dhobies' ghat, but Merivale was wondering if the hurdle-gap was still in the thick sloe hedge at Oakley Bottom. It was such an infernal nuisance going round as you walked upstream when the light was failing. One lost the best five minutes of the day.

'The road would be widened, no doubt, if the drain were removed to the other side,' the Municipal Secretary was saying.

Merivale made a movement of escape towards his friends at the farther end of the platform.

'It would necessitate the removal of sundry stalls for the barter of country produce.'

Merivale heard the patter of Siri Ram's feet behind him. The dejected youth had let go of the post, and was breaking into a shuffling trot to catch him up. Lala Ram Prasad was astonished to see him present his bouquet to the small of the magistrate's back. Merivale, swinging round, saw Siri Ram's face, and knew by a flash of intuition that the trout stream and buttercup meadows and the alders dipping their dingy twigs into the ripple were unattainable. He saw these things as through some dark green glass, which was splintering in on him with a resounding crash as the station roof and walls and girders swayed inwards, enveloping him. He sank to the ground on one arm, and tried to fix his gaze on Siri Ram and Lala Ram Prasad, who were swinging past him automatically. He wondered if they were riding bicycles. The noise of a train entering the station suggested to his flickering senses the idea of wheels. Then the supporting arm gave way under him, and he felt a twinge like a hot needle in his back.

'Bit of glass,' he murmured. His bewildered eyes closed and his head collapsed.

Siri Ram stood at bay, drunk with achievement, and waved his sinister bouquet in rapid circles like a bacchanal. His fingers still clutched the trigger. Another bullet hit the stone coping at his feet and ricocheted into an empty goods train. Lala Ram Prasad, taking cover behind an iron pillar, cried out to him—

'Place it down, place it down. It is heinous, abominable!'

The bouquet was hanging from the trigger guard. For a moment these two had the drama to themselves. In the din of shrieking engines and the clang of couplings, no one recognized the sound of the revolver shot. Mrs O'Shaughnessy was the first to see Merivale down and realize what had happened. She ran forward like a bull and struck at the murderous yellow Catherine-wheel. She threw her whole weight on Siri Ram and hurled him to the ground and knelt on his neck and wrenched the garland from him. A bullet was flung high over her head into the girders of the roof.

The crowd rushed in and pinioned him.

Merivale had not stirred. The bullet had struck him in the spine. It was the only time in Siri Ram's fruitless little life that chance had intervened to help his aim.

'Did he say anything?' Skene asked Lala Ram Prasad; 'you were there.'

'He talked something about a glass. I did not understand. It is a crying crime indeed. All India will be shocked.'

Skene lifted Merivale's head. He and Dean and Hobbs and O'Shaughnessy carried him on their shoulders to the gate. A parallel procession halted to let them pass. Skene watched Siri Ram with disgust; the miserable youth had a jaunty air: he looked ahead with an effort at complacency as if expecting an ovation, and then aside at the spectators; he would have strutted if he had not been so roughly handled. He tried to address the crowd. Shrill sentences were jerked out of him as he was dragged along between two constables.

'Oh yes, you may put me in prison, but you will see. English are not long for this country.'

A lanky policeman followed, carrying the bouquet and the disclosed pistol.

They carried Merivale to Innes' brougham, which was to have taken them back to the Club, and drove him to his bungalow. Skene laid his friend's helpless head on his shoulder and steadied him with a strong arm round the waist. Hobbs leant over from the back seat and held his knees. He had not spoken a word. The Bombay Mail with its freight of homeward-bound passengers rattled over the railway arch as they drove under. The metallic throb as it became faint in the distance sounded to them both like the knell of everything.

# 5

Siri Ram showed a calm spirit in gaol. He had gone through the trial with credit to the conspirators. Banarsi Das wondered at his coolness. He was imperturbable; he betrayed no one; he held his head up even when he was told that he would be hanged by the neck until he died. And he had learnt by heart the defiant heroic little speech he was to make to the Judge.

'You may hang me tomorrow, but you cannot destroy my spirit. That will pass into another frame, and in fifteen years if there are any Mlecchas left, it will be fighting against them then as now. The usurpers are doomed. They—'

But Siri Ram was led out declaiming. His vision of triumph had come to pass, the handcuffs and the gaol, the sacrifice and martyrdom, the sea of upturned faces, the witness-bearing in the crowded court. He was apotheosized. They were selling his picture in the street. Banarsi Das was in the crowd that pressed round him. He said that Siri Ram was looking glad.

'I saw my brother coming in a company of police. The scene passed before my eyes; he was a martyr going to stake and saying 'I am glad.' I was very proud to see him strong. His face was so bright on account of his innocence that I could not recognize him. In contrast the faces of the guards were pale and moroseful.'

Siri Ram had purchased eternal fame, and the price might not be called for. The army of young men were tarrying, but if Ramji Das had spoken the truth he would be garlanded and not hanged. The bunniah and his friends alone understood the secret of his calm. His counsel who had visited him daily in the lock-up had explained that 'the day' had been put off. There had been a hitch, but the end was the more sure. Ramji Das had tried to stop Siri Ram, but the messenger had come too late. The rising would be in fifteen days. The European gaolers would be the first to be killed, and the prisoners would be set free.

As the days passed, Siri Ram nourished a lean hope. In the long evenings in his cell he used to listen for the guns. He would ask the warder if the English were still lords. A rumour spread that he was mad, and his friends put up the plea of insanity. The vernacular papers demanded a medical board. Siri Ram noticed a change in the manner of the prison staff.

The superintendent who had passed on his rounds with a bare word to him or none, would spend a few minutes in his cell every morning. At first Siri Ram thought he was spying. He answered no questions, fearing to betray his companions. Then he became sure that it was interest in himself that attracted him. It was natural enough. He was hero, martyr, patriot. The thoughts of millions were centred on him. The Major could no longer pass him by.

He would stop and talk ethics with him, and ask him a dozen questions every day.

'Were you glad when you struck? Do you think it right to do wrong that good should come?'

Siri Ram answered these questions in the same set phrase of the tyrannicide, proud, obstinate, impenitent. They awoke the witness-bearer who had answered the judge. He was primed in that catechism.

The Major was so impressed that one day he brought another gentleman to see Siri Ram, a taller gentleman who was addressed as Colonel. The Colonel was more interested in Siri Ram than the Major. He spoke to him with gentle respect, thinking no doubt that he was some *avatar*, the embodied scourge of his country's foes.

'Do you ever hear voices?' he asked. 'Have you ever been visited at night in your cell? Is it true that you received a messenger who told you to kill this Englishman?'

Siri Ram was insensibly flattered. When they left him, he heard their voices in the corridor outside. One of them said, 'All right,' and the other, 'No trace of it.' And after that nobody took any interest in him again. He listened day and night for the guns. The warder grinned when he asked if the English were still lords.

In his condemned cell he could not look out on his fellow creatures.

His heavy bars opened on a small, solitary yard shut off from the world by a black door. He could see the kites through his iron clerestory window, which shut to with a sudden clang in the afternoon when he was not expecting it, and drew his mind, which had been mercifully ranging, back to the thoughts of solitude and death. Then he would circle round his cell like a revolving bird, his dull thoughts shot with vague apprehensions which gathered into images of fear and pain. In the plaster of the wall by his bed, some doomed soul had scratched his last calendar. Siri Ram counted twenty-one notches. Did they lead him out after that, he wondered; did he keep his tally to the end? He himself had reckoned eighteen nights and mornings, or was it nineteen?

He threw himself down on his brick bed and felt for the little wafer which he had hidden in the crevice under the plaster. He had carried it in his ear from the court; it was a precaution he had learnt from Mohan Roy. As he was feeling for it he heard the warder's step, and started guiltily. To his 'Are you there?' he answered, 'Yes, I am here. How many days have I been here?' But the automaton passed on indifferent to his term of life, and the night wore on in silence, broken only by the frightful cries for liberty of a lunatic in a distant cell, shrill and spasmodic like an enraged orang-outang. The man had wits enough to know that he was caged and helpless and alone.

As the days passed he became the prey of fear. He forgot politics. Hope deserted him. Everything slipped away from him but the bare walls of his cell. The universe and his Bharat Mata had sunk to that. He sought escape in Yoga, but could not concentrate his mind. He thought of Narasimha chanting his holy song.

'Beings are manifest in their origin; manifest in their midmost state. Unmanifest are they likewise in their dissolution. What room is there then for lamentation?'

There was no longer comfort in the words. Solitude and the cold fear of death strip formulas bare. The doomed trunk is paramount, the mind its shrunken attendant. Siri Ram saw himself with infinite pity, a lone spirit fearful of damage to its shell, caught in a whirl of unsympathetic matter which swept it slowly to its end, the cruel man-ordained ejection with violence in the chill of the morning when the sun had barely risen.

One evening the attendant reminded him that it would probably be in three days. Siri Ram slept, overcome with weariness. Early in the morning before it was light a tramping warder awoke him. The abyss of emptiness still yawned round him, and a mist of the spirit through which the vanity of the physical world loomed like a mountain. Often had he lain thus in doubt and fear, and consciousness of self slowly returning, the spirit stretching out in vain for hope and warm comfort in the grey interval before the magic lantern in the brain has time to throw its coloured pictures on the wall.

But on this morning there were no pictures to cheat him till he slept again. The sense of identity gathered slowly out of the mist with cruel definiteness. 'I am Siri Ram,' he thought. 'Though I am alive, I am dead. My body feels the bed, its hard and soft. Once more, perhaps, shall I sleep. After tonight my body will lie somewhere, but there will be no hard or soft. Iron spikes or wood or down will be one.' The thought of the flames was comfortable. He put his hand over his heart to feel the throbbing. He tried to revive the warmth of pride. He reminded himself that he was already haloed. He thought of Kamala Kanta and the Shop of Fame. His features were well known; thousands of cheap prints of him would be circulated in Bengal; the ladies in the zenanas who had given up wearing silk would be weeping for him. He was the equal of Mohan Roy, but—

Voices outside sent the ice into his blood. He heard a thin, hungry, mocking howl, tasting of teeth and worms and the last indignity of human clay. It was the jackal chorus which in a land of shallow graves makes men fear God more than they love Him.

While his spirit cowered, Siri Ram thought of instant escape with relief. He felt in the crevice of the bed for the little wafer of poison. He was calm and master of himself; the horror he had feared had gone. He opened the packet almost indifferently. A grain or two fell on the blanket, and he licked it up with his tongue, afraid that there might not be enough. Part had become paste and stuck to the folds of the paper. He detached it carefully with his finger. Then he threw his head back in the way Mohan Roy had showed him and shook it down his throat.

## 6

A rainless June had succeeded a rainless April and May at Gandeshwar. The thermometer was 116° F in the shade. Work in the College began at six and ended at eleven, but there was not a cool breath of air at night or even in the early morning. The *Ode to the Nightingale* had come round again with the revolving year, inevitable as the season.

It was a stifling June morning when Skene entered the classroom to lecture on 'the immortal bird'. The crows outside were open-mouthed with the heat. Every now and then a burning blast of air broke through the Venetian blind, filling the room with glare and dust and the breath of a furnace. The punkah rope swung idly on an unoiled pulley. The sickly scent of the khuskus pervaded the air and filled the room with a tepid, ineffectual moisture. As Skene passed to his desk, a student's notebook caught his eye, scribbled over with some Hindu annotator's ruthless logic. At the top of the page was written—

Title. Nightingale, a bird that sings in thicket.

Skene told the student, a sleepy youth with large calves, stockings with embroidered flowers and patent leather slippers, to read the first stanza. He read raucously with the grating undulations of a saw—

> My heart aches, and a drowsy numbness pains
> My sense as though of hemlock I had drunk,
> Or emptied some dull opiate to the drains
> One minute past, and Lethe-wards had sunk:
> 'Tis not through envy of thy happy lot,
> But being too happy in thine happiness,—
> That thou, light-winged dryad of the trees,
> In some melodious plot,
> Of beechen green, and shadows numberless,
> Singest of summer in full-throated ease.

The words carried him away far in a daydream to a hazel copse festooned with dog-roses and traveller's joy, the murmurous haunt of flies on summer eves—in which the rasping voice of the unhappy young man who read became a subconscious menace. Then he was wading through deep hedge-parsley under the elms to a brook where the pike lay motionless among the water-weeds in the sun. The scent of water-mint and willow-herb perfumed the air, and all along the banks of the osier bed a forest of lush umbelliferous weeds starred with convolvulus and hemp-agrimony and purple loosestrife.

When he awoke to reality after this merciful anæsthetic of associations, the profane monotone had ceased, and the student had relapsed into the cocksure accent of exposition which he employed in prose.

'The poet calling nightingale "light-winged druid of the trees" says further, "I am not sad because of envy a low person might feel with bird for its sweet song." '

'Yes. You have got the idea,' Skene said. 'But you must remember it is 'Dryad,' not 'Druid,' and he explained the difference.

Then he read some notes which he had written on the stanza years ago. He could not consciously murder the piece again. In every stanza flowers withered, embodied loveliness was mortified, the ghosts of passion were dissolved in pain. So he read mechanically, and let his thoughts wander far away. Thus only could he escape remorse.

The hot reek of stable manure came to him from the cricket field, which he had been returfing, and the smell was homely and welcome. It carried with it sweet early-morning memories of hunting days in Devon when he used to get up in the frosty starlight and find his mare ready saddled in the stable, her coat warm and sweet-smelling like a morocco-bound book; the long ride to the meet in the late autumn, the glistening scarlet of the wild cherry and the guelder rose, the babbling brook in the wood with its ferny banks under the holly trees and the naked silver birches.

Necessity had taught Skene to let his mind set three ways at once. Mixed with these images, which were intermittent with the business of dictation, he had a sense of being watched which was associated somehow in his mind with a feeling of deep depression that had hung over him for weeks. Some one was peeping into his classroom from behind a pillar in the verandah. Between the approach and retreat of the punkah he caught a glimpse of a brown cap and spectacles, and thought he recognized the penitent, uneasy figure of Banarsi Das, long forbidden the College precincts. He was going to drive him to the gaol to bid farewell to Siri Ram, and he had promised to take him back into the College afterwards. Skene could not think of Banarsi Das as a serious menace to the British Raj, or believe that he had the stomach for conspiracy. If he had, the condemned cell would lay any ghost in him of missionary or proselyte.

He looked at his watch. There were twenty minutes to the end of the lecture. He would take Banarsi Das then.

The student who had been reading had stopped, and was speaking in unrhythmical prose. The change into the expository accent warned Skene that he must be an accessory to the murder of another stanza.

'Fly away and I will dog thy steps, but I will not come to thee by taking seat in the carriage of God of Wine and Leopard. I will accompany you in flying by reciting and writing poetries.'

'You have misunderstood the second line,' Skene said. 'What is the literal meaning of "not charioted by Bacchus and his pards?" '

The youth looked blankly at him, and as he hesitated, another student, the most daring adventurer in those unfamiliar lands, rose and volunteered.

'Sir, may I? The poet says boastfully, "I will not intoxicate myself like drunkard in order to be with nightingale in the jungle. I will go to sweet songster on wings of the poetry." '

'Yes. That is the idea.'

Skene smiled sadly. His physical discomfort was an anodyne. It was gathering for a dust-storm outside, and a thin draught reached him from the chink of a window at his back like the hot puffs of air a dentist blows into the roots of a tooth from his india-rubber bulb. The sweat stood on his face. When he wrote he moved a blotting-pad up and down with his hand: the contact of skin and paper meant pulp. The ink was smudged in his register and notebook where his finger had touched the page. The little pocket edition of Keats on his table was warped like a dry leaf.

The next stanza carried him far away—

> I cannot see what flowers are at my feet,
> Nor what soft incense hangs upon the boughs,
> But in embalmed darkness, guess each sweet
> Wherewith the seasonable month endows
> The grass, the thicket, and the fruit tree wild;
> White hawthorn, and the pastoral eglantine;
> Fast fading violets covered up with leaves.

After the first lines he heard nothing. He was in a canoe in Byron's pool under the dappled shade of a willow. The fragrance of meadowsweet permeated the air, and the river smell rose from the weedy shallows. A water rat was performing his toilet on a crooked alder stump, and he pinched the leaves of the book he was carrying— the pocket Keats on the table—lest a rustle should disturb him. Nearby a mill wheel ceased suddenly, and a distant echo of children in the Grandchester meadows rose and fell and seemed to be connected in his mind somehow with a patch of buttercups on a shelving bank. He was wondering how long it would be before the shelf tumbled over into the pool when he saw the College chaprassie pass the window towards the gong.

'Read the next stanza,' he said, and shut his ears to the lines which enshrine romance for all time—

> Perhaps the self-same song that found a path
> Through the sad heart of Ruth, when, sick for home,
> She stood in tears among the alien corn:
> The same that oft-times hath
> Charmed magic casements, opening on the foam
> Of perilous seas, in faery lands forlorn.

The gong struck knell-like. Skene took up his warped Keats. He had found a midge pressed between the leaves in the middle of the stanza where

> haply the Queen-moon is on her throne
> Clustered around by all her starry fays.

It had once danced with the motes of a sunbeam on a June morning in Grandchester.

He rose and threw the bar down which had kept the door shut against the growing typhoon. The hot air rushed in. The students crowded round him from behind, begging to be allowed to go to their homes before the storm could come to a head. He let them go, and beckoned to Banarsi Das, who had been shivering by his pillar, to follow him. They drove off on their miserable errand to the gaol.

As they entered the passage Skene was surprised to see the door of the outer cell open. The Superintendent met them on the threshold and drew Skene aside. Banarsi Das heard them talking in low tones. He began to be afraid that they had already hanged Siri Ram; he almost hoped they had. A hospital assistant came out of the cell as he waited with a basin and a bottle and a long tube. Banarsi Das was sick with fear. He heard the Superintendent say, 'Perhaps you had better let his friend see him.'

He entered the inner cell with Skene. Siri Ram was lying quite still on his hard bed. Banarsi Das spoke to him, but he did not answer. He took him by the shoulder and swayed him gently to and fro, but his head fell over inertly on one side. He bent over him and shouted in his ear.

'Siri Ram! Siri Ram! Siri Ram!'

He shook him almost roughly, and called again, raising his voice each time—

'Siri Ra-am! Siri Ra-am!'

But Skene laid his hand on the boy's arm. 'We are too late,' he said. Banarsi Das's voice broke, and he began to weep.

'He has shaken off mortal coil! He has shaken off mortal coil!'

'Poor little devil,' was Skene's inward comment. 'He never had a dog's chance.'

He led Banarsi Das out of the cell. The storm had spent itself in a few drops of rain, just the scent of it without the relief. The air was hot and gritty. Ineffectual thunder rumbled in the distance. As they drove back to the College without a word, Banarsi Das was shaken with silent weeping.

# The Arya Samaj

Some of the chief instigators of the troubles in the Punjab of 1907-8 were members of the Arya Samaj, and the name of the society has become associated with sedition. This does not mean that every Samajist is plotting against the British Government. The Samaj stands for reform; it represents a revival, religious and national, which we cannot but admire, though it is our business to see that it does not threaten the stability of the British rule. In December 1909 the Aryas, themselves anxious about their position, approached the Lieutenant-Governor of the Punjab for an announcement of Government's attitude to the community. They were informed that membership of the Samaj would not be allowed to tell against them, and that any charges that were brought against them would not be prejudiced on account of such membership unless and until the Samaj was proved and declared to be a seditious body.

# Indigo*
## Christine Weston

* First published by Charles Scribner's Sons
New York 1943

To
My parents

# Foreword

*Indigo* was written in a big New England kitchen of my home in Brewer, Maine. This was after an absence of twenty-five years from India and despite philistine comments from my in-laws and husband. Before writing I read a great deal about India and about indigo, and I took my names Mrs Lyttleton and Madame de St Remy, the Macbeths, Boodrie, and others from the clear blue sky. I also, like any novelist, invented the incidents depicted in the book.

*Indigo* made two book clubs: the Literary Guild in the United States and the Book Society in Britain. It also received very good reviews in all major newspapers. Although my agent Henry Volkening and my editor Max Perkins had warned me about replying to any letter or review, I wrote a ferocious letter to the reviewer of a Massachusetts newspaper who had given *Indigo* a fulsome review, but she had panned my first novel stating among other things, that while I knew a great deal about India, I knew nothing about Maine. I wrote her that while *Indigo* had been written by me after an absence of twenty-five years, I had lived in Maine most of my adult life and therefore knew more about it than she did. To this letter I received no reply and did not expect one.

Before *Indigo*, I had written and published several novels. I was also writing short stories for *The New Yorker* magazine and other papers. As I look back on it all now, in the summer of 1987, I marvel at my past industry and dedication to my work; I marvel, too, at the patience of my agents Russell and Volkening and my editor Maxwell Perkins.

I have just heard of the death of Indira Gandhi and was not prepared for the storm of emotion which overtook me by the news of her death. I have not wept for a closer and dearer friend as I have wept for her. I only hope that India will weather this crisis as it has done others.

I cannot get Indira Gandhi out of my head. She was so gentle, shy, and mild in her appearance and manner, although I suspect that she got much of her strength from the crowds that came to hear her, like her father, the late Jawaharlal Nehru. I knew them both well and went on an election excursion with him in 1956 when he told me that when a man or woman chose to live the life he and his daughter did, they lay their life on the line, and assassination was something they live with every day of their lives.

But to turn to pleasant and humble things, I was born on 13 August 1903, in a small up-country station called Unao. The Boer War was just over in South Africa, and in India the monsoon was in full blast. My mother's doctor had to come by train and by bicycle through pouring rain to attend to her. And old Abdul, my father's bearer, who had been my grandfather's before him, crouched at the foot of my mother's bed, massaging her feet and proffering endless cups of tea—the English panacea for all emergencies in India.

My father, who was then Superintendent of the Indian Police (he later became a lawyer), taught me my English alphabet on his typewriter, and I was writing stories and poems when I was four years old. None of these have survived, to my sorrow, because they would surely have made interesting reading today! There were five children in our family but each had a different story to tell about our combined childhood, which often happens.

I was married to an American, Robert Weston, at the age of nineteen, in India. We came to the United States a year later. After Robert's death, I was married for the second time to Roger Griswold, a great friend of my first husband and his family. I have been back to India several times and stayed with Indian friends which put me in the position of being in the inside looking out instead of the other way around.

I am now living permanently in Maine, although I hope to go back to India for one last visit sometime. As far as my nomenclature is concerned, my father was French by the name of deGoutiere. My married name at the time was Mrs Robert Weston. I wanted to take back my French name, but after consultation with my publisher, we decided that since I had published my books under the name of Weston, I should continue to do so as long as the family had no objection.

Bangor, Maine, U.S.A.                                    Christine Weston


[Written by Christine Weston, specially at my request, towards the end of her life. Though in failing health, she yet managed to send a draft of some 1500 words and asked me to do with it as I thought best. This Foreword is reproduced from her original with some deletions, but no changes.—Editor]

# PART I

## 1

It was a February afternoon and they were watering the garden; the smell of water among the flowers reached young Jacques St Remy where he stood in his bedroom door, lazily allowing himself to be dressed. This was his fourteenth birthday and for fourteen years this fragrance had come up from the garden into his body, stirring a precious disquiet. Perhaps at the hour of his birth, this same fragrance had touched his mother's face and his own.

'Lift thy foot,' said Hanif sharply. He knelt before Jacques, tying the laces of his white buckskin shoes. 'The other one—place it here, on my knee.'

Jacques laid his hand on Hanif's head for support, but he did not take his gaze from the garden which lay in a haze of sunlit dust, twittering leaves, and odours of moisture and flowers. Beyond the boundary of cactus and lantana bushes rose the dark mass of the mango grove whose limp russet leaves would soon turn a crisp green. Beyond that stretched the fields. The vats and huts and boiler-rooms of his mother's factory lay out of sight beyond the trees, but as he listened Jacques could hear, above the creak of a well wheel and the voice of the gardener, a distant hum and stir of machinery.

'Must you pull all my hair out at once?' inquired Hanif plaintively.

Jacques' gaze drifted to the young man who knelt at his feet. Hanif was twenty, slender, beautiful in his own way. A velvet cap set off his curled and jet-black hair; he wore a velvet waistcoat over his white kurtha, and his long legs were hidden in immaculate pantaloons. Hanif was a dandy who spent all his wages on clothes when he did not squander them on luxuries less innocent. An orphan whose parents had died in the last great famine, he came from Monghyr where they speak a shriller tongue than up-country, but when he sang his voice dropped to a minor key, and he sang a good part of the time.

'This cap,' murmured Jacques. 'It makes seven at least. There is the red one and the purple one and the grey one and. . . .'

Hanif replaced the boy's foot on the ground and rose, setting the cap at an angle above his black velvet eyes. 'It was bought solely in honour of your birthday. Shall I proceed about my duties looking no better than a chamar, or am I to appear decently clad in your mother's sight?'

'Where is the butterfly you promised me?'

Hanif removed the cap and from its perfumed interior plucked a crumpled object which he laid on the dressing-table.

'That!' exclaimed Jacques scornfully.

'I chased it until I was exhausted. I ran and I ran.'

'The only time I saw you run was when the buck goat chased you.'

Hanif retorted with an unquotable jest on the character of buck goats, then gravity descended on him once more. 'Alas! Your hair, my child.'

Jacques regarded himself in the glass. His own face always interested him, for it appeared always as the face of a stranger. He wondered sometimes what his soul looked like—his soul, that hidden separate self. He had discussed this question with his friend Hardyal but they never arrived at any satisfactory explanation. 'My father,' said Hardyal, 'is not orthodox. He does not believe in the persistence of the soul as Father Sebastien believes or as Madame St Remy believes. My father has made his ideas quite clear to me and he is happy that I share them.'

'But your family!' Jacques had reminded him. 'Your grandmother and your aunts! Aren't they always afraid that if they misbehave they might be born again as fleas, or turtles?'

Hardyal shrugged scornfully. 'What can one expect from women?'

Hardyal's heresy did not trouble Jacques very much; nothing about his friend troubled Jacques, except perhaps an occasional twinge of fear lest something happen to separate them.

'Stand still,' commanded Hanif. 'You cannot appear thus before the photographer.'

'I don't want to appear before him at all—in these disgusting clothes.' His bottom itched in the new, tight drill.

Hanif dipped a comb in a bowl of water and drew it through the boy's light brown hair. Jacques knew that in her own room his sister Gisele was also being tricked out for the occasion. The ayah squatted on her haunches with Gisele crouched on a stool before her, and clawed the girl's golden fleece, eliciting screams of wrath.

The house was filled with the excitement of a party; bare feet pattered over the china-matting, bead curtains clashed and tinkled, there was a scurrying between the cookhouse and the back veranda. Jacques heard the familiar sound of Father Sebastien's arrival and saw the priest's fat pony led away to the stables. In a few hours, he thought, this day will have ended like all the days I can remember. When light fades, the crows will fly westward to roost and the flying foxes will flap across the garden to feed on the tamarinds. From all over the plain dust will rise into the air, stirred by homeward moving feet; there will be a smell of wood smoke and food cooking, and all the special evening voices. The Hour of Cowdust, Hardyal called it.

'There!' exclaimed Hanif. 'Now you are beautiful!'

Jacques' hair stuck to his head as if it had been varnished. Singing under his breath Hanif began to set the room in order, shaking the mosquito curtains above the bed, picking up and smoothing the discarded clothes.

In an hour the guests would be here: Mr Wall the Engineer, Doctor and Mrs Brown, Hardyal, and the railway inspector's two dull little girls, invited because there were no other white children in Amritpore. The inspector's little girls were not wholly white, and neither Jacques nor Gisele liked them, but Madame St Remy insisted that their company was better than nothing. Perhaps they would all bring presents, thought Jacques, brightening. Except for Hardyal he didn't care whether they came or not. Hardyal and Mrs Lyttleton. . . he wandered across the room to examine his collection of butterflies. In the cork-lined case under heavy glass they looked like a jeweller's window, and for some minutes he stared at the great Cat's Eye moth which Mrs. Lyttleton had given him.

Hardyal and Mrs Lyttleton! These were his friends. Why, why since he loved them equally had he not been allowed to invite Mrs Lyttleton this afternoon? He knew that his mother disliked her, but his understanding stopped there. It confused him to feel that he must not love Mrs Lyttleton, that he was not even supposed to be friends with her. She was old and kind and full of marvellous stories. She lived in a fascinating house from which he was allowed, at any time, to take anything he liked. She was the sort of friend one might dream about . . . and yet, and yet . . .

Wheels ground up the long avenue of shisham and he saw an ekka jerk to a stop, its dejected pony hanging its head. A shrill duet started up between the driver and his passenger, and Jacques began to laugh. Hanif joined him and they watched delightedly as Mr Boodrie the amateur photographer dismounted from the ekka. In his anxiety to unload the camera and its apparatus safely he'd managed to entangle himself in the black cloth; blind and frustrated he groped about under it while the ekka-wallah sat callously grinning.

Jacques exclaimed: 'I hope it all goes to smithereens!'

Hanif laid his hand on the boy's neck. 'No running off. No climbing trees. Come!'

# 2

In a corner of the veranda overlooking her rose garden Madame St Remy sat talking with her old friend and confessor, Father Sebastien, a tall, stout Franciscan with shrewd eyes and ruddy cheeks above his black beard. Ten years before, Father Sebastien had acquired Auguste St Remy's taste for Trichinopoly cigars and Madame obtained them for him regularly, long after her husband's death. Father Sebastien smoked one of these now while he listened to her clear, quick voice.

'I think Ganpat Rai is mistaken in putting so much faith in Aubrey Wall.'

'Why?'

'Because Wall is an Englishman and the English have a quality of maggots. They devour everything they come in contact with.'

If in 1757 the Frenchman Dupleix had triumphed over the Englishman Clive it is possible that a historic effulgence might have warmed and sweetened somewhat the character and destiny of Madame St Remy, one hundred and fifty years after the Battle of Plassey. But on this February afternoon she still cherished resentment against that ancient humiliation: whenever she was ill or angry her antipathies escaped into the open disguised as history.

The priest, who rather liked Aubrey Wall, said gently: 'Your judgment is sometimes very sweeping, Madame.'

'That is because I know them so well.'

Madame could not afford to be wrong; mistakes and shortcomings were reserved for God, via the accommodating ears of Father Sebastien. God and His vicar knew her to be chaste, a devoted mother, loyal to her traditions, and bedded in her faith. Believing in God, cynical of men, she managed to combine submission to the Church with a refined tyranny over human beings. But Father Sebastien knew that she was a lonely woman, capable of a mysterious increase of spirit to any degree which ambition might demand of her. When Auguste St Remy died, leaving her his two children and his indigo, Madame's genius for enterprise had emerged to astonish all who knew her. The indigo industry was wavering under the threat of German coal tar inventions, but to Madame it seemed inconceivable that anything so ancient and so well established as indigo should lose its market. She had learned much from the misfortunes of other planters, many of whom were Indians, and she was convinced that the European's flexibility was what made for his success against the native. She had observed, also, the waste and tedium of old methods, and two years after Auguste's death she imported machinery from England and built a new factory with a steam plant for the tanks and power for stirring and pumping. She bought up the pulse and millet fields of her neighbours and put them to indigo; nor did she forget the old cry of the peasants: If you sign an indigo contract you won't be free again for several generations! It was an echo from the days when men inherited their fathers' and their grandfathers' debts. So Madame wrote a new contract by which she bought, not their product, but their labour. Under her genius the factory prospered and five years after Auguste's death she was rich enough to build a chapel for Father Sebastien, and a year later, a school for his Indian converts.

In the big green-washed drawing-room of Madame's house there hung a portrait of Auguste St Remy made ten years ago. Fish ants had channelled down one aquiline nostril, down the lips into his beard; but his eyes, which his son had inherited, gazed across the room to a pencil drawing of his birthplace above Nonancourt in Normandy. Madame St Remy, never in love with her own middle-class heritage, sometimes confused her children by references to Nonancourt as her own birthplace and to the stone house among the plane trees as her father's house. In France, measured by her own standards and mislaid among her own kind she might not have stood a fair chance, but in India it was different. Indians were impressed by greatness, nurtured on arrogance; India was a vast theatre for the struggle of the Church—and of Madame—against the usurping Bloomsbury British. And when she spoke of the British, Madame used the word *sinister*, and the word *formidable* with ominous French sibilance.

She returned to the subject of Hardyal. 'They are determined, between them, to send him to England and turn him into a sahib.' She laughed, but Father Sebastien frowned. After a slight hesitation he said: 'We must not forget that there is a ruling power in this country. For better or for worse it is part of our own power. It is our protection too. We must not forget that Jacques must not be allowed to forget it.'

'On the contrary nothing would please me better than that Jacques might one day become lieutenant-governor of the Province!'

He gave her a quick glance, then laughed. 'Ah, Madame!'

Madame stared into her garden where the most fragile of her roses had shed their petals under the day's heat. She said: 'Talking of Aubrey Wall, you understand I am not inspired by rancour. It is just that I mistrust his intentions. One can never be sure what he is thinking. But you know as well as I that the most insignificant Englishman never loses sight of his object, which is the extension and preservation of the empire. They never submerge their identity, as we are always willing to submerge ours, in the soil and culture of a foreign land. The English will not even learn to speak another

language with the proper accent. They actually pride themselves on
their incapacities. Have you ever heard Wall trying to speak French?
*Execrable!*'

'Yet he has taught Hardyal to speak excellent English.'

'Yes,' she sneered. 'And boxing—and cricket!'

Father Sebastien surveyed his sandalled feet. 'This question of race
. . . how then do you account for a woman like Laura Lyttleton?'

Madame's hands clenched in her lap. 'I am not obliged to account
for her. I am not obliged to invite her into my house. I am in no way
responsible for her existence. . . nor am I constrained to admit, even,
that she does exist!'

Her passion alarmed him. 'But Madame, whoever suggested . . .'

'Jacques!'

He stared. 'Jacques?'

Madame brought her feelings under control. 'Yesterday there was a
scene. I asked Jacques whom besides Hardyal, he would like to invite
here for tea. I realize how little Amritpore has to offer in the way of
amusement and companionship for the children. And you know . . . for
his age . . . how serious he is, how discriminating. It is not natural in a
child, this quality, this capacity for love. It has always troubled me, for
my feelings are deeply maternal.'

He nodded, and she continued rather breathlessly: 'What was I to
think when he looked into my eyes and asked for Mrs Lyttleton?'

Father Sebastien was silent, frowning in his turn. He would have
liked to say that he understood Jacques, that he knew the boy as
intimately as she knew him, but the truth was he did not know
Jacques. Gisele yes, he knew Gisele; knew her mind, her heart, even
her fate. He was himself, in a sense, the instrument of that fate. But on
Jacques' account he suffered strange forebodings.

Madame went on: 'You know that I have scolded him for running
over there as he does behind my back. I have warned Hanif to see to it,
but Hanif is lazy. I have an idea that he might even connive.'

'Then you should dismiss Hanif.'

'It would accomplish nothing. Jacques can turn any servant round
his little finger.'

Father Sebastien chewed his cigar. He would not, if he could
prevent it, lose the son as he had lost the father. 'You believe then, that
Jacques really cares for Mrs. Lyttleton?'

She forced herself to say it: 'Yes.'

'It would be fatal for him to come under her influence!'

'As his father did,' murmured Madame St Remy with stinging
bitterness. Presently she said in a calmer voice: 'In a little while
Hardyal will be gone and Jacques will feel deserted. Though he does

not confide in me, though he tries to exclude me from his thoughts, I can read them. But what is one to do? Children are so unpredictable.'

The priest tossed his cigar into the garden. 'Perhaps it would be better, then, if we were to do what I have often suggested—send him to France for his education.'

She made a small, despairing gesture. 'Ah, not yet! When he is older . . . when I have taught myself to bear the thought of parting from him!'

Father Sebastien started to say something, but he was interrupted by the appearance of Boodrie. 'Madame! Will you please come to assist me in taking Jacques' photo? I have tried and tried. He will not stand still. He will not do one single thing which I ask. He falls down. He crosses his eyes. He makes indecent motions. He laughs. Hanif laughs. Gisele laughs. Junab Ali comes all the way from the cookhouse to laugh. They all laugh. Ah, Madame! Father!'

Madame rose, and she and the priest followed the demoralized half-caste into the house.

# 3

The guests assembled on a veranda which faced the big pipal tree in the centre of the lawn. They sat in cane chairs and sipped tea and nibbled sandwiches and cake. Madame had taught her Mohammedan cook something of the art of making French pastry, but how he did it in an unventilated kitchen over a reeking charcoal stove in a black hole of an oven remained a mystery bordering on the miraculous.

Every one talked in English, but the voices of the St Remys were distinguished by a quirk of accent which lent their English and even their Hindustani a separate character. Father Sebastien sat at Madame's right and was waited upon by Gisele and Hanif. Mr Wall the Engineer sprawled in his chair; slight, sandy, genial, always at ease, always like most Englishmen taking up as much room as he possibly could. Madame St Remy's ill-concealed antagonism amused him. He had never brought himself to like her, but he was fond of her children. Their beauty had a curious effect upon him: it touched and moved him as few things had ever touched or moved him in his life.

Doctor Brown and his wife were kind and prosaic, washed out after five summers on the Plains. Their children were in England, and something wistful crept in and out of Mrs Brown's eyes as she looked at Gisele or Jacques. At other times her gaze rested wonderingly upon their mother. A remarkable woman, reflected Mrs Brown, without envy. Indigo was planted in March and harvested in June when the heat was at its worst. She had seen Madame under an enormous mushroom of a solar topi, supervising the carting of the green crop by bullock cart to the factory; she knew that Madame spent hours in the blanching heat, that she left very little to the discretion of her foreman or her coolies. When the drying and pressing of the dye was finished she rushed to the hills for a brief respite, but in August she was back for the second crop. How did she manage it without breaking down? Doctor Brown thought he had the answer. 'Ambition, my dear—ambition!'

The Railway Inspector's two little girls had arrived, escorted by a tyrannical servant; they now sat huddled together, munching or retreating into a trance when they were spoken to. Jacques attended to them with a stiff, drilled politeness, but he felt sick at heart. Hardyal had not come. What could have happened? Perhaps it was just that he had misunderstood the time, perhaps even the date. But that was not like Hardyal. At any rate he should have sent word, declared Madame, and to this every one agreed.

'Perhaps the little devil ran off to the bazaar,' suggested Wall.

'Hardyal's father,' said Madame, 'does not permit him to frequent the bazaars. The family is exceedingly superior.'

Gisele stared at Aubrey Wall. Whenever he spoke she made a tiny, involuntary movement, almost a start. There was nothing particularly arresting about him, yet she could never be indifferent to his presence. Perhaps she sensed the effect of her own presence on him. She thought of his unfailing sweetness to herself and to Jacques, and how once, last year, he had kissed her. It was at Christmas time and she had not been able to get the incident out of her mind.

Hanif, demure in his finery, handed round plates of pastry and pink toffee. In passing through Madame's dressing-room on his way to the veranda he'd paused long enough to anoint himself with her Eau de Cologne.

One of the Railway Inspector's little girls suddenly shrilled: 'There was an accident to-day at the junction. My father said.'

Jacques revived momentarily. 'What sort of accident?'

'An awful accident. A woman threw herself under the train and it cut her up into mince. My father said.'

'Mince?' echoed Gisele.

'Potted meat, don't you know,' said Wall. Madame frowned and the little girl retreated into another trance.

Hanif passed the sandwiches and the petits-fours and the Napoleons. He passed cigars to the men. A trivial and well-bred hum set up around them. Evening sank towards the garden, sifting the glare of the sky, and to take his mind off Hardyal Jacques began to think about his presents. They had, on the whole, been disappointing, except for the beautiful little riding crop which Mr Wall had given him. Even while Madame thanked him she was annoyed that she had not thought of this herself, for it was impossible to miss Jacques' dazzled smile.

Gisele looked up suddenly. 'Here is Hardyal.'

They watched a phaeton drawn by a bay horse come down the drive, Hardyal's green-coated coachman riding high. Relief surged through Jacques as the phaeton stopped and Hardyal alighted. He was, perhaps, six months older than Jacques, a little stronger and taller. Like the other he'd assumed an especial finery for the occasion, and now he came towards them in his white dhoti and gold-bordered shirt, an embroidered cap on his head, and crimson slippers on his feet. Behind him walked a servant carrying a flat basket filled with fruit and flowers, globes of sugar spun on a thread, little boxes of white Persian grapes nestling in cotton wool, and a dish filled with Jacques' favourite sweets, the sugar-coated *gulab jamuns* about which he sometimes dreamed.

All whiteness and brownness and lightness and brightness, Hardyal approached and Jacques went to meet him. Side by side they walked back to the veranda, and Hardyal paused to discard his shoes before the lowest step. He was perfectly poised as he salaamed the company with both hands, and Madame St Remy thought, with regret: What a pity he is not a Christian! But Aubrey Wall reflected complacently: How well the English training stands out!

# 4

They played games until it got dark and the mosquitoes began to bite, then—gorged and exhausted—the party broke up and Father Sebastien's pony was brought round. He tucked his brown skirts round his waist and trotted massively away between the shisham trees, his groom loping barefoot after him, brandishing a fly whisk.

When they had gone—all except Hardyal—Madame took Gisele's hand and retired to the house. For the next hour Gisele would sit beside her mother's couch, patting Madame's forehead with Eau de Cologne and reading aloud in French.

Jacques turned to Hardyal. 'Let's go to the mango grove.'

They walked down the garden as the stars exploded along the

length and breadth of the sky. It was dark under the trees; bats flitted everywhere, the gloom was sweet with the scent of flowers. The boys came out at the end of the grove and sat down on a crumbling brick wall. Before them the plain lay dim in the vanishing light. To their left were the sheds, the huts, and the chimneys and vats of the factory. Some of the powdered blue carried by wind or on human feet lay in the dust beside them; it was in the sky above them, too—the vast indigo sky which sloped towards the farthest limit of the plain. Fires glittered among the distant buildings, figures passed and repassed before the flames. They heard voices, a smell of the evening meal reached them with the scent of smoke which, as they watched it, ascended in a fine web between plain and sky.

'Why were you so late?' asked Jacques. He spoke Hindustani as a relief from the precise English which he'd used all afternoon.

'I stopped to see Mrs Lyttleton, and she delayed me.'

'Oh.'

'She asked for you, she sent you her love. Shall we go there for a little while this evening?'

Jacques stared at the distant fires, knowing that each warmed and fed a small human clot. He felt, in all his pores, the still, warm, sensuous night, and out of it there emerged suddenly the face of Mrs Lyttleton with the special look which was, he knew, for him alone.

He said thickly: 'I can't go there this evening.'

'But why not?'

'I don't know . . . yes, I do know.' He ducked as a tiny bat flitted past his head. 'Maman doesn't want me to go to Mrs Lyttleton's. There was a scene yesterday. I promised that I would not see her to-day, though I said nothing about other days.'

'Mrs Lyttleton made lemonade with wine in it. We were to drink your health.'

'There is no use to speak of it.'

'No use?'

'Not today.' He plucked restlessly at the breast of his new suit. The plain darkened as the sky deepened in colour and each star spread its fire. Jacques longed to confide in Hardyal, to ask him questions, but loyalty to his mother came between them now as it had in the past. They sat, each wondering about the other's thoughts; then the mosquitoes set upon them and they rose. 'Will you ride tomorrow?' asked Jacques. He felt the great day slipping into oblivion, and he hated to let it go.

'Tomorrow I must spend with my grandmother.'

'Oh.' Blankness.

'But I could ride the day after tomorrow.'

Jacques' spirit lifted. 'Early, then—before breakfast. Before anybody is awake.'

The thought exhilarated them. They left the grove and came out into the lighter air of the garden. Lights were shining in the house, and Hardyal's coachman was waiting.

'Goodnight, Jacques!'

'Goodnight . . .'

# 5

Next day a light shower drifted across the plain and laid the dust for an hour. Aubrey Wall, riding home from an inspection of the new government canal, turned in through the gateless pillars of Mrs Lyttleton's compound and trotted up a grass-grown drive between flower-beds turned to jungle. In Amritpore, allusions to Mrs. Lyttleton usually centred on one of the three adjectives: Extraordinary, Eccentric, Impossible. They might with equal justice have applied them to her house, a huge sandstone affair which she had acquired for a song and a touch of blackmail from its original owner, a maharaja deposed by the English more than forty years ago. General Lyttleton had supplemented the torture chamber and the harem with bathrooms, gunrooms, pantries, and an aviary. When he died, his widow buried him near the loquat tree in the north-west corner, beside his infant daughter and his three favourite dogs.

As Wall dismounted under the porte-cochère a slovenly servant appeared and led away his horse. He went up the sandstone steps into a veranda crammed with furniture in varying stages of dilapidation. From the walls an assortment of stuffed heads stared down at him; oakum and cotton-wool oozed from their seams, here and there a glass eye drooped from its socket, little gray lizards played among the antlers.

As Wall came up the steps, an Indian in European clothes rose from one of the crumbling settees. 'Oh, hallo, Wall!'

'Ganpat Rai, how are you?'

Wall sat down and stared at the transmogrified menagerie. 'Lord!'

Ganpat Rai the barrister smiled. 'Cheer up! Yesterday when the water buffalo fell down and burst, we discovered a nest of scorpions.'

Mrs Lyttleton appeared and greeted her visitors. 'How kind of you to come! Has that lazy swine offered you anything to drink?' Without waiting for an answer she lifted her voice piercingly: 'Jalal!'

The men had risen, and waited until she was seated. She looked at the barrister. 'Well, what luck?'

There was an expression of restrained triumph on his dark, intelligent face. 'I won my case.'

'Ah, congratulations. But I never doubted that you would.' She turned to Wall. 'And what have you been doing?'

'Sweating as usual. They mixed *kankar* with the cement and an entire sector had to come down.'

'What did you do?'

'I told the contractor he could go to hell, I fined my headman, and gave his deputy a dammed good hiding.'

She frowned. 'Aren't you rather free with your hidings, Aubrey?'

'Well, it works, it works.' He stretched his legs. 'Since then I've dreamed of the long cold brandy-peg which awaited me here!'

'Jalal!' screamed Mrs Lyttleton again. 'Jalal!'

He appeared, dirty, red-eyed, with a slightly demented look about him.

'Brandy,' said Mrs Lyttleton. 'In the cut-glass decanter on the sideboard. And water. And the cigarettes which are beside my bed. And hasten lest death overtake you suddenly!'

She sat back with a sigh. 'Opium. I'm sure of it. You can see it in his eyes, but what can I do?'

'Kick him out,' suggested Wall lightly.

'His grandfather served my father. How could I kick him out?'

'You are a fearful sentimentalist.'

Ganpat Rai shook his head. 'No, it is just that her heart is golden.'

'Thank you, Ganpat Rai!' Mrs Lyttleton laughed. 'I've often wished it were—then I might live for ever.'

Mrs Lyttleton had lived in India most of her life. Now, at seventy, she was shrunken and brittle, the blood had thinned in her veins but it had not soured. Her once bright hair was sparse and white, pinned to her head by a tortoise-shell comb set with rubies. No one remembered, now, whether she had ever possessed beauty, but she gave that impression and they took it for granted. Because she had never fought India, India had preserved her from much of the bitterness of exile and the contradictions of the usurper. Essentially feminine, she had not ruined her complexion or her system by exaggerated exercise and unnecessary exposure to a ferocious climate. Aristocratic, it had never occurred to her that she had anything to lose by adapting herself to a way of life scorned and feared by her compatriots. Now in her old age she felt more comfortable in native dress, and kept better health by eating native food, and she was less lonely because she could speak their language as well as she spoke her own. No wonder that in Amritpore there were people who considered her eccentric, extraordinary, and by their standards, impossible. She had been altogether too high-spirited to escape slander, but she was fond of remarking that whereas in her youth she might have resented the tales which were told about her, now that she was old she rather enjoyed them. She would, herself, have been the last to deny that she had always liked men and that she preferred warriors to all others. And if beauty had vanished, her spirits died hard. She missed people, she missed the excitement of days when Amritpore was a garrison and the sentry-boxes at the fort housed soldiers instead of bats. She could, of course, have returned to England, but the prospect of eking out her old age on an Army pension in Norwood or Chelsea was not to be thought of. India was in her bones, and her bones would remain in India to sweeten, a little, some corner of its tortured soil.

Ganpat Rai had known her for twenty years. She was the only white woman with whom he could feel wholly at ease, although there were occasions when her directness disconcerted him. He had spent some years in England and greatly admired the English; he was eager that his son Hardyal grow up as nearly like an Englishman as possible, but he was slow to realize that the English are a race of contradictory elements, profoundly, even tragically, paradoxical. Ganpat Rai sometimes found it difficult to believe that Mrs Lyttleton and Aubrey Wall should belong to the same *jat*. Wall himself, though long since won over to a grudging admiration, never quite forgave Mrs Lyttleton her native ways, nor could he understand that—in her own way—she remained as true to the paradox as he did in his.

Age and climate had tired her bodily, and she cared little now for her garden or for her rambling, magnificent rooms through whose lonely reaches she wandered by herself, tinkling and twinkling in her priceless jewels at all hours, attended by a retinue of dogs and cats, tame squirrels, and the birds which flew loose through the hours. In addition to her pension she enjoyed the revenue of several villages which bordered the estates of Madame St Remy, and which Madame would have liked to own if Mrs Lyttleton had not been so perverse about selling. Mrs Lyttleton's villagers trespassed on the indigo fields; they stole Madame's mangoes and threw their dead grandmothers into her wells to save funeral expenses. Mrs Lyttleton, when she heard of these outrages, rolled her eyes piously and derived a secret zest from the situation.

Jalal appeared with a tray and Wall sighed with pleasure.

'I must admit that this is more to my taste than yesterday afternoon.'

'What about yesterday afternoon?' She refused the brandy but selected one of her Egyptian cigarettes.

'I went to Jacques St Remy's birthday party.' He glanced at her quizzically. 'Why were you not there?'

'I was not invited.' She smiled. 'Madame honours me with her mistrust!'

They laughed, and Ganpat Rai said: 'But that Jacques . . . he is charming.'

'Both children are charming. I feel sorry for them.' She hesitated, frowning. 'One cannot help wondering what will become of them.'

'Madame is rich, her children are clever and beautiful. Why wonder?'

Mrs Lyttleton shrugged. 'You have no imagination.'

Ganpat Rai waited tactfully for the conversation to proceed. He never felt quite as much at ease in Wall's presence as he did in Mrs Lyttleton's. Observed together, the English struck sparks from each other's armour; their wit, which lacked his conception of delicacy, sometimes bothered him, though for this he blamed himself, his own ignorance and slowness of understanding. With Hardyal it would be different. Hardyal would grow up among them, he would learn to know them in their own country. Even now they were impressed by the boy's manners, his quickness and intelligence.

Mrs Lyttleton said abruptly: 'Poor little Jacques!'

'Oh, I don't know!' Had she said 'Poor little Gisele' Wall might have aspired to know more. Mrs Lyttleton's face had a gentle, bemused look. 'I miss him. But perhaps when Hardyal has gone, Jacques will come to see me more often.'

Wall laughed. 'Do you know, I believe you are in love with him!'

'I have never tried to conceal it.'

'No wonder Madame St Remy . . .'

Mrs Lyttleton studied the diamonds on her hands. 'It is a case of history repeating itself, isn't it? Madame has never abandoned her suspicion that I might at one time or another have tried to seduce her husband.'

'Well,' said Aubrey Wall slyly, 'nor have we!'

Mrs Lyttleton laughed, her clear blue eyes meeting his. 'Auguste St Remy was twenty years younger than I.'

'And like the rest of us he liked to come here and talk and listen, in the long afternoons during the rains.' The barrister smiled at her. 'You are always gay, always kind. With you we are free to speak our hearts. It is natural that women should be jealous of you.'

Wall was a little put out by this fervour and by the flush which it brought to Mrs Lyttleton's unregenerate cheek. A compliment could make her look a dozen years younger.

'Madame,' said Mrs Lyttleton slowly, 'is really a fool. Imagine wanting to bury one's only daughter in a convent!'

Wall put down his glass. 'I don't think she meditates doing that, does she?'

'I am sure of it. After all, it would solve the problem of Gisele, would it not? Short of putting her in purdah with Ganpat Rai's ladies.'

The barrister laughed. 'Purdah solves no problems, I assure you. It is itself a problem.'

Wall was frowning. 'I don't believe . . .'

'I do. I've seen it coming. Gisele's beauty, Gisele's youth . . . here in India . . . how would you expect a woman like Madame to cope with the situations which—in Gisele's case—are almost bound to arise?'

Wall persisted obstinately: 'What situations, for instance?'

'Adolescence, love, marriage—all the rest of it.'

'But good Lord ! Why is Gisele's case unique? I don't see it.'

'Given her mother's temperament—given her own, and her quite extraordinary beauty, you still don't see it?'

'Ah,' said Ganpat Rai, nodding. 'Were she one of us she would already be married, her life—her future, secured.' When the others remained silent he added rather shyly: 'With us, beauty is never a problem. It is an asset, a treasure.'

'Yes,' agreed Mrs Lyttleton, rather sombrely. 'There are many things in which you are wiser than we.' She turned suddenly to Wall.

'I wish you would use your influence to have Jacques sent to England with Hardyal.'

'My dear lady, I have no influence with Madame.'

'With Father Sebastien, perhaps?'

'Hardly!'

She made a gesture of despair. 'They'll send him away to be educated among all those twittering priests, I know!' For a second or two she brooded unhappily. 'I believe in secular education. After all, what is possible for a Brahmin should be possible for a Catholic.'

'You must remember that I am not orthodox,' replied the barrister. 'And Catholicism is not an exclusive educational system as Brahminism is.'

She brushed this aside with a glitter of diamonds. 'What has all that mumbo-jumbo to do with governing India?'

'Perhaps everything,' said Ganpat Rai softly. It was during these conversations that pride in his own achievement, his own liberation, rose to comfort him. Enlightened though he was, modern, a sceptic, he had his secret hours of doubt, even of terror. True, he had accepted the West with all its promise—but had the West accepted him? And he remembered other conversations, not as happy as this one—conversations with his friend and colleague Abdul Salim. 'The English,' he once said with bitterness, 'belong to the category of men who leave welts on the flesh of history.'

But Ganpat Rai believed that a lasting civilization must come from the West, and that the East must go to meet it. Religion—Salim's own religion—was the great stumbling block, as it had always been. Three hundred years ago Akbar the great illiterate tried to solve the problem by welding Hinduism, Mohammedanism, and Christianity into one. He concocted a new faith and died its only convert.

'Perhaps,' said Ganpat Rai, hopefully, 'perhaps Jacques and Hardyal will provide a solution.'

'Perhaps,' assented Mrs Lyttleton. She looked at Wall. 'But in the meantime they will go away. You too will go away. India is the scene of farewells.'

He shrugged. 'Of course, one goes home.'

There was a brief silence, then she threw off her gloom and turned gaily to the barrister. 'Now do tell us about the case of Naiko versus Empress.'

# 6

Jacques awoke in the cocoon pallor of his mosquito net and saw the stars framed in the upper half of the Dutch doors. It was still night, but from the colour of the sky he guessed that it would soon be morning. He heard the jackals crying and remembered Hanif's interpretation of their refrain:

> Ek murra Hindu!
> Ka-hahn? Ka-hahn?
> Ya-hahn, ya-hahn, ya-hahn!

> One dead Hindu!
> Where? Where?
> Here, here, here!

Jacques pictured the gaunt shapes skulking outside sleeping villages or nosing among the funeral pyres beside the river. Mr Wall and Doctor Brown had promised to take him on a jackal hunt. This meant riding them down with hog spears and a pack of dogs. Perhaps Hardyal would come, though he was not very fond of killing things.

Jacques thought of Hardyal: then, more wide awake, he thought of Father Sebastien, who had talked to him for a long time after lessons yesterday. Queer, that all he should be able to remember now was the sound of Father Sebastien's voice, and nothing else. He clasped his hands behind his head and stared into the gloom of the mosquito net; he liked sleeping in a net, which made him feel mysterious, like a little spider. It brought him the same sense of inscrutability which he'd attained by accident a year ago when he found that he was never, actually, obliged to answer questions. At that time his mother had taxed him with some minor wrong-doing: confused, he engaged in a private summing up of facts and circumstances, but misreading his silence, she had broken into expostulations and accusations. Jacques' silence held, it took root, it grew. He found himself contemplating it with a sort of impersonal wonder. Madame went on and on, mystified, aware with a little inward shock of fright that he had discovered a means of eluding her.

The same thing happened yesterday with the priest. Jacques could not remember the question which had brought on his own sudden refusal—for that was what it amounted to, a deliberate refusal to commit himself. The question was not important, it was no more than one of those small prying remarks to which Father Sebastien was sometimes given. He'd repeated it in the form of a query; then, arrested by the new quality in Jacques, made the question direct. The boy stood before him, silent, listening to an inward pæan: 'Even if they were to light a fire on my stomach I wouldn't answer!'

Jacques knew that they would come back to it; not his weakness but his strength would set his fate in motion, forcing those who controlled it to take steps. In the meantime Father Sebastien's voice continued in the distance; it went on and on like the hum of a mosquito, and Jacques' eyes closed. When he opened them again he knew that it was time for him to get up.

Dawn was just emerging and a ribbon of colour rested on the garden's edge as he hurried across the compound to the stables. A cock crowed; his dogs barked and were answered by a pi-dog in the distance, but it was still another hour or two before a general rousing.

Jacques went into the stable and led his horse into the open; it whinnied and laid back its ears as he slid the bridle over its head and eased the bit between its soft lips. Then Hardyal appeared, cantering along the turf which edged the drive. He had exchanged his gold and muslin, his crimson slippers, for English boots and breeches and a solar topi. They greeted each other, then turned to see a figure emerge from the house. It was Gisele, also dressed for riding. She came up, pale, her eyes still heavy with sleep. 'I heard you. I'm coming, too.'

Her hair was braided and she carried the skirt of her habit over one arm. 'Will you saddle the mare, Jacques? I'll hold Robin.'

A change fell on the boys' spirits; neither liked Gisele, but Jacques felt sorry for her. Hardyal had dismounted, and between them he and Jacques led Gisele's half-breed Arab from its stall and saddled and bridled it. The three animals greeted each other in an electrifying whinny, and from the servants' quarters burst a medley of groans and coughings. Hardyal held the mare while Jacques helped his sister to mount. She flew upward like a bird, her spine resilient to the mare's lightning turn. Then all three trotted across the compound through a break in the cactus and lantana bushes. The plain lay in sallow light and a smell of dew rose from it as the horses sprang forward, a night's energy stored in their marrow.

They rode without speaking until the house faded into the trees behind them. Now there was nothing but the unending plain, the gallows-structure of wells and darkness of mango groves. They passed a village swathed in smoke; there were other villages hidden in contours of the earth, yet the plain seemed empty of life except for a quail which flew under the horses' feet, and a jackal which stole away among the shadows.

Gisele pulled ahead, her mare stiffening into a canter, and the boys followed, one on each side. They exchanged brief smiles, sheer physical exhilaration drawing all three into a simple comradeship. The Fort, their favourite objective, lay five miles away in a bend of the Gogra River. They swept three abreast over sown fields, recklessly aware that they should not. The earth flew behind them, and with a sudden tremendous clatter two peafowl rose and clambered into the air, the cock's tail streaming fire.

In a little while they were riding knee to knee and the first ray of light struck their faces and glittered on the chains and buckles of their harness; it brought forth, unaccountably, shivering half-clad figures of myth and testament. White bullocks swished their tails beside a well, a naked child salaamed, crying 'Maharaj!'

Women repairing the little canals which fed the fields rested their bangled arms and smiled, the younger ones instinctively drawing their veils over their eyes. The children rode on and their passage left a dark ripple in the acres sown and unsown. More than a hundred years ago the peasant folk had watched these children's ancestors ride across the plain to give battle at the Fort. Their own fathers had taken part in the ceaseless struggles for the plain and the ghat and the nullah and the prince's house among the trees. Portuguese and Dutch, Danish and French and English—and before these, stalwart hordes from the North-West, and the elite from everywhere, all converging upon the rich and inviting centre. For gold or for jewels, for that fertile strip or for this strategic temple, for shittim wood or for cotton to bind up wounds; for silk, for pepper, for jute and tobacco, and for the blue dye of sailors' livery. It had always happened; it would go on happening though those about to die exhorted otherwise, and for these at any rate it was the last time.

The Fort was built of unbaked brick crumbling everywhere but still impressive above its shallow moat. The children rode across a hollow-sounding bridge under the portcullis, into a quadrangle broken into doorless rooms and quarters whose original use was lost to their ghost-believing eyes. The sun had risen, and under it the Fort lay silent and deserted. Here in the middle of the last century Mahrattas under their French officers had fought and lost to the English. The children had long since explored every cranny for old bullets and bloodstains but all that remained to them now were scorpions and the sloughed off skins of snakes.

They hitched their horses to a thorn tree and wandered across the courtyard to a ruined stair which led to a favourite sentry box. Below them lay the moat, green and formal as a park, under stunted acacias where a child was grazing a flock of goats whose bleating mingled with the incessant whistle of green pigeons.

Gisele said: 'I'm going to see if I can find a snakeskin. I want one with the eye-holes complete.'

'Look out you don't find one with the fangs all complete, too,' Hardyal warned her jokingly.

He always found it difficult to joke with this girl, whose coldness chilled him. Her beauty, her sex were, for him, mysterious and remote. The boys sat on a crumbling balustrade beside the sentry box and watched her walk away. At fifteen she was almost a woman, and though neither mentioned it they were glad when she left them. They removed their hats and the breeze stirred their hair.

Jacques said suddenly: 'Next year we shall come here for my birthday.'

Hardyal's eyes had a heavy look. 'Next year!' He was in an odd mood. 'Do you remember the day we watched a cobra stalk a dove down there in the moat?'

'Hanif killed it with a stone.'

'And the year when Father took us to see the Magh Mela at Allahabad?'

'Yes,' said Jacques, looking at him. Hardyal would not meet his eyes, but went on in the same strange voice: 'You wanted to bathe in the Jumna with all the others but Hanif wouldn't let you. I remember . . .' He broke off, frowning. 'I've been remembering and remembering . . . sometimes it seems as if there was nothing that I had forgotten . . . nothing.' Jacques waited, troubled by his friend's manner.

'I remember an evening when we went to Mrs Lyttleton's and she told us about the Mutiny and how on certain days in broad daylight, guns are heard here in the Fort. I remember so much . . . so much!'

Jacques watched Gisele, who was walking along the pediment below them. She had found her snakeskin and wore it draped about her shoulders; he heard her singing under her breath, and as she passed below them she glanced up. 'Let's ride out to the river. I'll wait for you near the horses.'

Jacques bent to examine a small funnel-shaped contrivance in the dust beside him. It was the circumference of a man's thumb and of finest sand. At its steeple sloping bottom something minute and alive lay hidden. He captured an ant and rolled it down into the funnel; at once there followed a microscopic upheaval as a pair of tiny fangs appeared, and the lion-ant seized the bait and snuggled down with it out of sight.

When Jacques looked up he saw that Hardyal's eyes were full of tears.

'What?' he whispered. 'What is it, Hardyal?'

"I must tell you. . . . Father said I should not, because he promised Madame . . .'

Jacques sat motionless, and Hardyal went on in a thick voice: 'You know that I was supposed to go to England soon . . . but I didn't know . . . I didn't even think, how soon. Now I know. It is to be in a week. I shall spend this summer with Mr Wall's people in Sussex, then I shall go to school. In a week . . . in a few days.'

Jacques captured another victim and fed it to the lion-ant.

Suddenly Hardyal broke down. 'Hum nahi jana mungtha!'

I shall remember this, thought Jacques. I shall forget nothing, nothing, least of all that cry: I do not want to go! And suddenly everything that was familiar to him rushed away and stood at a distance. Hardyal was his earliest friend; he has slept in Hardyal's house, they had talked and walked and ridden together, and although he'd been told often enough that the day would come when Hardyal must go away, Jacques had never quite believed it. "I remember so much,' Hardyal had said, '. . . I remember so much!' Jacques, too, remembered, for in a flash memory had become more important than the future, more important than the present. He thought of the summer when they had not gone to the hills as usual, and the loo had blown red and scorching across the plains, while he and Hardyal played chess in the drawing-room and shouted to the punkah coolie to pull harder on the great frilled punkah over their head; he remembered the lazy swims in Hardyal's swimming pool among shoals of startled goldfish, and Krishna, Hardyal's servant, bringing them a dish of ripe figs as they emerged cool and dripping into the warm air. He would remember a summer when a break came in the rains and millions of tiny red velvet spiders appeared from nowhere, and all the frogs in creation chanted together: Port, Port, Port! White Wine, White Wine, White Wine! Sherry, Sherry, Sherry! Seasons would come and go but one's friend stayed beside one for ever!

Gisele's voice reached them from the courtyard. 'It's getting hot. We better start home.'

As they rose, Hardyal whispered: 'Do not speak of this.'

Gisele was waiting for them beside the horses. Jacques looked at her questioningly. 'What's the matter? We've only just come.'

'My head aches.'

She looked white, and as Hardyal held the stirrup for her he felt her blue flowerlike glance on his face; her lithe weight rested for a second on his shoulder, but the warmth which this contact kindled in him died at once. He dared not weep before her, he dared not touch her, nor dared he respond when she touched him, for the world which was soon to come between Jacques and himself had always stood between himself and Gisele.

They rode out into the bright sun and left the Fort to its cobras and its ghosts.

7

Madame St Remy, on her way to the factory, paused at her son's door. Jacques was bending over his collection of butterflies and for a moment she stood quietly watching his absorbed face. There were occasions when his remoteness frightened her and she suffered the jealous pang of an intruder. 'Jacques?'

He rose and faced her. 'I'm going to the factory. Would you like to come with me?'

'I have my geography lesson, Maman.'

She came and put her arm round him, the scent of her clothes touched his face. When she was gentle as she was now, Jacques was flooded with a passionate love. He was not proof against tenderness, but the storm was always interior—he contained it and remained still.

'Did you have a pleasant ride this morning with Gisele and Hardyal?'

He murmured something, and she put her hand under his chin, lifting his face. 'What is it, Jacques?'

'Nothing.'

'You looked as though you were going to say something.'

When he stayed silent she asked. 'What did you three talk about?'
'Talk? We didn't talk, much, about anything.'

His eyes could look like the eyes of a young lion. Madame
hesitated, then said lightly: 'I had a note from Hardyal's father. He
wants you to play tennis at his house tomorrow. You may go if you
like.'

'Thank you, Maman.'

On her way to the door Madame paused to admire the butterflies in
their cork-lined case. 'Where did you get that big one in the centre?'

'I caught it.'

He could not bring himself to tell her that Mrs Lyttleton had sent it
to him by Hanif, but when she had gone away his mind pursued her,
knowing how she must look sitting upright on the black leather seat of
her carriage, her brown eyes concentrated on the eternal problems of
dye, taxes, wages, revenue. He suffered a slight twinge of conscience:
perhaps he should have gone with her to the factory. He knew that she
liked to have him show an interest in the business, liked to have him
ask questions and to appear excited when she spoke of the future
when he would be old enough to help her. But Jacques hated the
factory, he hated the smell of indigo, the steamy smell of the machines,
the reek of coolies and attendants. He did not as yet fully understand
his own aversion to all this, nor why he shrank from the tired look of
the men and women who worked for his mother.

Madame St Remy drove briskly over the short dusty distance to the
factory, which stood in a large compound bordered by trees. On cool
days she transacted much of her business under the shade of these
trees, on an elevated structure called a chabutra. The process of hiring,
of dismissing, paying off and making cash advances to her labourers
sometimes consumed several days and invariably left her with a
splitting headache. She might have spared herself by delegating
authority to her factory foreman, but it was against her principles to
trust subordinates. Madame knew that when her workmen were paid
Mr Boodrie exacted his commission—a percentage which bought or
preserved his goodwill. After Boodrie loomed the figure of Ramdatta
the moneylender, without whom no one could hope to survive, since
there never was a wage which, of itself, did more than keep breath in
one's body. Madame knew this moneylender well, and rather liked
him. He was not really a villain—he was part of India, its fifth limb.
Not for nothing do her gods and goddesses boast a plethora of arms
and legs, for to endure at all one must sprout desperate tentacles.

Ramdatta was a big suave man who reminded Madame of
Frenchmen she had known at home; he was, in fact, thoroughly
bourgeois. Orphaned at fourteen, penniless, he left his village and

disappeared in the general direction of Bombay and its cotton mills. There among the gins and shuttles he worked as a sweetmeat vendor and somehow managed to save money. Naturally, inevitably, he slipped into the role of usurer, and when he was forty he came back to his native village and set up as moneylender, charging a 75 per cent interest. Gradually but by no means sluggishly he acquired his neighbours' fields and their flocks, even their homes. A gloss appeared on his skin, benevolent dimples at the corners of his full, childish lips. He cherished a profound admiration for Madame St. Remy's acumen and longed to lend her money, to install himself in her graces, for like all parvenues when a certain opulence has been reached, he now craved prestige. Madame was rich, she stood well with the local government; his lands adjoined hers, and he permitted his miserable tenants to work for her during the sowing and harvesting of indigo. As for Madame, although she heard numerous stories to his discredit, she had always found him deferential and obliging.

Above the earth and the tops of the ripening crops, above the preoccupation of struggle and death, stood the Burra Mem; beyond her hovered the carrion figure of the factory foreman, and beyond him again, the moneylender, and staunchly behind all three of them towered the invisible and all-powerful Sircar. No, there was nothing Madame St Remy could do about that look in her labourers' eyes; there was nothing that the moneylender could do about it, for he too had to live, and it is never enough just to live—a fact which he'd discovered for himself. There was nothing that Boodrie the foreman could do about it: he longed for a new and expensive camera. And the ryots and the coolies and the unschooled mechanics who were always putting Madame's machines out of order could do nothing about it either. There were too many of them, too many just like them. Unlike the land itself, which had reached a degree of exhaustion beyond which it could not go, the end for these people was the burning-ghat or the grave—and even to die involved expense. One's children took up the burden where one left off. There remained the Sircar and the Sircar did what it would here and there: it set up a dispensary, built a canal, staved off famine, fought cholera, and made a stab or two at education. But its exponents were a handful in a territory of roughly one million seven hundred miles, among a population of three hundred million. The Sircar lifted its precise English voice in a huge unlettered silence; it attempted in clumsy Christian fashion to impose incidental welfare on these miles and these millions, but when all was said and done the Sircar remained in India for reasons that were not very different from those of Ramdatta the moneylender himself. Madame St Remy, too feminine to mark the illogicality of her own point of view, often remarked to the Father Sebastien that the Sircar was simply old John Company in metamorphosis . . . not entirely unrecognizable.

This morning a big table was set on the factory chabutra under the trees. Madame seated herself and one of the factory servants held a parasol over her head. Beside Madame stood Mr Boodrie, arranging and rearranging ledgers, dispatch cases, fingering big braided sacks filled with coins. Nearby—relaxed but watchful—lounged two stalwart Sikhs, the factory policemen who wore Madame's livery.

Mr Boodrie spilled the coins from their sacks and arranged them in symmetrical towers the length of the table. These towers varied in height, and behind the first row stood another—the lesser coin of annas and pice. The eyes of every one except Madame flickered like bees over this metal architecture. Brooding, speculative, their glances computed the sum of rupees, annas, and pice in each tower, but the total remained a cloudy dream which had little relation to individual lives—wealth beyond computation, beyond imagination.

They gathered, men, women, and children, barefooted, their clothing splashed with the olive and orange and the final intense blue of indigo. They arranged themselves in a semi-circle before Madame's table and there squatted, coughing, murmuring, exchanging glances and small signals of expectancy, complacence or despair. Some of the women had brought their babies, and the spleeny stomachs of these little creatures stood out brown and naked, their great eyes opened like wet black flowers.

Madame St Remy took her spectacles from their velvet case and drew a ledger towards her; Boodrie tilted his dirty helmet back from his forehead, revealing his greasy curls, and the people massed in the dust before him swayed as though the wind had moved them.

Boodrie consulted his roster. 'Mirban!'

An elderly man rose and advanced towards the chabutra. The foreman deftly sliced the top off one of the pyramids of rupees and counted them into Mirban's hand. Mirban too counted them, counted them with passionate attention as though he might by sheer excess of hope multiply them into a sum adequate for his limitless burden. Of the ten silver coins which Boodrie handed him, one would go back to Boodrie, who had engineered the advance; five would go to Ramdatta to pay back a fleabite on the mortgage which the moneylender held on his millet field; the remaining four rupees must somehow be spread over food for Mirban, his wife, his mother, his two sons, and his bullock. And when the advance was used up Mirban must work for a month for nothing, unless the foreman would obtain a further advance, or unless Ramdatta would make a further loan. In the meantime

Mirban knotted his money in a corner of his shawl and retired into the crowd to brood.

'Adhira Bhai!'

The name rose, fell, rose again. A slight scuffle ensued, followed by a reassuring voice: 'Go, go, child—no one will hurt you.'

'Adhira Bhai!' cried Boodrie again, impatiently.

A little boy crept from the protective mass and one of the Sikh policemen volunteered: 'Adhira is ill. This is her son.'

Madame glanced at the child. 'Come,' she said gently. 'Can you be trusted to take your mother's money?'

Dumb with terror, he stood before her.

'Hold up your head—the Burra Mem does not eat children!' cried the policeman encouragingly.

'What is your name, little one?' inquired Madame. He reminded her distantly of Jacques, and as her son's face rose before her Madame picked up Adhira's share of rupees and gave them to the child. 'Don't be afraid. Take these to your mother.'

He gave her a single desperate glance, then took the money and bolted back to the safety of the crowd.

A pock-marked Mohammedan wearing a cast-off English jacket rose and thrust himself towards the chabutra. He began to talk in a high, excited voice, but Boodrie cut him short. 'Hakim Ali, you are dismissed. It is of no use for you to keep coming back. Now go!'

'My wages! I am owed seven rupees eight annas in arrears. . . .'

'You are not owed a single damnable cowrie. Go. Depart!'

Murder stood out in Hakim Ali's face, but before he could take a step, a lathi blow caught him behind the shoulders. The Sikhs closed in and he was shoved and hoisted across the compound and flung through the gates into the road. The crowd watched passively. Two or three laughed.

'Golam Hosain.'

No one answered, no one came forward.

'Golam Hosain!' repeated Boodrie. 'Where is Golam . . .?'

'He is dead.'

There was brief silence. Then Boodrie stared at the crowd.

'Dead?'

'Dead.'

Madame removed her glasses and wiped them on her handkerchief. Over her head in the branches of a nim tree, a green pigeon whistled. One of the policemen turned aside and spat into the dust. He said in a sonorous voice: 'Golam Hosain is dead. He died last night.'

Boodrie reached across the table and removed an inch of silver coin from one of the pyramids, setting it aside.

'Kullu!'

It would go on through the morning, through the afternoon, it would go on throughout the next day. Small lines would engrave themselves on Madame's features and her attention would waver, then from that reservoir which remained a mystery to the people who knew her best would spring a fresh resolution, a new strength, and the business would proceed unflaggingly, relentlessly. Boodrie might wilt in his stiff drill suit, Golam Hosain die of the consumption which had racked him for the past three months, but all the life in Madame would gather to burn with renewed vitality in her dark, expressive eyes.

She thought, now, about Jacques. Perhaps if he showed signs of missing Hardyal too much she would send him to the Hills earlier this year. But already he seemed stronger than he used to be; like most Frenchmen he would mature early, unlike the hooligan English who clung so to their youth. When Madame thought of her son's future she saw the circumstances and surroundings as remaining unchanged, herself still young and in full possession, while round his head flowered all the blessings and all the banners.

'Behari Lal! You are fined fourteen annas for permitting water to drip on a seed rack. Behari Lal!'

# 8

When his mother had gone Jacques stood looking down at his butterflies and making unselfish resolutions. Then the bead curtains chimed in their arched doorways and Gisele came in. 'Are you busy?' His glance went at once to her bare feet. 'You might step on a scorpion or get a splinter.'

She went to his bed and sat down, drawing her feet under her. She said slowly: 'The punkah coolie's baby is dying.'

'Which punkah coolie?'

'Kanhya. It's been sick and it's dying.' Her voice trembled. Jacques said: 'Does Maman know?'

'She says there isn't anything to be done about it now. It's too little and too sick. Jacques . . .' She broke off, staring at her hands, and Jacques hoped that she would not cry. Her crying always unnerved him. There was a strange quality to it, a grown-up quality.

'Jacques, it's terrible that anything so little should die unbaptized.'

'Perhaps Father Sebastien . . .'

'He told me not to worry. He said that God's infinite mercy would take care of Kanhya's baby.'

'Well, then.'

'I know. But it won't nurse any more. It doesn't even cry. It just lies there panting . . . .'

He saw the tears fill her eyes. "It looks like a little dry twig, except that its heart . . . its heart . . .'

'Shall we send for Maman?'

'No one can stop it dying now.'

He was silent, thinking about Kanhya, the casteless Habura, and his black wife. They were semi-nomadic, untrustworthy people, but Madame employed them out of pity. Gisele went on: 'I've prayed and prayed, I've even walked about without shoes.'

'Ah! You shouldn't.'

She stared at him with tear-filled eyes. 'One must make an offering. I didn't see how God could refuse. Look!' She thrust out a foot and he saw that there were spots of blood on the white skin. 'It's an act of faith, but it isn't enough. I even kept myself awake all night, on purpose. And when I was dying to go to sleep I forced myself to get up and ride with you and Hardyal.'

He stirred uneasily. 'If you've done all that . . . '

She shook her head. 'You could help if you wanted to.'

'I'll pray,' said Jacques. 'Now, if you like.'

'Would you do more than pray? Would you do something really difficult?' When he was silent she went on quickly: 'Make an act of faith. Give something you love . . . something it would hurt you to give up. Perhaps if we both did, He'd hear us and take pity.'

Jacques asked gently: 'Well, what, for instance?'

'Would you be willing to give up Mrs Lyttleton?'

'What do you mean?'

'It would hurt you, wouldn't it, never to see her again? But if by doing so you could persuade Our Lord to save Kanhya's baby?'

'I'll give up something else.'

'No, that. It would hurt you, it would be a true sacrifice. Please, Jacques!'

His eyes were suddenly hard as beryls. 'Is this . . . did Maman . . .?'

But he saw from her expression that his suspicion was unjust. Now suddenly he hated Gisele, he hated this situation, and everything behind it. They were always driving him into corners, making impossible demands on him. How different they were from Hardyal, from Mrs Lyttleton, who asked nothing, who gave so much . . . whose mere existence was in the nature of a gift!

Gisele was watching him. "I see. Then tell me this: Do you adore Him, as you should? Would you die for Him, as He died for us?'

Jacques stayed silent, staring at the floor.

'You don't,' said Gisele. 'You wouldn't.'

He wanted to speak, to protest, but his will remained quiescent as he listened to the sound of her voice falling away inside him.

'You've always loved other things too much,' said Gisele. 'You love Mrs Lyttleton and Hardyal and Maman. You love your horse Robin. You loved that baby bat you once had, that the spiders ate. You love anything, everything—but you do not love Him.'

Jacques knew that he should answer this, but her words bore his denial downward into a void.

'You know that if Kanhya's baby dies, it will be your fault in a way. At least I've done everything . . . everything. But you don't care. You won't lift a finger even for a little sick helpless baby.'

He burst out at that: 'I'm not God!'

She went on inexorably: 'You leave Him out on purpose for fear that He may interfere with what you want to do. And every time you take Communion you commit a sacrilege.'

Revulsion swept through Jacques. He got up and went to the door, seeing the garden lie there colourless under tides of sun. Presently he heard Gisele get up and leave the room; he heard the bead curtains clash softly behind her and knew that she was going away to cry. Left alone he felt a slight prickle on his skin. On Sunday it would be his turn to be one of the servers for Father Sebastien: he would carry the cruet of wine and water and ring the bell at the Elevation. But if it were sacrilegious to accept Communion without belief, was it not proof of belief to reject Communion for fear of sacrilege? Besides, he did believe . . . he did ! It was only when Gisele came to him with her accusations that he felt doubt and confusion rise up within him.

He sat down and tried to go on with his geography lesson.

# 9

That night Kanhya's baby died, and in the morning Gisele carried the little body into the house and dressed it in her old doll's clothes and laid it in a white cardboard box. She had watched while the parents dug a hole under a tamarind tree at the edge of the compound. 'Deeper,' she exhorted them, thinking of the jackals. 'Deeper, deeper!' Madame had made her *orgeat* and bathed her forehead in cologne and put her to bed, but Jacques was unable to escape the sound of Gisele's weeping, nor could he forget the look she'd given him when she came into the house with the tiny body clasped against her breast.

It was a relief when Ganpat Rai's carriage came to fetch him and they drove away, Hanif perched aloft beside the driver, and Jacques reclining on the hot leather seat. Hanif, decked out to kill in a sapphire waistcoat, glanced over his shoulder. 'Do we stop at the bazaar for sweets?'

"First we stop at Mrs Lyttleton's.' Jacques stiffened as he spoke, anticipating an argument though he knew he could always cow Hanif by a display of autocratic fury. The coachman however, interposed by informing them that Mrs Lyttleton would be at Ganpat Rai's house this afternoon.

Jacques sat back, suffused with happiness. For him these moods of anticipation were the purest luxury; no matter that reality seldom measured up to hope, his imagination was kindled, and the thought of Hardyal's departure, remembrance of Gisele, his own guilty doubts—all lost their importance and their torment. He knew well enough that they would return, at any rate, but this afternoon was his own.

To reach the Hindu barrister's house one drove through the bazaar, and before that one drove along a white road under dusty nim and mango trees. One skirted the sun-baked Maidan where native youths were playing cricket, and glimpsed the English club set among palms and green lawns. One passed Mrs Lyttleton's house, its sandstone minarets towering above the tangled garden which used to be the boast of Amritpore. Then one saw the Indian houses, and these had gardens also, though they were different from those of Madame St Remy and Mr Wall and the Browns—different even from Mrs Lytteton's where the jungle failed to obscure an original formality. The Indian gardens suffered from a sort of architectural miscegenation; they were broken into cubes and lozenges, the flower-beds set out in coleus and marigolds, porte cochères muffled in bougainvillea or the even uglier purple railway creeper. But after this came the bazaar, which Jacques loved. He loved its aromatic smells, its swarms of yellow wasps, its starved dogs, its privileged bull, and its insolent monkeys which slipped down the trees and helped themselves to sweets and parched gram under the owner's nose. He loved the turgid vitality which survived filth and disease and starvation. Here, everything that lived was sacred. The boy's innocence was proof against these contradictions: so little was ever concealed, it would have been strange indeed that he should have been called upon to marvel or to protest. When a beggar, half blind and covered with sores, held up supplication hands, Jacques looked away not because he was horrified but because he knew that this was one of a million such beggars. Once when he and Hardyal had driven through the bazaar they bought peanuts and bread to feed the infant monkeys whose tender sunlit ears caught their fancy while, nearby, the beggars and the dogs looked on.

The coachman halted the carriage beside a sweetmeat stall and Hanif leaped down to buy a big cone-shaped leaf filled with syrupy stickiness. They usually paused at this vendor's, for motives which were not always connected with the purchase of jelabies or gulab jamuns. An upstairs window was ajar and from behind the shutter feminine voices hailed Hanif. Chaff of a dubious nature flew back and forth, and the coachman's ears twitched. Jacques listened; although his education on these lines pursued a dim and reluctant course, not all the jokes were over his head. Presently he looked up and cried: 'Do not be misled by his beauty—he is knock-kneed!'

Laughter rained down and there was a great tinkling of silver and glass: Jacques knew that he was being keenly scrutinized from behind the shutters.

'Proceed!' cried Hanif, springing up beside the driver. 'If the Memsahib were to learn of this, it would be as much as my life is worth.'

'Rather late in the day for the awakening of your conscience,' said the coachman, flourishing his whip. Hanif burst into song as they left the bazaar behind them and turned down a road which wound towards the river and Ganpat Rai's house. Parrots rose from the poppy fields. Sometimes Jacques had seen these birds hang drowsy with opium among the white flowers and once Hardyal caught one in his hand. 'Look!' he exclaimed. 'The little drunkard!'

Ganpat Rai's house was painted blue with pillars and arches of a dazzling white among the date palms and banana fronds which bounded his garden. Anxious to evade the vulgarity of his less educated friends, the barrister had taken European advice on the laying out of his garden. Here were no funereal marigolds, no coleus border, no bougainvillea, no atrocious magenta roses. Beyond the tennis court, beyond the embankment of Mr Wall's new canal, lay the river which, when the sun rose and when it sank, turned to the colour of pearls. On its muddy banks at almost any hour of the day, there rose the smoke of a funeral pyre, and Jacques and Hardyal sometimes followed the funeral parties when they went down to the water's edge with their burden. 'Ram Ram!' breathed Hardyal in a troubled whisper, and Jacques, out of deference to something of which he was not quite sure, echoed: 'Ram Ram!'

He saw now that the big blue stop-curtains were raised on the tennis court, and as he left the carriage he heard the thud of tennis balls and Hardyal's voice calling the score. Ganpat Rai, wearing flannels and a striped blazer, emerged from the house and greeted Jacques.

'They are playing singles. Later, you and I will take on Mr Salim and his son.' He put his hand on the boy's shoulder and they strolled towards a group of chairs drawn up beside the courts. There were some of Ganpat Rai's colleagues whose wives were in purdah, but who had brought their young sons. Jacques saw Mrs Lyttleton. As a sop to public opinion she'd compromised with her costume to the extent of adding a pair of kidskin boots and a hat overflowing with chenille roses. From under its faded brim her mischievous face peered out at Jacques. 'You have not been near me for a week!'

She made love to every one, even to children. He gave her a bright look. 'I was going to stop at your house this afternoon, but they told me I'd find you here.'

He lowered himself on the grass beside her chair and they watched Hardyal and Wall engage in a spirited volley. Mrs Lyttleton said softly: 'You and I are going to miss Hardyal.'

She managed, somehow, to make almost anything bearable when she spoke of it; he had never known her to dodge a painful subject or to launch into discussions from a dry sense of duty. Why had his mother not spoken of Hardyal's going? Why had she been at such pains to prevent others telling him?

Now Mrs Lyttleton spoke to Jacques of her conversation with Hardyal's grandmother and his aunts and the numerous female cousins who kept strict purdah and who violently opposed this breaking caste and going away across the black water. Hardyal's mother was dead, but that didn't simplify matters for Hardyal or Ganpat Rai. Mrs Lyttleton repeated what she had already said to the inconsolable women: 'It will not be for long, and he will come back for the holidays.'

Jacques thought of Hardyal's words when they had gone to the Fort:

'First a whole year must pass.'

'Years are not long,' said Mrs Lyttleton, laying her hand for a moment on his head.

'Well, even if they were what could one do?'

She glanced at the young cheek, at the deep hazel eye near her. There was, in Jacques, something which stirred a troubled tenderness in the old woman; sometimes she thought she recognized the child of fortune to whose singularity all men bow, whose way is always made a little easier. But she could not be sure, for to her as to Father Sebastien and even to his mother, the boy was still an enigma. How strange, now, to remember Auguste St Remy and their old affection! Auguste had not possessed this latent fire, this brooding. His charm had been of a different order—a melancholy, questioning spirit. When

Jacques was two years old Auguste had carried him in to see her and had expressed the hope that his son might be different from himself.

'I hope that he will be ambitious,' said Auguste. 'Ambitious and even ruthless. He will suffer less—those who will love him will suffer less.'

Auguste brought her his verses and his drawings and played for her on the cracked piano in her drawing-room. They talked of an England and a France which both had left behind them a long time ago; each was drawn to the other by an ineradicable loveliness. Mrs Lyttleton had said of Auguste that he was one of those delightful ineffectual men produced by a great civilization, but for whose special talents no government seems yet to have found a function. Poor Auguste! So far from being a fool, so far from being ruthless, or even ambitious.

Wall and Hardyal finished their game and came over to the chairs, flinging themselves on the grass near Jacques. The other Indians drew a little closer and a murmur rose, hesitant, a little guarded because of the presence of the English. There was a flush on Hardyal's cheek and his black eyes shone. The first shock of his impending departure had passed; it recurred only at intervals between the excitement and bustle of preparation. He took pride in siding with his father against the women, although when, at night, he reviewed this angle of things, fear and grief drowned him in tears. But Ganpat Rai had ordered trunks of clothing from Calcutta; there were presents, letters, farewells, speculations on the new life which awaited him in England. Of his father's friend the Mohammedan Abdul Salim alone held aloof from the prevailing air of congratulation. 'You will take much luggage with you, and you will come back with much,' said he to Hardyal, and tapped his own forehead with a cryptic gesture. 'If you succeed in putting any of it to use afterwards—you will be a lucky man.'

Hardyal knew that Salim disliked the English and this fact made the big, black-bearded Mohammedan interesting in his eyes. 'Why do you not come with me, Salimji? We will walk in Hyde Park and look at the Thames River. . . .'

'I would rather walk on the Maidan and look at the Ganges,' Salim interrupted with a flash of temper. 'I have little use for piebald personalities, English or Indian. Were you my son you would stay at home and grow up like the rest of us.'

Hardyal was not offended, for he had listened to endless wrangles between Salim and his father on the same question. Afterwards Ganpat Rai gave it as his opinion that Salim was a jealous and frustrated man. 'He is his worst enemy, for he is totally without discretion.'

Now Abdul Salim sat at a little distance from the others, listening with an air of sardonic boredom to their trivial chatter. Hardyal leaned over and whispered to Jacques: 'Do come and look at all my new things.'

They rose and walked away towards the house, followed by the other little boys, and Ganpat Rai lifted his hands and groaned. 'Such a day! My mother and my sisters! I shall be thankful when it is over and he is gone.'

'Will it be over then?' asked Mrs Lyttleton gently.

'Merciful heavens, I hope so. It is so bad for Hardyal, all this weeping and grieving.'

'But consider your pride when he comes home a pukka sahib!' observed Abdul Salim sarcastically from his corner.

'You would not send your own son to Cambridge if you could, perhaps?' inquired another Indian, with equal sarcasm. Ganpat Rai intervened with a suggestion that they made up a foursome for tennis, and a cousin of his rose tactfully to the occasion. 'Salim, you and I will play against Mr Narayan and Mr Ram Chand. They are fat, but you and I are old. Is that fair enough?'

Tension dissolved, and when the game was under way Mrs Lyttleton turned to Ganpat Rai. 'Do not fret about Hardyal. He will like England.'

'Of that I am not afraid. But I wonder . . . will he adjust himself quickly and successfully? I did, but then, I was older.'

'The English are easy to adjust to, in their own country. They are perhaps the most aped people in the world.' Aubrey Wall caught himself up swiftly. 'Hardyal is young—there is more danger of his being spoiled than homesick.'

Mrs Lyttleton stared across the garden. 'What is all this?'

A little procession was approaching across the lawn, white-turbaned men bearing baskets and garlands. Ganpat Rai went to meet them, and after a short conversation waved them towards the house and returned to his guests. 'They were from my old client Naiko. He insists on sending me presents though I have asked him to stop.'

'Naturally, he is grateful to you for getting him off!'

The barrister smiled. 'Naturally, considering his guilt.'

They stared, then laughed. Ganpat Rai shrugged. 'That is our English law. But those presents should really go to the prosecuting counsel. *He* deserves them.'

Ganpat Rai watched his guests playing tennis. The little half-clad ball boys scurried beside the stop-curtains, the players' voices rose cheerfully on the warm and pleasant air. Abdul Salim seemed to have forgotten his bad temper and already in his heart Ganpat Rai had forgiven his friend's sarcastic remarks. After all, Salim was poor and could not afford to send his own son to England to be educated; he was also a man of intelligence and energy, and he felt himself to be wasted in a small cantonment station like Amritpore. Ganpat Rai thought, generously: 'I shall give him Naiko's dalis to take home. He is proud, but I shall put it on the score of his children, and he will not refuse.'

The boys reappeared, Abdul Salim's young son capering rapturously. Two walked sedately ahead, and their appearance arrested the conversation. 'What on earth . . .' began Aubrey Wall, and he began to laugh. Hardyal and Jacques had exchanged clothing; now Hardyal wore Jacques' white drill suit which was too tight for him, and Jacques was resplendent in Hardyal's gold embroidered muslins. Wall stared at Ganpat Rai's son. By Jove, he thought, the boy will make a very presentable Englishman when we've done with him. But Hardyal's garments on Jacques seemed to him effeminate and unbecoming.

Mrs Lyttleton gazed at them long and intently. Their youth, their vitality, their extraordinary good looks stirred her to the depths. Where were they going, and what was to be their fate? At the moment they gave her the impression that they were equal to anything, but she was old, and she had seen the beginning and the end of youth, of vitality, of beauty. When Jacques' eyes met hers she caught her breath, unable, for a moment, to utter the necessary trivialities.

Wall broke the spell. 'I'll tell you one thing, my boy,' he drawled, looking at Jacques. 'You simply can't play tennis in a dhoti!'

# 10

The corrugated tin on the station roof cracked from accumulated heat and a variety of smells and sounds escaped from the population which milled about on the platform. Threading this polymorphic mass were the usual complement of starving dogs and veiled, sidling women. The hot breath of the train and the steaming breath of humanity rose to a blue heaven where the everlasting kites wheeled and circled.

Hardyal stood beside his father; his heart was beating violently, his smile was fixed, great tears kept rising and subsiding in his eyes. Ganpat Rai would accompany his son to Calcutta and there Hardyal would be placed in the care of friends who were taking the same steamer to England.

'You'll like Colombo,' Wall had told him, encouragingly. 'The Galle Face, where a brown sea rolls up the beach . . . and when you pass the Island of Socotra think of the pirates who still prey on coastal shipping.

You'll go up the Red Sea into Suez, and you'll look at the Mediterranean, and the Straits of Messina with the land olive-green in the early morning and Naples. . . .' Homesickness had made Aubrey Wall poetic. But to Hardyal everything seemed very far away. The tennis party of a few days ago might have happened last year. An age had rolled over him, he felt stranded on a reef of loneliness.

The train was disgorging passengers and freight in an intense panic-stricken confusion directed by a fat white station-master and his thin black assistant. Water-carriers and food-peddlers wandered through the crowd, their voices rising in the peculiar cries of another species—they sounded like birds, or like frogs after the rain. In a flash of anguish, Hardyal remembered the farewell to his grandmother, who, now that the inevitable had arrived, found herself dry of tears. She had caressed his face with her jewelled hands and stared at him with unbelieving eyes. 'I am old. I shall not see thee again.'

'Yes, yes! Soon—next year!'

'Nay, I shall never see thee more. Our lives part on this moment. Let me touch thee, let me bless thee!' He felt that she was dying in his arms, this old familiar woman who had nurtured him all the years of his life. His father's oldest sister had cried bitterly: 'What good can come of this separation? You will come back to us changed, a stranger, as your father came back years ago. You will look upon us with scorn for our ignorant ways—what is worse, you will try to change us, too! And for what reason? Why? Why?'

One by one the servants came and fell at his feet, Krishna, his favourite, clinging to his knees, begging him not to leave them. Then Ganpat Rai appeared and scattered them with a look. 'Come, my son.'

Hardyal did not look back as the carriage rolled past the tennis court between the gardenia hedges, past the women's arbour where all was silent, through the gates, past the poppy fields and the bazaar, to the station. Now he stared past the end of the train to a tossing grey-green of trees. Beyond them lay Amritpore and everything he knew and had ever known, but already it had passed out of his reach, already it was immersed in itself, excluding them. How cruel the world is, thought Hardyal for the first time. Babies go on crying and sucking, children scream in the dust, women tinkle their glass bangles, men wash their teeth and spit beside the well . . . I am forgotten, forgotten!

The crowd near him parted and he saw Mrs Lyttleton and Mr Wall and Abdul Salim coming towards him, wearing determined smiles and waving gaily. He sensed his father's pleasure: How good of these friends, what an honour!

But where was Jacques?

Mrs Lyttleton put her arm round Hardyal. 'Don't dare to cry

because if you do I shall, and that would disgrace me in the eyes of the
world.'

He tried to smile. 'Why would it disgrace you?'

'Because I put rouge on my cheeks and tears would make it run.'

Wall thrust a package under Hardyal's arm. 'Something for the
journey. You must write me news of my family. Make them take you to
see Arundel when the daffodils are out.'

Abdul Salim smiled at Hardyal. 'I shall look for changes when I see
you again, my child!'

Where, where was Jacques?

Mrs Lyttleton tightened her clasp of his shoulders. 'He will come.
He would never let you go without saying goodbye.'

Ganpat Rai interposed. 'Madame St Remy sent me a note this
morning, saying that perhaps it would be better if Jacques did not
come, since the farewell might be too painful for both of them. Hardyal
knows this . . . it is silly for him to go on expecting.'

Mrs Lyttleton had flushed under her rouge. 'Damn Madame St
Remy!'

The others looked utterly shocked by this outburst, but she turned
and clasped Hardyal in her arms. 'I know how Jacques will feel about
this. Can I give him a message, Hardyal?'

He tried to think of something to say, but his head and his heart
were in confusion. Ganpat Rai and Salim were talking in hurried
undertones about some case; Aubrey Wall, dreading a scene, lighted a
cigarette and began to hum. Only Mrs Lyttleton, then, really cared . . .

'Tell him . . .'

A shudder ran through the train, a flexing of all its iron muscles,
and with a despairing howl the crowd surged towards it.

'Tell him . . .' whispered Hardyal. Suddenly he forgot everything
except that he did not want to go away.

'Come,' said Ganpat Rai. Their luggage was already installed in a
carriage which they would share with a venerable Hindu gentleman
on his way through Amritpore to Calcutta. For the past few minutes,
this pundit had leaned on his window watching the little scene. He
was touched to observe the happy mingling of English and Indian,
though he was too much of a sceptic to place much faith in its
significance. Still, how delightful, really, to see tears on that old
woman's face under the preposterous hat, and the sensitive expression
of the Englishman.

'Good bye, Hardyal!'

'Tell him . . . tell him . . .'

The sound of a whistle tore the moment into shreds as the train
began to move. Those who were not going fell back and watched the

great thing crawl over the rails and steady into its meshed and intricate flight. A cry rose from it and pierced their hearts with its strange, perpetually disturbing and incomprehensible message.

'I'll take you home,' said Wall, giving Mrs Lyttleton his arm. They turned to look for Abdul Salim, but he had disappeared; the thread which tied their awareness to him and his to theirs had stretched and thinned: now it snapped in the final glitter of the vanished train.

Gisele laid her hands on the organ keys and the voices of Father Sebastien's native choir swelled and died round her. Below the carved teakwood balcony she could see the kneeling figures of her mother and the Browns. Jacques, in gown and surplice, knelt on the altar steps beside Mr Boodrie. The candlelight swayed under the weight of the hymn and the incense-laden air was as close-woven as silk. Every head bent for the moment of Benediction: Jacques raised the censer and its fragrance drifted towards his bowed face. From under his lashes he saw Father Sebastien, in alb and chasuble, lift the gold monstrance. Except for the thin voice of the bell in Boodrie's hand there was no sound. Then Jacques heard the train far away, its voice flung in an arc, a rainbow of sound across the brown miles.

> *Laudate Dominum omnes gentes;*
> *Laudate eum omnes populi. . . .*

Outside in the oleander-bordered compound Madame St Remy and her daughter waited for Jacques and Father Sebastien, who were changing their vestments. As she watched the little congregation drift away, Madame smelled the nim blossoms and knew that the hot weather would soon begin. Beside her on the carriage seat Gisele sat rapt and bloodless.

'You played beautifully this afternoon, darling,' said Madame.

Father Sebastien appeared, followed by Jacques, and they seated themselves on the little seat facing Madame and Gisele. The coachman twitched his reins and they wheeled out of the compound into the road towards Madame's house where Father Sebastien would dine tonight.

Madame linked her arm in Gisele's. 'The nim flowers!' she exclaimed.

Father Sebastien lighted a cigar. 'Summer's in the air. I heard the brainfever bird.'

Jacques said suddenly, 'I shan't be able to go to you for study tomorrow, Father. Hardyal is going away and I promised to say good-bye to him at the station.'

Father Sebastien took the cigar from his lips and held it in his strong plump fingers; each finger wore a little overcoat of black hair, but the nails were like polished almonds.

Something in the silence which followed his words made Jacques look from one face to the other. 'May I not, Maman?'

It was Gisele who answered him suddenly, in a stifled voice: 'Hardyal has gone.'

'Don't be silly. He doesn't go until tomorrow.'

'He has gone. Ganpat Rai had business in Calcutta, so they went a day sooner than they had arranged.' Her blue eyes stared at him from the pale oval of her face. 'Hardyal has gone . . . gone!'

Madame pressed the girl's arm against her own, then she too looked at Jacques. 'I would have told you . . . but I thought it better to spare you and Hardyal the grief of parting.'

Jacques stared at them with utter disbelief. 'But how could he have gone without my knowing it? He would have told me.'

'Ganpat Rai sent me a note . . . I replied that there was hardly time . . . we all thought it best to avoid a scene.' It was costing her more than she had expected, as Father Sebastien had known that it would. He looked quietly at Jacques. 'Had we heard in time perhaps something could have been arranged. On the other hand, your mother is right: these partings are unnecessarily upsetting.'

Jacques replied in a stony voice: 'I don't care if they are upsetting . . . he is my friend. . . . I wanted to see him again.'

'Jacques, darling. . . .'

'How could you have done it. Maman?'

Gisele began in a high, excited voice: 'It serves you right! You're too fond of people! Anyway Hardyal had gone. You won't see him again . . . not for years, for ages.'

The boy sat quite still and stared at the brown hummocks of Father Sebastien's knees. Grief and rage had ignited him, he felt that his very blood was on fire.

Madame leaned forward and touched his hand. 'Jacques, darling!'

But he sat like a stone, not looking at any of them. He listened to the sound of the horses' hoofs on the hard road and their rhythm knocked dryly against his heart. Madame and the priest engaged in a discussion of church affairs, Gisele sat and watched her brother's white face.

Clip, clop, clip clop, went the hammer strokes against Jacques' heart. The carriage turned into the shisham avenue and its misty columns met over their heads. Down this familiar avenue Hardyal had ridden to see him, and he had ridden back along its flickering shadow to call on Hardyal. They had grown up together, sharing laughter, sharing thoughts, visions, hopes. Who, now, would there be to talk with, to confide in? He saw the house, white and low and thatched, and memory blew through him softly like the sound of a horn. He leaped from the carriage and without once turning his head or heeding the plaintive cries which pursued him he ran through the lantana bushes and the cactus, across the quelds towards the road and Mrs Lyttleton's house.

Father Sebastien glanced at Madame and shrugged. 'Let him go. Later, we shall have to come to some decision.'

Jacques took all the short cuts and at last, dry in the throat, he found himself in Mrs Lyttleton's garden. She was there, as he'd known she would be—as his father had often found her walking under her trees in the brief Indian twilight. When she saw Jacques she waited, a palm-leaf fan hanging lightly from her hand.

For a little while he stood before her, trying to get his breath, then he stammered: "Hardyal . . . they let him go . . . they never told me.'

'I know.' She took his arm and turned him towards the house; they went up the steps together, greeted in silence by all the stuffed relics of that great hunter, the General her husband. On a little table beside her chairs were set glasses and a big jug of sherbet: there were little cakes, and a plate of Jacques, favourite sweets. She had known he would come, and now as he sat down beside her she smiled, humour and tenderness making her face young again. 'Do you remember the day you and Hardyal stole my cigarettes? This time you and I shall smoke one together.'

# 11

There were still two weeks before the break of the south-west monsoon; the earth lay breathless under heat which seared the fields and seeped up the brown trickles of water which fed them. Buffalo carts and bullocks creaked between acres of indigo, lugging the freshly cut stock to the tanks where air and water would combine to beat it into a primary orange and ultimate blue. Everywhere people crawled like fleas seeking the living blood.

On the headwork of his canal, at a point where the river eddied past the locks, Aubrey Wall was fishing for crocodiles. It was an original sport, one invented by him in the deep boredom of the season. A coolie crouched above the locks and dangled a dead pi-dog at the end of a rope. Hideously enticing, the dog hung just above the brown water, while the hunter sat on a camp stool with his rifle across his knees, waiting for a glimpse of the blunt snout and hooded eyes of his quarry. Wall's cotton suit was dark with sweat, he felt brittle from weeks of intense heat. Now a cool breath rose from the water and there were fragile shadows under the acacias which had sprouted beside the embankment. Night, when it fell, would fall abruptly, but it would bring little respite to the overburdened air.

Father Sebastien sat nearby, smoking his cigar and taking an occasional sip from a bottle of lemonade which stood in a bucket beside him. A little distance away under the trees Wall's tonga waited, the syce stretched on the ground beside his unharnessed ponies. Wall watched a few Pity-to-do-its dipping and nodding along the shore; they looked like women with painted eyes and coifs of shiny black hair stepping fastidiously among the charred pyres and refuse of the river. Beyond, the fields rolled towards the pallid sky; mango groves rested like dark clouds on its edges and the mud walls of villages trembled as though they might collapse under the impact of human vision. The canal cut its rigid line towards Amritpore; its tributaries fed the tanks of Ramdatta the moneylender, the cisterns of Madame St Remy, the reservoirs of the bazaar, and the railway station. It revived with a lukewarm sweetness the few miles of exhausted soil which still continued, miraculously, like a buried corpse, to put forth a sort of subcutaneous verdure.

Wall stared at the glittering line which his labour had traced across the parched land. Well, there it stood, for whatever it might be worth. There were days when he felt well pleased with what he'd accomplished, but to-day was not one of them. With the approach of the hot weather just before the rains broke, his nervous system suffered a kind of accumulated shock, a reverberation of all the dis-appointments, dreams, hopes, despairs, and resignations which had piled up during the year. Now loathing possessed him, loathing for the place, for the climate, for his work which he saw as a mere drop in this bottomless bucket of poverty, superstition, and disease. He was haunted by memories of his home in Sussex, of his kind and civilized family, by tastes and sounds and familiar scenes. Their inaccessibility made him hate his exile.

Father Sebastien tilted his topi and mopped his rosy forehead with a large silk handkerchief. He'd been silent for some time, musing on the sacrament which he'd recently administered in the village whose grove of mangoes he could see from here. The recipient was young, a widow, and out of terror of the new God her family had sent for Father Sebastien. The priest knew well enough what would happen as soon as his back was turned—they'd carry her down to the river and complete the rites after their old fashion, and tie bits of rag to poles stuck in the sand—thus leaving nothing undone to pacify her restive shade. He sighed and hitched his camp stool close to the headwork. 'Raise the animal somewhat—do not let it sink out of sight,' he admonished the coolie, who roused himself and gave the bait an enticing wriggle.

'There were three of the brutes last week,' said Wall. 'But they've probably become wary.'

'Would you like some lemonade? Not cold, but refreshing just the same.' He poured the liquid into a cup and gave it to the Engineer, noticing, without appearing to, the slight tremor of the other's hand.

The coolie gave an exclamation and all three craned forward, Wall lifting the big double-barrelled Greener. Something moved sluggishly in the water, slid up against the masonry headwork, rolled over and bared its devastated human face. A charred arm saluted them from the current, then sank.

'No mugger this time,' sighed the priest, relaxing.

'Neither *Crocodilus Palustris* nor *Gavialis Gangeticus*,' Wall agreed, in disgust. 'Merely Homo Sapiens somewhat the worse for wear. One of your flock?'

'Hardly. We bury ours.'

'In consecrated ground, no doubt.'

'Naturally!'

'Do the jackals respect it?'

'Well, we do employ a watchman.'

Both smiled, amused by their grisly exchange. Then Wall rose.

'God, if only the rains would break!'

'But the malaria,' murmured Father Sebastien. He stood, impressive in his white summer robes, and stared at the river. 'I cannot persuade the children to swallow quinine. They hate the bitter taste.'

'Perhaps they'll find that death tastes sweeter,' remarked Wall, with unaccustomed irony. He had little sympathy with the priest's calling, but both men respected each other and got along well.

The syce had come to and harnessed the tonga ponies; the coolie hauled in his ugly bait and cut it free. It fell and disappeared, then rose a little distance away, and vanished in a vicious swirl that was not resurrection. Wall fingered his rifle. 'Damn! I knew that brute was somewhere. We'll get him next time.'

They slid down the embankment to the waiting tonga, followed by the coolie carrying their camp stools and the rope. Wall took the reins and the priest sat beside him, while the servants rode behind. They started down the road in the late sunshine, and passed Madame St Remy's creaking bullock carts laden with indigo. Boodrie, driving a dogcart, passed them at a smart pace and they had a glimpse of his shoddy tussore suit and his face like a melting chocolate-drop. Wall closed to allow the dust to settle. 'Swine! I can't stand these half-castes.'

Father Sebastien realised that there were many thing and many people Wall could not stand these days. He ventured, gently: 'Boodrie is a good servant. It's hardly his fault that he is a half-caste.'

'They're no good. I've never met one I'd trust round the corner.'

'Nevertheless, you will admit their social predicament?'

'Oh yes, I know, I know! The sins of the fathers and all that. But it isn't my fault either.'

Father Sebastien glanced at him. 'Come to my house and have dinner. I am alone. I would like it.'

'Thanks, Father, but I must get home. I have work to finish and I go into camp tomorrow.'

'Camp in this weather?'

'I have no choice.'

The priest nodded. 'No, we have no choice. We must sacrifice, suffer, endure, forgive.' He sounded contemplative rather than minatory, and Wall laughed. 'I belong to the opposition shop, if to any. But there are times when I wish I could share your charity. You fanatics possess an endurance the rest of us lack.'

The priest smiled. 'Well, you dig the canals and leave the rest of it to us fanatics.'

One of the ponies pecked a little and Wall lashed it with his whip. They tore along for a few minutes, then he muttered in a choking voice:

'This bloody country!'

The priest remained silent. Presently the green of the little civil station opened before them—carefully plotted gardens, shady trees, a scent of flowering hedges, and watered grass. They drove past Madame St Remy's factory and saw her carriage waiting inside the gates. Wall asked abruptly: 'Tell me, what news of the children?'

'Jacques seems to have adjusted himself to St Matthew's School. Gisele, as you know, is with the Sisters of St Mary, in Gambul.'

'Rather young, isn't she, for all that?'

'Fifteen? And she is, I think, mature for her age.'

Wall hesitated for a moment, then: 'I miss them—the children. They made this place endurable.'

'You should marry,' said the priest kindly. 'You'd make a good father.'

'Marry?' He laughed. 'Leave my wife and children in England or in the hills, or force them to swelter down here with me?'

The priest shrugged. 'There are many who have learned to make the best of it.'

'There is no best. There is merely compromise and boredom. I know. I've watched it. No, thanks . . . I'll wait until I retire, if I don't pop off with dysentery or enteric before then.'

He suffered from a curious onset of emotion which speech could not relieve. Presently they were at Father Sebastien's little house in the church compound, where a water-carrier was sprinkling the ground before the dusty oleanders. Father Sebastien got out of the tonga and stood for a moment looking at the Englishman. 'I enjoyed our little expedition. If you should want me at any time, I shall come. At any time, and always as a friend.'

Wall smiled dimly. 'Thanks, I'm all right, you know.'

He wheeled out of the compound and drove home. After the day's heat he craved a bath, a drink, the month-old newspapers at home—an unequivocal surrender to his mood.

The Civil Engineer's bungalow was government-owned, well kept but rather bleak. Wall had left it much as he found it, a state of mind typical of men who have been brought up by devoted women and who have never learned the knack of making themselves comfortable. There were several whitewashed rooms filled with tasteless cane furniture, yards of stiff matting and rep curtains out of which scorpions and tarantulas tumbled at unsuspected moments. Lizards stalked flies along the floors or fell and lost their tails which went on wriggling for an hour afterwards. The drawing-room mantelpiece was crowded with photographs to which Wall had recently added another, one of Hardyal in striped blazer and snake-buckled belt, a straw hat tilted over his eyes.

Bathed and refreshed, Wall examined this photograph with a faint smile. It had been taken by the village photographer at Bognor, under the supervision of his sisters. They had written how much they liked Hardyal, and Wall could picture them—well bred and kindly, hovering over the small dark stranger. After three months Hardyal showed the faint signs of integration and response: his eyes had the level focus of English eyes, his lips seemed less full and sensuous, his whole face seemed thinner and keener—or so Wall believed. The photograph had induced a wave of remembrance, and he saw himself at that age; youth surged upon him with its reminders of time flying, of life slipping, slipping away like that poor charred relic of the fires, down the Gogra River to the crocodiles and the sea.

He carried Hardyal's picture to an armchair and stretched his legs on the wide leg-rests. Over his head the frilled punkah flapped jerkily and he heard his servants moving about the other rooms, lighting the lamps, rattling dishes. In a little while his Mohammedan bearer brought him brandy and cigarettes, rolled up the cane screens, and closed the lower half of the Dutch doors.

'Do not light the lamps in here for a little while,' Wall ordered. 'And tell that brute of a coolie to *pull*!'

When the man had gone and the punkah had taken a new lease of life, Wall sat quietly, refashioning the past. He was a lonely man and whatever was most important to him seemed to have receded beyond his reach for ever. What he'd said to Father Sebastien was true—he missed the St Remy children, who had gone to the hills soon after Hardyal's departure. Something sweet and indefinable had fled Amritpore with them, and what remained seemed stale and hopeless. He found himself bored by his own generation—the Browns, Madame St Remy, even by Mrs Lyttleton whose age had seemed to set her in a special category. But the children had been like bees rifling what honey there remained in this parched country. He had not dreamed that he would miss them like this . . . that he would miss Gisele, dream about her, conjure up her face at odd moments of the day. Something vivid sprang through him when he thought of Gisele.

One evening before they had gone away he went to dine at Madame St Remy's with the Browns and Father Sebastien. It had been a pleasant evening, pleasanter than many evenings Wall could remember. Madame exerted herself to be friendly, and after a while it had dawned on him that the shadow of the children's departure hung over them all. When it came time for Wall to take his leave he walked out through the back verandah, past their two little beds shrouded in mosquito netting. Obeying a friendly impulse, he'd stopped beside Gisele's bed and peered through the snowy screen, seeing her lying there mysterious and wide awake. Her hair, all loose, stood about her head like the love dance of some strange bird, and he bent closer, murmuring:

'Gisele?'

She stirred, her eyes huge in the surrounding pallor, and it seemed to Wall that she lifted her arms towards him. He raised the mosquito curtain and knelt down to bid her a friendly goodnight, as he had done once or twice before in their casual acquaintance. But she put her arms round his neck and drew his face towards her and offered her lips, cool and sweet. She held him so he smelled the lovely youth of her neck and breast, the perfume of her extraordinary hair, and before he knew it he had kissed her again and again, felt her trembling in his arms. Then he freed himself and went away, shaken and thoughtful, more than half inclined to turn round and go back. But go back . . . to what? And why?

The punkah flapped at slower and slower intervals and stagnant heat swarmed upon him. He shouted at the punkah coolie to pull harder, and the punkah jerked madly to life again. Somewhere in the outer darkness a drum rattled, a voice sang for a minute then fell silent. Wall finished his brandy, desire, and despair flushing and draining him. Presently he called his bearer, and after a slight hesitation, gave him curt instructions. The servant stared discreetly at the dim outlines of his master's feet. He'd often wondered why this sahib had seemed different from others; perhaps he attributed the difference to eccentricities hidden in white flesh. Now, reassured and privately amused, he took his orders and went away to the bazaar, to a shuttered room above the sweetmeat stall, a room well known and dear to the heart of Jacques' servant, Hanif.

## 12

Hanif and Gisele's old ayah accompanied the children to the hills. They left Amritpore just as the hot winds were starting to blow, and their train came from a direction opposite to the one which had carried Hardyal to the sea.

From his slippery leather bunk beside the window Jacques watched the brown plain unroll; seen thus the country was both familiar and strange. He'd gone to the hills in other years but this time it was different; when he and Gisele had been delivered over to their fate, the servants would return to Amritpore—Jacques would be alone. He brooded over the drab miles with their interminable mango groves, their wells, their mud-walled villages. Amritpore was soon lost, but there gleamed the river, and in another minute he saw the Fort: how thin the acacias looked from here, how toylike the sentry-boxes where he and Hardyal liked to sit and watch the goats grazing in the moat below! Jacques more than half expected to hear a salute from those silent guns, and to catch a glimpse of the torn banners and the warriors so often resurrected by Mrs Lyttleton.

The train dashed into a gully, plumed grass brushed the windows, and the earth came up close like something seen through a magnifying glass. He had a glimpse of a separate, teeming world which went its way indifferent to trains and the life which they carried in their angry bellies.

Hanif prepared tea and produced a tin box of sugar-coated biscuits, smuggled into the compartment at the last minute by Mrs Lyttleton. The train's rocking spilled the tea into their saucers and sent suitcases skidding across the floor. It slammed the lavatory door tight shut with the ayah inside it, and Hanif laughed heartlessly at her panic-stricken outcries as he worked on the lock. 'You will be there until we reach the hills, Umma! That is, unless you suffocate.' Gisele did not share in their merriment. She sat, by herself, in a corner of the compartment, staring out at the flying miles. Jacques saw that she was crying—not the familiar childish tears of homesickness, but in a strained, suffering, grown-up way which hurt him.

At night Hanif retired to his own third-class compartment, leaving the liberated ayah in charge. Jacques lay staring at the round glow of the ceiling light behind its green baize cover; he listened to the wheels singing their monotonous song and imagined the shining tracks stringing events on their bright cord. The metal tracks joined land with land and life with life, and the thought brought him a sudden sense of being utterly at their mercy, at the mercy of people, and of circumstance: no matter what he said or did, he was powerless— powerless! He wondered whether that was the thought which troubled Gisele, and longed to ask her, but the sound of her crying held him motionless on his own bunk. He thought of Kanhya's baby and wondered whether the jackals had burrowed after the tiny body in its white cardboard box. He closed his eyes and saw the Fort, and then he thought of the soldiers who died there in some forgotten cause, blood bursting from their bodies and drying as he'd seen blood dry, swiftly in the famished dust. He felt that he was part of these mysterious events whose memory persisted into the present; the sensation became frightening, became unbearable, and he pressed his face to the window and saw the Indian sky alive with stars.

He had not intended to fall asleep, but he did, at last; and when he woke again the air tasted fresh on his lips. He rose and lowered the dash and peered out. The train had described a perfect arc and he could see the little engine puffing up a gradient through low-growing forests of dhak. The flowers were open, fiery among their pale silver leaves, and he knew that men came here to hunt tigers. But now all he could see were the flowering trees and little sandy openings and patches of plumed grass. Slowly the mountains materialized under his gaze, and then they came striding towards him out of the mist— towering, imperial. He lost them as they rose far above the angle of his vision and the train crept at a lowered speed under their shadow.

# 13

While Madame St Remy moved among her scorching fields and Father Sebastien and Mr Wall angled for crocodiles off the canal locks, Jacques sat behind his desk in the fifth standard classroom, waiting with bored longing for the dinner bell. He listened to his neighbour, the Raja of Johri, read aloud from a history of the Plantagenet kings. The Raja was the titular head of a tiny kingdom in the south-west, and his own ancestry was a matter of purest conjecture; but he accumulated learning as a parrot accumulates swear-words, and he loved to read and to write long sentences in English.

Jacques' thoughts were elsewhere. It was almost three months since he left Amritpore and came to St Matthew's College. Nostalgia had given way by degrees to the fascination which people and places always aroused, but of one thing he was quite certain: he detested St Matthew's and almost every one in it. Perhaps it was inevitable that he should find, in this heterogeneous collection of boys—white, native, and Eurasian—something essentially hostile to his own nature and his own way. On the day of his arrival they had ducked him in the great drinking cistern and almost drowned him. Jacques was not unprepared for what might lie in store for him; he'd listened while Mr Wall instructed Hardyal in the peculiarities of public-school behaviour, and Father Sebastien had dropped a few additional hints. Nevertheless, Jacques was not prepared for the ducking. For hours afterwards he'd brooded on this first violent affront to his youthful dignity, wondering what Hardyal would have thought, wondering whether the same outrage had been practised on his friend. No one had ever struck Jacques, no one had shouted at him, laughed at his clothes or sneered at his accent. Nor did he consider himself less of a man because of these deficiencies in his experience. He'd lived among adult human beings and friendship had come to him all too easily. Now he found himself forced to strike and to strike hard against strangers whom he'd come prepared to like. When, later, they approached him with overtures of reconciliation, he had nothing to say to them, and they went away disgruntled.

There were about two hundred boys at St. Matthew's; the school was run by a Catholic order of Irish Brothers, and from a distance Jacques rather admired this group of apple-cheeked men who looked like sportsmen and who joked and laughed a great deal while they strove to beat a semblance of scholarship into their charges. But if Jacques was no longer prepared to like he was more than prepared to hate, and it was not long before he found an object in his class-master, Brother Doyle. This man was unlike the other Brothers; he was lean and sallow, his features were coarse and his eyes like cold blue stones. Between Brother Doyle and Jacques there sprang an antipathy which, as the weeks passed, developed into outright antagonism.

Viewed from the perspective of St Matthew's, life at Amritpore recurred in a happy carefree glow. At St Matthew's there was no freedom, no privacy, no solitude. His letters were read, he moved in an inquisitorial atmosphere of study, prayer, pranks, and hostility. At night he slept in a long bleak dormitory with twenty-five other urchins before whom he was obliged to dress and undress, wash, brush his teeth. Sometimes he wondered whether all this was visited upon him by way of retribution for the death of the punkah coolie's baby.

Gisele's convent stood across the lake from St Matthew's, and on alternate Sundays Jacques was expected to visit his sister, although neither enjoyed these meetings. He would have liked to compare notes with Gisele but they were separated, now, by more than physical distance. Gisele adored her convent, and from Madame St Remy, Jacques learned that his sister enjoyed special privileges among the good Sisters. No, Gisele would have little interest or sympathy with his tribulations. On his rare Sunday visits their conversation was confined almost entirely to accounts of her studies, her devotions, her aspirations—all seemed dizzyingly beyond his reach or his desires. Once she had given him a letter and asked him to post it for her; turning it over in his hand, he saw that it was addressed to Aubrey Wall at Amritpore, but when he was leaving Gisele suddenly asked for the letter back. She had changed her mind about sending it—then.

After a long silence a letter came to Jacques from Hardyal who was spending his midsummer holidays in Sussex. 'We are on the sea and when the tide goes out we can hardly see it—it lies like a piece of wet string under the sky, and the sands come to life with very small crabs and things. I now find that I can swim quite well. We ride when I stay with Mr Wall's cousins, on the Downs. I wish you were here. In school some of the fellows call me 'Wog'. A Wog is a kind of black doll with button eyes and hair of wool. I do not think that I look like a Wog. I wish you were here.'

The original occupant of the seat which Jacques had usurped now returned and Jacques moved down the aisle to a seat at right angles from the prodigal whose profile was sometimes visible between all the others. Jacques was too self-absorbed to pay much attention to John Macbeth who, like the Raja of Jhori and a few others, was lucky enough to be a day scholar. But in a little while his sensibility registered a change in the atmosphere—something fresh, humorous, singular, animated it and attracted his attention. He drew his breath and cast about him for a cause and a reason, and immediately encountered a pair of grey, incurious eyes. As their eyes met, Macbeth smiled. That was as far as their acquaintance progressed for the time being. As suddenly as he had appeared Macbeth disappeared, and a note was brought by a mounted orderly from Colonel Macbeth, to say that his son was again indisposed and would not attend class for two or three days. Funny, reflected Jacques; Macbeth didn't look in the least delicate. Now that indefinable Something which had stirred this stale

and defeated air vanished once more, and he found himself staring at
the empty seat across the aisle and trying to refashion the shape of a
neat brown head and a sharply tilted profile.

A week passed and Macbeth returned, but still they did not meet.
Perhaps a mutual attraction interposed its queer barrier; at any rate
Jacques was still too disillusioned and suspicious to venture an
overture. What was more, he thought he recognized in Macbeth a trait
which Madame St Remy would instantly have stigmatized as
*formidable*, even *sinister*. Just as there are certain plants and certain
animals which enjoy a peculiar invulnerability, Macbeth was held in
obvious respect by his fellows; even Brother Doyle treated him
differently. Jacques himself was in no mood to take chances, and
between Macbeth and himself there grew a self-conscious reserve—
they went out of their way to ignore each other; but before the logic of
their relation could declare itself Macbeth disappeared once more, and
once more the mounted orderly appeared with the by now familiar
crested note for Brother Doyle.

'What's the matter with Macbeth?' Jacques so far demeaned himself
to inquire of his neighbour, the Raja.

'They say he has worms.'

'No, fits,' said someone else.

The situation between Brother Doyle and Jacques was becoming
steadily worse. Jacques suffered spasms of terror, fear of the Brother,
fear of some invisible force which operated against him through
Brother Doyle and perhaps without Brother Doyle's awareness. Hanif
would have said that the man possessed the Evil Eye and certainly
there were moments when Jacques was sure of this. As for the rest of
the class, the unequal struggle provided them with a happy release
from boredom. They had a taste of Jacques' spirit, now they watched
with vengeful fascination while Brother Doyle dealt with that spirit.
Jacques' accent came in for special attention: 'This is not a French
lesson, Remy. If you want to show off your abilities as a linguist, save
them for Brother Vincent.' Or it was: 'Remy, have you filled the
inkpots? Ah, I forgot! St Remy. Naturally you can't be expected to fill
inkpots.'

One day the nagging had gone on for the better part of an hour and
class waited feverishly for something to happen. Jacques looked as
though a touch would shatter him, and perhaps Brother Doyle
recognized the extent to which he'd succeeded, for he played the
dogged little fish to a standstill, then prepared to let him go. Jacques
had been summoned to the dais and stood now in full view of the
class. Brother Doyle smiled at him with sudden radiance. 'Very well,
that will be all. You may go back to your seat, Remy.'

Jacques did not obey at once; he lifted his head and gave his class-master a long, steady stare. Brother Doyle flushed.

'Wait a minute. What was it you were about to say?'

Jacques was silent.

'Did you hear my question, Remy?'

Silence grew in Jacques, it obsessed him.

'Remy!'

The windows sparkled and Jacques could see butterflies fluttering in the school gardens.

'Will you answer me, Remy?'

The others craned forward as Jacques' silence fed theirs, fed their silence as a spring feeds a lake, increasing with every second, deepening, involving them all in its conspiracy. But Brother Doyle had no intention of drowning in it himself. He struck Jacques a light, glancing blow. Reeling, the boy caught the edge of his master's desk and his fingers closed on a round glass inkpot which stood there. What happened then happened as inevitably as the arc of a reflex—his hand flew upward and the inkpot crashed against the blackboard, missing Brother Doyle by a few inches.

Then Jacques fled, down the aisle between the desks, and out through the great doors across the terrace. He fled as a deer flees, or a colt. The terrace ended in a steep drop which he took in his stride, flying through the air for an intoxicating second which ended in a bed of bracken. Through this he scuttled, twisting and turning until he found himself on the little path which ran below the playgrounds to the hill road below. He had no idea of where he was going or what he intended to do, but he was sure that there could be no more St Matthew's for him.

The path along which he was half running, half walking, dipped between the rhododendrons to the road below, and sauntering towards him, carrying a butterfly net, was John Macbeth. They came to an abrupt halt, doubt and suspicion drawing a resemblance between them. But some genius for gauging situations must always have distinguished Macbeth; he shot a swift glance up and down the road, then said:

'Come on, I know a place where they can't find us.'

They scrambled up the path, Macbeth in the lead. Here the trees were heavy and their feet made scarcely a sound on the leafy ground. The school was out of sight, they heard a voice or two in the distance, and the singing of a hillman far down the road.

Macbeth paused, glanced at Jacques over his shoulder, then plunged down the hillside into a mass of ferns. They were now amongst an outcropping of rocks where purple orchids clung to the moss blanket;

here, suddenly, Macbeth vanished as though jaws had swallowed him. His voice reached Jacques from a green dimness at his feet: 'Jump!'

Jacques jumped, landing beside Macbeth in a sort of dell through which a little stream rustled on its way to the lake. The ferns had closed over their heads and the sun filtered down in splinters of light; there was heat, and a smell of leaf mould and flowers. Macbeth crouched beside the stream and drank, and Jacques crouched beside him, plunging his face into the water. Then they sat back on their heels, embarrassment engulfing both. Macbeth took the initiative:

'I often come here when I'm fed up. No one else knows about it.'

'How did you happen to find it?'

'By accident one day when I was chasing a moth.'

Jacques saw the butterfly net propped against the wall of their den. 'I have a collection at home.'

The ice was broken and they made themselves comfortable. Macbeth removed his hat and took a butterfly from under the sweatband. As Jacques examined the exquisite creature remembrance took him by the throat. His birthday . . . Hanif taking a butterfly from his cap and laying it on the dressing-table. His mother, Hardyal, Amritpore. . . . He laid his head on his knees and stayed motionless, holding on to his tears.

Macbeth waited. He recognized homesickness when he saw it, and he had, from the very moment of setting eyes on Jacques, liked him and determined to know him. In a little while the paroxysm had passed and Jacques sat up. He smiled waveringly at his new friend. 'I thought you were supposed to be ill.'

'I was, but I'm all right now.'

'Jhori said you had worms.'

'He's the one that has worms!'

'Well, but what can it be, then? You're absent so often.'

The tacit admission that his absence had been noticed and regretted thawed Macbeth completely. "If I tell you, do you swear not to give me away?'

'I swear!'

'I just take Cascara.'

'Cascara?'

'It's quite harmless, but it makes you go to the bathroom like anything.'

'Cascara,' repeated Jacques, entranced. 'Fancy!'

'At first my family kept sending for old Das, the assistant surgeon. He gave me things to stop it and I had to go back to school. It doesn't worry them as much as it used to, and I'm very careful not to take too much at a time.'

Jacques gazed at him in admiration. Then Macbeth said suddenly:
'But what about you? Shouldn't you be in class?'
'I should, but I threw an inkpot at Doyle.'
'What?'
'An inkpot.'
'Heavens! Did you hit him?'
'No, worse luck.'
'Heavens'. It was Macbeth's turn to stare in wonder: 'You did, actually? Then you'll probably be expelled.'
Jacques was startled. Somehow the thought of expulsion had never entered his head, he had not really thought of anything except blind escape. He began to see, now, some of the angles of his predicament.
'They can't very well expel me if I don't go back.'
Macbeth was frowning. 'I say, you could put the fear of God into old Doyle if you liked. You could write him a letter—I'd post it for you—saying that you'd decided to commit suicide.' His grey eyes glittered with excitement. 'You could leave your shoes and coat on the shore near the lake. Someone would be sure to find them. Just think what it would do to that—' And he used an expressive native epithet.
Jacques revelled in the thought for several seconds, then cold reason intervened. 'What would be the use? In the end they'd find out that I hadn't committed suicide.'
'Yes. I suppose they would.' Macbeth relinquished the idea with evident reluctance. 'Well then, what are you going to do? You're in a proper fix, you know.'
They were silent as little by little the ominous and reasonable world intruded its logic upon them. 'Of course,' Macbeth said finally, 'you might be let off with the most terrific bumming.'
'Bumming?'
'Thrashing. Duane, the head, always gives the important ones.'
Jacques turned white. 'No, I couldn't . . .' He jumped to his feet. 'I couldn't . . . couldn't stand that.'
Macbeth stared. 'Lots of the chaps have had it. Is isn't so awful, you know. Better than being expelled.'
'No!' Jacques' reassurance had vanished completely, and Macbeth rose too, startled out of his complacence. 'Look here, I don't mean to say that you *will* get a bumming. As a matter of fact Duane hardly ever thrashes any one. It's only for chasing after the Convent girls or for stealing and things like that.'
Jacques was not listening. He seemed to feel once more the grasping hands of enemies when they hurled him into the tank and held him under the water until his breath was ready to die in his lungs. But those enemies, at least, had been his equals. How could he expect to

stand up to giants like Brothers Duane and Doyle? He had heard about those public thrashings—they would take down his trousers and whip him with a leather strap, and yet, it was not really the prospect of pain which frightened him. He remembered something that had happened a long time ago in Amritpore when he and Hardyal watched Aubrey Wall thrash a groom for stealing the horses' grain. It was not a spectacle which either he or Hardyal had ever been able to forget. The man offered no resistance as Wall beat him almost senseless with a riding crop. Jacques remembered his own feelings as he watched—feelings of terror, of queer, creeping excitement that was not wholly disagreeable. He'd even laughed rather hysterically when the groom's turban fell off, but Hardyal had turned away, shivering. Ah, to be beaten oneself, to submit to a beating—he couldn't stand it, he couldn't, he couldn't!

He stared at Macbeth. 'I'm going back to ask them to expel me.'

'What?'

'Yes. I won't let them touch me. I'd rather be expelled.'

He turned and scrambled up the side of the little dell and ran down the path towards the school. Again as when he'd bolted half an hour ago he had no very clear plan of action: he merely followed the dictate of his blood, which warned him that anything was better than indignity. There was still an hour before the class ended, and no one had been sent in pursuit of him. Round the end of the buildings and across the gravelled yard he ran, under the bored eyes of a few strolling Seniors.

Brother Doyle was standing beside the blackboard as Jacques walked down the aisle to the dais and faced his class-master. A stir went round the room, but no one spoke as Brother Doyle looked at this single envelope of flesh and blood.

'I came back to ask you to expel me. If you try to—to touch me I shall kill you, or kill myself. But you can expel me, if you want to.'

The saving grace to which his vows and his black robe fully entitled him, now came to Brother Doyle's rescue—and perhaps also to Jacques'. The Brother laid his hand on the boy's steamy forehead. 'Go to the infirmary and tell Nurse I sent you. You're to stay there until tomorrow.'

When Jacques had gone, Brother Doyle addressed the stupefied class:

'We shall hear no more of this incident. It is finished. I think that our young friend had just a touch of fever.'

# 14

A pair of Scotch missionaries struggling over the final hill of their long journey were, it is said, the first white men to look down on Gambul's bright blue lake. That was many years before Victoria became Empress, but news of the latter event and of all the ferocious events which had preceded it were long in reaching this shadowy crypt set half-way up the ladder of the Himalayas. It was in May that the missionaries came, with their noses like pointer-dogs lifted unerringly in the direction of strayed souls. They retrieved a few, although competition must have been rather one-sided, a native faith having got there first.

On the north-western shore of the lake, a Hindu temple rounded itself like a fat pearl on the rim of a blue shell, and the missionaries who pitched their tent at a discreet distance went to bed with the sound of conches in their ears and awoke to the same summons. There were no real houses, merely huts of mud and stone with grass roofs, and little paths beaten clean by generations of bare feet. People kept goats and sheep and planted a few crops on their rough terraces; they fished from rafts or waded with spears after the mahseer whose shapes the missionaries could see when they gazed down from the nearby cliffs. No one molested the newcomers although theirs were the first white faces to appear in the region. The hill people were too busy with their own affairs and the temple priest too preoccupied with his to indulge in inquisitive attitudes. The missionaries spoke only English and the natives spoke only Pahari, so a braying of temple conches, the plangent voice of the sambhur, and the short grunting cough of leopards were for a long time the only argument heard in Gambul. There was room, then, not only for the houses of men but for an architecture which would house their ideas. Sambhur and leopard watched the builders from afar, and in a little while strange reverberations disturbed the ancient solitude and pealed echoes from the hills. The missionaries had brought firearms and they lived well off the pheasants which flew and roosted everywhere. Then everything wild, everything lively and incurious, lifted its head and retreated a step. New and restless gods had arrived just in time to praise a vision of rhododendron flowers shed by the wind, floating above the dark shallows of the lake, and to bring a bundle of flower-tinted feathers hurtling out of the sky.

But all this was a long time ago. Years exercised a sort of molecular action and before Queen Victoria was dead Gambul had gathered to itself much of the substance of a self-conscious civilization. No one remembers what happened to the missionaries. More came after them. Paradise retreated another step or two but the idea of it remained captive in several churches and within the original undisturbed temple on the shore. When men had put their notions and their families safely under cover they set out after fresh adventure and further problems. Leopards and deer, birds and beetles were, unknown to themselves, invested with identities in Latin; rocks acquired dynasties, trees assumed titles, and Paradise faded—mute and intestate.

Colonel Macbeth had built his house on a speck of Empire which once supported only the missionaries' tent. He pushed away the deodar forest and laid out his English garden. A plum tree flowered suddenly among the primeval ferns, ivy swarmed up the north wall, a chastened sunlight distilled the perfume from great purple pools of heliotrope. Whenever the Colonel returned from his campaigns he discovered some patch of earth which might be persuaded to yield something better than stones or lizards.

The house itself was large and two-storied, and stood on a small hill flanked by larger hills. Here, all through the day, cicadas made music and fat moths hung damply beside their discarded chrysalises. Behind the house the hillside fell in terrace after terrace and one could see, through a cleft in the farther hills, a side view of the plains two hundred miles away. Among the grasses and rocks of the lower terrace Jacques and Macbeth lay, resting their exhausted bones after a long afternoon in the sun. It was a Saturday and the morning classes had ended with the Raja of Jhori stammering his way through English history. Today was a half-holiday, theirs to waste as they would.

Jacques had leave to spend the week-end with his new friends, and the boys had exchanged butterfly nets for catapults; each wore on his hat the bright wings of some murdered bird. Far below them the monsoon clouds were gathering, leagues of vapour shaped by wind into immense and intricate architecture. Wherever a warmer current of air pierced this mass, the boys had a glimpse of the lower hills, the thickets of the Terai jungle and beyond them the tense level of the plains. Somewhere in its indistinguishable patterns lay Amritpore where people were dissolving in their own sweat, where their minds tightened like wet bowstrings. But for Jacques Amritpore was already retiring to a limbo out of which in his decreasing moods of loneliness he plucked an occasional bitter fruit. His mother wrote that her foreman Boodrie had come down with dysentery and as a consequence she saw no prospect of escape to the hills until later, perhaps not at all. Father Sebastien, too, had been ill; the Browns had gone to England, Aubrey Wall sometimes called to ask after the children, and she had seen Ganpat Rai, who spoke of Hardyal's life in England. Hanif had boils, which made him irritable and sulky. Never mind, the summer would pass, and early in December Jacques and Gisele would come back to Amritpore.

Mrs Lyttleton had not written, but Jacques did not expect that she would, for he remembered her declaring once that pen and ink were poor substitutes for flesh and blood. He was, however, learning to draw the past close to him, to turn over the hoarded occasions and to ask himself just what it was, now, that he wanted. Did he really yearn for Amritpore? To return and find Hardyal gone, himself cut off from Mrs Lyttleton and confined to the companionship of his mother and Father Sebastien? To go back—to June's white heat and a long-drawn existence inside the house under a flagging punkah, reading for the hundredth time *The Count of Monte Cristo*, or arranging his butterflies, or riding along in the early mornings and late afternoons? The truth was that for Jacques life at St Matthew's had taken a turn for the better. The Macbeths, of course, were the deciding element in this. John had brought his new friend home one week-end after the episode of the flung inkpot and had presented him to his parents. Jacques found Colonel Macbeth to be a tall, angular soldier with drooping moustaches and pale eyes like his son's. The Colonel combined a passion for soldiering with a passion for gardening, and it was difficult for Jacques to picture this gentle giant killing anything larger than an aphis or a caterpillar.

Mrs Macbeth was a tiny woman with big eyes and numerous golden freckles. She fluttered from room to room, from house to garden, rather like one of the moths which her son was for ever pursuing, or like the little bird which he brought down with his catapult. For Jacques, busily engaged in building his secret honeycomb and storing up his secret honey, life at the Macbeths was as far removed from the uncouth existence at St Matthew's as St Matthew's was remote from life at home in Amritpore. With the Macbeths he had discovered a different charm, something which he was later to define as character grown out of the accumulation of history at its deepest point. From the very beginning he detected in it a resemblance to another character which he knew very well: a kinship to that authority which was larger than men. For the Macbeths this authority was history—it was, essentially, English history. For Madame St Remy it was French *esprit* and French *espoir* inescapably merged with God. Whatever it may have been for Colonel Macbeth's sepoys in their curled beards, their fringed turbans, and gold-frogged chapkans, was not for any one to say—not yet. History had not accumulated to a point where they, or Jacques, were finally to stand and say it.

In the meantime there were gay happenings in the big house up there on the hill; much playing of the piano and singing of Braga's Serenade by Mrs Macbeth and any one who would sing with her. There was a great deal of coming and going of the younger officers from the garrison, some as mild as milk, others as fierce as wart-hogs. Macbeth was himself the centre of much of this attention, which had the effect of making him a possessive and jealous friend—lacking in generosity, but poised, vain, and intelligent. He hated to hear others praised, something which Jacques had discovered at the very beginning of their friendship when he spoke of Hardyal.

'Hardyal?' Macbeth frowned.

'His father is a barrister in Amritpore. A—a very enlightened man,' added Jacques, not quite sure what that might mean, though he'd heard the term often enough.

'Ah, *educated*!' Macbeth shrugged. 'Father says that the educated native is worse than all the others put together.'

'Well, what about your father's soldiers—doesn't he like them?'

'They are different. They are men.'

Jacques tightened. 'So are Hardyal and Ganpat Rai men. So is my bearer Hanif a man.'

Macbeth replied coldly: 'There's no use in sticking up for natives. Sooner or later they let you down.'

'So do a lot of white people. Those beasts at school, for instance.'

'How would you have liked it if they'd been natives?'

'Don't be silly. No native has ever touched me.'

'If it wasn't for the Army, they might.'

They argued, now, as children argue—and as they had heard their elders argue. Jacques stammered: 'Well, what about the Mutiny? They gave us a run for our money then, didn't they? And they nearly beat us, too.'

Macbeth's smile became tense. 'A lot of howling niggers—beat *us*? I suppose your Hardyal, for instance, could beat *me*?'

It was a challenge, but Jacques missed it. Quite suddenly he felt the question to hold an interest above and beyond his friend's vanity. Could Hardyal have beaten Macbeth? Would he have tried? He thought of his Indian friend, slender and very strong. When they wrestled Hardyal could throw him on his back, but in boxing Jacques had the advantage. The argument with Macbeth ended there, and on this Saturday afternoon the air was clear between them as they lay propped on their elbows and watched the great clouds foregather. Sounds reached them strained by distance or magnified on the nearer winds—the high note of a bugle-call from the barracks and from the road directly below the guttural voices of Bhotiyals driving borax-laden sheep down to the foothills.

Macbeth removed his hat and examined the plumage of a Paradise flycatcher which adored it. 'That was a damned good shot I made.'

Jacques agreed, rather sleepily.

'Once,' said Macbeth, glancing at him sideways, 'once I killed a pigeon on the wing.'

'Jove! '

'And once on the plains when I was quail-shooting with Father, I got a right and left which he missed.'

'Did he like that?'

'Oh, he was sporting about it. But don't mention it before him, will you? I'd hate him to think that I was bragging.'

After a brief pause Macbeth said: 'Wonder what it feels like to kill a man?'

Jacques replied that he had no idea. 'Has your father killed a man?'

'Hundreds.' For Macbeth numbers were infinite. 'Only don't mention that I told you. He's frightfully reserved about such things.'

Jacques was, by now, fairly accustomed to these emendations.

'I dare say,' Macbeth continued, 'that some time I may have to kill men myself.'

'Good Lord, why?'

'If I go into the Army, like Father.'

'I thought we were both going to be taxidermists!'

'I haven't quite made up my mind.'

Slowly, the clouds travelled up the mountainside and the retreating sun bathed them in colour. Presently they must collide with the higher peaks, shatter, and rain down to the earth. Already from a single escaped cloudlet directly over their heads, the boys felt the first hard, cold drops. Macbeth got up and stood on the edge of the terrace, stretching his arms. 'Look!' he cried. His shadow was flung far across the sea of vapour and as Jacques rose and stood beside him they stared in awe at their two slight bodies extending and growing ominous in the freakish light.

Macbeth exulted. 'We're huge! Look at us! Look at us! We're miles!'

Jacques rose on his toes and watched the elastic air add a cubit to his stature. Were his head and shoulders at this moment in Amritpore? Down there on the plains could those crawling fleas look up and see the dark, gigantic angels?

More rain fell and from the pulsing mass below them a mutter rose, a vein of light played and vanished. The boys turned and scuttled for the shelter of the house.

# 15

That evening the Colonel and his lady were dining at Government House. Mrs Macbeth had spent the greater part of the afternoon in bed, with the curtains drawn, and later when Jacques saw her emerge from an arbour of still, white orchids into the golden light of the drawing-room, he gasped. She looked ethereal, hardly human, reminding him more than ever of some rare and fragile moth.

'Do you like me, Jacques?' she asked, and tilted her head so the tiny jewels in her hair gave off sparks of fire. He could not have said whether he liked her or not, whether she pleased or frightened him; her femininity was too complete and self-sufficient for his understanding.

She turned to her son. 'Do *you* like me, darling?'

'Yes—except for your earrings.'

'My earrings?' She raised her hand to touch one, an emerald giving off its strenuous fires. 'Why don't you like my earrings?'

He stared at her with concentration. 'I don't quite know. Whenever you wear them you look as if you were going away and never coming back.' At once Jacques saw what he meant; the earrings changed her expression, her whole air, they transformed her china delicacy into something dubious and disturbing.

She had flushed at her son's remark, but now she laughed. 'Silly! These are very precious. When I'm dead you shall give them to your wife.'

He replied coldly: 'I won't have a wife.'

'No? But I thought you intended to marry your cousin, Elizabeth.'

Conscious of his friend's embarrassment, Jacques turned away, glancing as he did so at a portrait which stood on the piano; it was a photograph framed in silver of a young girl, and now her eyes seemed to meet his and to hold them in a close and subtle glance.

Mrs Macbeth smiled from one face to the other. 'Go along,' she said. 'Both of you. Help your father tie his kummerbund, John.'

They left her for the Colonel's dressing-room which smelled of leather and brilliantine. Jacques perched unobtrusively in a corner and watched the Colonel's servant helping his master to dress, while John Macbeth lounged round the room touching things and asking questions. The Colonel, in blue trousers with a red stripe, and a stiff white shirt, stood before the mirror tying his little bow tie. Behind him the servant was carefully smoothing the starched collar of a mess jacket, and suddenly Jacques found himself remembering Father

Sebastien vesting himself for the Mass. First came the amice, then the alb. . . .

The Colonel turned, lifting his arms, and his son wound the crimson sash round the Colonel's lean waist. The cincture . . . ('Gird me, O Lord!') then the maniple and the stole. The Colonel clutched his stiff cuffs in his fists and turned his back on the servant, who slid the jacket deftly over the extended arms and eased it up the straight back.

'Receive the priestly garment, for the Lord is powerful to increase in you love and perfection . . .'

Jacques felt the Colonel's eye on him. 'What are you thinking about, young 'un?'

Jacques came to. 'Nothing, sir.' But he had been thinking of the sacred corn of the Brahmins, of amulets containing passages of the Koran, carried by some Moslems, and of the copper bangle worn on the left wrist of the Sikhs.

The Colonel was dressed at last—booted, spurred, armed against a world unarmed, his own impressiveness like his wife's beauty, a shield between them and the devil. Jacques felt that he himself had absorbed much of this splendour: he felt the sparkle sift down into him, lighting him like phosphor.

The rain had stopped. A rickshaw with hood raised waited, its runners in regimental livery squatting on the gravel beside it. A groom was walking the Colonel's horse to and fro under the trees.

Mrs Macbeth embraced the children. 'Goodnight, my darlings!'

They had gone at last, lighted by a runner with a lantern, and their passage glittered away like a swarm of fireflies down the road under the trees. The boys turned back to the house, all theirs, now. The sense of liberation went to their heads, and Macbeth rushed to the piano. 'I'll be Mother's friend Mrs Sykes,' he announced. 'You can be Captain Ponsonby. Here goes!'

Neither he nor Jacques could play or sing a note between them. Macbeth brought his hands down on the keys in a frightful discord and Jacques struck an attitude beside him.

'O qua—li mi ri-sve—glia-no . . .' Jacques bellowed after the style of Captain Ponsonby.

'Dol-cis-si-mi con-cen—ti non li o-di O . . .' shrieked Macbeth.

They were applauded from several doors by the grinning servants, and from her silver frame on the piano Macbeth's cousin Bertie Wood seemed to smile and to listen.

# 16

The school year ended in December. After Christmas Macbeth came down to Amritpore to stay with the St Remys. Madame was curious to meet her son's new friend, but she found little to reassure her. Macbeth's precocious self-possession and rather lordly manner were an offence in her eyes, for she read in him every vice which she held as being peculiar to the English. What was worse, he was not Catholic and his influence on Jacques might lead to almost anything. But happiness in her son's return tided Madame over her disappointment in his choice of a friend, and she exerted herself to be gracious. During meals she discoursed at length on the charms of her estates at Nonancourt, of Jacques' ancestors, of her own, and of the prosperous future of indigo. The children listened respectfully as Hanif handed round the silver dishes and interrupted the conversation with comments on the food and reminders to Jacques of this or that event, past and to come. Macbeth was cautious and slightly puzzled, but he betrayed nothing. He had taken an instant dislike to Madame and to Gisele and looked with suspicion on Hanif, for he was not accustomed to servants who behaved as though they were members of the family. Living with the St Remys was like living in another country; their mixture of prosperity and piety fascinated Macbeth, for although it had a foreign character he felt that it was a character which merged more steeply in this Indian setting than did his own or his parents'. Except when he was alone with Jacques, conversation with the St Remys struck him as being dull and strained. This was not like being at home where people said what they liked and usually like what they said. Jacques and Hanif seemed to be the only people who really laughed, and to Macbeth there was something wrong about that also, for one does not hobnob with one's servants.

'You don't understand,' said Jacques afterwards. 'Hanif isn't exactly a servant. My mother adopted him when his parents died in the great famine. He's been with us since he was five years old.'

'Is that any reason why he could give you a shove when we were leaving the dining-room?'

'Oh, that? Well, I did step on his foot.'

'Give them an inch and they'll take an ell,' said Macbeth, quoting something he'd heard from a disgruntled elder. 'And why on earth does Hanif cover himself with *scent*?'

Jacques was reflecting: 'It's a different life. Macbeth's life is the Army, all cut and dried, where no one dreams of going beyond certain limits. Every one has his appointed place, they don't have to make

allowances or to try hard to understand anything. For us it's different
. . . for us this means home. This is our country. Hanif is our friend.'
But although Jacques felt these things keenly enough he was unable to
translate them into a language which would be acceptable to his
friend. Macbeth liked his own world and had no intention of
exchanging it for another—faced with such a prospect he became more
than ever himself, hard, clear, and assured. He found the factory far
more exciting than Madame's household, but Jacques, though pleased
by his friend's interest, suffered the old revulsion as soon as he entered
the gates and smelled the acid dye. Boodrie bustled round the two
boys, pushing the coolies out of his way, cursing them when they were
slow to move.

'It belonged to my father,' Jacques explained to Macbeth. 'I suppose
it will belong to me eventually.' He looked depressed at the thought.
Boodrie gave a short laugh. 'If the bowels don't fall out of indigo in
the meantime. In which case, who will pay for the boilers, I'd like to
know?'

'Aren't they paid for?' inquired Jacques, surprised.

'Oh my! With last year's *gaud* still lying unsold in the Calcutta
godowns?'

'Then shall we plant as much this year as we did last year?'

'Madame says yes, but it depends on whether that old bitch Mrs
Lyttleton will sell her chunna fields.'

It was late afternoon when the boys left the factory and took a short
cut across the grounds towards the house. Jacques was smarting under
the foreman's insult to his old friend; he had longed to make a fierce
retort, but Macbeth's presence restrained him. Now he said with a
sudden air of desperation: 'Would you like to call on Mrs Lyttleton?'

'The old bitch?'

'She's my friend. I'm going to see her. You can come if you like.'

He had waited ever since his return from St Matthew's, waited
perhaps unconsciously for something like this to happen, for some spur
to his love and his loyalty.

Macbeth looked at him in surprise. 'You've never mentioned her
before.'

'I can't explain, exactly, but I'm not supposed to know her.'

'But doesn't your mother know her?'

Jacques hesitated. 'They don't like each other. It doesn't matter, does
it? She has always been my friend and Hardyal's.'

The thought of forbidden fruit made Macbeth's face light up. 'I say,
is she pretty, or something?'

'I don't know about that. Let's go and see her.'

They sauntered unobtrusively in the direction of the road, taking pot-shots at jays and hoopoes on the way. Macbeth's catapult hung from his hand as they passed between the sandstone pillars of the garden; there, perched enticingly on a branch, was a small green parrot. Macbeth brought it down with a perfect shot just as Mrs Lyttleton came down the steps of her house to greet them. She rushed forward and picked up the crumpled bunch of feathers, turning a face of fury upon the murderer. 'How could you?'

He recoiled, and she turned to Jacques. 'Couldn't you have stopped him?'

Jacques explained incoherently that he'd not had time and that upon his word his friend intended no harm. Macbeth, flushed and frightened, looked on with a defiant air, then pulled himself together and apologized. Mrs Lyttleton listened grimly, stroking the dead bird and twisting the tiny silver bracelet on one of its feet. 'I'd had him for years,' she said at last, bitterly. 'He knew my name, and always greeted me by shouting 'Laura, Laura,' when he saw me. He almost died last year when he had the moult, but I saved him. I gave him brandy and did him up in flannel and he slept beside my pillow. Now you've killed him. How could you? Oh, how could you?'

Jacques trembled. 'He didn't mean to . . . he just didn't know it was a tame parrot. Did you, Macbeth?'

Macbeth mumbled something, and Mrs Lyttleton lifted her fierce gaze to his. 'Macbeth? Where do you come from?'

He told her, and her face softened a little. 'There was a Macbeth who was killed at Kabul, with Major Cavagnari.'

'That was my uncle.'

'Ah!' Tension lessened. 'That Macbeth had a brother; as I remember. Tall, fair?'

'He is my father,' said Macbeth, secretly wondering how he might gain possession of the dead parrot and remove the offence from her sight.

Mrs Lyttleton said reflectively: 'I remember the Macbeth brothers when they were young—very young. But heavens! There were so many, and they have all vanished.'

She smiled faintly. 'There, I forgive you, you little brute. But first we must bury Arthur.'

They paused beside a weedy flower-bed and the boys knelt, scraping a hole with their hands. They worked diligently and with intense seriousness while she looked on; then, the grave completed, Jacques laid Arthur in it and covered him with earth. Macbeth toyed with the idea of plucking a flower for the hallowed spot, but a revived self-respect intervened. They rose, brushing off their knees, and Mrs Lyttleton led them up the driveway to the veranda. She put her hand through Jacques' arm. 'I knew you had come home. Now it will be like old times, except for Hardyal's absence.'

As they reached the veranda Macbeth stood in respectful contemplation of the stuffed heads. 'Someone *did* kill things,' he observed, pointedly.

'My husband was a great sportsman, but not given to knocking off little birds with a stone.'

'My father has a lot of horns too.' And he added, generously— 'Though not as many as your husband.'

She gave a sudden laugh. 'It's all a matter of luck, my dear.' over their heads. Then she conducted them into the house where canaries fluttered and a new generation of dogs and cats frisked over the tattered matting. Macbeth had never seen such a house; it smelled rather like a zoo, and it was crammed with weapons and trophies of all kinds. She showed them the underground zenana where the original owner had hidden his womenfolk when Amritpore was stormed by the Moslem hordes, and the torture chamber where he had practised on his captured enemies. These ancient events seemed to have left their echoes among the damp walls and crevices, and the precise English voices sent them fluttering and whispering into dim corners, and roused a sonorous protest from the heavy stones.

When the boys had seen all that there was to be seen, Mrs Lyttleton led them back to her favourite corner in the veranda, where her servant brought them refreshments. Macbeth stared when his hostess lighted a cigarette; it was the first time he had seen a woman smoke and the spectacle rather scandalized him. She caught his eye and laughed. 'Have one yourself. They're quite mild.'

Both boys had smoked before, making themselves ill on cheap native tobacco. Now they lighted up and lolled in their chairs like old roués while Mrs Lyttleton told them stories of what had happened in Amritpore during the past few months. Like most people who live much alone, she loved to talk, and like most children Jacques and Macbeth loved to listen. Now she recounted the story of a dacoity at Ramdatta's village, when thieves broke through the wall of Ramdatta's house, beat Ramdatta's servant to death with a brass pot, and escaped with much booty. The police gave chase, and the thieves took to the trees in a big mango grove. It was a dark night, and they bided their time until the constables with their high-caste inspector tracked them down—then they all excreted into their hands and rained the foul volley down upon the lordly heads in the darkness below. The policemen all fled in disorder, and the dacoits were still at large.

There was another story about the Assistant Magistrate's horse. A thief crept into the stable and burrowing under the straw and litter, managed to loosen the wooden peg to which the beast was tethered. But the horse stirred, wakening the groom who slept beside the door; he rose and finding the peg loose drove it in again with a mallet—right through the extended hand of the thief, who remained motionless. Then the groom returned to his slumbers and the thief, using his good hand, freed himself and rode away on the horse. He was caught later and given a stiff sentence, a fate deplored by Mrs Lyttleton, who admired courage and resource even among thieves.

She talked on and on, and the boys listened, forgetful of time. Shadows lay down on the overgrown garden, and the graves under the loquat trees shone in the waning light. Presently her slovenly servant, Jalal, appeared with his prayer mat, which he spread towards the west. They watched him remove his shoes and prostrate himself three times, crying upon Allah, and they knew that all over Amritpore men were praying like this, with their faces towards the setting sun.

When at last the boys had finished their cigarettes they rose, and Mrs Lyttleton walked with them to the gates. She had apparently forgotten about the parrot, and no one made any allusion to it as they passed the little raw spot in the ground where Arthur lay. When she bade them goodbye she kissed them both lightly, and Macbeth received, as others had received before him, a sense of warmth, an impression that she must, at one time, have been beautiful.

# 17

They rode to the Fort, and standing beside the sentry-box where last year Jacques had stood with Hardyal, Macbeth stared across the plain and made a sudden exultant gesture of his arms, as though he sought to embrace the landscape and everything it contained. 'Funny, when you come to think of it. . . .'

'What's funny?' Jacques had found a snakeskin and wore it round his neck like a scarf.

'That this should be ours. We won it—just a handful of us against the whole boiling lot. Imagine!'

Jacques watched the thin, nervous face with its burning eyes. Macbeth's intense possessiveness in such matters always astonished him.

'Perhaps,' Jacques suggested slyly, 'Perhaps someone will come along and take it away again, some day.'

'Not now, it's too late and we're too strong.' He always used the imperial *we*. 'Father says that if they had wanted to a little while ago they could have risen and polished us off. And what could we have done?'

'Well,' persisted Jacques, 'what could we do now?'

'Finish *them* off!'

'There are still more of them than there are of us.'

'But they're not armed as they used to be. Father says we must see that what happened in the Mutiny never happens again.' But Macbeth looked as if he would not be very sorry if 'it' did happen again, for he was in a warlike mood, and the Fort with its ruins and its reminders had fired his imagination.

They watched goats grazing down in the moat, they listened to the doves, and Jacques felt at peace with himself and with the world. A letter had come to him from Hardyal, yesterday's visit to Mrs Lyttleton had passed undetected by his family, and last night Aubrey Wall had come back to dinner and had promised to take the boys hunting black buck. That night when his mother came to kiss him goodnight Jacques had put his arms around her. 'Maman, have the copper boilers been paid for?'

She stared at him in surprise. 'What do you mean, darling?'

'Boodrie said something about their not being paid for.'

She laughed. 'Don't you understand that investments like that can't be paid for at once? They will be, of course, eventually.'

He hesitated, then said in a low voice: 'Unless the bottom falls out of indigo.'

Her surprise gave way to uneasiness. 'Where did you hear that, Jacques?'

'Oh, I don't know. But if that did happen we'd be—we'd be ruined, wouldn't we?' He'd brooded on it, visualizing strange nightmares. Madame St Remy touched his hair. 'Don't you trust me, Jacques?'

It was his turn to be surprised and he flushed a little under her pained glance. 'Trust you? Yes, of course. That wasn't what I meant. . . . I meant . . . I wondered . . .'

She bent and kissed him. 'I shall be glad when you have grown up, when we can work together, and I can rely on you. That will be my reward.'

Her sweetness, her air of strength, restored his sense of security, and it was from this sense that he now felt equal to challenging Macbeth. 'I don't believe that there ever will be another Mutiny. They like us too much, they are our friends.' He thought of Hardyal and of Ganpat Rai and of the mild, intelligent, friendly men and women he had always known. Dacoities and murders were not uncommon, of course—but they merely helped to make life more exciting and to provide Mrs Lyttleton with additional wealth of material for her stories. Revolt and mutiny were different things—what had they to do with this sun, with the bleating of the goats under the stunted acacias, with the throbbing sound of the doves?

Macbeth stretched. 'I'm thirsty. Let's go.'

Riding home they skirted the village of Ramdatta the moneylender, who saw them and came forth, all smiles and cordiality. 'Ah, back from school and filled with learning! Tell me, Sahib—how many bears did you slay up there in the mountains?'

'Many, many,' replied Jacques. He liked Ramdatta, who was always jolly and who brought Madame presents every Christmas. 'Could we have water? My friend has a thirst.'

'You shall have water and whatever else is mine to give.'

He led the way to the courtyard before his house, which was the most imposing in the village; it was two-storied and leeped in yellow, with a vermilion tiger painted above its arched door. Trees shaded it, and the breeze made a pleasant rustle in the leaves. Buffaloes were milling about in an adjoining pen, and a swarm of children appeared as Ramdatta waved the boys to a string bedstead set under the trees. One of the children was sent in search of the water-carrier, another disappeared into the house and emerged again carrying a brass platter heaped with sweets. While the boys ate the forbidden food and drank the thrice-forbidden, unboiled water, Ramdatta told them about the dacoits who had broken into his house, killed his servant, and robbed him of his valuables. They begged to be allowed to examine the wall, which had been repaired so not a trace of the break remained. One of the dacoits had been captured by the police, and Ramdatta regaled them with a description of how the captors had stripped their victim, placed a large and very active dung-beetle on his bare belly, bound a cloth tightly round it, and waited. Five minutes of activity on the part of the beetle had elicited much valuable information, and the police declared that it was a mere matter of days before they rounded up the remainder of the gang.

The moneylender squatted cross-legged on his string charpoy facing his guests, and told them stories about his early life in Bombay, of the factories and the mills, and the ships which he had seen steaming in and out of the harbour. Friends and relatives appeared and squatted on the ground in an attentive semicircle before the great man; someone fetched him his silver-plated water pipe, and one of his children curled like a soft brown puppy against his legs. Sunlight sifting through the leaves touched naked brown bodies, danced off a woman's anklet, shone on a child's shaken skull or on the wet nose of a big black buffalo. There was a continuous murmur of life, heightened by a shrill or a bout of violent coughing. Ramdatta was probably one of the most hated men in his neighbourhood; there were many who owed him money and the grudge that goes with owing, yet here he sat, the picture of benevolence, varying his tales of sophisticated splendours with nearer and more plausible accounts of ghosts and evil spirits.

When at last the boys rose to go he escorted them to their horses and entrusted Jacques with elaborate greetings for Madame St Remy. Then he looked keenly at Macbeth. 'Come again and visit me—Burra Sahib!'

'I say, did you notice the ring on his left hand?' asked Macbeth as they trotted homward. 'It was a ruby, as big as your thumb.'

The following day Aubrey Wall took them hunting antelope. They rode out in a cool dawn with Hanif pounding after them on a frowsy pony, his long legs almost touching the ground, a water-bottle strapped to the saddle, a long and murderous knife hanging from his belt. The sky lightened and the plain swam upward from the mists, revealing the land and a little herd of black buck hard as iron against the sky. The creatures saw them and were off at once, bounding into the air like horned gods. The riders raced across the plain with the air whistling in their ears and frightened crows making a din above them. They outflanked the antelope and hid in a gully, their horses hitched out of sight. Hanif passionately nursing his unsheathed knife. Wall brought down a young buck and as it lay kicking in the dust Hanif ran up to it and cut its throat with a loud cry of 'Allah Bismillah!' Blood spouted in a thin fountain, dyeing his arm and his loose white shirt. Then with the dead buck strapped across Hanif's pony and Hanif's song rising and falling, they rode home, warm, tired, friendly.

As they approached Madame's boundary Gisele came out to meet them. She was riding her little half-breed Arab, and her hair was heaped on her shoulders, her face shadowy under the brim of her hat. Wall had been laughing with the others, but when he saw Gisele he fell silent.

The boys rode ahead with Hanif, and Wall reined his horse beside Gisele's. 'I wish you had come with us,' he said. 'We had good sport.'

'I don't like to see them killed.'

As if by accord, they held their beasts to a walk until the others had disappeared. Wall saw little of Gisele these days, and when they met something intense and unquiet came between them, a self-consciousness which neither could conceal. To the man it seemed as if her beauty had passed beyond the boundaries which divide the mere glow of youth from the beginnings of an exquisite maturity. There were moments when her sudden appearance took his breath away, when it blinded him as though it were a lamp flashed in his eyes. She cast his thoughts, his feelings, into an uproar, although it is not easy to say what those thoughts were, or what the emotion behind them. He was not a man of strong imagination or subtlety; discontented, unhappy in his exile, he turned with a sense of longing towards the girl whose glow, whose promise, shone against the arid background of a land which he hated.

They rode a little distance without speaking, then she said: 'Do you know that old garden behind the Club? The one with the pomegranate trees and the Pir's grave? I'd like to see it, now.'

Wall hesitated. 'A bit late, isn't it?'

She gave him a strange, appealing glance, and he managed to smile. 'All right, of course. I'd love to see the garden.'

They wheeled and cantered over the unsown fields, skirting the edge of the cantonment itself and approaching the ancient garden by a long circuit. Wall felt a fever rising in his veins as he watched her controlled and charming body riding a little ahead of him. In a little while they were among the tangled pomegranates, and he saw the grave, built of crumbling masonry, with a few sweets placed on it by the faithful as an offering to the forgotten spirit.

Gisele reined her mare. 'Our ayah used to bring us here when we were little. I remember I used to steal the sweets!'

'How wicked of you,' said Wall. He dismounted, then went to her side and held out his hands. Gisele freed her feet from the stirrups and slipped lightly into his arms. He held her on his breast and her hair, blown upward by the sudden descent, drifted against his mouth; he tasted its sweetness and felt, through his jacket, the pressure of her little breasts. When he looked at her he saw that her eyes were closed, that her lips were raised towards his own. The appeal was unmistakable, his own desire no less so. Why not? he asked himself recklessly. This would not be the first time that he had kissed her, but it might be the last. Yes, he vowed it silently as he bent and pressed his mouth upon hers.

They stood motionless beside the anonymous Pir whose masonry bed the jackals had been undermining. Round them the doves muttered unseen among the pomegranates and a lizard watched them from under a leaf.

'Gisele, Gisele!'

'Take me away with you, Aubrey.'

Incredulous, he lifted his head to stare at her. 'Gisele, my darling . . .'

'Yes, take me away. Both of us, you and I . . . somewhere, anywhere.'

She clung to him and he held her fast, whispering incoherently:

'I can't . . . how can I? You're only a child . . . a child, Gisele!'

'No.' Her hands went up and clasped his head, drawing his cheek against hers. 'No, I'm not a child, Aubrey. You know I'm not . . .

you've known for a whole year that I am not a child.'

He led her to the shade beside the tomb, where they sat down; then he took her in his arms as if she had been a child, trying to assure himself that she was, after all, no more than a child and he a hundred years older. But her hair had settled in a gold cloud about him, her arms clasped him under his jacket and he felt the aroused tumult of her heart against his own.

'Gisele, my dear, let us talk a little.'

'Take me away. You could if you wanted to. I'll go with you, anywhere, anywhere.'

'But there is your mother, and I . . . and I . . .' He held her as though in defiance of his own reason, his own words. Her warmth flowed into him and he knew that a little more of this and he would be lost.

'Gisele, listen to me. You must be sensible, my darling.'

'Then if you won't take me away, love me.'

'Ah, I love you.'

'No, I mean love me, Aubrey!'

The ants were busy transporting morsels of sugar from the tomb to their own mysterious cities, and there was scarcely a sound except for the doves and the horses grazing nearby. Wall rose at last and drew her to her feet. He passed his hand tremblingly over her hair, then lifted her and set her back in the saddle, standing for a moment with his face buried against the skirt of her habit.

They rode back to Madame's house and Madame watched them from the veranda, her quiet eyes missing nothing in her daughter's face, missing nothing of the man's despair. When he had gone away Madame followed Gisele into her bedroom and helped her to unhook the heavy loped habit. In the adjoining bathroom the ayah was setting out soap and towels and testing the bath water by plunging her wizened arm into it.

Madame took Gisele's face between her hands. 'Where did you go, my dear?'

'To the old garden behind the Club.'

Gisele's eyes grew deeper, bluer under her mother's scrutiny, and her face was like a saint's face, limpid, expressionless.

'The bath is ready,' cried the ayah, jingling all her bracelets.

Gisele put her hands behind her neck and unfastened the hooks which fastened her blouse. Slowly, she began to undress, and Madame picked up the discarded clothes and laid them, one by one, on the foot of the bed.

# 18

Mrs Lyttleton listened to the drums. The procession had just passed and she had watched it from her gates, the gilt and paper tazias carried high on men's shoulders, long columns of boys and men beating their breasts and shouting the names of the martyred brothers in a passionate rhythm: 'Hasan! Hosain! Hasan! Hosain!' The festival of Mohorrum always moved her strangely, stirring, as it seemed, the very air to violence. She knew that all over Amritpore the police were anxiously watching the Hindu population. Just let the procession approach too close to a Hindu temple or let a Hindu pipe compete with the Moslem drums, and there was the making of a battle royal. Well, thought Mrs Lyttleton impatiently, let them have their fight and be done with it. Then she smiled: as though men were ever done with fighting! Of the twenty-odd wars fought in India by the English she could remember four in which her husband had participated. However, she was convinced that an occasional brisk little war was far healthier than the dry scab of bureaucracy imposed on the raw stuff of passion. And in the end these people know more about self-discipline than we can ever expect to teach them. Let any white man attempt the Fast of Ramadan! Let him attain—for a day— the contemplative ecstasy of the humblest saddhu! Mrs Lyttleton brooded contemptuously on the frightened precautions of the local police led by a single harassed Englishman. Mercenaries, all of them. If we are going to be conquerors then let us be conquerors, thought Mrs Lyttleton, hearing the drums throbbing in her heart.

She settled down in her accustomed chair with last week's newspapers and a greyhound puppy in her lap. The front page carried a report of a case argued by Ganpat Rai before the High Court, and presently she put the paper down and fell to thinking of the gentle, intelligent barrister, and his family. She had gone yesterday to call on Ganpat Rai's mother, and the old lady had entertained her with interminable accounts of the family's history, of pilgrimages and sacrifices, and with new and elaborate plans for the betrothal of Hardyal.

Mrs Lyttleton had protested, laughing: 'Give him time! He is only fourteen!'

Vijaya Bhai, squatting cross-legged on her enamelled bedstead, surrounded by sisters and nieces and poor relations, shook her earrings in great excitement. 'I was betrothed when I was five, my son when he was ten.'

Later, when Ganpat Rai walked with her across the garden to her carriage, he said: 'My mother is preparing endless puja for the purification of Hardyal when he returns. To placate her I have gone twice to the temple to offer players. I have given a thousand rupees to the family priest, not to mention gifts for sacrifice and for the poor.'

Mrs Lyttleton laughed, remembering his reputation as a hard-headed lawyer, but he went on gloomily: 'She is determined that Hardyal must marry as soon as he returns from England.'

'It sounds almost as silly as if one were to insist on a marriage for Jacques St Remy.'

He nodded. 'I tried to explain to my mother that Hardyal himself may well have different ideas by the time he comes home. Naturally, such reasoning is beyond her.'

'You are Hardyal's father,' Mrs Lyttleton reminded him. 'It is for you to decide.'

He clasped his mild brown hands. 'Ah! But it is not easy. I feel alone in the midst of my own family, for they are all against me. Even my brothers disapprove of my permitting Hardyal so much independence. They will not see that our world is not going to be the same, twenty years from now. I want to free him from the shackles of the past—free him from six thousand years of tradition, so that he may face his future without a burden.'

She was touched by his sincerity. 'Yes, I can see that it is not easy for you, and that it will not be easy for him.'

He responded eagerly to her friendly tone. 'You have always been our friend and you love Hardyal. In my position, what would you do?'

She hesitated, thinking of the women back there in the house, those doting women who clung so frantically to the past; she had, herself, seen too much to dismiss, lightly, the complexities of such a situation.

She said, at last: 'Hardyal seems happy in England. He writes that he has made friends, he likes the life. Why not let him stay there for another year? It could do no harm and it might well be for the best as far as he is concerned.'

'Yes, yes! As far as he is concerned. That is what matters, is it not?' His voice trembled and she saw the emotion in his eyes. 'Hardyal shall stay in England for another year. I had hoped that you, too, would advise it.'

The noise of the drums had retreated and Mrs Lyttleton was on the point of dropping into a light doze when she heard, in the road beyond the gates, the musical double-note of a carriage bell. She opened her eyes in time to see Madame St Remy's phaeton pass between the gates and bowl up the weedy driveway.

Mrs Lyttleton rose, instinctively smoothing her dress and shaking down her numerous bangles and bracelets. Her mind was a riot of conjecture: communication between herself and Madame had been conducted by channels as devious as Mrs Lyttleton, with a perverse sense of mischief, could possibly devise. For twenty years they had neither spoken nor set foot in each other's house. What, now, could be the purpose of this extraordinary visit?

The carriage drew up under the porte cochère and Mrs Lyttleton heard Madame tell the coachman to wait. Then she alighted, gowned in black, her white topi draped in fine crêpe. 'Concierge!' thought Mrs Lyttleton bitingly.

There was a flush on the faces of both women when they confronted each other across the crumbling furniture. Mrs Lyttleton spoke first.

'Madame St Remy, this is a great surprise, a great honour!'

Madame bowed, then stood with her gloved hands clasping the gold knob of her parasol. Twenty years of hostility divided them: only a triviality could bridge that abyss, and Mrs Lyttleton supplied it:

'Won't you sit down? I'd offer you tea, but my servants have gone to the Mohorrum and God knows when they'll come back.'

Madame selected the least ramshackle chair and removed her tight kidskin gloves. She missed no detail of her surroundings as she thought with mingled disgust and satisfaction: 'Just as shoddy as I expected.'

Mrs Lyttleton settled herself in her chair and arranged her skirts. 'You must have just missed the procession. Do you think we shall have the usual row?'

'If we do,' returned Madame stiffly, 'it will probably be the fault of the police. They are always looking for trouble, Mohorrum or no Mohorrum.'

'Ah yes, *divide et impera*, of course. Is that chair really comfortable? The dogs sleep in it.'

Madame's eyes met hers. 'Perhaps it would be just as well if I came straight to the point?'

Mrs Lyttleton shook her head. 'I should be most disappointed. I am delighted to see you. I love visitors and I've scarcely set eyes on another woman since Mrs Brown went back to England.'

There was a slight pause. Mrs Lyttleton thought: She's lost her looks. She used to be very pretty in her sharp little French way. I wonder what in the devil she is after?

Madame was reflecting: She's as dry and yellow as tarantula. What does Jacques see in her? What did Auguste see?

'Will you have a cigarette?' asked Mrs Lyttleton, opening the box of Egyptians beside her chair. Madame declined with a stony glance, and Mrs Lyttleton selected a cigarette for herself, her rings giving off a minor conflagration. No doubt, thought Madame, her lovers kept her in jewels. The vulgarity of it, wearing such things at this hour!

'I came,' she began, 'to ask whether you would consider selling the doab lands by the river. Perhaps I should have written to you, but I was given to understand that you never answer letters.'

'On the contrary, I carry on a voluminous correspondence. For instance, I had—just before you came—just finished writing a long letter to Hardyal. Did you know that his father wants him to go into the Civil Service? My own opinion is that the Army is the place for young men. But then I'm prejudiced naturally.'

'Naturally,' agreed Madame. She took a deep breath. 'But to return to the matter of the doab. I am anxious to extend my crop next year, and I cannot make plans for hiring additional labour until I know where I stand in regard to acreage.'

'You intend to put more land to indigo?' inquired Mrs Lyttleton with an air of surprise.

'Why not?' Madame's voice was crisp. 'Last year was most successful. This year should be even better, in which case I hope very much that I may be able to send my children home next year.'

'Home, Madame?'

'Gisele is eager to enter the convent at Bruges, and Jacques must have a few years of travel before he comes into the factory with me.'

'I see that you have many burdens and expenses, Madame.'

Their thoughts moved between them, subtle, inimical. Mrs Lyttleton continued: 'It's funny that you should ask me about the doab. I had a call a few days ago from that rascal Ramdatta. He wanted it himself to buy or to lease. I have my suspicions about him, however.'

'Suspicions?'

'I don't believe he wants it for himself. He already has more land than he knows what to do with. I think he is acting as go-between for one of his shady friends. He has many! It may be for one of those big zamindars from Lucknow, and they can easily afford to pay more than they are willing to offer.'

Madame stared at her hands. It was at her instigation that Ramdatta had approached Mrs Lyttleton, on the understanding that the land should be resold or subleased to Madame herself.

Mrs Lyttleton continued light-heartedly: 'He is clever, that Ramdatta. Nevertheless, I told him to go to Jehannum.'

'Then,' said Madame coldly, 'we come back to my question: will you sell to me?'

Mrs Lyttleton's eyes were suddenly hard as prisms. 'Certainly, Madame—but at a price.'

Madame St Remy named it without hesitation, aware that Ramdatta had offered less. Mrs Lyttleton continued to gaze at her. 'I was not thinking of money, Madame.'

'What?'

'My price is Jacques.'

The name exploded between them like a rocket. Madame flushed.

'What has Jacques to do with this?'

'Much. Shall we be clear with one another, just for once?'

'Mrs Lyttleton, I have come to discuss a purely business transaction . . .'

'We shall do so, but let us first discuss something that lies near both our hearts.'

Madame relapsed into silence, and Mrs Lyttleton continued, rather breathlessly: 'I am old, Madame St Remy, and I have not much to lose, now. You know something of my history, and I know something of yours. Whatever I once had and loved, lies buried over there.' She nodded towards the garden. 'I know you have always disliked me, even hated me, and I can guess why. Slanderous absurdities are bound to accumulate round a woman as unconventional as I, and women as conventional as you are bound to believe them. I don't care. I never have cared, much. And now that I am old I feel that there is very little left that I can lose. However, that little matters to me, considerably.' The greyhound puppy returned and clambered into her lap. Madame stared at it fixedly as Mrs Lyttleton continued: 'Madame St Remy, I love Jacques. I love him as only old and lonely women can love . . .' she laughed faintly. 'As they love the promise of eternal life. Can I make you see what I mean? I know what you're thinking, that I'm incorrigible, that I have had lovers and that the taste for love hasn't died in me as it should have died years ago. Well, you're right—it hasn't died. It will die when I die, not before. You must often have asked yourself what your child can see in an old woman like myself . . . ah, you're asking it at this moment! Well, he sees in me the equivalent of what I see in him—qualities which men and women desire in each other—forgiveness, variety, passion, and humour. Those were lessons you scorned to learn. No, please don't go yet. I've been dying to say these things to you . . . hoping for an opportunity which I never dreamed *you* would give me!'

Madame, who had half-risen, sank back in her chair. 'You are very eloquent,' she said dryly. 'But I still fail to see what Jacques has to do with the business that has brought me here.'

'Then I'll explain. If you will give Jacques permission to visit my house whenever he likes, without hindrance or stealth, I shall sell you that doab at any price you choose to name.'

Madame laughed for the first time. 'Really, your frankness disconcerts me! You believe, then, that I would accept your offer in exchange for my son's corruption?'

Mrs Lyttleton was silent, then she smiled. 'What a compliment from one woman to another! Somehow I did not expect that from you.'

Madame looked at her with detestation. 'May I now speak my mind? I too am glad of the opportunity. You and I have misunderstood each other for too long. Years ago, Mrs Lyttleton, when I came to Amritpore as a bride, young, innocent, and in love with my husband, you lost no time in trying to deprive me of his love. No, please do not interrupt. I was in a strange land, among strange people. I felt desperately alone. Auguste was all I had in the world, all I cared for. *Please* permit me to finish! You have just outlined your philosophy . . . You love life, you love youth!' Her voice was bleak with horror. 'I do not doubt that your friend Aubrey Wall subscribes to the same philosophy. He, too, prefers youth and innocence . . . as though we need to be told what it is you love! You have nourished yourself on other people's jealous misery, other people's love. You won Auguste away from his work, from his home, from his children, from his wife. You taught him to come to you with his difficulties and his disappointments—not to me, his wife! You sympathized with his weakness and condoled with his imaginary sorrows. But in the end what could you give him that I could not? Shall I tell you? It is very simple—every courtesan understands the formula. You provided Auguste with opportunities for vice, and vice, naturally, is not an asset which even libertines knowingly relish in their own wives! But I could forgive him, and you, had it not been for something greater and far more terrible.' Her eyes blazed. 'There is something neither God nor I will forgive. You destroyed Auguste's faith. Your influence was so strong that even when he was dying he refused the sacraments.' Her voice seemed to splinter, to fall everywhere in shrill fragments. Mrs Lyttleton sat in astounded silence.

Then Madame St Remy rose, collecting her parasol and gloves. As swiftly as she had lost her self-control she now regained it. 'And you have the superlative insolence to demand my son's friendship! Let me tell you, Mrs Lyttleton, that I would rather have my children dead and buried where much vultures will never dare to search them out!'

Mrs Lyttleton lifted herself rather stiffly to her feet. She was divided between mirth and fury, but before she could find words to conclude the interview Madame had turned on her once more. 'I know very well that Jacques has come to see you during these winter holidays. I have seen that your poison has already started to work in him . . . but he will not come again. He and Gisele are going back to the hills tomorrow.'

Mrs Lyttleton's temper gave way at last. 'Well, Madame—allow me at least one claim to mercy. *I* waited until my daughter was dead before I buried her!'

She turned and walked into the house, and long after the carriage had rolled away through the gates she stood alone in her great empty drawing-room, listening to the drums beating in the distance, and to the closer, painful beating of her heart.

# 19

The Raja of Jhori, in strawberry-coloured tweeds and bright yellow shoes, greeted Jacques and Macbeth on their return to St. Matthew's.

'Here we are, all together again! Jollee, isn't it?'

'We do not think it is so damned jollee.'

'Oh, I say. The same old snobs as of last year. I see.'

They gave the unfortunate prince a deadly stare, then went their way.

'I wonder why we don't like him?' Jacques murmured as they strolled across the playground.

'He's a swot, always trying to outdo every one else. It isn't even as though he were a real prince. Government put him on the throne when they found out that the real ruler was a rotter—he kept boys in cages.'

'What?'

Macbeth gave him an amused glance. 'Don't you know?'

'Know what?'

'Well,' Macbeth hesitated, waiting for a little group of third standard infants to kick a football out of range. 'Notice young Hicks over there? Looks like a girl. *He* ought to be in a cage.'

Study, prayers, games—the routine caught them up and strove to press and polish them all into the semblance of so many little ciphers, but it remained a semblance. The miracle of personality survived, assertive, defiant. A young Afridi chieftain taking special tutoring from Brother Duane found himself bored, he departed leaving a note in Pushtu: 'Thanks for kindness and patience. My brain wearies, and I go now to avenge the death of my sister's husband. Perhaps I shall return, perhaps not.'

He did not return, and spurred by this example young Leggatt, chronically homesick, ran away and was captured at the railway terminal and brought back. For the rest of the year he remained solitary and brooding. Edmonton was caught during a nocturnal visit to the Convent where he had gone to meet young Holtby's sister, and both were expelled amidst a flurry of partisan excitement.

Then one morning in May young Hicks was reported missing, and two days later they found his body lying in ten feet of water near the most sequestered part of the lake. He could not swim and someone said that he had waded beyond his depth, some that he must have fallen from a raft while fishing for minnows . . . others whispered suicide. He was a queer little fellow, not much liked, but his death struck on Jacques' nerves. He had seen death before, down by the ghats in Amritpore, but the death of Indians had not seemed specially significant. But after they had found little Hicks, Jacques could not sleep. He was one of the servers at the Mass for the Dead, and as he knelt beside the coffin and heard the hymns peal over his head, as he watched the priests in their black vestments, a terrible protest swelled in his throat. He felt that he alone challenged God's incomprehensible savagery, that he alone stood up to Heaven with the inaudible question: 'How dare you?' Tears burned his eyes as he listened to the choir, to the indescribable sweetness of boys' voices.

The day after the funeral was Sunday, and as Jacques climbed the hill towards the Macbeths' house he heard a koel whistle in the valley, and the guttural conversation of Bhotiyals driving their sheep towards the plains. He'd passed these cheerful Mongols on the road and they hailed him merrily in a language which he couldn't understand, but which he recognized as being friendly. Their eyes slanted upward at the corners, they wore their long hair braided with coloured wool, and as they disappeared in clouds of dust he could hear them admonishing their sheep with barking noises, like dogs.

The Macbeths' spaniel came wagging to meet him, and a big bearded orderly saluted jocosely as he ran up the veranda steps. The drawing-room seemed deserted, then he saw a figure rise from a chair beside the piano and an unknown voice greeted him. 'Are you Jacques?'

He did not answer at once, but stared through the gloom.

'You must be Jacques,' said the voice calmly. 'And I am Bertie Wood.'

He had known that she was coming, but he had forgotten. He went towards her as she rose—a girl of about his own age, with one of those faces which is more English than anything else about them—a face fashioned out of the alloy of generations, Saxon and Norman tempered by a perverse Mediterranean strain encountered Heaven knows where or when. Bertie's eyes were a light brown like the eyes of an orange cat, her skin but a few shades lighter, her hair a luxuriant black. She was not beautiful nor even pretty, but her face was full of light and movement, her body slight, poised, and eager. But shyness, it seemed, was not part of her accoutrements, for she held out her hand and as

Jacques took it she stared at him with a critical thoroughness. 'John has done nothing but talk about you since I arrived. I tried to make him describe you to me, but he couldn't.' Jacques dropped his hand on the piano keys and struck an inadvertent note. 'Well, he described you to me.'

'Go on, do tell me!'

'I don't remember, exactly.'

'Did he say he thought I was pretty?'

'Oh no, he didn't say that. Besides, he didn't have to, did he? I've seen your photograph.' He picked it up from the piano and examined it, glancing from the pictured face to the living one.

'Well, do you think I'm pretty?'

He put the photograph back in its place. 'Well no—not exactly.'

She sank on a chair arm, swinging her foot, and he went on quickly:

'All I meant was, you don't look like my sister Gisele.'

'Yes, I know all about your sister Gisele, and about your mother, and your servant Hanif, and about Amritpore. John has told me everything. But I wish the dickens . . .' She broke off, and on Jacques there dawned the extraordinary feeling that he had known her all his life. She finished explosively: 'I wish the dickens I was lovely . . . really, really lovely!' She stared at him intensely. 'You know, *devastating!*'

'Oh, well,' he murmured, rather at a loss. There was a brief pause, then he asked: 'Does it really matter?'

Bertie sighed deeply. 'Before you came I was thinking: how wonderful it would be if, when you entered the room and saw me for the first time, I could just bowl you over. You know, completely bowl you over.' When he remained discreetly silent she rose with a sudden, brave air, and taking his arm led him to the big window which gave on a view of the Colonel's rose garden. With her arm linked in Jacques', Bertie gazed at the sparkling hills. 'No one ever told me that India could be like this—all light, all green, all sky!'

He listened to her clean accent, so different from the polyglot of St Matthew's.

She went on: 'I'd like to live here for the rest of my life.'

'So would I.'

'It's a pity that one cannot, isn't it?'

'Why not?'

'Well, eventually one has to go away.'

He frowned. 'Lots of people stay. Hundreds! They live here and die here.' He thought of Mrs Lyttleton and of poor little Hicks. Bertie shook her head. 'This isn't our country. I haven't been here very long, but I can see that already. And some one was talking about it last night at dinner—Captain Ponsonby, I think. He said something about how essential it is for people to stick to their own culture.'

'But,' he objected, rather uncertainly, 'isn't culture something that is made up of lots of things? I mean, what is one to do if one *prefers* to live in a place that isn't one's country?'

She thought this over. 'I think that what Captain Ponsonby meant was—that if one stays here too long one loses one's sense of—of identity. That was the word. He said something about people going native.'

Jacques nodded. 'I wonder if Hardyal will go native in England, if he stays there long enough?'

'Hardyal?'

Jacques explained, glad that she showed none of Macbeth's reaction to that cherished name.

'Do you mean to say you have a Hindu friend, really? A friend like John? If I'm here next year shall I meet him?'

Before Jacques could answer, Colonel Macbeth entered the room behind them. 'Ah, so you've met!' He looked from one face to the other.

'Jacques, you don't know it yet but you will before long: this is a most unusual woman.'

'I know. She can ride and shoot and sail a boat and stand on her head and talk four languages and see in the dark!'

Colonel Macbeth laughed. 'I see that your cousin John has prepared the ground for you, Bertie, my dear.'

She tossed her dark head. 'What a liar John is! Does he still take cascara when he wants to dodge classes?'

'So that was it!'

'He wrote and told me all about it. He was frightfully pleased with himself. And he told me about all the leopards he'd shot. Has he ever killed anything more dangerous than a grasshopper, Uncle Jack?'

'There is a chance that he may, next week. I've been talking with Lal Singh, my old shikari, and he tells me that a leopard has been stealing goats from a village not far away. Would you like to come—and you, Jacques?'

Both replied excitedly that they would, and for Jacques St Matthew's had already receded into the distance. Mrs Macbeth entered, and now her fluttering delicacy seemed to clash with Bertie's dark presence. She kissed Jacques, then asked for her son.

'He's upstairs taking the insides out of beetles,' explained Bertie.

'Oh, dear!' Mrs Macbeth's gaze rested fleetingly on the girl.

'Bertie, darling, shouldn't you do your hair for lunch? Do put on a ribbon—the red velvet one.'

Jacques' ear caught something a little off-key in her tone, a sort of exaggerated persuasion, and he wondered rather innocently why she should suggest an accentuation of Bertie's charm. He had not failed to observe that charm was an asset by which the Colonel's lady set great store—she outshone every woman who came here, outshone, out-fluttered, out-sang. But he was still too innocent to guess that youth alone could place Mrs Macbeth at a disadvantage and that by her peculiar genius she would rise above even that disadvantage by conniving, in a fraudulent spirit, at the enchantment of a rival's charm. But if the boy failed to grasp entirely this little by-play, Bertie did not fail. She danced out of the room, to return a few minutes later not only with the bow in her hair but with the hair itself piled and knotted on top of her head: the transformation made her at once delectable, at once a rival. Colonel Macbeth put his arm round her, and at that moment John Macbeth came into the room behind Captain Ponsonby and two other officers from the garrison. Macbeth glanced at Bertie, then gave Jacques a triumphant stare which said as plainly as words: 'Now you see what *I* can produce at a moment's notice!'

A servant announced lunch, and as they all streamed into the dining-room Jacques wondered whether he would not, after all, be a soldier and wear a handsome *putto* coat with leather buttons when he was not wearing the blue and gold of his chosen regiment.

## 20

'Will you,' murmured Bertie, 'please kill that wasp?'

It was after lunch and the children lay on the terrace below the house. Bertie had provided herself with a rug and a cushion; Jacques was propped on his elbow beside her, and Macbeth sprawled at her feet. She had been reading aloud from *Vanity Fair*, but now she lay with the book upside down on her breast, her eyes seeping liquid vistas of sky and leaf. Jacques slew the wasp with his hat, and asked tentatively:

'Do you think we can beat the Boers?'

He had listened, during lunch, while Colonel Macbeth and his officers discussed the South African War. All were eager to go.

Macbeth repeated slowly: 'Beat them? Of course—eventually.'

'But think of Colenso,' said Bertie, with a shiver. 'And Spion Kop. I wish it would end. I hate it.'

Macbeth said abruptly: 'I wouldn't mind if Ponsonby went, though.'

She smiled faintly, watching Jacques from under her lashes. 'Nor would I. It would be nice if he went and the Boers took him prisoner, wouldn't it?'

There was a long pause, during which each was busy with his own thoughts, then Bertie said: 'You know, reading this book makes me think of my governess Fraulein Eberhard. She used to make me read it to her, and she always went to sleep after the first five minutes.'

'What happened to her?' asked Jacques, politely abandoning the Boer War in favour of a more personal topic.

'She died. That's why I'm here—she would never have let me come without her and she wouldn't come herself, so it's just as well that she died.'

Bertie reflected without remorse and without rancour on that miraculous deliverance. Like her cousin John, she was an only child, but unlike him she was an orphan whose parents were drowned in a yachting accident on the Norfolk Broads when she was six years old. Bertie spent her childhood with alternate sets of relatives, under the personal care of Fraulein Eberhard—one of those devoted leeches known as a governess-companion. Lying here now and gazing at this Indian sky, Bertie remembered those interminable London winters; she remembered Fraulein's nocturnal terrors, her fits of crying, her bullying, her passion for taking walks in cemeteries, her jealousy, her moods. Then Fraulein Eberhard died and Bertie, elated by freedom, found herself bored by all her English relatives. They were prigs who looked with a stern eye on her high spirits. She thought yearningly of her favourite uncle and of the happy times which she had spent when the Macbeths were on their rare furloughs in England. Finally she wrote a supplicating letter to Colonel Macbeth, and a month later she was on her way to India.

Now she retraced that journey from Southampton to Bombay—her first voyage, her first great adventure as the watery leagues slid under the ship's keel. She thought of the ocean as a transfusing element which bound India and England together, and this idea grew as she saw the reflections of Bombay breaking on the shallows of the Arabian Sea. The Macbeths had sent their servants to escort her to the hills, and she shared her first-class compartment with two missionary ladies from America. One was middle-aged and nervous and made a great to-do about boiling everything she drank; the other was young, brisk, and talkative. Bertie soon learned all the details about their home in Iowa and the fact that they were returning to India on the conclusion of what they called their Sabbatical. They were curious about her and looked disapproving when she explained that she had come to India for no better reason than to enjoy herself.

'This is hardly the country for play,' observed the elder of the two with a severe glance. 'But you will doubtless find that out for yourself after you've spent a summer in the plains.'

'I am not going to spend a summer on the plains. I'm going to the hills.'

'Even in the hills you will find discomfort,' the younger lady informed Bertie with an air, almost, of satisfaction. 'One cannot escape it. There are no proper cooking facilities, no fly screens, no refrigeration. To equip our mission we have had to import everything from America.'

'Even the simplest things,' added the elder lady, not without pride. 'There is no question that you English have been very backward about educating the natives. With all these great forests and all the water power, think what could have been done!'

'Yes, when I think of the settling of our great South-West!'

Bertie, who felt that her country's shortcoming could hardly be laid at her door, remained silent, watching with covert fascination as the middle-aged lady tied her bootlaces with two little pieces of toilet paper wrapped round her fingers.

'Why do you do that?' she inquired at last, unable to curb her curiosity.

'One hates the idea of germs.' She stared at Bertie. 'I trust you brought your chlorodyne?'

'I don't play it,' replied Bertie politely.

The younger missionary laughed. 'It's a medicine, my dear—not a musical instrument. We use it to ward off cholera. Goodness, you *are* ignorant, aren't you?'

Bertie resented this but felt that she had asked for it, so said nothing more. It was at Benares station that something happened to disturb her enchantment with the journey. There she saw a tall and dapper Englishman throw a young Indian out of a first-class compartment and get into it himself with his wife, his luggage, and all his dogs. The performance—it was necessarily brief—was watched by an interested but passive audience of natives and Eurasians, and Bertie stared in wonder as the Indian picked up his scattered belongings and walked quietly away to a third-class compartment. A passing guard explained to the missionaries' queries: 'Onlee one first-class and that native absolutely refused to give it up. True, he had a ticket, but onlee one first-class available, so what was the Sahib to do?'

'Why couldn't he share it with the Indian gentleman?' demanded the younger lady, who had flushed with indignation. The Eurasian guard looked at her, then shrugged and went his way. He knew from experience that it was impossible to explain some things satisfactorily to American ladies.

As the train drew away from the platform, the elder lady murmured:

'Dear me, so distressing . . . that poor Indian.'

'But I don't understand!' exclaimed Bertie. 'Why didn't he stand up for his rights?'

'Perhaps he doesn't have any,' suggested the other, in a dry voice.

'But there were all those other Indians standing there—why didn't they go for the Englishman?'

The Americans regarded her silently, then the younger one smiled.

'Goodness, you *are* ignorant, aren't you?'

'I don't see . . .' began Bertie, but the other interrupted, gently enough: 'Natives don't strike white men, my dear. Don't forget that!'

Bertie retired behind *Vanity Fair*, but the scene on Benares platform continued to haunt her. She simply could not understand why the Indian, who looked young and strong, had not defended himself against the uncouth Englishman. She thought of all the men she had known at home and she knew that not one of them would have put up with such treatment. In the first place people did not behave like that unless they were drunk or mad. Yet the Indian had submitted . . . and with this thought there rose an angry contempt for him. She put down her book and glanced once more at the younger of the Americans. 'Why do you keep telling me that I'm ignorant? I don't feel ignorant. I just want to know . . .'

The other hesitated for a moment, then said frankly: 'It's not so easy to explain. It's all mixed up with history and with your way of looking at things.'

'*Our* way?'

'The English way, then.'

The conversation suddenly embarrassed Bertie, for it was rather like talking about God or about love, or walking about in public showing too much leg. She hesitated, marshalling her thoughts, then decided to come out with them. 'I think I know what you mean. We are conquerors, and you don't like the way we behave about it. But after all hasn't every one been conquered at one time or another. The Romans conquered England, and that was very good for us.'

The other shrugged. 'I suppose it depends on where we decide to stop.' When Bertie remained silent, she asked. 'Have you ever been to America?'

Bertie said no, she had not had the pleasure.

'But you remember what happened there, don't you? We kicked you out. While Warren Hastings was busy saving India for the English, Lord North was losing America.'

Bertie felt that something was up to her—though she was not

entirely sure just what it was. She asked, in a cool voice:

'What about your own Red Indians? They can't even vote, can they?' She had heard this somewhere, and thanked her stars that it now recurred to her memory.

The elder lady interposed with an air of dignity. 'That is quite true, my dear. But there are many, many of us in America who lament the tragedy of the American Indian. Life is a very difficult thing . . . a very, very difficult thing.' And she gazed steadfastly into space.

Later, when Bertie mentioned this episode to her uncle, he frowned.

'Don't run away with the idea that we are all like that Englishman. I've lived in India for twenty-five years and I've never raised my hand against a native.'

'But you have fought them!' And she examined the little white scar on the back of his hand. He smiled down at her with his gentle eyes. 'My dear! There is a difference, you know. *That* was war.'

Now as she lay on the terrace and stared at the immense shadowless sky, England, the American missionaries, Benares Station all seemed very far away, their importance diminishing like a beetle's wing in great tides of sunlit air. She heard the boys discussing the leopard hunt on which they were all going the following week, and she interrupted lazily: 'I wish one didn't have to do all this killing.'

'You've killed pheasants, yourself,' her cousin reminded her.

'I know. It's fun, and that's what makes it so awful.'

'Oh well,' said Jacques, 'think of all the things we eat—the sheep and the chickens and the fish, even the eggs.'

'And even a potato must have some feeling,' Macbeth went on. 'And plums! How would you like to be a nice ripe plum and have someone come along and take a bite out of you?'

'And then spit you out because you were full of worms?' added Jacques.

'And back you go on the rubbish heap, and along comes a hyena and turns you over with his hideous snout . . .'

'Then lifts its head and gives a howl like this: BERTIE!'

Bertie listened to the echo which pealed away from the nearer hills.

'Now tell me how I'd feel if I were an antelope bounding over the mountains!'

Macbeth replied crushingly that antelope didn't live on mountains.

'But you could be a wild pig,' suggested Jacques.

'Or,' said Macbeth, 'one of those big black-faced monkeys. *Then* you could have a little black-faced monkey hanging on to you in front . . .'

Bertie rolled over, burying her face on her arms, and Jacques lay beside her, watching the sunlight play on her hair. It had been a long time since he had felt so happy.

# 21

'It's been ages since I've seen you,' said Gisele. She and Jacques sat in the vast cheerless room of the Convent, where the girls were permitted to receive visitors. Portraits of long departed Mothers and Sisters of the Order stared at them from the walls; outside, a hot sun beat on the gravel and on the leaves of the horse chestnuts.

Jacques stirred uneasily on the hard slippery chair where he sat facing Gisele. An abyss divided them—she struck him as being even more unapproachable than one of her own beloved martyrs.

'I've meant to come before this, but . . .'

She interrupted coolly: 'You, haven't really. You know you'd rather see the Macbeths. Isn't that true?'

He took refuge in defiance. 'Yes, it is true!'

'I'm glad that at least you don't try to lie. I always know when you're lying.' When he remained silent she went on: 'You're on your way to them now, aren't you? For the holiday?'

'Why not?'

'What will you do when Maman is here? She'll be here very soon. And when she comes she will want us to be with her. You won't be able, then, to run off to your friends whenever you please.'

Jacques felt something white-hot flower in his heart. Why had he come here? He should have stayed away. Gisele did not love him, she did not really want to see him, and she saw through his brotherly pretence to the sense of guilt which brought him. 'Why don't you like the Macbeths? Why won't you come with me sometimes when I go to see them?'

'Thank you, I can live without friends.'

'But why should you?'

'Because they take one away from God! You don't mind being taken away from Him, do you? You've never been very happy in His presence.'

He clenched his hands. 'Why do you want to talk about it all the time?'

'Because you are my brother and because I keep wondering what will become of you. So does Maman wonder.'

His heart was pounding angrily. 'I don't see why you want to talk about it. I don't see why.'

'You could if you tried, but you don't want to try. Oh, it's all very well to love. One should love one's mother, one's family, even one's friends.' Her eyes brooded on his face. 'I could love just as you do, perhaps even more than you can dream of loving. God doesn't blame us for that, but He cherishes those who renounce love for His sake.'

Jacques sat in stony silence, and after a slight pause Gisele went on: 'I had a letter from Maman in which she said that she was worried about you. Maman has always told me everything.'

Jacques was thinking that he had never really known Gisele, that she could not be his own sister, someone he'd grown up with, someone who used to play with him in the garden at home, who even laughed, sometimes, at the same jokes.

He burst out suddenly: 'Can't I have friends?'

'Why do you care so much whether you have friends or not?' When he made no answer to this she asked abruptly: 'Would you think of marrying someone who was not a Catholic?'

'I'm not going to marry.'

'But would you?'

He stared stubbornly at the floor.

'You would, of course. You'll let nothing stand in your way.'

'Then why do you ask?'

'I don't really need to ask. I know. I know everything, because Maman told me. She has always told me everything because I am the eldest and there was never any one for her to confide in. I am much closer to Maman than you are, because I have always understood . . .'

He listened, conscious of the growing hysteria in her voice. Gisele was staring at him fixedly. 'Maman has always been afraid that what happened to Papa would happen to you.'

'What happened to Papa?'

'He abandoned God. He left the Church and died without taking the sacraments. You didn't know that—Maman didn't want you to know.'

'Then it's wicked of you to tell me!'

She looked at him with eyes that suddenly terrified him. 'It was all because of your friend Mrs Lyttleton. She took Papa away from Maman. She took him away from us, and from God. Maman may have told you certain things about Mrs Lyttleton, but I don't think she told you that.'

'No, she didn't—she didn't, because it isn't true. People don't do such things . . . Mrs Lyttleton couldn't take Papa away . . . she didn't . . . she wouldn't . . .'

'Why not?'

'Because . . . because he wouldn't have let her . . . and because she would never have tried. People don't . . . not grown-up people.'

'They do. I know they do.'

A shadow passed before the doors and a Nun entered. This was the

Mother Superior, a tall, handsome, clear-eyed woman. The children rose as the impressive figure paused before them, its full black skirts falling into still lines like the plaster folds of a statue. 'Ah, Gisele! This is your brother.' She looked from one face to the other.

'You have a beautiful sister, my dear. We are proud of our Gisele.' She touched the girl's cheek with a plump hand. 'How nice that you should spend the afternoon together. God bless you.'

She swept away, and Jacques saw that his sister's cheek still bore, like a stigma, the pale imprint of the Nun's caress.

Something broke loose inside him. 'I hate you,' he whispered. 'I hate you, Gisele! You spoil everything. . . .'

'I know you hate me, but I don't hate you. I feel sorry for you. I shall pray for you as I pray for Papa, every day and every night.'

Jacques made a frantic gesture. 'Don't pray for us! I don't care, I tell you—I don't care!'

He seized his hat and with a wild glance at her pale, composed face, ran out of the room, across the sunlit gravel to the road.

The chapel was full of warm, sweet dusk as Jacques went forward and took his place in the confessional. Through the lattice-work screen he could see the red glow of the sanctuary lamp and four candles lighted on the altar. He knelt and crossed himself: 'Father, forgive me, for I have sinned!'

In the little window before him he could just see the priest's withered cheek and the grey hairs which grew in his ear. He heard the whispered intercession and a soft creaking of wood as Father Englebert leaned towards him on the other side of the confessional.

'Father, forgive me, for I have sinned!'

His throat, his lips, were dry with a dryness that went all the way down to his entrails, and he could hear the heavy thumping of his own blood. He stared at the little window which framed the priestly profile, a withered chin supported on four bent knuckles, and he wondered whether the uproar in his breast was audible to that attentive listener. He thought desperately on his sins, but they flew like leaves in every direction—fragmentary visions and images, small visceral murmurs drowned in the silencing flood from his heart. How and where had he sinned? And what was Sin—a great Raven hopping through heaven, or all remembered sweetness, all hope, all desire?

'Father . . .'

'Yes, my child. Go on.'

But he couldn't go on, he couldn't even begin, for all the words he had ever learned blew away when he sought to clutch them. 'I don't know . . . I don't believe . . . I don't understand!'

He saw his own father, the portrait in the drawing-room at

Amritpore, the faded brownish portrait which white ants had eaten, but from which the eyes stared back with indifference, and he thought: In the cemetery behind Father Sebastien's church those eyes have melted away. 'There is nothing left, nothing . . . nothing!' Ice seemed to trickle down his limbs as he heard himself whispering: 'To think like this is a sin. Nothing is a sin, a sin is nothing . . . nothing . . . nothing . . .'

Father Englebert leaned against the window and murmured: 'You are not prepared, my child. Go now, prepare yourself. Come to me later.'

Jacques left the chapel and came into the afternoon sunlight. Silence swelled and settled on all the half-hearted activities of a school week-end: he heard the sound of a piano, someone playing scales over and over again, and the click of hockey sticks on the playground. The world seemed to stand away from him, to ignore his existence.

# 22

A week later Jacques arrived at the Macbeths' to find the household excitedly preparing for the hunting trip which the Colonel had promised them. Tents and baggage had already gone and the party were waiting for Jacques to join them before setting out on the twenty-mile ride to the camping ground. Bertie rushed to meet him. 'We were afraid you were not coming after all!' She clutched his arm and he could feel the excitement running through her like a current.

Macbeth sauntered up. 'We've got a gun for you. It's gone with the baggage. Father says I can use his.'

Mrs Macbeth appeared with the Colonel and Captain Ponsonby, the latter a slight, dark young man with a silky black moustache. Mrs Macbeth was all dove-grey with a blue feather in her hat. 'I'll take care of Pedro,' she declared in her high, birdlike voice. "I shan't let him out of my sight. Poor darling, he'd hate to be left behind, leopards or no leopards.'

'Well,' said the Colonel, shrugging, 'remember what happened to Pongo!'

'And to Dumdum,' added Captain Ponsonby darkly. 'And to Gypsy!'

Leopards had at one time and another made off with all three dogs. But Mrs Macbeth refused to be separated from her special pet, a fat breathless spaniel now miraculously in his fifth year.

'Pedro can ride in the dandy with me, and the children will see that he doesn't wander too far when we get there.'

Jacques tasted the vagrant thrill which an expedition brings to an unjaded spirit, and he saw that the others shared with him this primitive lust for faring forth, for leaving all that is known and stale and turning one's face in a new direction. Bertie was watching him intently. 'Yes,' she murmured, pressing his arm. 'We're going, Jacques! We're going to ride all afternoon, lunch under the trees, then there'll be the camp and the coolies' voices coming out of the darkness, and the nighthawk going like this!' She pursed her lips and made the hollow gong-like note of the Himalayan nighthawk as it floats out from a silent valley.

He looked at her curiously. 'How do you know it will be like that?'
'Oh, I know, I know!'

'Come along, every one,' cried the Colonel. Mrs Macbeth was already seated in her dandy with Pedro slavering like a gargoyle on her lap. Four grunting coolies swung the dandy-poles on their shoulders, and their muscular brown legs vanished down the slope among the trees, pursued by the Colonel and Captain Ponsonby. The children mounted their ponies and followed, and after them straggled the grooms and a man with a straw lunch basket balanced on his head.

Their road fell away from the semi-civilization of Gambul towards the lower hills, and presently they were in the warmer air of cultivated terraces and a village of thatched roofs and bleating goats. They passed a little temple with a red-painted stone beside it, and jostled and were jostled by strings of starved-looking pack ponies coming from the opposite direction. Wizened old women with babies slung in rags on their backs smiled up at Bertie and in passing laid their gnarled hands on her skirts. 'Bhao! Bhao!' they cried, and held their babies up to her saddle.

'What do they want?' asked Bertie, laughing down at the gnomelike faces which laughed back at her.

'They're calling you their sister, and they'd like some money,' explained Jacques. 'Don't give them any or they'll be all over us.'

'Luckily I haven't any,' said Bertie, though she hated to refuse.

She and Jacques rode together and at every turn of the road ahead they caught glimpses of their companions—Mrs Macbeth's parasol bobbing above her white dandy, the Colonel's tall back, and the slighter figure of the young officer. Macbeth kept scurrying between one end of the procession and the other, a sort of self-instituted emissary, and presently they realized that he was engaged in a game of his own, a game in which he lorded it over these separate destinies, bringing them under his control, holding them, secretly, in the hollow of his hand.

Bertie laughed suddenly. 'It's queer about John. Whenever he is happiest he seems to be most alone. Have you noticed?'

He had noticed but had not thought of putting it into words.

'Now I,' continued the precocious girl, 'I am happiest when I am not alone.' She glanced at Jacques as their ponies came together in a narrowing of the road. 'You know, I'm glad we're friends—you and I and John. Don't you think it's funny, how people come together from the ends of the earth? It's as though a magnet had drawn us together. I've never had friends like this—not ones I wanted and chose for myself.' She tossed her fine dark hair. 'And yet I've always known what I wanted. It used to make me happy to think about it, but I know now that that was not really happiness.'

'Then what was it?' asked Jacques. He did not, as yet, fully understand her, for she seemed older than himself, infinitely more sure of herself. But her exuberance charmed him, he felt himself trembling on the brink of his one great love.

'I think it was my imagination. You know I have a terrific imagination. In England I used to imagine that I was happy. Haven't you, sometimes?'

He thought it over. 'No.'

She went on dreamily: 'I even used to imagine that I was sorry. I hate being sorry. I was, just a bit, when Fraulein died—I mean I was sorry because I knew that I couldn't love her as she wanted to be loved. Once, long ago, I loved someone, really, and that didn't make me sorry. At least not until afterwards.' She gave him a brilliant glance. 'Would you like to hear about it?'

Jacques suffered from a severe pang of jealousy, but without waiting for his grudging nod, Bertie went on: 'It was last summer just before Fraulein died. We were staying in Wales, on the coast. There was a boy there whose father was a fisherman. He was a very nice boy and took me swimming and fishing. Afterwards we used to lie on the rocks and practise staring at the sun to see who could do it longest. He always won. He taught me how to tie knots in ropes and the names of the different fishes. He was much older than I, but very good to me, and I would have liked to stay in Wales and be friends with him for ever.'

She fell silent, and Jacques waited, his mind vivid with the visions which she had created in it. Then Bertie continued: 'One day Fraulein saw us on the beach. My hair had got wet in the sea and he was holding it for the wind to blow through it. Fraulein didn't like that, and she took me away at once. She took me back to London, but first she said things to both of us in front of each other, and that is something which I shall never forgive Fraulein. Never!'

Jacques felt that he understood this in the very marrow of his bones.

'She didn't want me to love any one but herself,' said Bertie. 'And that was something I couldn't help. I'm glad she died. I knew I was going to be glad even before she died.'

'Then did you see your friend again?'

'No. I didn't want to see him again. I didn't even write to him. You see, the things that Fraulein said that time stayed in my mind. I could not forget them, and I was afraid that he could not forget them, either.'

'Yes,' Jacques murmured slowly, 'yes, I know.'

Macbeth came tearing back, his horse in a lather. 'I say, wouldn't it be fun if we should get a man-eater!'

Bertie wailed in terror, but Jacques explained that leopards do not attack people. Macbeth gave him a superior glance. 'They have been known to. They climb trees after you and even force their way into houses. Oh, not often, of course. But sometimes.' And with this contribution to natural history he scampered away at top speed, all hat and horse.

They rode beside a shallow valley under a sky of interminable blue; from a sunlit terrace a black partridge called as it had called to Marco Polo: '*Shir dharam ke shakrak!*' ('I have milk and honey!') Then they begin to climb and sprays of yellow dogwood brushed their hats as the ponies snorted and toiled up a slippery pine-spilled slope. Hills rising on either side flung heavy shadows on their road and the harsh cadenza of the partridge died behind them. The road widened and slipped out of sight round the edge of a gorge which seemed to open on nothing but an ocean of sky. Bertie suddenly reined in her pony and sat motionless, staring at a jagged rampart of quartz and cobalt which cut the world in half.

Jacques, reining his pony to a halt beside hers, said softly: 'Tibet.'

# 23

The tents were pitched in a semicircular glade with a fragment of the snows before and a densely wooded slope behind. Underbrush had been cleared and a shelter of boughs erected for horses and men. As the frail blue evening spiralled into darkness, a bonfire sprang up in the centre of the semicircle and a charcoal brazier glittered in the dark triangle of the cook's tent. Here on this pin-point of the continent, the nomadic English once more found home. But it was not enough, for like their poet who held eternity in an hour, their consciousness streamed towards the outer fringes of the firelight and embraced the brown hillmen who squatted there smoking their *chelums* and spitting on the stones.

The Macbeths and their guests sat round a table improvised out of a packing-case, and in the fire-glow and the flicker of a smoky lantern, they ate their tinned sardines and heard their own voices disperse in the starry air. When dinner was finished Lal Singh the old tracker squatted beside Colonel Macbeth, and they discussed plans for the next day's shoot. Lal Singh was tall and spare with a greenish beard and the bright, eternally youthful eyes of the hunter. 'I have arranged with the headman of a village not far from here to tie out a young goat. Tomorrow he will bring me word of the kill.'

'Must it be killed?' inquired Bertie plaintively.

The Colonel laughed, and Captain Ponsonby smiled, tilting back his camp chair. In the firelight their faces and hands shone like gold, their gestures were like abrupt portents flung upon the screen of darkness. Jacques, coming suddenly from his tent, saw Captain Ponsonby's hand lightly brush Mrs Macbeth's, saw their fingers twine and cling. The furtive intimacy sent a pang through him; he hesitated, then took his place between Bertie and Macbeth.

Bertie whispered: 'This is just as I said it would be. Listen!'

He listened, and heard the nighthawk strike its copper notes, two high and two low, and as though in answer to a signal, the fire fell together in a burst of sparks which perished, in their turn, under the full avalanche of night. Long after Macbeth had tumbled into sleep on the cot next to his own, Jacques lay awake, attentive to the Indian darkness where there is not such thing as silence—only a subtle shift of key and volume dividing the sound of night from the noise of day. Man is against nature, his thought is death to everything else that dares to move. Perhaps the child half-way between animal and man felt this without the necessity of words as, propped on his elbow, he stared through the opening of the tent across miles of starlit foliage to the pointed and luminous snows. And as he felt the other world stretch and stir around him he shared with nocturnal creatures an awareness of night and its meaning, for as human consciousness retreats the wilderness revives: it opens its golden eye, sets its soft black paw on the expectant stone. To be an animal is to be a thing as it is, not something inscribed in meaning, but a form without future, a palpitating and singular heart.

Jacques fell asleep and slid gently on to his pillow, the faint light touching his head and lying on his closed eyes. The shriek which woke him awoke, with its shrill stroke of terror, the whole camp. A little clot of humanity leaped and gesticulated, crying vengeance against the intruder who had outraged their temporary innocence. Every one

collected outside the Colonel's tent, and into their midst stalked Lal
Singh, to appropriate and to magnify his moment. 'A leopard has
taken the Memsahib's dog!'

It was true, Pedro had vanished. Leaving the foot of his mistress's
bed he had paddled forth to investigate the midnight stones, and in a
single weighted flash his pampered little spirit had bubbled into red
silence in the gully behind the camp. Now all the whistling and crying
in the world would not bring him wagging out of the darkness.

'By Jove!' exclaimed Captain Ponsonby, rushing out of his tent in
pyjamas. 'I thought the tribesmen had risen!'

His glance sought Pedro's mistress, who sat weeping on the edge of
her bed, with Bertie beside her. The Colonel stalked outside to quell a
babble of grooms and coolies, then he addressed Lal Singh. 'You're
quite sure it was a leopard?'

'The dog is dead, Sahib. Not a hundred yards away. I ran at once to
see, and the leopard, hearing me, dropped the body and made off. But
he will come back. We must, at once, build a *machan*.' And he vanished
into the shadows, trailed by two shivering hillmen carrying axes.

The Colonel looked at his wife. 'Poor darling! But you know Pedro
always was a fool. . . .'

'I should have chained him!'

Bertie shuddered. 'It must have been awfully sudden. He couldn't
have suffered.'

'How do you know?' demanded Macbeth. In the feeble lantern light
his face was white and drawn. 'That scream . . . of course he suffered!'

'Oh, don't!' wailed Mrs Macbeth. 'Don't, don't!'

Colonel Macbeth broke in decisively: 'We had better toss up for the
first shot. Anybody got a rupee?'

'You needn't bother about me,' said Bertie. 'I'm not going to sit up
for the thing. Wild horses wouldn't make me.'

'Then it's between us four. All right, Ponsonby?'

The coin spun upwards and fell on the Colonel's outstretched palm.

'I'm with you, Bertie,' said the Captain. He sat down beside her and
lighted a cigarette.

The Colonel looked at the two boys. 'All right, Jacques?'

'Heads,' said Jacques, his voice sounding odd in his own ears.

'Heads it is. Now it's between you and John.'

'Heads,' said Jacques again, presentiment gripping him.

The coin described its broken arc and landed once more on the
Colonel's hand. He smiled at Jacques. 'You win!'

Jacques watched the colour flow slowly back into Macbeth's face,
and he thought with a queer, inward thrill. '*He* was frightened too!'

Colonel Macbeth picked up a rifle which stood at the foot of his own cot, and Jacques watched stiffly as the brass cartridges slid into the breech. 'It's a bit long for you, but I think you can handle it. Better cock one barrel at a time. You may only need one unless you just wound him, in which case try and get in the second shot as fast as you can. Aim for the shoulder, or just a fraction behind the shoulder, unless you're sure of a good head shot.' He peered into the boy's face. 'What's up, old chap? You're trembling.'

'Excitement,' murmured Captain Ponsonby, who had been watching Jacques steadily.

Jacques took the rifle. 'I . . .' He broke off, meeting the Colonel's cool blue eyes. 'Shall we go?'

They were preceded by a coolie carrying a lantern which shed its silly little varnish on the nearer leaves and the big pale boulders of the gully. They found Pedro lying on the stones; his throat was torn open and his tongue hung horribly from a corner of his mouth. Colonel Macbeth whispered sharply: 'Don't touch him. We want to leave as little scent as possible. Ah, they've got the *machan* ready. Good work, Lal Singh!'

The *machan* comprised two short planks lashed between the branches of a tough little oak which leaned out towards the gully about twenty feet above Pedro's body. Lal Singh had contrived a screen of boughs which made a perfect eyrie for the hunter, and into this Jacques was pushed and hoisted, with a handful of extra cartridges and a few final instructions. 'Don't move. Keep your fingers off the hammer until you're ready. The moon may come up before he decides to return. Now, good luck!'

They left him there and he watched the lantern dance away among the trees and vanish with their voices and the sound of their cautious feet. With their going the night surged upon him like a tide; he was alone with the bleeding corpse below him and murder stalking among the shadows. He was alone, and in a little while the camp, which he could not see, settled into indifferent silence. They had cut him adrift from their warmth and the comfort of their bodies, they had abandoned him utterly.

A breath of wind rustled the stiff leaves of the oak in which he sat and he felt the sweat steal down his face, felt it wet the palms of his hands, gripping the rifle barrel. The unrelenting steel thrust against his flesh. Use me, it said, for that is what I mean, that is what I am. Holding his breath, he practised drawing back the hammers, then releasing them, feeling their sinewy strain against the ball of his thumb. All I have to do is to pull the triggers and the hills will rock in uproar and every living thing go to earth. Well, why not ? Tell them that I aimed at a shadow or at a flitting owl, and let them laugh. Then he saw Colonel Macbeth's offended eyes and behind those eyes a succession of others, the eyes of men who abhor a coward. And yet, he thought, I am not really a coward, not really afraid. But to be alone, to be left out, to be abandoned. . . . How far away the morning seemed!

One of his feet went to sleep and he stared earnestly at the sky, which seemed to change as the moon thrust invisibly past a barrier of hills. The silence had become a tensile web which stifled him. Pedro lay limply dark on the lighter stones, he might have been a stone, a furred stone from which the blood escaped with a lively logic. I wonder, thought Jacques, what is fear? Is it mauling, uproar, struggle, pain? And he remembered Pedro's dying shriek.

He clutched the rifle, reminding himself that its destructive force was a matter dependent on his own will. God of death, he sat waiting to destroy, and the terror of the destroyer fluttered in his body. All that was demanded of him was that he press the curled metal tooth under his hand and shattering death would cleanse the darkness before him. Out of man's brain had come this miracle, this beautiful little shining capsule which injects death into life's unsuspecting body. He was trembling, then his trembling ceased as he heard the sound for which he'd waited—the tiny creak of a dry leaf. It was as though the earth had drawn a faint extra breath, and this breath stirred the hairs along the back of his neck. There was no further sound, but a stone which had been dark now appeared light, and another which had been light concealed itself. Just as when, an hour ago, he had known that he was about to win the toss, he now knew that his presence was detected, that he was being pondered and judged, his fate meditated by a stealthy and humid god.

Silence crouched in the slow fire of the rising moon as Jacques, beside himself with terror, reached forward to tear away the screen of leaves before him; a twig brushed against the triggers and he caught in his left hand the full roar of the exploding charge.

# PART II

## 24

Striking eastward across Ceylon, the monsoon burst and divided like a pair of arms, one arm clasping the peninsula to the west and the other to the east, and in this cataclysmic weather men pondered their fields and returned thanks to God for the blessed reprieve of rain. Weather, they would have you know, was invented by God for men alone: it starts or stunts their crops, stalls a war, incites cholera, or allays, for a spell, the sprue. When weather misbehaves, men read in its defection a retribution for their wrongdoing; no wonder that, in gratitude for these tons of liquid, humanity returns thanks in appropriate fashion. It harnesses up a flowery cart and submits its body to the grinding wheels, it plunges into a river formed of Divine sweat, and remembers that when Juggernaut appeared in the guise of man he caused the prosaic nim tree to put forth champak flowers. If there were no weather there would be no God; He'd diminish, attenuated to a philosophical concept, or relapse into memory until the day when nature decided upon a further outrage against the human race. As Aubrey Wall drove towards Mrs Lyttleton's house where he was to dine for the last time, he watched rain drench the road and knew that everywhere humble people were praising the Lord as they paddled through the downpour, guiding it in crude channels to every plot and *bigha* of soil. But he was incapable of sharing in the jubilation of these god-infested folk—their joys and their griefs were on too vast a scale for his participation.

He drove between the sandstone pillars of Mrs Lyttleton's compound and drew up under the porch. The garden, stimulated to undreamed-of luxuriance, spewed forth frogs and fragrance and an occasional cobra. Only round the graves under the loquat trees was there any semblance of order.

His groom led the tonga away towards the stables, and Wall went up the steps to greet his old friend. She took his hand and stared into his face. 'I can't believe that this is the last time I shall see you.'

'I am only going on furlough, you know!'

They sat as usual on the veranda under the stuffed heads. Wall poured himself a brandy from the decanters which waited beside his chair, and played with a glass eye which had popped out from a mouldering socket above him.

'Well,' murmured Mrs Lyttleton, the sense of parting hanging over her like a cloud. 'Can it be two years since we said goodbye to Hardyal and you longed to go with him?'

'Two years! Hardyal and I will probably pass each other in the Mediterranean.'

They were silent, their thoughts branching at this point. For Aubrey Wall these two years were memorable less as sequences in time than as accidents which bore little relation to his past but which must in some indefinable way colour, or discolour, his future. For Mrs Lyttleton they were the final wave of the last century, carrying her forward and depositing her neatly within the boundary of the twentieth. She congratulated herself on a sense of achievement, for just as everything in her experience retained its vivid aura, so for her, now, did time retain it. Each year that she survived assumed the character of a personal possession, to be cherished as in the past she had cherished intenser pleasures.

To her companion she presently remarked that the years were like journeys which seemed shorter between certain points than between others, but for this phenomenon she held the human moon entirely responsible. 'After our forties time picks up speed and we know where we're headed, and that, my friend, is the age of resignation.'

'Resignation? To what—the end?'

'Oh no, I am not at all sure that there is an end.'

'Then to what else is one resigned?'

'Well, let's say to the consolatory role of the bystander.'

He laughed. 'You—a bystander! You will always be instrumental.'

She gave him a grateful smile. 'After all, I'm long past seventy.'

'Yet you are still not sure that there is an end. That sounds like a Hindu.'

'I am one at heart.'

'God forbid!'

'Ah, but just consider the mercies of rebirth.'

'Not for me, thanks. One life is enough.'

She gave him an acute glance, appropriating in all their details changes which the years had wrought in him. Not that she had ever thought him distinguished, but he interested her now as he had not interested her before. One life, he'd just said, was enough. Might it not perhaps have been almost too much? She knew that in every life there comes a sort of *crise*, after which anything is possible. Where and when had his *crise* occurred? He had never struck her as being specially inflammable, yet she was sure that something must have ignited him: something still smouldered there within a feverish glow.

She murmured: 'Perhaps for you England will constitute a rebirth.'

Two years ago—even a year ago—he would have kindled at the prospect, today he shrugged. 'Oh, perhaps.'

'But you are glad to be going?'

'I suppose so.'

'And you will come back to India?'

'It's my bread and butter, you know.'

'What a dull way of looking at it!' She laughed, then said gravely: 'I shall miss you, Aubrey. One by one my friends are disappearing.'

He gave her a gentle and understanding glance. 'You're thinking of Jacques St Remy. But it's your own fault, you know. If you were a more forgiving woman . . .'

She interrupted with an angry flash of her diamonds. 'Yes, yes, if I were more forgiving I would be less lonely! But after all, if one cannot forget one cannot forgive, no matter how cleverly one pretends. I have pretended, often, in love—but never in hate.'

He shrugged. 'Feuds bore me.'

'Yet they can be a means of preserving contact,' she reminded him, with an incorrigible laugh. After a brief silence, he said:

'Well, at any rate, you will soon have Hardyal, with whom you have no feud. Be good to him, won't you? Keep him up to the mark. They lose it . . . so easily.'

She did not need to be reminded what it was that 'they' lost so easily, for she was familiar with his ideas on the subject. Wall went on: 'Yes, I think . . . perhaps . . . to get away will be a sort of rebirth. I'm tired.' He broke off, then finished on a note of temper: 'I'm fed up!'

This was obvious, but Mrs Lyttleton had heard too many rumours about him to venture even a discreet inquiry, so she changed the subject by inquiring after the health of friends on whom she knew he had been paying farewell calls.

'I saw Father Sebastien, who gave me his blessing.' Wall smiled wryly. 'The good man seemed to think I needed it. When I called on Madame St Remy, she gave me *durwaza bund*.' He used the uncompromising Hindustani term for the English Not at Home.

'And the children, what news of them?'

Wall hesitated, staring at the glass eye which lay in his palm.

'Well, Father Sebastien informed me that Gisele is happily established in her Belgian cloister.'

'Ah! They would have seen to that.'

'Perhaps she saw to it herself.'

'That child? Hardly.'

'They sometimes marry, don't they, at her age?' His flippant tone surprised her and she replied: 'I thought you felt as I did, that Gisele's decision was a tragic one.'

He tossed the glass eye in the air and caught it again. 'Oh tragedy, tragedy! That's an overworked horse.'

Mrs Lyttleton shook her head. 'I had a glimpse of her last year. I have never seen a more beautiful girl.'

Wall drained his brandy. 'I have, though I must confess . . . somewhat duskier, somewhat muskier!'

The words, the tone, troubled Mrs Lyttleton. She hesitated, then asked for Jacques.

'Father Sebastien said that this was his last year at St Matthew's. Do you think they'll make a monk out of him?'

She frowned. 'To be fair, I don't think they ever intended that.'

'If not, it is only because Madame has other plans.' The glass eye slipped from her fingers and fell in a corner, where it lay balefully glaring. 'She will bring him back to Amritpore and set him to work in her factory, which he loathes. In due time she'll import a meek little wife for him from her so-aristocratic France. Oh, I think we can rest assured that Madame will attend to everything.'

Mrs Lyttleton looked at him curiously. 'I sometimes think that you must dislike Madame almost as much as I do.'

'If I do, it is because she frightens me, rather.'

She laughed at that. 'Frightens you? She doesn't frighten me.'

'Well, she frightened Gisele, and she has tried, I imagine, to frighten the boy.'

'By the exercise of power?' Mrs Lyttleton nodded slowly. 'I see. But after all, they are her children, and I suppose that in a sense she redeems herself by her love for them. I don't see, though, why she should frighten you.'

'Perhaps because I realize that she can have no redeeming love for me!'

'Well, neither can she have any conceivable power over you,' objected Mrs Lyttleton.

'Nevertheless, the spectacle of any one exercising tyrannical power over others is revolting, don't you agree? Especially in women.'

'Why especially in women?'

He brooded for a minute. 'Perhaps because women are not, as a rule, subject to the same discipline as ourselves. Power doesn't go to a woman's head as it goes to a man's—it goes straight to her emotions.'

'What you are trying to say is that power doesn't make for greatness in women as it very often does in men?'

'For intellectual greatness, no. They usually end up by becoming victims.' Mrs Lyttleton, remembering some of the stories which she had heard of his brutality to his servants, wondered silently whether he, too, had not fallen victim to his own power.

She gave him a keen glance. 'However, you don't deny that Madame St Remy is intelligent.'

He looked, suddenly bored. 'Oh, intelligent—yes.'

'I don't know whether you meant to, but you have given me a distinct impression that you regard her as a thoroughly immoral woman.'

'I never said so.'

'Tyrannical power,' Mrs Lyttleton repeated slowly, 'unredeemed by intellectual greatness . . .'

'Oh, that!'

'Yes, that.' She watched him pour himself another brandy. 'And what's more, I agree with you.'

There was a brief pause, then she wondered aloud: 'Do you think that Jacques will stand up?'

'I can't see that it signifies.'

'It will signify for him if not for us. I know you've accused me of reading too much importance into minor matters, but I think that Jacques' struggle is important, though he himself is hardly aware of it, as yet. Whenever I see youth break with the part I know that the future will feel the shock.'

He smiled sceptically, but she went on: 'I cannot help wondering about these children. It might have been a different story if they all stayed in their own country, but in India they—like you and I—will be on trial.'

'On trial?'

'Lately I have felt more and more this sense of being on trial—not only that we are being judged for our shortcomings as rulers, but for our capacities as human beings.'

Wall frowned, but she went on quickly: 'You have always seen the natives as a mass, with an occasional shining example of loyalty, and that is how you judge them. But doesn't it ever strike you as odd how well we've succeeded in elevating the natives' loyalty to a major virtue?'

'What's so odd about it?'

'That we should appraise the loyalty purely from the point of view of its relation to our own good.'

Wall disliked the turn which the conversation had taken. He enjoyed Mrs Lyttleton's wit and her malice just so long as she confined herself to more or less airy and personal affairs, but he had a horror of the controversial soul-searching to which she seemed increasingly given. By cutting herself away from most of her own people she had come to question and to criticize them more and more from the Indian standpoint—a dangerous and a futile attitude. The General's widow was a relic of days when it was still possible for an Indian and Englishman to meet on an autocratic footing. She had more than once laughingly described herself as the last of the English Begums, and declared that had she not had the luck to live in Victoria's time she would have chosen that of Queen Elizabeth, thus unconsciously, perhaps, identifying herself with an age of imperial and matriarchal vitality. What she seemed unable or unwilling to grasp was the fact that those reigns were over and done with: there was a brand-new spirit in the air. Aubrey Wall, for one, felt out of step with this new spirit; lately he'd begun to question whether he should ever have left England, to wonder whether his was an organism which survives transplanting. The question remained unanswered, for what would have been his chances in England, where every one jostled every one else and where the possession of brains—when not allied to birth and money—was considered an unfair advantage? You were invited to take them elsewhere and to be careful how you used them. Naturally it never occurred to Wall to question this state of affairs—he was essentially English, with a dyed-in-the-wool attitude towards social inequalities. But personal frustration and bitterness found their inevitable release in contempt and dislike of exile, and the land of the exile. In India he'd found a poverty so deplorable that millions sipped life rather than lived it—and he saw them tamely submitting to their fate. Wherever an oasis occurred the starving hordes closed in and the oasis diminished. The white man created his own oasis, ruthlessly aware that he must, while his conscience-stricken mind bore the notion of an inherent superiority, the myth of the self-anointed.

Mrs Lyttleton's problem had been simpler, for she had accepted exile with an aristocratic philosophy and the knowledge that one undertook a voyage round the Cape of Good Hope once in a lifetime. She had come to India with her mind made up and she had never unmade it; but for Aubrey Wall the psychic grudge of separation was kept alive by periodic leaves spent in England. Not India, but England was his home; he could not forget that, he did not want to forget it. And what after all did Mrs Lyttleton know of *his* India, the new India with its developing social consciousness? What did she know of the official India composed of time-servers, petty subordinates, cravens, conspirators, and sycophants? For five years he had had to do with Indians and although he'd liked several, even loved a few, the feeling was never deeper than a sentiment which they shared with his horses and his dogs. Even in the self-effacement of debauchery he was bitterly conscious of the difference between himself and them, for the dark skin was aromatic with it.

## 25

As night fell, the rain paused then stopped, and out from the obscurity burst the frogs' voices. Aubrey Wall could imagine the countless pallid throats swelling in chorus, and a sense of suffocation came upon him: there seemed no respite from the country's fecundity, no crevice which did not house some musician-snout, some fixed eye, some coiled spring of venom, or a fistful of feathers cheeping with lust. He conjured up visions of home, of England's antique serenity, and the effort brought him to the brink of revelation. He no longer felt alone and spectral but part of the solid structure of a tried and rational whole. Another second and the mystery of his own plight would have ended, he would understand all things—then Mrs Lyttleton broke the spell;

'Where is that boy with the lamps?'

A deliquescent light which bathed the garden stopped short at the veranda steps. 'Jalal!' screamed Mrs Lyttleton in the sudden fury of autocracy neglected. '*Butti jalao!*' ('Light the lamps!')

There was no answer except from the frogs, who renewed their chorus.

She peered at Wall through the gloom. 'I'm so sorry. He thought we were talking, so decided not to interrupt us. But the lights, the lights! It's getting as dark as pitch.'

'No doubt Jalal will come in his own good time.'

'I shall dock his pay!'

'You won't. You know you won't. You have never punished him and that's what's the trouble with him. It's what's the trouble with all of them!'

She realized that her guest was somewhat drunk. 'I'll go and find Jalal,' she murmured placatingly. 'I won't be a moment.'

But Wall rose suddenly. 'I'll go. I know my way.'

There was something menacing about him, and she demurred: 'I wish you would let me, Aubrey.'

'Don't worry, I'll find him.'

Mrs Lyttleton suffered from the sudden helpless fear which assails old people, for she had caught the note of temper in his voice and she knew that tone, having heard it often enough in her long life.

'Aubrey . . .'

But he walked across the veranda and disappeared into the darkened drawing-room. She heard his feet on the matting, heard him bump into a chair, then she guessed that he had entered the dining-room beyond. Darkness swallowed him as it had swallowed everything in the great empty house; only in the garden did forms remain and retain their meaning. She fumbled for her cigarettes, assuring herself that she was a fool to be anxious on Jalal's account. Either he was drunk in some remote nook, or wide awake to see the Sahib coming and to make his escape, for Wall's temper was a byword among the servants of Amritpore.

Wall felt his way through the dark rooms to the veranda where dishes were washed and lamps trimmed. Beyond it stretched an untidy compound and a line of servants' quarters, where a light or two glimmered. At sight of them his formless anger flared into rage. He had always detested Mrs Lyttleton's servants, who epitomized—for him—everything that was typical in the native character: inertia, instability, opportunism, filth. He'd settle them!

He started across the veranda and immediately fell over a large bundle which lay in the shadow of a meat safe. The bundle was Jalal, snoring in the deep oblivion of his favourite drug. Wall, in falling, cracked his elbow on a corner of the meat safe and a white heat exploded inside him. Pulling himself together he kicked the supine figure twice, with the precise weighted kick of an athlete. Jalal groaned and rolled sluggishly on is side; he did not waken but lay snoring on a changed note, with his knees drawn up like a trussed fowl.

Wall turned away and shouted into the gloom for his syce to fetch the tonga, and when a faint answering shout reached him, he made his way back to the front veranda. 'I found your faithful servant, but he is so stuffed with *bhang* that I doubt very much whether you will get any dinner, or any breakfast for that matter.'

'Did you try to wake him?'

'I have him a couple of kicks, but he merely snored.'

'You kicked him.'

'Not hard enough, apparently.'

They heard the jingle of harness and watched the soft beam from the carriage lamps bloom on the puddles. Mrs Lyttleton felt sad that they should part on such an ugly note, but Wall was silent, staring into the darkness where rain was beginning to fall again. He had a sudden strange feeling about the rain, a personal feeling, as he thought of it falling all over north-western India, swelling the rivers and the reservoirs, rushing along his canals into the great retaining tanks, and spilling over into the arid, wasted land. The violence of a few minutes ago had calmed him, his blood flowed cool in his veins, he was conscious of a revived sense of generosity and well-being.

The tonga drove up under the porch and his coachman leaped out and ran to the horses' heads. Mrs Lyttleton put out her hand and said in a firm voice: 'Well, Aubrey!'

He took the dry, wrinkled fingers. 'Au revoir, Laura.'

'Yes,' she murmured. 'Au revoir.'

# 26

'Come in, come in!' cried Ganpat Rai, catching sight of his visitor behind the bamboo screen. 'Come in, Abdul Salim!'

'I see you are busy. I can wait.'

'Wait then, in the drawing-room. I shall join you in a moment.'

Salim retired, stepping cautiously among an array of shoes outside Ganpat Rai's study. Within, clients were squatting on the floor round the barrister's English desk, and Salim could hear their droning voices punctuated by the nasal interruptions of Ganpat Rai's clerk taking down depositions. Salim knew that study, its bookcases stacked with works on jurisprudence, it walls hung with engravings of famous English judges and lawyers. All the paraphernalia of success was here, paraphernalia so dear to the eyes of harassed miscreants out on bail.

As he loitered on the veranda Salim watched servants hoist the curtains on the tennis court; rain had soaked them and they travelled stiffly on their pulleys. Nearby, a gardener was clipping a hedge, another raking the gravel.

Salim reflected grimly on his own house, a stone's throw from the bazaar, a house with no garden, no tennis court, and no punkah in the hot weather; he thought of the drab and dusty compound invaded by cats and pi-dogs and smells. From the study behind came a nasal whine: 'Wherefore your humble servant petitioneth . . .'

He wandered down the veranda to the drawing-room with its muddle of English and native furnishings, a muddle for which he had no particular fondness since he'd become a convert to the new school of Swadeshi and would not permit foreign things in his house. Here were altogether too many brass and teakwood tables, cane settees, a Chippendale mirror. There were too many photographs in ornamental frames—photographs of Hardyal taken during the successive stages of his sojourn in England. Hardyal standing before a low stone house in the uncertain English sunlight; Hardyal on horseback with a row of little willows behind him; Hardyal taller, stronger, in flannels and the striped cap of his school. Hardyal, every inch the pukka sahib! Then, as he examined a recent portrait of Ganpat Rai in the black gown, curled wig, and notched collar of the High Court, something hot and unhappy flowed upward from his heart. It was not that he grudged his friend his success, yet how resist a pang of envy? True, a diploma from the Moslem College at Aligarh and an M.A. from Calcutta University were not to be despised, but they were *not* Balliol and the Inner Temple. Salim thought again of his own sons, young men with superior ambitions occupying inferior government positions. Where was the money to come from, or the opportunity for that matter, in a land where the English and their toadies had cornered all the jobs? As the Mohammedan brooded on his pet grudge he paused before the mirror and examined his features: bearded, black-eyed, the hair under his fez streaked with grey. He knew himself to be equal if not superior to many of his friends, yet nothing in his life gave evidence of this fact. He was poor, his house was shabby, himself and his sons frustrated at every turn. Salim's forefathers had been officers in the court of the last Mughal, something which he found impossible to forget and painful to remember. Pride sustained him, pride which fed on a temper which in its turn sucked the bitter core of resentment.

He turned impatiently to a bookcase filled with history and biography, with the novels of Thackeray and Dickens and Balzac, and Dante's *Vita nuova*, which last the white ants seemed to prefer beyond all others. Too many books, Salim decided, sliding one back into its place. Men can glut themselves on learning and remain chained.

Ganpat Rai appeared in the door behind him. 'Which do you prefer, the garden or the house? Both are yours.'

The garden was damp and full of ants; Salim preferred the house. Free from European eyes, they sat on cushions on the floor and a servant brought them *pan supari* and cigarettes.

Salim said: 'I came to thank you for sending me the Khwaja case, though I hoped you would have come in on it with me.'

'What need? You have far greater skill than I in handling these police prosecutions.'

'You mean I understand their methods! Well, I fancy I left the Assistant Magistrate with very much the same impression.' He stroked his beard with a studied air of triumph. He had enjoyed too few in his time, and this one had been exceptionally sweet—it lasted.

'That was a witty remark of yours to the sub-inspector,' said Ganpat Rai. 'Wherever your exalted footsteps have fallen, there has an informer been born'!'

Both men laughed, reliving the splendid moment of the policeman's discomfiture. They were in native dress and their postures were characteristic: the Hindu all repose, the Mohammedan austere and intense. The latter's air of triumph waned a little as he asked, presently: 'I take it you have not heard that judgment was delivered yesterday on the Khwaja case?'

'I have heard nothing.'

'Well, it is true that I made them squirm—I made them squirm! But in his summing up that *badzat* Jones chose to indulge in sarcasm at my expense. "Mr Abdul Salim," said he'—and here the Mohammedan veered into a passable Oxford drawl—'"Mr. Abdul Salim has seen fit to inject political considerations into this case, considerations which are bewildering, to say the least of it, and to say the worst—irrelevant"!'

'Ah!' an expression of keen disappointment passed over Ganpat Rai's face. 'Case dismissed? No!'

'Case dismissed.'

There was a disturbance in the veranda and they watched a mob of clients drift down the steps and cross the drive towards the gates. The light changed subtly, a servant came in and rolled up the screens. When he had gone Ganpat Rai inquired gently: 'You attribute the judgment not to your own but to Jones's political bias?'

'Isn't it obvious?'

To the Hindu what was obvious was his friend's readiness to seize upon what, in this case, was not obvious at all. Salim shrugged with affected unconcern. 'What matter? Jones is an ignoramus. He has fallen under the spell of his snobbish friends.'

Ganpat Rai nodded soothingly. 'Perhaps he will be transferred.'

'Would that God might transfer every mother's son of them to Jehannum!'

The other smiled. 'To make room for another Mahmud of Ghazni?' He alluded to the first great Mohammedan conqueror of India. Salim shrugged. 'Why not?' When his friend remained silent the Mohammedan burst out: 'Allah! How tired I am of them all! You do not see it, you do not feel it! But we are like sheep, we are slaves, for ever obeying, salaaming, fawning!'

'Let us be honest, you do not fawn—neither do I.'

'I would be naught but honest. Let us all be honest, then, and force honesty upon them. Let us share in such honesty as would make the affair of 1857 look like a garden party!'

'No, my friend, no.'

'Why not? That is the sort of honesty they best understand. It is something we all share, for blood draws men together.'

'Yes, blood draws men together, yet everywhere else in the natural world extinction comes from ripeness, dropping heavy with life.'

'You speak as if we were rotten apples!'

'And what are we but rotten flesh?'

He sat sad-eyed like one of his own Bhakti saints, for he knew very well that in Amritpore there were many, Hindus and Mohammedans, who shared Salim's feelings; men with grievances festering like bamboo slivers in their flesh, honest men with the everlasting dream flowing in their veins.

Salim regained his composure. 'We see things differently. I have not your forbearance, for I cannot believe that in life changes occur of themselves. Nothing comes of itself but sickness.'

They were silent, their thoughts running close but divided. In character and in mentality both were diametrically opposed; both knew this and had ceased to resent it, yet much as they had learned to understand each other, psychologically they remained unreconciled. Like cloth which has been deeply dyed, their separate traditions clung to them: to the militant unswerving Moslem and the speculative, peace-loving Hindu.

Ganpat Rai offered his friend another cigarette and attempted, with a lawyer's skill, to divert the conversation into less stormy channels. Had Salim heard the story of Ramdatta's attempt to bribe the new Superintendent of Police? The moneylender had sent an emissary with an offering of mangoes, several of which had been cunningly opened and gold coins inserted in place of the big centre seed. But it seemed that the Englishman had received some warning of what to expect: a humorist in his way, he received Ramdatta's gift with a great show of geniality, admired the mangoes, then regretfully explained that he was himself unable to eat the fruit, which gave him diarrhoea. However, since it was out of the question to return such a gift he would presume to share credit with Ramdatta in an act of grace; and sending a constable to round up a group of itinerant beggars, the policeman distributed the fruit amongst them. The story diverted Salim, who hated the moneylender only a little less than he hated the English. And speaking of Ramdatta—had Ganpat Rai heard the rumour of Madame's indebtedness to the moneylender? This was mere gossip, but plausible enough. The world, always excepting poor Madame, knew that indigo was done for, yet last year she had put another three hundred acres to the crop while her foreman openly stated that they could no longer dispose of what they had on hand.

Ganpat Rai looked grave. 'So she is borrowing from that *gid*?' (Vulture)

'Birds of a feather!' said Salim. 'Let her ruin herself. If it were not indigo it would be something else. The country is a treasure house for these people. And by the way, I met your friend Wall's successor the other day.'

'How did he impress you?'

'You should know by now that your English friends do not impress me—they depress me.' He gave the other a sidelong glance. 'Since we gossip, what do you happen to know about the strange death of Mrs Lyttleton's servant, Jalal?'

'Nothing stranger than that he died of a fall.'

'I heard whispers that he was beaten to death.'

'By Mrs Lyttleton?' And Ganpat Rai laughed.

'Feroze the assistant surgeon is my cousin, as you know. He was present at the autopsy and he tells me that Jalal's spleen was ruptured by what looked like a sharp blow. Feroze assured me that it could not possibly have been self-inflicted.'

Ganpat Rai gazed at his friend. 'I know Jalal was a co-religionist of yours. Can that be the reason for this morbid concern?'

'It doesn't happen to be the reason. But mysteries amuse me, especially when they implicate the English. I'm not suggesting that Mrs Lyttleton was responsible or even that she knows how it happened. However, there are certain points which intrigue me: Jalal was a stupid fellow, he had no enemies, nor was he athletically given to rushing about inviting physical injury. And Feroze tells me emphatically that the spleen was ruptured. He has seen malarial spleens in people who have been beaten or kicked.'

Ganpat Rai frowned. 'I fail to see just what it is you are driving at.'

Salim lighted another cigarette. 'The local authorities have made their customary efficient investigation, and their verdict is death due to accidental causes. Jalal was only a poor servant and there were no witnesses. However, I have gone to the trouble to make a few inquiries on my own account. The results turn out to be rather interesting. The gardener, the scullion, the sweeper all assure me that Jalal was far too lethargic to have become involved in a brawl. He had not left the premises for several days nor had his friends visited him during that time. Yet according to Feroze death must have followed almost immediately after the blow.'

'Truly, a mystery!' Ganpat Rai spoke sarcastically, but he felt a sudden uneasiness. Salim was no fool and his little discoveries were often of a disquieting nature.

'Another thing,' continued the Mohammedan. 'The night they found Jalal dead in Mrs Lyttleton's house, your friend Aubrey Wall was there. It was the evening before he left Amritpore for Calcutta.'

He had the Hindu's attention now, all of it. 'Why on earth should Wall's presence have any bearing on Jalal's death?'

Salim hesitated for a moment, then spoke with bitterness: 'I know that Wall is your friend, that you like him greatly. Perhaps I should not speak of him to you. But we all share the same idea of justice, do we not? You and I, Wall himself. No, listen . . .' he put out a hand as the other seemed about to interrupt. 'He is your friend, but he was never mine. Nor was he ever friendly to many whom he knew as well as he knew you, and who might be said to have as much claim as you on his kindness. He disliked me, and for good reason—I disliked him. Perhaps for that reason I am better informed of his character than you could be, for I have kept a little dossier on him ever since he came to Amritpore.'

'You spied on him?' The Hindu's voice was suddenly hard.

'It was not necessary to spy. The English rarely descend to concealment—they are above that sort of thing. But I must say I think Wall was more indiscreet than most men. For instance, he had prostitutes brought into his house.'

'An indiscretion even in a lonely bachelor, I grant you!' And Ganpat Rai laughed, not very happily.

'Did you not know that he was diseased?'

'That I will not believe!'

'Come now, as a man of the world . . .'

Ganpat Rai interrupted in a troubled voice: 'I speak as a man of the world.'

'Don't worry. It will all be charged up to our account.' He was back on his favourite ground and Ganpat Rai listened in despair. 'Not enough white women to go around so we must take what we can get—black, brown, or tea-coloured. This beastly country, don't you know, quite unfit for white men.'

'Oh hush!' Ganpat Rai implored. He rose and walked to the door, peered out, then came back. 'Abdul Salim, sometimes I think you are quite mad. I cannot understand your feelings, I cannot!'

The Mohammedan looked at him sombrely. 'You mean you *will* not. You love these people,' he said in a heavy voice. 'I wonder why? I have tried to see them through your eyes, but I cannot. You say you do not understand my feelings, but there are many who do. There are more and more, every day, who feel as I feel.'

'Do not misunderstand me! I do not scorn your feelings—there is much in you that I admire and respect. But when you tell me that I love the English, you are right. We shall be governed by someone—by Hindus or Moslems or by the English. What does it matter?'

'Nevertheless the English do not love you, Ganpat Rai.'

'You are mistaken. They have proved it.'

Salim shook his head. There was, suddenly, something prophetic about him, and ominous dignity. 'No, they do not love you. They do

not love any of us. They have done us too much wrong ever to be able
to love us. It is easier for us to love them, for us to forgive them.' He
gazed at his friend. 'Beaten people have but two alternatives to
humiliation—they can hate or they can love.'

'I do not consider myself a beaten person!'

'That is because you have chosen one alternative.'

Ganpat Rai was about to break into a sharp rejoinder, then the spirit
went out of him and he sighed. 'Perhaps you are right. You are very
subtle. But there is nothing very subtle about affection and gratitude.
Aubrey Wall is my friend and I have eaten his salt. For two years his
family have befriended my son. I cannot—I will not listen to you.'

'Then I shall say no more about his personal life. Let us confine
ourselves to his public actions. You know that he was given to
thrashing his servants on the slightest provocation? On the night of
Jalal's death he drove to Mrs Lyttleton's and sent his syce to the stables
while he talked with Mrs Lyttleton on the front veranda. Later, the syce
was summoned to bring the tonga to the front of the house, and he
tells me that Wall shouted to him from the back veranda—from the
very place where Jalal was later found dead.'

'And it is on the strength of these flimsy details that you try to build
a case against Wall? Remember, you have yet to show cause.'

As the Hindu took up the cudgels, Salim smoked with an enigmatic
air.

'Let us for a moment,' said Ganpat Rai, 'ignore the all-important
why and wherefore and stick to your story of circumstantial evidence.
I am, as you know, familiar with the general plan of Mrs Lyttleton's
house. The distance which separates the front from the back veranda is
roughly a hundred feet. There are no doors, not even curtains in
between, merely open arches. On your own showing there were but
two people present on that evening, Wall and Mrs Lyttleton.
Presumably, there was not much noise going on. Had Wall for any
reason whatsoever attacked Jalal, there must surely have been a scuffle,
and outcry. Do you imagine that Mrs Lyttleton would have allowed
any one to lay a hand on her servant? She told me herself what
occurred that evening. Wall had come to dine with her, but Jalal never
appeared and she was obliged to let her guest depart supperless. When
he'd gone she found Jalal on the back veranda, fast asleep, as she
thought. She summoned a scullion and between them they tried to
rouse Jalal, but on taking his pulse Mrs Lyttleton realized that
something was wrong. She sent for the doctor, who pronounced the
man dead. The autopsy revealed that he was saturated with opium,
and they arrived at the perfectly justifiable conclusion that in his
drugged state he'd walked into some sharp object like the corner of a

table or a packing case, and had driven it into his stomach, which in its relaxed condition put up no resistance to the blow. There never was any question of foul play. Why should there be?' He stared at his companion. 'Come now, confess that you are by nature suspicious! Any excuse to pin guilt on your bugbears, the English!' And he laughed, laying his hand on Salim's knee. But the Mohammedan sneered. 'After all, you are staking your argument entirely on the word of Mrs Lyttleton.'

'I would stake my life on her word.'

The conventional statement, intended merely to clinch the argument, induced a curious effect in the speaker; for as he uttered the words they seemed to release a shock of intense, spontaneous joy which illumined him through and through. He would stake his life on her word! How pure and how simple the truth, yet how overwhelming! He could not, now, have borne to hear a word spoken against her, so he rose, saying firmly: 'Come, let us go into the garden.'

Salim responded, less to the command than to the tone, for he sensed the emotion which inspired it, and it was always easier for him to respond to emotion than to cold logic. They went out and the scent of damp earth rose against their faces, refreshing them. As they strolled between glossy hedges, their separate suspicions and rivalries dissolved and they fell into easy talk of local affairs, of their work, of their families. In a little while Salim asked for news of Hardyal, and Ganpat Rai took a letter from his pocket and handed it to him. Salim read it, smiling.

'What a beautiful hand! And how splendid it will be to have him back.' This was brought out fully and generously, and Ganpat Rai's eyes filled with tears. 'Yes, I shall be glad to have him back. I have missed him.'

They came to the end of their path and saw before them a sort of arbour whose walls were screens of the same blue stuff which served as backstops on the tennis court. From behind this screen came a sound of women's voices and the music of a sitar. Salim knew that purdah was a source of irritation to Ganpat Rai, who would have preferred his sisters and aunts to come into the open like white women; but at first sound of those voices the Mohammedan averted his eyes, striving also to avert his ears. His own feelings on this subject were contradictory; he saw himself as a modern man opposed to iron tradition, resenting the tyranny yet psychologically incapable of resisting it.

He said, slowly: 'Hardyal will miss his grandmother.'

'Yes.' And Ganpat Rai thought of the old woman who had died six months ago. She had always declared that she would not see her grandson again, and in grief and remorse Ganpat Rai had performed *shradda* for her; he touched her forehead with the sacred mud of the river and walked seven times round her pyre with a blazing torch. Through the night and all through the next day, the pyre burned, fed with oil and sandalwood.

Love, Mrs Lyttleton had assured him, transcends ceremonies and systems; love makes memory intelligible, love is what we must remember.

'I wonder . . .' mused Salim, and hesitated.

'Yes?'

'I wonder what changes we shall find in Hardyal.'

'I too wonder,' said Ganpat Rai, and he saw form in the air before him the young, unforgotten face of his son.

## 27

It was on the day of the Coconut Festival, when men celebrate the abatement of the monsoon, that Hardyal landed at Bombay. No one met him, and for a little while he felt solitary and elated as he stood on the Apollo Bunda among a mob of tongues and races and stared at the ship which had brought him home. Passengers were still disembarking in tenders rowed by blue-trousered Lascars; the ship itself stood at a distance, its reflections breaking and mending on the dirty sea. Wondering whether he dreamed, Hardyal now concentrated on this hour of his return and on all the small events to which it seemed intimately related. Already the *City of Sparta* whose throbbing existence he had shared for the past four weeks seemed about to dissolve in its own reflections, a creature casting off its robes one by one and with them, particle by particle, its flesh and its bone.

Some of the passengers whom he had known on the boat passed him with absent-minded greetings and were immediately lost in the crowd. He remembered how well he had seemed to know them: the jolly Scotch engineer, the dour captain, the genial doctor with his bright red moustache, the Civil Servant and his family from Agra, and two young officers back from leave in Ireland. These had been his familiars, and it was with a mixture of joy and melancholy that Hardyal watched them disappear, the same feeling which had moved him when he said goodbye to his English school, to Miss Bella, and Miss Margaret Wall, to the receding English shore; a feeling of sweetness, of resignation. Something of himself stayed with them, for had they not looked in his eyes and touched his hand and uttered his name? But now, with a single breath, India drew these last friends into her body, and only he—being Hardyal—stayed aloof.

Tall, slender, dressed in English clothes, he passed for a sunburned English boy as he stood there in the gale of voices and a rich profusion of smells. Wherever he turned he encountered the expressive stares of the East, where curiosity is a legitimate function of human intelligence. Touts and pedlars whined their enticements in his ear, Parsee gentlemen wearing shiny black hats stalked past, bent on large affairs, and Hardyal's glance was caught by the vision of a Parsee lady in a sari the colour of a canary's wing.

Presently, not aware himself that his movements had adjusted themselves to the tempo of his own land—a tempo which even in emergencies remains the tempo of leisure—Hardyal turned to make inquiries about his luggage, and found himself gazing into the eyes of his father's servant, Krishna. They regarded each other silently, each marking the passage of time whose tiny signals were more visible in the boy than in the man. Krishna clasped his hands with thumbs against his breast in the characteristic Hindu salutation, which does not rely on contact or garrulity. It was two years since Hardyal had seen a man weep for joy, and the sight of Krishna's tears loosed a responsive emotion in his own breast. 'Ah, Krishnaji!'

'My lord!'

'But where is Bapu, why did he not come to meet me?'

'He could not come, but he had sent these letters.' And Krishna combed his numerous shawls for the letters which he'd brought. One was from Jacques St Remy, the other from Ganpat Rai explaining that he had been detained by an important case, so sent Krishna instead. Money was enclosed and instructions for their journey to Amritpore. While Hardyal read his father's letter and listened to Krishna's welcoming monologue he felt the pressure of an immense and increasing familiarity. It was in the air about him, in his ears and in his nostrils, but some instinct urged him to fend it off, to preserve a little longer the consciousness of his own unique identity and of the other men and other places. It was in this instinctive clinging to a mood that, after slight hesitation, he put Jacques' unopened letter in his pocket and said to the servant: 'Let us go.'

They completed arrangements for the disposal of Hardyal's luggage, then elbowed their way through a storm of humanity to the street beyond the Bunda, where Krishna had a hired landau waiting. The coachman in a dirty pink turban saluted Hardyal with a flourish of his whip.

'Whither, Sahib?'

Sudden and irrepressible gaiety poured through Hardyal. 'I care not! Just drive. Drive until I tell you to stop.' He sat back on the lumpy cushions and sniffed the waterproof lining of the hood which sheltered himself and Krishna from a blaze of the afternoon sun. The landau wheeled away from the pier and headed towards the city where the tops of trees moved against a chaotic design of walls, arches, and domes. Hardyal had glimpses of the sea, of the outline of the Malabar Hills, and the sepia-tinted earth of Bombay. And while Krishna talked of home and of family affairs Hardyal engaged in the secret task of reviving much that had lain dormant in his memory. How often he'd dreamed of this homecoming! But now the dream itself claimed him, the dream contained him as a detail in its complex pattern; he no longer controlled it nor could he escape it.

Great streets opened before him as the landau threaded between other carriages, between ekkas and bullock carts and bicycles. He smelled the fading freshness of the sea as it lost itself in the city's spicy breath and knew that at last he'd reached a stage in his life when to look back is to count experience as golden. A youth with long black hair and an hibiscus flower tucked behind one ear pedalled beside the carriage, eyeing him with eyes like a dove's and crying in birdlike tones. Krishna spat an imprecation and the male Apsaras, losing heart, veered off down a side street. 'Everywhere one finds them,' murmured the servant philosophically. 'Tell me, didst thou not also find them in Belait?'

Hardyal considered, then smiled. 'There also, but they did not wear hibiscus flowers in their ears.'

'Where then did they wear them?' inquired the coachman, genially flicking a passing bullock with his whip.

The landau moved northward through the sprawling Crawford Market, where Hardyal suddenly ordered the coachman to stop, that Krishna might buy *pan supari*. Leaning on his elbow, he watched the shopman pick a wet green leaf from a square of folded linen, smear the leaf with lime and betel-nut, and press it in a triangle to fit the human mouth. The taste of *pan* on his tongue brought a sort of intoxication to Hardyal; he chewed, while every pore in his body exclaimed in delight. The coachman volunteered over his shoulder: 'The Sahib-log who come to Bombay for the first time ask always to be taken to see the Towers of Silence on Malabar Hill.'

Krishna interposed quickly: 'That is no place to celebrate a homecoming! Let us wait and go instead to the Coconut Festival, down by the sea.'

Hardyal cried: 'We have time for both. I would like to see the Towers of Silence.'

Krishna looked glum, he was a good Hindu, and the funeral customs of other people did not interest him; but this was his young master's first day at home and he did not have the heart to demur. As they drove towards the outskirts of the city, past the great balconied houses of Bombay's Parsee merchants, Hardyal was thinking of a day in Sussex when, over the breakfast table, he listened to Aubrey Wall's sister argue about the Towers of Silence.

'It is where they keep the outcastes,' insisted Miss Margaret, always the more forceful and the less accurate of the two. 'I ought to know because I was reading about it just the other day.'

'But Aubrey *told* me that the Towers are where they put their dead,' Miss Bella had contradicted her sister with a flatness which for forty years had availed nothing. Both ladies then appealed to Hardyal: 'Am I not right?' And he answered gravely: 'When I am in Bombay I shall go myself and see, and I will write and tell you.'

Rain had beautified those strange gardens on Malabar Hill, where the Parsee *dhakma*s rise under a massed shade of trees. As the landau stopped, Hardyal got out, noticing everywhere the droppings of the vultures. Several of these feathered monsters stalked about in the sun, their wings drooping, an air about them that was not all bird. He examined the low roofless towers where the Parsees bring their dead for these birds to translate into eternity, and something of his young optimism faded when, continuing his glance upward, he saw in the soft blue sky a ceaseless wheeling flight of wings silvered a little by the sun.

'Yes,' observed a voice in English, close beside him. 'Barbarous, I call it!'

The speaker, a sallow man in shabby clothes and a stained yellow, topi, appeared suddenly from behind a bed of canna lilies. Hardyal, who in his dealings with Englishmen had acquired something of their reserve, smiled non-committally. The other smiled back, revealing a row of bad teeth. 'Two thousand years of Christianity, two hundred years of civilized rule—and look at them!'

Which does he mean, wondered Hardyal—his teeth, the vultures, or the Towers? The other elucidated by a wave of his arm. 'I must say, I'm disappointed. First time I've been in Bombay and I paid a gharry-wallah two dibs to drive me here, expecting that I'd see at least one corpse. But no! We're not even allowed to go into the bloody things.'

'I don't think I'd care to,' said Hardyal. His voice caught the other's attention and he turned upon Hardyal an eye as seedy as everything else about him. 'Oh, you wouldn't, wouldn't you?' The eye narrowed, concentrated, 'I say, are you English or what?'

The boy, always disconcerted by bad manners, remained silent and after further point-blank staring the stranger shrugged. 'Of course, I see! One of our young rajas. You do look so damnably English in that get-up, I must say.'

Some imp of mischief entered Hardyal, who presented himself
briefly as the Raj Kunwar of Amritpore. The other frowned.
'Amritpore? Can't say that I've ever heard of it. One of those little up-
country States, I suppose. Does your Highness happen to know the
Raja of Jhori? He is, I should say, about your age.'

'Afraid I don't.'

'He has a salute of eleven guns. And your Highness?'

'But seven,' murmured Hardyal modestly.

'Ah! Well, I'm Jhori's secretary. That is, I am his Secretary's
secretary. My name is Smythe.' He spelled it. 'My young Raja is
visiting relatives not far from here and I got a few days' leave in order
to see Bombay. Must say I'm disappointed. Not a patch on Calcutta,
especially the statues. Do you know the Octerlony statue in Calcutta?'

'I don't think I remember it.'

'One of my uncles served with Colonel Octerlony in the Gurkha
War. I myself was born in Bihar, but my family goes all the way back
to the time of John Company.'

Hardyal listened politely, repelled though he was by the man's
spurious inflection and by his manner, at once intimate and arrogant.
He recognized the native-born white, poor, thwarted, full of weird
conceits, and fantastic aspirations, and suddenly he felt sorry that he
had embarked on this silly masquerade. He listened guiltily while Mr
Smithe jabbered on: 'What a piece of luck to have met your Highness!
You see, my gharry-wallah ran away because I refused to pay him
three rupees instead of the two which we'd agreed on at the start.
These damned natives . . .' He checked himself. 'I hope you'll let me
cadge a lift back to the city?'

Hardyal had no desire to share his privacy with the under-secretary
to the Raja of Jhori, but he could hardly refuse. It became evident that
Mr Smythe had no intention of letting him out of sight. He took
Hardyal's arm and, talking in the jocular tone of an old and
experienced mind to a young and inferior one, conducted him on a
tour of the gardens. They admired the flowers and studied the
architecture of the Towers from every angle, while Mr Smythe enlarged
in scornful amusement on the funeral customs of the Parsees. 'Your
Hindu custom of cremation is, I must say, practically civilized. The
next best thing to burial as we practise it. Give me the good old
ground every time, worms and all! Imagine exposing the body of
someone you loved to these carrion-eaters!'

Hardyal, who had been imagining exactly that, stood quite still and
stared at the grass and pebbles at his feet. He suffered a sort of seizure
to which he was occasionally subject, when it seemed that everything

that he had ever known, and a premonition of things not yet experienced, flowed with a bitter flavour into his mouth.

Mr Smythe was tugging at his elbow. 'What about the Coconut Festival? Does your Highness intend to see it this evening?'

The spell was broken and Hardyal raised his eyes. 'The Coconut Festival?'

'They all gather on the beach and chuck coconuts into the sea as offerings to—who is it, Varuna?' He nudged the boy's arm and winked with inexpressible lewdness. 'Afterwards there are places I could take you . . .'

'My train leaves at midnight.'

'Oh, you'll have time. I'd be glad to go with you to the Festival, if I could be of any assistance.'

Hardyal's brown eyes met his at last. 'I must tell you, sir . . . I'm not really the Raj Kunwar of Amritpore.'

'Eh?' He reddened.

'I'm not a prince at all. I was just joking.'

'The devil you were!' He dropped Hardyal's arm.

'I do beg your pardon, sir.' It was the English schoolboy who spoke, but Smythe's bewilderment hardened into anger. 'Damned cheeky even for a native, aren't you? Or is it part of your education?'

This was brought out in the sudden temper of an upstart deprived of all his little props, and for a moment Hardyal was afraid that the man would strike him. But the threat passed. Smythe glared, then shrugged. 'Well, you can jolly well give me a lift back to the city, just the same.'

They returned to the landau, where Smythe stared at Krishna.

'There is room on the box beside the driver.'

The servant hesitated and glanced at his master; for a second the air seemed to stretch and to become brittle with tension, then Hardyal nodded, 'Do so, my brother.'

Krishna got out of the landau and climbed up beside the coachman, whose sophisticated features had assumed a sudden blandness. While Mr Smythe arranged himself over the greater part of the seat under the hood, Hardyal perched on the smaller one facing him. Access to authority exerted a soothing effect upon Mr Smythe's feelings; he produced a cheroot, and leaning well back propped his feet on the seat beside Hardyal. The landau swung down the hill and under the big gates, then turned towards the city. Hardyal, to avoid meeting the eyes of his fellow passenger, watched the shadows of the vultures making arabesques on the red, sunlit earth.

# 28

Pride's natural reluctance to concede its hurt prevented Hardyal from brooding too long on that little adventure on Malabar Hill, and Mr Smythe dropped out of his life on the instant that the landau deposited him, with his topi and his cheroot, on the outskirts of the Crawford Market. There, with a perfunctory nod, he vanished into the heaving mass of India just as earlier in the day Hardyal's fellow passengers had vanished. The encounter was trivial, but it left a faint troubled stir, a tiny whirlpool which required a larger disturbance for its eventual stilling. So it was with a conscious resolve to put Mr Smythe in his proper place among the insignificant items of experience that Hardyal decided to attend the Coconut Festival in Hindu dress, a yearning which he had not felt this morning as he stood on the Apollo Bunda and struggled to preserve the unique sense of his own identity—not as Englishman or as Hindu, but simply as Hardyal.

Accompanied by Krishna he sauntered among the native shops, and brought a white dhoti, a muslin shirt with silver studs, a flowered waistcoat, a cap of Kotah cloth, and sandals which rasped his feet after two years of English wool and leather. Krishna had hired a room in the respectable Hindu quarter and here Hardyal bathed and changed his clothes. As he assumed the friendly garments his limbs seemed to take on independent life; memory gave a little stir, and he remembered an afternoon in Amritpore when he and Jacques St. Remy had exchanged their clothing and presented themselves before his father's guests. He stood motionless on the mud floor of the hired room, watching Krishna fold the discarded garments, and lay them on a string charpoy. A grey lizard crawled on the wall and from a mitred niche beside the window a crude and glossy picture of Varuna stared back at him—Varuna, god of the elements, his eyes beaming fire, his hair streaming like a hatch of serpents.

Krishna said: 'Here is the letter, which you did not open.'

It was Jacques' letter, but a childish instinct to postpone pleasure moved Hardyal to put the envelope back in his pocket. 'I shall save it to read on the train.'

They had commanded their original charioteer to drive them to the shore, and it was dusk when they stepped into the tremors and the marigold smells of a little street where lamps were glimmering behind ironwork grilles and bamboo blinds. The landau picked its way southward this time, skirting the docks and warehouses, and the pointing fingers of mills. Swarms of people were pushing in the same direction and progress was slow, with a great commotion of tikkagharries, carriage bells, bicycles, the cries of touts and vendors and sporadic yells which splintered against the brusque commands of city policemen. Hardyal gazed at the lights of Bombay. The city had ignited in a fine transparence of balconies and cupolas, in spidery lattice-work and the stern flat line of rooftops all laced together in a web of glittering telegraph wires. As the city glowed with a sustained and intense preoccupation Hardyal felt that it was solitary and complete, and that the millions who lived in it were the fleshy pores through which it drew its enormous breath.

The coachman drove through by-streets and disgraceful slums in whose sudden convulsive darkness and rancid odours Hardyal's throat seemed to close up. Beggars and lepers seeped from black crannies and staggered, whining, beside the wheels; children with old miserly faces capered in thin slivers of light, crying for pennies. Shutters creaked, spit flew, and a conglomeration of mangy cats, descending from nowhere, struck the cobbles and exploded like fire-crackers, shooting off into the hideous night. Hardyal held his nose and cried: 'Why must you bring us by this route?'

'Why not? It's a short cut, isn't it?'

But he whipped his browbeaten horse to a sprightlier gait, almost mowing down a knobby, noseless Something upon whose half-human face the carriage lamp flung its single revealing ray.

At last they were free of the slums and on the road towards the sea, with the celebrating crowd billowing round them like foam. A drum rattled and a man's voice soared into the serene, expressionless sky. Hardyal had never seen the Coconut Festival. He thought: 'I must write about this to Miss Bella and Miss Margaret.' And he started composing a long letter to his friends, including them in to-night's magic, conversing with them in small, lordly, expository gestures, his eyes aglow with generous light.

Then the carriage lurched and slowed to a crawl as it ran abreast a perfect avalanche of humanity. Hardyal stood up, clinging to the little rail behind the driver's seat. Below were the shore and the sea quivering in leagues of moonlight which broke into shadows amongst the moving crowd. Driving through the city he had forgotten the moon, but he saw it now as it hung in the sky between himself and Arabia; its cool radiance flowed over his hand, twinkled on the drop at the end of Krishna's nose, and lingered for a second on the scrofulous ear of their tired horse.

They ordered the coachman to wait for them on this spot, for they must get back to the city in time to catch their train, and Krishna followed Hardyal down the sands into the crowd which ebbed and flowed like the sea itself, a tide of dark limbs and glistening heads and sudden apparitional faces. Hardyal struggled to the water's edge and stood there with the sea nibbling his feet, where moonlight slid like mercury over a surface littered with bobbing coconuts; Krishna brought him one and Hardyal flung it with all his force, a prayer going out with it from his heart, a voiceless prayer which he left to the god to interpret as he would. Half a day had passed since he stepped ashore on the Apollo Bunda and sent a final glance at the ship which had brought him home, but he felt that he was not the Hardyal who had gone away, nor was he, quite, the Hardyal who had come back. Broodingly, he slipped two fingers of his right hand into his shirt and felt, under his nails, the delicate hairs on his breast, the steady beating of his heart. Beside him moaned and swayed a thousand other bodies like his own; they brushed against him, he smelled their human sweat, he felt their life. A woman laughed and the sound trembled in his ear with the articulateness of a song, but when he turned to look for her, he faced a thousand eyes and lost her voice in a hoarse murmur of invocation from uncounted lips. Then something cool and white struck his thigh and fell to the ground, and as he stooped to pick up a garland of flowers their scent rushed through his body, thrilling him. He held the garland and cast about for the owner, but no one approached to claim it. Men brushed past, and a little group of children, as brown as coconuts and as bare, dashed under his arm towards the sea, in whose smallest wave they skipped with tiny splashes and infinitesimal cries.

Hardyal caressed his flowers and smiled to himself. He no longer thought of writing to his friends of this adventure, for he no longer saw them as essential to his mood. In a passion of joy and reverence he stooped and laid his garland on the sea, watching it as minute by minute the accepting tide bore it away.

Hardyal read Jacques' letter as the train carried him northward through the night, towards Nasik and Khandwa, on towards the goldfields of Indore. Folded in a Scotch travelling rug whose fringes tickled his chin, he swayed luxuriously with the train's motion while on the next berth Krishna slept rolled up in blankets like a corpse, his snores drowned in the humming wheels.

'In ten days,' wrote Jacques, 'you will be back in India! Now that you are on your way home I find it hard to write because when I start to think about things they suddenly become not so very much. This is one reason why I've never got a great deal out of books: words make time seem all queer and wrong, for when you are alive everything that happens takes a proper length of time—minutes, hours, days. And in two years so many things have happened—things I can put into a few sentences. Last spring Macbeth's mother ran away with Captain

Ponsonby. No one speaks of it now, except Bertie. She's told me a lot. Macbeth was awfully cut up, but the Colonel behaved very quietly. He always behaves quietly and sometimes you wonder whether he notices anything except his garden and his soldiers. I like him because I can never forget the night when I was hurt and he lifted me down from the tree and bent over me, telling me over and over that I was all right, that there was nothing to be afraid of. So, you can see it is not really surprising that he should have behaved like a gentleman when Mrs Macbeth ran off with Ponsonby. Bertie is living in Gambul with the Macbeths. It's queer, you know, the feeling that Mrs Macbeth is still with us. I feel that she might walk into the room at any moment, and I know that Macbeth feels it too—more than any of us. He hangs around looking as if that was what he was waiting for.

'Mr Wall must be nearing England now. And you won't see Gisele. Have I told you that this is my last year at St Matthew's? I shan't sit for the Cambridge exams—what would be the use? Maman says I know enough as it is, so after this year I shall be in Amritpore learning about the factory. Father Sebastien will go on giving me Maths and Latin, and I suppose I can get the rest out of reading.

'Here is a story which Hanif has just told me. Mrs Lyttleton's servant died a few days ago, and Hanif says that a devil entered into him and killed him, and that now he haunts Mrs Lyttleton's house. Hanif won't walk past the gates after dark, though he is very brave in broad daylight!'

'I keep wondering what you will think of Bertie Wood. I must tell you, in strictest confidence, that I am going to marry her eventually, perhaps in two or three years. No one knows of this, not even Maman, but Bertie and I have decided.'

'The rains have broken and this evening there is a sunset which makes everything look like a lighted room. There is so much to tell you, so much to ask you—I can't believe that we shall be seeing each other soon . . . soon! Well, *mon chère*!'

Hardyal finished the letter and lay for some minutes with the loose pages on his breast, feeling the urgent rhythm of the wheels as they rushed through the darkness. Then he rose and pushed the baize cover over the ceiling light, plunging the compartment into gloom, and at once the sound of the wheels turned into a song which Krishna had taught him when he was a little boy:

> Eke eke anna,
> Doh doh pisa!
>
> Teen teen pisa,
> Doh doh anna!

He fell asleep with the childish refrain running through his head.

## 29

One afternoon, three months after Hardyal's return to Amritpore, Madame St Remy sat on the same veranda where she had sat with Father Sebastien on the afternoon of Jacques' fourteenth birthday. Time had wrought no striking change upon Madame, for whom shocks and mutations were always of an interior order. Her features, more sculptural than pictorial, concentrated vitality in her brown eyes, which missed nothing except that which the brain behind them had never cared to recognize. Mrs Lyttleton often asserted that Madame had inherited the instincts of a French *concierge*, but the charge was hardly just; Madame had cultivated stoicism as an attribute of good breeding, she had, through sheer will power, acquired much of the literary lumber of aristocracy—lumber which Mrs Lyttleton had long since cheerfully thrown overboard. Madame's metamorphosis might have been complete but for her secretiveness, that hallmark of *banias* the world over. However, she never lacked force, a fact which Mrs Lyttleton was to discover too late when Madame intervened between herself and Jacques.

Madame might well preen herself on having scored, for there was no doubt that Jacques' affection for his old friend had been effectively nipped in the bud. Madame had indeed won that round as in the past she had won others, yet when she paused to ponder on her victories her reflections were followed by others of a less triumphal nature. There had, of course, been a succession of rounds, and even if she were not prepared to admit defeat in all of them, she could not in any honesty claim unconditional surrenders. Madame St Remy was always most candid with herself when she was least observed as she happened to be at this moment, alone on her veranda overlooking the rose garden and the trees which massed their airy green between her and the flat brown plain. She had need of candour, since for the past two hours she'd engaged in a process of recapitulation—mental, spiritual, and financial. The materials for this process were spread before her on a table: letters, account books, bills of sale, receipts, beside a black-and-gold japanned box with an intricate lock which only she knew how to open. It was a marvellous box, composed of drawers and compartments and hiding-places, every one of which contained something that with the years had become as native to it as a seed is to its fruit. Locks of the children's hair tied with wisps of silk, a gold crucifix worn by Auguste St Remy when he was a child, a locket with portraits of Amèlie and Auguste at the time of their engagement, and a pair of diminutive enamelled foxes which Auguste had given his bride on her nineteenth birthday. For years Jacques and Gisele had coveted these foxes, but Madame explained sternly that they were not toys.

To the St Remy children these reminders of their own and their parents' past were the most fascinating things in the box, but it contained other reminders which they had never been permitted to see, and it was upon these that Madame had brooded with a sombre and unrewarding candour for the past two hours. Stacked in the largest compartment between locks of Gisele's hair and a package of her husband's letters lay several sheets of thin native paper covered with spidery Hindi, each bearing a three-anna stamp and flowing signatures. These were notes of hand to the credit of Ramdatta the moneylender, and a simple sum in arithmetic had started the pin-wheel of speculation spinning in Madame's head. Meshing with all its neighbouring wheels it wove an inevitable sequence of doubt, conjecture, and frustration, though nothing of all this was visible in her expression. Perhaps she realized that she faced ruin, but to fuss was not in her nature. Let the world make its own discoveries, she would rest upon her faith, which had carried her over every natural and artificial obstacle planted in her way by luck or by design. Nor was hers a blind faith; rather, like her intelligence, it was an intense and narrow one. Whenever she thought of the past she managed to revive the peculiar thrill of the self-righteous who glory in defeat, attributing it—as in her case—to the machinations of the Devil or of the English, both of whom she would have missed badly, since between them they kept her faculties alert and her faith radiant.

For Madame St Remy there never could be any acknowledgment of paradox, a concept which she feared was already exerting its heretical fascination upon the mind of her son. It was becoming increasingly difficult for her to guess what went on in Jacques' thoughts. How strange that Gisele's beauty and sensibility—and by these Madame meant Gisele's sex—should have posed a comparatively simple problem. Gisele was provided for, she was even provided against. Gisele was beyond all question safe. But Jacques was a different story, and at this point Madame's reflections changed; she seemed to exude shadow, making her body a separate world, separate climate almost. She suffered from the assault of a memory which occurred to her often when she found herself alone, as now, the empty garden before her and at her back the empty house.

Her servants were in their own quarters, Jacques had gone with Macbeth and Bertie to visit Hardyal, and it was with a sense of desolation that she found herself not only remembering, but intensely and actually reviving that day, two years ago, when she received Colonel Macbeth's telegram informing her of Jacques' accident.

Accompanied by Hanif she arrived at the Macbeths' house and they had taken her to see Jacques where he lay on the Colonel's bed, in that dressing-room which smelled of Pinaud's Brilliantine and boot polish. The Macbeths left her at the door, but Hanif followed her in and crouched at Jacques' feet, clasping them in his slender brown hands, weeping over them.

Madame drew a chair towards the bed and sat down, bending towards her son. His left arm lay across his breast under the sheet. His eyes, wide and steady, stared at her from the white pillows.

She whispered: 'Don't talk. Lie very still until you are well again.'

'But there is something I want to tell you.'

'I know everything.'

'I want to tell you myself.' He gazed at her with his young lion eyes. 'They had to cut off my hand at the wrist.' He said it in a cool, measured voice and she guessed that he must have lain here practising how to say it. She caught her breath. 'Yes, I was afraid. . .'

'The regimental surgeon did it. But it was Colonel Macbeth who saved me. He lifted me down from the tree and put a tight thing round my arm. He helped the dandy-coolies carry me back to Gambul. He and Bertie and Macbeth . . . and all the time when I felt I was going . . . you know, Maman? going . . . they held on to me as if they knew, as if they understood that I felt I was going.'

'Don't talk,' whispered Madame between dry lips. 'My darling, don't talk.'

'I want to. I must. You see, it wasn't any one's fault. It wasn't *their* fault. Maman, you must promise me . . .'

She strove, vainly, to read the question in his eyes. 'Promise me. . . .'

'We will talk tomorrow, Jacques. Now close your eyes. I am here. I shall stay beside you until you sleep.'

Dinner was brought to her on a tray and when at last the boy fell asleep she went downstairs to the strange, lamplit room where the Macbeth family awaited her. John Macbeth had disappeared, but Bertie stayed, curled like a tawny cat on the window-seat. Madame, with something of the air of a somnambulist, allowed her hand to be taken, and accepted the chair which the Colonel brought forward. Mrs Macbeth expressed her concern in faint, incoherent murmurs, then relapsed into unhappy silence, but the Colonel faced Madame, fixing her with his pale, luminous eyes.

'Nothing,' he declared, 'nothing could have upset me more than this, not even if it had happened to my own son.'

Madame St Remy returned his gaze expressionlessly. 'But it did not happen to your son, sir. It happened to mine.'

Seated beside the piano in a little pool of light, Mrs Macbeth stared at her hands, but the Colonel continued to withstand the icy shock of his visitor's gaze. 'At least, we know now that Jacques will recover. He is young and strong. We must thank God for that.'

'I shall never cease to thank God, but you, I think, have additional need to thank Him.' After a brief pause, she went on: 'Jacques was in your care. Now I realize that it might have been better had I acted on my first impulse, which was certainly not one of blind confidence.'

'Then what was your impulse, Madame?' inquired the soldier, gently.

'My first impulse was to forbid Jacques spending his holidays away from the authorities whom I had entrusted with his safety.'

Mrs Macbeth glanced up in distress, but it was Bertie who interposed in a high, excited voice: 'Good heavens! You couldn't leave him stuck in that horrible school all the time, could you?'

It was always difficult for Madame to lose her temper in English, and to have lost it in French would have made the situation ridiculous, since she was quite sure that these barbarians spoke nothing except their own language. Ignoring Bertie, she said swiftly: 'Of course I realize that the English have odd notions in regard to the training of their children, ideas of nobility and courage, virtues which you exact from mere infants. I suppose this is admirable. It is, no doubt, one reason for your great success as colonizers.'

The Colonel twisted his moustache. 'Well, upon my word, don't you know . . .'

'*Enfin*, Monsieur, not being English myself I have less exalted ideas. I do not believe in throwing my children to lions and panthers. I do not believe in compelling them to sit in trees with loaded guns, and in leaving them there for hours until they go insane with fright!'

Colonel Macbeth took a short step in one direction, changed his mind, and came back. 'By Jove, I never thought about it in quite that light. You see, it was all a matter of luck.'

'Luck?'

'*Qui porte bonheur!*' He smiled with an air of relief, as though he was sure that this succinct phrase must clear away all misunderstanding.

'Jacques, you see, won the toss.'

She smiled bitterly. 'You are wrong. He lost!'

'Oh no, he didn't!' As she spoke, Bertie crossed the room and took her uncle's arm. 'And if you were to ask Jacques, Madame, he would tell you, himself, that he won.'

Madame seemed to notice her for the first time; as a matter of fact she had met them all several hours ago but then she was conscious of little except of her son. Now, as the mist of terror and anxiety began to lift, she saw these cold-blooded English in the baleful light in which she had always judged them. Their composure, their acceptance of irresponsibility as something which involved no more than a stroke of 'luck' or a point in sportsmanship, roused the dormant hatred in her breast. They were in league, as usual; they stuck by each other even when they were in the wrong—perhaps never so loyally as when they were wrong! They forgot their differences and pooled their strength against the stranger, for this, too, was part of their code. And as she glanced from one face to another, Madame felt grateful to a chance to speak her mind—her poor, distraught mind.

She addressed herself to Bertie. 'I do not need to ask Jacques anything, Mademoiselle. I have been him, and that is enough. I have seen that he lost the toss, as you call it, and that he has permanently lost the use of his hand as a consequence. I am not interested in the details of how or why such a thing should have been allowed to happen. Do you not understand that this has made him a cripple for life?'

They winced, and the tiny convulsion drew all three faces into a single momentary likeness. Then Bertie's eyes filled with tears.

'Do you think that we need to be reminded? Do you think that after seeing him lying there . . . after watching him fight to keep alive, to do more than just that . . . to be a man about it . . .' She ignored a warning pressure of the Colonel's arm. 'We are not trying to dodge responsibility, as you seem to think. But it was up to each of us, that night. It was just as much up to Jacques.'

Madame stared at her. 'I am afraid that I do not understand you, my child.'

'But what is it that's so difficult to understand? Jacques did what any of us would have done. He couldn't back out of it, could he?'

'Had you been my child I should never have permitted you to get into such a dilemma.'

'You couldn't have stopped me.'

Madame smiled. 'I could, and would, have stopped Jacques.'

They exchanged a long, hard look, then Bertie asked: 'Would you have tried?' She did not wait for an answer. 'Because if you had, it would have been very unfair to him.'

Madame shrugged. 'Possibly.'

Bertie flushed. 'You would have made him look like a coward when he was trying his hardest not to be one. What's more, I don't think that he'd have let you.'

The Colonel put his arm round her shoulders. 'My dear Bertie, we mustn't forget that Madame has been through a frightful ordeal.' He looked, now, as though he were going through one himself. Of them all only Mrs Macbeth seemed exempt from suffering. Since she could not escape the embarrassment of this scene she divorced herself from it by retreating into a sort of trance.

Madame was silent for a minute then she shrugged with an air of resignation. 'For years I have lived among you people, but I confess that I have never understood you. I don't think that I shall ever understand you. Perhaps no one will understand you. Others will hate you and resent you, some may even try to ape you, but they will never understand you. For myself, I simply do not know what to make of you. You are—what shall I say?' She spread her hand despairingly. 'Impossible!'

They accepted this in silence, unprotestingly, with a sort of meditative gallantry that poor Madame recognized as one of the most *impossible* traits in their benighted racial character. The silence continued, it threatened to last for ever, and she realized that this was part of an unrehearsed collusion—she was to be permitted the full, triumphal satisfaction of the Last Word.

Conscious, suddenly, of her own fatigue, she rose, distributed fragmentary bows, and went out of the room. But in the dimly lighted hall she paused a moment to get herself in hand before going upstairs to Jacques. She stood in an angle of the staircase, her dark dress merging with the heavy shadow which fell about her. From here she had a partial view of the room which she'd just left, and of the tableau now being enacted there in the golden lamplight. Mrs Macbeth was not visible but the Colonel's figure was amply framed, his arm still round his niece's shoulder. Madame heard his deep indistinguishable murmur, followed by Bertie's voice as clear as a bell: 'I hate her! She's going to try and take Jacques away from us, you'll see.'

There were further murmurs from the Colonel, then Bertie's voice again: 'It *is* our business. I'll fight her if you won't. John and I will fight her together. We'll fight her—tooth and nail!'

Madame turned away, stepping from the shadow towards the foot of the stairs, and she saw then that she was not alone, that John Macbeth leaned against the newel-post facing her, racing past her towards the open doors of the drawing-room. From his expression Madame guessed that he'd heard what Bertie said and that he had caught her, herself, in the intolerable role of eavesdropper. As she prepared to pass him their eyes met, and she thought bitterly: 'Yes, they're in league, all of them, even the children!'

Her sense of desolation increased as she mounted the stairs and found Hanif squatting like a watchful genie outside Jacques' door. He rose, reassuringly strong and familiar in his elegant garments, and Madame waited a moment to get her breath. 'Does he sleep?' she asked at last, and raised her hand to her own tired eyes.

'He sleeps,' the young man replied softly. 'He woke but once, thinking you were near, and he asked something of you.'

Madame stared at her servant. 'He asked something? What was it?'

Hanif's eyes gleamed darkly in his smooth brown face. 'Perhaps he was not entirely awake, but it seemed to me that he begged a promise of you.'

She waited, and the deferential voice continued: 'Have I liberty to speak? You are my father and my mother, else how should I dare?'

Madame drew a deep breath. 'Oh, go on, go on!'

'Then you must know that he has set his heart on these friends. Do not take him away from them, for if he should come to believe that you intend to take him away, he may lose heart . . . and he must not lose heart!'

Madame hesitated, a strange emotion leaping and dying within her. Hanif waited, his hands clasped before him, his eyes lowered. Then with a curious little sigh Madame put her hand on the door and walked past him into her son's room.

# 30

A flock of crows alighted among the trees and their uncouth din roused Madame from her reverie. Imperceptibly, the tragic concentration dissolved in her features, and her thoughts retired into a privacy as inviolable as the secret compartments of the japanned box. If she had gained nothing by this short spell of retrospection neither had she surrendered anything; so long as she alone knew where and how she stood in her devious relationships, they must endure. Other people's minds might be as enigmatic as her own and behind the humdrum exchange of everyday life all sorts of conspiracies might be brewing, but these were dangers on which she dared not brood. As for Ramdatta . . . reaching forward with her fingernail, she snapped the hinged lid on the compartment which contained the *hundies*, knowing well enough that so long as she continued to owe him money he would continue to advance her more. The end remained hidden, as it should, according to God's will.

She heard a step on the gravel and presently Hanif appeared, sauntering among her roses. He did not see her at once, and as she watched him move like some painted and fastidious bird among the flowers Madame experienced the peculiar emotion which this young servant alone had power to evoke in her. It was, perhaps, less an emotion than a sort of vicarious thrill which other people derived from plays, from music, from books or from conversation. His loyalty touched her, his peccadilloes were an endless source of astonishment to her impeccable soul. She knew that he lied to her, that he stole tea and sugar from her godowns, that he helped himself to her perfume. He was a spendthrift, a gambler, with a weakness for fine clothes and loose women—vices which Madame would never have tolerated in a white man, nor dreamed of forgiving in any one related to herself. But Hanif was her periscope into another world; because he was not her son, she had never suffered for him, she had never troubled to change him, to correct him, to dull him. Nor, strangely, had she thought to convert him or to use her influence towards his conversion. He stood, for her, in the light of some rare and costly animal, absolved from Christian retribution as he remained, inevitably, exempt from Christian salvation.

It was something of the same feeling that she extended to Hardyal, even to Ganpat Rai, for although she would vehemently have denied prejudice in the matter of race or of colour, her sense of racial identity as something foreordained was so deeply ingrained as to have become practically unconscious. Unlike Aubrey Wall and Mrs Lyttleton who acknowledged the dilemma and hated it, unlike Father Sebastien who, in his own way, laboured to mitigate it, Madame never even paused to question its existence. She was simply not interested in natives as human beings and for this reason they had never posed a problem to her intelligence nor offered a challenge to her conscience. This, in fact, was the secret of her acceptance of Hardyal as Jacques' friend—she was no more capable of jealousy on Hardyal's account than she was capable of it on Hanif's. Throughout her life she remained supremely unaware of this contradiction, and she would have been scandalized had any one ventured to bring it to her attention. Her feeling towards Hanif had been intensified and somewhat complicated by that evening in Gambul when he begged her not to take Jacques away from the Macbeths. That appeal, which she had ignored but not neglected, recurred to Madame for days afterwards. She knew that she could never have brought herself to examine, let alone grant, such a plea had it been made by one of the Macbeths. Consciously or not, she was girded for that battle which Bertie Wood had declared as being joined—tooth and nail, and to the bitter end. Strange that it should devolve on Hanif to come forward with an alternative, one by which

Madame stood to lose nothing, nothing whatsoever of her dignity, her pride, her possessiveness. Jacques' life was what counted, and Jacques' life was what Hanif held up to her, not as a threat but as a reward. If God had saved Jacques then Hanif had saved Madame, and in her silent decision to ignore Bertie's challenge—for the time being— Madame was hardly likely to forget Hanif or to consider him the less because of his deft and innocent intervention.

Now as she watched him, resplendent in Baluchi trousers and a green velvet waistcoat, a velvet cap tilted to one side of his pomaded head, Madame smiled with a rare spontaneity. Dawdling among the roses, he caught sight of her from under his long lashes and at once a not too subtle change came over him. He twisted a long stem topped with a half-blown rose from its circling leaves and carried it, swooningly, to his nose. He hummed a song and moved with languorous grace towards the veranda.

Madame addressed him. 'I did not raise those flowers to be plucked by you and distributed amongst the bazaars, my friend!'

He mounted the veranda steps and laid the rose alongside the japanned box and the marbled account books. 'The Fair is soon, and I must have new trousers.' He glanced with abhorrence at his pantaloons. 'If I am to escort the children I cannot go dressed in these rags.'

She surveyed him critically. 'When you escort my son you will wear your livery.'

He smiled ravishingly. 'That still leaves the problem of trousers, and of shoes. Two weeks ago I saw a pair—blue leather worked in gold. Unfortunately I had bestowed my last pice on a beggar, else I might have persuaded the skinflint of a *mochi* to let me have the shoes on a small down-payment.'

Madame clasped her hands and rested her chin on them. 'You shall have the shoes. Tell me, where did the children ride yesterday?'

'To the Fort, as usual. It was hot. Allah, how I suffered!'

His manner had not changed but she saw at once that she could get little out of him. While his personal loyalty to her remained unswerving, she knew that with him Jacques came first; the knowledge both pleased and angered her.

'Well, what did they talk about?' she demanded bluntly, and he lowered his limpid gaze to the floor. 'They conversed in English, naturally, so how would I understand what they said?'

'You understand very well when you are not supposed to. Now tell me, were you present when Macbeth sahib fell from his horse? He assured me it was nothing, yet his knees were badly cut.'

Hanif made a bland gesture with pale, upturned palms. 'Ah, that

Macbeth! Difficult to tell which is rider and which is horse. He jumped the ditch beyond the canal and his horse came down, but when it stood up again Macbeth was still in the saddle.'

'I have given you authority to prevent such recklessness. Why do you not control them?'

'Macbeth is the reckless one. He has a devil, which drives him.'

'Devil or no devil, I want no accidents while they are my guests.'

Hanif put his head on one side and gazed at her. 'There will be no accidents—on that I pledge my life. But the shoes?'

Madame opened the box and took a little chamois leather bag, from which she extracted two rupees. 'These come out of your wages, remember.' She inclined her head slightly as he took the money and salaamed her deeply with both hands. Then she glanced at the little gold watch pinned to her blouse. 'It is late. The children should be returning.'

Hanif tucked the coins in his waistcoat pocket. 'You know what happens when they get among those Hindus. It is all jabber, jabber, and eat, eat.'

Madame heard, far away, the sound of Father Sebastien's church bell and knew that he was preparing for Benediction. She had hoped that Jacques might return in time to accompany her; his laxity in these matters was getting more pronounced, but some obscure fear prevented her from acknowledging it, even to herself. Ever since his accident she had been aware of a new strength growing in him, as though the loped branch of his hand had sent the vitality back into his spirit, steeling it.

Once more she glanced at her watch. 'We will wait half an hour. Then you shall go and bring them home.'

# 31

While Madame St Remy was poring over the contents of her despatch case, Bertie Wood sat rather shyly among the ladies of Ganpat Rai's household in their zenana at the rear of the house. It was here they spent their days, when they did not prefer the arbour at the end of the garden. The zenana itself, comprising several large rooms and the inevitable veranda, opened on a courtyard with high walls and rows of custard-apple trees. In its centre was a goldfish pond and a plot of grass on which grazed a tame antelope, its wicked horns capped with brass, a silver bell ringing at its throat. Suspended from the veranda ceiling was a large basket-work cage filled with *lals*, tiny coloured birds whose ceaseless fluttering and twittering transformed the upper air into a world of their own. Babies wearing silver amulets, and little else, stumbled or crawled everywhere, or finger in mouth, stood staring with kohl-painted eyes at the stranger. The ladies—there must have been twenty of them—crouched on rugs or perched cross-legged on enamelled charpoys, a silver anklet or be-ringed toe peeping under the deckled edges of their *saries*. The atmosphere, new to Bertie, seemed redolent of a femininity which tinkled, rustled, whispered, and giggled in a continuous minor orchestration, fanned by the breeze which moved from the courtyard into the house and emerged again, freighted with odours of sweet oil, warm flesh, and tinselled gauze. The air kept rising against Bertie's face, strangely disturbing and exciting her as she sat in the main chamber on a chair especially provided for her. She felt the women's liquid gaze cover every detail of her own person. Some returned her frank smile, others, overcome by shyness, turned aside their varnished heads and gave little deprecating tugs to their veils. They had, of course, seen other white women, but Bertie was the youngest ever to visit them and perhaps for that reason they vested her with additional glamour. Her Hindustani was still shaky but she ventured a few remarks which were received with instantaneous, charming attention. How unlike us, she reflected, ruefully remembering her own and her cousins' squeals of mirth when foreigners mauled the Queen's English.

But for Bertie, creature of the open air, the zenana was like walking straight into a dream. Draperies and screens fell behind her, shadows grew like forests in every corner and from their gloom demure figures emerged to greet her, their little narrow hands touching vermilion-starred foreheads. She had a confused impression of flashing glass and metal, of fire spurting from the centre of priceless jewels, and of the concentrated gaze of these denizens of a culture six thousand years old. Ganpat Rai had explained to her that Hindu women borrowed the custom of purdah from their Mohammedan conquerors. 'Before that time they were as free as you,' he told her, sadly. 'Now they shrink from a freedom that is always within their grasp.'

It was several minutes before Bertie could reconcile Ganpat Rai's female establishment with the rest of his household, with the barrister himself and with his charming son. Now she found herself surrounded by a palpitating community of aunts and great-aunts, cousins, and the wives and sisters of cousins. She allowed herself to be touched, to be gazed upon, to be addressed in exquisite Hindi to which she made overloud and inadequate replies. Ganpat Rai's aunt, a blue-eyed woman from Kashmir, who spoke a little English and understood more, touched Bertie's skirt and exclaimed: 'Pure wool, yes!'

When Bertie nodded and smiled, the others exploded in little cries of admiration and wonder. The aunt's blue eyes lingered on Bertie's face. 'Husband? Marry? Engage?'

'I'm afraid I'm too young yet.'

The aunt smiled, and corresponding smiles flowered everywhere.

'Too young? I was married when I was twelve. My daughters are all married. The youngest, fifteen, has her first child.'

'I think perhaps we are rather backward about such things,' Bertie ventured, and assisted her meaning with vague explanatory gestures.

The statement was received by a musical clashing of bangles and bracelets. Mirana Bhai nodded approval. 'I've been told that in past times in Belait it used to be with you as it has always been with us, folks married young and lived long. But no matter how long one may live, time is too short. I have ten children,' she added complacently, 'ten children and eighteen grandchildren.'

There was a further outburst of trills from the gauzy audience, and the aunt shifted her *pan* to the other cheek. 'I suspect that in your country you waste much time. The best years are the years of our youth, yet I am told that among you many wait until middle-age, even until old age, before they take husbands. Many, I hear, never marry at all.'

A moan of compassion and bewilderment eddied through the room as Bertie assented to this melancholy fact. Mirana Bhai looked at her keenly. 'But you have a young, strong body, and beautiful breasts. What is it you wait for?'

Taken aback by the directness of the question and the frankness of the admiration, Bertie coloured up; then half-laughing, she attempted an explanation while the others listened, fixing her with tender and inquiring glances. Mirana Bhai shook her head. 'Nay, I have heard that white women set great store by something they call their independence. My nephew has explained this term to me, but I still have difficulty understanding it. For if women will not bear children they must assume some other responsibility. Would they be teachers and servants rather than mothers?'

Her *sari*, slipping from her head, revealed a coiffure varnished smooth with coconut oil, tasselled with bright threads which, passing behind her ears, supported clusters of heavy silver earrings. She went on with an air of authority. 'As for us, we perform our duties better if we are not distracted by matters which, in the end, cannot have any great importance. I understand these things, for I have heard much about them. We are born with bodies, with wombs, and nothing can ever change their meaning. Now, tell me, little one, wilt thou, also, wait until thou art an old back-toothed hag before thou bearest a child?'

Bertie laughed. 'I don't know. I hope not!' But she felt a heat in her face and an unexpected sting of tears in her eyes. In the brief ensuing pause she thought, confusedly: 'They live for this—for their dark, inscrutable men, and their fruitlike children, for this hushed, dim existence. . . .'

Mirana Bhai rose suddenly. 'Now we shall have *tee*. Do you like hulwa? Do you like batasas?'

Jacques had warned her not to refuse the hospitality with which she was bound to be showered, and for some time she'd been aware of mysterious preparations going on in the background. Now, as Mirana Bhai clapped her hands, various curtains shuddered and parted, and three female servants appeared carrying vast platters of food. There was tea in a massive china teapot, there were English biscuits, sardines, and bowls of Hindu sweets strewn with almonds, and glimmering with silver foil which melted when she helped herself.

Bertie ate without self-consciousness; she was still young enough for food to constitute a vital if not an æsthetic pleasure. And presently as they watched her and urged her to try this dish and that, the women relaxed and settled into unconstrained postures, as though they had but waited for a signal, a spontaneous acceptance of friendship. Now the true significance of hospitality dawned on Bertie; it was an intimacy, a sacrament almost.

The ladies all began to talk at once, teasing each other, shooting bold little questions at her, examining with passionate interest her net stockings and the French lace on her petticoat. They cried 'Aré!' and 'Wah wah!' at her feeble attempts at wit, and when, finally, she relapsed with a groan, declaring that she could not possibly eat another morsel, they fell upon her with outcries and urgent recommendations that she swallow just one more trifle of this or another fragment of that. 'I cannot!' she protested, despairingly. 'I simply can't!'

Nature, coming to the rescue, supplied the essential note of sincerity and she gave a loud hiccup. It was the magic sign, one which she would never have known how to render unaided. The platters were borne away to be distributed among the hand-maidens, and Mirana Bhai produced a box of Egyptian cigarettes given her by Mrs Lyttleton.

The conversation continued for some time, but for Bertie the air seemed to thicken, and she gazed longingly at the little courtyard where the antelope tossed its head and charged a blowing leaf. She felt suddenly sated, as much with food as with the overladen atmosphere, but she knew that she must stay the appropriate length of time, for to do otherwise would constitute an unpardonable breach of etiquette. So she stayed, nodding and smiling, answering interminable questions and offering fragmentary observations while minute by minute her attention strayed from her surroundings to the mysteries which bounded them. Then, as the sense of intimacy which had first kindled in her began to wane, it struck her that these voices lacked a dissonance to which her ears were accustomed and for which she now listened with increasing nervous impatience. This, she felt, was the conversation of caged beings, the conversation of the little *lals* whose ceaseless flutterings and chirpings provided a diminuendo to a theme perversely tuned to the minor key.

When at last she rose to take her leave, the ladies rose too in a great upsurge of gauze and tinsel, a climax of tinkling anklets and bracelets dying away on long-drawn sighs of farewell.

Mirana Bhai put her arm around Bertie. 'Come, you may pass through the courtyard into the garden, and join your friends.'

In the veranda Bertie paused to admire the *lals*. 'Isn't it a pity to keep them shut up like that?' she inquired, for something to say.

Mirana Bhai smiled. 'Look again. You see, there are no doors. They are free to come and go as they wish.' She put out her hand and a crimson tuft of feathers the size of a thimble alighted on her finger.

'See he knows me! Sometimes he takes sugar from my lips. There now; fly, little one, fly!'

The bird left her finger and fluttered back to join its companions in their cage. Mirana turned, smiling, to Bertie. 'There are many of them loose outdoors, but these know each other. They are happier, living together like this.'

As they walked across the courtyard to a heavy door set in the wall among the custard-apple trees Bertie wondered whether Mirana Bhai's comment was intended as an observation, or as an intimation.

## 32

When the zenana gate closed behind her Bertie found herself standing in an unfamiliar corner of Ganpat Rai's garden, where she could see the river coiling between muddy shores and the sun poised on the edge of a plain already swathed in bluish haze. This, she had been told, was the Hour of Cowdust when cattle wander back to their pens, and smoke from cooking fires rises above mud roofs under the mango trees. She stood with her hard, clear little mind at a loss to understand the sudden pain which touched her heart. From the day of her arrival in India there had been recurrences of this mood; a breath of wind could inspire it, a flash of colour, a voice singing.

Across the river a light glimmered, a dog howled on the long-drawn immemorial note of village dogs; in the courtyard she heard a child's fretful whimper and pictured the small face turned expectantly to its mother's round, brown breast.

The Hour of Cowdust when men and beasts turn their faces towards some fragment of earth known to them for a thousand years! Behind her in the zenana life persisted unchanged, a humid existence from which she was excluded, and the thought left her feeling vaguely homesick. Then three figures appeared in the path before her: Hardyal, Jacques, and her cousin. They were in tennis flannels and as she walked towards them Bertie felt the tension increasing within her, felt an indefinable urge towards tears. But by now the light was going fast and no one noticed her strange distress.

'You've been ages,' exclaimed Jacques. 'Hanif has come to fetch us home.'

He stood with his left hand thrust into his pocket, a posture which had become habitual. Hardyal said: 'Father thought you must have decided to adopt *purdah nashin* yourself, Bertie!'

'Did I stay too long?'

'Oh no. My aunts will be very pleased. They will pester you to come again, to come often.'

'What was it like?' asked Macbeth. 'Did they wear those nosebag things they wear travelling?'

'They were all very kind, but I ate far, far too much.'

Eager to take Jacques' arm, she took Hardyal's instead, missing Macbeth's swift, disapproving glance. As they moved up the path between the glossy hedges, Jacques asked: 'Would you like to live like that, Bertie?'

Hardyal answered for her, forcibly: 'I hope not! Father and I disapprove of purdah, but my aunts have always lived like that and nothing will persuade them to change, though many of their more enlightened friends have given it up. Abdul Salim says that only a revolution will shatter our customs, and his!'

'Would Salim like to start a revolution?' asked Macbeth. He lopped off a budding gardenia with his racquet.

'I think he was just talking,' said Hardyal. He stooped and retrieved the flower, handing it to Bertie. The smell of the bruised petals caught her throat, and feeling her hand tremble Hardyal glanced at her curiously. 'Did the tea party make you ill, Bertie?'

She shook her head, and anxious to distract attention from herself, inquired what Abdul Salim meant when he spoke of revolution.

'Well, he has all manner of ideas.' Hardyal hesitated. 'He believes that a country as ancient and hidebound as ours must have what he calls an internal revolution. It is the only way to break down our absurd religious tyrannies and to bring enlightenment.'

'He sounds like a cut-throat,' observed Macbeth scornfully. 'If he were in the Army and talked like that he'd be jolly well shot.'

'But he is not in the Army,' returned Hardyal, quietly. 'And I am fond of him. He is our good friend.'

'But do you agree with him?' asked Bertie. Hardyal fascinated her; seeing him for the first time through Jacques' eyes she had quickly learned to accept him on his own merits. Macbeth had put up a more determined struggle against the same attraction, and although he had never surrendered as Bertie had, to the young Indian's charming and gentle spirit, he had succumbed to admiration for his skill at games.

'Not a bit like a native,' Macbeth wrote to his father a few days after meeting Hardyal, and this accolade was to place Hardyal in that peculiar category of beings isolated much as a collector's specimen is isolated, from its own and from every other genus.

'Do I agree with Salim?' Hardyal considered Bertie's question. 'Perhaps, though I don't like his idea of violence.'

'Violence, violence! What is this talk of violence?' Ganpat Rai emerged suddenly out of the gloom. 'What are you young conspirators talking about?'

'Hardyal thinks that your ladies need a revolution to bring them out of purdah,' exclaimed Bertie. She liked to watch this father and son together; there was something rare, something subtle, and alive in their relationship.

'Perhaps Hardyal is right,' observed Ganpat Rai, lightly. 'But if we wait for revolution I fear my aunts and sisters will not be here to reap the benefits. Tell me, Bertie, how does purdah affect you?'

'They will seem very comfortable and happy.'

'But you would not change places with them?'

'Change places? That is hardly possible, is it? One can go forwards, but can one go back?'

He peered at her keenly. 'Perhaps if you were to come more often to see my aunts and sisters you would inspire them with healthier ideas.'

She hesitated. 'They are happy, and that is the main thing.'

'Is it the main thing?' He shook his head. 'Come, be frank. Purdah is an anachronism. Salim, good Moslem though he is, agrees with me on that—but like myself, he feels helpless to do anything about it. Indian women have far greater power than is generally believed—their fate is largely their own fault. But if I could bring my ladies into closer communion with you, with Madame St. Remy and with Mrs Lyttleton, perhaps something would come of it. We all learn from one another.'

'But suppose your ladies should succeed in persuading *us*?' asked

Bertie, laughing. Standing beside her, Jacques felt flowing between them a warm and intoxicating current. Then Hanif's voice reached them from the gates. 'For the love of heaven! Am I to wait here all night?'

As they rode home through the dusk Bertie listened to Hanif's singing; he sang always of love unrequited, despairing wails bursting from him and dying in the darkness. Macbeth, unconsciously affected by the song, hummed under his breath while his hunter's eye explored the shadows for a glimpse of some passing hare or fox. And when Jacques' hand discovered hers Bertie felt her blood swarm towards him, and wished that this ride might last forever. She dreaded the evening which she knew must follow the pattern of other evenings passed under Madame's roof; she dreaded the elaborate formulæ, the mistrust and concealment which for the past two years had characterized her relations with Jacques' mother. Although pretence was unnatural to Bertie she sometimes wondered whether it were not, after all, second nature to Madame.

This evening the conversation struck her as being more than ever forced and irrelevant, for although Madame and Father Sebastien talked, in French, of matters dealing with the church and the factory, she felt that both adults were secretly far more preoccupied with conjectures about herself and the boys.

When dinner was finished they all gathered in the drawing-room, where the boys played chess, and if Bertie had doubted the importance of her own presence here she might have derived a sort of amusement from the situation, for it was obvious that with one exception, all were embarrassingly conscious of one another. Like creatures in a wood, half fearful and half curious, they awaited only the crackle of a twig to freeze into immobility or dive into silence.

The exception was Macbeth. Crouched over the chessboard, his features drawn in characteristic lines of concentration, he remained as he was to remain for much of his life, oblivious to everything which lay beyond the circle of his own interest. This was the most childlike, the most touching of all his traits, and in this room, on this evening, he constituted, all by himself, a sort of caduceus, a touchstone, for to look at him and to be reminded of him was in a sense to acquire reassurance.

But later that night when they had all retired, Bertie found it impossible to sleep. She lay in Gisele's bed in the room which used to be Gisele's, where everything remained just as its owner had left it; her prie-dieu stood in one corner under a portrait of the Sacred Heart, and on the dressing-table were her comb and brush with a few golden hairs still tangled in them. The Dutch doors were open and Bertie watched the stars blaze through the pale cloud of her mosquito net. Though she'd bathed before going to bed she could still smell on her hands the tincture of attar, and her brain was filled with fragments and echoes of the afternoon's adventure.

When a breath of wind rattled the loose hinge of the door she sat up, remembering the noise which the wind had made among the oak leaves on the night when Jacques was hurt and she stood in the gully watching her uncle lift the unconscious body down from its tree. It had made her think of the Crucifixion; it had shaken her, changed her. She longed now for the assurance of joy; she could not bear the thought that people come into one's life and endear themselves, only to vanish. Nor could she yet believe that indifference resembles death, that it sometimes supplants death. Did those women in the zenana understand these things better? Did Mirana Bhai, in the saturated wisdom of her kind, realize that life is frightful, impossible to endure alone? And can that be the reason why we turn to the humid warmth of corners and convents and zenanas, even to the balm of death, so we may forget for a little while how lonely we are?

This thought had occurred to Bertie on a morning when John Macbeth came into her room at Gambul and drew aside the curtains at her window. Standing with his back to her he said: 'Listen to the partridge, Bertie!'

'*Shir dharam ke shakrak!*' cried the black partridge from its terrace below the garden. '*Shir dharam ke shakrak!*'

'Do you know what it's saying?' Bertie asked her cousin. He turned, his face working painfully.

'Yes, it's saying that Mother has gone away with Captain Ponsonby.'

This had been Bertie's first glimpse of the human creature as a victim, and the vision stirred a pity which, in her impetuous judgment, passed for love. What was she to say when, later, her uncle came to her with his new, tightened smile, and murmured: 'Don't *you* desert us, Bertie.'

What was she to say or do but what she did—fling her arms round him and cry in passionate assurance: 'Oh, as if I could!'

So, where her aunt had succumbed to the occasion Bertie rose to it, rose on a generous scale which they, bruised and inarticulate, accepted as wounded men accept a crutch or a cup of water.

But as for Bertie, pity had broken away from her like an untamed pet; it eluded her until, at last, she could pursue it no further, and it was at this point, almost a year after her aunt's elopement, that she realized her own exhaustion, a sort of weakness as though she'd risen from an artificially induced fever. Now she longed for food that was not medicine and for emotion that was not pity. Perhaps it was inevitable that she should turn to Jacques, to find in him what had been there from the day of their first encounter in Gambul. He restored something of the exuberance which she expended on others, he gave back in richer measure echoes for which she provided the evocative note.

At midnight the wind drifted against her curtains and she opened her eyes, seeing Jacques standing beside the bed. For a moment she lay wondering whether this were not a continuing figment of her dream, but then he knelt, pressing his face against the net, and when she put out her hand she felt the thrust of his nose, his breath warm against her fingers.

'Bertie, did I wake you?'

He loosened the curtains and crept in, head and shoulders first, until he perched on the edge of the bed. 'I couldn't sleep,' he whispered. 'I kept wondering what happened to upset you at Ganpat Rai's.'

'To upset me?' She dropped her hand on his bare feet, strong and slender on the sheet beside her. 'What do you mean?'

'Oh, I don't know. I thought you seemed upset.'

'I was,' she admitted. 'A little. It was because of the *lals*, I think.'

'The *lals*?'

'Those silly little birds all hopping about outside their cage, trying to get in.'

He had caught the contagion from her heart, and laughed breathlessly.

He leaned across her body, supporting himself on his elbow, his crippled hand hidden among the bedclothes. 'They were only birds, Bertie . . . Mirana's tame birds.'

She stared at his face poised above her own, and something whispered to her that this was how one really studies, really understands, the fascination of the human face. He put his hand on her head in a trembling caress. 'Bertie . . . how silly . . .'

'I know I'm silly, and it wasn't only because of the birds. All those women made me wonder . . . Jacques . . . why are lives so different? Why are we all so separated from one another?'

Both talked to gain time, to delay for a second the cataclysm which they felt closing upon them, but their youth, the weight of the smoky night, and the flight of stars beyond the net conspired against coherence and pathetically acquired restraints. Their breath mingled, their lashes brushed each other's cheeks; they smelled like daffodils, faintly rank, as their virginial limbs sought and discovered each other in the darkness. Then Jacques drew the mosquito curtains and, blindly turning, felt under his good hand the hard globe of her breast, and against his face the enveloping richness of her hair. They lay for a long time silent and motionless, almost dead with terror.

## 33

Hardyal, playing the piano with concentration, did not hear Abdul Salim until he had crossed the drawing-room and presented himself suddenly at the boy's elbow. There he stood smiling down at the absorbed young face until Hardyal suddenly dropped his hands from the keys and swung round on the piano stool. 'Ah, Salim Sahib! I did not hear you come in.'

'I told Krishna not to announce me. I heard you playing and I could not forbear to listen.' His brilliant, restless glance appraised the new upright piano. 'Have I seen this before?'

'Father sent for it, from Calcutta.'

Salim examined his young friend with a fresh curiosity. No one had told him that Ganpat Rai's son had brought home such expensive attainments. A year ago he would have resented the discovery, a few months ago he could not have refrained from gibes, but since Hardyal's return they had seen much of each other, and each recognized the other's sincerity. Now it pleased Salim that his friend's son should possess European accomplishments, for not only did it place Hardyal on a footing with his English friends, in Salim's estimation it placed him on an even higher level, for while to the English these gifts came as a matter of course, to an Indian they were prizes won only by painful struggles against long odds—or so he liked to believe.

'I came to inquire whether you would drive with me to the village where I have business. It is early and we would be gone one or two hours.'

Hardyal was flattered by the invitation, but when he made as if to rise Abdul Salim waved him back and sank, himself, into a nearby chair.

'Play again what you have just played. I should like to watch you.'

Hardyal turned to the keyboard. His playing was amateur but he possessed a sure touch and a particular feeling for this music, which appealed to something complex and inarticulate in his nature. Aubrey Wall's sisters had taught him the piano, but what he had learned was largely of his own choice—a little English ballad, a Mozart sonata, Handel's Largo, a Brahams waltz. He had memorized them with the boyish hope of impressing his father and his aunts. Ever since the

arrival of the piano a few days ago he had been unable to tear himself
away from it, recapturing moods and visions which he'd left behind in
England. His nature, emotionally rich, had developed fresh
complexities under the reserve which two years of English life had
taught him. But when he read poetry or listened to music, the reserve
crumbled and outward expression became one with inward dreams
and desires. Now as he played, once more, the Mozart sonata, his face
and manner assumed a sort of raptness; watching him Salim thought:
'He has taken in, through his pores, the best that they have to give.
What will he do with it?'

Hardyal finished playing and turned once more, smiling as Salim
clapped his hands. 'Even in my ignorance I know that that was
beautiful!'

'It is my European side,' said Hardyal, pleased by the compliment.
'You know, I wish more of us understood these things.'

The Mohammedan lighted a cigarette. 'I agree. We should develop
our own art.' He blew smoke through his nose. 'We are a huge land
with a diverse culture, like Russia. But look at us!' He gestured
somewhat theatrically. 'Where is our music? Where our painting, our
literature? Oh yes, we have our mosques and our temples and our
palaces. We have our Ramayana, our Bhagavad-Gita, our Koran. But
Allah! When my friends come to me with their boastings of Hindu and
Moslem attainments, what do I say? I am cruel. You, I remind them,
have been stopped short in your cultural development long before the
time of Asoka. But Europe has never even paused. I fling Shakespeare
in their teeth. I fling Racine and Molière, I fling Chaucer, Spenser,
Dryden, Pope. I fling Voltaire and Hugo. I fling Wagner. But it is all
wasted. Most of the poor devils cannot even read English, let alone
French or German. We are subjugated and poverty-stricken, so how
should we expect a high degree of artistic development which is, itself,
the result of ages of prosperous civilization?'

While Salim talked with the fluency of a man who has thoroughly
rehearsed his part and who believes in it, Hardyal listened. He could
not resist a glow of pride in the thought that he had been singled out
to be this man's confidant and friend. Ganpat Rai had cautioned him
against taking these radical conversationalists too seriously, but
although Hardyal listened respectfully to his father's warnings he
could not agree with him on this score, certainly not on Salim's score,
for he felt, instinctively, the man's sincerity and passionate conviction.
Salim could not be lightly dismissed by friends or enemies, simply
because as a fearless man he posed a special problem. It was this
quality of fearlessness which attracted Hardyal. He had met courage in
the English, oh, many times! But in them it had become a national

trait, an abstraction, almost. Fearlessness as an inherent attribute was something he had not yet learned to appraise, not even in his father, whom he loved with an intimate, sensual love. During Hardyal's childhood Salim had loomed as a somewhat forbidding figure, all black beard and flashing teeth, one of many men who came and went in his father's professional life, yet one who in the child's eyes moved always with a special distinction. Now he realized that Salim lacked what musicians call *pitch*—he was quite unable to inject the tame note into any social gathering; instead, he disrupted accepted themes, threw every one off key, and struck a dissonant chord in every breast. But it was not until they met again after two years that the boy experienced that shock of recognition, that pang, with which a sensitive mind receives its friend.

Never a creature of repose, the Mohammedan suddenly sprang to his feet. 'Come, let us go before your father returns from the courts. He might object to your being seen in my company.'

'What?'

'Well, I happened to be *persona non grata* with the authorities, and Ganpat Rai is very much in the opposite case.'

Hardyal protested. 'Abdul Salim, you should not say such things! You are our friend, we are yours.'

The tall, testy Mohammedan hesitated, then shrugged. 'One cannot help one's moments of doubt. But forgive me!'

A dogcart, old and shabby, with an uncurried pony between the shafts, waited in the driveway. They got in and Salim picked up the reins. 'My cousin Feroze lent me this trap, in your honour. Ordinarily I hire an ekka. This vehicle belonged to your friend Aubrey Wall, and Feroze bought it from Wall when he auctioned off his things before going back to England.'

They wheeled between the gates and Salim glanced at his young companion. 'You must miss Wall. He was quite a friend, was he not?'

'I never felt that I knew him very well, but I have always looked upon him as one of my very best friends.'

'His family were kind to you in England, then?'

'Yes . . . they treated me like a son or a nephew.'

'And you had no unfortunate experiences with the English?'

Hardyal hesitated, frowning. 'A few, perhaps. But they do not count.' He was sorry that Salim should have asked the question, for it stirred a train of recollections . . . small slights and insignificant occasions among his schoolmates and others; the occasions had been few as he said, and they did not really count. Nevertheless he was sorry that Salim should have asked the question.

They drove towards the river and after a brief silence Salim murmured: 'This question of friendship . . . it can be tragic, don't you agree?'

'Tragic?' Hardyal repeated the word gingerly.

'Ah, how young you are!' It came on a sigh, impatient, envious. 'You love your friends Macbeth and Jacques—even the girl, Miss Wood.'

Hardyal watched the flies which clustered round the pony's ears.

'Tell me,' said Salim abruptly, 'do you find yourself attracted to her?'

'To whom?' He slightly averted his head.

'To Miss Wood, to Bertie. I confess she appeals to me.'

'I am fond of her.'

'But you do not desire her?'

The boy hesitated, not from embarrassment, for in matters of sex his thought was free from romantic taints, but for subtler reasons. He was not in love with Bertie, no; but he remembered that on the evening of the purdah party when she came out from the zenana she had taken his arm, and he had experienced a sudden warmth in his veins and had spent much of the night thinking of her. Now he tried to find words that would once and for all excise the doubts in Salim's mind and in his own. 'I do not, I never have desired her.'

'Because you think that Jacques does?'

'Simply because she does not attract me.'

And having said it, he was comforted, feeling it to be true. The older man nodded. 'I am glad, otherwise it might have made for great unhappiness.'

Hardyal laughed suddenly. 'I have loved only one white woman— Mrs Lyttleton!'

Salim thrust out his beard in an angry *moue*. 'Ah yes, I know. Well, so far as love is concerned she is too old to be dangerous. Nevertheless I do not trust her.'

The boy turned to stare at him. 'You do not trust Mrs Lyttleton?'

'Do not forget that she is English.'

'Ah, Salimji! . . . That is not fair of you.'

'Fair, fair!' He exploded. 'What has reason to do with fairness? What sort of logic is it that holds up an individual virtue as being synonymous with a whole race? She and Wall—they are the same *jat*. They stick together, I tell you—they stick together!'

Viciously, he slapped the reins on the pony's matted back.

'But,' objected Hardyal, timid yet compelled by loyalty to speak out, 'but do you not find the admirable in them, that they do stick together?' He added slyly, 'And would it not be better for us if *we* stuck together?'

'Yes, yes, it would be better for us, but it would be worse for them—oh, far, far worse!'

Hardyal remained silent; Salim's ferocity sometimes confused him. Now he thought of Mrs Lyttleton, who had welcomed him home with tears, clasping him in her arms, making him think of his own grandmother.

Salim glanced at the boy, and moved by a generosity that came as naturally to him as passion, he laid his hand on Hardyal's knee.

'Come, you and I will not quarrel. Life is short. These things will all resolve themselves.'

As they skirted the bazaar with its beggars and its monkeys and drove on a narrow rutted road towards the canal, Hardyal sniffed the dusty air and watched a tide of green parrots tilt, shrieking, across the sky. He never felt, as he knew Jacques felt, and as Macbeth felt, any particular sense of intimacy or ownership in the countryside, and lately he had begun to question this lack in himself. He loved his home, his father, and his family with an intense and personal love which stopped short with its immediate object; but beyond that, life and land seemed huge and shapeless and impersonal, matters for wonder, but not for curiosity or love.

Salim was explaining the purpose of their ride; they were going to the village of Ramdatta the moneylender where he expected to meet two men who had offered to stand as sureties for his client Ganga Singh, at that moment lodged in Amritpore's new red-brick jail. Once the sureties had been found and their pledge accepted by the magistrate, Ganga Singh would be bound over to be of good behaviour, and released.

'The men are caste-fellows of my client, but they are likewise Ramdatta's tenants, and the police have been at some pains to make it difficult for us to obtain sureties anywhere. You know how our lathi-wielders batten on convictions!'

'But what about the Superintendent, Crichton?' Hardyal remembered the able, red-faced Scot.

'Oh, Crichton is all right,' Salim's tone was grudging. 'But even he cannot know all that goes on. If he did he'd be obliged to suspend half his police force!'

The village appeared under its umbrella of trees; a white temple and raised water tank gleamed in the sunlight, shadows striped the walls and the threshing floors and danced on the flat roofs. As Salim drove up, a whole battalion of dogs rushed forth barking and snapping at the pony's legs. Salim, who generated temper while he talked, rose from his seat and laid about him with the carriage whip. The dogs fled howling, and Hardyal saw a figure appear in an opening of the low

mud wall which bounded the village. Although they had not met for
some time he recognized Ramdatta the moneylender. Ramdatta wore a
voluminous dhoti, his head and body were bare, glistening with
coconut oil. He was accompanied by a little group of men and boys
and as Salim, still brandishing the whip, pulled his frightened pony to
a halt, Ramdatta hailed him. 'Ah, my friends! I apologize for these
curs.'

He came forward, smiling, and Hardyal wondered as he had often
wondered in the past, why so many people detested this man.
Ramdatta's good-nature never faltered; his person reminded Hardyal
of some rich and succulent sweet.

Without waiting for Salim's reply, the moneylender turned to
Hardyal.

'On my word, this is twofold honour! Come, both of you— come to
my house. I have fruits and tobacco and my sons shall wait on us.'

At sight of the man, a sort of vibration had set up in Abdul Salim.
He put the whip back in its socket but kept the reins in his hands. His
eyes, like two vivid and fiery stones, stared down at Ramdatta.

'We are pushed for time. Tell me, Protector of the Poor, how is your
servant?'

'Which servant ? I have many.'

'I refer to one whose head I broke when I threw him out of my
brother-in-law's house.'

Ramdatta pondered, then slapped his thigh, laughing. 'That
numbskull, Govind! It was not with my permission that he went to
collect interest on your brother-in-law's debt, my friend! Govind has an
officious temper. You would have done me a service had you finished
him completely.'

'It will be a pleasure, at any time,' rejoined Salim.

There was a brief pause, charged on all sides with a sort of
passionate attention. Then Salim said: 'I have an appointment with two
men of your village—Ram Prasad and Munnu Singh. Would you of
your kindness tell me where I might find them?'

Ramdatta, his strong legs planted in the stance of meditation, his
brown arms folded across his hairless breast, put his head to one side
and frowned. 'Ram Prasad? Munnu Singh? You expected to meet them
here?'

'That was our arrangement. If you would send a boy to fetch
them . . .'

A voice interrupted from the group behind Ramdatta. 'They are not
here. Ram Prasad went to Lucknow for the funeral of his wife's
mother, and Munnu has gone away to the hills.'

Hardyal felt that the air around him gathered suspense; he had not looked for it, he had not expected it. Intent on the scene, on the village which nested among the trees, on the figure of the priest whose orange robe shone like a flame against the temple wall, he was prepared only for one of those long, boring conversations by means of which most grown-up people waste their time. But now, sitting beside Salim on the narrow leather seat, he felt the air grow still and tight. It was Salim who shattered the silence: 'You must be mistaken, brother. Ram Prasad sent me word that he would meet me here this very noon. Had he changed his plans I would have been the first to know.'

Ramdatta turned masterfully to the little crew behind him. 'I have, myself, been absent for a day or two. Are you sure that Ram Prasad and Munnu are not here? Go, my son,' he addressed a small boy. 'Go to Munnu's house and find out.'

The boy, who had been standing on one leg like a stork, shook down the other and squirmed deferentially. 'My lord, I myself saw Munnu depart. He rode away in the same cart with Ram Prasad, late yesterday evening.'

Salim burst out in a sudden terrific laugh. 'Nay then, do not put yourselves to any further trouble. I see that others have been here before me. . . . Mighty ones, walking on their flat feet and shaking the gold fringes on their turbans. The very thud of their big toes can slay a man's mother-in-law and raise a fever in the lungs of a prize-fighter like Munnu Singh, making it imperative that he depart into the hills. Wah! What heroes! Allah, no—what gods!'

Under this pelting sarcasm the little crowd swayed and fell back; but Ramdatta remained, his sandalled feet firmly planted in the dust, one hand resting on his hip, the other hanging at his side. His face, smooth, with full lips and mocking eyes, reflected an imperturbable composure. 'If you would honour me by setting forth in my village we might discuss, in peace and amity, the strange disappearance of your friends. Had I known that you were coming I would have used what influence I have to delay them. Nay, I would have insisted that they wait until you had concluded your business with them. However, who is this Ram Prasad? Who is Munnu Singh?' He snapped his plump fingers disdainfully. 'Unreliable souls from their birth? But there are other men of worth and goodwill, as you will doubtless find, for Abdul Salim, as I well know, is a lawyer of stupendous talents. Come, my friends—Come, Hardyal. Wah! Thou hast grown.'

Hardyal listened, hypnotized by a voice which oozed rather than spoke. Glancing at Salim he had a glimpse of a single blazing eye; Salim's fingers gripped the reins as though he were in the act of strangling something. 'You are most hospitable, Maharaj,' said the Mohammedan. 'But then, why should that surprise one to whom your name has long been a byword for charity? One who dispenses golden mangoes to the poor, and before whose august face the police bow down like grass in the wind? Hardly a man breathes but to pray for your long life and continued health. May you live to conceal many gold mohurs inside mangoes and melons, and may the echoes ring with the guffaws of your brothers, the English. But come, this is not a farewell. You and I occupy a restricted area upon the earth—too restricted, alas, to allow for fat! We shall meet again, without doubt.'

The moneylender shrugged a glossy shoulder, and replied, mockingly:

'Salute your client for me. I am told that in the jail yard there is a mango tree whose fruit is always sour!'

Salim, suddenly jerking the off rein, pulled the trap round so that it brought him several feet closer to the moneylender, and leaning forward he spat over the wheel into the dust at Ramdatta's feet. At this insult a small boy, popping out from behind his elders, flung a stone at the pony, which promptly whirled about and bolted. Salim swore, plied the whip, and hauled on the reins in a paroxysm of fury; thanks to some miracle they regained the road where, after a final defiant buck, their pony lapsed into its habitual decorous gait.

In a voice gone suddenly flat and ominous Salim declared: 'I should have killed the fat swine.'

They were nearing the canal locks where Aubrey Wall and Father Sebastien used to fish for crocodiles. Hardyal saw one of the cold beasts slumbering at the water's edge, while Pity-to-do-its stepped like privileged spirits beside it motionless jaws.

'Yes, I should have killed him. Do you know what would have happened had I stuck a knife in his soft brown belly? It would have spewed forth a gutful of rupees, annas, and pice!'

Hardyal stirred uneasily. 'Yet he does not look to me like a bad man.'

Salim seemed not to hear. He laid the reins on the pony's back and lighted a cigarette. 'In my grandfather's time we threw our enemies to the elephants. Once, when even I was a boy, I saw a big durbar elephant kill its mahout. It caught the man as he was about to mount and drew him slowly, slowly down, then knelt on him. It knelt on his head, on his belly, his genitals, and all its weight and all its hatred were in its crushing knees. Then it lowered its forehead, all painted for ceremony, and set it squarely on the man's body and flattened him out like a taxidermist's hide. Never have I seen a job of death better done.'

Behind them a cloud of dust rose and settled, and before their eyes stretched the level fields, a young green the colour of evening skies.

## 34

E ven in the resplendent days of her youth Mrs Lyttleton was not
famous for displays of public spirit, nor was she given to
excesses of neatness and order. It came, therefore, as something
of a shock to her ragtag and bobtail crew of servants when, a day
before the opening of the Agricultural Fair, she suddenly commanded
them to set to and clean up her garden. It was a jungle, no less, but it
had been a jungle for more than thirty years, and the fact had never
weighed very heavily on her spirits. In fact she had taken a rather
perverse pleasure in the contrast afforded by her own compound and
those of her more conventional neighbours. That she should out of a
clear sky elect to bring order out of chaos stupefied her ancient
gardener, who had scarcely lifted a finger since the death of his master,
the General.

'Truly, she has lost her mind,' declared the old man to his colleagues
in the servants' quarters. 'For a month, now, one dare not cross her
path. She is bewitched, or the food no longer sits well on her stomach.'

'It has nothing to do with the food,' replied the cook, grinding the
day's supply of spices on his basalt grindstone. 'I, too, have watched
her closely. One day she appears to be her old self, praising my
kedgeree, asking for gossip. Then without warning this silence
descends on her and she shrinks in her chair like a sick child. Or she
will suddenly turn on me and curse me for a down-at-heel wastrel!
However,' he shrugged, 'as I have said before, I have my own ideas on
the mystery.'

'I also,' observed the syce thoughtfully. 'It all dates from the death
of Jalal.'

The cook lowered his eyes. 'I am not one to spread or to listen to
rumours.'

'She grieves for him,' said the syce. 'That, I believe, is at the bottom
of it. She has a heart of sugar.'

'And a tongue steeped in acid,' mumbled the gardener. 'Where am
I to procure labour for this task? I shall have to hire half-wits and
paralytics not already engaged by the Fair Committee. If they cut
down the wrong tree or uproot the wrong vine, who will be to blame?'

In spite of the mali's misgivings a platoon of coolies presently
descended on the garden, and with their arrival a general exodus took
place as multitudes of rats, snakes, lizards, and toads debouched into
the road and into adjacent compounds. The hoopoes, used to strutting
unmolested near the graves under the loquat tree, suddenly fled. Blue-
jays flew, chattering angrily, with the parrots and the seven sisters, and

the garden's aromatic breath dispersed on the winter air as Mrs Lyttleton, smoking her Egyptian cigarettes, supervised the exhumation from her chair on the veranda.

Madness, grumbled the gardener, untangling himself from a rose tree which he'd planted heaven knew how many years before; now its hooked talons ripped the flesh from his legs. The lilies had rotted, the orange trees and the limes were dead, but a laburnum twisted to a travesty of itself bore amidst its yellow flowers the wreath of cuckoo-lantana and the wild palm. To the gardener this rifling of time's palette was a sacrilege, no less; since neglect had claimed the garden, spirits dwelt here, good and evil foregathered to compare notes; to let in the sunlight was once more to separate the two and to invite retribution from both.

'Fool!' cried Mrs Lyttleton, rattling her bracelets. 'What spirits there are crawl on their bellies and carry poison in their fangs. Others hop on two legs and keep me awake all night with their infernal croakings. Chop down the cactus! Pull up the vines, uncover the roses and the sandstone basin of the lotus pond, and the old paths where I used to walk. They must still be there. Stones do not walk away of themselves, do they? Have I kept you in food and blankets fifty years for nothing?'

By the end of the second day the garden had exchanged its crazy charm for complete confusion. Whole patches were whittled down to raw soil flanked by mounds of decaying vegetation. Weeds, rain, and drought had usurped every vestige of an original architecture, and of the lotus pond all that survived was a blackened pit which oozed delegations of pale, nameless worms.

As Mrs Lyttleton roamed among the clearings her dogs followed her, stepping gingerly as if the denuded earth hurt their feet, pausing to sniff an alien stone or to examine some naked stump or to retreat, growling, from the edge of the lotus pond. They sought, unfailingly, to keep their mistress's petticoats between themselves and the spectral air of these unfamiliar vistas.

On the third day it rained slightly, big drops pocking the dust and stirring a troubled breath from the bruised weeds. Mrs Lyttleton watched her coolies as one by one they wrapped their rags over their heads and retired to await a clearing sky. Then she summoned her gardener and as abruptly as she had ordered the assault upon the garden she now ordered him to cease. 'I was a fool,' she said in a tired voice. 'A fool, to imagine that we could bring it back as it used to be.'

He stood before her on legs as bowed and knotted as an old acacia. 'I do not understand. Are we to wait until the rain has ceased?'

'Tell them to cart away the rubbish and dismiss them.'

He shook his shrivelled head. 'I am too old, now, to relish such jokes.'

'It is no joke. I wish the garden to be left as it is.'

When he turned away she called him back and said gently: 'Pardon me for having spoken roughly to thee. I also am old, but I had no cause to upbraid thee.'

She had always been a generous mistress, but this was going far, even for her. He fell at her feet, crying: 'You are my father and my mother! How can there be talk of forgiveness between us?'

When he'd gone at last she stood motionless, gazing at her ravaged garden, watching the rain fall in delicate spears from a sky that was still partly blue above the trees. 'What a fool I am,' she mused, striving by the admission to allay a far deeper disquiet. 'What a fool!'

A bicycle bell chimed down the road and she saw Hardyal pedal between the gates, saw him swerve wildly to avoid the rubbish which littered the driveway. He propped his machine against the veranda steps and came running up, breathless, to greet her. 'Heavens! What have you been doing?'

He stared at the garden, then at her, his eyes big with inquiry. Mrs Lyttleton lighted a cigarette. 'I have been playing the snob, Hardyal . . . attempting, at my time of life, to impress my neighbours!' And she laughed on a stilled note.

Hardyal dropped into a chair and clasped his hands between his knees.

She went on in an affected voice: 'Amritpore will be filled with distinguished visitors for the Fair, and it suddenly occurred to me that I had no wish to pose as an exhibit on their agenda . . . the Old Woman who lives in a Jungle, don't you know?'

He stared at her uncomprehendingly, and she went on: 'So I decided to astound them all by putting my house in order. I thought that it might impress them as a sign of my regenerated soul. They would wonder whether perhaps, after all, they had not been mistaken in me? Perhaps I was really quite all right in spite of my eccentricities. Perhaps they would now accept me as one of their own *jat*.'

It was a weird and uncharacteristic speech and the boy continued to gaze at her with unfathomable eyes. Then he asked: 'Who do you mean by *they*?'

'Oh, Mr Crichton and Mr Swan, Mr and Mrs Burrows, and . . . good lord, yes! Madame St Remy, Father Sebastien and his Christians, Macbeth, Miss Wood, Jacques!'

His lashes fell slowly, then he raised them in a fierce, direct look.

'So for that you have spoiled your garden?'

'I meant only to restore it.'

He turned once more to survey the ruins. 'I feel that I have never been here before!'

'Ah, but you have been here before, Hardyal.'

'I know, I know . . .' Suddenly he seemed on the verge of tears, and she said quickly: 'Never mind, my dear, it will grow again. Everything turns to jungle sooner or later.'

Hardyal shook his head. 'It was lovely as it used to be. I loved it. I remember when Jacques and I used to come here and play among the bushes. It seemed like our own, and now it's gone.'

'It will come back,' she insisted, troubled by his emotion. 'Give it one monsoon and it will come back.'

But he was inconsolable. 'No, it won't come back.'

She thought silently: He is right, he sees something that I have not wanted to see: it won't come back, no monsoon will ever bring back his innocent and imaginative love for it.

After a brief pause she remarked with a false air of gaiety: 'You came in time to cheer me, for I was beginning to feel neglected.' Inwardly she thought, bitterly: There I go, making a bid for pity! She pulled herself together and reached for her cigarettes. 'Remind me to give you a box of these for Mirana Bhai.'

His face cleared. 'And that reminds me why I am here. Mirana has sent you a present, too.' He reached in a pocket and fished out a little heart-shaped box of brass and enamel, intricately chased.

Mrs Lyttleton took it, exclaiming: 'But I know this box! It is one in which Mirana keeps her betel-nut. Surely she cannot intend it for me?'

'You know she would be hurt if you were to refuse it.'

Mrs Lyttleton guessed that there was something special in the nature and the manner of this offering. The chill which had touched her heart a little while ago touched it again. She met Hardyal's eyes, and he nodded, smiling faintly. 'Yes, Mirana thinks that you have neglected her lately. The box is a reminder . . . a token. . .'.

'I have not been very well. Will you tell her that I shall see her very soon, and that I shall reserve my gratitude until I can thank her myself?'

'Father, too, has missed you. You know he has a conspiracy in mind. He believes that if only he can persuade English ladies to visit our house constantly they will fire my aunts with an ambition to come out from purdah. Already they ask Father to buy them stockings like Bertie's, and a piano like mine. But while Father plots from outside, Mirana Bhai plots from within!'

Mrs Lyttleton laughed. 'Which do you think will win?'

'I don't know. Abdul Salim insists that persuasion is a waste of time. He believes that such matters should not be left to individuals but should be decided politically.' The last word was brought out with a hesitant, conscious pride, and she looked at him keenly.

'Salim said that? He is quite a friend of yours, then?'

'He has always been our friend.'

'Yet I know that your father does not wholly approve of him.'

'Oh, Father does not share many of Salim's views, but he admires him, as I do also.'

She glanced away from his young, serious face. 'I know Salim only slightly. He is an avowed seditionist.'

Hardyal rose eagerly in his friend's defence and she listened, troubled by his loyalty. It troubled her that she was unable to share his enthusiasm as she had shared others. The truth was, she did not like Abdul Salim; she had never found him sympathetic, and she mistrusted his truculence. She was more weary of violence and of violent characters than she would have believed possible a year ago, even a few months ago. Time compresses events into narrow channels, decisions are precipitated in seconds, even in split-seconds. I'm old, she reflected, bleakly. Old . . .

Now as she listened to Hardyal speak of his Moslem friend she remembered what Aubrey Wall had once said to her: 'Hold on to Hardyal! Keep him up to the mark, won't you? They lose it so easily.'

She wished that it was not Aubrey Wall who had said that; she wished that she could forget Wall; but he, too, had forced a decision whose consequences were still in the making. And while Hardyal talked with affection and admiration of his Mohammedan friend Mrs Lyttleton studied the boy's face and reflected on all that she knew about him, all that she had thought and hoped for him, remembering him as a brown seraph with silver *kurras* on his wrists, and his disconcerting infant's gaze. Hardyal was inextricably part of her love for the country as he was in a sense part of her love for Jacques. She had lost Jacques: was she, now, to lose Hardyal? She saw him suddenly beset by new forces—forces inimical to her philosophy, her experience. She caught the virile note in his voice when he said: 'It is nice to be treated as an equal by a man like Salim. Father and I talk, but we seem never to disagree about anything!'

Mrs Lyttleton imagined the nature of conversations which must give rise to such disagreements. Here, then, was an allegiance which had already claimed him. Would there be others, infections and contagions of whose exact scope she could never hope to learn? The thought startled her with its intimation of the distance that separated her sphere from his. She might guess at the forces which conditioned Jacques' life or John Macbeth's, but in Hardyal's case she remained in the dark! She felt suddenly the need to make some possessive gesture without which everything that had happened until now would become meaningless. She, who had always insisted that she knew where she stood and, by that token, to a large measure, where others stood, she, who had kept her spirit free, submitted at last, reluctantly enough, to the necessities of that freedom, to its inexorable paradox. She felt that she must exert herself to hold Hardyal up to that mark which not only Aubrey Wall and herself, but which his own father had set for him, the mark which, should he miss it, or abjure it, would result in incalculable dismay. But the moment was too portentous, too delicately in balance, its springs still too deeply hidden for her to dare risk anything but subtlety. Whatever her gesture, it must be equal in portent, equal in delicacy, its springs as carefully concealed as the fear which prompted it.

She said presently, with an air of lightness: 'Of course you know that Salim loathes us?'

The boy hesitated, frowning. 'Salim is a very honest man. He knows that like others he is bound by silly customs and prejudices against which he alone can do little. That is why he always insists that great changes must be enforced by law rather than by personal whims. He hates the English because he thinks that they are immoral.'

Mrs Lyttleton gasped slightly. 'Oh, he does, does he? And he'd enforce his own brand of morality by throwing his enemies to the elephants, as his forefathers used to do?'

The boy smiled.

'That's only his way of talking. Father says that Salim's bark is much worse than his bite.'

'I must say that I don't personally fancy either.'

Hardyal remembered the Mohammedan's judgment of Mrs Lyttleton. Young and generous himself, he was filled with a desire to have everything straight between his friends. It was towards this end that he'd conspired with Jacques for Macbeth's good graces; he had compelled Macbeth to accept him, just as in England he'd compelled others. You have but to loom a little larger, a little deeper, in all your capacities, for people to lose their differences in you. This belief had gradually assumed the proportions of a characteristic in Hardyal, whose Hindu nature was learning the subtlest lesson of the Christian, at a point where both were nearest each other, at the point where they had first diverged.

He said gently: 'If you and Salim were really to know each other, you could not help liking each other.'

She was touched by his artlessness. Tenderness reinforces her resolve to hold on to him, and the resolve rekindled her spirit. There had been a time when she felt equal to everything, when she had in fact proved herself equal to a great deal. This was such a time, and her eyes shone with the realization.

'Well, I shall take your word for Salim, my dear boy. Why don't bring him to call on me one of these days?'

The degree to which she found herself equal revealed itself to her conscience, which did not flinch before Hardyal's responsive pleasure. 'Do you mean that, honestly, honestly?'

'Honestly!' She went on quickly—'And now since we are on the subject of friendship, what do you hear from your friends the Walls?'

His radiance faded somewhat. 'I have had only one letter from Miss Bella, nothing from Mr Wall.'

It was her moment, and she rose. 'I have heard from Aubrey, and there is a letter I'd like to read you, from him.'

When she had disappeared into the house Hardyal turned with a deliberate exercise of will to confront the desolate garden. All through the conversation he'd kept his back towards it, but now it recurred like an unhappy dream. He was horrified at sight of the raw branches and castrated soil, at the defeated look of familiar old trees and the rags of creepers which still clung to them. Whatever was creative in Hardyal sprang from a submerged religious source, from an almost superstitious dread of destruction. He remembered his first fox-hunt in England, and the unuttered and unutterable sensation which filled him when the Master had 'blooded' him with the raw stump of the fox's brush. He had in that instant resurrected the creature's agony, while his intelligence insisted that this feeling was irrelevant and sentimental, that in the civilized world death and desecration had a waning importance. But the confusion could still take him unawares, as it had taken him at first sight of Jacques Remy's mutilated hand, as it took him now at sight of Mrs Lyttleton's mutilated garden.

It was with a sigh of relief that he greeted her when she reappeared carrying a bundle of letters. Like most old women, she could never bring herself to destroy letters. Now she paused, staring at him in surprise. 'Hardyal, what is it? You look frightened.'

He laughed, turning aside. 'I was afraid that there might be *bhut*s in the garden.'

She laughed, too. 'You're too old, now, to see *bhut*s. Sit down and let me read you Aubrey's letter.'

He sat at a little distance from her, gazing eagerly at the bundle which she untied and spread on the wicker table before her. She skimmed through one and then another, and he had no means of reading the expression which increasingly tightened the corners of her mouth, which seemed to cause a sort of shrinking in all her features, as if a drop of acid had fallen somewhere within their calm and familiar mask.

'Ah,' she said at last. 'Here it is.'

She did not, however, begin to read it at once. Instead, she read the first page to herself, then the second, and it was only when she was half-way down the third that she glanced up and said: 'This is the part that will interest you . . .' She began to read in a clear, almost a ringing voice: 'When you see Hardyal give him my love and tell him I think of him often and look forward to the day when we shall meet again. I have heard nothing but good reports of him from my sisters, who miss him badly, as do most of his friends here. Every one has been charmed by his manners and his spirit. I have always believed, myself, that he was one of our best, like his father. We need more like them, for they are the stuff and the hope of the future. Perhaps I shall see Hardyal when he comes back to England, or at any rate, surely when I come back to India.'

She read a few more sentences, picking them out from the body of the letter, then folded, it and replaced it in its envelope, which she laid on the table among the others. 'I thought you ought to hear that, Hardyal.'

He was glad to have heard it. An extraordinary elation filled him as he listened, a sense of pride, affection, and justification. Naturally modest, flattery tasted to him like a sip of forbidden wine—and it went to his head. Watching his face Mrs Lyttleton saw that she had indeed achieved a victory: for the moment at any rate she and Aubrey Wall had caught up with, had perhaps even passed, Abdul Salim. Yet while she talked, putting little touches and flourishes to the victorious moment, laying the ground for its further development, her heart grew heavier and heavier. If only it had not been through Aubrey Wall that she should have recaptured Hardyal! If it could have been through Jacques or John Macbeth—through any one else! The thought of Wall bit into her soul, poisoning it, numbing it, so that presently Hardyal saw that she wore an expression of extraordinary fatigue. He'd been on the verge of asking her to let him see the letter, even of asking whether he might take it home with him to show his father and Abdul Salim. He'd known Aubrey Wall to be friendly, but he had experienced the man's reserve, and the tone of this letter surprised him—it profoundly stirred him. He was too shy to suggest that Mrs Lyttleton read it again, and while he hesitated he became obsessed by an almost mystical longing to possess the letter, to make a talisman of it. But he sat quietly, with his eyes fixed on the grey envelope where it lay on the table between the cigarettes and a folded newspaper, a few feet away from him. If only she would read his mind and offer it herself, saying: 'Ah, Hardyal! This really belongs to you, for in a sense it was written to you. Won't you take it and keep it?'

The request trembled on his lips, he longed to speak out, but with every second the words became more difficult to utter: he was too shy, insistence would have seemed immodest and conceited—worse, she might chaff him! Indecision paralysed his tongue, and he finally rose.

'I must go now. I will tell Mirana Bhai that you will come soon to see her.'

Mrs Lyttleton rose too, putting her hand on his shoulder. He felt her slight weight lean on him, felt her strange tiredness when she murmured: 'Yes, soon, very soon.'

He went down the steps and picked up his bicycle, and as he threaded his way down the littered driveway he kept thinking of Wall's letter, thinking of it with a passion which, as a child, he used to feel towards certain objects and certain people, vesting them with an impossible value. When finally he reached the gates he knew that he could go no further, for his legs had become dead weights, all the purpose accumulated in his shoulders and his arms. He swung the handle-bars round and once more faced the tall, dark arches of the veranda. He'd go back, he would ask Mrs Lyttleton outright whether she would give him the letter to keep. She would give it to him, of this he had no doubt. She would understand, as in the past she had never failed to understand, everything! He dismounted by the steps, but the veranda was empty. He called her name, softly at first, then a little louder, but when his voice died away on the unresponsive silence he thought: 'She has gone to the bathroom.'

He hesitated, while from their places on the wall the stuffed heads brooded upon him, and past him on the garden, where the rain had ended in a burst of saffron light. Then Hardyal turned to the wicker table where the letters still lay; he had no difficulty in picking out the one which she had read to him, and he trembled slightly, not from doubt or fear but from the excitement of doing something which he had never thought of doing before. He picked up the letter and for a full minute stood motionless, waiting for Mrs Lyttleton to appear in the dim and silent doorway. She did not appear, and the house stood before him, echo-less and wrapped in shadow. He tucked the letter into his breast pocket and went down the steps to his bicycle. No one had seen him come back; no one, now, saw him go.

## 35

He did not read the letter at once; he did not, as a matter of fact, read it for several days. It remained untouched in his pocket and the thought of it lay in his consciousness like a dry shard, slowly, mysteriously germinating an independent life. While his memory retained the gist of what Mrs Lyttleton had read to him, Hardyal could not have explained the instinct—it was obscure enough to be called instinct—which prevented his satisfying himself of its contents, once and for all. Perhaps he felt that to do so would disrupt the charm and break the spell, and he was still of an age and of a kind which more than half-believes in spells.

As the days passed he found himself thinking long and intently about Aubrey Wall, a man like a hundred other Englishmen yet one who by virtue of a certain sensitivity, a certain force, has been saved from the category of 'type'. And that particular virtue, as Hardyal realized, was what he now sought to recover—that singularity, that difference. Because Wall had expressed a special liking for him, Hardyal felt bound to uncover an equivalent feeling for Wall—a feeling which had not hitherto distinguished their relationship. He set himself to recall all the things that Aubrey Wall used to do and say, his likes and his dislikes, his kindnesses, his explosions of temper, every manifestation of a character with which he'd at one time been familiar. Yet, in the end what did it amount to, that familiarity, that understanding? Nothing more than a handful of ashes which a fire leaves below the ghats when wood and oil have done their work. Nevertheless, there must have been something that he'd missed until this moment; some current, some depth which he'd been too young or too careless to fathom. Wall had liked him, had liked him more than he'd known how to express, more than he could bring himself to reveal except through the medium of letters! How queer the English were! Only an Englishman could have written a drama like *King Lear*, and built a tragedy on the inanity of a single tongue-tied maiden!

But Aubrey Wall had been instrumental in Hardyal's destiny; that was an unforgettable fact, one which made them in a sense belong to each other, an exchange like the clasp of hands or the mingling of a glance. For Hardyal, the Oriental, intimacy carried a profound responsibility, and he began to reflect with remorse on his own possible shortcomings.

'Aubrey was reserved and rather cold, giving little of himself even to his sisters. And now I discover, in that inexpressive spirit, this small flame of warmth and affection for me. And I, what did I give in return? Nothing! I took him for granted, I was even a little bit afraid of him. I must have let him down a hundred times without knowing it. I must have hurt him, disappointed him, puzzled him by neglecting to let him see that I understood.'

At this point in his broodings Hardyal suffered from a stab of memory. He had a vision of Malabar Hill and of the shabby Englishman he had encountered there beside the Parsee *dhakma*s under the trees. He remembered the man's face, the dingy freckles, and seedy eye, the whole offensive personality, and he was shaken by fear lest something in his own behaviour might at one time or another have given Wall to reflect, with a fatal shrug: 'Damned cheeky, even for a native!' But not once in the days which followed his visit to Mrs Lyttleton did Hardyal suffer from a twinge of conscience in having taken the letter itself. He was convinced that it belonged to him in the first place; his intention had been innocent—the act could not be less so! And when, a few days afterwards, he saw Mrs Lyttleton again—this time when she came to call on his aunt Mirana Bhai—he ran out to greet her and to help her alight from her carriage. She put her hand on his shoulder, and he knew at once that she had not missed the letter. From this knowledge there budded instantly the conviction that she knew he had taken it, that she had intended all along that he should take it, and therefore found it superfluous to remark on its disappearance. This sort of rationalization could not, perhaps, have occurred in the minds of either Jacques St Remy or of John Macbeth, for in both the sense of guilt would have been inevitable, followed by a breakdown into contrition and a final confessing. But in Hardyal the whole thing originated in a completely different point of view, the Oriental view which sticks to essentials and which regards most Occidental ideals as hypocrisy or convention. Two years in England had not taught Hardyal to demur in such matters when his emotions were deeply involved, nor had his own sense of honour suffered by contrast.

When Mrs Lyttleton emerged from the ladies' quarters and asked him to play for her he whirled gaily on the piano stool and asked: 'What would you like to hear?'

Anything, she assured him, would please her. She sat on the chair where Abdul Salim had sat, and as she watched Hardyal she became aware, once more, of the man growing within him, visible in the thickening muscles of his neck, in the strength of the profile where a short strong nose jutted above sensuous lips. He wore half-native dress, a dhoti with an English jacket; the folds of the dhoti slipping to one side revealed a leg which swelled in a single sinewy curve from calf to ankle, ending in a well-shaped dark foot cased in a rope sandal. Mrs Lyttleton was no great admirer of Oriental beauty; instinctively she, like others, sought what was foreign in Hardyal—sought the impress of her own country and her own standards. She thought she saw it in his eyes when he glanced up at her, and in his quick and fluent hands.

He finished at last, and turned, dropping his hands on his knees.

She applauded with the characteristic native exclamation: 'Wah, wah! It makes me homesick for the past, to see a man play the piano. I never have understood why music, any music, can make one vaguely unhappy.'

He walked with her to the door of the drawing-room. 'I don't feel like that at all. I like to play, I have all kinds of fancies and visions—visions of fountains and of clouds, of strange birds flying through purple light, and sometimes I see a temple where the sun falls like an offering of little coins on Shiva's body, and thousands of tiny bells speak with separate tongues, announcing the arrival of Kali!'

She turned to gaze at him. 'That comes from your heart, doesn't it?'

'From my heart? Yes, and from my mind also.'

A little while after she had driven away in her ancient carriage Abdul Salim and Ganpat Rai appeared riding in a hired ekka, and as it drew up before the veranda steps Salim leaped out, laughing and offering his hand to help his friend alight.

'Ah, Hardyal! Your father condescended to accept a lift in my humble equipage! It is, I believe, many years since he has so far demeaned himself. But after all, isn't the true measure of a man's greatness his willingness to descend to the level of obscure friends? You,' he waved imperiously at the ekka-wallah. 'Withdraw a little distance and wait for me.'

The ekka creaked away, and they turned to the drawing-room where all three cast themselves on cushions upon the floor, and Krishna brought them the usual offerings of *pan* and cigarettes. Hardyal saw at once that both men were in good spirits. Ganpat Rai had just won a case, and his satisfaction expressed itself in numerous small gestures of affection towards his son and his guest, while his kind, shrewd face beamed with content. Salim was exuberant, for he, too, had passed a successful morning in court, where he had finally obtained the release of his client Ganga Singh.

Hardyal sat facing the two men with his arms clasping his knees. As any well-bred boy must, he listened more than he spoke, and felt himself secreting a special delight in his father's success and his friend's good humour.

Ganpat Rai slapped Salim lightly on the shoulder. 'You know, you ought to write a treatise on Section 110 of the Criminal Procedure Code. You have made it your special study, and by publishing it you would be doing us all a great service. I would find a publisher for you, in Calcutta or in Bombay. Easily.' He blew an elegant spiral of smoke.

Salim folded his white-pantalooned legs under him; the silk tassel of his fez swayed slightly above his right eye. 'You believe that any publisher would glance twice at what an obscure up-country pleader has to say?'

'Pooh! You are full of false modesty. Any publisher would seize on what you have to say, for you write well—yes, exceedingly well.'

Salim inhaled luxuriously, his black eyes softer, kinder than Hardyal had ever seen them. 'The Subordinate Police would not like to read what I would like to write!' He laughed. 'Crichton would not like it, the Inspector General would not like it! And for that reason . . . who knows? Yes, yes—for that very reason perhaps I shall write a treatise on Section 110 of the Indian Criminal Procedure Code.'

Ganpat Rai smiled. 'It would be a relief to me to know that you were devoting your talents to such an end. Writing would be a worthy substitute for indiscreet speech and misdirected energy. Yes, it would be a service to the country and a great load off my mind.'

An air of fraternal well-being coursed between them. For Hardyal, the moment seemed complete; he related it to a sensation which he sometimes experienced, half-way between the allurement of a dream and the languor which washes gently against the shore of consciousness. He felt drowsy with happiness.

Ganpat Rai turned once more to Salim. 'My aunt has been in consultation with Mrs Lyttleton on the problem of selecting a wife for our young friend here.' He glanced shyly at his son. 'They have found one at last. She is fat beyond belief, pockmarked, and with defective vision. But she is of good family and some wealth. Tell me, son, did Mrs Lyttleton use her good offices to persuade you?'

'Mrs Lyttleton is my friend. She would not stoop to such a low trick.'

'Yes, yes, we all know how you feel towards Mrs Lyttleton!' And Salim shook his head, the black silk tassel waving wildly.

Hardyal laughed. 'I repeat, I do not intend to marry until I am so old that I have need to lean on a woman.'

Salim could not refrain from making a rather crude little joke, and all three laughed. Then Hardyal repeated, firmly: 'I will do as other civilized men do, marry whom and when I please.'

'Then you will fare better than many of us,' said Salim. 'Perhaps even better than some of our rulers. I have just seen the wife of the Deputy Commissioner. I could not be sure, at first sight, that she was a woman. She looked like a giraffe, with enormous teeth. Were I her husband I should be terrified to sleep with her for fear she might become hungry in the night and mistake me for a cabbage. By the way, what *do* giraffes live on?'

'Their husbands, like every one else,' replied Ganpat Rai gravely. He glanced at his son. 'By the way, your friend Miss Wood has made a great impression on Mirana. She is now determined to find a husband for Bertie, too. Truly, the thought of marriage is a plague with these women.'

'Hardyal assures me that as far as Miss Wood is concerned, he has no designs,' Salim observed. 'Personally, I think he errs in taste. She is admirable in many ways, though I do not approve of her wanton manners.'

Ganpat Rai said quietly: 'Hardyal has too much sense to let himself be attracted towards white women.'

'Ah, but there are always the landlady's daughters, and one is not obliged to marry them,' replied Salim with his incorrigible sarcasm. 'When they meet what in England they call a black man, they jump to the conclusion that he must be a prince or a nawab. Then, when he brings them back to India—wah! They find that he is nothing more than some nondescript pleader like myself or a starveling medical student like Feroze. Also, it transpires that we have seraglios filled with beauties of our own preferred blackness, so the washed-out little landlady's daughter pines away with T.B. or else we seal her up in a cupboard, or stake her out on the plains for red ants to devour.'

He finished this flight of fancy on a burst of laughter, echoed by Hardyal. Ganpat Rai shook his head. 'Nevertheless, I hope that when Hardyal marries he will find one who will be a companion as well as a wife.'

'Talk with the old ones, sleep with the young,' Salim admonished the young man, with mock gravity. 'But come! I feel in the mood for music! Play for us, child. Play for us as you would play for two angelic females who recline here upon our pillows, their hips swelling like the Himalayas, their breasts like melons!'

Hardyal was laughing helplessly. 'I have played enough for one day. I was playing for Mrs Lyttleton just before you arrived.'

'Ah!' his good humour died like a flame. 'So you play for your English friends, but not for us?'

Ganpat Rai met his son's eyes. 'Play, Hardyal. We are weary. We have worked all day.'

Hardyal rose at once and went to the piano. Behind him he heard Salim's voice: 'I confess I was taken aback by her affability when we met on the road a little while ago. She greeted me as though we were old friends, a courtesy which I do not recall ever receiving at her hands.'

'She is a woman of rare sensibility,' said Ganpat Rai.

'She also is somewhat mad,' returned the Mohammedan, shrugging. 'They tell me that she has completely destroyed her garden, that she has cut down her choicest trees, and ploughed up her rosebeds. They say it is because she desires to make the place uninhabitable for ghosts.'

Hardyal turned on the piano stool. 'Ghosts!'

'For the particular ghost of Jalal, her servant—who died under mysterious circumstances.'

'What circumstances?'

Salim started to speak, but Ganpat Rai interposed almost roughly:

'I beg of you, my friend!' He turned imperatively to his son: 'Play for us, Hardyal.'

Hardyal struck the opening measure of a waltz, but there were now no visions of flying clouds, no sound of bells speaking each with a separate tongue, no thought of the sun caressing Shiva's prostrate form nor lighting with its vibrant fire the hair of the goddess Kali. He played, thinking of Mrs Lyttleton's garden as he had last seen it, full of melancholy and confusion, haunted by a discontented spirit whose face remained hidden from him.

When he had finished, both men clapped and asked for more.

'What would you like?' he asked Salim. 'The piece which I played for you the other day?'

The Mohammedan seemed oddly to have regained his humour. 'I care not! It all sounds alike to me—a beautiful noise.'

Hardyal played on, though spontaneity had died within him.

'Wah, wah!' exclaimed Salim, when at last he finished and rose from the piano stool. 'That was beautiful, it was impressive.' But he looked bored and did not ask for more. Hardyal left the piano and came back to his cushion. As he sat down he felt his father's presence beside him, felt it as warm and as powerful as the attraction between lovers, and although their glances did not meet nor their bodies touch, he knew that Ganpat Rai had read his heart.

Presently Salim began to talk of the Fair which opened on the following week, of the merchants whom he'd seen streaming into Amritpore from outlying districts, and of all the small and fascinating squabbles and intrigues without which no communal event can be considered complete. Hardyal only half-listened. He stretched himself on the floor and clasped his hands on his breast, staring at the ceiling where the wasps were building their little nests of mud. He heard, flowing round his head, the voices of his father and of his friend, and he began to think of the Fair where he would buy gifts for Jacques and for Macbeth and Bertie. He would spend all the money he had, he would spare no expense, and he would watch their faces as they uncovered his gifts from their wrappings and turned to him with astonishment and delight. He shut his eyes, and his face had the passive sweetness of one who dreams.

# 36

Jacques sat in his mother's whitewashed office at the indigo factory, and laboriously copied four columns of figures from one ledger to another. He hated every stroke of the ink-caked pen which reminded him of St Matthew's and of a sedentary existence which he'd hoped that he had put behind him forever. He was aware too that this was wasted labour, a form of penance, a calculated attempt to divert his energies into a routine which they were expected to pursue for the rest of his life. On this score he was not in the least deceived; he knew that the hours spent in this cool white room were hours which in the end must amount to little or nothing, since these ledgers had long since been audited and put away for future reference. He was not permitted to examine the later accounts, kept under lock and key in his mother's safe.

Today, if Jacques submitted to boredom it was simply because he felt the necessity of making some return to Madame for favours received, favours which she had conferred with tact, even with grace. The truth was that Madame had truly endeavoured to live up to the letter of her agreement with Hanif, tacit though that agreement had been. She had not tried to come between her son and his friends as once she had come between him and Mrs Lyttleton. The visible cost of this self-effacement was not lost on Jacques, and to preserve its grace he felt that he must somehow prevent its deterioration into mere bribery. Therefore he could accept with gratitude whatever margin of liberty and privacy she accorded him, and he would take care to make a scrupulous accounting of it—scrupulous to a degree which Madame might never suspect. Jacques had no intention of becoming a party to further schemes and arrangements; certainly, now he had no intention of becoming a victim.

Madame had explained that when he mastered the complexities of book-keeping and management it would be his privilege to preside over the future prosperity of the factory, but that time was not yet, for it could scarcely be said that he had until now displayed any notable talent for such responsibility. He had not actually displayed a talent for much of anything beyond the companionship of his friends, for long rides across the plains hunting blackbuck or stalking crocodiles on the river bank, and for occasional inexplicable lapses into what Madame impatiently described as *ennui*.

On the table before him, a table on whose surface uncounted generations of white ants had traced their muddy dynasties, Jacques noticed a sample cake of *leel*, the finished product of the factory done up in thin yellow paper. It made him think of Bertie; he remembered the first time that he'd taken her on a tour of the factory and she held a square of this substance in her hand, examining it with the childish curiosity which she brought to everything new and unexplored. She'd remarked then that the little cake of indigo reminded her of the sky above Gambul that first year when she came out from England. The oblong of powdery blue shaped like a tessera revived, she said, all her first impressions, her first enthusiasm for a new land. But she was unable to find the word, or the symbol, which might preserve for herself and for Jacques the past and the present, and which might project them, together, into the future.

Now as he played with the fragment of indigo Jacques thought, not of mountain skies, that saturated distance upon which the clouds moved with vast invisible intention, but of the thing itself, the residium of seed and soil and moisture, of thought and idea, deed and ambition, all concentrated in a cube of colour so intense that it burned in the mind long after the eye had discarded it. He thought of men hunting gold and diamonds, mining for coal, killing for fur and ivory; seeking, seeking everywhere, indefatigably, feverishly—the precious thing, the precious word, the precious experience.

He sighed and stirred as he became aware of a pair of dark eyes watching him from across the room where Boodrie the foreman sat at another desk, beside a large tin clock which ticked like some ferocious insect. 'I have been observing,' said Boodrie, severely. 'I would bet that you have not performed one stroke of work for the past five minutes.'

'I finished what you gave me to do, twenty minutes ago.'

'That is so? Why, then, did you not tell me? You will have to learn initiative. There is always something more to do, in this life.'

Jacques yawned, for he wasted little ceremony on the poor Eurasian, whom he had always disliked. He'd learned that an occasional overture served only to dislodge an avalanche of attentions, half servile and half insolent, in keeping with everything else about the man. Boodrie was half-and-half, black-and-white, a zebra personality. When unobserved he slid into the path of least resistance and went native with a vengeance, but on public occasions he remained offensively, pervasively *white*, an ubiquitous reminder of man's sexual democracy, despised by the natives and deplored by the whites.

'It will shortly be time and you may proceed to join with your friends. Where, exactly, do you propose to conduct your amusements, if I might presume to ask?'

'Ask, and ye shall receive,' murmured Jacques indifferently.

Boodrie lighted a cigar which Father Sebastien had given him that morning. 'You know, you are occasionally exceedingly bad-tempered. I think you have learned such from your friend Macbeth. I do not like that Macbeth. He is a snob and cheeky even when he does not open his mouth. How in the world either of you ever got through St Matthew's I fail to comprehend.'

'We cheated.'

'Oh my! You are also getting to be a great liar. It is not funny to lie. And that reminds me, we have not had the honour of your assistance at Mass or at benediction for I don't know how long.'

Jacques was drawing a caricature of the foreman's profile on a corner of the ledger. He replied: 'I have become a freethinker.'

'That is purest heresy. What if Father should hear you, or Madame?'

'Why don't you tell them? It's part of your job, isn't it?'

'You do not believe that I am a pure common or garden sneak.'

Boodrie's eyes had filled with slow, greasy tears. When Jacques remained silent he retreated into a silence of his own and pretended to busy himself with his account books. In his heart he wished that he possessed the arrogance of this white man's son. He wished that he cared as little of *hisab kitab*, for all the sweat and tedium, the thankless expenditure of mind and energy on the mere necessity of earning a living. He envied this boy his pale skin and curling, light brown hair, his clear features, his clear eyes, his clear soul; envied him, in fact, every item of spiritual and physical good fortune. It must be wonderful, thought Boodrie, whose mother was a low-caste Hindu and his father a low-class white—it must be wonderful to be wholly, wholesomely Some One. And for a single bitter moment he longed for a state of mind, a state of being, which might make such bitterness unnecessary.

Jacques, conscious of something unusual in the other's long silence, glanced up to encounter tear-filled eyes. His own cheek flushed slightly.

'Oh, good heavens! Must you *blub*?'

Boodrie produced a handkerchief and blew his nose. 'You have fractured my feelings.'

'Well, I didn't mean to.'

'You always treat me as though I was dirt.'

'I don't.'

'All the time you are nicer to the coolies than you are to me. You treat Hanif as though he were your brother, and he is altogether a native. Hardyal also. But as for me . . .' He began to snivel.

'Oh, good heavens!' Jacques whirled angrily on his office chair, glaring at the floor, secretly ashamed of himself. Boodrie watched him covertly. 'I do only my duty, as I am bound to do. Madame has told me that I must make you attend to your work. How can I help it if she and Father Sebastien are worried about you? I am not the only one who notices how you have changed.' His glance crept, in unwilling fascination, to the boy's crippled hand which rested on the open ledger. 'Changed in many ways. You do not, for instance, go to church as you should, as you always used to.'

'Shut up, will you?'

'It is a serious matter! Can you blame us because we care? Can you? It is only because we love you.'

'I don't wish to be loved by you or any one!' Jacques burst out in fury.

'You cannot prevent people from loving you if they want to. Even I love you. I have watched you grow up, you and Gisele. You never watched *me*. Oh, no; after all, who am I that you should bother your heads about me? But you cannot prevent my looking upon you as though I were one of your family. Gisele has been saved . . . yes saved! But you, you make me think of your father, Monsieur Auguste.' He drivelled away into murmurs and Jacques rose, slamming the ledgers. Words crowded to his lips, but he did not utter them. In a flash of discernment he realized that this relatively insignificant scene held a far deeper importance, that it had been brought about less by Boodrie's lacerated feelings than by Boodrie's fortuitous use of those feelings. I am on trial, thought Jacques. I am being watched and tested, and for a price, no doubt. Today it is a cigar, tomorrow some other form of *baksheesh*. Anger died and a rather cruel amusement took its place. He rose and picked up his hat. 'Eleven o' clock!' As he passed the Eurasian's chair he paused and said in Hindustani: 'Brother, your cigar has gone out.'

Outside, the air was clear, with a sparkle of dust and a noise of crows in the trees. A water-carrier was sprinkling the ground nearby, and his water-skin made a pleasant gurgling as he hitched it on his shoulder, tendrils of water sprayed from the pale arc of his hand. Jacques' bad temper vanished; even the subdued hum of the factory possessed a charm, now that he was leaving it for a little while. Poor Boodrie! He permitted himself the luxury of pity, but it could not survive in the rush of relief and expectation. As he crossed the compound towards the gates, coolies shuffled past, some bare-footed, others in heavy shoes, making for the vats and the boiler rooms. They salaamed him, some with smiles, others with a dim, primordial gaze. The bare bodies of these last ones, the Haburas, had a dusty bloom on their thick sweatless skins; the others shone like copper, muscled like Greeks. The rags of all were splashed with the separate shades of dye, olive and ochre which had eaten into the cloth, and the feet and hands of some were steeped in brilliance as though they served still another god in their endless calendar of deities, a god who demanded pigment as offering and who made return in those varying towers of silver coin at the month's end.

The big Sikh policemen who squatted in the shade, smoking and throwing dice, rose lazily as Jacques approached. They greeted him with jocular salutes, and he read the liking in their eyes.

'Thy friend waits,' said one, nodding towards the gates where Hardyal sat on his bay mare, holding Jacques' horse by its bridle. Strolling towards him Jacques thought: 'There is a difference nowadays in the way they greet me.' He knew why, and he knew that they knew, a fact which would have disturbed him in his own people. But it did not trouble him in Hanif, in Gisele's old ayah, in these policemen, and in Hardyal. In its celebration of concupiscence the East retains its respect for a man's personal privacy. Jacques knew that his was safe in the keeping of his Indian friend and his Indian servants. Coming out of Bertie's room at dawn he had met the ayah, a woman who had served his mother for thirty years, who had scolded and spoiled him from babyhood. Now she stood aside and drew her veil over her eyes as he passed. Hanif looked at him as he might have looked at a brother. 'You are man,' said Hanif's black glance, and his voice, when he spoke of other matters, had a little ring of possessive pride in his master's coming of age. This was an accolade, silent, tacit, but Jacques felt a tingle in his veins and springing in his feet.

Hardyal walked the horses to meet him. 'I brought Robin because I thought it would save time. Bertie and Macbeth are to meet us at the Fort.'

They trotted through the gates, the horses sidling and prancing as the white road opened before them. Hardyal was in high spirits and talked of plans for the next day, when they would all attend the opening of the Fair and return, afterwards, to his father's house for a grand repast. 'All manner of people have been invited, Hindus and Moslems, the Collector and his wife, Mr Crichton and his guests. My aunts have been cooking, cooking, cooking for days. The place smells like a *barwarchikhana!*'

Jacques thought of those mounds of food, of platters of rice cooked with raisins and saffron, of vegetable curry, of chutneys and sauces, sweets, pastries, syrups, spices; of all the gorging and belching, the happy surfeit. He adored native meals and always ate until—as Hardyal said—the grease stood out all over him like a fried cake.

'Do you think Bertie will enjoy it?' inquired Hardyal, anxiously.

'Of course—why not?'

'I just wondered.'

Hardyal could not have explained this sudden anxiety on Bertie's account, for, ever since Abdul Salim's ill-considered remarks, his attitude towards her had suffered a faint, indefinable change. Now when he found himself in her company he experienced a sense of loss; he found it difficult to meet her gaze, and shrank from her friendly touch. All this pained him and he longed to make amends to her and in a sense through her to Jacques. Hardyal had accepted Bertie as, in England, he'd accepted other girls, and as they had apparently accepted him. His response had been friendly, merry, even sexless. But Salim's jesting observations had transformed this innocence to something which at times amounted to an aversion. Confused by his own reactions, Hardyal was at infinite pains to conceal them, but they escaped from him disguised as small erratic gestures and exaggerated concern for the comfort and happiness of his friends. It was, in other words, another facet of his new attitude towards Aubrey Wall. It sprang from anxiety, from a passionate desire to meet and to measure up their undeclared opinion of himself.

As they rode under the portcullis Jacques and Hardyal fell silent, for they were never quite able to resist their own sensations as they emerged from under the shadowy arch into the arc of walled sunlight. The silence which awaited them here seemed sudden and premeditated, an invisible retirement took place, and their flesh tingled under a close and imagined scrutiny. Ruins are more than history; like shells they belong to a huge oceanic process. Stranded, the life in them falls dormant but it does not die, it persists in our idea of it. At any moment this suspense might give way and an invisible barrier release the pent-up years.

The boys rode into the courtyard and dismounted, hitching their horses to the same gnarled acacia where they had once hitched their own and Gisele's ponies. Bertie and Macbeth were nowhere to be seen, there was scarcely a sound except the plaintive crying of the doves. Then Jacques saw their wicker lunch-basket perched on a rampart beside a sentry-box, and beside it, like a flag, Bertie's long blue veil which she had unpinned from her hat as a signal.

'They've gone down the river,' said Jacques. 'Let's climb up and have a look.'

They strolled across the courtyard and climbed the ruined stair to the rampart, and standing beside the little sentry-box shaped like a medieval helmet, they stared across the plain towards the river. It glittered flat and straight like everything in the landscape. Tiny creatures moved under their gaze: a pair of bullocks so white they shone like mica, threads of water fed by wells into little channels, men and women patching the channels and guiding the precious trickles to the yearning soil.

Hardyal stretched, feeling the sun hot on his back. 'There they are!' He pointed, and Jacques saw the riders, small and active in the distance.

'Let's go and meet them,' he suggested, but Hardyal shook his head.

'You go, I'll wait for you here.'

He watched Jacques ride under the portcullis and disappear, and as the silence rose about him once more he was half-tempted to follow. Instead, he seated himself resolutely beside the sentry-box to wait for Jacques' appearance beyond the farther reaches of the moat. Macbeth and Bertie had vanished in some fold of the land, the sun, signalling the river, drew a single answering flash, and a multitude of crows clamoured above a dead something half a mile away. Above the crows wheeled the kites, their shrill whistles falling through the void, and above them circled the vultures.

Jacques appeared, galloping, but it seemed no more than a second before he, too, had become a detail in the intricate pattern of the plain. Then an unaccountable loneliness descended on Hardyal. The scene, as familiar to him as a room at home, stretched now in an alien light. It was too vast, too impersonal—his eye could contain it, but it could not contain him—he felt lost within it. He turned away to look down at the courtyard where his mare stood quietly in the shade of the acacia, but beyond her placid, insentient form rose a series of broken doors and the arches of what used to be officers' quarters and shelters for horses and men. In the piercing light these dim unexplored interiors grew shadows and as he gazed they deepened and darkened and generated within themselves other shadows; these seemed to stir, to move beyond the penumbra, to press against it as a hand might press, or a shoulder, in the movement of figures which pass secretly behind a heavy curtain. What if that curtain should suddenly part and all the dead, with all their unfulfilment, come trooping out towards him?

Hardyal's nerves trembled in a sort of arterial protest against the developing magic. He rose, crossing his arms on his breast in the unconsciously pathetic attitude of a man about to be shot; and he felt under his fingers the firm edges of Aubrey Wall's letter in his pocket. The contact restored, in a flash, the known and ordinary world. He sat down again and took out the letter, surprised by its thickness until he remembered that when Mrs Lyttleton read it she had skipped much. Now he would read it all, read it from the beginning, and so recapture each coveted phrase, and thrill again, without shame, to the praise.

Wall wrote a small but clear hand and for several minutes Hardyal read with a purely visual sense, scarcely grasping the full import of the words. The letter was more than a month old, postmarked from

Bognor, in Sussex, and he was sure he knew the room in which it had been written, and the view, from a window, of the lazy sea beyond.

'My dear Laura,

'Your letter has reached me and if I did not answer at once it was because I wanted to give myself time to understand, to reconstruct the situation which you have put before me. But perhaps you yourself have not waited, perhaps you have already taken the course which indignation would prompt you to take, in which case this letter must prove wholly irrelevant. However, I have a feeling that you will wait for my answer, for—shall I call it my confession?—which is likewise my defence; that is if, in accord with your rather incoherent insistence, I am at least entitled to a defence. How fantastic this sounds here, in these surroundings, in this unbelievably tender England where, although doubt and horror exist, they wear a recognizable face. You voiced the hope, once that in England I might find a rebirth. You guessed, apparently, that I stood in need of one, and you were right. Can you blame me now if I hesitate to exchange the mercy of that rebirth for the damnation of exposure by law and the inevitable end of all my hopes? Perhaps I am mistaken, but can you blame me for placing my own fate on a level somewhat higher than your servant Jalal's? And if I choose, as I do choose, to put my fate in your hands, I do so with a conscious pride in its value, and because I believe in your judgment. Of your mercy I know nothing, as yet. I can only trust you, as I would trust you had you been my mother.'

Hardyal came to the end of the page and looked up. Far across the plain he could see his friends converging on each other; in a few minutes they would meet, and turn to ride back to the Fort. He wondered whether they saw him up here beside the sentry-box, a living speck among the dun-coloured ruins. Then he returned with a growing heaviness to Wall's letter.

'I have been thinking and trying to remember. You tell me that your servant Jalal is dead and that I killed him. You make the picture very clear, for you write with such bitterness and anger that I wonder you have kept this knowledge to yourself, that you have not carried it to the authorities.'

Hardyal stopped short. 'No!' he gasped. 'Oh, no, no, no!'

A butterfly hovering near him was not alarmed; it settled on a stone and spread wings the colour of buttercups.

'No, oh, no—no!' repeated Hardyal wildly. But it was impossible, now, to leave it at that. He felt compelled towards a final, frightful discovery. The letter continued.

'Has it occurred to you to question your own reasons for such a delay? You must know that you've not exactly strengthened your position, for by hesitating, by waiting, you, in a sense, condone if you do not connive at the whole predicament. I know you to be a fearless woman; I know that once you have made up your mind you will act, heedless of consequences to yourself or to me. Yet the fact remains that three months have passed since Jalal's death and you have not acted. Why not? Can it be that in spite of our conventional morality you and I share something more profound, a kinship which, in our precarious moments, we dare not deny? You've asked me for an accounting, for an explanation of what you describe as my unspeakable act on that last evening of my visit to you. You remind me that when I returned to the veranda after having gone in search of Jalal I callously remarked that I had twice kicked him while he slept. Well, my answer, if not my explanation, is that the act was neither unspeakable nor inexplicable: with no desire to extenuate the circumstances, I must make them clear to you, as they are, at this moment, clear to me.

'It was raining that evening. I had come from Father Sebastien's and you greeted me, as usual, on your veranda. We talked, and I poured myself several brandy pegs from your decanters. We talked of the St Remys and of Hardyal and of the future, we talked of India as though the country were something we held in our hands, pliable, intimate. I drank a good deal of brandy, and I remember feeling that much of what happened to me while I lived in India had the character of a drunken dream. I have always felt, while there, as if I were contained in a dream, and that is the extent of my feeling towards the damned country, the total of—what shall I call it?—*my committedness*. And here I must mention something which you do not know and which I, myself, don't yet really understand. I was unhappy. I had been unhappy for a couple of years; the reason for that unhappiness won't interest you, since it has ceased entirely to interest me. It is not important now but it was important then. Brandy helped me as it has helped many men, it helped to put the world in a light which made existence just a shade or two more endurable.

'Well, on that evening you called for your servant and he did not appear. I went in search of him and found him asleep in the darkness of the back veranda. I say I found him—but as a matter of fact I stumbled over him, and it seemed to me that the insensible clod lying there at my feet symbolized India, drugged and snoring, wrapped up in its own idea of itself, unimpressionable, indifferent to everything else. I saw this as one sometimes sees a single monstrous detail in a landscape or in a crowd. And I lashed out with the instinct to destroy whatever it was that I had seen—a fragment of something unclean, sub-human, parasitical. Well, then—I killed Jalal, and perhaps by doing so I have killed myself. I have no remorse, I have no emotion, I have hardly any feeling for Jalal. I cannot even now remember what he looked like, although I know that he did exist.

'Can I make you see, Laura, that I am not afraid of the consequences of this action: I just cannot bring myself to believe that I have done another human being out of his life. There is, in me, something which makes it impossible to 'believe' in Indians. You have assured me fiercely that they are human beings, but I have known horses and dogs almost as human, and I have loved them better. You will resent this, you will hate me for saying it, but let me say it, for I must. I do not believe in Indians, I do not hold with the sentimentality of treating dark people as one treats even the lowest, the humblest white. I do not believe that there will ever be equality of race—why should there be when there is not equality between one white man and another? Our Christian teaching and humanitarian policy have between them made a mess of our honesty. We simply do not begin to understand Indians. They never will approximate our civilization, even our individual accomplishment. If they should do so, so much the worse for us: it will be from imitation, and it will be of the worst kind of imitation. Oh, I know what you'll say to all this—I can hear you saying it: We all sprang from the same root, originally. Possibly. But *we* have gone a long way from there, and *they* have not. They are where we started from and there they will stick. For every Ganpat Rai and Hardyal there are a thousand—no, ten thousand Jalals. Whatever good has come to them has come from us, and what have they given? Rather, what have they to give? They have tried to adopt our ideals, even our ideas; above all, this very justice before which they would be the first to summon me. They know their own inadequacy and they hate us because they know we know it. There is in every one of them an ember of hatred; blow on it and it will make our feeling towards them appear as a smile of mercy by comparison. And in the end they will turn against us, yes even our charming Hardyal will turn against us, the enlightened Ganpat Rai himself will turn against us. When one lives amongst them one makes the best of them, for not to do so would be stupid. But between them and ourselves there can be only one relationship, the relationship of our mastery over them.'

There were a few additional sentences but Hardyal did not read them. Before him, the plain reeled in a glare devoid of shade or boundary, an abyss of light. From it emerged three figures which cantered towards him, waving, but he made no attempt to respond. He rose, staggering a little, and stumbled down the steps to his horse, clambering into his saddle like a wounded man. The mare bore him under the portcullis and her hooves struck a hollow note from the

bridge above the moat, where the little doves were crying ceaselessly.
When, a few minutes later, Jacques with Bertie and Macbeth rode into
the Fort, they shouted and looked for him in vain.

## 37

A cloud of dust hung over Amritpore. For two days people had
been streaming towards the Fair grounds which lay just
outside the cantonment. They came in ekkas, in bullock carts,
in carriages, in fine fast dog-carts. A few rode bicycles, but most of
them trudged on foot, carrying bundles on their heads, babies on their
hips, and leading tottering infants by the hand. They brought their
dogs and their grandmothers, even their great-grandmothers, and
invalids who flatly refused to be left behind. All were dressed in their
best, all wore the expectant smiles of incorrigible celebrants in this land
of festival. There was not one who did not intend to buy something,
there was not one who did not come with a whole-hearted
determination to enjoy the occasion to the utmost.

There would be buying and selling, looking and longing, wanting
and going without. There would be cheating, beating, exchange and
assignation, sighing, lying, intrigue. For this was more than a fair
where the industrious and the virtuous brought their wares and
inducements; there would be more to marvel at than the largest turnip
and the fastest gelding in a hundred miles; the whitest bullock, the
smallest dog, the maddest saddhu, and the Government Agricultural
Station's most successful experiment with artificial fertilizer. Besides
these things there would be countless others, things as yet unseen,
even undreamed of, by villagers who worshipped a pot-bellied god
named Ganesh, and who marked progress by the simple revolutions of
an ancient wooden wheel. There would—above all things—there
would be people, hundreds of people, for this was a *mela*, a coming
together of all one's fellows. It was not necessary to be Hindu or
Moslem, Christian or hedonist, black, yellow or brown: for full
enjoyment one had merely to want to be here.

The authorities had taken precaution—riots have a way of breaking
out—but in this crowd there seemed to move a deep, sweet current of
good-nature. Their gods, looking down on them, must have observed
that mass itself possesses an incipient order, every individual stirred by
a private design, intent upon his own discovery. The women's kirtles
swayed above silver anklets, and a touch of gold or silver on a humble
*sari* added its pennyworth to the pounds of tinkle and glitter. Bare feet

trod the dust as their owners carried new shoes strung on sticks over their shoulders, to save wood or leather for the proper moment of ceremony. They tramped in the soft dust and left the hard middle for wheeled craft which rattled and creaked at a speed somewhat beyond that of the traditional snail's pace. The purse-proud swept by with a flurry of bells and swaying curtains, drawn by ponies with beads round their necks, driven by conceited servants. Ramdatta the moneylender rode in his own ekka, one with a black-and-gold canopy, under which he sat in splendour, his stout legs gleaming with oil, his muslin cap encrusted with pearls.

At night the outskirts of the Fair grounds had twinkled with the fires of those who arrived early. All ages and all castes converged upon the flat shadeless plain which the Municipality had bedecked with beds of drooping petunias and blatant canna lilies. The booths with concrete floors and tin roofs were gaudy with paper streamers and banners of every description, and here the visiting merchants made themselves at home. They had come from the great cities of Allahabad and Lucknow and Benares, from Agra and Fyzabad and Bareilly. Some still worked feverishly among their boxes and bundles and bales, putting temporary quarters in as seductive an order as their calculating imaginations could devise. Others, earlier birds, squatted portly and expectant, marking down the nearest rival and the likeliest prey.

There were shoe-sellers and cloth-merchants, gold- and silver-smiths, purveyors of brass and enamel and cane-work, of toys made from painted clay, and little boxes which fitted into one another and ended in one so minute it had to be picked out with a pin. There were furred animals made from the pelts of real beasts—camels and leopards and tigers. There were jewellers with their wares, real and fake, blazing under keen and wary eyes. Beside these sat the workers of marble and inlay, and next to them the makers of clothing in every colour and of every design, the corners of their stalls hung with great fans of plumed grass dyed and embroidered like the tails of peacocks. Scattered among them were the sellers of food, where sunlight danced off enormous, plated cauldrons and vast platters stacked with intricately shaped breads and pastries and sweets. Here the flies and the wasps collected in swarms, and women waved palm-leaf fans with brown, languid arms strapped to the elbows in silver and coloured glass. Their new *saries*, slipping from their pomaded heads, revealed tassels of bright silk, and the ears of some of these women were torn in strips from the weight of silver earrings. All displayed the gay red or yellow tikka between their brows, and the hands and the gestures of almost every one were beautiful, like the hands of dancers, like the posturing of a perpetual creative impulse.

The stalls were arranged in two rows that faced each other across a baked expanse which had been watered and swept and rolled flat by the Municipal servants. Alleys and byways opened off the main channel and here were the side-shows, little tents of canvas or matting; within lurked the fortune-tellers and exhibitionists (these with one eye on the quality and probable tastes of their clients, the other on the police). This was a happy-hunting-ground of jugglers and the trainers of parrots and monkeys. There was even a tiny circus which comprised a single haggard tiger and a small old elephant whose only role seemed to be the feat of balancing himself—with every indication of reluctance—on a board laid across the belly of a fat man. The fat man was depicted on a poster outside the marquee; he was almost as big as the elephant and easily twice as strong, with blazing eyes and bulging arms crossed on enormous feminine breasts.

Children were almost as ubiquitous as the flies and wasps; they hung round the side-shows and the sweet-stalls while their elders roamed among more serious attractions.

The Fair opened in the morning with a formal address by the Collector. It was the usual speech, delivered first in beautiful precise English and then in beautiful sonorous Hindustani by a dried-up little Englishman wearing a morning coat and striped trousers, a large pipe-clayed topi, and a *har* of jewelled tinsel round his neck. Behind him on the dais stood his orderly supporting a large red umbrella, and on a semicircle of hard varnished chairs were his wife, their friends, and a sprinkling of local and visiting dignitaries, waving away the flies and trying to look interested in what the Collector had to say.

To the unjaded sensibility there are two pronounced elements in a native crowd—noise and smell. These break upon one's awareness as unfamiliar music breaks for the first time on uneducated ears—disturbingly, even frighteningly. The police had been to some trouble to exclude professional beggars and the prowling bazaar dogs, but no sooner had the crowd thickened into its fullness than every beggar, ever leper, every cripple, and every pariah for miles reappeared as if they had been squeezed from the pores of the earth. The noise, like the dust and the smell, seemed more substance than sound, it lay within, round, and about, pricked by sudden dissonant notes which rose straight up like the thrust of a sword—the scream of a stallion in the stables set up by Pathan horse-dealers, the clear singing of a bugle from the police station a quarter of a mile away, the shriek of a baby with colic; and under these combined noises the beating of the eternal drums, the little tinpot drum of the professional singer, and the cavernous throbbing of a drum from a Sikh regimental band.

# 38

It was afternoon and the dust, the heat, and the smell were at their height when Jacques drove to the Fair with Bertie and Macbeth, Hanif riding as usual beside the driver. Madame St Remy had said that she might join them later when the air cooled a little. Crowds annoyed her and noise always gave her a headache.

Hanif, wearing brand new finery from the crown of his cap to the fantastically curled toes of his shoes, twisted in his seat to smile at the young people. 'Does my appearance reflect glory upon the household?'

'You are dazzling,' Jacques assured him. 'Simply dazzling.'

The driver flourished his whip. 'Ah me, the wenching in store!'

'Nay,' protested Hanif gaily. 'Not for me, not this afternoon. Have I not instructions not to let these untrustworthy ones out of sight?'

'We also have instructions not to let you out of our sight. Maman has no desire to pay compensation to outraged husbands.'

The driver chuckled. 'Ah, if there be talk of outrage. . . .'

Hanif gave his elbow a jolt. 'Fie!'

They drove under the shisham avenue and out on the hard white road. Bertie slipped her hand through Jacques' arm. 'I adore fairs!'

'Let's hope there'll be some good side-shows,' said Macbeth. 'I want to see the two-headed man and the six-legged sheep.'

'No side-shows,' said Hanif firmly. 'I have express orders to that effect.'

'You know you like them as well as we do!'

'Nevertheless I have my orders.'

'Nevertheless you will take ours.'

'Or shall we tell Rahat Ali where you were last night?'

'I do not know any one named Rahat Ali.'

'But you do know Mrs Rahat Ali!'

The driver laughed, and Macbeth grinned. 'Why don't we tell all the men where Hanif is when *they're* away from home?'

Hanif was quite unabashed by these jokes. He adored attention.

'Such talk! If the Memsahib should only hear.'

They drove smartly along the road, passing small companies of late-comers, when Hanif exchanged taunts with the men and brilliant glances with the girls. He had produced a large pink rose from somewhere in the folds of his clothing, and now tucked it behind one ear. Jacques stared at the bobbing flower. 'That is Maman's new Queen Victoria rose—you picked the only flower on it!'

Hanif replied without turning his head. 'Pruning brings strength to the roots, so the *mali* tells me.'

They drove between tall plaster gateposts which marked the main entrance to the grounds, and were immediately engulfed in the crowd. The driver plied his whip and the crowd made way for the carriage and its freight of white folk guarded by supercilious servants. Jacques looked everywhere for Hardyal. Ever since yesterday when he had ridden to the Fort and not found his friend, Jacques had been puzzled and anxious. There seemed no explanation for Hardyal's disappearance, and it was not in his nature to indulge in moods or in silly jokes.

Later that afternoon Jacques had ridden over to Ganpat Rai's house, but Hardyal was not at home, nor was his father. A servant assured Jacques that his young master was well and that all was tranquil in the house. Jacques left a message and rode away, more bewildered than anxious, but reassured by thoughts of the next day, for Hardyal would be at the Fair—had they not talked of it and looked forward to it, together?

Inside the Fair grounds they dismissed the carriage and, accompanied by Hanif, plunged into the crowd. Bertie clung to Jacques' arm; once, finding her crushed against him in an amalgam of hot and happy strangers, he turned and kissed her. She whispered: 'I would like to buy you something beautiful and expensive!'

They were beside the gayest and richest stall, surrounded by people who pushed and shoved in their anxiety to see everything at once. The box-wallah who squatted among his wares saw the young white folk and waved invitingly. 'What will Your Magnificence have? Name it . . . name your wish. Behold, ten yards of gold tissue with birds of Paradise flying upon it. Two rupees per yard. For others, rupees three—but because you are young I make it only two. Nay, reflect: two rupees for thread which is pure gold, and birds . . .'

'Which are *not* birds of Paradise,' Macbeth broke in, coldly. 'Whoever saw a bird of Paradise with a short tail?'

The cloth merchant, a genial man from Benares, and used to the ways of Englishmen, gave the boy a friendly smile. 'Others I might deceive, but thee—never! Well, these are even better than birds of Paradise. They are earthly birds, my lord; they live among the passion-flower trees of Assam, and are rare indeed, else surely you would have seen them. I doubt not that you miss nothing—nothing, indeed.'

Bertie stared at the glowing silks, at the bales and bundles and bolts of brocade and cotton amongst which the merchant sat like some queer persuasive deity. He had already taken up his steel measuring staff and was peeling off yards of material, his practical hands unwinding the heavy bolt and stripping it in loose, glistening lengths.

'Nay,' cried Jacques. 'We never said we wanted it. Do we, Bertie?'

She wanted it, she wanted everything in the shop. The richness, the peculiar odour of native cloth spun or woven by clever fingers in close spice-tinctured interiors fascinated her. It was unlike the characterless product of machines, it had substance, and a life of its own. The merchant glanced at her and smiled. 'I have others. I have shawls from Kashmir, muslin from Dacca, silk from Kotah. I have *saries* with a hand's breadth of silver for selvedge and others which I sell by weight for the metal in them. Which does the lady prefer? Point out the bale. This one? That? Or here . . . this, which only maharanies and princes can afford to buy. Look!' He rose and taking the loose end of a bolt drew it out to his own height, standing to one side and shaking the stuff gently as a dancer might, so it gathered the light and broke in constellations of fire and colour.

'How much?' asked Bertie.

He stared at the material draped on his arm as a man might stare at his beloved, and for a moment he made no answer. When he did, it was in a soft, almost an indifferent voice: 'How much? How should I say? This is not for ordinary folk. It is for those who never need to ask how much!'

'Cheek!' exclaimed Macbeth. 'We don't want your old cloth. Besides, I don't believe that is real gold and silver any more than that those birds are birds of Paradise. Come on, Bertie.'

They strolled away, followed by Hanif. The rose had wilted and one by one the petals fell on his shoulder.

Jacques was looking everywhere for Hardyal.

'Perhaps he is here and we just haven't run into him,' suggested Macbeth.

'I would have seen him. We never miss each other.'

'Oh, look out!' gasped Bertie, and sprang aside as a naked, legless man strapped to a board on four wheels, using his hands as fulcrums, skittered past them like some monstrous beetle.

Then the crowd parted and Mr Crichton the Superintendent of Police strode forward, followed by a little company of constables. Crichton was big and burly. He paused to exchange greetings with the children, then went his way, his men pattering after him. The crowd closed in again like the sea in the wake of a ship, and Jacques felt Bertie's hand tremble a little on his arm. She smiled faintly when he glanced at her. 'I wish he'd stay!'

'Mr Crichton! Why?'

She was unable or unwilling to explain that she found something reassuring at sight of the big Englishman, and later in the presence of the Collector himself. She felt that both officials would not be indifferent to her presence in this upheaval of a diverse and, to her, vaguely inimical humanity. It was a new feeling, one which disturbed her by its unheralded arrival.

Macbeth sauntered beside her with his hands in his pockets. He was secretly debating what to buy for his mother, wondering how he might accomplish the transaction in private. The thought of his mother was a constant ache, a spot of decay in his healthy youth. It made him shy and sometimes cruel; it tended, year after year, to add salt rather than sweet to his nature.

Jacques was thinking: 'Hardyal, Hardyal! Where *is* Hardyal!'

Bertie noticed his disquiet and for the first time she experienced the cramping pangs of jealousy. 'Why worry about Hardyal? He'll turn up. Perhaps he doesn't want to come, after all. Perhaps he's gone off somewhere with his Mohammedan friends.'

'Rot.'

'Well, I do think it was funny his running away as he did, yesterday.'

'Something must have happened.'

'He's only a native, after all.'

Jacques stopped dead and stared at her. 'What did you say?'

She saw the temper in his eyes. 'Oh, Jacques, I'm sorry! I didn't mean to say it. I shall never say it again.'

Hanif and Macbeth had fallen behind, but now they came up and Macbeth said: 'I just saw that barrister chap, Salim. He's over there with his friends.'

'Is Hardyal with them?'

'I didn't see Hardyal.' He added impatiently: 'Look here, I'm not going to hang round waiting for Hardyal. Let him hunt for us. I want to see the side-shows.'

Hanif attempted a firm stand. 'No side-shows! I was given express orders . . .'.

They ignored him, and with a sigh that was part despair and part relief, he followed them down one of the noisome alleys where drums rattled and barkers chanted inducements through their noses.

Hanif managed to steer them past the Two-headed Baby, the Siamese Twins, a group of hermaphrodites and the Six-legged Sheep. They selected a tent devoted to the antics of trained animals. As the children entered with their retainer, the little crowd inside the tent fell back, and the owner greeted them with a burst of nasal chanting while his assistant beat a feverish tattoo on the drum. Hanif spoke swiftly to the master of ceremonies: 'No indecencies, please. These are exalted persons.'

The young people stood near the entrance where the air was somewhat less murky, and stared in fascination at a little group of monkeys dressed in kirtles and quilted jackets. There was also a parrot, whose duty it was to walk up to a tiny cannon, seize the lanyard, and make the gun go off. The master of ceremonies addressed the parrot in loud encouraging tones and gave it a poke with his wand. There was something indescribably lewd in the bird's eye as it tilted its head and sidled forth. It seized the lanyard in its beak, braced its little grey feet, and pulled. The cannon went off with quite a respectable plop and a smell of gunpowder, while the crowd clapped and exclaimed: 'Wah wah!'

Bertie gazed at the talented bird with some pity. 'Poor thing! It has hardly any feathers.'

'Make him do it again,' commanded Macbeth, infatuated.

The owner adjured the parrot and his assistant rattled the drum in a fresh overture. The bird's bleached lid slid upward, then suddenly lowered, revealing a bright gold orb. It sidled up to the cannon once more, then in a sudden access of temperament it dropped the lanyard and stood with a stubborn air, sealing up its eyes. The master chanted, commanded, cajoled, the assistant thumped his drum, but the moody creature refused to budge.

'The monkeys,' cried Macbeth. 'Let's have the monkeys!'

Hanif gazed doubtfully at the monkeys, but their owner seemed to have them well under control. He dismissed the parrot and picked up the leading-strings of his monkey troupe. The drum rattled and a horrid little dog dashed into the arena. One of the monkeys sprang on his back, another climbed up behind him, and they raced in circles while the others looked on, their depraved little faces and listless gestures reminiscent, for all the world, of a troupe of passée prima donnas. The dog act came to an end and was followed by a dance, by handsprings and tumblings, amidst the plaudits of the crowd. In a little while it was the parrot's turn again and the monkeys retired to their corner to misbehave in a bored fashion among themselves.

'Come!' cried Hanif, with authority. 'It is finished. Let us go.'

They flung a few coins to the master of ceremonies and made their way out into the wider if not fresher air of the alley. Once in the crowd, Macbeth slipped away from his friends and singled out a jeweller from Agra, a little pale man with a cast in one eye and the still, sweet smile of a child. He sat alone behind his showcase of jewels, and catching sight of the English boy, saluted him with a deferential air.

'I don't want anything,' said Macbeth, flushing, fearful lest one of his friends find him here. 'That is, I'm not sure. What've you got?'

The man studied his client with a single keen glance.

'Everything,' he sighed. 'Everything! What does the Sahib desire? What I have not I can procure, no matter the price, no matter the gem.'

His serious manner reassured Macbeth, who had dreaded an outburst of chaff. The man leaned forward and unlatched a flat case, felt among the contents, and picked out a single fat uncut stone. 'Take this in your hand. No, don't be shy—take it.'

Macbeth took the strange stone, which felt like a piece of butter, but it did not melt in the warmth of his fingers, rather it seemed to thicken and to increase. He stared at it, rubbing it with the ball of his thumb, and an indefinable pleasure passed from the stone into his flesh. He looked at the owner. 'That's funny stuff, what is it?'

'White jade. But you do not want that. Try this.'

It was an amber necklace smooth and slippery as a live serpent, but the weight and colour did not appeal to Macbeth. 'No, something small, something bright.'

'Something for your sister?' suggested the jeweller in his soft voice. Macbeth shook his head. He was intent on an amethyst brooch shaped like a butterfly.

'For thy mother, then?'

The boy's head jerked upward and he gave the man a suspicious stare.

'It is none of your business for whom. Let me see that one, that purple thing.'

The jeweller handed it over. 'Seventy-five rupees. It has seed-pearls for its eyes, and is, as you see, cunningly mounted in gold.'

'Seventy-five rupees!' He handed it back precipitately, staring with increasing indecision at the glittering wealth before him. He had no idea of the value of precious stones, no idea what he should pay for the smallest piece of silver or the smallest garnet. But his mother had loved jewellery and now he remembered her as she had appeared on that last evening before she left him. She came into his room to say goodnight, and she wore a white dress, with her favourite earrings.

He saw the jeweller's eye fixed upon him. 'Have you any emeralds?'

The man's expression did not alter. 'Emeralds? Assuredly, I have emeralds.'

He plunged his hand into the confusion of treasures and found one, a ring with a square stone set in silver. Macbeth took it, his heart beating painfully. How beautiful it was, how green and bright, and how terribly it reminded him of her! He saw her now as she stood before the looking-glass in his room, adjusting the fine fish-hook which fastened the emerald to the lobe of her pretty ear, turning her golden head sideways to smile at him as if he, too, were a lover.

Macbeth was not aware that he was under the steady scrutiny of one besides the jeweller. A little distance off at the next booth Ramdatta the moneylender waited for one of his relatives to conclude some transaction. He'd seen Macbeth approach the jeweller and he had not missed a word that passed between them.

Macbeth, drawing his breath, held up the ring and looked its owner in the eye. 'How much?'

'You are young to be buying emeralds, and the fact makes me hesitate.'

Macbeth frowned. To him an emerald was an emerald, no more and no less. He said in a strained voice: 'I may not be able to pay you in full, but if you will take part of the price I will give you a chit for the remainder. I will give you references. My father is Colonel Macbeth, and I have friends in Amritpore.'

The man interrupted with a wave of his hand. 'Could I live a day without trusting my clients? And shall I presume to demand references from the son of a Colonel Sahib?' He lowered his voice confidentially: 'What can you pay me on account? Perhaps if I cannot sell you that very stone I may have one a trifle smaller, for less.'

'I'll give you fifty rupees,' said Macbeth at once. He had been saving his pocket money for months in anticipation of his mother's birthday.

The man leaned back with an air of profound deliberation. 'Fifty rupees . . . fifty . . .'

Macbeth turned the ring in his hand, making it catch the light. Then a shadow fell across the showcase and he looked up to find Ramdatta standing beside him. The moneylender smiled. 'You remember me, Sahib?'

Macbeth remembered him. He felt at once, in the air which surrounded this man, the warmth of a particular, protective vitality. Gently, with an exquisite gesture of respect, Ramdatta took the ring from him and held it to the light, turning it in his plump fingers in a way which even Macbeth realised must be the way of the true connoisseur. Ramdatta's hand was full of knowledge, one felt that his flesh, like a turning fork, rang truth from the prized object. The jeweller sat motionless, his smile vanished behind the set mask of his face.

'Fifty rupees for an emerald, an emerald the size of this, an emerald of the first water!'

Macbeth looked at him eagerly. 'That's just on account. What do you think it's worth?'

'That is not easy to say at first glance,' returned Ramdatta. He had not so much as glanced at the jeweller. Suddenly fumbling at his breast, he found a chain to which was attached a little silver toothpick. So swiftly that Macbeth hardly followed the movement, Ramdatta bent back the tiny claws which held the stone, picked the emerald out with his nail, and scratched away the square of green paper which was pasted on it.

The 'emerald' a piece of ordinary glass, lay wanly on his palm.

As Macbeth turned on the jeweller Ramdatta laid a restraining hand on the boy's shoulder. 'Do not curse him, Sahib. He shall make redress.'

The jeweller burst into violent explanations, but Ramdatta silenced him with a look. 'Do you wish to attract the attention of the police?'

The man relapsed into growls, his one good eye burning like a spent match. The moneylender turned to Macbeth. 'Let us select a stone for you. What do you say to a pearl? See, here is one. A real pearl.'

The owner of the real pearl craned forward in anguish, but Ramdatta waved him aside. 'Or, failing pearls, here are some little rubies. Like drops of blood pricked from a woman's finger! Do you fancy rubies?'

Macbeth saw that he stood in the centre of a minor clash of personalities; with every second Ramdatta seemed to increase in stature, in imposing tower of flesh and authority.

'Moonstones are not considered precious, but they have beauty. What do you say to a double string of moonstones with earrings to match?'

Macbeth peered at the nearest case and his glance fell on the little amethyst butterfly. 'There, that. I like that. Are they real stones?'

Ramdatta signalled the jeweller. 'The amethyst butterfly,' he commanded sonorously. 'That with the seed-pearls. What is the matter with thee? Hast thou a stroke?'

'I will not sell,' replied the other, sullenly. 'I am not obliged to sell. Go elsewhere for thy gems.'

'And send the police for thine?'

Speechless, the man lifted the cover of the jewel case and extracted the amethyst butterfly. Macbeth felt an intense amusement. 'Yes, I like this. Is it real?'

'It is real,' said Ramdatta, who had given the thing a single cursory glance. 'Men do you waste such workmanship on an unreal stone. But amethyst! Is there not something else you would prefer? What of the sapphire there in the corner, next the gold earrings?'

'Nay!' wailed the jeweller despairingly. 'That is a true sapphire! I have but three.'

'What, only three? But these others . . .' He shrugged and turned to Macbeth. 'Take the amethyst if it pleases you. Pay this blackguard five rupees.'

'Five rupees! My God! Five? It's worth ten times five.'

'Since when have amethysts and emeralds been the same price?' Ramdatta's big face glistened with benevolence. 'Before the city magistrate your fine would be ten times ten, with ten years in jail.

Come, be sensible if you cannot be honest. The amethyst goes to the young Sahib for rupees five, cash. Give him the money, Sahib, and take your jewel.'

## 39

Dusk was falling when Ganpat Rai's guest, assembled in the garden. The light still lingered in the sky and on the river, and great cranes were flying homeward two by two, their harsh cries falling towards the submerging plain as regiments of flying-foxes emerged to feast in the nearer branches. Servants had sprinkled the drive and the garden paths and strung paper lanterns among the trees, where they glowed like fruit, already attracting big soft-winged moths. One by one carriages and bicycles wheeled through the gates, delivered their passengers, and were taken away to the rear of the house. Tables had been set on the lawn between the tennis court and the arbour where Hardyal's female relatives listened and peeped excitedly between their shielding curtains. Here, later, they would receive the visiting ladies, Indian and English.

The Collector and his wife had arrived, and in honour of this official presence Ganpat Rai was wearing European clothes, a jasmin in his buttonhole. It surprised him when, at the last minute, his son appeared in native dress.

'I feel more comfortable in these,' explained Hardyal. Puzzled by the boy's manner, Ganpat Rai put a hand on his shoulder.

'You are not ill, my son?'

'Ill?' he stood, gazing heavily at his sandalled feet.

'All yesterday you hardly spoke and to-day you did not want to go to the Fair. Naturally, I wondered.'

Neither was given to prying, and when Hardyal answered: 'It is nothing,' the father let him go, deciding to postpone inquiries until later.

Hardyal went down the steps, making his away between groups of friends towards the St Remy phaeton which had just swung between the gates.

'We missed you!' cried Jacques.

'I was so sorry. I was detained.'

The formal word astonished them. '*Detained*?'

'First you run away from the Fort, then you don't turn up at the Fair.'

'Beast!'

'We missed you . . . we missed you!'

For a moment he said nothing, his expression that of a deaf man to whom meaning comes one beat after the sound of words. Then he repeated in a detached voice: 'I was detained.'

He stood before them, slender, white-clad, and it was Jacques who first felt the difference in him. It was more than a difference of dress and of manner, for these had not troubled him before. He felt, now, a creeping chill. When at last Hardyal lifted·his dark gaze and their eyes met, Jacques knew that something had gone wrong.

Hardyal said: 'I think that perhaps I had a touch of the sun yesterday. That is why I went away.'

'You might have waited. We couldn't have missed you by more than a few minutes!' Bertie sounded friendly enough, but she, too, had read something in the air. She read it, not in Hardyal but in Jacques. Were they, then, so close that they could commune without speech? She felt again the swift clutch of jealousy, and turned away, followed by her cousin.

A cloud of voices, Indian and English, drifted among the flowers and the darkening hedges; they seemed to continue in a humming monotone among the glowing Chinese lanterns.

For a moment neither boy spoke, then Jacques said: 'Hardyal . . .'

Hardyal lifted his hand, and said softly, in Hindustani: 'Do not let us talk now. Perhaps, later.'

More guests were arriving, and hearing his name called, Hardyal went away to join Abdul Salim and a group of young Mohammedans who wore the black coat, white trousers, and red fez of Aligarh College.

Jacques felt vaguely sick as he used to when he was a child and something frightened him. He realized that the sensation had been gathering might ever since yesterday, when the morning's pleasure had been spoiled by Hardyal's disappearance from the Fort. All afternoon at the Fair he waited with an increasing nervous impatience for this moment when they were sure to meet in Hardyal's own house . . .when surely the air would be cleared, for the simplest explanation must clear it. Then: 'I was detained!' The stilted sentence was more confusing than no explanation at all. Jacques kicked the gravel, and felt a hand laid on his arm. He turned to find Mrs Lyttleton standing beside him. 'More than ever, you remind me of Auguste!'

He stood rooted. It was a long time since they had spoken, and the years had crowded out his old affection and cast it into a half-shamed memory. He gave her a troubled smile, saying nothing.

'I won't keep you,' she said in a tart voice. 'I know your mother is here and that she would object to my speaking with you . . . that is, beyond the bounds of common politeness. Or would she resent even so little?'

Her irony had a stab to it and he winced. She released him with a harsh little laugh. 'I am glad that you look like Auguste, though I had hoped you would show a sterner spirit. You will certainly have need of it, my dear.'

Jacques felt completely miserable. Somewhere behind a storm of conflicting thoughts shone the remembrance of all his previous anticipations. Youth, when it does not live completely in the present, looks forward. Now it seemed as if everything he loved was twisting into deformity under his eyes. As a child he had acquired perceptions natural to animals, but which in men are considered psychic. He knew that the change which he now observed in his old friend owed less to time itself than to some other cause: it was as though age, bored with stepping softly, had made a sudden pounce. He had never thought of her as being old, as being cruel, or even unkind. He had never thought that she could change. But now her head trembled in the pathetic vertigo of age, her eyes had lost their humour, her movements had the groping hesitancy of blind people. It shocked him, he felt the crumbling away of some structure within himself. What had happened to her, to himself, to Hardyal? What were the forces at work behind the familiar everyday world?

They stood together, the boy and the old woman, watching a crowd of figures move singly and in pairs, listening to civilized accents speaking together under the Chinese lanterns which glowed with an intensity they lost when one looked up at the deepening sky.

Mrs Lyttleton asked querulously: 'Where is he?'

'Where is who?'

'Hardyal, of course. I must see him. I must talk to him.'

Her voice cracked, and Jacques winced. Then he forced himself to look at her directly. Was he seeing her for the first time, this wrinkled, yellow, shivering old woman who was also perhaps somewhat mad, as many described her who had never known her?

He asked gently: 'Shall I find Hardyal for you?'

'Ah, you would welcome the excuse to escape, wouldn't you?'

His lips trembled. 'No, I . . .'

She interrupted with extraordinary bitterness. 'Don't lie to me. I'm sick of lies. It's a lying world . . . even children . . . lying, stealing!'

He felt a little thrill of aversion. "Won't you let me fetch you a chair?'

'One must dissociate oneself from liars and cowards. But the world is full of them. They are all murderers . . . murderers, I tell you!' She peered at him from under her hat. 'You too, you too!'

'Please! Take my arm. Let me fetch you a chair, and some ginger beer!'

She gave a shrill cackle of laughter. 'Ginger beer! Yes, do. Find me some ginger beer. It is exactly what I need, exactly!'

Horrified, Jacques slipped away in search of a servant. Everywhere, people were sitting at little tables, eating, drinking, talking. Individual had gravitated to individual, group to group. Propinquity, sympathy, drew them together. Macbeth and Bertie were laughing with a young Englishman, the guest of one of Amritpore's officials. Madame St Remy sipped tea with Father Sebastien and the English doctor. The Collector had removed his white helmet and his tinsel *har* and was smoking a cigarette, surrounded by barristers and lesser fry. He was apparently telling a funny story, for bursts of laughter and a great slapping of thighs and shoulders indicated both sincere and sycophantic appreciation. Many of the ladies had disappeared into the arbour, from whose discreetly drawn curtains there escaped an occasional peal of laughter and crisp, English voices.

Jacques watched Ganpat Rai move from group to group; he had the air of a proud, wise, and happy man. Everyone, reflected Jacques . . . every one is happy except Mrs Lyttleton and Hardyal and I. Once or twice when he passed Bertie he had a feeling that she deliberately averted her glance. He saw Hardyal in the distance—always in the distance!

Standing for a moment near Abdul Salim, Jacques could not help overhearing the Mohammedan's emphatic speech: 'Crichton is not here. I doubt whether we shall see him this evening. There was some sort of a row at the Fair grounds. I didn't see it, but Feroze told me. I met Feroze on his way to the hospital. It seems there was a beating or something . . . and our friend Ramdatta was involved. Feroze could tell me only the little he had learned for himself. The story is, Ramdatta tried to cheat some poor devil of a jeweller out of a gem. There was an argument, and as Ramdatta was leaving the grounds sticks and *kanker* were thrown, and several people were hurt. Oh, no, Ramdatta was not hurt. He never is! From all accounts the police arrived just in time to check the makings of a nice little riot. Naturally, Crichton cannot very well leave in the middle of a riot!'

A group of musicians appeared and spread their mats a little distance from the guests. Glad of a diversion, Jacques wandered towards them. The ripple of a *zitar* and the soft growl of rice-bowl drums brushed against the subdued hum of voices and clatter of plates and knives. A young man sitting cross-legged between the *zitar* player and the drums sang in a high minor key and his voice, soaring above all the other voices, had the special sweetness of an awakened bird.

A man standing near Jacques spoke to another in a low tone:

'You heard Salim? It is true. I was near the south gate and I saw it happen. Ramdatta drove past in his ekka and a man tried to jump on the wheel and drag him out. Others closed in. I saw one throw a large stone. It was the signal—you know how these things happen! I removed myself. It seemed unwise to linger.'

Afraid that they might suspect him of eavesdropping, Jacques moved away. Now he noticed that a sort of segregation was slowly taking place; Hindus had gathered in a loosely knit group under the trees, while the red fezzes and astrakhan caps of the Mohammedan contingent seemed to gravitate towards a summer-house beyond the tennis courts. Between these recognizable islands flowed the other guests, a few English and Eurasian, servants preoccupied with their duties, and those perennially unattached characters who seem always to wait for some signal before deciding where it is they belong, if they belong anywhere.

A clatter of dishes and the hum of voices rose into the darkening air which, as it darkened, struck chords of light from the doors and windows of the house. The Chinese lanterns bloomed golden among leaves which took on sharpness like details etched in iron, round whose stillness the white moths came and went. Beyond the garden the plain fell away into a dark blue haze and the cooling air captured all the essence of evening, distilling it in keener breaths of wood-smoke and of flesh trying hard to be discreet, to remain immune to its own secret agitation. The closer all these diverse elements were drawn together, the nearer they approached towards ultimate unity, the more urgent became their unconscious resistance. It seemed as if some perverse and original memory asserted itself to remind them that moths are moths and bats are bats that the devoted cranes which desert their crimson pools at sunset obey a wisdom which has determined to put more than space—to put form and substance—between life and life. The closer these people came to resembling one another the more strenuously they strove to separate. Only in the orgasm of love or of death could they ever forget their identity, and between themselves and this forgetfulness they had raised their fantastic barriers.

## 40

Hardyal had seen Mrs Lyttleton; he had, as a matter of fact, waited intently for her arrival. He saw her approach Jacques and watched them as they talked together; then Jacques went away and for several minutes she stood there alone, staring at the crowd. A servant brought her something on a tray, but she waved him aside and walked slowly across the lawn towards the tables, and he lost sight of her.

> Down by the river
> When at night on the pyre of sleep
> You burn with decreasing fire
> And the very sky melts towards you
> With longing, with longing
> Love with his hand shall part the sacred water.
> And revive you with showers from his hair.

Hardyal listened as the song threaded its nasal syllables between drum and *zitar*. He did not linger more than a few minutes with any group of friends, but moved quietly from one to another, keeping a little space around himself. His mind ached from the chimera of a recurring, feverish dream in which the unbelievable sentences from Wall's letter alternately blazed and faded. Other words, other voices detached themselves from figures which moved round him in the gloom. He heard Abdul Salim wondering aloud whether Mrs Lyttleton and Madame St Remy would come to blows here in Ganpat Rai's charming garden. A friend hushed him, and they disappeared among the shadows. Another voice spoke suddenly, with nervous emphasis: 'I trust Crichton. He has tact and force—a good man in a situation. I think perhaps the story may be exaggerated, for had any one been hurt we must have learned of it by now.'

Hardyal stood in the golden light of a lantern and watched the musicians. They sang on, indifferent to the crowd to whom they sang.

> Love with his hand shall part the sacred water
> And revive you with showers from his hair!

He heard Macbeth explaining impatiently to Bertie: 'Moths *don't* love the flame! The light cramps the muscles of their eyes and blinds them . . .'

Then he saw Mrs Lyttleton coming towards him where he stood apart under the trees. He waited until he was sure that she had recognized him, then stepped forward to meet her.

'Hardyal! I have looked everywhere for you.'

'I have been here.'

'But you never even came to greet me!'

'I am sorry. There are so many guests, some who do not know me as you do, and whose feelings would be hurt were I to neglect them.'

She stood in the frail light of a paper lantern, peering at him.

'Are you trying to hurt my feelings, Hardyal?'

'How should I?' His heart was beating strangely, as though he had taken an anæsthetic.

She shuddered. 'Don't . . . don't prevaricate! Don't lie . . . I can't bear it. I won't bear it!' She went on harshly: 'You have avoided me and now you make excuses. Why? You never used to.'

He turned aside and found a chair, which he carried forward and set down for her. She sank into it and he saw her hands move tremblingly on her old silk parasol. 'Hardyal . . . what has happened to every one ? They are all changed . . . all, all, are changed!'

He stood beside her, his face half hidden in the gloom of the leaves, the folds of his white dhoti shining like the sculptured folds of a marble robe. They were alone except for the musicians who sat a few yards away. The song had ended but the *zitar* sent an occasional melancholy note into the darkness, and the drummer's pliant hands stirred a murmur from his drums.

'Answer me, Hardyal!'

'I do not yet know what it is you wish me to say.'

She cried brokenly: 'Tell me the truth!'

He bowed slightly, his brown hands clasped before him.

'I have lost Aubrey Wall's letter. Hardyal, did you take it?'

'Yes.'

The sigh which escaped her was half groan and she lifted one hand shakily to her eyes. 'You took it! You of all people, you!'

'You read it to me, do you remember? You read me things out of it. Things about myself and my father. Do you remember?' He had himself in hand now, and the words came readily enough, though his heart still beat painfully. 'It pleased me to hear those things. They made me feel proud and happy.'

She dropped her hand from her eyes and her frail old body seemed to gather itself together in a frenzy of protest. 'But the letter, the letter! Don't you know that you should never read people's letters? It's most dishonourable. You didn't read it, did you?'

'Yes, I read it.'

'Oh, no, no!'

'All of it.'

Silence fell heavily and at that instant it touched, or seemed to touch, the entire garden and all the preoccupied people in it. Hardyal heard the moths whispering round the nearest paper lantern, he saw their eyes glow like rubies in the dark.

When Mrs Lyttleton spoke at last her voice had regained something of its old acerbity. 'I might have believed it of any one else, but not of you.'

'Was it so wrong? I did not mean to be dishonourable. I meant only to keep the letter a little while because of the things that were in it. Like—like a tikka.'

'What do you mean?'

'A charm, a touchstone. It had made me so happy and so proud to think that there were people who felt . . . happy and proud on my account. Then I discovered that I was wrong . . . that everything was wrong, that the letter . . . the letter was a lie.'

'And you read it, you read it! You know, now, everything that was in it. How many people have you told? How far have you broadcast that horror?'

He was silent, listening to Ganpat Rai bid the Collector and his lady goodnight.

'I suppose you have told your father and all your friends, and that untrustworthy Salim! By this time, it must be all over the bazaar.'

He moved, putting his hand inside his shirt and bringing out the letter, which he laid gently in her lap. 'I have told no one. I have said nothing. There is the letter.'

As her fingers closed upon it all her rings glittered like water.

'What good to return it to me now? You know what happened, and no doubt it is a mere matter of time before the whole world knows!'

'I have told no one. No one has seen the letter, no one except you and me.'

'You expect me to believe you?' Then when he remained silent she cried again: "Why did you? How could you? I should have destroyed it, but I was confused. I thought I should keep it as a sort of—a sort of threat over Aubrey. I didn't know what to do . . . I don't now know what to do.'

'Nor do I.'

A carriage bell twanged, a pair of yellow lamps disappeared between the gate-posts as another pair appeared.

'You read it to me yourself,' said Hardyal in a low voice. 'But what I do not understand is, why the things that you read to me were not in the letter.'

She made a despairing gesture. 'Oh, I was a fool . . . a sentimental fool? I wanted to spite Aubrey Wall . . . to use the evil he had done, and to make some good come of it. It was perverse of me . . . it was wicked, stupid of me! But I didn't think.'

'Then when you read me those things, those things which made me feel proud and happy . . . tell me now, were they there, or perhaps in another letter? Or did you make them up?'

'Yes,' she replied coldly. 'I made them up. With his beastly words under my eyes, I made up the things that I said to you. It pleased me to do so.'

'But why?' His voice was suddenly desolate, and the sound of it went straight to her heart. She lifted her hand and took his, drawing him down on the grass beside her. 'Oh, Hardyal, what have we done, between us?'

She laid her hand on his rich, dark hair. 'I hate Aubrey Wall. I hate everything he stands for, everything he is! But I know that hate is not the answer. I have behaved like an idiotic, romantic old woman, simply because I wanted to make amends to you . . . to you and to others, for another's brutality. I was confused. I felt old and powerless, yet I could not escape the responsibility which he had thrust on me. I have been too long out of step with my own kind, who think me mad and disloyal. And I even tried to retrace my steps, to conciliate them by showing that I cared what they thought. I wanted to put some tiny fragment of the world to rights, starting with my own garden!' He felt her fingers tremble on his head. 'What a fool!'

He sat like a stone, not moving an eyelash when a big sphinx moth darted out from the shadows and hung on electric wings beside his cheek.

'Ah, Hardyal! This damnable violence in men! Why, why?'

'I don't know.'

'But what are we to do? Jalal is dead, and Aubrey . . . what can it prove, now, to betray him?'

'Betray?'

'A friend, a countryman—and he couldn't have known what he was doing. I hate him. I detest him. He has destroyed the last few years of peace left to me. But what am I to do? What am I to do, now?'

She leaned towards him, the old woman towards the young boy, who turned his head aside as though he heard another voice.

'Who am I, to tell you what you should do?'

'But if you were I, Hardyal?'

'What could I do, even then? And he didn't like me. He said I . . . was not to be trusted.'

Mrs Lyttleton was trembling violently. 'Oh, that letter, that letter!'

'I do not know, now, whether I should even trust myself. He did not trust any of us. He said that we would turn against him in the end. But he didn't wait, did he?'

'Wait ? Wait for what?'

'For the end, for the proof. He liked horses and dogs better. They were more human, he said.'

'Oh, don't, don't!'

'I wish I understood. You see, I don't really understand at all.'

'Ah, Hardyal, do not think of it. There are others who are not like Aubrey Wall. You have known many! There is Jacques, there is myself.

We love you . . . yes, yes, we love you! Do not turn away from us, forgive us, Hardyal!'

He sat without speaking, and she went on eagerly: 'See, I shall destroy the letter. I shall burn it, and when it has vanished, everything it contained will have vanished. To tell any one, make it public . . . what would it bring except more misery?'

'You need never fear that I will speak of it. Do you think that I would dream of hurting my father, or others, as I have been hurt?'

Her shame was complete and for a moment she was unable to speak, feeling age sweep upon her in a deafening wave. Then Abdul Salim's voice boomed through the darkness. 'Hardyal, where are you, my child?'

'Help me,' murmured Mrs Lyttleton, and put out her hand in a blind gesture. He rose, drawing her gently to her feet. She felt light and dry, like last year's leaf, as he led her back to the other guests.

# 41

A canopy of firelit dusk hung above the Fair grounds as night brought an accentuation of gaiety and excitement. Booths twinkled in the glow of charags and lanterns, drums throbbed, pipes shrilled, colour melted into colour or flared in strokes of crimson or gold as the darkness beat towards the edges of light, spilled, and receded.

A file of red-turbaned police arrived to relieve their fellows; their shoes clumped noisily and the brass knobs of their *lathies* gleamed like wands of ceremony. The afternoon's disturbance had scarcely affected the general turmoil of gaiety and good humour. Fewer than fifty people had seen the scuffle, the volley of stones and the broken head of one of the participants. Mr Crichton congratulated himself and his men on averting a row of far more serious proportions, and after posting guards and increasing his normal contingent, he went home to bathe and to dine.

The cause of the outbreak was still more or less of a mystery. Crichton had listened to contradictory accounts: one had it that Ramdatta used his whip on a group which attempted to bar his passage through the south gate. A one-eyed vendor of jewels was seen egging on the stone-throwers. Mohammedans joined in, singling out their ancient enemies, and the police arrived in time to break up the party. But the man with the cracked head would probably die, for Feroze, the assistant surgeon, held out little hope. Should he die, the news must somehow be kept quiet until the Fair was over and the crowds safely dispersed. Crichton had no intention of permitting communal violence to mar the success of the Agricultural Fair.

Hanif had missed the fight, but as he moved among the crowd rumours of it filtered through to him, a word here, a whisper there. Two little Hindu boys capered up to him, making insulting gestures. A big Punjabi spat in the dust and shook his fist, for a piece of *kankar* had caught him in the eye. But the mass remained unaffected, and like a rock at high tide that single moment of bloodshed sank under a preoccupied human sea.

Hanif had decked his ear with a fresher rose; now he made his way past the food stalls, past the humid byways, and the strong-smelling purlieus given over to prize-winning goats and the rampant stallions of the Pathans. The young man's expensive elegance excited an occasional smile or a bawdy quip, and he retaliated in kind. The night was his, he breathed its exhilaration and felt its invitation in his warm and gentle blood. The pearls in his new cap and the intricate pattern of his new shoes filled him with satisfaction. He laid his hand on the silk of his waistcoat and played with the silver chain and the links which fastened his shirt. His own beauty, his own youth went to his head: he turned his face to the smoky sky and flung his song to the stars.

'Wah!' exclaimed a fellow Moslem at his elbow. 'Congratulations—but must you tell the world?'

They laughed together, then Hanif glided unobtrusively down an alley which branched away from the main body of the grounds. Here were the sellers of birds, a little arena where the grey partridges fought each other, and a thousand caged canaries contributing their silly din to the general uproar.

Hanif headed towards a *chhatri* at the end of the lane, pushed aside the heavy plaited screen, and went in.

'You are late,' came the inevitable tender reproach, and he felt the cold caress of her glass bracelets against this neck.

'I had duties, but they are finished.'

Inside the *chhatri* the floor was freshly leeped and immaculate; there were no windows, and charags burned at the corners. The outside world beat against this impermanent abode which housed everything that is permanent in human life. She was a girl of perhaps thirteen, still fresh and firm, her hair threaded with jasmin, her round arms laden with glass. Hanif carried her to a heap of coloured quilts in a corner of the room, then came back and stooping, blew out the charags. He was quite sure that he was in love, and the knowledge made his knees tremble as he groped his way back to the bed. He was always sure that he was in love and the knowledge always made his knees tremble.

More than an hour later he stepped forth into the pulsing air, and the tireless voices of the birds rose about him. He bought a cigarette made of black, sticky native tobacco, set his cap at an angle, and sauntered towards the nearest gate and a short-cut across the fields towards the road. Once or twice he stopped to smile and to raise his left wrist upon which he'd managed to squeeze a single glass bangle. Remembering her little hands, he laughed huskily, his blood and brain filled with drowsy sweetness. Well, there was tomorrow. He must invent a sick friend.

As he walked away from the Fair grounds, the noise fell behind him in a soft roar from which smaller, keener sounds escaped like raindrops stroking the leaves closest to one in a storm. People passed him, coming and going. A bullock cart creaked its wooden wheels, a boy on a bicycle veered by with an important shrilling of a nickel bell. An old man loped past, riding a bedraggled horse.

As Hanif reached the road he met the little orchestra which had played for Ganpat Rai's guests. The singer strolled happily in the dust and his song caught Hanif's ear as they passed each other:

> And the very sky melts towards you
> With longing, with longing. . . .

The voice dimmed and died, but Hanif hummed the verse, as he walked, smoking his cigarette, alone now on the white road. It was half an hour's walk from here to the cantonment and the gates and gardens of Madame's neighbours. He was in no hurry, for the night smelled delicious in his nostrils and the cigarette had a special savour.

A tiny eye of light flickered in the darkness and as he approached he saw it was the ember of a fire, beside a cart drawn by two bullocks. From behind the cart stepped a little group of men. They hailed him:

'Where goest thou?'

He answered them gaily, but as he prepared to pass they strung out across the road, barring his path. He saw now that they were Hindus; he saw also that something was amiss, and his mind worked fast.

'Do you spend the night beside the road, my brothers?' he inquired in friendly accents. No one replied and for a moment they confronted him in a silence whose menace was unmistakable. He loosened his feet in his shoes, preparing to kick them off at a second's notice and to make a run for it.

One of the men spoke up at last: 'What business is it of yours where we spend the night? Who are you, a police spy?'

'I am the servant of a great lady. Make way!'

Another laughed. 'The servant of a great lady, dressed up like a pimp!'

'Where is thy badge, thy livery?'

'Perhaps he is wearing it,' suggested a third, and they laughed, a sound unpleasantly devoid of mirth. Hanif glanced round him out of the corner of his eye. On either side of the road were a few trees, and beyond them the open fields. Once in the fields the darkness might hide him. Silently, he cursed the glittering whiteness of his new pantaloons.

A voice burst from the gloom: 'I would swear this one was amongst them!'

'Amongst whom? I have been to the Fair with my friends and masters.'

'And know you that my brother is dead? He died an hour ago at the Government dispensary. That dog of a Mohammedan doctor killed him.'

'And it was you threw the stone!'

Hanif stood his ground. 'I know nothing of all this. I have never seen your brother, nor you. Now let me pass.'

But they were keyed up and half frantic with passion; and they had waited some time for their revenge. What did it matter whether this lad had been present at the beating, or whether he had not? A Mohammedan had thrown the stone, and here was a Mohammedan, defying them. He was one and they were many. They moved nearer and Hanif began to back, but he kept his head, sure that could he but get a good start he would outstrip them.

'Fools!' he cried, his voice firm and strong. 'I have never set eyes on you, your brother or your uncles! Lay a hand on me and you will live to regret it.'

His young voice stayed them for a moment. Then one spoke on a changed note. 'Perhaps he tells the truth. We don't punish innocent men.'

There was a slight, enigmatic pause, then the same voice addressed Hanif. 'Go, then. Go your way, but hurry before we change our minds.'

Hanif threw away his cigarette and stepped forward. His heart was beating faster than he liked, but he was no coward. The men parted as he strode towards them and he saw that they all carried sticks, and one of them a heavy brass *lotah* or drinking vessel bought, no doubt, that very day at the Fair. He walked past them with a resolute step, and they let him go. Then they closed in behind him, and he who carried the *lotah* whirled it suddenly and sent it flying through the air. It caught Hanif between the shoulders, making him stumble. A short heavy stick flew between his legs and he fell face down on the road. They were upon him in a minute, and he gathered himself together with his head in his arms and his knees drawn against his stomach, bracing his muscles against the rain of kicks and blows. They tore his shirt from him and his trousers and beat him until the breath sagged in his chest and his head lolled helplessly in the dust. Then they withdrew a little and provided themselves with stones. Forming a semicircle about him and leaving room so they would not hit one another by mistake, they threw stones, every sort and weight of stone they could lay hands on. And while they worked they made short grunting sounds, the spittle running from their mouths. No one spoke—the only noise was the grunting and the soft thud of stones striking Hanif. At last one man, the tallest, moved away to the edge of the road and returned with a boulder. He straddled Hanif's body, lifted the boulder, and let it fall squarely on the glossy head. An hour passed before they were finished with him, and when at last they moved away, staggering a little from their orgy, all that was recognizable of Hanif under his coverlet of stones and rubble was one hand, darkly articulated against the white dust.

# PART III

## 42

Bertie Wood, coming out of the house one hot July afternoon, found her uncle standing in rapt contemplation of a new flower-bed on the eastern edge of the terrace. When she approached and linked her arm in his, he murmured: 'Cottage tulips, I think. They flower early.'

'I still don't see, if you are going to retire next year, why you should bother to plant them.'

He was silent for a minute, and she examined his profile which in this diamond light had the character of rock, and much of its changelessness. It was always difficult for her to guess what her uncle was thinking; his gentleness never failed to surprise her, well though she knew it. But she had learned that professional soldiers sometimes possess a peculiar simplicity and a tenderness often lacking in subtler men. Colonel Macbeth had remarked on this trait in his comrades but he seemed unaware, or unimpressed, by the same quality in himself. His love for flowers, for animals, for women, was entirely without affectation. It seemed at times as though consecration to the doom of war had bred in him and in his kind a wistful hunger for everything ephemeral in life. He had no talent for tortured intellectuality, no time for doubt, and very little for hate. Because he had never spoken of it, because she never would know his thoughts or his feelings when his wife deserted him, Bertie never ceased to wonder about her uncle. He had killed men and men had tried to kill him, yet here he stood, pulling the ends of his grey moustache, meditating on the virtues and disadvantages of an experiment in cottage tulips.

He repeated her question with an air of surprise. 'Why should I bother to plant them? Why not?'

'They'll be wasted if you sell the house.'

'Oh, I don't think so.' He straightened his great height and stared at the house which had been his home for thirty years. It never occurred to him that he would not leave it, in the end, for a remote and less familiar England.

Bertie said slowly: 'I hate to think of your selling it. Must you?'

'Well, I can't afford to keep the place for John. A colonel's pension is hardly a fortune, and I intend to live at home when I retire.'

'If there isn't a war,' she reminded him, frowning.

'If there isn't a war.'

They turned and began to saunter up and down the terrace before the house, Bertie's arm linked in her uncle's, their feet keeping step. 'If there isn't a war,' he repeated. 'If Grey can persuade them all to meet and talk it over.'

'You don't really think there will be a war, do you?'

He hesitated, then removed his hat and struck with it, lightly, at a flock of brown spaniels which emerged from the house to greet them.

'Yes, I think there will be war, and soon.'

'Yet you want to plant all those tulips, and you talk about retiring and living in England.'

'Life goes on, doesn't it? One can't very well stop in the middle.'

'But what makes you think there is going to be a war?'

He shrugged. 'I'm a soldier. I've been a soldier all my life. War is in the air. My men feel it. I can see it in their eyes.'

She drew him to a halt and turned to stare at him. 'Do you mean it? You are never said this before.'

'One hates to put some things into words. But there is a stir . . . a stir.'

They resumed their walk, and she burst out suddenly: 'Life goes on! It's been going on, everywhere, for years and years! And all the time there is always some one calmly plotting a war! Isn't it funny?'

He glanced at her with his pale, gentle eyes. 'It is funny, you know. Awfully!'

They came to the end of the terrace, then turned and walked slowly back. Bertie said: 'If there should be a war, do you think that John will try and transfer from the Police into the Army?'

'Why should he? He will have his work cut out for him here. The Police in India are every bit as important as the Army. More so now than ever, with these Swaraj-wallahs on the rampage. There was a speech in yesterday's *Pioneer*, by Gokhale. I do not intend to read it.'

She kicked the gravel. 'Just the same, I'm glad that if war should come, the people I love won't be in it. Jacques because of his hand, John because he will have to stay in India, and you . . .' she pressed his arm, 'you because you are an old Methuselah.'

He smiled faintly. 'Women have no shame.'

'You mean we don't always pretend to be heroic.'

'On the contrary, you never stop pretending all sorts of things until you're faced with a moral issue. Then you behave realistically.'

'Well, I certainly don't pretend to like the idea of war.'

He laughed. 'As long as you don't make a scene, I shall forgive you anything.' He tilted her face towards his. 'Do you know, I never believed that you'd grow into a lovely woman. Do you remember how you used to want to be told that you were lovely? You are. Is Jacques responsible?'

Her animation gave way to brooding. 'Jacques! You said just now that life went on, but it seems to me that only situations go on. On and on! It seems to me that the situations which I found here when I first arrived have never really been resolved. We've all changed, grown older—but how far are we from where we started? It frightens me to think about it. Nothing seems to happen, nothing.'

He looked away. 'Next year you and Jacques will be married, and you'll find, then, that life has taken a turn. Hold on to your vision of the future, my darling.'

'Oh, the future, the future!' Her voice sounded brittle. 'These delays . . . sometimes I think that time can strangle everything just by itself.'

Impatience had become increasingly a characteristic with Bertie, though she seemed unconscious of this. Eagerness, anticipation were transmuted to a nervous craning, and an indifference towards all that was not immediate. Colonel Macbeth knew that she was thinking of Jacques, of their long engagement, of all the obstacles which necessity had set in their path. Both lovers were beginning to show the strain of a difficult and too delicate relationship, both seemed more and more obsessed by their difficulties than by their passion.

He reminded her, tenderly: 'You will see him very soon. Perhaps there'll be a letter from him, to-day.'

'I'm going down to the post office now. Uncle Jack . . .' She stared at him rather shamefacedly. 'I never used to be a coward . . . I don't want to sound like one now, but you know . . .'

'I know. Sometimes it's rather beastly, isn't it, just to be young?'

Every afternoon from her window Bertie watched for the mail-carrier on his way up from the railway terminus thirty miles below. He was always heralded by a jingle of bells on a short iron spear, and she had learned to catch the first sound of those bells while the man was still out of sight. Presently he would appear on the semi-circle of road across the lake, a dirty mail sack on his back, its leather strap supported on his brows, his unbelievably thin and wiry legs covering the miles up hill and down at an undeviating trot.

Bertie had been on her way to the post office when she met her uncle in the garden. Now she left him and walked down the hill to the Mall, past the European shops and the band-stand to the stuffy little post office. There she waited in a white heat of impatience while native clerks squatted on the cement floor and sorted the letters into tidy heaps. They were supervised by the postmaster who wore European clothes offset by a filthy cap and a Kashmir shawl draped across his consumptive chest. Bertie spied Jacques' writing among all the others being pawed over by dilatory black fingers.

'There it is in the grey envelope.'

'It is not yet stamped,' objected the postmaster, and spat blood into a brass spittoon.

'Never mind the stamp.'

'But that is strictly against regulations!'

They could not live without their regulations. Temper flared in Bertie: 'Hand it over, Babuji.'

'Oh, very well,' murmured the postmaster resignedly. He took the letter, fumbled about for the date seal and pressed it with artistic deliberation on the envelope. It passed through several pairs of hands into her own, and the additional delay fed her impatience. My God, what sloths! How slow life was, how incredibly careless and indifferent these minute processes of civilization! Anything might have happened to Jacques, he might be dead or become cold towards her, he might this very second be on his way from Amritpore to Gambul, and she torn by suspense while these leisurely apes mooned about with their miserable official scruples. Damn them, damn all natives.

The afternoon was hot and still and when she came to a turn in the path she stopped and leaned against a wall where bunches of pink sorrel grew among the rocks. It was along this path that Jacques St Remy had come a long time ago on his first visit to the Macbeths. It was down this path that Captain Ponsonby had ridden away with Mrs Macbeth.

Bertie, trembling with the almost painful happiness which Jacques' letters always brought her, opened the envelope and took out the thin grey sheets. Her joy receded slowly, giving way to a stupefaction of despair; the blood seemed to drift from her face to her feet, leaving her cold in the clear blaze of sunlight. She stood with the letter in her hand while the words repeated themselves over and over in her mind: Jacques is not coming, Jacques is not coming!

A sailboat stood motionless on the indigo blue of the lake. Round her the cicadas droned, the oak leaves rattled, a spider the size of her hand clambered from branch to branch, spreading its net for little birds. She thought dimly: Inanimate forms survive, while round them the whole performance of life falls and rises. One is always alone, always, always.

When she got back to the house her uncle had disappeared. Slowly, she made her way upstairs to her cousin's bedroom. Macbeth lay thin and narrow in the light of an open window, and for a moment she thought he must be sound asleep, But when she hesitated on the threshold he spoke without moving his head. 'That you, old girl?'

Bertie came in and sat on the edge of his bed, taking his hand. She said, mechanically: 'The fever's broken, hasn't it?'

'I think so. But I've had the damnedest dreams.'

'Dreams?'

'You know the kind one has when one has fever—huge landscapes and very small people. The feeling of unimportance.'

'Dreams,' she repeated sombrely. 'I think that I prefer them, sometimes, to reality.'

He opened his eyes. 'Anything up?'

Bertie was holding back her tears, but they filled her voice. 'Jacques writes that he is not coming to Gambul, after all. Madame St Remy has broken her leg.'

'Oh, the dickens! No!'

'Yes,' said Bertie. Then, explosively: 'I wish she were a centipede and would break all her legs!'

Macbeth clasped his fingers tightly round hers, but said nothing. He watched her, seeing her as he often saw her after a pause in their communion, seeing her as something fresh and strong and desirable, all of a colour, everything he knew and understood.

As for Bertie, she had not yet learned to see him as man sprung clear of his boyhood. Her love for Jacques had kept the world at a distance, it had kept other men at a distance. Little by little now the world and its occupants were beginning to intrude upon and to challenge her indifference.

She said suddenly: 'Do you mind if I talk? I'll burst if I don't.'

'Fire away.'

'Madame is going to be my mother-in-law, and I know I ought to be feeling sorry for her this very minute. But what's the use of pretending? To say that I love her would be a lie. To love her at all would be fantastic. Whenever anything happens to her, whether it is good or bad, comes between Jacques and me.'

'Perhaps later, when she is well again . . .'

'She'll take jolly good care not to get well in a hurry. She'll keep him down there among her coolies and her half-castes. I know.'

'Not if he makes up his own mind.'

'He's had *years* to make up his mind.'

They avoided each other's glance, then Macbeth said gently: 'It's just as rough on him, you know. Don't forget that.'

'Oh, heavens, forget? Oh, damn her, damn her soul!'

Bertie sprang up and walked to the window and he watched her as she stood there crying to herself. His fever had gone, leaving him clear and composed, even his love for her a special and clairvoyant thing.

He said softly: 'Bertie, fetch me a cigarette, will you?'

She came back to the bed and found his silver case, lighting a cigarette for him and one for herself. He said: 'After all, there is only this summer. You'll see him in Amritpore, and next year you'll be married.'

'Will we? That's what we've all supposed. Madame gave her gracious consent. Oh, that graciousness! Like a thin Persian cat. She knows I don't trust her, that I never have trusted her. Not from the day when Jacques was hurt and she came up here to this very house and tried to take him away from us. She knew then that she was in for a fight. We have seen through each other from the very beginning, like two women in love with the same man.'

'Oh, look here!'

'Yes, and we've played the game that women in love always play, pretending to be friends, trying to buy each other off with bribes and hypocrisy.'

He was silent, strangely disturbed by her excitement.

'Nothing, no one, was ever to be allowed to stand in her way. Not even Gisele, her own daughter. Gisele was beautiful, Gisele was a problem, perhaps even a rival! And if she permitted Gisele happiness she could hardly deny it to Jacques, could she? So Gisele was stuffed away in some convent, and Jacques . . .'

He stirred uneasily. 'My dear, your imagination . . .'

'Oh, don't be silly!'

Both were silent, while she struggled to get herself under control. Presently she went on. 'Madame has no intention that Jacques and I should marry. She is very clever. She is making time work for her. And with every year, with every month, with every week, she comes closer to winning.'

'She can't win.'

'Do you know why I went to England last year? It wasn't just to buy my trousseau. It was because I was frightened.'

Again, he took her hand. 'Frightened of what, Bertie?'

'You know perfectly well of what! I was frightened because I thought if we went on seeing each other I might have a baby.'

Their hands lay together numbly on the blanket. He said in a thick voice: 'Well, if you had, it would have pretty well settled everything, wouldn't it?'

'It might have settled everything except for Madame's cleverness.'

He looked at her questioningly, and Bertie went on with a rush:

'She saw what troubled me, she knew that being young, being decent, I was bound to be frightened. She knew that I'd have to go away, that I'd have to put space as well as time between Jacques and myself.'

He pressed her hand. 'Bertie, why worry now? You're going to marry him. Never mind the past, never mind the present. Think of the future. Think of the future, Bertie!'

'That's what Uncle Jack said. Think of the future! But when have I had a chance to think of anything else?'

She got up again and began to walk round the room and he followed her with an aching glance, noticing her strong, lithe movements, the despairing pride in her carriage.

'You see, John, the trouble is that Madame loves Jacques. Mothers must love their sons. It is absolutely right and natural and nice. The greater her love for him the more praiseworthy every one thinks it. The trouble with me is that I love him too. The greater and more unbearable my love, the more praiseworthy. But do you know, I sometimes catch myself wondering whether there is really much difference between Madame and myself?'

'Rot.'

'Is it?' She came and stood beside him, looking down at him wistfully. 'I wish I could be as sure as you seem to be. I can't be sure of anything any more. I don't want to hurt Jacques. We have never hurt each other, at any rate not intentionally. Yet how am I going to endure seeing him put his mother before me? You know, it's because of what happened to her once. Her husband was unfaithful to her, with, of all people, old Mrs Lyttleton.'

'It's what they say, and it's ancient history, rather, isn't it?'

'It's what Madame believes, and she doesn't regard it as ancient history. Jacques is determined that she shan't be hurt again. That's why he goes on making concessions, why he goes on putting off our marriage, why, in the end, he will be forced to hurt me rather than hurt her.'

Macbeth drew a long breath. 'You talk as if all this were final, but you do intend to marry him, don't you, after all?'

She brooded on his face. 'After all? After we've finished caring about each other? Madame will certainly have won then, won't she?'

There was a long silence. A dog scratched himself on the gravel outside; far away in the barracks a bugle sang and sang, its music breaking against their thoughts. Then Macbeth changed the conversation to a less painful subject. 'What were you and Dad talking about a little while ago? I could hear you as you walked outside.'

'We were talking about war.'

He raised his brows, and she repeated: 'War.' But she was not interested in war. Obsession with her own problems made everything else insignificant. Let the world cut its own throat. People were beastly, really. Beastly.

Macbeth said: 'The Germans?'

'I suppose so, and the French.'

'And us.'

'I don't see why.'

'Well, can you see a war without us?'

Bertie sighed, coming to the surface for air. 'Oh, why not?'

'We couldn't keep out. Any one else might, but we couldn't. Old Grey can try and try but he can't stop it.'

'He's a peaceful man. He loves birds.'

'He can't stop it. Think of the German Navy!'

'But after all, Queen Victoria was the Kaiser's grandmother.'

'He hates us just the same. They all hate us.' He pondered the fact, dispassionately. 'When you stop to think of it, the Germans are really unspeakable parvenues.'

She made a gesture of impatience. 'How silly it all is, how childish!'

He shook his head. 'War isn't childish. It's very grown up. It's the most grown-up thing we ever do.'

She stared at him with sudden attention. 'If it should come, will you try to get into the Army?'

He moved restively. 'I'd like to, but Dad thinks I ought to stay here, in the Police. We are probably in for trouble, war or no war.'

She smiled sceptically. 'Another Mutiny?'

'Lord no, the Army is loyal. All it needs is someone to fight against. The Police are trustworthy. But there are lots of others. . . . Men like Tilak. But he's in the Andamans. I wish all the others were. You simply can't trust these educated natives . . . they're bent on making trouble. If the Army goes abroad the Police will have to take over its job.' He frowned. 'Things have started, as a matter of fact. Have you heard of a man called Jagnath Singh?'

Bertie shook her head. 'I can never remember one from another.'

'He's one of the political leaders in my district. Personally, I rather like him. Impersonally, I think he ought to be shot.'

'Perhaps you'll get a change to shoot him,' Bertie suggested. Something in the recesses of her mind gave a little twist of pain. Could she have brought herself to say such a thing a few years ago?

Macbeth went on: 'You must remember Abdul Salim, Hardyal's friend?'

'What about Salim?'

'He's a great admirer of Jagnath's. Between them they're spreading the gospel of Non-co-operation far and wide. My district borders on Amritpore, so I have a dossier on Mr Salim. He has been busy organizing the ryots to strike against paying their rents. Not very successfully; so far it's a pretty minor affair, but it could easily spread. You know how these things do spread in India. Like fire carried by the wind. They are all so emotional, and so poor that the silliest promise inflames them. Jagnath Singh and Abdul Salim are both clever, tenacious men, and they are only two of God knows how many more. If war should break out they'll think it a God-given opportunity to make things hot for us. And that's where the Police come in.'

She said slowly: 'And Hardyal, what about him?'

'Oh, Hardyal is all right.'

'You really trust him?'

'Trust Hardyal? Good God, why not?'

'He, too, is Salim's friend.'

'But we mustn't forget that he is also Jacques' friend, and ours.'

She shook her head, flushing a little. 'I don't know. I feel that Hardyal has changed from the time when we first knew him. Why did he never go back to England? Imagine, when he had the chance, when his father wished it, he preferred to tutor with some obscure Eurasian professor, and chose Calcutta University instead of Oxford. There are other things about him that I don't quite understand . . . I can't even tell you what they are. But I'm conscious, whenever I see him, of a . . . of a . . .'

'Yes?' He was looking at her attentively.

'A coldness.'

'You mean, towards you especially?'

She hesitated. 'Yes, I suppose so.'

Macbeth was silent for a moment, then he said gently: 'There is something you must bear in mind. You are an Englishwoman and Hardyal is an Indian. No matter how warm his friendship for you, there must always be a barrier, and he understands that. He can't do anything about it, even if he should want to.'

She brushed this aside impatiently. 'Men stick together. You have loyalties which we women can never quite understand.'

'Perhaps we are not as possessive as you are.'

The remark, coming from him, surprised her. Once more she sank down on the bed beside him. 'I don't know. It's only when one feels one cannot have something that one becomes possessive. Strong people are hardly ever possessive, are they? I wonder whether my love for Jacques isn't based on the suspicion that I don't really possess him. No one will possess him, not even his mother.'

He clasped her hand. 'Jacques is awfully decent. Really too decent.'

'Can one be too decent?'

'I think so. Father is. Jacques . . . Hardyal.'

She withdrew her hand. 'I don't share you view of Hardyal. I used to. I don't now.'

'Aren't you, perhaps, a bit jealous of Jacques' friendship for him?'

For a moment she looked as though she might burst into violent denials, then she shrugged. 'Oh, I'm sick of pretending! I suppose I am jealous of everything that concerns Jacques. Everything, every one!'

He nodded. 'I understand. But you know, a chap like Jacques is a sort of accident in society. I've often thought of it. You wonder and wonder how they happen, why they are born into the same circumstances as the rest of us, and in our time. They are really not one of us, at all. They don't seem to need us as we need them.'

She looked at him strangely. 'I wonder! I wonder whether Jacques' whole nature isn't on a different plane from ours. Whether, because his need, like his generosity, is much deeper than ours, he has put a curb on himself, knowing that he can never receive a quarter of what he gives.'

Macbeth accepted this without comment and for a long time the cousins remained silent. But their faces wore happier expressions, they felt drawn towards each other, warmed and comforted by this exchange of confidence.

## 43

As the August sun forced its way through a bank of cloud above Amritpore, it sucked a scalding breath from the sodden plains. The river, like a gorged yellow serpent, crept past fields and jetties, swallowing funeral pyres and more than one unwary life. A few birds fluttered, a crocodile rose from the flood, bellowed its hellish message, and sank. A man standing on the ramparts of the Fort would have seen spread beneath and around him, a brown pastiche slowly giving way to tides of delicate, timid green.

But today rain and sun had made a yellow puddle of the factory yard where the nim trees laid their fragile shadows. The noise of the factory was on a diminished scale, for half the vats remained unused and two of the great boilers had been sealed off. Beyond, the compound acres which in the past grew indigo were now reverting gradually to millet and pulse. Familiar, discarded forms revived and moved with a tentative air.

Jacques St Remy, strolling between the empty vats, wondered why he was not depressed by this atmosphere of desuetude. But he found a strange charm in the muted sound of the place, in the phases of dye which peeled away from the vat walls and lay like petals on the bottom, where a lizard blinked in a morsel of shade. The boiler rooms had a different smell; there the machines were shedding their scale, an invisible principle converting them to another fate. In the midst of life we are in death: he had never thought of the words as possessing a coherent meaning but now he felt that he understood them for the first time. The energy of death embraced this cold plaster and inert metal while the energy of life throbbed ceaselessly in a farther corner of the plant. He picked up a crumb of dye and threw it at the lizard which lifted its head and steered away like a tiny battleship battling an invisible sea.

Jacques left the vats and walked slowly towards his office. A few coolies eating their noon meal under the trees turned modestly aside when they saw him. A factory policeman squatting near the well put down the vernacular paper which he'd been reading, and rose, saluting with a listless air. Heat like a steaming lid hung above these human heads, and Jacques felt it pressing on his shoulders as though it sought to crush him to the ground.

He stepped from the glare into his office and found Boodrie collapsed across a desk. The man lifted a pallid face, locks of grey hair falling over his eyes. 'I am completely done up. The assistant surgeon says I am coming down with dysentery if I do not look out.'

Jacques regarded him critically. 'You do look seedy, I must say. Take a week off, old man.'

The Eurasian gave a feeble laugh. 'A week off!'

'Why not? There's not much going on just now.'

Boodrie pulled himself together and wiped his face on his sleeve.

'The minute your back is turned, or my back, wah!' The native exclamation escaped him before he could check it. 'The bloody coolies go to sleep or they steal something.'

Jacques took off his hat. His drill suit clung to him like a second skin; he felt light and transparent, but well enough. These unrelenting summers had accentuated his remarkable looks, which reminded Boodrie, suddenly, of a little picture he had of the youthful St Anthony of Padua. It struck Boodrie as extremely unfair that any one should retain youth and resemble St Anthony when he, himself, felt old, ugly, and ill.

He said querulously: 'I should go to the hills.'

Jacques was looking among the letters and papers on his desk, hoping to find a letter from Bertie. 'Yes, you should. Why don't you?'

'And who will pay, may I ask?'

'Oh, Lord! Put it on the factory account and stop grousing.'

'The factory account? Oh, my? And the factory will pay with

what—with cowries? With *kankar*?'

Jacques sat down and lighted a cigarette. He felt the sweat slip down his body, leaving a chill. The indefatigable white ants had built a new set of tunnels under the edge of his desk and he held a match against the little mud structure, baking it until it crumbled and the disgusting little occupants tumbled out. 'No letters have come for me, I suppose?'

'Nothing from Miss Wood, if that's what you mean. She is too busy enjoying herself in Gambul, no doubt. He ha!'

Jacques looked at him. 'Trot along home, why don't you?'

Boodrie's eyes glittered with fever. 'I have been thinking and thinking. This war ought to help us. It is bound to bring back indigo. All German dyestuffs will be cut off. What a chance; my God, what a chance!'

Jacques smiled. 'An irony, isn't it? When we need new boilers, new linings for the vats—for all the vats. New pressure-gauges, new this, new that, new everything. But you know, when something has started to die you can't bring it back.'

'Bosh!' retorted the Eurasian angrily. 'What has started to die? We have the factory. All we need is money.' He stared at the young man, who sprawled in his chair across the room. 'Twenty-five thousand rupees would make all the difference. When I was at Calcutta two weeks ago every one said that this was our great chance. You will make lakhs, they told me, lakhs!'

A yellow wasp floated into the room and attempted to settle on his face. He brushed it away violently. 'Lakhs!' He continued to stare at Jacques. 'Why in God's name do you not ask your friends?'

'Ask my friends for what?'

'For a loan. There is Ganpat Rai and Colonel Macbeth. They love you. There is Miss Wood. She has money of her own. Not one of them would refuse you.'

Jacques watched the stricken wasp crawl along the matting. He said slowly: 'No, not one of them would refuse me.'

'Then why do you waste time like this? Why . . . why . . . when you could do something. . . .'

Jacques remained silent, and Boodrie gestured despairingly. 'I do not understand you. I have never understood you. You do not care about anything. You do not go to church. You do not go to confession. You are utterly without ambition and responsibility. Everything is going to pot and there you sit smoking cigarettes!'

Jacques said nothing, but he was thinking: The poor blighter has hit on the truth: everything is going to pot and here I sit smoking cigarettes.

He thought of the disused vats and the rusting machines, objects used and forgotten, ancient ideas, lost battles. Catastrophe's perverse beauty obsessed him as he remembered the breaking of the monsoon in Gambul, the splitting crash of lightning as it struck a tree, the look of a hillside as it careered downward into the lake. Then he thought of the ghats by the river where once he and Hardyal had seen a body rear up and confront them from its convulsion of flame. And now, now the war! There was a secret here, a fascination in the paroxysm of death.

Boodrie's voice interrupted his thoughts. 'You should go and see Ramdatta the moneylender.'

'Why Ramdatta?'

'You should speak with him.' Boodrie played with pencils on the desk. 'He would be flattered if you were to stop and see him some day when you are riding past his village.'

'Why should I bother to flatter Ramdatta?'

Boodrie dropped the pencils in agitation. 'Ramdatta is influential. Should we ever find ourselves in a fix, he might be useful. It is just as well to keep in with him. And you do not keep in by hobnobbing with others such as that scoundrel Abdul Salim.'

Jacques was amused. 'What on earth have you got against Salim?'

'I have nothing against him, personally. But Government has. You know that he has been making trouble among Ramdatta's tenants?'

'I can't see that it has anything to do with you or me.'

'Sometimes you talk like a fool. If Ramdatta's people won't pay him, well then . . . what is he to do, pray?'

'Oh, pray away—don't ask me!'

'But it is very important to ask you. We are all in the same boat with men like Ramdatta.'

Jacques shrugged. 'I think you need a pill or something. Why don't you go home and take one? Take several.'

When the Eurasian had gone, muttering and mysterious, Jacques tried to concentrate on his work, but it was too hot and his thoughts kept breaking away. He was consumed with unrest and uneasiness. War! For three weeks Europe had been at war. The Germans were sweeping everything before them—and here he sat smoking cigarettes! He laid his useless left arm on the table and stared at the smooth, blunt stump of flesh. He was young, and the thought of war filled him with inexpressible emotion. But what could he do? What was he good for? All yesterday afternoon he had sat and listened while his mother and Father Sebastien discussed the war. The Germans were in Belgium, headed towards the Channel ports. Madame thought of Gisele in her convent at Bruges. '*Impossible!*' she exclaimed, while the impossible was taking place before her. '*Impossible!*'

War was ridiculous. This one must surely end before it had really got under way. Who cared about Serfia? Who, really, cared about anything enough to go to war for it? This was a typical Prussian gesture. Bismarck was dead and there was not another man in Germany equal to the task of winning such a war. The Kaiser's generals would betray him. The French army was invincible. The English would never permit the situation to pass out of their control. The Pope himself would intervene and the whole Catholic world rise against this affront to the peace of God.

But Liége had fallen, and in Father Sebastien's little church the candles burned for the succour of France and for the souls of those already dead. As far as they were concerned, certainly, the war was over almost as soon as it had begun, and for those who had loved them hope itself was over. But the little dark-faced Christians lifted their chi-chi voices and their prayers to mingle with the chirrup of squirrels and the echo-less voice of the brain-fever bird.

War!

Outside Madame's house the pipul leaves rustled in the hot air and shutters of heat stirred the parched flowers. It was difficult for Jacques to believe that the world was not moribund under this siege, that it was not here in its entirety—naked, sweating, burning in its native fevers.

War!

He thought of Bertie. It was ten days since she had written and her last letter had seemed to him cold and detached. She wrote about the war, about impersonal things. He knew she was bitterly hurt and angry that he had not gone to Gambul, but he had counted on her forgiveness and understanding. Now he thought: She does understand, but she won't forgive. She wants to hurt me, to force me. His love had become a perpetual ache, a chronic longing compounded of desire and the instinct towards inviting and inflicting injury. Well, if she would not write, then neither would he. Let her suffer too, let her wonder what had happened to him, let her wake up in the night and lie sleepless, twisting under the hot sheets, limbs and brain on fire with memory.

Now as he sat before his desk in the whitewashed office he brooded over the past. There seemed to be an incredible aura of innocence and serenity about those days which war had thrust into a distance as a storm sometimes thrusts a fragment of landscape, and one sees it shining beyond one's reach. Those days in Gambul when they walked or rode together along the narrow mountain roads. Nights when the moonlight seemed to inclose them in its special substance as they lay on the terrace below the Macbeths' house and listened to the nighthawk sound its copper gong in the valley. Her body lying beside him took on something of the moon's pallor as it stirred, cool and fragrant, under his touch.

He relived that last year of her absence in England; it had been a strange experience during which both contrived, somehow, to banish the actual for the future, and to exist in a state of physical suspense which had held them both in an identical mood. But this exaltation, in the end, proved unequal before the breathless hour of their reunion. Separation had bred desperation, it fed their appetite but not their love. The truth was, something was dying within them; they were obsessed by unconfessed fears, and stared blindly towards a hope which was gradually becoming dull and inadequate.

Jacques decided that concentration on mundane affairs was beyond him. He flung the papers into a drawer and left the office. Outside, the heat fell upon him like a tiger, and he gasped. The thought of home was repugnant, for there as everywhere, life had passed into a coma. Across the sea a world was splitting apart, but in Amritpore the brown horde drowsed, starved, scratched itself, shrugged. In the developing struggle, what could there be for them? They breathed as best they might under an accumulation of years which had no memory, no clangour, no echo. Their own past had been lost to them—and it was left to strangers, to intruders, to revive it.

Jacques craved the company of youth, the feeling of the storm just as when he was a child he longed to run out into the downpour and the lightning. A servant brought his bicycle and he rode through the gates towards Hardyal's house. The roads were still deserted, since several hours must pass before Amritpore came to life in the cool of the evening. As he approached the gates of Mrs Lyttleton's house he slowed, more than half tempted to go in and call on his old friend. They met rarely and had little to say to each other. Jacques knew that her mind was failing and the knowledge hurt him, for when they did meet the mists before her lightened and lifted and he encountered the old, clear, familiar glance. What, he wondered, would she have to say about this war, she who had lived through so many? He wheeled in an indecisive circle before the sandstone pillars, then continued on his way. What Mrs Lyttleton or any one else had to say about the war could make no difference. War had come. No one had been able to stop it, no one!

He pedalled unhurriedly under the shadow of the mango trees which bordered the road, and presently found himself near the spot where Hanif had been killed. Beyond the trees lay the soggy fields where a few big blue buffaloes were grazing. Jacques dismounted and laid his machine against a pile of kankar beside the road. It was here, on this spot, that the police had found Hanif's body. Madame St Remy bought the plot of ground nearby, and there they buried him. Now Jacques walked to the grave to make sure that the rain and the jackals had not been at work. The simple white-limed surface bore Hanif's same and his age. and under these a single word: *Khatm*, which is the Moslem *Finis*.

# 44

Jacques found his friends gathered as usual in Ganpat Rai's drawing-room. They sat or reclined among a welter of cushions and goat-hair rugs, under a frilled punkah which barely stirred the warm, spicy air. Besides himself there were several visitors, two young Mohammedans, and a trio of Hardyal's cousins. When Jacques was announced they rose, and he had an impression of embarrassment swiftly dissimulated, as though a conversation had been abruptly nipped in the bud.

Ganpat Rai, clothed in a thin dhoti and holding a palm-leaf fan, put his arm around Jacques' shoulder. 'Do you know Mr Mahmud Ali and Mr Hosain? You have, I think, met our cousins.'

The young men exchanged salutes. 'Sit,' Ganpat Rai commanded them, genially. 'It is only our young friend, Jacques.'

Hardyal patted a cushion beside him. 'Tell us what you think of the war. Will the Germans reach Paris?'

'Will they take the Channel ports?'

'Ah, if they do—England is lost!'

'Shall we have conscription in India?'

'If so, I shall most certainly resist.'

'Ha! Easy for you to talk so big just now, Sheo Dyal! But when the time comes we shall do as we are told, just as usual.'

'Yes, like Salim's cousin Dr Feroze.'

'Feroze was not told to do anything—he went of his own free will.'

'Salim says he always was a lickboot of the Government.'

'My brother Shaukat is no lickboot, but he too has gone into the Army.'

'However, Jacques, here, will not have to go. You are lucky, Jacques!'

'Am I?' He lowered himself on a cushion between Hardyal and one of the young Mohammedans. He liked to sit on the floor, a posture which makes formality difficult. 'I'm glad someone thinks so.'

Hardyal repeated impatiently: 'Tell us! Tell us what you have heard about the war!'

'You know as much about it as I do.'

776 • A RAJ COLLECTION

'How can that be, Sahib? We are told little or nothing.'

The speaker was Mahmud Ali, a teacher in Amritpore's High School. Ganpat Rai looked at him. 'Come now, Mahmud! You read the papers, do you not? For myself I refuse to worry too much about the war at this early date. We must not forget the French Army. But Jacques, my poor boy! It is your France that is overrun. Ah, how it must feel to be a Frenchman!' His eyes were moist, and the young men lowered theirs out of deference. This emotional coming-to-the-point would have been impossible among Englishmen, but among these Indians it seemed natural enough, since with them sympathy, pity, curiosity are not ingredients to be deliberately excluded from conversation.

Jacques shrugged. 'Good Lord, what difference does it make whether one is French or what? In the end, we're all human.'

Hosain said quickly: 'Yet if India were invaded the English would fight only to preserve their own skins. The rest of us would have to shift for ourselves.'

'Assuming you would not fight for yourselves,' observed Jacques, coolly. He spoke, not from any honest objection to Hosain's remark, but from an instinctive dislike of the young man whose appearance was unprepossessing and who never failed to inject the note of grievance.

Ganpat Rai interposed: 'What, after all, is the question? Men are right or they are wrong. It is essential that we choose our own side and stick to it.'

'That would be easy were the issues clear,' said Hardyal in a low voice. 'I admit that for myself they are not so clear.'

'They are clear to me,' returned his father, giving him a troubled glance. 'Surely you and I know where we stand?'

There was a brief silence, and Jacques wondered whether this had been the point under discussion when he entered. Mahmud Ali now cleared his throat. 'But do we stand, sir? Sometimes it seems to me that we spend much of our time in crawling.'

A murmur, half protest and half approval, greeted this remark. Ganpat Rai made a gesture of impatience. 'Why must you young men always exaggerate? Why must you, in particular, exaggerate the wrong things? What is important to-day is the scope and the significance of this war. We stand in as grave peril as the rest of the world. On that we are agreed, are we not?'

'*Be shak!*' came the swift Urdu response in one voice. The young Hindus stared anxiously at their host, but said nothing. Ganpat Rai went on: 'It is important that we see, or try to see, what it is that we all want. For myself I have found that what men want, what they think, and what they do, remain for the most part widely separated things.'

'Nevertheless, they work together towards an end,' said Hardyal.

These discussions always interested Jacques. He knew that they originated in a deep inner discontent from which few of his Indian friends seemed immune. Yet it seemed to him that when men argued politically what emerged was their smallness, their egocentricity, their pitiable assumption of clairvoyance. With Indians a sort of hysteria was added to all this, making it difficult to debate with them without at the same time wounding their susceptibilities and exciting their passionate resentment. Would Hardyal, he wondered, escape the infection? Jacques met Ganpat Rai's glance and read the same question in his kind, expressive eyes. He's seen it coming, too, thought Jacques, and suffered a pang of love and fear for his friend, as he would have suffered had someone told him that Hardyal was doomed to an incurable disease.

Ganpat Rai turned to Mahmud Ali. 'Now tell me, Mahmud, do you and Hardyal desire the same things?'

'Certainly, certainly we do! What else? We want only our rights.'

'That is most original. I live in your world. What is available to me, is, surely, available to you.'

'Oh, sir! How can you say so? I am not even able to procure for myself a university education.'

'And how many Englishmen or Frenchmen do you imagine enjoy that advantage?'

Hardyal answered for his friend: 'If all may not, then Mahmud is still right!'

'Also it is well known that under English rule Brahmins get all the good jobs,' complained Mr Hosain, with dreadful tactlessness. Every one laughed, and Mahmud Ali gave his co-religionist a sarcastic glance.

Ganpat Rai pursued his advantage. 'We always get back to the beginning, do we not? Hosain would substitute Islam for England and call that a fair solution.'

'Why not?' muttered Hosain. 'Islam has a better right than some others.'

'That also I have heard. If one listens long enough one hears always the same things.'

'But that is because there is no change, no reform, no justice!' Hosain was becoming excited. 'One of our leaders has said that if we Moslems are not careful we shall become like the Jews, a religion without a country.'

'You more resemble the Catholics,' observed Ganpat Rai, slyly, 'with your vicar in Turkey.'

There was a scandalized pause, but they were too young and too much in awe of his age and superior wisdom to do more than step gingerly aside from the dynamite which he proffered. Then Mahmud Ali began humbly: 'Myself, I cannot be altogether sure of these matters, but Salim says. . . . '

'What says Salim?'

A shadow moved behind the screen and the tall bearded Pleader came in. He had kicked off his shoes in the veranda, now he stooped and laid a hand on Ganpat Rai's shoulder. 'Do you, my friend, permit these whippersnappers to discuss their betters?'

The barrister reached up and pulled the big man down on a cushion beside him. 'They quote you as an oracle.'

'Hardyal my child, a cigarette!'

He folded his legs under him and his bare, strong toes stuck out on either side. Ganpat Rai watched him closely as he lighted the cigarette. 'Tell me, from where have you come?'

'From the Collector Sahib's.'

'Ah, I thought so!'

'But you are not surprised? Why should you be? This is not the first time I have been summoned to such a conference.'

Jacques felt the gathering tension. It was Mahmud Ali who spoke first: 'Did he threaten you?'

They leaned forward, their eyes stony. But Salim laughed. 'How little you understand these people! He offered me a cigar. Allah, how it burned my unsuspecting tongue.'

'But what happened?' demanded Hardyal impatiently. 'Tell us what he said. Speak frankly, we are all friends here.'

Salim glanced at Jacques, then shrugged. 'What does it matter who hears? There were Government chuprassies listening at every door. Well, the Collector was affable, even friendly. You know how disarming they can be when they are sure neither of themselves nor of you. We talked of this and that. He spoke of the increasing seriousness of the war. It would, he declared, be prolonged, for the Germans were proving themselves far more formidable than any one had dreamed. Had they not been preparing for this for the past twenty years? Their frank boasting had thrown dust in the eyes of the world. Ah, yes, it looked serious, most serious. On this point the Collector and I agreed, *ad nauseam*. From there he went on to emphasize the necessity of free men sticking together, but I thought it best to let the injunction pass, for the moment. He dwelt at some length on the loyal support which the Government was receiving from the public, and how charmingly he alluded to the patriotism of my cousin Feroze, now with a regiment of Punjabies, and also of your brother Shaukat, training at Nasik!

When an Englishman desires to flatter you, the process is so delicate, so subtle, that you are in gravest danger of not discovering what has befallen your virtue until nine months afterwards!'

They met this with laughter, Jacques joining with them. Then Hardyal asked: 'But where did all this lead you, Sahib?'

'Well, it led me charmingly to believe that for the first time in my humble career I have attained a certain eminence in the eyes of high officialdom. I, a mere Pleader in the district court; poor, practically unknown beyond the limits of my native town! It seems that I now constitute something of a splinter in the august flesh of the Raj. I ventured to point out the absurdity of my position *vis-à-vis* his own. After all, I reminded him, my personal history during the past few years could scarcely be described as lurid. I have lost a good half of my practice—clients do not incline naturally to one who stands in doubtful odour with the authorities. My touts report a distinct falling away in all quarters. In order to live I have had to sell some of my belongings. Several of my close friends have dropped me. True, I have made others, I have even accumulated what in a larger arena might be described as a political following. But Allah! What can the sum total of these activities amount to in an insignificant segment of Empire such as Amritpore?'

His sarcasm stirred the uneasy silence. No one seemed to know what to say next, and it was Ganpat Rai who made the first move, his profound gaze challenging the other's. 'In the end, did you part friends?'

Salim did not reply at once, but when he did it was with electrifying passion. 'Friends! He offered me his hand, there in the open door of his office, before the eyes of his servants! And I, too late I recognized the manoeuvre designed to put me in the position of a fellow sportsman pledged not to deliver a foul blow. My God! These English.'

'And you, did you take his hand?'

'Why not? I am an Oriental. These gestures mean nothing.'

'Why did you not oppose him frankly?'

'Because I am not an Englishman.'

The barrister slammed his palm-leaf fan on his knees. 'Bah, how you quibble!'

Salim spoke on a quieter note. 'I do not believe that what is in store for the world is just another game of football on a universal scale, nor do I hold that political immorality can be palmed off on us disguised as political necessity. We are not fools. "Stand beside us in our hour of need", cry our masters, "and when the common danger is past you shall have your reward!" But I would ask our Collectors and Policemen, our Lat Sahibs, this question: "Why can you not bring yourselves to forget the military rebellion of 1857, and in order to enable us to stand beside you, and beside each other, make colonels and generals out of our sepoys, and train them in the use of heavy artillery and the complexities of modern warfare? If death is the final equality between men, then we must first learn to live together".'

'Bravo!' exclaimed Ganpat Rai, sarcastic in his turn. 'Why did you not visit this eloquence upon the Collector when you had the opportunity?'

'I do not choose to waste my eloquence on dunderheads.'

Ganpat Rai made a wild gesture of the fan. 'You are utterly without judgment!'

The other's temper rose once more like wine to the surface, and a responsive tremor went through the listeners. 'I tell you, the Raj will use this war as an excuse for thrusting us back from where we started. It will appeal to our patriotism, even to our venality, in face of a common enemy. Time enough, says the Raj—time enough after the battle has been won. And it will make the same vague promises which have not changed for the past sixty years. The Raj will remain sole judge of the ripeness of time. The Raj will decide when, if ever, adult human beings are to emerge from kindergarten.'

'But can you honestly hold that the intrigues and squabbles of a handful of illiterate ryots are reason for inciting to unrest, to violence even, at such a time?'

Salim looked at him. 'Why not? Does the Raj give a damn about the ryots? It is far too busy fighting its war abroad and supporting its moneylenders at home, to worry about the ryots. If this is not the time to force the issue, then there never will be a time. Not for us. For the Raj, yes. For the Raj, endless time. Listen, in Ahmedabad, Mohandas Gandhi is actually recruiting for the Government! Everywhere men who should have learned their lesson succumb like fish to the same rotten bait. The time to strike is now, when the iron is hot. Else we shall wake up to find it cold and heavy on our wrists and ankles.'

Ganpat Rai replied sombrely: 'Men are going to die like flies before this war is finished. There is going to be violence enough for the most bloodthirsty amongst us.'

Salim's hands closed into fists as they rested on his knees.

'You have surrendered to the virus of the West, my friend. It has made you sentimental.'

The young men held their breath for as long as the silence lasted, then Ganpat Rai turned and laid his hand across Salim's shoulder. He said gently: 'You and I disagree, as always, but do not let us quarrel. There are others . . . leave it to them. This is my house and you are my friend—for me, that is sufficient.'

It looked for a moment as though the fiery Mohammedan would resist this appeal, but Hardyal came to the rescue.

'It is sufficient for all of us that you remain friends! As for me, I am stiff from long sitting.' He turned to Jacques. 'It is cooler outside, now. Shall we walk?'

They rose and Hardyal smiled at his friends. 'There are matters I wish to discuss with Jacques. We shall return very soon'.

# 45

Heat rose from the ground and crawled towards them from every side as they strolled past the zenana gate to the end of the garden. A flock of mynas twittered beside a flooded tank and there was a hint of freshness in the air, but Jacques felt the sweat start out on him at every step. He was glad, however, to escape from the argument, which had become oppressive.

Hardyal had brought a palm-leaf fan which he waved before them as they walked, Jacques in his crumpled drill suit, Hardyal in a loose muslin shirt and dhoti. Where the garden ended on a slight eminence they could see the river changing colour with the changing light. Clouds were heaped in an ornate mass whose edges glowed with subdued fire.

The young men said little until they reached the boundary of the garden, where under a row of eucalyptus trees they found a stone bench and sat down. The panorama before them contained little that seemed important; they watched an umbrella supported on two naked brown legs bob along a soggy road, and two humped grey bullocks dragging a *ruth*. Life was everywhere, but it remained concealed, muted, awaiting a signal to declare itself in the sudden spark of village hearths and the homeward flight of birds.

Hardyal said at last: 'You must not misunderstand Abdul Salim.'

'On the contrary, I understand him very well.'

'If what he said to-day were to reach the ears of a Government official. . . .'

'You mean through me? Surely you know me better!'

'Forgive me. The war has made us all unsure of ourselves, and of one another.'

Both were silent, then Hardyal asked: 'You like Salim?'

'You always ask me that and I always reply: Yes, I like him. What is more, I admire him, though I fear he will not get very far.'

'Because he is too outspoken?'

Jacques nodded, then he said: 'In a way I envy him. There is always something thrilling about a man who will not back down.'

'I like to hear you say it. People do not, as a rule, admire Salim. His brand of courage makes demands on them—it makes them uncomfortable.'

Jacques pondered. 'He is revolutionary, of course, and that is unique in India.'

'Yet I sometimes think that he is not wholly aware of his own tendency. Revolt is instinctive with him.'

'Yet he remains a good Moslem.'

'Well, liberal compromise doesn't offer much scope to the Moslems, does it? Salim realizes that. He realizes that they are still stuck with their limitations.'

'Like the Brahmins.'

'And the Catholics.'

'Not to mention the Jews!'

Both smiled, feeling the air clear between them. Jacques shook his head. 'Damn it, I wish I had it in me to be a political animal!' Hardyal gave him an affectionate look. 'Sometimes your incapacity for faith troubles me. Then again, I seem to understand a little. You are essentially Gallic, and they were the first to ripen.'

'And will be the first to rot.'

'That I did not say. Certainly they are proving themselves vigorously now. You say you do not believe, that you are not "political", yet if you were able, you would fight?'

'Of course.'

'Then I do not understand.'

'One hates to be left out.'

Both were conscious of a difference between them, a difference not in love or in sympathy, but in passion, Jacques tried to explain:

'It's like having one brick after another knocked away from under you. Hanif's death did not help. . . . I have thought and thought about that death, its stupidity, its waste. Then, when I listen to your father and Salim argue. . . .'

Hardyal interrupted quickly: 'Ah, Hanif's death was cruel, but it was in the nature of an accident.'

'Was it? He was murdered. Behind it all lies the intention. If I could ever bring myself to believe that the intention stems from men's essential sanity, their morality. . . .' He shrugged and laid his crippled arm on his knee. 'Was this an accident? Here again, I find myself wondering. I was up in that tree. I felt deserted, friendless, as poor Hanif must have felt.'

Hardyal ceased waving the palm-leaf fan; he rested his head on his hand, gazing sideways at his friend. Jacques went on meditatively:

'I remember distinctly how it felt to be left in that tree all by myself. I thought the leopard was stalking me. Pretty soon I was sure. And I was so bloody frightened. . . .' He drew a sharp breath, then laughed. 'Anyhow, the damned rifle went off. I don't know, I wouldn't swear, now, that I pulled the trigger in order to break the suspense and release myself, or whether it happened of itself.'

'And you think that what you call your faith has suffered a similar fate?'

'Doesn't it happen, more or less, to almost every one?'

Hardyal nodded broodingly. 'For me, too, there was a leopard. . . but it came out of the sunlight, like a friend.'

Jacques waited for the confidence, but Hardyal said no more. They watched the clouds build and rebuild vast citadels of light and purple, a single shaft striking the distant line of the canal. Hardyal broke the silence at last: 'However, I did not bring you here to talk of Abdul Salim or of the past, but to tell you that I am to be married very soon.'

Jacques' surprise crept upon him by degrees. 'Married? Good Lord, you've never so much as hinted. . . .'

'I thought it better not to speak until I had made up my mind. Now I am sure. Father is pleased, and so are my aunts.'

Jacques stared at him. 'I don't quite know what to say. If you're happy, then so am I.'

Hardyal held the fan before him as though it were a book. 'It is something I should have done long ago, but then I was filled with different ideas and aspirations. She is a splendid girl. Our families have known each other for many years.'

'Are you in love with her?'

The other waited a moment, then smiled. 'They are strictly orthodox, so naturally I have not set eyes on her nor she on me.'

'Oh, good Lord!'

Hardyal laughed. 'What does it matter? This question of love . . . you know that in India romance does not enjoy the exaggerated importance it does elsewhere.'

Jacques hated the false note. 'I don't understand! When we used to discuss these things you agreed that a strong mutual attraction was the best basis for marriage, no matter what happened afterwards.'

Hardyal continued to study the fan. Something of its blankness was reflected in his face. 'Perhaps the attraction will follow on marriage. It is a safer bet.'

Jacques said bitterly: 'You sound as if you'd succumbed to the domination of all your aunts!'

'It is not easy, at a moment's notice, to throw aside the traditions of many thousands of years.'

Jacques made a gesture of hopelessness. 'A moment's notice! What people! Politically, spiritually, you are a match for the world. Socially, you stagger along under the abracadabra of centuries. Hardyal, be honest, tell me. . . .'

The other turned a face that was full of emotion. 'Yes, I can tell you, but I can tell no one else—not my father, not Salim. You insist that you do not believe in much of anything, but in love you must believe. That is something which has not died in you, as I sometimes think it has died in me. Tell me, now, where in my society shall I find, for instance, a woman like your Bertie? There are some, of course, but I know none. I do not look for equality and companionship among the women from whom I must choose. Try to understand! I must marry. I have tried the other thing, for sex becomes a problem only when one tries to live without it. I have responsibilities towards my family. But I am not in love, how can I say that I shall ever be in love? It is a state of mind, a condition which depends on many other things.'

Jacques was moved by his friend's emotion. 'On what other things?'

Hardyal seemed to grope for words; they came at last, breathlessly: 'It depends on everything that goes to make up a society. You are right when you say that politically and spiritually we can be a match for the world, and you are also right when you remind me that we stagger under the abracadabra of centuries. This has made us sensual rather than passionate, mystical rather than rational. But isn't that bound to happen when the form of a society is stronger than its individuals? There are times when life seems clear and good, other times when I wonder whether it is not a colossal blunder from beginning to end!'

Jacques was struck, as he had been struck before, by something that almost invariably occurred when he talked with Indians: they seldom failed to relate their personal problems with larger, indeed with universal considerations, and he wondered whether this were not the inevitable concomitant of a country ruled by outsiders. He found himself at a disadvantage, and, unable to think of anything omniscient, or even comforting, he reverted to the familiar note. 'Well, so we are both to be married. Do you think our wives will like each other?'

Hardyal's features cleared slowly of their strange discontent. He smiled, but said nothing, and in a little while they heard, in the garden behind them, the voices of the other guests. 'Jacques! Hardyal! Where are you?'

'It is almost cool enough for a game, if Hardyal will lend me his tennis shoes.'

'How provident of you always to forget to bring your own!'

'Why should I bother when my cousin has fourteen pairs, all of which fit me to perfection?'

# 46

One afternoon in mid-September Ramdatta the moneylender lay on a string cot under his favourite tree. The air was warm and moist, but a light breeze stirred the mango leaves. Beside Ramdatta's cot squatted a little company of his neighbours; a Kyeth, or scribe, perched on a camp stool, reading aloud from a pink-tinted vernacular newspaper. He was reading about the European war and the others listened as only natives can listen to the printed word: they listened with an entire concentration of their bodies. Ramdatta's youngest son, a boy of ten, stood behind his father, fanning him with a wand of plumed grass.

The Kyeth's singsong voice mingled with a creak of well-wheels and the sound of water gushing from its big leather sack. Sundry tinklings and jinglings escaped from the arched door of the house, figures appeared and vanished with a twinkle of feet and a flash of anklets. Nearby, strutted Ramdatta's tame peacock, spreading its tail in a patch of sun. Village life established its peculiar fabric of sound which scarcely varied from day to day or from evening to evening; an attentive ear would have picked up the running-stitch of birds and squirrels, the steady champing of cattle chewing dry cornstalks in their pens behind their owners' houses, and the soft, incessant crying of a sick child. From fields beyond the village, a voice rose high and keen above all the others: 'Oh, Allah Din! Allah Din, oh!' But the Gift of Heaven, whoever he was, chose to make no reply. The voice wailed on plaintively, then gave up.

'The English ships *Aboukir, Hogue,* and *Crecy* have been sunk by the Germans,' read the Kyeth, and a stir went round the listeners.

'Tobah,' exclaimed one, and turned aside to spit.

Ramdatta snapped his plump fingers. 'That is nothing. We have many ships, all of them superior. When I was at Bombay in the old days I saw them—like great birds they were, resting on the water. There is no cause for anxiety. We have many, many more, all bigger and better than the Germans.'

The Kyeth waited respectfully for his master to finish, then went on reading. Ramdatta's son, bored, changed the wand from one hand to the other and watched a pair of razor-horned lizards manoeuvring for battle on a nearby branch. The sun, slipping west of the village, laid its patina on mud walls covered with little pancakes of cow dung, each with its imprint of a hand. An emaciated cur nursing a row of puppies dragged herself to her feet and wandered away, panting, pursued by her insatiable brood. Tired of watching the lizards Ramdatta's son transferred his attention to an ant-hill near his feet. He gave it a poke with his toe and watched the startled inhabitants scurry about, clinging tenaciously to their bundles.

'Art thou asleep, my son?' asked Ramdatta softly, and the boy, swallowing his yawns, fanned with renewed vigour.

The moneylender was recovering from an attack of fever which still lingered in his bones; but except for a slight dullness of his eye and a peeling of the lips he showed little sign of illness. The brown flesh grew as firm and as glossy as ever on his big frame, his shaven head shone like a bullet. Hieratic, impressive, he reclined among his cushions, attended by his son, admired by the sycophants who crouched round him.

Jacques St Remy, riding in through an opening in the village wall, saw this tableau set against the white wall of the house where a rampant tiger had been freshly painted in vermilion. The sound of hooves struck on Ramdatta's ear and he sat up, spilling his shawls and waving the Kyeth into silence. 'Behold, a Sahib comes to visit me! Depart, all of you. Send one to take the Sahib's horse.'

Jacques dismounted and surrendered his beast to a servant who came running. Ramdatta's coterie melted away but the boy remained, staring shyly as the young man approached. 'Hallo, Ramdatta! I come, bringing you quinine.'

The moneylender rose and salaamed. There was scarcely a change in his expression, but he was well aware of the many curious and admiring eyes that watched from shadowy doorways; there was something imposing, even noble, in his bearing as he greeted his visitor.

'Huzoor, this is an honour.' He turned to his son. 'Go and tell them to fetch the chair—the European chair. Hurry!'

The boy scampered off and Jacques gazed quizzically at the moneylender.

'Boodrie gave me to understand that you were practically at death's door!'

'These *Keranies* always exaggerate. They must, to make up for their own lack.'

The boy reappeared, proudly ushering two men who staggered under a huge chintz-upholstered chair which they set down a little distance from Ramdatta's cot. This chair was the pride of his heart; he had sent for it several years before, from Bombay, and it was produced only on state occasions. Jacques, assuming a fitting air of dignity, lowered himself into the ample seat and crossed his legs. He wondered a little at all this ceremony. Boodrie, with an air of excitement, bordering on panic, had passed on Ramdatta's invitation, adding the mysterious injunction that Madame was on no account to be told.

'He is a sick man, or he would have come himself to see you.'

Jacques, enjoying an afternoon's canter across the plain, saw no reason why he should not drop in on the moneylender. The man had always exercised a sort of fascination over him in spite of the loathing in which he was generally held in Amritpore. Now, as the young man lighted a cigarette Ramdatta returned to his cot, on which he sat cross-legged, the shawls draped over his shoulders. His little son was dismissed and departed, dragging his feet, glancing back at the pale young Sahib who smiled after him. White men were certainly not rare in the village, but Jacques' beauty affected Indians even more profoundly than it did his own kind.

Ramdatta said presently: 'It is considerate of you to accept the invitation of a sick and ageing man, Sahib.'

Jacques lighted a cigarette and smiled. He knew better than to congratulate his host on his recovery or to compliment him on his appearance, for to do either would have been a breach of etiquette and a direct provocation to the Evil Eye.

Ramdatta crossed his sleek arms on the folds of his shawl.

'I have grave responsibilities and it is sometimes a relief to speak of them to an intelligent and well-informed person. My sons are all devoted and good, but quite without worldly knowledge or ambition. That seems to be the fate of fathers like myself. By our own labours we deprive our children of an essential initiative.'

'You can always cut them off with a pice,' suggested Jacques, slyly.

The other smiled. 'They would straightway become beggars, or worse. No, there is no solution to the problem. One must accept it.' His glance slid off Jacques to the ground. 'One learns to accept much. There are, however, men who abjure the doctrine of resignation. They believe that by a mere wave of the hand they can move mountains.'

Jacques waited, silently enjoying the situation and the taste of his cigarette. He was filled with happiness, because Bertie had written with a renewed passion and yearning, and her letter had fired him with responsive ardour. The reassuring effect of love was to put a distance between himself and his immediate surroundings; he felt immune from all their uncertainties.

Ramdatta heaved a sigh. 'Madame is indeed fortunate in her possession of a son such as you. You have but to marry and produce sons of your own, and you will complete her happiness.'

The peacock reappeared. Sumptuous, arrogant, it put its head on one side and listened, aware, as all pampered creatures are, of an alien presence.

Ramdatta went on conversationally: 'I have heard that in the holy book of the Christians it is written that when a child is born he comes into the world with his hands empty, and empty-handed leaves it. But we put it differently: we say that a child comes into the world with hands closed, clutching all his hopes and all his gifts. It is when he dies that he goes forth empty-handed.'

Jacques said: 'I think I like your version better.'

'One must use one's gifts while one has life. One can but conduct oneself according to the potentialities one brings with one from the past creation. Not to do so would be sinful. Nevertheless, I have not found it easy, for the world is full of envious men.'

Jacques, realizing at once that the conversation had arrived at a crucial stage, schooled his features to a cautious impassivity.

'You and I, Sahib, are in the same case. We were born into a category of men who, to survive, must work, and who by working cannot help but accumulate fortunes which rouse the jealousy and greed even of our friends. But that is the way of the world, is it not? Even on isolated and forgotten islands there are some who have and some who have not.'

'And there are likewise those of whom it is said that there shall be taken from them even that which they have not,' observed Jacques with an absent-minded air.

The moneylender gave him a keen glance. 'Ah! That I had not heard, but I believe it.'

'However, there are scholars who insist that the statement applies not to worldly wealth but to the attribute of wisdom,' Jacques finished, gravely.

A golden smile spread over Ramdatta's features. 'Would that you were my son! There is none other with whom I can converse in such a vein. My family are dunces, my friends liars and worse.'

'God forbid!'

'Nay, it is true.' He leaned forward, fixing Jacques with an eye that was suddenly as cold and steady as a cobra's. 'But perhaps I am luckier than you, after all, for I at least am not deceived.'

Jacques lighted another cigarette as Ramdatta straightened up and stared round him. The courtyard was empty, the arched door under its vermilion tiger framed only a bluish, smoky interior.

'Draw your chair closer, Sahib, that we may not have to raise our voices.'

'Must we be so mysterious?'

Ramdatta arranged his plump, well-shaped legs under him.

'There is no mystery, except perhaps where you are concerned. Innocence is often a shield in one's childhood, but in men it is folly. I asked you to come here so that I might, with your permission, exercise

for a little while the prerogatives of a father and extend to you a word
of warning and advice.'

The young man shrugged resignedly. 'Well?'

'Let us not beat about the bush. You are a friend of Ganpat Rai's
son Hardyal. Ganpat Rai I have always admired. Hardyal also. But
men change with the times, and time has most strangely changed
Hardyal. No, do not be offended if I venture to suggest that in
Hardyal's case the change has not been for the best.'

'The suggestion offends me, nevertheless.'

'Would that I could withdraw it! But Hardyal has fallen into the
wrong hands. He is seen everywhere with Abdul Salim, and Salim, as
you know, or should know, is under police surveillance.'

Jacques felt a stab of anxiety. 'Since when?'

'For months past. It is not secret—Salim himself knows it. But he is
a fanatic, and nothing short of a jail sentence will cure him.'

Jacques started angrily. 'He is, I believe, fully entitled to his
convictions!'

'Ah, Sahib! You talk like a child. What are Salim's convictions? He is
an obstructionist. Sooner or later the Government will lose patience
and clap him into jail, but in the meantime he is at large, he is vocal
and popular, and becomes increasingly so. Young men like Hardyal
are attracted by his teaching because it is novel. But Salim will end by
carrying all his friends off to jail with him.'

'And what, exactly, is this teaching to which you so violently
object?' Jacques spoke sarcastically, in an attempt to cover his real
concern.

The moneylender shrugged. 'You must have heard as much about it
as any one, for you see him often. You meet at the house of Ganpat
Rai, and Hardyal himself carries Salim's words of wisdom into your
home, does he not? They use your friendship as a blind. Nay! Do not
lose your temper with me, Sahib. I speak for your own good. Salim has
been warned repeatedly by the Collector himself. Yet he continues to
hold meetings in his house, he even addresses public gatherings on the
Maidan and in the bazaar. He has toured the Province with that
notorious agitator Jagnath Singh. Well, I say let him risk his own neck
if he so desires—who cares? But what right has he to involve young,
idealistic, and inexperienced men like Hardyal in these criminal
activities?'

'You use strong language, my friend!'

'I have strong feelings. You must forgive me, Sahib—I speak for us
all.'

'Speak for yourself, if you must. I fail to see where I come in.'

Stillness descended on Ramdatta, then he made a strange gesture of his hands, bringing the palms together in an attitude of prayer, and letting them fall in his lap. 'Well, then, Sahib—hear me out. Two days ago Abdul Salim was at the village of my brother-in-law. He collected the people around him and outlined to them a plan for the non-payment of their rents and taxes. In my brother-in-law's village, and indeed in my own, there are a certain number of Moslems. They are shiftless, in debt almost to a man, yet they kick and scream against paying interest. Why? Because to charge or to pay interest is contrary to their religious code. Every Hindu pays his interest, or at least accepts the responsibility even when he is unable to meet it. Well, Abdul Salim has exploited this situation to such an extent that he has succeeded in rousing, everywhere, something approaching organized revolt in the villages. The Police are worried, so are the district magistrates. Salim is poisoning the public mind against the landlords and even against the Sircar. He has succeeded so well that many Hindus have banded with Moslems in a flat refusal to meet their obligations or to work them off in labour. In some cases they have resisted lawful attempts at eviction or confiscation. And do you know what Salim tells these people? He tells them that before the English came, the land was free, tilled, and tended in common. But, says Salim, the conquering English, finding no documents or proofs of ownership, parcelled out the land as they pleased and distributed it amongst their favourite Zamindars, who hold it in perpetual ownership. It is easy, is it not, Sahib, to guess the effect of such talk on unlettered peasants? But what Salim is unable to explain is this: If the peasants will not pay their dues to the Zamindars, how are the Zamindars to pay the yearly revenues to the Government? If we moneylenders cannot collect our legal rate of interest, on what basis are we to continue making loans?'

While he talked, the sweat had started out afresh on Ramdatta's flesh and his eyes began to glow with fever. Jacques had listened attentively, less to the man's complaint, the sense of which caused him no great surprise, than to a special subterranean quality in his voice. It was a quality which he was sure had not been there earlier in the conversation, one which seemed to develop gradually like a fissure under the fluent speech. His own thoughts hidden under an air of judicious consideration, Jacques smoked in silence, turning over the possible significance of that odd, unfamiliar note. It came to him suddenly that what he'd caught was the note of fear. It is not a human note, for like a child's cry of pain or a lover's unintelligible mutter it lies quite outside the subtle inclosure of language. Jacques had heard that note before: hearing it now he was moved to a curious excitement, a sense almost of revulsion.

Ramdatta was afraid. Afraid of Abdul Salim, afraid of Hardyal!

Ramdatta the Great, the omnipotent Ramdatta, friend of the Police, privileged crony of officialdom, sumptuous, engaging old sophisticate . . . there he sat, secretly frightened out of his clever wits! To Hardyal, Jacques had observed that there is always something thrilling about a man who will not back down. The thought recurred to him now as he saw the moneylender for the first time as more than a familiar figure, more even than a symbol: saw him as that opponent against whom Abdul Salim would not, would positively never, back down.

Ramdatta broke the silence which had followed his last question.

'So now perhaps you can see, Sahib, what I mean when I insist that I speak for all of us, for you as well as for myself.'

'You mean to say that you think we're all in the same boat?'

'Can you doubt it?'

'And that Salim may attempt to capsize the whole bloody *sub cheez*?'

'It is no joking matter, Sahib.'

'For you, no—I can see that. But what I still fail to see is where Madame and I—where I specially—come into the picture, or shall we stick to the simile of the boat?'

Ramdatta gazed at him thoughtfully. 'You believe that Abdul Salim would not dare to encroach on your preserves? Does the thought reassure you?'

Jacques laughed. 'Good Lord, man! I feel under no compulsion to strike attitudes.'

'You may find yourself compelled to strike an attitude, sooner or later.'

'Against my friends?' Jacques leaned forward in the chair of state. 'Would you like to hear the truth as far as I'm concerned, Ramdatta? If my mother's half-starved coolies decided to burn down the factory tomorrow, I wouldn't lift a finger to stop them.'

The other smiled faintly. 'So Boodrie has informed me many times.' He hesitated, the smile melting into the corners of his full, childish mouth. 'I was a coolie once, in Bombay. I sweated. I starved. But I survived. It was an instructive experience, one well calculated to cure a man of any illusions he may have cherished about his fellows. I have learned that there are but few complete human beings in society, Sahib. The rest are cattle.'

The smile had vanished and from the rich brown oval of his face his eyes gazed piercingly at Jacques. 'That is my attitude, if you wish to call it one. And I repeat, Sahib, that sooner or later you will yourself be forced to assume an attitude which, in the nature of things, must be opposed to such men as Abdul Salim and Hardyal.'

'In the nature of what things, Ramdatta?'

'You are not really obtuse, Sahib.'

'I do but ask enlightenment.'

Ramdatta hesitated, then he said slowly: 'It distresses me that I should be the instrument of your enlightenment. I do not hope to be forgiven, but I have no alternative.'

Jacques cried impatiently, 'Must we talk riddles all afternoon?'

Ramdatta made no answer. He rose from the cot and reaching under it pulled out a highly decorated tin box fastened with a brass padlock. From somewhere in the folds of his clothing he produced a bunch of keys. Jacques watched him unlock the box and lay back the lid; he was reminded of his mother's japanned dispatch case with all its little compartments, the locks of hair, the letters, the pair of tiny enamelled foxes.

Ramdatta grouped among the contents of his box and lifted out a large package covered in oilskin and tied with black tape. This he opened and after a glance at the contents, laid them on Jacques' lap.

'Read them, Sahib. Take your time. There is no hurry.'

He retired to his cot, folding his legs under him, clasping his shawl across his breast. Shade lay heavy on the ground and there was a pleasant smell of cooking in the air. The peacock, struck by an athletic notion, shot suddenly upward and alighted on a neighbouring roof, where it perched motionless as the light died slowly, reluctantly, on its jewelled breast.

# 47

An hour later as Jacques rode away from the village he met the returning herds driven by children whose shrill voices pierced the dusty haze. Smoke hung in the air, life seemed to concentrate once more on the few hours of daylight which promised change and refreshment. As Jacques pulled his horse from the path of wet black snouts and tossing horns, the herdsman—a child of perhaps six or seven—smiled up at him and cried: 'Salaam, Maharaj!'

The title struck ironically on Jacques' ears. The child himself could scarcely have understood its meaning, yet he lisped it out in mimicry of his elders. Jacques pictured the infant's panic were he to pause and explain, in grown-up language, that he was no longer a Maharaj, that in fact, possessing nothing, he had become nobody. The knowledge brought a curious elation; he tried to capture it, to pin it down, but it eluded capture and he remembered how once as a boy he'd broken a clinical thermometer and the mercury, running loose between his fingers, had fascinated him by its silvery substance which seemed related more to magic than to matter.

The papers which Ramdatta had given him to read were *hundies*, or notes of hand, to the tune of uncomputed sums. The thin sheets of native paper bearing signatures in English and in Hindi—all up-to-date, businesslike and unmistakable—were proof enough to Jacques that his mother had pledged herself far beyond the limit of her resources. He thought: 'Possessions, like numbers, are infinite; they begin in a man's flesh and work outward through his clothing to every artifice of his incorrigible brain.' And he studied his own hand, his sunburnt wrist, the hard contour of his knees in their riding breeches. Were his flesh and blood his in fact? Or was his breath and the tide which pumped in his heart pledged, likewise, to Ramdatta the moneylender?

Ramdatta had explained, sonorously: 'Years ago I promised your mother that I would not reveal the truth to you. She hoped, as I did, that by the time you were grown she might have managed to pay off these obligations. There is no one whom I admire more than Madame. We have always understood each other, for we are in a remote sense, of the same *jat*. I kept my promise faithfully until today. But what can it profit Madame, or yourself, for you to remain in ignorance any longer? Should creatures like Abdul Salim succeed in wrecking my livelihood what recourse would I have but to call upon you to fulfil your obligations? Alas, this is not a new situation, Sahib. We all must live.'

Jacques listened, his voice garnering the expected, the ordinary, the dry crumbs on which all mice must feed. He wondered why he was not more surprised, why this moment came to him rather as a vague, distant memory.

'We are in the same boat, Sahib. You, however, are in a position to help yourself and by so doing to help me. In the first place because you are a Sahib, in the second place because you are a friend of Hardyal and Ganpat Rai, both of whom exercise considerable influence over Abdul Salim. Men will sometimes do for love what they would scorn to do from other motives. Not that I expect wonders—I know that Salim! He and I are old enemies. We were enemies before we were born. Yet, were he brought to realize that your fate must, in a measure, depend on mine, who shall say that he would not think twice, or even thrice?'

Jacques spoke without glancing up from the papers. 'He has threatened you, then?'

'His very existence is a threat to me.'

'But your friends the Police, what about them?'

'Yes, there is always the Police. But Salim knows that as well as I do. He has his methods, and subtle ones they are. You must remember that the Police can step in only after a situation has been created.'

'True, I was forgetting. And in the meantime your house might be burned over your head and your crops trampled into the ground.'

Ramdatta winced. 'We deal with unscrupulous men!'

'True. Salim has a determined nature. Suppose I were to approach him as you suggest, and he refused to hear me. What then?'

'It is a chance, a hope only! I know men well, I have known them to do remarkable things out of affection and chivalry. Ah, I could tell you stories!' He moved his glossy shoulders. 'But do I need to tell you? You are yourself young and full of illusions. Salim speaks well of you in public. He likes you, trusts you.'

'You hear much.'

'I hear everything!'

'So you would have me go to him and tell him of these. . . .' Jacques tapped the package on his knee. 'And say to him, "Salim, my friend! Ramdatta has me in his clutches. He can in the wink of an eye deprive me of my home, my factory, my very shoes! Stay your hand, Salim, my fire-eating friend. Do not breathe brimstone into the ears of Ramdatta, nor try to inspire courage in the breasts of his miserable victims—for by doing so, see where you will land *me*"!'

Ramdatta stared at the young man, and round them the silence seemed to settle, to thicken, as if the whole village had become conscious of something extraordinary taking place in its midst.

The moneylender said at last: 'You misunderstand me. I am not trying to blackmail you. I too have a code of friendship. Have I not for twenty years kept my word to your mother? Have I once come to her with whinings, with a single demand for what, after all, are my just dues? Come, Sahib! A little while ago you spoke scathingly of attitudes. It is not necessary that you strike one now, with me.'

When the young man remained silent he went on urgently: 'Jacques! Work with me, let us be friends! Let me serve your interests as I have always served Madame's. This war will bring wealth to many—why not to you and to me? Salim is an obstructionist, a troublemaker, a fool. He thinks that this is the moment to oppose men like myself and to force concessions from the Government. He cannot last long, but he can do much harm while he lasts. Is it not better for us to try and win him over to our side—rather, to shame or to frighten him into retreat? I don't demand that you succeed with Salim, I merely ask that you try, that you use your good offices through Ganpat Rai and Hardyal. If you fail, then no matter. We shall be no better off and no worse off than before.'

While Ramdatta was talking Jacques reflected on the familiar pattern of all accepted themes, all normal preoccupations. He replaced the *hundie*s in their oilskin cover, and rising, flung the package on the cot beside Ramdatta, who looked up at him eagerly, like a child.

'Well, Sahib?'

'No.'

'Ah, come! That is sheer foolishness.'

Jacques stood under the flickering shadows of the mango leaves and his stillness was matched by that of Ramdatta's son, who appeared in the doorway and watched them with big, inquiring eyes.

'Sahib,' Ramdatta repeated in a voice which had lost most of its resonance.

Jacques glanced at the boy. 'Tell them to fetch my horse.'

He turned to Ramdatta. 'Salim is your enemy, not mine. As for this other affair. . . .' He shrugged. 'It has rested in your hands for a long time. The decision is yours. I leave it to you.'

The man rose in agitation. 'Then give me your word that you will never tell Madame! It would blacken my face before her were she to know that I have spoken of this to you.'

Jacques looked at him curiously. 'For a man of substance you are full of quaint humours! Why should I tell my mother? What has this matter—any of it—to do with me?'

He left his horse at the stables and walked round the end of the house to the garden where he found his mother walking with Father Sebastien. Madame leaned on a stick; she still limped slightly from her injury, but it was with eagerness, almost with anxiety, that she greeted her son. 'It has been so hot, and you were gone for ages.'

He had taken off his hat and the brown hair clung to his head, giving him for a moment, in that afternoon glow which holds all the humid tints of evening, an air of something bronze and permanent. His beauty troubled the priest, who looked away as some men look away when confronted by just this conjunction of youth and perfection in their own sex.

'I missed you,' said Madame, her eyes fixed upon him.

Jacques said nothing.

# 48

A late October somnolence hung above the Terai jungle; once in a while the hint of a breeze strayed down from the mountains, themselves invisible in the haze, and overhead wheeled a few kites, alternately black and brilliant in the sun. The Government rest-house stood in the shade of a sal grove that did little to soften the glare which rose off the empty ravine a few hundred yards away. Beyond the ravine stretched a level plain of plumed grass and beyond that again the jungle and the farther crouching forms of the lower hills.

A woodpecker was hammering in an old stump and green pigeons kept up a ceaseless whistling in the sal trees. Bertie Wood, lying in one of the Government's long veranda chairs, stared from the dazzling stones of the ravine to the wheeling kites, and reflected that here was an air, a place, which made speculation difficult but which with every breath and every mutation of light and shadow, stirred afresh the slow pain of realization.

Pale, inert from the heat, she found herself at the mercy of her own discontent, which had settled like a sullen fever in her bones. Part of the pathos of intelligence is its impotence before such moods, and as she listened to the subtle overture which in India heralds the changing hour, she thought bitterly: 'Every note of the pigeons' whistle, every answer from the kites, the whisper of wind in the grass, and the savage dance of sunlight on stones, used to mean something—once! Even as late as yesterday they meant something. Now they don't. My mind and heart are closed up tight like an idiot's.'

Her features had the drawn look of a child who has cried itself to sleep, and this thought occurred to John Macbeth as he stepped from a room farther down the veranda and came towards her. Bertie heard him and turned her head, meeting his gaze with the false directness which he had learned to interpret.

'Pat and I are taking a stroll. Coming?'

'In this heat?'

'It will cool off. We'll take the elephant if you like.'

She shuddered. 'God no! I had enough of the elephant yesterday. So did Diana.'

Macbeth leaned against the veranda pillar. He looked cool and comfortable in khaki shirt and shorts, the little fringed tassels of his garters showing under the ribbed tops of his stockings. Sinewy, slender, he had at such moments a stillness which belied a capacity for sudden unerring movement. Bertie's gaze rested on him with a sort of gratitude for his appearance, for his calm.

She said: 'I'll go if you really want me to.'

'Better not. Pat says Diana won't move. She's lying down, full of aspirin and moans. Hadn't you better do the same?'

'Moan?'

'I meant, take some aspirin.'

'No, I'll just lie here and wait for you.'

'That's nice. I'll remember it.'

She looked away. 'I may go for a little walk, later.'

'It's quite jungly, but there's a good path which takes you towards that little village, we saw yesterday. It's shady most of the way.'

'Don't worry, old boy. I'm all right.'

'Honestly?'

'Honestly.'

He came close and bent over her. 'Bertie!'

She caught the clean smell of his clothes and his flesh, and when she lifted her hand to touch him he took it and pressed his lips to the palm. 'Bertie,' he murmured. 'Bertie, Bertie!'

There was a disturbance down the veranda and a young man appeared, walking clumsily on tiptoe. 'Hallo!' he exclaimed. 'Bertie down and out, too?'

'It must have been that shandygaff after lunch, yesterday,' said Macbeth. 'That, and the sun.'

Captain Harding shook his head. 'Diana has her own theory. In the first place it isn't her fault, in the second place it's mine. But this time I share the blame with that damned *hathi*. She says it had a motion like a Messagerie Maritime steamer during a storm in the Bay of Biscay. Never again will she ride a pad elephant, never!'

A crew of orderlies and gunbearers appeared round a corner of the house, and Macbeth glanced at Bertie. 'Sure you won't come, after all?'

She shook her head, and Captain Harding nodded approval. 'If I wasn't sure that this time next week my Sikhs and I will be en route in quest of different game, I'd stay and bear you company.'

Bertie watched them stride away across the compound followed by their retinue. They disappeared over the edge of the ravine; then she saw them again, the sunlight leaping off their gun barrels. As the sound of their feet died away she became aware once more of the recurring diminuendo of the afternoon and felt, on her face, a breath from the invisible snows.

'Bertie, are you there?'

Bertie rose and walked down the veranda to the Hardings' room. A dark-haired girl lay on one of the beds. She opened her eyes as Bertie came in. 'I suppose I should have gone with Pat. There is so little time left, and I hate to be unsporting.'

'You're not in the least unsporting,' said Bertie. She sat on the edge of the bed and gazed at its occupant. 'Feeling better?'

The other stared at her with troubled eyes. 'You, know, it wasn't the heat that upset me. It wasn't the shandy either, nor the elephant.'

'I understand. It's the baby.'

'No.'

Bertie waited, She had met the Hardings a month before at Gambul, where Captain Harding was spending his leave before going to France with his regiment. It had been Macbeth's idea that they come to Lal Bagh together for a few days' shooting, for he knew that the soldier was an ardent sportsman. 'Hardly the season for good shooting—grass too high, foliage too thick, sun too hot! But it's all you'll get for some time.'

Diana went on: 'It's the war. I try not to think about it or about Pat going, but there it is, all the time. When I wake up and when I go to sleep, whenever I start to feel happy.' She stirred uneasily. 'I'm a coward. Pat would hate to hear me talk like this, he'd hate me to have such thoughts.'

Bertie touched the dark hair gently, but found nothing to say. The other continued: 'There are actually times what I catch myself wishing that there was something the matter with Pat, that he might have a game leg or something, so he'd be unfit for active service.' She looked at the girl beside her. 'That's sinking pretty low, isn't it?'

'I think I understand.'

'Well, there's nothing the matter with him. He's young and strong and fit. He's exactly what they want.'

Both were silent, listening to the faint crepitations of the house, to the voices of the pigeons outside. Both felt the presence of an irrelevant, almost an irresponsible peace, and it was Diana who remarked:

'When I'm able to keep the thought of war out of my mind for just a minute, everything that used to be, everything warm and friendly, everything familiar, comes back. Like the uninterrupted sound of those birds, who have been singing for hundreds of years . . . singing on the same note, among the same kind of trees. Then it seems as if nothing could happen to interrupt my life, that it is still here—the past and the future—the hope . . . the hope . . . the hope of all known things going on quietly until one dies as one has a right to die, as all gentle things die. Although at such times one doesn't even think of dying.'

'Don't think of it now.'

'I'm Irish, you know. That means I'm full of presentiment.'

'And imagination!' Bertie tried to sound rallying.

'And hate, I'm full of hate. You don't have to be Irish to hate, you just have to be a woman. Pat doesn't hate the Germans. He just wants to kill them without making too much mess. It's left to me to hate them.'

Bertie thought of her uncle, who had left India six weeks before with his Indian regiment. Diana was staring at her. 'Yesterday, out there in the sun, in the jungle, whenever I looked at you I was conscious of your vitality, your happiness. You looked as if you expected joy to fall from every thorn tree or to come stepping from behind every tuft of grass. And I remembered that it was only a little while ago that I used to feel the same.'

Bertie said impulsively: 'You will, again!'

'No, it won't be quite the same. Nothing will ever be quite the same for any of us.'

Bertie left her, and went back to her own room. She found her leather writing-case and drew out Jacques' last letter which had come the evening before, brought with the three-day-old newspaper and other letters, by runner from the post office at the nearest railway junction. Macbeth, glancing at the envelope, had handed it to her without comment, and she had carried it to her own room to read. She stayed there a long time, and when she emerged at last he asked no questions, nor did he look at her. It dawned on her then that he had learned to dread Jacques' letters almost as much as she was learning to dread them herself.

She returned to the veranda. The sun was draining towards the farther grasses; it bathed the ravine in a flood of greying light beyond which the tallest plumes rose in a host of spears. Bertie sat down and reread Jacques' letter. He wrote briefly, almost brutally, of his financial predicament, and as she read, Bertie understood something of the savage spirit in which he had forced himself to state the bleak truth.

'God knows when, if ever, we shall be able to marry. You will suggest, as you have before, that we live off your income 'until' and 'unless.' If it were merely a question of pride I wouldn't hesitate, for pride in money matters is the attribute of *bania*s and to my sorrow, and perhaps also to yours, I am not and never will be a *bania*. However, until I have brought some sort of order into my life I cannot—in fact I will not—ask you to share it. Nor can I ask you to go on forever waiting and waiting for something to happen. Neither of us asked for this. Neither of us has done anything to deserve it. It all began a long time ago, before we were born; in a way it's like this bloody war. Someone was planning it while we were innocent and happy. But what's the use? There you are and here am I . . . and I suppose that the priests and the politicians, the bunglers and the *bania*s, all have their explanations. You and I just don't count.'

Bertie did not finish the letter. She laid it on the arm of her chair and sat staring before her. The flashing light ignited, it seemed, an equivalent fire in her veins. Far away stood the little dark hills and behind them she thought she glimpsed the mountains tipped with ice, but it must have been her imagination, for as she stared the sun gathered itself together and struck her between the eyes, so there were no longer mountains, nor the cool breath of mountains, but instead the lesser figures of malevolent hills beyond the harsh plain. India! The name held everything that had been important in her life; it had taken her up in its dark hand, caressed her, enchanted her. It had exacted from her every impulse of fervour and generosity and she scarcely knew when the loving grasp relaxed, when her eyes first began to clear of their childish dream, when the hills ceased to be miracles and became, instead, beasts which stalked her along the horizon. She thought of yesterday before Jacques' letter had reached her, and a line from the Persian poet recurred to her: 'Tomorrow I may be, myself, with yesterday's seven thousand years.' A trite sentiment, but truth and triteness seem always to be one and the same thing.

Perhaps what burned and blistered more than anything was the knowledge that what had happened to her and to Jacques was an ancient story; they had simply not been able to muster sufficient force or sufficient originality to evade a commonplace fate. She had believed that because one lived in a different country, one's life could be different too, that it could approach nearer to the dream, the vision.

Yesterday, hunting cheetul from the back of an elephant, the will to happiness, like the will to beauty, had palmed itself off on her as the real thing. She felt like a goddess as she stared down at the tall grass which waved above the elephant's knees, and watched a covey of peafowl scuttling with outstretched necks. The elephant had carried them past small sandy openings covered with the tracks of wild pig; it stopped, and with its trunk plucked a green bough with which to fan away the flies, while its passengers climbed down to examine the pugs of a tiger in the soft sand. Then from out of the sal jungle crashed a cheetul herd and fled like ghosts under a splitting volley which left one of them kicking and twisting in the grass. Life, thought Bertie, has its special, its personal direction—there could be no other; and her happiness faltered as she stared for a moment at the creature's brilliant, dying eyes.

# 49

There was still an hour before sundown as Bertie crossed the compound to the path Macbeth had indicated. She heard a shot in the distance and decided that by skirting the little village she might waylay the hunters on their way home. The light in which she walked was no longer perpendicular; it lay on acres of plumes of grass or struck a tentative note on a twig, a leaf, a stone. The pigeons had fallen silent at last; the woodpecker uttered its terse note and darted down the path before her, leaving a trail of blue. She heard something pad away into the brush on the other side of the trees, and a slight qualm assailed her. Life was everywhere, she felt its breath, she was aware of its unseen eye, and for a moment she thought she heard it talking to itself under the crisp sound of her own feet among the dry leaves.

The peace of the hour and of her surroundings struck her even more forcibly than it had done a little while ago in the bungalow, for the indifference of nature had never seemed more irrelevant in face of human realities. It spumed up from the earth, it whistled with the pigeons, it was implicit in the paw which had left its seal in the mud beside the drinking-pool. It was a mood, too, which dwelt in the flimsy huts of the villagers and which keyed and coloured their flimsy lives. Certainly its indifference bore little resemblance to the mood of her own world, stumbling towards eclipse and spitting blood at every step. One does not require the approach of death to see pass before one's eyes a retinue of departed days; one needs only to come to the end of a vital experience, and with this confession Bertie repudiated, not her private universe, but this other, this monstrous, terrestrial indifference.

Before her the path stretched in a stream of golden dust and presently she heard goat-bells and caught a glimpse of a woman striding through the grass, carrying an earthen pitcher on her head. The village was out of sight, but now the path widened and the land on either side had a cleared look. The sun struck fire from something beyond the frieze of sal and cactus, and Bertie saw a temple so small that a child might have built it. It seemed deserted and for a moment she wondered whether some shy god—perhaps the genial Ganesh himself—had melted into the jungle at her approach.

Then she saw him, or rather his image. Made of stone painted a deathly white, his red hair plastered with cow dung, he sat cross-legged under a baobab tree, the shadows playing over his stony nakedness. At his back the trunk of the baobab hung in smooth pschydermic golds, like the sheltering knees of a vaguer, vaster deity. Bertie pushed aside the intervening leaves and stepped to the edge of the clearing. No one challenged her and for a long time she stared at the stone god, motionless under the caressing shadows. A chain round his loins supported a sort of tray, and on this reposed the godly genitals amidst an offering of jungle fronds and flowers. The silence was complete, but as she stood there Bertie imagined that the shadows whispered together in their evening dance over the god's breast and shoulders. The fantasy lingering in her mind inspired wonder as his painted eyelids opened and he stared back at her with drugged and crimson eyes. Fantasy completing itself, the stone came to life and rising to its feet made a rush towards her.

Bertie turned and fled through the screening leaves to the path. Light-headed, she flew down its glistening channel and saw her cousin walking towards her. Macbeth stopped and held out his arms and she flung herself on his breast, clinging to him like a creature distraught. 'Hold me . . . hold me . . . hold me.'

'Bertie, what on earth!'

'Don't let me go, don't ever let me go!'

He stared at the path stretching innocently before him. Somewhere along its empty length a woodpecker hammered, then ceased. Could that sudden sound have frightened her?

'Bertie, what is it? What happened?'

But she clung, shivering and muttering incoherently, and he led her to a patch of grass. There he sat, drawing her into his arms. He stroked away the hair which had fallen across her eyes and his own hand trembled against her warm skin.

'Tell me, Bertie, tell me.'

She tried to explain in hysterical sentences, and presently the light broke on Macbeth. 'Oh, good Lord, that *saddhu*! I forgot all about him. He's supposed to be mad, so the villagers keep him tied up to his tree. But he's quite harmless. . . .'

Bertie was not listening, and presently, frightened himself by this hysteria, Macbeth laid her down on the grass and leaned over her, cradling her head on his arm.

'Don't let me go. Swear that you will never let me go.'

'I swear I shall never let you go.'

She opened her eyes and he saw himself reflected there, leaning down as though to drink. 'Bertie. . . .'

She lifted her arms, drawing him down to her breast.

# 50

As Madame St Remy stepped from the church door into the light of the church compound she felt that she left behind her, like a forgotten cloak, the charmed oblivion of the past hour. All the emergencies of her life seemed to wait for her in the brighter air, already tinctured by winter. Behind her rose the voice of Father Sebastien's native choir practising a Christmas hymn, and in Madame's mind there lingered a prayer which she had just uttered, a prayer for the return of peace to the world. She felt the weight of the unanswered appeal lie heavy on her heart, for the Battle of Ypres was just ending, but not the war. Yet here in the oleander-bordered compound was peace indeed. Difficult to believe that its grace paused on the fringes of the land, difficult to acknowledge that upon all the earth those nasal voices were not singing 'Noel, Noel!' to the surging optimism of the church organ.

Father Sebastien emerged from the vestry. 'Shall I send for your carriage, Madame?'

'It is waiting for me at the gate.'

'Then I will walk there with you.'

As they fell into step she said: 'Jacques has gone to Mrs Lyttleton's funeral. They tell me she desired to be buried in her garden, near her husband and child.'

He nodded. 'I called at her house, out of respect. I found her servants weeping.'

Madame said grudgingly: 'No doubt she had her virtues, but it would be hypocrisy to pretend that I care one way or another.' When he remained silent she exclaimed: 'All I care about is Jacques! He has been hurt enough. If her death is to hurt him more, then I shall find it harder than ever to forgive her.'

He said in a low voice: 'Ah, Madame, let the dead past bury its dead. She can do you no further injury, nor you her. And as for Jacques, you have news which will, I imagine, divert something from his sorrow for Mrs Lyttleton.'

'I know, I know! I have thought of little else, and all day I have felt like a coward, all day since I read the announcement of Bertie's marriage in the *Pioneer* and knew that Jacques had not yet seen it. Why must these things always fall to a mother's lot? No, I don't mean that. I'm glad, happy that it should be my task to have to tell him, and to be with him when he learns of it. But I dread it just the same.' Her eyes hardened. 'One would have supposed that people who call themselves civilized might have found a civilized method of conveying such news. Why did Bertie not write to Jacques himself to tell him about her marriage? Why didn't Macbeth write?'

'It was Jacques who asked to be released from his engagement,' the priest reminded her, gently. 'Under the circumstances one can hardly blame the Macbeths.' When she said nothing, he asked: 'Jacques has never explained to you, has he, why the engagement was broken?'

'Never,' said Madame bitterly. 'Never! He explains nothing. He asked me not to speak of it, and naturally I have respected his wish. But I, his own mother, am told nothing, nothing.'

As she bade the priest goodbye and drove away she felt more than ever conscious of a fading of that solemn charm which never failed her in the house of her God. Faced, now, with a return to her own house, foreboding descended on her. The thought of meeting her son, a thought which used to bring its special delight and anticipation, brought instead the pang of some mysteriously acquired bruise. A month had passed since the day when he came to her with the news of his broken engagement, and remembrance of that scene was still vivid. She had thrown her arms around him, and he stood in the circle, submitting but not responding to her embrace.

'Jacques, my poor child! She has deserted you.'

He looked at her then and through the blur of her own tears she saw that his eyes were hard and clean as stones. Gently, he freed himself and led her to a chair, and in a voice which somehow matched his eyes he said: 'Bertie has not deserted me. It is I who have deserted her. Please understand this, then promise me that you will never speak of it again.'

For Madame the weeks had passed in an atmosphere of bewilderment and incredulity. Every morning Jacques rode to the factory and stayed until afternoon; then he changed his clothes and bicycled to Hardyal's house where he played tennis and often stayed for dinner. It seemed as if his whole nature had suffered some catastrophic change, it had become elusive, elliptical, at no point could she grasp it. He no longer offered to kiss her nor did he display any more the charming little attentions which she had learned to expect from him. When, rather timidly, she tried to force them upon him he submitted with averted eyes.

'One would suppose,' she confided bitterly to Father Sebastien, 'one would suppose that it was all my fault!'

'Give him time,' urged the priest. 'He is young and he has suffered. Give him time and he will come back to you.'

Madame did not voice the thought which sprang into her mind: '*You* gave him time, but he has never come back to you!'

As confusion increased, hope diminished; unable, now, to win a word or a glance of tenderness from him she began to brood on her wrongs, to recall with tears the hundred and one griefs and sacrifices which she had endured for his sake. Right was on her side, God was on her side, and if the world only knew, the world itself would be on her side. This exercise in self-pity assumed a curiously familiar pattern, but Madame's subjective intelligence barred her from the recognition that here was an experience almost identical with one she had suffered years before on discovering that Auguste no longer loved her. What followed was to follow inevitably the lines laid down for it. Denied possession, her vitality sought its only expression, and she dwelt with a sweet and secret satisfaction on Jacques' physical and economic handicap. She felt increasingly secure in the knowledge that she had lost her two most formidable rivals, Bertie, and at last and forever—

Mrs Lyttleton.

The carriage stopped and she got out, making her way slowly up the steps to the veranda. It was not yet dusk and the lamps had not been lighted. She heard her servants talking as they went about their evening duties, and the sound of her carriage as it rolled across the compound towards the stables. At the door of the drawing-room Madame paused. The room was empty, vagrant flickers of light touched familiar objects—the ormolu clock, a bowl of flowers, the gilt frame of her husband's portrait. She stared round her, affected by the stillness and the air of expectancy which hangs about an empty room. Then the bead curtains moved and Jacques appeared, his figure in its white suit slender as a shaft before her. They stared at one another, then Madame inquired gently: 'When did you get back, my dear?'

'An hour ago.' His voice was colourless.

'Were there many people at the funeral?'

'Just her friends.'

'You, Hardyal, Ganpat Rai. . . . '

'Ganpat Rai has not returned from Agra.'

It might have been the conversation of mere acquaintances. Madame removed her hat, stabbed the hatpins through the crown, and laid it with her gloves on a chair. Both continued to stand in the curious indecision which beset them, nowadays, when they found themselves together. She said, presently: 'I wonder what will happen to her property. She had no relatives that one ever heard of, unless there are some in England.'

'Ganpat Rai handled her affairs, and I understand that there are cousins in England.'

His voice sounded absent-minded, and she asked, with a tentative smile: 'Tell me, Jacques, would it have pleased you if I'd gone with you to Mrs Lyttleton's funeral?'

'I think it might have amused Mrs Lyttleton, could she have known!'

Madame flushed. 'So, in spite of your expressed disbelief in such matters, it did occur to you that Mrs Lyttleton *might* know. . . .'

He shrugged. 'She was always so much alive when she lived, I now find it difficult to believe that she is dead.'

'Nevertheless, she is dead.'

'Yes.' He stood at a little distance, the oval of his face somewhat darker than the rest of him, his wounded hand in his pocket. There was something apparitional about him, and Madame's heart beat with a sudden frenzy. 'She is dead, Jacques, dead! She has gone out of your life, as completely as though she had never come into it.'

He shook his head. 'No, for I shall never forget her. Nor shall I ever feel my conscience to be clear again.'

She started. 'Your conscience!'

'That I should have neglected her in the end . . . that I should have listened . . . believed ill of her . . . allowed myself to be persuaded.'

Madame St Remy controlled her emotion with a visible effort.

'So, both the women you professed so to love have left you!'

He made no reply. A servant came into the room carrying a lamp and hung it on its ornamental bracket against the wall, then withdrew. Silence, that immeasurable silence which she knew of old, deepened between them. Madame clenched her hands. 'Jacques there is something I have to say to you. . . . You must find out sometime, and though it hurts me. . . .'

He interrupted calmly: 'If you are trying to tell me about Bertie's marriage, she wrote and told me about it, herself, two days ago.'

Madame felt, flow back on her, all the heat and exaltation of this prepared moment. 'She told you? You know? And you said nothing to me?'

'What did you expect me to say?'

'I would expect you to behave like a human being . . .'. She struggled to repress a detestable shrillness. 'I would expect you to show a decent indignation . . . feeling . . .'

'If you were looking forward to telling me, yourself, then I'm sorry I deprived you of the opportunity.'

Her passion flared into fury. 'Mon Dieu! You speak to me in such a tone? You, who have squandered your affections and are now paying for it. . . . Bankrupt in your love, you turn against me, your own mother?'

He looked at her steadily. 'Must we use the language of banias, Maman? If so, have you ever considered what might happen were Ramdatta to take it into his head to press for payment of his bills?'

Madame grasped the back of a chair. 'Ramdatta! What do you mean?'

Jacques hesitated, then in a few curt sentences told her of his interview with the moneylender more than a month ago. He felt a vague astonishment at the sound of his own voice, but was powerless to check himself; the things were there, they uttered themselves. Inside him all was darkness, a continent obscured by a new climate. He finished at last, coldly: 'And that is why I broke my engagement with Bertie. I might have asked her to share my poverty, but you'd scarcely expect her to share my penury?'

Madame felt crumble within her the fantastic structure which she had been twenty-five years in building. She broke into breathless explanations while he stood impassively before her: Some day the factory would take a new lease on life. Indigo would come back as it had come back in the past. And after all, had she not been right? The war was not her responsibility—God knew how long and how passionately she had prayed for its end. But war had come and with it a renewed demand for indigo. Ah, could she but find a few paltry thousands of rupees she would put the factory back on its feet! At the end of the year Ramdatta would be paid back. While she talked, eagerly and at times incoherently, Jacques stared at the floor. When she paused for breath and he made no move to speak, to comfort her, she cried in despair: 'Whatever I did, I did for your sake! If I made mistakes they were no worse than any you might have made in my place. One cannot read the future, one cannot give up just because circumstances are temporarily against one. And what would you have had me do? Let the factory go? Sell the property? What would we have lived on? If I've kept the truth from you all this time it was not because I was ashamed. It was because I wanted to save you anxiety.'

'You should have told me when I left school and came home to work for you.'

'And what could you have done that I was unable to do?'

'At least I would have known where I stood. I would not have become engaged to Bertie.'

'Ah!' Her voice was charged with bitterness. 'Bertie! Because Bertie has shown that she has not the strength of character to share your misfortune, you blame me?'

He replied in a gentler voice: 'No, I don't blame you.'

She stammered: 'Oh, Jacques, if you would return to God. . . .'

'Let us not speak of that, Maman. I realize how fortunate you are in your faith. I understand how people can be persuaded into any belief. Perhaps to be constituted as I am is a sign of stupidity; I don't know, I can't be sure of anything any more.'

'You would live on air,' she retorted angrily. 'You are like your father. He, too, despised *banias*. He thought money was mean and vulgar. He gave up his wife, his children, his church, everything, because he acquired instead a pride in what he was pleased to call his free intelligence.'

'You would prefer that I give up everything even before I have attained it, then?' He turned to look at her and she saw how pale he seemed, how remote. 'Sometimes it seems as though my father's problem and mine are the same.'

At a loss, she hesitated, and he went on: 'You have explained that he hated meanness and vulgarity. Perhaps his hatred taught him how little choice a man has, and he chose the little for whatever it was worth to him. Well, I choose it too, but for myself only. It is far too meagre to ask someone I love to share it with me.' When she remained silent he added: 'You are quite right . . . the women whom I so professed to love have left me. You should now be quite content.'

'Do you realize to whom you are speaking?'

'I know very well that I am not speaking to Mrs Lyttleton or to Bertie.'

'Ah, yes, with them you would use a very different tone!'

He murmured distractedly: 'One loves . . . one loves . . . irresponsibly. It's the only love. I can't explain and you cannot understand. Let us not discuss it.'

'I shall discuss it!' The passion which had been generating in her breast broke free at last; her face had a distorted, sexless look. 'I shall discuss it! You cannot deceive me, it has never been in your power to deceive me, in these matters which you now say you cannot explain and that I cannot understand. I understand very well. You already know that your father was unfaithful to me with Mrs Lyttleton. Perhaps you do not know that he was her lover before you were born. Ah, you did not know that! You cannot believe it! Well, it is true. Before you were born. And I think that in his diseased mind he formed some hideous notion that you were in a sense—ah, in what a sense!— his and Mrs Lyttleton's child. They had their way, but I was resolved that their way would stop short of my children. Gisele's case was easy, she was naturally mild and virtuous. You were not, you never have been. When Auguste died Mrs Lyttleton tried to appropriate you as she had appropriated him. Perhaps she shared his monstrous idea that you were, in that sense, her child too. She did her utmost to make you so, but she reckoned without your true mother. And when I saw Bertie that first time in Gambul I saw in her something of the look of Mrs Lyttleton. They had that same air, that frightful pride of the English, that sinister force which makes them believe that there is nothing they may not appropriate if they so desire! And Bertie, your loyal and beautiful Bertie, coming here to stay under my roof when you were both hardly more than children. Do you imagine that I was blind to what went on? Do you think that I was ever taken in by your cleverness and by the complicity of the servants?'

He said harshly: 'Then why did you not interfere? It was your chance . . . we were young, what could we have done?'

'I refrained because I loved you. I loved you more than any stranger could have loved you. I wanted you to trust me, I wanted you to feel that I trusted you. It seems that I was mistaken. And Bertie . . . ah! Bertie. . . . In the years after Mrs Macbeth ran away from her dolt of a husband, what sort of life did Bertie live, unchaperoned, with her uncle and cousin? Your father had taught me to be suspicious—nothing that has happened has gone unobserved by me. One loves irresponsibly . . . what a delightful idea! But not always, not always.'

The breathless sentences came to an end and in the silence which followed, it seemed as if the servants, the whole house, must be waiting tensely for what was to come. Outside, dusk had fallen; it crept into the room, but its freshness had no power over their human fever.

Madame said in a calmer voice: 'Let us not talk of love or understanding since you seem to have so little need of either. Let us confine ourselves to more practical matters. You are still my son, though no doubt you consider yourself to be fully a man. You scorn a man's natural responsibilities, and it does seem rather as if they, in a manner of speaking, scorn you.'

She broke off, distracted by his silence, by his almost spectral stillness. He had remained like this throughout the strange interview, unconscious of the clock's faint strokes. Madame waited for him to speak, to move, and when he continued to stand motionless she was taken by a storm of shivering. 'Jacques, Jacques, forgive me!' She held out her arms. 'This is fantastic. . . . Don't look like that . . . don't stand there like that, like a ghost! My dear, my son. . . .'

He made no move towards her, and, denied the impetus which such a move would have invited, she gazed at him with a sort of terror.

'You cannot treat me like this, you cannot!'

His figure against the glinting beads which, years ago, Gisele had threaded on linen cords, blurred and melted under Madame's eyes. When her vision cleared again he had gone, and the bead curtains trembled slightly, giving off little spurts of colour and light, their faint music the only sound in the room.

# 51

'I hope,' said Abdul Salim, 'that your father will not be angry with me when he learns that I have taken you to Berari to hear a political speech!'

Hardyal was amused by his friend's misgivings; the fiery Mohammedan cared so little, as a rule, for another man's anger.

'Abdul Salim, must I remind you that I am no longer a child? Besides, Father has too much affection for you to be angry.'

'He has, however, little affection for Jagnath Singh.'

'You think, then, that there might be a row over this speech?'

Salim hesitated. 'I understand that he has obtained permission from the magistrate, Mr Sheldon, who is one of the most liberal of our Civil

Servants. But one can never be sure even with the best of them . . . nor,' and he laughed, 'nor can one always be sure with Jagnath! Government is now embarked on a policy of forgive and forget. The loyal response of the Princes and of our rich industrialists has rather gone to the Government's collective head. It feels that it can afford to be lenient with men like Jagnath, the Ali brothers, and the rest—not to mention such insignificant fry as myself.'

There was nothing insignificant in Salim's appearance; tall, rugged, with an iron grey beard, he looked more like a distinguished soldier than like a struggling pleader of the lower court. Both men wore native dress. They had a second-class compartment to themselves and reclined on a long leather-covered bunk, smoking and watching the shadow of the train hurtle alongside. The green plain unfolded like a carpet, villages and mango groves loomed and faded, camels grazed, and children capered derisively.

Hardyal was glad to be with Salim, glad to lose himself for a little while in the Mohammedan's restless existence which seemed so impersonal, so divorced from everything that was self-centred and stale. They were on their way to Berari, a city twice the size of Amritpore and a day's journey distant, where they were to hear Salim's friend Jagnath Singh discuss the Government's recruitment policy for the Indian Army. Jagnath Singh was a barrister of great ability and an old enemy of the Raj. He had in the past served several terms in jail, but remained uncompromising, and it was largely due to the Government's recent policy of conciliation that he was not now languishing in prison. Salim spoke of the man with admiration, even with veneration. 'The truth is, Government would give much to have Jagnath's support of the war effort. They have done everything except offer him bribes. They would welcome, in him, recreance which they condemn in one of their own skin! Now, because their existence as Englishmen is threatened by Germans, they demand that an Indian forthwith rush to the English side. In other words, Jagnath Singh must conduct himself like an English patriot—after he has three times been sent to jail for preaching English logic to the English.'

They talked of politics, of the war, and their conversation seemed strangely at variance with the traditional, peaceful landscape which unrolled before their eyes. Presently, Salim asked why Hardyal had not asked Jacques to accompany them, but Hardyal shook his head.

'You know that Berari is Macbeth's station. It would have been embarrassing, should they have met.'

Salim agreed, then added impatiently: 'These intimacies bore me! Macbeth has married the charming Bertie. Jacques, I expect, will eventually marry someone else. The world is full of white women dying for someone to marry them. What does it matter? There are more important things in life. You know, there is in your Jacques a disillusionment which I cannot understand.' He went on quickly: 'I do not understand, nor do I condone. He refuses responsibility. He has denied his religion, he declares that he has passed beyond persuasion. What now? I tell you, he is an example of the dry rot which has infected the European spirit.'

Hardyal said sadly: 'It is what he believes, himself.'

'Yet these are the people who profess superiority! Allah! But I feel sorry for Jacques. He, at least, has honesty. He knows.'

'Yes,' Hardyal repeated. 'He knows.'

'Poor boy! Did he not even have a chance to sleep with his lovely Bertie? Ah, to know, now, that his friend is in possession. That must be painful, it must be unbearable. But they are a disorderly lot, these English and French. Unable to manage their own lives, they turn on each other. Let them bleed to death, who cares?'

Hardyal stared out of the window. The train was passing a big *jheel*, glassy under the sun, and as the engine sang its hollow song, birds rose, clamouring and glittering, into the air. Only the *sarus* remained motionless, studying their black-and-white images in the water.

Presently, Salim drowsed and Hardyal turned to his own reflections. He was coming closer and closer towards sharing Salim's ideas and attitudes, and the knowledge brought him a peculiar thrill, half fear and half surprise at himself. He knew that this impulse must have resided in him for a long time, that it had been growing silently, unobtrusively, like some tough and fluid sea-plant. Nevertheless love, which Mrs Lyttleton had once said transcended politics, still held him faithful to the few whom he knew well. It held him faithful to her memory, faithful to the spirit which he had seen in her. But now the great war had swamped individual concepts, it made personal considerations appear as mean and slight, it thrust past glories into a background lighted only a little by nostalgia; it imposed distance, like a no-man's-land of dreams, between generation and generation. Perhaps he should have gone back to England and finished his education, then gone into English service, or studied for the Bar as his father had wished him to do. Instead, he had chosen his own way, in his own country, among his own people. What troubled him now was the suspicion that the choice had not been his own, but that it had been forced upon him by accident, and that he had reacted to the accident by striking an attitude at once defensive and defiant. Mrs Lyttleton argued as women argue but the bitter truth remained: love never has and never will transcend politics . . . not until politics have broken down the barriers which transcend love.

He began to think about Mrs Lyttleton. Like all Indians, he was profoundly affected by death because he saw it as void and expressionless. Coming home after her funeral he had gone to his piano, and, moved to pay her some secret tribute, he sat down and tried to play. But his talent proved too small for his emotion. What was the use? Getting up, he stood frowning at the keyboard and a song began to run in his head, a tune half remembered: he thought of the Fair at Amritpore and the garden party at his father's house, of Mrs Lyttleton asking him for Aubrey Wall's letter. There were Chinese lanterns hanging in the trees and the musicians had played their *sitars* and rice-bowl drums, and one had sung:

> Love with his hand shall part the sacred water
> And revive you with showers from his hair!

That night, Jacques' servant Hanif had been stoned to death, and now Mrs Lyttleton, herself, was no more. Hardyal understood at last why he mourned for her: she had been part of his innocence, part of vanished time.

In a few weeks he would be married. He had not seen his prospective bride, but prayers and purifications and the terrific excitement of all his female relatives, were beginning to affect him. Day and night the house trembled with preparations, with snatches of song, laughter suddenly stifled, sibilant whispers, jinglings, tinklings, heady scents. Every day there arrived gifts and deputations, and strange circulars from medical firms in Calcutta and Bombay, documents offering marvellous elixirs for the restoration or promotion of virility. Hardyal laughed when he read them, but his blood was already stirring, a strangeness opened before his eyes, and he knew that his life would no longer be what it had been.

The train jolted over a level-crossing and he sighed, glancing at his bare forearm where it rested on the sill. Suddenly he wised that his grandmother had lived to see his marriage and to receive his first-born son into her arms. His son! Strange that at this moment the woman who must bear that son was unknown to him as a creature of flesh and blood, one he would hold in his arms, one whose hair would lie warm as woodsmoke round his throat. He had been told that she was lovely; he knew that she was young, much younger than himself. He was far from ignorant in matters of sex, for, as he had told Jacques, he had not denied himself the essential experience. But the idea of marriage with its august ramifications had seemed remote enough. He knew that it would be decisive, that it would seal him away, forever, from his childhood. Happiness! He closed his eyes and at once the mysterious image of his wife appeared under his eyelids. Motionless, he waited, feeling her presence increase, feeling her breath against his face, her breath scented with cardamoms as he had once smelled them on a woman's breath a year ago at Allahabad. He saw the shape of her face with the little red tikka between her brows, the thin arch of her nostril with its turquoise stud, the unbearable slow lifting of her lashes under his own.

He opened his eyes to find Abdul Salim watching him with friendly amusement. 'Wake up! We shall be in Berari in a little while.'

# 52

Berari platform was large and imposingly modern; there were no monkeys and very few beggars, and the red turbans of the police bobbed like flowers among the drab and dust of the crowd. Europeans in khaki or pipe-clayed helmets appeared and vanished, and everywhere squirmed the ubiquitous pedlars whose cries sounded like birds' or like frogs' during the monsoon.

Missionary ladies were buying *The Tatler* and the *Illustrated London News* at Wheeler's big roll-top bookstand; a palanquin containing a sick begum swayed towards the exit on the shoulders of four staggering bearers, and a troop of Eurasian school children home for the holidays chattered shrilly like a troop of mynas. Salim and Hardyal were jostled and butted by the stream of passengers disembarking from the train and an opposing stream clambering on to it.

'I will find a tonga,' said Salim, elbowing his way through the mob. 'We will go straight to Jagnath's cousin's house. It is Number Three Tamarind Road, behind the European quarter.'

Hardyal followed the tall Mohammedan but he had not gone far before his arm was touched and he was saluted by a police orderly, who handed him a note. 'This is the son of Ganpat Rai of Amritpore? A letter for you from the Captain Sahib of Police.'

Hardyal stopped in surprise. 'For me?'

'For you, from Macbeth Sahib.'

Salim, missing him, had fought his way back. 'What is it? What has happened?'

The orderly stood a few paces away, respectful and aloof, as Hardyal tore open the envelope. With Salim peering over his shoulder he read the letter:

'Dear Hardyal,
'I have learned that you are expected in Berari and I thought that

814 • A RAJ COLLECTION

with luck I might catch you as you got off the train. I do not wish to
interrupt your plans, but if you can spare an hour will you come and
see me? The orderly who carries this note will direct you to my house.
I should like very much to have a talk.

'Yours sincerely,

'John Macbeth.'

'Wah!' Salim's exclamation was full of jealousy and suspicion. 'Had
you told him you were coming to Berari?'

'How should I? We have never corresponded.'

'Then Jacques. . . . '

'Hardly, under the circumstances.'

They looked at each other, and Salim's eyes hardened. 'I made no
secret of our plans. Every one knows that Jagnath Singh is to speak this
evening. However, you and I are not such exalted persons that we
should be followed with this devotion.'

'My servants knew where I was going,' said Hardyal. 'I, too,
mentioned it casually, here and there.'

'The Police were intrigued,' muttered Salim. 'No doubt we were
watched from the moment we left our homes.' His lawyer's mind was
working swiftly, and he turned to the orderly. 'Tell me, brother, how it
happened that you recognized my friend? Had you seen him before?'

The man answered respectfully: 'His appearance, and yours, were
described to me by the Sahib. To make sure, I inquired of the guard.'

It could mean but one thing: they were objects of official
surveillance. Suddenly, Salim laughed. 'Go, Hardyal. Call on your
friend the Captain Sahib. Convey my salaams and congratulate him on
his efficiency.'

'He means no harm. This is a friendly invitation.'

'Is it so friendly? Why then did he not write to you at Amritpore?
Why does he have you accosted thus, by a police constable, on a
public platform? Nay, you cannot refuse, for this is a command, my
boy—a command!'

For the first time in his life Hardyal experienced the shock of
knowing that his actions were under a mysterious scrutiny. His privacy
had been invaded, he was no longer an anonymous figure. He stared
about him with a new feeling, encountering glances which a moment
before had seemed merely inquisitive or casual, but which now became
sly and inimical. He turned to Salim. 'I will do whatever you say.'

The other's hard face softened a little. 'I would rather you did what
your father would have you do. Go, my son. Perhaps, after all,
Macbeth's intentions are friendly. You will soon find out.'

Followed by the policeman they made their way through the crowd out on to the broad courtyard behind the station. Here Salim hailed a tonga, and turned once more to Hardyal. 'For the time being our ways lie in opposite directions. When you have seen Macbeth, come to Jagnath's cousin's house. Do not be late, for the meeting is at six, and it is now four o'clock.'

They parted and Hardyal climbed into another tonga with the police orderly. They rattled out of the courtyard, and left to his own reflections Hardyal's spirits began to lift. Salim always affected him powerfully; the man's optimism or his pessimism was alike contagious. But now, reading Macbeth's note for the second time and judging from the deferential manner of his escort, it was far easier to believe that nothing particularly sinister could be afoot. After all, Macbeth was an officer in one of the most efficient police systems in the world; all kinds of information must reach him, and the merest accident might have put him in possession of the fact that Hardyal had taken the train from Amritpore with Abdul Salim. And in any event, although Jagnath Singh might temporarily enjoy the good graces of the Government it did not follow that his movements or those of his admirers were ignored by the authorities. Learning of Hardyal's destination Macbeth might easily have acted on a friendly impulse. Hardyal began to feel much better. He wished now that he had thought this sooner and spoken of it to Salim; it might have spared that irascible person an hour or two of anger and anxiety.

His mind more at ease, Hardyal looked about him with renewed pleasure and curiosity. He had never been at Berari, and he decided that he liked its trim and prosperous air. As they swung into the main channel of traffic, the orderly pointed out the line of the distant barracks and parade ground, the Municipality buildings, the woollen mill, the new High Court with its lawns and flowers. Flags floated from their turrets and cast leisurely shadows on the white streets. There were palms and oleanders and a fountain in the little park which served as a boundary between the commercial side of the city and the beginnings of the residential quarter. A car with its hood down whisked past, and Hardyal had a glimpse of rugged soldierly faces.

'Look, Huzoor,' said his companion suddenly. They were seated at the back of the tonga; from a side-street at right angles to their path a troop of horsemen appeared, Indian lancers in the khaki of battle dress, with their lances at rest and pennons fluttering. They drew abreast of the tonga and Hardyal gazed at the erect and magnificent figures led by a young prince whose saddle-cloth was a leopard-skin and whose profile under his tightly wound turban might have come off a coin discovered on the upper reaches of the Indus valley where, once upon a time, Alexander the Great had paused.

The troopers drew away and Hardyal exclaimed: 'I did not know they were in Berari.'

'We had a regiment of Punjabies, but they have gone. The cavalry came last week. They, too, will go, but others will come. While the war lasts there will be soldiers in Berari.'

That glimpse of warriors had an odd effect on Hardyal. They had, inexplicably, engraved themselves on his mind, and he knew that it was one of those vignettes, of no particular importance, which sometimes lodge in one's memory and which are never forgotten. He wondered what passed in the minds of those men. Dare he claim them as brothers? He would have liked to touch them, to have looked for a moment into their aloof eyes, for he had the conviction that men who look like that, who ride like that, do not come home from battle.

They left the busy precincts of the town and turned off down a side-street bordered with trees, beyond which he caught glimpses of big, attractive houses. All this was familiar enough, the ekkas and hired rattletrap carriages, the ayah wheeling a white baby in a pram, the figure flying past on a bicycle.

Would Macbeth ask for Jacques? Instinctively, Hardyal dismissed the question; Englishmen do not as a rule discuss one another before an Indian. He wondered about Bertie. Would she be there, would she greet him as a friend? He was filled with a pleasurable stir of excitement and anticipation.

The tonga turned in through a pair of handsome gates and rolled up a neat driveway, accompanied by a flock of barking spaniels. It stopped before a deep veranda furnished in chintz and wicker. On a table were books and a bowl of flowers which no *mali* could have arranged. A woman lives here, thought Hardyal, remembering the bleak quarters inhabited by bachelors, white or brown.

He commanded the tonga-wallah to wait, and got out, giving his name to the sentry who stood beside the steps. But Macbeth appeared at once from a door farther down the veranda. 'Hardyal, this is good of you!'

Momentarily embarrassed, Hardyal said simply: 'I came.'

They shook hands, each observing the other with a sense of relief. He looks less secretive, less arrogant, decided Hardyal, and wondered whether Bertie was responsible for the change.

Seems damned decent, as he always did, thought Macbeth. Aloud, he said: 'Let's go into my *duftar*.'

The *duftar*, the official sanctum. . . . Hardyal suffered a momentary recurrence of suspicion. Why the *duftar*? Why not the drawing-room or the veranda? But Macbeth put a hand lightly on his shoulder and they walked down the length of the veranda into a large bright room furnished like an office. A native clerk was typing at a desk, but at a word from Macbeth he gathered up his papers and left the room.

Macbeth offered Hardyal a cigarette, took one himself, and they sat down on cool leather-covered chairs. Macbeth looked at him and smiled, his eyes friendly and tranquil. 'How are you? It's ages since we met.'

'The last time was two years ago.'

'It seems longer.' There was a tiny pause, then he added: 'I hear you are to be married. Congratulations!'

Hardyal smiled. 'Will you accept mine?' Then, before Macbeth could speak, he said, lightly: 'There seems little you do not know about me—about my forthcoming marriage, my departures, my arrivals!'

'My note must have surprised you. But the explanation is really quite simple. You were travelling with Abdul Salim, and you must know, as I am sure he does, that his movements are more or less under official surveillance. But as far as you are concerned my information was purely fortuitous.'

Hardyal persisted banteringly: 'But my marriage! Who could have told you of that?'

'My dear chap, Amritpore isn't on the other side of the world. One meets people, occasionally, and one exchanges news. As a matter of fact I learned of your marriage from an old and mutual friend—Ramdatta the moneylender.'

'Ramdatta?' Uneasiness returned, but vaguely.

'The old scamp did me a good turn once long ago, and we correspond occasionally. If you should see him when you return to Amritpore, give him my salaams.'

Hardyal thought, yes, but first I shall speak of this to Abdul Salim. So Ramdatta is in communication with the Superintendent of Police of Berari. They are friends, they exchange news, information. A gleam, still not clear, touched the edges of his mind.

Macbeth went on: 'Tell me about your father.'

'Father is well. He has been in Agra for several weeks, on a riot case.'

'And I take it you have come to Berari to hear Jagnath Singh?' It was put lightly, almost absent-mindedly, and without waiting for an answer he went on: 'I am told he is a fine speaker, though I have never heard him.'

'Perhaps you will hear him this evening?'

'I dare say.' He dropped his hand on the head of the spaniel which had come in and lay at his feet. In a tone which was somehow unexpected he asked: 'Did your father know that you were coming here with Salim?'

'I don't think I mentioned it to Father.' This was the simple truth but it sounded like equivocation in his own ears.

'Had he known, do you think that he might have tried to dissuade you from coming.'

'Why should he? Salim and I are not children.'

Macbeth laughed. 'Right you are! And all this must sound to you like prying, but honestly, I speak out of friendship for your father as well as for you. I've often thought of those long rides and the games of tennis and the garden parties at Amritpore.'

Hardyal, feeling that he had been churlish, replied: 'I, too, think of them. I appreciate your motives in asking. . . .' He did not, quite, yet he felt that he had to say it.

'As a matter of fact,' Macbeth continued, 'there is no reason why you shouldn't go to hear Jagnath Singh, provided he *does* speak. What I wanted to discuss is your association with Salim. He is unquestionably heading towards trouble. You could not prevent it, nor, I imagine, could he, at this stage of the game. That is why I was sorry to hear that you had travelled to Berari in his company. Duty, if nothing else, would compel me to speak of it to you.'

Hardyal hesitated, then began confusedly: 'But you know that Salim has been our friend for many years! And as for Jagnath Singh, the authorities have agreed to let him speak, have they not? Where, then, is the difficulty? You said just now "provided he *does* speak"! May I ask what that can mean?'

Macbeth stroked his spaniel's smooth brown head. 'Since we talk as friends I may as well tell you that a difficulty *has* arisen. You probably don't know our Magistrate, Mr Sheldon. He is in many ways a remarkable man, what people call a liberal, a dyed-in-the-wool sympathizer of—of Indians, a stickler for free speech and all that sort of thing. Perfectly all right, of course. He is immensely popular as a consequence, and that is undoubtedly why Jagnath Singh selected Berari for his speech-making.'

To Bertie, an hour before, Macbeth had unburdened himself of a more forthright and exasperated version of the situation: 'Sheldon, the infernal idiot, will end by getting us all into the devil of a hole before we know where we are. He's so full of his brown-brotherly notions, prides himself on talking their *boli* even better than they themselves, likes to imagine that he thinks like them, hobnobs with them all over the place, and generally inspires them with the belief that there is nothing they cannot say or do while under his aegis. But if things get out of hand and there's a row, I shall have to go in with my men and stop it. Damn Sheldon!'

To Hardyal, he continued with a friendly, confiding air: 'You know we have troops stationed in Berari. Their commanding officer, Colonel Gordon, has of course nothing to do with the civil administration. However, he is a friend of mine and of Mr Sheldon's and he has privately expressed his disapproval of public controversy in the neighbourhood of troops at such a time. You can't blame a soldier for having little patience with such things, for while Jagnath Singh talks and talks, Gordon and his *sowar*s go out and do the fighting and the dying. To put it in a nutshell Colonel Gordon is not a bit keen on having his men filter into Perron Park to listen while a fellow-Indian lambastes the Raj which they are pledged to defend. He could, of course, confine his men to barracks, but that would rather take the edge off Mr Sheldon's gesture of confidence, wouldn't it?'

It would, as Hardyal perceived instantly and vividly. He was flattered by Macbeth's friendly candour. No matter what one's own view might be, here was a situation too delicate, too implicit with danger, to be lightly shrugged off.

Macbeth went on quickly: 'The speech itself is harmless enough—I've read it, so has Colonel Gordon. It's quite innocuous in fact.'

'Well, then . . .' murmured Hardyal, hopefully.

'That's just the point—it's too damned innocuous to be worth giving. But you don't know Jagnath Singh, do you? He's a genius in his way. Once he starts to talk it will be in the vernacular, full of twists and turns, images, innuendoes—all idiomatic and impossible to pin down. His presence by itself rouses a strong response in the crowd. Berari is literally overrun since the news got about that he was coming. And those who have come to hear him are hardly going to be content with milk and water from such a source, are they? Questions will be asked, challenges flung by men like your Abdul Salim. And that is exactly what Jagnath hopes for . . . someone to throw him the ball so he can throw it back, weighted. Whatever has been forbidden or agreed upon between us will go by the board, and it will, of course, be nobody's fault!'

In the pause which followed, Hardyal, feeling suddenly important and responsible, smoked and pondered while Macbeth reviewed the argument in which he had joined the night before, after dinner at Henry Sheldon's. Colonel Gordon had suggested that Jagnath Singh's speech be arbitrarily called off, that notices be pasted on every wall and policemen posted at every strategic corner. 'They won't like it but they'll have to lump it, and once you've made a decision there's damned little they can do about it.'

Sheldon had replied without hesitation: 'You simply can't do things like that.'

He was a scholar, a man of mild appearance, but obstinate,

820 • A RAJ COLLECTION

idealistic, visionary, immovable in his conviction that East and West are one and that individuals alone barred the path to reunion. Indians loved him; his own kind, with but few exceptions, regarded him as a lunatic when they did not stigmatize him as something much worse. 'Sooner or later,' they prophesied with bitter satisfaction, 'sooner or later Saint Sheldon will pay for his sentimentality and will make the rest of us pay with him.'

'Sooner or later,' thought some Indians, with an equivalent bitterness, 'sooner or later he will let us down. It may not be his fault. He won't be able to help himself.'

But for more than twenty years Henry Sheldon had let no one down. How should he have bargained for the complexities and contradictions of a vast European war?

Macbeth had volunteered, mildly enough: 'As a matter of fact, at any other time it wouldn't make any difference, would it? Jagnath Singh could talk his head off, as usual. But now . . . with the Turkish-German mission at Kabul, under our very noses . . . the possibility of spies, enemy agents and all the rest of it. . . .'

'Precisely!' interposed Colonel Gordon. 'It's all the purest rot, Sheldon the purest rot, allowing that swine to talk against us at this stage of the game!'

Sheldon looked at them mildly. 'What do you want me to do, rescind my permission at the last moment?'

'Why not wire Government House and put it up to Sir William?'

'Why should I?'

'Damn it, man! It's an emergency, isn't it?' The Colonel was nervous and angry. He had been nervous and angry for several days. 'If Sir William backs you, naturally no one can have anything further to say.' He did not add his private hope that the Lieutenant Governor would refuse point blank to back this amiable crackpot, that Sir William would telegraph his immediate and unequivocal demand that the whole business be called off. It should never have been called on; no one but Sheldon would have dreamed of carrying tolerance and conciliation to such lengths.

It was with maddening good temper that Sheldon replied: 'I don't see it as an emergency. We've all read the speech. There is nothing in it to provoke a row.'

'Then why does he want to give it?'

'God knows. He's probably no different from other men who like the sound of their own voices.'

'Just the same,' objected Macbeth, 'I'm thinking of the audience. We all know the sort who'll gather to listen to him.'

'Yes,' exclaimed the soldier, angrily. 'It's the audience that I'm thinking about, myself.'

'Jagnath Singh has given me his word. . . .'

'His word!'

'. . . His word,' Sheldon repeated, equably. 'I foresee no trouble. Had I done so I certainly would not have been fool enough to give my permission in the first place.'

There was a brief pause, then the soldier said, heavily: 'There will be Mohammedans present. Someone will ask a question about Turkey: Why should Indian Moslems be expected to fight against their co-religionists, in a foreign war?'

Sheldon shrugged. 'Moslems have volunteered to fight and are now fighting, in such a war. Isn't that your answer?'

Colonel Gordon ignored this as mere quibbling. 'Damned if I see why you don't put the whole thing up to Sir William.'

'Damned if I see why you should expect me to. This is my show, you know.'

'Oh, good Lord, I know that! I'm not trying to barge in where angels fear to tread. On the other hand. . . under the circumstances . . . with troops quartered next door . . . I think you'll find that Macbeth agrees with me.'

Sheldon turned to his young colleague. 'Do you?'

'Afraid I do, rather.'

Sheldon heaved a sigh. 'You sound like a pair of old women. Will it set your minds at rest to hear that Sir William *does* know? I had a letter from him last week, and I answered at once, telling him about Jagnath, and I stated that, considering the remarkably loyal response we have received from all over the country, there could be little risk in allowing these public addresses. Since then, I haven't had a word from Sir William. I think it's safe to assume that he shares my views.'

They looked at him. 'Why in the devil didn't you tell us this before?'

Sheldon merely smiled. 'And that,' Macbeth observed afterwards to Bertie, 'is his idea of humour.'

## 53

Hardyal broke the long silence. 'I do appreciate your confidence, although I don't quite see what I can do about it. I'm a nobody, after all.'

'There's precious little any one can do about it now, except perhaps where oneself is concerned.'

'You mean, it would please you if I were to absent myself from this meeting?'

Macbeth met candour with candour. 'It would please me. I'm pretty sure that it would please your father. I, too, can do little, for I'm hardly more of a somebody than you. One can only stand by or advise one's friends, to the best of one's ability.'

He has changed, decided Hardyal. He carries force and authority, but love—and perhaps war—which embitter many, have sweetened him. He was silent for a moment, and Macbeth was thinking: 'If I can keep this one from becoming infected it will be something. Little enough, God knows, but something.'

'You realize,' said Hardyal, with a smile, 'that the implications of your request are not exactly flattering?'

Good-nature flowed between them, making it possible for him to add, with a laugh: 'I make no promises!'

'Nor would I dream of asking for one. Cigarette?'

They smoked and talked for a little while about the war and its problems. Macbeth, grateful that Hardyal had not brought Bertie's name or Jacques' into the conversation—grateful for the considerate restraint on many subjects whose mention he'd dreaded—leaned forward and said: 'Would you care to hear my point of view? It isn't very great or very grand. As a matter of fact, it's almost entirely a personal one. My father is a man of sixty-five. He is now in France with his regiment. At an age when most men look forward to peace, he is fighting, simply because he held an idea, or an ideal if you prefer it, which has tried to bar the path of unfairness and indecency all over the world. It has tried to bar it here in India. I see this not so much as a problem of race or of government but as something far more important. I see it as a question whether or not a fundamental sense of decency should be allowed to grow and prevail. Personally, I couldn't breathe without that sense. There are lots of things about us that are not so very decent, but these things do not happen to be fundamental.'

Hardyal was moved by this frankness, by this sincerity. He realized that he must often have misjudged an earlier, inarticulate Macbeth. Somehow, somewhere, a miracle had taken place, making a new man.

He said in a low voice: 'You and I would not disagree about those ideas.'

'No. But one of us might, out of a confusion of values, acquire substitutes. They might be palmed off on one, like fake emeralds.'

'Not when one has known the real!'

Instinctively, now, both relapsed into Hindustani. Macbeth said: 'To know the real, one must first have experienced the false, and that is far more difficult in the realm of ideas than it is in the matter of gems.'

'Nevertheless, both have reality. What it all comes down to in the end is, as you say, value . . . value. . . .' His eyes became luminous. 'Not the real or the unreal, for there is nothing unreal in that sense. There is but the true and the untrue. . . .' He felt, powerfully, the force of this idea, of this difference. 'And I have known both, yes—both!'

'You mean the personal and the impersonal,' said Macbeth, watching him curiously.

The tensions of the past hour, indeed of the past few weeks, were working towards expression. Hardyal, with extraordinary intensity and with the voice of one who conjures up a spirit outside himself, repeated: 'Both, both! I have seen them, I have known them!'

'Name me one, for I, too, should like to know!'

'Mrs Lyttleton.'

'That queer old lady!'

'She is dead.' He had forgotten, but now he remembered and a protest rose in him. He saw her quite clearly, a strong and limpid presence declaring itself in the very teeth of that falsehood, Death.

'Dead?' exclaimed Macbeth. 'I hadn't heard. I wish I'd known . . . another friend was asking about her just the other day. Aubrey Wall.'

Stillness fell on Hardyal. One spirit had conjured up another, and if he had asked for any proof of his vision, here it was.

'Wall? Aubrey? Aubrey Wall?'

'One of your old pals, wasn't he? He's been stationed at Berari for the past few months. His wife and child are here, too, for the winter. He retires next year.'

'He has children?'

'One, a little girl.'

Macbeth felt the tension of the past minute without understanding its cause. He went on conversationally: 'Wall spoke of the old days at Amritpore. He asked for you and for the—for the St Remys, and of course for old Mrs Lyttleton. I'm sure he will be saddened to hear that she is dead. But she must have been quite old.'

He became increasingly conscious of a coldness interposing between them. There was something new in Hardyal's silence; his eyes, once filled with intelligent animation, were now veiled in the obscurity one sometimes sees in the eyes of very young children or of Orientals. At a loss to account for this changed mood, Macbeth persisted in his easy, friendly manner: 'You stayed with Wall's people in Sussex, didn't you?'

Hardyal nodded. He stared at his feet, thrust into light sandals which he had not remembered to take off before coming into the house.

'Wall wondered—and so, as a matter of fact, did I—why you never returned to England.'

'Did the talk about that?'

Macbeth hesitated. Wall's remarks had not been complimentary: they were the remarks of a disappointed patron turned indifferent.

'Well, he just wondered.'

Hardyal drew a deep breath. 'I came home for the holidays. I felt, then, that my place was at home.'

It was not convincing, and Macbeth had the impression that it was not intended to be. But he went on, agreeably: 'Well, what have you been up to since, anything important?'

Hardyal answered without looking up. 'Important? What could I do that might be considered important? You know that when I came back from England I studied with a tutor. He was an Eurasian, and clever. Then I took my B.A. at Calcutta University. It was easy . . . everything has been fairly easy. Since then I have helped my father somewhat with his work.'

'And soon you are to be married.'

'Yes.'

'And the future, have you thought about that?'

A slight tremor passed over his dark, impassive features. 'I have thought of it, often, often!'

'You've never considered getting into Government service, I suppose? A nomination to the Police. . . .'

'It does not appeal to me.'

There was another silence and Macbeth thought: Mentioning England was, somehow, a mistake. I wonder what happened. Could he have fallen in love with some girl, and it ended unhappily? That was the usual thing. . . . Hardyal sat before him, silent as a clod, and Macbeth, who had seen other natives go through these strange metamorphoses, knew that there was nothing to be done about it. He asked gently: 'How long will you stay at Berari?'

'I return to Amritpore early tomorrow.'

'With Abdul Salim?'

'With Abdul Salim.'

So, it was ended. Not by words, not by declarations and gestures, but by the incomprehensible accident which at some unguarded moment had come between them. It was Hardyal who rose at last; he could not have borne, now, to be politely or even kindly given the hint that it was time for him to go. Macbeth, grateful for the other's initiative, rose too, rubbing out his cigarette on a silver tray.

'Well, Hardyal. . . .'

He tried to meet the other's eye, to accost without peril of direct inquiry, a spirit which for a little while had seemed to march with his, but instead he met a darkness in which his own cheerful glance was swiftly drowned.

The trivial preoccupation of navigating chairs and tables brought them safely to the door and there, for a moment, they stood.

'Whenever you are in Berari . . .' said Macbeth, his friendliness straining for survival, 'do come and see me.'

He held out his hand and Hardyal took it, his own nerveless. He did not look round as he walked down the veranda to the steps, but he felt that his body, like his spirit, was suddenly unclothed, that he took upon his flesh the stab of hostile glances, the harsh breath of unspoken summations. Memory winced under its old, tight scars.

His tonga was waiting and when he walked down the steps he was sure as he would have been had his eyes guaranteed her, that Bertie's eyes followed his departure. She must have known that he was with Macbeth in the *duftar*, yet she had not come out to meet him. She had eaten his salt, she had walked in his father's garden, she had, without doubt, slept with his closest friend, Jacques. But now she let him came and go without greeting.

'Whither, Huzoor?' asked the tonga-wallah as his passenger climbed in beside him.

Hardyal made a vague motion of his hand. 'Drive a little way, and I will tell thee.'

## 54

As they drove through the gates and into the road, the tonga-wallah looked once more at his passenger. 'Which way, left or right?'

Hardyal clasped his forehead. 'Drive . . . drive . . . till I tell thee.'

The man whipped his pony and settled back contentedly. So long as he had a fare what did he care how far or how long he drove? The young man had a prosperous and respectable air, he was evidently in the good graces of local officialdom. All would be well, with probably a handsome baksheesh at the journey's end. They struck off down a side-street.

Hardyal lifted his head and stared about him with superstitious eyes. Aubrey Wall was here, in Berari. Wall, whom he had not seen for years, whom he had hoped never to see again. Wall was here . . . within reach, perhaps within a few paces of himself. He might now be strolling behind that clump of oleanders, he might be the figure reclining in a chair on the veranda of that house just visible between the trees. Perhaps this white man bicycling towards him in grey flannels and sun-coat. . . . Ah, if they should meet and their eyes encounter! Hardyal's muscles were rigid as an Englishman pedalled by. Their eyes met fleetingly—but it was not Aubrey Wall.

Hardyal sat back and tried to reconstruct the half-remembered, rather colourless figure of his old friend and patron. But what recurred, what Macbeth's casual reference to the Engineer had sharply revived, was the memory of Mrs Lyttleton and the finality of her death. A little while ago that death had seemed to set a seal upon his youth, now in an aching second it ripped bare the knowledge that he had inherited the full weight of a terrible responsibility. Aware that he and Wall, now, stood together in the baleful light of that responsibility, Hardyal felt at one and the same instant threatened and threatening. He was caught up in the contradictory impulse of longing yet dreading to meet his unconscious adversary, not to talk with him or to be seen by him, but to catch him unawares, to scrutinize from a safe distance the enigma that was Wall. This is an instinct shared by lovers and enemies, the fatal attraction which seeks to shatter an unbearable suspense. Yet in all this the pathetic figure of Jalal had not once intruded; he was as lost to Hardyal's memory as he was lost, now doubly lost, to Mrs Lyttleton. He had emerged but once from his brief and inconsequential existence—an obstacle, a stone against which a man stumbled and fell. But the thought of that fall and of what it had brought down with it excited a sort of delirium in Hardyal. A sweat of fear broke over him and he turned his face aside, seeking the unknown wife who would comfort him, who would receive him into her heart, believing him supreme among men. He would lay his head between her breasts and generate a son who would be different from himself and from her, different from his own time and from his fate: he would generate a hope, a future. To be thought supreme, to know oneself supreme, to rise once in one's life above all others, to breathe into one's nostrils the promise of one's own tried and trusted gods! Forget the Walls and the Macbeths, forget—forget! He closed his eyes and felt the warm sea washing his feet, he saw the white moon above Arabia and the offerings to Varuna moving out with the accepting tide. He heard, somewhere, the faint sweet sound of a woman's laughter.

'In that house,' said the tonga-wallah, pointing with his whip, 'resides the District Magistrate. The other, the big white one, is the house of the Deputy Commissioner.'

Hardyal's fever broke; the conscious world thrust itself before his startled eyes. 'Driver, what time is it?'

The man consulted the air, sniffed, meditated, then replied, with reasonable accuracy: 'Going on six.'

'Oh, good heavens! My friend . . . I must meet my friend. Turn and let us go back as we came.' He racked his brain. The number and name of the street which Salim had given him had completely vanished from his memory. He stared at the tonga-wallah. 'Where is Jagnath Singh staying?'

The man started. 'Jagnath Singh? He who is to speak this evening?'

'I was to meet my friend at the house of Jagnath's cousin.'

The driver, with Jehu's dry wit, suggested that they drive to the nearest jail. 'If Jagnath and his cousin and all their friends are not already there, they will be shortly.'

Hardyal hailed a man trudging along in the dust with a bundle of sugar-cane on his shoulder. The man stared, shook his head, opened his mouth, and made a mewing noise.

'He is mute, he hath no tongue,' said the driver in disgust.

'Then let us drive to the city and make inquiries there.'

'Better to go straight to the park. Jagnath is to speak there in half an hour. If your friend is with him, you are sure to meet.'

Hardyal thought confusedly: Suppose Salim waits for me and misses the speech? Suppose he imagines that I have been arrested and goes to Macbeth's house to make a scene? It would be like him . . . No, they must somehow find the cousin's house. He searched his memory in an agony of humiliation. Salim had told him clearly enough. . . . Something Avenue . . . Something Road. He stared anxiously round him as the tonga wheeled and headed back as it had come.

'Someone is sure to know where Jagnath Singh is staying. Let us ask a constable.'

The driver spat over a wheel. 'Do not be sure that a constable will tell you anything.' He glanced at his passenger. 'I would not be too sure that Jagnath will speak, at that.'

'What are you talking about?'

'Do not be impatient with your humble servant. While you were with the Captain Sahib, I listened to his minions. Those flatfeet know everything and they cannot resist showing off their knowledge if it suits them to do so. It seems there is a chance that Jagnath's speech may be called off. There is disagreement in high places.'

'Called off—at this hour?' scoffed Hardyal. He was obsessed by the thought of Salim waiting for him, perhaps fuming and disgusted, perhaps darkly suspecting the worst. 'Drive to the city. I shall ask at the post office.'

The driver had taken a short-cut down a dusty ally, and they now emerged on the main thoroughfare which ran in a straight line from the railway station, past Perron Park, towards the European Club.

'Look,' said the driver. 'All these folk are going to the park. Let us go with them.'

A stream of traffic flowed along the main channel—ekkas, carriages, a motor car or two, bicycles, people on foot. They were in holiday mood, raising clouds of dust, some lifting their voices in a half defiant, half jocular shout: 'Jagnath Singh ki jai!'

The tonga-wallah smiled dourly. 'They better take care. Here come the Police.'

With the eerie suddenness of their kind, a company of khaki-clad, red-turbaned figures appeared riding bicycles, led by a short, powerful, red-faced English sergeant. The crowd made way for them, genially or timidly according to their separate natures or consciences.

'Let's ask them,' cried Hardyal. 'Stop, let me speak to the sergeant.' He leaned out and shouted as the Englishman pedalled alongside.

'Can you tell me, please, where Mr Jagnath Singh is residing?'

The man did not answer, nor did he turn his head. Grim, thick-necked, he flashed past, followed by his retinue.

Hardyal subsided on the shabby seat. 'Drive to the park,' he said, his voice not quite as assured as it had been. 'Hurry, hurry!'

'Be calm,' urged the driver, gently. He had, with the peculiar sophistication of his calling, already gauged his young fare's innocence, which inspired a protective condescension. 'Let them go. Perron Park is no distance, and without doubt that is where you will meet your friends, or someone who will direct you to them.'

The tonga merged with a flux of vehicles and pedestrians, and was forced to slow down. The city lay directly behind them, and Hardyal saw the bright green of the little park which he had noticed when he drove from the station to Macbeth's. The crowd was orderly enough, and he saw numerous policemen armed not only with their truncheons but with the brass-bound *lathies* which come as close as anything can to being India's national weapon. Once, he caught sight of the white police sergeant and thought: Undoubtedly that one has not changed since he was born . . . that face, incapable of expression, was cast in stone rather than in flesh.

'Jagnath will speak from the bandstand at the farther end of the park,' explained the tonga-wallah. 'It is wider there, and there are benches.'

Hardyal watched the crowd, knowing that many had come from a distance, others from the suburbs, from the bazaars and alleys of the city itself. Members of an amateur band straggled by, wearing the cast-off tunics of some long-demobilized regiment. The late sun struck gold from a battered trumpet; a drum, cheerfully thumped by some urchin, emitted a thunderous growl. Voices and the rattle of vehicles, the tinny warnings of bicycle bells, all rose on a mounting wave towards the higher, clearer air.

'The world and its wife are here,' observed the tonga-wallah. He interrupted himself to engage in foul genealogical compliments with an ekka driver whose near wheel threatened to tangle with the tonga. 'Well, perhaps I heard wrong there at the Captain Sahib's. Or else his chuprassies were talking through their turbans. No one would prevent this gathering at this hour.'

A policeman pressed through the crowd. 'Vehicles may not proceed nearer the park. You will have to walk from here.'

Hardyal paid the driver, adding a generous tip, then got out, and was instantly swallowed up by the crowd. Pushed, jostled, his feet stepped on, his cap knocked off, he felt exhilaration well up inside him. Here was the same sweating, craning, genial crew which brought to the scene of political controversy the incorrigible *tamasha*-loving spirit of the country. They came with minds and hearts prepared for anything, for everything. Such occasions were all too rare in their lives; what matter if this turns out to be a dull party, nothing but vague chit-chat and impossible visions presided over by the police, with nothing to buy or to covet, and little to look at except one another? Take what the gods offered . . . and be happy.

A casteless man bumped into Hardyal, and recognizing their separate stations, backed away with abject salaams and muttered 'Maharaj!' Hardyal saw groups of students in the black coats, white trousers, and red fezzes of the Moslem High School, others in the less formal haberdashery of Hindus. Everywhere moved the red turbans of the police, enlivened here and there by dashes of braid and the bobbing gold fringes of subordinate officers.

Agile and athletic, he had little difficulty in making his way through the congestion to the park gates. The enclosure was shaped roughly in the form of a square, bounded by an irregular masonry wall of perhaps five feet. He saw at once that he had no chance of reaching the bandstand from which Jagnath Singh was to speak, so he decided to wait until after the speech before going in search of Abdul Salim. Perhaps Salim would accompany Jagnath to the speaker's stand, in which case, thought Hardyal, it might be possible somehow to attract his friend's attention.

# 55

Trees grew at intervals along the wall nearest the main road; boys swarmed up their trunks and swarmed down again when their dangling legs were spied by the police who, however, offered no objection to people taking up positions of vantage on top the wall itself. Someone gave Hardyal a hand and hauled him up, another steadied him when he was almost precipitated over the other side. He felt their excitement, their good humour. 'We may not hear anything, but we'll get a good view,' observed one, philosophically.

The whole scene might have been a circus or a pantomime. Hardyal, longing for a sight of Abdul Salim, studied the milling and leisurely crowd. The bandstand was a couple of hundred yards distant and he could see little beyond the ornamental palms and the European hats of some of its occupants.

'Will Jagnath Singh be in European dress?'

'Never fear, you will recognize him,' declared a neighbour. 'He is tall and stout, with white hair. He always wears European dress. He is said to have observed once, that in a scuffle the police might find it child's play to steal one's dhoti, but it would be less easy for them to deprive one of one's trousers.'

'He hath a tongue, that Jagnath.'

'I heard him once, in Lucknow. He can make a stone laugh or a tree burst into tears.'

'Aye, and he has been known to raise blisters as big as plovers' eggs on the police, before now.'

'What will he tell us to-day, know you?'

'About Turkey and the great war.'

'A thorny subject.'

'Nay, he is to explain about the new taxes.'

'Why should he waste time on such matters! It is more likely that he will explain why the Raj needs our sons to wage war against the Germans.'

'You mean,' drawled a sour voice, 'why we should refuse to send our sons anywhere to wage war against any one.'

'Let us wait and listen.'

Hardyal felt happy among them. The man who had given him a hand on to the wall was youngish, with a leathery black face and sparkling eyes. He wore an English jacket with his dhoti and clutched the rough stone wall with bare, muscular toes. From his pocket he now extracted a piece of sugar-cane, chewed the rind off it with his teeth, and offered a fragment to Hardyal, who accepted it with thanks. They champed, enjoying the sweet liquid, spitting the pith between their feet. Hardyal could see various comings and goings on the bandstand, but there was no sign of Abdul Salim nor of him whom they had described as Jagnath Singh.

'It is early yet,' said the man in the jacket. He was a clerk in the Municipality. Now, with a self-conscious flourish, he produced a nickel-plated watch and consulted it. 'Ten minutes. These affairs are always late.'

Hardyal watched the evening crows fly in squadrons across the deepening sky. Where, where was Salim?

Behind him in the road a carriage bell shrilled imperiously. He heard important shouts from the police, cries of 'Hut jao! Hut jao! Make way for the Sahib's carriage.'

Craning round, Hardyal had a glimpse of a smart dogcart driven by an Englishman. The police were clearing a way for its passage. The Englishman looked as though he was keeping his temper with an effort, but he was also keeping his foot on the bell, which shrilled and shrilled. Behind him on the syce's stand his groom brandished a horsehair switch over the heads of scurrying urchins.

'Hut jao!' bawled the policemen, shoving people out of the way.

'Dolts, owls, brothers-in-law of untrustworthy women, make way for the Sahib's horse!'

'It is the Engineer of Canals,' volunteered the clerk at Hardyal's elbow. 'It is Wall Sahib himself.'

Hardyal's heart grew huge, he was almost stifled by its sudden pounding. Aubrey Wall, intent on keeping his horse and his temper under control in this melling, milling mob, saw no one in particular. They were natives, heterogeneous, unmannerly as usual, a bloody bore . . . and he was on his way to the Club for a game of billiards and a drink before dining with friends.

'Hut jao! Hut jao!'

The bell shrilled again, sharp, insistent, imperious, then the dogcart and its occupant disappeared and the crowd surged upon the space where it had been, as the sea surges upon the site of a dislodged pebble. Hardyal's eyes were blazing. He was possessed by an emotion which seemed to fill his veins with light. He put his hand on the shoulder of the Municipal clerk, and steadying himself thus, stared across the shifting throng. Then he lifted his voice in a shout which carried high above the muted uproar:

'Jagnath Singh ki jai! Jagnath Singh ki Jai!'

The cry, evocative, traditional, first stilled, then stirred the fickle mob; it harnessed their disorderly limbs, focused their attention, channelled and directed their ready emotions. The clerk put his arm round Hardyal and added his own undistinguished voice to the plangent cry: '*Ki jai! Ki jai!* Jagnath Singh ki jai!'

Accented like this, the words surrendered their purely evocative appeal and became at once militant, emphatic, intense. The crowd took it up, took it up with a roar as only people reared and nurtured in the single current of tradition, religious or otherwise, could take it. The amateur drummer lost somewhere in the mass rub-a-dub-dubbed wildly, a trumpet squealed, small boys concealed among the higher branches gave themselves away with shrill cries. Then all these human throats instinctively discarded whatever was trivial or individual: Moslem and Hindu, and the outcastes among them, settled as marching men settle into that throbbing primordial chant which for force and rhythm depends on the upward, outward stroke of the heart's concerted beat. 'Ki jai! Ki jai! Jagnath Singh ki jai!'

By the gates, the policemen moved towards each other, forming up two by two or in fours, slipping their truncheons from the leather holsters. Those who carried *lathies* held their right palms against their mouths for a second before grasping anew the polished bamboo staves topped with brass.

The people nearest Hardyal had taken their stroke from him and relayed it to others farther along. It travelled, not in eddies and trickles, but in an increasing wave, as one voice and then another—waiting only the penultimate note—came crashing home on it. The young, unknown voice which had struck the note where and when a forgotten carriage bell left off, now merged and became one with the larger, the growing, the formidable voice of the mob.

Light flung its final spear among the trees; falling, it dazzled for a moment the eyes and the hearts of the multitude. This was the heroic moment, and they acclaimed it, every one poised on the brink of instant, obedient silence should their hero show himself. But he did not show himself. Instead, the bandstand suddenly swarmed with strangers, like a piece of sugar with ants.

A figure wearing a dark suit and a white topi detached itself from the group and walked quietly to the edge of the platform. As he held up his hand for silence those nearest him, recognizing Henry Sheldon, their Magistrate, became silent, and that silence rolled back as the sea might have rolled back for King Canute . . . had Canute been lucky.

Hardyal craned forward in a passion of concentration, but he caught only a word or two of an utterance which lasted, at most, not more than three minutes. The gist of it reached him several minutes after Sheldon and his companions had left the bandstand and disappeared. It reached him through exactly the same channels as news reaches the unlettered and the far-away—it reached him strained and modified through the minds and mouths of a hundred intervening human beings.

'Jagnath Singh will not speak to you to-day. A difficulty has arisen which makes it necessary to postpone his speech. The Lieutenant Governor himself ordered the postponement, but in due time the public will be notified as to the reason for this delay. Until then they will be so good as to disperse with the least possible disturbance of the general peace.'

The pause—the indecision rather—which followed the collective digestion of this announcement endured for a few minutes, then a ripple passed over the crowd, another and yet another—the loud formless humble characteristic of surprised and disappointed citizenry. In a vague, unhurried fashion they began to drift towards the separate exits. Packed fairly tight, they still maintained proportion, density, and centre, and it was from this centre that a voice, hoarse with rage, suddenly yelled: 'It is a put-up job! Shame on them, Shame! Shame!'

The new voice, as Hardyal's voice had done earlier, carried no farther than the depth of ten or fifteen standing men, but that was far enough. Tempers were ignited or extinguished by the sheer heat of contact and example, and a tremor shuddered through the single sympathetic nerve which Hardyal's voice had first touched and set quivering.

'They don't dare let Jagnath Singh speak to us!' This from one of the Moslem students.

'It's the truth! Jagnath was going to tell us that we have no quarrel with our brothers in Turkey.'

'He was going to tell us how Government backs the Marwaries and the *banias* against us. . . .'

'. . . Things which he felt we should understand . . . but they prevented . . . they prevented!'

'They gave their word, then broke it!'

'Cheats! Liars! Cowards!'

Hardyal stayed on his wall. The tumult poured in and out of his veins; he shivered a little from excitement, although his brain worked fast and clearly. Jagnath Singh and Salim had not come to the park—of this he was increasingly sure. It was hardly likely that the authorities would allow the speaker and his entourage to appear before an angry and disappointed audience. No, if they were not already in jail they must still be at the address which Salim had given him at the station. Something Road, Something Avenue. . . .

A voice near him yelled: 'Let Jagnath appear before us and explain!'

'Let us see him, and we will go quietly.'

'See him? What do you wager the police had already hustled him off to jail?'

A gruff voice spoke suddenly behind Hardyal. 'Move on, move on.'

It was the police sergeant, mounted now on a tough cavalry charger, carrying his wand of office—a short, stout leather quirt.

'Move on, I said. *Chello*, you!'

Those below the wall began to move a little faster. Children scuttled like frightened beetles; women, pulling their veils over their eyes, clung silently to their men.

'*Chello*,' repeated the rasping voice, its Cockney lending an indescribable accent to the vernacular word. 'Go on, go on!'

One by one, the people on the wall began to jump down and mix with the crowd. Hardyal gave a final sweeping glance over the massed heads. There was just a bare chance that Salim might have come in search of him.

A voice muttered: 'The whole thing is a police trap. They've put Jagnath in jail.'

'If you ask me, they got us all here so they could arrest us, too.'

'Better get out. They've sent to the nearest *chauki* for more men. You know what happens when they start picking people up. All they want is a couple of dozen innocents to swell their bag and maintain their reputation!'

The voice behind Hardyal reiterated: 'Didn't you hear what I said, you cheeky swine? *Chello!*'

The Municipal clerk, who had been addressed thus, leaped swiftly from the wall and disappeared into the crowd.

'You too,' said the sergeant, staring at Hardyal. 'Get down from the wall and move along.'

Hardyal answered mechanically in English: 'I am looking for a friend.'

'Then look for him somewhere else. You can just bloody well *chello* off that wall and hurry up about it.'

Hardyal climbed down—he dared not jump because of the congestion. Nor did he see what happened immediately afterwards. He did, however, hear a sudden scream as the sergeant's horse, pricked by a vicious spur, reared and brought its iron-shod hoof down on a man's foot.

'God blast your soul! Why don't you get out of the way?'

There was the sound of a scuffle, blows, shouts. Somewhere a police-whistle shrilled and was answered, mockingly, by a terrific thumping on the band's invisible drum. Hardyal pushed his way along the wall and presently found himself pressed up against his friend the Municipal clerk. They exchanged grins. 'If we get out without broken heads, we'll be lucky,' murmured the clerk, quite cheerfully. 'I just had a glimpse of the Captain Sahib himself. They're afraid of a riot.'

'Then let us give them one,' muttered an infuriated voice close beside him. The speaker was a strapping man with the look of a Pathan. 'Jagnath Singh is right—they herd us like cattle, like cattle!'

Hardyal pushed ahead and when he believed himself to be out of reach of the sergeant, hoisted himself on to the wall once more, realizing that to make his way along its undisputed length was his only chance of rapid progress. But the noise of the scuffle seemed to dog his heels. A voice cried passionately: 'They even train their horses to kill us!'

'He's not dead, you fool! Pick him up. Make way there, make way!'

The whistle shrilled again, and he saw coming towards him a phalanx of constables led by Macbeth on horseback. His face under the severe brim of his helmet wore an assured expression; he was talking quietly to the people, who crushed aside to give him and his horse ample room. Pale, erect, he bored through the mass, with his constables shouldering their way behind him. The light was now almost gone; it struck the gilt spike on Macbeth's helmet and the metal knobs of the police *lathies*, it ran eerily along the battered trumpet of the native bandsman and lost itself like quicksilver in the drab and defeated mob. Hardyal, momentarily arrested by the sight of Macbeth, saw something fly through the air and for a split second took it for a frightened bird or a bat. But it was a shoe which, hurtling over the intervening heads, struck a red turban. Then something viperous whipped out, struck, vanished. The turbanless constable fell, with blood spuming from his nostrils. On top of him, his head split like an egg, lay the big man who looked like a Pathan.

Hardyal was caught in a sort of trance by the sheer unexpectedness, the sheer perfection of this detail set in a generally formless and indifferent whole. Perhaps a dozen people had actually seen the thing happen, certainly very few more were to witness what so swiftly followed. As Macbeth rose in his stirrups and began to lay about him with his riding-crop, a figure leaped on to the wall and Hardyal saw the uplifted hand which clutched, for missile, a green, broken, jagged bottle. Hardyal's warning cry reached Macbeth who ducked as the murderous glass flew past his face, but the sound of that English: 'Look out!' never reached the ears of the white sergeant and his escort. They struck Hardyal from behind, and he and the thrower of the bottle went down together under a rain of *lathi* blows and the high, thin piping of the whistles.

# 56

Three days later Jacques left his bicycle on the gravel of the driveway and ran up the steps of Ganpat Rai's house, where Krishna, the old servant, came to meet him. The man's eyes were inflamed, his voice harsh from weeping. 'My master will receive you in his study.'

The barrister, wearing a kurtha and dhoti, rose as his visitor appeared in the door. For a moment they stared at each other, then as Jacques went to him, the older man clasped the younger to his breast.

'Ganpat Rai, why in God's name didn't you send for me at once?'

'There was little time, and much confusion.' Gently, Ganpat Rai released him. 'Let us sit. I am very tired, I feel old.' He smiled, but his face had a worn, yellowish look. 'First let me set your heart at ease: Hardyal was badly hurt, but he is out of danger. In a few days he will be out of jail.'

Jacques felt that they moved, spoke, listened in a dimension which had somehow lost all its familiar characteristics. 'In jail!'

'In jail. It was there that he recovered consciousness, it was there that we found him—Salim and I—two days ago.'

As Jacques stared, unable to speak, the older man went on heavily.

'I was at Agra when Salim wired me of Hardyal's disappearance. I took the first train to Berari, where I arrived on the morning after the affair. I went at once to see Henry Sheldon, who has always been my friend. He is in very bad odour with his colleagues and with most of the European community, who hold him directly responsible for what happened at Perron Park. You know that two men were killed and several badly hurt, among the latter, Hardyal.' His eyes moved in a troubled way, as though he were trying to peer through a veil. 'From the chorus of 'I told you so!' and 'What can you expect?' one would suppose that they are really delighted at what occurred. It justifies their attitude.'

Looking at him, Jacques realized that here was a wound that would never mend. 'And Hardyal?' he murmured, sick at heart.

'There are certain formalities, but he will be released within a very few days. Sheldon has promised, so has Macbeth.'

'Macbeth!'

'We had a long talk. I found him sympathetic. You see, he is convinced that it was Hardyal's shout of warning which saved him from serious injury. Others have testified to this, among them a clerk from the Municipality, who saw the whole thing.'

'Then,' said Jacques, drawing his breath, 'Hardyal has a clear case?'

'As far as that goes, yes. But there are things which I myself do not find so clear. Salim and I spent hours making inquiries and questioning people. If, after leaving Macbeth's house, Hardyal had gone straight to the address which Salim gave him, he would have found Jagnath Singh and Salim there, for Sheldon had already notified them of the Governor's last-minute intervention. But when I questioned Hardyal about this he was very evasive: he declared that he had completely forgotten the address which Salim gave him. Realizing how such an excuse might sound in court, I protested that such forgetfulness was foreign to him, whereupon he turned away his face, saying: 'It was fate.' Ganpat Rai laughed. 'Fate! To speak of fate to me, who have learned that there are but two implements to human action—intention and accident. However, I did not want to disturb him then with arguments and expostulations. But when I was leaving him I tried to cheer him up by saying that Macbeth himself had interceded for his speedy release—that it would be a mere matter of days before he was free. At that he gave me a strange look and replied: 'There is no hurry. Let me lie here and get used to these walls. I have a feeling that I shall see them again, often, often.'

'What did he mean?'

Ganpat Rai hesitated, and Jacques sensed his deep disquiet. It expressed itself at last, haltingly. 'I think we both know what he means. Some men are born into the path of revolt, as Salim was. Others are thrust into by accident—or by another's fault. I can tell you, who have known him all his life, who have always loved him, that I find myself wondering whether we have lost Hardyal.'

'Lost him?'

'You must know that more than his body suffered at Perron Park.'

'Yes, I understand.' Then, afraid lest the understanding contribute to the other's distress, he added: 'But if the whole thing was an accident . . . surely he will see it that way for himself!'

'What is happening in Hardyal's mind and spirit is no longer accidental. It is, I believe, the culmination of something that has been long in coming. I don't know when or where it had its beginnings. I have often wondered, but he has never confided that secret to me, and I have never brought the technique of the courtroom into my home. Once, years ago, Hardyal and I quarrelled. I was eager for him to return to England to finish his studies, but he refused. He gave as excuse the fact that he could not bring himself to leave home again. Although at the time I was sure that there was more to it than that, I said no more. I hoped he might one day come to me with the truth, but he never has.'

'Nor,' said Jacques, 'has he confided that mystery to me.'

'Then you, too, feel that there is a mystery?'

'I have been sure of it for a long time.'

Both were silent, then Jacques asked: 'What can we do? There must be something.'

Ganpat Rai shrugged his tired shoulders. 'We must wait. I think that just now he moves in a sort of darkness. He has ceased, temporarily, to see men as friends or enemies. The shock has numbed, in him, the faculty of discrimination—he is aware only of forces, immense, impersonal, and hostile. He sees himself caught up by these forces, victimized by them, even aggrandized by them. I have seen it happen to witnesses and to men whom I have defended in court. By identifying themselves with a cause, or with a friend or a lover, they succeed in depersonalizing themselves to such a degree that they can endure any situation. It is this detachment from himself which moves one man to confession, and which breeds impregnable silence in another.'

'Is that what you meant when you said, just now, that we had lost Hardyal?'

'Yes, and it is what I mean when I say that Hardyal must not lose us.'

Jacques exclaimed unhappily: 'But if he should no longer want us!'

'Remember, he is the wronged one, the sufferer. He will make demands he has never made before, demands on our love, on our patience, on our understanding. On you, perhaps, more than on any one.'

'Why on me especially? I should think that he could take me for granted.'

'I do not think that Hardyal will ever again take a man for granted.'

Jacques gave him a straight look. 'Tell me what it is you really mean, Ganpat Rai.'

The older man stared at his hands, folded on the desk before him.

'I mean that he may never again bring himself to take a white man for granted.'

'As a friend?'

The other bowed his head a little, and Jacques thought: This has brought the years upon him; he looks twenty years older.

'As enemies?'

Ganpat Rai made a sudden despairing gesture. 'My God, how can I say? I do not know . . . I cannot see. . . .' He clenched his hands. 'I cannot resign myself! Do you know what they did to him? Macbeth himself told me this when he was trying to explain how it all happened. He never saw Hardyal, he thought he must have disappeared into the crowd after that warning shout. But there was good reason why no one saw Hardyal, for the police had beaten him senseless behind the wall. They broke his arm and his teeth. They manacled him between two others, and left him all night chained to the floor of his cell, without water, without attention. They did this, to Hardyal, to my son!'

As swiftly as his composure had deserted him, it returned.

'Excuse me. It is stupid to lose one's temper.'

Jacques rose impulsively. 'Ganpat Rai, my friend. . . .'

Ganpat Rai rose too, and put his hands on the young man's shoulders, staring into his face. 'We are friends . . . friends?' It was asked wonderingly, and Jacques was made to feel the full weight of his own misery with this additional, vicarious shame.

'Can you doubt it, Ganpat Rai?'

The other dropped his hands with a sigh. 'No, for you and I are the same kind of man. We are not like Hardyal, not like Salim. We were not cut out for faith or for destiny.' A glimmer of his old humour appeared for a moment on his face. "For that reason, perhaps, we shall always remain friends—loving, but incapable of illusion!'

Jacques said gently: 'Take me to Berari with you, when you go to see Hardyal.'

They exchanged a long glance, then Ganpat Rai's face cleared.

'We will go together and bring him home. But in the meantime, here I have sat talking, talking only of my troubles, when all the while there is a matter which concerns you and which I had almost forgotten. I would have written you from Agra if all this had not happened to drive it from my mind.'

He crossed the room to a small green safe set against the wall, and returned carrying a large brown envelope. 'This is Mrs Lyttleton's will.'

Jacques scarcely heard. He was thinking of Hardyal.

'She did me the honour of entrusting me with her affairs. I felt bitterly that I was not in Amritpore when she died, that I was unable, even, to attend her funeral.' He opened the envelope and withdrew its contents. 'This was written five years ago. In it she has made you her heir.'

Jacques stared at the document which the barrister spread before him on the desk. 'There are a few bequests to her old servants. Everything else—and there is a great deal, for she was a wealthy woman—everything else goes to you.'

Jacques picked up the crisp bluish paper and examined its elaborate phraseology with almost casual attention. Neither surprise nor pleasure moved him, only a sort of painful mirth, as though he'd taken a draught of slightly poisonous nectar. Ganpat Rai was watching him. 'This will make a difference to you. It will take a little time for you to get used to the idea that you are now . . . independent.' He smiled. 'I, for one, shall observe the outcome with interest.'

So, thought Jacques, shall I.

Both men were silent, meditating on a future whose sudden, sumptuous contours even Madame St. Remy could scarcely have visualized, let alone have achieved; on a revenge so exquisitely contrived that it must leave her, irretrievably and to the end of her days, to the subtle mercy of her dead rival.

'You are not going to refuse?' Ganpat Rai asked at last, puzzled by his companion's long silence.

'Refuse?' Jacques repeated. 'No, how could I refuse?'

How could he refuse his old friend her long-delayed triumph, or deny her, from this distance, the rewards of this ironic moment? And because he glimpsed, now, the first bright outlines of this moment which she had long ago conceived and foreseen—a moment whose eventuality must intensely have amused and sustained her—Jacques began to laugh, convinced in his heart that from somewhere on her point of vantage she laughed with him.

'Good!' said Ganpat Rai. 'Take it, my child. Take it, use it, be happy.'

'Happy? I'm not sure about that. . . .'

'Yes, I understand. If only there were no war, if only we could carry forward into life the innocence and the generosity of childhood!' His brown eyes filled with light, like pools at evening. 'You are young . . . you, Hardyal, Bertie, Macbeth. Whatever the future holds will belong to you.'

'I wish I knew!'

'One must go on living, Jacques. For you children, as well as for us who are old, the end remains hidden.'

# The Wild Sweet Witch*

## Philip Mason

*In the most iron crag his foot can tread*
*A dream may strew her bed*
*And suddenly his limbs entwine*
*And draw him down through rock as sea-nymphs*
*might through brine.*
*But unlike those feigned temptress-ladies who*
*In guerdon of a night the lover slew,*
*When the embrace has failed, the rapture fled,*
*Not he, not he, the wild sweet witch is dead!*
*And though he cherisheth*
*The babe most strangely born from out her death—*
*Some tender trick of her it hath, maybe—*
*It is not she!*

FRANCIS THOMPSON

---

* First published by Jonathan Cape as *The Wild Sweet Witch*
by Philip Woodruff 1947

# CONTENTS

# Preface

It was not until I was an adult that I read my father's book *The Wild Sweet Witch*. I had been aware of it since my childhood as one of the first books he had written, and I liked the title. However, when my elder sister read it and found to her disappointment that there was no witch in the story, I did not think I would enjoy it either.

When eventually I did come to it, I found much of it astonishingly familiar. My father, Philip, and my mother, Mary, had spent three years in Garhwal when they were first married. During this period my father was Deputy Commissioner, and he and my mother always spoke of their time in Garhwal with great enthusiasm. We had heard about their adventures in the mountains, their life in camp, the rigours of having a bath in a tent when it is freezing outside, and how carefully you have to time taking your clothes off when the water is hot and how quickly you have to dress afterwards to keep warm. We had, as in the novel, even heard stories of men who turn into man-eating panthers at night. We had seen photographs that my parents had taken of mountains, villages, and pilgrims on their way to Badrinath; we had shuddered at photographs of rope bridges over vast chasms, which I imagined to be rather like the one over which Kalyanu is carried on a stretcher in *The Wild Sweet Witch*. My mother still had some of the paintings she had done in Garhwal to illustrate the countryside described in the novel. She painted the design for the cover for the first edition which showed the triumphal dance after the bear is killed; she also drew the map of the novel's locale for the endpaper.

My sister, Susan Janie, was born in Garhwal soon after the outbreak of World War II, and at the party for her christening the Garhwali officers proclaimed her a Garhwali and named her Sundari Devi. My father was pleased; he liked things associated with Garhwal and later, when we returned to England, he would use a *kukri* for chopping undergrowth in our garden. Although my parents' stay in Garhwal was before my time, we had acquired a kind of folk memory from tales often told and repeated.

*The Wild Sweet Witch* was written in 1946 when the family was reunited in Europe after the war. My mother had brought us three children (my brother George was born in Delhi in 1944) back to England in what must have been one of the last convoys from India. We stayed in a cottage near our grandparents at Charmouth, and in 1946 my father, who had been transferred to the War Department in Delhi, had four months' leave from India and was able to join us there. After the frightening times of the war, and the long separations, *The Wild Sweet Witch* was written in a happy interlude when we were all together briefly for an English summer. His correspondence of the time reveals he was full of optimism and hope. The favourable notices for *Call the Next Witness*, published in 1945, encouraged him to believe that he could make a career in writing, and he began trying out new ideas for stories in letters to my mother.

*The Wild Sweet Witch* is dedicated to my mother and her copy is inscribed 'Here at last is your book, built up from all we remember together'. In the novel he brings their Garhwal experiences back to life with the lyrical descriptions of the mountains, woods, streams, terraces, and the warm and affectionate accounts of the people they grew to know. He speaks of the simple peasants like Kalyanu and his brothers, who struggled to grow enough on the steep hills to provide for themselves; of the Doms, 'the dark faced aboriginals' who work as serfs of Kalyanu and his brothers and who play drums for their dance; of the Marchas, 'half-Tibetan people', who use the time when their homes are buried deep under snow in winter to trade in the lower hills of India, and who return to their homes just in time to sow a crop before descending into Tibet to sell the goods they have acquired in India.

Like Christopher Tregard in *The Wild Sweet Witch*, my father always intended to come home and lead a different life after his time in India. He wanted to live in the country and take up writing as a profession. The plan appealed to us all, especially as it meant living in the lovely Dorset countryside near our grandparents. The first book that we were aware of his writing was one that he wrote for my sister. *The Sword of Northumbria* is an exciting adventure story set in the countryside around Sedbergh, my father's school in Yorkshire. It is about a boy who has been brought up as a farmer's son but is told that he is in truth the king of Northumbria, then under foreign rule. He must reclaim his kingdom and make it free. My father read it to us in instalments, as he wrote it. There is a great deal of fighting in it, and when it came to my turn to have a book written for me I told him I did not want any killing in it. He wrote a much gentler, but equally exciting story, *Hernshaw Castle*, set in the Dorset countryside. The plots of these books, like that of *The Wild Sweet Witch*, are very closely grounded in the local terrain. And like the novel, each book has a map of the setting on the endpapers to clarify the plot. It was exciting for us to wander around the Dorset countryside and trace the footsteps of the characters in my book. There was a wood nearby where we always felt nervous and spoke in whispers because we knew there were wolves and wild boar hiding in the thickets. It is here that one of the children in *Hernshaw Castle* is captured and tied up by mysterious strangers. . . .

We all loved living in Dorset, but after a short time we had to move nearer to London as my father needed to spend more time there. He realized that he could not make enough money through his writing and our smallholding, and he looked for some paid employment which would allow him to continue his own writing. When he joined Chatham House as Director of Studies of Race Relations, and later set up the Institute of Race Relations, he was pioneering an altogether new field of study. His work in India had involved settling disputes between individuals and groups; now he was producing scholarly work on the causes of ethnic hatred. He was still writing, but not fiction. His work involved raising money to run the Institute, appointing researchers, commissioning studies, and giving lectures as well as travelling and meeting people all over the world. It was the period of decolonization in Africa and he wrote a major historical study of Rhodesia (now known as Zimbabwe), *The Birth of a Dilemma: The Conquest and Settlement of Rhodesia*. This was followed by *Patterns of Dominance*, which compares the development of racial intolerance in diverse and geographically distinct societies. At weekends we frequently had guests he had met through his work. When he was at home he maintained a very strict timetable for writing, and visitors were asked to come to a meal so that he could see them without making inroads on his writing time.

After retirement from directorship in 1969, he continued to write on a variety of subjects that interested him and it was a very happy period of his life. He became blind in old age, and it was a great sadness that he could no longer write, or even read. His memories of India, however, remained vivid and he derived profound spiritual insights from them. In an article in *The Tablet* he wrote of his time in Garhwal: 'I was almost half a Hindu, for was I not in the home of the Hindu gods? It seemed the most natural thing in the world to look on the junction of two rivers as holy or to leave an offering of grains or nuts at the little stone doll's house shrine that stands by the path where it crosses a ridge. . . .'

In another of these articles, my father refers to a discussion he had read about whether there is, anywhere in fiction, a record of one perfectly happy day. He says that although he has had many happy days, they are not individually memorable. However, 'moments to remember are quite another thing'. He tells of one in particular when, at the end of the day's march, 'we had reached our destination and were waiting for supper. I sat down on a rock and gazed across miles of space at a group of fluted peaks, still silvery in the sun but beginning to show here and there the more mellow gold of evening and in shadow turning grey and lilac. I was overwhelmed—dwarfed by their vastness.' This idea of recalling a perfect moment seems to relate to Hugh Upton's discussion with Margaret and later Christopher's with Susan about the difficulty of recapturing the happiness and the loveliness of time spent together. Through describing many happy moments in *The Wild Sweet Witch*, my father had recreated in large measure the joyful period he and my mother spent together among the Garhwalis.

Cambridge, U.K.                                                          Sarah Irons

# Author's Foreword

G arhwal is a real district, whose hills and people, so far as they come into this story, I have described as well as I can. Since the district is quite different from any other in India, it would be silly to try to hide it under a changed name and most of the places are drawn just as I remember them; but the story itself is fiction. None of the characters are drawn direct from any single living person, although Mr Bennett unites in himself some of the characteristics of three Deputy Commissioners in the nineteenth century whose names are still remembered.

Readers of recent fiction about India may think that my pictures of Mr Bennett and his successors are too kind, but one can only write from one's own experience. Perhaps I have been lucky in the people I have known and the visitors who write books after a six months' stay have been unlucky.

The incidents which make up the story come more directly from experience than the characters, but they are usually based on tales heard from villagers which have been worn by time from their original shape, like pebbles in a stream, and they have been further modified to suit the main purpose. For instance, all I know about the forced labour is that there was an agitation against it after the war of 1914–18, and it was abolished. I have no idea what the Deputy Commissioner of that day thought about it nor what course the agitation took. There was certainly no Jodh Singh. Again, there really was a panther which killed human beings once or twice a week for some years; the villagers did think he was a man by day, who turned into a panther at night; and the Deputy Commissioner of the day did take a man into protective custody to prove he was not the panther. But my knowledge is based on hearsay; the true story of this panther is, I believe, being written by Major Jim Corbett, the author of *Man-eaters of Kumaon*, who eventually shot him.

The word I have translated 'warlock' really means a person who may turn into either a panther or a bear and some of the stories I have heard seem to indicate that the same person may turn into either and does not even know which form he is going to take when he starts his spell or incantation.

I have never cared for what Peter Fleming calls the 'nullah' school of writing, and expect other people to dislike Indian words they do not understand as much as I do the *'m'bongos'* and *'b'wanas'* in books about Africa. I think there are only three Indian words in this story: kukri, the heavy Nepalese chopping knife, which has been made familiar by the doings of Gurkha and Garhwali troops in two wars; *tahsildar,* a magistrate and revenue officer, who in the hills is a police officer as well; and *patwari,* a junior revenue official. He too in the hills is also a policeman.

Names, however, cannot be avoided, and the easiest way of explaining the pronunciation is to say that vowels are as in Italian, except the short *a* which has the sound of *u* in the English word butter. Thus Kalyanu is pronounced Kull-yah-noo, the first syllable rhyming with hull. 'Garhwal' is very difficult to pronounce well, but for all practical purposes the first syllable rhymes with 'her', and the second with 'marl'. By the same rough standard, 'Jodh' may be taken to rhyme with 'goad'.

I have a clear conscience about crops, states of the moon, and seasons; but the feast of lights mentioned in Part III would really have come a few weeks earlier in relation to other events, and I suspect that the rope festival really took place in the spring, in order to fertilize the millet and maize crop. But it fitted this story to relate it to the winter crop of barley and I doubt whether anyone can say this is wrong, because there is no one living who has seen it.

Philip Mason

# PART I

The Uprooting, 1875

# 1

Everyone in the hills knows that when the snow has melted and the flowers are in their first glory, the scent in the high pastures is so strong that it makes a man drunk and he is likely to do strange things and wake with a headache. Kalyanu knew the feeling well, for it was his custom every year to climb many thousands of feet to the summer alps and to stay there with the sheep and goats for the lambing. But now he was in the fields below the forest where the homestead stood; and yet it was the same constriction of the throat and lightness in the head, the same impulse of wild unreason, that rose and choked him as he stood looking at his field of ruined millet.

As soon as he had come down from the pastures, he had been round the fields to see how his brothers had managed while he was away. It was a hard life they led, here between the mountains and the river, and they had not much reserve if a crop failed them. The autumn millet fed them for most of the year, and they added to it any barley they were lucky enough to get if there was good snow or rain in the winter. But the millet was their life, and here were the best fields ruined by a bear. Rage filled him; it swelled in his chest and head, a drunkenness of rage as suffocating as that other drunkenness of height.

As the worst of it passed and he became conscious of more than blind fury, he spoke aloud:

'The bear must be killed,' he said.

He looked at the sun. It would soon be behind the mountains to the west; daylight is short in the high steep valleys. The bear would come again when the sun had gone and he must quickly get his brothers together for the fight. No one could be certain that the bear would come to the same field, but there was a chance. He looked at the damage, and the drunkenness rose in him again when he saw how the beast had rolled in the crop after eating its fill. But he fought it down and looked for tracks in the moist soil which was never wholly dried by the brief warmth of midday. It was one bear, only one. It would be an old strong male. It would come again, that night or the next or the one after; they must wait every night till it came and then they would kill it. He went quickly down the hill to fetch his brothers, planning as he went.

His problem was not an easy one. Weapons were his first thought. There was not much iron in the upper hills of the Himalayas in the year 1875, because every ounce had to be carried up from the plains on the buyer's back and the journey took twelve days. As the buyer had to take his own food for the journey too, the less iron he carried the better. What there was, soft untempered stuff, would not take an edge and was most of it beaten into short blunt sickles or trowels. Wood and stone were the two materials of which there was plenty and they were used for almost every purpose. The only arms Kalyanu possessed were one degenerate kukri used for beheading goats, one axe, and several heavy wooden poles. The kukri was really quite unsuitable for a fight with a bear. It was small and involved coming to very close quarters before it could be used. The axe was better and would be invaluable in the last stage, but it was short and clumsy. Kalyanu had decided before he found the first of his brothers that they must stun the bear with poles and then use the axe to finish him off.

The four brothers were all working in the fields near the homestead and it did not take long to find them nor to collect their heavy poles and the axe and kukri. They started at once on the climb back to the damaged field. The path was one they had made themselves in their goings and comings to their fields, and to the forest above the fields where the women went to cut grass and collect sticks, and where they drove the cattle to graze. The way led first through the home fields, little shelves of ploughed land a few yards in width, with a slanting scramble after each shelf up a bank, about the height of a man, faced sometimes with stone, sometimes with the natural turf. The twisted triple ears of the green millet near the farm, like the plaited tails of tiny shire horses, were beginning to turn yellow for the harvest; farther up the patches of red millet were already a deep madder, ear and leaf and stalk alike. The air was moist with the fruitfulness of autumn and the scent of vegetation was heavy.

The path left the fields and struck up slanting across a long hillside too steep for cultivation, deep in grass which the women would cut before it was buried by the snow. But it was easy walking because the feet of themselves and their goats and their ancestors for generations had worn a firm ledge, seldom as much as six inches wide, but not difficult for anyone who did not think of the depth below. For the almost precipitous grassy side gave way farther down to a sheer rocky scarp, which fell away in cliff on cliff to the river, boiling in ice-fed spate in its narrow channel. The steady roar of tormented water and rolling boulders made a background to every other sound that Kalyanu and his brothers heard, although the river was thousands of feet below them.

The way led below a sheer rock face with a spring at the foot and then turned to zigzag directly upwards to the less extreme slopes which lay at the top of the cliff. Here the labour of their fathers and grandfathers and themselves had driven back the pines and gradually cleared a patch of snaky terraced fields, sloping outwards between rocky walls, fields a few feet wide that nothing could have ploughed but the little mountain bullocks as high as a man's waist, and that no one but a hillman would have thought worth the heart-breaking labour. But on this side of the river there were only two patches of ground where the slope was not so steep as to forbid even this hard-won cultivation, one near the homestead and the second up here, where the bear had rolled in the millet.

The sun was already behind the mountains as the brothers climbed the hill, but there would be reflected light from the sky for some time. The fight had to be very carefully planned, because one man with a pole is no match for a bear and if the bear was able to attack one of the brothers alone, that one would probably be killed. Kalyanu was thinking hard as he climbed. If all the brothers were close together from the start, hiding behind one rock, the bear would probably get away. A bear can move fast for a short distance and it would not stay to fight five men if it saw them all close together in a group. But if the brothers surrounded the field and were too far apart, one of them might be left to face the bear alone. It must eventually make away up hill, towards the forest, for there was a sheer drop on the lower side. A subtle plan was needed, based on the lie of the ground.

The three fields that were damaged were at the top of the patch of ploughed land and from Kalyanu's point of view at present they were well placed, for there was only one natural line for a retreat to the forest above, and that was fairly narrow. On one side was a bluff with a rock cliff fifty feet high, up which not even a goat could go, and on the other the debris of some fall of rock in forgotten times, huge fragments as big as a cottage, over which a bear could scramble, but which he would not willingly choose as his path. His natural line would be between the bluff and the fall of rock. He could, of course, go down and traverse below either of these obstacles, but he would not do this unless he realized that he had something formidable to face. And this was unlikely, for firearms were almost unknown and as a rule the men of the hills feared a bear more than the bear feared them. Once the bear was committed to the way between the cliff and the fall of rock, he would not easily be deflected. The plan must, therefore, be to make him start on that path, and then to take him in the narrow place, all arriving there at the same moment.

Kalyanu did not formulate this reasoning even to himself. He

• A RAJ COLLECTION

certainly could not have put it in words, but by a swift subconscious
appreciation of the nature of the ground and the mentality of his
enemy, he saw that it was the best course to take. And since his
brothers gave him unquestioning obedience, he did not need to explain
his reasoning to them. He hid two of them among the rocks to the east
of the narrow place and two in the bushes in the thick shadow below
the cliff on the west. He himself would be farther down, below where
he thought the bear would be, and it would be his first task to make it
move towards the narrow place. He explained to his brothers what
they had to do. They were to lie still, even when they heard him shout.
He would not show himself when he first shouted, but would try to
make the bear think it had more than one man to deal with, so that it
would start for the narrow place, but it must not be frightened, it must
be slow and unhurried. Only when Kalyanu showed himself and
shouted a definite word of command—'Strike'—were they to leap out
from their hiding places and rush upon the enemy. And then they must
make sure to arrive all at the same moment. They must not lose their
heads in the excitement and rush in without thought. He made each of
them repeat what he had to do.

The waxing moon rose early, but it was some time before it cleared
the eastern hills and shone on the fields and rocks of Kalyanu's upper
farm. The forest above the ploughed ledges was of blue pine; the trees
nearest to the fields glistened with little points of light, but the mass of
the forest made a black menacing shadow. Inky black were the
shadows below the rocks and among the thick bushes at the foot of the
cliff. The silvery light on the narrow fields seemed clear as day by
contrast, but it was deceptive. You could not distinguish detail, and it
was the shadow rather than the object that could be seen. Black and
silver, forest and cliff and rock, the stage was set.

Kalyanu waited with fast-beating heart, a sick feeling in the
stomach. He strained his eyes to see their enemy. Surely that shadow
had not been there before? It was just the shape of a bear. It was very
still. No, it was moving; a tiny movement. It looked different; it had
moved as he blinked his eyes. It was the bear. Wait and see which way
it goes. Wait. Wait. No, it has been still too long. No, it is nothing, a
rock. Things look so different in the moonlight. Quiet, more waiting,
and then again the heart pounds, the breath comes quick, the palms of
the hands are wet on the polished wood of the staff, at a stone rolling
down from above; the bear must have dislodged it. Wait again; wait
and see; no, it was nothing.

Disaster might have overtaken the brothers if they had missed the
bear that night and had tried a second night with senses dulled by lack
of sleep and the boredom of waiting. But they were lucky. The bear

came early, while they were still keen and alert, keyed and poised by Kalyanu's talk, their eyes bright, their bowels still conscious of the nearness of danger. The black bulk rolled forward in the moonlight, black as a moving shadow. Kalyanu waited till it was well into the field and then he yelled. He did not show himself, but shouted and moved from one bush to another and shouted again; he beat the bushes, threw stones at other bushes, and rolled boulders down the hill. The bear stood still suspiciously; then slowly it began to move uphill towards the narrow place. Still Kalyanu did not show himself; he waited, watching, forgetting to breathe, judging his moment; then he shouted: 'Strike!' and ran with all his strength and fire for the narrow place. The four brothers sprang from their tense muscles and dashed forward, hurling insults at the bear.

It was perfectly timed. The four younger brothers reached the centre of the narrow place a fraction of a second before the bear; Kalyanu was close behind, in a position of great danger if it should turn. But it did not turn; it swung clumsily but with incredible quickness to its left towards the cliff, meaning to pass between the two brothers coming from that side and to maul both as it passed. But the men it had to deal with were not trying to get away as it had expected; their stout poles swung high above their shoulders and came down with all their force, almost in the same second as those of the two on the right. Three blows fell on the head and neck and the fourth, that of the brother on the bear's extreme right, on the backbone. And at the same moment Kalyanu flung aside his pole and made his axe bite deep into the back above the root of the tail. Such a volley of blows, all at once like a clap of thunder, stopped the bear for the blink of an eyelid, but he shook his head and rose on his hind legs to strike right and left with the curved claws of his forepaws. But again that shattering volley of four blows fell on head and shoulders and a second time Kalyanu struck with his axe and this time the axe reached the backbone. The bear fell; at once all five were on him, yelling wildly, striking again and again till their poles were splintered and broken. The bear lay stunned and battered; with all his strength Kalyanu swung the axe and split its skull. He drew the kukri and cut its throat.

'He's dead,' they said.

'He's dead!'

They could not believe it. They were silent, looking at each other and panting. Then they all began to talk at once.

'Did you see how I hit him the moment he turned our way?'

'Well, he's dead now, and he won't roll in our crops again.'

'That was a fine blow Kalyanu caught him with the axe!' And so on.

At last Kalyanu stilled the chatter and said:

'Let us drag this sod of a bear out of our field into the forest and leave him to the vultures. Then we will go home and eat. We will kill the home-fed sheep. And we will eat raw game. And when we have eaten we will dance. We will dance *Bakhtuwar Wins*.'

They did certain things to the corpse and then they dragged it out of the field and they went back down the little twisty path to the homestead. The moon silvered the grass on the steep side below the bluff, as the wind sighed over it in a long ripple, like a caress on the skin of a panther. The wind sighed again and the blue pines breathed deep in reply. The roar of the torrent below rose to them faintly and the wind sighed in the pines, the five men chattered of their triumph, but behind all trivial sound, behind the roar of the torrent, was the deep positive silence of the mountains, the silence, and the silver of the moonlight.

The chatter broke out in a fresh spurt of excitement when they came to the little cluster of houses where they lived, a stone-paved terrace with circular paved pits for treading out the corn, and round the terrace little stone cabins on three sides of a square, some for men and some for beasts. The women heaped up the fire and they dragged out the home-fed sheep. It had been in the dark and fed on grain for six months. The grain made it fat; it was kept in the dark so that the sun should not melt its fat. Its feet had grown so that they curved up before it like fantastic medieval slippers. Autaru, the second brother, led it up to Kalyanu. There was no Brahman in the little community of Bantok, but Kalyanu was priest of the godling they propitiated from time to time, a power who had ruled over this hillside before the Hindus came up from the plains. The godling lived in a tiny stone house at the foot of a cedar tree. They led the sheep before him and marked its forehead with a daub of colour and a few grains of barley. Then Autaru seized the sheep by the horns and leaned back, stretching the neck while another brother held the hind-quarters. Kalyanu struck once with the kukri and Autaru staggered one pace back with the head in his hands. A spurt of blood fell on him and he laughed, and they all laughed at him. They cut the sheep to pieces without skinning it, and singed the raw meat in the flames. Then they ate it with handfuls of salt. The liver they did not even singe in the fire but rolled little pieces of it in salt and red pepper and ate it. This is 'raw game'; for in Garhwal all meat is called 'game'.

They piled up the fires higher and stuck torches of pinewood round the paved courtyard. Then they began to dance the dance of *Bakhtawar Wins*. There was a family of aboriginals, the dark-faced Doms, who lived farther down towards the river and worked as the serfs of Kalyanu and his brothers. One of the children had gone to fetch them as soon as the triumphant party returned. They had brought the drums, one a great vessel of copper shaped like an egg with the top cut off, the severed end bound over with stout buffalo skin, the other smaller, with a narrow waist, a percussion surface at either end, bound with thinner goatskin. The drums were beaten with a curved and polished stick held in the right hand; the second man played also with his fingers and the butt of his left palm on the reverse end of his small tenor drum. There was no other instrument but the drums, and so no tune, only the cadence of the voice singing a ballad and the odd exciting syncopated rhythm of the drums, quickening and quickening to intolerable broken speed, dropping again to a slower throb, throbbing and pulsing in slow broken rhythm, quickening again, pulsing faster and faster at a climax in the story.

There was silence and silver moonlight on the cliffs and the hanging bulk of the hills, but in the paved yard before the houses the flicker and waver of torches and the broken pulse of the drums and a man's voice singing. The figures moving in a circle were short and square, the woollen blankets that they wore looped round their bodies and over their shoulders like a plaid, accenting the angle of the shoulder. They stamped and bowed in the dance, their arms rose and gesticulated, as they circled between the torches. The little circle of fire and human joy was as small as one star among the myriads of heaven.

The ballad to which they danced was the story of a king from over the passes in Tibet who crossed the high range and came down with his slant-eyed men into the valleys of Garhwal. They came with their felt boots, their barbarous furs, round copper shields studded with turquoise and silver, with spears and swords and bows, and they were very many. But Bakhtawar called together the people of the valleys and led them against the invaders. When they told him that the odds were against him, for the men of Garhwal were few and poorly armed, he told them that this was a land beloved of the gods, where the sacred Ganges rose, and where the gods had played and journeyed when the world was young; the gods will help us, he said. And sure enough, when they came close to the armies from across the mountains, the gods sent on the Tibetans a madness, that drunkenness that comes in the high pastures when the flowers are in bloom. They ate stones and grass and snow and turned their weapons upon each other; and the people of Garhwal fell upon them and killed many of them and drove the rest back over the passes. So to this day they dance the dance of *Bakhtawar Wins* to celebrate victory.

The dancers are first the people of Garhwal, marching up the narrow valleys to unequal battle; and then in turn they are the Tibetans on whom the madness has fallen. They become possessed by the gods and the drums quicken and quicken again, till it seems beyond belief that nerve and muscle can keep up the speed, and each dancer twirls away in a wild *pas seul*, twirling and spinning till he falls breathless and dizzy. Then on hands and knees he fills his mouth with grass or stones, and foaming and champing joins the dance again, till at last the rhythm drops and all sink exhausted to the ground. Then again the steady throbbing approach of Bakhtawar's army, and again the drums quicken to the climax of action and victory and defeat.

The drums died, the torches burnt low, the serfs went back to their hovels below and the people of the homestead turned to sleep. Kalyanu was happy. Like Bakhtawar, he had triumphed over impossible strength. He had earned his rest. The little homestead clung to the cliff's edge and there was only the silver moonshine, the roar of the torrent below, the sigh of the wind in the pines and the deep silence of the mountains.

# 2

The mood in which Kalyanu and his brothers danced and feasted after killing the bear lasted for some days. They had indeed done something worthy of note. As a rule the people of the high valleys looked on the damage done by wild beasts as an act of the gods, something against which it was little use to fight. They took some precautions, just as they went through certain ceremonies to avert calamity, but with no very fervent belief that anything would come of it. They put up scarecrows and primitive booby-traps and, if things got too bad, would build themselves a little hut raised high above the ground on poles and in this would watch all night with the object not of killing but of scaring the marauder; but that was as far as they usually went. Gun-licences were rare and were usually given to pensioners from the army or to the descendants of the barons who had ruled the land for the Rajas in the days before the Gurkhas swept over the hills and conquered the country. And if Kalyanu had asked for a gun-licence, which he was not so presumptuous as to do, he would certainly have been told that he was not the most important person in his village, no account being taken of the fact that the rest of the village was on the other side of the river and the nearest bridge was thirty miles downstream. The bow was forgotten, though it had been the weapon of the heroes of Hindu story and ballad. And for some strange reason the pitfall was not used. The truth was that the hill folk were not a hunting people and knew little of the ways of beasts.

So it was a great thing to have killed a bear with clubs and an axe. Kalyanu woke next day with something of the exaltation of a young man successful in his first love affair. He regarded the world with the same feeling of confidence in himself and mastery over external incident; he could shape events as he wished them and make others dance to his piping. And just as the happy youth feels himself irresistible to all women, so Kalyanu believed that he had nothing more to fear from wild beasts. Bears were easy.

This confidence and self-satisfaction were still with him a week later when he decided to climb to the upper patch of ploughland and see how the crops were ripening. In the fields round the homestead, his brothers and the women were all at work, getting in the yellow millet. Men and women alike moved stooping through the crops, reaching out the left hand to gather together a bunch of stalks, cutting with a stroke of the blunt sickle in the right hand; there was none of the orderly division of labour that went with the work on an English farm at the same period, no sweeping line of scythes with the women picking up. Each worker drove his own path into the crop and collected the fallen corn when there was a load he or she could conveniently manage; each carried it on his own back to the homestead. Kalyanu regarded their activities with satisfaction and thought of the work still to be done. The snow had already fallen on the high pastures in a light powdering that would melt by day. Up there the ground would freeze hard every night and the clefts and corries where no sun came would gradually fill with snow; but it would be two months yet with any luck before it would lie on the upper fields. There would be time to finish the harvest in the lower fields, then to get in the millet from the higher; then to plough into some of the upper fields the rotted bracken that had been stored during the summer and sow the barley before the snow covered it. Next would come the ploughing and sowing of the lower fields. It was a great convenience that everything on the upper farm was so much slower; one could cut later and sow earlier up there; the labour force at Kalyanu's disposal would not have been enough to deal with the same acreage if the land had been all at one level and the crops had all ripened at the same time.

He turned from the busy scene in the fields round the homestead and set his face to the path leading to the upper farm. He climbed easily and quickly; indeed it was hardly climbing to him, for his muscles were so attuned to rough paths on the hill face that they would have been more quickly tired on the level. But he had never walked on the level.

Kalyanu had no ears for the roar of the river below, no eyes for the scene he knew so well. His thoughts were on practical matters, the harvesting of crops and the work he should set his brothers to do. To an observer on the hillside beyond the river he would have seemed a minute dark point moving steadily across the grass slope below the bluff. Even the ploughed land below him made only a tiny patch of colour against the immensity of the hillside. Its snaky terraces, the crimson of the red millet, the yellow of the green millet, the brilliant orange of the drying heads of maize, were touches with the point of the brush, hardly to be picked up by the eye in the vastness of rock face, grass slope, and forest. Grass clothed the hill where it was not sheer rock; forest poured into every corrie, glen, or hollow where a tree could stand. Below the homestead were long-leaved pines, the light sparkling on their dancing upturned needle-points, their airy glitter interspersed with the darker masses of cedar or contorted oak scrub; higher, the blue pine turned its closer darker fingers to the sky with the same exultation. Even where the trees could grow, the line of the ground was nearer the vertical than the horizontal; it was a landscape crazily tip-tilted out of the plane familiar to the world of men and the tiny evidence of man's presence could hardly be distinguished against those impending precipitous masses.

When Kalyanu reached the first field he plucked an ear of millet and rubbed it between his fingers to see how it was forming. He was pleased at the progress it had made. It should be possible to start cutting this patch from the bottom upwards as soon as the work below was ended. He climbed up from terrace to terrace, appraising the crop in each narrow shelf. Half way up he stopped and stood, gazing at the ruins of one field where a bear had again eaten its fill and rolled.

The anger he felt this time was quite different from that of a week ago. This was no surging of uncontrollable fury, because he no longer felt helpless. He knew how to deal with a bear. He would show the swine. He went quickly over the remaining fields, to see the extent of the damage, and he looked at the footprints. Not so large a beast as last time. Probably a female. His confidence needed no strengthening but his contempt was increased. He followed the tracks up through the crops to the narrow place at the top, where the first bear had been killed. This was where the female too had come in from the forest. Then he turned to go back and fetch his brothers.

It was a pity that Kalyanu did not examine the tracks more carefully or apply his mind more thoroughly to the problem. Had he done this, he would have seen that the tracks did not return to the forest by the narrow place, as they had come in. He had hunted heel, following the tracks back in the direction from which they had come; but though they came in by the narrow place, they went right through the crops, going on, not back. After eating and rolling, the bear had wandered downwards and westwards, passing out of the cultivated patch below the cliff that formed one flank of the narrow place. If he had noticed this, Kalyanu might have remembered the thicket of wild raspberries that lay beyond the plough on that western side. If he had troubled to think how a bear lived, it would have occurred to him that it must find much other food besides his crops and an occasional goat or bullock. He might then have reflected that this beast must have enjoyed the wild raspberries and that where a bear has gone once, it may go again; and had he thought thus, the story of his life, his son's, and his grandson's, might have been changed. But the Himalayan peasant is unobservant of the ways of beasts and birds except as they affect him directly. He does not even know of the strange habits of the cuckoo, whose word of fear rings through his hills in May and June just as it does in England. Kalyanu assumed that this bear would come in by the narrow place and could be made to go out by the same way, just as the first bear had done a week ago. He did not hesitate but went at once to fetch his brothers.

The five men stopped work in the fields, leaving it to the women to go on till dark, and climbed up the hillside once more to the ambush. But they did not come as they had a week before, full of wonder at their own daring, breathless, with a queer empty feeling in the bowels. They were only a little keyed up by the thought of what they had to do. They could joke among themselves quite naturally, for they knew now that bears were easy.

Kalyanu arranged them just as he had done before and they took up their stations. The moon had not yet risen, so that waiting should have been more nervous work than last time. But the tension that had made the heart pound at every moving stone and crackling leaf had gone when victory was achieved and, far from being on edge, as the night wore on, the younger brothers were inclined to doze. Kalyanu being separate from the others did not know this, but Autaru, the second brother, had to speak several times to his companion, the youngest, to keep him awake. They had all worked a long day in the fields.

No bear came that night and it was a weary and dispirited party who came back to the homestead in the dawn. They worked badly in the fields that day and when Kalyanu told them they were to watch for the bear again, Autaru was the only one who did not grumble. But there was no question of disobedience and they hid once more in the appointed places, Kalyanu agreeing, however, at Autaru's suggestion, that one of each pair of brothers should sleep.

The moon had risen and her silvery light made long inky shadows below rocks and terrace walls, when, an hour after this watch began, Kalyanu rose carefully to his feet, taking care to make no sound. He glanced over his shoulder to the east and saw the pines on the next ridge cut out in rigid black silhouette against the growing radiance; then turned again to look at the fields before him. As he looked, he stiffened in sudden attention. There it was. Yes, there was no doubt. There was the bear, right in the middle of the crops. That shadow had not been there before; it was moving slowly, very slowly, but undoubtedly moving, as the beast nosed here and there, making up its mind where to begin.

For about ten heart beats Kalyanu was flustered. The bear was below him. How had it got there without his knowledge? Had it crept past him in the dark? It seemed now to be moving upwards; was it already retreating? But the moment of indecision passed. However the bear had got there, whatever irrelevancies it had introduced, the original plan must stand. It was moving upwards. He would wait till it was level with him and then he would hurl rocks and shout, and it would make upwards for the narrow place.

The bear moved very slowly and Kalyanu's patience began to wear thin. He was very short of sleep; and all the time this sod of a bear was spoiling his crops. He did not stick to his decision to wait till it was level with him. The bear was still on a terrace lower than his own when he let out his first yell and began to throw stones at the bushes and send them crashing down the hillside.

The bear raised her head at this sudden commotion and began to move away, slow and unhurried, for she was disturbed, not frightened. But she did not go towards the narrow place as Kalyanu had expected. She went back the way she had come, towards the wild raspberries, downwards and westwards. Kalyanu sprang to his feet.

'Strike!' he shouted at the top of his voice, and ran after the bear in a frenzy lest she should escape and the hours of waiting be wasted. He sprang down from the top of a terrace-wall into the field across which the bear was moving with rolling unhurried gait. He swung his pole and brought it down with all his strength on the hairy black hindquarters. The bear turned with incredible speed; Kalyanu struck again with his shortened staff as she came at him on all fours, but quite ineffectively; the bear's quick lunge with mouth and paw went home. Her right paw broke his left leg below the knee; her teeth crunched deep in his right thigh.

As Kalyanu fell back at the foot of the terrace wall, Autaru arrived at the top with a yell and struck downwards with his staff at the beast below. It was a blow into which he could put no strength, for she was too far below him, and in a blind red fighting lust he sprang down beside her. His blow had been just enough to distract the bear from Kalyanu and to infuriate her. She rose on her hindquarters and struck with both forepaws a fraction of a second quicker than he could. Her left stripped the flesh from the side of his face and glanced off his shoulder; but before he could feel the agony her right fell with its full force on his head, crushing the skull and breaking his neck.

The youngest brother had been sharing the watch with Autaru in the bushes below the cliff and had been asleep when Kalyanu first shouted. He was only a few yards behind when he saw his brother drop lifeless, but he was fully awake by now and he acted with sense and courage. He did not leap down at once to the bear's level, to drop almost into her arms as Autaru had done, but moved off a few paces, dropped to her level and approached her warily, poised on his toes, ready for flight or fight. The bear had hardly noticed him, for she was still wholly unafraid, and was actually sniffing at Autaru and considering his possibilities as a meal, when he struck. Her lunge towards him with curved left forepaw was made almost as one might brush away a fly; she returned to her interest in Autaru. But her hooked blow had done all that was necessary; the youngest brother had sprung back and had dropped his staff as a guard, but the bear's strength and quickness were such that the staff was torn from his hands and broke his shin-bone where it struck him. He pulled himself away from the enemy with his hands, trailing his useless leg.

The third and fourth brothers arrived as the youngest fell. They had run as fast as they could and were wildly excited. They too would have flung themselves at the bear, no doubt with the same result, if Kalyanu had not spoken. But lying there sick with pain, he still knew what was happening and from the shadow below the terrace wall had seen the fate of his two brothers. He heard the others shout as they came up and called up all his strength to cry:

'No! Do not fight! You must look after us. Do not fight!'

Then he fainted.

The two remaining brothers pulled up at Kalyanu's voice. For a second they hesitated, but they were used to obeying Kalyanu, and once they paused a strong natural inclination came to the aid of his instructions. They shouted abuse and threw stones but kept their distance. The bear paused, grunted, then slowly made off towards the wild raspberries. The two brothers returned to pick up their wounded and take home the dead.

The youngest brother had a cracked shin-bone which needed nothing but rest. Kalyanu's case was more serious. His left leg required to be set before nature could begin the work of healing; and more serious still was his mangled thigh, with multiple wounds from the bear's teeth. He and his brothers knew well enough that a wound can go septic, but their only means of preventing this was to apply cow-dung to exclude the air and in this method they had, rightly enough, no great faith. Kalyanu lay tossing in agony while the two brothers who were still whole debated with the women of Bantok what they should do. No one really had any plan, until one of the outcast Doms mentioned that the day before he had met another Dom from ten miles down the river who had come their way in search of a stray goat. He had heard that the Deputy Commissioner would soon be coming to camp on the other side of the river, near the bridge thirty miles downstream which was their only link with the outside world. Everyone's face lightened; they were not used to responsibility but to doing what Kalyanu told them, and here was someone else on whom the responsibility could be placed.

'We will take him to the District Sahib,' they said. Kalyanu was lying on a bed, made of tough oak roughly shaped with the axe and strung with hemp string they had twisted themselves, but it was too wide for the paths they would have to follow. They must make a litter hardly wider than their own shoulders or it would catch on the cliff walls and throw them all over the edge. The women set to work quickly to make a hammock which could be slung from one stout pole, whilst the two brothers worked feverishly to get in what they could of the millet and to leave the farm in such trim that the women could manage without them. Ten or twelve miles on a hill path is a good day's stage for a loaded man, but they could not afford to take three days to reach the bridge. They must hurry, because they had to get back to see to the harvest and because if they were to save Kalyanu he must be in better hands than theirs as soon as possible. And before they went they had to burn Autaru.

It was not till the morning of the second day after the disaster that they started, taking with them food for three days only. They could get more on the other side of the bridge and they took with them some of their precious store of silver, a hoard into which they usually dipped twice a year to pay their few rupees of land revenue; once every year or two when one of them went across the river and down towards the plains to Chamoli to buy salt and iron; a few times in a generation to buy a bride. They started very early, after a drink of milk and no more, meaning to get as far as they could before they stopped for food. The women watched them move away, their reddish-brown legs naked to the thigh, their sturdy bodies square in the dark homespun blankets draped across the shoulders, Kalyanu swinging in his hammock between them. Then the women turned to get on with the work of the farm, the feeding of the children, the animals, and Darshanu the youngest brother, and the harvesting of the millet, their life blood for the winter.

The path the brothers had to take followed the river and, since the river for most of its course ran in a precipitous rocky gorge, it was not an easy path. It went down to the river for an easy crossing of a tributary torrent where there were stepping stones, renewed every year after the autumn spates, and then across the shingly debris brought down from the hills in the course of years. The roar of the river here was deafening. You had to put your mouth to a man's ear and shout to make yourself heard. The water was milky-green with the ice-ground dust of glaciers and melted snow; it swept and churned and stormed; spouting high where it dashed against a bastion of the cliff, breaking with the shattering weight of Atlantic rollers over a rock in midstream, rolling and grinding the boulders in its bed, a stream of ceaseless, furious energy, seeking the centre of the earth with swifter force, but the same remorseless purpose, as the upthrusting green of trees and grass and corn.

Then the path went up, zigzagging up a narrow edge between two arms of the tributary torrent, then out on to the face of the sheer rock cliff over the main river, following a crack that led up and up for two thousand feet; then on to a long grass face, so steep that if one stretched out a hand to the bole of a pine below the path, the fingers touched a point twice the height of a man from the roots. Across this face the tiny track made by the feet of goats and men lay like a single hair. Down again, to a tributary crossing and a stretch of shingle; up, to go over another bluff with an impassable face; a long, long, tiring journey in which the mind after some miles could not disentangle the steady succession of cliff and torrent, corrie and grass slope, rock and pine.

The brothers kept going all day, except for a halt in the middle of the morning to eat. They had fresh water to drink at every torrent, ice-cold, and they were in hard condition, but they were very tired by the evening, for they had covered twenty miles, a long march over such country and with such a load. They gave Kalyanu water; he wanted nothing else; they put him by their side on a bed of leaves in the shelter of an overhanging rock, much used by goats and shepherds, where they rolled themselves up in the blankets that had covered their shoulders by day.

They reached the bridge at midday on the third day after the disaster. Near this point on the northern bank, there was a village, not an isolated homestead, for a larger tributary had made a valley in which there were slopes that could be terraced and ploughed. Here the banks of the river approached each other in two leaning cliffs, on each of which there was a convenient ledge on which a man could stand. From each side had been thrust out three pine trunks lashed together, the butts firmly wedged in hollows carved deep in the cliff face, the angle of the ledge pushing them steeply up, so that the space between the tips could be bridged by a pair of lashed trunks. The drop from the bridge was two hundred feet to the frenzy of the milky torrent below. It was not easy to walk over the two pine trunks with such a burden as Kalyanu in his hammock, but the two brothers did it. Fortunately Kalyanu was conscious at that point and they made him understand that he must lie quite still, for a sudden movement would destroy them all.

When they got him over, they looked at each other and grinned.

'That was worse than the bear,' said Amru, the elder.

They went on to the first village and began to ask questions. It was true. The Deputy Commissioner's camp was only five miles away up the hillside. In two more hours, his tents were in sight, but their hearts sank. They would have to talk and explain, to superior people, who would laugh at them because their hair was long and their speech barbarous. But their luck had turned. They met the District Sahib himself as he was coming back to camp and he stopped to ask them questions.

At first they were speechless, shifting from one leg to another. Then Amru said:

'Lord, it is our brother. It was a bear. We have brought him to you.'

And after more questioning at last the strange man understood them. His face was strange, sharp and light coloured, but kindly; still more strange was his speech; but he had understood. He would look after Kalyanu. They could go back to the farm.

# 3

Mr Bennett, the Deputy Commissioner of Garhwal in 1875, was an amateur surgeon and physician of some repute. His methods were simple and usually drastic but they suited the people with whom he had to deal. Castor oil was the basis of his physic, warm water and carbolic of his surgery.[1] With a people who did not wash much and lived in highly insanitary villages, the moderate degree of surgical cleanliness he was able to achieve worked

---

[1]Lister's discoveries were only ten years old, and Mr Bennett was somewhat ahead of the average of medical practice at this date. He owed his knowledge to a regular correspondence with a medical friend of his year at Oxford, a keen disciple of Lister.

wonders, for, when it was released from the great majority of the foes it was accustomed to deal with, the injured flesh flourished and clove together with startling rapidity.

It did not need great skill to see that Kalyanu's left shin-bone would have to be set and Mr Bennett set it and bound it to a splint of oak, an unshaped branch that happened to be the right shape and size. The bitten thigh was more difficult. The bone did not seem to be broken but was probably bruised; the flesh was terribly lacerated. There was really nothing to do but to clean up the oil and cow-dung which the people of Bantok had applied, wash the wounds generously with hot water and carbolic and tie them up again, continue the treatment, and hope for the best.

So Kalyanu's pole and hammock joined the considerable assemblage that moved round with Mr Bennett's camp. Rest in one place would of course have been much better, but the business of the district could not be held up for one man and Mr Bennett could not trust anyone but himself to look after the patient. The addition of a load that was now usually carried by four men made little difference to his arrangements, because his tents and bedding and gear and that of his many servants were carried by the people of each village to the next halting-place. This was an ancient feudal service due to the Rajas which had been continued by the Commissioners of Kumaon because there was no other way of getting about. Kalyanu was moved every two or three days and the journeys were not pleasant, but then he was not used to anything pleasant and he was being looked after better than ever before in his life. Mr Bennett's orderlies were charged with the duty of feeding him at Mr Bennett's expense and, being hill-peasants only one degree less unsophisticated than Kalyanu himself, they did as they were told. It never entered their heads to underfeed him for their own benefit, or to overcharge their master. Once a day Mr Bennett himself came and took off the bandages and washed the wounds. After the first day or two, as he began to mend and his mind grew clearer, Kalyanu tried to struggle to his feet when this strange ruler came to see him but it was made clear to him that this was forbidden. His first feeling of surprise and fear at being waited on by someone who was practically a king was gradually replaced by veneration and a deep devotion. If it is love to wish ardently for an opportunity to serve and be near the object of one's devotion, then Kalyanu loved Mr Bennett.

Mr Bennett in his turn felt an increasing liking for the man who grew to health under his care. For a generous nature, there is a natural inclination towards affection for anyone to whom a kindness has been done; and to this was gradually added an interest in Kalyanu himself. It was difficult at first to get him to talk. 'Yes, lord,' and 'No, lord,' and

'It was a bear, lord,' were the most that could be got from him, but gradually he told more and more of the story. His dialect was difficult to follow, for speech differs from village to village in Garhwal; but Mr Bennett had been ten years in the hills, and he had applied himself seriously to the dialects when he first came. And Kalyanu himself gradually acquired a rather more sophisticated vocabulary. When his story had been fully explained, an impression was left of courage and initiative that was enhanced by his cheerfulness in pain and his obvious gratitude.

Mr Bennett was not ambitious for an outwardly successful career ending in high office and many decorations, but he was by no means an ordinary man. He was a solitary, a poet, and a mountaineer. Had he been ambitious in the conventional sense, he would not have exerted himself in his early days to get on the Kumaon Commission, which could lead to no great post; had his recreations been those of most men, he would have preferred to his present loneliness the life of the plains, where there would be polo, pigsticking, and racing, and brandy and soda at the club. But he loved the hills. He would perhaps never be the kind of mountaineer who writes books, or of whom books are written, but his love for mountains had guided his life. His long vacations in Oxford days had been spent in Switzerland, and it was to Switzerland he went on his first leave. He taught himself to climb in the Alps without a guide and he then began to experiment in the Himalayas, not with any object of making a name for himself or of achieving what had not been done before, but because the silence of the snows in high places raised his clear spirit to a wordless delight which nothing else could equal. As for poetry, every mountaineer is a poet at heart, though few have been poets in execution. Mr Bennett might have been called a poet by virtue only of his pleasure in singing water, rock and cliff, and flower and icy peak, but he was also a lover of the English poets, and of a most catholic taste. He read them all, and not the old masters only, for he had a standing order with his booksellers in Oxford for the latest works of his contemporaries. He might perhaps have been called uncritical, for he did not take sides in the controversies of his day, but found a stimulating pleasure in wrestling with Browning or Coventry Patmore and yet turned-with an equal anticipation of happiness to the smooth melodies of Tennyson and Matthew Arnold. But this argued wide interests, not lack of standards; for he burnt his own efforts remorselessly.

Mr Bennett did a good deal of reading in his lonely evenings in camp but he was conscientious in allowing himself only a limited amount of time for his other recreation of mountaineering. His duties as Deputy Commissioner of Garhwal need not have been exacting, for although he was judge, policeman, and chief executive officer in one, the administration could really have been suspended for a few months without anyone noticing much difference. Crimes against property were unknown, murder and assault were rare. There were so few Muslims that communal trouble was not even thought of. The only local official of whom the villager had any knowledge was the patwari, who with the help of one servant collected the land revenue—almost a token rent—and administered criminal justice for some sixty to a hundred villages, with no sanction but the authority of the Government and the possession of a shotgun. There was not even much scope to the patwari for rapacity, for every villager paid him annually a gift of grain which was a fixed proportion of his crop. Although this amounted to ten times the trivial wages paid him by government, neither the patwari nor anyone else regarded the practice as dishonest, as indeed it was not, for, since everyone paid regularly, he was on the whole as fair as his intellect and training permitted him to be.

For Mr Bennett, therefore, the constant effort to prevent extortion which in those days made up most of the life of his colleagues in the plains hardly existed. His checks of the work of minor officials were little more than a formality. He could have spent his winters shooting tigers where the hills break down into the plains, his spring and autumn fishing, and his summer mountaineering, without anyone being actively the worse. Indeed, this was just what some of his predecessors had done. But he was a man with an essential goodness of heart who believed with no shadow of doubt that he was where he was for the good of the people he ruled. He made no attempt to change their way of life beyond putting an end so far as he could to certain practices which were repugnant to Christian morality and which orthodox Hinduism would have disowned. But he did think deeply about the welfare and the administration of his people and he came to the conclusion that, since most of the troubles which came to him were disputes about the ownership of land, the most beneficent boon that good government could bestow would be maps of the fields and a record of every man's rights.

After some months of correspondence he managed to convince his government that this was so and a survey expert was sent to make experimental maps. The expert made an accurate trigonometrical survey of one village and took two months to do it. His maps showed every terrace and every field. But he calculated that to cover the whole district would absorb four times the annual revenue received from the district for ten years. Government shook its heavy head.

So Mr Bennett invented an ingenious form of survey of his own, which could be carried out with no equipment but a few ropes for measuring distances and which concerned itself with no trigonometrical pedantry. By this means he could make sketch-maps that would serve his purpose in one-eighth of the time taken by the expert and at one-thirtieth of the cost. And to this, after more months of correspondence, his government did agree; and so Mr Bennett camped in every village of the district, worked ten hours a day to make his maps, and was happy.

When Kalyanu was well enough to walk, he felt no desire to go back to Bantok. Life there would not be the same without Autaru, and they seemed to be getting on fairly well without him, for Amru had developed unsuspected powers of leadership. Also, Kalyanu had tasted something of a more varied and, on the whole, rather less arduous life. But behind these superficial reasons was a warm positive desire to be near the man who had saved his life, and for whom he felt a real devotion and affection. He could not formulate these wishes to himself, much less tell them to anyone else. He hung about the camp, trying to bring himself to go to the District Sahib and ask to be allowed to serve him; but he was too shy to come to the point.

He was brought to the point, however, by external circumstance. And this happened at the one moment most opportune for himself. Had it happened on any other day, Mr Bennett would have told him he had no place vacant and advised him to go back to Bantok; and Kalyanu and his son and grandson would have lived out their lives in the yearly struggle to harvest enough grain to feed the homestead for another year. But the chances of this one day were to lead to the uprooting of himself and his family from Bantok and to the complex revenge which his grandson Jodh Singh was to take on society for uprooting him.

There were three threads of chance that twisted together into a pattern and altered Kalyanu's life. The first was that Mr Bennett changed the plans for his march without warning, a thing he did from time to time to make sure that he saw what was normal and not something specially prepared for the occasion; the second was that having varied his plan he made a further variation within it because he was a mountaineer and felt he deserved a holiday; and the third was that Keshar Singh, one of his orderlies, had a friend in the village of Marora.

Mr Bennett was moving eastwards along the south side of a steep ridge which varied between nine and ten thousand feet in height. There was a well-established route along the south side about three thousand feet below the crest of the ridge, with regular halting-places. If you went three days' march along it, everyone assumed you would take the next step and go on to the fourth halt. It was for this very reason that Mr Bennett decided that he would leave it and go over the ridge to look at some map-making which was going on among the lower villages on the north side of the ridge. The locals shook their heads when he told them he was going to cross the ridge.

'There is no path suitable for your Honour,' they said.

'But there is a way?' persisted Mr Bennett.

'There is a way that goats and shepherds take,' they admitted, 'but it is not a suitable path and there will be snow.'

Mr Bennett pointed out that there was not much snow yet, only a sprinkling, and that where a shepherd could go, so could he. He gave orders that next morning his camp should cross the ridge by the goat-path.

They had packed the first loads and the first porters were moving off when he started next morning. He came out of his tent and stamped his feet and clapped his hands for warmth in the diamond sunshine. The breaths of men and mules came in puffs of steam. There was still frost in the shadows of the bushes and behind the tent. To the south, the hillside was cultivated right down to the stream; every arm and root running downwards and outwards was wrinkled by the terraced fields like the skin of some very ancient and scaly beast. Looking down on them from above they were as regular and orderly as the rings in the stump of a great tree, or the scales on a butterfly's wing. They were ploughed and sown for the winter crops.

Mr Bennett turned and looked up to the north. From about the level of his camp to the crest, there was thick forest, from which, here and there along the ridge, peaks of rock or grass-clad domes stood out, sprinkled with the first powdering of snow. There was no wind and the smoke from the village to the east hung in a blue mist over the pines and oak scrub, sparkling with refracted light. A frosty, sparkling, diamond morning, thought Mr Bennett, and his spirit rejoiced at the thought that he would see the snows of the main range when he reached the crest.

His three orderlies approached, Amar Singh, the senior, with his square competent face serious, his black pillbox hat tilted over one eye as he had pushed it when considering some problem about the loading of a tent; Keshar Singh, humorous, his crinkled brown face waiting to widen to a grin at the first excuse; Bharat Singh like a small boy unexpectedly grown up, with his ears standing straight out from his head, and his terrier air of wanting to be taken for a walk. No one had ever got more than 'Yes, lord' and 'No, lord' out of Bharat Singh, Mr Bennett reflected. He smiled at them all with affection.

'Who is coming with me today?' he asked.

'Keshar Singh, lord,' replied Amar Singh. 'Bharat Singh is going on ahead as quickly as he can, and I shall see the last loads off and come with the coolies to see they do not rest too much.'

Mr Bennett nodded and turned to go. The path at first was not difficult, for it was the way to one of the main village grazing grounds and led on to another village. It ran through patches of pine forest, where the reddish boles of the long-leaved pine stood up like the straight limbs of prehistoric animals, coated in plates of scaly bark, and the sun lighted the brown floor of needles; then through patches of evergreen oak scrub and rhododendron; and then began to climb, the long-leaved pine giving way to the blue pine and a few deciduous trees appearing. In one glade, Mr Bennett stopped for a moment entranced. Through a tangle of rusty bracken and patches of bright couch-grass ran a little brown stream, tinkling happily over a dozen tiny falls. Alone in the glade stood one chestnut-tree, naked against the wintry blue of the sky, in a pool of its ruddy fan-shaped leaves. There was an autumn smell of dying leaves and frost and moisture. It was home, the English autumn, the English woodland. Mr Bennett shook his head and went on.

Keshar Singh had enlisted a local man to show the way, whom he now led forward to introduce. He pointed out with his usual crinkly grin that here they must leave the main path and begin to climb. It was not easy going, overgrown with trees and scrub and extremely steep. All three men had to use their hands to pull themselves up and there was no more walking. After about two hours of this, they were on the saddle. The ground was comparatively level for a few yards and then began to descend. The path, if it could be called a path, for it needed some skill to see where it ran, led straight on, and by that road the porters and the camp would go. But Mr Bennett wanted to see about him and on the saddle he was still among trees which obscured his view. He had noticed before starting that to the west of the saddle there was a sharply pointed peak, which seemed to be about ten thousand feet or rather more, with a rock face which might have possibilities; and he felt he owed himself some recreation, for there were no Sundays in camp. So he turned sharply westward.

In another hour he was out of the trees and only a few hundred feet below the little peak. It would be possible to walk to the summit if one kept on the north side but Mr Bennett wanted some exercise on rock to keep him from getting rusty. He sent Keshar Singh and the local man by the easy route and himself spent a happy half-hour clinging by toes and fingers to the rocky southern face. There was a refinement of pleasure in this, because as he climbed he could not see the snows of the main range. He saved them up, like a child with sweets, until they burst upon him when he reached the summit. There they were, icy dome and snowy cliff, fluted ridge and needle, blue and white and silver, clear and hard in the diamond air, calm in the gay sunshine. Mr Bennett held his breath in wonder and happiness, as he had done the first time he saw them, as he would do the last. Keshar Singh and the local man also sat and gazed.

After eating some sandwiches, Mr Bennett began to discuss the way down. Keshar Singh and the local man wanted to go back to the saddle as they had come and follow the goat-track. It was the obvious route and Keshar Singh was particularly anxious to get into camp early because he had a friend in Marora village, an old comrade who had served with him in the 3rd Gurkha Rifles.[2] But Mr Bennett disliked doing the obvious, partly from temperament and partly because if he went by the obvious route everyone he met was expecting him. He favoured following a spur which ran due northward and reckoned that once they got down from that spur to the level of their camp they would find a lateral path that would take them the right way. Keshar Singh argued that the spur would end in precipice and the local man backed him, but had to admit he had never been on it and did not know the villages below it. Mr Bennett was not to be persuaded and they started along the spur.

It was fairly easy going at first, through open country rather like a Westmorland fell, except for the forest immediately below them on all sides. But where the spur broke its smooth line, at the first knobbly knee, Keshar Singh and the local man both registered expressions which plainly said: 'I told you so.' For ahead to the north was sheer rocky cliff, and to the east, the side to which they wanted to turn, was a grassy slope on which none of the three would have trusted themselves. The only way down was to the west, and this they took.

The slope of the ground brought them into a side glen with cultivation among the trees. There was the smoke of a village up the glen to their left. They found a path leading downwards and out of the glen to the north and hurried along it, hoping for a more frequented path that would take them eastwards. Their path was little used and they met no one till they turned a corner and saw a small figure weeping in an utter abandonment of grief, one arm raised to lean against a boulder the size of a cottage, her forehead bowed on that raised arm, her whole body shaking with her sobs. She wore the uncomely blanket dress of the hills, which conceals the figure, and of the head nothing could be seen but matted dark hair, bleached here

[2]Two companies of this regiment formed the beginnings of the Royal Garhwal Rifles twelve years later.

and there to auburn.

Mr Bennett approached her gently. It would be very difficult to find out what her trouble was. If Amar Singh had been with him, he would have deputed him to find out, but Keshar Singh, who was kept on as an orderly mainly for his humorous expression, was unreliable. He was in a hurry, and if he were left to find out the truth, he would put words into her mouth and report them as though her sobs had confirmed them. Mr Bennett must talk to her himself and try not to frighten her. He sat down on the ground, not too close, not too far away.

'What is the matter, daughter?' he asked.

There was no answer, and he repeated the question gently.

'She is only a Dom, lord,' said Keshar Singh. Mr Bennett told him to be quiet, and repeated his question.

'My master,' she sobbed. She meant her husband, and Mr Bennett felt it was going to be more difficult than ever. But for once Keshar Singh was helpful.

'He has been beating her,' he said with a grin, in a voice which might just pass as an aside to the local man.

'No, no,' sobbed the girl, raising her head and showing a smooth round chin and a snub nose that would have been attractive in a face less disfigured by tears. She was young, almost a child. 'They are going to kill him.'

'Why are they going to kill him?' Mr Bennett asked gently.

'The rope festival,' she wept, her head falling again on her raised arm.

'When will it be?' Mr Bennett asked still more gently. He was very near something important, and he silenced Keshar Singh with his hand.

'Tomorrow, in the afternoon.'

'And where? Here in this village?'

Between her sobs came a just distinguishable yes.

Mr Bennett rose to his feet.

'Do not tell anyone you have seen us,' he said. 'Do you understand? If you tell no one at all, I will save your husband. Do you understand?'

She was lost in her sorrow and did not answer. Nothing would save her man. But Mr Bennett judged she would not be likely to talk, while if he took her with him, the cat would be out of the bag and things might later be unpleasant for her. He left her and pressed on. It was after dark when they found the camp.

The girl by the rock stayed on. She was hardly conscious that they had been there; if she had been asked she could only have said that she had spoken to strangers, without knowing who they were, for there was no room in her heart for anything but her grief. At any other time, she would have been tongue-tied in the presence even of men from another village, but her defences were down, she reacted without resistance. She had given them the one thought in her mind — 'My master' — and then Keshar Singh's lucky brutality had stung her to protest. For her husband was kind to her. He did not beat her and she loved him dearly.

She stayed there by the rock with her grief till she suddenly realized that she was cold and it was getting dark. She had come out to get sticks and had only collected a few when her sorrow suddenly became more than she could bear. She dabbed at her eyes with her blanket skirt, pushed back her hair, blew her nose with her fingers, picked up her sticks, and started for home.

Her husband was in the house and had begun to cook the cakes of millet flour.

'You are late, Padmini,' he said.

She did not answer, but turning her face away from him, put a pot of porridge on the side of the fire and squatting down beside him, took over the patting and tossing and roasting of the coarse pancakes.

Sohan Das himself was less disturbed than might have been expected by the thought of the ordeal he had to face tomorrow. It was not true that the villagers had decided to kill him. What they had decided was to hold the rope festival. This had been forbidden by the British Government but they felt sure that no one would come to hear of it. Theirs was a lonely and isolated glen, which the patwari did not often visit. He had been there recently and now he was busy in the villages down by the river where the maps were being made. He would not be in their village again for a month at least. So it would be safe to hold the festival, which was exciting to watch and fun for everyone but the victim, and was besides a sure way of making the fields fertile. Everyone knew that the fields used to be more fertile when the festival was held every year; nobody remembered that there were then fewer people and more land and the fields were left to lie fallow occasionally. So the villagers decided to hold the feast and the young men were sent up to the top of the cliff above the village from which the victim began his descent. They looked at the tree to which the rope had always been tied. It was still quite firm and strong; they fixed a post in the fields below and began to make the rope, two hundred and fifty yards long, and the wooden saddle on which the victim would sit.

It was a form of human sacrifice which combined the pleasures of a simple exercise in geometry with a sporting gamble, a free-for-all rough-and-tumble in which nothing was barred, and a lucky dip. The top of the precipice was about five hundred feet above the level of the fields and the post to which the lower end of the rope was fastened was about the same distance from the foot of the precipice; the rope when tied at both ends therefore made an angle of about forty-five degrees. The victim sat on a piece of wood shaped like an inverted Y, the inner angle of the fork being polished till it was smooth and slippery. He held the upright in his hands and put his legs over the branches of the fork. Stones were tied to his feet and to the lower forks of the saddle so that it should not overturn. There was a simple ritual; his forehead was marked with a splash of colour in which a few grains of rice were stuck. Then he was released. He would shoot down the curving rope with growing speed, and one of three things would happen. The rope might break, which happened seldom; it might catch fire, which happened frequently; or he might reach the lower end with nothing more than a few bruises or a broken leg, which happened less often. If the victim fell, the crowd at the lower end of the rope raced for his body, each man eager to pluck a fragment of his hair or beard, even his clothes, to bury in the fields and bring fertility. If the victim reached the ground alive, there was no race, but there was an added zest in the struggle for fragments of his hair or clothes, partly because there was less that was detachable and partly because the detaching was painful to the victim.

The prospect of being the victim was not one which would have much general appeal, but to Sohan Das it did not seem more unusual or alarming than the birth of her first child seems to a peasant woman. His community, a sub-caste among the aboriginal Doms, had always provided the victim for this festival and they were rewarded at the time of the festival by gifts of grain from all the shareholders in the village. It had hit them hard when the festival had been forbidden and they had been the most eager that it should be held again. They chose the victim on each occasion by lot, but a survivor, like the member of a jury, was exempt from service until there was no one else available. Sohan Das regarded the whole business as part of the course of nature, something which ought to happen and which must happen to him sooner or later. The fact that the festival had not taken place in the last few years seemed to him something impious, an interference with the seasons and the ways of God.

But it was different for Padmini. She was younger, and she came from another village where the festival had stopped earlier. She had only seen it once. She had seen the rope smoke and break into flame; she had seen her father falling, slowly, slowly, it seemed for a protracted second of time, his hands clutching at the air above his head; she could remember the distorted angles of his limbs when the villagers had left him and she followed her mother to what remained.

To her, the warm kindly man with whom she shared her life was already broken, stripped, and lifeless. She lay down in sorrow and her young face was wet with tears when she fell asleep.

Mr Bennett, on the other hand, lay down to sleep with a pleasurable anticipation of excitement next day. His only fear was that Keshar Singh or the local man who had been with him might give away the fact that it had been the girl who had told him the secret. The local man, however, lived on the other side of the ridge and he would send him back first thing in the morning. Keshar Singh was more of a problem; either of the other orderlies could be trusted to keep their mouths shut if they were told, but not Keshar Singh. Mr Bennett wondered whether he should send him back to headquarters and get another man in his place, as he had often wondered before, only to forgive him for his impudence and grin. He fell asleep without making up his mind.

It was next morning that the affairs of Padmini and Sohan Das impinged on those of Kalyanu. The latter shared a tent with the three orderlies, and it was a small tent in which the presence of an extra man was an inconvenience. Nobody minded much as a rule, but on the morning when the rope festival was to be held Keshar Singh had a hangover. As soon as he had been dismissed the night before, he had slipped away to see his friend in Marora and they had sat up over a bottle of spirits till far into the night. He woke up in a bad temper and grumbled at Kalyanu because he was in the way.

'Why does this son of a bitch live in the tent with us?' he said. 'Who asked him to stay on in this camp for ever?'

'I have a petition to the District Sahib,' said Kalyanu, on the defensive, for the same point had been on his conscience for some time.

'Then why don't you give him your petition and go?' Keshar Singh spoke with ill-humour because that was how he felt about everything this morning, but there was confirmation for his point of view in the silence of the other two. Kalyanu saw that he must bring the matter to the touch at once.

The orderlies knew that camp was not to be moved that day, and on a halting day no specific duties were assigned to the man who had gone with Mr Bennett on the day before. Keshar Singh was therefore justified in assuming that he would have nothing to do that day. Ordinarily, he would have asked Mr Bennett before he went to see his friend. But today he was afraid that if he showed himself the traces of his carousal would be evident; besides, he was very anxious to get back for the opening of the second bottle, which he thought might make him feel better, and he did not want to risk being stopped. He took a chance and slipped away.

Mr Bennett meanwhile was just ready to start. He calculated that the sooner he got to the village in the glen the better. The girl by the rock had said the afternoon; he would get there by noon, which was as soon as he could without arousing interest by a specially early start, for it was between three and four hours' march. By that time the situation should not have developed to a stage at which it would be difficult to stop. If he arrived when the victim was decked and on the altar, so to speak, things would be more likely to be awkward. He did not anticipate any difficulty, but it would be as well to take the patwari and two orderlies, instead of the one who usually came with him. It was Bharat Singh's day, and Bharat Singh presented himself. The patwari was also standing by.

'I want another orderly,' said Mr Bennett. 'Whose day is it to look after the camp?'

'Amar Singh's, lord.'

'Then call Keshar Singh.'

Bharat Singh looked exactly like a small boy asked to sneak on a pal.

'He is not here, lord,' he said.

'Where is he?'

'He has gone to the village, lord.'

At this moment, Kalyanu arrived. He came forward sheepishly and stood first on one leg and then on the other, with that air of one about to ask for something with which Mr Bennett was familiar. Mr Bennett was irritated and was about to snap angrily at Kalyanu, as the first object within reach, but he restrained himself with an effort and remembered that Kalyanu had never asked him for anything before. It was a point of conscience with him that he should force himself never to be in too much of a hurry to listen to anyone who had anything to say. He swallowed his anger, counted ten, and produced an encouraging smile.

'What is it?' he asked.

'I am better now, lord,' said Kalyanu.

'Yes, I am glad. What is it? Do you want to go back to your village?'

'No, lord. I want to stay with you.'

'What, doing nothing?'

'No, lord. I want to be your servant. With you. To work for you. Not for anyone else,' said Kalyanu, swallowing hard several times, and with long pauses.

Mr Bennett was about to say he had no place for him, when he remembered the story of the bear and thought Kalyanu might be a useful man to have with him at an awkward moment. Then he remembered Keshar Singh's absence from duty.

'Well, you can come with me today,' he said, 'and we'll see later on. Bring a stick. You'd better both bring sticks. Have you eaten? No, of course not. Get something you can eat on the way. You give him something, Bharat Singh. Be quick, and catch us up. I am starting, with the patwari.' And he was off.

Kalyanu went with Bharat Singh to the orderlies' tent and collected a handful of roast barley, a lump of molasses, and a stick, and a few minutes later was following the path Mr Bennett had taken at a slow jog-trot. He was in a private heaven of his own. He was going to be Mr Bennett's servant.

Soon after the party from the camp had started, a council of war was summoned at the village in the glen. The news that the District Sahib was camping only three hours' march away had reached the shareholders of the village, though they did not know he had actually been through part of their own glen. Ought they to go on with their plan of holding the festival? The priest had said very clearly that this was the one auspicious day, so that there could be no question of postponement. It was now or never. They had not told the surrounding villages, so there was no reason to suppose the District Sahib would hear of it, and everyone knew he was going down to the villages near the river to look at the maps. Yes, they decided they would hold the festival. But to make quite sure there was no interruption, they would hold it earlier than they had planned. They would hold it at noon. Someone was deputed to tell Sohan Das.

Both Sohan Das and Padmini took the news with calm. A few hours one way or the other made little difference, and indeed to Sohan Das there was even a feeling of relief. It would be the sooner over. For Padmini it was another knife into a heart numbed with grief. They finished cooking the morning meal and ate it together in silence. Then they started for the temple of the little godling who ruled the glen. Sohan Das was led before the godling's house and decked like a ram or a buffalo for the sacrifice. Then he was led away by four men, younger brothers of the shareholders who would stay below and who would make sure of a portion to bury in the fields they owned jointly. Padmini watched him go in stony misery. For her he had died already when the lot fell upon him.

As Sohan Das's procession went into the thicket by the side of the cliff, through which a path zig zagged to the top, Mr Bennett and his three companions were coming up the glen and nearing the village. Their path was strewed with stones, winding along the course of the brook, which was attenuated by many irrigation channels. The slope was not steep, and the terrace-walls were low; but the fields were small because of the many rocks, huge boulders among which the little terraces wandered like paths in a petrified maze. It seemed an unfriendly and inhospitable landscape as it lay deserted under the bright sun, and Mr Bennett quickened his steps. He ought to be in good time, but he did not like the absence of men and women from the fields, of smoke from the village.

He had marked the night before the cliff from which the victim's descent would obviously be made; there was only one near at hand; and he found his way without difficulty to where the villagers were standing, between the house of the godling and the post to which the rope was fastened. He noted the rope and the group of villagers, and realized at once that the sacrifice had not yet taken place. But there was another small group at the top of the rope, where Sohan Das's attendants were adjusting the weights of the saddle; it was just the situation he had hoped to avoid. The victim was decked and laid upon the altar, the priest's hand raised to strike.

He stepped forward and said:

'Who is the headman of this village?'

For the first time since he had been in the hills, the eyes turned towards him were sullen and hostile. There was a murmur in the crowd and a tall man of middle age stepped forward.

'You are trying to hold the rope festival,' said Mr Bennett. 'It is forbidden. You know that. You are to stop it.'

A young man sprang suddenly on to a boulder by the godling's house. In his hand was a coloured scarf, such as is used in the village dances.

'Stop that man!' said Mr Bennett, over his shoulder.

Kalyanu, Bharat Singh, the patwari, moved in that order. Kalyanu got there first. He brought the young man down by clutching his leg and pulling as he began to raise his arm. The signal was not sent.

The crowd surged forward angrily, sullen, undecided, wanting a lead.

'Stop!' said Mr Bennett. 'Listen to me!'

He spoke to the headman, but in tones that all could hear.

'If that man slides down the rope, I shall make a new headman from another village. And if the rope breaks, I shall hang you, and the men up there. All of them. Do you understand? I shall hang you. And you will no longer be headman unless you stop this at once. Do you hear?'

The headman shifted from one leg to the other. After a long pause:

'How am I to stop it? They are too far away,' he muttered, sullenly and rudely. But Mr Bennett knew that he had won.

'You can make them hear well enough if you want to,' he said. 'You know how it can be done. Tell them now.'

There was another moment of indecision. Then the headman said to a villager:

'Tell them it is stopped and they are to come down as they went up.'

There was another pause, while the villager wondered whether to obey. But he felt it was better to do as he was told, and moved to another tall flat boulder, three times his own height. He leaned his back against it, made a funnel of his hands, and sent a long call up to the top of the cliff. The patwari moved over to his side as he called. Wild echoes rang from cliff to cliff, and as they died away, an answering hail came from above. The caller below made his words very slow, he drew out the vowels of each syllable and waited till the echoes had died before he sent the next.

'It is stopped. Come down by the path.'

There was a pause and discussion at the top. Then the group withdrew from the edge of the cliff. Someone officiously untied the rope at the bottom.

'I want that rope,' said Mr Bennett. 'Bring it to me, cut in pieces please.'

Then he sat down and began to talk to the headman.

He left the village some hours later, when he had seen the rope cut to bits. He knew it would take a week to make another, but to make sure he ordered the patwari to stay in the village for a few days. As he went down the glen, he turned to look back. Smoke was rising again from the village; people were moving about gathering sticks. Perhaps for this reason, perhaps because the sun was lower and the trees and boulders now stood in variegated patches of shade, the whole look of the valley seemed to him more friendly and human than it had in the stony glare of noon. It might on the other hand be due only to his own gratifying consciousness of something done. It would, he reflected with a smile, be something to put in his fortnightly report, a document over which he always felt difficulty, for nothing positive ever seemed to be achieved, one struggled eternally with intangibles.

He stopped to rest as he turned eastwards below the spur down which he had come yesterday. The snows of the high range were there, softer now in the evening light, rising serene, ineffably lovely and remote, against the dark glowing indigo and scarlet of the nearer hills. He wondered whether when he left it all he would be able to remember the beauty he had seen and recapture the happiness of the life he had lived, sunshine and snow and wet, the fatigue and responsibility, his gipsy wandering, the smell of cows and wood smoke. He tried to remember his days in the Alps, and concluded with a wry smile that

memories were a poor substitute for the actual. As poor a substitute, he
thought, as the artist's achievement when it is compared with his
dream. His own attempts at verse had taught him this before he
burned them; and surely it must be so even with the masters. He
thought:

> Oh how feeble is man's power
> That if good fortune fall
> Cannot add another hour
> Nor a lost hour recall!

When he got back to camp, Keshar Singh presented himself. He was
very much the old soldier in the orderly room. Mr Bennett however
had made up his mind. He said:

'You are going back to headquarters. Kalyanu Singh is my orderly
now.'

Kalyanu slept happily that night. So too did Padmini, her head on
her husband's breast, and his arms about her.

## 4

Kalyanu was now Mr Bennett's orderly, and he wore a short coat
of serge, trousers, and a black pill box hat instead of a folded
homespun blanket. He was gradually learning to speak a
language which would have been moderately intelligible to a visitor
from the plains. But his son was still at Bantok and his prospects of
ever getting away depended on his father. So avid is man of his own
unrest that neither of them would for a moment have questioned the
desirability of leaving the homestead for any job in the world outside.
Kalyanu thought much about this, but it would have cost money to
bring Govind Singh to headquarters and send him to school there.
Kalyanu himself seldom stayed at headquarters more than a few days
and it would have meant setting up house separately there as well as
in Bantok. Besides, Govind Singh's mother was a unit of labour at
Bantok and could not be spared. There really seemed no way of getting
the boy educated until Kalyanu had saved some money, and that
would take a long time, and by then it might be too late.

But the opportunity to get what he wanted did come, about a year
after he was taken on as an orderly. It was due to no planning on
Kalyanu's part, nor to blind chance, but to his own character and Mr
Bennett's. Mr Bennett, as has been already explained, was troubled by
conscience about his mountaineering. He did not like to give himself

what amounted to leave and disappear into the snows on a long expedition; even when he did concede himself a few days, he liked to feel that he was carrying out an exploration of some practical value. He was therefore deeply interested in the persistent stories that there was once a direct route through the snows between the two great shrines of Badrinath and Kedarnath, to which people come on pilgrimage from all over India. Each is well within the high range, several days' march up a side valley from the main stream of the Ganges. It takes fourteen ordinary stages for a loaded coolie to walk down the valley from Kedarnath, up the main river, and up again to Badrinath. Yet on the map they are quite close. To find a way across through the snow might not have much practical value, for few would be bold enough to follow such a path; but it was a very attractive idea to Mr Bennett.

He decided accordingly to make a reconnaissance from Kedarnath, in the west. It would be no more than that, the first day. He would go up and see how far he could get and gather some idea of what lay in the way; and he would come back to Kedarnath in the evening and decide whether or not to make a determined attempt. No local man would be any help to him, for they had no knowledge of anything above the snowline. He decided to take with him Kalyanu, to whom he had given some elementary lessons on snow and ice during the summer. It did not look as though there would be any rock work.

They started next morning an hour before dawn, and walked over peaty turf that by midday would squelch with water at every step but now was frozen hard. They made for the snout of the glacier, but before reaching it they turned eastwards on to a long slope leading to a cup-shaped corrie far above. At the foot of the slope they came on to snow. It was late in the season, and the snow was old. It had been melted by day and frozen by night a hundred times, and was like rough frosted glass. Their nailed boots rang on the snow. It was not bad going at present, while the slope was easy, but they moved slowly, for they had only just come up, and at first even twelve thousand feet should be treated with respect. It was a clear night, but there was a mistiness about the waning moon which Mr Bennett did not like.

Kalyanu was a perfect companion for such an expedition, for he had utter confidence in his leader and in his presence would never show fear; he did exactly as he was told; and he did not speak unless spoken to. Mr Bennett revelled in the feeling of release from the responsibilities and decisions which usually beset him. He savoured every sniff of the frosty air, and rejoiced in the sweat which soon began to trickle down his spine beneath the sweaters and leather jerkin he wore.

It grew lighter. The world of moonlight, where there is an unreally simple choice of black or silver and no half-tones, began to give way to reality, with its infinite gradations of colour and meaning. Rocks ceased to be shadows and took on shape. The line of the crests above grew clear; the peaks to the west were suddenly gay with sunlight. Mr Bennett and Kalyanu were still in the shadow of the eastern heights, a shadow which ran across the cliffs and glacier to the west, and moved slowly downwards and towards them. Suddenly, unbelievably, a rim of molten metal appeared above the eastern crest. The glassy snow at their feet was dimpled with sun and shadow; for a few magic minutes the tiniest hummock threw long blue fingers of darkness towards them. Then the sun was up and all was glittering light.

The first gentle slope was now ended and they were on the floor of the corrie, at about fifteen thousand feet. It was almost level here, but on three sides the cup-shaped walls rose about them. To the west was the least abrupt slope; it was not too formidable and would bring them up on to the rim in about a thousand feet. They roped up, and proceeded to climb steadily, cutting shallow steps as they went, each with a single cut of the axe. Mr Bennett led. They were on the rim in an hour and a half.

This was one of the moments for which Mr Bennett lived. The valley with the temple was far below them, far and tiny, the torrent from the foot of the glacier twisting like a green and silver thread down the glen. Westwards the snow ridge stretched on above them to the sky; north, there was a valley whose depths could not be seen and beyond it a wall of rock reaching up to twenty thousand feet, over whose edge the snow bulged in a gigantic cornice like the thick icing dripping over the side of a rich black Christmas cake; to the east, peak and glacier, needle and serrac, a fantastic tangle of ice and rock in frozen loveliness. This was really what he had come for, to gaze, and fill his memory with beauty; but he did want to see if he could get any farther. He must think whether any way led through all this to the east.

The rim of the cup on which he stood could be followed eastward without difficulty. At the point where he stood, what had been from below the skyline and had seemed the top was only a change in the angle of slope; but farther north it was a true rim, a col leading to a dome-shaped snow peak to the east from which he would be able to see farther. The first step was a traverse to the col, and from there it looked as though it should be easy to reach the summit of the dome, which he reckoned must be about eighteen thousand feet.

The slope above the rim was not acute and the traverse to the col was easy going. They could kick steps in the snow without much exertion and they made good progress, the chips of snow that they dislodged slithering down a few yards to the rim of the corrie and then dropping a thousand feet to the floor of the cup. Mr Bennett thought of the possibility of establishing a hut on the col, as the first stage in the route he hoped to find. It would certainly be a good place for his own first camp, if he made a serious attempt, though rather a short first stage. If there was another easy col beyond the dome, it might be possible to push on to that; but that might make rather a long first stage. A short one was better to begin with.

Mr Bennett glanced from time to time at the sky while he thought of these possibilities. There was cloud about, but it was high, and it did not seem to be moving fast. His view of the western sky was blocked. He judged that the weather might break next day, but that it would hold for at least another twelve hours. It was not till they were beyond the col and making their way up the dome that it began to look alarming. Clouds from the west at their own level began to drive down the main glacier towards the valley and the temple, shapeless wet nimbus that came with frightening speed in ragged wisps. Drifts of it curled round the mass of rock and snow to the west that had concealed the evidence of what was coming. It swept over their heads and hid the sun. In ten minutes, a world of glittering snow, sunshine, and blue sky, had turned to a grey and chilling landscape, full of menace to men with neither a tent nor a blanket. Mr Bennett turned round and began to go back. He had led on the way up, mainly from natural exuberance, meaning to make Kalyanu take a turn when he grew tired of kicking steps. Now he had to lead, because he was much the quicker and it was important to get across the col and down the steep slope before the clouds came down on them. He regretted that he had not saved himself at the start.

But they were still on the col when the clouds came, and with them snow began to fall. It was not a blizzard. The wind was not strong and the snow fell lightly. The cloud was intermittent, and they could always see a few yards, sometimes more. After a few moments' reflection, Mr Bennett decided to keep moving. He was doubtful whether either of them would survive a night on the col without a tent. There was no climbing worth the name by the route they had followed and it should not be difficult to find; nothing but care was needed on the steep thousand feet down to the floor of the corrie. The danger was fresh snow on top of old; but at present it was only a light feathering. He pressed on as quickly as he could, feeling his way along the rim of the cup which lay on their left hand.

The film of new snow made it more difficult to find the firm old snow beneath the boot and kick a step. And the step had to be a better step now than it had been coming up, because of that treacherous slippery coating. They did not get on so fast as he would have liked and he was getting increasingly anxious about the point at which to turn and cross the rim to the steeper slope below that led to the floor of the corrie. There was only one place where the slope could properly be tackled by two men in a hurry, and he began more and more to fear that he might pass it. There was no way of comparing the pace at which they were now moving with that at which they had come up, and he could not reckon with any accuracy when they ought to be at the top of the one negotiable slope. Half a dozen times he moved down to his left to the rim and peered over, only to find that he was peering over a cornice that would have been dangerous for anyone, out of the question for Kalyanu and himself. Reason kept assuring him that he could not have passed the place, but the nagging fear was there. If they did pass it, they would find themselves on an impossible rock face, and much time would be wasted in getting back; and they could not afford to waste time. In the best case, it would be dark before they were off the snow.

The seventh or eighth time that he peered over the edge, he found the slope definitely less steep. A few paces farther on and there was an improvement. He moved on till it began to get worse again. When he was sure he had found the best place, he turned to speak to Kalyanu.

'We shall go down as we came up,' he explained. 'I shall lead and cut the steps. All you have to do is to be careful. Make quite sure each foot is firm before you put your weight on it. Use your ice-axe all the time. If you do slip, drive it into the snow at once. Keep the rope tight and do not come down to me even if I am slow. Remember I have to cut the steps.'

That was Kalyanu's only fault. He was inclined to come on too fast and Mr Bennett had more than once turned to find Kalyanu close behind him with the rope dangling uselessly between them. But he seemed now to be sufficiently impressed by the seriousness of the situation and he kept his distance, paying out the rope as Mr Bennett went over the cornice and following slowly and carefully at the right distance. He did not find it easy because it was difficult to see in falling snow and wet mist; most of the time he had to watch the rope and move as soon as its tightening showed that Mr Bennett had moved.

Coming up, one action had been enough to cut a step; one swift blow of the axe at the right angle nicked out a slice of snow just big enough to take the boot placed sideways. Now, three movements had to be made; one, to scrape away the fresh snow where the step would come and clear the firm frozen snow beneath; the second, to make the step; a third short one, to make it deeper because they were both tired now and it was slippery. It was slow work. Mr Bennett wished he had not led in the morning and he told himself he ought to have waited another day at eleven thousand feet before doing this. His head was aching. He ought not to be so tired; it was the height, and coming up so soon. Scrape, cut, half cut; step; scrape, cut, half cut; step; scrape, cut, half cut; he went on mechanically, but he knew he was very tired.

They were still about two hundred feet above the floor of the corrie when they reached the steepest part of the whole slope. Mr Bennett did not remember it on the way up; but in that light he could not see whether it could be avoided by traversing either way and he simply had nothing to spare, either time or energy, for a fruitless traverse. There was about twelve feet of almost sheer snow, and then again the steep but negotiable angle on which his scrape, cut, half cut, had been sufficient. This twelve feet would need more than that, but it was very hard snow. He decided to take it. He shouted to Kalyanu to come down to him, but the wind took the words from his mouth. They had never been out in a wind together before and had developed no system of signals by tugs on the rope. He began to cut deep steps. He panted at every blow of the axe and his head throbbed worse than before, much worse. When he got to the bottom of those twelve feet, he relaxed; he felt they were safe now. Just a little more of the old scrape, cut, half cut, and they would be able to walk. His head was throbbing less, but it felt as though it was full of hot liquid, hot blood, and nothing else. He laughed. The Vikings used to drink from skulls. He wouldn't mind a drink from his own. Nothing like a warm drink. A minute's rest, he thought. He drove the axe into the snow, took off his glove, and put his hand in an inner pocket for raisins.

At the other end of the rope, Kalyanu was worried. He had been following the steady tighten and dip of the rope, tighten when Mr Bennett took a step, dip when he took a step himself. It went to the rhythm of the leader's scrape, cut, half cut, step. Tighten, step, dip, tighten, step, dip, was Kalyanu's slower tune. Suddenly it stopped. Mr Bennett was considering whether to traverse or go straight down the steep place. Kalyanu shouted to ask what was the matter, but he heard no answer. Then the rope tightened, Kalyanu took a step, it dipped, but there was a long pause before it tightened again, while Mr Bennett hacked the next difficult step. Kalyanu was worried. The pauses seemed to grow longer and longer. At last there came a pause that seemed to last for ever. Kalyanu now felt sure that Mr Bennett had suddenly become exhausted, had managed to pull himself together to cut a few more steps very slowly, and was now collapsed, anchored by his axe. He went down to see what was the matter.

Mr Bennett had eaten some raisins and was wishing he could give some to Kalyanu. Quite light-headed he had been for a moment, he thought, but he was better now. And now it would all be plain easy work, and in less than two hours he would be drinking hot rum and cocoa in his tent. He heard his name called and looked up to see Kalyanu peering down over the steep place. Mr Bennett gave him a kindly smile, and quite simply stepped back into space to get a better view.

He had his hand on the axe, and the moment he felt himself falling he came out of his temporary loss of reason and grabbed it with his other hand. It came away, and he found himself slithering and rolling with increasing speed down the slope of glassy snow at an angle of more than fifty degrees. He tried to turn over on his face and make his axe bite into the snow. There was a sudden tremendous jerk. He had come to the end of the rope. Kalyanu had braced himself for the shock and driven his axe in as far as he could, but he could not have been in a worse place nor in a worse position, peering over a twelve-foot drop. The jerk was too much for him and he came over the drop and hit the slope beyond with a jar that knocked all the breath out of his body. But the momentary check had been enough for Mr Bennett to get his axe into the snow; he rolled over on his face and kicked his toes in as deep as he could, bracing himself for the moment when Kalyanu's weight should come on him. But he had not time to get sufficient grip. He too was torn away and both went down the slope, each desperately trying to get a purchase with his axe and slow up his fall.

Kalyanu was more successful. He did get his axe to bite and he reached the floor of the corrie, ploughing a deep furrow behind him, without serious damage. But Mr Bennett, a few yards to his left, had not managed to brake his descent at all and he was stopped by a crevasse, not a wide one, at the foot of the slope. His axe jammed across the top of it and he was clinging to the axe when Kalyanu came to pull him out. When he was out, he could not put one foot to the ground and there was a pain in his side which could only be a broken rib. Kalyanu propped him up against a boulder and stood waiting for orders.

'Leave me here,' said Mr Bennett. 'Go back to the camp and fetch men to carry me down.'

When he had said this, he lost consciousness.

Kalyanu reflected. It would be dark before he got to the camp. He was doubtful whether he would be able to find the place again. By the time he did, the Sahib might be dead. He decided to disobey him. He picked Mr Bennett up and managed to get him on to his back, although Mr Bennett was two stones heavier and six inches taller than he was; he brought his arms over his shoulders and held them firmly at the wrists with his left hand. He took his axe in his right hand. Then he saw Mr Bennett's axe; it did not occur to his frugal peasant's mind to leave it and with some difficulty he burdened himself with that as well, passing it below the injured man's arms and across his chest. Then he started to go down.

It was an hour before midnight when he got off the snow. There were men there with lanterns; Amar Singh had brought them out, but they could not go any farther because they did not know which way the party had gone. Kalyanu could not speak, but they helped him to the camp, where Mr Bennett's bearer took upon himself the responsibility of giving them both rum and hot milk and sugar.

Kalyanu was himself again next morning. About midday, Mr Bennett sent for him. Kalyanu went rather guiltily, conscious only of his disobedience. Mr Bennett was propped up as well as he could be in a camp bed. He said:

'Kalyanu, I think you saved my life. What would you like me to do to reward you?'

'Lord—' said Kalyanu, and was silent.

'Yes? What would you like?'

'Lord, my son—' Kalyanu was silent again. What he wanted was too much to ask.

'Something for your son? What?'

Then it came in a rush:

'Lord, please make him a patwari!'

Mr Bennett laughed.

'Very well,' he said. 'I will send him to school, and if he is good enough, I will make him a patwari.'

So Govind Singh, the son of Kalyanu, left Bantok and went to school.

# PART II

The Uprooted, 1923

# 1

Jodh Singh, son of Govind Singh, son of Kalyanu Singh of Bantok, was coming back to Garhwal in a complicated state of mind. His father's sudden death was not the most important element in his emotions, because he had never been able to feel any deep affection for that careful and narrow soul. His real love had gone to his mother and his grandfather. Nor did the fact that he would be too late for the funeral rites worry him so much as it would have done had he been entirely orthodox in his beliefs. The hill peasant, at heart the servant of older gods, is less concerned with the externals of Hinduism than the plainsman; and he only becomes deeply interested in rites and ceremonies when he is the victim of a snobbish desire to show that he is really just as good a Hindu as anyone else, an affliction which usually attacks the first generation removed from the peasant. The second generation is inclined to look at such things with tolerance or contempt; this had certainly been the effect on Jodh Singh of his English education at Lucknow University.

No, he was concerned with thoughts of himself, not of his father, and at the same time he was excited by the prospect of smelling the hill air and drinking hill water again. At school and college, Jodh Singh had been a disappointment to himself, though not to his father or to his teachers. Outwardly he had been moderately successful. He had taken his BA with second class honours in philosophy and English literature; he had played football for his university and hockey for his hostel; he had held office, though not the highest, in debating societies; he had been a scout and a patrol leader. The tin trunk under the seat of his intermediate class compartment contained a generous bundle of certificates from his teachers saying that he bore a good moral character, had taken part in all forms of college life, and had every right to look forward to a brilliant career. But he knew himself that his achievements were in no way distinguished; and he thought they should have been.

It was not so much with the results of his examinations or with his games that he was dissatisfied. He felt that he ought to have cut more ice with his contemporaries. He was sure that none of them experienced the burning zeal which often filled him, the intense desire to put something right, no matter what, the ardent love for the idea of India, the indignation at her wrongs. If only some magic could press the catch and release the spring, he would soar above them all. If just that something would happen that would put him in the lead, everyone would follow him, and recount with bated breath what he had said and done. But somehow it had never happened. Like most hill-boys, he was later in developing than is usual with Indians and he had been handicapped because he looked younger than he was. He was rustic and unsophisticated when he first went to school in the plains, compared with other boys of his age, and they laughed at him. And the diffidence born of that laughter had never quite left him. When he spoke at the debating society, his eyes wandered over the faces before him, searching for a look of derision, and he had never been able to lose himself in his subject and speak without self-consciousness, from his heart. And so he had never carried conviction.

All this would be very different in Garhwal, he thought. There were not many young men from the district with a college education and those few were almost all in government service, away in the plains. If he stayed in the district, he would have few rivals and no fear of laughter. Should he not make this his object, to be the leader of the district and guide his people from their backwardness and ignorance to something higher? He ought perhaps to qualify as a lawyer, but he did not intend to practise regularly. He could leave that to lesser men who had to earn their living.

His father, Govind Singh, had been rich by the standards of Garhwal, for his career as a patwari had been a long one. For forty years he had lived on the bounty of the villagers in his jurisdiction and had saved much. And every penny of his savings had been put to good use, being passed to a younger brother who had carried on a conservative and very profitable business as a money-lender under Govind Singh's direction. Govind Singh had been very wise and had avoided making enemies. No one had ever thought it necessary to tell the Deputy Commissioner about the money-lending. None of this worried Jodh Singh. It had simply never occurred to him to think where the money came from, although he was filled with burning indignation when he thought of the Government's failure to prevent corruption and put down malpractices, their connivance at the spoliation of the peasant. All that his father's wealth meant was that he had not to work for his bread but could devote himself to righting wrongs. Yes, that was what he would do! He would give his life to the district. His eyes filled with tears as he thought of the devotion with which he would toil for the simple peasants of his native land. But he could not afford to be sentimental, he told himself. Energy and courage were what he would need. He knew he had energy: he was burning to begin the fight at once. And he was sure he would have courage. He would be ready to face anything, torture, starvation, prison, death!

The train slowed up to stop at the junction from which the narrow-gauge line took off for the hills. As Jodh Singh sprang down from the carriage and pulled out his tin trunk and roll of bedding, he became for a moment the universal schoolboy coming home. He could see the hills from the station, but it was more important to him that the people on the platform were many of them hill-folk. Merely to look at them brought memories of clear running water, rock and pine and gravel, the smell of wood smoke and rotting leaves and frosty mornings. All these things he wanted, as every hill-man does when he is in the plains. But he reminded himself that he had a purpose, an aim in life. He must not be deflected by thoughts of simple homely things into forgetting his mission. There was nobody on the platform that he knew, but he was going to be their leader and impress them from the start. He would travel first-class for the few miles of his train journey that remained. Nothing would impress them so much as that.

But rich though he was by his own standards, Jodh Singh was too close to the peasant not to be careful about money. He had bought an intermediate ticket as far as the junction, rejecting the third class as fit only for peasants and the first and second class as recklessly extravagant. After the junction there was only upper class, consisting of first and second class ticket-holders; and lower class for the rest. It was, therefore, obviously a waste of money to buy an intermediate ticket right through; you were no better off in the last stage of the journey than if you had a third class ticket. At Lucknow, it had been his intention to get a third class ticket when he reached the junction and travel lower class. He now decided to buy a third class ticket and travel upper class. This he would do by the simple expedient of getting on the train at the last minute, knowing well that no one looked at tickets on this line once the journey had begun and that the ticket-collector at the other end would not notice what sort of carriage he had got out of. It occurred to him that the ticket-collector would probably hear in the evening, when word went round the little town at the terminus that young Jodh Singh had travelled upper class; but then, he reflected, no official would talk about that because it might get him into trouble. So he bought his third-class ticket, and hung about on the platform with his two pieces of luggage till the train was just starting; then with an air of lordly impudence he strolled forward with one in either hand to the empty carriage he had marked. There were always several upper-class carriages empty on the line to Garhwal. He settled down in his corner with a grin on his face that was purely boyish.

At the terminus, two miles inside the district, he got out sufficiently slowly to let any idlers on the platform see him, but did not delay long enough to attract the attention of officialdom. It was perfectly timed. He decided again to do something lordly, although this time he would have to pay for it. He strolled up to the lorry that would carry him ten miles farther into the hills, giving one anna to a coolie to carry his bundles, and bought a place on one of the two front seats, where he would be divided by brass rails from the common herd at the back, just as though he were an Englishman. Then he bought something to eat from a shop kept by a Brahman, for he was not sufficiently emancipated to disregard caste prejudices about food.

They drove the first stage of the journey up a savage and precipitous gorge, to a village where the traffic for the higher hills changed its motive power from petrol and steel to grain and muscle. You had the choice of walking or riding, your goods went on a mule's back or a porter's. Jodh Singh hired a porter and started to walk.

The valley up which he went was not beautiful. A stream boiled and foamed below him, but the channel through which it ran was a gutter into which poured from the hills on either side the debris of many landslides. The slopes of shaly rock were tortured and broken by the action of water as though by the explosions of a battlefield. Here and there a few fields hung together, shored up by the moraines of two converging scars of scree, but it seemed strange that such a country could support human life. The principal vegetation was the fantastic and inhospitable cactus.

The path wound slowly upwards and the ground became firmer, the slopes less extreme. Cactus began to give way to pine, there was grass and oak scrub, and fields became more frequent. About the middle of the afternoon, when heat and fatigue had begun to suggest a rest, Jodh Singh came on a dejected-looking group of villagers. In the steady toil of the ascent, he had almost forgotten that he had a mission. Now he remembered. He would talk to them and find out why they had assembled and why they looked so cheerless.

They would hardly have understood the patois of Upper Garhwal, but he had no difficulty in making himself clear in a dialect of Hindustani which would pass throughout the district. What were they doing, he asked, and why were they gathered here on a fine morning when there was so much to be done in the fields?

Their leader, a disreputable figure in an old army tunic and a pair of shapeless black cotton trousers, pushed a greasy black pill box hat farther on to one side of his head and spat. He took a long pull through a funnel made by his hands at a clay pipe-bowl and passed it on to his neighbour.

'That sod of a patwari,' he said, 'has ordered us to be here. The tahsildar is coming on tour, and we are to carry the tents and gear.'

'But when is he coming?' asked Jodh Singh.

'God knows. He was to have come yesterday. The villagers from Deokhal were to bring the stuff here and we are to take it on to Dwarikhal. He will camp there. We waited here all yesterday. We may have to wait all tomorrow.'

Jodh Singh's blood began to boil. Indignantly he said:

'But this is a great hardship.'

They all began to talk at once.

'It is a great hardship. We lose three days' work on the fields for one day's pay. And it is beggar's pay. We are not coolies, we are share-holders in our village, and the land belongs to us. It is not our work. Why doesn't the Government pay coolies to do this work? It is not for us.'

'It is a great tyranny,' said Jodh Singh. 'It is like the days of the Gurkhas. Why do you not refuse?'

They looked at each other. They had not thought of this; it had simply not occurred to their submissive natures. But the leader, rather shamefacedly, knew the answer.

'It is written in the settlement,' he said, 'we are to pay so much land revenue and work for the Government for pay whenever we are ordered. All but me. I am the headman. I do not have to work. But it is just as bad for me, this waiting. I lose three days' work in the fields, just like the rest.'

No one thought much of this.

'The settlement was fifty years ago, in the time of Mr Bennett,' someone said.

'Times have changed,' said another. 'We are not coolies. It is a great tyranny.'

Jodh Singh had listened with growing anger and excitement. Now he began to talk. They were all squatting on the ground, and he did not rise, but spoke eagerly and earnestly, as he would have done to his friends, sitting in a circle. The words poured out, driven from his heart by the anger he felt. He spoke of the wrongs of India and the tyranny of the British, the wealth and corruption of tahsildars and patwaris, the poverty of the peasants, and now this, a burden not to be borne, an intolerable insult to their dignity.

'Are we not men?' he cried. 'Are we different from the tahsildar? Is there not blood in our veins too? Are we animals and beasts of burden? Why should we live on coarse millet bread while the Deputy Commissioner eats meat every day and drinks wine and lives like a Raja? He should be the servant of the people but it is we who are his servants. We sweat in the fields to pay him land revenue and he loads us like beasts and does not care what becomes of us.'

He had never spoken like this before, forgetting himself and his dignity and the fact that people might laugh at him. The villagers listened breathless with interest, anger rising in their hearts as they shared his emotion, his own passion feeding on the power this new gift of speech gave him, the sense of mastery, the unity of his whole self in the endeavour to persuade them of what he knew was right.

He ended on a note quieter and more intense.

'Why do you not refuse?' he asked. 'Show that you are men. Go home to your village. Let there be none here when he comes.'

Then he rose to his feet and the villagers rose too, all talking confusedly. They began at once to pick up their belongings and to go. The headman made no attempt to dissuade them, but stood by dejectedly.

'What am I to do?' he asked, 'I shall be dismissed.'

'Go back to your village,' said Jodh Singh, still in the flush of his new-found authority. 'Be bold with the patwari and tell him none of you going to be coolies any longer. Soon every village in Garhwal will say the same. They cannot dismiss all the headmen.'

Jodh Singh watched the last man start back for the village and then he too went on his way. It was eight stages to his home and he did not hurry but spent the full eight days on the journey, asking questions of the villagers as he went. He heard everywhere the same tale of discontent at the way the corvee was levied. If it had been one day's work and one day's pay, that would have been no grievous burden, though even so there would have been grumbling. But it was often two days' hanging about for nothing and then one day's work for one day's pay, and sometimes, if an official changed his mind, two days' hanging about for nothing at all. And it might come at the time of harvest or sowing, and the corn would be spoilt in the fields or the right moment pass for scattering the seed. Nobody liked it; but so strong was the habit of obedience that no one had thought of refusing the service till they heard Jodh Singh talk. It was not often that he found a gathering like the first, which he could harangue; but he spread, wherever he went, the tale of the village which had refused to give the service and he hinted that every other village where he had been had declared their intention of doing the same. The word spread outward from his track like water through thick dust, here slowly and doubtfully, there faster, but everywhere gaining ground, turning the powdery white dust to a paste of mud, colouring and changing men's minds.

On the eighth day, he reached the big house which Govind Singh had built on the south side of the river, below the bridge leading to Bantok. It was a very different house from the cabin where Kalyanu had lived originally, two-storied, with deep eaves to shoot the snow clear and leave a warm path round the house, with balconies on the upper floor that would be cool in summer, with deep carving in the wood round the door and intricate ornament on the under side of the eaves. But Jodh Singh did not stay long to take possession of his patrimony. It was a pleasure to see the familiar fields and hills again and to be greeted with respect by his relations, but he had never had any intention of settling down among ignorant villagers; and now he had a mission. He greeted his mother with affection and explained that he must be away at once on important affairs. He did not explain what they were. He knew he could safely leave the money-lending business to his uncle and cousins, and to them also the management of the land, the shares in surrounding villages in which Govind Singh had from time to time invested. In three days, he set out again, taking with him as servant and companion one man to carry his blankets for the night and to cook his meals, a second cousin who was one of the exports of Bantok, where the holding could not be extended to keep pace with the population.

Jodh Singh and his cousin went north-eastwards up the river, and then struck off south and west up a tributary stream. Here in the upper hills his success was less obvious than nearer the plains; discontent there was at being kept hanging about, but time was on the whole less precious, and there was the compensation that when an officer did come their way, they were glad to see him. They were all ready to agree with Jodh Singh that the government ought to employ coolies but they did not fire at his talk of the injustice of life in general. It was only right, they felt, that the Deputy Commissioner, who was a kind of Raja, should live a very different life from theirs. It was part of the nature of things. And at his talk of refusing the service they shook their heads and went away considering.

So he turned south, to the lower hills, where he would, he knew, be able to find more enthusiastic audiences. But he realized before long that it was no good merely stumping the country. He could fire a village in the southern areas to a state of fervour when they were ready to defy the authority of the patwari and would do so at once if he should arrive while Jodh Singh's glowing periods were still hot in their minds; but the mood would not last long after he left them. In a few days, the habit of centuries would reassert itself, and whatever discontent they might feel, they would do as they were told. Even if he could contrive to be in the village just before one of the tahsildars and persuade the villagers to leave him stranded with no one to move his tents, he would not have achieved a decisive blow. He must do something more than this. He must make things uncomfortable for the Deputy Commissioner, the District Sahib himself. Only by this means would the Government be made to feel their discontent and the grievance be righted.

Once he had reached this conclusion he sat down to think out the best way of tackling the problem. Should he be there himself at the moment of crisis? If he were not, the villagers might weaken before the authority of so great a man as the Deputy Commissioner. On the other hand, he might be arrested. He did not stop to consider whether this would be legal or not; he assumed it could be done if the Deputy Commissioner wished. He was not afraid of arrest, he told himself, but he did not want the work he had begun to be stopped. Perhaps it would be better to keep just one stage ahead of the Deputy Commissioner and not actually meet him. But the more he thought of this course, the less he liked it. There would be no doubt everyone would say he was afraid; and once that story went round, his influence would be lost. No, he would meet the danger. It was the course that appealed to his youth and fervour, when an older man would have prepared the way more carefully, waited, and not brought all to the touch at once. He would make for a village where the District Sahib was expected, incite the villagers to passive resistance, and stay there, come what might.

Having decided on his general course, he proceeded to make a more detailed plan. It was easy to get information of the Deputy Commissioner's next tour, for the present head of the district believed in advertising his tours and sticking to his plans. He argued that by this means people knew where to find him and could come and tell him anything they wanted. If no one knew he was coming, they might not hear of his presence till he had gone. And his methods would be much more convenient to his staff and to the villagers who had to carry his gear than the erratic and unexpected excursions of a genius like Mr Bennett. Jodh Singh studied his programme and chose a large village, not far from the plains, where a large proportion of the population had been employed outside the district and were thus more sophisticated and volatile material than the peasant who had never left home. He decided to arrive some ten days before the Deputy Commissioner was due and sow the seed; he would go away and let it mature; and he would return on the critical day. And having made his plans, he went ahead with them.

Jodh Singh was very happy. Action and excitement brought out the best in him; he was delighted with the new power that came to him when he faced an audience, the thought that he was in danger and defying authority was a perpetual and agreeable stimulant. And at the same time he was sustained by the consciousness that he was doing something noble and striking a blow for his oppressed people. Add to this the physical well-being that came from living in the hills, walking from village to village, sleeping and eating where he could, and what more could a young man want, except to be in love as well?

## 2

Hugh Upton, Deputy Commissioner of Garhwal in 1923, looked at his watch. Half past four, and the last appeal of the day finished. Very satisfactory.

'Anything else, Gobardhan?'

'No, Sir, nothing that requires your attention.'

He left his court room with a sense of deep contentment. He was well abreast of his work and for the first time in his service was without the gnawing irritation of knowing that he had a pile of arrears with which he could never catch up because he was doing three men's work. He was fitter than he had ever been in his life and the immediate prospect of tea by the fireside with Margaret on a frosty November evening was as pleasant as anything he could visualize. He put his hands in his coat pockets and strode steadily up the steep and narrow cobbled bridle-path, that was the main street of his headquarter town— by courtesy, but it was really only a village—of Pokhra. He passed through an avenue of spruce, cedar and pine, planted fifty years before by Mr Bennett, through the little bazaar of thirty or forty shops, which sold headstalls with scarlet tassels and bells for mules, brass pots and pans, grain and sweetmeats and vegetables, and cloth from the plains for those who had become too sophisticated for the native blanket. The shopkeepers squatting by their wares rose to their feet and saluted him reverently as he passed, all but one or two who were politically minded and ostentatiously ignored him. He regarded this ceremony as a bore, because it meant taking his hands out of his pockets to return the salute; but nevertheless noted carefully who omitted it. Any such knowledge might be useful one day.

In a few minutes he was out of the bazaar and he turned aside, from the bridle path which led westward over the hills, to the winding path which led up through the forest to his house at Pokhrakhal. It was a path he took every day when he was at headquarters and it was therefore in good order, but automatically his eye looked for drains that would need repair if a big bill for repairs after the rains was to be avoided, for shrubs that needed cutting back, and boughs that might cause damage if a heavy fall of snow brought them down. He was a practical man with a tidy mind, no visionary or reformer. He had seen most of his service in the big cities, where his level-headed competence had saved much bloodshed, and he regarded a short spell in the hills as a well-earned respite from heat and riots.

He turned into the big pleasant sitting-room with bay windows on two sides and found Margaret kneeling before the fire, doing things with the copper kettle and spirit stove which she always managed to produce in the most unlikely places. The tea things were on a low table. There was a blazing wood fire. Hugh was not an emotional man, but as he saw her kneeling there, her cheeks rosy from the fire, her blue eyes between black lashes that always seemed to be smiling, he felt, as he always did, a sudden quick excitement, somewhere deep in his body a pang of wonder and joy, and sorrow too.

She looked up and regarded him, big and smiling, his face red from the frosty air, with the scar running down his face from a stone in a riot at Cawnpore, a nice ugly face, she thought, nicer and uglier than when she married him. She thought for a moment of Ronald, and put the thought from her like a dutiful wife.

'Tea?' she held up the cup to him. 'Anything interesting this afternoon?'

'Usual sort of stuff in court,' he answered, sipping at once while it was still scalding hot and thinking that Margaret was the only woman in India who seemed able to produce a decent cup of tea. 'But there's a rather interesting thing happening in the district.'

'Do tell me,' she said.

'Yes, I think you should know about this. It may affect our next tour and make things rather uncomfortable.' He settled into an arm-chair. 'Do you remember the story I told you about the man who beat a bear to death with sticks?'

'And afterwards he saved somebody's life, didn't he? Who was it? I forget.'

'Somebody's life? It was Mr Bennett's—the great Mr Bennett, who made the maps we curse for being so inaccurate—but it was a good job he made of them all the same—and planted all the trees and made the house. Well, Mr Bennett rewarded the man who saved his life by making his son a patwari, and the son was a success and made money and sent his son to a university in the plains; and now the grandson has come back and he's raising hell.'

'Doesn't his grandfather tell him to behave?'

'The old man's dead, and so is the father. There's no one to control the boy. He seems to speak well and he's calling meetings everywhere and asking the villagers why the Deputy Commissioner should be better off than they are—when Adam delved and Eve span—that kind of thing.'

'But no one in Garhwal would listen to that,' said Margaret incredulously.

'They seem to be listening in the lower hills. And he's got hold of one genuine grievance that he's having a lot of success with. You know the villagers carry our tents and baggage on tour?'

'They always seem very cheerful about it. Don't they get paid?' she asked.

'They get paid all right, at least they do in my camp, and I don't think they mind doing it for me very much, because I always say in advance where I am going and when, and I stick to it. But the tahsildars make a plan and then change their minds—sometimes they can't help it, something else crops up. Anyhow, the patwaris collect the villagers and keep them hanging about, sometimes for two or three days, and of course they don't get paid for that, and they hate it. And in the lower hills they're beginning to think it's beneath their dignity to carry a load at all. I've tried to make the tahsildars be more considerate, but it doesn't work. It's no use trying to make water run uphill, or a tiger go the way he doesn't want to.'

'And what exactly do you mean by that, you old cynic? Have you got a cigarette?'

'I mean, it's the way of the country and it's no use trying to tell junior officials to be thoughtful for peasants. They won't, unless you're there to make them. The only thing is to change the system.'

'Well, how can you?' Margaret settled herself again on a cushion on the floor, leaning back against the chair opposite Hugh's. She looked idly at the smoke of her cigarette as he talked; she had learnt long ago to keep him talking about the things that interested him; it did not need much effort.

'Oh, it would be quite easy. We could run a transport company. We might get a contractor to take it on and find the coolies. Or perhaps it might be difficult to get a contractor up here. In that case, we could do it ourselves and hire coolies for the whole tour. But of course that would cost money to begin with.'

'It sounds easy enough.'

'I've suggested it before, but Smith wouldn't put it up. He didn't like suggesting anything that would cost money, and he said anyhow it was all nonsense—they've always done it and why shouldn't they go on? I wish now I'd put it stronger.'

'Do you think there'll be trouble?'

'I think there will. This boy—Jodh Singh his name is—has persuaded one village to refuse to carry the tahsildar's camp gear, and he's telling them all to refuse. In fact he's trying to organize a sort of general strike.'

'But will he be able to do it?'

'Not a general strike perhaps, but he'll get some villages to do it. I've done what I can to discourage them, but there's not much I can do. Even dismissing the headman will take months—he'll have to be given an opportunity to give his reasons and he'll engage counsel and make as much delay as he can. When we go into the lower hills next month we may have some trouble.'

'Well, that'll be fun,' said Margaret. 'Couldn't you beat him by just not going to the villages where he was expecting you? Then you could finish your tour quite happily and everyone would laugh at him.'

Hugh shook his head. He said:

'That would be no good. He'd have scored. Everybody would know that I'd run away from Jodh Singh and that I couldn't go where I wanted in my own district. The real trouble is that I agree with him about this, but I mustn't say so till I've convinced Smith and the government that I'm right. Lucknow will probably begin by advising me to hire bullock-carts. They never seem able to realize that we haven't any roads or any carts.'

'Having to go on being loyal about something you don't agree with always seems very hard to me. However, I suppose you must.'

'Of course we must,' said Hugh. 'If we weren't loyal we shouldn't be here; and if we didn't go on being loyal, we shouldn't stay.'

'Have you time to come for a walk, or must you do your old files? Do come.'

'Yes, I can manage a stroll round. I'll write a report on all this after dinner.'

'Cheers. Come on.'

They went out on to the narrow lawn in front of the house. They could see clear across through a gap in the pines to the snow peaks forty miles away, flushed with rose in the last light of evening, a few tiny puffs of cloud high above them still a tender lucid gold. The nearer hills were warm scarlet and orange; the distant loveliness of the snows swam up from deepest glowing blue.

Margaret caught Hugh's arm.

'If I could only paint that!' she said. 'But no one would believe it. Hugh, do you think we shall be able to remember it? The lovely things we've seen and the fun we've had?'

'When we're playing golf at Cheltenham, d'you mean? We shall be able to remember that we've had a good time, but you can't live it over again. Memory's a poor thing. I've often tried to live over again a good day's shooting or fishing. You can't do it.'

'No,' she said, 'you're right. I can remember England in May, the bluebells and the primroses, and the hedges white with may. But I can only remember it and want it. I can't really see it.'

She sighed, and they went on. He said:

'I must tell them to cut back the undergrowth along this ride. These brutes of hill pheasants won't get up unless you make them. They creep right up to the open and then scuttle across, and you can't get a shot. If we cut it back ten yards they'd have to fly.'

# 3

Jodh Singh had chosen the village of Chopta in the south-eastern part of the district as the scene for his crucial test of strength with the Deputy Commissioner. It was in the right area, only two days' march from a railway station, it was a large village for the hills, with over a hundred families, a post office and primary school, and the younger brothers usually made their way to the plains to take service of some kind, the humbler as messengers or private servants, the better educated as postmen or typists. And there were many Brahmans, who would offer better material on the whole than the Kshatriyas, the Rajputs, the warrior class. The village was too close to the plains to be favoured by the army, who preferred the simpler peasant from the higher hills, the man whose knowledge of the outer world was all learnt in the regiment; and to Jodh Singh this was an additional recommendation. He did not want any danger of an opposition party of old soldiers whose life long habit of obedience to authority would be hard to break. It was of course impossible to find any village in the district in 1923 which had not sent someone to the army, but from Chopta they would be hospital orderlies, mule-leaders, and the like, not riflemen from the infantry. And if the soldiers did venture on criticism of his ideas, the sting would be drawn by the fact that they themselves were exempt from the corvee.

By the time Jodh Singh reached Chopta, he had already made a good deal of progress in the technique of his approach to a new village. He had found that if he began his propaganda among the villagers without first going to the headman, almost invariably the full weight of traditional authority was turned against him. The headman more than anyone else had something to fear, for his post depended on his behaving as officialdom thought he should, and he could be dismissed. Whereas, if he comported himself correctly and his heir was not obviously disqualified by deformity, idiocy or bad behaviour, the appointment was hereditary. It brought him slight material advantage but much honour, and he did not want to lose it. He was, besides, himself exempt from the corvee and the headman was therefore in every village liable to be distrustful of Jodh Singh's persuasions. If to this natural disinclination was added jealousy because his influence was being undermined, he would usually turn hostile. It was true that by approaching him direct, Jodh Singh risked an initial rebuff, for the headman might commit himself to an opinion before he realized the weight of popular feeling and it might then be difficult to make him change. Jodh Singh, however, had by now decided that the risk was almost always worth taking, although, with a foresight beyond his years, he would make inquiries at the next village before he arrived and suit his approach to circumstances.

In the case of Chopta, he learned nothing from his preliminary inquiries to make him vary his usual method and he went straight to Ram Dat Naithani, the headman. Ram Dat, being the eldest brother, had managed the land and taken over the duties of headman from his father and he had never been far away from the village. Being a Brahman, he could read and write Hindi and had some knowledge of Sanskrit, but he knew that both in education and knowledge of the world he was a long way behind his own younger brother, who was a sub-assistant surgeon in the plains, and many other younger brothers who had served as postmen or clerks. This made him cautious and suspicious and increased his Brahmanical preference for the indirect. He had of course already heard rumours of Jodh Singh's teachings and thought the matter out with some care. He was not a man of impulse who would be guided by his heart. He had made up his mind as to the line he would take before he saw Jodh Singh.

As a Brahman, he was naturally suspicious of a Rajput, for in the old days the Brahmans had enjoyed a monopoly of learning, and had held all the civil posts. Now the Rajputs were claiming a share and every Brahman resented it, the more so as the army still preferred the Rajput. Again, as an old man he regarded with reserve the arrogance of a youth straight from college who was telling his elders what to do. But already everyone in the district was talking about Jodh Singh and he might perhaps stand for election as their representative in Lucknow. If he was successful in this he would indubitably be a great man with whom it would be well to be in favour. If the Brahmans decided to support him, and they might, for they had no good candidate of their own, and the sitting member was a militant Rajput who hated Brahmans, it would more than ever be desirable to have helped him in his early days. He would have to reward the Brahmans and naturally the best he had to give would go to old friends. All this, perhaps, was looking a long way ahead, but it touched on the immediate problem, which was the line to take about compulsory labour. It would be no use going all out against a movement to end the corvee. It was bitterly unpopular, particularly so in such a village as this where there were many unused to bodily labour. To oppose the movement whole-heartedly would kill the headman's influence in the village. On the other hand, to support the strike openly might mean dismissal from being headman; of course, if refusal to work became general, it would probably be impossible to dismiss all the headmen—but it would be remembered against him always. No, everything led to one conclusion; he must avoid offending Jodh Singh and let both him and the villagers know that he was on their side, but outwardly, he must appear to help the patwari.

Jodh Singh greeted Ram Dat respectfully. He placed his hands together in the attitude of prayer and addressed him as 'Pandit,' the Brahman's title of respect. He treated him with the deference due to an older man and asked for a blessing. All this increased Ram Dat's suspicion of him as a Rajput, but he responded graciously, and the conversation proceeded with extreme courtesy and goodwill.

When Jodh Singh at last came to the point and asked Ram Dat whether he would mind if he arranged a meeting in the village—he was careful to explain that he did not expect the headman himself to call the villagers together—the Brahman began to explain his difficulties. He was after all the headman, and he had to think of his son as well as of himself. He saw the justice of Jodh Singh's arguments and sympathized entirely with his point of view. He would do everything to help him but he had to think how this could best be done. If he were to act openly, the patwari would report against him and much of his influence would be lost. To give the maximum help, he must seem to be acting with the patwari. It might perhaps appear as though he were not being entirely helpful, but everyone would know he did not mean anything he might say in the presence of the patwari. He would take good care of that. Privately, he would be using his influence the other way.

Jodh Singh was accustomed to this attitude, though it was not usually stated so explicitly. The first time he had met it, he had exploded with anger, for his nature was impetuous and direct; but that had got him nowhere, and eventually he had been forced to regard that village as one of his failure. He had learnt to curb his impatience and contempt at an expedient which he regarded as cowardly, because he knew it was the only way he could get what he wanted. He felt his anger mounting as Ram Dat talked, it seemed almost to choke him; but he would not give way to it. He must force himself to be calm. He nodded wisely as Ram Dat made his points and it was with all the courtesy and deference at his command that he said he entirely understood and agreed that this would be far more helpful than open support. He knew that the real struggle with Ram Dat would be over the amount of secret support that he could get. Whatever the Brahman might decide as a matter of policy, he would never get over his suspicion of Jodh Singh as a Rajput, and he was perfectly capable of playing a game with three tiers of duplicity—in public, supporting the patwari, and in private appearing to encourage the villagers to refuse the customary service, but qualifying all he said with hints of evil consequences that would undo much of Jodh Singh's work. And this, reflected Jodh Singh, was almost certainly what he would tell the patwari he was doing. He would know that the patwari would not be such a fool as to be deceived by his public utterances, and so he would probably explain to him that while he would uphold his position and satisfy the decencies in public, in private he would not be able to declare himself strongly as a supporter of government, or he would lose all his influence. So in private, he would say, I shall pretend to be backing Jodh Singh, but everything I say will be so craftily qualified. Jodh Singh could see it all, and his anger again began to rise, but again he beat it down. He felt that it would take someone very clever indeed and far more experienced than himself to know what the old man was up to. Much, he felt, might depend on the impression he made and he tried, therefore, to be not only polite and deferential but to give an impression of judicious calm and a reason and understanding beyond his years. He had to do this mainly by silence and by nods for he could not trust himself to speak. Inwardly, he boiled with impatience to get out and to talk to the villagers.

The upshot of his talk was that Ram Dat agreed with him that he should call a meeting, at which the headman would ostentatiously appear and tell everyone to go home; but no one would take any notice because the word would have been privately passed round beforehand that they should not. And what else would they be told at the same time, Jodh Singh wondered; but he was not really worried, for the headman's hold on the shareholders of the village was tenuous. Apart from his government post, he was only the first of equals, the president and managing director of a board. His influence depended on his never cutting directly across the popular will; he must guide rather than command; and Jodh Singh felt sure that Ram Dat had seriously underestimated the power of his eloquence and his ability to fire the villagers to action in a cause to which they were already strongly inclined.

When he rose to go, Ram Dat suggested that he should stay with one of the Rajput shareholders, but Jodh Singh politely declined an offer which he knew to be a trap. If he stayed with a Rajput, all the Brahmans would believe that they were plotting together and Ram Dat would use the suspicion to throw further confusion into the minds of everyone as to which side he was really backing. No, said Jodh Singh, he would sleep in the village school, which was commonly used as a guest-house. No one could question the right of the villagers to use it in this way, as they had built it themselves, the District Board having undertaken to pay for a teacher if they would do so. He would sleep in the school and perhaps the shareholders would be so kind as to send him some food; he realized that with his position to consider, the headman could not be expected to send food from his own house. But perhaps he would see no objection if some of the others did. Ram Dat gravely agreed and so it was arranged.

Next day Jodh Singh went with confidence to the meeting, which was held in a field close to the village. All the shareholders were there, Brahman and Rajput, elder brother and younger brother, for all were in theory equal in the management of village affairs, although in practice one had authority in the village and one in each family above the others. There were no women. The Doms, such of them as had come, were in a separate group, on a higher terrace above the main gathering. As arranged, Ram Dat appeared and in a loud voice but with a very unconvincing manner told everyone to go home and not to listen to this dangerous and seditious person. No one took any notice and Ram Dat then went home himself. One of his brothers however remained.

By this time, Jodh Singh had his speech perfect and it slipped off his tongue very smoothly, with impressive pauses at the right places, with mounting emphasis as he completed a point, a quiet resumption of the argument as he started a new one. But beneath his perfected technique was real emotion, which mounted steadily as he spoke. His heart burned within him and the fire spread and warmed his audience. He began by speaking of all the district had done in the war, how their blood had been poured out in generous response to the appeals of the British, of how freedom had been promised to India in return for her help, and of the falsity of every promise made.

'Has freedom been given us, now that the war is over?' he cried. 'No, the British are laughing at our simplicity. They know us for the simple and credulous fools we are. They know that they can go on, living in luxury while we toil in the fields, sweating to feed them with wine and meat and to clothe their women with costly silks, while we live on millet bread and porridge and wear blankets.'

He went on from the general to the particular and to the grievance of the corvee. Here was something which would show whether the British were sincere in what they said of freedom. Would they go on forcing the peasant to toil for them, carrying camp gear as though they were mules or coolies, instead of free shareholders, Brahmans and Rajputs, twice-born? There would be no difficulty in arranging for coolies; it was simple for the government, with all the power and the money and the prestige in the world at their disposal, to arrange anything they wanted. But they would not do it. Their devilish policy was to oppress the peasant and debase his spirit by making him carry loads. Thus he would show the world that he was a slave and would keep for ever the slave spirit; and so long as he knew he was a slave who had to carry burdens he would never rise against his oppressors.

So it went on. Jodh Singh believed every word of it. As he spoke, his hearers became more and more moved; and when he ended they crowded round him asking him what they should do. He told them that their duty was simple. They had nothing to do but to refuse politely when the patwari told them to carry the Deputy Commissioner's camp gear.

'I shall be here to help you,' he said. 'I am going now to all the villages nearby, to make sure they do not come to the Sahib's help; but I shall come back the day before the Deputy Commissioner comes and I shall be here if there is trouble. There is nothing for you to fear. If anyone is sent to prison, it will not be you, for you are too many. I am the only one who is in danger and I shall be here if they want me. But there must be no violence. Not yet. No violence, that is what our Mahatma has said.'

His eye was roving round among the crowd as he spoke. He wanted to find the natural leaders, the men of energy and character to whom the others would listen. He must take those men aside and talk to them, he must leave behind lieutenants working for the cause with something of his own ardour and determination. He picked on three, one of whom was Ram Dat's younger brother, and he detached them after the meeting and talked to them long and earnestly. In the evening, he paid a polite and ceremonious call on Ram Dat, but he came by night, and explained very tactfully that he had taken care no one should see him come. This would make it possible for Ram Dat to tell the patwari that he had reproved Jodh Singh at their first interview and refused to have anything to do with him. Next morning he saw his three lieutenants again and satisfied himself that they were solidly behind him. Then he left, to spread the word among the neighbouring villages and make sure there were no blacklegs.

# 4

On the same day that Jodh Singh first arrived at Chopta and talked to Ram Dat, Hugh and Margaret Upton started on their tour to the south-east. Their road lay in a huge half-circle round the end and side of a wide shallow valley. Below the road the ground fell steeply, mostly rough pasture on which only a hill beast could find sustenance, with patches here and there of pine or oak scrub, remnants of the forest that had once clothed all the hills but had been gradually eaten down to the few surviving areas, jealously preserved now by villagers who began to realize the value of what they had destroyed. Below the pastures, where the slope became gentler, the cultivation began, terrace on wrinkled terrace, writhing over every fold of ground, outlining every contour, a finely reticulated net over the whole floor and lower slopes of the valley. Not a yard of land was wasted here, for the population was three or four times what it had been in the days of the Rajas and Gurkhas.

Above the road, the hillside swept up to low down-like crests, with outcrops of rock here and there among the short, golden grass, and here and there the dry bed of a stream, its sides clothed in dark scrub. Hugh had to stop several times on the way to deal with people who wanted him perhaps to check the monstrous tendency of the next village to encroach on their preserves of grazing-land or forest, perhaps to restrain one of their own shareholders from defying the village community and taking more than his share of the common land. When she saw that familiar sight, a figure standing by the side of the road, petition in hand, Margaret looked round for a convenient seat and settled herself to rest, looking back to the north at the snow peaks, or watching the faces round her husband. Sometimes sketch-book and pencil would come out and she would try to catch the look on a wrinkled face, or the angle of a gesticulating arm, but quite as often her eyes would rest in endless wonder on the serrated line of ice and snow. Those who knew her superficially would have said she was a brisk practical woman, for all her beauty emphatically a Martha; but it was not because the externals of life were her only interest that she was concerned with them, but because she was determined to let no one know that life had not given her what she had dreamt of and what she had now decided she could never have. She would make a good job of her marriage and her life, and she would enjoy both.

There were fewer interruptions and discussions than usual on the road today, because it was near headquarters and almost everyone who had anything to plead had already come in to see Hugh and tell him about it. As they came to the last stretch of the journey, for about a mile the track lay in the shadow of the hillside. All morning the sun had blazed upon it and the surface had been beaten by the feet of mules and men into powdery white dust, two inches deep. In the late afternoon, when the shadow of the hill fell on the path, a fine covering of dew had formed over the dust; and an hour later this had frozen. The road before them stretched shining and dimpled, like old snow in the early morning after a frost; but with every step they broke the thin crackling surface and plunged into dry feathery white dust.

They were not using the tents the first night, but were to sleep in a rather dilapidated bungalow built in the old days by the Deputy Commissioner as a rest-house for travellers and now maintained intermittently by the District Board, to whom it had been transferred as a measure of self-government. Margaret had sent a servant ahead and he was waiting for them by a blazing wood fire, with her inevitable copper kettle and spirit stove. The water was hot already and she had a cup of tea in Hugh's hands within five minutes of arrival. While he was drinking it, she moved quickly about the room, putting up brightly coloured curtains and throwing cushions on the chairs.

'There!' she said, coming back to the fire side, 'that's a little more cheerful and homelike. And may I remind you once more that the proper place for your boots when you take them off is neither the table nor the chairs. At heart you're still a bachelor who happened to get married. I ought to have caught you younger.' And that, she thought, is true, oddly enough. If I had met him first—she brushed away the thought, and went on:

'Well, there wasn't any trouble with the porters today, was there?'

'Not actual trouble for us,' said Hugh, 'they did the job all right. But the patwari says he had a difficult time getting them together. There was a good deal of argument and discussion and he had to use all his influence.'

'What are you doing about it?' Margaret asked.

'There's nothing I can do, except tell the patwaris to persevere and do the best they can, and at the same time tell the government about it. I've written to Smith again, and I'm expecting the letter for signature this evening. We shall run into trouble in a few days and that will convince him that there's something in it. Nothing else will. Ah, here's Tara Dat with my letter.'

The lamps had been lighted, and Hugh read over the letter he had dictated that morning before starting. He had said:

'I hope you will forgive me for writing again on this subject so soon after my official letter, but all my reports indicate that Jodh Singh is having very general success with his propaganda and I think I should be failing in my duty if I did not warn you of what I fear the results may be. You are of course aware of all the facts about this agitation and I know that there is nothing new that I can tell you about the district, but I think it is worth restating some obvious points which have a bearing on the situation.

'The main point I want to make is that there are no police and we hold the hills entirely by bluff. There is one patwari for every sixty villages on an average—about one to every eight thousand of the population. The headman is a shareholder in the village first and a government servant second—a very poor second. Our only assets are the prestige of the Deputy Commissioner and the patwaris, and the habit of obedience. Once that habit is broken, things would be very different. In other words, with the present arrangements, we can only carry on the administration if we have the general goodwill and backing of the people. This we still have, as we always have had in the past, because we have never done anything they regarded as seriously unjust or unfair and because we started with the initial advantage of being their deliverers from Gurkha oppression.

'I do not mean by this argument that we ought to give in to anything which the people of the district might demand. But I do wish to suggest that if it ever did come to a show-down, we ought to be on very firm ground. In this particular case I do not think we are. There would not be so much objection if it could be ensured that the system of forced labour would be administered considerately and with a minimum of inconvenience to the villager, but as I have explained in my official letter, I do not think it will ever be possible to make sure of this. And even if this difficulty could be overcome, I venture to think there would still be an objection to the system. Forced labour does not sound well in modern times. It is a feudal survival and I think it would be very difficult to justify calling in outside force to maintain it.

'If it is decided to continue the present system, I have no doubt that it will be necessary to call in force from outside. Perhaps not much would be needed. We might arrest Jodh Singh for obstructing a public servant in the execution of his duty, though I have not taken legal advice, and we might restore the situation in a few villages with the help of say a hundred armed police. But I think that this would leave behind a legacy of mistrust and dislike which would lead to more trouble before long, and would eventually mean that the cost of administering the hills, at present very low, would be increased considerably, with no corresponding increase in revenue. I advise most strongly against it.

'I sent you with my official letter a scheme for starting a transport company, with an estimate of cost. This does not include any estimate of receipts, but I see no reason why the public should not come to use such an agency, which might then in a few years become self-supporting. The outlay should therefore be small and I believe that if it could now be announced that we were about to introduce such a scheme, all the sting would be taken out of Jodh Singh's attack. His general political propaganda is dangerous because it is associated with a practical grievance, which I venture to think is genuine. Remove the grievance and I believe the political propaganda would fall on deaf ears.

'Once again, I hope you will forgive me if I seem to press my own views strongly. But I think it is essential you should be in no doubt of what I fear the consequences may be before you take a decision. If it is decided that I am wrong and that Jodh Singh should be arrested, he will undoubtedly get the best lawyers he can, for he has money, and they will probably come from the plains. In that case, the whole business will get into the press and I think the matter is certain to be brought to the notice of government by questions in the legislature.'

Hugh read through what he had written and made some alterations. Margaret said:

'May I see? Or is that being an interfering wife?'

'Of course,' he said, 'I'd be glad to hear what you think of the last paragraph. Does it sound too much like a threat? You see, I know Smith, and he doesn't like putting anything to government at all. He thinks that the best district officer is the one you never hear of, and he believes everything will always come right in the end provided you're firm but not provocative. And he will say of course that my arguments cut both ways. If everything in the hills depends on the prestige of the patwari, then you should never give in to agitation or the habit of obedience will be lost. His instinct on getting my letters will be to say I'm belly-aching and to do nothing about it. But if he thinks government are going to hear about it anyhow, he may be forced to tell them in advance. I hope that my last paragraph will make him send on copies of my letters to Lucknow, with his own opinion in a covering note. But I'm afraid his covering note will be against what I advise.'

She read the letter through.

'I think you're right,' she said. 'Though I don't expect he'll love you. You're not quite such a fool as you look, are you, my funny old ugly?'

He grinned cheerfully.

'Oh, I don't expect to be loved,' he said. She was sure there was no second thought behind his words. She was sure he had no inner problems of his own and was not aware of hers. She did not even glance at his face to see what he was thinking when he used that ambiguous phrase. He sent for the clerk to dispatch his letter.

They moved on next day towards the south-east and for a few days marched through low hills, rolling down-like country with steep short valleys in between. The tops were short golden grass; there were few trees; a windy, open country, in which there were many disputes for Hugh to attend to, because the pressure on the land was great and the few remaining trees were quite insufficient for a people whose inherited way of life was built on inexhaustible forests. It was only occasionally that Margaret caught a glimpse of the high snows, for the view to the north was blocked by another range, the same Mr Bennett had unexpectedly crossed to find the rope-sacrifice preparing on the other side. But it was a country which had many attractions; little tinkling streams which they would cross after a steep stony descent, friendly corners where the fields, beautifully terraced and faced with stone to make a level surface for irrigation, made clear clean patterns below the rounded golden tops, villages clustered in a huddle of tiled roofs and a blue mist of wood smoke, on which you looked down as if from the air, stacks of golden straw, a pond with willows round it from which the buffaloes rose slowly one by one, a hundred little intimate pictures to be sketched.

As usual, the porters turned up to carry the loads, villagers came out with petitions, schools lined the road and sang songs of welcome; but there was a difference, difficult to define, but noticeable. There was not the usual air of spontaneous pleasure in their coming; in camp at evening everyone had come strictly for business; there was no cheerful crowd of spectators and those who clustered round Margaret for medicines and plasters were fewer. And everywhere the patwaris reported that it was only by the exercise of all their powers of tact and patience and persuasion that they had collected porters.

On the tenth day they reached Chopta. Their gear had been brought by men from the last village and the tents were pitched, but Dewan Singh, the senior orderly, came to meet Hugh as soon as he arrived, his round face serious.

'Lord,' he began, 'the villagers here will do nothing for us. I got the men from the last village to stay and put up the tents, and they helped us to get wood for the fires and water for the baths; but there was nearly a fight because the Chopta people tried to stop them, and I had to call the patwari. Now the men from Deora have gone and these men from Chopta will not help us at all. We shall not be able to move on tomorrow.'

'Then we must stay here,' said Hugh cheerfully. 'Where is the patwari?'

'He is in the village, lord, trying to persuade them. Shall I send for him?'

'No, he will be coming to report when he is ready. Don't hurry him.'

He went on to the tent where Margaret was already making tea. There were two tents, each just so big that you could stand up in the middle if there did not happen to be a lantern swinging from the ridge-pole, as there generally was. At the far end of each tent there was an alcove within the outer fly, divided from the main tent by a curtain. This made a pantry for one tent, a bathroom for the other. In the living-tent were two small tables, two canvas chairs.

'Tea as usual is the first thing I want,' said Hugh. 'I never really knew how good tea could be till I came here. After a day scrambling about these hills, it's meat, drink, and tobacco in one, the staff of life, absolutely. Well, the trouble has come.' He told her what he had heard from Dewan Singh.

'What are you going to do?'

'I shall stay here tomorrow and talk to them. I've plenty of written work to keep me busy in between. I shall ask Master Jodh Singh to come and have a chat. It will be much better to do nothing at all to-night. I don't want to seem excited or worried. Calm and good-humoured and rather amused, that's me. Meanwhile, I shall have a bath. It may be the last we'll get for a day or two. Mind if I go first? Then I shall be finished by the time the patwari comes up to report.'

He shouted for his bath and went into the other tent. It was cold at five thousand feet in November and the business of bathing needed careful timing. He undid his boots but waited till he heard the bath being poured before he tore off coat and shorts as quickly as possible and crept through the flaps into the little alcove, which smelt strongly of the damp straw on the floor. It was just not possible to stand up here and it was essential not to waste a minute between the pouring of the bath and getting in, because the water cooled so quickly in a tent; for the same reason, it was very important to get into the flat zinc tub when the water was just a little hotter than it could be borne. Having adjusted the temperature of the almost boiling water by adding cold from an old paraffin canister, Hugh stepped in delicately. It was agony, the water was so hot; and the part of his flesh not in the water was like a newly plucked fowl from the cold air. There was a band of deep mahogany colour round his knees and on his forearms to the elbow, from day-long exposure. Drying was difficult, because it was necessary to crouch, and there was a penetrating wind that blew down one side of the tent between the outer and inner fly and through the bathroom. But once it was over, he was in a happy glow and he hurried to pull on warm clothes, long felt boots, and a dressing-gown over everything, which gave him the appearance of a gigantic Tibetan.

He was on his way back to the living-tent when the patwari arrived, to confirm Dewan Singh's report. He had done everything he could to persuade the villagers but he could not shake them. The headman was pretending to help him but in secret he was certainly using his influence in quite a different way. Jodh Singh himself was here and he had managed to get considerable influence.

Hugh smiled cheerfully, thanked him, and told him to come back in the morning with any fresh news; he said that he was going to invite Jodh Singh to come and see him. When he lay down two hours later in the narrow camp bed by the side of Margaret's, he fell asleep the moment his head touched the pillow.

Next morning, Hugh had a talk with the patwari, who told him there was no change in the attitude of the villagers, and then he wrote a letter of invitation which he sent to Jodh Singh by one of the orderlies. Next he sent a telegram by a special runner to the nearest office for dispatch to Mr Smith.

His telegram said: 'As expected villagers of Chopta have refused to carry my camp gear or fetch wood and water for camp. stop. My advice is still to announce immediately government's intention of forming transport company. stop. If decision is against this consider only alternative course will be to arrest Jodh Singh if he proves obdurate and request immediate dispatch ten repeat ten armed police. stop. Consider this may lead to situation demanding dispatch one hundred repeat hundred armed police. stop.'

When the telegram had gone, Hugh considered again very carefully for a few minutes. He decided it would be no use talking to the villagers collectively himself. If they had made up their minds to this extreme step and the patwari could not shake them, it was unlikely he could persuade them to change. And if he tried and failed he would only make things worse. He must make alternative arrangements, and accordingly he wrote another letter and dispatched another man on urgent business to the west. He then settled down to a morning of correspondence, dealing with various questions he had put aside while travelling. He felt he was unlikely to be interrupted until after lunch and could allow himself the rare luxury of working slowly and thoughtfully. He had considerable powers of concentration and in any case he was in no way excited by the crisis which had arisen, for he felt himself quite detached from what was happening. He had given advice which he was sure was right and now the decision lay with someone else.

Jodh Singh's frame of mind was very different. This he was sure was the big crisis of his life. He was sitting on the veranda of the school house, where he was lodging, when one of the Deputy Commissioner's orderlies came and asked if Jodh Singh was there. His heart pounded and his stomach turned to water. Perhaps this man had come to arrest him. It must be that. He was not going to resist arrest, but he would go slowly, and collect a crowd, and address them before he was bundled away to he knew not what dreadful torments. But all the orderly did was to hand him a letter. He took it with surprise and confusion. His hands still trembled as he opened it. There would be threats in it and anger. But he would not be browbeaten or frightened. What he read was this:

'Dear Thakur Jodh Singh, I hear that you are in the village of Chopta and as there are one or two things I should like to talk over with you, I wonder if you could come up to my camp and have a cup of tea with me this afternoon about four o'clock. I hope you will be able to come. Yours sincerely, Hugh Upton.'

Jodh Singh was so taken aback by this that when the orderly asked him if there was an answer he replied automatically:

'Say I will come.'

But as soon as the orderly had gone, he began to wonder whether he had done the right thing. He had always heard that Englishmen were haughty and contemptuous and usually angry; those he had seen, it was true, had usually appeared utterly careless, seeming not even to notice the crowds about them, talking to each other as if in their own homes. The only Englishman he had really known had been a professor at the university, a shy grey man whom the students regarded with affectionate contempt. But everyone said he was not really like an Englishman at all. Jodh Singh's picture of the Deputy Commissioner was of a stout red-faced angry man; he had expected a letter either abusive and threatening or curt and official. This polite note, written as if to an equal, and as if there were nothing of importance in the air, was the last thing he had imagined. It did not even ask him to come at once. It was probably a trap. The English were cunning behind their careless appearance. The sahib would try to melt Jodh Singh's heart with tea and kind words. Would it be better even now not to go?

The danger in going was not physical. They could arrest him when they wanted. It was that he might melt. Well, he would steel his heart and make up his mind not to melt. Was there any other danger? He could not see it. And to be asked to tea was a score; there was no question of that. He was negotiating on equal terms—but would it appear like that? Would the district say that the Deputy Commissioner had called him, and he had gone at once, like an obedient spaniel? Ought he not to try to make the Deputy Commissioner come to him?

His imagination quailed at this stupendous thought. It will come to that, he told himself; one day I shall make him come to me; but for the present, it is enough that he has asked me to tea. Yes, I will go.

He passed the rest of the day in a fever of excitement. He had to meet a man older and more experienced than himself, and of a race whom his forebears for several generations had regarded as masters and superiors. And he had to play on his adversary's ground. He would be hampered by social problems. He would not know what to do with his cup and saucer. And he would be talking a foreign language. It was as though a boy from a labourer's cottage in Victorian England had been asked to sit down to tea with an earl and discuss important affairs in which he alone had to use Ciceronian Latin, while the earl spoke his mother tongue. At a quarter to four, he began to walk up the hill. He said to himself:

'I will not give way. I will not be worried about my tea-cup. I know I am right. I will remember India's wrongs. I will not give way.'

He was sweating when he arrived and ran his hand over his hair, which he wore long and well-oiled, cut in a European style. An orderly, with a faint air of wondering what the world was coming to, led him to the two larger tents, and Hugh came out to meet him, grinning cheerfully, and unbelievably large. His face was not red but a clear healthy brown, not much lighter than Jodh Singh's own; and he was neither fat nor angry.

'Come and sit down,' he said. 'This is my wife.'

'How do you do, Mr Rawat,' said Margaret. She was wearing a magenta silk shirt with a dark blue skirt, fitting closely to her hips and flared out at the knees to suit her slim figure and to free her movements. The colours brought out her vivid colouring, dark hair, eyes of a sunny blue, cheeks flushed with the sun and the hill air. To Jodh Singh she was unbelievably beautiful, and his confusion was increased.

'I am very well, mem-sahib,' he replied bending over her hand as he had seen Europeans do in the cinema. It immediately occurred to him that he should have said Mrs Upton, not mem-sahib, as though he were a servant, and his shyness increased. 'I hope you are well.'

She gave him tea and asked him with a friendly smile whether he was glad to come back to the hills after the university in the plains. They talked of Lucknow for a little. He thought she must be insincere in saying that she was happier in Garhwal; she could not like this rough, lonely life. He was very shy and stilted, but spoke with an obvious desire to please and to he polite. She liked him. At last she said:

'Well, you want to talk business, so I must leave you. Goodbye, Mr

Rawat; I hope we meet again soon.'

She had been kind and friendly and it had delighted him to look at her, but he was more at ease when she left, though his emotion increased. His heart beat fast and painfully, for now the moment had come.

'I must not give way,' he said to himself. 'I must not give way.'

But Hugh did not come to the point at once. He spoke of the high esteem in which Jodh Singh's grandfather had been held and of his father's good record as a patwari. It was a great thing for the district, he said, that there were now more educated young men; and he asked Jodh Singh what were his plans for the future.

This put Jodh Singh in a difficulty, for he did not want to be rude. His every instinct was to repay courtesy with courtesy, for he had been charmed and flattered by his reception and he liked this big man. He did not wish to say that he was going to devote his life to driving out the English. It was haltingly, therefore, that he began to explain that he meant to lead the people of the district to higher things and a better way of life, but as he spoke he warmed and spoke more fluently. Hugh made encouraging noises from time to time and suggested that there could really be nothing more helpful than persuading the villagers in those areas where they still had forests to preserve them carefully. They might thus avoid the fate of the lower hills, where they not only had no fuel but were beginning to see their fields swept away by torrents because there were no forests on the hilltops to act as sponges, to soak up the rain and release it slowly. Jodh Singh cleared his throat nervously and began to say that this was really work for an official; but his courage came back to him and he said:

'But we shall make no real progress in that or anything else until we are free. We must have a government of our own.'

'I agree there's a great deal to be done that only an Indian government can do,' said Hugh. 'We only differ as to the date on which an Indian government will be able to take over from us. But surely there's a great deal of progress that can be made in the meantime and much on which we should be agreed and on which you could help.'

'But it is the first duty of every Indian who is not an official to work as hard as he can to bring the day of freedom to birth. Other things must wait,' said Jodh Singh seriously, and so the argument proceeded.

At last Hugh began to talk about the corvee. He told Jodh Singh that he thought he understood his case and explained very fully what he believed that case to be.

'Now, in the first place, is that your case and have I put it fairly? Is there anything I have left out—apart from the political background?'

Jodh Singh agreed that as regards the forced labour, nothing had been forgotten.

'All right. Now I have told the government that that is what you want and why you want it. I have told them what I think it would cost to run a transport company. What I have to ask you now is to wait patiently for their decision and meanwhile not to make it difficult for me to get on with my job of running the district. After all, what I do on these tours of mine is all for the benefit of the peasants, you know. Now, will you help me? Call off your strike now and let me get on. If the decision is as you want it to be, well and good. If not, our bargain is ended and you start again, and then it is my job to stop you. I don't want to threaten—but in that case I should have to do whatever I could to restore discipline and it might be unpleasant for you. To be frank, I should probably have to arrest you, much as I should dislike doing it.'

Everything in Jodh Singh warmed to this man. He wanted with all his emotional nature to be friends with him and help him. He wanted to accept this offer at once, though he knew he had not had time to think about it. But astonished and distant, as if he were far from his body, he heard himself say in a small obstinate voice:

'No, I will not give way.'

Hugh paused. Then he said:

'Are you quite sure, Jodh Singh? I should like to be friends and we could do a lot for the district together.'

Jodh Singh shook his head. He was almost in tears. He could not trust himself to speak again. He shook his head, stretched out his hand to the Englishman in friendship, and walked away.

'I take off my hat to that boy,' said Hugh to Margaret. 'I was really very unsporting and did everything I could to make him take the wrong decision. But he stuck to his guns, though he wanted desperately to be friends. He's an emotional creature. They all are, of course, particularly when young. That's the mistake we make. Too cold. But it's our nature to be aloof with them, just as it's theirs to need that emotional appeal.'

They are like women in that, thought Margaret, and you make the same mistake with women. She said:

'But why do you say you tried to make him take the wrong decision?'

'From his point of view it would be wrong. They'd start a file at Lucknow and argue about the thing for a year. Nothing would be done. And if he tried to start it again, he'd have lost the right moment. He'd have no way on his ship and you know what it's like trying to bring a boat round into the wind once you've lost way.'

'Then why did you try to make him take it?' she asked.

'I had to try every means of taking the pressure off government. It's my job to advise them, but I must do everything I can to give them the chance of an unforced decision. It would be disloyal not to. I had to try it.'

Margaret looked at him seriously.

'Oh, dear, how public-school we are,' she said. 'I liked him. I hope you won't have to arrest him. Do you think you will?'

'I don't know. Fifty-fifty chance, I should say. The government seem only to think of money and in the long run I believe it would be cheaper to start a transport company. And morally it's the right thing to do. If it wasn't for Smith, I think they'd take my advice. But he's a pugnacious old devil. He loves a row and hates giving way, and he has this idea of prestige on the brain. Give way on one thing and they'll ask for another; that's what he'd say, I know. I don't say he's not right; it's point of view. But our feet are on the slippery road of giving way already. We've said we're going, and it seems to me much more dignified to go with a good grace and meanwhile to carry on loyally, doing what we feel's the right thing for the future.'

'Can't you do anything else? I'm sure there's a lot of good in that boy.'

'I don't see that I can do anything more. I've put my views as plain as I can.'

'Why not go to Lucknow and talk to them?' Margaret asked.

'Well, in the first place, we seem to be stuck here. In the second, I can't short-circuit Smith and rush off to Lucknow to talk to the Chief Secretary direct. It would be frightfully disloyal. Of course, if it was the summer—they'd all be in Naini Tal in the hills. I could go to talk to Smith—and I'd be in duty bound to call on the Chief Secretary and he'd be sure to ask me what I'd come for.' He grinned. 'No one could complain about that. But it isn't the summer. Smith's in Naini Tal and the Chief Secretary's in Lucknow. It can't be done, I'm afraid. I must go back to work.'

He thought how beautiful she looked in that shirt, the dark hair swept back from her temples, her lovely slim figure standing at the door of the tent in the last sunshine. But he did not say what he thought. He went to his files.

Half an hour later he was back, a letter in his hand.

'Funny what you said about Lucknow,' he said. 'Here's a letter, a week old of course, telling me that Smith has been suddenly called to Lucknow for a conference of all Commissioners about the political situation. He must have got there today.'

'Then you could go to see him? Oh, do go. It would be grand to save that boy and make him see reason.'

Hugh was doubtful.

'I suppose I might. I shouldn't have thought of it myself. I don't quite see that anything new has happened to make me want to go. Seeing Jodh Singh hasn't really changed the situation.'

'You could pretend it had.'

'Yes, I suppose so. I've never been much good at pretending. But you're right. It would disturb the district for a long time if they went wrong on this. It's the district I'm worried about, not the boy. All right, I'll go. You'll come, of course?'

She shook her head. She knew who was in Lucknow. She was not going to tear her heart again.

'I should only be a nuisance. You go by yourself. But how will you get away from here?'

He was disappointed. It would have been fun to have gone together. But he did not argue about that. He had made it a rule never to ask her for anything twice.

'Oh, I've got a scheme which may come off for getting away from here. We might get away tomorrow night and it's only three marches to Ramgarh. I could get a slow train from Ramgarh and then catch the night mail from Ramnagar, stay Thursday and Friday, back in Ramgarh Saturday morning. You could stay in Ramgarh.'

'Yes,' said Margaret. It wouldn't be a very happy two days she thought, as Hugh went off to send a telegram to the Commissioner. There was one phrase in that last letter that to her seemed scorched on steel, something she could never forgive. She hadn't thought of that for a long time, consciously. Funny how this came in waves, like a headache, only there wasn't any aspirin. Sometimes you'd hardly know it was there, and then it would suddenly start again. Wonder what started it this time. It began before there was any talk of going to Lucknow. Something Hugh had said, perhaps. Nice old Hugh. He might see Ronald and know nothing. She would paint like mad for those two days; it might help her to paint a decent picture. Hugh said memory was a poor thing. Well, it didn't do her much good.

Next day towards evening an old gentleman, from two days' march to the west, came to see Hugh. He wore narrow trousers of white wool and a full-skirted white woollen coat, falling to the knees, collarless and fastening right up to the neck with tape. He had been born before the Mutiny, and his grandfather—they were a stock who seemed to beget eldest sons late in life—had been one of the barons to whom the Rajas had delegated feudal power before the Gurkhas came. When the British sent the Gurkhas back to Nepal and took over the country, Raghubir Singh's grandfather had been in hiding with his peasantry; he reappeared and the British restored his lands, but they took away his feudal powers and he no longer exercised the high, low, and middle justice. But he kept much of his influence. Among Raghubir

Singh's most cherished possessions was a parchment dated 1857, addressed to his father, signed by the Deputy Commissioner of the day and sealed with his seal, which, when shorn of elaborate formal phrases and imposing calligraphy, said quite simply: 'If any strangers come into your villages from the plains, kill them.' Raghubir Singh was far from a man of blood, being a very gentle old person indeed, but he mourned the simplicity of those days when an order was an order.

He placed his small hand in Hugh's large grip and left it there affectionately. It was the wrinkled hand of old age, the skin still fine because it had never driven a plough or carried a load, but it was warm and alive.

'Have no care, sahib,' he said. 'My villagers will listen to me before they hear the words of an orderly's grandson from the upper hills. They will be here tonight, and they will come after dark as you say, and they will leave tomorrow before it is light. They will take you all the way to Ramgarh. They will do it for love of me and of the government.' He paused and laid his left hand on Hugh's, which still enclosed his right. His gentle old face became sad. 'I am old and you are young,' he went on. 'Bring back the old ways.'

Hugh too was sad, because there was nothing he could do for him except betray him to the new age he did not like.

It was barely light next morning when Jodh Singh was wakened by a villager who came to tell him that the Deputy Commissioner's camp was already on the move. The first porters had started already and soon the whole long bobbing line would be winding in a string of dots towards the plains.

'Shall we stop them? We could easily catch them for they are loaded and we should have nothing to carry but our sticks.'

'Wait,' said Jodh Singh, scrambling to his feet. He must think for a moment about this new problem.

He had left Hugh's camp two evenings before, deeply stirred by the necessity for refusing an offer that seemed to be made in friendship. He had wondered whether he had been right, but not for long. Only his previous resolve, impressed on himself till it was stronger than his conscious mind, had stopped him from giving way to his emotions and saying yes. But as he went down the hill, he had time to think and he saw as clearly as Hugh had done that he would have been wrong. And his feeling of friendship for the big man who had seemed so friendly, but had really used all his charm of manner and his social prestige to deceive him, turned to anger, a sick envious anger that made him unhappy. For he envied Hugh his ease, his certainty, his wife, the possession of everything whose use had almost undone him. His anger had grown yesterday and he had talked with much bitterness to his lieutenants in the village. But he had made up his mind once more to resist sudden impulse and the pull of his heart.

Now the sahib had again deceived him and escaped him. His anger rose and choked him. He would stop him! He would send the village to beat up his blackleg porters, found by some lickspittle. But he stopped himself. I must think what would happen then. We should all be prosecuted. The village would suffer and be punished. We should be in the wrong. And there is to be no violence till we are forced to it. He told me he had written to the government. We must not fight till they have decided against us. Then we will fight to the death.

But his anger rose again; he wanted to show his power, to stop this superior being from escaping him and laughing at him. But if he struck, it would really be a victory for the Government. They would be in the right and the villagers in the wrong. And as it was, the Deputy Commissioner had had to run away. That was the important thing to remember; he had had to run away. Jodh Singh decided to let him go. Of all he did in this matter of the corvee, nothing showed so clearly as this decision the possibilities of wise leadership that were in him; but it cost him much, more than his youth could afford.

He went outside the school house and looked towards the village. There were others hurrying down the path to ask for instructions. He told them to wait, and would not let them know his mind till a small crowd had collected. Then he spoke.

He spoke well, as he always did now, with passion and bitterness. He spoke bitterly of the sahib who had tried to deceive him once, and had now sneaked away in the night, though even as he spoke he saw again the brown kindly face, the beautiful lady who had smiled and given him tea, and a pang of regret mingled with his bitterness. He brought in much of his stock-in-trade, now familiar to his hearers, though still capable of stirring them, and he stressed again and again the fact that by making the Deputy Commissioner run away they had scored a victory.

'Let them go,' he said, 'let them go. Soon all the district will think as we do and the Government will give in and put an end to this tyranny.'

And at that moment he saw on the edge of the crowd Ram Dat the headman. Ram Dat did not speak, but in his face Jodh Singh saw all the cynicism and indifference of age, the contemptuous knowledge that the young cannot make the world to their own pattern; and something seemed to snap within him and he forgot his wisdom and patience, worn thin by the effort of his previous restraint.

'Yes, we shall win,' he cried, 'we shall win, whatever you may think, Ram Dat, and whatever you and your kind may do, lickspittles, trencher-hounds, cowering before the hand that beats you.'

As he began to speak, Ram Dat turned to go, but the crowd turned too at Jodh Singh's abuse and looked at the Brahman with hostility. He turned on the defensive, and in a moment of panic, cried:

'I have done nothing. All the world knows the part I played.'

' "I meant to be virtuous, said the mule's mother",' mocked Jodh Singh, and he quoted another proverb: ' "Yes, we know the part you played. You were the washerman's dog, that belongs neither to the house nor the washing-place. You eat at both if you can." '

The crowd laughed. Ram Dat went home. Jodh Singh finished his harangue and felt better. But he had made the first of the enemies who were to undo him.

When Hugh came back to the district five days later, Jodh Singh was moving northwards, back towards his own country, revisiting the villages where he had been most successful in his journey south. Although he had rejected the Deputy Commissioner's offer of a truce he could put no heart into further fiery preaching. He was exhausted by the strain of the last few days, and needed the relaxation of going back over ground already broken. He was in a particularly friendly village when the news came through that government had announced that the corvee would be ended and a transport company started in its place.

Jodh Singh could hardly believe it. It was ended. It really was ended. He had won. He had won against the English government and the Deputy Commissioner. He had killed his bear. His face suddenly lighted:

'Let us dance the dance of *Bakhtawar Wins* tonight,' he cried. 'Let us eat raw game. Is there a home-fed sheep in this village that I can buy?'

Among those who circled that night in angular dance among the flaring torches, in a tiny patch of flame and movement against the dark stillness of the hills, none was so wild as Jodh Singh. When the time came for the madness to enter the dancers, it seemed as though he was indeed possessed by that drunkenness which the gods send on men who venture into the high places, when the snow has melted and the flowers are in their first glory.

5

In the months immediately after the corvee was remitted, Jodh Singh's mood was very like his grandfather's after killing the bear, allowance being made for difference of age and upbringing. He too was like a young man in love who knows himself admitted to favours shared with no one else and believes he has every woman at his feet. There was nothing he could not do; but while in his grandfather there was no outward manifestation of the inner feeling of mastery, because he had to get in the harvest and had no time to waste, the grandson did not wait for them to come but went out looking for bears. He went from one to another of the larger villages of the district, preaching the wrongs of his country and looking for a concrete grievance to which they could be linked.

As a triumphal progress his reception was gratifying, but as a basis for further achievements, it was disappointing. He was successful in interesting his audiences and he was everywhere greeted with great honour as the man who had ended the forced labour; but that was usually as far as he got. No one was going to be enthusiastic about mere words and until he could find genuine grievance no one regarded his talk as anything but words. It was no use telling anyone in Garhwal about the fiscal policy of the British in India in the nineteenth century; they had never seen the sea or a train and many had never seen a bullock-cart or a five-rupee note. As for the heavy burden of defence expenditure, they prayed for war as others pray for rain, so that employment could be found in the army for all the younger brothers. No, their grievance must be local; and the nearest approach to a genuine local grievance was that in the north, where there were still plenty of trees, there was some resentment that the government was protecting them, while in the south, where there were hardly any trees left, there was a strong feeling that they should have been protected sooner. In fact, Jodh Singh was beginning to despair of ever raising the district to political manhood, when at last he came on a bear, a small one, it is true, and one he could regard with contempt, but it had the advantage that it came from the headquarters of the district at Pokhra.

Pokhra was originally a village of no particular importance on a fairly extensively used route which ran east and west along a low range of hills. But the first British officers did not care for the old capital of the Rajas, which lay in hot and steamy valley, so they chose as their capital the nearest hill village of any size, which happened to be Pokhra. The first Deputy Commissioner built his office and courts of justice by the side of the bridle-track round which the houses clustered. It would at the time have been strange and pointless if he had not. But as time wore on and the traffic on the road increased, there came a Deputy Commissioner to whom it seemed intolerable that mules with their bells should jangle past the door of his office, raising clouds of white dust and bringing flies and smells and the loud cries of muleteers, offending not only himself but the waiting petitioners and litigants, the lawyers and stamp vendors and the contractors who offered sweetmeats and tea to all these people. He built a wall in front of his office, enclosing a large space, and deflected the road in a detour down the hill. But at either end of the enclosure, where the old road used to enter, was a stile for pedestrians and an iron gate which was usually kept closed but could be opened for an official procession on the occasion of a jubilee or the coronation of a monarch. Everyone could remember that the gates had been open and a procession had gone through to celebrate the end of the war; and most people could remember a previous occasion, at the time of the coronation of King George V.

Now there was in Pokhra a small but fairly vigorous branch of the Congress party. Its members, like Jodh Singh, found that most of their teaching fell on very stony ground and took no root at all, but they had a certain number of secret adherents who were afraid to come out in the open; the majority of the villagers, and of those who came in from the neighbourhood for litigation or the payment of revenue, were indifferent to politics of any kind. However, the party persevered with a fine persistence and they held a public meeting once a week on the one open space in the village, where they harangued each other and a sprinkling of schoolchildren and loafers who came from curiosity. It was usually a disappointing audience, because they seldom had anything new to say, and the figures of attendance sent in to their provincial headquarters looked bad, even though they were strikingly larger than those sent in by the patwari to the Deputy Commissioner. Their leader was one Ram Parshad Singh, a lawyer with a long narrow face and a drooping moustache who on six days of the week wore a check knickerbocker suit, while on the day of his weekly meeting he put on snowy homespun cotton, the uniform of the Congress party. His moustache and his knickerbockers would have automatically qualified him for the part of the squire's wicked son in a rustic melodrama. Ram Parshad Singh was worried about his poor audiences; he decided that he must attract a better house and it occurred to him that this could be done by organizing a procession through the village which would end at the meeting. If there were flags and drums, people would follow and stay to listen.

So a procession was organized. It assembled outside the village to the east and marched with beating drums and a host of flags, green, yellow, and white, by the detour below the courts and along the bridle-path right through the village, and then turned down the hill to the meeting-ground. It was undoubtedly a draw to begin with and audiences increased considerably; but they soon drooped off again when people found that at the end of the march there was nothing to look at or listen to but Ram Parshad Singh talking as usual about tyranny and fiscal policy and imported cotton goods. Ram Parshad Singh felt he must liven up the proceedings; and he thought he could best do this by being in some way openly provocative to the officials of the district. He was encouraged in this idea by the remission of the corvee, which he interpreted as having been conceded by a reluctant government solely because they were afraid of the agitation started by Jodh Singh. He knew nothing of the part played by the Deputy Commissioner. After some thought, he came to the conclusion that it would probably be a good way to begin the provocation if he took his procession straight through the court enclosure, making as much noise as possible on the way. No one could call the detour a burning popular grievance, but it could be worked up a little and it could be argued that if the route was available for an official procession it ought also to be open to the one political organization in the district, particularly as that organization claimed to represent the whole of India. Whatever the merits of the case, someone could be found to support it; and it would certainly annoy the Tahsildar. 'Anything to give pain,' was really Ram Parshad Singh's thought.

Before he made up his mind to adopt this particular form of irritation, Ram Parshad Singh considered the method. He might write a letter asking, in words sufficiently insolent to ensure refusal, that the gate should be opened for his next procession. Or the next procession might climb over it, for it was a simple five-barred field gate of iron. If he chose to climb over, he would certainly get away with it the first time and there would probably be a show down next time he tried it. If he wrote a letter, it would mean a show down the first time.

He had come to this point in his deliberations when a letter reached him from Jodh Singh, who had not yet been to Pokhra since the decision about the corvee and wished to include the headquarters of the district in his triumphal progress. Ram Parshad Singh thought this over carefully. He was not an idealist and an enthusiast as Jodh Singh was; he was a careerist, a political adventurer. He wanted to represent the district at Lucknow and Jodh Singh was a dangerous rival whom it would be pleasant to discredit. On the other hand, he was a draw and his presence would send up the numbers at Ram Parshad's weekly meeting. How could he be used to the best advantage? Could he be connected with the gate agitation?

Suddenly a smile lightened Ram Parshad Singh's long sallow face, making it for the moment almost attractive. He would take his procession over the gate before Jodh Singh arrived. The Tahsildar would know nothing of this until they were right in front of his court-room and by then it would be too late for him to stop them. They would bring it off the first time. Next day, he would write to the Tahsildar complaining that his procession had been obstructed by a gate. 'A gate,' he repeated to himself with relish; he would write as though he had lived in Pokhra all his life; he grinned at the idea, for a hill man is seldom without a sense of humour. He would invite the Tahsildar to have it open for his next procession. The reaction, he could be certain, would be sharp; the Deputy Commissioner, who was a less predictable factor in any situation, was as usual away on tour and the Tahsildar in charge was a fire-eater. Then Jodh Singh would arrive. Ram Parshad Singh, with a fine show of deference to so successful an agitator, would hand over the situation to him. There would be a sharp tussle and Ram Parshad Singh did not think victory would be achieved quickly. Jodh Singh would not want to stay in Pokhra for ever; he would leave when nothing was settled and everyone was tired of the whole affair. Then Ram Parshad Singh would tidy it up. His friends could be trusted to use the incident to the best advantage in a whispering campaign, which would show him as uniformly successful and Jodh Singh as having fumbled. Yes, that would be how it would go. He wrote a letter to Jodh Singh cordially welcoming him to the headquarters, and a week before he was due to arrive led the procession over the gate and through the court enclosure.

Bhola Nath, the Tahsildar[3] of Pokhra, was a Brahman from the plains who regarded all hill men as dirty, a condemnation which bulked so large in his mind that he was not impressed by their courage, simplicity, and humour. He had plenty of courage himself, and a liking for the direct old-fashioned way of dealing with trouble. He liked a government to govern, no doubt for the good of the people, but as the government conceived the good, standing no nonsense. He did not like conciliation. And he hated the Congress, partly because they were agitators and he was a ruler, and partly because he was a landowner in the plains and they made it difficult for him to collect rent. He disliked Ram Parshad Singh more even than he did other Congressmen, the reason he gave being that he liked a man to come out in the open and show himself for what he was; and he held it against Ram Parshad that he did not wear his Congress uniform every day.

When Bhola Nath heard the drums and shouts of the procession pass the door of his office, he was furious. It was the grossest

[3]Actually, the magistrate in charge when the Deputy Commissioner was away would have been a grade higher than Tahsildar. But the titles of civil officers differ in various parts of India and are all confusing. I have eliminated this higher grade for the purpose of this book.

impertinence to come that way at all, and for a few minutes he could not hear himself speak in his own court. His first impulse was to rush out and stop the procession at once, but a moment's thought convinced him that this would merely make him look ridiculous. A procession of avowed Congressmen could not stop at his bare word without becoming a laughing-stock themselves; and he could not in the time available collect enough force to ensure obedience. There was no police administration, but there were a dozen armed police at Pokhra who provided the guard for the treasury, a few hundred yards away, and he could muster twenty or thirty orderlies if he had a day's warning, but at a few minutes' notice, not more than five or six. He had no alternative but to sit and fume. All the same, he was not going to put up with this kind of thing. He published an order before he went home, prohibiting the taking of processions through the court enclosure, a practice which he stated was dangerous to public order and tranquillity. He had copies of this posted on both gates and gave instructions for other copies to be served on Ram Parshad Singh and his principal henchmen.

This order anticipated Ram Parshad's impertinent letter, which reached Bhola Nath next day and increased his anger, as it was meant to; he repeated phrases from it to himself all day with growing irritation.

' "Found his way obstructed by a gate," indeed! As if he hadn't lived here all his life! And I am to "be so good as to see that this obstruction is removed", am I? You wait till next Wednesday, my friend, and just try it on again. You'll see what you'll get.'

He would collect old soldiers as well as orderlies and his handful of police. They would soon knock the stuffing out of a handful of half-hearted Congressmen. He began at once to make arrangements to collect them, and it was not till the evening that it occurred to him that he ought to tell the Deputy Commissioner what he was doing. By this time, the patwari had ferreted out the news that Jodh Singh was expected during the week and Bhola Nath added this to his letter, which he sent off with the rest of the day's work by a runner who would hand it over by a system of relays and cover the four stages to the camp in a day and a half.

Hugh was fishing when the runner reached his camp and he did not open the bag till the evening. He was not a man to look for work, as Mr Bennett had done, and since he regarded his time in the hills as a pleasant interlude in which to recuperate from the burden of responsibility he had borne in the plains, he was scrupulous to allot one day in seven to recreation. If there was no fishing or shooting in the neighbourhood on the seventh day, he went on working till he was somewhere more suitable, but he saved up every day due to him. There had been three days owing to him which he was working off in a fishing holiday, of which this was only the second day. He had not done badly so far and hoped to do better tomorrow; but even if he didn't it was a good river to fish.

Nothing released him more completely from the cares of the world than to see the arrowy curve of his line in a good cast, to feel his lure swimming home smoothly across the tail of a long pool as he wound steadily in; nothing gave him the same unmixed thrill of excitement and pleasure as the tug of a heavy fish. Margaret too enjoyed the days by the river. Her enthusiasm for fishing was intermittent, but she revelled in the colour of the valleys in winter and spring, the translucent green of deep pools that glowed with inner light like chrysoprase, the silver and diamond of glancing rapids, the bleached white of little beaches of sun-soaked sand, the black of wet rocks and stranded driftwood. She liked the scrunch of pebbles under her feet and the bobbing of the quick wagtails as they prinked and perked and flitted. And after vain attempts to paint wide hillsides and snow mountains, it was a joy to turn to the closer, more intimate pattern of glowing pool, dark bank, and glittering cascade.

They walked back to camp together to a late tea. Hugh opened his bag of mail at once, and looked through it quickly to see what could wait and whether there was anything he must look at now. Bhola Nath's letter was marked urgent. He read it with an expression of disgust.

'What's the matter?' asked Margaret.

'Bhola Nath and the Congress have started a quarrel at Pokhra and the old man wants to beat them up. It's the most trivial thing—but it might cause a lot of trouble if he did. Damn! It means I ought to go back to Pokhra tomorrow, I suppose.'

'Curse them!' said Margaret. 'Why can't they agree among themselves?'

'I suppose it would leave me out of a job. Let me see, I could take a horse most of the way. It's Saturday, I think, isn't it? Then I could be there Monday evening and I should have Tuesday to try to settle it. If anything happens it will be on Wednesday.' Hugh was thinking as he talked.

Margaret said:

'What's it all about? Or is it too secret to tell me?'

'It's really complete nonsense. Last Wednesday the Congress people took a procession in front of the courts, where we had the party to celebrate victory, making what Bhola Nath calls great uproar and intolerable commotion. He's forbidden them to do it again and they've formally applied to him to open the gate, in what he says is a highly scurrilous and impertinent letter. So they're both committed up to the hilt. He wants to collect an army and stop them by force. The trouble is I've just had a letter to say the Viceroy is engaged in very delicate negotiations with Gandhi and we're to do nothing to provoke the Congress just at the moment. It's the usual sort of letter of course; "while on the one hand", do nothing, "on the other hand" don't let anyone else do anything. Nice easy instructions to follow. Well, I'm not going to lose my day's fishing. I'll come back and have it later. Would you like to stay and finish your picture?'

'No, I'll come with you if you can arrange so that it won't slow you up. But I'm afraid that pool won't look the same to me when we get back. It's a pity because I was liking that picture. Are you sure you must go? It does seem silly. What can you do?'

'I'm afraid I must. They're sure to make a fuss about it if Bhola Nath does beat them up and I can't very well stand aside and leave him to take the blame later. Your old friend Jodh Singh's going to be in Pokhra too, which will add to the excitement. The whole thing's absurdly trivial, but it's the kind of thing that does happen in India. Both sides are committed to something they don't really mind about much in itself, but it becomes a life and death affair because prestige will suffer if either gives way.'

'Well, if it doesn't matter, give way and have your day's fishing,' said Margaret flippantly.

Hugh shook his head.

'Bhola Nath would think I'd let him down, and not a patwari in the district would have any confidence in me. Nor would I in them. They'd always be afraid to do anything without my written orders for fear I should let them down again.'

'Where do we sleep tomorrow?' was all she asked.

Four stages could easily be done in two days with the help of ponies, but it was hard on the porters. Still, it was done, and Hugh was in Pokhra on Monday evening.

Meanwhile Jodh Singh had arrived and found the tracks of his small female bear. Ram Parshad Singh had used considerable skill in leading him to them. The local leader had heard enough to realize that he had to deal with an enthusiast, a youthful idealist to whom it would be no use to present the issue as it appeared to himself, a move in the game, a simple matter of profit and loss. On the other hand, Jodh Singh could hardly be such a fool that he would think it a matter of burning public importance that a small procession should have to make a detour of a few hundred yards. Ram Parshad Singh acknowledged that the detour in itself meant nothing.

'But it's a principle that's at stake,' he went on earnestly. 'This is a
test case. Are the British really sincere when they say they are going to
give us freedom and show us how to become a democracy? They talk
of giving us power when we're fit for it—but actually they look on
every political meeting as a danger. Why is there a patwari at every
meeting we hold to take down what we say and report it to the
Deputy Commissioner? They mean to cling to every vestige of power
and suppress every sign of awakening nationhood. That's why they
oppose it. They don't want my brave volunteers, who are ready to face
prison and torture rather than be slaves, to corrupt the toadies and
lickspittles who hang round the courts.'

Jodh Singh agreed eagerly. This was the language he had been
brought up on and used himself. He accepted without demur Ram
Parshad Singh's suggestion that he should take over the conduct of the
affair, and he made several fiery speeches. People came to hear him.
They came the first time out of curiosity, to see the grandson of old
Kalyan Singh whom they had all known, and to thank him for what he
had done in the matter of the corvee. They came a second time because
they found his speech exciting. He spoke with warmth and obvious
sincerity, and what he said was dramatic; he lowered his voice at
critical points till every ear was strained to hear him, he raised it again
to heighten and then release the tension, and their emotions rose and
fell as he intended. He did not talk about fiscal policy; it was simple
but emotional stuff about freedom and tyranny. He told them stories
(mostly quite imaginary) of oppression when the Gurkhas ruled the
land and the courage of those who had fought against them, of brave
Garhwalis who charged to their death, with the name of their great
temple on their lips in the war-cry of 'Jai Badri Bisal!'; and then
skilfully he transferred to the present the ardour he had roused. But
though it was good entertainment and a fine purging of the emotions,
it led very few to think it worth risking either a broken head or arrest
by defying Bhola Nath's order and taking part in the procession which
was to march past the court-rooms. To the practical peasant, there
seemed no point in it.

Jodh Singh came away from his first meeting in a glow of triumph.
He had carried his audience with him; they would follow him
anywhere. Ram Parshad Singh fed his vanity with compliments and
the other local men picked up the cue and said the same. But talks next
day with secret sympathizers who might have been expected to come
into the open were disappointing. And when at the end of his second
meeting he asked for a show of hands and promises of attendance,
only the little band of regulars, mostly briefless lawyers and
unemployed, showed their hands, while the body of the meeting began

to melt. A stream began to flow out from the meeting-ground through the narrow lane that led steeply up to the bazaar.

Fury and disappointment filled Jodh Singh's heart. He sickened with disgust at the cowardice of men and the strength of custom and tradition. He forgot for the moment everything but his fury; he wanted to hurt, to smash, to revenge himself on the world which had disappointed him. He clenched his fists; his eye circled the meeting and it fell on the patwari Uma Nand Naithani who was standing quiet and observant at the back of the audience.

'It is you who make men cowards,' he cried, 'you and the likes of you, Uma Nand, dogs who are ready to lick any trencher, who will sell their own brothers to the English for fourteen rupees a month. Once you take up this shameful bondage of government service, there is no infamy too base for you. How much money did you take in the matter of Dewan Singh Rawat's house? And how much for Vidya Dhar's shop? Corrupt and faithless, will you stop at nothing?'

There was a thrill of horror among the crowd. It was a shameless breach of convention to speak in public of such transactions. It had never been done before. The flow to the lane increased. No one could tell what might come next. The patwari himself stood frozen and motionless. If his superiors heard such talk, something would stick whether they believed it or not. He dared not look on either side of him at the faces of the crowd. He stared fixedly towards Jodh Singh.

Jodh Singh recovered himself. He announced that the meeting was over, but that there would be another tomorrow; and on the following day the procession would take place. Ram Parshad Singh and his friends said nothing about his outburst against the patwari. They felt it was in rather bad taste and the less said about it the better. But secretly they were glad because Jodh Singh's stock had gone down.

When he heard Jodh Singh say that the meeting was over, Uma Nand the patwari drew himself together and took a long breath. He turned and went up the steep lane towards the bazaar with the others, but he was careful to catch no one's eye. He looked at the ground and walked slowly. He had next to go to the Deputy Commissioner's house to meet him on arrival and tell him the latest position. He was a fattish man, with a long body and short legs; his long face was broad at the temples and jaw so that it looked oblong and blockish at first sight, but there was nothing stupid about his wrinkled eyes or wide sad mouth. His skin was greyish over its brown, as though dusted over with flour. He walked with his shoulders bent, slowly, thinking of Jodh Singh.

He had felt unfriendly to the young man before he saw him. He had recently had a short spell of leave and had revisited his native village of Chopta in the south-east, where he had talked much with his cousin

Ram Dat Naithani, the headman. Ram Dat had spoken bitterly of the insults heaped upon him by Jodh Singh, on him, the headman, in public, in the presence of his own villagers.

'They are all the same, these Rajputs,' Ram Dat had said. 'They hate all Brahmans. Sometimes they try to hide it, but it breaks out like this. He is not to be trusted. He is plotting something against us. If he stands to represent the district at Lucknow, he must not have our backing.'

Well, Ram Dat was clearly right. Jodh Singh must be bitterly hostile to all Brahmans, and particularly against the clan of Naithani. He had done the same thing at Pokhra as at Chopta, hurled abuse at the patwari in public, before the people of his own area. Uma Nand was filled with horror and anger. Dirt had been heaped on his head. He could not be happy until he had put things right and he could only do that by bringing disgrace upon the boy who had injured him. He would do that in good time. He would think later what he would do. Meanwhile, he must consider what he should say to the District Sahib. If he said nothing of the accusations made against him, he could be sure that someone else would, and though there would be no proof—.

He stopped and cast back anxiously in his mind. He was not a particularly corrupt or extortionate man, but the pittance he received from government of fourteen rupees a month (that is one guinea or four dollars) was much what it had been in Mr Bennett's time. And while the cost of living was ten times what it had been, it was no longer the rule for every peasant to pay the patwari a fraction of his crop, except in some isolated parts of the high hills where life had not changed. The patwari now had to make what he could on disputes and reports. Uma Nand liked to take something from each party and send in a report that was substantially accurate, and he had therefore the reputation of being an honest man and a good patwari. But sometimes of course one had a more difficult course to steer and could hardly help oneself. As easy to pass through the eye of a needle as to be an entirely honest patwari. No, his conscience was reasonably clear and whatever gossip might say about those particular cases, he was confident there could be no proof. There was always a fear—but it was better in any case to avert suspicion in advance by making a clear confession of what had been said. If the Tahsildar had been a hill-man, he would have gone to him first, in spite of his orders to be present when the sahib arrived.

He was coming up by the forest path now and in a few more minutes he was at the house. He did not have to wait long before Hugh and Margaret arrived and he was able to make his report at once. He said that if Jodh Singh led the procession past the courts he would have with him the dozen or so of Congress regulars and perhaps thirty or forty others, not more. He ended by telling of the attack on himself.

'And at the end, lord, he said much against me. He gave me very bad abuse. He said I had taken bribes. What am I to do, lord?'

Hugh thought this over. At last he said:

'You need do nothing. I shall make inquiries. If you have not taken bribes, you need fear nothing.'

'No, lord never, never.'

'Then do not fear.'

Hugh went to his desk and wrote a letter to Jodh Singh:

'I hear you are in Pokhra and are planning to defy the Tahsildar's orders. I hope very much that before you do something which will certainly lead to violence, you will have a talk with me on the subject. Your party and the government both wish to avoid violence, so let us talk it over before it is too late. A talk can do no harm and may do good. So please come and see me tomorrow morning.'

That night the moon rose late and in the darkness Uma Nand the patwari went to the house of Ram Parshad Singh. He tapped quietly on the door and would not say who he was or show his face until the Congressman in person came to see him. When he knew who it was Ram Parshad Singh smiled to himself. Things were going his way and he was amused. He led the patwari into a very small side-room in which there was just sufficient space for an empty string bed. Both had to stoop to get through the low door. They sat on the bed side by side, uncomfortably; the room was lighted only by the yellow light of a hurricane lantern; the walls and beams were of wood blackened with smoke. They talked of nothing for a few minutes. Then Uma Nand said:

'You were at the meeting. You heard what Jodh Singh said to me.'

'Yes, I heard. He is young and hot-tempered and impetuous,' said Ram Parshad Singh soothingly.

'I think perhaps he is not altogether a good person to stand for the district,' said Uma Nand.

'He is my colleague. As to who will represent the district'—a modest pause—'that rests with the public.'

'Still, I think it would be better if he did not. Perhaps you think the same. And if at any time you need my help—' Uma Nand left the sentence unfinished and rose to go. 'I do not wish him well.'

'Of course, of course, I understand,' said Ram Parshad Singh. He did understand perfectly, and he was more amused than ever. The bargain was sealed, as firmly as it could be between two people who distrusted each other thoroughly.

Next morning at breakfast Hugh remarked to Margaret:

'I've asked your friend Jodh Singh to come and see me this morning.'

'Oh, have you? Do send him along to me if I'm here. I'd like to talk to him for a few minutes. He seemed so young and full of life and enthusiasm.'

'Yes, I like him too, but he's riding for a fall, annoying people unnecessarily. He's really too young, years too young, for the position he's got himself into.'

'What shall you say to him?' she asked.

'There's not really much I can say to him, except ask him to be sensible. I don't expect much from that, though I have to make the attempt. But there's just one fly I shall put down on the water over his head very, very gently, just within reach, which may appeal to his impetuous nature. And if he takes it, we might avoid a scrap. Otherwise, we'll have to have one, but there couldn't be a worse moment.'

'What's your fly?'

He laughed.

'I'll tell you later.' He went to his desk.

She watched him go with a smile. He's really quite subtle about his work, she thought. Odd that he should be so unsubtle in other ways. Is it because he's never loved anyone but me? Or is it just that he's a different sort of man? I suppose most men are that kind really, but you don't find out about that kind till you've married one. How very different. Much more worthy and reputable; the kind of man the world admires; and so do I admire him. Only—. Come on, woman, see the cook; order stores by post for the next tour; go down to that new women's hospital; would there be time to see that unfortunate girl guide woman? I ought to try.

Jodh Singh read his letter with mixed feelings. His mood of triumph and mastery was already beginning to alternate with one of irritation and despair when he came to Pokhra. Most of the time he was full of elation at what he had done, but the wonder was beginning to wear off, the almost stunned feeling 'Can it really be true? Have I, Jodh Singh, done this, pulled off this unbelievable triumph?' And from time to time he was plunged in the blackest depths at the strength of the forces of custom and inertia with which he had to contend. When his enemy seemed to be that abstraction, the foreign government, then he could be joyful in the fight; but when it was his own countrymen with whose muddy spirits he had to contend, there was no strength or joy in him, and all things beneath the sun seemed to him futile and pointless. He was in such a mood of despair now and it was coupled with irritation because he knew he had failed himself and made things worse by his outburst of fury.

But his spirit lifted as he read the letter. He was the leader, and the District Sahib wanted to treat with him. He was Jodh Singh, who had ended the forced labour, and on whose word all men hung. And here was a problem to be considered. Should he go? It could do no harm and he would like to see that big man again. And it was true that the Mahatma said violence should be avoided. He would be glad if it could be avoided by the other side giving in. But he would not give way himself. Yes, he would go.

He started at once, pleased by the prospect of action. He thought of his last meeting with Hugh, and how nervous he had been, and how he had said over and over again to himself that he would not give in. Well, he would not be nervous this time and there was no question of giving in. But he would like to know what that big man would say to him. He knew that last time he had done Hugh an injustice. When he went to Lucknow, the Deputy Commissioner must have spoken for the district and advised the government to give up the forced labour; it was a fair deduction that they would not have given it up against his advice and in any case a certain amount of what he had said in his letters was now known, having leaked out partly from the camp staff in the district and partly from relations in the secretariat staff at Lucknow. But why did that big man not say that he was on the side of the people? If only he had said that, the two of them could have made a plan together. Jodh Singh's heart swelled at the thought. He could have worked with that man happily. But he had not been trusted and brought into partnership. He could not forgive that. It was quite outside his training and experience to perceive, or even to understand if it had been pointed out to him, that Hugh would have regarded it as deeply disloyal to his superiors to express his own thoughts fully to Jodh Singh.

This time Hugh came straight to the point with a directness that appealed to Jodh Singh's temperament. He expanded the point he had made briefly in his letter. No one wanted violence. Why provoke it over so trivial a matter?

Jodh Singh said:

'But if it is trivial, why does the government insist? I agree, Sir, it is nothing, this matter of the gate. But it is the attitude to our party that is important. If we are to be a nation, we must develop political consciousness.'

Hugh could not say what he thought about the difficulty of carrying out a policy conceived in Westminster by means of officials in India who disliked it, nor could he say that with him the main consideration was that he must back up the Tahsildar. He said:

'We cannot get on with our work and administer the law if there is so much noise in front of the courts that we cannot hear what the witnesses say.'

'But it is only for a few minutes once a week; that cannot make any difference.'

'It would not make much difference if it was only that. But if we let one party and one procession through, we should have to let the others. We couldn't discriminate. And it wouldn't end with processions. The next thing would be meetings.'

'But you already discriminate. You let a government procession go through, to celebrate the end of a war into which we were forced without the will of the people being consulted.'

So it went on. They could get no further without one or the other giving way, and since neither had any such intention, no progress was made. At last Hugh said:

'Well, I see it's no use trying to make you change your plans. But about your future, if you will allow me to talk about it. I still think you could be doing far more valuable work for the district if you would turn to something constructive. I know you think politics must come first, but you could talk politics at the same time and they'd listen to you if you had something practical to talk about. Last time we talked I suggested you could help the district over forests; but there are lots of other things if that doesn't appeal to you. I'm sure the system of agriculture here could be improved if someone would really do some work on it. Or teach the villager some sideline that would pay him, such as bee-keeping. And look at all the work that could be done on primary education.'

'It is very bad,' agreed Jodh Singh.

'Now let me be frank with you,' said Hugh. 'You people want India to be free and manage her own affairs at once, but what sort of a showing do you make at managing a district, let alone a country? The deputy commissioners may not have been enthusiasts for education but they did keep roofs on the schools and see that the teachers were paid. How many schools are there that are falling down and how many teachers are there who are more than six months in arrears with their pay, now that the district board has taken them over? You could become a member of the District Board and make education your special subject. They'd make you chairman of the education sub-committee. You could do immense good. But it'd be real work, not just talking about national consciousness and freedom and tyranny, if you'll forgive me for putting it like that.'

He spoke with so cheerful and friendly an air that Jodh Singh could not be hurt. He went on:

'Or if it's social reform—what about the Doms? What are they but serfs? They're a feudal survival if you like. Your own Mahatma talks about helping the depressed, but no one else does anything about them. Which of your Congressmen here would stir a finger to help them? Would you dare to go and get Mangi Das, their leader, here, and put him at the head of your procession tomorrow riding on a horse? Of course you wouldn't. But that's something you could do at once, to day, and it's something that only you can do, yourselves; I can't help in that, nor can any British government. You must do it. But you won't. No, Jodh Singh, I'll believe in your new India when I see you getting down to something practical.'

He stood up:

'Forgive me my long lecture. Will you come and speak to my wife? She'd be glad to see you again.'

'There is nothing to forgive, Sir. I am very thankful for your advice. It is very good, but I am not sure it is right for me. I must think more about it. Thank you very much; I am very thankful.'

They went together to the next room, where Margaret was making out a list of stores. They both thought how lovely she looked, tall and slim, in a tweed riding coat and Jodhpurs, a dove-grey shirt, an emerald tie. Hugh left them and went back to see other visitors. Jodh Singh was desperately shy, but he thawed as she talked to him about the beauty she loved in the hills and showed him some sketches she had made near his home in the upper district. She told him too about the women's hospital she was going to visit, and the pathetic shortage of stores and equipment. There was not much he could say to her, because they had so little common ground. He thought the poverty of the hospital a reproach to the government and therefore to every English person; she could only see the indifference of everyone about her, the fact that no one would help with gifts, or time, or interest. She would have said it was a reproach to every Indian. But each was conscious of the other's liking. He was shy because he did not know how long to stay or how to go; she perceived his embarrassment and at last said she must say good bye as she had to go to the hospital. He left her in a mood of sadness. How could he find a wife like her among his own people, he asked himself. I shall always remember her and think more kindly of the English, he thought. She was kind to me, she liked me.

He was halfway down the hill before it occurred to him that he had no business to be thinking of a wife, for tomorrow night he would be in prison. He was overcome with self-pity and sat down on the boundary wall of the Deputy Commissioner's forest to contemplate his own heroism and wretchedness. If only there was someone near who loved him and understood him and would be sorry for him. But he was alone, for his mother did not understand him, and as for the mem-sahib—he used the word to himself with sarcasm—she would be sorry for him for a minute, but it would not make her lose her sleep. She must look very beautiful when she was asleep. He thought of her husband. He shook himself; he must think about other things.

It had been a very unprofitable talk with her husband. He had not got much there. But there was something in what he had said at the end. It is true that we are unpractical, visionaries, dreamers, he thought. It is because we put the spirit first, and these Europeans always think of the material. That is why they are our masters, but the things of the spirit are more important, and there they are children. But there was much in what he had said about the Doms. It is true that only we can help them. It would be a great thing, to make it my next mission to help the Doms. It was the teaching of the Mahatma. It would show her husband how wrong he was to despise Indians.

But it is too big for me, he thought in another wave of depression. There would be no one on my side. No one. No help anywhere. It was no use. His eyes travelled across forty miles of limpid sun-filled air to the square snowy tower of Chaukamba, the crown-shaped peak that stands above Badrinath and is called that name by Europeans. The home of the gods. His eyes travelled from peak to peak; thought left him; he felt more calm.

A man trudging outwards from Pokhra with a load on his back stopped at the top of the hill for a rest. He leaned back and let the weight of his load come on the wall, lowered himself gradually till he was sitting on top of the bank that rose to the wall's foot, and then allowed the load to slide down until it was resting on the bank. He looked up at Jodh Singh, joined his hands as if in prayer as a sign of respect for his sophisticated clothes and style of haircut, and said:

'Maharaj!'

Jodh Singh was miles away in the home of the gods. He muttered something impatiently, but the man with the burden was not to be deterred. He told with easy garrulity how he had come to Pokhra to pay the land revenue for his elder brother the headman who was sick and whose son was still small; he recounted the things he had bought for his friends and relations and the prices he had paid, and compared present prices with those before the war. Then he asked Jodh Singh who he was and what he did for his living and whether he was married and had any children.

'I am Jodh Singh Rawat, son of Govind Singh son of Kalyan Singh.' The man with the burden scrambled to his feet.

'Jodh Singh that stopped the forced labour?' he cried. 'Maharaj!'

And he made a sweeping gesture of obeisance as though to touch the ground at Jodh Singh's feet.

It was more than enough to restore Jodh Singh's confidence. He came down from the clouds and talked to his admirer for a few minutes. Then he stood up to go. He looked again at the snowy crown of Chaukamba and muttered aloud the war-cry which he had invented for his Garhwali heroes in the Gurkha wars:

'Jai Badri Bisal!'

Yes, he thought, I will do it. I am Jodh Singh and I can do it. I will raise the name of the Doms and end their serfdom. I will show her husband that we can do something practical.

He did not delay but went straight down through the little town to the Domana where the Doms lived. He asked for Mangi Das, found him, and took an instant dislike to his dark skin, insolent manner, and coarse appearance. However, he had made up his mind and there was no going back. He wasted no words but told Mangi Das that he was determined to carry out the wishes of the Mahatma and treat the Doms as brothers. He would begin by asking Mangi Das to lead his procession tomorrow.

'On a horse?' asked Mangi Das. He was lying on a string bed and did not rise but propped himself up on an elbow. The burning grievance with his community was that the Brahmans and Rajputs forbade the bridegroom to ride on a horse or the bride to go in a litter at their weddings.

Jodh Singh hesitated. Then:

'Yes,' he said firmly, 'on a horse. As far as the gate, of course. You'll have to get off at the gate. But the horse can be led round.'

Mangi Das reflected. He had become a leader because he was clever and insolent and had served in a labour corps during the war, but the root principle of his life was laziness. This might involve trouble and going to prison. He could avoid blows by giving himself up without resistance. He might avoid prison by saying he was only a Dom and knew no better. And in any case, he knew about prison, and there was plenty of food there, almost as much as in the army. And to have been in prison for one's politics gave one a distinct cachet. To ride on a horse at the head of a procession would be a great stroke, establish him firmly as a leader.

'Yes,' he said. 'I'll be there.'

Jodh Singh looked at his wrist-watch; he really did want to know the time, but there was also a consciousness that the movement would impress Mangi Das. He had to meet Ram Parshad Singh and his committee and would be late unless he was quick.

When he told the committee that Mangi Das was to ride at the head of the procession, they looked down their noses. Ram Parshad Singh exulted; it was all going far better than he had hoped and this silly boy was making every possible mistake. But his face was serious and deferential as he said:

'But are you sure that would not be a mistake? I know it is the teaching of the Mahatma that we should regard these people as brothers, but we have had no official orders from the party.[4] And here in this district which is so backward politically—we have so much to contend with. It will only turn people away. But of course it is the Mahatma's teaching.'

Jodh Singh flared up. This was time-serving; these mean-souled calculations brought the party into disrepute. They must do what was right, fearlessly.

Ram Parshad Singh paid a tribute to these high ideals and said that of course Jodh Singh was the leader. The other members of the committee were sullen; they did not like Doms, who were dirty and black and servile, and least of all did they like Mangi Das, who was insolent instead of servile; and they were sure this new move would alienate the public. But Jodh Singh had made up his mind; opposition merely infuriated him, and Ram Parshad Singh, while outwardly gently demurring, fanned the flame of his resolve.

Jodh Singh held another meeting that afternoon. The attendance to start with was poorer than at any he had yet held; it grew less and less when he began to talk about making brothers of the Doms. He came away with his chin up, determined to go on, but his boy's heart was once again in the depths. He knew it was going to be a failure.

Next day, at the gathering point for the procession that was to defy the Tahsildar, there were present Jodh Singh, Mangi Das with his horse, a handful of the Congress regulars, and some twenty or thirty others who had come out of curiosity. A small boy brought a letter written by Ram Parshad Singh's schoolgirl daughter to say her father was sick with fever and could not come and so she was writing for her mother. Jodh Singh read it with a bitter smile. He knew what that meant. He began to arrange his procession.

When they saw that Jodh Singh was persisting in his intention of putting Mangi Das in front on a horse, the spectators began to melt away and the Congressmen became unaccountably shy. They found every kind of excuse. The procession that eventually reached the gate consisted of Mangi Das on his horse and Jodh Singh holding the bridle, his heart bursting, but his head still high. There was a crowd of small

[4]The Congress party did tackle this issue fifteen years later, and lost some ground in the district thereby.

boys and loafers following to see what would happen, but they kept at a distance to show they were not part of the procession.

In silence Mangi Das dismounted and they climbed the gate together. Together they walked in silence across the court enclosure to the gate on the other side. A way was left for them. Litigants, spectators, stamp vendors, onlookers, let them pass and laughed. Bhola Nath and his army stood on the veranda to watch, let them pass, and laughed.

'Two does not make an unlawful assembly,' cried Bhola Nath. 'Let them go.'

So the sticks and handcuffs were idle and nothing happened to mar the negotiations between the Viceroy and Mr Gandhi. Mangi Das enjoyed it all. He had seen from the start that with only the two of them in it there was no danger of blows or prison and his fears had gone. And it was amusing to be attended by a Rajput and walk by his side. He grinned insolently at the crowd.

Jodh Singh did not let a muscle of his face move but before he reached the second gate, big tears were forming one by one and rolling down his stony cheeks. Once over the gate, he turned in a fury on Mangi Das.

'Take that grin off your face! Get out of my sight! I never want to see you again.'

Then he ran as fast as he could to his lodging and burst into a storm of weeping. If only crying could help! There was no one who could help him. He was all alone.

'Roll up the bedding and everything inside. We are going at once,' he said to the cousin from Bantok as soon as the fit began to abate.

'Where to?' asked the cousin.

'North, north, to the high hills,' cried Jodh Singh. 'I don't know where. Yes, I do know, to Bantok. Yes, to Bantok.'

# 6

It was the sight of his cousin's face that made Bantok occur to the conscious part of Jodh Singh's mind, but the will to go which responded immediately to that slight stimulus came from something very deep indeed. It was only as a boy that he had been there and his memories of the place were vague. He had still been small when Govind Singh had built his fine new house to the south of the river and that was the home he remembered. He had not gone back to Bantok for the same reason that had made his father desert the place, because of that contempt for peasant mentality and peasant habits which usually colours the conscious mind of anyone of peasant stock who has recently found another way of life. But when he was hurt it was the place to go; it was the hole to which the wounded animal drags itself, to lick the rankling part in silence. No one would laugh at him there.

And he was hurt, badly hurt. He was not quite sure whether or not the Englishman had deliberately put into his mind the thought of helping the Doms in the hope that he would act on it and wreck his plans. Most of the time he felt sure that this had been the intention and then he was very bitter in his mind against the man he thought of as her husband. On the other hand, he was quite sure that Ram Parshad Singh had deliberately kept away from the fiasco and had rejoiced at his discomfiture. Therefore, he was bitter also against Ram Parshad Singh and against the Congressmen and the people of Pokhra; he raged against them because they were cynical and selfish and greedy. But his thoughts came back again and again to his own failure, his own lack of control. He had been ruled by his emotions. He ought not to have given way to bad temper and abused the patwari; he should not have given way to the wave of feeling that had made him decide to take up the case of the Doms. He ought to have considered the whole question carefully and rationally, but no, it had all been emotion. First he had been depressed and felt he could not do it; then a chance meeting with a stranger had filled him with confidence and he had committed himself immediately to Mangi Das without consulting anyone else first. He was not old enough to be a leader; he had failed and spoilt everything; he kept coming back to the thought, to torture himself as one presses with the tongue on an aching tooth. It was no use; he had failed himself by giving way to emotion and the people of this world had planned and plotted and conspired together against him, and the world had been too strong for him. Somewhere to lick his wounds where no one would laugh at him, that was his need.

When he could for a few moments get his mind away from its twofold bitterness, against himself and against the world, he reasoned that if he was ever to take up his work again, he ought to know more than he did know about the peasants of the district and their way of life; and that there was no better place to learn about them than the homestead from which he drew his being. But this was his reasoning; his reasons were quite another matter.

It was towards the end of March when he left Pokhra and the deep pools in the river still glowed a tender lucid green, the rapids still flashed silver. Soon the snows would begin to melt and the water to curdle with ice-ground dust, the torrent rise till the black rocks were hidden in a milky grey-green smother, but in March there was still the colour and beauty of winter. Jodh Singh marched steadily for ten days. He would not talk at meetings, he would hardly speak to the headmen of the villages through which he passed. His cousin had to make excuses for him, to explain that he was sick and tired. He would not even stop at his own home at Gadoli, but went straight past it to Bantok. He crossed the perilous bridge, unchanged since Mr Bennett's time, on the eighth day, and very early on the eleventh he reached the homestead where his father and grandfather and his fathers' fathers had been born.

It was not long before he tired of living in the low smoky cabins of the homestead. He was used to a diet that to a European would have seemed simple and monotonous, but here there was not even rice, only flat thick pancakes made from coarse millet flour, or occasionally from barley as a treat, eaten sometimes with porridge and sometimes with potatoes. There was meat on feast-days only; and there was honey, mixed with grubs and wax and bees' legs, such as a bear might eat; and sour buttery cheese. He missed the rice and the rich spices to which he had become used, but he could put up with the coarse simple food. What he did dislike was the dirt and the communal life, a whole family herded together into a tiny room. There were neither chimneys nor windows and the smoke found what egress it could, by leaks and cracks or in the day time by the open door. There were dung-heaps within a few feet of the doors of the cabins, and when it rained, the water that trickled under the door and through the cabin was impregnated with farmyard manure. Until the regular rains began, Jodh Singh decided to live out, building a hut of leaves as a protection against occasional thunderstorms.

There was practically no level ground except the fields of the upper and lower farms, but he set out to look round the edges of the crops for somewhere flat enough for a hut. The thin straggly barley was not yet cut in the lower fields and would not ripen in the upper for a month; he found the place he wanted in the upper farm at the top of the bluff which made one side of the narrow place where his grandfather had killed the bear. There was a spring in the woods above and a stream ran down through the narrow place which his kinsmen told him never failed. The top of the bluff ran out into a flat table of rock ten yards square; there was a sparse covering of grass and pine-needles, but you came to the rock in an inch or two inches and so it had never been cultivated. One great pine had thrust its roots deep into crevices in the rock and drew its nourishment from some hidden source.

Jodh Singh and his servant-cousin cut a forked stick from the forest and prodded about near the pine till they found a pocket of earth in which they could make it stand upright. Then they lashed a pole from that to the pine and with that as the ridge of their roof they made a thatched hut that would keep out any but the heaviest rain. Autaru, the cousin—there are very few names in Garhwal and they are repeated from generation to generation—was good at this, for he had been brought up at Bantok and was well used to making such huts in the high pastures where they took the sheep and goats in the rains.

It was cold up there in April. There was still snow in the hollows, where there were clusters of pink and white saxifrage, like dwarf spires of horse-chestnut bloom on plump red stems, and here and there little purple primroses and earth-loving violets. The oak was only just putting out new leaves, tiny crumpled buds of pink and bronze and yellow. But the sun shone by day and at night they made huge bonfires from the inexhaustible forest above them. To Autaru it was madness, for they might have been warm in the smoky cabins a thousand feet below them; but Jodh Singh was happy, released from the bitterness that preyed on him, the fear of scorn and laughter. His cousins in the homestead treated him with deference, almost with reverence, for he had escaped from the hard bondage of the daily life that bound them, he was educated, a great man. But he did not see much of them, for when the work of building the hut was finished, he explored the forests by himself, coming back in the evening to the bonfire and the food Autaru had cooked.

In the mornings, when the water had been fetched and the fire lighted and the breakfast eaten, he would sit gazing across the river at the great hillside opposite. The river had begun to rise and the water was curdling to the milky green of summer; he could hear its roar above the silence of hill and forest; from here it was a little snaky streak of greyish-green showing here and there between the gorges. Across the river, the hill rose steeply at first, in rocky bluff or precipice or a velvet green side of grass. Then the slope grew less and there were villages and cultivation; brown fields where there would soon be rice, green fields of barley yellowing to the harvest. And above the fields, the forest stretching up to the skyline, pouring down into the corries, between the fields, wherever the ground was too steep for terraces.

There was a great contrast between his own hillside and that other across the river. Here there was essential silence, and the noise of the river and the breath of the pines; the tiny evidence of man was an intrusion. Over there, man was everywhere, it was the forest which thrust down and intruded among the fields. But that world of men and defeat and laughter that hurt, was a long way from Jodh Singh in his eyrie, with the blue smoke of the fire curling up in the still morning air and the pines about him throwing back the sunlight from a million dancing needles.

Jodh Singh's was not a nature that could be idle long. After the work of making the hut and the first few days of solitary rambling and exploration, he made two decisions. First of all, he would not be beaten; he would not give up; he would go back to the world of men; he would be a leader and would represent the district in Lucknow; but before that he would go on to the District Board and he would work for a practical end as well as educating the people to want the nationhood that was their right. But not just yet; he would spend the summer here in Bantok and get to know the way of life here in the lonely homestead, and he would grow older, and give people time to forget his defeat at Pokhra. And perhaps he would forget it himself. The second decision was to build a house for himself here, on this rocky bluff, a house that would be all his own and that he could come back to when the world of men sickened him. And some day, but perhaps not yet, he would marry and there would be a wife and a son to come back to. This idea of marriage was only a vague intention. He knew that he needed a wife, but where could he find a wife who was fit for him? For was he not Jodh Singh, who was different from other people and would one day be a great leader? He had met no educated girl of his own people; he did not want to marry a peasant girl, a cutter of grass and gatherer of sticks. He put the idea away as something to be thought of later.

As soon as he had made up his mind about the house he wrote to his uncle for money and carpenters and masons. Here in Bantok they could build a house of a kind, but they could not afford to be specialists in anything and it would be a rough affair indeed; in any case, they were busy just now with the spring harvest. He sent off Autaru with the letter, and while he was away, busied himself with planning his house and marking out the foundations; when this was more or less to his liking, he set to work to make huts for the carpenters and masons.

The money-lending uncle was disturbed by the idea of building a new house at Bantok when there was already a house big enough for everyone at Gadoli. He feared that Jodh Singh would be a serious embarrassment to him and business was already not so good as it had been in the days when Govind Singh was alive. He considered whether it would not be a wise move now to separate from Jodh Singh and partition the family fortunes which were all held in common. But he had too much money out; he could not find Jodh Singh's share if there was a partition. If it were not for that bridge, he would go to the boy and try to make him see reason. But he did not like the thought of crossing the bridge, so instead he wrote a letter which he hoped would dissuade Jodh Singh from the plan.

It brought Jodh Singh to Gadoli in a fury. He did the journey in less than three days; when he returned he took with him the money and the men he wanted. His energy and determination would have overcome his uncle's timidity and lethargy in most circumstances and he did not have much difficulty on this occasion because he had the whip hand. He could always demand a partition and his uncle dared not face one.

The days spent in building the house were very happy. It was warmer now and Jodh Singh, Autaru, and the four workmen camped together in their leafy huts in luxury. Autaru cooked and kept house for everyone. Jodh Singh made plans and altered them, but no one was irritated or minded how often he changed his mind; he learnt too, to shape a block of stone or a beam in the rough and he worked hard with the men. In the evening he joined them round the fire and they told stories, wonderful stories told simply, as a child tells them, without detail or emotion, but with an occasional vivid touch.

'—And his wife said to him: "I know you have the power to turn yourself into a panther. Let me see you do it." And he said "No", because he did not know what he was doing when he was a panther and he might hurt her. But she worried him to do it, and at last she worried him so often and so much that he took her out into the forest and told her to climb a tree to be safe, and watch. And then he changed himself into a panther. And she watched from the tree and saw him. And the panther saw the woman in the tree and climbed the tree after her. And it killed the woman and ate her up. And then it changed back into a man. And he did not know what he had done. And he looked for the woman everywhere, but could not find her. So he went back to the village and said he had lost his wife in the forest. And they came with him to look for her. And they found what was left of her body and they knew the man had turned into a panther and killed her, but he did not know what he had done. . . .'

They were happy days, and Jodh Singh was a boy again, laughing and working and forgetting that people had laughed at him. But the rains came before the house was finished, and they were miserable in their leaf huts, and the masons could not make mortar and the carpenters did not like to work with damp wood. So the workmen went back to Gadoli, promising to come again in the autumn and finish the job, and Jodh Singh and Autaru went up with their kinsmen to the high pastures with the sheep and goats.

They climbed up through the forest, winding about the line of the stream that ran past the homestead, making a path as they went, for last year's tracks had been buried for eight months and the grass had sprung up under the snow. Blue pine gave way to silver birch and spruce and silver fir and then to creeping rhododendron, with great glooms of purple and creamy white and rose-pink. The slope grew less and the stream which had poured over the boulders and mantled the cliffs with sheets of spray ran more gently, a brook of clear water hurrying over brown pebbles, fringed with rushes and fern. Then they were out, above the trees, on grassy golden fells, with streaks of snow still lying in the corries, and bridges of snow across the streams. The flowers had burst into their first radiance, dwarf iris carpeting the ground in sheets; blood-red anemones; primulas pale as lady's-smock; potentillas, scarlet, white and purple; and great clusters of the flowering thistle, five feet high, a cathedral spire of blossom, pink and white and gold. In the miles and miles of high pasture, there were millions of flowers and butterflies of which perhaps one in a thousand would ever be seen by the eye of man or beast, surging upwards to life in a prodigal gaiety that proceeded from sheer joy in creation, the mood in which the stars sang together. The grass was knee-deep and every armful was rich in colour and scent, a heavy spicy fragrance. Jodh Singh knelt and buried his face in it. When he stood up, he was dizzy, his head swam in circles, his throat was constricted. One of his kinsmen caught his arm.

'It is the drunkenness,' he said. 'It comes from the scent of the flowers. Sit down by a rock and rest. There will be pain in your head tonight and again tomorrow, but after that you will get used to it.'

In one place up there in the high alps there was a low cliff of grey stone, with the heavenly blue of the Himalayan poppy growing here and there in the crevices. Beneath this cliff were caves, not deep, but sheltered from rain and wind, with encircling walls built to keep off wild beasts and to throw back the warmth of the fire; it was here that the colony from Bantok made their headquarters. Here they sat at night with the sheep huddled round them, telling stories of ghosts and gods and godlings and warlocks who turned at night into bears or panthers. The fire shone back from the eyes of the sheep; it flickered on the ruddy faces of the men, their long hair hanging out from under round caps of unbleached wool. Men and sheep alike smelt of damp wool, and there was the raw bitter smell of wood-smoke, the drip of water outside in the mist, and the small sounds of the sheep stamping or changing their ground.

In the daytime, Jodh Singh wandered about with the sheep and learnt their ways. Sometimes the whole day there was white mist in wreaths swirling in the hollows and round the rocks, rain and mist and the sound of running water and the squelch of fine tussocky grass under the feet. The men would come back to the caves with the moisture standing on every hair of their woollen blankets like tiny diamonds, just as it stood in the sheep's wool, for the wool of the blankets held the natural grease of the sheep and kept out the rain. Sometimes in the early morning the sky was clear, the sun shone, and then you could gaze away to the south towards the plains, over ridge on scalloped ridge, hill and peak and forest, the dark green of the nearer hills melting to indigo blue, and then fading, fainter, to the smoky blue of the distance. Or you could look north to the icy majesty of Dunagiri and Nilkanta's graceful spire of silver, or east to the long ice slopes and snowfields of Nanda Devi and Trisul, or west to the square snowy crown of Chaukamba. They stood waiting, glacier, peak and snowfield, glittering in the diamond sun, icy, joyful, remote.

As the day grew older, clouds would billow up and their shadows play across the blue hills to the south; they would pile themselves in mountains of white radiance. Evening would stain them angry red, with long jagged bars of grey against the crimson, touches of glowing gold, orange, and the pink of a flamingo's breast. And when the splendour died, the bloom would linger on peak and snowfield till it was lost in the enveloping night.

Jodh Singh was happy, he was a boy, he forgot his cares and bitterness. But it began to grow cold at nights as the rain grew less frequent and when the first frosts came at the beginning of September the men and sheep moved down again to Bantok. Jodh Singh sent Autaru to Gadoli to make sure the workmen returned and when they came, he finished building his house. Early in October, he went to Gadoli, planning to come back to Bantok again in the summer.

His uncle met him at Gadoli with a suggestion. Jodh Singh's mother had been worrying the old man to arrange her son's marriage. He did not feel he could do anything in the matter without his nephew's consent, but was it not time he married? He must have a son and now he was a man ripe for marrying. If Jodh Singh agreed, there was the daughter of a lawyer from Chamoli who had been to a middle school and knew a little English. Secretly he thought that a wife would be a steadying influence that was badly needed.

Jodh Singh felt that the world had come upon him again, at once. It had sprung on him the moment he showed it his face. He did not want a wife of his own people, for none of them were fit for him. If his father had been living and had been secure in a comfortable post, something better than a patwari, he might have been able to arrange a marriage with an educated girl from the city of Dehra Dun, someone who might have been a companion, but by himself he could do nothing. A wife who was beautiful, who could talk and paint and think, like the Deputy Commissioner's wife—but it was no good dreaming of any such thing. It is because of the foreign government that our women are so backward, he thought.

A sick numbness filled him at the grip of the world. It was no good, he must take what was offered. He agreed. His uncle could arrange what he liked. He would be there on the day. Meanwhile, he was off to wander about the district, to talk to the villagers about politics, to find out what their schools were like, and to see what could be done to improve them.

He let it be known that he was going to stand for the District Board, and went into the villages in the neighbourhood. He was greeted everywhere with honour and gratitude for what he had done in the matter of the corvee. His failure at Pokhra had hardly been heard of here, and what they had heard meant nothing to peasants who had not been there. His confidence began to return.

He went through the ceremonies of his marriage and the beginning of his married life with indifference. His wife could read and write Hindi; she knew a little English of the standard of 'The cat sat on the mat'. She was a prodigy of female learning for Upper Garhwal but she had never been ten miles from her home and she had no understanding of the ideas in Jodh Singh's mind. She was shy in his presence and could not talk to him, but she was ready to love him and worship him as a Hindu wife should do. She was sturdy and not uncomely; she had the smooth skin and firm muscles of youth and health; he took her as he took his food and left her without regret. She made no impression on his mind. He went away to his self-appointed work. She could stay at Gadoli for the present; in the summer, unless she was expecting a child, she should go to Bantok and start to keep house there. She might as well learn to cut grass and gather sticks, he thought bitterly; she was fit for nothing else.

It was about the time that Jodh Singh came back to Gadoli from Bantok that the panther began to kill in the river valley. There were always a dozen ordinary panthers, of course, up and down this stretch of the river, but they confined their diet as a rule to wild animals, the barking deer, the little chamois or a young pig, with an occasional goat or dog. But this was no ordinary panther.

The first news came from a village called Bhainswara, twenty miles from Gadoli, and it so happened that Jodh Singh was in the village that night. One Deb Singh, a young peasant on an isolated homestead above the village, had just married, and he felt that with an extra pair of arms to cut grass from the forest and help in the fields, he could manage to increase his stock by another bullock. He knew the beast he wanted, in a village two miles below Bhainswara, and one day early in November he determined to go to see the owner and bring off the deal. After the morning meal he said goodbye to his wife and sent her up into the forest to bring back a bundle of grass. He thought of her with pleasure as he went down the hillside with the easy gait of the hill-man, loose at knees and ankles. She pleased him well, for she was young and strong, smooth of skin and firm of muscle and a child still who could laugh and play with childish things. She was not shy with him. She laughed much, and when she laughed there was a dimple in her cheeks, below the high cheekbones and slightly slanting eyes, a broad comely merry little face. He had given her father three hundred rupees. Deb Singh was very happy and he sang as he went down the hill, at the top of his voice, a song with few words, a long and rather mournful cadence, though he was singing for joy. He had done his business by midday, but he sat some time smoking and talking with the seller and it was towards evening when he got back to his own little homestead. Sita Devi was not back yet and he was rather surprised, but he went about the work of the farm near at hand and did not trouble his mind till darkness began to fall. Then he became anxious; she would not fall, but she might have met a snake or a bear. He took a torch and went up the hill, but it was no use, for she might have taken any of a dozen branching cattle tracks. He came back without her and spent an anxious night; as soon as it was light, he went down to the village to get help. Jodh Singh had slept that night in the village and he came with the rescue party.

It was the vultures that told them where she was, what was left of her. Deb Singh wept bitterly. A panther had killed her, there was no doubt of that. They found blood on the path, for he had attacked her in the open, she had not stumbled on him in the grass by accident. He had dragged her up the hill into a thicket to make his meal. It was the deliberate murder of a man-eater, not the panic-stricken act of a beast suddenly disturbed.

Jodh Singh was moved by Deb Singh's grief and he determined to have revenge on the panther. He would sit up for it over a goat. He borrowed a double-barrelled muzzle-loader from the headman and made himself a platform of a few sticks in a tree near the place where the body had been found. He tied a live goat to a stump in a glade through which a cattle-path led and settled down to wait. But he was by temperament the worst person in the world for such a vigil. He was impatient and excitable; every movement of a bird, every falling leaf, was a panther; his hands would grow wet with excitement and his breath come faster. And he was physically restless and undisciplined; he could not keep still when his leg was pricking where the blood was checked. There was never half an hour when his tree did not shake and the leaves chatter with a change of position. After two sleepless and tiring nights, he gave up. He put in one good night's sleep and then he resumed his wanderings and moved on.

On the fourth night, the panther killed again, on the outskirts of a village ten miles away. This time the victim was a man; he had spent too long smoking with a neighbour before he went to fetch home the cattle. His wife had just been delivered of a child or she would have gone, but tonight he had to do it and he had forgotten until it was late. It was dusk when he passed the big rock outside the village and he got no further. The panther must have been on top of the rock; it sprang on him as he came out from the rock's protection, and dragged him up the hillside into the scrub. The frightened cattle ran on into the village and clustered round the shed. His wife heard them and managed to get up; when she saw they had come home without their master, she called the neighbours. They went out along the path towards the grazing ground with torches, but they did not go very far. They had heard of Sita Devi's death and no one would leave the path and venture into the scrub.

After that there was terror in the valley. The panther went from village to village; he never killed twice running in the same area; he seldom came back to a kill. For one thing the kill was seldom there if it was a human being, the relations being scrupulous to burn what remained and to throw the ashes in the river. And it was usually a human being, although he did not keep himself exclusively to man but would occasionally take a goat, a dog, or even a cow. Most often it was a woman, for it was the women who brought home the cattle and fetched the grass, and the kills were made in lonely places near the forest, not in the fields where the men did their ploughing. But the panther was very bold and its tracks were often found in the morning in the farmyard muck in front of the houses. Every three or four days the story would run up and down the valley of a fresh killing, ten, twenty or thirty miles from the last. Thirty miles up-stream from Gadoli, thirty miles down, in a wide belt from the river below to the forest above, men made for their homes before twilight and slept with barred doors and every living thing shut safely within.

Hugh Upton came up from Pokhra and spent some time in pursuit of the beast, until he had to move on to other parts of the district. Before he left, he wrote to men well-known as good shots and keen followers of wild beasts, and asked them to take up where he left off. Several came at different times, but it was no use. They sat up over carcasses of animals and even over a human corpse if the relations could be persuaded to leave it; but the panther never came near a guarded kill. They lost their sleep and stiffened their limbs over live baits, but he seemed to know they were there. There are no hunting people in the hills and there was no one to track him, even if it had been possible in that precipitous country. They tried poison, but the panther seldom came back to a kill and when he did, he seemed to know that poison was there. Only once did he eat of the poisoned carcass of a cow and then, before he had taken ten paces from it, he vomited up every fragment he had swallowed and was none the worse.

The villagers baited their clumsy wooden drop-traps for him with live dogs, but he would not go near them. Hugh tried spring traps. But here too there was the difficulty that relations would not leave out a human corpse a second night, while goats and cows were rare victims and in any case were seldom revisited. A dozen times the big steel traps were cunningly hidden in grass and leaves; anxious hours were spent to make sure nothing was left that would betray them to eye or even nose, although the panther is almost without the sense of smell; but a dozen times, the work went for nothing, because next morning the tale would come in of a fresh kill twenty miles away. Three or four times the panther came to a trap, but he seemed to know it was there and they would find from his tracks that he had walked once round it and made off. Once and once only he stepped within the steel circle. That day there were half a dozen spring traps set on every approach and on the carcass itself. It did not seem possible for anything bigger than a cat to touch the meat and escape. In the night there was a sudden scream of fury, horrible to hear, yet the morning party of inspection found only one trap sprung, and that at first sight empty. The dust showed that the panther had leapt lightly over the traps and stepped delicately to his meal as though he had known where every spring lay; he had torn a few mouthfuls only, as if not in hunger and with the sole object of showing his scorn for men; but when he turned to go he had sprung one trap and left his toe in it. There was a blood track which they were able to follow with great trouble and patience for about a mile before it was lost, and this showed that he had travelled very fast, in great bounds.

Further news soon came in of that night when he lost a toe. In his fury he had gone through village after village, travelling thirty miles before dawn, going right up to the houses in his search for something on which he could be revenged. But every man and animal was behind barred doors, except in one village. There a traveller passing through had left the dozen goats he was driving in a pen below a leaning rock on the outskirts of the village. He could find nowhere else to put them and had not dared to stay with them. The panther had come through that village. He had sprung into the pen and slain them all. He had not eaten. The torn bodies lay there as witness of his rage.

As the tale of his killings grew, the story of his cunning and boldness passed from mouth to mouth. He seemed to have more than natural cunning, and whenever two men sat down to smoke and gossip, heads shook and the same word was spoken. He was more than a beast. A panther by night, he must be a man by day. There was a story of someone walking home in the evening hand in hand with a friend and suddenly he felt the hand in his grow furry, the nails grow sharp and long and cruel . . . . All the better to grip you with, my dear . . . . People began to look at their neighbours with sidelong eyes. Can it be he? But at first there was no name to which the horror could be linked.

Now at this time the patwari in the lower half of the panther's country was that same Uma Nand whom Jodh Singh had abused at Pokhra. Hugh Upton had made inquiries as he had promised. He had looked up the two cases of bribery which Jodh Singh had quoted. But there was nothing that suggested unfairness in the reports the patwari had made. The parties to both disputes had been questioned but though in both cases the losing party said the decision was unfair, neither had anything to allege against Uma Nand. He was exonerated, but all the same Hugh thought it better to move him. And he came to the area south-west of Gadoli.

It was he who first hinted who the panther might be. He had finished an investigation about a piece of grazing land on the borders of the forest which the owner of the nearest fields wanted to plough. The shareholders of the village objected; it was common land, and they were short of grazing. Uma Nand came and heard their story and wrote his report. When they had fed him, he sat smoking with the leaders of the village, passing the clay pipe-bowl to and fro, for there were Brahmans here with whom it was lawful for him to consort. Each man made a funnel of his hands and drew the smoke cunningly from the bowl; it would have been pollution to touch the clay with the lip. Talk turned on the panther, and who he could be. No one doubted he was a man.

'It will be someone who moves about,' mused Uma Nand aloud. 'No one who stays always in one village. Look how far up the river the killings go.'

There was a long pause, and the pipe-bowl passed. Heads nodded slowly. It sounded sense.

'It began at Bhainswara,' he went on. 'Was there a stranger in the villages near Bhainswara that night? I do not know. It is not my circle.' He rose to go. 'It is late. It is not well to be abroad in the evening these days.'

It was enough. The seed was sown. The whisper went round. It was Jodh Singh who did not sleep in his bed at nights. Everything fitted.

He had more than human energy. He was restless. He did not live quietly in his house like a reasonable man, but wandered from village to village. He did not even stay at home a week after his marriage. Everyone had heard of the sudden rages into which he would fly at the most reasonable remarks. He had been in Bhainswara the first night. And there had been no killing at Gadoli. It was Jodh Singh.

The last two people to hear this story were Jodh Singh himself and the Deputy Commissioner. To Jodh Singh the change in the attitude of the villagers came suddenly. One day men had crowded round him to thank him for what he had done in the matter of the corvee and had listened respectfully to what he had to say. Next day, in another village, there were sullen looks and averted eyes. As soon as the whisper reached them, everyone had accepted it; there was no one else but Jodh Singh who filled the bill. There were very few in the villages of the upper hills who had sufficient education to question the idea that a man could turn into a panther by night. Even those few were not sure. They might laugh deprecatingly if an Englishman asked them questions and say it was a superstition of the peasants, but they had heard tales round the wood fires in the evening too often to be sure. There might be something in it; queer things happened. And whatever they might think of the rumour, few of those with education had much love for Jodh Singh. He had not borne his honours meekly. He had not been patient with those who temporized and were ready to make a bargain with the world. His following was among the simple peasants, who knew only that he had sympathized with them and fought their battle and won; and it was they who believed the whisper without question.

When he saw the changed faces, Jodh Singh asked no questions. He went quietly to the lodging where he was to stay and, pretending to notice nothing, kept to himself as much as possible. But he sent Autaru to find what was in men's minds.

It did not take Autaru long to get to the bottom of it. He was a simple peasant himself, simpler and less sophisticated than anyone brought up to the south of the river. His approach was blunt and direct. He met silence from a few but before long found someone as direct as himself, for the hill-peasant in his native state is direct, as the most illiterate plainsman is not. Autaru came back to Jodh Singh in fear.

'Yes,' said Jodh Singh, with his usual impatience, 'what is it?'

'Lord,' began Autaru. 'Brother.' He was silent. He could not say it.

'Come on,' said Jodh Singh. 'Tell me. You will get no milk from looking at my feet.'

The homely phrase brought it out. Autaru said all in a breath:

'They say you are the panther.'

Jodh Singh sprang to his feet. He was furious, astonished, incredulous, hurt, deeply hurt, all in a moment. His people. His own people. They could not believe such a thing. He would go and talk to them. Now, at once. But he stopped. He must think. He must hold on to himself and not act in a rage. He turned his back on Autaru and sat down to think. Autaru waited in silence and sorrow. And when he began to think, Jodh Singh saw how it fitted, how everything about him lent to the story. He had been at Bhainswara at the time of the first killing. There had been no deaths at Gadoli. And he was different from everyone else. It was true he was different from everyone else. They were tame and he was wild. He belonged to the forest not the villages. Then a new thought came to him. They said such men—warlocks— knew nothing of what they had done when they were beasts. Could one turn into a beast without knowing it? It was nonsense of course, a peasant superstition. No educated person would believe a man could turn into a panther. But science and common sense and the West did not know everything. And things were different in the hills. What was that story of the man who devoured his own wife and knew nothing of what he had done? It was all nonsense of course. But that they should believe it of him! His own people, whom he loved, who knew how much he loved them, who loved him because of what he had done for them. He had done so much and was going to do so much more.

Rage and grief and hurt pride, and a haunting ridiculous fear—but it must be nonsense—and then the odd feeling that it was somehow appropriate, for he was truly different from other people—chased through his mind in confusing and illogical sequence. For a moment he hardened his jaw; at least it was better to be feared than to go unnoticed. Then self-pity overcame him and he wept; but again he braced himself and tried to think what he should do. One thing was clear; it was no use trying to talk politics while this was in men's minds. He must leave his work in the villages till it had cleared. He would go to Gadoli first and on the way he would think what to do next. He turned and gave his orders to Autaru. Then he said suddenly:

'Have you ever known me go out in the night when I seemed to be asleep?'

'No, lord, no,' cried Autaru. 'Never.'

But there was a new look of fear and horror in his eyes.

It was two days' stage to Gadoli, and the way lay through the village which was the headquarters of the patwari. Uma Nand himself was away on one of his inquiries, for there were only two or three nights a month when he slept under his own roof. But his son Dharma Nand was home on half-term leave from the middle school fifteen

miles away. Half-term was an important institution in the middle
school because most of the children lived a full day's march or more
away and the parents could seldom afford boarding fees in cash. So
they sent each child with a sack of flour and he came home to
replenish it at half-term. Dharma Nand was naturally feeling ebullient
because of his holiday and since his father was away, there was no one
to restrain him. He had heard of course the rumour about Jodh Singh
and, though he did not know it had started with his father, he did
know that there was some enmity between them. When he saw Jodh
Singh and Autaru going through the village, he ran after them, and
with the instinct that makes little birds mob an owl in daylight or a
crowd stone a woman in the pillory, he shouted as loud as he could:

'There he goes! There goes the panther, the man-eater!'

People left their houses and ran to see what the shouting was about.
Other boys joined in. Jodh Singh hurried on, his heart bursting with
fury and shame. Those who saw him read his guilt in his looks. They
watched him with hatred and sullen anger. They did not do anything;
no one had yet suggested action against the warlock. Jodh Singh
hurried on. Outside the village and away from the noise and men, he
still hurried, trying to make his legs take him away from his heart.
Hatred for Dharma Nand surged up in his breast; he knew he was
Uma Nand's son and he hated Uma Nand because he could read in his
looks resentment at the injury done to him at Pokhra, because he was
a patwari, because he was grey and cynical. And now he hated
Dharma Nand too.

'I will be even with him,' he thought. 'I will be even with him. One
day I will show him that I am not called a panther for nothing.' He
hurried on towards Gadoli.

Hugh Upton had just come back to the valley for a further attempt
to settle the panther when he heard the rumour about Jodh Singh, from
another patwari, not Uma Nand. He told Margaret that evening after
dinner.

'I'm rather anxious about it,' he said. 'They all seem sure it's Jodh
Singh and it will be difficult to convince them it isn't. It would be no
use telling them men don't turn into panthers. They'd think to
themselves that that's just one of the things Englishmen don't know,
though of course they wouldn't say so. And they'd think it is one of
the things they do know, because it's something they've been brought
up on.'

'But what will they do?' she asked.

'Heaven knows. They're frightened and angry and people do very
funny things when they're frightened. It's odd that people who make
such gallant soldiers should be so frightened of wild beasts and ghosts.'

'Not odd they should be frightened of ghosts or anything they don't understand, is it?'

'Well, perhaps not. But they were very frightened and angry about the panther even before this idea got into their heads. Perhaps because it's the women who get killed. Ordinarily, they're the most law-abiding people on earth, but I should hate to predict what they might do now.'

'You mean, you think he's in danger?'

'I think he may be in very serious danger. Perhaps from a mob of villagers who've lost all reason in a sort of collective funk, or perhaps from one man who's had his wife killed.'

'Poor boy. It'll be terrible for him if he finds out what they think, even if they don't do anything to him. He's a sensitive creature. And so unsure of himself for all his cocksureness about politics. What a predicament for a young intellectual! Can't you do anything?'

'I don't know. I'm thinking what I can do. I must do something. There'd be a fuss if a leading political agitator was murdered by mob violence. Much more than if he was a supporter of government, I feel sure. As you say, it'll be a shock to him and he may be the one to make it most difficult to do anything. If he turns haughty and won't co-operate with me in disproving the idea, it'll only make them more certain.'

'A Coriolanus complex,' said Margaret. 'New to science. He hasn't shown much sign of that in the past. Well, do think hard. I go on liking that boy, and feel very sorry for him.'

Hugh tucked the problem neatly away in his mind and bent his thoughts for two hours to problems of the promotion of clerks, the transfer of patwaris, and the grant of gun-licences. Next morning he lighted a pipe and set himself seriously to consider it. He figured that he must give as many villagers as possible ocular proof that Jodh Singh was asleep in his bed on a night when the panther killed elsewhere. It would not be easy, for as Margaret had said, the boy would probably be in a complicated frame of mind and would not be likely to respond if he received a message summoning him to the camp. Hugh would have to go to Gadoli himself. Then there was the problem of getting the panther. The trouble was that it always had the initiative. There was a kill and Hugh moved to the place, saw the remains if he was in time and set his traps, or watched over the kill or over a live goat, in the hope that one day its habits would change and it would come back to the same place. But he was always one kill behind it. He had only fourteen days in the valley; he could not spare more at present. Would it be justifiable to spend some of these precious days in dealing with the Jodh Singh problem? He decided that he had a reasonable chance of proving that Jodh Singh was not the panther, while judging on past performance he had very little prospect of getting the panther by any means used so far. And since the panther always went somewhere new and it had never yet killed in Gadoli, right in the centre of its country, Gadoli might be as good a place to go as any other. He might for once catch up with it and be there when a kill occurred. Not that that would help Jodh Singh, who had just gone there.

There was one risk in the Jodh Singh affair. Suppose Hugh persuaded him to co-operate in a test, with men sleeping by him and others on watch by his side at night. And suppose by a freak of chance that the panther chose that moment to live for a fortnight on wild game or on dogs that no one missed. Things would be worse than ever for Jodh Singh if it stopped killing men just when he was under observation. But it had been almost as regular as clockwork so far. There was no reason to suppose it would chance. The risk would have to be taken. He called the patwari and his orderly Dewan Singh and gave orders for the camp to move to Gadoli, and for all the headmen in the neighbourhood of that village to be summoned to a talk with the Deputy Commissioner in Gadoli the day after he arrived. He wrote a letter to Jodh Singh asking him to tea in his camp on the day of his arrival, sat and considered it for a moment, slowly tore it up with his square blunt fingers, and wrote another asking Jodh Singh if he and Margaret might call when they arrived and drink tea with him. That, he thought, would do more to show the villagers what he thought of this nonsense than anything else he could possibly do.

'Horrid tea we shall get,' said Margaret when he told her. 'All buffalo milk and sugar. Never mind, it's all in a good cause, and we can have some more when we get back to camp.'

Jodh Singh was bitter when the letter reached him.

'The Deputy Commissioner is being kind to me,' he thought. 'He is doing me this honour to show the people he does not believe this story. Well, I will be grateful and flattered.'

But all the same, though he would not admit it to himself, he really was grateful and flattered. He began to make arrangements. If it had not been for the hostility of the villagers, he would have received his guests on the roughly paved terrace before his house and everyone in the village would have crowded round to watch the great man and his visitors drink their tea. But he dare not risk that now and must ask them indoors. So a room was made ready, with two undyed woollen rugs and the skins of a panther and two chamoix on the floor. The skins had been dried, not properly cured and the hair was beginning to come out. There were three rather rickety chairs and a table that was both clumsy and weak. Govind Singh had not aspired to European customs and Jodh Singh had never given any thought to his home.

Three chairs, however, were enough; he was not going to let her see his wife; she would pity him for marrying such a woman and her husband would despise him. He would not show it, but in his heart he would despise him. There was no china and the visitors would have to drink from brass tumblers without handles, that would be too hot both for their fingers and their lips. The tea would be boiled, tea, milk, and sugar together, in a round brass pot without a lid and would taste of wood-smoke. And what could he give them to eat? Unleavened barley bread in pancakes would not be suitable. Autaru was dispatched to intercept the camp on its way and beg some bread from Hugh's servants. White buffalo butter could be provided, and hard-boiled eggs. Englishmen always ate eggs. And bananas. Jodh Singh's mouth curled in scorn when he saw the best he could do and thought of the Uptons' neat camp arrangements. But they must take us as we are, he thought fiercely; we are a poor and oppressed and backward people and it is well they should see us as we are. Ignorant, backward hill-folk, and I am one of them.

Hugh and Margaret were familiar with this sort of reception. They wished people would give them what they liked themselves, and not try to imitate customs foreign to them, but it was seldom any use suggesting such a thing. They were also used to embarrassing apologies for the inadequacy of what was put before them, but not to the tone into which Jodh Singh slipped for a moment. He began conventionally. He came to meet them and said very politely:

'It is very good of you to honour my humble house. I am deeply grateful to you, Sir, and especially to Mrs Upton. It is very poor and backward.'

Then he led them to the house and showed them into the room prepared, and when he spoke again, his voice was harsh with pride and pain.

'This is all I can offer you. We are poor and backward people. It is shameful, the way we live.'

Then he was the polite young man again. They talked of nothing while Autaru poured out the tea from the round pot. He did not spill much, and Margaret, although she was trained by now to accept anything, was pleased that he did not stir the tea in their brass tumblers with his fingers, nor insist on shelling the eggs and handing them the grubby result. After a little, Hugh said:

'Jodh Singh, I want to talk to you about this ridiculous story that's going round. You needn't worry about my wife; she knows all about it and wants to help you as much as I do.'

Jodh Singh sat forward on his chair and looked at the floor. He had known this would come. It was all very well for her husband to want to talk about it; he didn't; it would blow over. He could go to Bantok earlier than he had meant and people would forget. But he knew that peasants have so little to remember that they do not forget. He did not say anything.

Hugh went on:

'I think it may be serious for you unless we do something to show the villagers how silly it is. Don't you?'

'I shall go to Bantok,' said Jodh Singh gruffly to the floor.

'Well, that might be a good thing if all else failed. It would save you from immediate danger.'

'Danger?' said Jodh Singh, completely surprised.

. 'Yes. Hadn't it occurred to you that someone whose wife had been killed might want revenge, thinking as you know they do think? Or a whole village might take things into their own hands.'

'No, I had not thought of that. No, Sir, they would not do that.' But he remembered some of the stories he had heard and did not feel sure.

'Well, you see what I mean. By going to Bantok, you escape immediate danger—at least, probably you do, though someone might follow you. But what would it be like when you came back? You'd never live it down. The real answer is to disprove it.'

Jodh Singh was still sullen. He had forgotten most of his shyness in thinking of his own problem. He said:

'How can we—how can I disprove it?'

He paused, but before Hugh had time to speak, he went on:

'If I thought they wanted to kill me, I would go to them and talk to them.'

'I think it would only make things worse if you were to talk to them. I suggest the best thing would be if I were to talk to them and ask them to agree to a test. You would come and sleep in my camp and I would get men from several villages to watch you while you slept. That's all.'

Jodh Singh suddenly looked up at him like a child.

'You do not believe it, do you?' he asked quickly. But the mask was back in place at once; his eyes sought the floor. 'No, no, of course, you do not. No educated man believes these silly tales.'

Hugh leaned back in his chair. Poor little snipe, he thought; he half believes it himself. He said:

'I know very well that it is a perfectly ordinary panther, which one day I shall kill, or someone else perhaps may. But you and I know it's no use trying to explain that to the villagers. We have to prove that it isn't you. And that should be easy. Once it has killed, somewhere else, twenty miles away, when there are men standing round your bed watching you, no one will think it's you.'

Jodh Singh was silent. He hated the thought of being watched at night. He was going to be a great leader, one day. How could he give in to this and submit to such an indignity? But he would never be a leader if he didn't. But suppose—suppose—it was ridiculous even to suppose it—and it wasn't a thing he could say to this big man.

Margaret's clear voice broke in:

'Please do,' she said. 'It's the only way to clear you completely.'

He looked at her for a second only, for the first time since Hugh had spoken of this thing. How lovely she was. But for the moment she was only an irritation. He ignored her and spoke to Hugh:

'What shall you tell them they are to do if it is—if I do—if I do turn into a panther? What shall you tell them? We—I know it is not true, but they believe it, and they will want instructions.'

'I shall tell them to kill any panther they see.'

'And what if they kill me and show you my body—and say I turned back into a man when I was dead?'

'In that case, they would be arrested, and tried for murder. And in my opinion they would be hanged.' How much nicer if I could say I will hang them, thought Hugh.

Jodh Singh stood up.

'I think that is what they will do, but I will do what you say,' he said. 'Thank you very much, Mrs Upton, for your interest. I—I know I am a very interesting case.' He suddenly turned his back on them both, for his eyes were full of tears.

'Good man,' said Hugh. 'Well done; I'm sure you're right. Come to my camp tomorrow before the meeting. Thank you for our tea.' He hurried Margaret away with his eyes. She said:

'I wish I could help you. I'm glad you've decided that way.'

They went out together, leaving him alone. There was a small group of villagers outside, all men, no women or children. They were quite silent and expressionless. Hugh and Margaret took the path to their camp, an orderly going ahead to show the way. There is no room to walk abreast in Garhwal and Hugh made his wife go first because he liked watching her. No one can talk intimately in single file, so they waited till they reached the tents and were drinking the promised brew of real tea. Then he said:

'He's quite right. There is a risk of the guards killing him. But it's got to be taken. What he's really afraid of is that the story's true.'

She said:

'I don't know when I felt sorrier for anyone. He seems so completely alone. Hasn't he got a wife?'

'He was married this winter, I heard, to a local girl. I don't suppose she's much of a companion.' He felt, as he said it, that little ache that the thought of Margaret always gave him, of wonder and joy because she was his, and of pain because she was not and she never could be his.

She said:

'How little we know of other people, and how less than nothing of these people.'

Next morning was the first for some time that they had not been either marching or setting traps or preparing to sit up for the panther. Margaret got out her paint box and slipped out after breakfast; she was glad to find the kind of subject she wanted close to the camp, in a place from which she could see the gathering of the headmen Hugh had summoned. She would try to paint the sunlight falling through the twisted limbs of an oak on to the ground by the end of a tiled cow-house; it was not going to be easy to deal with in one morning and the light would have changed completely by the afternoon. She worked as fast as she could all morning. But when she came back after lunch, there was no need for hurry and before she settled down to what little more she could do, she spent a few minutes idly contemplating all that was before her and letting her mind go where it would. Beyond her oak and cowshed were the steep hills on the north of the river, not so precipitous here as at Bantok and showing more signs of human life, but little enough even so; there were three little patches of terracing in the whole stupendous sweep of grass and cliff and forest. The hills went straight up from the river for four or five thousand feet. From Gadoli, which was only about two thousand feet above the river, nothing could be seen of the snows behind them. But eye and mind tire with immensity, she thought; what would I not give for the chalk downs, and a little winding lane! She tried to picture such a lane in late spring, the hedges starred with may, every branch crusted with the stiff blossom, the white petals on the wet soil at her feet; she tried to see the long bank below the hedge; bluebells and campion and fool's parsley, misty blue and pink and foamy white; she tried to see a little patch at closer range, fronds of bracken beginning to uncurl, palest green and rusty bronze, eyebright, flowering nettle, a constellation of primroses. She put down her face to the blooms and tried to inhale the faint earthy scent of the primroses. But it isn't the same, she cried. What was it Hugh had said? Memory's a poor thing. The headmen were beginning to arrive from the meeting. She started to paint again.

Hugh had given a few moments' thought to stage management. If he put Jodh Singh in a chair and sat in a chair himself, the two of them would be isolated in grandeur and separated from the headmen, who of course would have to sit on the ground. But he wanted Jodh Singh near him and after inviting himself to tea with the boy yesterday, he could hardly make him sit at his feet on the ground. They are so sensitive about such things, he thought. He spoke to Jodh Singh beforehand and asked him to sit on a rock, a little in advance of the chair where he would sit himself, and to face both him and the audience. He kept the boy in his tent till the patwari told him that the headmen were assembled. Then he came out, bringing Jodh Singh with him, and motioned him to sit on his rock. He himself sat in the chair, looking rather like a teacher conducting an infant class in the open air. He began to speak, slowly and clearly. He was not one of the very few Englishmen who have learnt the language with the care needed for a diplomatic appointment. He knew the simpler grammatical forms and had a small vocabulary; he was neither fluent nor idiomatic, but he was good at putting his thoughts into the form of simple sentences that were within his powers and for that reason what he said was perfectly clear. He spoke the Hindustani of the plains, but the headmen at least could understand that, if many villagers could not. He said:

'Headmen of villages, I have called you together because I have heard a strange story. I have heard that you think the panther who has been killing here is not a panther, but a man. I myself believe it is an ordinary panther and that one day I shall kill it, but in such a matter what is the use of words? No man will change what he believes in his heart for words. He will believe what his eyes see. Now I am told you believe that the man who becomes a panther is Jodh Singh here. It is a strange thing to me that you should believe this, for you know he has done much for you. The village folk have heard that he has worked for them with great eagerness of heart. But since some of you believe this thing which to me is foolishness, I want to give you proof that it is not so. Let us put the matter to proof and see with our eyes. Let each headman find me two men from his village, full-grown men, not children, and men who are shareholders in the village and fathers of families. No one whose relation has been killed by the panther. Let those men come to my camp here and come with me for a week, bringing their food. From them we will choose a guard every night of eight men who will watch Jodh Singh as he sleeps. There will always be four who are waking and watching. We will mount guard as they do in the battalions. Then we shall know in the morning that he has slept in his bed all night. And if we hear that the panther has killed in the body while Jodh Singh was sleeping here in his bed in the body, we shall know this thing is foolishness. What do you think of this test? Would it not then be proved?'

He waited, and let them talk among themselves; but not for long, because while he did not want to let them feel they were being rushed, he did not want the meeting to get out of his hand. There might be one obstinate old man who would sour them all if he were given the chance. When he judged the moment had come, he went on:

'There are two other things to explain. The guard will be armed with poles and axes or kukris—'

'No guns?' asked someone.

'No,' said Hugh, who had thought of this before, 'guns are well enough in the army where each man knows his duty and the punishment if he does wrong; but not here in civil life where everyone follows the wish of his heart. I do not want to be shot in my bed by a guard who becomes excited.'

'It will be very dangerous, lord,' said the man who had asked about guns.

'What, with eight guards, four awake and four ready to spring to their feet, all with axes ready to strike? Nonsense. And I shall be sleeping a few yards away with a rifle. Now, the second thing. If the guards see a panther, they are to kill it. But they are not to touch a hair of any man's head. If they attack a man they will be hanged. Is that understood? If they see a man behaving strangely, they are to wake me. Is that understood? Now, is there anyone here who does *not* agree to this test?'

He sent the patwari among them to see if there were any objections. Someone said:

'Lord, let Jodh Singh also be handcuffed to the bed.'

Hugh had thought of this, and felt it was a humiliation to be avoided. He said quietly:

'To what profit? If the hand becomes a paw, it will slip through a handcuff.' But he was not at all sure that it would. Probably a panther's wrist was thicker than a man's. Anyway, it did not seem to convince the audience, who muttered among themselves, until someone said:

'It would be safer, lord.'

Jodh Singh spoke for the first time. He had sat with bowed head, looking at the ground, never moving. Now he said:

'I have no objection. I am on trial. It is very suitable that I should be handcuffed.'

'Then it is settled,' said Hugh getting up. 'See that your men are here to night. They are to report to the patwari, each man bringing his food and blanket, and a pole, and an axe or kukri.'

Hugh set the guards himself that night and explained what would happen if any harm came to Jodh Singh in his own body. The guards were submissive and frightened. Jodh Singh was silent, his face frozen and grey. He looked ill, his cheeks fallen in. He suffered himself to be handcuffed to the bed without a word, then turned on his side and pulled the blanket over his head.

For four nights the guard was set and nothing happened. It was a different group of men every night, but the others, those who had served their turn or were still to serve it, Hugh kept in the camp to spread the news when proof should be obtained. By day, Hugh travelled, with the help of a pony where possible, to every village in the neighbourhood where the panther had killed, to see the place, to talk to the people, to make sure that everyone understood the curfew order which was the only preventive action that could be taken. Every night he explained their orders to the new guards, who had their post only a few yards from his tent, so that he could be awakened if necessary. Every morning he went to see them and dismissed them. The fourth morning someone bolder than the rest, a man who had been a soldier and therefore was not afraid to talk to an Englishman, said:

'Of course nothing has happened, lord. What would he be likely to do when he is watched? He is too cunning. He has stopped killing now. Consider, how long it is since he killed.'

It was just what Hugh had feared. The panther had stopped killing at the wrong moment. When the test began, there had been no kill for a week, so that news of a fresh kill was now long overdue. It was worrying. Jodh Singh seemed in a kind of stupor. Hugh himself was becoming irritable; he had seldom stayed in one place so long as this since he came to the district and he was really doing nothing useful; he felt that time was slipping through his fingers and getting the better of him. But there was nothing he could do until the panther killed again. Sitting over a live bait in the hope that the panther might wander up to that particular spot, out of the sixty miles by ten that was his beat, would really be asking too much of change.

But after breakfast on the fifth day there was sensational news. A man panted up the hill from a village ten miles away, which was on the main road running up the bank of the river. He had been sent to tell a story, but it took some time to piece it together by questioning and even then only the barest outline emerged. It was not till later, when Hugh saw the place, that he understood exactly what had happened. There was a shopkeeper, one Hukm Singh, who had a two-storied house, a shop below and living-rooms above, close to the road. He came from a village higher up the hill, but he was a younger brother and he had first been in the army and now he had started this shop. There had been some sickness in the house and as it was getting warm down there by the river, the shopkeeper had started to sleep out of doors on his veranda rather earlier than he usually did. Last night his stomach was not well and he had got up in the night, gone down

by the staircase and walked a little way from the house and the road to
an open field to relieve himself. He was nervous because of the
panther and kept well away from any bushes or shadows in the bright
moonlight. He came back with several anxious looks over his shoulder,
but when he reached the top of the stairs he sighed with relief. Now he
was safe. He put his hand on his bed to get in and at that moment
heard the stairs creak behind him.

Hukm Singh turned and saw the panther come softly up the stairs.
He would never have heard its step, but the stairs moved under its
weight. He jumped back to the head of his bed, which was placed with
one side close under the rail of the veranda, the other side facing the
head of the stairs. The panther was at the top of the stairs facing the
foot of the bed. Hukm Singh stood beyond the head of the bed against
the veranda rail. He stood staring at the panther, which did not move.
He was looking out of the corner of his eye for a weapon, but there
was nothing within reach except a round stool of plaited cane near his
hand. He picked that up as a shield. The panther did not attack him,
but sprang lightly on to the bed, and continued to look at him. It was
playing with him before the ecstasy of death, as a lover plays with his
mistress before the ecstasy of love. Still on the bed, it took a step
towards him. But he did not recoil. Instead he thrust the stool into its
face with all his strength and at the top of his voice began to shout.
The panther was surprised; no man had ever before anticipated its
attack and taken the initiative himself. It half rose on its quarters and
gripped the stool with mouth and paws together. That gave Hukm
Singh the fraction of a second in which to fling all his weight on the
stool, and it was in just that particular moment of time, less than the
blink of an eye, that the panther's weight was wrongly disposed,
because it was surprised. Its muscular strength was four times that of a
man, but it was not balanced to use its strength; and with a hoarse
scream of indignation it vanished over the veranda rail. Hukm Singh
did not waste any time. He was inside the upper room with the door
barred before the panther was back on the veranda. He heard it pace
up and down. Once it flung its weight against the door; he could hear
its breath, as it stood motionless, panting after the effort; he could smell
the reek of it. Then it made off. It was too cunning to stay there long.

When Hugh heard this, he said to Margaret, who had been listening
to the story as it was gradually squeezed out of the messenger:

'This is the best chance yet. It hasn't killed and must be hungry and
wanting revenge. It may be hanging round that same place again to
night; and I shall be waiting for it. And incidentally it lets Jodh Singh
out.'

He gave his orders. All the guards on Jodh Singh, both those who had served their turn and those still to come, were to be collected at once, and he would talk to them. Immediately after that he would start with a rifle and his orderly Dewan Singh for Hukm Singh's house. Camp would move to somewhere more convenient, but not too close. He chose a village less than three miles this side of Hukm Singh's shop, feeling that to move the camp any closer might disturb the panther.

The guards agreed gravely when he spoke to them. They had to admit that Jodh Singh had been sleeping quietly in his bed when Hukm Singh was wrestling vigorously with the panther.

'He did not even talk in his sleep,' one of them volunteered.

'Then he cannot be the panther,' Hugh argued relentlessly, and they agreed rather doubtfully that this must be so. But they were not utterly convinced, the weak spot in the defence being that if your powers of wizardry are strong enough to turn yourself into a panther, it should not be beyond your art to be in two places at once. Thus there were no congratulations to Jodh Singh on the fortunate end of his ordeal; the guards drifted away, undertaking to tell the villagers that Jodh Singh had been asleep when Hukm Singh's adventure took place, but both Hugh and Jodh Singh knew that something would stick.

'At first people were saying Jodh Singh was a warlock and turned himself into the panther; later on they were saying he wasn't. God alone can say what the truth of it all may be.' That was what they would be saying in the villages for many years.

Jodh Singh came to thank the Uptons before they left. He made Hugh uncomfortable by saying:

'Sir, you have been very kind to me. You have been like my father to me. I wish to thank you. I thought bad thoughts of you before, but now I know you have always been kind. I do not want any foreign rulers, but I thank God that He has sent us such a ruler as you.'

He did not seem to expect a reply, but turned to Margaret and said to her:

'Please try to think well of me whatever you may hear. Thank you very much, Mrs Upton, because you have been kind. You are my only friend.'

'Of course, I'll think well of you,' she said. 'I do already and you know I do. And in any case, I expect we'll be seeing you soon. You seem to get about nearly as much as we do.'

Hugh was impatient to be after the panther and they left at once. Jodh Singh never saw either of them again. A month later, Hugh was unexpectedly transferred to a city of the plains, where he resumed the life of continual crisis and overwork he had come to regard as normal. He went without question, without expressing a personal preference, just as he tried to carry out unquestioningly the policy set him from above. The district had to learn the ways of a new master who also had not a little to learn. Since it was before the days when English-women decided that they could after all work in the plains in summer, Margaret had the choice of a lonely hill station or England. She spent the summer in London. There she reopened that wound she had hoped was scarred over.

Jodh Singh was left without a friend. He stuck to his plan of going to Bantok. He needed the healing airs of that lonely place more even than he had after the affair at Pokhra. Politics must wait till the memory of his ordeal had died.

# PART III

The Uprooted, 1938

# 1

When the runner arrived, the men were just beginning the business of pitching camp. The mules came jingling in, hung about with bells and red tassels, with big blue and white beads round their necks. The drivers lifted off their loads and their curious saddles, like a thin tube of matting doubled back on itself so as to give a line of padding on either side of the backbone. As each mule was freed, it rolled its gaunt sweaty back on the turf, turning over from one side to the other with the uncouth effort which all the horse tribe seem to need for this simple act. The drivers, the idlest and most feckless of mankind, lighted cigarettes and sauntered off to make themselves comfortable. There were porters as well as mules, for the camp sometimes split when Christopher Tregard, Deputy Commissioner in 1938, wanted to go to a village where the paths were too difficult for mules. The porters were mostly Nepalese, for since the forced labour ended there were not many local villagers who were willing to carry loads for other people. Each porter went his own pace; they were less gregarious than the mules, who came in groups of two and three with a common driver. The loaded men came one by one; each one as he reached the camp sat down with a deep grunt, let the weight of his burden on to the ground, and then eased the ropes and webbing that held it to his shoulders and head. Then he lifted off the pad of sacking that protected his back, a simpler affair than the type the mules used, moved off for a drink and a few minutes' rest, and then came back to help the orderlies with the tents.

The camp was at the foot of a bank of forest that ran steeply up in an unbroken sweep for four or five thousand feet, till the trees thinned out and gave way to bare fells. Where the steepness of the slope broke below the forest, there was a shelf of green turf before the cultivated terraces began. At one point in this shelf a small stream ran out, making a break in the forest; if you stood facing the camp, you looked at a gently rising stretch of turf on either side of the stream, with tall trees closing in behind. Facing the other way, you looked through miles of space straight across the valley to the majesty of Dunagiri's twenty thousand feet, her snowfields and cliffs of ice. The vastness of the valley and its ice-fed streams was something the mind could not comprehend; and to that was added the mountain, revealed in her entirety from crown to roots. There she was; you just looked at her and were filled with wonder. Christopher and Susan stood gazing for a few moments without speech. Then they turned towards the camp.

Christopher smiled:

'I like that site,' he said. 'It might be in the New Forest. Chestnuts, do you see? And turf—have you ever thought of the thousands of miles of this planet where there's no turf? Oh, and there's the first yew. Red berries and all. D'you remember. "Colour threads the darkness as yewberries the yew"?'

Susan did remember, and was just saying so when the runner arrived. The bag had been passed on from man to man, but they were eleven stages from headquarters and it had taken four days to reach them. An orderly hurried up to break the seals and cut the string. He took out two big bundles of files, which were put aside till there should be a tent to work in, a table, and a stenographer; he gave Christopher a bundle of newspapers and some letters. Christopher sorted out Susan's letters and sat down on a rock to read his own.

Christopher and Susan had started out that morning of September 1938 from Vishnumath, on the first day of a new world. The rains were over, the sky was washed and bright, the air was crisp. They had left the tiny bungalow at eight o'clock, feeling exhilarated by the prospect of brisk walking. But it had happened as it always did. Immediately outside the gate a man appeared, hurrying towards them. He said:

'Lord, come and look at my wall!'

'Where is your wall?'

'Just down there, lord. Only ten steps. Close to your road. Please look at it, Presence. There is great tyranny. I am a very poor man.'

They reached the wall. There was a house on the upper side of the mule-track and on the lower side an orchard. In front of the house, the track, which was usually of the natural gravel, rock, or clay from which it had been cut, was cobbled with rough stones, so that the surface was much more durable than elsewhere; on the valley side of the stretch of cobbling, for its exact length, ran a low wall, two feet high, built of roughly shaped stones, mortared, with carefully-cut flat stones on the top. A pleasant wall to sit on; obviously part of one plan, the house, the cobbled stretch of track, the wall, the work of a man who wished to make himself a settled home and did not want half the width of the track washed down into his orchard by heavy rain.

'Well,' said Christopher, 'I see your wall. What is your trouble?'

The owner of the wall stretched out his hands over it in a protective, almost caressing gesture. His hands said that the wall was his wife and little children, that he loved it dearly, that it was in danger. But his mouth made only an inarticulate sound, and then said:

'Lord—my wall—. . . .'

'Can anyone explain what the trouble is?' Christopher asked.

'Yes, Presence, I can,' said the patwari, who had arrived as if attracted by some telepathic knowledge. 'The Public Works Department say that this is their track. They have to mend it and it all belongs to government. And they say this wall is not shown on their records, and therefore this man built it without permission, and it is an encroachment, and must be removed. And when this man wouldn't move it, they reported it to the court, and the court has ordered him to move it at once or be fined.'

Christopher gave a deep sigh.

'Well, now, how old would you say this wall was?' he asked.

The patwari put his head on one side.

'I cannot say, Presence.'

'But does it look to you new?'

'No, it does not look new.'

'And who built this wall and this house? It is all one work—look at the carving on the stone at the corner of the house and the corner of the wall; it is the same pattern.'

'It was my grandfather,' said the owner, who was a man of more than fifty.

'Yes, it was his grandfather,' agreed all the bystanders.

'Is that true?' Christopher asked the patwari.

'Lord, I have only been here three years. It was here when I came.'

'Well,' said Christopher, 'I do not go only by what I am told, but here what I am told agrees with what I see. There's no doubt this is old. Look at this carving! Do you carve stone doorways like this if you build a house now? And what sort of roof would you put on your house if you built one now? Corrugated iron—but this is all tiled. No one who built a house this size would put tiles on it now. No, I think this house and this wall were here before the Public Works Department had any records—and that's not very long in any case. All right, old man; don't be afraid; no one shall touch your wall. I will see to it. Have you written me a petition? No. Then write it quickly and give it to the patwari here, and he will bring it to me this evening. Do you understand?' he added to the patwari. 'I want his petition brought to me at the next camp and you are responsible for bringing it. Bring it this evening when all the petitions come.'

Susan and Christopher started again.

'But *why*,' asked Susan, 'why should anyone want to destroy his wall? It looked a very useful wall, and it was holding the track together. I should have thought there ought to be a wall like that all the way along.'

'Well,' said Christopher, 'the Public Works people say that walls on the lower sides of these tracks turn them into torrents, and the water runs along them instead of across them and tears up the surface. But in this case it was just red tape, blind obedience by some junior chap to general orders from Naini Tal or Lucknow. Most unintelligent.'

They walked on, along a winding path that followed the contour of the hill, but rising slightly. It was pleasantly varied. There were patches of terraced cultivation, with men ploughing the little shelves of fields for the winter crop at the same time as others were cutting the maize and the autumn crop, so that there was green and brown and gold and the deep crimson of the red millet, smiling in the sun. But the cultivation soon gave way again to forest and they were in the deep shade where the smell of rotting leaves and moisture pricked their nostrils. Every leaf in the brown carpet at their feet was rimed with frost on the underside. There would come the sound of running water and they would cross a steam, clear water chattering happily over brown pebbles, or white water at the foot of a fall scooping hungrily at the stone in whose hollow it churned; the chill of the fresh water would strike them, and then they would be past it and out in the sun again, gazing across that immense valley to the snowfields. But they never got very far without interruption. Up would bob a blanket-clad figure, his legs in thick shapeless trousers of handwoven wool, almost like felt, his body swathed in a plaid of the same stuff, fastened by a pair of strong iron pins, chained together so that one of them could not be lost without the other.

'Lord, look at my field.'

'Where is your field?'

'Over there, lord. There—there—there—' the reddish-brown face between the locks of long hair would screw up into still more intricate convolutions of wrinkles with the effort of pointing out the place.

'All right, I see it. What about it?'

'Lord, it is a very dangerous place. Look at the forest all round. It is full of animals. Pigs—deer—bears—' a pause between each, and a long-drawn hiss of intaken breath to show how big and many and dangerous the animals were—'panthers—monkeys—porcupines—tigers. . . .'

'You want a gun-licence, I suppose. But which is your village? Aren't there any guns there?'

'There is my village, there—there. *Very* far from my fields, and there is a gun there, but he uses it to guard his own fields. He won't come to mine.'

'And where is your house? Out by the fields? I see. All right, I've seen where it is. Come to the camp this evening and we'll see what the other people in your village have to say and whether you've got a good character.'

They went on, and came to a village. It was tiny, twenty or thirty houses round an old stone temple, and a stone tank into which the clear water shot in a bright sunlit curve from two spouts roughly carved to the shape of a cow's head. There was a school, and the two went gravely round it while ragged little tots sang a shrill song of praise.

Outside the village, again there was the cry:

'Lord, look at my field.'

'Where is it?'

'Just down there, lord, only ten steps.'

'Ten steps? All right—one, two, three—ten. Am I there?'

'No, lord, not that sort of ten steps. Farther than that.'

'Below that village?'

'Yes, lord, a very little way below that village.'

'About three miles, and two thousand feet down, in fact. And why do you want me to look at your field?'

'Lord, there is a dispute!'

'What is the dispute about?'

'About my field, lord. Just look at it, lord, and then I shall get justice. Only if you come can I get justice.'

'But tell me, now,' said Christopher, 'what good would it do if I saw the field? Would the field speak to me? Would the crops lift up their voice and tell me the truth?'

'No, lord, but you would see what a good field it is.'

'But I should have to go and see the other man's field too. I should have no time for anyone's business today but your business. And just by seeing I cannot give you justice. I must have your opponents there. Have you made a suit before the courts?'

'No, lord, but the other man has.'

'Well, if you can bring the other man to my camp this evening, I will try to give you justice and make an agreement between you.'

'I will bring him; but there will be no justice if you do not look at my field, lord!'

All morning they heard the cry: 'Look at my field, lord,' and several times if it really seemed that it would do some good Christopher scrambled down or up the hillside. But usually the cry was born simply of a pathetic belief in personal rule. Each man wanted a direct order. No abstract business of law in a court miles away, but an order on the spot, after inspection.

But at last the camp was reached, and the runner panted up with the letters.

'Anything interesting?' Susan asked when Christopher had skimmed through the more urgent and personal.

'Nothing very startling,' he said, 'but there's one thing that is rather interesting to me at any rate: you remember that man Jodh Singh I was telling you about?'

Susan wrinkled her brows.

'Jodh Singh? Which Jodh Singh was that? There aren't enough names to go round here; there seem to be only about a dozen and there are so many people.'

'Yes, but this one's rather special. Don't you remember the story Margaret Upton told me about how everyone thought he turned into a panther? I was telling you when we came through his village.'

'Oh, yes, of course I remember that. A lovely story. Has he turned into anything else?'

'No, but I have a feeling he may be going to, or at any rate, that I may be going to hear quite a lot of him. I've been interested in him ever since Margaret told me the story; she obviously thought there was a lot in him, and felt desperately sorry for him, and I felt, in the way one does, you know, a special sort of interest in him because she was so interested. . . .'

'If I'd known Margaret was going to be there, I shouldn't have let you go to Naini Tal by yourself,' said Susan.

Christopher put out his tongue at her.

'I regard her as an elder sister,' he said. 'A very nice and decorative one. The kind that's an asset. But as I was saying when you so rudely interrupted, Margaret talked about him and I was interested, but I wanted to hear Hugh's side, so I got hold of him in the bar one night and asked him. Now Hugh wouldn't strike you as a chap with much imagination. . . .'

'None whatever, I should have thought. But I don't know him as well as you do, of course,' said Susan thoughtfully.

'More than you might suppose, as a matter of fact. At least, I think so, even from a woman's point of view. I sometimes wonder whether even Margaret quite realizes how sensitive he is. He pretends not to be. Anyhow, he had imagination as a district officer. More than anyone who's been here since—'

'Until you came, darling?'

'Until I came, as you so rightly say. Well, Hugh told me that he strongly suspected, though he never had any proof or shadow of it, that the panther story was started by a patwari who'd been accused of bribery by Jodh Singh. And that patwari's son, one Dharma Nand, has just come to be tahsildar of the Northern Circle, which is Jodh Singh's home country.'

'Dramma,' said Susan appreciatively.

'Well, setting for dramma, or so I thought when I heard it. And so I expect did Dharma Nand. Poor devil! It's not much of a plum anyhow, the Northern Circle, seven days' march from a road, no decent schools, and everything double the price it is in the plains; and anyone would be a bit nervous of coming to Jodh Singh's part of the world. . . .'

'Why?' Susan was interested in everything about the district. It was Christopher's work.

'Well, now,' said Christopher thoughtfully, 'how can I explain fairly? He obviously impressed Margaret as fundamentally a nice and honest person, and an idealist. Hugh thought the same, though he put it differently. Hugh said his ideas were half-baked and unpractical and he was a bit of a visionary, but full of enthusiasm, and full of guts. But terribly emotional and quick-tempered. Now every other district officer since has described him as a pest, because he will start complaints about officials which have usually nothing in them. I reckon, from what they've written about him, and what I've heard and seen myself, that he's completely honest in the sense that he's not interested in money or just making himself important; but he's intolerant, can't see any point of view but his own and flares up if people disagree with him, and highly emotional. Someone comes and pitches him a yarn about some patwari taking a bribe and he gets in a passion and rushes off to start a war at once, without attempting to hear the other side of the case. Well, if you throw mud long enough, some of it sticks, and there's hardly an official in the district who doesn't bear him a grudge for some accusation that has never been proved, perhaps, but has been worrying and harmful.'

'Doesn't sound as if he'd be very popular,' said Susan.

'Not with the patwaris. And there's hardly a member of the District Board he hasn't fought. But the villagers—well, they're a little frightened of him, because they don't understand him. I shouldn't wonder if the panther story sticks, you know. Peasants have long memories. And he does have these unaccountable rages. But although they're frightened, they do look on him as a champion when they're in trouble. They don't forget what he did for them over the forced labour. And he has great charm. He so obviously feels and believes what he says. I can't help liking him whenever I meet him. He's trying in a way to do the same kind of thing as I am; his blood boils at the same things as mine—only I wait to make sure they're true before I let it boil.'

'Oh, yes, I remember you telling me about the forced labour. But tell

984 • A RAJ COLLECTION

me more about the panther part. Do they really still believe in were-wolves or were-panthers, or what would you call them?'

'It's very difficult to know what they do believe. I think that most of them in the villages do believe it's a thing that does happen. And if you believe it may happen and meet someone to whom it is supposed to have happened, and who is obviously not quite like other people— well, it just adds a little extra something the others haven't got. I should think that now it probably rather adds to his prestige than otherwise. The reformed warlock. You could never be quite sure, you see, that the panther that was eventually killed was the one that was doing the killing. The killing stopped, but that might be just because the warlock turned over a new leaf.'

'Y-e-e-s, I wonder—do you think, Christopher, that the panther story might have had an effect on him? Mentally, I mean. Still?'

'Bound to have some effect. Both Hugh and Margaret said that the most pathetic thing was that he seemed half to believe that it might be true. You mean that he might go on half believing, or perhaps about one-eighth believing, that it had been true?'

'Yes—I hadn't put it to myself as definitely as that—but that was the kind of idea at the back of my mind.'

'I dare say. In fact, I should say you're probably right. It would encourage him to think he was different from other people and in a way flatter his vanity. He certainly is different; a sort of scourge of God, the self-appointed champion of the oppressed. So you see why a tahsildar in these parts is not on a bed of roses. And this poor devil has the added complication of a family feud with the scourge.'

'Most worrying for him. Well, anyhow, what's happened?'

'Well, trouble between them has started at once, though in a minor way. Jodh Singh goes into a sort of retreat every summer to a lonely village on the north side of the river, a most inaccessible place, where he communes with nature, certainly with nothing else. And the moment he comes out of his retreat—in fact, I didn't know he was out till today—he sends in a complaint about Dharma Nand taking bribes. He says Dharma Nand went to a village where there was a dispute and they feasted him on goats and wine—he means spirits, of course; no wine here, worse luck—and made their women dance naked before him and supply all his needs. He adds a little note here that Dharma Nand is a young man and notoriously gluttonous of women. And then they gave him five hundred rupees. And then he made an order in their favour.'

'But if Jodh Singh's honest, as you say he is, why does he send in a complaint like that? It isn't true, is it?'

'Well, you can't be sure, of course. I shall have to make inquiries.

But I must say, it doesn't sound true to me. Dharma Nand's a young chap with a good reputation and this is his first independent post. And he's only officiating. He's bound to be on his best behaviour. I expect it's the story the other side told Jodh Singh. I've had this kind of thing from him before and I've talked to him about it. My impression is that people come to him with a yarn and he gets so worked up and full of indignation that he really believes every word of it. Then he gets committed to it and simply won't accept any arguments on the other side. He really is incapable of understanding them, once he's excited about a case; he hasn't the mental detachment. He has a sort of reservoir of moral indignation which is always ready to come to the boil. And being a creature of emotions, the fact that he doesn't like Dharma Nand to start with will only make him more ready to believe anything against him. And incidentally, the complainants are the Marchas, who are great pets of his.'

'Oh, the Marchas. Yaks and things. Why does he like them? Is he fond of beetle porridge?' Susan had once wandered up to the skin tents of a Marcha camp and looked into the cooking-pot.

'Well, it's rather typical of him, as I picture him. You see, they're wanderers, not really settled folk. Their villages are under the snow most of the year. And they're nobody's baby. All the settled villages hate them because they eat up all the grazing and waste firewood. They're always getting into trouble over that. And it's like Jodh Singh to take them up; there's no political advantage in it, in fact, the opposite. He's done a lot for them. Look, the tents are up. I must go and do petitions. But I think we shall hear more of Jodh Singh and Dharma Nand before long.'

Christopher called one of the orderlies and Susan went to the tent to get her box of medicines. Christopher sat on a tree-stump and the orderly shouted at the top of his voice that justice was available for anyone in the neighbourhood who wanted it.

They came, a dozen or twenty wild figures, with long hair and blanket plaids made from the coarse black wool of their little horned sheep. Among them were most of those he had seen in the morning and all had troubles of much the same kind. Gun-licences, fields, wood from the forest to build houses and cowsheds, leave to break new ground, those were the kind of things they wanted. And that individual want had always to be balanced against something else, the right of the village, who did not want all the grazing land cut up for cultivation; or the good of the forest, which must be protected for the sake of future generations and because it is the forest that holds together the hills and stores the water. At last they were finished, orders given, and peace made where possible. Christopher stood up:

'The court is closed,' he said. 'Now, medicines?'

Most of the petitioners wanted medicine. And a number of other people were already getting doses and powders from Susan. The petitioners moved over to join the group of patients and Christopher came too in case he could help. Susan listened gravely to their troubles, with some assistance from an orderly when the dialect became too obscure.

'Castor oil,' she would say. And an orderly would pour out castor oil from an enormous bottle in incredibly large doses. But there was no shirking. The patient drank it slowly, as though he enjoyed it, and ran his finger round the inside of the brass cup and licked it to make sure that not a drop was wasted.

'Quinine and aspirin, for you, my friend—'

'Tannofax on that burn—but you must take it to hospital if it doesn't begin to heal in two days—can you make him go, Christopher?'

'Cough lozenges for you, but really, you know, I can't cure asthma—'

'And as for you, what you've got is either an appendix or duodenal ulcer—' She glanced quickly at a first aid book, 'Yes, I'm sure that's it. Don't you think so, Christopher? We can't cure you, brother. You must go to the hospital at Vishnumath. The doctor will cure you. The sahib will give you a letter to him.'

The patient looked sad. He turned to Christopher.

'Please cure me, lord,' he said. 'Your medicine is better than the doctor's. You *can* cure me.'

'I'm very sorry,' said Christopher, 'but honestly, I can't do it.'

The patient sighed.

'Well, lord,' he began, 'I've got another illness too. A dreadful sore throat. Can you give me some medicine for that?' The last man swallowed his dose, the last little party went away with precious bundles of pills or stoups of castor oil or bottles of disinfectant for distant friends and relations. The light began to fade. The bulk of Dunagiri grew vaster, her snowfields flushed with rose, as the colour died from trees and grass. A little icy wind crept across the valley.

'Tea,' said Christopher. 'Hot, strong, and sweet like a kiss. That's a Russian proverb.'

'It's no use your pretending you learnt that from a Russian girl friend because I know about your past and you never had one,' said Susan.

'Well, I know someone who did and I got it from him. And anyhow, you only know as much of my past as I've told you.'

'You'd have told me that,' said Susan.

Susan was slim and young. Christopher Tregard had met her in

Delhi, where he was bidden to decorous dinner parties given by kind mammas and aunts, from which eligible young men and nice young things would troop away to dance together. She laughed at the same things as he did, and she spoke to him of England, the downs and meadows, bluebells in the clear green light of the beech woods, the damp bracken, birdsong in spring, and cowslips in the banks of the soft south-west. They danced together, they rode together; at each party he looked first to see if she was there.

There is a magic moment in Delhi between the seasons, when the winter is past, before the heat begins. It comes overnight, it goes without warning. Suddenly the green stems in the gardens are crowned with flowers and the evenings are heavy with their scent. Their life is short; soon the hot winds will wither them and the earth will be dusty beneath the searing sun. But for those few days, the hollyhocks nod their pink and white sun-bonnets; the tender blue of larkspur melts against the dancing cornflower; the snapdragons are gallant yellow and glowing orange; the rose scatters her petals; pansies hold up their faces like happy children on the floor at a party; and the poppies are cups of liquid light, floating in purest colour, scarlet, white, and gold.

On such a day, Christopher turned away for a moment from a group of people chattering in the sunshine before lunch. He saw Susan leave the house and come towards him through the flowers, fresh and cool and dark. His heart turned over within him; he knew that she was his and he must never let her go.

They were married six weeks later and in the autumn Christopher was posted to Garhwal. Susan and he held hands and danced when they heard the news; they could have hoped for nothing better. That was two years ago and they were still sure there would never be anywhere in India where they would sooner be. They went everywhere together; when they first came to the district, the villagers in some particularly inaccessible spot would ask incredulously:

'But will the lady be coming too?'

And the orderly sent on ahead would reply:

'Why not? Where the needle goes, does the thread not follow?'

This evening Christopher finished his tea and settled down for a couple of hours to the files and letters which the runner had brought. After dinner, Susan curled up on a camp chair in a dark blue jersey and slacks. She said:

'You know, really this is the life for us. Why do we ever want anything else?'

'Well, yes, if it could go on for ever. It has been fun, hasn't it? Do you remember our first march, when they brought you a sheep, and you came to me with tears in your eyes and said: "But it's alive! The poor thing looks so trusting!" Now you come stamping with fury and say: "Look at this skinny creature they've brought today! Nothing on it at all! Feel these ribs!" '

'Yes, and do you remember all the times we've come into camp late, in the dark, cold or wet or both? The time when we had to cross the river on stepping-stones by the light of one lantern; and the smooth water gleaming and slipping away like a mill-race? And that night on Dudhatoli when the tents got lost because you would go by a new way no one had ever been before, and it poured with rain all night, and we had to keep warm as well as we could by a bonfire?'

'Weren't the men nice about that? Never the sign of a grumble or an I-told-you-so. That's one of the nicest things about being here; everyone is so cheerful.'

'And us being gipsies,' said Susan. 'And in being able to hear about all you're doing. I don't think I could ever go back to being folk in housen.'

'We'll have to sometime. This can't last for ever. At the end of three years they'd move me to some Dustypore in the plains. And then it will be time to go.'

'Was it so very dreadful in the plains? I don't mean Delhi, because that's different; I mean in a district.'

'Oh, no, I don't regret a minute of it. I feel about all those years rather as I did about going to school. One hated the thought of going back at the end of the holidays; I hated it so much that I used to be sick; and yet if anyone had suggested never going back again, I should have been appalled. The hot weather wasn't very nice, of course, but even about the hot weather there is something attractive, at least in retrospect. You count the days till it's over, but there's something tough and astringent about it; everything is stripped bare, no curtains on the windows, no mattresses on the beds, no women. You have a feeling that you really are earning your keep and are in the front line, which is good for one's self-conceit. But I've done it. I don't want any more. It can't be good for one to go on being abroad when one wants so much to be in England. And from the point of view of duty—no one seems to want us to stay.'

'But, Christopher, how can you say that? You know I want to be home more even than you do, but these people, the villagers, they do want you.'

'Yes, I know. What I feel may be self-deception; I suppose my reason is not to be trusted because I want so much to see the English country and to be among English people again; but it seems to me wrong for us, the English, as a people, to take refuge behind the peasant and say we must stay because he wants us. Every people must express itself through its vocal classes; we shouldn't dream of saying that American opinion was exclusively what the farmer thinks in the Middle West; and the vocal classes in India want us to go. It's true they're out of touch with the peasant, but that is just because we're here. It's a thing which can't right itself so long as we are. It was different for people like Hugh. They'd had the best part of their life under the old tradition and when changes came it was their plain duty to carry on, and they did. But for our generation, the good we can do has to be balanced against the harm to our own lives. And for me, the point is approaching when the balance tips over against staying. Once I'm out of this district, my value goes down sharply. Frustration is the key note in the ordinary district now. You have to acquiesce in much you hate and can't achieve anything you want. No, we must go where we belong and settle down and make a home for the children, and drive our roots deep into the soil. We shall have to be folk in housen some day.'

'Well, of course, I know that; and I don't mind so long as it's folk in nice housen, not little horrors in rows. A nice rambling farmhouse with lots of bedrooms where people can come and stay, and lofts with apples in them, and places for playing trains. And I see what you mean about the vocal classes, but it's hard to believe they want us to go. It's so easy to forget the rest of the world when one sees only these nice people who come to you for everything and live almost exactly the same life as they did in Mr Bennett's time.' She stopped, then said:

'But tell me about camp in the plains. I mean the nice part, not the frustration. What did it feel like and smell like? You see, I wasn't with you and I want to know what it was like when I wasn't there. I can't picture it a bit because I only know Delhi.'

Christopher tried to tell her. He talked of one of his camps down by the river, where he went every year in the spring because the stream changed its course in the floods, washing away the fertile fields and replacing them with sand, so that a fresh record had to be made every year. He tried to recall a day, seeing as he relived it the pictures he had seen then. Called by lamplight; a cup of tea and some bread and jam before you start—but Susan was used to that—and then you were out in the cool morning, on Sweet Janet or Corvette, cantering easily along a sandy road to the first village. The light was sweet and fresh, there was a sense of infinite space, sand and water and sky, with milky clouds in clear smooth bars on the horizon, and here and there the aromatic fragrance of crops. It was light soil and peas were a favourite sowing; their white blossom, sparkling with dew, repeated the tones of sky and sand. At dawn, it was a country for the Dutch and English water-colourists, space, emptiness, cool colours; but later, when the sun was high, it was beyond the power of painter. You found a sandy bank with a tamarisk bush above, and sat in that tiny patch of shade to eat a large late breakfast. It was not really hot, for there was always a breeze by the river, but sand and water flashed and glittered, it was bright sky and blinding sun, light trembling and glittering and incandescent, the flashing flight of the white river tern, and the cry of the water-fowl. Back to the tents in the early afternoon, and then, in the cool of the evening, the villagers would collect and for two or three hours you would try to settle their troubles on the spot, by word of mouth.

Then there was the winter camping, when the morning ride was sharp with cold, the level green fields wet with dew or touched with hoar frost; the smell of sugar-cane juice, rich and warm, as they boiled it into brown toffee-like molasses on the edge of the field where it had grown; the return to camp in the evening when the smoke lay in level blue lines above the villages and the peafowl were settling for the night with noisy flappings in the treetops, the air chilling the arms that had been bare in the sunshine; and the smell of the camp, smoke and straw and bullocks.

'But it's no use,' said Christopher, 'I can't recapture it to myself, let alone make you see it. Try to remember for yourself a day on the downs or in the Alps. You try, but memory can only call up a shadowy sort of ghost, one of the strengthless heads of the dead which have no reality till they drink some blood. Go to the place again, and it all comes back with the first breath of wind that carries the scent of thyme, or of pine woods in the sun.'

Susan sighed. She said:

'Oh dear, I'm afraid you're right. Shan't we be able to remember all the loveliness we've seen here?'

'We can help each other. But not much. You can't really call things back.'

'You can call them back a little way,' said Susan, 'but your memory's inadequate. What was that thing in Francis Thompson we liked, about the wild sweet witch? Read it to me, will you, Christopher?'

Christopher found it and read:

> In the most iron crag his foot can tread
> A dream may strew her bed
> And suddenly his limbs entwine
> And draw him down through rock as sea-nymphs
>     might through brine.
> But unlike those feigned temptress-ladies who
> In guerdon of a night the lover slew,

When the embrace has failed, the rapture fled,
Not he, not he, the wild sweet witch is dead!
   And though he cherisheth
The babe most strangely born from out her death—
Some tender trick of her it hath, maybe—
   It is not she!

Christopher looked up when he had read it. He said:

'He's talking about the poet, of course. Every poet there's ever been. I suppose everyone who tries to paint or write must have that feeling. He has an idea, but when he puts into paint or words, the result is pitifully inadequate compared with what he dreamed it might be.'

'What I meant,' said Susan, 'was that the memory of anything lovely is inadequate in the same kind of way. If you were a perfect artist, you could make your past days, and your dreams, both live. But I suppose lots of people have had the same thought before.'

It was Mr Bennett's thought of sixty years earlier, but he had lacked Francis Thompson's words to express it.

'Yes,' said Christopher. 'I don't think memory and what the artist makes are really the same, but they are inadequate in the same kind of way. It's odd you should have thought of those lines. Because I'd been thinking about them too, after we read them the other night. Only my thought was a little different; I thought that for many people, who don't paint or write or express themselves in that way, the same is true of their lives. What you make of your life—well, it's usually very different from the dream that strewed her bed for you as a young man. If you had dreams at all, of course. That must be true of my friend Jodh Singh, whom we were talking about this afternoon, if I'm at all right in my picture of him.'

'Yes, poor man,' said Susan. 'What sort of trouble do you expect about him?'

'Oh, I don't know. I just feel it's an electric sort of atmosphere in which anything might touch off a disturbance. Something that was nothing to do with either him or Dharma Nand might happen, some dispute, and those two get sucked in on opposite sides, and gradually get absorbed in it, till the whole district was excited about it. But I dare say I'm talking rot. Let's go to bed.'

It was cold outside the tents and the stars had a frosty twinkle. The moon was just rising over the eastern shoulder of Dunagiri, lighting a long slope of snow with milky radiance. Vastness and cold and silence, the stars, and the icy bulk of the mountain; a wind breathed in the trees and they swayed against the clear sky.

'Let's try very hard not to forget,' said Susan.

## 2

In the fifteen years since the episode of the panther, Jodh Singh had kept only one of the resolutions he had made when he was younger. He never missed going to Bantok for some part at any rate of the summer. It seemed to him that only when he was there could he really be himself, as he wished to be. During the rest of the year, as he wandered about the district from his headquarters at Gadoli, with no companion but his servant Autaru, he was continually being forced by the world and the pressure of events into words or actions which he did not feel were really his. He had never realized himself again as he had done in those first days of the agitation about the corvee. When he spoke to the villagers now, there was always somewhere a tiny corner of his mind that remembered the jeering faces at Pokhra, when he had walked past the court-room with the Dom in a procession of two, the handcuffs and the guard set over him in the night at Gadoli.

In the villages they looked on him with respect and even fear. He was not like other people. You never knew how he would take things. Someone would suggest what was obviously the wisest course, a judicious attempt to delay throwing oneself completely into the fray until it was clear which way it would go, and he would flare up in a rage that was terrible to see. There was hardly a member of the District Board who had not winced under his tongue at some time or another. Hot-tempered, sometimes raging like a wounded panther, unaccountable to the worldly mind, moody and solitary; but all the same, he was a champion to be sent for by the weak when they were in trouble. Every villager knew that if Jodh Singh took up his cause, or the cause of his village, there would be no lack of courage or of energy in the way it was fought.

But when he was at Bantok, or better still, in the high pastures with the sheep, and could sit gazing south over the blue foothills, or north towards the icy peaks, he felt like a god, remote from passion. He could see then how year by year his emotions had led him, and how again and again they had led him wrong, and he would resolve that when he went back to the world of men he would let them dominate him no more. Nor would he again lose himself in drink when he was miserable, inflaming the passions from which he was trying to escape. And then one day there would come that opportunity for which he still waited, the chance that he would seize as he had once seized it in the days of the corvee, a chance that would let him show what was really in him. For he still knew that he was capable of more than he had yet shown the world. His moment would come, and it would make him truly a leader. They had recognized already that he was different from other people; everyone in the district knew that he was set aside for something special. It had been that which they had recognized in an obscure way when they thought he was the panther; and indeed in a sense it was true, for he was a panther, a whip, a purge, to cleanse the land of evil. And one day his hour would come and his full stature be revealed.

These were his thoughts when he was alone; and then he would forget thought and live in the body, enjoying flowers and sunlight and the clean air, or he would play with his son as if he were himself a boy again. But when he went back to the world of men, there it was, ready to pounce on him; it would spring before he was poised to receive it, and his passions would mount and push him into swift action. He would be back in the current again, hurled from wave to wave with no time to recover his breath between one crest and the next.

This was just what had happened when he came back from Bantok for the last winter of his life. The world had sprung on him at once. There was waiting for him one of the Marchas from the upper valleys, with a tale of tyranny and oppression. It was two years now since Jodh Singh had extended the favour of his special patronage and protection to the Marchas, the half-Tibetan people who live in the valleys leading to the passes to Tibet. They are a folk who lead a strange life. Half the year their villages are buried twenty or thirty feet deep in snow. They move down in autumn when the first snow falls, men, women, and children, with herds of strange creatures, half yak and half cow, and flocks of sheep and goats, pitching their black skin tents at the camping-places prescribed by long usage. Their beasts carry their tents and cooking gear and food, the women carry their babies on their backs, queer little mummified bundles slung between Tibetan tubes for mixing tea and butter, and a host of oddities; and the goats and sheep carry panniers of the salt and wool and borax and the rare skins they have brought from Tibet. They move down towards the plains, trading as they go, selling sheep and goats and the goods in their panniers, buying grain and sugar in the plains to carry back to Tibet. They depend for food and fodder on the forests and the grazing grounds of the villages where they camp. After mid-winter, they start to move back and they reach their own villages just as the snow begins to melt. Even then, they do not live long in houses. They plough the fields and sow the barley, and a small buckwheat with a pink flower like London Pride, which will not grow below eight thousand feet. Then in July, when the snow melts in the passes, the men move on to Tibet, where they sell their grain and sugar and refill their panniers for next winter. They are a hardy folk and a Marcha woman will drop her child one evening and move on with the flocks next day, carrying her bundle, like a ewe from her own flocks.

This way of life had been all very well in the old days, when there was plenty of grass and fuel for everyone, but as people grew more and forests less, there were more and more villages which resented watching the Marcha flocks and herds eating their jealously preserved grass and the Marcha women recklessly burning wood from their forests. It was for help in one of the quarrels arising from this resentment that the Marchas first turned to Jodh Singh. He had never been one to wait and consider and weigh the arguments, for and against; and as he grew older he grew more impatient. The story the Marchas told appealed to him, because they were wanderers like himself and opposed to vested interests. He took up their cause without waiting to hear what the villagers had to say on the other side. When he did hear the villagers, he regarded their arguments as selfish. He came very quickly to look on the Marchas as his people, especially committed to his care, because they had no other friends.

While he was fighting their case, they told him of their need for a trade agent and general store at Vishnumath, the last village of any size before the climb to the passes begins; and he had spoken of this to a cousin of his át Gadoli, another Govind Singh, who was becoming increasingly restive at the control of his father, Jodh Singh's money-lending uncle. Govind Singh and Jodh Singh in alliance had decided to start a shop at Vishnumath, to be run by Govind Singh. They had carried the day against the uncle, as in the last resort Jodh Singh always could, and had set up the shop, thus strengthening Jodh Singh's bond with the Marchas.

That had been two years ago. Now, when Jodh Singh came back to Gadoli from Bantok for the last time, he was met by one of the Marchas who had come on in advance of their main camps to tell him of fresh trouble. Last year, there had been a quarrel with one of the villages where they pitched their tents, but there was no doubt that by old custom the Marchas had a right to camp there and the Tahsildar had decided the case in their favour. But there had been unpleasantness and threats of violence. The Marchas were peaceful folk, nomad traders, not soldiers; they did not want trouble. They were afraid the villagers would not respect the Tahsildar's decision and so this year they had camped nearby in another village, where they thought the villagers would be more amenable. They said that this was a place where they had always camped, but this was not true; and Dharma Nand, the new Tahsildar, soon got to the truth and turned them out. Now they came running to Jodh Singh, with a sad tale of corruption and intrigue.

As soon as he had heard the name of Dharma Nand, Jodh Singh had felt that suffocating uncontrollable anger that constricted the throat and filled the head with blood, a drunkenness of anger like the drunkenness of the high pastures that he knew so well. He remembered the boy who years ago had run after him and called him a panther; and now that same boy had come to lord it over him here, in his own country, among his own people, a creature from the lower hills who looked down on the people of the upper hills as backward, a lickspittle, a toady who had taken the safe course of government service instead of helping his country by opposing foreign rule. And the Marchas' tale showed him corrupt and unfair, as bad as the rest of them. Jodh Singh did not stop to consider. He would show the swine that he was not called a panther for nothing. He sent the Marcha to wait outside and sat down at once to write his complaint to the Deputy Commissioner.

But he regarded that complaint as no more than the opening shot of his cannonade. He went about looking for material for further attacks on a man whom he was firmly persuaded was extortionate and tyrannous. He found material of a kind and sent in one petition after another. The atmosphere in the Northern Circle became indeed, as Christopher had said, electric and charged with tension. A trivial incident would be enough to release that tension in storm.

It was not long before it occurred. The murder of Raghubar Dat, the high priest's cook, was a sordid and petty affair in itself, but one of which the consequences spread wide.

It happened in Vishnumath, when the first snow had fallen. The high priest and his retinue had come down from Badrinath, the great temple, some six weeks earlier. The temple was deep in snow all the winter, and twice a year the acolytes and thurifers and choristers moved between Badrinath and Vishnumath, and with them the shopkeepers and the keepers of hostels and lodgings and all who lived on the pilgrim traffic. Down they came in autumn to Vishnumath, moving up again in the spring when the snow began to melt. But they were dull in winter, with no pilgrims; they felt the need for a relaxation which it was hard to find in Vishnumath, a hill village where the snow lay for two months, though not so deeply nor for so long as at the temple. This particular night, Raghubar Dat wanted a drink. He was a hill Brahman, a Dimri, and it was the custom of his caste to drink spirits, one reason for the contempt in which a Brahman of the plains would hold him. There was no liquor in his own quarters and in any case he wanted company as much as drink. He was bored, he wanted to be cheerful and excited. He had cooked the high priest's evening meal and there was nothing more he had to do that night. He went out to look for amusement.

Outside in the snow, he paused. There was really only one place where he could be certain of finding drink and that was in the Marchas' cabin. It was true the Marchas were almost as repulsive a caste as the aboriginal Doms; it was said, though they denied it, that in Tibet they would eat yak's meat and a yak is practically a cow. But they always had liquor, because they had a special dispensation from the government to follow their age-long practice of distilling their own drink from barley. They were not supposed to sell it or give it to anyone else, but no one worried much about that. There was one family of Marchas who did not go down to the plains with the rest, but stayed behind in Vishnumath, and there was always drink to be had there. And one of the women was an attractive piece. That was the place. Raghubar Dat's pause lasted only a moment and then he moved off to the Marchas' cabin.

The Marchas were not particularly glad to see him. He had been there before, and their private opinion was that he was not sufficiently free with his money to make up for his bad manners. In fact, Keshar Singh, the leader of the community, had told them that next time Raghubar Dat came, they should refuse to let him in. Tonight, however, Keshar Singh was out and not one of the others felt sufficiently sure of himself to be rude to a Brahman. And Raghubar Dat gave them no chance to deny him entrance. He banged on the door of the smoky little hut and when they opened to see who was there, he stooped at once and came straight in, crouching as one had to, for the door was not four feet high.

It was snowing again outside and there was a sharp wind, which whistled in the cracks of the cabin and in the cedar overhead, a noisy blustering night, when one would be glad to be indoors. The Marchas, two women and three men, clustered round the fire of yak's dung and wood. They squatted on the floor; it was their lifelong habit, but in any case it was the only way to be comfortable because the ceiling was too low to stand upright and the smoke was much thicker in the upper part of the room. It you kept near the floor, you avoided the worst of it. They were smoking tobacco, handing round the pipe-bowl, men and women taking their turn alike.

Raghubar Dat slipped quickly into the place of the man who had opened the door. The others surlily made more room. Raghubar Dat knew them, and greeted the men by name. Then he looked sideways at Tara Devi, the woman sitting next to him. She was the elder of the two, the wife of Keshar Singh, but she was young. She was the one who took his fancy. He asked her for a drink.

She replied shortly and sulkily.

'There is no drink,' she said. 'We finished it yesterday. We are making some more tomorrow.'

'Ah, come now,' said Raghubar Dat. 'It's no use telling me that. You people are never without a drink. I know you're not supposed to sell it, but between friends now, on a night like this—'

'There isn't any,' she said, still more sulkily.

Raghubar Dat put down a rupee, a whole rupee.

'Come now,' he said, 'give me a little. Just a little.'

'Give him some,' said one of the men. He thought it would save trouble to give in to one so importunate. Tara Devi looked at him. The firelight shone on her wide-boned face, the clear whites of her slanting eyes. Her cheeks beneath the grime of smoke and cooking were as firm and red as the flesh of a ripe apple. Her look said that the man who spoke was a fool and had let her down, but she said nothing. She rose crouching and turned to get the bottle. She wore a full red petticoat over trousers and felt boots. As she squatted again with the bottle in her hand, Raghubar Dat looked with pleasure and desire at her squareness, the swell of her breasts beneath the close-fitting bodice, the silver ornaments round her neck, and the smooth skin beneath them. A woman of the villages would have been swathed in shapeless blanket. He took his drink; and they all drank.

Raghubar Dat asked for more. He produced another rupee. The party began to mellow and to talk. Keshar Singh, the leader, the husband of Tara Devi, came in. He looked at Raghubar Dat with a scowl, but said nothing. They made room for him in the circle and he too drank, but he would not talk. He saw with anger the looks Raghubar Dat cast on his wife. The drink inflamed his sullen anger, but there was nothing he could say; he sat and glowered.

Raghubar Dat grew bolder and his tongue bawdier. His jokes grew more and more shameless; it could not be said that he was making direct advances to Tara Devi, but all were conscious of the thought behind the words. The other Marchas laughed at his sallies, but shamefacedly, their eyes on Keshar Singh. Tara Devi grew more angry and more silent. She passed the bottle as she was asked, with no further protest. It was for her men to say when the visitor had had enough.

Then Raghubar Dat's hour came. With his fourth drink he grew bolder still. He leaned forward and turned towards Tara Devi, sitting on his left.

'You are beautiful, beloved,' he said. And his right hand passed across his body and caressed her left breast, and then strove to enter her bodice.

Keshar Singh was sitting on his right. He put back his hand to a wooden butter tube that stood against the wall behind him. He pulled out the plunger. It was eighteen inches long and as thick as a rolling-pin, of maple-wood polished by years of use till it was hard and smooth. Keshar Singh half rose from his squatting position and with one violent movement swung the plunger over the head of the man beyond him and brought it with all the strength of his arm on to the back of Raghubar Dat's head, below his cap as he bent towards Tara Devi. Raghubar Dat toppled forward. He fell with his head on Tara Devi's lap, and a thin trickle of blood ran from his nose on to her red skirt. His cap fell off towards the fire and someone automatically picked it up to save it from burning.

They lifted him and laid him on his back.

'He is badly hurt,' said one.

'He is dead,' said another.

Keshar Singh looked at his head. He put a hand on his heart and listened for his breathing.

'He is not dead,' he said, 'but the bone of his skull is broken. He will die. But he might talk first. We must take care he does not talk.'

The others nodded.

'Give me a blanket,' said Keshar Singh. He put the folded blanket over Raghubar Dat's mouth and nose and pressed. When he moved the blanket, he listened again. Then he said:

'Now he is dead.'

'We must hide him,' said one of the other men.

Keshar Singh thought for a little.

'We must take him out and push him over a cliff,' he said. 'Then they will think it was an accident.'

'It would be better if they did not find him at once,' said Tara Devi. 'They will take him to the doctor at Chamoli and he will cut him up and find liquor in his stomach and then they will guess he had been here. It would be better if the vultures found him first before the doctor.'

Keshar Singh thought again. He said:

'They will look for him tomorrow when he does not come back. Let us hide him now, then throw him over a cliff tomorrow night when the search is over. Then they will not find him till the vultures have been at him.' He paused and thought. 'We will take out his stomach anyhow, and it will look as though the vultures had done it.'

'Where shall we hide him?' asked one of the younger brothers. 'There is no room here and people come here all day, all kinds of people.'

Keshar Singh considered again. Then he said:

'There is Jodh Singh Ji's shop. There is the place underneath it where we put the liquor. We might try that.'

They continued the discussion for some time before they opened the low door and lifted out the body, rolled in a blanket. It had stopped snowing, and the wind had dropped, but the stars were hidden.

'Do not put it down,' whispered Keshar Singh. 'Keep it off the snow.'

The three men moved away over the fresh snow, carrying the body between them.

## 3

On the second morning after the death of Raghubar Dat, that is, some thirty-six hours after Keshar Singh had struck his blow, a young man was driving out the family flock of sheep and goats into the snow from his home about two miles from Vishnumath. It was no use taking out the cows in the snow, but until it grew deeper, it was worth sending the smaller and hardier beasts. They would find leaves on the bushes and would scrape away the snow from patches of grass and find a certain amount of nourishment, not enough to keep them, but enough to reduce the demands on the stored hay that had been cut from the forests by the women during the summer and laboriously carried down to the village on their backs. And there was a small sheltered grazing-ground, where the drifts would not lie deep, to which no other flocks had access and which Pancham Singh had been reserving for just this purpose. It was a shelf in the face of a cliff and could not be reached from the Vishnumath side. There were precipices above and below and the only path to it was a narrow track along the face of the hill from the lonely homestead where Pancham Singh lived with his brothers. He had come there every day since the first snow fell, and, with the wind as it had been, not much had lain there. It would be worth going for some time yet.

Pancham Singh tramped along cheerfully, his feet warm in fragments of old blanket bound with a network of grass rope. Coming and going was all right, but it was not much fun waiting while the animals grazed. He would collect sticks, of course, to take home, and also to make himself a fire. It was women's work really, but they were very short of women. They were a stock who bred males and the last two generations had had to expend all their hoard of rupees on wives; this generation would have to save before they could marry. He reached the grazing-ground and at once collected sticks to make a fire on the ashes of yesterday's. The wood was soaking wet, of course, but he had some dry grass and chips with him. He squatted down and pulled out a brass cartridge case with a wooden plug, full of tinder made from lichen collected on the high pastures. He struck his steel, shaped like a tiny knuckleduster, on a flint, and soon had his tinder glowing. When the smoke of his fire was rising in the still air, he strolled round the little shelf to see how his flock was getting on.

He went up first towards the upper cliff, and there he stopped. Half among the bushes, half on the open snow, lay something dark. For a fraction of a second he thought it was a bear, but it was quite still and it was too small for a bear. A black sheep had fallen over the cliff perhaps; that might mean a meal of meat. He went closer. It was a man. He was quite dead.

Pancham Singh did not wait to look at him closely. He saw that this was not a peasant like himself, for he was wearing a suit of shaped clothes, not a blanket plaid. He covered him with branches to keep the vultures from seeing him and decided he could leave the flocks to itself for the half hour or so that would be needed to get to the homestead and back. There was obviously neither a panther nor a bear lying up on the shelf, or the flock would have winded him by now and would be huddled together in a frightened circle. He had with him a black long-haired dog with a wide brass collar studded with spikes. He left the dog to guard the flock and went as quickly as he could to tell his brothers.

Amar Singh, the patwari, reached the grazing-ground by midday. He was a short man, almost completely square, with a hooked nose and a reddish-brown face. He was a good patwari, intelligent and conscientious, who did his best to be honest within reason. He recognized the body at once as Raghubar Dat's, for he knew the man well by sight. He had of course suspected that it would be he, for he had heard yesterday that the high priest's cook had not come home and that the retinue had been out looking for him. He had not worried very much, supposing that he had fallen over a cliff when drunk. Raghubar Dat's reputation was not a good one.

When he heard of the corpse, however, he began to suspect something more serious. He asked questions as he walked up the narrow path towards the grazing-ground. Pancham Singh was positive there had been no corpse there yesterday. Now it was credible, though not very likely, that Raghubar Dat might have fallen over the cliff in his cups the night he disappeared. Not very likely, because it was difficult to see why he should have gone to the top of that particular cliff, a mile from Vishnumath, on a snowy night. It had not been the sort of time or place one would be likely to choose for either a drinking-bout or a love affair; and drink and women had been his interests. Still, he might have agreed to meet someone outside the village and lost his way. It was just possible.

But to suppose that he should have disappeared, near his home, and remained alive for twenty-four hours, and then fallen over a cliff by accident—that was surely stretching probability too far. It looked at once as though he had been killed the night he disappeared, his body concealed, and only now pushed over the cliff to make the death appear an accident.

This was Amar Singh's simple reasoning as soon as he heard Pancham Singh say the body had not been there the day before. And when he saw it, his reasoning was at once confirmed, because while the rest of the body was untorn, the stomach had been taken out. If the vultures had done this, they would have torn at least the face and eyes as well, but they had not; and again, Pancham Singh had been positive that there had been no vultures when he found the corpse. It looked as though someone, for some reason of his own, wished to make sure the stomach was not examined.

The patwari hunted in the bushes, but he could find nothing else connected with the body. No hat. Hardly anyone in India goes about with his head uncovered. In the hills, everyone wears a round cap; the villager has a shapeless woollen affair, woven from the yarn he has spun himself; those who have employment away from the village usually wear a black pill box. It is worn indoors and out. There was no cap with this body.

Amar Singh had the body dispatched to Chamoli for post-mortem with a brief report. He could not form any opinion on how long it was since death, nor on how the wound on the back of the head had been caused. He himself went back to Vishnumath and began to ask questions from the high priest's household. But he got nothing there. No one had seen Raghubar Dat go out, nor heard him say where he was going. But they could make a guess why he had gone out. There were bottles in his quarters which had contained spirits, but they were empty.

He must have gone out for a drink, and that meant the Marchas' cabin. There the patwari went. He was met with stony denial. They had not seen Raghubar Dat that evening. Well, yes, he had been to them in the past. Not for a drink, no. They could not imagine why he had come. They had not wanted him to come again and had not been friendly with him. They had seen nothing of him that evening; nothing at all.

Amar Singh felt sure they were lying. Most of the answers came from Keshar Singh or Tara Devi, the other three keeping silent. Amar Singh sat back and looked at them, their high Mongolian cheek bones and slanting eyes, their long hair. Their glances were downcast, there was a positive sulkiness and resentment about them all, and fear, he was sure. But were they frightened only because this might bring to light their activities in the matter of liquor, or had they something more serious to hide? He had of course long known that they peddled small quantities of liquor and had a shrewd suspicion that they had rather larger dealings in which Govind Singh, Jodh Singh's partner in the shop, was involved. But was there something more?

He began again to question Keshar Singh and Tara Devi. He asked them the same questions all over again, quickly, any question that came into his head. He did not pay much attention to their answers. The corner of his eye was all the time ready to dart a glance at the others, the silent three, of whom he asked nothing, but he was careful not to release that glance. He waited, talking and bullying. Then he said:

'I shall have to search this room.'

And then at last he let his eye flick to the youngest of the three men, quick as the dart of a lizard. And he caught the look he had hoped for, a half turn of the head toward a corner where there was a pile of gear, clothes, a butter-mixer, cooking pots.

He felt he was safe in making a search. These people were not the kind to hire lawyers and make a fuss, they were too simple. And in any case there was no doubt they were on the wrong side of the law over liquor. He went straight to the corner where the youngest man's eye had turned.

He looked at the butter-mixer with curiosity and pulled out the plunger, but pushed it back again. He had hoped for a weapon, but there was nothing of that kind. There was a folded blanket. He looked at it carefully. There were dark stains of something that had gone hard. It looked like blood. He asked about it.

'That's the blanket we carried the goat in,' said Tara Devi. Amar Singh wrote down her reply. It did not sound very convincing. Why should anyone carry a goat in a good blanket? But they might have a gun they had no licence for, and they might have shot a chamois and smuggled it home in a blanket.

Then he found a cap, a round black cap. Keshar Singh said it was his. He wore it when he went to Chamoli. It was not the sort of cap he usually wore, but it was difficult to say he had never worn it and Amar Singh saw at once that it would be impossible to prove it was Raghubar Dat's. It was, for instance, indistinguishable to the ordinary eye from the cap he wore himself. If Raghubar Dat had had a wife living with him in his quarters she might have been able to identify it, though even that was doubtful, but she was in his village three days' march away, looking after the farm.

But even without the cap, Amar Singh felt he had the rudiments of a case. He took the Marchas out into the snowy track. He looked at their clothes. There might be some blood there. Sure enough there was, on the front of Tara Devi's red skirt. She said it was from the goat, the same goat that had been in the blanket. But the doctors would be able to say whether it was goat's blood, and Amar Singh said he must take possession of her skirt, a demand which caused a good deal of delay, because Tara Devi maintained she had no other skirt. At last someone lent her one. Amar Singh then arrested Keshar Singh and Tara Devi; as he had only two pairs of handcuffs and nowhere but his own quarters to lock them up, he felt that two were as many as he could manage.

The body of Raghubar Dat had been sent with a team of eight porters, who had orders to waste no time on the way and they covered the thirty odd miles to Chamoli within the twenty-four hours. As soon as they arrived, the Tahsildar, Dharma Nand, read the report that they brought; he decided that a possible case of murder in which the corpse belonged to the high priest's household was too important to be left to a patwari and he sent his assistant to take over the investigation. The Assistant Tahsildar also wasted no time. He arrived on the fourth day after the murder.

He set to work to get a confession.

# 4

About a fortnight after the murder of Raghubar Dat, Susan and Christopher were sitting out of doors in the clear starlight, muffled to the ears in all the clothes they possessed. They were camped on a bluff in the middle of a wide shallow valley and they could see the hillside on either side of the stream, up and down, for ten miles each way. There were perhaps thirty villages in their view. It was the feast of lights, and as they gazed at the dark bulk of the forest-clad hills, below the clean line where the ridge cut the stars, one by one, from every village, there crept a winding golden caterpillar, which crawled down the hillside and then broke into fiery clusters. From the nearest village a caterpillar came directly towards them. Every male in the village was carrying a torch, a blazing bundle of resinous splinters tied together with a grass rope, of which an end several yards long was left free. As the long winding line reached the open fields below Christopher's camp, each man flung his torch from him to the full length of the rope and then, as it checked, tightened the strain, and leaning backwards swung the tangled flames in planetary circles round his head. Each man had to dodge his neighbour's torch and keep his own swinging; twenty circles of flame and sparks crossed and curved and intersected amongst a wild confusion of leaping figures, with here and there a face lighted for a momentary glimpse as a torch passed close. When he tired of making others jump over his Catherine wheel, each man broke off into a pas seul in which the rope was shortened and the flaming brand made to spin in a smaller circle over which the performer skipped himself, while next, in even smaller circles, it would flash under one leg, over an arm, back in an inverted curve, under the other leg, behind the back.

The torches burnt themselves out, the men stood panting and happy, waiting for congratulations on their skill and vigour. Then a bonfire was made, and the drums began their stammering syncopated rhythm; the men danced a story of the Pandavas, heroes of old Hindu legend, and the wars they had fought in the hills. They moved round the fire in contorted attitudes, their arms and hands accenting the rhythm in angular motion; then the drums quicken, the knees bend more sharply, the angles of elbow and shoulder become more acute, like the knotted limbs of the hill oak; the dancers are ecstatic; the rhythm sinks again, the dancers shuffle less violently.

In such a lull, a figure pushed forward from the darkness towards the two camp chairs where Susan and Christopher were sitting. This was not a blanket-clad peasant, but a man wearing a shaped suit, a shopkeeper or a minor official. He stooped and laid his hands on Christopher's feet.

'Lord, forgive me,' he said.

Christopher removed his feet out of reach under his chair and cautiously asked what there was to forgive.

'Lord, it is Jodh Singh Ji.'

'What has happened to him?'

'Lord, he has been arrested and locked up.'

'Why?'

'Because the Tahsildar is his enemy.'

'But why does the Tahsildar say he has locked him up?'

'They say he hid the body of Raghubar Dat. But it is false, lord. Why should he? It is all for enmity.'

'I see. Well I can do nothing about it tonight. In any case, I expect he has been released on bail. I have had no reports on this yet and must wait till I have. If there is reason to suspect him, I cannot interfere with justice.'

'But, lord, it is Jodh Singh Ji. You know him. You know his temperament. I am afraid. I do not know what he will do.'

'Whoever he is,' said Christopher, 'it cannot make any difference to the law if he has done this.'

'But he has not done it. He is innocent.'

'Well, we shall see. I promise to look into it and see what I think. Come again tomorrow morning. I may have had a report by then. Who are you, in any case?'

'Lord, I am his cousin, Govind Singh. We have a shop at Vishnumath.'

'Oh, yes, I see. Well, come again in the morning.'

Christopher suggested to Susan that they should leave the dancing now. He gave the headman of the village the price of a goat for the dancers and they went into the tents. There he undid the bags of mail, which had arrived late that evening, and looked through them for a letter from the Northern Circle. It was there sure enough, and also a letter from Jodh Singh and he read them both without delay.

'Now,' said Susan when he had finished, 'tell me all about it. Or do you want to do something important?'

'No, I can't do anything tonight. It would be a help to talk about it. You be Watson.'

Susan was wearing a dark blue sweater, slacks the colour of the sails in a Breton fishing-smack, a long camel-hair coat. She curled herself up in a big camp chair and pulled up to her chin a honey-coloured blanket that left nothing to be seen but a tangle of dark curls and a small round face that by nature looked always amused but was now serious.

'Now,' said Christopher, 'I told you about this rather sordid affair, the murder of the high priest's cook—the title of the crime's the best part of it. Well, since I last heard, the Assistant Tahsildar has got a confession from the younger of the Marcha women, who has turned King's evidence. Better not ask how he got it. Jodh Singh says they did extremely intimate things to her with red pepper and also made her lie in the snow with nothing on till she talked, but he is inclined to believe rather exaggerated stories. I shall have to look into that separately.'

'I suppose they must have done something, or she wouldn't have confessed,' said Susan.

'Yes. And for that reason I don't expect her confession will help much in court—even if she sticks to it, which she probably won't. But it may all the same be true. She says that Raghubar Dat came to them for a drink and got fresh with the other woman, her sister. Apparently he had rather a reputation for that kind of thing. And under provocation her husband hit him on the head. They thought there would be a search next day and so they hid the body till after the search and then pushed it over a cliff, hoping it would look like an accident.'

'Wait a minute,' said Susan. 'Was that really any good? Because if the searchers didn't look in the place where the body was going to be tipped, there would have been nothing gained by hiding it; but if the searchers did look in that place and it was empty, and then next day the body suddenly appeared there, it would be worse for the murderers? Or wouldn't it?'

'You're being much too clever for Watson. And also for the Marchas. You must remember they've never read any detective stories. They haven't had that thorough grounding in crime that every young Anglo-Saxon has the right to expect. Anyhow, that's what she says they thought. And she says they went with the body to Jodh Singh's shop, and he was staying there, and they asked if he would help, and he agreed, and they put the body under the shop in a sort of secret cellar that they knew about and had used for smuggling liquor.'

'I see,' said Susan. 'But—oh well, you tell me what you think about it.'

'Well first the murder, apart from the Jodh Singh part. Raghubar Dat went out somewhere, on a snowy night; the only place anyone can suggest he could have gone to is the Marchas, because he was a drinker and he often did go there for drink. His body is found two mornings later. There's a wound on his head which might have been caused by a blow or by a rock. The doctor says he had been dead about thirty-six hours when found; and a shepherd whom no one sees any reason to disbelieve says the corpse was not in the place where it was found the morning after death took place. Also the stomach had been removed with a knife.'

'Disgusting,' said Susan. 'And I can't see why.'

'Well, the only reason I can think of is that they thought a post-mortem would show his stomach was full of drink, which would point to them. But it wasn't very clever really. Anyhow, all that makes it pretty clear the body was concealed somewhere. Therefore, the presumption is murder, though there may have been an accident which they were afraid might be taken for murder.'

'Yes. How silly people are when they try to hide things. It always seems to land them in trouble.'

'I don't know what I should do myself if I suddenly found a corpse on my hands in suspicious circumstances. I've never tried. It might take a lot of courage to come clean. However, that's beside the point. Now—it looks very much like murder. The next question of course is, who did it? And it looks very like the Marchas, even if you disregard the confession. They were the only people he was likely to visit that anyone can suggest. No one else seems to have seen him. There was a blanket in their hut with blood on it, and blood on the elder woman's skirt. They say it was goat's blood, but the doctors say it's human. There is an extra cap in the cabin, of the kind Raghubar Dat wore, but it can't be positively identified. It seems to me ten to one that he did go to their hut and died there; no, more, a hundred to one; and the real doubt in my mind is whether they meant to kill him, or whether he was killed by accident and they decided to hush it up. They might even have been justified in killing him if he really assaulted the woman and that was the only way they could protect her—but that's most unlikely. No, as far as the murder goes, I'd say it was a clear case. Really, from my point of view, the problem is whether Jodh Singh was concerned in hiding the body. The first evidence for that is the confession. It may be that the rest of the confession is true, and that the bit about waking Jodh Singh and asking him to help was dictated, just to implicate Jodh Singh. The patwaris don't love him a little bit.'

'Do you think that—what's his name? The Tahsildar—would really go as far as that?'

'I must say all my instinct is against believing he would. But his Assistant, or the patwari, might have done what they thought he'd like them to do. You know, Thomas à Beckett—who will rid me of this turbulent priest—that kind of feeling.'

'It doesn't sound very convincing to me, but I don't begin to understand the official mind.'

'And long may you not,' said Christopher. 'As a matter of fact, Dharma Nand has written here that he finds this very embarrassing because of his known enmity with Jodh Singh, and he asks me to have the formal magistrate's inquiry done somewhere else. He also says he's going up to Vishnumath himself to hear what the witnesses say and to make sure they're not under pressure. That sounds all right, and I want to believe him; but of course the defence would say he was going to make sure the witnesses don't recant. But to return to the story. Of course, it's possible they hid the body in the smuggler's cellar without telling Jodh Singh. In fact, I shouldn't have expected Jodh Singh even to know that the cellar existed; it was used only as a smuggling depot, and the only entry was from outside the house at the back: it was a concealed entrance. And it's most unlikely to my mind that Jodh Singh knew about the smuggling. It wasn't his kind of racket at all. I should have expected that Govind Singh was doing the smuggling, without Jodh Singh's knowledge. I've always heard Jodh Singh never concerned himself at all with the way his cousins did business. He just wasn't interested. And it's a mean niggling sort of way of breaking the law; most unlike him. But it would be quite in character for him to make up his mind that the Marchas weren't morally guilty and decide to help them. I don't think he has much abstract respect for the law, and his arrogance—in one kind of way—is terrific.'

'Perhaps it was really Govind Singh who helped them and they changed it to Jodh Singh because the patwari told them to.'

'The only thing against that,' said Christopher, 'is that a shopkeeper, who's always thinking of profit and loss, isn't really very likely to run the immense risk involved in hiding a body on the premises for someone else's benefit. Jodh Singh of course never counts the cost of anything. Only you'd think he might have seen your point, that it was silly to hide the corpse anyhow.'

'Well,' said Susan, 'if there's nothing against Jodh Singh but the confession, and you don't think that's any good—have they really got anything on him?'

'What I think about the confession is that it'll be retracted. When she gets into court, she will say she didn't really mean it and it was all extorted from her under pressure. But there is something else, as well as the confession. There's a man who lives on one of those little solitary farms you find in the upper part of the district, about a day's march from Vishnumath. He says he came in to do business with a man who has a shop in Vishnumath, as he does once a year, and stayed the night. Well, that's quite plausible. The shopkeeper confirms that he spent the night there. Jodh Singh says rather vaguely that they're both enemies of his, and I happen to know it's true of the shopkeeper. He's a member of the District Board, and Jodh Singh accused him about a year ago of having got himself a contract to build a school and of having made a very good thing of it. I think Jodh Singh was right. Anyhow, they had a flaming row, and I remember hearing about it. Well, the other man, Dharam Singh his name is, was staying in this shop, and he had a pain in the night, one of those convenient calls of nature, as they say, that witnesses always do have when there's something interesting going on. He went outside and while he was there he heard some men come and knock on the door of Govind Singh's shop. And he says Jodh Singh came and spoke to them. He recognized his voice and saw his face by the light of a lantern he was carrying. He couldn't see the men because it was too dark.'

'Fishy,' said Susan.

'I agree; very fishy. It's too good to be true. But I must say I should be hard put to it to give really convincing reasons for disbelieving it. Well, there it is; undoubtedly, there is a case of a kind made out against Jodh Singh. I'm inclined to suspect it, but I don't see that I can do much beyond making sure he's given bail and having the magistrate's inquiry held in another circle. I shall warn the magistrate to sift it all very thoroughly, though I must take care not to influence him. But every official is prejudiced against Jodh Singh; and in any case, even if he's discharged from the magistrate's court, he'll have been put to a lot of trouble and will have lost a great deal of prestige. I'm afraid it'll drive him into a furious, irresponsible kind of mood; and he still has immense influence. It may cause a lot of trouble. I told you something would happen. This is just the kind of thing I imagined. Let's go to bed.'

Next morning, Christopher told Govind Singh his conclusions. He could not interfere but he would make sure that bail was allowed and would have the inquiry held in another circle. Govind Singh seemed dazed. He could only say:

'Lord, it is Jodh Singh Ji. I do not know what he will do. He will be very angry. And it is false. It is all enmity. Why should any man be so mad as to keep a corpse in his house for someone else? He will be very angry.'

# 5

Jodh Singh was sitting on a bluff above the village of Vishnumath. It was a steep rocky promontory, uncultivated, where nothing grew but sparse grass and a few pines. He could see from here a long way up and down the river, and across it to a peak that was visible from his home at Bantok.

His heart was full of anger and despair. Anger at the meanness of his enemies, despair at the wreckage of his life. And there was shame because his name was fallen low. He had been released on bail in the end, but for two nights he had been handcuffed and locked up in a back room of the patwari's quarters, eating his heart out, consumed with fury and impatience. Anger flamed up in a quick bright blaze when he thought of the way he had been treated, he, Jodh Singh, the leader of the district, the champion of the oppressed. Arrested and handcuffed, not for any political offence, but for concealing evidence of a most sordid murder. And whatever doubts the Deputy Commissioner might feel, Jodh Singh himself had none as to who was responsible. He knew it was all a plot. Dharma Nand and all his enemies had banded together against him. Dharma Nand had told them what to say. It was he who had planned this. Dharma Nand had schooled his assistant and the patwari, and those two had taught the Marcha woman what to say. The drunkenness of anger filled his heart and constricted his throat; his head felt as though it would burst.

And then he plunged into an abyss of misery when he thought of the plans he had made for his life. Year by year he had fallen below what he had hoped, but until now his feet had been turned the right way, even though he struggled aimlessly with the cactus and the boulders at the foot of the snow-clad peak that some day he would climb. The child born of his dream had up till now some tender trick of its mother, though the wild sweet witch herself was dead. But now he would never rear it; the child too lay dead at his feet. He could no more hope to lead the district after this. He saw before him nothing but a long dreary prospect of charge and counter-charge, inquiry in this court, trial in that court, the hired lawyer and the perjured witness, all the meanness his soul hated. For now his enemies would never be content. If he escaped from this, they would dig another pit about his feet. They would compass him about for fear lest he should strike back at them first. He would be locked up again, to rage baffled at the bars and pine for freedom, as he had in the patwari's quarters. He could not bear captivity.

Then there was money. Things had not gone well with the money-lending uncle, and now that Jodh Singh was down his creditors would make for him like vultures on a corpse. Debt would be their portion, and all its degradation.

He looked across the river towards Bantok and thought of his happiness there, the home he loved and his son. He looked at the track winding away from Vishnumath towards the bridge that led there. That was the way to his home, but it was not for him to tread it. He would never go there again. Tomorrow he must go south to face his judges.

His mind turned to the witnesses against him. Lachchman Parshad, the shopkeeper whose corrupt contract he had exposed, mean, money-grubbing, a foreigner from the next district, a sneaking sophisticated Kumaoni, an intriguer like every one of his race. And Dharam Singh, who had no cause to hate him except that he had taken the part of the Marchas. Dharam Singh had not even the personal excuse for a grievance that the shopkeeper had. But Dharma Nand was the worst. From the day he had shouted in the village street that Jodh Singh was a panther and a man-eater, Dharma Nand had hated him and plotted against him, like his father before him. And this was his latest plot. Well, they should feel his fury. They should know what it was to anger a panther.

He had a kukri with him. He drew it and looked at the sharp heavy blade. He felt its edge. Years ago someone had given it to him, someone he had helped. He remembered the serious wrinkled face of the old man who had come to him when the case was won and given him the kukri, laying his hand on his arm and begging him to keep it and to take it with him wherever he went, because his enemies were many and he travelled in lonely places. He had kept it ever since, with his few belongings, in the basket covered with goatskin which Autaru carried for him on his travels. He had never used it for anything, but he liked to have it, partly because he had not often been given a present in return for what he had done, and partly because he felt a pleasure in the thought that he had to go armed because of his enemies. Its presence made life more exciting, and Jodh Singh more important. It had been there in his basket when they came to arrest him, but as soon as they led him away, Autaru had hidden it, with an obscure feeling that if they found it they might regard it as incriminating. They had not found it when they searched and now that he was released he had it again. He did not usually carry it on his person, but this morning he had slipped it under his coat and brought it with him, he could not tell why.

He thought of his enemies again. He knew where they were. They were to start tomorrow for the south, like himself, for the inquiry before a magistrate. Dharma Nand had gone up to Seragad Tok to question the main witness against him, Dharam Singh. Jodh Singh knew the place, for he had been there in the Marchas' quarrel about the camping-place. The Tahsildar would be in a tent near Dharam Singh's house. The shopkeeper, Lachchman Parshad, was in his shop in Vishnumath.

Again the drunkenness of anger swelled and mounted in his veins, suffocating, intolerable. There was a roaring in his ears, lights danced before his eyes. Something seemed to happen in his brain like the shift of pattern in a kaleidoscope, and suddenly he was lighter, clearer, cooler. He could see the world very small and very clear and far away, as though through the wrong end of a telescope. His body seemed to dance and sing; he could hardly feel it. He knew now what he would do. He would go and see them. He would show them what his anger meant. He would make them see how wrong they had been. They should understand everything, all he ought to have been. And he would take his kukri in case he needed it. He stood up and moved towards the path for Seragad Tok.

That evening, Dharam Singh and his son Man Singh, a boy of about twelve, were sitting quietly talking after their evening meal. Dharam Singh was going away next day, to give evidence in the south, and he was telling Man Singh what to do in his absence. Most of the work would be done by Makar Singh, Dharam Singh's younger brother, who lived in the other dwelling house, which with a huddle of cowsheds made up the buildings of the homestead; but there would be plenty for the boy to remember too. Dharam Singh was recently a widower and the two of them slept alone, but his brother's woman cooked for him. Father and son chatted quietly. There was no light except the fire, but it was a good fire, and they were warm and happy talking together.

There came a tap at the door and a low voice.

'Who is there?' said Dharam Singh. He could not hear the answer and went to the door to listen. The boy rose to his feet.

'Let me in, Dharam Singh,' said a quiet voice outside. Dharam Singh thought it was a message from the Tahsildar camped nearby. He opened the door.

The boy Man Singh could never properly remember what happened after that. He heard the stranger speak, and something in his voice must have frightened him, for he stepped back out of the light of the fire and stood in the shadow of a corn-bin, and then there were more words, not loud but angry, and suddenly a blow and his father uttered a choking cry. Man Singh sank to the ground in his dark corner. He covered his eyes with his hands. He heard a dreadful chopping noise, and a harsh panting, and then he heard the door close. He crouched trembling, not daring to move.

He did not move for a very long time. Then the door opened again and he crouched closer and stiller. A voice said:

'Oh Dharmu!'

Someone came in and said:

'Where are you both? Are you asleep?'

Man Singh knew the voice but his brain was too frozen to tell him who it was and he kept quiet. He heard a step go to the fire and the sounds of wood being thrown on the ashes being raked together. The voice spoke again, slow and wondering:

'My feet are wet and sticky!'

And then the voice cried in horror:

'What has happened! He's been killed!'

He heard a quick rush of steps and then the door slammed. He crouched still.

Makar Singh, Dharam Singh's brother, had been at the Tahsildar's camp talking to the orderly about the arrangements for the move next day. He had come back to tell Dharam Singh what had been decided. When he found his feet wet with blood, and the fire blazed up to show his brother lying with his head almost severed from the body, he ran out into the courtyard and stood still for a moment panting with fear and horror. There was no one in his own home but the women and children. He ran to the door and called:

'Are you awake? It is Makru.'

They answered sleepily and he told them to bar the doors quickly and open to no one but himself. Then he ran to the Tahsildar's camp. He found the orderly whom he had just left. The orderly was already in bed, but when he heard what had happened he said at once that the Tahsildar, Dharma Nand, must be told. The moon was at the end of its

first quarter and had just risen. By its light they could see the
Tahsildar's tent glimmering fifty yards away. There was no snow here
yet.

They stopped outside the tent and asked permission to enter. There
was silence and they called louder. There was still no answer, and at
last they went in. They found Dharma Nand fallen forward across a
table at which he had been writing. He must have half risen to speak
to his visitor, and dropped without a sound when the first savage blow
fell on his skull and split the bone. Blows had been rained on his head.
There was blood everywhere.

Early in the small hours of that morning, Lachchman Parshad, the
shopkeeper at Vishnumath with whom Dharam Singh was supposed to
have stayed, was roused by a voice calling his name. He slept on the
upper floor of his house, above the shop, and he could hear someone
on the veranda, which was reached by an outside staircase. There was
a small window by the door, a tiny opening not a foot across with a
wooden shutter, and before he unfastened the door he looked out to
see who was there.

The moon by this time was high in the clear sky, and its light was
reflected from the snow. He recognized Jodh Singh with a kukri in his
hand.

'Let me in,' said Jodh Singh. 'I want to talk to you.'

Lachchman Parshad was frightened by his voice, his look, the
weapon in his hand. He thanked the gods his door was barred and
told Jodh Singh to come in the morning if he had anything to say. He
crept into bed again, but did not dare to sleep, and as he lay trembling
he too, like that other shopkeeper fifteen years ago, heard feet like an
angry beast's pad back and forth on the veranda seeking entrance.
Once the door was seized and rattled, and he heard it shake with the
weight of a heavy body; blows were showered on the lock; it held, and
he heard the breath of his enemy come in gasps as he stood motionless,
panting after the effort. Then he heard steps going quickly and softly
away.

In the morning, he found that the door of the shed where his goats
were kept had been broken. Jodh Singh had burst his way in, and slain
them all. Twelve goats lay decapitated. He had not taken their flesh for
meat. The headless bodies lay there as witness of his rage.

## 6

Christopher was moving south and was several days' march away when he heard the news that Jodh Singh had disappeared and that two of his enemies had been killed in a night. There was nothing for it but to cancel the rest of his tour and turn north again. He arrived to find that terror had come to that part of the valley round Vishnumath, and that as in the days of the panther men slept with barred doors and did not go out after dark. Jodh Singh had taken the Tahsildar's gun from his tent and some cartridges known to be loaded for large game. He had fired once at the patwari, but had missed him and had escaped into the forest. The patwari was sure that food was being taken to him by villagers he had helped in the past, but it was impossible to find who was sending it or how it was sent. The patwari had taken Autaru and Govind Singh into custody as obvious links between the outlaw and the means of life, but this had not stopped the supply and he could not hold them long when there was no charge against them. Christopher ordered their release, although he had not the men to have them kept under continuous watch.

The difficulty was the same for the hunters of the man as it had been for the hunters of the panther. Until he revealed his whereabouts by some open act, a kill or a murder, the hunt was always far behind. The initiative lay with the hunted. There were hundreds of miles of forest where a man could lie hid; there were caves and shelters without number, and unlimited fuel with which a man might keep himself warm. Jodh Singh had influence all over the district; there were a score of villages in the Northern Circle alone that remembered him with gratitude. He could descend on any one of these and demand food and be ten miles away by morning. To the villagers' gratitude to their old champion and their natural sympathy with any breaker of the law was added the powerful cement of fear, plain bodily fear and a superstitious horror that Jodh Singh was something more than a man. He seemed to place everyone who met him under a spell of terror.

Christopher sent for a force of armed police. He moved in patwaris from elsewhere and left quieter circles in the hands of probationers. He kept a small mobile force with himself and stationed men in any village which he thought likely to be helping the fugitive, hoping that somewhere someone would catch an echo of his flying footsteps and make it possible to pick up the trail. But it was no use. For nearly a month he heard nothing. He made up his mind he would have to go away to the south and leave it to the new tahsildar to avenge the murder of his predecessor.

But just as he had reached this decision, something happened. He was staying in a bungalow on the edge of the forest, at the head of a shallow valley, just below the snow. After dinner he did some work he had neglected all day; then he stepped out of the bungalow to look at the stars before going to bed. The moon was at the end of its first quarter and had just risen. The forest lay still in the windless cold; from far away a wind sighed and crept nearer over the tree tops as though the night was turning in its sleep. There was the sound of a stream close by, but behind the running water he could hear the silence of frost and snow and the stars and millions of leaves. There came the sharp bark of a fox; he shuddered in the cold and turned to go; and as he turned there came a voice crying in the night from beyond the stream.

'Lord!' it cried, 'lord! Can you hear me?'

Christopher was silent. He listened intently.

'Lord! Can you hear?'

'I hear you,' Christopher called and moved behind a tree.

'Listen, lord. It is I, Jodh Singh. Come and see what has happened here by the shop on the track beyond the stream. Come and see what has happened.'

It was the first time Christopher had known Jodh Singh address him in Hindustani.

'I wonder if it's a corpse or an ambush,' he thought to himself, and called for the patwari and the six armed police whom he kept with him as a mobile squad, to be put on the trail if anyone should pick it up.

Ten minutes later they were stumbling down the hill together. The track and the shop were beyond the stream and there was no path leading that way directly, the usual route being round the head of the valley. They went straight down through the forest, pines, scrub oak, scarlet rhododendrons and thorn bushes. It would have been difficult ground in daylight; by the light of a half moon it was frightful; they tripped over bushes and rocks, tangled themselves in briars, fell into holes. Christopher felt that if it was an ambush they were making all the noise Jodh Singh could want. He must know just where they were. But if he was lying up to shoot them, he must be near the shop on the track. He had not got a rifle, but a shotgun, and in the moonlight he was unlikely to fire at anything more than twenty yards away. The only thing to do was to move as though going straight to the shop, and then when fifty yards away make a detour and reach the track well below it. There would then still be an anxious moment as one approached the shop but at least it could be done comparatively quietly, and at the same time distracting noises could be made by flanking parties.

They crossed the stream and struggled breathless up the farther slope. Christopher swung the whole party sharp to his left, down the valley; then a last burst straight up and they were on the track about a hundred yards below the shop, without misadventure.

Christopher thought his feelings must be exactly those of an experienced tiger approaching last night's kill, wondering when a tree would spurt death. He decided to take a lesson from the tiger. Circle round before approaching; stop and wait and listen—those were the tiger's maxims. But it's no use trying to listen for Jodh Singh when I've got this gang of heavy-footed policemen with me, he thought.

After some consideration, he decided to send the patwari and one policeman in a detour above the shop, to strike the track fifty yards beyond it. They would whistle when they reached the track. Two policemen would take up a position thirty yards below the shop, two more thirty yards above. Each of these parties would also whistle, so that each knew where the other was. After the whistles there would be ten minutes' complete silence, in which everyone would be trying to hear Jodh Singh move if he was there.

At the end of ten minutes, on a whistle from Christopher, everyone would start making a noise, beating bushes, throwing stones. In the middle of this, Christopher would walk up the track to the shop, with a constable ten yards behind him ready to fire at the flash if there should be one.

The parties moved off, crashing and stumbling as before. It was remarkable how quickly the noise died. What had seemed deafening when one was in the middle of it dropped to no more than the snap of an occasional stick as the distance increased. The three parties whistled to show they had taken their stations. Then came the silence.

There was a spring near the shop and water overflowed on to the track so that the black leaf mould of its surface was always wet. It was trampled by the feet of men and animals into a bog of tiny patches of water, interspersed with black points and hummocks, both glittering in the light of the moon, which shone directly down the track. Christopher gazed at that broken path of glistening black and silver up which he would soon have to walk. He strained to hear a sound that might be an excuse for doing something else, but he knew the sound would not come and there would be no way out. He had often waited in silence before, to take the life of a beast; he knew the pounding heart that comes at every sound that may be the tread of a tiger. But for the moment, he was the hunted; it was his life that might be taken this time. This time there was no false alarm, only the sickening certainty that he must walk up that path.

He looked at his watch. Only five minutes. I wish it would be over and I could start. I wish it would be over. Six minutes. Seven. Eight. I wish it would be over. Nine. Ten.

Christopher swallowed twice and blew his whistle. Crashings began in the forest above, below, beyond the shop. He waited a last wait of thirty seconds, his eyes on his watch. Then he walked slowly up the track towards the shop. He felt better at once. Now it was settled. It was to be or it was not to be his death; there was no more to worry about.

Nothing happened. He reached the shop without sound from man or beast. He banged on the door.

'Who is there?' he called. 'Oh, shopkeeper! Let me in.'

There was silence inside. The constable who had been following Christopher came up, and the others came crashing through the bushes. The patwari called:

'Open the door, you fool. It is the Deputy Commissioner.'

Still there was silence.

'They've been murdered,' said one of the constables. 'All of them.'

No one else spoke. No one had thought of bringing an axe; the head constable doubtfully drew his bayonet, but the patwari had a kukri which was obviously more suitable, and he set to work to chop a hole in the door by the latch.

'Wait,' said Christopher. 'The door is locked from the inside. He must be inside with them. Come back with me.'

He led them away from the shop to a point where his talk could not be heard by anyone inside and gave his orders. When the door was opened, everyone must be on one side or the other, to give a clear line of fire through the door; and in the doorway against the moonlight there must be something that looked like a man, to draw Jodh Singh's fire. The constables set about making a dummy. But it was a double-barrelled gun and no one would fire twice at a dummy, Christopher reflected; he would lose one man with the second barrel, and it would be himself. He did not fancy the thought of a shotgun fired at short range into his stomach. He explored the back of the shop. But there was no entrance big enough for a man's body.

The dummy was made, something that would pass for a man in the moonlight if it moved quickly before the eyes. Operations on the door began again. Snap. The last fragment was chopped through. Nothing remained but to thrust in a hand, draw the latch, and open the door. Christopher looked round to make sure that the man with the dummy was ready.

'Now!' he said.

The door was flung open. The dummy swung out for a second

across the open doorway and darted back.

Nothing happened.

'Again!' said Christopher.

Again, nothing. The dummy had failed. The next step seemed a concerted rush. If Jodh Singh was inside it would almost certainly mean the loss of two men; surely it would be better to wait till morning? And then to consider whether to fire the hut. Christopher decided that it would. Four pairs of men, at the four corners of the hut; one man of each pair to sleep. One man to go now and get blankets. He moved round to post the sentries.

As he came to the upper side of the shop, he noticed a cattle-track leading up the hill at an acute angle with the main track. He would have seen it before if all his thoughts had not been concentrated on the hut. The patwari's encircling party must have crossed this. But had they? They would have thought it was the main track and had probably come straight down it to the shop, and if that was so, no one had explored the main track. The patwari confirmed his surmise, and Christopher, expecting nothing in particular, moved up the main track in case something had been missed.

Twenty yards up was a forked stick, on which there was a paper and a sealed letter, addressed to himself, and at the foot of the stick was a packet. He struck a light and set it to a lantern. Then he read the papers. They were written with a blunt indelible pencil.

The open paper said:

I, Jodh Singh, son of Govind Singh, son of Kalyan Singh Rawat, of Bantok, the deliverer of Garhwal from the forced labour, formerly a member of the Legislative Assembly at Lucknow and a member of the District Board, killed my enemies Dharma Nand and Dharam Singh because they were liars and had borne false witness against me. Now I have decided to kill no more of my enemies and I will surrender to the Deputy Commissioner and to no one else on the fourth day from today at midday, at the shop on the track near the bungalow, where this paper was found. Let the Deputy Commissioner be present to accept my surrender.

The letter said:

Dear Mr Tregard,

At the foot of this stick is a packet of personal belongings which I wish to be sent to my son at Bantok. I do not wish that they should be handled by the police and dragged into court. They are personal papers and a ring. There is nothing that has to do with this case, and I shall plead guilty, so it does not matter. I beg you to send them to my

son at Bantok as you believe in Almighty God. I trust no one but you.
There was an English lady who was my friend and believed in me and
so I trust you. I trust no one else. I have not meant to do any harm, but
to lead a good life. I do not understand what has happened to me.
Please believe me, that I meant no harm.

Yours sincerely,
Jodh Singh Rawat.

Christopher opened the packet. There was a ring and a bundle of
letters, certificates of good conduct from school and college, letters of
thanks from villagers, two letters from Hugh Upton written in the days
of the forced labour, all the carefully treasured evidence of Jodh Singh's
successes against the world that laughed at him. Christopher put them
in his pocket and said:

'I think there is no one in the hut. Let us see.'

They went together to the hut. Christopher opened the door and
walked in. There was a bed inside and a man lying on the bed. His
head was covered with the blanket. Christopher pulled back the
blanket gently, moved the hands that covered the face. To his surprise,
they were warm. The man said:

'I know nothing. I saw nothing. I heard nothing.'

That was all they could get out of him. So powerful had been the
spell that Jodh Singh had put upon him that he had lain quite still,
frozen with terror, throughout their operations on the door and their
planning outside.

They went back to the forked stick and looked for tracks. But many
men had been that way during the past day and they had no tracker
who could have puzzled out such a trail. It was two hours since Jodh
Singh had called across the valley. There was nothing for it but to take
him at his word and wait for his surrender on the fourth day.

At noon on that fourth day, Christopher was at the shop with the
patwari and six armed policemen. The stage was set; it was a familiar
scene. The surface of the track, black with leaf mould, stretched before
them. It was puddled with water. There was a leaden sky that looked
like snow. On the hill above them, and again across the stream, the
forest swept up to that lowering sky. Only the wet black track and the
tiny clearing round the hut were free from trees. Christopher's heart
was beating fast; he could not have said why he was so stirred. He
lighted a cigarette to show that he was calm and waited till he had
smoked it before he acted. Nothing had happened. He called, loudly,
slow and clear:

'Jodh Singh! Are you there?'

There was silence. He called again.

This time there was an answer:

'Yes, lord. I am here.'

Christopher waited a moment. An order might frighten him away. He called:

'I am here to meet you.'

There was silence again. Christopher called:

'Are you coming down to surrender?'

There was a long silence. Then the voice cried, suddenly and very loud:

'No! No! Never!'

There were two shots from above and a few slugs whistled over their heads and spattered on the trees beyond. They heard a crashing above and a shout:

'Jai Badri Bisal!'

The muskets of the police were loaded. Christopher said:

'Get ready to fire!'

The crashing of bushes and branches came straight down the hill towards them. Jodh Singh burst out of the trees into the clearing by the hut, his kukri in his hand, running as hard as he could. He made straight for the line of police. Christopher said:

'Fire!'

The body of Jodh Singh rolled to his feet.

# 7

There was a new Kalyanu at Bantok, a great-grandson of that first Kalyanu who had fought the bear. He was the leader of the little community at the homestead and it was he who planned the sowing and harvesting and the paying of land revenue. He had gone across the bridge to Gadoli to talk business with his kinsmen and he was there when the news came of Jodh Singh's death. A special messenger had come from the Deputy Commissioner with a packet of papers for Jodh Singh's son. The messenger put them into Kalyanu's hand.

Kalyanu went back sadly, for at Bantok they had loved and reverenced Jodh Singh. He crossed the bridge, and made the three days' journey, cliff and torrent, corrie and grass slope, rock and pine. There were fresh crossings to the streams, where the spates had washed the old stepping-stones away, but except for this, the way was unchanged since his great-grandfather had travelled it in the opposite direction in his hammock, leaving Bantok. The young Kalyanu reached Bantok on the third day and decided he must go at once to the upper farm and tell the news to the household. Snow was lying up there, but it had not yet reached the lower homestead.

As he climbed, he thought of the things to be done on the farm. Among the narrow shelves of ploughed land near the homestead, he thought of the weeding and hoeing that was needed, and the spring harvesting and ploughing. He wondered how soon snow would fall, it was badly wanted, for these lower fields were dry; but it did not look like snow today. The sky was clear. Then he was above the little snaky fields, out on the long hillside of grass, where the feet of his ancestors and their goats and sheep had worn a path like a thread through the golden grass. He moved slowly across the vast hill, a tiny dark point. He wondered if the stocks of hay cut in the summer would last them through the winter. He thought they would.

The way led below the rock face and turned to zigzag directly up the hill. Here he came into the snow, but there was a beaten track, and it was easy going to feet wrapped in blanket tied with grass rope. Through the tiny terraced fields of the upper farm, through the narrow place where the first Kalyanu had killed the bear, to the rocky spur where Jodh Singh had built his house.

He gave the news. The widow wept, though she had lost nothing of Jodh Singh, for he had never been hers. The son took his papers and went away to read them, dry-eyed. They kept Kalyanu late and it was dark when he went back. The moon was in its third quarter and had not risen. He ate his evening meal and went to bed. The dark lay close as a blanket over the homestead and the hills and there was silence behind the distant roar of the torrent. It was very still and the trees too were silent.

But towards morning, when the moon had risen, there came a little wind. The moon silvered the grass on the steep side below the bluff, as the wind sighed over it in a long ripple, like a caress on the skin of a panther. The wind sighed again and the blue pines breathed deep in reply. The roar of the torrent rose faintly and the wind sighed in the pines, but behind all sound was the silence of the mountains, silence and the silver of the moonlight.

Charmouth, Dorset
May–July 1946

# Biographical Notes

EDMUND CANDLER (1874–1926): Born in Harleston, Norfolk, he was educated at Repton School and Emmanuel College, Cambridge, where he received a classics degree in 1895. Between 1896 and 1914 he earned his living primarily as a teacher in India, his longest appointment being that of Principal of Mohindra College in the princely state of Patiala. In 1900 he published his first book, *A Vagabond in Asia*, and in January 1902 he married Olive Mary Tooth in Calcutta. Two years later he joined the Younghusband Mission to Tibet as a special correspondent of *The Daily Mail*. His account of the expedition, in which he lost his left hand, appeared in 1905 as *The Unveiling of Lhasa*. There followed another travel book, *The Mantle of the East* (1910), a book of short stories, *The General Plan* (1911), and the novel for which he is best known, *Siri Ram—Revolutionist* (1912).

Candler spent the war years as a correspondent. His account of the Mesopotamian campaign, *The Long Road to Baghdad*, appeared in 1919, the year in which he was appointed Director of Publicity for the Punjab. In his new post he came to know and respect Gandhi, whom he portrays in *Abdication* (1921). Four years later he published his unconventional autobiography, *Youth and the East* (the 1932 edition carries a useful 'Introductory Memoir' by his brother Henry). Candler had suffered from diabetes for years and had bought a villa in the French Pyrenees to recover his health. He died there in his fifty-second year.

RACHAEL CORKILL: Granddaughter of Edmund Candler, and the only child of Candler's daughter, Audrey. She made a study of Candler's life and works as part of her MA in English Literature.

PHILIP MASON (1906–99): Born in London and educated at Balliol College, Oxford, from where he took a first in Philosophy, Politics, and Economics. He joined the Indian Civil Service in 1928 and served as Assistant Magistrate in the United Provinces, now called Uttar Pradesh. In 1935 he married Eileen Mary Hayes, and the following year was appointed Deputy Commissioner of Garhwal—the job he prized above all others and where he spent some of the most satisfying years of his life. During the war years he held senior appointments in the Defence and War Departments in Delhi, finally retiring from service in 1947 with the end of the Raj.

His literary career began in earnest with his return to England. He had already published a novel about India, *Call the Next Witness* (1945), which he followed up with two others: *The Wild Sweet Witch* (1947) and *The Island of Chamba* (1950). In England he got involved in race relations and, as Director of the Institute of Race Relations for twelve years, he travelled extensively in Africa and Latin America and authored many books on the subject. But his interest in India remained steadfast, and in 1953 and 1954 appeared his monumental study in two volumes, *The Men Who Ruled India*. Twenty years later came another notable study, this time on the Indian Army, called *A Matter of Honour* (1974). Among others, Mason wrote books for children, a much-admired biography of Kipling, and two autobiographies, *A Shaft of Sunlight* (1978) and *A Thread of Silk* (1984). In all, he wrote some thirty books, of which the first nine were published under the pseudonym Philip Woodruff. Among the recognitions he received were the Companion of the Indian Empire (1945), a D.Sc. from the University of Bristol, and a D.Litt. from Oxford.

SARAH IRONS: Daughter of Philip and Mary Mason. She was born in Simla and recently retired as librarian at the African Studies Centre in Cambridge, U.K.

FLORA ANNIE STEEL (1847–1929): Born at Sudbury Park, Harrow, she was one of eleven brothers and sisters. Her education was spasmodic and left in the hands of governesses, but she was an avid reader with an exceptionally good memory. In 1867 she married Henry Steel of the ICS and left for the Punjab (India), where she was to spend more than twenty years. Unlike most Anglo-Indian women of the time, she learned the Indian language and managed to establish relations with Indians of all classes. She took active interest in the welfare of women and children and in 1884 was appointed Inspectress of Schools for Girls. While in India she co-authored two books: a collection of folk tales called *Wide-Awake Stories* (1884) and a guide to newly arrived English ladies to India, *The Complete Indian Housekeeper and Cook* (1888). The guide is often cited to show Steel's autocratic and imperialistic attitudes in dealing with Indians.

Known primarily for her fiction on India (she wrote novels on British life as well), Steel's writing career began with her husband's retirement and return to Scotland in 1889. She wrote some of the finest short stories on India, collected and published in five volumes (for a selection, see *The Oxford Anthology of Raj Stories*, 1998), as well as six novels of Indian and Anglo-Indian life. Her best-known work is *On the Face of the Waters* (1896), with *The Potter's Thumb* (1894) running a close second. She also wrote four historical/biographical novels on the Mogul dynasty, four children's books, and a frank and fascinating autobiography towards the close of her life called *The Garden of Fidelity* (1929). Though she was Kipling's equal in many ways, her works, unlike those of Kipling, are not easily available.

LADY VIOLET POWELL (1912–2002): Daughter of the Fifth Earl of Longford, she was married to the novelist Anthony Powell. Herself a well-known writer, her *Flora Annie Steel: Novelist of India* (1981) did much to draw attention to Anglo-Indian fiction.

CHRISTINE WESTON (1904–89): Born in Unao in the United Provinces (now Uttar Pradesh) in India, her father was a member of the Imperial Police, who later took to law, and her mother the daughter of an English army officer. She considered herself fortunate in her parents 'whose attitude towards the natives was quite different from the attitude of most English people.' Her early schooling was in a convent run by Irish and German nuns, which she came to hate, but she loved the convent's location in the Himalayan hills and regarded that country as a fine place for children to grow up. She had learned to read and write at the early age of four, and later had the run of her father's professional library which included a whole series of famous English trials. In 1923 she married an American, Robert Weston, and went to live in Maine. After Robert's death she married a close friend of his, Roger Griswold, but continued to use the Weston name by which she was known to her readers.

Like most Anglo-Indian writers, she took to fiction after leaving India and, like many of them, her best works deal with India. Her principal novels are *Be Thou My Bride* (1940), *The Dark Wood* (1946), *The Devil's Foot* (1942), and *The World is a Bridge* (1950). She also wrote some non-fiction and children's books. But it was with the publication of *Indigo* (1943) that she gained immediate recognition. Here was a work that could stand comparison with Forster's *A Passage to India* for its authenticity and compassionate understanding of India's problem. A work of no less importance is her collection of short stories, *There and Then* (1947). Many of the stories in this volume were first published in *The New Yorker* and can challenge the best of Kipling, Flora Annie Steel or Alice Perrin. Though the book has been long out of print, a selection from it can be viewed in *The Oxford Anthology of Raj Stories* (1998).

# Glossary of Indian Words and Phrases

*agni hotri*: one who prepares the sacrificial fire. *Agni* is the Vedic god of fire

*alakh! alakh!*: an invokation to the ascetics

*anna*: one-sixteenth of a rupee; coin no longer in use

*ari, aree*: a common exclamation, like oh!

*Arjun*: brother of god Rama in the epic *Mahabharata*

*Arya Samaj*: a religious reform society founded by Dayananda Sarasvati in 1875

*Asura*: an evil spirit; an enemy of the gods

*atta*: flour

*ayah*: Indian nanny; lady's maid

*babajee*: term of respect for an elderly man; *baba* often used for a young boy

*baboo-jee, babujee*: a learned man; a term of respect

*backsheesh, baksheesh*: tip, present

*badzat*: rascal, rogue

*banyan tree*: Indian fig tree, *Ficus indica*, venerated by Hindus

*baobab*: also called *kikar*, a tree with sharp thorns common in India

*bawarchi-khana*: kitchen

*be-shak*: without doubt, certainly

*Bhagavad Gita*: celebrated Sanskrit philosophical poem in the *Mahabharta*

*bhakti*: salvation through devotion to God

*bhang*: an intoxicating drink

*Bharat Mata*: Mother India

*bhisti*: native water-carrier

*bhut*: ghost

*bibi*: term of respect for a native woman.

*Bismillah*: 'in the name of Allah'—a pious expression used by Muslims

*boli*: language

*Brahm*: supreme god of the Hindu Trinity, the second being Vishnu and the third Shiva

*Brahmin*: member of the highest caste among Hindus
*budmash*: rogue
*bukh*: to talk nonsense
*bullah*: an exclamation
*bunniah, bunnia*: shopkeeper; member of the merchant class
*burrah*: high ranking; big

*chamar*: one of the inferior castes of leather-workers, a cobbler, etc.
*channa*: chick-pea
*chappati, chupatti*: Indian pancake; unleavened bread
*chaprassi, chuprassi*: office servant, messenger
*charas*: a narcotic
*charpoy*: light wooden string bed
*chela*: a pupil, a disciple
*chhatri*: a monumental structure in the shape of an umbrella; a large
    building
*chiragh, charag*: a simple earthenware oil-lamp
*chupkun*: long frock coat or cassock
*chumbaeli*: a creeper bearing fragrant white flowers

*dâk*: postal service; mail
*dali*: basket or tray of presents
*dandy*: a sort of *dooli* used in the Himalayas to carry people
*Devi*: goddess; a term of high respect for a woman.
*dhak*: the Hindustani name for the palasa tree
*Dhakma*: Parsi Towers of Silence
*dharma*: religion
*dhobi*: washerman
*dohai!*: an exclamation for seeking redress or justice
*Dom*: member of a low Dravidian caste often performing menial jobs
*dooli, dhooli*: a swinging litter for carrying women or sick person
*dhoti*: loin cloth worn by Indian men
*durbar*: royal court
*durwaza bund*: the door is closed

*ekka*: two-wheeled pony cart, inferior to a *tonga*

*fakeer, fakir*: Muslim religious mendicant
*feringhi, feringhee*: European; literally foreigner
*fez*: cap worn usually by Muslims

*gayatri, gyatri*: the name of a metre and verse composed in that metre
    in the *Rig-Veda*

*gharami*: a thatcher or maker of mat houses
*ghari*: a cart or carriage
*ghat*: steps on the bank of a river; a wharf
*Ghâzee*: a Muslim warrior against infidels
*Granth*: sacred scripture of the Sikhs
*ghee*: clarified butter
*guru, gooroo*: a teacher, master
*gymkhana*: club; a sports ground

*hakeem*: an Indian physician
*har*: garland
*haveli*: palace; a large house. Also land attached to a capital town
*havildar*: a native army officer about the rank of a sergeant
*hisab kitab*: keeping account; book work
*hom*: possibly *homa*, the act of oblation by pouring clarified butter on
   fire
*hundi*: bill of exchange
*hut jao*: move away
*huzoor*: sire; also, abstractly, the government

*jat*: caste
*Jatni*: a female *Jat*. *Jats* are mostly Hindus, found in northwest India
*jee, ji*: term of respect, often used as a suffix to a name
*jehad*: a sacred war of the Muslims against the infidels
*jehannum*: hell
*jemadar*: subaltern officer in the Indian Army, ranking below a *soubadar*
*jheel*: swamp, a sheet of shallow water

*kangar, kangri*: a clay-lined pot in which fire is lit
*kankar*: small stone
*Kali*: black Hindu goddess requiring propitiation through blood
   sacrifice
*Kali Yug*: the present iron age, according to Hindu cosmology
*kedgeree*: an Indian dish of rice cooked with lentils
*Khalsa*: means pure, real, proper. Stands for militant Sikh theocracy
   founded by Guru Gobind Singh
*khansâman*: cook
*Khidmutgar*: a male servant who waits at table
*khuskhus tattis*: screens of aromatic fibrous roots used in hot weather
   to keep cool
*ki jai*: victory to
*kikar*: Indian name for a species of acacia yielding gum arabic

*kukri*: a curved knife used by Gurkhas
*kurras*: bracelet

*lathi*: bamboo pole; any strong stick
*lat-sahib*: a high official, a governor or viceroy
*Lingayat*: a member of a sect whose adherent wear the *linga* (a phallic symbol) round the neck
*logue*: people
*loh!*: an exclamation
*loquot*: a Chinese and Japanese fruit-tree naturalized in India
*lota, lotah*: a small metal pot or tumbler
*lumbardar*: headman of an Indian village

*machan*: shooting platform generally built on a tree
*Magha Mela*: February festival; the Hindu month *Magha* corresponds to February
*Maharaj*: a title of some of the Indian princes; also used as a term of high respect
*mai*: mother; term of respect for an elderly woman
*mai-baap*: mother-father
*mali*: gardener
*mantra*: an incantation; a magic formula
*Manvantara*: the period or age of a Manu or cosmic deity, held equal to 4,320,000 years
*mata*: mother
*mem*: wife of a sahib
*mofussil*: rural; up-country
*mlechcha*: a foreigner; one who is not a Hindu
*mohalla*: a locality in a town
*mohur*: gold coin worth Rs 15 during the Mutiny
*moonshi, munshi*: a scribe, a teacher, an interpreter
*moulvie*: Muslim religious teacher
*muazzim*: Muslim mosque official

*nameste*: a Hindu mode of greeting with joined palms of both hands
*nautch*: a combination of dancing and gesticulating by women
*neem*: a tree common to India and often planted on roadsides
*nulla, nullah*: narrow river-bed

*Om*: a sacred Hindu utterance of assent, or *mantra*

*Padishah*: emperor/empress of India

*palkee*: more commonly palankeen

*pan supari*: betel-leaf with *areca*-nut and other ingredients

*pandal*: temporary structure erected for a special occasion such as marriage or lecture

*patwari*: village official and junior revenue officer

*peepul*: a large Indian tree sacred to Hindus and Buddhists

*pice*: one of the lowest denomination Indian coin no longer in circulation

*Pir*: Muslim saint; a spiritual guide

*poojarni*: female worshipper or temple assistant

*poorbeah*: person from upper India

*pranayan*: the Hindu (*yoga*) system of breath control

*pucca*: ripe, full-fledged, dependable

*pugri*: light Indian turban

*punkah*: fan usually suspended from ceiling and pulled by hand

*Puranas*: sacred poetical works containing the myths and legends of the Brahmins

*purdah*: curtain screening women's quarters; veil worn by Muslim women

*purdah nashin*: in *purdah*

*putto*: coarse Cashmere goat hair; tweed


*rath, ruth*: native carriage drawn by a pony or oxen

*Ram-Ram-Sita-Ram*: invocation to the Hindu god Rama and his consort

*rishi*: an ascetic, a sage, a saint

*ryot*: a peasant; cultivator tenant


*sabha*: conclave, assembly

*sadhini*: a female *sadhu*

*sadhu*: holy man, an ascetic

*sahib*: sir; often used for Whites. Also used as a suffix to names

*salaam*: Indian salutation with bow of head and right palm raised to the forehead

*sannyasi*: an ascetic

*saras*: Indian red-headed grey crane

*sari*: a long wrapping garment worn mostly by Hindu women

*sarangi*: Indian string musical instrument resembling a violin

*serai*: lodging for travellers

*shahbash*: well-done, bravo

*shaitan*: devil

*Shastras*: any one of the sacred writings of the Hindus

*shisham*: Indian timber tree, used for house building and furniture
*Shiva, Shiv-jee*: one of the three deities of the Hindu Trinity, the other two being Brahma and Vishnu
*Shivala*: temple to god Shiva
*shradda*: ceremonies performed on occasions of grief as well as rejoicing
*sircar, sirkar*: government; also high government official
*sitar*: an Indian guitar
*soubadar*: chief Indian officer of company of sepoys
*sowar*: a native cavalryman
*sutaras*: possibly *sitars*
*suttee*: the act of immolation; the supreme act of wifely fidelity
*swadeshi*: a political and national movement advocating the boycott of foreign goods
*swami*: often used as a title for a holy man. Also as a prefix to a name
*swaraj*: freedom
*swarga*: heaven

*tahseeldar, tahsildar*: a revenue officer of a *tahsil*—a subdivision of a district
*tantra*: one of a class of Sanskrit religious works, chiefly of a magical and mystical nature
*tamasha*: fair, amusement, entertainment
*turi*: pulse

*Vedas*: the ancient sacred book of the Hindus
*Vishnu*: the second of the great Hindu Triad—the Preserver

*wah!*: an exclamation
*Wahabis*: Muslim reformers called after their leader Shaikh Abdul Wahab (1691–1787)
*wilaiti*: English; foreign

*yagna*: religious mortification in Hinduism
*yogi*: Hindu ascetic

*zenana*: secluded female quarters of residence
*zemindar*: well-to-do landowner
*zitar, sitar*: an Indian guitar